Falco on the Loose

Lindsey Davis was born in Birmingham but now lives in
Greenwich. After an English degree at Oxford she joined the
Civil Service but now writes full time. Her novel *Two for the
Lions* won the first CWA Ellis Peters Historical Dagger Award.

Also by Lindsey Davis

The Course of Honour

The Falco Series

The Silver Pigs
Shadows in Bronze
Venus in Copper
The Iron Hand of Mars
Poseidon's Gold
Last Act in Palmyra
Time to Depart
A Dying Light In Corduba
Three Hands in the Fountain
Two for the Lions
One Virgin Too Many
Ode to a Banker
A Body in the Bath House
The Jupiter Myth
The Accusers

FALCO
ON THE LOOSE

Last Act in Palmyra
Time to Depart
A Dying Light in Corduba

Lindsey Davis

arrow books

Published by Arrow Books in 2003

1 3 5 7 9 10 8 6 4 2

Last Act in Palmyra © Lindsey Davis 1994
Time to Depart © Lindsey Davis 1995
A Dying Light in Corduba © Lindsey Davis 1996

Lindsey Davis has asserted her right under the Copyright, Designs
and Patents Act, 1988 to be identified as the author of this work

Arrow Books
The Random House Group Limited
20 Vauxhall Bridge Road, London SW1V 2SA

Random House Australia (Pty) Limited
20 Alfred Street, Milsons Point, Sydney
New South Wales 2061, Australia

Random House New Zealand Limited
18 Poland Road, Glenfield
Auckland 10, New Zealand

Random House (Pty) Limited
Endulini, 5a Jubilee Road, Parktown 2193, South Africa

The Random House Group Limited Reg. No. 954009

www.randomhouse.co.uk

A CIP catalogue record for this book
is available from the British Library

Papers used by Random House
are natural, recyclable products made from wood grown in
sustainable forests. The manufacturing processes conform to
the environmental regulations of the country of origin

ISBN 0 09 945199 9

Printed and bound in Great Britain by
Cox & Wyman Ltd, Reading, Berkshire

List of Contents

Last Act in Palmyra   1

Time to Depart   415

A Dying Light in Corduba   795

LAST ACT IN
PALMYRA

For Janet
('Six o'clock; first there bags a table . . .')
with neither gunshots nor simulated rape
– and only one insult to lawyers!

LAST ACT IN PALMYRA

PROLOGUE: *ROME*   11
ACT ONE: *NABATAEA*   37
ACT TWO: *THE DECAPOLIS*   127
ACT THREE: *PALMYRA*   307
EPILOGUE: *PALMYRA*   403

'There comes a time in everyone's life when he feels he was born to be an actor. Something within him tells him he is the coming man, and that one day he will electrify the world. Then he burns with a desire to show them how the thing's done, and to draw a salary of three hundred a week . . .'

Jerome K. Jerome

'And let those that play your clowns speak no more than is set down for them; for there be of them that will themselves laugh, to set on some quantity of barren spectators to laugh too; though, in the mean time, some necessary question of the play be then to be considered . . .'

William Shakespeare

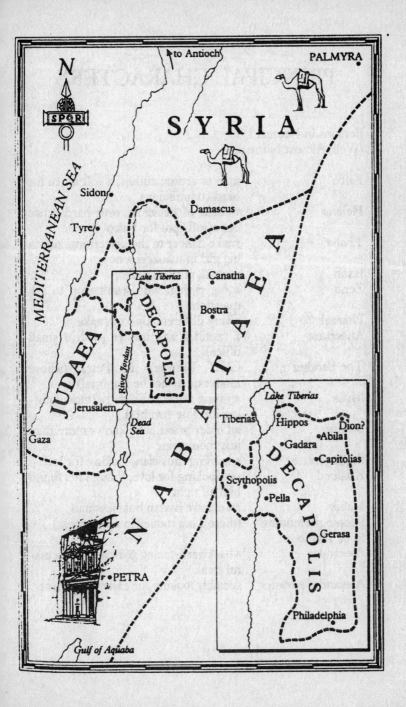

PRINCIPAL CHARACTERS

Persons in Normal Life
(Well, Almost Normal)

Falco	man of action; author; a soft touch for hard commissions
Helena	woman of decision; with hard sense but a soft spot for Falco
Thalia	snake dancer to the discerning; now a big girl in management
Jason	a small, curious python
Zeno	a big python who won't stop to ask questions
Pharaoh	a very different kind of snake
Anacrites	a reptilian spy master (with a small office)
The Brother	Chief Minister in Petra (whose motives may not be fraternal)
Musa	a young priest of Dushara (moonlighting for The Brother)
Shullay	an older priest, who knows more than just moonshine
Sophrona	a missing musician, looking for love
Khaleed	not looking for love, though it's found him all right
Habib	an elusive Syrian businessman
People pretending to be Habib	(there's big money in elusiveness)
Alexander	a backward-facing goat; an unsuccessful freak
Alexander's owner	sensibly looking for early retirement

DRAMATIS PERSONAE

The Company

Heliodorus	a jobbing playwright (dead); not much of a contributor
Chremes	actor-manager of an itinerant theatre group; a hopeless type
Phrygia	an actress of stature (a tall woman); Chremes' wife
Davos	who appears so reliable he can't be
Philocrates	a small handsome package heading for a big fall
Philocrates' Mule	another lively performer looking for a break
Byrria	a very beautiful girl who just wants a career (that old story!)
Tranio	a sophisticated clown (a contradiction in terms)
Grumio	a clever stand-up comedian (another contradiction?)
Congrio	a billposter with big ideas (another comic?)

From the Orchestra

Ione	a tambourinist
Afrania	a tibia-player } not a trio to mess with
Plancina	a panpipe girl }
Ribes	a lyre-player who hasn't found his muse

From 'The Spook who Spoke'

'Moschion'	a prototype

PROLOGUE

The scene is set in Rome, in the Circus of Nero and in a small back room at the Palace of the Caesars on Palatine Hill. The time is AD 72.

SYNOPSIS: *Helena*, daughter of *Camillus*, is a young girl disappointed by *Falco*, a trickster, who seemed to have promised her marriage. He now claims he has been let down by *Vespasian*, an Emperor, his patron. In the nick of time *Thalia*, a high-class entertainer, and *Anacrites*, a low-class spy, both suggest ways in which Falco may escape from this predicament, but he must prevent Helena discovering what he is up to, or a Chorus of Disapproval is bound to ensue.

I

'Somebody could get killed here!' Helena exclaimed.

I grinned, watching the arena avidly. 'That's what we're meant to be hoping for!' Playing the bloodthirsty spectator comes easy to a Roman.

'I'm worried about the elephant,' she murmured. It stepped tentatively forwards, now at shoulder height on the ramp. A trainer risked tickling its toes.

I felt more concern for the man at ground level who would catch the full weight if the elephant fell. Not too much concern, however. I was happy that for once the person in danger was not me.

Helena and I were sitting safely in the front row of Nero's Circus, just across the river outside Rome. This place had a bloody history, but was nowadays used for comparatively staid chariot racing. The long circuit was dominated by the huge red granite obelisk that Caligula had imported from Heliopolis. The Circus lay in Agrippina's Gardens at the foot of the Vatican Hill. Empty of crowds and of Christians being turned into firebrands, it had an almost peaceful atmosphere. This was broken only by brief cries of 'hup!' from practising tumblers and rope dancers and restrained encouragement from the elephant's trainers.

We were the only two observers allowed into this rather fraught rehearsal. I happened to know the entertainment manager. I had gained entrance by mentioning her name at the starting gates, and was now waiting for a chance to talk to her. Her name was Thalia. She was a gregarious character, with physical attractions that she did not bother concealing behind the indignity of clothing, so my girlfriend had come to protect me. As a senator's daughter, Helena Justina had strict ideas about letting the man she lived with put himself in moral danger. As a private informer in an unsatisfactory job and with a shady past behind me, I suppose I had asked for it.

13

Above us soared a sky that a bad lyric poet would certainly have called cerulean. It was early April; midmorning on a promising day. Just across the Tiber everyone in the imperial city was twisting garlands for a long warm springtime of festivals. We were well into the third year of Vespasian's reign as Emperor, and it was a time of busy reconstruction as burnt-out public monuments were rebuilt after the civil wars. If I thought about it, I was in a mood for some refurbishment myself.

Thalia must have despaired of proceedings out in the arena for she threw a few harsh words over a barely decent shoulder, then left the trainers to get on with it. She came over to greet us. Behind her we could see people still cajoling the elephant, who was a very small one, along the ramp that was supposed to bring him to a platform; from this they had hopefully stretched a tightrope. The baby elephant could not yet see the rope, but he knew he did not like what he had discovered about his training programme so far.

At Thalia's arrival my own worries became wilder too. She not only had an interesting occupation, but unusual friends. One of them lay around her neck like a scarf. I had met him at close quarters once before, and still blenched at the memory. He was a snake, of modest size but gigantic curiosity. A python: one of the constricting species. He obviously remembered me from our last meeting, for he came reaching out delightedly, as if he wanted to hug me to death. His tongue flickered, testing the air.

Thalia herself took careful handling. With commanding height and a crackling voice that cut right across this huge arena, she could always make her presence felt. She also possessed a shape few men could take their eyes off. Currently it was draped in silly strips of saffron gauze, held in place by gigantic jewellery that would break bones if she dropped any of it on your foot. I liked her. I sincerely hoped she liked me. Who wants to offend a woman who is sporting a live python for effect?

'Falco, you ridiculous bastard!' Being named after one of the Graces had never affected her manners.

She stopped in front of us, feet planted apart to help

14

support the snake's weight. Her huge thighs bulged through the flimsy saffron. Bangles the size of trireme rowlocks gripped tightly on her arms. I started to make introductions, but nobody was listening.

'Your gigolo looks jaded!' Thalia snorted to Helena, jerking her head at me. They had never met before but Thalia did not trouble with etiquette. The python now peered at me from her pillowing bosom. He seemed more torpid than usual, but even so something about his disparaging attitude reminded me of my relatives. He had small scales, beautifully patterned in large diamond shapes. 'So what's this, Falco? Come to take up my offer?'

I tried to look innocent. 'I did promise to come and see your act, Thalia.' I sounded like some stuffed green fig barely out of his toga praetexta, making his first solemn speech in court at the Basilica. There was no doubt I had lost my case before the usher set the water clock.

Thalia winked at Helena. 'He told me he was leaving home to seek employment taming tigers.'

'Taming Helena takes all my time,' I got in.

'He told *me*,' Helena said to Thalia, as if I had never spoken, 'he was a tycoon with big olive vineyards in Samnium, and that if I tickled his fancy he would show me the Seven Wonders of the World.'

'Well, we all make mistakes,' Thalia sympathised.

Helena Justina crossed her ankles with a swift kick at the embroidered flounce on her skirt. They were devastating ankles. She could be a devastating girl.

Thalia was giving her a practised scrutiny. From our previous encounters Thalia knew me to be a low-life informer, plugging away at a dismal occupation in return for putrid wages and the public's contempt. Now she took in my unexpectedly superior girlfriend. Helena was posing as a cool, quiet, serious person, though one who could silence a cohort of drunken Praetorians with a few crisp words. She also wore a stunningly expensive gold filigree bracelet that by itself must have told the snake dancer something: even though she had come to the Circus with a dried melon seed like me, my lass was a patrician piece, backed up by solid collateral.

15

Having assessed the jewellery, Thalia turned back to me. 'Your luck's changed!' It was true. I accepted the compliment with a happy grin.

Helena gracefully rearranged the drape of her silken stole. She knew I didn't deserve her, and that I knew it too.

Thalia gently lifted the python from her neck, then rewound it around a bollard so she could sit down and talk to us. The creature, which had always tried to upset me, immediately unravelled its blunt, spade-shaped head and stared balefully with its slitted eyes. I resisted the urge to pull in my boots. I refused to be alarmed by a legless thug. Besides, sudden movement can be a mistake with a snake.

'Jason's really taken to you!' cackled Thalia.

'Oh, he's called Jason, is he?'

An inch closer and I was planning to spear Jason with my knife. I was only holding off because I knew Thalia was fond of him. Turning Jason into a snakeskin belt was likely to upset her. The thought of what Thalia might do a person who upset her was even more worrying than a squeeze from her pet.

'He looks a bit sick at the moment,' she explained to Helena. 'See how milky his eyes are? He's ready to shed his skin again. Jason's a growing boy – he has to have a new outfit every couple of months. It makes him go broody for over a week. I can't use him in public appearances; he's completely unreliable when you're trying to fix up bookings. Believe me, it's worse than operating an act with a troupe of young girls who have to lie down moaning every month – '

Helena looked ready to reply in kind, but I interrupted the women's talk. 'So how's business, Thalia? The gateman told me you've taken over the management from Fronto?'

'Someone had to take charge. It was either me or a damned man.' Thalia had always taken a brutal view of men. Can't think why, though her bedroom stories were sordid.

The Fronto I referred to had been an importer of exotic arena beasts, and an organiser of even more exotic entertainment for the smart banqueting crowd. He met with a sudden indisposition, in the form of a panther who ate him.

16

Apparently Thalia, a one-time party-circuit dancer, was now running the business he left behind.

'Still got the panther?' I joked.

'Oh yes!' I knew Thalia saw this as a mark of respect for Fronto, since parts of her ex-employer might still be inside the beast. 'Did you catch out the grieving widow?' she demanded of me abruptly. In fact, Fronto's widow had failed to grieve convincingly – a normal scenario in Rome, where life was cheap and death might not be random if a man offended his wife. It was whilst investigating the possible collusion between the widow and the panther that I had first met Thalia and her collection of snakes.

'Not enough evidence to bring her before the courts, but we stopped her chasing after legacies. She's married to a lawyer now.'

'That's a tough punishment, even for a bitch like her!' Thalia grimaced evilly.

I grinned back. 'Tell me, does your move into management mean I've lost my opportunity to see you do your snake dance?'

'I still do my act. I like to give the crowd a thrill.'

'But you don't perform with Jason because of his off-days?' Helena smiled. They had accepted one another. Helena for one usually gave her friendship reluctantly. Getting to know her could be as tricky as mopping up oil with a sponge. It had taken me six months to make any headway, even though I had wit, good looks and years of experience on my side.

'I use Zeno,' said Thalia, as if this reptile needed no other description. I had already heard that Thalia's act involved an immense snake that even she spoke of with awe.

'Is that another python?' Helena asked curiously.

'And a half!'

'And who does the dancing – him or you? Or is the trick to make the audience think Zeno is taking a greater part than he really does?'

'Just like making love to a man . . . Smart girl you've picked up here!' Thalia commented drily to me. 'You're right,' she confirmed to Helena. 'I dance; I hope Zeno doesn't. Twenty feet of African constrictor is too heavy to lift, for one thing.'

'Twenty feet!'

'And the rest of it.'

'Goodness! So how dangerous is it?'

'Well . . .' Thalia tapped her nose confidentially, then she seemed to let us in on a secret. 'Pythons only eat what they can get their jaws around, and even then in captivity they're picky eaters. They're immensely strong, so people think they're sinister. But I've never known one to show the slightest interest in killing a human being.'

I laughed shortly, considering my unease over Jason, and feeling conned. 'So this act of yours is pretty tame, really!'

'Fancy a dance with my big Zeno yourself?' Thalia challenged me caustically. I backed down with a gracious gesture. 'No, you're right, Falco. I've been thinking the act needs pepping up. I might have to get a cobra, to add a bit more danger. Good for catching rats around the menagerie too.'

Helena and I both fell silent, knowing cobra bites to be generally fatal.

The conversation took a turn in a different direction. 'Well, that's my news!' Thalia said. 'So what job are you on now, Falco?'

'Ah. A hard question.'

'With an easy answer,' Helena joined in lightly enough. 'He's not on any job at all.'

That was not quite true. I had been offered a commission only that morning, though Helena was still unaware of it. The business was secret. I mean not just that it would involve working under cover, but that it was secret from Helena because she would strongly disapprove of the client.

'You call yourself an informer, don't you?' Thalia said. I nodded, though with only half my attention on it as I continued to worry about keeping from Helena the truth of what I had just been offered.

'Don't be shy!' Thalia joked. 'You're among friends. You can confess to anything!'

'He's quite a good one,' said Helena, who already seemed to be eyeing me suspiciously. She might not know what I was hiding, but she was beginning to suspect that there was something. I tried to think about the weather.

18

Thalia tipped her head on one side. 'So what's it about, Falco?'

'Information mostly. Finding evidence for barristers – you know about that – or just listening for gossip, more often than not. Helping election candidates slander their opponents. Helping husbands find reasons to divorce wives they've grown tired of. Helping wives avoid paying blackmail to lovers they've discarded. Helping the lovers shed women they've seen through.'

'Oh, a social service,' Thalia scoffed.

'Definitely. A real boon to the community . . . Sometimes I trace stolen antiques,' I added, hoping to impose an air of class. It sounded merely as though I hunted down fake Egyptian amulets, or pornographic scrolls.

'Do you look for missing persons too?' Thalia demanded, as if she had suddenly had an idea. I nodded again, rather reluctantly. Mine is a job where I try to prevent people getting ideas, since they tend to be time-consuming and unprofitable for me. I was right to be wary. The dancer exploded gleefully. 'Hah! If I had any money, I'd take you on for a search-and-retrieve myself.'

'If we didn't need to eat,' I replied mildly, 'I'd accept the tempting offer!'

At that moment the baby elephant spotted the tightrope and realised why he was being taken for a walk up the ramp. He began trumpeting wildly, then somehow turned around and tried to charge back down. Trainers scattered. With a mutter of impatience, Thalia rushed out into the arena again. She told Helena to look after her snake. Evidently I could not be trusted with the task.

II

Helena and Jason watched keenly as Thalia strode up the ramp to comfort the elephant. We could hear her berating its trainers; she loved animals, but evidently believed in producing high-class acts by a regime of fear – in her staff, that is. Like me, they had now decided the exercise was doomed. Even if they could entice their ungainly grey acrobat out over the void, the rope was bound to snap. I wondered whether to point this out. No one would thank me, so I stayed mum. Scientific information has a low rating in Rome.

Helena and Jason were getting on well. She had had some practice with untrustworthy reptiles, after all; she knew me.

Since nothing else was required, I started to think. Informers spend a lot of time crouching in dark porticos, waiting to overhear scandals that may bring in a greasy denarius from some unlikeable patron. It's boring work. You are bound to fall into one bad habit or another. Other informers amuse themselves with casual vice. I had grown out of that. My failing was to indulge in private thought.

The elephant had now been fed a sesame bun, but still looked dismal. So did I. What was on my mind was the job I had just been offered. I was thinking up excuses to turn it down.

Sometimes I worked for Vespasian. A new emperor, sprung from a middle-class background and wanting to keep a canny eye on the nasty snobs of the old élite, may need the occasional favour. I mean, a favour of the kind he won't be boasting about when his glorious achievements are recorded in bronze lettering on marble monuments. Rome was full of plotters who would have liked to poke Vespasian off the throne, so long as they could make the attempt with a fairly long stick in case he turned round and bit them. There were others annoyances, too, that he wanted to be rid of – dreary men fastened into high public positions on the strength of mouldy old pedigrees, men who had neither brains nor energy nor morals, and whom the new Emperor intended to replace with brighter talent. Somebody had to weed out the plotters and discredit the idiots. I was quick and discreet, and Vespasian could trust me to tidy up loose ends. There were never repercussions from my jobs.

We first took each other on eighteen months ago. Now, whenever I had more creditors than usual, or when I forgot how much I loathed the work, I agreed to imperial employment. Though I despised myself for becoming a tool of the state, I had earned some cash. Cash was always welcome in my vicinity.

As a result of my efforts Rome and some of the provinces were more secure. But last week the imperial family had broken an important promise. Instead of promoting me socially, so I could marry Helena Justina and appease her disgruntled family, when I had called to claim my recompense from the Caesars they kicked me down the Palatine steps empty-handed. At that, Helena declared that Vespasian had given me his last commission. He himself failed to notice that I might feel slighted by so small a thing as mere lack of reward; within three days here he was, offering me another of his diplomatic trips abroad. Helena would be furious.

Luckily, when the new summons to the Palace came, I was heading downstairs from our apartment on my way to pick up gossip at the barber's. The message had been brought to me by a puny slave with coarse eyebrows joined together above hardly any brain – up to standard for Palace messengers. I managed to grab the back of his short tunic and march him down to the ground-floor laundry without Helena seeing him. I paid a small bribe to Lenia, the laundress, to keep her quiet. Then I hurried the slave back to the Palatine and gave him a stern warning against causing me domestic inconvenience.

'Stuff you, Falco! I'll go where I'm sent.'

'Who sent you then?'

He looked nervous – with reason. 'Anacrites.'

I growled. This was worse news than being asked to attend Vespasian or one of his sons.

21

Anacrites was the official Chief Spy at the Palace. We were old antagonists. Our rivalry was the most bitter kind: purely professional. He liked to see himself as an expert at dealing with tricky characters in dangerous locations, but the truth was he led too soft a life and had lost the knack; besides, Vespasian kept him short of resources, so he was beset by pathetic subordinates and never had a ready bribe to hand. Lack of small change is fatal in our job.

Whenever Anacrites bungled some sensitive commission, he knew Vespasian would send me in to put his mistakes right. (I provided my own resources; I came cheap.) My successes had aroused his permanent jealousy. Now, although his habit was always to appear friendly in public, I knew that one day Anacrites meant to fix me for good.

I gave his messenger another piece of colourful career advice, then stomped in for what was bound to be a tense confrontation. Anacrites' office was about the size of my mother's lamp store. Spies were not accorded respect under Vespasian; he had never cared who might be overheard insulting him. Vespasian had Rome to rebuild, and took the rash view that his public achievements would sufficiently enhance his reputation without the need to resort to terror tactics.

Under this relaxed regime Anacrites was visibly struggling. He had equipped himself with a folding bronze chair, but sat crushed up in one corner of the room in order to make space for his clerk. The clerk was a big, misshapen lump of Thracian sheep's fat in a flashy red tunic that he must have stolen off a balcony parapet whilst it was hanging out to air. His huge feet took up most of the floor in their ungainly sandals, ink and lamp oil spilled on their thongs. Even with Anacrites sitting there, this clerk managed to suggest that *he* was the important person visitors ought to address.

The room gave off a faintly unprofessional impression. It had an odd scent of turpentine corn plasters and cold toasted bread. Scattered all around were crumpled scrolls and wax tablets that I took to be expenses claims. Probably claims by Anacrites and his runners which the Emperor had refused to pay. Vespasian was notoriously tight, and spies have no sense of discretion when requesting travel refunds.

22

As I went in, the master of espionage was chewing a stylus and staring dreamily at a fly on the wall. Once he saw me, Anacrites straightened up and looked important. He hit his knee with a crack that made the clerk wince, and me too; then he sank back pretending to be unconcerned. I winked at the clerk. He knew what a bastard he worked for, yet openly dared to grin back at me.

Anacrites affected tunics in discreet shades of stone and buff as if he were pretending to merge into backgrounds, but his clothes always had a slightly racy cut, and his hair lay oiled back from his temples so precisely I felt my nostrils curl. The vanity in his appearance matched his view of himself professionally. He was a good public speaker, able to mislead with easy grace. I never trust men who have nicely manicured fingernails and a deceitful way with words.

My dusty boot knocked into a group of scrolls. 'What's this? More poisonous accusations against innocent citizens?'

'Falco, just you attend to your business, and I'll look after mine.' He managed to imply that his business was deeply relevant and intriguing, while my motives and methods smelt like a barrel of dead squid.

'A pleasure,' I agreed. 'Must have received the wrong message. Someone claimed you needed me – '

'I *sent* for you.' He had to act as if he were giving me orders. I ignored the insult – temporarily.

I pressed a small copper into his clerk's hand. 'Go out and buy yourself an apple.' Anacrites looked furious at me interfering with his staff. While he was still thinking up a countermand, the Thracian skipped. I slumped on to the clerk's vacant stool, spreading myself across most of the office, and grabbed a scroll to look through nosily.

'That document is confidential, Falco.'

I carried on unrolling the papyrus, raising an eyebrow. 'Dear gods, I hope it is! You won't want this muck being made public . . .' I dropped the scroll behind my stool, out of his reach. He went pink with annoyance at not being able to see which secrets I had been looking at.

Actually, I had not bothered to read it. Nothing but nonsense ever came through this office. Most of the sly

23

schemes Anacrites was pursuing would sound ludicrous to the average stroller in the Forum. I preferred not to upset myself by finding out.

'Falco, you're making my office untidy!'

'So spill the message and I'll go.'

Anacrites was too professional to squabble. Pulling himself together, he lowered his voice. 'We ought to be on the same side,' he commented, like a drunken old friend reaching the point where he wants to tell you just why he shoved his elderly father over the cliff. 'I don't know what makes us always seem so incompatible!'

I could suggest reasons. He was a sinister shark with devious motives who manipulated everyone. He received a good salary for working as little as possible. I was just a freelance hero doing his best in a hard world, meanly paid for it, and always in arrears. Anacrites stayed in the Palace and dabbled in sophisticated concepts, while I was out saving the empire, getting filthy and beaten up.

I smiled quietly. 'I've no idea.'

He knew I was lying. Then he hit me with the words I dread to hear from bureaucrats: 'Time we made it all up, then! Marcus Didius, old friend, let's go out for a drink . . .'

III

He hauled me off to a thermopolium the Palace secretaries use. I had been there before. It was always full of ghastly types who liked to think they ruled the world. When secretariat papyrus beetles go out to socialise they have to burrow among their own kind.

They can't even find a decent hole. This was a shabby stand-up wine bar where the air smelt sour and one glance around the clientele explained it. The few pots of food looked caked with week-old crusts of gravy on their rims; nobody was eating from them. In a chipped dish a dry old gherkin tried to look impressive beneath a pair of copulating flies. A misshapen, bad-tempered male skivvy flung herb twigs into pannikins of hot wine boiled down to the colour of dried blood.

Even halfway through the morning, eight or ten inky blots in dingy tunics were crammed up against one another, all talking about their terrible jobs and their lost chances for promotion. They swigged drearily as if someone had just told them the Parthians had wiped out five thousand Roman veterans and the price of olive oil had slumped. I felt ill just looking at them.

Anacrites ordered. I knew I was in trouble when he also settled the bill.

'What's this? I expect a Palace employee to dash for the latrine door whenever a reckoning hoves into view!'

'You like your joke, Falco.' What made him think it was a joke?

'Your health,' I said politely, trying not to sound as if actually I wished him a plague of warts and Tiber fever.

'Yours too! So, Falco, here we are . . .' From a beautiful woman slipping out of her tunic, this could have been a promising remark. From him it stank.

'Here we are,' I growled back, intending to be somewhere

else as soon as possible. Then I sniffed at my drink, which smelt like thin vinegar, and waited in silence for him to come to the point. Trying to rush Anacrites only made him dawdle more.

After what seemed like half an hour, though I had only managed to swallow a digit of the awful wine, he struck: 'I've been hearing all about your German adventure.' I smiled to myself as he tried to insinuate an admiring tone into his basic hostility. 'How was it?'

'Fine, if you like gloomy weather, legionary swank, and amazing examples of ineptitude among the higher ranks. Fine, if you like to winter in a forest where the ferocity of the animals is excelled only by the bad mood of the trousered barbarians who are holding spears to your throat.'

'You do love to talk!'

'And I hate wasting time. What's the point of this fake banter, Anacrites?'

He gave me a soothing smile, meant to patronise. 'The Emperor happens to want another extraterritorial expedition – by somebody discreet.'

My response may have sounded cynical. 'You mean he's instructed you to do the job yourself, but you're keen to duck? Is the mission just dangerous, or does it involve an inconvenient journey, a foul climate, a total lack of civilised amenities, and a tyrannical king who likes his Romans laced on a spit over a very hot fire?'

'Oh, the place is civilised.'

That applied to very few corners outside the Empire – the one thing these tended to have in common was a determination to *stay* outside. It led to an unfriendly reception for our envoys. The more we pretended to arrive with peaceful intentions, the more certain they felt that we had their country earmarked for annexation. 'I don't like the sound of that! Before you bother asking, my answer's no.'

Anacrites was keeping his face expressionless. He sipped his wine. I had seen him quaff fine fifteen-year-old Alban, and I knew he could tell the difference. It amused me to watch his strange, light eyes flicker as he tried not to mind drinking this bitter brew in company he also despised. He asked,

'What makes you so certain the old man instructed me to go myself?'

'Anacrites, when he wants me, he tells me so in person.'

'Maybe he asked my opinion, and I warned him you were unreceptive to work from the Palace nowadays.'

'I've always been unreceptive.' I was reluctant to mention my recent kick in the teeth, though in fact Anacrites had been present when my request for promotion was turned down by Vespasian's son Domitian. I even suspected Anacrites was behind that act of imperial graciousness. He must have noticed my anger.

'I find your feelings perfectly understandable,' the Chief Spy said in what he must have hoped was a winning way, apparently unaware he was risking several broken ribs. 'You had a big investment in getting promoted. It must have been a bad shock being turned down. I suppose this spells the end of your relationship with the Camillus girl?'

'I'll handle my own feelings. And don't speculate about my girl.'

'Sorry!' he murmured meekly. I felt my teeth grind. 'Look, Falco, I thought I might be able to do you a favour here. The Emperor put me in charge of this; I can commission whoever I want. After what happened the other day at the Palace, you may welcome an opportunity to get as far away from Rome as possible . . .'

Sometimes Anacrites sounded as though he had been listening at my doorlatch while I talked life over with Helena. As we lived on the sixth floor, it was unlikely any of his minions had flogged up to eavesdrop, but I took a firmer grip on my winecup while my eyes narrowed.

'There's no need to go on to the defensive, Falco!' He could be too observant for anybody's good. Then he shrugged, raising his hands easily. 'Suit yourself. If I can't identify a suitable envoy I can always go myself.'

'Why, where is it?' I asked, without intending to.

'Nabataea.'

'Arabia Petraia?'

'Does that surprise you?'

'No.'

I had hung around the Forum often enough to consider myself an expert in foreign policy. Most of the gossipmongers on the steps of the Temple of Saturn had never stepped outside Rome, or at least had gone no further than whichever little villa in central Italy their grandfathers came from; unlike them I had seen the edge of the Empire. I knew what went on at the frontier, and when the Emperor looked beyond it I knew what his preoccupations were.

Nabataea lay between our troubled lands in Judaea, which Vespasian and his son Titus had recently pacified, and the imperial province of Egypt. It was the meeting point of several great trade routes across Arabia from the Far East: spices and peppers, gemstones and sea pearls, exotic woods and incense. By policing these caravan routes the Nabataeans kept the country safe for merchants, and charged highly for the service. At Petra, their secretively guarded stronghold, they had established a key centre of trade. Their customs levies were notorious, and since Rome was the most voracious customer for luxury goods, in the end it was Rome who paid. I could see exactly why Vespasian might now be wondering whether the rich and powerful Nabataeans should be encouraged to join the Empire and bring their vital, lucrative trading post under our direct control.

Anacrites mistook my silence for interest in his proposal. He gave me the usual flattery about this being a task very few agents could tackle.

'You mean you've already asked ten other people, and they all developed sick headaches!'

'It could be a job to get you noticed.'

'You mean if I do it well, the assumption will be it can't have been so difficult after all.'

'You've been around too long!' He grinned. Momentarily I liked him more than usual. 'You seemed the ideal candidate, Falco.'

'Oh come off it! I've never been outside Europe!'

'You have connections with the East.'

I laughed shortly. 'Only the fact my brother died there!'

'It gives you an interest – '

'Correct! An interest in making sure I never visit the damned desert myself!'

I told Anacrites to wrap himself in a vine leaf and jump head first into an amphora of rancid oil, then I derisively poured what remained in my winecup back into his flagon, and marched off.

Behind me I knew the Chief Spy wore an indulgent smile. He was sure I would think over his fascinating proposition, then come creeping back.

Anacrites was forgetting about Helena.

IV

Guiltily I recalled my attention to the baby elephant.

Helena was looking at me. She said nothing, but she gave me a certain still, quiet stare. It had the same effect on me as walking down a dark alley between high buildings in a known haunt of robbers with knives.

There was no need to mention that I had been offered a new mission; Helena knew. Now my problem was not trying to find a way of telling her, but sounding as if I had intended to come clean all along. I disguised a sigh. Helena looked away.

'We'll give the elephant a rest,' Thalia grumbled, coming back to us. 'Is he being a good boy?' She meant the python. Presumably.

'He's a treat,' Helena answered, in the same dry tone. 'Thalia, what were you saying about a possible job for Marcus?'

'Oh, it's nothing.'

'If it was nothing,' I said, 'you wouldn't have thought of mentioning it.'

'Just a girl.'

'Marcus likes jobs involving girls,' Helena commented.

'I bet he does!'

'I met a nice one once,' I put in reminiscently. The girl I once met took my hand, fairly nicely.

'He's all talk,' Thalia consoled her.

'Well, he thinks he's a poet.'

'That's right: all lip and libido!' I joined in, for self-protection.

'Pure swank,' said Thalia. 'Like the bastard who ran off with my water organist.'

'Is this your missing person?' I forced myself to show an interest, partly to insert some professional grit but mainly to distract Helena from guessing I had been called to the Palace again.

Thalia spread herself on the arena seats. The effect was dramatic. I made sure I was gazing out towards the elephant. 'Don't rush me, as the High Priest said to the acolyte . . . Sophrona, her name was.'

'It would be.' All the cheap skirts who pretended to play musical instruments were called Sophrona nowadays.

'She was really good, Falco!' I knew what that meant. (Actually, coming from Thalia it meant she *was* really good.) 'She could play,' Thalia confirmed. 'There were plenty of parasites taking advantage of the Emperor's interest.' She was referring to Nero, the water-organ fanatic, not our present endearing specimen. Vespasian's most famous musical trait was going to sleep during Nero's lyre performances, for which he had been lucky to escape with nothing worse than a few months' exile. 'A true artiste, Sophrona was.'

'Musicianship?' I queried innocently.

'A lovely touch . . . And looks! When Sophrona pumped out her tunes men rose in their seats.'

I took it at face value, not looking at Helena, who was supposed to have been politely brought up. Nevertheless I heard her giggling shamelessly before she asked, 'Had she been with you long?'

'Virtually from babyhood. Her mother was a lanky chorus dancer in a mime group I once ran into. Reckoned she couldn't look after a child. Couldn't be bothered, more like. I saved the scrap, fostered her out until she was a useful age, then taught her what I could. She was too tall for an acrobat, but luckily she turned out to be musical, so when I saw that the hydraulus was the instrument of the moment I grabbed the chance and got Sophrona trained. I paid for it, at a time when I wasn't doing so well as nowadays, so I'm annoyed at losing her.'

'Tell us what happened, Thalia?' I asked. 'How could an expert like you be so careless as to lose valuable talent from your troupe?'

'It wasn't me who lost her!' Thalia snorted. 'That fool Fronto. He was showing some prospective patrons around – Eastern visitors. He reckoned they were theatrical entrepreneurs, but they were time-wasters.'

'Just wanted a free gawp at the menagerie?'

'And at female tumblers with no clothes on. The rest of us could see we hadn't much hope of them hiring us for anything. Even if they had done it would have been all sodomy and mean tips. So nobody took much notice. It was just before the panther got loose and munched up Fronto; naturally things grew rather hectic after that. The Syrians did pay us another hopeful visit, but we pulled down the awnings. They must have left Rome, and then we realised Sophrona had gone too.'

'A man in it?'

'Oh bound to be!'

I noticed Helena smiling again as Thalia exploded with contempt. Then Helena asked, 'At least you know they were Syrian. So who were these visitors?'

'No idea. Fronto was the man in charge,' Thalia grumbled, as if she were accusing him of seedy moral habits. 'Once Fronto ended up inside the panther, all we could remember was that they spoke Greek with a very funny accent, wore stripy robes, and seemed to think somewhere called "the ten Towns" was the tops in civic life.'

'I've heard of the Decapolis,' I said. 'It's a Greek federation in central Syria. That's a long way to go looking for a musician who's done a moonlight.'

'Not to mention the fact that if you do go,' said Helena, 'whichever order you flog around these ten gracious metropolitan sites, she's bound to be in the last town you visit. By the time you get there, you'll be too tired to argue with her.'

'No point anyway,' I added. 'She's probably got a set of twins and marsh fever by now. Don't you have any other facts to go on, Thalia?'

'Only a name one of the menagerie-keepers remembered – Habib.'

'Oh dear. In the East it's probably as common as Gaius,' said Helena. 'Or Marcus,' she added slyly.

'And we know *he's* common!' Thalia joined in.

'Could the girl have gone looking for her mother?' I asked, having had some experience of tracing fostered children.

Thalia shook her head. 'She doesn't know who her mother was.'

'Might the mother have come looking for her?'

'Doubt it. I've heard nothing about her for twenty years. She might be working under a different name. Well, face it, Falco, she's most likely dead by now.'

I agreed the point sombrely. 'So what about the father? Any chance Sophrona heard from him?'

Thalia roared with laughter. 'What father? There were various candidates, none of whom had the slightest interest in being pinned down. As I recall it, only one of them had anything about him, and naturally he was the one the mother wouldn't look at twice.'

'She must have looked once!' I observed facetiously.

Thalia gave me a pitying glance, then said to Helena, 'Explain the facts of life to him, dearie! Just because you go to bed with a man doesn't mean you have to look at the bastard!'

Helena was smiling again, though the expression in her eyes was less charitable. I reckoned it might be time to halt the ribaldry. 'So we're stuck with the "young love" theory?'

'Don't get excited, Falco,' Thalia told me with her usual frankness. 'Sophrona was a treasure and I'd risk a lot to get her back. But I can't afford the fare to send you scavenging in the Orient. Still, next time you have business in the desert, remember me!'

'Stranger things have happened.' I spoke with care. Helena was watching me thoughtfully. 'The East is a lively arena at present. People are talking about the place all the time. Since Jerusalem was captured, the whole area is opening up for expansion.'

'So that's it!' Helena muttered. 'I knew you were up to something again.'

Thalia looked surprised. 'You're really going to Syria?'

'Somewhere close, possibly. Proposals have been whispered in my direction.' For a moment it had seemed easier to break the news to Helena with a witness who was strong enough to prevent me from being beaten up. Like most of my good ideas, I was rapidly losing faith in this one.

33

Unaware of the undercurrents, Thalia asked, 'Would I have to pay you if you did some scouting for me?'

'For a friend I can be commissioned to be paid on results.'

'What about your fare?'

'Ah well! Someone else may be persuaded to come up with the fare – '

'I thought so!' Helena exclaimed, breaking in angrily. 'This will be someone called Vespasian?'

'You know I was intending to tell you – '

'You promised, Marcus. You promised to refuse the work next time.' She stood up and stalked out across the arena to pat the elephant. The set of her back implied it was safer not to follow her.

I watched her go, a tall, dark-haired girl with a straight carriage. Watching Helena was as pleasant as hearing Falernian glug into a winecup, especially when it was my own cup.

Mine she might be, but I still had serious second thoughts about upsetting her.

Thalia was eyeing me shrewdly. 'You're in love!' People always said this with a mixture of wonder and disgust.

'You have a keen grasp of the situation!' I grinned.

'What's the problem between you?'

'There's no problem between us. Just other people who think there ought to be.'

'What other people?'

'Most of Rome.'

Thalia raised her eyes. 'Sounds as if going somewhere else could make life easier!'

'Who wants an easy life?' She knew I was lying about that.

To my relief, once her temper cooled Helen strolled back, leading the elephant, who was now devoted to her. I assumed he realised he would have to shift me before it could do him any good. He nuzzled her ear in a way I liked to do myself, while she bent her head away resignedly, just as if avoiding annoying attentions from me.

'Helena doesn't want you to leave her,' observed Thalia.

'Who said anything about leaving her? Helena Justina is my partner. We share danger and disaster, joy and triumph – '

'Oh very nice!' Thalia commenced, with a sceptical rasp.

Helena had listened to my speech in a way that at least allowed me to make another: 'At the moment I wouldn't mind putting myself a long way from Rome,' I said. 'Especially if the Treasury pays for it. The only issue is whether *Helena* wants to go.'

She accepted my gaze quietly. She too was searching for ways we could live together without interference or pressure from others. Travel was one method we had found that sometimes worked. 'So long as I do have a say in the decision, I'll go where you go, Marcus Didius.'

'That's right, dearie,' Thalia agreed with her. 'Always best to trot along and keep an eye on them!'

ACT ONE : NABATAEA

About a month later. The scene is set initially in Petra, a remote city in the desert. Dramatic mountains dominate on either side. Then on rapidly to Bostra.

SYNOPSIS: *Falco*, an adventurer, and *Helena*, a rash young woman, arrive in a strange city disguised as curious travellers. They are unaware that *Anacrites*, a jealous enemy, has transmitted news of their visit to the one man they need to avoid. When an unpleasant accident befalls *Heliodorus*, a theatrical hack, their help is enlisted by *Chremes*, an actor-producer, but by then everyone is looking nervously for a quick camel ride out of town.

V

We had been following the two men all the way to the High Place. From time to time we heard their voices ringing off the rocks up ahead of us. They were talking in occasional short sentences, like acquaintances who kept the politeness going. Not lost in a deep conversation, not angry, but not strangers either. Strangers would have either walked along in silence or made more of a sustained effort.

I did wonder if they might be priests, going up for a ritual.

'If they are, we should turn back,' Helena suggested. The remark was her only contribution so far that morning. Her tone was cool, sensible, and subtly implying that *I* was a dangerous idiot for bringing us here.

A staid response seemed called for; I put on a frivolous manner: 'I never intrude on religion, particularly when the Lord of the Mountain might demand the ultimate sacrifice.' We knew little of the Petrans' religion, beyond the facts that their chief god was symbolised by blocks of rock and that this strong, mysterious deity was said to require bloodthirsty appeasement, carried out on the mountaintops he ruled. 'My mother wouldn't like her boy to be consecrated to Dushara.'

Helena said nothing.

Helena said nothing, in fact, during most of our climb. We were having a furious argument, the kind that's intensely silent. For this reason, although *we* heard that the two men were toiling up ahead of us, *they* almost certainly failed to notice that we were following. We made no attempt to let them know. It seemed unimportant at the time.

I decided that their intermittent voices were too casual to cause alarm. Even if they were priests they were probably going routinely to sweep away yesterday's offerings (in whatever unlikeable form those offerings took). They might be locals making the trip for a picnic. Most likely they were fellow visitors, just panting up to the sky-high altar out of curiosity.

So we clambered on, more concerned about the steepness of the path and our own quarrel than anybody else.

There were various ways to reach the High Place. 'Some joker down by the temple tried to tell me this route is how they bring the virgins up for sacrifice.'

'*You've* nothing to worry about then!' Helena deigned to utter.

We had taken what appeared to be a gentle flight of steps a little to the left of the theatre. It rapidly steepened, cutting up beside a narrow gorge. We had the rock face on both sides at first, quarried intriguingly and threatening to overhang our way; soon we acquired a narrow but increasingly spectacular defile to our right. Greenery clung to its sides – spear-leafed oleanders and tamarisk among the red, grey and amber striations of the rocks. These were most eye-catching on the cliff face alongside us, where the Nabataeans had carved out their passage to the mountaintop taking their normal delight in revealing the silken patterns of the sandstone.

This was no place for hurrying. The twisting path angled through a rocky corridor and crossed the gorge, widening briefly into a more open space where I snatched my first breather, planning several more before we reached the uppermost heights. Helena paused too, pretending she had only stopped because I was in her way.

'Do you want to get past me?'

'I can wait.' She was gasping. I grinned at her. Then we both turned to face out across Petra, already a fine view, with the widest part of the gravelly road in the valley below snaking away past the theatre and a bunch of tasteful rock-face tombs, then on towards the distant town.

'Are you going to fight with me all day?'

'Probably,' growled Helena.

We both fell silent. Helena surveyed the dusty thongs of her sandals. She was thinking about whatever dark issues had come between us. I kept quiet too, because as usual I was not entirely certain what the quarrel was about.

Getting to Petra had been less difficult than I had feared.

Anacrites had taken great pleasure in implying that my journey here posed intolerable problems. I simply brought us by sea to Gaza. I had 'hired' – at a price that meant 'bought outright' – an ox and cart, transport I was used to handling, then looked around for the trade route. Strangers were discouraged from travelling it, but caravans up to a thousand strong converged on Nabataea each year. They arrived in Petra from several directions, their ways parting again when they left. Some toiled westwards to northern Egypt. Some took the interior road up to Bostra, before going on to Damascus or Palmyra. Many crossed straight to the Judaean coast for urgent shipment from the great port at Gaza to the hungry markets in Rome. So with dozens of merchants trekking towards Gaza, all leading immense, slowly moving strings of camels or oxen, it was no trouble for me as an ex-army scout to trace back their route. No entrepôt can be kept secret. Nor can its guardians prevent penetration of their city by strangers. Petra was essentially a public place.

Even before we arrived I was making mental notes for Vespasian. The rocky approach had been striking, yet there was plenty of greenery. Nabataea was rich in freshwater springs. Reports of flocks and agriculture were correct. They lacked horses, but camels and oxen were everywhere. All along the rift valley was a flourishing mining industry, and we soon discovered that the locals produced pottery of great delicacy, floral platters and bowls in huge quantities, all decorated with panache. In short, even without the income from the merchants, there would be plenty here to attract the benevolent interest of Rome.

'Well!' Helena let slip. 'I reckon you can report back to your masters that the rich kingdom of Nabataea certainly deserves inclusion in the Empire.' She was insultingly equating me with some mad-eyed, province-collecting patriot.

'Don't annoy me, lady – '

'We have so much to offer them!' she quipped; beneath the political irony was a personal sneer at me.

Whether the rich Nabataeans would see things our way might be a different cask of nuts. Helena knew that. They had

41

guarded their independence with skill for several centuries, making it their role to keep the routes across the desert safely open and offer a market to traders of all kinds. They were practised in negotiating peace with would-be invaders, from the successors of Alexander to Pompey and Augustus. They had an amiable monarchy. Their present king, Rabel, was a youth whose mother was acting as regent, an arrangement that seemed to be non-controversial. Much of the routine workload of government fell to the Chief Minister. This more sinister character was referred to as The Brother. I guessed what that meant. Still, so long as the people of Petra were flourishing so vibrantly, I dare say they could put up with somebody to hate and fear. Everyone likes to have a figure of authority to mutter about. You can't blame the weather for all of life's ills.

The weather, incidentally, was fabulous. Sunlight streamed off the rocks, melting everything into a dazzling haze.

We continued our climb.

The second time we stopped, more desperately out of breath, I unhooked a water flask I was carrying on my belt. We sat side by side on a large rock, too hot to fight.

'What's the matter?' Something Helena had said earlier had struck a nerve. 'Finding out that I'm acting for the Chief Spy?'

'Anacrites!' she snorted with contempt.

'So? He's a slug, but no worse than the other slime lovers in Rome.'

'I thought at least you were working for Vespasian. You let me come all this way thinking that – '

'An oversight.' By this time I had convinced myself that was true. 'It just never came up in conversation. Anyway, what's the difference?'

'The difference is, Anacrites when he's acting inde-pendently is a threat to you. I don't trust the man.'

'Neither do I, so you can stop erupting.' Hauling her up here had been an inspired move; I could see she had lost her energy for bickering. I gave her more water. Then I kept her

42

sitting on the rock. The soft sandstone made a tolerable backrest if your back was muscular; I leaned on the rock and made Helena lean against me. 'Look at the view and be friends with the man who loves you.'

'Oh him!' she scoffed.

There was one good thing about this argument: yesterday, when we left the outer caravanserai and entered Petra itself down the famous narrow gorge, we had been squabbling so bitterly none of the guards gave us a second glance. A man listening to his woman complaining about him can ride pretty well anywhere; armed retainers always treat him with sympathy. As they had waved us along the raised causeway and into the rocky cleft, then hurried us on under the monumental arch that marked the way, little did they know that at the same time as she harangued me Helena was reconnoitring their fortifications with eyes as sharp and a mind as acute as Caesar's.

We had already passed enough rock-hewn tombs, free-standing blocks with strange, stepped roofs, inscriptions and carved reliefs to strike a sense of awe. Then had come the forbidding gorge, along which I noticed sophisticated systems of water pipes.

'Pray it doesn't rain!' I muttered, as we lost sight of the entrance behind us. 'A torrent rushes down here, and people get swept away . . .'

Eventually the path had narrowed to a single gloomy track where the rocks seemed ready to meet above our heads; after that the gorge suddenly widened again and we glimpsed the sunlit façade of the Great Temple. Instead of exclaiming with delight Helena muttered, 'Our journey's superfluous. They could hold this entrance against an army, using just five men!'

Emerging through the crack in the rocks, we had drawn up abruptly in front of the temple, as we were intended to. Once I got my breath back from gasping with awe, I commented, 'I thought you were going to say, "*Well, Marcus, you may never have shown me the Seven Wonders of the World, but at least you've brought me to the Eighth!*" '

We stood in silence for a moment.

'I like the goddess in the round pavilion between the broken pediments,' said Helena.

43

'Those are what I call really smart entablatures,' I answered, playing the architectural snob. 'What do you think is in the big orb on top of the goddess's pavilion?'

'Bath oils.'

'Of course!'

After a moment, Helena carried on where she had left off just before we reached this fabulous spectacle: 'So Petra lies in a mountain enclave. But there are other entrances? I had the impression this was the only one.' Dear gods, she was single-minded. Anacrites should be paying her instead of me.

Some Romans get away with treating their womenfolk like mindless ornaments, but I knew I stood no chance of that so I answered calmly, 'That's the impression the cautious Nabataeans like to give. Now gape at the opulent rock carving, sweetheart, and try to look as if you just popped this side of the mountain to buy a pair of Indian earrings and a length of turquoise silk.'

'Don't mix me up with your previous trashy girlfriends!' she rounded on me crossly, as a Nabataean irregular who was obviously checking for suspicious faces wandered past. Helena took my point. 'I may buy a bale in its natural state, but I'll have it bleached a good plain white at home . . .'

We had passed muster. Easily fooled, these guards! Either that, or they were sentimentalists who could not bear to arrest a hen-pecked man.

There had not been, yesterday, much time for me to sort out what lay behind Helena's wrath. Nervous about how long we could keep up our act as innocent travellers, I had taken us very hastily into town along the dry dirt track that curved away past numerous cliffside tombs and temples. We noticed that although this was a desert, there were gardens everywhere. The Nabataeans possessed spring water, and made the most of conserving rainfall. For people still close to their nomadic roots, they were surprisingly fine engineers. All the same it *was* a desert; when it did rain on our journey, a shower had covered our clothing with fine reddish dust, and when we combed our hair, black grit had worked in right to the scalp.

At the end of the track lay a settlement, with many fine houses and public buildings as well as a tightly packed

44

lower-class habitation full of small square dwellings, each set behind its own walled courtyard. I had found us a room, at a price that showed the Petrans knew exactly what a room was worth in the middle of the desert. Then I spent the evening scouting the walls to the north and south of the city. They were nothing spectacular, for the Nabataeans had long preferred to make treaties rather than physically resist hostility – a trick made easier by their custom of offering to guide invading troops through the desert, then taking the longest, most difficult route so that the troops arrived at Petra too exhausted to start fighting. (Most armies lack Helena's stamina.)

She was looking at me now in a way that made her considerably more attractive than most armies. She was completely wrapped in stoles against the heat, so she looked cool, though I could feel her warmth as I held her against me. She smelled of sweet almond oil.

'This is a wonderful place,' she conceded. Her voice had dropped to a murmur. Those rich dark eyes of hers still flashed, but I had fallen in love with Helena when she was angry; she was well aware of the effect it still had on me. 'I certainly see the world with you.'

'That's generous.' I fought back, though with a familiar sense of imminent surrender. At even closer quarters our eyes met. Hers were not scathing at all when you knew her, but redolent of good humour and intelligence. 'Helena, are you following the local rule of suing for peace?'

'Better to safeguard what you have,' she agreed. 'It's a good Petran system.'

'Thanks.' I favour the laconic in negotiation. I hoped Helena had not heard of the Nabataeans' other political custom: sending away their won-over opponents with large quantities of treasure. The Falco purse, as usual, was not up to it.

'Yes, you can skip the exorbitant gifts,' she smiled, though I had said nothing.

Asserting my rights, I slid my other arm around her. It was accepted as a term in the treaty. I started to feel happy again.

The sun beat down on the glowing rocks, where huge clumps of dark tulips with dusty leaves clung tenaciously. The voices ahead of us had passed out of earshot. We were alone in the warm silence, in what seemed a not unfriendly place.

Helena and I had a history of friendly relations near the tops of famous mountains. Taking a girl to see a spectacular view has only one purpose, to my mind, and if a man can achieve the same purpose halfway up the hill, he saves some energy for better things. I gathered Helena closer and settled down to enjoy as much playful recreation as she was likely to allow us alongside a public footpath that might be frequented by stern-visaged priests.

VI

'Anyway, was it really an oversight?' Helena asked some time later – a girl not easily deflected. If she was thinking that letting me kiss her had softened me up, she was right.

'Forgetting to mention Anacrites? Certainly. I don't lie to you.'

'Men always say that.'

'Sounds as if you've been talking to Thalia. I can't be held responsible for all the other lying bastards.'

'And usually you say it in the middle of an argument.'

'So you reckon it's just the line I use? Wrong, lady! But even if that were true, we do need to preserve a few escape routes! I want us to survive together,' I told her piously. (Frank talk always disarmed Helena, since she expected me to be devious.) 'Don't you?'

'Yes,' she said. Helena never messed me around playing coy. I could tell her that I loved her without feeling embarrassed, and I knew I could rely on her to be equally frank: she thought I was unreliable. Despite that she added, 'A girl doesn't come this far across the world with a mere Thursday-afternoon dalliance!'

I kissed her again. 'Thursday afternoons? Is that when senators' wives and daughters have free run of the gladiators' barracks?' Helena wriggled furiously, which might have led to more playfulness had our baking rock seat not lain right alongside a well-beaten track. A stone fell somewhere. We both remembered the voices we had heard, and were afraid their owners might be coming back. I did wonder if I could take us off up the hillside, but its steepness and stoniness looked unpromising.

I loved travelling with Helena – except for the frustrating series of small cabins and cramped hired rooms where we never felt free to make love. Suddenly I was longing for our sixth-floor tenement apartment, where few interlopers struggled up the stairs and only rooftop pigeons could overhear.

'Let's go home!'

'What – to our rented room?'

'To Rome.'

'Don't be silly,' scoffed Helena. 'We're going up to see the mountaintop.'

My only interest in the mountaintop had been the possibilities it offered for grappling Helena. Nevertheless I put on my serious traveller's face and we continued uphill.

The summit was announced by a pair of unequal obelisks. Perhaps they represented gods. If so, they were crude, mysterious, and definitely alien to the human-featured Roman pantheon. They appeared to have been created not by transporting stones here, but by carving away the entire surrounding rock-bed to a depth of six or seven metres to leave these dramatic sentinels. The effort involved was staggering, and the final effect eerie. They were unidentical twins, one slightly taller, one flared at the base. Beyond lay some sort of strongly built building that we preferred not to investigate in case it was occupied by priests honing sacrificial knives.

We climbed on, reaching the ceremonial area by a steep flight of steps. This brought us out on to a windswept promontory. On all sides the high, airy rock offered staggering views of the circlet of harsh mountains within which Petra lies. We had emerged on the north side of a slightly sunken rectangular court. Around it had been cut three benches, presumably for spectators, like the triple couches in a formal dining room. Ahead of us lay a raised platform on which were displayed offerings that we tactfully ignored. To the right, steps led to the main altar. There a tall column of black stone represented the god. Beyond him lay another, larger, round altar like a basin cut from the living rock, connected by a channel to a rectangular water tank.

By now my imagination was working at a hairy pace. I hoped I was impervious to awe-striking locations and sinister religions, but I had been to Britain, Gaul and Germany; I knew more than I wanted about unpleasant pagan rites. I grasped Helena's hand as the wind buffeted us. She walked fearlessly out on to the sunken court, gazing at the spectacular views as if we were on some balustraded vista provided for the convenience of summer tourists above the Bay of Surrentum.

I was wishing we were. This place gave me a bad feeling. It aroused no sense of reverence. I hate ancient sites where creatures have long been slain for the grim delight of monolithic gods. I especially hate them when the local populace like to pretend, as the Nabataeans did with great relish, that some of the creatures they sacrificed could have been human. Even at that point I felt alert, as if we were walking into trouble.

There was trouble at Dushara's shrine all right, though it did not yet directly involve us. We still had time to avoid it – though not for much longer.

'Well, this is it, my darling. Let's go back now.'

But Helena had spied some new feature. She pushed her hair back out of her eyes and dragged me over to look. To the south of the ceremonial area lay another rectangular reservoir. This one apparently drained the summit to provide an ample supply of fresh water for the rites of sacrifice. Unlike the rest of the High Place, this cistern was occupied.

The man in the water could have been taking a swim in the sunlight. But as soon as I spotted him I knew that he was not floating there for pleasure or exercise.

VII

If I had had any sense I would still have convinced myself he was just bathing peacefully. We could have turned away without staring too closely, then a rapid stroll downhill would have taken us back to our lodging. We should have done that anyway; I should have kept us out of it.

He was almost submerged. His head was under water. Only something bulky, caught under his clothing, was holding him afloat.

We were both already running forwards. 'Unbelievable!' Helena marvelled bitterly as she scrambled down from the sacrificial platform. 'Just two days here, and look what you've found.'

I had reached the rock-formed tank ahead of her. I lowered myself over the edge into the water, trying to forget I couldn't swim. The water came above my waist. The chill made me gasp. It was a large cistern, about four feet deep: ample to drown in.

The swirl of water as I entered caused the body to move and start sinking. I managed to grab at the garments that had helped buoy him up. Arriving a few moments later, we could have avoided this trouble. He would have been lying out of sight on the bottom as the drowned do – assuming, of course, that drowning was the real cause of his death.

Slowly I pulled my burden to the side. An inflated goatskin floated out from under his tangled cloak as I manoeuvred him. Helena leant down and held his feet, then helped me haul him half out of the water. She had the nice manners of any senator's daughter, but no qualms about helping out in an emergency.

I climbed out again. We completed the operation. He was heavy, but together we managed to remove him from the cistern and flop him face down. Without more ado I turned his head sideways. I leaned on his ribs for a respectable period, trying to revive him. I noticed my first shove seemed to expel air rather than water. And there was none of the froth I had seen with other corpses who had drowned. We get plenty in the Tiber.

Helena waited, at first standing above me with the wind blowing her clothes against her body while she gazed thoughtfully around the high plateau. Then she walked to the far side of the cistern, examining the ground.

As I worked I was thinking things through. Helena and I had been climbing quite slowly, and our pause for recreation had taken up time. But for that, we would have arrived at the crucial moment. But for that, we would be sharing the fabulous windswept views with two men, both alive.

We had come too late for this one. I knew even before I started that my efforts would be useless. Still, I gave him the courtesy. I might need to be resuscitated by a stranger myself one day.

Eventually I rolled him over on his back and stood up again.

He was fortyish. Too fat and flabby. A wide, berry-brown face with a heavy chin and thuggish neck. The face looked mottled under its tan. Short arms; broad hands. He had not troubled himself with shaving today. Lank, rather long hair merged with coarse black eyebrows and dripped sluggishly on to the rock floor beneath him. He was dressed in a long, loose-weave brown tunic, with a more sun-bleached cloak tangled wetly around him. Shoes knotted on top of the foot, a toe-thong apiece. No weapon. Something bulky under his clothes at the waist, however – a writing tablet, not written on.

Helena held out something else she had found beside the cistern – a round-bottomed flask on a plaited leather cord. Its wicker casing, stained brown with wine, made me pull out the stopper: wine had been in it recently, though only a couple of drops shook out on to my palm. Maybe the goatskin had contained wine too. Being tipsy could explain how he came to be overpowered.

His attire was Eastern, protecting him from the burning heat. Those swathes of cloth would have impeded his movements if he had been struggling to escape an attacker. I had no doubt he had been attacked. His face was grazed and cut, probably where he had been pushed bodily over the edge of the water tank. Then someone must have jumped in alongside, probably not to hold his head under; marks on his neck looked more like strangulation to me. Helena showed me that in addition to the ground that had been soaked when I clambered out, beside the tank on the far side was a similar wet area where the killer must have emerged sopping wet. The sun had made his tracks faint already, but Helena had found them leading back towards the ceremonial platform.

We left the body and recrossed the summit in front of the altar. The trail petered out, already evaporated by sun and wind. To the north we found a moon god's shrine with two crescent-crowned pillars flanking a niche; beyond that lay a wide staircase leading downwards. But now we could hear voices approaching – a large number of people, intoning a low ceremonial chant. This was plainly a major ceremonial route to the High Place. I doubted whether the killer could have rushed down that way, or the procession now winding up the stairs would have been disturbed.

Helena and I turned away and climbed back by the same steps that had brought us up. We scrambled down as far as the priests' house or guardpost. We could have knocked and asked for help. Why take the easy way? Still loath to encounter anybody with a sharp implement who might view me as an easy catch for the altar, I convinced myself the murderer would have crept past anonymously too.

Now I noticed a second path. This must be the one he had taken; he had certainly not passed us while we were canoodling. Helena was a senator's daughter after all; she was supposed to know the meaning of modesty. We had been alert for voyeurs.

I never know when to leave well alone. 'Go down,' I commanded Helena. 'Either wait for me near the theatre, or I'll see you back at the lodging. Go down the same way we came up.'

She made no protest. The sight of the dead man's face must have stayed in her mind. Anyway, her attitude mirrored my own. I would have done this in Rome; being a visiting flea on the rump of civilisation changed nothing. Somebody had just killed this man, and I was going after whoever did it. Helena knew I had no choice. Helena would have come with me if she could cover ground as fast.

I touched her gently on the cheek and felt her fingers brush my wrist. Then without a second thought I started down the path.

VIII

This path was much less steep than the one we had come up by. It seemed to be heading into the city, a much longer way down. Sudden wicked turns forced me to watch my footing above astounding aerial vistas that would have made me quake if there had been time to look at them properly.

I was trying to be quiet as I hurried. Though I had no reason to think the fleeing man knew pursuit was hot on his tail, murderers rarely hang about studying the view.

I was passing through another valley gorge cut by watercourses, like the one that had brought Helena and me to the summit. Flights of steps, inscriptions in the cliff face, sharp corners and short stretches of narrow corridor led me downhill as far as a rock-carved lion. Five strides in length and pleasingly weathered, he served as a fountain; a straight channel brought fresh water down through a pipe and out of his mouth. Now I was certain the killer had come this way, for the sandstone ledge beneath the lion's head was damp, as if a man with wet clothing had sat there snatching a drink. I splashed water hastily over my own forehead, thanked the lion for his information, and rushed on again.

The water that had flowed through the lion now trickled downhill in a waist-high runnel cut into the cliff face, keeping me company. I stumbled down a steeply winding flight of steps then found myself in a secluded stretch of the wadi. Overhung by oleanders and tulips, its peaceful stillness nearly made me abandon my quest. But I hate murder. I strode on. The path came to a pleasant temple: two free-standing columns in a pilastered frame, with a shrine behind, darkly dug out of the mountain like a cavern. The portico was approached by wide steps, a parched garden in their base. There I saw an elderly Nabataean priest and a younger man, also a priest. I had the impression they had just come out from the temple sanctum. Both were gazing downhill.

My arrival made both of them gape at me instead. In Latin first, automatically, then in careful Greek I asked the elder man if anyone had just passed that way in a hurry. He merely stared at me. There was no way I could attempt the local Arabic tongue. Then the younger man suddenly spoke to him as if translating. I explained briskly that somebody had died at the High Place, apparently not by accident. This too was relayed, without much result. Impatient, I started walking on again. The elder priest spoke. The younger one came straight out from the garden, and loped downhill alongside me. He said nothing, but I accepted his company. Glancing back I saw that the other had turned to go to the place of sacrifice and investigate.

My new ally had a dark desert-dweller's skin and intense eyes. He was wearing a long white tunic that flapped around his ankles, but he managed to shift along pretty fast. Although he never spoke I felt we had shared motives. So, feeling slightly better than strangers, we hurried downhill together and eventually reached the city wall, far over in the western precincts, where the main habitation lay.

We had passed no one. Once we entered by the city gate there were people everywhere, and no way of discerning the man we sought. His clothes must be dry by now, as mine almost were. There seemed nothing else I could do. But the young man with me still strode ahead, so I found myself drawn along with him.

We had emerged close to the public monuments. Passing through an area of impressive homes built from well-dressed sandstone blocks, we reached the craftsmen's quarter on the main thoroughfare. The gravelled street cried out for decent paving and colonnades, but possessed its own exotic grandeur. Here, the great covered markets lay to our left, with an area of casual stalls and tethering posts between them. The main watercourse ran along-side this street, about ten feet below. Poky stairways ran down to that lower level, while handsome bridges spanned the gulley to reach important buildings on the far side – the royal palace, and one of the monumental temples that dominated this part of the city. These lay on wide terraces and were approached by spectacular flights of steps.

We were heading purposefully past them to the large terminal gate. This, I knew, was the heart of the city. Impressive temples stood back from the street on either side, though the greatest temple lay ahead of us within the sanctuary area. We reached and crossed a small piazza, then went through the tall gateway, which had massive doors folded back. Immediately inside were administrative buildings. My young priest stopped there and spoke to someone in a doorway but then pressed on, waving me to accompany him. We had entered a long open space, enclosed by a high wall on the watercourse side – a typically Eastern temple sanctuary. Stone benches ran around the perimeter. At the far end on a raised platform was an open-air altar. This lay in front of Petra's main temple, dedicated to Dushara, the mountain-god.

It was a colossal structure. We clambered up to an immense, marble-clad platform approached by wide marble steps. Four plain but massive pillars formed a portico, deep in welcome shade, below a rather static frieze of rosettes and triglyphs. The Greeks had been to Petra, possibly by invitation. They had left their mark in the carved work, yet it was a fleeting influence, quite unlike the domination they exerted on Roman art.

Within, we came to a vast entrance chamber where high windows lit elaborately moulded plasterwork and wall frescos of architectural patterns. A character who was evidently a very senior priest had noticed us. My companion marched forwards in his dogged way. I would have had about two seconds to turn around and make a run for it. I had done nothing wrong, so I stood my ground. Sweat trickled down my back. Hot and exhausted, it was difficult to assume my normal air of confidence. I felt far from home, in a land where mere innocence might be no defence.

Our news was relayed. There came a sudden upsurge of chatter, as there normally is when an unnatural death has been announced unexpectedly in a public place. The sacrilege had caused a shock. The senior functionary jumped, as if it were the most alarming event of the last six months. He gabbled away in the local dialect, then appeared

to reach a decision; he exclaimed some formal pronounce-
ment, and made a couple of urgent gestures.

My young companion turned and finally spoke: 'You must
tell this!'

'Certainly,' I answered, in my role as an honest traveller.
'Whom shall I tell?'

'He will come.' To sensitive ears it had an ominous ring.

I recognised my predicament. A person of extreme
consequence was about to interest himself in my story. I had
been hoping to remain unobtrusive in Petra. As a Roman who
was not a valid trader my presence here would be awkward to
explain. Something told me that drawing attention to myself
might be a very bad idea. Still, it was too late now.

We had to wait.

In the desert, extremes of climate and distance encourage a
leisurely attitude. Quick settlement of crises would be bad
manners. People like to savour news.

I was led back outside: Dushara's temple was no place for a
curious foreigner. I regretted this, for I would have liked to
appreciate the fantastic interior with its striking ornamenta-
tion; to explore beyond the high arch leading to the dim inner
sanctum, and climb up to the intriguing upper-storey
balconies. But after one swift glimpse of a tall dark god with
clenched fists gazing out towards his mountains, I was hustled
away.

From the first I realised that hanging about for the
anonymous great one was going to be a trial. I wondered
where Helena was. I gave up on the idea of sending her a
message. Our address would be difficult to describe and I had
nothing to write on. I wished I had brought the corpse's
note-tablet; he had no use for it now.

The young priest had been designated my official minder.
That failed to make him communicative. He and I sat on one
of the benches around the sanctuary, where he was
approached by various acquaintances, but I was studiously
ignored. I was growing restless. I had a strong sensation of
sinking into a situation I would very much regret. I resigned

57

myself to a lost day, with trouble at the end of it. Besides that, it was clear I would miss lunch – the kind of habit I deplore.

To overcome my depression, I insisted on making conversation with the priest. 'Did you see the fugitive? What did he look like?' I asked firmly in Greek.

Addressed so directly it was hard for him refuse me. 'A man.'

'Old? Young? My age?'

'I did not see.'

'You couldn't see his face? Or only his back disappearing? Did he have all his hair? Could you see its colouring?'

'I did not see.'

'You're not much help,' I told him frankly.

Annoyed and frustrated, I fell silent. In the slow, aggravating way of the desert, just when I had given up on him, my companion explained: 'I was within the temple. I heard footsteps, running. I went out and glimpsed a man far away, as he passed out of sight.'

'So you didn't notice anything about him? Was he slight or tall? Light or heavy?'

The young priest considered. 'I could not tell.'

'This fellow will be easy to spot!'

After a second the priest smiled, unexpectedly seeing the joke. He still felt disinclined to communicate, but he was getting the hang of the game now. Softening up, he volunteered brightly: 'I could not see his hair – he wore a hat.'

A hat was unexpected. Most people around here wrapped their heads in their robes. 'What sort of hat?' He gestured a widish brim, looking slightly disapproving. This was a definite rarity. Since Helena and I landed at Gaza we had seen lolling Phrygian caps, tight little skullcaps, and flat-topped felt circles, but a brimmed hat was a Western extravagance.

Confirming my own thoughts, he then said, 'A foreigner, alone and in a great hurry near the High Place, is unusual.'

'You could tell he was a foreigner? How?' The man shrugged.

I knew one reason: the hat. But people can always tell if they get a proper look at someone. Build, colouring, a way of walking, a style of beard or haircut all give a clue. Even a glimpse for a fraction of a second might do it. Or not a glimpse, but a sound: 'He came down whistling,' said the priest suddenly.

'Really? Know the tune?'

'No.'

'Any other colourful details?' He shook his head, losing interest.

That seemed to be as far as I could take it. I had a tantalising impression, from which nobody would be able to identify the fugitive.

We resumed our boring wait. I started to feel depressed again. The hot golden light, bouncing back from the stonework, was giving me a headache.

People came and went; some sat on the benches chewing or humming to themselves. Many ignored the seats but squatted in the shade, giving me a sharp feeling of being among nomads who despised furniture. I told myself not to feel complacent. These leathery men in dusty cloaks looked only one step up from beggars and one stride short of the grave; yet they belonged to the richest nation in the world. They handled frankincense and myrrh as casually as my own relatives inspected three radishes and a cabbage. Each wrinkled old prune probably had more gold in the saddle-bags of his camel train than Rome possessed in the whole Temple of Saturn Treasury.

Thinking ahead, I tried to plan an escape. I realised I stood no chance of sliding out of trouble with the traditional diplomacy; the meagre funds at my disposal would make an insulting bribe.

We were under obvious scrutiny, though it was polite. If you sat on the steps of the Forum Basilica for such a length of time you would fall prey to rude comments and be openly accosted by pickpockets, poets and prostitutes, sellers of lukewarm rissoles, and forty bores trying to tell you the story of their lives. Here they just waited to see what I would do; they liked their tedium bland.

The first hint of action: a small camel was led in through the arch of the great gate, carrying over its back the man I had found drowned. A quiet but curious crowd came following.

Simultaneously someone strode out from a great doorway cut through the enclosure wall. I never found out what lay behind it, whether the area beyond that impressive-looking portal housed the quarters of the priestly college, or was this high official's own stately residence. Somehow I knew he was important even before I looked at him directly. He carried the aura of power.

He was walking straight towards us. He was alone, but every man in the place was aware of him. Apart from a jewelled belt and a neat, high head-dress with a Parthian look to it, little marked him out. My priestly companion hardly moved or changed expression, yet I sensed a frantic upsurge of tension in him.

'Who is it?' I managed to mutter.

For reasons I could guess, the young man could barely croak out his answer. 'The Brother,' he said. And now I could tell that he was terrified.

IX

I stood up.

Like most Nabataeans the Petran Chief Minister was shorter than me, and slighter. He wore the usual full-length, long-sleeved tunic with other robes in fine material folded back over his upper arms. That was how I could see the glittering belt. There was a dagger thrust through it, with a ruby set in the hilt that barely left room for the handle's ornate metalwork. He had a high forehead, his hair well receded under the head-dress, and his manner was energetic. The wide mouth gave an impression of smiling pleasantly, though I did not fall into the trap of believing it. He looked like a friendly banker – one with his heart set on diddling you on your interest rate.

'Welcome to Petra!' He had a deep, resonant voice. He had spoken in Greek.

'Thank you.' I tried to make my accent as Athenian as possible – not easy when you've been taught your Greek under a ripped awning on a dusty street corner near the neighbourhood middenheap.

'Shall we see what you have found for us?' It was like an invitation to open a basket of presents from an uncle in the country.

His eyes gave the game away. The lids were so deeply pouched and crinkled that no expression was visible in those dark, faraway glints. I hate men who hide what they think. This one had the difficult manner I normally associate with a vicious fornicating fraud who has kicked his mother to death.

We walked to the camel, which thrust its head towards us unnervingly. Someone grabbed the bridle, hissing at its disrespect for my companion. Two men lifted down the body, fairly gently. The Brother inspected the corpse just as I had done previously. It appeared an intelligent scrutiny. People stood back, watching him earnestly. Among the crowd I

61

recognised the elder priest from the temple with the garden, though he made no move to contact his young colleague, who was now standing behind me. I tried to believe the youngster was there in case I needed support, but help seemed unlikely. I was on my own with this.

'What do we know of this person?' The Brother asked, addressing me. I gathered that I was expected to take responsibility for explaining the stranger.

I indicated the writing block at the dead man's waist. 'A scholar or clerk maybe.' Then I pointed to the grazes on the broad, slightly puffy face. 'He had clearly suffered violence, though not an extreme beating. I found empty drinking vessels at the scene.'

'This occurred at the High Place?' The Brother's tone was not particularly angry, but the careful posing of the question spoke volumes.

'Apparently. Seems to be some drunk who fell out with his friend.'

'You saw them?'

'No. I had heard voices, though. They sounded amiable. I had no reason to rush up after them and investigate.'

'What was your own purpose in visiting the Place of Sacrifice?'

'Reverent curiosity,' I stated. It sounded unconvincing and crass, of course. 'I had been told it is not forbidden?'

'It is not forbidden,' agreed The Brother, as if he thought that in a just world it should have been. Legislation seemed likely to emanate from his office later that afternoon.

I took a stand. 'I believe that is all the help I can give you.' My remark was ignored. If a foreign visitor foolishly came across a drowned man in the Basin of Fundanus in Rome, he would be thanked for his sense of civic duty, given a public reward of modest proportions, and led quietly out of town – or so I told myself. Maybe I was wrong. Maybe he would be flung into the worst jail available, to teach him not to malign the Golden Citadel with sordid discoveries.

The Brother stood back from crouching over the corpse. 'And what is your name?' he enquired, fixing me with those pleasant dark eyes. From deep in their wrinkled pouches of weariness those eyes had already noted the cut of my tunic and style of my sandals. I knew he knew that I was Roman.

'Didius Falco,' I answered, with a more or less clear conscience. 'A traveller from Italy – '

'*Ah yes!*' he said.

My heart sank. My name was already known here. Somebody had warned the King's Chief Minister to expect me. I could guess who it was. I had told everyone at home that I was going to the Decapolis on a seek-and-retrieve for Thalia's water organist. Apart from Helena Justina, only one person knew I was coming here: Anacrites.

And if Anacrites had written ahead to the Nabataeans, then as sure as honey makes your teeth rot, he wasn't asking The Brother to extend me any diplomatic courtesies.

X

I would have liked to punch The Brother in the solar plexus and make a run for it. If, as I guessed, he was hated and feared in Petra, then the crowd might let me through. If he was hated and feared even more than I suspected, however, it might be to their advantage to avert his wrath by stopping me.

We Romans are a civilised nation. I kept my fists at my sides and faced him out. 'Sir, I am a man of humble origins. I am surprised you know of me.' He made no attempt to explain. It was vital that I found out his source of information, and quickly. There was no point trying to bluff. 'Can I guess that you heard about me from a functionary called Anacrites? And did he ask you to put me top of the list for sacrifice in Dushara's High Place?'

'Dushara requires immolation only from the pure!' commented The Brother. He had a gentle line in sarcasm — the most dangerous kind. I was in a tricky situation here, and he liked the fact that I was aware of it.

I noticed him make a surreptitious gesture to tell the surrounding crowd to stand off somewhat. A space promptly cleared. I was to be interrogated with a modicum of privacy.

Ignoring the disturbance, I answered him lightly: 'No doubt Petra has other quick and easy systems of disposal?'

'Oh yes. You can be laid out on an offering block for the birds and the sun.' He sounded as if he would enjoy giving the order. Just what I always wanted: to die by being frizzled like offal, then picked clean by a clan of vultures.

'I look forward to the privilege! And what have you been told about me?'

'Naturally that you are a spy.' He appeared to be making a polite joke of it. Somehow I felt no urge to grin at the pleasantry. That was information on which he would certainly act.

'Ah, the usual diplomatic nicety! Do you believe it though?'

'Should I?' he asked, still giving me the dubious courtesy of appearing open and frank. A clever man. Neither vain nor corrupt: nothing to bite back against.

'Oh I think so,' I replied, employing similar tactics. 'Rome has a new emperor, an efficient one for once. Vespasian is taking stock; that includes surveying all the territory which borders on his own. You must have been expecting visitors.'

We both glanced down at the body. He deserved more personal consideration. Instead, some tawdry domestic quarrel had made him an opportunity for this unexpected high-flown discussion of world events. Whoever he was, he had wound himself into my mission. His fate was welded to mine.

'What is Vespasian's interest in Petra?' The Brother asked. His eyes were sly, deceptive slits in that passionless face. A man so astute must know exactly what Rome's interest would be in a rich nation that controlled important trade routes just outside our own boundaries.

I can argue politics as fiercely as the next man who is standing around the Forum with two hours to fill before dinner, but I did not relish putting the Empire's point of view in a foreign city. Not when nobody at the Palace had bothered to instruct me what the Empire's foreign policy was supposed to be. (Nor when the Emperor, being pedantic about such trifles, was likely to hear about my answer sooner or later.) I tried to escape. 'I can't answer you, sir. I'm just a humble information-gatherer.'

'Not so humble, I think!' It sounded elegant in Greek, but was not a compliment. He could sneer without the slightest change of expression.

The Brother folded his arms, still staring down at the dead man lying at our feet. Water from the sodden body and its clothing had seeped into the paving. Every fibre within the cadaver must be growing cold; soon flies would be coming to look for egg-laying sites. 'What is your quality? Do you have many possessions?'

'My house is poor,' I answered. Then I remembered Helena reading out to me a passage from a historian who said the Nabataeans particularly prized the acquisition of

65

possessions. I managed to make my remark sound like polite modesty by adding, 'Though it has seen feasting with the son of the Emperor.' The Nabataeans were supposed to enjoy a good feast, and most cultures are impressed by men who dine freely with their own rulers.

My information left The Brother looking thoughtful. Well it might. My relationship with Titus Caesar had its puzzling aspects, plus one that was perfectly clear: we both hankered for the same girl. Unsure of the Nabataean attitude to women, I kept quiet on this subject.

I thought about it aplenty. Every time I went somewhere dangerous abroad, I wondered if Titus was hoping that I never came back. Maybe Anacrites was not merely plotting to get rid of me for his own reasons; perhaps he had sent me here on prompting from Titus. For all I knew, the Chief Spy's letter to The Brother had suggested that Titus Caesar, the heir to the Empire, would deem it a personal favour if I stayed at Petra for a very long time: for ever, for instance.

'My visit has no sinister implications,' I assured Petra's minister, trying not to look depressed. 'Rome's knowledge of your famous city is somewhat thin and out of date. We rely on a few very old writings that are said to be based on eye-witness reports, chief among them an account by Strabo. This Strabo had his facts from Athenodorus, who was tutor to the Emperor Augustus. *His* value as an eye-witness may be tempered by the fact that he was blind. Our sharp new Emperor distrusts such stuff.'

'So Vespasian's curiosity is scholarly?' queried The Brother.

'He is a cultured man.' That was to say he was on record as once quoting a rude line from a play by Menander concerning a chap with an enormous phallus, which by the standards of previous emperors made Vespasian a highly educated wit.

But it was Vespasian the crusty old general who must preoccupy foreign politicians. 'True,' The Brother pointed out. 'But he is also a strategist.'

I decided to stop feinting. 'And a pragmatic one. He has plenty to occupy his energies within his own borders. If he believes the Nabataeans are interested only in pursuing their

66

own affairs peacefully, you can rely on it that he will elect, like his predecessors, to make gestures of friendship to Petra.'

'And were you sent to say that?' queried The Brother, rather haughtily. For once I saw him tighten his mouth. So the Petrans *were* afraid of Rome – which meant there were terms we might negotiate.

I lowered my voice. 'If and when Rome chooses to assimilate Nabataea within its Empire, then Nabataea will come to us. This is a fact. It is no treachery towards you, and perhaps not even an unkindness, to state it.' I was taking a lot upon myself here, even by my risky standards. 'I am a simple man, but it seems to me that time is not yet here. Even so, Nabataea might do well to plan ahead. You lie in an enclave between Judaea and Egypt, so the questions are not *will* you join the Empire, but when and on what terms. At present these are within your own control. A partnership could be achieved both peacefully and at a time that suited you.'

'This is what your Emperor says to me?' queried The Brother. Since I had been told by Anacrites to avoid official contact, I had of course been given no instructions about speaking for Vespasian.

'You will realise,' I confessed frankly, 'I am a fairly low-grade messenger.' The hooded eyes darkened angrily. One lean hand played with the jewelled dagger at his belt. 'Don't be insulted,' I urged him quietly. 'The advantage to you is that a higher-powered embassy would necessitate action. Important men sent on delicate missions expect results; they have careers to found. The day you find a Roman senator measuring your civic monuments, you'll know he's trying to find a space for a statue of himself in a laurel wreath, looking like a conqueror. But any report *I* make can be filed away in a casket if Vespasian wants to preserve the status quo.'

'Assuming you make a report!' The Brother rejoined, going back to the fun of threatening me.

I was blunt. 'Best that I do. Pegging me out on top of one of your crow-step altars could rebound on you. The peremptory death of a Roman citizen – which I am, despite shabby appearances – might be a neat excuse for sending in a Roman army and annexing Nabataea immediately.'

67

The Brother smiled faintly at this idea. The death of an informer, travelling without official documents, was unlikely to justify world-scale political initiatives. Besides, Anacrites had told him I was coming. Apart from his personal hatred of me, in diplomatic terms that was probably meant as a warning to the Nabataeans: *Here's one observer you know about; there may be others you fail to detect. Rome feels so confident, she's even spying on you openly.*

My own fate was not a diplomatic issue. Anyone who took a dislike to my face could safely cast my corpse on their local rubbish tip. Accepting it, I smiled back peacefully.

At our feet the man who really was dead still waited for attention.

'Falco, what does this unknown body have to do with you?'

'Nothing. I found him. It was coincidence.'

'He brought you to me.'

Coincidence has a habit of landing me in tight situations. 'Neither the victim nor his killer knew me. I have merely reported the incident.'

'Why did you do that?' enquired The Brother sedately.

'I believe his killer should be traced and brought to justice.'

'There are laws in the desert!' he rebuked me, his deep voice soft.

'I was not suggesting otherwise. For that reason I alerted you.'

'You may have wished to remain silent!' He was still niggling about my role in Petra.

Reluctantly I conceded: 'It might have been more convenient! I'm sorry if you have been informed I'm a spy. To get this in perspective, let me tell you that your helpful informant is also the man who paid me to come here.'

The Brother smiled. More than ever he looked like somebody you wouldn't trust to hold your purse while you were undressing at the baths. 'Didius Falco, you have dangerous friends.'

'He and I were never friends.'

We had stood talking in the open outdoor area for much longer than could be customary. At first it must have appeared to the onlookers that we were speculating about the dead man. Now people in the crowd were growing restless as they sensed more going on.

This corpse had become a useful cover for The Brother. It could well be that at some future date the sensible Nabataeans would hand themselves over to Rome on negotiated terms – but there would be ample preparation. No disturbing rumour would be permitted to ruffle commerce prematurely. At this stage The Brother needed to hide from his people the fact that he had been talking with an official from Rome.

Suddenly my interview reached its end. The Brother told me that he would see me again tomorrow. He stared at the young priest for a moment, said something in Arabian, then instructed him in Greek to conduct me to my lodging. I understood that all too well: I had been released on parole. I was being watched. I would not be permitted to inspect places they wished to keep secret. I would not be allowed free talk with the populace. Meanwhile, a decision on whether or not to let me leave Petra would be taken without my knowledge and without leave to appeal.

From now on, the Chief Minister would always know where I was. All my movements and even my continued existence, were at his whim. In fact, it struck me he was the sort of unreliable potentate who could well send me off now with a smile and a promise of mint tea and sesame cakes tomorrow – then dispatch his executioner after me in half an hour's time.

I was escorted from the sanctuary. I had no idea what was intended for the corpse. I never did find out what happened to it.

But that would not be my last connection with the man I had found on the High Place of Sacrifice.

XI

Helena was waiting in our room. Expecting trouble, she had dressed her hair neatly in a decorated net, though she covered it demurely with a white stole when we entered. Discreet strands of beads were evenly hung on her fine bosom; hints of gold glinted at the tips of her ears. She was sitting very upright. Her hands were folded; her ankles crossed. She looked severe and expectant. There was a stillness about her that spoke of quality.

'This is Helena Justina,' I informed the young priest, as if he ought to treat her respectfully. 'I am Didius Falco, as you know. And you are?'

This time he could not ignore it. 'My name is Musa.'

'We have been adopted as personal guests of The Brother,' I stated, for Helena's benefit. Maybe I could impose duties of hospitality on the priest. (Maybe not.) 'Musa, at The Brother's request, is to look after us while we are in Petra.'

I could see that Helena understood.

Now we all knew everyone. All we had to do was communicate.

'How are we off for languages?' I asked, making it a matter of politeness. I was wondering how to shake Musa loose and drag Helena safely out of here. 'Helena is fluent in Greek; she used to kidnap her brothers' tutor. Musa speaks Greek, Arabic and I presume Aramaic. My Latin's low class but I can insult an Athenian, read the price-list in a Gallic inn or ask what's for breakfast of a Celt . . . Let's stick with Greek,' I offered gallantly, then switched to Latin, using an impenetrable street dialect. 'What's the news, beautiful?' I asked Helena, as if I were accosting her in an Aventine fish market. Even if Musa understood more Latin than he was letting on, this ought to fool him. The only problem was, a respectable young noblewoman born in a Capena Gate mansion might not understand me either.

I helped Helena unpack some olives we had bought earlier that day; it seemed like weeks ago.

Helena busied herself dividing salad into bowls. She replied to me off-handedly as if discussing dressed beans and chickpeas: 'When I came down from the High Place, I reported what had happened to a man who looked in authority who was standing outside the theatre – ' She peered at some strangely white cheeses.

'Ewe's milk,' I said cheerfully, in Greek. 'Or camel's!' I was not sure that was possible.

'People nearby must have been listening in,' Helena continued. 'I overheard speculation from a company of actors that the drowned man might belong to them, but I was so exhausted I just said they could contact you if they wanted more information. They seemed an odd lot; I don't know if we'll hear from them. The official collected his favourite cronies and went up to see about the body.'

'I saw it later,' I confirmed.

'Well, I left them to it and slipped away.'

We sat on rugs and cushions. Our Nabataean guardian seemed shy of small talk. Helena and I had a lot to think about; the apparent murder at the High Place had upset both of us, and we knew we were in a sticky predicament as a result. I stared into my supper bowl.

'Didius Falco, you have three radishes, seven olives, two lettuce leaves and a piece of cheese!' listed Helena, as if I was checking the equality of our rations. 'I divided it fairly, so there would be no quarrelling . . .'

She had spoken Greek herself this time as a courtesy to our silent guest. I switched back to Latin, like the man of the house being stubborn. 'Well, that's probably the last we'll hear of the drowned man, but you will gather you and I are now the subject of a tense political incident.'

'Can we shed this overseer?' she queried in our own tongue, smiling graciously at Musa and serving him the burned segment of our flat Petran loaf.

'Afraid he sticks.' I spooned him some mashed chickpeas.

Musa politely accepted our offerings, though with a worried air. He took what he was given – then did not eat. He probably knew he was the subject under discussion, and given the brevity of his instructions from The Brother he may have been feeling anxious about being alone with two dangerous criminals.

We tucked in. I wasn't his foster-mother. If Musa chose to be picky, as far as I was concerned he could starve. But I wanted my strength.

Knocking summoned us to the door. We found a gang of Nabataeans who did not look like passing lamp-oil salesmen; they were armed and determined. They started jabbering excitedly. Musa had followed us to the threshold; I could tell he disliked what he heard.

'You have to go,' he told me. His startled tone seemed genuine.

'Leave Petra?' It was amazing these people managed to conduct so much lucrative commerce if everyone who came to their city got sent away so promptly. Still, it could have been worse. I had been expecting The Brother to decide we should stay – probably in custody. In fact I had been pondering ways I could sneak us down the Siq to collect our ox-cart from the caravanserai in secret, then dash for freedom. 'We'll pack!' I volunteered eagerly. Helena had jumped up and was already doing it. 'So this is goodbye, Musa!'

'Oh no,' replied the priest, with an earnest expression. 'I was told to stay with you. If you leave Petra, I shall have to come.'

I patted his shoulder. We had no time to waste in argument. 'If we're being asked to leave, no doubt somebody forgot to countermand your orders.' He was unimpressed with this reasoning. I didn't believe it myself. If my corns had been in The Brother's boots, I too would have made sure an underling followed us to the Nabataean borders and put us firmly on board ship. 'Well, it's your decision.'

Helena was used to me acquiring eccentric travel companions, but looked as if this one had stretched her tolerance. Grinning unconvincingly, I tried to reassure her: 'He won't come with us far; he'll miss his mountains.'

Helena smiled wearily. 'Don't worry. I'm quite used to handling men I could do without!'

With as much dignity as we could muster we allowed ourselves to be marched out of Petra. From shadows among the rocks, dark figures watched us leave. The odd camel did us the honour of spitting after us disparagingly.

Once we stopped. Musa spoke almost crossly to the armed escort. They didn't like waiting, but he darted into a house and came back with a small baggage roll. Equipped with Nabataean underwear and toothpicks, presumably, we were hurried on.

By then night had fallen, so our journey took place by the light of flares. Their pallid flames flickered eerily on the lower carvings of the rock tombs, sending long shadows up the sandstone. Columns and pediments were glimpsed, then quickly lost. Square-topped doorways assumed a menacing air, their openings like mysterious black cave mouths. We were on foot. We let the Nabataeans carry our baggage across the city, but when we reached the narrow gorge through the mountains it was clear we were being sent on alone – almost. Musa definitely intended to stick all the way. To reach the outside world, I had to grapple with our baggage while Helena lit our way with a flaming brand. As she strode ahead of us in high annoyance, she looked like some devastating sibyl leading the way down a cleft into Hades.

'Lucky I hadn't spent my inheritance on a lifetime's supply of bales of silk and incense jars!' muttered Helena, loud enough for Musa to hear. I knew she had been looking forward to what ought to have been an unrivalled chance to make luxury purchases. If her mother was as efficient as mine, she had come with a three-scroll shopping list.

'I'll buy you a pair of Indian pearl earrings,' I tried offering to her stately back.

'Oh thanks! That should overcome my disappointment . . .' Helena knew the pearls would probably never materialise.

We stumbled down the rocky path between cliffs that now craned together in complete blackness overhead. If we stopped, occasional tumbling stones were all that broke the silence of the Siq. We kept going.

I was now feeling mild despair. I always like to accomplish my tasks for the Emperor with dispatch, but even by my economical standards spending barely one day in Petra was not a good basis for briefing His Caesarship on the usual dire subjects (topography, fortifications, economics, social mores, political stability and mental state of the populace). I could just about manage to tell him the market price of radishes – information Vespasian probably knew from other sources, and not much use for helping a war council decide whether to invade.

Without hard information to offer, my chances of screwing a fee from the Palace must be slim. Besides, if Anacrites had sent me here in the hope that it would be a terminal journey, I could assume he had never budgeted for a large outlay. Probably nobody expected to see my happy grin at the accounts kiosk again. It meant that not for the first time I was nose to nose with bankruptcy.

Helena, who discovered her sense of discretion whilst she was trying to handle a wildly flaring torch, found little to say about our situation. She had money. She would, if I allowed it, subsidise our journey home. I would let her do it eventually, if that was the only way to spare Helena herself discomfort. Biting back my pride would make me pretty short-tempered, so for both our sakes she refrained from asking pointedly what plans I had now. Maybe I could extricate us myself. More likely not.

Most likely, as Helena knew from experience, I had no plans at all.

This was not the worst disaster of our lives, nor my worst failure. But I was dangerously angry about it. So when a small group of camels and ox-carts came rattling down the gorge behind us, my first reaction was to stay in the middle of the gravel track, forcing them to slow and stick behind us. Then, when a voice called out offering a lift on a cart, irrational frivolity took over. I turned round, dumping my load. The first cart stopped, leaving me gazing into the dolorous eyes of an edgy-looking ox.

'Your offer's welcome, stranger! How far can you take us?'

The man grinned back, responding to the challenge. 'Bostra, perhaps?' He was not Nabataean. We were talking in Greek.

'Bostra's not on my itinerary. How about dropping us at the caravanserai here, where I can pick up my own transport?'

'Done,' he said, with an easygoing smile. His intonation had the same overlay as mine; I was now sure of it.

'You from Italy?' I asked.

'Yes.'

I accepted the lift.

Only when we were ensconced on the waggon did I notice what a raggle-taggle company had picked us up. There were about ten of them, split between three carts and a couple of moth-eaten camels. Most of the people looked white-faced and anxious. Our driver caught the question in my eyes. 'I'm Chremes, an actor-manager. My company has been ordered to depart from Petra. We saw them lift the curfew to let you out, so we're doing a quick flit before anybody changes their mind about us.'

'Might somebody insist you stay?' I asked, though I had already guessed.

'We lost a friend.' He nodded to Helena, whom he must have recognised. 'You are the couple who found him, I believe. Heliodorus, who had the unfortunate accident up on the mountaintop.'

That was the first time I heard our drowned man's name.

Immediately afterwards I heard something else: 'Bostra might be an interesting town to visit, Marcus,' suggested Helena Justina in a speculative voice.

That young lady could never resist a mystery.

XII

Of course we did go to Bostra. Helena knew she was doing me a favour by suggesting it. Having discovered the drowned man, I too was fascinated to have met up with his companions. I wanted to know much more about them – and him. Being nosy was my livelihood.

That first evening, Chremes took us to recover our own stabled ox, the sad beast I had taken on at Gaza, together with the shaky contraption that passed for our hired vehicle. The night was really too dark now to travel on further, but both our parties were keen to put distance between ourselves and Petra. For added security and confidence we drove on in convoy, sharing our torches. We all seemed to feel that in the desert chance encounters are important.

After we set up camp I approached the actor-manager curiously: 'Are you certain the man Helena and I discovered was your friend?'

'Everything fits from your description – same build, same colouring. Same drinking habits!' he added bitterly.

'Then why didn't you come forward and claim the body?' I sprang at him.

'We were already in enough trouble!' twinkled Chremes like a conspirator.

I could understand that. But the situation intrigued me all the same.

We had all made our tents by hanging black goat-hair covers on rough wooden frames and were sitting outside these shelters by firelight. Most of the theatricals were huddled together, subdued by Heliodorus' death. Chremes came to join Helena and me, while Musa sat slightly apart in a world of his own. Hugging my knees I took my first good look at the leader of the theatre troupe.

He was, like the dead man, broadly built and full of face. More striking, however, with a strong chin and a dramatic nose that would have looked good on a republican general. Even in normal conversation he had a powerful voice with a resonance that seemed almost overdone. He delivered his sentences crisply. I did not doubt there were reasons why he had come to talk this evening. He wanted to judge Helena and me; maybe he wanted more than that from us.

'Where are you from?' Helena enquired. She could draw out information as smoothly as a pickpocket slitting a purse-thong.

'Most of the group hail from southern Italy. I'm a Tusculum man.'

'You're a long way from home!'

'I've been a long way from Tusculum for twenty years.'

I chortled. 'What's that – the old "one wife too many and I was cut out of my inheritance" excuse?'

'There was nothing there for me. Tusculum's a dead-and-alive, ungrateful, uncivilised backwater.' The world is full of people slandering their birthplaces, as if they really believe that small-town life is different elsewhere.

Helena seemed to be enjoying herself; I let her carry on. 'So how did you end up here, Chremes?'

'After half a lifetime performing on rocky stages in thunderstorms to provincial thickheads who only want to talk among themselves about that day's market, it's like a drug. I do have a wife – one I hate, who hates me back – and I've no more sense than to carry on for ever dragging a gang of tattered strutters into any city we find on our road . . .'

Chremes talked almost too readily. I wondered how much was a pose. 'When did you actually leave Italy?' Helena asked.

'The first time, twenty years ago. Five years back we came east again with Nero's travelling sideshow, his famous Greek Tour. When he tired of receiving laurel chaplets from bribed judges and packed up for home, we kept on drifting until we floated into Antiochia. The real Greeks didn't want to see what the Romans have done to their stage heritage, but so-called Hellenic cities here, which haven't been Greek since Alexander, think we're presenting them with masterpiece theatre. We found we could scrape a living in Syria. They are drama-mad. Then I wondered what Nabataea was like.

77

Worked our way south – and now thanks to The Brother we're working north again.'

'I'm not with you?'

'Our offer of culture was about as welcome in Petra as a performance of *The Trojan Women* to a family of baboons.'

'So you were already departing even before Heliodorus was drowned?'

'Seen off by The Brother. Happens often in our profession. Sometimes we get driven out of town for no reason. At least at Petra they produced a passable exuse.'

'What was that?'

'We were planning a performance in their theatre – though the gods know the place was primitive. Aeschylus would have taken one glance and gone on strike. But we were going to give them *The Pot of Gold* – seemed appropriate, given that everyone there has plenty. Congrio, our poster-writer, had chalked up details all round the city. Then we were solemnly informed that the theatre is only used ceremonially, for funeral rites. The implication was that if we desecrated their stage, the funeral rites might be our own ... A strange people,' Chremes stated.

This sort of comment normally produces a silence. Adverse remarks about foreigners make people remember their own folk – temporarily convincing themselves that those they have left at home are sensible and sane. Nostalgia seeped into our circle gloomily.

'If you were all about to leave Petra,' Helena asked thoughtfully, 'why had Heliodorus gone for a walk?'

'Why? Because he was a constant menace!' Chremes exclaimed. 'Trust him to lose himself when we were set to leave.'

'I still think you should have identified him formally,' I told him.

'Oh it will be him,' Chremes insisted airily. 'He was the type to inflict himself on an accident, and at the worst possible moment. Just like him to die somewhere sacrilegious and get us all locked in an underground dungeon. Having dozy officials argue for years about who caused his death would have struck Heliodorus as a fine joke!'

'A comedian?'

'He thought so.' Chremes caught Helena smiling, so added instructively, 'Someone else had to write the jokes for him.'

'Not creative?'

'If I told you exactly what *I* thought of Heliodorus it would sound unkind. So let's confine it to, he was a shabby, shambling dissolute with no sense of language, tact or timing.'

'You're a measured critic!' she answered solemnly.

'I try to be fair!'

'So he won't be missed?' I enquired quietly.

'Oh, he'll be missed! He was employed to do a certain job, which nobody else can undertake – '

'Ah, you mean no one else wants it?' I was speaking from experience in my own career.

'What was it?' Helena asked, with the light, careless inflection of a girl whose close companion needs to earn a crust.

'He was our jobbing playwright.'

Even Helena sounded surprised by that. 'The man we found drowned had written plays?'

'Certainly not!' Chremes was shocked. 'We are a respectable troupe with a fine reputation; we only perform the established repertoire! Heliodorus *adapted* plays.'

'What did that entail?' Helena Justina always asked the direct question. 'Translations from Greek to Latin?'

'Anything and everything. Not full translations, but pepping up turgid ones so we could bear to speak the lines. Modifying the story if the cast did not suit our company. Adding better characters to liven up proceedings. He was *supposed* to add jokes, though as I told you, Heliodorus wouldn't recognise a funny line if it jumped up and poked him in the eye. We mainly put on New Comedy. It has two painful disadvantages: it's no longer new, and quite frankly, it's not comic.'

Helena Justina was a shrewd, educated girl, and sensitive to atmosphere. She certainly knew what she was risking when she asked, 'What will you do about replacing Heliodorus now?'

At once Chremes grinned at me. 'Want a job?' He had an evil streak.

'What are the qualifications needed?'

'Able to read and write.'

I smiled diffidently, like a man who is too polite to say no to a friend. People never take the hint.

'Marcus can do that,' Helena put in. 'He does need a job.'

Some girls would be happy just to sit under the stars in the desert with the love of their heart, without trying to hire him out to any passing entrepreneur.

'What's your trade?' Chremes asked, perhaps warily.

'In Rome I am an informer.' It was best to be frank, but I knew better than to mention my imperial sponsorship.

'Oh! What are the qualifications for *that*?'

'Able to duck and dive.'

'Why Petra?'

'I came east to look for a missing person. Just a musician. For some unaccountable reason The Brother decided I must be a spy.'

'Oh don't worry about that!' Chremes reassured me heartily. 'In our profession it happens all the time.' Probably when it suited them, it could be true. Actors went everywhere. According to their reputation in Rome, they were not fussy who they spoke to when they got there and they often sold much more than tasteful Athenian hexameters. 'So, young Marcus, being whipped out of the mountain sanctuary leaves you a quadrans short of a denarius?'

'It does, but don't put me on the payroll before I've even heard your offer and its terms!'

'Marcus can do it,' Helena interrupted. I like my girl-friends to have faith in me – though not that much faith. 'He writes poetry in his spare time,' she revealed, without bothering to ask whether I wanted my private hobbies publicly exposed.

'The very man!'

I stood my ground, temporarily. 'Sorry, I'm just a scribbler of lousy satires and elegies. Besides, I hate Greek plays.'

'Don't we all? There's nothing to it,' Chremes assured me.

'You'll love it!' gurgled Helena.

The actor-manager patted my arm. 'Listen, Falco, if Heliodorus could do this job, anybody can!' Just the sort of career proposal I look for. It was too late for resistance, however. Chremes raised a fist in greeting and cried, 'Welcome to the company!'

I made one last attempt to extricate myself from this lunatic jape. 'I still have to look for my missing person. I doubt if you're going where I need to be – '

'We are going', pronounced Chremes elaborately, 'where the desert-dwelling populace barely recognise their sophisticated Greek heritage and are overdue for some permanent theatre-building, but where the founders of their paltry Hellenic cities have at least provided them with *some* auditoria that purveyors of the dramatic arts are allowed to use. We are going, my fine young informer – '

I knew it already. I broke in on the long-windedness: 'You are going to the Decapolis!'

Leaning against my knee and gazing up at the mysterious desert sky, Helena smiled contentedly. 'That's convenient, Chremes. Marcus and I already had plans to travel to the same area!'

XIII

We were going to Bostra first, however, for we had to pick up
the rest of the theatre group. That meant we were travelling
right past the region where I wanted to search for Sophrona,
well east of the Decapolis towns. But I was used to making
journeys backwards. I never expected a logical life.

Trekking to Bostra gave me a clear idea of what I would say to
Vespasian about this region if I ever reached home safely and
had the chance. This was still Nabataea – still, therefore, outside
the Empire, if Helena and I really wanted to frighten ourselves
by thinking about how remote our location was. In fact, even on
the well-maintained Nabataean roads, which had once
belonged to the great Persian Empire, the trip turned out to be a
dreary haul and took a good ten days. Northern Nabataea ran up
in a long finger beside the Decapolis, making geographical
neatness yet another reason for Rome to consider taking over
this territory. A straight frontier down from Syria would look
much better organised on a map.

We were heading into a highly fertile region; a potential
grain basket for the Empire. Given that Rome was keen to
gain control of the incense trade, I reckoned it would make
good sense to shift the trade routes eastwards to this northern
capital, ignoring the Petrans' insistence that all caravans turn
aside and stop there. Running the country from Bostra
instead would provide a more pleasant centre of government,
one with a kinder climate and closer links with civilisation.
The people of Bostra would be amenable to such a change
since it would enhance their current back-row status. And the
uppity Petrans would be put in their place.

This wonderful theory of mine had nothing to do with the
fact that the Petrans had bounced me out of town. I happen to
believe that when you take over any new business, your first
task should be to change the personnel so you can run things
your own way, and with loyal staff.

The theory might never be implemented in my lifetime, but devising it gave me something to think about when I wanted to stop reading comedies.

Leaving behind us the harsh mountain barrier that enclosed Petra, we had first climbed through the sparse local settlements, then reached more level ground. The desert rolled easily to the horizon on all sides. Everyone told us it was not real desert, compared to the wilderness of Arabia Felix – ironically named – or the terrible wastes beyond the River Euphrates, but it seemed barren and lonely enough for me. We felt we were crossing an old, old land. A land over which varied peoples had rolled like tides for centuries, and would continue to do so in war or peaceful settlement as long as time lasted. A land in which our present journeying was insignificant. It was impossible to tell whether the little crooked cairns of stones beside the road that marked the graves of nomads had been set up last week or several thousand years ago.

Gradually the rocky features diminished; boulders gave way to stones; the stones, which had spread the landscape like acres of roughly chopped nuts on a cooking board, turned into scatters, then were lost altogether in rich, dark, arable soil supporting wheat fields, vineyards and orchards. The Nabataeans conserved their meagre rainfall with a system of shallow terracing on each side of the wadis: wide shelves of ground were held back by low walls some forty or fifty feet apart, over which any surplus water ran off to the terrace below. It seemed successful. They grew wheat as well as barley. They had olives and grapes for oil and wine. Their eating fruit consisted of a lush mixture of figs, dates and pomegranates, whilst their most popular nuts – amongst a handsome variety – were almonds.

The whole atmosphere was different now. Instead of long nomad tents, hump-backed as caterpillars, we saw increasingly pretty houses, each set within its garden and smallholding. Instead of free-ranging ibex and rock-rabbits, there were tethered donkeys and goats.

Once we hit Bostra we were supposed to be meeting up with the remainder of Chremes' company. The group Helena

83

and I had met in Petra were the chief members of the troupe, mainly actors. Various hangers-on, with most of their stage equipment, had been left behind in the north, which did seem friendly, in case the rest found a hostile welcome in the mountains. As far as the murder was concerned, I could virtually ignore them. It was on the first group that I needed to concentrate.

Quite early in the trip I had asked Chremes, 'Why did Heliodorus really go for that walk?' The scenario was still bothering me.

'It was like him to wander off. They all do it – minds of their own.'

'Was it because he wanted a drink, quietly, on his own?'

'Doubt it.' Chremes shrugged. He showed a distinct lack of interest in this death.

'Someone went with him anyway. Who was it?' A long shot, since I was asking the name of the killer.

'Nobody knows.'

'Everyone accounted for?' Needless to say, he nodded. I would check that later for myself. 'Someone else must have fancied a tipple though?' I pressed.

'They'd be out of luck then. Heliodorus never reckoned to share his jar.'

'Might the companion have had his own jar – or goatskin – that Heliodorus had his eye on?'

'Oh yes! That makes sense.'

Maybe the playwright had had an acquaintance nobody else knew about. 'Would Heliodorus have made friends with anybody in Petra, anybody outside your group?'

'I doubt that.' Chremes seemed fairly definite. 'The locals were reserved, and we don't mix much with merchants – or anyone else. We're a close-knit family; we find enough squabbles among ourselves without looking outside for more trouble. Besides, we hadn't been in the city long enough to make contacts.'

'I heard him going up the mountain. I felt he knew the person he was with.' Chremes obviously realised where my questions were heading. 'That's right: what you say means he was killed by somebody from your group.'

84

That was when Chremes asked me directly to keep my eyes and ears open. He did not exactly commission me; that, with a fee at the end of it, would have been too much to hope for. But despite his initial reluctance to involve himself, if he was harbouring a killer he wanted to know who it was. People like to feel free to insult their companions or let them pay all of the wine bill without having to worry that it could annoy the kind of man who shoves his travelling companions face down in cold water until they stop breathing.

'Tell me about Heliodorus, Chremes. Did anyone in particular dislike him?' It had seemed a simple question.

'Hah! *Everyone* did!' scoffed Chremes.

That was a good start. The force with which he said it convinced me that every one of the group from Petra must be a suspect for killing the playwright. On the journey to Bostra, therefore, Helena and I had to think about all of them.

XIV

Bostra was a black basalt city built in this blackly ploughed land. It flourished. It had commerce, but it generated much of its own prosperity. There was a fine town gate in distinctly Nabataean architecture, and the King owned a second palace here. To Romans it was alien in flavour – yet it was the kind of city we understood. Irascible donkey-drovers cursed us as we tried to decide where we were going. Shopkeepers looked out from ordinary lock-ups with calculating eyes, shouting at us to come in and see their merchandise. When we arrived, near evening, we were greeted by the familiar scent of woodsmoke from baths and ovens. The tempting odours from hot-food stalls were spicier, but the reek of the leather tannery was as disgusting as any at home, and the stuttering lamp oil in the slums smelled just as rancid as it does all over the Aventine.

At first we were unable to find the rest of the company. They were not at the caravanserai where they had been left. Chremes seemed reluctant to make enquiries openly, from which Helena and I gathered it was likely there had been trouble in his absence. Various members of our group set off to look for their colleagues in the city while we guarded the waggons and luggage. We set up our tent with Musa's silent help. We ate supper, then sat down to wait for the return of the others. It was our first chance to talk over our findings so far.

During the journey we had managed to survey individual members of the group by judiciously offering lifts on our waggon. Then, when Helena grew weary of my efforts at controlling our temperamental ox, she hopped off and invited herself into other transport. We had now made contact with most of them, though whether we had also made friends was less certain.

We were considering everyone for possible motives – females too.

'A man did it,' I had explained cautiously to Helena. 'We heard him on the mountain. But you don't have to be cynical to know that a woman may have provided his reason.'

'Or bought the drink and devised the plan,' Helena agreed, as if she herself regularly did such things. 'What sort of motive do you think we are looking for?'

'I don't believe it can be money. No one here has enough of it. That leaves us with the old excuses – envy or sexual jealousy.'

'So we have to ask people what they thought of the playwright? Marcus, won't they wonder why we keep enquiring?'

'You're a woman; you can be plain nosy. I shall tell them the killer must be one of our party and I'm worried about protecting you.'

'Load of mule-dung!' scoffed my elegant lady with one of the pungent phrases she had picked up from me.

I had already seen what the theatre troupe was like. We were dealing with a fickle, feckless crowd here. We would never pin down any of them unless we set about it logically.

It had taken most of the trip just to work out who everyone was. Now we sat on a rug outside our tent. Musa was with us, though as usual he squatted slightly apart, not saying a word but calmly listening. There was no reason to hide our discussion from him so we talked in Greek.

'Right, let's survey the tattered cast list. They all look like stock characters, but I'm betting that not one of them is what they seem . . .'

The list had to be headed by Chremes. Encouraging us to investigate might exonerate him as a suspect – or it might mean he was cunning. I ran through what we knew about him: 'Chremes runs the company. He recruits members, chooses the repertoire, negotiates fees, keeps the cash box under his bed when there's anything in it worth guarding. His sole interest is in seeing that things run smoothly. It would take a really serious grievance to make him jeopardise the company's future. He realised that a corpse in Petra could land them all in jail, and his priority was to get them away. But we know he despised Heliodorus. Do we know why?'

'Heliodorus was no good,' Helena answered, impatiently.

'So why didn't Chremes simply pay him off?'

'Playwrights are difficult to find.' She kept her head down while she said it. I growled. I was not enjoying reading through the dead man's box of New Comedy. New Comedy had turned out to be as dire as Chremes had predicted. I was already tired of separated twins, wastrels jumping into blanket chests, silly old men falling out with their selfish heirs, and roguish slaves making pitiful jokes.

I changed the subject. 'Chremes hates his wife and she hates him. Do we know why? Maybe she had a lover – Heliodorus, say – so Chremes put his rival out of the way.'

'You would think that,' Helena sneered. 'I've talked to her. She yearns to star in serious Greek tragedy. She feels dragged down by having to play prostitutes and long-lost heiresses for this ragged troupe.'

'Why? They get to wear the best dresses, and even the prostitutes are always reformed in the last scene.' I was showing off my research.

'I gather she gives her all powerfully while longing for better things – a woman's lot in most situations!' Helena told me drily. 'People tell me her speech when she gives up brothelkeeping and becomes a temple priestess is thrilling.'

'I can't wait to hear it!' In fact I'd be shooting out of the theatre to buy a cinnamon cake at a stall outside. 'She's called Phrygia, isn't she?' The players had all taken names from drama. This was understandable. Acting was such a despised profession any performer would assume a pseudonym. I was trying to think up one myself.

Phrygia was the company's somewhat elderly female lead. She was tall, gaunt, and flamboyantly bitter about life. She looked over fifty but we were assured by everybody that when she stepped on stage she could easily persuade an audience she was a beautiful girl of sixteen. They made much of the fact that Phrygia could really act – which made me nervous about the talents of the rest.

'Why does Chremes hate her?' I wondered. 'If she's good on stage she ought to be an asset to his company.'

Helena looked dour. 'He's a man, and she is good. Naturally he resents it. Anyway, I gather he's always lusting after more glamorous bits.'

'Well that would have explained it if *he* had been found in the pool, and we had heard *Phrygia* luring him uphill.' It seemed irrelevant to Heliodorus. But something about Chremes had always bothered me. I thought about him more. 'Chremes himself plays the parts of tiresome old fellows – '

'Pimps, fathers and ghosts,' Helena confirmed. It didn't help.

I gave up and tried considering the other actors. 'The juvenile lead is called Philocrates. Though he's not so juvenile if you look closely; in fact he creaks a bit. He takes on prisoners of war, lads about town, and one of the main set of twins in every farce which has that gruesome identity mix-up joke.'

Helena's summary was swift: 'A dilettante handsome jerk!'

'He isn't my chosen dinner companion either,' I admitted. We had exchanged words on one occasion when Philocrates had watched me trying to corner my ox to harness it. The words were cool in the circumstances – which were that I asked his assistance, and he snootily declined. I had gathered it was nothing personal; Philocrates thought himself above chores that might earn him a kicked shin or a dirty cloak. He was high on our list to investigate further when we could brace up to an hour of insufferable arrogance. 'I don't know who he hates, but he's in love with himself. I'll have to find out how he got on with Heliodorus. Then there's Davos.'

'The opposite type,' Helena said. 'A gruff, tough professional. I tried to chat with him, but he's taciturn, suspicious of strangers, and I guess he rebuffs women. He plays the second male lead – boasting soldiers and such. I reckon he's good – he can swagger stylishly. And if Heliodorus was a liability as a writer, Davos wouldn't think much of it.'

'I'll watch my step then! But would he kill the man? Davos might have despised his work, but who gets shoved in a pool for bad writing?' Helena laughed at me suggestively.

89

'I rather took to Davos,' she grumbled, annoyed with herself for being illogical. Somehow I agreed with her and wanted Davos to be innocent. From what I knew of Fate, that probably put poor Davos at the top of the suspects list.

'Next we have the clowns, Tranio and Grumio.'

'Marcus, I find it hard to tell the difference between those two.'

'You're not meant to. In plays that have a pair of young masters who are twins, these two play their cheeky servants – also identical.'

We both fell silent. It was dangerous to view them as a pair. They were not twins; they were not even brothers. Yet of all the company they seemed most inclined to carry over their stage roles into normal life. We had seen them larking about on camels together, both playing tricks on the others. (Easy to do on a camel, for a camel will cause trouble for you without being asked.)

They went around in tandem. They were the same slim build – underweight and light-footed. Not quite the same height. The slightly taller one, Tranio, seemed to play the flashy character, the know-all city wit; his apparent crony, Grumio, had to make do with being the country clown, the butt of sophisticated jokes from the rest of the cast. Even without knowing them closely I could see that Grumio might grow tired of this. If so, however, surely he was more likely to put the boot into Tranio than strangle or drown the playwright?

'Is the clever one bright enough to get away with murder? Is he even as bright as he likes to think, in fact? And can the dopey one possibly be as dumb as he appears?'

Helena ignored my rhetoric. I put it down to the fact that only senators' sons have rhetoric tutors; daughters need only know how to twist around their fingers the senators they will marry and the bathhouse masseurs who will probably father those senators' sons.

I was feeling sour. An intellectual diet of *The Girl from Andros*, followed by *The Girl from Samos*, then *The Girl from Perinthos*, had not produced a sunny temperament. This turgid stuff might appeal to the kind of bachelor whose pick-up line is asking a girl where she comes from, but I had moved on from that two years ago when a certain girl from Rome decided to pick me up.

Helena smiled gently. She always knew what I was thinking. 'Well that's the men. There's no particularly striking motive there. So maybe the killer we heard was acting for somebody else. Shall we reconsider the women?'

'I'll always consider women!'

'Be serious.'

'Oh I was ... Well, we've thought about Phrygia.' I stretched luxuriantly. 'That leaves the eavesdropping maid.'

'Trust you to spot the beauty at the bar counter!' Helena retorted. It was hardly my fault. Even for a bachelor who had had to stop asking strange women where they hailed from, this beauty was unmissable.

Her name was Byrria. Byrria was genuinely young. She had looks that would withstand the closest inspection, a perfect skin, a figure worth grabbing, a gentle nature, huge, glorious eyes ...

'Perhaps Byrria wanted Heliodorus to give her some better lines?' wondered Helena far from rhapsodically.

'If Byrria needs anyone murdered, it's obviously Phrygia. That would secure her the good parts.'

I knew from my reading that in plays which could barely support one good female role, Byrria must be lucky to find herself a speaking part. Such meat as there was would be snaffled by Phrygia, while the young beauty could only watch yearningly. Phrygia was the stage manager's wife so the chief parts were hers by right, but we all knew who *should* be the female lead. There was no justice.

'In view of the way all you men are staring,' said my beloved icily, 'I shouldn't wonder if *Phrygia* would like *Byrria* removed!'

I was still searching for a motive for the playwright's death – though had I known just how long it would take me to find it I should have given up on the spot.

'Byrria didn't kill Heliodorus, but good looks like hers could well have stirred up strong feelings among the men, and then who knows?'

'I dare say you will be investigating Byrria closely,' said Helena.

I ignored the jibe. 'Do you think Byrria could have been after the scribe?'

'Unlikely!' scoffed Helena. 'Not if Heliodorus was as disgusting as everyone says. Anyway, your wondrous Byrria could take her pick of the pomegranates without fingering him. But why don't you ask her?'

'I'll do that.'

'I'm sure you will!'

I was not in the mood for a squabble. We had taken the discussion as far as we could, so I decided to abandon sleuthing and settled down on my back for a snooze.

Helena, who had polite manners, remembered our Nabataean priest. He had been sitting with us contributing total silence – his usual routine. Perhaps restraint was part of his religion; it would have been a tough discipline for me. 'Musa, you saw the murderer come down the mountain. Is there anybody in this group of travellers whom you recognise?'

She did not know I had already asked him, though she ought to have guessed. Musa answered her courteously anyway. 'He wore a hat, lady.'

'We shall have to look out for it,' replied Helena with some gravity.

I grinned at him, struck by a wicked possibility. 'If we can't solve this puzzle, we could set a trap. We could let it be known that Musa saw the murderer, hint that Musa was planning to identify him formally, then you and I could sit behind a rock, Helena, and we could see who comes – hatted or hatless – to shut Musa up.'

Musa received the suggestion as calmly as ever, with neither fear nor enthusiasm.

A few minutes later somebody did come, but it was only the company bill-poster.

XV

Helena and I exchanged a surreptitious glance. We had forgotten this one. He had been in Petra and ought to have been included in our list of suspects. Something told us that being forgotten was his permanent role. Being constantly overlooked could give him a motive for anything. But maybe he accepted it. So often it is the people who *have* who think they deserve more. Those who *lack* expect nothing else from life.

Such was our visitor – a miserable specimen. He had appeared around a corner of our tent very quietly. He could have been lurking about for ages. I wondered how much he had overheard.

'Hello there! Come and join us. Didn't Chremes mention to me that your name is Congrio?'

Congrio had a light skin covered with freckles, thin straight hair, and a fearful look. He had never been tall to begin with, and his slight, weedy body stooped under burdens of inadequacy. Everything about him spoke of leading a poor life. If he was not a slave now he probably had been at some stage, and whatever existence he snatched for himself these days could not be much better. Being a menial among people who have no regular income is worse than captivity on a rich landowner's farm. No one here cared whether Congrio ate or starved; he was nobody's asset, so nobody's loss if he suffered.

He shuffled near, the kind of mournful maggot who makes you feel crass if you ignore him or patronising if you try to be sociable.

'You chalk up the advertisements, don't you? I'm Falco, the new jobbing playwright. I'm looking out for people who can read and write in case I need help with my adaptations.'

'I can't write,' Congrio told me abruptly. 'Chremes gives me a wax tablet; I just copy it.'

'Do you act in the plays?'

'No. But I can dream!' he added defiantly, apparently not without a sense of self-mockery.

Helena smiled at him. 'What can we do for you?'

'Grumio and Tranio have come back from the city with a wineskin. They told me to ask whether you wanted to join them.' He was addressing me.

I was ready for bed, but put on my interested face. 'Sounds as if a sociable evening could be had here?'

'Only if you want to keep the caravanserai awake all night and feel like death tomorrow,' Congrio advised frankly.

Helena shot me a look that said she wondered how the town-and-country twins could tell so easily who was the degenerate in our party. But I did not need her permission – or at least not when this offered a good excuse to ask questions about Heliodorus – so off I went to disgrace myself. Musa stayed with Helena. I had never bothered to ask him, but I deduced that our Nabataean shadow was no drinking man.

Congrio seemed to be heading the same way as me, but then turned off on his own. 'Don't you want a drink?' I called after him.

'Not with that pair!' he responded, vanishing behind a waggon.

On the surface he spoke like a man who had better taste in friends, but I noticed a violent undertone. The easy explanation was that they pushed him around. But there could be more to it. I would have to scrutinise this bill-poster.

Feeling thoughtful, I made my own way to the Twins' tent.

XVI

Grumio and Tranio had put up the uncomplicated bivouac that was standard in our ramshackle camp. They had slung a cover over poles, leaving one whole long side open so they could see who was passing (and in their case commentate rudely). I noticed that they had bothered to hang a curtain down the middle of their shelter, dividing it precisely into private halves. These were equally untidy, so it couldn't have been because they fell out over the housekeeping; it hinted instead at aloofness in their relationship.

Surveyed quietly at leisure they were not in the least alike. Grumio, the 'country' twin who played runaway slaves and idiots, had a pleasant nature, a chubby face, and straight hair that fell evenly from the crown. Tranio, the taller 'townee', had his hair cut short up the back and swept forwards on top. He was sharp-featured and sounded as though he could be a sarcastic enemy. They both had dark, knowing eyes with which they watched the world critically.

'Thanks for the invitation! Congrio refused to come,' I said at once, as if I assumed the poster-writer would have been asked too.

Tranio, the one who played the boasting soldier's flashy servant, poured me a full winecup with an exaggerated flourish. 'That's Congrio! He likes to sulk – we all do. From which you can immediately deduce that beneath the false bonhomie, our joyous company is seething with angry emotions.'

'I gathered that.' I took the drink and joined them, relaxing on sacks of costumes alongside the walkway that ran through our encampment. 'Almost the first thing Helena and I were told was that Chremes hates his wife and she hates him.'

'He must have admitted that himself,' Tranio said knowingly. 'They do make a big thing of it.'

'Isn't it true? Phrygia openly laments that he has deprived

her of stardom. And Helena reckons that Chremes frequently wanders from the hearth. So the wife is after a laurel wreath, while the husband wants to stuff a lyre-player . . .'

Tranio grinned. 'Who knows what they're up to? They've been at each other's throats for twenty years. Somehow he never quite manages to run off with a dancer, and she never remembers to poison his soup.'

'Sounds like any normal married couple,' I grimaced.

Tranio was topping up my beaker almost before I had tried it. 'Like you and Helena?'

'We're not married.' I never explained our relationship. People would either not believe me, or not understand. It was no one else's business anyway. 'Do I gather that inviting me tonight is a shameless attempt to find out what she and I are doing here?' I taunted, probing in return.

'We see you as a Hired Trickster,' grinned Grumio, the supposedly dopey one, unabashed as he named one of the stock characters in New Comedy. It was the first time he had spoken. He sounded brighter than I had expected.

I shrugged. 'I'm trying my hand with a stylus. Finding your playwright's soused body got me pitched out of Petra. It also happened at about the time I ran out of travelling funds. I needed work. Your job was the soft option: offering to scribble for Chremes looked easier work than straining my back lifting barrels of myrrh, or catching fleas driving camel trains.' Both twins had their noses deep in their winecups. I was not sure I had deflected their curiosity about my interest in the playwright's death. 'I've agreed to replace Heliodorus provided I'm not asked to play a tambourine in the orchestra and Helena Justina never acts on a public stage.'

'Why not?' queried Grumio. 'Does she come from a respectable family?' He ought to be able to see that. Maybe pretending to have a few brains was just a pose.

'No, I rescued her from slavery, in return for two bags of apples and a nanny goat . . .'

'You're a take-off merchant!' giggled Grumio. He turned to his friend, who was wielding the wineskin again. 'We're on to a scandal.'

Ineffectively shielding my cup from Tranio, I rebuked the

other quietly: 'The only scandal Helena was ever involved in was when she chose to live with me.'

'Interesting partnership!' Grumio commented.

'Interesting girl,' I said.

'And now she's helping you spy on us?' Tranio prodded.

It was a challenge, one I should have been waiting for. They had brought me here to find out what I was doing, and they would not be deterred. 'We don't spy. But Helena and I found the body. Naturally we'd like to know who killed the man.'

Tranio drained his winecup in one gulp. 'Is it true you actually saw who did it?'

'Who told you that?' Not to be outdone, I quaffed my drink too, wondering whether Tranio was just nosy – or had a deadly earnest reason for wanting to know.

'Well, everyone's keen to know what you're doing with us now – assuming you were just a tourist in Petra,' Tranio insinuated.

As I had started to expect, my refill came immediately. I knew when I was being set up. After years as an informer, I also had a clear idea of my limit for drink. I set down my overflowing cup as if I was carried away by strong feelings. 'A tourist who made the journey of a lifetime only to get thrown out – ' My rant as a disappointed traveller was received fairly coolly.

'So where does your sinister Arab fit in?' Tranio demanded bluntly.

'Musa?' I acted surprised. 'He's our interpreter.'

'Oh of course.'

'Why,' I asked with a light, incredulous laugh, 'are people suggesting Musa saw the killer or something?'

Tranio smiled, answering in the same apparently friendly tone that I had used: 'Did he?'

'No,' I said. For all useful purposes it was the truth.

As Grumio prodded the fire I too picked up a twisted branch and played with it among the sparks. 'So are either of you going to tell me why Heliodorus was so stinkingly unpopular?'

It was still Tranio, the exponent of mercurial wit, who

97

enjoyed himself making up answers: 'We were all in his power.' He twirled his wrist elegantly, pretending to philosophise. 'Weak parts and dull speeches could finish us. That crude bastard knew it; he toyed with us. The choice was either to flatter him, which was unspeakable, or to bribe him, which was often impossible, or just to wait for somebody else to grab him by the balls and squeeze till he dropped. Before Petra no one had done it – but it was only a matter of time. I should have taken bets on who would get to him first.'

'That seems extreme,' I commented.

'People whose livelihood depends on a writer exist under stress.' As their new writer, I tried not to take it to heart. 'To find his killer,' Tranio advised me, 'look for the despairing actor who had suffered one bad role too many.'

'You, for instance?'

His eyes dropped, but if I had worried him he rallied. 'Not me. I don't need a set text. If he wrote me out, I improvised. He knew I would do it, so being spiteful lost its fun. Grumio was the same, of course.' I glanced at Grumio, who might have been patronised by the afterthought, but his cheerful face remained neutral.

I grunted, sipping wine again. 'And I thought the man had just borrowed somebody's best silvered belt once too often!'

'He was a pig,' Grumio muttered, breaking his silence.

'Well that's simple! Tell me why.'

'A bully. He beat the lower orders. People he dared not attack physically he terrorised in more subtle ways.'

'Was he a womaniser?'

'Better ask the women.' Grumio was still the speaker – with what could have been a jealous glint. 'There are one or two I'll help you interrogate!'

While I was at it, I checked every possibility: 'Or did he chase young men?' They both shrugged offhandedly. In fact nobody in this company was young enough to appeal to the usual ogler of boys in bathhouses. If more mature relationships existed, I might as well look first for evidence here with the Twins; they lived closely enough. But Grumio seemed to have straightforward female interests; and Tranio had also grinned at his interrogation joke.

As before it was Tranio who wanted to elaborate: 'Heliodorus could spot a hangover, or a pimple on a sensitive adolescent, or a disappointed lover at twenty paces. He knew what each of us wanted from life. He also knew how to make people feel that their weaknesses were enormous flaws, and their hopes beyond reach.'

I wondered what Tranio thought his own weakness was – and what hopes he had. Or might once have had.

'A tyrant! But people here seem pretty strong-willed.' Both Twins laughed easily. 'So why', I asked, 'did you all put up with him?'

'Chremes had known him a long time,' suggested Grumio wearily.

'We needed him. Only an idiot would do the job,' said Tranio, insulting me with what I thought was unnecessary glee.

They were an odd pair. At first glance they had seemed closely bonded, but I decided they hung together only in the way of craftsmen who work together, which gave them some basic loyalty, though they might not meet socially from choice. Yet in this travelling company Tranio and Grumio had to live under one goat-hair roof with everyone presuming they formed one unit. Perhaps sustaining the fraud set up hidden strains.

I was fascinated. Some friendships are sounder for having one easygoing partner with one who seems more intense. I felt that this ought to have been the case here; that the stolid Grumio ought to have been grateful for the opportunity to pal up with Tranio, to whom frankly I warmed more. Apart from the fact that he kept refilling my winecup, he was a cynic and a satirist; exactly my kind of fellow.

I wondered if professional jealousy had come between them, though I saw no signs. There was scope on stage for both of them, as I knew from my reading. All the same, in Grumio, the quieter of the clowns, I sensed deliberate restraint. He looked pleasant and harmless. But to an informer that could easily mean he was hiding something dangerous.

The wineskin was empty. I watched Tranio shake out the

very last drops, then he squashed the skin flat, clapping it under his elbow.

'So, Falco!' He seemed to be changing the subject. 'You're new to playwriting. How are you finding it?'

I told him my thoughts on New Comedy, dwelling with morose despair on its dreariest features.

'Oh you're reading the stuff? So you've been given the company play box?' I nodded. Chremes had handed over a mighty trunk stuffed with an untidy mass of scrolls. Putting them together in sets to make whole plays had taken most of our journey to Bostra, even with help from Helena, who enjoyed that kind of puzzle. Tranio went on idly. 'I might come and have a quick look sometime. Heliodorus borrowed something that wasn't left among his personal things . . .'

'Anytime,' I offered, curious, though not in my present condition wanting to pay too much attention to some lost stylus knife or bath-oil flask. I swayed to my feet, suddenly anxious to stop torturing my liver and brain. I had been away from Helena for longer than I liked. I wanted my bed.

The sharp clown grinned, noticing how the wine had affected me. I was not alone, however. Grumio was lying on his back near the fire, eyes closed, mouth open, dead to the world. 'I'll come back to your tent now,' laughed my new friend. 'I'll do it while I think of it.'

Since I could use an arm to steady me home, I made no protest but let him bring a light and come with me.

XVII

Helena appeared to be sound asleep, though I noticed a smell of snuffed lamp wick. She made a show of waking drowsily: 'Do I hear the morning cockerel, or is that my stupefied darling rolling back to his tent before he drops?'

'Me, stupefied . . .' I never lied to Helena. She was too sharp to delude. I added quickly, 'I've brought a friend – ' I thought she stifled a groan.

The light of Tranio's flare wavered crazily up the back wall of our shelter. I gestured him to the trunk of plays while I folded up on a baggage roll as neatly as possible and let him get on with it. Helena glared at the clown, though I tried to persuade myself she looked more indulgently on me.

'Something Heliodorus pinched,' Tranio explained, diving into the depths of the scroll box unabashed. 'I just want to dip into the box . . .' After midnight, in the close domestic privacy of our bivouac, this explanation fell short of convincing. Theatricals seemed a tactless lot.

'I know,' I soothed Helena. 'Little did you think when you found me in a black bog in Britannia and fell for my soft manners and sweet-natured charm that you'd end up having your sleep disturbed by a gang of drunkards in a desert khan – '

'You're rambling, Falco,' she snapped. 'But how right. Little did I think!'

I smiled at her fondly. Helena closed her eyes. I told myself that was the only way she could resist either the smile or the frank affection in it.

Tranio was thorough in his search. He delved right to the bottom of the trunk, then replaced every scroll, taking the opportunity to look at each a second time.

'If you tell me what you're looking for—' I offered blearily, longing to get rid of him.

101

'Oh, it's nothing. It's not here, anyway.' He was still searching, however.

'What is it? Your diary of five years as a sex slave in the temple of some Eastern goddess with an ecstatic cult? A rich widow's will, leaving you a Lusitanian gold mine and a troupe of performing apes? Your birth certificate?'

'Oh much worse!' he laughed.

'Looking for a scroll?'

'No, no. Nothing like that.'

Helena watched him in a silence that may have passed for politeness to a stranger. I like more alluring entertainment. I watched her. Tranio finally banged down the lid and sat on the chest kicking his heels against its studded sides. The friendly fellow looked as if he intended to stay chatting until dawn.

'No luck?' I asked.

'No, damn it!'

Helena yawned blatantly. Tranio gave a flourishing gesture of acquiescence, took the hint, and left.

My tired eyes met Helena's for a moment. In the weak light of the flare Tranio had left us, hers looked darker than ever – and not devoid of challenge.

'Sorry, fruit.'

'Well, you have to do your work, Marcus.'

'I'm still sorry.'

'Find anything out?'

'Early days.'

Helena knew what that meant: I had found nothing. As I washed my face in cold water she told me, 'Chremes dropped in to tell you he has found the rest of his people, and we're performing here tomorrow.' She could have announced this while we were waiting for Tranio to go, but Helena and I liked to exchange news more discreetly. Discussing things together in private meant a lot to us. 'He wants you to write out the moneylender's part Heliodorus used to play. You have to make sure that omitting the character doesn't lose any vital lines. If so – '

'I reallocate them to someone else. I can do that!'

'All right.'

'I could always go on stage as the moneylender myself.'

'You have not been asked.'

'Don't see why not. I know what they're like. Jove knows I've dealt with enough of the bastards.'

'Don't be ridiculous,' Helena scoffed. 'You're a free-born Aventine citizen; you're much too proud to sink so low!'

'Unlike you?'

'Oh I could do it. I'm a senator's offspring; disgracing myself is my heritage! Every family my mother gossips with has a disgruntled son no one talks about who ran off to scandalise his grandfather by acting in public. My parents will be disappointed if I *don't*.'

'Then they will have to be disappointed, so long as I'm in charge of you.' Supervising Helena Justina was a rash claim; she laughed at me. 'I promised your father I'd keep you respectable,' I finished lamely.

'You promised him nothing.' True. He had more sense than to ask me to take on that impossible labour.

'Feel free to carry on reading,' I offered, fumbling with my boots.

Helena removed from under her pillow the scroll I guessed she had been peacefully perusing before I turned up like trouble. 'How could you tell?' she demanded.

'Smut on your nose from the lamp.' In any case, after living with her for a year I had deduced that if I left her anywhere near forty papyrus scrolls she would scoot through the lot in a week like a starved library beetle.

'This is pretty grubby too,' she remarked, gesturing to her bedtime read.

'What is it?'

'A very rude collection of anecdotes and funny tales. Too saucy for you, with your pure mind.'

'I'm not in the mood for pornography.' I took several chances in succession, aiming myself at the bed, inserting my body under the light cover, and winding myself around my lass. She allowed it. Perhaps she knew better than to argue with a hopeless drunk. Perhaps she liked being enveloped.

'Could this be what Tranio was looking for?' she asked.

103

Sick of Tranio, I pointed out that he had said quite decisively his lost item was not a scroll.

'People do sometimes tell lies!' Helena reminded me pedantically.

We too, like the Twins, had our tent divided up for privacy. Behind the makeshift curtain I could hear Musa snoring. The rest of the camp lay silent. It was one of our few moments of solitude, and I was not interested in a risqué Greek novel, if that was what Helena had been studying. I managed to extract the scroll from her and tossed it aside. I let it be known what mood I was in.

'You're not capable,' she grumbled. Not without reason, and perhaps not without regret.

With an effort that may have surprised her I wrenched myself sideways and up-ended the flare in a pitcher of water. Then, as it hissed into darkness, I turned back to Helena intent on proving her wrong.

Once she accepted that I was serious, and likely to stay awake long enough, she sighed. 'Preparations, Marcus . . .'

'Incomparable woman!' I let her go, apart from annoying her with delaying caresses as she struggled over me on her way out of bed.

Helena and I were one, a lasting partnership. But due to her fears of childbirth and my fears of poverty, we had taken the decision not to add to our family yet. We shared the burden of defying the Fates. We had rejected wearing a hairy spider amulet, as practised by some of my sisters, mainly because its success seemed doubtful; my sisters had huge families. Anyway, Helena reckoned I was not sufficiently frightened of spiders to be driven off her by a mere amulet. Instead, I faced the deep embarrassment of bribing an apothecary to forget that controlling birth contravened the Augustan family laws; then she endured the humiliating, sticky procedure with the costly alum in wax. We both had to live with the fear of failing. We both knew if that happened we could never allow a child of ours to be killed in the womb by an abortionist, so our lives would take a serious turn. That had never stopped us giggling over the remedy.

Without a light, I heard Helena cursing and laughing as she rummaged for her soapstone box of thick cerate ointment that was supposed to keep us childless. After some muttering she hopped back to bed. 'Quick, before it melts – '

Sometimes I thought the alum worked on the principle of making performance impossible. Instructed to be quick, as every man knows, the will to proceed is liable to collapse. Following too many winecups this seemed even more likely, though the wax at least helped provide a steady aim, after which maintaining a position, as my gymnasium trainer Glaucus would call it, did become more difficult.

Applying care to these problems, I made love to Helena as skilfully as a woman can expect from a man who has been made drunk by a couple of crass clowns in a tent. And since I always ignore instructions, I made sure that I did it very slowly, and for the longest possible time.

Hours later I thought I heard Helena murmur, 'A Greek and a Roman and an elephant went into a brothel together; when they came out, only the elephant was smiling. Why?'

I must have been asleep. I must have dreamed it. It sounded like the sort of joke my tentmate Petronius Longus used to wake me up to howl over when we were wicked lads in the legions ten years before.

Senators' nicely brought-up daughters are not even supposed to know that jokes like that exist.

XVIII

Bostra was our first performance. Certain aspects stick in the memory. Like an acrid sauce repeating after a cut-price dinner party given by a patron you had never liked.

The play was called *The Pirate Brothers*. Despite Chremes' claim that his notable company only tackled the standard repertoire, this drama was the product of no known author. It appeared to have developed spontaneously over many years from any bits of business the actors had enjoyed in other plays, expounded in whatever lines from the classics they could remember on the night. Davos had whispered to me that it went best when they were down to their last few coppers and seriously hungry. It required tight ensemble playing, with despair to give it an edge. There were no pirates; that was a ploy to attract an audience. And even though I had read what purported to be the script, I had failed to identify the brothers of the title.

We offered up this dismal vehicle to a small crowd in a dark theatre. The audience on the creaking wooden seats was swelled by spare members of our company, well drilled in creating a vibrant mood with enthusiastic cheers. Any one of them could have earned a good living in the Roman Basilica egging on prosecuting barristers, but they were having a hard time breaking the morose Nabataean atmosphere.

At least we had an increased complement to give us confidence. Helena had nosed about the camp to see who the additions to our company were.

'Cooks, slaves and flute girls,' I informed her before she could tell me.

'You've certainly done your reading!' she replied, with admiring sarcasm. She was always annoyed at being fore-stalled.

'How many are there?'

'Quite a tribe! They're musicians as well as extras. They all double up making costumes and scenery. Some take the money if the performance is ticketed.'

We had both learned already that the ideal ruse was to persuade a gullible local magistrate to subsidise our play, hoping to trade on the crowd's goodwill next election time. He would pay us a lump sum for the night, after which we needn't care if nobody bothered to come. Chremes had managed to swing this at towns in Syria, but in Nabataea they had not heard of the civilised Roman custom of politicians bribing the electorate. For us, playing to an empty arena would mean eating from empty bowls. So Congrio was sent out early to chalk up enticing notices for *The Pirate Brothers* on local houses, while we hoped he didn't choose to annoy any householders who were keen theatregoers.

In fact, 'keen' was not an epithet that seemed to apply in Bostra. Since our play was ticketed, we knew in advance that there must be some rival attraction in town: a snail race with heavy side-bets, or two old men playing a very tense game of draughts.

It was drizzling. This is not supposed to happen in the wilderness, but as Bostra was a grain basket we knew they must get rain for their corn sometimes. Sometimes was tonight.

'I gather the company will perform even if the theatre is being struck by lightning,' Helena told me, scowling.

'Oh stalwart chaps!'

We clung together under a cloak among a thin crowd trying to make out the action through the miserable mist.

I was expecting to be hailed as a hero after the play. I had taken a great deal of trouble with my adaptation and had spent all morning perfecting new lines, or tinkering with tired old ones as much as time allowed. I had proudly presented the revisions to Chremes at lunch, though he brushed aside my eager offer to attend the afternoon rehearsal and point out significant changes. They called it a rehearsal, but when I stationed myself on a back row at the theatre, trying to overhear how things were going, I was dismayed. Everyone spent most of their time discussing a flute girl's pregnancy and whether Chremes' costume would last in one piece another night.

The actual performance bore out my disquiet. My laborious redraft had been tossed aside. All the actors ignored it. As the action evolved they repeatedly referred to the missing moneylender, even though he would never appear, then in the last act they improvised a few haphazard speeches to get around the problem. The plot, which I had so wittily resurrected, dwindled into ludicrous tosh. For me, the most bitter insult was that the audience swallowed the gibberish. The sombre Nabataeans actually applauded. They stood up politely, clapping their hands above their heads. Somebody even threw what looked like a flower, though it may have been an unpaid laundry bill.

'You're upset!' Helena observed, as we fought our way to the exit. We barged past Philocrates, who was hanging around the gateway, showing off his profile to admiring women. I steered Helena through a smaller group of men with entranced expressions who were waiting for the beauteous Byrria; she had taken herself off promptly, however, so they were looking over anything else in a long skirt. Having my nobly reared girlfriend mistaken for a flute girl was now my worst nightmare. 'Oh, don't let it worry you, Marcus my love . . .' She was still talking about the play.

I explained to Helena succinctly that I didn't give a damn what a group of illogical, illiterate, impossible thespians did on stage or off it, and that I would see her in a while. Then I strode off to find somewhere I could kick rocks in decent solitude.

XIX

It came on to rain more heavily. When you're down, Fortune loves stamping on your head.

Tearing off ahead of everyone else, I reached the centre of our encampment. That was where the heavier waggons were drawn up in the hope that our encircling tents would deter sneak-thieves. Hopping over the nearest tailboard I took shelter under the ragged leather roof that protected our stage properties from the weather. It was my first chance to inspect this battered treasure trove. After I had finished swearing about the performance, I devised a ferocious speech of resignation that ought to leave Chremes whimpering. Then I fetched out my tinderbox, wasted half an hour with it, but eventually lit the large lantern that was carried on stage in scenes of night-time conspiracy.

As the pale flame wandered around dangerously in its ironwork container, I found myself crouching up against a small shrine (large enough to hide behind for overhearing secrets). Stacked opposite were several painted doorways, meant to distinguish the neighbouring houses that featured in so much of the New Comedy. These had not been used in tonight's *Pirate Brothers* in order to save them from the wet. Instead the scene, which was originally 'A Street in Samothrace', had been redesignated 'A Rocky Coast' and 'The Road to Miletus'; Chremes had simply played Chorus and announced these arbitrary locations to his hapless audience.

I struggled to settle more comfortably. Under my elbow was an old wooden log with a greying shawl nailed to it (the 'baby'). Sticking out above my head was a gigantic sword of curved design. I assumed it was blunt – then cut my finger on the edge while testing out my assumption. So much for scientific experiment. Wicker baskets mostly overflowed with costumes, shoes and masks. One basket had toppled over, showing itself nearly empty apart from a long set of rattly chains, a large ring with a big red glass stone (for recognition of long-lost offspring), some parcels of shopping, and a brown jar containing a few pistachio shells (the ever-present Pot of Gold). Behind it were a stuffed sheep (for sacrifice) and a wooden pig on wheels that could be towed across the stage by Tranio in his role as a merrily wittering Clever Cook who cracked thousand-year-old jokes about preparations for the Wedding Feast.

Once I had finished gloomily surveying the torn and faded panoply with which I was sharing this waggon, my thoughts naturally turned again to issues like Life, Fate, and however did I come to end up in this tip being paid zero for an unappealing job? Like most philosophy it was a waste of time. I noticed a woodlouse and began timing his progress, taking bets with myself about which direction he would wander in. I had grown cold enough to think I would now return to my own bivouac and allow Helena Justina to bolster my esteem, when I heard footsteps outside. Somebody stamped up to the waggon, the end flap was beaten aside, there came a flurry of irritated movement, and then Phrygia hauled herself inside. Presumably she too was seeking privacy, though she did not appear bothered by finding me.

Phrygia was as long as a leek; she could overtop most men. She increased her advantage of height by wearing her hair in a coronet of frizzled curls, and by teetering about on frightful platformed shoes. Like a statue that had been purposely designed to stand in a niche, her front view was perfectly finished, but her back had been left in the rough. She was a model of immaculate face paint, with a whole breastplate of gilt jewellery that crackled in layers upon the meticulous pleats of the stole across her bosom. Seen from behind, however, every bone pin pegging down her hairstyle was visible, the frontispiece jewellery all hung from a single tarnished chain that had worn a red furrow in her scrawny neck, the stole was rumpled, the shoes were backless, and her gown was hoicked together and pinned in clumps in order to provide the more elegant drape on her frontal plane. I had seen her walk down a street with a sideways glide that preserved her public image almost intact. Since her stage presence was strong enough to entrance an audience, she did not care if the louts behind the back wall sneered.

'I thought it might be you skulking here.' She threw herself against one of the costume baskets, flapping her sleeves to shake off drops of rain. Some fell on me. It was like being joined on a small couch by a thin but energetic dog.

'I'd better be off,' I muttered. 'I was just sheltering – '

'I see! Don't want that girl of yours to hear you've been closeted in a waggon with the manager's wife?' I settled back weakly. I like to be polite. She looked fifteen years older than me, and might be more. Phrygia favoured me with her bitter laugh. 'Consoling the ranks is my privilege, Falco. I'm the Mother of the Company!'

I joined in the laughter, as one does. I felt threatened, wondering briefly if accepting consolation from Phrygia was an obligation for men in the troupe. 'Don't worry about me. I'm a big boy – '

'Really?' At her tone, I shrank mentally. 'So how was your first night?' she challenged.

'Let's say I can now see how Heliodorus might have turned his back on society!'

'You'll learn,' she consoled me. 'Don't make it so literary. And don't waste time sticking in political allusions. You're not bloody Aristophanes, and the people who are paying for tickets are not educated Athenians. We're acting for turnips who only come to talk to their cousins and fart. We have to give them a lot of action and low-level jokes, but you can leave all that to us on stage. We know what's required. Your job is to hone the basic framework and remember the simple motto: short speeches, short lines, short words.'

'Oh, and I foolishly thought I would be handling major themes of social disillusionment, humanity and justice!'

'Skip the themes. You're handling old envy and young love.' Like most of my career as an informer, in fact.

'Silly me!'

'As for Heliodorus,' Phrygia went on, with a change of tone, 'he was just nasty to begin with.'

'So what was his problem?'

111

'Juno only knows.'

'Did he make enemies with anyone in particular?'

'No. He was fair; he hated everyone.'

'And everyone was even-handed with their loathing in return? What about you, Phrygia? How did you get on with him? Surely an actress of your status was beyond reach of his spite?'

'My status!' she murmured drily. I sat quiet. 'I've had my turn. I was offered the chance to play Medea at Epidaurus once . . .' It must have been years ago, but I did not disbelieve it. Tonight she had given a crisp cameo performance as a priestess that had let us glimpse what might have been.

'I'd like to have seen that. I can visualise you raving at Jason and bashing the children . . . What happened?'

'Married Chremes.' And never forgave him. Still, it was premature for me to feel sorry for him when I had no idea what other crises had distorted their relationship. My work had long ago taught me never to judge marriages.

'Heliodorus knew about you missing this Medea?'

'Of course.' She spoke quietly. I had no need to probe for details. I could imagine the use he must have made of the knowledge; a world of torment lay in her very restraint.

She was a great actress. And maybe she was acting now. Maybe she and Heliodorus had really been passionate lovers – or maybe she had wanted him, but he rebuffed her, so she arranged his swimming accident . . . Luckily Helena was not present to pour scorn on these wild theories.

'Why did Chremes keep him on?' Even though she and her husband were not speaking to each other generally, I had a feeling they could always discuss the company. Probably it was the sole factor that kept them together.

'Chremes is too soft-hearted to boot anyone out.' She grinned at me. 'Plenty of people rely on that to keep their position with us!'

I felt my jaw set. 'If that's a jibe at me, I don't need charity. I had a job of my own before I met up with you people.'

'He tells me you're an investigator?'

I let her probe. 'I'm trying to find a young musician called Sophrona.'

112

'Oh! We thought you must be political.'

I pretended to be amazed by that idea. Sticking with Sophrona, I went on, 'It's worth a parcel if I track her down. All I know is she can play the water organ as if she had lessons direct from Apollo, and she'll be with a man from the Decapolis, probably called Habib.'

'The name should help.'

'Yes, I'm relying on it. The Decapolis region sounds ill-defined, too large for wandering about clueless like a prophet in the wilderness.'

'Who wants you to find the girl?'

'Who do you think? The manager who paid the fee for training her.'

Phrygia nodded; she knew that a trained musician was a valuable commodity. 'What happens if you don't?'

'I go home poor.'

'We can help you look.'

'That seems a fair bargain. It's why I took this job. You help me when we get to the Decapolis, and even if my scribing is crude, in return I'll do my best to identify your murderer.'

The actress shivered. It was probably real. 'Someone here . . . Someone we know . . .'

'Yes, Phrygia. Someone you eat with; a man somebody probably sleeps with. Someone who may be late for rehearsals yet turns in a good performance. Someone who has done you kindnesses, made you laugh, sometimes irritated you to Hades for no reason in particular. Someone, in short, just like all the rest in the company.'

'It's horrible!' Phrygia cried.

'It's murder,' I said.

'We have to find him!' It sounded as if she would help if she could. (In my long experience that meant I should be prepared for the woman to try to jeopardise my search at every turn.)

'So who hated him, Phrygia? I'm looking for a motive. Just knowing who he had dealings with would be a start.'

'Dealings? He used to try out his luck with Byrria, but she kept away from him. He hung around the musicians some-times – though most of them would tell him where to put his little implement – but he was too wound up in his own black personality to have been involved in any special affairs.'

'A man who bore grudges?'

'Yes. He was bitter against Byrria. But you know she didn't go up the mountain. Chremes told me you heard the killer talking, and it was a man.'

'Could have been a man defending Byrria.' When I see an attractive woman, I'm seeing motives for all kinds of stupid behaviour. 'Who else hankers after her?'

'All of them!' said Phrygia, at her most dry. She pursed her lips thoughtfully. 'Byrria has no followers, I'll say that for her.'

'There were plenty of oglers waiting here for her tonight.'

'And was she visible?'

'No,' I conceded.

'That surprised you! You thought Byrria was young enough to listen to them and only I was old enough to see through their flattery!'

'I think you have plenty of admirers – but you're right about the girl. So what's with Byrria if she turned down Heliodorus and she can live without cheap popularity?'

'She's ambitious. She doesn't want one short night of passion in return for the long disillusionment; she wants to work.' I was reaching the conclusion that Phrygia hated the beauty less than we had supposed. Clearly she approved of intense dramatic ambition; perhaps she wished the younger woman well. It could be for that classic reason: Byrria reminded Phrygia of her younger self.

'So she studies her art, and keeps to herself.' That could easily drive men mad. 'Is anyone particularly soft on her? Who loves the dedicated Byrria from afar?'

'I told you: all of the bastards!' Phrygia said.

I sighed gently. 'Well, tell me if you decide there was somebody who might have been prepared to kick Heliodorus out of her path.'

'I'll tell you,' she agreed calmly. 'On the whole, Falco, taking action – especially for a woman – is alien to men.'

Since she still seemed prepared to talk to me, although I was one of those feeble specimens, I went through the list of suspects in a businesslike way: 'It has to be someone who

114

came with you to Petra. Apart from your husband—' No flicker of emotion crossed her face. 'That leaves the two clowns, the wonderfully handsome Philocrates, Congrio the bill-poster, and Davos. Davos looks an interesting case – '

'Not him!' Phrygia was crisp. 'Davos wouldn't do anything stupid. He's an old friend. I won't have you insulting Davos. He's too sensible – and he's much too quiet.' People always believe their personal cronies should be above suspicion; in fact the chances are high that anyone in the Empire who dies unnaturally has been set on by their oldest friend.

'Did he get on with the playwright?'

'He thought he was mule dung. But he thinks that about most playwrights,' she informed me conversationally.

'I'll bear it in mind when I talk to him.'

'Don't strain yourself. Davos will tell you quite freely himself.'

'I can't wait.'

By now I had heard one put-down too many about the creative craft. It was late, I had had a miserable day, Helena would be fretting and the thought of soothing her anxieties grew more appealing every minute.

I said I thought the rain had stopped. Then I bade the Mother of the Company a gruffly filial goodnight.

Hardly had I entered my tent when I knew that I should have been somewhere else tonight.

XX

Something had happened to our Nabataean priest.

Davos was holding Musa up as if he was going to collapse. They were in our section of the tent, with Helena in attendance. Musa was soaking wet and shuddering, either with cold or terror. He was deathly pale and looked in shock.

I glanced at Helena and could tell she had only just started extracting the story. She turned aside discreetly, attending to the fire while Davos and I stripped the priest of his wet clothes and wrapped him in a blanket. He was less sturdily built than either of us, but his physique was strong enough; years of climbing the high mountains of his native city had toughened him. He kept his eyes downcast.

'Not much to say for himself!' muttered Davos. With Musa, that was hardly unusual.

'What happened?' I demanded. 'It's peeing down outside like customers in a cold bathhouse privy, but he shouldn't be this wet.'

'Fell in a reservoir.'

'Do me a favour, Davos!'

'No, it's right!' he explained, with an endearingly sheepish air. 'After the play a group of us went looking for some wineshop that the clowns thought they knew about – '

'I don't believe it! In a storm like this?'

'Performers need to unwind. They persuaded your man to come along.'

'I don't believe that either. I've never seen him drink.'

'He seemed interested,' Davos insisted stolidly. Musa himself remained clammed up, shivering in his blanket and looking even more strained than usual. I knew I couldn't trust Musa, since he was representing The Brother; I scrutinised the actor, wondering whether I trusted him.

Davos had a square face with quiet, regretful eyes. Short, no-nonsense black hair topped his head. He was built like a cairn of Celtic rocks, basic, long-lasting, dependable, broadly based; not much would topple him. His view of life was dry. He looked as if he had seen the whole spectacle – and wouldn't waste his money on a second entrance fee. For my purposes, he seemed too bitter to waste effort on pretence. Though if he did want to delude me, I knew he was a good enough actor to do it.

Yet I could not see Davos as a killer.

'So what exactly happened?' I asked.

Davos continued his story. In his voice, which was a magnificent baritone, it seemed like a public performance. That's the trouble with actors; everything they say sounds completely believable. 'The Twins' fabulous entertainment spot was supposed to be outside the rampart wall, on the eastern side of the city – '

'Spare me the tourists' itinerary.' I was kicking myself for not having stayed close. If I had gone on this crazy tour myself I might at least have seen what had happened – maybe have prevented it. And I might even have got a drink out of the trip. 'Where does a reservoir come into this?'

'There are a couple of great water cisterns to conserve rain.' They must be full enough this evening. Fortune was now dumping a whole year's rainfall on Bostra. 'We had to go around one. It's built within a huge embankment. There was a narrow elevated path, people were larking about a bit, and somehow Musa slipped into the water.'

It would have been beneath him to trail off; Davos paused portentously. I gave him a long stare. Its meaning would have been obvious, on stage or off. 'Who exactly was larking? And how did Musa come to "slip"?'

The priest lifted his head for the first time. He still said nothing, but he watched Davos answer me. 'Who do you think was larking? The Twins for two, and several of the stagehands. They were pretending to push one another about on the edge of the walkway. But I don't know how he slipped.' Musa made no attempt to inform us. For the moment I left him alone.

Helena brought a warm drink for Musa. She fussed over him protectively, giving me a chance to talk to the actor apart. 'You are sure you didn't see who pushed our friend?'

117

Like me, Davos had lowered his voice. 'I wasn't aware I needed to look. I was watching my step. It was pitch-dark and slippery enough without fools playing up.'

'Was the accident on the way to the wineshop, or on the way back?'

'The way there.' So no one had been drunk. Davos understood what I was thinking. If somebody had tripped up the Nabataean, whoever it was had fully intended him to fall.

'What's your opinion of Tranio and Grumio?' I asked thoughtfully.

'A mad pair. But that's traditional. Being witty all night on-stage makes clowns unpredictable. Who can blame them when you listen to the standard of playwrights' jokes?' Shrugging, I accepted the professional insult, as I was supposed to. 'Most clowns have fallen off a ladder once too often anyway.' A stage trick, presumably. I must have looked bemused; Davos interpreted: 'Dented heads; not all there.'

'Our two seem bright enough,' I grunted.

'Bright enough to cause trouble,' he agreed.

'Would they go as far as killing?'

'You're the investigator, Falco. You tell me.'

'Who said I was an investigator?'

'Phrygia mentioned it.'

'Well do me a favour, don't pass on the news any further! Blabbing isn't going to help my task.' There was no chance of making discreet enquiries in this company. No one had any idea of how to hold their tongue and let you get on with it. 'Are you and Phrygia close?'

'I've known the gorgeous old stick for twenty years, if that's what you mean.'

Beyond the fire I could sense that Helena Justina was watching him curiously. Later, after observing him here, the intuitive girl would tell me whether Davos had been Phrygia's lover in the past, or was now, or merely wished to be. He had spoken with the assurance of an old acquaintance, a troupe member who had earned himself the right to be consulted about a newcomer.

'She told me about being asked to play Medea at Epidaurus.'

118

'Ah that!' he commented quietly, with a soft smile.

'Did you know her then?' In reply to my question he nodded. It was a reply of sorts – the kind of simple answer that leads down a dead end. I tackled him directly: 'And what about Heliodorus, Davos? How long had you known him?'

'Too long!' I waited, so he added more temperately: 'Five or six seasons. Chremes picked him up in southern Italy. He knew an alphabet or two; seemed ideal for the job.' This time I ignored the arrow.

'You didn't get on?'

'Is that right?' He was not truculent, merely secretive. Truculence, being based on simple motives such as guilt and fear, is easier to fathom. Secrecy could have any number of explanations – including the straightforward one that Davos had a polite personality. However, I did not ascribe his reserved manner to mere tact.

'Was he just an awful writer, or was it personal?'

'He was a bloody awful writer – and I bloody loathed the creep.'

'Any reason?'

'Plenty!' Suddenly Davos lost patience. He stood up, leaving us. But the habit of making an exit speech overtook him: 'Somebody will no doubt whisper to you, if they haven't yet: I had just told Chremes the man was a troublemaker and that he ought to be dropped from the company.' Davos carried weight; it would matter. There was more, however. 'At Petra I gave Chremes an ultimatum: either he dumped Heliodorus, or he lost me.'

Surprised, I managed to fetch out, 'And what was his decision?'

'He hadn't made any decision.' The contempt in his tone revealed that if Davos had hated the playwright, his opinion of the manager was nearly as low. 'The only time in his life Chremes ever made a choice was when he married Phrygia, and she organised that herself, due to pressing circumstances.'

Afraid I would ask, Helena kicked me. She was a tall girl, with an impressive length of leg. A glimpse of her fine ankle gave me a *frisson* I could not enjoy properly at that moment.

The warning was unnecessary. I had been an informer long enough; I recognised the allusion, but I asked the question anyway: 'That, I take it, is a dark reference to an unwelcome pregnancy? Chremes and Phrygia have no children with them now, so I assume the baby died?' Davos screwed up his mouth in silence, as if reluctantly acknowledging the story. 'Leaving Phrygia shackled to Chremes, apparently pointlessly? Did Heliodorus know this?'

'He knew.' Full of his own anger, Davos had recognised mine. He kept his answer short and left me to deduce for myself the unpleasant follow-on.

'I suppose he used it to taunt the people involved in his normal friendly manner?'

'Yes. He stuck the knife in both of them at every opportunity.'

I didn't need to elaborate, but tried it to put pressure on Davos: 'He ragged Chremes about the marriage he regrets – '

'Chremes knows it was the best thing he ever did.'

'And tormented Phrygia over the bad marriage, her lost chance at Epidaurus, and, probably, over her lost child?'

'Over all those things,' Davos answered, perhaps more guardedly.

'He sounds vicious. No wonder you wanted Chremes to get rid of him.'

As soon as I said it I realised that this could be taken as a suggestion that *Chremes* had drowned the playwright. Davos picked up the implication, but merely smiled grimly. I had a feeling that if Chremes was ever accused, Davos would cheerfully stand by and see him convicted – whether or not the charge was a just one.

Helena, ever quick to smooth over sensitivities, broke in. 'Davos, if Heliodorus was always wounding people so painfully, surely the company manager had a good excuse – and a personal motive – to dismiss him when you asked for it?'

'Chremes is incapable of decisions, even when it's easy. This,' Davos told Helena heavily, 'was difficult.'

Before we could ask him why, he had left the tent.

XXI

I was beginning to see the picture: Chremes, Phrygia, and where Davos himself fitted in as the old friend who had mourned for their mistakes and his own lost opportunities. When Helena caught my eye, I checked with her: 'What do you think?'

'He's not involved,' she answered slowly. 'I think he may have meant more to Phrygia in the past than he does now, but it was probably a long time ago. After knowing her and Chremes for twenty years, now he's just a critical but loyal friend.'

Helena had been warming some honey for me. She rose and fetched it from the fire. I took the beaker, settling down more comfortably and giving Musa a reassuring smile. For a while none of us spoke. We sat in a close group, considering events.

I was aware of a change in the atmosphere. As soon as Davos left the tent, Musa had relaxed. His manner became more open. Instead of huddling under his blanket he ran his hands through his hair, which had started to dry and curl up at the ends ridiculously. It made him look young. His dark eyes had a thoughtful expression; the mere fact that I could judge his expression marked a change in him.

I realised what was up. I had seen Helena looking after him as if he belonged to us, while he accepted her anxious attentions with little trace of his old wariness. The truth was clear. We had been together for a couple of weeks. The worst had happened: the damned Nabataean hanger-on had joined the family.

'Falco,' he said. I could not remember him addressing me by name before. I gave him a nod. It was not unfriendly. He had not yet attained the position of loathing I reserved for my natural relatives.

'Tell us what happened,' Helena murmured. The

121

conversation was taking place in low voices, as if we were afraid there might be lurking figures outside the tent. That seemed unlikely; it was still a filthy night.

'It was a ridiculous expedition, ill-conceived and ill-planned.' It sounded as if Musa had viewed his jolly night on the town as some military manoeuvre. 'People had not taken enough torches, and those we had were waning in the damp.'

'Who asked you to go on this drinking spree?' I broke in. Musa recollected. 'Tranio, I think.'

'I guessed it might have been!' Tranio was not my chief suspect – or at least not yet, because I had no evidence – but he was first choice as a general stirrer-up of trouble.

'Why did you agree to go?' Helena queried.

He flashed her an astonishing grin; it split his face apart. 'I thought you and Falco were going to be quarrelling about the play.' It was Musa's first joke: one aimed at me.

'We never quarrel!' I growled.

'Then I beg your pardon!' He said it with the polite insincerity of a man who shared our tent and knew the truth.

'Tell us about the accident!' Helena urged him, smiling.

The priest smiled too, more wickedly than we were used to, but immediately grew intense as he told his story. 'Walking was difficult. We were stumbling, our heads low. People were grumbling, but nobody wanted to suggest turning back. When we were on the cistern's raised embankment, I felt somebody push me, like this – ' He suddenly aimed a hard blow with the flat of his palm against the lower middle of my back. I braced my calves to avoid falling into the fire; he had quite a shove. 'I fell down over the wall – '

'Jupiter! And of course you can't swim!'

Unable to swim myself, I viewed his predicament with horror. However, Musa's dark eyes looked amused. 'Why do you say that?'

'It seemed a reasonable deduction, given that you live in a desert citadel – '

He raised a disapproving eyebrow, as if I had said something stupid. 'We have water cisterns in Petra. Small boys always play in them. I can swim.'

'Ah!' It had saved his life. But somebody else must have made the same mistake as me.

'It was very dark, however,' Musa went on in his light, conversational way. 'I was startled. The cold water made me gasp and lose my breath. I could not see any place to climb out. I was afraid.' His admission was frank and straightforward, like everything he said or did. 'I could tell that the water below me was deep. It felt many times deeper than a man. As soon as I could breathe, I shouted out very loudly.'

Helena frowned angrily. 'It's terrifying! Did anyone help you?'

'Davos quickly found a way down to the water's edge. He was roaring instructions, to me and to the other people. He was, I think . . .' Musa searched for the word in Greek. 'Competent. Then everyone came – the clowns, the stagehands, Congrio. Hands pulled me out. I do not know whose hands.' That meant nothing. As soon as it became obvious he hadn't sunk and would be rescued, whoever tipped Musa into the water would help him out again to cover his own tracks.

'It's the hand that shoved you in that matters.' I was thinking about our suspects list and trying to envisage who had been doing what on that embankment in the dark. 'You haven't mentioned Chremes or Philocrates. Were they with you?'

'No.'

'It sounds as if we can eliminate Davos as perpetrator, but we'll keep an open mind on all the rest. Do you know who had been walking closest to you beforehand?'

'I am not sure. I thought it was the Twins. A while before I had been talking to the bill-poster, Congrio. But he had fallen behind. Because of the height of the walkway and the wind, everyone had slowed up and strung out more. You could see figures, though not tell who they were.'

'Were you in single file?'

'No. I was alone, others were in groups. The walkway was wide enough; it only seemed dangerous because it was high, and in darkness, and made slippery by the rain.' When he did talk, Musa was extremely precise, an intelligent man talking in a language not his own. A man full of caution too. Not many people who have narrowly escaped death remain so calm.

There was a small silence. As usual it was Helena who faced up to asking the trickiest question: 'Musa was pushed into the reservoir deliberately. So why', she enquired gently, 'has he become a target?'

Musa's reply to that was a precise one too: 'People think I saw the man who murdered the previous playwright.' I felt a slight jar. His phrasing made it sound as if merely being a playwright was dangerous.

I considered the suggestion slowly. 'We have never told anybody that. I always call you an interpreter.'

'The bill-poster may have overheard us talking about it yesterday,' said Musa. I liked the way his mind worked. He had noticed Congrio lurking too close, just as I had, and had already marked him as suspicious.

'Or he may have told somebody else what he overheard.' I swore quietly. 'If my light-hearted suggestion that we made you a decoy brought this accident upon you, I apologise, Musa.'

'People had been suspicious of us anyway,' Helena rebutted. 'I know there are all sorts of rumours about all three of us.'

'One thing is sure,' I said. 'It looks as if we have made the playwright's murderer extremely jumpy merely by joining the group.'

'He was there,' Musa confirmed in a sombre tone. 'I knew he was there on the embankment above me.'

'How was that?'

'When I first fell into the water, no one seemed to hear the splash. I sank fast, then rose to the surface. I was trying to catch my breath; at first I could not shout. For a moment I felt entirely alone. The other people sounded far off. I could hear their voices growing fainter as they walked away.' He paused, staring into the fire. Helena had reached for my hand; like me she was sharing Musa's dreadful moment of solitude as he struggled to survive down in the black waters of the reservoir while most of his companions carried on oblivious.

Musa's face stayed expressionless. His whole body was

still. He did not rant or make wild threats about his future actions. Only his tone clearly told us that the playwright's killer should be wary of meeting him again. 'He is here,' Musa said. 'Among the voices that were going into the darkness, one man had started whistling.'

Exactly like the man he had heard whistling as he came down from the High Place.

'I'm sorry, Musa.' Apologising again I was terse. 'I should have foreseen this. I should have protected you.'

'I am unharmed. It is well.'

'Do you own a dagger?' He was vulnerable; I was ready to give him mine.

'Yes.' Davos and I had not found it when we stripped him.

'Then wear it.'

'Yes, Falco.'

'Next time you'll use it,' I commented.

'Oh yes.' Again that commonplace tone, belying the compelling words. He was a priest of Dushara; I reckoned that Musa would know where to strike. There could be a swift, sticky fate awaiting the man who had whistled in the dark. 'You and I will find this hill bandit, Falco.' Musa stood up, keeping the blanket around him modestly. 'Now I think we should all sleep.'

'Quite right.' I threw his own joke back at him: 'Helena and I still have a lot of *quarrelling* to do.'

There was a teasing glint in Musa's eye. 'Hah! Then until you have finished I must go back to the reservoir.'

Helena scowled. 'Go to bed, Musa!'

Next day we were setting off for the Decapolis. I made a vow to keep a watchful eye out for the safety of all of us.

ACT TWO: THE DECAPOLIS

The next few weeks. The settings are various rocky roads and hillside cities with unwelcoming aspects. A number of camels are walking about watching the action curiously.

SYNOPSIS: *Falco*, a jobbing playwright, and *Helena*, his accomplice, together with *Musa*, a priest who has left his temple for rather vague reasons, are travelling through the Decapolis in a search for Truth. Suspected of being imposters, they soon find themselves in danger from an anonymous *Plotter* who must be concealing himself amongst their new-found friends. Somebody needs to devise a sharp plan to penetrate his disguise . . .

XXII

Philadelphia: a pretty Greek name for a pretty Greek town, rather knocked about at present. It had been pillaged a few years earlier by the rebelling Jews. The inward-looking fanatics of Judaea had always hated the Hellenistic settlements across the Jordan in the Decapolis, places where good citizenship – which could be learned by anybody at a decent Greek city school – counted for more than inheriting a stern religion in the blood. The marauders from Judaea had made it plain with vicious damage to property what they thought of such airy tolerance. Then a Roman army under Vespasian had made it plain to the Judaeans what *we* thought about damage to property by heavily damaging theirs. Judaea was pretty quiet these days, and the Decapolis was enjoying a new period of stability.

Philadelphia was enclosed by steep-sided hills, seven in number, though far more parched than the founding hills of Rome. There was a well-placed precipitous citadel, with the town spilling outwards and downwards on to a broad valley floor where a stream wandered attractively, doing away with any obvious need for cisterns, I was glad to see. We made camp, and sat down in our tents for what I gathered was likely to be a long wait while Chremes tried to negotiate terms for performing a play.

We had now entered Roman Syria. On our original journey between Petra and Bostra I had been working through the company play box, but on the way here to the Decapolis I had been able to give more attention to our surroundings. The road from Bostra to Philadelphia was supposed to be a good one. That meant a lot of people used it: not the same thing.

To be a travelling theatre group was not easy in these parts. The country people hated us because they identified us with the Greekified towns where we played, yet the townsfolk all thought we were uncivilised nomads because we travelled about. In the villages were the weekly markets, where we had nothing to offer that people valued; the cities were administrative centres where we paid neither poll tax nor property tax and had no voting rights, so we were outsiders there too.

If the cities despised us, there was a certain amount of prejudice on our side as well. We Romans viewed these Greek-founded towns as hotbeds of licentiousness. Philadelphia offered little promise of that, however. (Believe me, I looked hard for it.) The city was thriving in a pleasant way, although to a Roman the place was a backwater.

I sensed that this was typical. Had it not been for the great trade routes, the East would never have been more to Rome than a buffer against the might of Parthia. Even the trade routes could not alter the impression that the Ten Towns were mostly *small* towns, often in the middle of nowhere. Some had gained status when Alexander noticed them on his progress to world domination, but they had all achieved a position in history when Pompey first liberated them from the recurrent Jewish plunderers and established Roman Syria. Syria was important because it was our frontier with Parthia. But the Parthians were smouldering on the other side of the River Euphrates, and the Euphrates lay many miles from the Decapolis.

At least in the cities they all spoke Greek, so we could haggle and pick up the news.

'Are you going to send your "interpreter" home now?' quipped Grumio rather pointedly when we arrived.

'What, to spare him another ducking?' With Musa scarcely dry from his near-fatal dip I was angry.

Helena answered him more quietly: 'Musa is our travelling companion, and our friend.'

Musa said nothing as usual until the three of us were in our tent. Then his eyebrows shifted upwards again in teasing wonder as he commented, 'I am your friend!'

It carried a world of gentle amusement. Musa had the sweet-natured charm of many people in this region – and he was wielding it to notable effect. He had grasped that belonging to the Didius family conferred the perpetual right to play the fool.

To liven up Philadelphia, Chremes was planning to give them *The Rope* by Plautus. In the plot rope hardly features; the important item of interest is a disputed travelling trunk (more of a satchel in the Greek original; we Roman playwrights know how to think big when we adapt). There is, however, a protracted tug of war for possession of the trunk, to be performed in our staging by Tranio and Grumio. I had seen them rehearsing the scene already. Their hilarious performance had a lot to teach a budding playwright: mainly, that his script is irrelevant. It's the 'business' that brings the crowd to its feet, and however sharp your stylus is, you can't write 'business' down.

I wasted some effort in Philadelphia asking about Thalia's missing person, without luck. Nor did anybody recognise the other name I was touting: Habib, the mysterious Syrian businessman who had visited Rome and expressed a questionable interest in circus entertainment. I wondered if his wife knew that while he was acting the world traveller he liked to make friends with bosomy snakedancers. (*Oh don't worry about it*, Helena assured me. *She knows all right!*)

On my return to camp I saw Grumio practising dramatic stunts. I asked him to teach me how to fall off a ladder, a trick for which I could see plenty of uses in daily life. It was stupid to try; I had soon landed badly on a leg I had broken two years previously. It left me bruised and limping, worried that I might have shattered the bone a second time. While Grumio shook his head over the incident, I hopped off to recover in my tent.

As I lay complaining on my bed, Helena sat outside with something to read.

'Whose fault was this?' she had demanded. 'You being stupid, or somebody putting you out of action?'

Reluctantly I admitted I had asked for the lesson myself. After a sketchy murmur of sympathy, she rolled down the tent-flap and left me in semidarkness, as if I had been concussed. I thought her attitude was a little satirical, but a nap seemed called for anyway.

The weather had grown hot. We were taking things extremely gently, knowing we would be baked far hotter later on; you have to beware of exhaustion when you are unused to desert conditions. I was all ready for a long snooze, but as I drowsed on the verge of it, I heard Helena call out 'Hello there!' to a passer-by.

I might have taken no notice, had not the masculine voice that answered her been laden with self-satisfaction. It was a handsome rich-toned tenor with seductive modulations, and I knew to whom it belonged: Philocrates, who thought himself the idol of all the girls.

XXIII

'Well, hello!' he responded, evidently overjoyed to find he had attracted the attention of my highly superior bloom. Men didn't need an exploratory chat with her banker before they found Helena Justina worth talking to.

I stayed put. But I had sat up.

From my dim hiding place I heard him tramp closer, the smart leather boots that always showed off his manly calves crunching on the stony ground. Footwear was his one extravagance, though he wore the rest of his threadbare outfit as if he were in regal robes. (Actually, Philocrates wore all his clothes like a man who was just about to shrug them off for indecent purposes.) From a theatre seat he was extravagantly good-looking; stupid to pretend otherwise. But he turned into a ripe damson if you peered into the punnet closely: too soft, and browning under the skin. Also, though his physique was all in proportion, he was extremely small. I could look right over his neatly combed locks, and most of his scenes with Phrygia had to be played with her sitting down.

I imagined him striking a pose in front of Helena – and tried *not* to imagine Helena being impressed by the haughty good looks.

'May I join you?' He didn't mess about.

'Of course.' I was all set to thunder out and defend her, though Helena seemed to be making a brave effort to cope. I could hear from her voice that she was smiling, a sleepy, happy smile. Then I heard Philocrates stretching out at her feet, where instead of looking like a smug dwarf he would simply look well honed.

'What's a beautiful woman like you doing here all on her own?' Dear gods, his chat line was so old it was positively rancid. Next thing he would be flaring his nostrils and asking her if she would like to see his war wounds.

'I'm enjoying this lovely day,' replied Helena, with more

serenity than she had ever shown with me when I first tried getting to know her. She used to swat me like a hornet on a honey-jar.

'What are you reading, Helena?'

'Plato.' It put a quick stop to the intellectual discussion.

'Well, well!' said Philocrates. This seemed to be his pause-filler.

'Well, well,' echoed Helena placidly. She could be very unhelpful to men who were trying to impress her.

'That's a beautiful dress.' She was in white. White had never suited Helena; I repeatedly told her so.

'Thank you,' she answered modestly.

'I'll bet you look even better with it off . . .' Mars blast his balls! Wide awake now, I was expecting my young lady to call out to me for protection.

'It's a paradox of science,' stated Helena Justina calmly, 'but when the weather gets as hot as this, people are more comfortable covered up.'

'Fascinating!' Philocrates knew how to sound as if he meant it, though somehow I thought science was not his strong point. 'I've been noticing you. You're an interesting woman.' Helena was more interesting than this facile bastard knew, but if he started to investigate her finer qualities he would be sent on his way with my boot. 'What's your star sign?' he mused, one of those pea-brained types who thought astrology was the straight route to a quick seduction. 'A Leo, I should say . . .'

Jupiter! I hadn't used 'What's your horoscope?' since I was eleven. He ought to have guessed Virgo; that would always get them giggling, after which you could cruise home.

'Virgo,' stated Helena herself crisply, which should put a blight on astrology.

'You surprise me!' She surprised me too. I had been thinking Helena's birthday was in October, and was mentally making up jokes about Librans weighing up trouble. Trouble was what *I* would be in if I didn't learn the correct date.

'Oh I doubt if I could surprise you with much, Philocrates!' she answered. The annoying wench must think I was asleep. She was playing up to him as if I didn't exist at all, let alone lying behind a tent wall growing furious, barely a stride away.

134

Philocrates had missed her irony. He laughed gaily. '*Really*? In my experience, girls who appear terribly serious and seem like vestal virgins can be a lot of fun!'

'Have you had fun with a lot of girls, Philocrates?' asked Helena innocently.

'Let's say, a lot of girls have had fun with me!'

'That must be very gratifying for you,' Helena murmured. Anyone who knew her well could hear her thinking, *Probably not so much fun for them!*

'I've learned a few tricks with the pleasure pipe.' Two more words, and I would spring from the tent and tie up his pleasure pipe in a very tight Hercules knot.

'If that's an offer, I'm flattered, naturally.' Helena was smiling, I could tell. 'Apart from the fact that I couldn't possibly live up to your sophisticated standards, I'm afraid I have other commitments.'

'Are you married?' he shot in.

Helena loathed that question. Her voice acquired bite. 'Would that be a bonus? Deceiving husbands must be so amusing . . . I was married once.'

'Is your husband dead?'

'I divorced him.' He *was* dead now in fact, but Helena Justina never referred to it.

'Hard-hearted girl! What was the fellow's crime?'

Helena's worst insults were always delivered in cool tone. 'Oh he was just a normal arrogant male – deficient in morals, incapable of devotion, insensitive to a wife who had the good manners to be honest.'

Philocrates passed it over as a reasonable comment. 'And now you're available?'

'Now I live with someone else.'

'Well, well . . .' I heard him shifting his ground again. 'So where is the happy scribbler?'

'Probably up a date-palm writing a play. He takes his work very seriously.' Helena knew I had never done that, whatever job I was pretending to hold down. However, I did have an idea for a completely new play of my own. I had not discussed it with Helena; she must have noticed me thinking and guessed.

Philocrates sneered. 'Pity his skill doesn't match his dedication!' What a bastard. I made a note to write him out of at least three scenes in my next adaptation. 'I'm intrigued. What can this Falco have to offer a smart and intelligent girl like you?'

'Marcus Didius has wonderful qualities.'

'An amateur author who looks as if he's been dragged through a thicket by a wild mule? The man's haircut should be an indictable offence!'

'Some girls like raffish charm, Philocrates ... He's entertaining and affectionate,' Helena rebuked him. 'He tells the truth. He doesn't make promises unless he can keep them, though sometimes he keeps promises he never even made. What I like most,' she added, 'is his loyalty.'

'Is that right? He looks as if he knows his way around. How can you be certain he's faithful?'

'How can anyone ever be certain? The point is,' Helena said gently, 'that I believe it.'

'Because he tells you?'

'No. Because he never feels he needs to.'

'I suppose you're in love with him?'

'I suppose I am.' She said it unrepentantly.

'He's a lucky man!' exclaimed Philocrates insincerely. His mockery was evident. 'And have *you* ever betrayed *him*?' His voice held a hopeful note.

'No.' Hers was cool.

'And you're not going to try it now?' At last he was catching on.

'Probably not – though how can anyone ever be certain?' responded Helena graciously.

'Well, when you decide to try sipping from a different bowl – and you will, Helena, believe me – I'm available.'

'You'll be the first candidate,' she promised in a light tone. Ten minutes beforehand I would have burst from the tent and wrapped a guy rope around the actor's neck; instead I sat tight. Helena's voice hardly changed tone, though because I knew her I was ready for her new tack. She had finished with whimsy; she was taking charge. 'Now may I ask you something very personal, Philocrates?'

His big chance to talk about himself: 'Of course!'

'Would you mind telling me what your relations with the drowned playwright used to be?'

There was a brief pause. Then Philocrates complained spitefully, 'So this is the price for being permitted to converse with your ladyship?'

Helena Justina did not balk. 'It's simply the price for knowing someone who has been murdered,' she corrected him. 'And probably knowing his killer too. You can refuse to answer the question.'

'From which you will draw your own conclusions?'

'That would seem reasonable. What have you to say?'

'I didn't get on with him. In fact we damn nearly came to blows,' Philocrates confessed shortly.

'Why was that?' She hardly waited before adding, 'Was it a quarrel over a girl?'

'Correct.' He hated saying it. 'We both received a put-down from the same woman. I did less badly than him, though.' He was probably boasting to console himself. Helena, who understood arrogance, did not bother pursuing it.

'I'm sure you did,' she flattered him sympathetically. 'I won't ask who it was.'

'Byrria, if you must know,' he told her before he could stop himself. The poor rabbit was helpless; Helena had moved effortlessly from an object of seduction to his most confidential friend.

'I'm sorry. I doubt if it was personal, Philocrates. I've heard she is extremely ambitious and declines all approaches from men. I'm sure you rose above the rejection, but what about Heliodorus?'

'No sense of discretion.'

'He kept on pestering her? That would make her all the more obdurate, of course.'

'I hope so!' he growled. 'There was better sport on offer, after all.'

'There certainly was! If *you* had done her the honour . . . So

137

you and the playwright had an ongoing rivalry. Did you hate him enough to kill him though?'

'Great gods, no! It was only a tiff over a girl.'

'Oh quite! Was that his attitude too?'

'He probably let it rankle. That was his kind of stupidity.'

'And did you ever tackle Heliodorus about him bothering Byrria?'

'Why should I do that?' Philocrates' surprise sounded genuine. 'She turned me down. What she did or did not do after that was no concern of mine.'

'Did other people notice that he was being a nuisance?'

'Must have done. She never complained about it; that would have made him worse. But we all knew he kept putting pressure on her.'

'So the man had no finesse?'

'No pride, anyway.'

'And Byrria was constantly avoiding him. Did he write her bad parts?'

'Stinkers.'

'Do you know of any other admirers Byrria might have?'

'I wouldn't notice.'

'No,' Helena agreed thoughtfully. 'I don't expect you would . . . Where were you when Heliodorus took his fatal walk to the High Place?'

'The last afternoon? I'd packed my bags for leaving Petra and was making good use of some spare time before we left.'

'What were you doing?'

Helena had walked straight into it. He turned triumphantly vindictive: 'I was up in one of the rock tombs with a frankincense merchant's pretty wife – and I was giving her the screwing of her life!'

'Silly of me to ask!' my lass managed to rally, though I guessed she was blushing. 'I wish I'd known you then. I would have asked you to ask her the proper rate for buying incense gum.'

Either her courage or simply her sense of humour finally broke through to him. I heard Philocrates laugh shortly, then there was a sudden movement and his voice came from a different level; he must have swung himself to his feet. His

138

tone had changed. For once the admiration was unfeigned and unselfish: 'You're incredible. When that bastard Falco ditches you, don't weep too long; make sure you come and console yourself with me.'

Helena made no answer, and his small feet in their expensive boots scrunched away across the pebbly road.

I waited a suitable time then emerged from the tent, stretching.

'Ah here's the mellifluous bard awakening!' teased the love of my life. Her quiet eyes surveyed me from the deep shadow of a sloppily brimmed sunhat.

'You're asking for a very rude pentameter.'

Helena was reclining in a folding chair with her feet on a bale. We had learned the essential desert trick of pitching tent in the shade of a tree wherever possible; Helena had taken all the remaining patch of coolness. Philocrates must have been charcoal-grilled like a mullet as he lay out in full sun while he talked to her. I was pleased to see it.

'You look nicely settled. Had a good afternoon?'

'Very quiet,' said Helena.

'Anyone bother you?'

'No one I couldn't deal with . . .' Her voice dropped gently. 'Hello, Marcus.' She had a way of greeting me that was almost unbearably intimate.

'Hello, beautiful.' I was tough. I could cope with having my wrath undermined by female trickery. Then she smiled at me softly so I felt my resolve going limp.

It was later now. The burning sun was dropping towards the horizon and losing its power. When I took the actor's place lying at her feet the situation would be virtually pleasant, even though the ground was stony and the stones still hot.

She knew I had been listening in. I pretended to look her over. Despite an effort to appear nonchalant I could feel a tendon going rigid in my neck at the thought of Philocrates eyeing her then making suggestive remarks. 'I hate that dress. White makes you look washed out.'

Helen wriggled her toes in her sandals and answered peacefully, 'When I want to attract someone in particular, I'll

139

change it.' A certain glint in her eye held a private message for me.

I grinned. Any man of taste liked Helena wearing blue or red. I was a man of taste who liked to be frank. 'Don't bother. Just take the white one off.' I assumed my station on the ground like a loyal dog. She leaned down and rumpled my indictable curls, while I looked up at her thoughtfully. I said, in a lower voice, 'He was perfectly happy cruising the colonnades looking for a frolic with a flute girl. You didn't have to do that to him.'

Helena raised an eyebrow. Watching her, I thought she coloured up slightly. 'Are you objecting to me flirting, Marcus?' We both knew I was in no position to do that. Hypocrisy had never been my style.

'Flirt with whom you like, if you can handle the results. I meant, you didn't have to make that poor peristyle prowler fall in love with you.'

Helena didn't realise, or wouldn't acknowledge, her influence. Five years of marriage to a disinterested prig in a senatorial toga had crushed most of her confidence. Two years of being adored by me had so far failed to revive it. She shook her head. 'Don't be romantic, Marcus.'

'No?' I was on his side, partly. 'I just happen to know what it feels like to realise abruptly that the girl you are mentally undressing is staring back at you with eyes that can see your soul naked.' Hers were the eyes I meant. Rather than look into them at that moment I changed the subject flippantly: 'That's certainly not a scroll of Plato in your lap.'

'No. It's the collection of ribald stories I found among your box of plays.'

'What is this thing – some notes by Heliodorus?'

'I shouldn't think so, Marcus. There seem to be several handwritings, but none look like his awful scrawl.' I had been complaining about the dead man's revisions on the play scrolls, most of which were illegible. Helena went on, 'In places the ink has faded; it looks quite old. Besides, everyone says Heliodorus had no feeling for jokes, and these are very funny. If you like,' she suggested seductively, 'I'll read some of the rude ones out to you . . .'

The actor was right. Serious girls who look like vestal virgins can be a lot of fun – provided you can persuade them it's you they want to have fun with.

XXIV

The rope went well. We put it on for a second night, and nobody came. We left town.

Our next destination was Gerasa. It lay forty miles to the north – two days with decent transport, but probably twice that with our group of cheap camels and heavily laden waggons. Cursing Philadelphia for an uncultured dump and damning Plautus as an unfunny hack, we turned our backs on the town, flung the play to the bottom of the heap, and creaked on our way. At least Gerasa had a prosperous reputation; people with money might be looking for something to spend it on. (More likely, news that our production of *The Rope* was as stiff as cheese would run ahead of us.)

One way and another the pointers were strong for an urgent interview with Byrria. The dead playwright had been nursing his lust for her, and most of our male suspects seemed to be tangled in the same set. Besides, if Helena could flirt with the masculine star, I could allow myself a chat with his delicious female counterpart.

It was easy to arrange. A few nosy passers-by had spotted my darling's dalliance with Philocrates; already everyone knew about it. Pretending to quarrel with her about her diminutive admirer, I hopped off our cart and sat on a rock with my chin in my hands, looking glum. I had left Helena with Musa; protection for both of them. I was unwilling to leave either for long without cover.

Slowly the tired parade of our company went past me, all bare legs on backboards, bursting baskets and bad jokes. Those who had camels mostly led them on foot; if you've ever been up on a camel you'll know why. Those in the waggons were scarcely more comfortable. Some of the stagehands had given up having their ribs jolted and had chosen to walk. People carried cudgels or long knives in their belts in case we were attacked by desert raiders; some of the orchestra piped or banged on their instruments – an even more successful deterrent to nomadic thieves.

Byrria drove her own cart. That summed her up. She shared herself with no one, and relied on no one. As she drew level I stood up and hailed her. She didn't want to give me a lift, but she was almost at the end of the caravan and had to accept that if she didn't I might be left behind. Nobody thought they needed a writer, but people like keeping a target to mock.

'Cheer up!' I cried, as I sprang aboard with a lithe twist of the torso and a charming grin. 'It won't happen!'

She continued to scowl bleakly. 'Drop the antique routine, Falco.'

'Sorry. The old lines are the best – '

'Diana of the Ephesians! Put a lid on it, poser.'

I was about to think, *This never happens to Philocrates*, when I remembered that it had.

She was twenty, perhaps less. She had probably been on the stage for eight or nine years; it's one of those professions where girls with looks start young. In a different social circle she would have been old enough to become a vestal. There can't be much difference between being a priestess and an actress, except for public status. They both involve fooling an audience with a ritual performance in order to make the public believe in the unbelievable.

I did my best to be professional, but Byrria's looks were impossible to ignore. She had a triangular face with green eyes like an Egyptian cat set wide above high cheekbones and a thin, perfect nose. Her mouth had a strange lopsided quirk that gave her an ironic, world-weary air. Her figure was as watchable as her face, small and curvaceous, and hinting of unrevealed possibilities. To finish the business, she had a dramatic knack of looping up her warm brown hair with a couple of bronze hairpins, so it not only looked unusual but stayed in place, showing off a tantalising neck.

Her voice seemed too low for such a neat person; it had a huskiness that was completely distracting when combined with her experienced manner. Byrria gave the impression she was holding all the competition at arm's length while she waited for the right person to move in on her. Even though he knew it was a false impression, any man she met would have to try.

'Why the hatred of men, flower?'

'I've known some, that's why.'

'Anyone in particular?'

'Men are never particular.'

'I meant, anyone special?'

'Special? I thought we were talking about men!'

I can recognize an impasse. Folding my arms, I sat in silence.

In those days the road to Gerasa was a poor one, begging for a military highway to be thrust through to Damascus. It would be done. Rome had spent a great deal of money on this region during the Judaean troubles, so inevitably in peacetime we would be spending even more. Once the region settled down the Decapolis would be dragged up to decent Roman standards. In the meantime we were suffering on an old Nabataean caravan route that nobody maintained. It was a lonely landscape. Later we reached a level plain and crossed a tributary of the Jordan through more fertile pasture into thick pine forest. But this early stage of our trip involved a rocky track amongst scrubby hills with only occasional glimpses of low nomad tents, few of them with visible occupants. Driving was not easy; Byrria had to concentrate.

As I expected, after a short time the lady felt obliged to fire more arrows at me. 'I have a question, Falco. When do you intend to stop slandering me?'

'Goodness, I thought you were about to ask for the address of my cloak-maker or my recipe for tarragon marinade! I know nothing about any slander.'

'You're making out to everyone that Heliodorus died because of me.'

'I never said that.' It was only one possibility. So far it seemed the most likely explanation for the playwright's drowning, but until I had proof I kept an open mind.

'I had nothing to do with it, Falco.'

'I do know you didn't push him into the cistern and hold his head under. A man did that.'

'Then why keep hinting I was involved?'

'I wasn't aware that I had. But face facts: like it or not, you're a popular girl. Everyone keeps telling me Heliodorus was after you but you weren't having it. Maybe one of your friends tackled him. Maybe it was a secret admirer. It's always possible someone knew you would be pleased if the bastard was out of the way, and tried to help.'

'That's a horrible suggestion!' She was frowning bitterly. On Byrria a frown looked good.

I was starting to feel protective. I *wanted* to prove the murder was nothing to do with her. I wanted to find a different motive. Those wonderful eyes were working impossible magic. I told myself I was too professional to let a dainty little actress with a pretty set of wide-spaced peepers overcome me – then I told myself not to be such a fool. I was stuck, just as anyone would be. We all hate murderers to be beautiful. Before long if I did unearth evidence implicating Byrria as an accomplice I would find myself considering whether to bury it in an old hay sack at the bottom of a drainage ditch . . .

'All right, just tell me about Heliodorus.' My voice was rasping; I cleared my throat. 'I know he was obsessed with you.'

'Wrong.' She spoke very quietly. 'He was just obsessed with getting what he wanted.'

'Ah! Too pushy?'

'That's a man's way of putting it!' Now she sounded bitter, her voice rising. ' "*A bit too pushy*" almost makes it sound as though it was my fault he went away disappointed.'

She was staring ahead, even though the road was easier to travel at this point. Away to our right a teenaged girl watched over a small flock of lean brown goats. In another direction vultures wheeled gracefully. We had started out early on purpose; now the heat was beginning to reflect off the stony track with dazzling force.

Byrria was not intending to help me. I pressed for more details: 'Heliodorus tried it on, and you rebuffed him?'

'Correct.'

'Then what?'

'What do you think?' Her voice remained dangerously level. 'He assumed that saying "No" meant "Yes, please – with force".'

'He *raped* you?'

She was a person who showed anger by very carefully keeping her temper. For a moment, while I reeled at this new angle, she also stayed silent. Then she attacked me contemptuously: 'I suppose you're going to tell me that there is always provocation, that women always want it, that rape never happens.'

'It happens.'

We were raging at one another. I suppose I knew why. Understanding it did not help.

'It happens,' I repeated. 'And I don't just mean men attacking women, be it strangers or acquaintances. I mean husbands misusing their wives. Fathers having "special secrets" with their children. Masters treating their slaves like so much bought meat. Guards torturing their prisoners. Soldiers bullying new recruits. High officials blackmailing – '

'Oh be quiet!' There was no mollifying her. Her green eyes flashed and she tossed her head so the ringlets danced, but there was nothing charming in the gesture. Undoubtedly enjoying the fact that she had misled me, she exclaimed, 'It did not happen to me, in fact. He had me on the ground, he had my wrists pinioned above my head and my skirts up, and the bruises he made forcing his knee between my thighs were still showing a month later, but somebody came looking for him and rescued me.'

'I'm glad.' I meant it, even though something in the way she had forced me to hear the details was subtly disturbing. 'Who was the useful friend?'

'Mind your own business.'

'Maybe it matters.' I wanted to force her to say it. Instinct told me I ought to identify her rescuer. She knew something I wanted to hear, and I could easily have become as much of a bully as Heliodorus.

'What matters to me,' Byrria flared angrily, 'is that I *thought* Heliodorus was going to rape me. Afterwards I was living with the knowledge that if he ever caught me on my own he was bound to try again – but all you need to know is that I never, ever went near him. I tried to know where he was always, because I made certain that I kept as far away from him as possible.'

'You can help me then,' I said, ignoring her hysterical edge. 'Did you know he was going up the mountain that last day at Petra? Did you see who went with him?'

'You mean, do I know who killed him?' The girl was effortlessly bright – and deliberately made me feel like an idiot. 'No. I just noticed the playwright was missing when the rest of us gathered at the theatre ready to leave.'

'All right.' Refusing to be put off, I tackled it another way. 'Who *was* there – and when did they arrive at the meeting point?'

'It won't help you,' Byrria assured me. 'When we noticed your girlfriend telling an official a body had been found, we had already missed Heliodorus and were complaining about him. Allowing time for you to have found the body and Helena to have come back down the hill – ' I hate witnesses who have done my thinking for me ' – then he must have been dead before any of us gathered at the theatre. Actually I was one of the last to get there. I turned up at the same time as Tranio and Grumio, who were looking the worse for wear, as usual.'

'Why were you late?' I grinned cheekily, in the vain hope of reasserting myself. 'Saying a fond farewell to a manly paramour?'

Up ahead people were stopping so we could rest during the simmering heat of midday. Byrria reined in, then literally pushed me out of her cart.

I sauntered back to my own waggon.

'Falco!' Musa had his head-dress wrapped across his lower face in the Eastern manner; he looked lean, cool, and much wiser than I felt in my short Roman tunic, with my bare arms and legs burning and sweat rivuleting down my back beneath the hot cloth. Byrria must have worked her spell on him too; for once he seemed actively curious. 'Did you learn anything from the beautiful one?'

I burrowed in our lunch basket. 'Not much.'

'So how did you get on?' asked Helena innocently.

'The woman's incorrigible. I had to fend off her advances in case the donkey bolted.'

'That's the problem with being so witty and good-looking,' retorted Helena. Musa burst into a rare fit of giggling. Helena, having denounced me in her normal offhand manner, merely carried on with the more important work of cleaning dust from her right sandal.

Ignoring them both, I sat spitting out date stones like a man who had something extremely intriguing to think about.

XXV

Gerasa: otherwise known as 'Antioch on the Chrysorhoas'.

Antiochia itself had a reputation for soft living. My brother Festus, who could be relied on as a scandalmonger, had told me that as a legionary posting it was notorious for the routine debauchery of its happy garrison. Life there was continual festivity; the city resounded to minstrels playing harps and drums . . . I was hoping to visit Antiochia. But it lay a long way north, so for now I had to be content with its namesake. Chrysorhoan Antiochia had plenty to offer, though I personally was never offered much debauchery, with or without minstrels.

Gerasa had grown from a small walled town on a knoll into a larger suburban centre through which ran the River Chrysorhoas, the Golden River, a bit of a stream that, compared to the noble Tiber, could barely support three minnow-fishers and a few women slapping dirty shirts on stones. Pillaged by Jews in the Rebellion, and then plundered again by Romans because one of the main leaders of the Jewish Revolt was a Gerasene, the town had been fitted up recently with new city walls that sprouted a coronet of watchtowers. Two of these defended the Watergate through which the Golden River rushed out via a sluice that directed its water under some pressure over a ten-foot waterfall. As we waited to enter the city we could see and hear the cascade to our right.

'This looks like a fine place for accidents!' I warned anyone who would listen. Only Musa took notice; he nodded, with his usual seriousness. He had the air of a fanatic who for the sake of Truth might volunteer to stand beside the sluice waiting for our murderer to tip him into the racing stream.

We were held up at the Southern Gate, waiting for customs clearance. Gerasa lay conveniently at the junction of two major trade routes. Its income from caravan tributes was such that twice it had smoothly survived being plundered. There must have been plenty of raiders to pillage, then afterwards, in the Pax Romana, there remained ample cash for restoration work. According to a site plan we later saw pegged up in the cleared area that was to become the main piazza, Gerasa was in the grip of a spectacular building programme that had started twenty years earlier and was projected to continue for several decades. Children were growing up here who had only ever seen a street that was half roped off by stonemasons. A bunch of shrines on the acropolis were being given cosmetic attention; waiting at the town gate we could hear hammers clanging frenziedly in the sanctuary of Zeus; suburban villas were being knocked out by smiling contractors like beans from a pod; and surveyors' poles impeded progress everywhere, marking out a new street grid and an ambitious elliptical forum.

In any other city in any corner of the Empire, I would have said the grandiose plan would never happen. But Gerasa undoubtedly possessed the wherewithal to drape itself in colonnades. Our own interrogation gave an indication of what kind of tribute (a polite word for bribe) the citizens expected to extract from the thousand or so caravans that plodded up each year from Nabataea.

'Total camels?' barked the tariff master, a man in a hurry.
'Twelve.'

His lip curled. He was used to dealing in scores and hundreds. Even so, his scroll was at the ready. 'Donkeys?'

'None with saleable merchandise. Only private goods.'

'Detail the camels. Number of loads of myrrh in alabaster vessels?'

'None.'

'Frankincense? Other aromatics? Balsam, bdellium, ladanum gum, galbanum, any of the four types of cardamom?'

'No.'

'Number of loads of olive oil? A load equals four goatskins,' he qualified helpfully.

'None.'

'Gemstones, ivory, tortoiseshell or pearls? Select woods?'
To save time we simply shook our heads. He was getting the

150

picture. He ran through the straightforward spices almost without looking up from his list: 'Peppers, ginger, allspice, turmeric, sweet flag, mace, cinnamon, saffron? No . . . Dried goods?' he tried hopefully.

'None.'

'Individual number of slaves? Other than for personal use,' he added, with a sneer that said he could see none of us had been manicured or massaged by a sloe-eyed, sleek-skinned bondsman in the recent past.

'None.'

'What exactly,' he asked us, with an expression that veered between suspicion and horror, '*are* you dealing in?'

'Entertainment.'

Unable to decide whether we were daft or dangerous, he waved us angrily to a holding post while he consulted with a colleague.

'Is this delay serious?' whispered Helena.

'Probably.'

One of the girls from our scratch orchestra laughed. 'Don't worry. If he wants to cause trouble we'll set Afrania on to him!'

Afrania, who was a creature of wondrous and self-assured beauty, played the flute for us and danced a bit. Those who were not accompanied by fastidious girlfriends found other uses for her. As we waited she was flirting lazily with Philocrates but heard her name and glanced over. She made a gesture whose grossness belied her superbly placid features. 'He's all yours, Ione! Salting officials calls for an expert. I couldn't compete!'

Her friend Ione turned away dismissively. Attaching herself to us, she gave us a grin (minus two front teeth), then hoicked half a loaf from somewhere amongst her crumpled skirts, ripped it into portions and handed them round.

Ione was a tambourinist, and a startling character. Helena and I tried not to stare, though Musa gazed at her openly. Ione's compact form was swathed in at least two stoles, wound crossways over her bosom. She wore a snake bracelet covering half her left arm and various glass-stoned finger-rings. Triangular earrings, so long they brushed her shoulders, clattered with red and green beads, loops of wire and metallic spacers. She went in for whippy belts, thongy sandals, swoony scarves and clownish face make-up. Her wild crinkly hair flared back from her head in all directions like a radiate diadem; odd sections of the mass of untamed locks were braided into long thin plaits, tied up with wisps of wool. In colour the hair was mainly a tarnished bronze, with matted reddish streaks that were almost like dried blood after a messy fight. There was a positive air to her; I reckoned Ione would win all her fights.

Somewhere beneath these flash trappings lay a small-featured young woman with a sharp wit and a big heart. She was brighter than she pretended. I can handle it, but for most men that's a dangerous girl.

She had noticed Musa gaping. Her grin widened in a way that did finally make him look uncomfortable. 'Hey you!' Her shout was raucous and brisk. 'Better not stand too close to the Golden River – and don't go near the double pool! You don't want to end up as a soggy sacrifice in the Festival of Maiuma!'

Whether or not the Petran mountain-god Dushara demands that his priests be chaste, Ione's boldness was too much for ours. Musa rose to his feet (he had been squatting on his heels like a nomad while we were held up by the customs officer). He turned away, looking haughty. I could have told him; it never works.

'Oh bull's balls, I've offended him!' laughed the tambourinist easily.

'He's a shy lad.' It was safe for me to smile at her; I had protection. Helena was lolling against me, probably to annoy Philocrates. I tickled her neck, hoping he would spot the propietary gesture. 'What's Maiuma, Ione?'

'Gods, don't you know? I thought it was famous.'

'It's an antique nautical festival,' Helena recited. She always did the heavy reading-up when we were planning foreign trips. 'Of resonant notoriety,' she added, as if she knew that would catch my interest. 'Believed to derive from Phoenicia, it involves, amongst other shameless public practices, the ritual immersion of naked women in sacred pools.'

'Good idea! While we're here, let's try to take in an evening of sacred pond-watching. I like to collect a salacious rite or two to liven up my memoirs – '

'Shut up, Falco!' I deduced that my senator's daughter was not planning a plunge at the pleasure ground. She enjoyed herself being superior. 'I imagine there is a great deal of shrieking, plenty of overpriced sour red wine on sale, and everyone goes home afterwards with sand down their tunics and foot fungus.'

'Falco?' Whether it was Helena's use of my name that roused her, Ione suddenly bolted down the last of her bread. She squinted at me sideways, still with crumbs on her face. 'You're the new boy, aren't you? Hah!' she exclaimed derisively. 'Written any good plays lately?'

'Enough to learn that my job is to provide creative ideas, neat plots, good jokes, provocative thoughts and subtle dialogue, all so that cliché-ridden producers can convert them into trash. Played any good tunes lately?'

'All I have to do is bash in time for the boys!' I might have known she was a girl who liked innuendo. 'What sort of plays do you like then, Falco?' It sounded a straight question. She was one of those girls who seem to threaten abuse, then disarm you by taking a sensible interest in your hobbies.

Helena joked: 'Falco's idea of a good day at the theatre is watching all three Oedipus tragedies, without a break for lunch.'

'Oh very Greek!' Ione must have been born under the Pons Sublicius; she had the authentic twang of the Tiber. She was a Roman; 'Greek' was the worst insult she could hand out.

'Ignore the silly patter from the tall piece in the blue skirt,' I said. 'Her family all sell lupins on the Esquiline; she only knows how to tell lies.'

'That so?' Ione gazed at Helena admiringly.

I heard myself admitting, 'I had a good idea for a play I want to write myself.' We were obviously going to be stuck in customs for a long time. Bored and weary after the forty miles from Philadelphia, I fell into the trap of betraying my dreams: 'It starts off with a young wastrel meeting the ghost of his father – '

Helena and Ione looked at each other, then chorused frankly: 'Give up, Falco! It will never sell tickets.'

'That's not all you do, is it?' young Ione demanded narrowly. After my long career as an informer, I recognised the subtle air of self-importance before she spoke. Some evidence was about to emerge. 'They say you're sniffing out what happened up on the magic mountain in Petra. I could tell you a few things!'

'About Heliodorus? I found him dead, you know.' She presumably did know, but openness is inoffensive and fills in time while you gather your wits. 'I'd like to know who held him under,' I said.

'Maybe you should ask why they did it?' Ione was like a young girl teasing me on a treasure hunt, openly excited. Not a good idea if she really did know something. Not when most of my suspects were all close by and probably listening.

'So are you able to tell me that?' I pretended to grin in return, keeping it light.

'You're not so dumb; you'll get there in the end. I bet I could give you some clues, though.'

I wanted to press for details, but the customs post was far too public. I had to shut her up, for her own sake as much as for my own chances of finding the killer.

'Are you willing to talk to me sometime, but maybe not here?'

In response to my question she glanced downwards, until her eyes were virtually closed. Painted spikes lengthened the appearance of her eyelashes; her lids were brushed with something that looked like gold dust. Some of the expensive prostitutes who serviced senators at Roman dinner parties would pay thousands for an introduction to Ione's cosmetics mixer. Long practised in buying information, I wondered how many amethystine marbled boxes and little pink glass scent vials I would have to offer to acquire whatever she was touting.

Unable to resist the mystery, I tried suggestion: 'I'm working on the theory it was a man who hated him for reasons connected with women – '

'Ha!' Ione barked with laughter. 'Wrong direction, Falco!

154

Completely wrong! Believe me, the scribe's ducking was purely professional.'

It was too late to ask her more. Tranio and Grumio, who were always hanging about near the orchestra girls, came mooching up like spare waiters at an orgy wanting to offer limp garlands in return for a large tip.

'Another time,' Ione promised me, winking. She made it sound like an offer of sexual favours. 'Somewhere quiet when we're on our own, eh Falco?'

I grinned bravely, while Helena Justina assumed the expression of the jealous loser in a one-sided partnership.

Tranio, the taller, wittier clown, gave me a long dumb stare.

XXVI

The customs officer suddenly turned on us as if he could not imagine why we were loitering in his precious space, and shooed us off. Without giving him a chance to change his mind, we shot in through the town gate.

We had come about fifteen years too early. It was not much in the scheme of town planning, but too long for hungry performers who were gnawing on their last pomegranate. The site diagram of the future Gerasa showed an ambitious design with not one but two theatres of extravagant proportions, plus another, smaller auditorium outside the city at the site of the notorious water festival where Helena had forbidden me to go and leer. They needed all these stages – now. Most were still only architectural drawings. We soon discovered that the situation for performers was desperate. At present we were stuck with one very basic arena in the older part of town, over which all comers had to haggle – and there was plenty of competition.

It was turmoil. In this town we were just one small act in a mad circus. Gerasa had such a reputation for riches that it drew buskers from all the parched corners of the East. To be offering a simple play with flute, drum and tambourine accompaniment was nothing. In Gerasa they had every gaggle of scruffy acrobats with torn tunics and only one left boot between them, every bad-tempered fire-eater, every troupe of sardine-dish spinners and turnip jugglers, every one-armed harpist or arthritic stilt-walker. We could pay half a denarius to see the Tallest Man in Alexandria (who must have shrunk in the Nile, for he was barely a foot longer than I was), or a mere copper for a backward-facing goat. In fact for a quadrans or two extra I could have actually *bought* the goat, whose owner told me he was sick of the heat and the slowness of trade and was going home to plant beans.

I had a long conversation with this man, in the course of

which I nearly did acquire his goat. So long as he kept me talking, taking on an unconvincing sideshow freak seemed quite a decent business proposition. Gerasa was that kind of town.

Entering by the South Gate had placed us near the existing theatre, but it had the disadvantage of marking us out for hordes of grubby children who mobbed us, trying to sell cheap ribbons and badly made whistles. Looking serious and cute, they offered their wares in silence, but otherwise the noise from the packed streets was unbearable.

'This is hopeless!' shouted Chremes, as we huddled together to discuss what to do. His disgust with *The Rope* after its failed second outing at Philadelphia had faded so quickly that he was now planning for us to repeat it while the Twins were in practice for their tug of war. However, the indecisiveness Davos had complained about soon reappeared. Almost before we dug the props out, new doubts set in. 'I'd like you to brush up *The Arbitration*, Falco.' I had read it; I complained wittily that *The Rope* had much more pulling power. Chremes ignored me. Quibbling about the play was only half his problem. 'We can either travel on straight away, or I'll do what I can to obtain an appearance. If we stay, the bribe to the booker will wipe out most of the ticket money, but if we go on we've lost a week without earning – '

Clearly irritated, Davos weighed in. 'I vote to see what you can get. Mind you, with all this cheap competition it's going to be like doing The Play We Never Mention on a wet Thursday in Olynthus . . .'

'What's the unmentionable play?' asked Helena.

Davos gave her a shirty look, pointed out that by definition he wasn't allowed to mention it, and shrugged off her meek apology.

I tried another ploy for avoiding the manager's turgid idea of a repertoire: 'Chremes, we need a good draw. I've a brand-new idea you may like to try. A lad about town meets the ghost of his newly dead father, who tells him – '

'You say the father's dead?' He was already confused and I hadn't even reached the complicated bit.

'Murdered. That's the point. You see, his ghost catches the hero by the tunic sleeve and reveals who snuffed out his pa – '

157

'Impossible! In New Comedy ghosts never speak.' So much for my big idea. Chremes could be firm enough when crushing a genius; having rejected my masterpiece he went wittering on as usual. I lost interest and sat chewing a straw.

Eventually, when even he was tired of havering, Chremes stumped off to see the theatre manager; we sent Davos along to stiffen him. The rest of us moped around looking sick. We were too hot and depressed to do anything until we knew what was happening.

Grumio, who had a provocative streak, spoke up: 'The play we don't mention is *The Mother-in-Law* by Terence.'

'You just mentioned it!' Stung by Davos, Helena had become a literalist.

'I'm not superstitious.'

'What's wrong with it?'

'Apart from the off-putting title? Nothing. It's his best play.'

'Why the dirty reputation then?' I demanded.

'It was a legendary failure, due to the rival attractions of boxers, tightrope walkers and gladiators.' I knew how Terence must have felt.

We all looked gloomy. Our own situation seemed horribly similar. Our struggling little dramas were unlikely to draw crowds at Gerasa, where the populace had devised their own sophisticatedly ribald festival, the Phoenician Maiuma, to fill any quiet evening. Besides we had already glimpsed the street performers, and knew Gerasa could call on other entertainment that was twice as unusual and three times as noisy as ours, at half the cost.

Rather than think about our predicament, people started wandering off.

Grumio was still sitting nearby. I got talking to him. As usual when you look as if you're having a rich literary conversation, our companions left us severely alone. I asked him more about The Play We Never Mention, and quickly discovered he had a deep knowledge of theatrical history. In fact he turned out to be quite an interesting character.

It was easy to dismiss Grumio. His round face could be

taken for a sign of simplicity. Playing the dullard of the two clowns, he had been forced into a secondary role off-stage as well as on. In fact he was highly intelligent, not to mention professional. Getting him on his own, without the noisy brilliance of Tranio to overshadow him, I learned that he saw himself as an exponent of an ancient and honourable craft.

'So how did you get into this line, Grumio?'

'Partly heredity. I'm following my father and grandfather. Poverty comes into it. We never owned land; we never knew any other trade. All we had – a precious gift that most folk lack – was natural wit.'

'And you can survive by this?'

'Not easily any more. That's why I'm in a stage company. My ancestors never had to suffer like this. In the old days laughter-men were independent. They travelled around earning their meals with their varied skills – sleight of hand and tumbling, recitation, dancing – but most of all with a crackling repertoire of jokes. I was trained to the physical jerks by my father, and of course I inherited sixty years of family wisecracks. For me, it's a let-down to be stuck in Chremes' gang like this and tied to a script.'

'You're good at it though,' I told him.

'Yes, but it's dull. It lacks the edge of living on your wits; devising your patter on your feet; improvising the apt rejoinder; snapping out the perfect quip.'

I was fascinated by this new side to the country clown. He was a much more thoughtful student of his art than I had given him credit for, though it was my own fault for assuming that playing the fool meant he was one. Now I saw that Grumio had a devotee's respect for the practice of humour; even for our dreadful comedies he would polish his performance, though all the time he was hankering for better things. For him the old jokes really were the best – especially if he turned them out in a new guise.

This dedication meant he had a deep, private personality. There was far more to him than the sleepy character who yearned for girls and drink and who let Tranio take the lead as much in their off-duty lives as in some tiresome plot. Under that fairly lightly worn mask, Grumio was his own man.

159

Communicating wit is a lonely art. It demands an independent soul.

Being an informal stand-up comic at formal reclining dinners seemed a nerve-racking way of life to me. But if someone could do it, I would have thought there was a market for a satirist. I asked why Grumio had had to turn to lesser things.

'No call. In my father or grandfather's day all I would have needed in life were my cloak and shoes, my flask and strigil, a cup and knife to take to dinner, and a small wallet for my earnings. Everyone who could find the wherewithal would eagerly ask a wandering jokesmith in.'

'Sounds just like being a vagrant philosopher!'

'A cynic,' he agreed readily. 'Exactly. Most cynics are witty and all clowns are cynical. Meet us on the road, and who could tell the difference?'

'Me, I hope! I'm a good Roman. I'd take a five-mile detour to avoid a philosopher.'

He disabused me. 'You won't be tested. No clown can do that any longer. I'd be run out of town like a warty beggar by the idlers who hang around the water tower inventing slander. Now everyone wants to be the funny man himself; all people like me can do is flatter them silly and feed them material. It's not for me; I won't be a yes-man. I get sick of pandering to other people's stupidity.' Grumio's voice had a raw note. He had a real hatred for the amateur rivals he was deriding, a real lament for the deterioration of his trade. (I also noticed a strident belief in his own brilliance; clowns are an arrogant lot.) 'Besides,' he complained, 'There are no morals. The new "humour", if you can call it that, is pure malicious gossip. Instead of making a genuine point, it's now good enough to repeat any ribald story without a thought for whether it's even true. In fact, making up a spiteful lie has become respectable. Today's "jesters" are outright public nuisances.'

A similar charge is often laid against informers. We too are supposed to be amoral vendors of overheard dirt, gutter know-alls who fabricate freely if we cannot produce hard facts; deliberate mixers, self-seekers and stirrers. It's even regarded as a suitable insult for people to call us comedians . . .

Abruptly Grumio lurched to his feet. There was a restlessness about him I had overlooked before; perhaps I had caused it by discussing his work. That does depress most people.

For a moment I felt I had annoyed or upset him. But then he waved a hand amiably enough, and sauntered off.

'What was all that about?' asked Helena curiously, coming up as usual just when I had been assuming she had her head down in business of her own.

'Just a history lesson about clowns.'

She smiled. Helena Justina could make a thoughtful smile raise more questions than a dead mouse in a pail of milk. 'Oh, men's talk!' she commented.

I leaned on my chin and gazed at her. She had probably been listening, then being Helena she had done some thinking too. We both had an instinct for certain things. I found myself being niggled by a sensation she must have shared: somewhere an issue that might be important had been raised.

XXVII

To the great surprise of all of us, within the hour Chremes came rushing back to announce he had secured the theatre; moreover it was for the very next night. Obviously the Gerasenes had no notion of fair turns. Chremes and Davos had happened to be demanding attention from the booking manager just when that grafter received a cancellation, so for the proverbial small fee we were allowed to snap up the vacancy, never mind who else had been waiting around town.

'They like an easy life here,' Chremes told us. 'All the booker wanted to be sure of was that we'd pay his sweetener.' He told us how much the bribe had been, and some of us were of the opinion it would be more profitable to leave Gerasa now and play *The Arbitration* to a nomad's herd of sheep.

'Is this why the other troupe packed their traps?'

Chremes looked huffed that we were complaining after he had pulled off a triumph. 'Not according to my information. They were a sleazy circus act. Apparently they could cope when their chief trapezist had a fall that left him paralysed, yet when their performing bear caught a cold – '

'They lost their nerve,' Tranio broke in snappily. 'As we may do when all the groups who arrived here ahead of us find out how we jumped the queue and come looking for us!'

'We'll show the town something worth watching, then do a quick flit,' Chremes answered with a casual air that said just how many times the company had fled places in a hurry.

'Tell that to the Chersonesus Taurica weightlifting team!' muttered Tranio.

Still, when you think you are about to make some money, nobody likes to be too ethical.

We all had an evening to ourselves. Revived by the prospect of work tomorrow we pooled our food and ate as a group, then went our separate ways. Those with cash could spend it on seeing a classic Greek tragedy performed by an extremely sombre group from Cilicia. Helena and I were not in the mood. She sauntered off to talk to the girls from the orchestra while I had a few swift stabs at improving the scenes in *The Arbitration* that I decided the great Menander had left slightly rough.

There were things to be done during our visit and this seemed the night for it. I wanted an urgent talk with the tambourinist Ione, but I could see her amongst the group Helena had just joined. I then realised Helena was probably trying to arrange a discreet meeting. I approved. If Helena persuaded the girl to talk, it could work out cheaper than if Ione spilled the tale to me. Girls don't bribe one another for gossip, I assured myself cheerfully.

Instead I turned my attention to Thalia's missing artiste. Chremes had already told me he had managed to ascertain that the theatre manager knew nothing of any water organist. That reasonably put an end to my search in this city. A water organ is not something you miss if one ever comes to town; apart from the fact they are as big as a small room, you cannot possibly avoid the noise. I felt clear to forget Sophrona, though I was prepared to make a show of double-checking by taking a turn around the forum and asking whether anybody knew a businessman called Habib who had been to Rome.

Musa said he would come with me. There was a Nabataean temple he wanted to visit. After his enforced swim at Bostra I was not prepared to let him out on his own, so we joined forces.

As we were setting off we noticed Grumio standing on a barrel at a street corner.

'What's this, Grumio – found some old jokes to sell?'

He had just started his patter but a crowd had already gathered, looking quite respectful too. He grinned. 'Thought I'd try and earn back the bribe Chremes had to pay to get the theatre!'

He was good. Musa and I watched for a while, laughing along with his audience. He was juggling quoits and hand-balls, then performing wonderful sleight-of-hand tricks. Even in a city full of tumblers and magicians his talent was outstanding. We wished him good luck eventually, but were sorry to leave. By then even other performers had left their pitches to join his fascinated audience.

It was a superb night. Gerasa's mild climate is its chief luxury. Musa and I were happy to stroll about seeing the sights before we tackled our real business. We were men on the loose, not looking for lechery, nor even for trouble, but enjoying a sense of release. We had a quiet drink. I bought a few presents to take home. We stared at the markets, the women, and the foodstalls. We slapped donkeys, tested fountains, saved children from being crushed under cartwheels, were polite to old ladies, invented directions for lost people who thought we must be locals, and generally made ourselves at home.

North of the old town, in what was planned as the centre of the expanding new metropolis, we found a group of temples dominated by a dramatic shrine to Artemis, the ancestral goddess of this place. There was scaffolding around some of the twelve dramatic Corinthian columns – nothing new for Gerasa. Alongside lay a temple to Dionysus. Within that, since a synthesis could apparently be forced between Dionysus and Dushara, Nabataean priests had an enclave. We made their acquaintance, then I buzzed off to make extra enquiries about Thalia's girl, telling Musa not to leave the sanctuary without me.

The enquiries were unfruitful. Nobody had heard of Sophrona or Habib; most people claimed to be strangers there themselves. When my feet had had enough I went back to the temple. Musa was still chattering, so I waved at him and sank down for a rest in the pleasant Ionic portico. Given the abruptness of his departure with us from Petra, there could be fairly urgent messages Musa wanted to send home: to his family, his fellow priests at the Garden Temple on the mountainside, and perhaps to The Brother too. I myself felt a nagging guilt that it was time to let my mother know I was alive; Musa might be in the same trouble. He may have looked for a messenger while we were at Bostra, but if so I never saw him doing it. This was probably his first chance. So I let him talk.

When acolytes came to light the temple lamps, we both realised we had lost all sense of time. Musa dragged himself away from his fellow Nabataeans. He came and squatted beside me. I reckoned there was something on his mind.

'Everything all right?' I kept my voice neutral.

'Oh yes.' He liked his touch of mystery.

Musa drew his headcloth across his face and folded his hands together. We both stared out at the temple precincts. Like any other sanctuary, this temenos was full of devout old women who ought to be at home with a stiff toddy, swindlers selling religious statuettes, and men looking out for tourists who might pay for a night with their sisters. A peaceful scene.

I had been sitting on the temple steps. I adjusted my position so I could look at Musa more directly. With him formally wrapped, all I could see were his eyes, but they seemed honest and intelligent. A woman might find their dark, inscrutable gaze romantic. I judged him on his behaviour. I saw someone lean and tough, straightforward in his way, though when Musa started looking abstracted, I remembered that he had come with us because he thought it was what had been ordered by The Brother.

'Are you married?' Because of the way he had joined us, as The Brother's parole officer, we had never asked the normal questions. Now, although we had travelled together, I knew nothing of him socially.

'No,' he answered.

'Any plans?'

'One day perhaps. It is allowed!' A smile had anticipated my curiosity about sexual stipulations for Dushara's priests.

'Glad to hear it!' I grinned back. 'Family?'

'My sister. When I am not at the High Palace of Sacrifice, I live in her house. I sent her news of my travels.' He sounded almost apologetic. Maybe he thought I found his behaviour suspicious.

'Good!'

'And I sent a message to Shullay.'

Again, an odd note in his voice caught my attention, though I could not decide why. 'Who's Shullay?'

'The elder at my temple.'

'The old priest I saw with you when I was chasing after the killer?'

He nodded. I must have been mistaken about the nuance in his voice. This was just a subordinate worried about explaining to a sceptical superior why he had dodged off from his duties.

'Also there was a message for me here,' he brought out.

'Want to tell me?'

'It is from The Brother.' My heart took a lurch. The Decapolis had come under Roman authority, but the cities preserved their independent status. I was unsure what would happen if Nabataea tried to extradite Helena and me. You had to be realistic: Gerasa relied on Petra for its prosperity. If Petra wanted us, Gerasa would comply.

'The Brother knows you are here, Musa?'

'He sent the message in case I should come. The message is,' Musa revealed with some difficulty, 'I do not have to remain with you.'

'Ah!' I said.

So he was leaving. I felt quite upset. I had grown used to him as a travelling companion. Helena and I were outsiders among the theatre group; Musa was another, which had made him one of us. He pulled his weight and had an endearing personality. To lose him halfway through our trip seemed too great a loss.

He was watching me, without wanting me to see it. 'Is it possible I may ask you something, Falco?' I noticed his Greek was wandering more than normal.

'Ask away. We are friends!' I reminded him.

'Ah yes! If it were convenient, I would like to help you find this murderer.'

I was delighted. 'You want to stay with us?' I noticed he still looked uncertain. 'I see no problem.'

I had never known Musa so diffident. 'But before, I was under orders from The Brother. You did not have to take me in your tent, though you did so – '

I burst out laughing. 'Come along, Helena will be worrying about us both!' I leapt up, holding out my hand to him. 'You are our guest, Musa. So long as you help me drive the bloody ox-cart and pitch the tent, you're welcome. Just don't let anybody drown you while the rules of hospitality make me responsible for you!'

Back at the camp it turned out we need not have hurried home. There were three or four people talking quietly in a close-knit group outside Chremes' tent, looking as if they had spent the evening together. All the girls had gone off somewhere; that included Helena. I expected a consoling message, but no such luck.

Musa and I strolled out, intending to look for her. We assured ourselves we were not anxious, since she was in company, but I wanted to know what was going on. It might be something we would like to join in. (Wild hopes that the party Helena had disappeared to might involve an exotic dancer in some smoky den where they served toasted almonds in dainty bowls and the wine was free – or at least extremely cheap . . .) Anyway, we ourselves had been out in the city for several hours. I was a good boy sometimes; I was probably missing her.

At the same street corner as before, standing on the same barrel, we found Grumio. What looked like the same enthusiastic crowd was still clustering around. We joined them again.

By now Grumio had developed a close relationship with his audience. From time to time he pulled somebody out to assist with his conjuring; in between he tossed insults at individuals, all part of running jokes he must have set up before we arrived. This teasing had enough bite to tingle the atmosphere, but nobody was complaining. He was developing a theme; insulting the other towns of the Decapolis.

'Anyone here from Scythopolis? No? That's lucky! I won't say Scythopolitans are stupid . . .' We sensed an expectant ripple. 'But if you ever see two Scythopolitans digging a huge hole in the road outside a house, just ask them – go on, ask them what they're doing. I bet they tell you they've forgotten the doorkey again! Pella! Anybody from Pella? Listen, Pella and Scythopolis have this ancient feud – oh forget it! What's the point of insulting the Pellans if they're not here? Probably couldn't find their way! Couldn't ask. No one can understand their accent . . . Anyone from Abila?' Amazingly a hand was raised. 'That's your misfortune, sir! I won't say Abilans are daft, but who else would own up? Your moment of fame . . . Excuse me, is that your camel looking over your shoulder, or is your wife extremely ugly?' This was low stuff, but he was pitching it right for the street trade.

It was time for a mood change; he switched the monologue into a more reflective tone. 'A man from Gadara had a smallholding, nothing immodest, built it up slowly. First a pig . . .' Grumio did a farmyard impression, each animal in turn, slowly to begin with, then he changed to little dialogues between them, and finally a furious intercutting that sounded just like the whole group honking and mooing at once. He topped it off by introducing the farmer – represented by an elaborately disgusting human fart.

'What a swine . . . Hey, Marcus!' Musa grabbed my arm, but it was too late. Grumio must have spotted us earlier but he was ready now to turn me into embarrassing material. 'This is my friend Marcus. Come up here, Marcus! Give him a hand here.' A routine had been set for nervous volunteers; people reached for me as soon as I was identified and I was manhandled into the performance area without a chance. 'Hello, Marcus.' Jumping off his barrel to greet me, his voice dropped but his eyes twinkled wickedly. I felt like a herring about to be filleted. 'Marcus is going to help me with my next trick. Just stand there. Try not to look as if you've wet yourself.' He squared me up to the audience. Obediently I looked as dumb as possible. 'Ladies and gentlemen, pay attention to this boy. He looks nothing, but his girlfriend's a senator's daughter. So stiff that when they want to you-know-what, he just kicks her ankles and she falls straight on her back – '

Such disrespect for Helena from anyone else and I would have broken his neck. But I was trapped. I stood there enduring it while the crowd could feel the tension. They must have seen me colour up, and my teeth had set gratingly. Next time Grumio wanted a discussion of humorous history, I would be teaching him some very serious new words.

I had to get out of this first.

We started with illusions. I was the stooge, of course. I held scarves from which wooden eggs vanished, then had eggs discovered tucked into parts of my person that caused fits of giggles in the audience: an unsophisticated lot. I had feathers produced from behind one ear and coloured knucklebones from up my sleeve. Finally a set of balls appeared in a manner I still blush to remember, and we were ready for some juggling.

It was very good. I was given an improvised lesson, then every now and then Grumio made me take part. If I dropped the ball it raised a laugh because I looked ridiculous. If I caught it, people roared at my surprise. Actually I caught quite a few. I was meant to; that was Grumio's throwing skill.

Finally the handballs were exchanged one by one for an assortment: a knucklebone, a quoit, one ball, a flywhisk and a cup. This was much more difficult, and I supposed I was now out of it. But suddenly Grumio bent low; in a flash he had extracted my own dagger, which I kept hidden down my boot. Jove only knows how he had spotted it there. He must be damned observant.

A gasp ran through the crowd. By some terrible luck the knife had come into his hand unsheathed.

'Grumio!' He would not stop. Everyone could see the danger; they thought it was intentional. It was bad enough to see the blade flash as he spun it in the air. Then he started whizzing items at me again. The crowd, which had chuckled at my astonishment when the knife was produced, now leant forwards in silence. I was gripped by terror that Grumio would cut off his hand; the crowd all hoped he would hurl the naked blade at me.

I managed to catch and return the quoit and the cup. I was expecting the knucklebone or the flywhisk, then thought Grumio would finish the whole scene gracefully. The bastard was drawing out the final moment. Sweat poured off me as I tried to concentrate.

Something beyond the audience caught my eye.

Not a movement: she was absolutely still on the edge of the

crowd. A tall, straight-backed girl in blue with softly looped dark hair: Helena. She looked angry and terrified.

When I saw her my nerve went. I did not want her to watch me near danger. I tried to warn Grumio. His eyes met mine. Their expression was totally mischievous, completely amoral. The whisk flickered; the ball spooled up.

Then Grumio threw the knife.

IX

I caught it. By the handle, of course.

XXIX

Why the surprise?

Anyone who had spent five years in the legions, banged up in a freezing estuary fortress in western Britain, had tried knife-throwing. There was not much else to do. There were no women, or if there were they just wanted to marry centurions. Draughts palled after a hundred nights of the same strategy. We would bathe, eat, drink, some would fornicate, we would shout insults into the mist in case any British homunculi were listening, then, naturally, being young lads a thousand miles from our mothers, we tried to kill ourselves playing Dare.

I can catch knives. In Britain, catching a knife thrown after I had turned away was my speciality. When I was twenty I could do it blind drunk. Better drunk than sober, in fact, or if not drunk, then thinking about a girl.

My thoughts were on a girl now.

I put my knife back down my boot – in its sheath. The crowd was whistling ecstatically. I could still see Helena, still not stirring. Nearby, Musa was making frantic efforts to break through the crush to her.

Grumio was flapping: 'Sorry, Falco. I meant to throw the knucklebone. You caught me off guard when you moved . . .' *My fault, eh!* He was an idiot. I forced my attention back to him. Grumio had been bowing low in response to the crowd's applause. When he looked up, his eyes were veiled. He was breathless, like a man who had had a nasty shock. 'Dear gods, you know I wasn't trying to kill you!'

'No harm done.' I sounded calm. Possibly I was.

'Are you going to take the hat round for me?' He was holding out his collection cap, one of those woollen Phrygian efforts that flop over on top like wearing a long sock on your head.

172

'Something else to do – ' I hopped into the crowd leaving the clown to make the best of it.

As I barged through the press he was continuing the patter: 'Well, that was exciting. Thanks Marcus! What a character . . . Now then, anyone here from Capitolias?'

Musa and I reached Helena simultaneously. 'Olympus! What's wrong?' I stopped in my tracks.

Musa heard my urgency and drew back slightly.

There was a deep stillness about her. Knowing her best I interpreted it first, but our friend soon saw her agitation too. It had nothing to do with Grumio's act. Helena had come here to find me. For a moment she could not tell me why. The worst conclusions flashed into my mind.

Musa and I were both assuming she had been attacked. Gently but quickly I drew her to a quiet corner. My heart was pounding. She knew that. Before we moved far she stopped me. 'I'm all right.'

'My darling!' I clutched her, for once grateful to the Fates. I must have looked ghastly. She bowed her head on my shoulder briefly. Musa stumbled, thinking he ought to leave us alone. I shook my head. There was still some problem. I might yet need help.

Helena looked up. Her face was set, though she was in control again. 'Marcus, you must come with me.'

'What's happened?'

She was full of grief. But she managed to say, 'I was supposed to meet Ione at the pools of Maiuma. When I got there I found her in the water. She seems to have drowned.'

173

XXX

I remember the frogs.

We had come to a place whose calm beauty should bemuse
the soul. In daytime the sacred site must be flooded with
sunlight and birdsong. As darkness descended the birds fell
silent, whilst all around those still-warm, sensuous waters,
scores of frogs started a chorus mad enough to delight
Aristophanes. They were croaking their heads off frenziedly,
insensitive to human crisis.

The three of us had ridden here on hastily collected donkeys.
We had had to cross the whole city northwards, cursing as we
were held up twice where the main street, the Decumanus, hit
major crossroads; needless to say, both junctions had been
undergoing road maintenance, as well as being packed with
the usual aimless crush of beggars and sightseers. Emerging
through the North Gate, we followed a much less frantic
processional road along a fertile valley, coming through
prosperous suburban villas that nestled peacefully amongst
the trees on rolling hill slopes. It was cool and quiet. We
passed a temple lying deserted for the night.

By now it was growing too dark to see our way easily. But
when we emerged through an archway at the sacred pools we
found lamps hung like glow-worms in the trees and bitumen
torches screwed into the earth. Somebody must attend the
site, though nobody was visible.

Helena and I had ridden one donkey, so I could hold her
close. She had told me more about what happened, while I
tried not to rage at her for taking risks.

'Marcus, you know we needed to speak to Ione about her
hints regarding Heliodorus.'

'I'm not arguing with that.'

'I managed to have a word with her, and arranged to talk
privately at the pools.'

174

'What was this for – a promiscuous skinny-dip?'

'Don't be silly. Several of us were coming, just to see the site. We heard that people bathe here normally outside the festival.'

'I bet!'

'Marcus, just listen! The arrangements were fairly flexible, because we all had other things to do first. I wanted to tidy our tent – '

'That's good. Nice girls always do their housework before they slip off to a rude festival. Decent mothers tell their daughters, don't be dunked until you've done the floors!'

'Please stop ranting.'

'Don't alarm me then!'

I have to admit I was disturbed by the thought of my girl going near a lewd cult. No one would ever suborn Helena easily, but any informer of standing has been asked by distraught relations to try rescuing supposedly sensible acolytes from the clutches of peculiar religions. I knew too much about the blank-eyed smiles of brainwashed little rich girls. I was determined that my lass would never be sucked into any dirty festival. In Syria, where the cults involved women ecstatically castrating men then hurling the bits around, I felt uneasiest of all about exotic shrines.

I found myself gripping Helena's arm so tightly I must be bruising her; angrily I released my hold and buffed up her skin. 'You should have told me.'

'I would have done!' she exclaimed hotly. 'You were nowhere around to be told.'

'Sorry.' I bit my lip, annoyed with myself for staying out so long with Musa.

A girl was dead; our feelings were unimportant. Brushing off the quarrel, Helena continued her story. 'To be honest, it seemed best not to rush. Ione gave the impression she had an assignation.'

'With a man?'

'So I presumed. She only said, "I'll go ahead. I've some fun fixed up . . ." The plan was for me to meet her at the pools ahead of the others, but I didn't hurry because I was nervous about interrupting her fun. I hate myself now; it made me too late to help her.'

'Who else was going?'

'Byrria. Afrania had shown interest, but I was not sure she meant to turn up.'

'All women?'

Helena looked cool. 'That's right.'

'Why did you have to go at night?'

'Oh don't be silly! It wasn't dark then.'

I tried to stay calm. 'When you got to the pools Ione was in the water?'

'I noticed her clothes beside the pool. As soon as I saw her lying still, I knew.'

'Oh love! I should have been with you. What did you do?'

'No one else was about. There are steps at the edge for drawing water. She was there in the shallow water on the ledges. That was how I saw her. It helped me drag her out by myself; I don't think I could have managed otherwise. It was hard even so, but I was very angry. I remembered how you tried to revive Heliodorus. I don't know if I did it properly, but it didn't work – '

I hushed her soothingly. 'You didn't fail her. You tried. Probably she was already dead. Tell me the rest.'

'I looked nearby for evidence, then suddenly I became frightened in case whoever killed Ione was still there. There are fir trees all around the site. I seemed to feel someone watching me – I ran for help. On the way back to the city I met Byrria coming to join us.'

I was surprised. 'Where is she now?'

'She went to the pools. She said she was not afraid of any murderer. She said Ione should have a friend guarding her.'

'Let's hurry then . . .'

Not long after that we were among the same fir trees that had made Helena feel threatened. We rode under the arch and reached the pools, dimly lit and resonant with the frenzied croaking of the frogs.

There was a large rectangular reservoir, so large it must be used to supply the city. It was divided into two by a retaining wall that formed a sluice. On the long sidesteps led down into the water, which looked deep.

At the far end we could hear people cavorting, not all of them women. Like the frogs, they were ignoring the tragic tableau, too lost in their private riot even to be curious. Ione's body lay at the edge of the water. A kneeling figure kept guard alongside: Byrria, with a face that said she was blaming a man for this. She rose at our approach, then she and Helena embraced in tears.

Musa and I walked quietly to the dead girl. Beneath a white covering which I recognised as Helena's stole, Ione lay on her back. Apart from a heavy necklace, she was naked. Musa gasped. He drew back, shamed by the blatant bare flesh. I fetched a lamp for a close look.

She had been beautiful. As beautiful as a woman could wish to be, or a man yearn to possess.

'Oh cover her!' Musa's voice was rough.

I was angry too, but losing my temper would be no help to anyone. 'I mean the woman no disrespect.'

I made my decisions, then covered her again and stood.

The priest turned away. I stared at the water. I had forgotten he was not my friend Petronius Longus, the Roman watch captain with whom I had surveyed so many corpses destroyed by violence. Male or female made no difference. Stripped, clad, or merely rumpled, what you saw was the pointlessness of it. That, and if you were lucky, clues to the criminal.

Still appalled but controlling it, Musa faced me again. 'So what did you find, Falco?'

'Some things I *don't* find, Musa.' I talked quietly while I thought. 'Heliodorus had been beaten to overpower him; Ione shows no similar marks.' I glanced quickly around the spot where we stood. 'Nothing here implies the taking of drink, either.'

Accepting my motives, he had calmed down. 'It means?'

'If it was the same man, he is from our company and she knew him. So did Heliodorus. But unlike him, Ione was quite off her guard. Her killer had no need to surprise or subdue her. He was a friend of hers – or more than a friend.'

177

'If her killer was the person she had been prepared to name to you, it was rash to arrange to meet him just before she spoke of it to Helena.'

'Yes. But an element of danger appeals to some – '

'Marcus!'

Helena herself suddenly said my name in a low voice. A reveller with a conscience may after all have reported a disturbance. We were being joined by one of the sanctuary servants. My heart sank, expecting inconvenience.

He was an elderly attendant in a long striped shirt and several days' growth of whiskers. In one dirty claw he carried an oil flagon so he could pretend to replenish lamps. He had arrived silently in thonged slippers, and I knew staight away his chief pleasure in life was creeping about among the fir trees, spying on women frolicking.

When he shuffled into our circle both Musa and I squared up defensively. He whipped aside the stole and had a good look at Ione anyway. 'Another accident!' he commented in Greek that would have sounded low-class even on the Piraeus waterfront. Musa said something curt in Arabic. The curator's home language would be Aramaic, but he would have understood Musa's contemptuous tone.

'Do you suffer many deaths in this place?' My own voice sounded haughty, even to me. I could have been some stiff-necked tribune on foreign service letting the locals know how much he despised them.

'Too much excitement!' cackled the lecherous old water flea. It was obvious he thought there had been dangerous fornication, and he assumed Musa and I, Helena and Byrria, were all part of it. I ceased to regret sounding arrogant. Wherever they are in the world, some types cry out to be despised.

'And what is the procedure?' I asked, as patiently as I could manage.

'Procedure?'

'What do we do with the body?'

He sounded surprised: 'If the girl is a friend of yours, take her away and bury her.'

I should have realised. Finding a girl's naked corpse at the site of a promiscuous festival at the end of the Empire is not like finding a corpse in the well-policed city sectors of Rome.

For a second I was on the verge of demanding an official enquiry. I was so angry, I actually wanted the watch, the local magistrate, an advertisement scrawled in the forum asking witnesses to come forward, our own party to be detained pending the investigation, and a full case in court in half a year's time . . . Sense prevailed.

I drew the greasy curator to one side, palming across as much small change as I could bear.

'We'll take her,' I promised. 'Just tell me, did you see what happened?'

'Oh no!' He was lying. There was absolutely no doubt about it. And I knew that with all the barriers of language and culture between Rome and this grubby pleasure ground, I would never be able to nail his lies. For a moment I felt overwhelmed. I ought to go home to my own streets. Here, I was no use to anyone.

Musa appeared at my shoulder. He spoke out in his deepest, most sonorous voice. There was no threat, simply a clean-cut authority: Dushara, the grim mountain-god, had entered this place.

They exchanged a few sentences in Aramaic, then the man with the oil flagon slithered away into the trees. He was heading for the noises at the far end of the reservoir. The merrymakers' lamps looked bright enough, but he had his own unsavoury business there.

Musa and I stood. The night's darkness seemed to be growing and as it did the sanctuary felt colder and ever more sordid. The frogs' chorus sounded harsher. At my feet were the ceaseless, restlessly lapping waters of the reservoir. Midges swarmed in my face.

'Thanks, friend! Did you get the tale?'

Musa reported grimly: 'He sweeps up leaves and fir-cones, and is supposed to keep order. He says Ione came alone, then a man joined her. This fool could not describe the man. He was watching the girl.'

'How did you get him to talk?'

'I said you were angry and would cause trouble, then he would be blamed for the accident.'

'Musa! Where did you learn to bully a witness?'

'Watching you.' It was gently said. Even in a situation like this, Musa sustained his teasing streak.

'Lay off! My methods are ethical. So what else did you screw out of the poolside peeper?'

'Ione and the man were acting as lovers, in the water. During their passion the girl seemed to be in trouble, struggling towards the step; then she stopped moving. The man climbed out, looked around quickly, and vanished into the trees. The unpleasant one thought he had run for help.'

'The unpleasant one did not offer such help?'

'No.' Musa's voice was equally dry. 'Then Helena arrived and discovered the accident.'

'So it was this gruesome brushman whom Helena sensed was watching her . . . Musa, Ione's death was no accident.'

'Proven, Falco?'

'If you are willing to look.'

I knelt beside the dead girl one final time, drawing back the cover just as far as necessary. The girl's face was darkly discoloured. I showed Musa where the beaded chains of her necklace seemed to have dragged at her throat, leaving indented marks. Some pairs of the heavy stone beads were still trapping tiny folds of skin. Trickles of kohl and whatever other paint she used disfigured her face. Beneath the necklace burns and charcoal smears, numerous small red flecks showed on her flesh. 'This is why I examined her so closely earlier. The necklace *may* simply have dragged at her throat as she thrashed in the water, but I think it shows pressure from a man's hands. The tiny red clusters are what appear on the corpse of somebody who has died in particular circumstances.'

'Drowning?'

'No. Her face would be pale. Ione was strangled,' I said.

XXXI

The rest of that night, and the following day, passed in various struggles that left us exhausted. We wrapped the corpse as best we could. Helena and Byrria then rode together on one animal. Musa and I had to walk, one either side of the donkey that was carrying Ione. Keeping the poor soul decent, and firmly across the donkey's back, was tricky. In the hot climate her corpse was already stiffening fast. On my own, I would have strapped her methodically and disguised her as a bale of straw. In company I was expected to behave with reverence.

We stole lamps from the sanctuary to light our way but even before the end of the processional road we knew it would be impossible to recross the entire city with our burden. I have done flamboyant things in my time, but I could not take a dead girl, her hennaed hair still dripping and her bare arms outflung to the dust, down a packed main street while merchants and local inhabitants were all out strolling and looking for somebody else in an interesting predicament to gawp at. The crowds here were the type to form a jostling procession and follow us.

We were saved by the temple outside the city gate which we had passed earlier. Priests had turned up for night duty. Musa appealed to them as a fellow professional with colleagues at the Temple of Dionysus-Dushara, and they agreed to let the body rest in their care until the next day.

Ironically, the place where we left Ione was the Temple of Nemesis.

Unencumbered, we were able to travel more quickly. I was now riding with Helena side-saddle in front of me again. Byrria had consented to go with Musa. They both looked embarrassed about it as he sat extremely upright on his shaggy beast while she perched behind him, barely willing to hold on to his belt.

181

Squeezing back through the town was an experience I would have paid a lot to miss. We reached our camp in darkness, though the streets were still busy. Merchants play hard and late. Grumio was still standing on his barrel. With nightfall the humour had grown more obscene and he was slightly hoarse but gamely calling out endless cries of 'Anyone here from Damascus or Dium?'

We signalled to him. He sent around his collection cap one last time, then knotted the top on the money and joined us; we told him the news. Visibly shocked, he wandered off to tell the rest. In an ideal world I ought to have gone with him to observe their reactions, but in an ideal world heroes never get tired or depressed; what's more, heroes are paid more than me – in nectar and ambrosia, willing virgins, golden apples, golden fleeces, and fame.

I was worried about Byrria. She had hardly spoken since we found her at the sacred pools. Despite her original bravery, she now looked chilled, horrified and deeply shocked. Musa said he would escort her safely to her tent; I advised him to try and find one of the other women to stay with her that night.

Not being entirely hopeless, I did have something urgent to attend to. Once I had seen Helena back to our own quarters, I forayed among the orchestra girls to try and learn who Ione's fatal lover was. It was a hopeless quest. Afrania and a couple of other dancers were easy to find from the noise. They were expressing their relief that it was Ione who had ended in trouble and not themselves. Their hysterical wailing only varied as they opted to shriek with feigned terror when I, a man, who might be slightly dangerous, tried to talk to them. I mentioned the well-known medical cure for hysteria, saying that it would be smacks all round if they didn't stop screaming, so then one of the panpipe-players jumped up and offered to ram me in the guts with a cart axle.

It seemed best to retire.

Back at my tent, another crisis: Musa had failed to reappear. I had a look round, but apart from the distant rumpus from the orchestra (and even the girls were tiring), the whole camp now lay quiet. A light shone dimly in Byrria's tent, but the side flaps were rolled firmly down. Neither Helena nor I could imagine that Musa had managed close relations with Byrria, but neither of us wanted to look stupid by interrupting if he had. Both Helena and I lay awake worrying about him most of the night.

'He's a grown man,' I muttered.

'That's what I'm worried about!' she said.

He didn't come back until morning. Even then he looked perfectly normal and made no attempt to explain himself.

'Well!' I scoffed when Helena went outside to tend the fire and we were free to indulge in men's talk. 'Couldn't find a woman to sit up with her?'

'No, Falco.'

'Sat up with her yourself then?' This time he made no answer to my dig. He was definitely not going to tell me the story. Well that made him fair game for ribbing. 'Jupiter! This doesn't look like a fellow who spent all last night consoling a beautiful young woman.'

'What should such a man look like?' he challenged quietly.

'Exhausted, sunshine! No, I'm teasing. I assume if you had asked her, the famously chaste Byrria would have pitched you out into the night.'

'Very probably,' said Musa. 'Best not to ask.' You could take that two ways. A woman who was used to being asked might find reticence strangely alluring.

'Do I gather Byrria was so impressed, that *she asked you*? Sounds a good plan!'

'Oh yes,' agreed Musa, smiling at last like a normal male. 'It's a good *plan*, Falco!' Only in theory, apparently.

'Excuse me, Musa, but you seem to lead your life in the wrong order. Most men would seduce the beauty and *then* get shoved off an embankment by a jealous rival. *You* get the painful part over with first!'

'Of course you're the expert on women, Marcus Didius!' Helena had popped back without us noticing. 'Don't underestimate our guest.'

I thought a faint smile crossed the Nabataean's face.

Helena, who always knew when to change the subject, then soothed Musa adroitly. 'Your host carries out intrusive work;

183

he forgets to stop when he comes home. There are plenty of other aspects to investigate. Marcus spent some time last night trying to ask Ione's friends about her life.'

Musa ducked his head rather, but said, 'I have found some information.'

He sounded shy about his source, so I demanded cheerfully, 'Was this while you were sitting up all night comforting Byrria?' Helena threw a cushion at me.

'The girl who played the tambourine,' said Musa patiently, as reluctant to name the corpse he had seen naked as he was to specify his informant, 'had probably been connected with Chremes the manager and with Philocrates the handsome one.'

'I expected it,' I commented. 'Chremes exacted a routine dalliance, probably as the price of her job. Philocrates just thought it was his duty as a seducer to go through the orchestra the way a hot knife skims a dripping pan.'

'Even Davos probably liked her, I am told.'

'She was a likeable girl,' Helena said. There was a trace of rebuke in her tone.

'True,' Musa answered gravely. He knew how to handle disapproval. Somebody somewhere had taught him when to look submissive. I wondered if by chance the sister he lived with in Petra was like any of mine. 'It is suggested that Ione was most friendly on a regular basis with the Twins.'

Helena glanced at me. We both knew that it must be Byrria who had made these suggestions. I reckoned we could rely on her information. Byrria struck me as observant. She might not like men herself, but she could still watch the behaviour of other girls curiously. The others may even have talked freely to her about their relationships, though they were more likely to avoid a woman with Byrria's reputation, thinking her stuck-up and sanctimonious.

'It would fit,' I answered thoughtfully. 'The Twins were both at Petra. Both of them are already on our suspects list for killing Heliodorus. And it looks as if we can straight away narrow the focus to one, because *Grumio* was making the Gerasenes crack up with laughter by insulting their neighbours all night.'

'Oh no!' Helena sounded regretful. 'So it seems to be Tranio!' Like me, she had always found Tranio's wit appealing.

'Looks like it,' I conceded. Somehow I never trust solutions that appear so readily.

Instead of breakfast, which I could not fancy, I went out for an early prod at the personnel. First I cleared the ground by eliminating those who were least likely to be involved. I soon established that Chremes and Phrygia had been dining together; Phrygia had invited their old friend Davos, and for most of the evening they had also been joined by Philocrates. (It was unclear whether Chremes had deliberately brought in the arrogant actor, or whether Philocrates had invited himself.) I remembered seeing this group sitting quietly outside the manager's tent the night before, which confirmed their alibis.

Philocrates had had a later appointment too, one he readily mentioned. He was proud to tell me he had been chalking up a success with a female cheeseseller.

'What's her name?'

'No idea.'

'Know where to find her?'

'Ask a sheep.'

However, he did produce a couple of ewe's milk cheeses – one half-eaten – which I accepted at least temporarily as proof.

I was ready to tackle Tranio. I found him emerging from the flute-girl Afrania's tent. He seemed to expect my questions, and struck a truculent attitude. His story was that he had spent the evening drinking and doing other pleasant things with Afrania. He called her out from her tent, and of course she backed him up.

The girl looked as if she were lying, but I was unable to shake her. Tranio had an odd appearance too – but a strange expression won't convict. If he was guilty, he knew how to cover himself. When a winsome flautist declares that a man with all his faculties has been bedding her, any jury tends to believe it's true.

I looked Tranio straight in the face, knowing these

185

defiantly flashing dark eyes might be the eyes of a man who had killed twice, and who had attempted to drown Musa too. An odd sensation. He stared straight back tauntingly. He dared me to accuse him. But I was not ready to do that.

When I left them I was certain that Tranio and Afrania were turning back to each other as if to argue about what they had told me. If it had been the truth, of course, there should have been nothing to argue about.

I felt my morning's investigations were unsatisfactory. More pressing business loomed. We had to give Ione a funeral, and I was needed to arrange it. All I could add to my enquiries was a rapid chat with Grumio.

I found Grumio alone in the clowns' tent. He was exhausted and had the grandfather of hangovers. I decided to put the situation to him directly: 'Ione was killed by a man she was close to. I'll be straight. I hear that you and Tranio were her most frequent contacts.'

'Probably correct.' Gloomily, he made no attempt to dodge the issue. 'Tranio and I are on free-and-easy terms with the musicians.'

'Any intense relationships?'

'Frankly,' he admitted, 'no!'

'I'm plotting everyone's movements yesterday evening. You're easy to rule out, of course. I know you were delighting the crowds. That was all night?' The question was routine. He nodded. Having witnessed him on his barrel myself on two or three occasions last evening, that ended it. 'Tranio tells me he was with Afrania. But did he have a similar friendship with Ione too?'

'That's right.'

'Special?'

'No. He just slept with her.' Helena would say that was special. Wrong; I was being romantic about my beloved. Helena had been married, so she knew the facts of life.

'When he wasn't sleeping with Afrania?' I said dourly.

'Or when Ione wasn't sleeping with someone else!' Grumio seemed troubled about his partner. I could see he had a personal interest. He had to share Tranio's tent. Before he next passed out after a few drinks, he needed to know whether Tranio might stick his head in a water pail. 'Is Tranio cleared? What does Afrania say?'

'Oh she supports Tranio.'

'So where does that leave you, Falco?'

'Up a palm tree, Grumio!'

We spent the rest of that day, with the help of Musa's Nabataean colleagues, organising a short-notice funeral. Unlike Heliodorus at Petra, Ione was at least claimed, honoured and sent to the gods by her friends. The affair was more sumptuous than might have been expected. She had a popular send-off. Even strangers made donations for a monument. People in the entertainment community had heard of her death, though not the true manner of it. Only Musa and I and the murderer knew that. People thought she had drowned; most thought she had drowned *in flagrante*, but I doubt if Ione would have minded that.

Naturally *The Arbitration* went ahead that night as planned. Chremes dragged out the old lie about '*She would have wanted us to continue . . .*' I hardly knew the girl but I believed all Ione would have wanted was to be alive. However, Chremes could be certain we would pack the arena. The poolside voyeur in the filthy shirt was bound to have spread our company's notoriety.

Chremes proved to be right. A sudden death was perfect for trade – a fact I personally found bad for my morale.

We travelled on next day. We crossed the city before dawn. At first repeating our journey towards the sacred pools, we left by the North Gate. At the Temple of Nemesis once more we thanked the priests who had given Ione her last resting place, and paid them to oversee setting up her monument alongside the road. We had commissioned a stone plaque, in the Roman manner, so other musicians passing through Gerasa would pause and remember her.

I know that, with the priests' permission, Helena and Byrria covered their heads and went together into the temple. When they prayed to the dark goddess of retribution, I can assume what they asked.

187

Then, still before dawn, we took the great trade road that ran west into the Jordan Valley and on to the coast. This was the road to Pella.

As we journeyed there was one notable difference. In the early hours of morning, we were all hunched and silent. Yet I knew that an extra sense of doom had befallen us. Where the company had once seemed to carry lightly its loss of Heliodorous, Ione's death left everybody stricken. For one thing, he had been highly unpopular; she had had friends everywhere. Also, until now people may have been able to pretend to themselves that Heliodorus could have been murdered in Petra by a stranger. Now there was no doubt: they were harbouring a killer. All of them wondered where he might strike next.

Our one hope was that this fear would drive the truth into the light.

XXXII

Pella: founded by Seleucus, Alexander's general. It possessed an ancient and highly respectable history, and a modern,
booming air. Like everywhere else it had been pillaged in the
Rebellion, but had bounced back cheerfully. A little honey-
pot, aware of its own importance.

We had moved north and west to much more viable
country that produced textiles, meat, grain, wood, pottery,
leather and dyes. The export trade up the River Jordan
valley may have reduced during the Judaean troubles, but it
was reviving now. Old Seleucus knew how to pick a site.
Pella straddled a long spur of the lush foothills, with a
fabulous view across the valley. Below the steep-sided
domed acropolis of the Hellenic foundation, Romanised
suburbia was spreading rapidly through a valley that
contained a crisply splashing spring and stream. They had
water, pasture, and merchants to prey off: all a Decapolis
city needed.

We had been warned about a bitter feud between the
Pellans and their rivals across the valley in Scythopolis.
Hoping for fights in the streets, we were disappointed,
needless to say. On the whole, Pella was a dull, well-
behaved little city. There was, however, a large new colony
of Christians there, people who had fled when Titus
conquered and destroyed Jerusalem. The native Pellans
now seemed to spend their energy picking on them instead.

With their wealth, which was quite enviable, the Pellans
had built themselves smart villas nuzzling the warm city
walls, temples for every occasion, and all the usual public
buildings that show a city thinks itself civilised. These
included a small theatre, right down beside the water.

The Pellans obviously liked culture. Instead we gave them
our company favourite, *The Pirate Brothers*, an undemanding
vehicle for our shocked actors to walk through.

189

'No one wants to perform. This is crass!' I grumbled, as we dragged out costumes that evening.

'This is the East,' answered Tranio.

'What's that supposed to mean?'

'Expect a full house tonight. News flashes around here. They will have heard we had a death at our last venue. We're well set up.'

As he spoke of Ione I gave him a sharp look, but there was nothing exceptional in his behaviour. No guilt. No relief, if he was feeling he had silenced an unwelcome revelation from the girl. No sign any longer of the defiance I had thought he exhibited when I questioned him at Gerasa. Nor, if he noticed me staring, did he show any awareness of my interest.

Helena was sitting on a bale sewing braid back on to a gown for Phrygia (who in turn was holding nails for a stagehand mending a piece of broken scenery). My lass bit through her thread, with little thought for the safety of her teeth. 'Why do you think Easterners have lurid tastes, Tranio?'

'Fact,' he said. 'Heard of the Battle of Carrhae?' It was one of Rome's famous disasters. Several legions under Crassus had been massacred by the legendary Parthians, our foreign policy lay in ruins for decades afterwards, the Senate was outraged, then more plebeian soldiers' lives had been chucked away in expeditions to recapture lost military standards: the usual stuff. 'On the night after their triumph at Carrhae,' Tranio told us, 'the Parthians and Armenians all sat down to watch *The Bacchae* of Euripides.'

'Strong stuff, but a night at a play seems a respectable way to celebrate a victory,' said Helena.

'What,' Tranio demanded bitterly, 'with the severed head of Crassus kicked around the stage?'

'Juno!' Helena blanched.

'The only thing we could do to please people better,' Tranio continued, 'would be *Laureolus* with a robber king actually crucified live in the last act.'

'Been done,' I told him. Presumably he knew that. Like Grumio, he was putting himself forward as a student of drama history. I was about to enter into a discussion, but he was keeping himself aloof from me now and swiftly made off.

Helena and I exchanged a thoughtful look. Was Tranio's delight in these lurid theatrical details a reflection of his own involvement in violence? Or was he an innocent party, merely depressed by the deaths in the company?

Unable to fathom his attitude, I filled in time before the play by asking in the town about Thalia's musician, without luck, as usual.

However, this did provide me with an unexpected chance to do some checking up on the wilfully elusive Tranio. As I sauntered back to camp, I happened to come across his girlfriend Afrania, the tibia-player. She was having trouble shaking off a group of Pellan youths who were following her. I didn't blame them, for she was a luscious armful with the dangerous habit of looking at anything masculine as if she wanted to be followed home. They had never seen anything like her; I had not seen *much* like it myself.

I told the lads to get lost, in a friendly fashion, then when this had no effect I resorted to old-fashioned diplomacy: hurling rocks at them while Afrania screamed insults. They took the hint; we congratulated ourselves on our style; then we walked together, just in case the hooligans found reinforcements and came after us again.

Once she regained her breath, Afrania suddenly stared at me. 'It was true, you know.'

I guessed what she meant, but played the innocent. 'What's that?'

'Me and Tranio. He really was with me that night.'

'If you say so,' I said.

Having chosen to talk to me, she seemed annoyed that I didn't believe her. 'Oh, don't be po-faced, Falco!'

'All right. When I asked you, I just gained the impression,' I told her frankly, 'there was something funny going on.' With girls like Afrania I always liked to play the man of the world. I wanted her to understand I had sensed the touchy atmosphere when I questioned the pair of them.

'It's not me,' she assured me self-righteously, tossing back her rampant black curls with a gesture that had a bouncing effect on her thinly clad bosom as well.

191

'If you say so.'

'No, really. It's that idiot Tranio.' I made no comment. We were nearing our camp. I knew there was unlikely to be another opportunity to persuade Afrania to confide in me; there was unlikely to be another occasion when she needed rescuing from men. Normally Afrania accepted all comers.

'Whatever you say,' I repeated in a sceptical tone. 'If he was with you, then he's cleared of murdering Ione. I assume you wouldn't lie about that. After all, she was supposed to be your friend.'

Afrania made no comment on that. I knew there had been a degree of rivalry between them, in fact. What she did say amazed me. 'Tranio was with me all right. He asked me to deny it though.'

'Jupiter! Whatever for?'

She had the grace to look embarrassed. 'He said it was one of his practical jokes, to get you confused.'

I laughed bitterly. 'It takes less than that to get me confused,' I confessed. 'I don't get it. Why should Tranio put himself on the spot for a killing? And why should you be a party to it?'

'Tranio never killed Ione,' Afrania said self-righteously. 'But don't ask me what the silly bastard thought he was up to. I never knew.'

The practical joke idea seemed so far-fetched I reckoned it was just a line Tranio had come up with for Afrania. But I was hard-pressed to think of another reason why he would want her to lie. The only slim possibility might be drawing the heat away from someone else. But Tranio would need to owe someone a truly enormous debt if he would risk being accused of a murder he had not committed.

'Has anyone done Tranio any big favours recently?'

'Only me!' quipped the girl. 'Going to bed with him, I mean.'

I grinned appreciatively, then quickly changed tack: 'Do you know who Ione might have been meeting at the pools?'

Afrania shook her head. 'No. That's the reason she and I had a few words sometimes. The person I used to reckon she had her eye on was Tranio.'

Very convenient. Here was Tranio being fingered as a possible associate of the dead girl just when he was also being given a firm alibi. 'Yet it couldn't be him,' I concluded, with a certain dryness, 'because wonderful Tranio was doing acrobatic tricks with you all night.'

'He was!' retorted Afrania. 'So where does that leave you, Falco? Ione must have been up to it with the whole company!'

Not much help to the sleuth trying to fix who had murdered her.

As our waggons came in sight, Afrania rapidly lost interest in talking to me. I let her go, wondering whether to have another talk with Tranio, or whether to pretend to forget him. I decided to leave him unchallenged, but to observe him secretly.

Helena always reckoned that was the informer's lazy way out. However, she would not be hearing about this. Unless it was essential, I never told Helena when I had gathered information from a very pretty girl.

If the Pellans were baying for blood they held their vile tastes well in check. In fact they behaved with quiet manners during our performance of *The Pirate Brothers*, sat in neat rows eating honeyed dates, and applauded us gravely afterwards. Pellan women mobbed Philocrates in sufficient numbers to keep him insufferable; Pellan men mooned after Byrria but were satisfied with the orchestra girls; Chremes and Phrygia were invited to a decent dinner by a local magistrate. And the rest of us were paid for once.

In other circumstances we might have stayed longer at Pella, but Ione's death had made the whole company restless. Luckily the next town lay very close, just across the Jordan Valley. So we moved on immediately, making the short journey to Scythopolis.

XXXIII

Scythopolis, previously known as Nysa after its founder, had been renamed to cause confusion and pronunciation difficulties, but otherwise lacked eccentricity. It held a commanding position on the main road up the west bank of the Jordan, drawing income from that. Its features were those we had come to expect: a high citadel where the Greeks had originally planted their temples, with more modern buildings spreading fast down the slopes. Surrounded by hills, it was set back from the River Jordan, facing Pella across the valley. Once again, signs of the famous feud between the two towns were disappointingly absent.

By now the places we visited were starting to lose their individuality. This one called itself the chief city of the Decapolis, hardly a distinguishing feature since half of them assumed that title; like most Greek towns, they were a shameless lot. Scythopolis was as large as any of them, which meant not particularly large to anybody who had seen Rome.

For me, however, Scythopolis was different. There was one aspect of this particular city that made me both anxious to come here, and yet full of dread. During the Judaean Revolt, it had been the winter quarters of Vespasian's Fifteenth Legion. That legion had now left the province, reassigned to Pannonia once its commander had made himself Emperor and hiked back to Rome to fulfil a more famous destiny. Even now, however, Scythopolis seemed to have a more Roman atmosphere than the rest of the Decapolis. Its roads were superb. There was a cracking good bathhouse built for the troops. As well as their own minted coins, shops and stalls readily accepted denarii. We heard more Latin than anywhere else in the East. Children with a suspiciously familiar cast of feature tumbled in the dust.

This atmosphere upset me more than I admitted. There was a reason. I had a close interest in the town's military past.

My brother Festus had served in the Fifteenth Apollinaris, his final posting before he became one of the fatalities of Judaea. That last season before he died, Festus must have been here.

So Scythopolis does stay in my memory. I spent a lot of time there walking about on my own, thinking private thoughts.

XXXIV

I was drunk.

I was so drunk even I could hardly pretend I had not noticed. Helena, Musa and their visitor, all sitting demurely around the fire outside our tent waiting for me to come home, must have summed up the situation at once. As I carefully placed my feet in order to approach my welcome bivouac, I realised there was no chance of reaching it unobserved. They had seen me coming; best to brazen it out. They were watching every step. I had to stop thinking about them so I could concentrate on remaining upright. The flickering blur that must be the fire warned me that on arrival I would probably pitch face first into the burning sticks.

Thanks to a ten-year career of debauched living, I made it to the tent at what I convinced myself was a nonchalant stroll. Probably about as nonchalant as a fledgling falling off a roof finial. No one commented.

I heard, rather than saw, Helena rising to her feet, then my arm found its way around her shoulders. She helped me tiptoe in past our guests and tumble on to the bed. Naturally I expected a lecture. Without a word she made me sit up enough to take a long quaff of water.

Three years had taught Helena Justina a thing or two. Three years ago she was a primly scowling fury who would have spurned a man in my condition; now she made him take precautions against a hangover. Three years ago, she wasn't mine and I was lost . . .

'I love you!'

'I know you do.' She had spoken quietly. She was pulling off my boots for me. I had been lying on my back; she rolled me partly on to my side. It made no difference to me as I could not tell which way up I was, but she was happy to have given me protection in case I choked. She was wonderful. What a perfect companion.

196

'Who's that outside?'

'Congrio.' I lost interest. 'He brought a message for you from Chremes about the play we are to put on here.' I had lost interest in plays too. Helena continued talking calmly, as if I were still rational. 'I remembered we had never asked him about the night Ione died, so I invited him to sit with Musa and me until you came home.'

'Congrio ...' In the way of the drunk I was several sentences behind. 'I forgot Congrio.'

'That seems to be Congrio's destiny,' murmured Helena. She was unbuckling my belt, always an erotic moment; blearily I enjoyed the situation, though I was helpless to react with my usual eagerness. She tugged the belt; I arched my back, allowing it to slither under me. Pleasantly I recalled other occasions of such unbuckling when I had not been so incapable.

In a crisis Helena made no comment about the emergency. Her eyes met mine. I gave her the smile of a helpless man in the hands of a very beautiful nurse.

Suddenly she bent and kissed me, though it cannot have been congenial. 'Go to sleep. I'll take care of everything,' she whispered against my cheek.

As she moved away I gripped her fast. 'Sorry, fruit. Something I had to do ...'

'I know.' Understanding about my brother, there were tears in her eyes. I made to stroke her soft hair; my arm seemed impossibly heavy and nearly caught her a clout on the side of the brow. Seeing it coming, Helena held my wrist. Once I stopped flailing she laid my arm back tidily alongside me. 'Go to sleep.' She was right; that was safest. Sensing my silent appeal, she came back at the last minute, then kissed me again, briskly on the head. 'I love you too.' Thanks, sweetheart.

What a mess. Why does solitary, deeply significant thought lead so inevitably to an amphora?

I lay still, while the darkened tent zoomed to and fro around me and my ears sang. Now that I had collapsed, the sleep I had been heavily craving refused to come. So I lay in my woozy cocoon of misery, listening to the events at my own fireside that I could not join.

197

XXXV

'Marcus Didius has things on his mind.'

It was the briefest excuse, as Helena sank back in her place gracefully. Neither Musa nor the bill-poster answered; they knew when to keep their heads down.

From my position the three figures looked dark against the flames. Musa was leaning forwards, rebuilding the fire. As sparks suddenly crackled up, I caught a glimpse of his young, earnest face and the scent of smoke, slightly resinous. I wondered how many nights my brother Festus had spent like this, watching the same brushwood smoke lose itself in the darkness of the desert sky.

I had things on my mind all right. Death, mostly. It was making me intolerant.

Loss of life has incalculable repercussions. Politicians and generals, like murderers, must ignore that. To lose one soldier in battle – or to drown an unlovable playwright and strangle an unwanted witness – inevitably affects others. Heliodorus and Ione both had homes somewhere. Slowly the messages would be winding back, taking their domestic devastation: the endless search for a rational explanation; the permanent damage to unknown numbers of other lives.

At the same time as I was pledging a violent vow to right these wrongs, Helena Justina said lightly to Congrio, 'If you give me the message from Chremes to Falco, I will pass it on tomorrow.'

'Will he be able to do the work?' Congrio must be the kind of messenger who liked returning to source with a pessimistic announcement of 'It can't be done'. He would have made a good cartwheel-mender in a backstreet lock-up workshop.

'The work will be completed,' replied Helena, a firm girl. Optimistic too. I would probably not be able to see a scroll tomorrow, let alone write on it.

'Well, it's to be *The Birds*,' said Congrio. I heard this

impassively, unable to remember if it was a play, whether I had ever read it, and what I thought if I had done so.

'Aristophanes?'

'If you say so. I just write up the playbills. I like the ones with short names; takes less chalk. If that's the scribe's name who wrote it, I'll leave him off.'

'This is a Greek play.'

'That's right. Full of birds. Chremes says it will cheer everyone up. They all get a chance to dress in feathers, then hop about squawking.'

'Will anyone notice the difference from normal?' Helena quipped. I found this incredibly funny. I heard Musa chuckle, though sensibly he was keeping out of the rest of it.

Congrio accepted her wit as a straight comment. 'Doubt it. Could I draw birds on the posters? Vultures, that's what I'd like to have a go at.'

Avoiding comment, Helena asked, 'What does Chremes want from us? Not a full translation into Latin, I hope?'

'Got you worried!' Congrio chortled, though in fact Helena was perfectly calm (apart from a slight quiver as she heard his plans for artwork). 'Chremes says we'll do it in Greek. You've got a set of scrolls in the box, he says. He wants it gone through and brought up to date if the jokes are too Athenian.'

'Yes, I've seen the play in the box. That will be all right.'

'So you reckon your man in there is up to it?'

'My man in there is up to anything.' Like most girls with a strongly ethical upbringing, Helena lied well. Her loyalty was impressive too, though perhaps rather dry in tone. 'What will happen about these elaborate beak-and-feather costumes, Congrio?'

'Same as usual. People have to hire them off Chremes.'

'Does he already possess a set of bird costumes?'

'Oh yes. We did this one a few years ago. People who can sew,' he menaced cheerfully, 'had better get used to the idea of stitching feathers on!'

'Thanks for warning me! Unfortunately, I've just developed a terrible whitlow on my needle finger,' said Helena, making up the excuse smoothly. 'I shall have to back out.'

'You're a character!'

'Thanks again.'

I could tell from her voice Helena had now decided that she had sufficient details of my writing commission. The signs were slight, but I knew the way she bent to toss a piece of kindling on the fire, then sat back tidying her hair under one of its combs. For her, the actions marked a pause. She was probably unaware of it.

Musa understood the change of atmosphere. I noticed him silently shrink deeper into his headcloth, leaving Helena to interrogate the suspect.

'How long have you been with Chremes and the company, Congrio?'

'I dunno . . . a few seasons. Since they were in Italy.'

'Have you always done the same job?'

Congrio, who could sometimes appear taciturn, now seemed blissfully keen to talk: 'I always do the posters.'

'That requires some skill?'

'Right! It's important too. If I don't do it, nobody comes to see the stuff, and none of us earns. The whole lot depends on me.'

'That's wonderful! What do you have to do?'

'Fool the opposition. I know how to get through the streets without anybody spotting me. You have to get around and write the notices real quick – before the locals see you and start complaining about you ruining their white walls. All they want is space to advertise their pet gladiators and draw rude signs for brothels. You have to dodge in secretly. I know the methods.' He knew how to boast like an expert too. Carried away by Helena's interest, he then confided, 'I have done acting once. I was in this play *The Birds*, as it happens.'

'That's how you remember it?'

'I'll say! That was an experience. I was an owl.'

'Goodness! What did that entail?'

'In this play, *The Birds*,' Congrio expounded gravely, 'there are some scenes – probably the most important ones – where all the birds from the heavens come on the stage. So I was the owl.' In case Helena had missed the full picture, he added, 'I hooted.'

I buried my face in my pillow. Helena managed to stifle the laughter that must be threatening to bubble up. 'The bird of wisdom! That was quite a part!'

'I was going to be one of the other birds, but Chremes took me off it because of the whistling.'

'Why was that?'

'Can't do it. Never could. Wrong teeth or something.'

He could have been lying, to give himself an alibi, but we had told nobody Musa had heard the playwright's killer whistling near the High Place at Petra.

'How did you get on with hooting?' Helena asked politely.

'I could hoot really well. It sounds like nothing difficult, but you have to have timing, and put feeling into it.' Congrio sounded full of himself. This had to be the truth. He had ruled himself right out of killing Heliodorus.

'Did you enjoy your part?'

'I'll say!'

In that short speech Congrio had revealed his heart. 'Would you like to become one of the actors, some day?' Helena asked him with gentle sympathy.

He was bursting to tell her: 'I could do it!'

'I'm sure you could.' Helena declared. 'When people really want something, they can usually manage it.'

Congrio sat up straighter, hopefully. It was the kind of remark that seemed to be addressed to all of us.

Once again I saw Helena push up the side comb above her right ear. The soft hair that grew back from her temples had a habit of slithering out of control and drooping, so it bothered her. But this time it was Musa who punctuated the scene by finding sticks to twiddle in the embers. A rogue spark flew out and he stamped on it with his bony sandalled foot.

Even though he was not talking, Musa had a way of staying silent that still kept him in the conversation. He pretended being foreign made him unable to take part, but I noticed how he listened. At such times my old doubts about him working for The Brother tended to sneak up again. There still could be more to Musa than we thought.

'All this trouble in the company is very sad,' Helena mused. 'Heliodorus, and now Ione . . .' I heard Congrio groan in

201

agreement. Helena continued innocently, 'Heliodorus does seem to have asked for what happened to him. Everyone tells us he was a very unpleasant character. How did you get on with him, Congrio?'

The answer came out freely: 'I hated him. He knocked me about. And when he knew I wanted to be an actor he plagued me with it. I didn't kill him though!' Congrio inserted quickly.

'Of course not,' said Helena, her voice matter-of-fact. 'We know something about the person who killed him that eliminates you, Congrio.'

'What's that then?' came the sharp question, but Helena avoided telling him about the whistling fugitive. This brazen habit was still the only thing definite we knew about the killer.

'How did Heliodorus plague you about acting, Congrio?'

'Oh, he was always trumpeting on about me not being able to read. That's nothing; half the actors do their parts by guesswork anyway.'

'Have you ever tried to learn reading?' I saw Congrio shake his head: a big mistake. If I knew Helena Justina she was now planning to teach him, whether or not he wanted it. 'Someone might give you lessons one day . . .'

To my surprise, Musa suddenly leaned forward. 'Do you remember the night at Bostra when I fell into the reservoir?'

'Lost your footing?' chuckled Congrio.

Musa stayed cool. 'Someone helped me dive in.'

'Not me!' Congrio shouted hotly.

'We had been talking together,' Musa reminded him.

'You can't accuse me of anything. I was miles away from you when Davos heard you splashing and called out!'

'Did you see anyone else near me just before I fell?'

'I wasn't looking.'

As Musa fell silent, Helena took up the same incident. 'Congrio, do you remember hearing Marcus and me teasing Musa that we would tell people he had seen the murderer at Petra? I wonder if you told anyone about that?'

Once again Congrio appeared to answer frankly – and once again he was useless: 'Oh I reckon I told everyone!'

Evidently the kind of feeble weevil who liked to make himself big in the community by passing on scandal.

Helena betrayed none of the irritation she probably felt. 'Just to complete the picture,' she went on, 'on the night when Ione was killed in Gerasa, do you happen to have anyone who can vouch for where you were?'

Congrio thought about it. Then he chuckled. 'I should say so! Everyone who came to the theatre the next day.'

'How's that?'

'Easy. When you girls went off to the sacred pools for a splash, I was putting up the playbills for *The Arbitration*. Gerasa was a big place; it took all night. If I hadn't done my job like that, nobody would have come.'

'Ah but you could have done the bills the next morning,' Helena challenged.

Congrio laughed again. 'Oh I did that, lady! Ask Chremes. He can vouch for it. I wrote up bills everywhere in Gerasa the night Ione died. Chremes saw them first thing next morning and I had to go round to every one of them again. He knows how many I did and how long it must have taken. He came round with me the second time and stood over the job. Ask me why? Don't bother. The first time I did it, I spelt the word wrong.'

'The title? *Arbitration?*'

'Right. So Chremes insisted that I had to sponge off every single one next day and do it again.'

Not long after that Helena stopped asking questions so, bored with no longer being the centre of attention, Congrio stood up and left.

For a while Musa and Helena sat in silence. Eventually Musa asked, 'Will Falco do the new play?'

'Is that a tactful way of asking what is up with him?' queried Helena. Musa shrugged. Helena answered the literal question first. 'I think Falco had better do it, Musa. We need to insist *The Birds* is performed, so you and I – and Falco if he ever returns to the conscious world – can sit beside the stage and listen out for who *can* whistle! Congrio seems to be ruled out as a suspect, but it leaves plenty of others. This slim clue is all we have.'

'I have sent word of our problem to Shullay,' Musa said abruptly. This meant nothing to Helena, though I recognised

203

the name. Musa explained to her, 'Shullay is a priest at my temple.'

'So?'

'When the killer ran down the mountain ahead of Falco, I had been within the temple and only caught a fleeting sight of him. I cannot describe this man. But Shullay,' Musa revealed quietly, 'had been tending the garden outside.'

Helena's excitement overcame any anger that this was the first Musa had told us of it. 'You mean, Shullay had a proper view of him?'

'He may have done. I never had a chance to ask. Now it is difficult to receive a message from him, since he cannot know where I am,' Musa said. 'But every time we reach a new city I ask at their temple in case there is news. If I learn anything, I will tell Falco.'

'Yes, Musa. Do that!' Helena commented, still restraining herself commendably.

They fell silent for a while. After some time, Musa reminded Helena, 'You did not say what is troubling our scribe? Am I permitted to know this?'

'Ah well!' I heard Helena sigh gently. 'Since you are our friend I dare say I can answer.'

Then she told Musa in a few sentences about brotherly affection and rivalry, just why she supposed I had got drunk in Scythopolis. I reckon she got it more or less right.

Not long after that, Musa rose and went to his own part of the tent.

Helena Justina sat on alone in the dying firelight. I thought of calling out to her. The intention was still at the thought stage when she came inside anyway. She curled up, tucking herself into the curve of my body. Somehow I dragged one sluggish arm over her then stroked her hair, properly this time. We were good enough friends to be perfectly peaceful together even on a night like this.

I felt Helena's head growing heavier against my chest; then almost immediately she fell asleep. When I was sure she had stopped worrying about the world in general and me in particular, I did some more worrying for her, then fell asleep myself.

XXXVI

When I awoke the next day, I could hear the furious scratching of a stylus. I had a good idea why: Helena was reworking the play Chremes wanted from me.

I rolled off the bed. Stifling a groan, I scooped a beaker of water from a pail, put my boots on, drank the water, felt sick, managed to keep everything in place, and emerged from the tent. Light exploded in my head. After a pause for readjustment, I opened my eyes again. My oil flask and strigil had been placed on a towel, together with a laundered tunic – a succinct hint.

Helena Justina sat crossed-legged on a cushion in the shade, looking neat and efficient. She was wearing a red dress that I liked, with bare feet and no jewellery. Always a fast worker, she had already amended two scrolls, and was whipping through the third. She had a double inkstand, one belonging to Heliodorus that we had found in the play box. It had one black and one red compartment; she was using the red ink to mark up her corrections to the text. Her handwriting was clear and fluent. Her face looked flushed with enjoyment. I knew she was loving the work.

She glanced up. Her expression was friendly. I gave her a nod, then without speaking went to the baths.

When I returned, still moving slowly but now refreshed, shaved and cleanly clad, the play must have been finished. Helena had dressed up more with agate earrings and two arm bracelets, in order to greet the master of her household with the formal respect that was appropriate in a well-run Roman home (unusual meekness, which proved she was aware she had better look out after pinching my job). She kissed my cheek, with the formality I mentioned, then went back to melting honey in a pan to make us a hot drink. There were fresh bread rolls, olives, and chickpea paste on a platter.

For a moment I stood watching her. She pretended not to notice. I loved to make her shy. 'One day, lady, you shall have a villa crammed with Egyptian carpets and fine Athenian vases, where marble fountains soothe your precious ears, and a hundred slaves are hanging about just waiting to do the dirty work when your disreputable lover staggers home.'

'I'll be bored. Eat something, Falco.'

'Done *The Birds*?'

Helena shrieked like a herring-gull, confirming it.

Exercising caution I sat, ate a small quantity, and with the experience of an ex-soldier and hardened man about town, waited to see what would happen. 'Where's Musa?' I asked, to fill in time while my disturbed guts wondered what unpleasant tricks to throw at me.

'Gone to visit a temple.'

'Oh why's that?' I queried innocently.

'He's a priest,' said Helena.

I hid a smile, allowing them their secret over Shullay. 'Oh, it's religion? I thought he might be pursuing Byrria.'

After their night of whatever it was (or wasn't), Helena and I had surreptitiously watched for signs of romantic involvement. When the pair next met in public all they exchanged were sombre nods. Either the girl was an ungrateful hag, or our Musa was exceedingly slow.

Helena recognised what I was thinking, and smiled. Compared with this, our own relationship was as old and solid as Mount Olympus. Behind the two of us were a couple of years of furious squabbling, taking care of each other in crazy situations, and falling into bed whenever possible. She could recognise my step from three streets away; I could tell from a room's atmosphere if Helena had entered it for only half a minute several hours before. We knew each other so closely we hardly needed to communicate.

Musa and Byrria were a long way from this. They needed some fast action. They would never be more than polite strangers unless they got stuck in to some serious insults, a few complaints about table manners and a bit of light flirting. Musa had come back to sleeping in our tent; that would never achieve much for him.

Actually neither he nor Byrria seemed the type to want the kind of mutual dependency Helena and I had. That did not stop us from speculating avidly.

'Nothing can come of it,' Helena decided.

'People say that about us.'

'People know nothing then.' While I toyed with my breakfast, she tucked into her lunch. 'You and I will have to try to look after them, Marcus.'

'You speak as if falling for someone were a penalty.'

She flashed me a smile of joyous sweetness. 'Oh that depends who you fall for!' Something in the pit of my stomach took a familiar lurch; this time it had nothing to do with last night's drink. I grabbed more bread and adopted a tough stance. Helena smiled. 'Oh Marcus, I know you're a hopeless romantic, but be practical. They come from different worlds.'

'One of them could change cultures.'

'Who? They both have work they are closely tied to. Musa is taking an extended holiday with us, but it can't last. His life is in Petra.'

'You've been talking to him?'

'Yes. What do you make of him, Marcus?'

'Nothing particular. I like him. I like his personality.' That was all, however. I regarded him as a normal, fairly unexciting foreign priest.

'I get the impression that in Petra he is thought of as a boy with promise.'

'Is that what he says? It won't be for long,' I chortled. 'Not if he returns to the mountain fastness with a vibrant Roman actress on his elbow.' No priest who did that would stand a chance of acceptance, even in Rome. Temples are havens of sordid behaviour, but they do have some standards.

Helena grimaced. 'What makes you think Byrria would abandon her career to hang on *any* man's elbow?'

I reached out and tucked in a loose strand of hair – a good opportunity to tickle her neck. 'If Musa really is interested – and that's a debatable issue in itself – he probably only wants one night in her bed.'

'I was assuming', Helena asserted pompously, 'that was all Byrria would be offering! She's just lonely and desperate, and he's intriguingly different from the other men who try to nobble her.'

'Hmm. Is that what you thought when you nobbled me?' I was remembering the night we had first managed to recognise we wanted each other. 'I've no objection to being thought intriguing, but I did hope that falling into bed with me was more than a desperate act!'

'Afraid not.' Helena knew how to aggravate me if I pushed my luck. 'I told myself, *Once, just to know what passion feels like* . . . The trouble was, *once* led straight to *once again*!'

'So long as you never start feeling it's been *once too often* . . .' I held out my arms to her. 'I haven't kissed you this morning.'

'No you haven't!' exclaimed Helena in a changed tone, as if being kissed by me was an interesting proposition. I made sure I kissed her in a way that would re-enforce that view.

After a while she interrupted me: 'You can look through what I've done to *The Birds* if you like, and see if you approve.' Helena was a tactful scribe.

'Your revising is good enough for me.' I preferred to embark on extra kissing.

'Well my work may be wasted. There's a big question mark hanging over whether it can be performed.'

'Why's that?'

Helena sighed. 'Our orchestra has gone on strike.'

XXXVII

'Hey, hey! Things must be bad if they have to send the scribbler to sort us!'

My arrival amidst the orchestra and stagehands caused a surge of mocking applause. They lived in an enclave at one end of our camp. Fifteen or twenty musicians, scene-shifters and their hangers-on were sitting about looking militant while they waited for people in the main company to notice their complaint. Babies toddled about with sticky faces. A couple of dogs scratched their fleas. The angry atmosphere was making my own skin prickle uneasily.

'What's up?' I tried playing the simple, friendly type.

'Whatever you've been told.'

'I've been told nothing. I've been drunk in my tent. Even Helena has stopped talking to me.'

Still pretending not to notice the ominous tension, I squatted in the circle and grinned at them like a harmless sightseer. They glared back while I surveyed who was here.

Our orchestra consisted of Afrania the flautist, whose instrument was the single-piped tibia; another girl who played panpipes; a gnarled, hook-nosed old chap whom I had seen clashing a pair of small hand-cymbals with an incongruous delicacy; and a pale young man who plucked the lyre when he felt like it. They were led by a tall, thin, balding character who sometimes boomed away on a big double wind instrument that had one pipe turned up at the end, whilst he beat time for the others on a foot clacker. This was a large group, compared with some theatre-company ensembles, but allowed for the fact that the participants also danced, sold trays of limp sweetmeats, and offered entertainment afterwards to members of the audience.

Attached to them were the hard-labour boys, a set of small, bandy-legged stagehands whose wives were all hefty boot-faced wenches you wouldn't push in front of in a baker's

209

queue. In contrast to the musicians, whose origins were varied and whose quarters had an artistic abandon, the scenery-movers were a closely related group, like bargees or tinkers. They lived in spotless tidiness; they had all been born to the roving life. Whenever we arrived at a new venue, they were the first to organise themselves. Their tents were lined up in straight rows with elaborate sanitary arrangements at one end, and they shared a huge iron broth cauldron that was stirred by a strict rota of cooks. I could see the cauldron now, breathing out coils of gravy steam that reminded me of my stomach's queasiness.

'Do I detect an atmosphere?'

'Where've you been, Falco?' The hook-nosed cymbalist sounded weary as he threw a stone at a dog. I felt lucky he chose the dog.

'I told you: drunk in bed.'

'Oh, you took to the life of a playwright easily!'

'If you wrote for this company you'd be drunk too.'

'Or dead in a cistern!' scoffed a voice from the back.

'Or dead,' I agreed quietly. 'I do worry about that sometimes. Maybe whoever had it in for Heliodorus dislikes all playwrights, and I'm next.' I was carefully not mentioning Ione yet, though she must matter more here than the drowned scribe.

'Don't worry,' sneered the girl who played the panpipes. 'You're not that good!'

'Hah! How would you know? Even the actors never read the script, so I'm damned sure you musicians don't! But surely you're not saying Heliodorus was a decent writer?'

'He was trash!' exclaimed Afrania. 'Plancina's just trying to annoy you.'

'Oh, for a moment I thought I was hearing that Heliodorus was better than everyone tells me – though aren't we all?' I tried to look like a wounded writer. This was not easy since naturally I knew my own work was of fine quality – if anyone with any true critical sense ever did read it.

'Not you, Falco!' laughed the panpipe girl, the brash piece in a brief saffron tunic whom Afrania had called Plancina.

'Well thanks. I needed reassurance . . . So what's the black mood in this part of the camp all about?'

'Get lost. We're not talking to management.'

'I'm not one of them. I'm not even a performer. I'm just a freelance scribe who happened upon this group by accident; one who's starting to wish he'd given Chremes a wide berth.' The murmur of discontent that ran around warned me I had best take care or else instead of persuading the group back to work I would end up leading their walk-out. That would be just my style: from peacemaker to chief rebel in about five minutes. Smart work, Falco.

'It's no secret,' said one of the stagehands, a particular misery. 'We had a big row with Chremes last night, and we're not backing down.'

'Well you don't have to tell me. I didn't mean to pry into your business.'

Even with a hangover that made my head feel like the spot on a fortress gate that's just been hit by a thirty-foot battering-ram, my professional grit had stayed intact: as soon as I said they need not spill the tale, they all wanted to tell me everything.

I had guessed right: Ione's death was at the heart of their discontent. They had finally noticed there was a maniac in our midst. He could murder dramatic writers with impunity, but now that he had turned his attention to the musicians they were wondering which of them would be picked off next.

'It's reasonable to feel alarmed,' I sympathised. 'But what was last night's row with Chremes about?'

'We are not staying on,' said the cymbalist. 'We want to be given our money for the season – '

'Hang on, the rest of us were paid our share of the takings last night. Are your contract terms very different?'

'Too damn right! Chremes knows actors and scribes are pushed to find employment. You won't leave him until you're given a firm shove. But musicians and lifters can always find work so he gives us a fraction, then keeps us waiting for the rest until the tour packs up.'

'And now he won't release your residue?'

'Fast, Falco! Not if we leave early. It's in the trunk under his bed, and he says it's staying there. So now we're saying to him, he can stick *The Birds* in his aviary and tweet all the way

211

from here to Antiochia. If we've got to stay around, he won't be able to take on replacements because we'll warn them off. But we're not going to work. He'll have no music and no scenery. These Greek towns will laugh him off the stage.'

'*The Birds*! That was about the final straw,' grumbled the youthful lyre-player, Ribes. He was no Apollo. He could neither play well nor strike awe with his majestic beauty. In fact he looked as appetising as yesterday's ground-millet polenta. 'Wanting us to chirp like bloody sparrows.'

'I can see that would be a liberty to a professional who can tell his Lydian modes from his Dorians!'

'One more crack from you, Falco, and you'll be picked with a plectrum in a place you won't like!'

I grinned at him. 'Sorry. I'm employed to write jokes.'

'About time you started doing it then,' someone chuckled; I didn't see who.

Afrania broke in, softening slightly. 'So Falco, what made you venture here among the troublemaking low life?'

'Thought I might be able to help.'

'Like how?' jeered a stagehand's wife.

'Who knows? I'm a man of ideas – '

'He means filthy thoughts,' suggested another broad-beamed female whose thoughts were undoubtedly much grimier than mine.

'I came to consult you all,' I carried on bravely. 'You may be able to help me work out who caused the two deaths. And I believe I can assure you that none of you is at risk.'

'How can you do that?' demanded the leader of the orchestra.

'Well, let's take this slowly. I'll not make rash promises about any man who can take life in such a cruelly casual way. I still don't have any real idea why he killed Heliodorus. But in Ione's case, the reason is much clearer.'

'Clear as mud on a bootstrap!' Plancina declared. There was still much hostility, though most of the group were now listening intently.

'Ione thought she knew who killed the playwright,' I told them. 'She had promised to reveal the man's name to me; she must have been killed to stop her giving him away.'

212

'So we are safe so long as we all go around saying "I've absolutely no idea who killed them!" in loud voices?' The orchestra leader was dry, though not unbearably sarcastic.

Ignoring him, I announced: 'If I knew whom Ione was meeting on the night she died, I would know everything. She was your friend. One of you must have an idea. She will have said something about her movements that evening, or at some other time she may have mentioned a man she was friendly with – ' Before the jeers could break out I added hastily, 'I do know she was very popular. There must be some of you here she had banged her tambourine for on occasions, am I right?'

One or two present owned up to it freely. Of the rest, some declared they were married, which was supposed to imply they were innocent; at any rate, in the presence of their wives it gave them immunity from questioning. Those men who had not tangled with Ione had certainly thought about it; this was accepted by everyone.

'Well that illustrates my problem,' I sighed. 'It could be any of you – or any of the actors.'

'Or you!' suggested Afrania. She looked sullen, and developed a nasty streak whenever this subject was discussed.

'Falco never knew Heliodorus,' someone else pointed out fairly.

'Maybe I did,' I conceded. 'I *said* I found him as a stranger, but maybe I *had* known him, took against him, then attached myself to the company afterwards for some perverted reason – '

'Such as you wanted his job?' cried Ribes the lyre-player with a wit that was rare for him. The rest dissolved into roars of laughter, and I was deemed innocent.

No one could offer any useful information. That did not mean no one had any. I might yet hear a furtive whisper outside my tent as someone became braver and came to pass on some vital clue.

'I cannot advise you about staying with the company,' I declared. 'But look at it this way. If you withdraw your labour, the tour will fold. Chremes and Phrygia cannot put on comedy without music or scenery. Both are traditional and the audience expects them.'

'A Plautian monologue without enhancing flute music is a loaf made with dead yeast,' pronounced the orchestra leader sombrely.

'Oh quite!' I tried to look respectful. 'Without you, bookings would become harder and eventually the troupe would disperse. Remember, if we break up, the killer gets away with it.' I stood up. That meant I could see all of them and address each conscience. I wondered how often they had received appeals to the heart from a grey-faced, nauseous inebriate who had nothing substantial to offer them: quite often if they worked for actor-managers. 'It's up to you. Do you want Ione's death to be avenged, or don't you care?'

'It's too dangerous!' wailed one of the women, who happened to be holding a small child on her hip.

'I'm not so crass that I don't know what I'm asking. Each of you must make the choice.'

'What's your interest, Falco?' It was Afrania who asked. 'You said you're a freelance. Why don't you just cut and run?'

'I am involved. I cannot avoid it. I discovered Heliodorus. My girlfriend found Ione. We have to know who did that — and make sure he pays.'

'He's right,' argued the cymbalist reasonably. 'The only way to catch this man is to stick together as a group and keep the killer among us. But how long will it take, Falco?'

'If I knew how long, I would know who he was.'

'He knows you're looking for him,' warned Afrania.

'And I know he must be watching me.' I gave her a hard stare, remembering her odd claims about the alibi she had given Tranio. I still felt certain that she had lied.

'If he thinks you are close, he may come after you,' suggested the cymbalist.

'He probably will.'

'Aren't you afraid?' Plancina asked, as if waiting to see me struck down was the next best thing to a gory chariot race.

'Coming after me will be his mistake.' I sounded confident.

'If you need a drink of water during the next few weeks,' the orchestra leader advised me in his usual pessimistic tone, 'I should make sure you only use a very small cup!'

'I'm not intending to drown.'

214

I folded my arms, planting my feet astride like a man who could be trusted in a tight spot. They knew about decent acting and were unconvinced by this. 'I can't make your decisions. But I can make one promise. There is more to me than some jobbing scribe Chremes picked up in the desert. My background's tough. I've worked for the best – don't ask me names. I've been involved in jobs I'm not allowed to discuss, and I'm trained in skills you'd rather I didn't describe. I've tracked down plenty of felons, and if you haven't heard about it that just proves how discreet I am. If you agree to stay on, I'll stay too. Then you will at least know that you have me looking after your interests . . .'

I must have been mad. I had had more sense and sanity when I was totally befuddled by last night's drink. Guarding them was not the problem. What I hated was the thought of explaining to Helena that I had offered my personal protection to wild women like Plancina and Afrania.

XXXVIII

The musicians and stagehands stayed with us and continued
to work. We gave Scythopolis *The Birds*. Scythopolis gave us –
an ovation.

For Greeks, they were surprisingly tolerant.

They had an interesting theatre, with a semicircular orchestra
that could only be reached by steps. In a Roman play we
would not have used it, but of course we were doing a Greek
one, with a very large chorus, and Chremes wanted a flock of
birds to spill down towards the audience. The steps made life
difficult for anyone foolish enough to be acting while dressed
in a large padded costume, with gigantic claws on their shoes,
and a heavy beaked mask.

While we were there some cheapskate salesman was trying
to persuade the magistrates to spend thousands on an
acoustic system (some bronze devices to be hung on the
theatre wall). The theatre architect was happily pointing out
that he had already provided seven splendid oval niches that
would take the complex equipment; he was obviously in on
the deal with the salesman, and stood to receive a cut.

We tested the samples of the salesman's toys to the limit
with tweeting, twittering and booming, and frankly they made
no difference. Given the perfect acoustics of most Greek
theatres, this was no surprise. The taxpayers of Scythopolis
settled back in their seats and looked as if they were quite
content to place wreaths in the seven niches. The architect
looked sick.

Even though Congrio had told us it had happened before, I
never really understood why Chremes had suddenly abandoned his normal repertoire. With Aristophanes we had leapt
back in time about four hundred years, from New Roman
Comedy to Old Greek ditto. I liked it. They say the old jokes
are the best. They are certainly better than none at all. I want a

play to have bite. By that, speaking as a republican, I mean some political point. Old Comedy had that, which made a sophisticated change. For me New Comedy was dire. I hate watching meaningless plots about tiresome characters in grisly situations on a provincial street. If I wanted that, I could go home and listen to my neighbours through their apartment walls.

The Birds was famous. At rehearsal Tranio, always ready with an anecdote, told us, 'Not bad considering it only won second prize at the festival it was written for.'

'What a show-off! Which archive did you drag that one out of, Tranio?' I scoffed.

'And what play actually won then?' Helena demanded.

'Some trifle called *The Revellers*, now unknown to man.'

'Sounds fun. One of the people in my tent has been revelling too much lately, though,' Helena commented.

'This play is not half as obscene as some Aristophanes,' grumbled Tranio. 'I saw *Peace* once – not often performed, as we're always at war of course. It has two female roles for wicked girls with nice arses. One of them has her clothes taken off on-stage, then she's handed down to the man in the centre of the front row. She sits on his lap for starters, then spends the rest of the play going up and down, "comforting" other members of the audience.'

'Filth!' I cried, feigning shock.

Tranio scowled. 'It hardly compares with showing Hercules as a glutton, giving out cookery tips.'

'No, but recipes won't get us run out of town,' said Helena. She was always practical. Offered a prospect of wicked women with nice arses 'comforting' the ticket-holders, her practical nature became even more brisk than usual.

Helena knew *The Birds*. She had been well educated, partly by her brothers' tutors when her brothers slipped off to the racecourse, and partly through grabbing any written scrolls that she could lay her hands on in private libraries owned by her wealthy family (plus the few tattered fifth-hand items I kept under my own bed). Since she had never been one for the senators' wives' circuit of orgies and admiring gladiators, she had always spent time at home reading. So she told me, anyway.

217

She had done a good job on the script; Chremes had accepted it without change, remarking that at last I seemed to be getting on top of the job.

'Fast work,' I congratulated her.

'It's nothing.'

'Don't let having your adaptations accepted first time go to your head. I'd hate to think you're becoming an intellectual.'

'Sorry, I forgot. You don't like cultured women.'

'Suits me.' I grinned at her. 'I'm no snob. I'm prepared to put up with brains in an exceptional case.'

'Thank you very much!'

'Don't mention it. Mind you, I never expected to end up in bed with some learned scroll-beetle who's studied Greek and knows that *The Birds* is a famous play. I suppose it sticks in the mind because of the feathers. Like when you think about the Greek philosophers and can only remember that the first premise of Pythagoras was that nobody should eat beans.'

'Philosophy's a new side to you,' she smiled.

'Oh I can run off philosophers as well as any dinner-party bore. My favourite is Bias, who invented the informers' motto – '

'All Men are Bad!' Helena had read the philosophers as well as the dramatists. 'Everyone has to play a bird in the chorus, Marcus. Which has Chremes given you?'

'Listen, fruit, when I make my acting début, it will be a moment to memorise for our grandchildren. I will be a Tragic Hero, striding on through the central doorway in a coronet, not hopping from the wings as a bloody bird.'

Helena chortled. 'Oh I think you're wrong! This play was written for a very prosperous festival. There is a full chorus of twenty-four named cheepers, and we all have to participate.'

I shook my head. 'Not me.'

Helena Justina was a bright girl. Besides, as the adaptor she was the only person in our group who had read the entire play. Most people just skimmed through to find their own parts. Helena soon worked out what Chremes must have me down for, and thought it hilarious.

218

Musa, who had been silent as usual, looked bemused – though not half as bemused as when Helena explained that *he* would be appearing as the reed warbler.

So what was I playing? They had found me the dross, needless to say.

In our performance the two humans who run away from Athens in disgust at the litigation, the strife and the hefty fines were played by handsome Philocrates and tough Davos. Naturally Philocrates had grabbed the major part, with all the speeches, while Davos took the stooge who puts in the obscene one-line rejoinders. His part was shorter, though more pungent.

Tranio was playing Hercules. In fact he and Grumio were to be a long succession of unwelcome visitors who call at Cloud-cuckoo-land in order to be chased off ignominiously. Phrygia had a hilarious cameo as an elderly Iris whose lightning bolts refused to fulminate, while Byrria appeared as the hoopoe's beautiful wife and as Sovereignty (a symbolic part, made more interesting by a scanty costume). Chremes was chorus leader for the famous twenty-four named birds. These included Congrio hooting, Musa warbling, and Helena disguised as the cutest dabchick who ever hopped on to a stage. I was unsure how I would confess to her noble father and disapproving mother that their elegant daughter with the centuries-old pedigree had now been witnessed by a crowd of raw Scythopolitans acting as a dabchick . . .

At least from now on I would always be able to call up material to blackmail Helena.

My role was tiresome. I played the informer. In this otherwise witty satire, my character creeps in after the ghastly poet, the twisting fortune-teller, the rebellious youth and the cranky philosopher. Once they have come to Cloud-cuckoo-land and all been seen off by the Athenians, an informer tries his luck. Like mine, his luck is in short supply, to the delight of the audience. He is stirring up court cases on the basis of questionable evidence and wants some wings to help him fly about the Greek islands quicker as he hands out subpoenas. If anyone had been prepared to listen, I could have told them an informer's life is so boring it's positively respectable, while the chances of a lucrative court case are about equal with discovering an emerald in a goose's gizzard. But the company were used to abusing my profession (which is much mocked in drama) so they loved this chance to heap insults on a live victim. I offered to play the sacrificial pig instead, but was overruled. Needless to say, in the play, the informer fails to get his wings.

Chremes deemed me fit to act my role without coaching, even though it was a speaking part. He claimed I could talk well enough without assistance. By the end of rehearsals I was tired of people crying 'Oh just be yourself, Falco!' ever so wittily. And the moment when Philocrates was called upon to whip me off-stage was maddening. He really enjoyed handing out a thrashing. I was now plotting a black revenge.

Everyone else hugely enjoyed putting on this stuff. I decided that perhaps Chremes did know what he was doing. Even though we had always complained about his judgement, the mood lightened. Scythopolis kept us for several performances. The company was calmer, as well as richer, by the time we moved on up the Jordan Valley to Gadara.

XXXIX

Gadara called itself the Athens of the East. From this Eastern outpost had come the cynic satirist Menippos, the philosopher and poet Philodemos, who had had Virgil as his pupil in Italy, and the elegiac epigrammatist Meleager. Helena had read Meleager's poetic anthology *The Garland*, so before we arrived she enlightened me.

'His themes are love and death – '

'Very nice.'

'And he compares each poet he includes to a different flower.'

I said what I thought, and she smiled gently. Love and death are gritty subjects. Their appropriate handling by poets does not require myrtle petals and violets.

The city commanded a promontory above a rich and vital landscape, with stunning views to both Palestine and Syria, westwards over Lake Tiberias and north to the far snow-capped mountain peak of Mount Hermon. Nearby, thriving villages studded the surrounding slopes, which were lush with pasture-land. Instead of the bare tawny hills we had seen endlessly rolling elsewhere, this area was clothed with green fields and woodlands. Instead of lone nomadic goatherds, we saw chattering groups watching over fatter, fleecier flocks. Even the sunlight seemed brighter, enlivened by the nearby twinkling presence of the great lake. No doubt all the shepherds and swineherds in the desirable pastures were busy composing sunlit, elegantly elegiac odes. If they were kept awake at night struggling with metric imperfections in their verse, they could always put themselves off to sleep by counting their obols and drachmas; people here had no financial worries that I could see.

As always in our company, argument about what play to put on was raging; eventually, with matters still unresolved, Chremes and Philocrates, supported by Grumio, strolled off

221

to see the local magistrate. Helena and I took a walk around town. We made enquiries about Thalia's lost musical maiden, fruitlessly as usual. We didn't much care; we were enjoying this short time alone together. We found ourselves following a throng of people who were ambling down from the acropolis to the river valley below.

Apparently the routine here was for the citizens to flock out in the evening, go to the river, bathe in its reputedly therapeutic waters, then flog back uphill (complaining) for their nightly dose of public entertainment. Even if bathing in the river had cured their aches, walking back afterwards up the precipitous slope to their lofty town was likely to set their joints again, and half of them probably caught a chill when they reached the cooler air. Still, if one or two had to take to their beds, all the more room on the comfortable theatre seats for folk who had come direct from the shop or the office without risking their health in water therapy.

We joined the crowds of people in their striped robes and twisted headgear on the banks of the river, where Helena cautiously dipped a toe while I stood aloof, looking Roman and superior. The late-evening sunlight had a pleasantly soothing effect. I could happily have forgotten both my searches and relaxed into the theatrical life for good.

Further along the bank I suddenly noticed Philocrates; he had not spotted us. He had been drinking – wine, presumably – from a goatskin. As he finished he stood up, demonstrating his physique for any watching women, then blew up the skin, tied its neck, and tossed it to some children who were playing in the water. As they fell on it, squealing with delight, Philocrates stripped off his tunic ready to dive into the river.

'You'd need a lot of *those* to fill a punnet!' giggled Helena, noticing that the naked actor was not well endowed.

'Size isn't everything,' I assured her.

'Just as well!'

She was grinning, while I wondered whether I ought to play the heavy-handed patriarch and censor whatever it was she had been reading to acquire such a low taste in jokes.

'There's a very odd smell, Marcus. Why do spa waters always stink?'

'To fool you into thinking they are doing you good. Who told you the punnet joke?'

'Aha! Did you see what Philocrates did with his wineskin?'

'I did. He can't possibly have killed Heliodorus if he's kind to children,' I remarked sarcastically.

Helena and I started the steep climb up from the elegant waterfront to the town high on its ridge. It was hard going, reminding us both of our wearying assault on the High Place at Petra.

Partly to gain a breathing space, but interested anyway, I stopped to have a look at the town's water system. They had an aqueduct that brought drinking water over ten miles from a spring to the east of the city; it then ran through an amazing underground system. One of the caps to a flue had been removed by some workmen for cleaning; I was leaning over the hole and staring down into the depths when a voice behind made me jump violently.

'That's a long drop, Falco!'

It was Grumio.

Helena had grabbed my arm, though her intervention was probably unnecessary. Grumio laughed cheerfully. 'Steady!' he warned, before clattering downhill the way we had just come.

Helena and I exchanged a wry glance. The thought crossed my mind that if someone fell down into those tunnels and the exit was re-covered, even if he survived the tumble no one would ever hear him call for help. His body would not be found until it had decayed so much that townsfolk started feeling poorly . . .

If Grumio had been a suspect who could not account for his movements, I might have found myself shivering.

Helena and I made our way back to camp slowly, amorously intertwined.

Not for the first time with this company, we had walked into a panic. Chremes and the others had been gone too long; Davos had sent Congrio to wander round town in his most unobtrusive manner, trying to find out where they were. As we reached the camp Congrio came scampering back, shrieking: 'They're all locked up!'

'Calm down.' I made a grab at him, and held him still. 'Locked up? What for?'

'It's Grumio's fault. When they got in to see the magistrate, it turned out he had been at Gerasa when we were there; he'd heard Grumio doing his comic turn. Part of it was insulting Gadarenes . . .' As I recalled Grumio's stand-up act, *most* of it had involved being rude about the Decapolis towns. Thinking of Helena's recent joke, we were only lucky he hadn't mentioned punnets in connection with the private parts of their pompous magistrates. Maybe he had never read whatever scroll Helena had found for herself. 'Now our lot are all thrown into prison for slander,' Congrio wailed.

I wanted my dinner. My chief reaction was annoyance. 'If Grumio said the Gadarenes were impetuous and touchy and have no sense of humour, where's the slander? It's obviously true! Anyway, that's nothing to what I heard him say about Abila and Dium.'

'I'm just telling you what I heard, Falco.'

'And I'm just deciding what we can do.'

'Cause a fuss,' suggested Davos. 'Tell them we intend to warn our Emperor about their unkind welcome for innocent visitors, then beat the local jailor over the head with a cudgel. After that, run like mad.'

Davos was the kind of man I could work with. He had a good grasp of a situation and a down-to-earth attitude to handling it.

He and I went into town together, dressed up to look like respectable entrepreneurs. We wore newly polished boots and togas from the costume box. Davos was carrying a laurel wreath for an even more refined effect, though I did think that was overdoing it.

We presented ourselves at the magistrate's house, looking surprised there could be a problem. The nob was out: at the theatre. We then presented ourselves at one end of the orchestra stalls and hung around for a break in what turned out to be a *very* poor satyr play. Davos muttered, 'At least they could tune their damned panpipes! Their masks stink. And their nymphs are rubbish.'

While we fretted on the sidelines, I managed to ask, 'Davos, have you ever seen Philocrates blow up an empty wineskin and throw it into water, the way children like to do? Is making floats a habit of his?'

'Not that I've noticed. I've seen the clowns do it.'

As usual, what had looked like a pinpointing clue caused more confusion than it solved.

Luckily satyr plays are short. A few disguises, a couple of mock rapes, and they gallop off-stage in their goatskin trousers.

At last there was a pause to let the sweetmeat trays go round. Seizing our moment we leapt across the pit to beard the elected nincompoop who had incarcerated our gang. He was an overbearing bastard. Sometimes I lose faith in democracy. Usually, in fact.

There was not much time to argue; we could hear tambourines rattling as a fleet of overweight female dancers prepared to come on-stage next and titillate with some choric frivolity in see-through skirts. After three minutes of fast talking we had achieved nothing with the official, and he signalled the theatre guards to shift us.

Davos and I left of our own accord. We went straight to the jail, where we bribed the keeper with half our proceeds from performing *The Birds* at Scythopolis. Anticipating trouble, we had already left instructions for the waggons and camels to be loaded up by my friends the scene-shifters. Once we had organised our jailbreak, we spent a few moments in the forum loudly discussing our next move eastwards to Capitolias, then we met the rest of our group on the road and galloped off in the northerly direction of Hippos.

We travelled fast, cursing the Gadarenes for the indelicate swine they had shown themselves to be.

So much for the Athens of the East!

225

XL

Hippos: a jumpy town. Not as jumpy as some of its visitors were, however.

It was located halfway along the eastern shore of Lake Tiberias on a hilltop site – fine vistas, but inconvenient. The site set it back from the lake a considerable distance, with no nearby river, so water for domestic consumption was scarce. Across the lake lay Tiberias, a city that had been much more conveniently placed at shore level. The people of Hippos hated the people of Tiberias with passionate hostility – much more real than the vaunted feud between Pella and Scythopolis, which we had been hard-put to spot.

Hippos had its water shortage and feud to contend with, which ought to have left little time for parting traders from their money or spending that money on grandiose building schemes, yet with the tenacity of this region its people were managing both. From the gate where we entered (on foot, for we camped out of town in case we needed to flee again) ran an established main street, a long black basalt thoroughfare whose gracious colonnades travelled the length of the ridge on which the town stood, giving fine views of Lake Tiberias.

Perhaps due to our own nervous situation, we found the populace edgy. The streets were full of swarthy faces peering from hoods with an air that told you not to ask directions to the marketplace. The women had the guarded expressions of those who spend many hours every day jostling to fill pitchers with water; thin, harassed little pieces with the sinewy arms of those who then had to carry the full pitchers home. The men's role was to stand about looking sinister; they all carried knives, visible or hidden, ready to stab anyone they could accuse of having a Tiberias accent. Hippos was a dark, introverted huddle of suspicion. To my mind this was the sort of place poets and philosophers ought to come from, to give them the right tone of cynical distrust; of course none did.

In a town like Hippos, even the most hardened informer starts to feel nervous about asking questions. Nevertheless, there was no point coming here unless I carried out my commission. I had to try to find the missing organist. I braced myself and tackled various leathery characters. Some of them spat; not many directly at me, unless their aim was truly bad. Most gazed into the middle distance with blank faces, which appeared to be the Hippos dialect for 'No, I'm terribly sorry, young Roman sir, I've never seen your delightful maiden nor heard of the raffish Syrian businessman who snaffled her . . .' Nobody actually stuck a knife into me.

I crossed off one more possible destination for Sophrona and Habib (assuming he was the person she did the flit with), then took the long haul out of town to our camp. All the way back I kept looking over my shoulder to see if the people of Hippos were tailing me. I was growing as nervy as they were.

Luckily my mind was taken off my unease when halfway along the trail I caught up with Ribes the lyre-player.

Ribes was a pasty youth who believed his role as a musician was to sit around in a lopsided haircut describing plans for making vast sums of money with popular songs he had yet to compose. So far there was no sign of him being mobbed by Egyptian accountants keen to rob him of huge agency fees. He wore the sort of belt that said he was tough, with a facial expression that belonged on a moonstruck vole. I tried to avoid him, but he had seen me.

'How's the music?' I asked politely.

'Coming along . . .' He did not ask how the playwriting was.

We strolled along together for a short time while I tried to twist my ankle so I could fall behind.

'Have you been looking for clues?' he asked earnestly.

'Just looking for a girl.' Perhaps because he knew Helena, this appeared to worry him. It was not a concept that had ever worried me.

'I've been thinking about what you said to us,' Ribes offered after a few more strides. 'About what happened to Ione . . .' He tailed off. I forced myself to look interested,

227

though talking to Ribes thrilled me about as much as trying to pick my teeth at a banquet without a toothpick and without the host's wife noticing.

'Thought of anything to help me?' I encouraged gloomily.

'I don't know.'

'Nobody else has either,' I said.

Ribes looked more cheerful. 'Well, I might know something.' Fortunately, six years as an informer had taught me how to wait patiently. 'Ione and I were friendly, actually. I don't mean – Well, I mean we never – But she used to talk to me.'

This was the best news I had had for days. Men who had slept with the tambourinist would be useless; they had certainly proved slow to come forward. I welcomed this feeble reed with the bent stalk, in whom the girl could well have confided since he had so little else to offer.

'And what did she say, Ribes, that now strikes you as possibly significant?'

'Well, did you know that at one time she had dealings with Heliodorus?' This could be the link I was needing to find. Ione had implied to me that she knew more about the playwright than most people. 'He used to boast to her about what he'd got on other people – stories that would upset them, you know. He never told her much, just hints, and I don't remember much that she passed on.' Ribes was not exactly bursting with curiosity about the rest of the human race.

'Tell me what you can,' I said.

'Well . . .' Ribes ticked off some tantalising references: 'He reckoned he had Chremes in his power; he used to laugh about how Congrio hated his guts; he was supposed to be pals with Tranio, but there was something going on there – '

'Anything about Byrria?'

'No.'

'Davos?'

'No.'

'Grumio?'

'No. The only thing I really remember is that Ione said Heliodorus had been horrible to Phrygia. He found out she had once had a baby; she'd had to leave it behind somewhere and she was desperate to find out what had happened to it since. Heliodorus told her he knew somebody who had seen the child, but he wouldn't tell her who it was, or where. Ione said Phrygia had had to pretend that she didn't believe him. It was the only way to stop him tormenting her with it.'

I was thinking hard. 'This is interesting, Ribes, but I'd be surprised if it relates to why Heliodorus died. Ione told me very definitely that he was killed for "purely professional" reasons. Can you say anything about that?'

Ribes shook his head. We spent the rest of the walk with him trying to tell me about a dirge he had composed in Ione's memory, and me doing my best to avoid letting him sing it.

Contrary to our expectations, Hippos offered a warm welcome to theatrical performers. We easily obtained a booking at the auditorium, although we could not attract a local sponsor so had to play on a directly ticketed basis; however, we did sell tickets. It was hard to say who was buying them, and we went into the opening night with some trepidation. Every good Roman has heard stories of riots in provincial theatres. Sooner or later our turn might arrive to become part of disreputable folklore. Hippos seemed the place.

Our performance must have had a calming influence, however. We put on *The Pirate Brothers*. The townsfolk seemed to be genuinely informed critics. Villians were booed with gusto (no doubt on the assumption that they might come from Tiberias) and love scenes enthusiastically cheered.

We gave them two more performances. *The Rope* was rather quietly received, up to the scene with the tug of war, which went down superbly. This brought increased crowds the following day for *The Birds*. After much silly debate of the kind he loved and we all hated, Chremes had risked this as a gamble, since piquant satire was not obvious fare for an audience who spent their time seething with pent-up suspicions and fingering their daggers. However, the costumes swayed them. Hippos took to *The Birds* so well that at the end we were mobbed by members of the audience. After a moment of panic as they came swarming on to the

229

stage, we realised they all wanted to join in. Then ensued the fascinating spectacle of sombre men in long flowing robes all losing their inhibitions with joyous glee and hopping about for half an hour, flapping their elbows as imitation wings, like chickens who had eaten fermented grain. We, meanwhile, stood about rather stiffly, unsure what to make of it.

Exhausted, we crept away that night, before Hippos could demand even more excitement from our repertoire.

XLI

Approaching Dium we were told there was a plague. We retreated very fast.

XLII

Abila was not officially one of the fabled ten in the region of the Ten Towns. Like other places, this one claimed to belong in order to acquire prestige and the sense of mutual protection against raiders that was enjoyed amongst the true federation. If raiders turned up and asked to see their certificate of membership, presumably the claim failed and they had to submit to pillage meekly.

It did have all the qualifying features of the best of the Decapolis: a beautiful location, a rippling stream, good defensive walls, a Greek acropolis plus a more Romanised settlement, a huge temple complex honouring deities to suit every palate, and a theatre. The local architecture was a rich mixture of marble, basalt and grey granite. Abila was set on a high rolling plateau where a restless wind eerily seethed. There was something remote and lonely about it. The people looked at us thoughtfully; they were not directly hostile but we found the atmosphere unsettling.

Our thwarted trip to Dium, leading to an unexpectedly lengthened journey, had caused us to arrive at an awkward time of day. Normally we travelled through the night to avoid the worst heat, and tried to enter cities in the morning. Then Chremes could investigate the possibilities for a booking at an early stage while we others rested and complained about him among ourselves.

Having come on a poor track, we reached Abila well after noon. No one was happy. One of the waggons had had a broken axle, which held us up on a road that had seemed likely to be patrolled by brigands, and we were all shaken to bits by the roughness of the ground. On arrival we threw up tents, then straight away retired into them without wanting to make plans.

Outside our tent, Musa doggedly lit a fire. However tired we were, he always did this, and also always fetched water, before he would relax. I forced myself to co-operate and fed

232

the ox, having my foot stepped on by the ridiculous beast in return for my act of duty. Helena found food for us, though no one was hungry.

It was too hot, and we were too ill-tempered to sleep. Instead we all sat cross-legged and talked restlessly.

'I feel depressed,' Helena exclaimed. 'We're running out of cities but not solving anything. What are the places we have left to visit? Just Capitolias, Canatha, and Damascus.' She was in a brisk mood again, answering her own questions as if she expected Musa and me to stare into space lethargically. We did that for a while, not deliberately intending to annoy her but because it seemed natural.

'Damascus is big,' I offered eventually. 'There seems a good hope of finding Sophrona.'

'But what if she was at Dium?'

'Then she's probably caught the plague. Thalia wouldn't want her back.'

'Meanwhile we go on searching for her, though, Marcus.' Helena hated wasted effort. I was an informer; I was used to it.

'We have to do something, fruit. We're trapped at the ends of the Empire, and we need to earn our keep. Look, we'll go to the last three cities with the company and if Sophrona doesn't turn up then we'll know we should have tried Dium. If it happens, we can decide what we think about this plague.'

It was one of those moments that hit travellers, a moment when I reckoned our decision would be to take a fast ship home. I didn't say it, because we were both so frustrated and gloomy that even mentioning a retreat would have had us packing our bags that minute. These moods pass. If they don't, *then* you can suggest going home.

'Maybe there was nothing really wrong at Dium,' Helena fretted. 'We only have the word of a caravan we met. The men who told us may have been lying for some reason. Or it could be no more than one child with spots. People panic too easily.'

I tried myself not to sound panicky. 'Risking our own lives would be stupid – and I'm not going to be responsible for extracting a runaway musician from Dium if taking her to Rome might bring an epidemic there. It's too high a price for a water-organ fugue, however brilliant a player she is.'

233

'All right.' After a moment Helena added, 'I hate you when you're sensible.'

'The caravanners looked pretty grim when they waved us away,' I insisted.

'I said, all right!'

I saw Musa smile faintly. As usual he was sitting there saying nothing. It was the kind of irritating day when I could easily have lost my temper with him for this silence, so I covered by taking charge: 'Maybe we need to take stock.' If I thought this would perk up my companions, I was disappointed. They both remained listless and glum. Still, I pressed on: 'Looking for Sophrona may be pointless, I agree. I know the girl could be anywhere by now. We're not even certain she ever left Italy.' This was verging on too much pessimism. 'All we can do is to be as thorough as possible. Sometimes these jobs are impossible. Or you may run across a piece of luck and solve the case after all.'

Helena and Musa looked as impressed as a desert vulture who had flown down to an intriguing carcase only to find it was a piece of old tunic blowing against a broken amphora. I try to stay cheerful. However, I gave up on the girl musician. We had been looking for her for too long. She had ceased to seem real. Our interest in the creature had waned, along with any chances we had ever had of finding her out here.

Suddenly Helena rallied. 'So what about the murderer?'

Once again I tried to liven us up with a review of the facts. 'Well what do we know? He's a man, one who can whistle, who must be fairly strong, who wears a hat sometimes – '

'His nerve holds,' contributed Musa. 'He has been with us for weeks. He knows we are looking for him, yet he makes no mistake.'

'Yes, he's confident – although he does jump sometimes. He panicked and tried to put you out of action, Musa, then he soon silenced Ione.'

'He's ruthless,' said Helena. 'And also persuasive: he did make both Heliodorus and Ione agree to go somewhere alone with him. Ione even suspected he was a killer, though I presume that didn't apply in the playwright's case.'

'Let's think about Petra again,' I suggested. 'The chief

players went there and came back without the playwright. What have we found out about them? Who hated Heliodorus enough to turn his walk into a swim?'

'Most of them.' Helena ticked them off on her fingers: 'Chremes and Phrygia, because he plagued them about their unhappy marriage and Phrygia's lost baby. Philocrates because they were unsuccessful rivals for Byrria. Byrria, too, because he tried to rape her. Davos partly because of his loyalty to Phrygia, but also because he thought the man was . . .' She hesitated.

'A shit,' I supplied.

'Worse: a bad writer!' We all grinned briefly, then Helena carried on. 'Congrio loathed Heliodorus because he was bullied, but Congrio is let off because he can't whistle.'

'We'd better check that,' I said.

'I asked Chremes,' she whipped back crisply. 'As for the Twins, they have told us they disliked Heliodorus. But do they have a particular reason? A strong enough motive to kill him?'

I agreed: 'If there was one, we haven't unearthed it yet. They told me that Heliodorus couldn't succeed in doing them down on the stage. If he tried to write poor parts, they could improvise. Well, we know that's true.'

'So they were not in his power,' Helena mused. 'Yet they do say they despised him.'

'Right. And if we come forward in time, one at least – Tranio –has an unsatisfactory alibi for the night Ione died. Everyone else seems to be accounted for that night. Poor Congrio was running around Gerasa writing wrongly spelt playbills. Grumio was joking his heart out in the street. Chremes, Davos and Philocrates were all dining together – '

'Apart from when Philocrates says he left to bed his cheese-maker,' scowled Helena. She seemed to have developed an antipathy for her admirer.

I grinned. 'He showed me the cheese!'

Musa openly chortled too. 'I think the handsome one is too busy to find time for killing people.'

'Eating cheese!' I laughed abusively.

Helena stayed serious: 'He could have acquired the cheese at any time – '

'So long as the shop had a low counter!'

'Oh shut up, Marcus!'

'Right.' I pulled myself together. 'Everyone has an alibi except Tranio. Tranio ducks out by claiming he was with Afrania; I don't believe him though.'

'So we really suspect Tranio?' said Helena, pushing for a decision.

I still felt uneasy. 'There's a worrying lack of evidence. Musa, *could* Tranio be your whistling man?'

'Oh yes.' He too was troubled though. 'But the night I was pushed off the embankment at Bostra – ' If I ever forgot that incident, Musa never did. He thought about it again now, cautious as ever. 'That night, I am sure Tranio was walking up ahead of me. Congrio, Grumio, Davos – they were all behind. It could have been any one of them, but not Tranio.'

'You're quite certain?'

'Oh yes.'

'When I asked you about it straight after the incident – '

'I have thought about it a lot more since. Tranio was in front.'

I considered this. 'Are we still sure what happened to you that night was deliberate? Nothing else has been done to you.'

'I stay near you – I have perfect protection!' He said it deadpan, though I was trying to decide if there was a trace of irony. 'I felt the hard push,' he reminded me. 'Whoever did that must have known we had collided. He made no call for help when I fell.'

Helena weighed in thoughtfully. 'Marcus, they all know that you are trying to find the killer. Perhaps he is being more careful. He has not attacked you.' Nor had he attacked Helena herself, which at one time had been my unspoken fear.

'I wish he'd try,' I murmured. 'Then I'd have the creep!'

In my head I carried on thinking. This had a bad taste. Either we had missed something crucial, or it would be difficult ever to expose this villain. The vital proof was eluding us. The more time passed, the less chance we stood of solving the mystery.

'We have never seen anybody wearing the hat again,' Helena pointed out. She must have been thinking hard, like me.

'And he has stopped whistling,' Musa added.

He seemed to have stopped killing too. He must know I was utterly stumped. If he did nothing else he would be safe.

I would have to *make* him do something.

Refusing to give up, I nagged at the problem: 'We have a situation where all the suspects are ruled out on at least one of the attacks. That cannot be right. I still feel one person is responsible for everything, even what happened to Musa.'

'But there can be other possibilities?' asked Helena. 'An accomplice?'

'Oh yes. Perhaps a general conspiracy, with people providing false alibis. Heliodorus was universally loathed, after all. It is possible more than one of them was actively involved.'

'You don't believe that though?' Musa tackled me.

'No. A man was killed, for a reason we don't know, but we'll assume it made sense at the time. Then a possible witness was attacked, and another who intended to name him was strangled. This is a logical progression. To me, it fits one killer acting alone, and then reacting alone as he tries to escape discovery.'

'It's very confusing,' Helena complained.

'No, it's simple,' I corrected her, suddenly sure of myself. 'There is a lie somewhere. There must be. It cannot be obvious, or one of us would have spotted a discrepancy.'

'So what can we do?' Helena demanded. 'How can we find out?'

Musa shared her despondency. 'This man is too clever to change the lie just because we ask the same questions a second time.'

'We'll test everything,' I said. 'Make no assumptions, recheck every story, but asking somebody different whenever we can. We may jog a memory. We may drag more information to the surface just by putting pressure on. Then, if that fails, we'll have to force the issue.'

'How?'

'I'll think of something.'

As usual it had a futile ring, yet the others did not question my claim. Maybe I would think of a way to break this man. The more I remembered what he had done, the more I was determined to better him.

XLIII

For Abila, Chremes came up with another new play, an unfunny farce about Hercules sent down to earth on a mission from the other gods. It was deep Greek myth rendered as crass Roman satire. Davos played Hercules. The actors all seemed to know the work and there was nothing required of me beforehand. At rehearsal, while Davos, in a ridiculous rolling baritone, sailed confidently through his stuff needing no direction from Chremes, I took the opportunity to ask the manager for a private word some time. He invited me to dinner that evening.

There was no performance; we were having to wait for the theatre behind a local group who had the run of the stage for a week doing something proclamatory with drumbeats and harps. I could hear the throb of their music as I walked through the camp to attend my tryst. By then I was starving. Chremes and Phrygia dined late. At my own bivouac Helena and Musa, who were not included in my invitation, had made a point of tucking into a lavish spread while I hung about waiting to go. Outside the tents I passed on the way happy people who had already eaten were tipsily waving beakers or spitting olive stones after me.

It must have been perfectly obvious where and why I was going, for I had my napkin in one hand and the good guest's gift of an amphora under the other arm. I wore my best tunic (the one with least moth holes) and had combed the desert grit out of my hair. I felt strangely conspicuous as I ran the gauntlet of the rows of long black tents that we had pitched in nomad fashion at right angles to the track. I noticed that Byrria's tent lay in near-darkness. Both Twins were outside theirs, drinking with Plancina. No sign of Afrania tonight. As I passed, I thought one of the clowns stood up and silently stared after me.

When I arrived at the manager's tent, my heart sank.

Chremes and Phrygia were deep in some unexplained wrangle and the dinner was not even ready yet. They were such an odd, ill-assorted couple. By firelight Phrygia's face appeared more gaunt and unhappy than ever as she swooped about like a very tall Fury who had some harsh torments lined up for sinners. As she made desultory motions towards eventually feeding me I tried to be affable, even though my reception was offhand. Slouching outside with a furious scowl, Chremes looked older too, his striking looks showing signs of early ruin, with deep hollows in his face and a wine gut flowing over his belt.

He and I opened my amphora furtively while Phrygia crashed platters inside the tent.

'So what's the mystery, young Marcus?'

'Nothing really. I just wanted to consult you again over this search for your murderer.'

'Might as well consult a camel-driver's hitching post!' cried Phrygia from indoors.

'Consult away!' boomed the manager, as if he had not heard his jaded consort. Probably after twenty years of their angry marriage his ears were genuinely selective.

'Well, I've narrowed the field of suspects but I still need the vital fact that will pin this bastard down. When the tambourinist died I had hoped for extra clues, but Ione had so many menfriends that sorting them out is hopeless.'

Without appearing to watch him, I checked Chremes for a reaction. He seemed oblivious to my subtle suggestion that he might have been one of the girl's 'friends'. Phrygia knew better, and popped out of the tent again to supervise our conversation. She had transformed herself into a gracious hostess for the night with a few deft touches: a flowing scarf, probably silk, thrown over her shoulders dramatically; silver earrings the size of spoonbowls, daring swathes of facepaint. She had also switched on a more attentive manner as she produced our food with a lazy flourish.

Despite my fears, the meal was impressive: huge salvers of Eastern delicacies decorated with olives and dates; warmed bread; grains, pulses and spiced meats; small bowls of sharp pastes for dipping; plenty of salt and pickled fish from Lake

Tiberias. Phrygia served with an offhand manner, as if she was surprised by her own success in concocting the feast. Both hosts implied that food was incidental to their lives, though I noticed that all they ate was of the best.

Their travelling dinnerset was one of bold ceramics, with heavy metal drinking cups and elegant bronze servingware. It was like dining with a family of sculptors, people who knew shape and quality; people who could afford style.

The domestic quarrel had gone into abeyance; probably not abandoned, but deferred.

'The girl knew what she was doing,' Phrygia commented on Ione, neither bitter nor condemning.

I disgreed. 'She can't have known she would be killed for it.' Minding my manners, for the mood seemed more formal than I was used to, I scooped up as many tastings as I could fit in my feeding bowl without looking greedy. 'She enjoyed life too much to give it up. But she didn't fight back. She wasn't expecting what happened at the pool.'

'She was a fool to go there!' Chremes exclaimed. 'I can't understand it. She thought the man she was meeting had killed Heliodorus, so why risk it?'

Phrygia tried to be helpful: 'She was just a girl. She thought no one who loathed him could have the same reason for loathing her. She didn't understand that a killer is illogical and unpredictable. Marcus – ' we were on first-name terms apparently ' – enjoy yourself. Have plenty.'

'So do you think', I asked, manipulating a honey dip on my flat bread, 'that she wanted to let him know she had identified him?'

'I'm sure she did,' Phrygia answered. I could tell she had been thinking this through for herself; perhaps she had wanted to feel certain her own husband could not be involved. 'She was attracted by the danger. But the little idiot had no real idea this man would see her as a threat. She was not the type to blackmail him, though he would probably suspect it. Knowing Ione, she thought it was a good giggle.'

'So the killer would have felt she was laughing at him. The worst thing she could have done,' I groaned. 'What about the playwright? Did she have no sense of regret that Heliodorus had been removed from society?'

'She didn't like him.'

'Why? I heard he once made a play for her?'

'He made a play for anything that moved,' said Chremes. According to what I had heard, this was rich coming from him. 'We were always having to rescue the girls from his clutches.'

'Oh? Was it you who rescued Byrria?'

'No. I would have said she could take care of herself.'

'Oh would you!' Phrygia exclaimed, with a scornful note. Chremes set his jaw.

'Did you know about Heliodorus trying to rape Byrria?' I asked Phrygia.

'I may have heard something.'

'There's no need to be secretive. She told me herself.' I noticed that Chremes was stuffing his bowl with seconds, so I leaned forward too and gathered up more.

'Well, if Byrria told you . . . I knew about it because she came to me in great distress afterwards, wanting to leave the company. I persuaded her to stay on. She's a good little actress. Why should she let a bully destroy a promising career?'

'Did you say anything to him?'

'Naturally!' muttered Chremes through another mouthful of bread. 'Trust Phrygia!'

Phrygia rounded on him. 'I knew *you* would never do it!' He looked shifty. I felt shifty myself, without any reason. 'He was impossible. He had to be dealt with. You should have kicked him out then and there.'

'So you warned him?' I prompted, licking sauce off my fingers.

'It was more of a threat than a warning!' I could believe that. Phrygia was some force. But in view of what Ribes had told me, I wondered if she really would have kicked out the playwright while she thought he might know something about her missing child. She seemed definite, however. 'I told him, one more wrong move and he could no longer rely on Chremes to be soft; he would march. He knew I meant it too.'

241

I glanced at Chremes. 'I was growing extremely dissatisfied with the man,' he declared, as if it was all his idea. I hid a smile as he made the best of a losing situation. 'I was certainly ready to take my wife's advice.'

'But when you reached Petra he was still with the company?'

'On probation!' said Chremes.

'On notice!' snapped Phrygia.

I decided I could risk a more delicate subject. 'Davos hinted you had good reason to take against him anyway, Phrygia?'

'Oh, Davos told you that story, did he?' Phrygia's tone was hard. I thought Chremes sat up fractionally. 'Good old Davos!' she raved.

'He didn't pass on details. As a friend, he was angry about Heliodorus tormenting you. He only spoke to illustrate what a bastard the man had been,' I muttered, trying to soften the atmosphere.

Phrygia was still in a huff. 'He was a bastard all right.'

'I'm sorry. Don't upset yourself – '

'I'm not upset. I saw exactly what he was. All talk – like most men.'

I glanced at Chremes, as if appealing for help to understand what she was saying. He lowered his voice in a useless attempt at sensitivity. 'According to him, he had some information about a relative Phrygia has been trying to trace. It was a trick, in my opinion – '

'Well, we'll never know now, will we?' Phrygia blazed angrily.

I knew when to retreat. I let the subject drop.

I savoured some nuggets of meat in a hot marinade. Evidently the tattered appearance of the troupe as a whole belied how well its leading players lived. Phrygia must have invested lavishly in peppers while she travelled around, and even in Nabataea and Syria, where there were no middlemen to pay if you bought direct from the caravans, such spices were expensive. Now I could understand more fully the mutters of rebellion amongst the stagehands and musicians. Frankly, given the meagre cut I was awarded as playwright, I could have gone on strike myself.

I was developing a fascinating picture of my predecessor's

situation during those last days of his life. At Petra he had been a marked man. Davos had told me previously that *he* had given Chremes an ultimatum to dismiss the scribe. Now Phrygia said she had done the same, despite the hold Heliodorus had tried to apply using the whereabouts of her missing child.

Having taken over his job and gained some insight into his feelings, I almost felt sorry for Heliodorus. Not only was he badly paid and his work hated, but his career with the company was firmly under threat.

The atmosphere had relaxed enough for me to speak again. 'So really, by the time you hit Petra, Heliodorus was on his way out?'

Phrygia confirmed it. Chremes was silent, but that meant nothing.

'Did everyone know that he was being given the heave-ho?'

Phrygia laughed. 'What do you think?'

Everyone knew.

I found it interesting. If Heliodorus had been so visibly under threat, it was highly unusual that somebody had snapped. Normally, once a troublemaking colleague is known to have attracted attention from management, everyone else relaxes. When the thieving cook is about to be sent back to the slave market, or the dozy apprentice is to be packed off home to mother at last, the rest just like to sit back and watch. Yet even with Heliodorus on the hop, somebody still could not wait.

Who could hate him so much they wanted to risk all by killing him when he was leaving anyway? Or was it a case where his very leaving caused the problem? Did he possess something, or know something, that he was starting to use as a lever? *If I go, I take the money!* . . . *If I go, I tell all* . . . Or even, *If I go, I don't tell, and you'll never find your child?* The issue of the child was too sensitive to probe.

'Did anyone owe him a debt? One they would have to repay if he left?'

'He wouldn't lend a copper, even if he had one,' Phrygia told me.

Chremes added in a morose tone, 'The way he drank, if his purse ever contained anything, it all went on the wine.' Thoughtfully, we both drained our goblets, with that air of extreme sense men acquire when discussing a fool who can't handle it.

'Did he owe anyone himself?'

Phrygia answered: 'No one would lend to him, mainly because it was obvious they would never get it back.' One of the simpler, and more reliable, laws of high finance.

Something niggled me. 'Tranio lent him something, I believe?'

'Tranio?' Chremes laughed briefly. 'I doubt it! Tranio's never had anything worth borrowing, and he's always broke!'

'Were the clowns on good terms with the playwright?'

Chremes discussed them happily enough. 'They had an on-off friendship with him.' Again I had a sense that he was hedging. 'Last time I noticed they were all at loggerheads. Basically he was a loner.'

'You're sure of that? And what about Tranio and Grumio? However they look on the surface, I suspect both of them are complex characters.'

'They're good boys,' Phrygia rebuked me. 'Lots of talent.'

Talent was her measure for everyone. For talent she would forgive a great deal. Maybe it made her judgement unreliable. Even though Phrygia shivered at the thought of harbouring a murderer, maybe a usefully talented comedian with the ability to improvise would seem too valuable to hand over to justice if his only crime was eliminating an unpleasant hack who couldn't write.

I smiled pleasantly. 'Do you know how the Twins were applying their talent when Heliodorus went up Dushara's mountain?'

'Oh stop it, Falco! They never did it.' I had definitely offended against Phrygia's code of company behaviour: good boys never did bad things. I loathed that kind of short-sightedness, though in the world of informing it was nothing new.

'They were packing their bags,' Chremes told me, with an attitude that suggested he was being more impartial and reasonable than his wife. 'Same as everyone else.'

'Did you see them doing it?'

'Of course not. I was packing mine.'

According to this weak theory the entire group would have alibis. I did not bother to ask where he thought Davos, Philocrates and Congrio might have been. If I wanted to be bamboozled, I could ask the suspects individually in the hope that the murderer at least would be inventive in his lies. 'Where were you staying?'

'The others were in an indifferent rooming house. Phrygia and I had found a slightly better place.' It fitted. They always liked to pretend we were one big share-alike family; but they preferred to have their comforts. I wondered if Heliodorus had ragged them about this snobbery.

I remembered Grumio saying something. 'According to Grumio, all a clown needs are a cloak, a strigil and oil flask, and a wallet for his takings. On that basis, a clown's trappings could be flung together pretty rapidly.'

'Grumio's all fantasy,' Chremes mourned, shaking his head. 'It makes him a wonderful artiste, but you have to know it's just talk.'

Phrygia was losing patience with me. 'So where is all this getting you, Falco?'

'It's filling in the picture helpfully.' I could take a hint. I had been munching their wonderful titbits until I could hold no more. It was time to go home and make my tent companions jealous by happily belching and describing the goodies. 'That was quite a feast! I'm grateful . . .'

I made the usual offers of they must come over to us sometime (with the usual underlying suggestion that all they might get would be two winkles on a lettuce leaf), then I turned to leave.

'Oh, just tell me one more thing. What happened to the playwright's personal property after he died?' I knew Heliodorus must have owned more than Helena and I had acquired with the play box.

'There wasn't much,' said Chremes. 'We picked out anything of value – a ring and a couple of inkstands – then I gave his few rags to Congrio.'

'What about his heirs?'

Phrygia laughed her dismissive laugh. 'Falco, nobody in a travelling theatre company has heirs!'

XLIV

Davos stood behind the tree under which he had pitched his tent. He was doing what a man does when it's night, when he thinks there is nobody about, and he can't be bothered to walk further off into open countryside. The camp had fallen silent; so had the distant town. He must have heard my feet crunching up the stony track. After quaffing my share of my amphora, I was in dire need of relief myself, so I greeted him, walked up alongside, and helped water his tree.

'I'm very impressed with your Hercules.'

'Wait until you see my bloody Zeus!'

'Not in the same play?'

'No, no. Once Chremes thinks of one "Frolicking Gods" farce, we tend to get given a run of them.'

A huge moon had risen over the uplands. The Syrian moon seemed bigger, and the Syrian stars more numerous, than those we had back home in Italy. This, with the restless wind that always hummed around Abila, gave me a sudden, poignant feeling of being lost in a very remote place. To avoid it, I kept talking. 'I've just been for a meal with our gregarious actor-manager and his loving spouse.'

'They normally put on a good spread.'

'Wonderful hospitality . . . Do they do this often?'

Davos chuckled. He was not a snob. 'Only for the right strata of society!'

'Aha! I'd never been invited before. Have I come up in the world, or was I just lumbered originally with the backwash of disapproval for my scribbling predecessor?'

'Heliodorus? He was asked, once, I believe. He soon lost his status. Once Phrygia got the measure of him, that was the end of it.'

'Would that be when he claimed to know where her offspring might be?'

Davos gave me a sharp look when I mentioned this. Then he commented, 'She's stupid to look!'

I rather agreed with that. 'The child's probably dead, or almost certainly won't want to know.'

Davos, in his dour way, said nothing.

We finished the horticulture, tightened our belts in the time-honoured manner, casually stuck our thumbs in them, and sauntered back to the track. A stagehand came by, saw us looking innocent, immediately guessed what we must have been doing, got the idea himself, and vanished sideways behind somebody else's tent looking for the next tree. We had started a craze.

Without comment, Davos and I waited to see what would happen, since the next tent was clearly occupied and a desperate pee tends to be audible. A muffled voice soon shouted in protest. The stagehand scuttled guiltily on his way. Silence fell again.

We stood on the path while the breeze bustled around us. A tent roof flapped. Somewhere in the town a dog howled mournfully. Both of us raised our faces to the wind, absorbing the night's atmosphere contemplatively. Davos was not normally one to chat, but we were two men with some mutual respect who had met at night, neither ready for sleep. We spoke together quietly, in a way that at other times might have been impossible. 'I'm trying to fill in missing facts,' I said. 'Can you remember what you were doing in Petra when Heliodorus wandered up to the High Place?'

'I most certainly do remember: loading the bloody waggons. We had no stagehands with us, if you recall. Chremes had issued his orders like a lord, then taken himself off to fold up his underwear.'

'Were you loading up alone?'

'Assisted in his pitiful manner by Congrio.'

'He can't help being a flyweight.'

Davos relented. 'No, he did his best, for what it was worth. What really got up my nose was being supervised by Philocrates. Instead of shifting bales with us, he took the opportunity to lean against a pillar looking attractive to the women and passing the kind of remarks that make you want to spew.'

'I can imagine. He drove me wild once by standing about like a demigod while I was trying to hitch my damned ox . . . Was he there all the time?'

'Until he fixed himself a bit of spice and went up among the tombs with the skirt.' The frankincense merchant's wife; he had mentioned her to Helena.

'So how long did the lading take you?'

'All bloody afternoon. I'm telling you, I was doing it as a one-man job. I still hadn't finished the stage effects – those two doorways are a trial to lift on your own – when your girl came down the hill and word whizzed round that somebody was dead. By then the rest of our party had assembled to watch me struggling. We were supposed to be all ready for the off, and people were starting to wonder where Heliodorus was. Someone asked Helena what the corpse looked like, so then we guessed who it must be.'

'Any idea where the Twins were while you were piling up the waggons?'

'No.'

He made no attempt to offer possibilities. Whether they were under suspicion or in the clear, Davos left it up to me to judge them. But I did gather that if they were accused, he would not care. Another case of professional jealousy among the players, presumably.

Probably the Twins would give each other alibis. That would land me in the usual situation: none of the known suspects actually available to do the deed. I sighed gently.

'Davos, tell me again about the night Musa was shoved off the embankment at Bostra. You must have been walking behind him?'

'I was right at the back of the queue.'

'Last in line?'

'Correct. To tell the truth, it was such a god-awful night I was losing interest in drinking in some dive with the Twins, knowing we would have to walk back through that weather just when we had got dry and warm again. I was planning to peel off unnoticed and scamper back to my own tent. I had been dropping behind stealthily. Two minutes more and I would never have heard your Nabataean shout.'

'Could you see who was near Musa when he was pushed?'

'No. If I'd seen it I'd have told you before this. I'd like to get the villain sorted,' Davos chortled, 'so I can avoid being plagued by questions from you!'

'Sorry.' I wasn't, and I refused to give up. 'So you won't want to tell me about the night Ione died?'

'Dear gods . . .' he muttered good-humouredly. 'Oh all right, get on with it!'

'You were dining with Chremes and Phrygia, and Philocrates was there too.'

'Until he bunked off as usual. That was quite late. If you're suggesting he drowned the girl, then judging by the time we all heard the news after you got back from the pools, he must have sped there on Mercury's wings. No, I reckon he was with his dame when it happened, and probably still hard at it while you were finding the corpse.'

'If there ever was a dame.'

'Ah well. You'll have to check with him.' Once again the disinterested way he threw it back to me seemed convincing. Killers looking to cover their own tracks like to speculate in detail about how others might be implicated. Davos always seemed too straight for such nonsense. He said what he knew; he left the rest to me.

I was getting nowhere. I tried the hard screw. 'Somebody told me that *you* liked Ione.'

'I liked her. That was all it amounted to.'

'It wasn't you who met her at the pools?'

'It was not!' He was crisp in denying it. 'You know damn well that was my night for dining with Chremes and Phrygia.'

'Yes, we've been over that rather convenient tale. One thing I'm asking myself is whether your party at the manager's tent was a set-up. Maybe the whole gang of you were in a conspiracy.'

By the light of his camp fire I could just make out Davos' face: sceptical, world-weary, utterly dependable. 'Oh stuff you, Falco. If you want to talk rot, go and do it somewhere else.'

'It has to be thought about. Give me one good reason to discard the idea.'

249

'I can't. You'll just have to take our word.' Actually, Davos giving his word seemed fairly convincing to me. He was that kind of man.

Mind you, Brutus and Cassius probably seemed decent, dependable and harmless until somebody offended them.

I clapped Davos on the shoulder and was off on my way when another point struck me. 'One final thought. I've just had an odd conversation with Chremes. I'm sure he was holding back on me. Listen, could he have known anything significant about the playwright's finances?'

Davos said nothing. I knew I had got him. I turned back, square to him. 'So that's it!'

'That's what, Falco?'

'Oh come on Davos, for a man whose timing is so tight on-stage, you're lousy off it! That silence was too long. There's something you don't want to tell me, and you're working out how to be uncooperative. Don't bother. It's too late now. Unless you tell me yourself, I'll only press the matter elsewhere until someone gives.'

'Leave it, Falco.'

'I will if you tell me.'

'It's old history . . .' He seemed to be making up his mind. 'Was Phrygia there when you had this strange chat?' I nodded. 'That explains it. Chremes on his own might have told you. The fact is, Heliodorus was subsidising the company. Phrygia doesn't know.'

I gaped. 'I'm amazed. Explain this!'

Davos sounded reluctant. 'You can fill in the rest, surely?'

'I've seen that Chremes and Phrygia like enjoying the good life.'

'More than our proceeds really cover.'

'So are they peeling off the takings?'

'Phrygia doesn't know,' he repeated stubbornly.

'All right, Phrygia's a vestal virgin. What about her tiresome spouse?'

'Chremes spent what he owes to the stagehands and the orchestra.' That explained a lot. Davos continued glumly: 'He isn't hopeless with money, but he's scared that Phrygia will finally leave him if their lifestyle gets too basic. That's what he's convinced himself, anyway. I doubt it myself. She's stayed so long she can't leave now; it would make all her past life pointless.'

'So he put himself in hock to Heliodorus?'

'Yes. The man is an idiot.'

'I'm starting to believe it . . .' He was also a liar. Chremes had told me Heliodorus spent all his cash on drink. 'I thought Heliodorus drank all his wages?'

'He liked to cadge other people's flagons.'

'At the scene of his death I found a goatskin and a wicker flask.'

'My guess would be the flask was his own, and he probably drained it himself too. The goatskin may have belonged to whoever was with him, in which case Heliodorus would not have objected to helping the other party drink what it contained.'

'Going back to Chremes' debt, if it was a substantial sum, where did the money come from?'

'Heliodorus was a private hoarder. He had amassed a pile.'

'And he let Chremes borrow it in order to gain the upper hand?'

'You're brighter than Chremes was about his reasoning! Chremes walked right into the blackmail: borrowed from Heliodorus, then had no way to pay him back. Everything could have been avoided if only he had come clean with Phrygia instead. She likes good things, but she's not stupidly extravagant. She wouldn't ruin the company for a few touches of luxury. Of course, they discuss everything – except what matters most.'

'Like most couples.'

Obviously hating to dump them in trouble, Davos blew out his cheeks, as if breathing had become difficult. 'Oh gods, what a mess . . . Chremes didn't kill him, Falco.'

'Sure? He was in a tight spot. Both you and Phrygia were insisting that the inkblot should be kicked out of the company. Meanwhile, Heliodorus must have been laughing up his tunic sleeve because he knew Chremes could not repay him. Incidentally, is this why he was kept on for so long in the first place?'

'Of course.'

'That and Phrygia hoping to extract the location of her child?'

'Oh she'd given up expecting him to tell her that, even if he really knew.'

'And how did you find out about the situation with Chremes?'

'At Petra. When I marched in to say it was Heliodorus or me. Chremes cracked and admitted why he couldn't give the playwright the boot.'

'So what happened?'

'I'd had enough. I certainly wasn't going to hang around and watch Heliodorus hold the troupe to ransom. I said I would leave when we got back to Bostra. Chremes knew Phrygia would hate that. We have been friends for a long time.'

'She knows your value to the company.'

'If you say so.'

'Why not just tell Phrygia yourself?'

'No need to. She would certainly insist on knowing why I was leaving – and she'd make sure she heard the right reason. If she pressed him, Chremes would crumble and tell her. He and I both knew that.'

'So, I see what your plan was. You were really intending to stick around until that happened.'

'You get it.' Davos seemed relieved now to be talking about this. 'Once Phrygia knew the situation, I reckoned Heliodorus would have been sorted – paid off somehow, and then told to leave.'

'Was he owed a large amount?'

'Finding it would have hit us all very hard, but it was not unmanageable. Worth it to get rid of him, anyway.'

'You were confident the whole business could have been cleared up?' This was important.

'Oh yes!' Davos seemed surprised that I asked. He was one of life's fixers; the opposite of Chremes, who collapsed when trouble flared. Davos did know when to cut and run in a crisis (I had seen that when our people were in jail at Gadara), but if it were possible, he preferred to face a bully out.

252

'This is the crux then, Davos. Did *Chremes* believe that he could be rescued?'

Davos considered his answer carefully. He understood what I was asking: whether Chremes felt so hopeless he might have killed as his only escape. 'Falco, he must have known that telling Phrygia would cause some harrowing rows, but after all these years, that's how they live. She wasn't in for any surprises. She knows the man. To save the company she – and I – would rally round. So, I suppose you are asking, ought he to have felt privately optimistic? In his heart, he must have.'

This was the only time Davos actively sought to clear another person. All I had to decide now was whether he was lying (perhaps to protect his old friend Phrygia), or whether he was telling the truth.

XLV

We never did put on a show at Abila. Chremes learned that even when the local amateurs had finished impressing their cousins we would still be waiting in a queue behind some acrobats from Pamphilia.

'This is no good! We're not dawdling in line for a week only to have some damned handstand boys wobble on ahead of us –'

'They were already ahead,' Phrygia put him straight, tight-lipped. 'We happened to arrive in the middle of a civic festival, which has been planned for six months. Unfortunately, no one informed the town councillors that they needed to consult you! The good citizens of Abila are celebrating the formal entry into the Empire of Commagene –'

'Stuff Commagene!'

With this acid political commentary (a view most of us shared, since only Helena Justina had any idea where Commagene was, or whether well-informed men should afford it significance), Chremes led us all off to Capitolias.

Capitolias had all the usual attributes of a Decapolis town. I'm not some damned itinerary writer – you can fill in the details for yourselves.

You can also guess the results of my search for Sophrona. As at Abila, and all the other towns before, there was no trace of Thalia's musical prodigy.

I admit, I was starting to feel bad-tempered about all this. I was sick of looking for the girl. I was tired of one damned acropolis after another. I didn't care if I never saw another set of neat little city walls with a tasteful temple, shrouded in expensive scaffolding, peeping Ionically over them. Stuff Commagene? Never mind it. Commagene (a small, previously autonomous kingdom miles to the north of here) had one wonderful attribute: nobody had ever suggested M.

254

Didius Falco ought to pack his bags and traipse around it. No, forget harmless pockets of quaintness that wanted to be Roman, and instead just stuff the whole pretentious, grasping, Hellenic Decapolis.

I had had enough. I was sick of stones in my shoes and the raw smell of camels' breath. I wanted glorious monuments and towering, teeming tenements. I wanted to be sold some dubious fish that tasted of Tiber grit, and to eat it gazing over the river from my own grubby nook on the Aventine while waiting for an old friend to knock on the door. I wanted to breathe garlic at an aedile. I wanted to stamp on a banker. I wanted to hear that solid roar that slams across the racecourse at the Circus Maximus. I wanted spectacular scandals and gigantic criminality. I wanted to be amazed by size and sordidness. I wanted to go home.

'Have you a toothache or something?' asked Helena. I proved that my teeth were all in working order by gnashing them.

For the company, things looked brighter. At Capitolias we acquired a two-night booking. We first put on the Hercules play, since that was newly rehearsed; then, as Davos had prophesied, Chremes became keen on this horrible species and handed us a further 'Frolicking Gods' effort, so we did see Davos do his famous Zeus. Whether people liked it depended on whether they enjoyed farces full of ladders at women's windows, betrayed husbands helplessly banging on locked doors, divinity mocked relentlessly, and Byrria in a nightgown that revealed pretty well everything.

Musa, we gathered, either liked this very much indeed, or not at all. He went silent. In essence it was hard to tell any difference from normal, but the quality of his silence assumed a new mood. It was brooding; perhaps downright sinister. In a man whose professional life had been spent cutting throats for Dushara, I found this alarming.

Helena and I were uncertain whether Musa's new silence meant he was now in mental and physical agony over the strength of his attraction to the beauty, or whether her bawdy part in the Zeus play had completely disgusted him. Either way, Musa was finding it hard to handle his feelings. We were ready to offer sympathy, but he plainly wanted to work out his solutions for himself.

To give him something else to think about I drew him more closely into my investigations. I had wanted to proceed alone, but I hate to abandon a man to love. My verdict on Musa was twofold: he was mature, but inexperienced. This was the worst possible combination for tackling a hostile quarry like Byrria. The maturity would remove any chance of her feeling sorry for him; the lack of experience could lead to embarrassment and bungling if he ever made a move. A woman who had so ferociously set herself apart from men would need a practised hand to win her over.

'I'll give you advice if you want it.' I grinned. 'But advice rarely works. The mistakes are waiting to be made – and you'll have to walk straight into them.'

'Oh yes,' he replied rather vacantly. As usual, his apparent affirmative sounded ambiguous. I never met a man who could discuss women so elusively. 'What about our task, Falco?' If he wanted to lose himself in work, frankly that seemed the best idea. As a lad about town Musa was hard work to organise.

I explained to him that asking people questions about money would be as difficult as advising a friend on a love affair. He screwed out a smile, then we buckled down to checking on the story Davos had told me.

I wanted to avoid questioning Chremes about his debt directly. Tackling him would be useless while we had no evidence against him for actually causing either death. I had strong doubts whether we would find that evidence. As I told Musa, he remained a low priority on my suspects list: 'He's strong enough to have held Heliodorus down but he was not on the embankment at Bostra when you were pushed in the water, and unless someone is lying, he was also out of the picture when Ione died. This is depressing –and typical of my work, Musa. Davos has just given me the best possible motive for killing Heliodorus, but in the long run it's likely to prove irrelevant.'

'We have to check it, though?'

'Oh yes!'

I sent Musa to confirm with Phrygia that Chremes really had been packing his belongings when Heliodorus was killed. She vouched for it. If she still didn't entertain any notion that Chremes had been in debt to the playwright, then she had no reason to think we might be closing in on a suspect, and so no reason to lie.

'So, Falco, is this story of the debt one we can forget?' Musa pondered. He answered himself: 'No, we cannot. We must now check up on Davos.'

'Right. And the reason?'

'He is friendly with Chremes, and especially loyal to Phrygia. Maybe when he found out about the debt he himself killed Heliodorus – to protect his friends from the blackmailing creditor.'

'Not only his friends, Musa. He would have been safeguarding the future of the theatre group, and also his own job, which he had been saying he would leave. So yes, we'll check on him – but he looks in the clear. If he went up the mountain, then who packed the stage props at Petra? We know *somebody* did it. Philocrates would think himself above hard labour, and anyway, half the time he was off screwing a conquest. Let's ask the Twins and Congrio where they all were. We need to know that too.'

I myself tackled Congrio.

'Yes, Falco. I helped Davos load the heavy stuff. It took all afternoon. Philocrates was watching us some of the time, then he went off somewhere . . .'

The twins told Musa they had been together in the room they shared: packing their belongings; having a last drink, rather larger than they had anticipated, to save carrying an amphora to their camel; then sleeping it off. It fitted what we knew of their disorganised, slightly disreputable lifestyle. Other people agreed that when the company assembled to leave Petra the Twins had turned up last, looking dozy and crumpled and complaining of bad heads.

Wonderful. Every male suspect had somebody who could clear him. Everyone, except possibly Philocrates during the time he was philandering. 'I'll have to put pressure on the rutting little bastard. I'll enjoy that!'

'Mind you, Falco, a big-brimmed hat would swamp him!' Musa qualified, equally vindictively.

This clarified one thing anyway: Philocrates spent several scenes in the Zeus play cuddling up to the lovely Byrria. Musa's anger appeared to clinch the question of *his* feelings for the girl.

XLVI

A restless mood hit the company once we performed at Capitolias. One reason for it was that decisions now had to be taken. This was the last in the central group of Decapolis cities. Damascus lay a good sixty miles to the north – further than we had been accustomed to travelling between towns. The remaining place, Canatha, was awkwardly isolated from the group, far out to the east on the basalt plain north of Bostra. In fact, because of its remote position, the best way to get there was going back via Bostra, which added half as much again to the thirty- or forty-mile distance it would have been direct.

The thought of revisiting Bostra gave everyone a feeling that we were about to complete a circle, after which it might seem natural for ways to part.

It was now deep summer. The weather had grown almost unbearably hot. Working in such temperatures was difficult, though at the same time audiences seemed to welcome performances once their cities cooled slightly at night. By day people huddled in whatever shade they could find; shops and businesses were shuttered for long periods; and no one travelled unless they had a death in the family, or they were idiotic foreigners like us. At night, the locals all came out to meet one another and be entertained. For a group like ours, it posed a problem. We needed the money. We could not afford to stop working, however great a toll of our energy the heat took.

Chremes called everyone to a meeting. His vagabond collection squashed together on the ground in a ragged circle, all jeering and jostling. He stood up on a cart to give a public address. He looked assured, but we knew better than to hope for it.

'Well, we've completed a natural circuit. Now we have to decide where to go next.' I believe somebody suggested

259

Chremes might try Hades, though it was in a furtive undertone. 'Wherever is chosen, none of you are bound to continue. If needs be, the group can break up and reform.' That was bad news for those of us who wanted to keep it together in order to identify the murderer. That blowfly would be early in the queue for terminating contracts and flitting away.

'What about our money?' called one of the stagehands. I wondered if they had sniffed out a rumour that Chremes might have spent their season's earnings. They had said nothing to me when we discussed their grievances, but it would explain some of their anger. I knew they had been suspicious that I might be reporting back to the management, so they might well have kept their fears on this subject to themselves.

I noticed Davos fold his arms and gaze at Chremes sardonically. Without a blush Chremes announced, 'I'm going to settle up now for what you've earned.' He was absurdly confident. Like Davos, I could smile over it. Chremes had diced with disaster, and been rescued in the nick of time by the maniac who killed his creditor. How many of us can hope for such luck? Now Chremes had the satisfied air of those who are constantly saved from peril by the Fates. It was a trait I had never been favoured with. But I knew these men existed. I knew they never learned from their mistakes because they never had to suffer for them. A few moments of panic were the worst effects Chremes would ever know. He would float through life, behaving as badly as possible and risking everyone else's happiness, yet never having to face responsibility.

Of course he could produce the money his workforce was owed; Heliodorus had bailed him out. And although Chremes ought to have paid the playwright back, he blatantly had no intention of remembering the debt now. He would have diddled the man himself, if he could have got away with it, so he would certainly rob the dead. My question about heirs, and Phrygia's easy answer that Heliodorus was assumed to have had none, took on a dry significance. Not knowing about her husband's debt, even Phrygia could not understand the full irony.

This was the moment when I looked at the manager hardest. However, Chremes had been cleared as a suspect pretty convincingly. He had alibis for both murders, and had been somewhere else the night Musa was attacked. Chremes had a serious motive for killing Heliodorus, but for all I knew so did half the group. It had taken a long time for me to unearth this debt of Chremes'; maybe there were other lurking maggots if I turned over the right cowpat.

As if by chance, I had seated myself at our manager's feet, on the tail of the same cart. This put me staring out at the assembly. I could see most of their faces – among which had to be the one I was looking for. I wondered whether the killer was gazing back, aware of my complete bafflement. I tried to look at each one as if I was thinking about some vital fact he was unaware I knew: Davos, almost too reliable by half (could anyone be *quite* so straight as Davos always seemed?); Philocrates, chin up so his profile showed best (could anyone be so totally self-obsessed?); Congrio, undernourished and unappealing (what twisted ideas might that thin, pale wraith be harbouring?); Tranio and Grumio, so clever, so sharp, each so secure in his mastery of their craft – a craft that relied on a devious mind, an attacking wit, and visual deceit.

The faces returning my gaze all looked more cheerful than I liked. If anyone had worries, they had not been posed by me.

'The options,' stated Chremes importantly, 'are, firstly, to go around the same circuit again, trading on our previous success.' There were a few jeers. 'I reject this,' the manager agreed, 'on the grounds that it poses no dramatic challenge – ' This time some of us laughed outright. 'Besides, one or two towns hold bad memories . . .' He subsided. Public reference to death was not in his style of speechmaking. 'The next alternative is to move further afield in Syria – '

'Are there good pickings?' I prompted in a not very quiet mutter.

'Thanks, Falco! Yes, I think Syria still holds out a welcome for a reputable theatre group like ours. We still have a large repertoire which we have not properly explored – '

'Falco's ghost play!' suggested a satirist. I had not been aware that my idea for writing a play of my own was so widely known about.

'Jupiter forfend!' cried Chremes as raucous merriment erupted and I grinned gamely. My ghost play would be better than these bastards knew, but I was a professional writer now; I had learned to keep my smouldering genius quiet. 'So where shall we take ourselves? The choices are various.'

His options had turned into choices, but the dilemma remained.

'Do we want to complete the Decapolis towns? Or shall we travel north more quickly and tackle the sophisticated cities there? We won't want to go into the desert, but beyond Damascus there is a good route in a fairly civilised area, through Emesa, Epiphania, Beroia, and across to Antiochia. On the way we can certainly cover Damascus.'

'Any drawbacks?' I queried.

'Long distances, mainly.'

'Longer than going to Canatha?' I pressed.

'Very much so. Canatha would mean a detour back through Bostra – '

'Though there would be a good road up to Damascus afterwards?' I had already been looking at itineraries myself. I never rely on anyone else to research a route.

'Er, yes.' Chremes was feeling hard-pressed, a position he hated. 'Do you particularly want us to go to Canatha, Falco?'

'Taking the company or not is up to you. Myself, I've no option. I'd be happy to stay with you as your playwright but I have my own business in the Decapolis, a commission I want to clear up – '

I was trying to give the impression my private search for Sophrona was taking precedence over finding the murderer. I wanted the villain to think I was losing interest. I hoped to make him relax.

'I dare say we can accommodate your wish to visit Canatha,' Chremes offered graciously. 'A city which is off the beaten track may be ripe for some of our high-class performances – '

'Oh, I reckon they are starved of culture!' I encouraged, not specifying whether I thought 'culture' would be a product handed out by us.

'We'll go where Falco says,' called one of the stagehands. 'He's our lucky talisman.' Some of the others gave me nods and winks that proclaimed in a far from subtle manner that they wanted to keep me close enough to protect them. Not that I had done much on their behalf so far.

'Show of hands then,' answered Chremes, as usual letting anybody other than himself decide. He loved the fine idea of democracy, like most men who couldn't organise an orgy with twenty bored gladiators in a women's bathhouse on a hot Tuesday night.

As the stagehands shuffled and glanced around them it seemed to me the killer must have detected the widespread conspiracy building up against him. But if he did, he uttered no protest. A further quick scan of our male suspects revealed nobody visibly cursing. No one seemed resentful that the chance to shed me, or to break up the troupe altogether, had just been deferred.

So to Canatha it was. The group would be staying together for two more Decapolis cities, Canatha, then Damascus. However, after Damascus – a major administrative centre, with plenty of other work on offer – group members might start drifting off.

Which meant that if I was to expose the killer, time was now running out.

XLVII

The temperature was definitely bothering all of us now. Travel by day, previously inadvisable, had become quite impossible. Travel in the dark was twice as tiring since we had to go more slowly while drivers constantly peered at the road, needing to concentrate. Our animals were restless. Fear of ambush was increasing as we re-entered Nabataea and ahead of us lay expanses of desert where the nomads were by our standards lawless and their livelihood openly depended on a centuries-old tradition of robbing passers-by. Only the fact that we were obviously not a caravan of rich merchants gave us any protection; it seemed to suffice, but we could never be off guard.

All the time the heat grew daily. It was relentless and inescapable – until night fell abruptly, bringing fierce cold as the warmth lifted like a curtain under open skies. Then, lit by a few flares, we had to set off on the road again, on journeys that seemed far longer, more uncomfortable and more tiresome than they would have been in daylight.

The climate was draining and dehydrating. We saw little of the country, and met hardly anyone to talk to; Musa told us the local tribes all migrated towards the mountains in summer. At roadside stops, our people stood about stamping their feet to get the blood running, miserably taking refreshments and talking in hushed voices. Millions of stars watched us, probably all wondering just what we were doing there. Then, by day, we collapsed in our tents, through which the baking heat soon breathed with suffocating strength, killing the sleep we needed so desperately. So we tossed and turned, groaned and quarrelled with each other, threatening to turn around, head for the coast and go home.

On the road it was difficult for me to continue reinterviewing people. The conditions were so unpleasant everyone stuck with their own camels or waggons. The strongest and those with the best eyesight were always needed for driving. The quarrelsome were always bickering with their friends too angrily to listen to me. None of the women were interested in handing out personal favours, so none of them developed the kind of jealousies that normally bring them running to confide in a handy informer. None of the men wanted to stop threatening to divorce their wives long enough to answer rational questions, especially if they thought the questions might be about the generous Ione. Nobody wanted to share food or precious water, so hitching a lift on another waggon was discouraged. At stops on the road everyone was too busy feeding themselves and their animals or swatting flies.

I did manage one useful conversation, just as we were heading into Bostra. Philocrates lost the pin from one wheel of his waggon. Nothing was broken, luckily; it had just loosened and dropped out. Davos, in the cart behind, saw it happen and shouted a warning before the whole wheel fell off. Davos seemed to spend his life averting disasters. A cynic might have suspected it was some kind of bluff, but I was in no mood for that kind of subtlety.

Philocrates managed to halt his smart equipage gently. He made no attempt to ask for help; he must have known how unpopular this would be after all the times he had refused assistance to the rest of us. Without a word, he jumped down, inspected the problem, cursed, and started to unload the cart. Nobody else was prepared to help him out, so I volunteered. The rest drew up on the road ahead, and waited while I helped with the repair.

Philocrates had a light, zippy two-wheeler – a real fast chaser's vehicle – with flashy spokes and metal felloes welded on to the rims. But whoever sold him this hot property had passed on a salvage job: one wheel did have a decent hub that was probably original, but the other had been cobbled together with a museum-piece arrangement of a linchpin on the axle.

'Somebody saw you coming!' I commented. He made no reply.

I had expected Philocrates to be useless, but it turned out he could be a pretty handy technician if his alternative was to

265

be abandoned on a lonely road in Nabataea. He was small but muscular, and certainly well exercised. We had to unhitch his mule, which had sensed trouble, then we improvised blocks to support the weight of the cart. Philocrates had to use some of his valuable water supply to cool down the axle-bush. Normally I would have peed on it, but not with a jeering audience.

I pushed against the good wheel while Philocrates straightened the loose one, then we hammered in the pin. The problem was to bang it in hard enough to stay there. One of the stagehands' children brought us a mallet just when we were pondering how to tackle it. The child handed the tool to me, probably under instructions, and waited to take it straight back to her father afterwards. I reckoned I would be the best hitter, but Philocrates grabbed the mallet from me and swung down on the pin himself. It was his cart, so I let him. He was the one who would be stuck with a broken axle and shattered wheel if the pin worked loose again. He did have a small tent-peg hammer of his own, though, so I took that and put in alternate blows.

'Phew! We're a good team,' commented the actor when we stopped to take a breath and contemplate our work. I gave him a dirty look. 'I reckon that should hold it. I can get a wheelwright to look at it at Bostra. Thanks,' he forced out. It was perfunctory, but no less valid for that.

'I was brought up to pull my weight in the community!' If he knew this crack of mine was a hint, no flicker showed on his haughty, high-cheeked face.

We returned the mallet to the urchin. She scampered off, and I helped Philocrates reload his cart. He owned a lot of fancy stuff – presents from grateful women, no doubt. Next came the moment I had been waiting for all along: he had to rehitch the mule. This was exquisite. After having watched me chase my stupid ox that time, I felt he owed me the privilege of sitting at the roadside doing nothing while he stumbled around offering straw to his frisky beast. Like most mules, it applied all its high intelligence to leading the life of a bad character.

'I'm glad of a chat,' I offered, as I squatted on a rock. It was

266

not what Philocrates wanted to hear at that moment, but I was ready to have some fun. 'It's only fair to warn you, you're chief suspect in the murder case.'

'What?' Philocrates stopped stock-still in outrage. His mule saw its moment, snatched the straw and skipped away. 'I never heard such rubbish – '

'You've lost him,' I pointed out helpfully, nodding at his animal. 'Obviously you ought to be given a chance to clear yourself.'

Philocrates responded with a short phrase that referred to a part of his anatomy he overused. I pondered how easy it is to make a confident man flustered merely by saying something grossly unfair.

'Clear myself of what?' he demanded. He was definitely hot, and it had nothing to do with the climate or our recent labouring. Philocrates' life veered between two themes: acting and philandering. He was highly competent at both, but in other fields he was starting to look stupid. 'Clear myself of nothing, Falco! I've done nothing, and nobody can suggest I have!'

'Oh, come on! This is pathetic. You must have had plenty of angry husbands and fathers accusing you. With all that practice behind you, I expected a better-rehearsed plea. Where's your famous stage sparkle? Especially,' I mused thoughtfully, 'when these charges are so serious. A few adulteries and the occasional bastard may litter your off-colour past, but this is hard crime, Philocrates. Murder is called to account in the public arena – '

'You'll not send me to the bloody lions for something I had nothing to do with! There is some justice.'

'In Nabataea? Are you sure of that?'

'I'll not answer the case in Nabataea!' I had threatened him with the barbarians; instant panic had set in.

'You will if I make the charges here. We're in Nabataea already. Bostra's just up the road. One murder took place in its sister city, and I have with me a Petran representative. Musa has come all this way, on command of the Nabataean Chief Minister, specifically to condemn the killer who committed the sacrilege at their High Place!' I loved this sort of high-flown oratory. Incantations may be complete rubbish, but they have a gorgeous effect.

'Musa?' Philocrates was suddenly more suspicious.

'Musa. He may look like a lovelorn adolescent, but he's The Brother's personal envoy, charged with arresting the killer – who looks like you.'

'He's a junior priest, without authority.' Maybe I should have known better than to trust oratory with an actor; he knew all about the power of words, especially empty ones.

'Ask Helena,' I said. 'She can give you the straight story. Musa has been singled out for high position. This embassy abroad is a training job. He urgently needs to take a criminal back to preserve his reputation. I'm sorry, but you're the best candidate.'

Philocrates' mule had become disappointed by the lack of action. It strolled up and nudged its master on the shoulder, telling him to get on with the chase.

'How?' Philocrates spat at me; no use to a mule who was looking for entertainment. One ear up and one ear down, the fun-loving beast gazed across at me sadly, deploring its lot.

'Philocrates,' I advised him like a brother, 'you are the only suspect who has no alibi.'

'What? *Why*?' He was well equipped with interrogatives.

'Facts, man. When Heliodorus was murdered you say you were bunked up in a rock tomb. When Ione died in the pools of Maiuma, you came up with exactly the same shabby story – bumping a so-called "cheeseseller". Sounds fine. Sounds in keeping. But do we ever have a name? An address? Anyone who ever saw you with either of these bits of flotsam? A furious father or fiancé trying to cut your throat for the insult? No. Face it, Philocrates. Everyone else provides proper witnesses. You only hand me feeble lies.'

The fact that the 'lies' were completely in character should offer him a good defence. The fact that I also knew he had not been on the embankment at Bostra when Musa was attacked clinched his innocence for me. But he was too dumb to argue.

'As a matter of fact,' I continued the pressure, as he kicked his natty boot against a stone in helpless outrage, 'I do think you were with a girl the night Ione died – I think it was Ione herself.'

'Oh come on, Falco!'

'I think you were the lover Ione met at the Maiuma pools.' I noticed that every time I said Ione's name he jumped guiltily. Real criminals are not so nervous.

'Falco, I'd had a fling with her – who hadn't? – but that was long past. I like to keep moving. So did she, for that matter. Anyway, life is much less complicated if you confine your attentions outside the company.'

'Ione herself was never that scrupulous.'

'No,' he agreed.

'So do you know who her special lover in the company was?'

'I don't. One of the clowns could probably enlighten you.'

'You mean either Tranio or Grumio was Ione's special friend?'

'That's not what I said!' Philocrates grew snappy. 'I mean they were friendly enough with the silly girl to have heard from her what she was up to. She didn't take either of those two idiots seriously.'

'So who did she take seriously, Philocrates? Was it you?'

'Should have been. Somebody worth it.' Automatically, he swept one hand back across his sleek hair. His arrogance was intolerable.

'You reckon so?' I lost my temper. 'One thing about you, Philocrates: your intellect is nowhere near as lively as your prick.' I fear he took it as a compliment.

Even the mule had registered its master's uselessness. It came up behind Philocrates, gave a sudden shove with its long-nosed head, and knocked the furious actor face down.

A cheer went up from the rest of our group. I grinned and walked back to my own slow, solid-wheeled ox-cart.

'What was going on there?' Helena demanded.

'I just told Philocrates he's lost his alibi. He'd already lost his cartwheel, his mule, his temper and his dignity – '

'The poor man,' murmured Musa, with little sign of sympathy. 'A bad day!'

The actor had told me virtually nothing. But he had cheered me up completely. That can be as much use as any piece of evidence. I had met informers who implied that to succeed they needed not just sore feet, a hangover, a sorry love life and some progressive disease, but a dour, depressing outlook too. I disagree. The work provides enough misery. Being happy gives a man a boost that can help solve cases. Confidence counts.

I rode into Bostra hot, tired, dusty and dry. But all the same, every time I thought of Philocrates' mule flooring him, I felt ready to tackle anything.

XLVIII

Bostra again.

It seemed an age since we had arrived here the last time and performed *The Pirate Brothers* in the rain. An age since my first effort as a playwright was ignored by everyone. Since then I had grown quite used to critical hammerings, though when I remembered my early disappointment I still did not like the place.

We were all glad to stop. Chremes staggered off to see about a booking. He was plainly exhausted; he had no sense of priorities and was bound to bungle it. He would come back with nothing for us; that was obvious.

Nabataean or not, Bostra was a capital city and boasted good amenities. Those of us who were willing to spend money on comfort had been looking forward to leaving our tents on the waggons and finding real rooms to stay in. Walls; ceilings; floors with spiders in the corners; doors with cold draughts flooding under them. Chremes' no-hope aura cast a blight. I clung to my optimism and still meant to find lodgings for Helena, Musa and myself, a basic roost that would not be too far from a bathhouse and not noticeably a brothel, where the landlord scratched his lice discreetly and the rent was small. Being unwilling to waste even a small deposit on rooms we might not enjoy for long, I waited for the manager's return before I booked a place.

Some of the group were camping as usual. Pretending it was just my day for helping out, I presented myself as if by chance at the waggon that was driven by Congrio. Our weedy bill-poster had little equipment of his own. On the road he took charge of one of the props carts; then, instead of putting up a tent, he just hung an awning off the side of it and huddled under that. I made a show of lending a hand to unload his few bits and bobs.

He was not stupid. 'What's this for, Falco?' He knew nobody helps the bill-poster unless they want a favour.

I came clean. 'Somebody told me you came in for the stuff

271

Heliodorus left behind. I wondered if you'd be prepared to show me what his effects consisted of.'

'If that's what you want. Just speak up another time!' he instructed grumpily. Almost at once he started pulling apart his baggage roll, tossing some things aside, but laying certain items in a neat line at my feet. The discards were plainly his own originals; the kit offered up for inspection was his heirloom from the drowned man.

What Phrygia had passed on to him would not have raised much excitement at an auctioneer's house clearance. My father, who was in that business, would have dumped the dead playwright's clothes with his glassware porter for use as packing rags. Among the awful duds were a couple of tunics, now pleated on the shoulders with large stitches where Congrio had taken them in to fit his skinnier frame; a pair of disgusting old sandals; a twisted belt; and a toga not even I would have plucked off a second-hand stall, since the wine-stains on it looked twenty years old and indelible. Also a battered satchel (empty); a bundle of quills, some of them partly whittled into pens; a rather nice tinderbox; three drawstring purses (two empty, one with five dice and a bronze coin with one blank face, evidently a forgery); a broken lantern; and a wax tablet with one corner snapped off.

'Anything else?'

'This is the lot.'

Something in his manner attracted my attention. 'You've laid it out nice and correct.'

'Practice!' sniffed Congrio. 'What makes you think you're the first busybody wanting to do an inventory?' He was enjoying being difficult.

I lazily lifted one eyebrow. 'Somehow I can't see a finance tribune trying to screw you for inheritance tax on this lot! So who was so intrigued? Is somebody jealous because you came in for the hand-out?'

'I just took the stuff when I was offered. If anybody wants to look at it, I lets them see. You finished?' He started packing it all up again. Even though the items were horrible his packing was systematic and his folding neat. My question remained tantalisingly unanswered.

272

If Congrio was hedging, my interest grew. The clothes had a nasty, musky smell. It was impossible to tell whether this had derived from their previous owner or been imposed since they were taken over, but nobody with any taste or discretion would want them now. The other objects mostly made a sad collection too. It was hard to see in anything here either a motive or any other clue.

I shook two of the dice around in my hand then let them fall casually on a spread tunic. Both turned up six. 'Hello! Looks like he left you a lucky set.'

'You found the right two to test,' said Congrio. I lifted the dice, weighing them in my hand. As I expected they were weighted. Congrio grinned. 'The rest are normal. I don't think I've got the nerve to use those two, but don't tell anyone, in case I change my mind. Anyway, now we know why he was always winning.'

'Was he?'

'Famous for it.'

I whistled quietly. 'I'd not heard. Was he a big player?'

'All the time. That was how he gathered his pile.'

'A pile? That wasn't part of your hand-out. I take it?'

'Hah! No. Chremes said he would take care of any cash.'

'A nice gesture!' We grinned wryly together. 'Did Heliodorus play dice against the other members of the company?'

'Not normally. Chremes had told him it caused trouble. He liked to go off and fleece the locals the night we left a place. Chremes was always nagging him about that as well, afraid one day we'd be followed by an angry mob and set upon.'

'Did Chremes know why Heliodorus had such permanent good luck?' I asked, shaking the dice tellingly.

'Oh no! He never looked like a bent player.' He must have been a subtle one. From what I had already heard about his ability to judge people, cleverly finding their weak points, it made sense that he could also pull the old weighted-dice trick without being detected. A clever, highly unlikeable man.

'So Heliodorus knew better than to upset the party by cheating his own? Yet if Chremes issued a warning, does that mean it happened once?'

'There were a few rows,' offered Congrio, his pale face crinkling up slyly.

'Going to tell me who else was involved?'

'Gambling debts are private,' he replied. He had a cheek. I was not prepared to give him a bribe.

'Fair enough.' Now I had a clue to work with, I would simply ask someone else. 'Davos told me Heliodorus went through a phase of being friendly with the Twins.'

'Oh you know then?' It had been a lucky connection on my part; the bill-poster looked irritated by my guessing correctly.

'About them all drinking together at one time? Yes. Did they dice too? May as well tell it, Congrio. I can always ask Davos. So was there gambling going on among those three?'

'I reckon so,' Congrio agreed. 'Nobody tells me things, but I got the idea Heliodorus won too much off them, and that was when they stopped drinking with him.'

'Was this once? Was it a long time ago?'

'Oh no,' sneered Congrio. 'It was always happening. They'd pal up for a few weeks, then next thing they weren't speaking. After a bit they'd forget they had quarrelled, and start over again. I used to notice because the times they were friendly with Heliodorus was when the Twins caught his nasty habits. He always shoved me around, and while they were in league with him, I copped for it from them too.'

'What phase of this happy cycle were they all in when you went to Petra?'

'Ignoring each other. Had been for months, I was happy to know.'

I applied my innocent face. 'So who apart from me,' I enquired suddenly, 'has been wanting a perusal of your wonderful inheritance?'

'Oh just those clowns again,' scoffed Congrio.

'You don't like them?' I commented quietly.

'Too clever.' Cleverness was not an offence in Roman law, though I had often shared Congrio's view that it ought to be. 'Every time I see them, I get knotted up and start feeling annoyed.'

'Why's that?'

274

He kicked at his baggage roll impatiently. 'They look down on you. There's nothing so special about telling a few jokes. They don't make them up, you know. All they do is say what some other old clown thought up and wrote down a hundred years ago. I could do it if I had a script.'

'If you could read it.'

'Helena's teaching me.' I might have known. He continued boasting recklessly: 'All I need is a joke collection and I'll be a clown myself.'

It seemed to me it would take him a long time to put together enough funny stories to be a stand-up comic of Grumio's calibre. Besides, I couldn't see him managing the right timing and tone. 'Where are you going to get the collection, Congrio?' I tried not to sound patronising – without much success.

For some reason it didn't bother him. 'Oh, they do exist, Falco!'

I changed the subject to avoid an argument. 'Tell me, did the clowns come together to look at your property?' The bill-poster nodded. 'Any idea what they were looking for?'

'No.'

'Something particular?'

'They never said so.'

'Trying to get back some I-owe-yous, maybe?'

'No, Falco.'

'Did they want these dice? After all, the Twins do magic tricks – '

'They saw the dice were here. They never asked for them.' Presumably they did not realise the dice were crooked. 'Look, they just strolled up, laughing and asking what I had got. I thought they were going to pinch my stuff, or ruin it. You know what they're like when they're feeling mischievous.'

'The Twins? I know they can be a menace, but not outright delinquents, surely?'

'No,' Congrio admitted, though rather reluctantly. 'Just a pair of nosy bastards then.'

Somehow I wondered about that.

IL

He was right. The two clowns *were* clever. It would take more than a bland expression and a quick change of subject to trip them up. I was aware before I started that the minute they had any idea I was trying to squeeze particular information from them, fending me off would become a joyous game. They were seditious. I would need to watch for exactly the right opportunity to tackle them. And when I did, I would need all my skill.

Wondering how I could choose the moment, I came back to my own tent.

Helena was alone. She told me that as I had predicted, Chremes had bungled acquiring a booking here.

'When he was waiting to see the town councillor who runs the theatre, he overheard the fellow scoff to a servant, *"Oh, not the ghastly tribe who did that terrible piece about the pirates?"* When Chremes finally got in to see the big man, relations failed to improve. So we're moving off straight away – '

'Today?' I was horrified.

'Tonight. We get a day's rest, then go.' It was goodbye to booking rooms then. No landlord was going to screw me for a night's rent when I only had a few daylight hours for sleeping. Helena sounded bitter too. 'Chremes, with his nose put out of joint by a rude critic, does not dally for more insults. Canatha here we come! Everyone is furious –'

'That includes me! And where's Musa?'

'Gone to find a temple and send a message to his sister. He seems rather low. He never gives much away, but I'm sure he was looking forward to spending some time here, back in his own country. Let's just hope the message Musa is sending his sister doesn't say, *"Put out my slippers. I'm coming home . . ."* '

'So he's a homesick boy? This is bad news. He was miserable enough with mooning over Byrria.'

276

'Well, I'm trying to help out there. I've invited Byrria to dine with us the first time we stop properly. We've been doing so much travelling she must be lonely driving all by herself.'

'If she is lonely, it's her own fault.' Charity was not on my agenda at the moment. 'She could have had a lusty young Nabataean to crack the whip for her!' Come to that, she could have had pretty well any man in the company, except those of us with strict companions. 'Does Musa know you're brokering romance for him? I'll take him for a decent haircut and shave!'

Helena sighed. 'Better not be too obvious.'

'Really?' I grinned, grabbing hold of her suddenly. 'Being obvious always worked for me.' I pulled Helena close enough for my own obvious feelings to be unmissable.

'Not this time.' Helena, who had had a great deal of practice, wriggled free. 'If we're moving on, we need to sleep. What did you find out from Congrio?'

'That Heliodorus was a hardened gambling cheat, and his victims may just have included Tranio and Grumio.'

'Together or separately?'

'This is unclear.'

'Lot of money involved?'

'Another unknown quantity.' But my guess was, probably.

'Do you plan to question them next?'

'I plan to know just what I'm asking before I attempt anything. Those two are a tricky pair.' In fact, I was surprised that even a seasoned cheat had managed to mug them. But if they were accustomed to feeling sure of themselves, being fleeced might have come as a nasty surprise. Congrio was right; they had a streak of arrogance. They were so used to sneering at others that if they found they had been set up, I hated to speculate how they would react.

'Do you think they are hiding something?' Helena asked. 'Something significant?'

'More and more it looks that way. What do you think, fruit?'

'I think,' Helena prophesied, 'anything with those two in it will be even more complicated than it looks.'

On the way to Canatha I asked Davos about the gambling. He

277

had known it went on. He also remembered Heliodorus and the Twins arguing on occasions, though nothing too spectacular. He had guessed the playwright used to swindle local townsfolk. He himself had nothing to do with it. Davos was a man who could smell trouble; when he did he walked away.

I was reluctant to speak to Chremes about financial smears on Heliodorus. It touched too closely on his own problems, which I was holding in reserve at present. I did ask Phrygia. She assumed gambling was something all men did, and that cheating came naturally into the process. Like most disgusting male habits she ignored it, she said.

Helena offered to make enquiries of Philocrates, but I decided we could manage without help from him.

If Byrria was in a receptive mood, we would ask her when she came to dine.

L

Halfway to Canatha, on a high, flat, volcanic plain with distant views to the snow-capped peak of Mount Hermon, Helena and I tried our hands as matchmakers. For reasons we only found out later, we were wasting our time.

Entertaining two people who like to ignore each other's existence is quite a strain. As hosts we had supplied tasty wines, delectable fish, stuffed dates (stuffed by me, in my masquerade as an efficient cook), elegantly spiced side-dishes, olives, nuts, and sticky sweets. We had tried to place the romantic pair together, but they gave us the slip and took up stations at opposite ends of the fire. We sat side by side between them. Helena found herself talking to Byrria, while I just glared at Musa. Musa himself found a ferocious appetite for eating, buried his head in a bowl, and made no attempt to show off. As a wooer he had a slack technique. Byrria paid no attention to him. As a victim of his wiles, she was a tough proposition. Anyone who managed to tear this daisy from the pasture would need to tug hard.

The quality of the dinner did compensate for the lack of action. I helped myself to much of the wine while passing among the company, pointlessly trying to animate them with a generous jug. In the end I simply lay back with my head pillowed in Helena's lap, relaxed completely (not hard, in the state I had reached), and exclaimed, 'I give up! A man should know his limitations. Playing Eros is not my style. I must have the wrong kind of arrows in my bow.'

'I'm sorry,' murmured Byrria. 'I didn't realise the invitation was conditional.' Her reproach was light-hearted. The refills I had been plying her with had mellowed her somewhat. Either that or she was too practical to try flouncing off in a huff while she was tipsy.

'The only condition,' Helena smiled, 'is that all present quietly tolerate the romantic nature of their host.' Byrria tipped her winecup at me obligingly. There was no problem. We were all in a sleepy, well-filled, amenable mood.

'Maybe,' I suggested to Helena, 'Musa has perched so far from our lovely guest so he can gaze at her through the firelight.' While we talked about her, Byrria merely sat looking beautiful. She did it well. I had no complaints.

Helena Justina tickled my chin as she chimed in with my dreamy speculations. 'Admiring her in secret through the leaping sparks?'

'Unless he's just avoiding her because he hasn't washed.'

'Unfair!'

Helena was right. He was always clean. Given the fact that he had joined us in Petra so unexpectedly, and with so little luggage, it was a puzzle how Musa remained presentable. Sharing a tent, Helena and I would soon have known if his habits were unpleasant. His worst feature at the moment was a sheepish expression as I tried to set him up as a sophisticated lover.

Tonight he was turned out the same as always in his long white robe. He only had one, and yet he seemed to keep it laundered. He looked washed and tidy; he had definitely shaved (something none of us bothered with much on the road). On close examination there were one or two gestures to smart presentation: a soapstone scarab amulet on his chest, which I remembered him buying when he was out with me at Gerasa, a rope girdle that looked so new he must have picked it up in Bostra, and he was bare-headed in the Roman way. That made him look too boyish; I would have warned against it, but he had not asked for my sartorial advice.

Byrria, too, had probably dressed up slightly in response to our formal invitation. She was in green, rather plain if anything, with a very long skirt and long-sleeves against the flies which tended to descend on us at twilight. It marked a change from her spangled and revealing stage costumes, and signified that tonight she was being herself. Being herself also involved long bronze earrings that rattled all the time. Had I been in a less forgiving mood, they would have severely annoyed me.

Helena was looking sophisticated in a brown dress I had

not known she owned. I had favoured a casual approach, trying out a long striped Eastern robe I had brought to fend off the heat. I felt like a goat farmer and was in need of a scratch; I hoped it was just due to the newness of the material.

While we teased him, Musa put on a patient face but stood up, breathing the cool night air and gazing somewhere away to the south.

'Be kind to him,' Helena said to Byrria. 'We think Musa is homesick.' He turned back to her, as if she had accused him of being impolite, but stayed on his feet. At least it gave Byrria a better view of him. He was passable, though not much more.

'It's just a ploy,' I informed the girl confidentially. 'Somebody once told him women like men who have an air of mysterious sadness.'

'I am not sad, Falco.' Musa gave me the controlled look of a man who was just trying to ease his indigestion after eating too much.

'Maybe not. But ignoring the most beautiful woman in Syria is pretty mysterious.'

'Oh, I am not ignoring her!'

Well that was better. His sombre, deliberate manner of speech did make it sound vaguely admiring. Helena and I knew Musa always talked that way, but Byrria might read it as restrained ardour.

'There you are.' I grinned at her, encouraging this. 'You are quite right to be wary. Under the glacially aloof pose smoulders a hot-blooded philanderer. Compared to this man, Adonis was a ruffianly buck with bad breath and dandruff. In a moment he'll be tossing you roses and reciting poetry.'

Musa smiled politely. 'Poetry I can do, Falco.'

We were lacking the floristry, but he came to the fire, sitting opposite Helena and me, which at last brought him nearer to the girl he was supposed to be entrancing, though in fact he forgot to gaze at her. He dropped to a cushion (conveniently placed by Helena before the meal just where it would allow things to develop if our guests had wanted that). Then Musa started to recite. It was obviously going to be a very long poem, and it was in Nabataean Arabic.

Byrria listened with the faintest of smiles and her slanting green eyes well cast down. There was not much else the poor girl could do.

Helena sat still. Musa's posture for recitation was to stare straight ahead, which meant Helena was catching most of the performance. The soft pressure of her thumb on my windpipe warned me not to interrupt. Still lying in her lap I closed my eyes and forced myself to leave our idiotic tent guest to his fate.

Sooner than I had dared to hope, Musa stopped – or at least paused long enough for me to break in without upsetting him. Rolling over and smiling at Byrria, I said quietly, 'I think a certain young lady has just been favourably compared to a soft-eyed gazelle, running free on the mountains – '

'Falco!' Musa was tutting, fortunately with a laugh in his tone. 'Are you speaking more of my language than you pretend?'

'I'm a spare-time poet and I know how to guess.'

'You're an acting playwright; you should be able to interpret well-spoken verse.' There was a hard note in Byrria's voice. 'And how are your other guesses, Falco?' Without appearing graceless, Byrria had turned the conversation. Her long earrings tinkled slightly, though whether with amusement or embarrassment I could not tell. She was a girl who hid her thoughts. 'Are you any nearer identifying the person who killed Ione?'

Giving up on the priest now that I had seen his technique for seduction, I too welcomed the new subject. 'I'm still looking for Ione's unknown lover, and I'd be grateful for suggestions. With regard to the playwright, motives have suddenly started turning up as thick as barnacles on a boat bottom. The newest concerns Tranio, Grumio, and the possibility of bad gambling debts. Know anything about this?'

Byrria shook her head. She seemed very relieved that the talk had changed pace. 'No I don't, except that Heliodorus gambled in the same way he drank – hard, yet always staying in control.' Recalling it, she shivered slightly. Her earrings trembled, soundlessly this time, reflecting the fire in tiny

282

ripples of light. If she had been a girlfriend of mine, I would have reached to caress her earlobes – and deftly removed the jewellery. 'No one bettered him.'

'Custom-made dice!' I explained. She hissed angrily at the news. 'So how do you see Heliodorus relating to the Twins, Byrria?'

'I would have thought they were a match for him.'

I could tell that she liked them. On an impulse I asked, 'Are you going to tell me which of them pulled Heliodorus off, that time he jumped on you?'

'It was Grumio.' She said it without drama.

At her side I thought Musa tensed. Byrria herself sat extremely quietly, no longer showing her anger over the bad experience. All evening, in fact, she had behaved with reserve. She seemed to be watching us, or some of us. I almost felt that she, not Musa, was the foreigner at our fireside, subjecting our strange manners to curious scrutiny.

'You refused to tell me that before,' I reminded her. 'Why now?'

'I refused to be interrogated like a criminal. But here I am with friends.' From her, that was quite a compliment.

'So what happened?'

'Just at the right moment – for me – Grumio burst in. He had come to ask Heliodorus for something. I don't know what it was about really, but Grumio pulled the brute off me and started asking him about a scroll – a play I suppose. I managed to flee. Obviously,' she said to me in a reasonable tone, 'I am hoping you are not going to tell me Grumio is your main suspect.'

'The Twins have alibis, at least for Ione's death. Grumio in particular. I saw him otherwise occupied myself. For what happened at Petra, they're vouching for each other. Of course they may be conspiring – '

Byrria looked surprised. 'Oh, I don't think they like each other that much.'

'What do you mean?' Helena picked it up at once. 'They spend a lot of time together. Is there some rivalry?'

'Plenty!' Byrria replied quickly, as though it ought to be well known. Uneasily, she added, 'Tranio really does have more flair as a comedian. But I know Grumio feels that's merely a reflection of Tranio having more showy parts in plays. Grumio is much better at standing up to improvise, entertaining a crowd, though he hasn't done it so much recently.'

'Do they fight?' Musa put in. It was the kind of blunt question I like to ask myself.

'They have occasional squabbles.' She smiled at him. Must have been an aberration. Musa found enough spirit to mock himself by basking in the favour; then Byrria seemed to blush, though she could have been overheated by the nearness of the fire. I must have been looking thoughtful. 'Does that help, Falco?'

'Not sure. It may give me a way to approach them. Thanks, Byrria.'

It was late. Tomorrow there would be more travelling as we pressed on to Canatha. Around us the rest of the camp had quietened. Many people were already asleep. Our group seemed the only active party. It was time to break up. Glancing at Helena, I abandoned the attempt to bring the reluctant pair together.

Helena yawned, making the hint refined. She began collecting dishes, Byrria helping her. Musa and I confined our efforts to manly procedures such as poking the fire and finishing the olives. When Byrria thanked us for the evening, Helena apologised. 'I hope we didn't tease you too unbearably.'

'In what way?' Byrria responded drily. Then she smiled again. She was an extraordinarily beautiful young woman; the fact that she was barely twenty suddenly became more evident. She had enjoyed herself tonight; we could satisfy ourselves with that. Tonight she was as near to contentment as she might ever be. It made her look vulnerable for once. Even Musa seemed more mature, and more her equal.

'Don't mind us.' Helena spoke informally, licking sauce off her hand where she had picked up a sticky plate. 'You have to make your life as you wish. The important thing is to find and to keep real friends.' Reluctant to make too much of it, she went into the tent with the pile of dishes.

284

I was not prepared to let this go so easily. 'Even so, that doesn't mean she ought to be afraid of men!'

'I fear no one!' Byrria shot back, with a burst of her hot temper. It was a passing moment; her voice dropped again. Staring at a tray she had picked up, she added, 'Maybe I just fear the consequences.'

'Very wise!' quipped Helena, reappearing in an instant. 'Think of Phrygia whose whole life has been embittered and ruined by having a baby and marrying wrongly. She lost the child, she lost her chance to develop fully as an actress, and I think maybe she also gave up the man she should really have been with all these years – '

'You give a bad example,' Musa broke in. He was terse. 'I could say, look at Falco and you!'

'Us?' I grinned. Somebody had to play the fool and lighten the conversation. 'We're just two completely unsuitable people who knew we could have no future together but liked each other enough to go to bed for a night.'

'How long ago was that?' demanded Byrria hotly. Not a girl who could take irony.

'Two years,' I confessed.

'That's your one night?' laughed Byrria. 'How carefree and cosmopolitan! And how long, Didius Falco, do you suppose this unsuitable relationship may last?'

'About a lifetime,' I said cheerfully. 'We're not unreasonable in our hopes.'

'So what are you trying to prove to me? It seems contradictory.'

'Life is contradictory sometimes, though most times it just stinks.' I sighed. Never give advice. People catch you out and start fighting back. 'On the whole, I agree with you. So, life stinks; ambitions disappoint; friends die; men destroy and women disintegrate. But if, my dear Byrria and Musa, you will listen to one kind word from a friend, I should say, if you do find true affection, never turn your back on it.'

Helena, who was standing behind me, laughed lovingly. She ruffled my hair, then bent over me and kissed my forehead. 'This poor soul needs his bed. Musa, will you see Byrria safely to her tent?'

We all said our goodnights, then Helena and I watched the others go.

They walked uneasily together, space showing between them. They did stroll slowly, as if there might be things to be said, but we could not hear them talking as they left. They appeared to be strangers, and yet if I had given a professional judgement I would have said they knew more about each other than Helena and I supposed.

'Have we made a mistake?'

'I don't see what it can be, Marcus.'

We had done, though it was to be some time before I understood the obvious.

Helena and I cleared the debris and did what packing we needed, ready to drive on before dawn. Helena was in bed when I heard Musa returning. I went out and found him crouched beside the remnants of the fire. He must have heard me, but he made no move to evade me, so I squatted alongside. His face was buried in his hands.

After a moment I thumped his shoulder consolingly. 'Did something happen?'

He shook his head. 'Nothing that matters.'

'No. I thought you had the miserable air of a man with a clean conscience. The girl's a fool!'

'No, she was kind.' He spoke offhandedly, as if they were friends.

'Talk about it if you want, Musa. I know it's serious.'

'I never felt like this, Falco.'

'I know.' I let a moment pass before I spoke again. 'Sometimes the feeling goes away.'

He looked up. His face was drawn. Intense emotion racked him. I liked the poor idiot; his unhappiness was hard to contemplate. 'And if not?' he squeezed out.

I smiled sadly. 'If not, there are two alternatives. Most frequently – and you can guess this one – everything sorts itself out because the girl leaves the scene.'

'Or?'

I knew how low the chances were. But with Helena Justina asleep a few feet away, I had to acknowledge the fatal possibility: 'Or sometimes your feeling stays – and so does she.'

'Ah!' Musa exclaimed softly, as if to himself. 'In that case what am I to do?' I assumed he meant, *If I do win Byrria, what am I to do with her?*

'You'll get over this, Musa. Trust me. Tomorrow you could wake up and find yourself adoring some languid blonde who always wanted a flurry with a Nabataean priest.'

I doubted it. But on the off chance that he might be needing his strength, I hauled Musa to his feet and made him go to bed.

Tomorrow, if a cold blast of sanity seemed less likely to damage him, I would explain my theory that it is better to show off your multifaceted personality in their own language than to bore them stiff reciting poetry they cannot understand. If that failed, I would just have to get him interested in drinking, rude songs, and fast chariots.

LI

Canatha.

It was an old, walled, isolated city huddled on the northern incline of the basalt plain. As the only habitation of any substance in this remote area, it had acquired a special reputation and a special atmosphere. Its territory was small. Its commercial activity was greater, for a major trade route up from Bostra came this way. Even with the fine Hellenic attributes we had come to expect – the high acropolis, civilised amenities, and heavy programme of civic refurbishment – Canatha had strange touches. Hints of both Nabataean and Parthian architecture mingled exotically with its Greek and Roman features.

Though it lay too far out to be at risk of jealous Jewish incursions, there were other dangers lurking beyond the close clasp of its walls. Canatha was a lonely outpost in traditional bandit country. The mood here reminded me more of frontier fortresses in Germany and Britain than the pleasure-grasping, money-loving cities further west in the Decapolis. This was a self-reliant, self-involved community. Trouble had always lain not far outside the city gates.

We, of course, as a hapless band of vagabonds, were scrutinised keenly in case we were bringing trouble in with us. We played it straight, patiently letting them question and search us. Once in, we found the place friendly. Where craftsmen look long distances for influences, there is often a welcome for all comers. Canatha lacked prejudice. Canatha liked visitors. Canatha, being a town many people omitted from their itinerary, was so grateful to see travelling entertainers that its audiences even liked us.

The first play we gave them was *The Pirate Brothers*, which Chremes was determined to rehabilitate after the slurs cast upon it by the Bostra magistrate. It was well received, and we busily plundered our repertoire for *The Girl from Andros* and

Plautus' *Amphitryon* (one of Chremes' beloved gods-go-a-fornicating japes). I was anticipating thunder from Musa over *Amphitryon* but luckily the play had only one substantial female part, the virtuous wife unknowingly seduced by Jupiter, and this role was snatched by Phrygia. Byrria only got to play a nurse; she had one scene, at the very end, and no hanky-panky. She did get a good speech, however, where she had to describe the infant Hercules dispatching a snake with his chubby little hands.

To liven things up, Helena constructed a strangled snake to appear in the play. She stuffed a tube made from an old tunic and sewed on eyes with fringed, flirty lashes to produce a python with a silly expression (closely based on Thalia's Jason. Musa made it a long forked tongue, utilising a piece of broken belt. Byrria, who unexpectedly turned out to be a comedienne, ran on-stage with this puppet dangling limply under her elbow, then made it waggle about as if it was recovering from strangulation, causing her to beat it into submission irritatedly. The unscripted effect was hilarious. It caused a joyous roar at Canatha, but earned some of us a reprimand from Chremes, who had not been forewarned.

So, with the company funds restored at least temporarily, and a new reputation for the ridiculous among my own party, we travelled from Canatha to Damascus.

We had to cross dangerous country, so we kept our wits about us. 'This seems a road on which the unexpected could happen,' I muttered to Musa.

'Bandits?'

His was a true prophecy. Suddenly we were surrounded by menacing nomads. We were more surprised than terrified. They could see we were not exactly laden down with panniers of frankincense.

We pushed Musa, finally useful as an interpreter, up to speak to them. Adopting a solemn, priestly manner (as he told me afterwards), he greeted them in the name of Dushara and promised a free theatrical performance if they would let us go in peace. We could see the thieves thought this was the funniest offer they had had since the Great King of Persia tried to send them a tax demand, so they sat down in a half-circle while we sped through a quick version of *Amphitryon*, complete with stuffed snake. Needless to say, the snake received the best hand, but then there was a tricky moment when the bandits made it plain they wanted to purchase Byrria. While she contemplated life being beaten and cursed as some nomad's foreign concubine, Musa strode forwards and exclaimed something dramatic. They cheered ironically. In the end we satisfied the group by making them a present of the python puppet and providing a short lesson in waggling him.

We rode on.

'Whatever did you say, Musa?'

'I told them Byrria is to be a sacrificial virgin on a High Place.'

Byrria shot him a worse glance than she had given the nomads.

Our next excitement was being waylaid by a band of Christians. Tribesmen stealing our props was fair business, but cult adherents after freeborn Roman souls was an outrage. They were casually scattered across the road at a stopping place so that we had to go round them or submit to conversation. As soon as they smiled and said how pleasant it was to meet us, we knew they were bastards.

'Who are they?' whispered Musa, puzzled by their attitude.

'Wide-eyed lunatics who meet secretly for meals in upstairs rooms in honour of what they say is the One God.'

'One? Is that not rather limiting?'

'Surely. They'd be harmless, but they have bad-mannered politics. They refuse to respect the Emperor.'

'Do you respect the Emperor, Falco?'

'Of course not.' Apart from the fact I worked for the old skinflint, I was a republican. 'But I don't upset him by saying so publicly.'

When the fanatical sales talk moved to offering us a guarantee of eternal life, we beat the Christians up soundly and left them whimpering.

With the rising heat and these annoying interruptions, it took three stages to reach Damascus. On the last leg of our journey I did finally achieve a private talk with Tranio.

LII

Due to these disturbances, we had regrouped somewhat. Tranio happened to come alongside my waggon, whilst I noticed that for once Grumio was some way behind. I myself was alone. Helena had gone to spend some time with Byrria, diplomatically taking Musa. This was too good a chance to miss.

'Who wants to live for ever anyway?' Tranio joked, referring to the Christians we had just sorted out. He made the comment before he realised whose waggon he was riding next to.

'I could take that as a give-away!' I shot back, seizing the chance to work on him.

'For what, Marcus Didius?' I hate people who try to unnerve me by unbidden familiarity.

'Guilt,' I said.

'You see guilt everywhere, Falco.' He switched smartly back to the formal mode of address.

'Tranio, everywhere I run up against guilty men.'

I should like to pretend that my reputation as an informer was so grand that Tranio felt drawn to stay and challenge my skills. What really happened was that he tried hard to get away. He kicked his heels into his animal to spur it off, but being a camel it refused; a pain in the ribs was better than being obedient. This beast with the sly soul of a revolutionary was the usual dust-coloured creature with unsavoury bare patches on its ragged pelt, a morose manner and a tormented cry. It could run fast, but only ever did so as an excuse to try and unseat its rider. Its prime ambition was to abandon a human to the vultures forty miles from an oasis. A nice pet – if you wanted to die slowly of a septic camel bite.

Now Tranio was surreptitiously attempting to remove himself, but the camel had decided to lollop along beside my ox in the hope of unsettling him.

'I think you're trapped.' I grinned. 'So tell me about comedy, Tranio.'

'That's based on guilt mostly,' he conceded with a wry smile.

'Oh? I thought it was meant to tap hidden fears?'

'You a theorist, Falco?'

'Why not? Just because Chremes keeps me on the routine hack work doesn't mean that I never dissect the lines I'm revising for him.'

As he rode alongside me it was difficult to watch him too closely. If I turned my head I could see that he had been to a barber in Canatha; the cropped hair up the back of his head had been scraped off so close the skin showed red through the stubble. Even without twisting in my seat, I could catch a whiff of the rather overpowering balsam he had slopped on while shaving – a young man's mistaken purchase, which as a poor man he now had to use up. An occasional glance sideways gave me the impression of darkly hairy arms, a green signet ring with a gash in the stone, and whitened knuckles as he fought against the strong will of his camel. But he was riding in my blind spot. As I myself had to concentrate on calming our ox, which was upset by the bared teeth of Tranio's savage camel, it was impossible to look my subject directly in the eye.

'I'm doing a plodder's job,' I continued, leaning back with my whole weight as the ox tried to surge. 'I'm interested, did Heliodorus see it the way I do? Was it just piecework he flogged through? Did he reckon himself worthy of much better things?'

'He had a brain,' Tranio admitted. 'And the slimy creep knew it.'

'He used it, I reckon.'

'Not in his writing, Falco!'

'No. The scrolls I inherited in the play box prove that. His corrections are lousy and slapdash – when they are even legible.'

'Why are you so intrigued by Heliodorus and his glorious lack of talent?'

'Fellow feeling!' I smiled, not giving away the true reason. I wanted to explore why Ione had told me that the cause of the previous playwright's death had been purely professional.

Tranio laughed, perhaps uneasily. 'Oh come! Surely you're not telling me that underneath everything, Heliodorus was secretly a star comedian! It wasn't true. His creative powers were enormous when it came to manipulating people, but fictionally he was a complete dud. He knew that too, believe me!'

'You told him, I gather?' I asked rather drily. People were always keen to tell me too if they hated my work.

'Every time Chremes gave him some dusty old Greek master-piece and asked to have the jokes modernised, his dearth of intellectual equipment became pitifully evident. He couldn't raise a smile by tickling a baby. You've either got it or you haven't.'

'Or else you buy yourself a joke collection.' I was remembering something Congrio had said. 'Somebody told me they're still obtainable.'

Tranio spent a few moments swearing at his camel as it practised a war dance. Part of this involved skidding sideways into my cart. I joined in the bad language; Tranio got his leg trapped painfully against a cartwheel; my ox lowed hoarsely in protest; and the people travelling behind us shouted abuse.

When peace was restored, Tranio's camel was more interested than ever in nuzzling my cart. The clown did his best to jerk the beast away while I said thoughtfully, 'It would be nice to have access to some endless supply of good material. Something like Grumio talks about – an ancestral hoard of jests.'

'Don't live in the past, Falco.'

'What does that mean?'

'Grumio's obsessed – and he's wrong.' I seemed to have tapped some old professional disagreement he had had with Grumio. 'You can't bid at auction for humour. That's all gone. Oh maybe once there *was* a golden age of comedy when material was sacrosanct and a clown could earn a fortune raffling off his great-great-grandfather's precious scroll of antique pornography and musty puns. But nowadays you need a new script every day. Satire has to be as fresh as a

293

barrel of winkles. Yesterday's tired quips won't get you a titter on today's cosmopolitan stage.'

'So if you inherited a collection of old jokes,' I put to him, 'you'd just toss it away?' Feeling I might be on to something, I struggled to remember details of my earlier conversation with Grumio. 'Are you telling me I shouldn't believe all that wonderful rhetoric your tentmate exudes about the ancient hereditary trade of the jester? The professional laughter-man, valued according to his stock in trade? The old stories, which can be sold when in dire straits?'

'Crap!' Tranio cried.

'Not witty, but succinct.'

'Falco, what good have his family connections done him? Myself, I've had more success relying on a sharp brain and a five-year apprenticeship doing the warm-ups in Nero's Circus before gladiatorial shows.'

'You think you're better than him?'

'I know it, Falco. He *could* be as good as he wants, but he'll need to stop whining about the decline in stage standards, accept what's really wanted, and forget that his father and grandfather could survive on a few poor stories, a farmyard impression, and some trick juggling. Dear gods, all those terrible lines about funny foreigners: Why do Roman roads run perfectly straight?' Tranio quipped harshly, mimicking every stand-up comedian who had ever made me wince. 'To stop Thracian foodsellers setting up hot-and-cold foodstalls on the corners! And then the unsubtle innuendoes: What did the vestal virgin say to the eunuch?'

It sounded a good one, but he was cut short by the need to yank at his camel as it tried to dash off sideways across the road. I refrained from admitting my low taste by asking for the punch line.

Our route had been tilting slightly downhill, and now up ahead we could make out the abrupt break in the dry landscape that heralds Damascus, the oasis that hangs at the edge of the wilderness like a prosperous port on the rim of a vast infertile sea. On all sides we could see more traffic converging on this ancient honey-pot. Any moment now either Grumio would trot up to join his supposèd friend or Tranio would be leaving me.

It was time to apply blatant leverage. 'Going back to Heliodorus. You thought he was an untalented stylus-pusher with less flair than an old pine log. So why were you and Grumio so thick with him that you let the bastard encumber you with horrific gambling debts?'

I had struck a nerve. The only problem was to deduce which nerve it was.

'Who told you that, Falco?' Tranio's face looked paler under the lank fall of hair that tumbled forwards over his clever, dark eyes. His voice was dark too, with a dangerous mood that was hard to interpret.

'Common knowledge.'

'Common lies!' From being pale he suddenly flushed a raw colour, like a man with desperate marsh fever. 'We hardly ever played with him for money. Dicing with Heliodorus was a fool's game!' It almost sounded as if the clowns knew that he had cheated. 'We gambled for trifles, casual forfeits, that's all.'

'Why are you losing your temper then?' I asked quietly.

He was so furious that at last he overcame his camel's perversity. Tearing at its mouth with a rough hand on the bridle, he forced the animal to turn and galloped off to the back of the caravan.

LIII

Damascus claimed to be the oldest inhabited city in the world. It would take somebody with a very long memory to disprove the claim. As Tranio said, who wants to live that long? Besides, the evidence was clear enough. Damascus had been working its wicked systems for centuries, and knew all the tricks. Its money-changers were notorious. It possessed more liars, embezzlers and thieves amongst the stone-framed market stalls that packed its colourful grid of streets than any city I had ever visited. It was outstandingly famous and prosperous. Its colourful citizens practised an astonishing variety of villainy. As a Roman I felt quite at home.

This was the last city on our route through the Decapolis, and it had to be the jewel of the collection. Like Canatha, its position was remote from the rest, though here the isolation was simply a matter of long distance rather than atmosphere. This was no huddled bastion facing acres of wilderness – even though there were deserts in several directions. Damascus simply throbbed with power, commerce and self-assurance.

It had the normal Decapolis features. Established in a flourishing oasis where the River Abana dashed out through a gorge in the long mountain range, the stout city walls and their protecting towers were themselves encircled for a wide area by water meadows. On the site of an ancient citadel within the city stood a modest Roman camp. An aqueduct brought water for both public baths and private homes. As the terminus of the old, jealously guarded Nabataean trade route from the Red Sea and also a major crossroads, it was well supplied with markets and caravanserai. As a Greek city it had town planning and democratic institutions. As a Roman acquisition it had a lavish civic building programme, which centred on a grandiose plan to convert the local cult precinct into a huge sanctuary of Jupiter that would be set in a grotesquely oversized enclosure overloaded with colonnades, arches and monumental gates.

We entered town from the east by the Gate of the Sun. Immediately the hubbub hit us. Coming out of the desert, the cries of rapacious street sellers and the racket of banter and barter were a shock. Of all the cities we had visited this bore the closest resemblance to the setting of a lively Greek play, a place where babies might be given away or treasure stolen, runaway slaves lurked behind every pillar, and prostitutes rarely survived to retirement age. Here, without doubt, sophisticated wives would berate their enfeebled husbands for not coming good in bed. Wayward sons bamboozled doddering fathers. Dutiful daughters were a rarity. Anyone passing for a priestess was likely to have had a first career preparing virgins for deflowerment by off-duty soldiers in a damp quayside brothel, and anyone who openly admitted to being a madam was best avoided hastily in case she turned out to be your long-lost grandmother.

From the Gate of the Sun to the Gate of Jupiter at the opposite end of town ran the Via Recta, a street some surveyor with a sense of humour had once had named 'Straight'. An embarrassing thoroughfare. Not exactly the place to hire a quiet room for a week of contemplative soul-searching. It ought to have been a stately axis of the city, yet singularly lacked grandeur. In Roman terms it was a Decumanus Maximus, though one that took several demeaning wiggles around hillocks and inconvenient old buildings. It was a foundation line in what should have been a classical Greek street grid. But Hippodamnus of Miletus, who laid down the principles of gracious town planning, would have chucked up his dinner in disgust if faced with this.

It was chaotic too, and characterised by a forest of columns that held up cloth awnings. In the turgid heat that soon built up beneath the heavy roofing as the sun climbed, official traders worked from solidly constructed lock-ups. Numerous illegal stalls were also crammed in, spilling in unsupervised rows across most of the width of the street. A Roman aedile would have become apoplectic. Controlling the irreverent mayhem would be impossible. Traffic ground to a standstill soon after dawn. People stopped for long conversations, planting themselves immovably in the road.

We clapped our hands on our purses, clung together, and tried to forge our way through the impasse, wincing at the noise. We were assailed by entrancing scents from huge piles of spices and blinked at the glitter of tawdry trinkets hung in streamers on the stalls. We ducked to avoid casually wielded bales of fine-weave material. We gaped at the array of sponges and jewellery, figs and whole honeycombs, household pots and tall candelabra, five shades of henna powder, seven kinds of nuts. We were bruised. We were crushed against walls by men with handcarts. Members of our party panicked as they glimpsed an exotic bargain, some bauble in copper, with a twirl to its handle and an Oriental spout; they only turned round for a second, then lost sight of the rest of us among the jostling crowds.

Needless to say, we had to traverse almost the whole of this chaotic street. The theatre where Chremes had secured us a booking was at the far end, slightly south of the main thoroughfare, near the Jupiter Gate. It stood close to the second-hand clothes-sellers, in what people had honestly named the louse market.

Since we were to have the honour of performing at the monumental theatre built by Herod the Great, we could live with a few lice.

We never did find out how Chremes pulled off this coup. With a slight sign of awareness that people despised his powers as an organiser, he clammed up proudly and refused to say.

How he did it ceased to matter once we ascertained the local rate for theatre tickets and started selling them. At that point we cheered up tremendously. We had a smart venue (for once), and found no difficulty filling the auditorium. In this teeming hive of buyers and sellers people handed over good money regardless of repertoire. They all prided themselves on driving a hard bargain; once off the commodities in which they were experts, most of them became easy touches. Culture was merely a facet of retailing here. Plenty of brokers were looking to impress clients; they bought tickets to entertain their guests without bothering what might be on. Commercial hospitality is a splendid invention.

For a couple of days we all thought Damascus was a wonderful place. Then, as people started to realise they had been rooked by the money-changers and as one or two purses were lifted in the narrow alleys off the main streets, our views cooled. Even I went out on my own one morning and bought as a present for my mother a large quantity of what I believed to be myrrh, only to have Musa sniff at it and sadly tell me it was bdellium, a much less pure aromatic gum that should sell at a much less aromatic price. I went back to challenge the stallholder; he had disappeared.

Our booking was for three nights. Chremes settled on performing what he regarded as the gems in our repertoire: *The Pirate Brothers*, then a fornicating gods farce, and *The Girl from Mykonos*. The last sparkler had been cobbled together by Heliodorus some time before he died: maybe he should have died of shame. It was 'loosely based' on all the other *Girl from . . .* comedies, a teaser for lustful merchants who were on the razzle in a big city without their wives. It had what the Samos, Andros and Perinthos plays all lacked: Grumio's falling-off-a-ladder trick, Byrria fully clothed but doing a revealing dance while pretending to be mad, and all the girls in the orchestra playing topless. (Plancina asked to be paid a bonus after trapping a nipple between her castanets.)

Chremes' choice caused groans. He had no real sense of atmosphere. We knew these were the wrong plays and after a morning of muttering, the rest of the company, led by me as their literary expert, gathered to put matters right. We allowed *The Girl from Mykonos*, which was obviously a runner in a bad city, but overruled the other two; they were altered by democratic vote to *The Rope*, with its ever-popular tug of war, and a play Davos liked that enabled him to show off in his Boasting Soldier role. Philocrates, so in love with himself and public adulation, would probably have argued as his own part in the latter was minimal, but he happened to be hiding in his tent after spotting a woman he had seduced

299

on our visit to Pella in the company of a rather large male relative who looked as if he had something on his mind.

That was the trouble with Damascus. All roads led there.

'And lead away,' Helena reminded me, 'in three days' time. What are we going to do, Marcus?'

'I don't know. I agree we didn't come to the East to spend the rest of our lives with a cheap drama company. We're earning enough to live on – but not enough to stop and take a holiday, and certainly not enough to pay our fares home if Anacrites won't sign for it.'

'Marcus, I could pay those.'

'If I lost all self-respect.'

'Don't exaggerate.'

'All right, you can pay, but let me try to complete at least one commission first.'

I led her into the streets. Uncomplainingly she took my arm. Most women of her status would have frizzled up in horror at the thought of stepping into the public hubbub of a loud, lewd foreign metropolis with neither a litter nor a bodyguard. Many citizens of Damascus eyed her with obvious suspicion for doing so. For a senator's daughter Helena had always had a strange sense of propriety. If I was there, that satisfied her. She was neither embarrassed nor afraid.

The size and liveliness of Damascus suddenly reminded me of the rules we had left behind in Rome, rules that Helena broke there, too, though at least it was home. In Rome scandalous behaviour among senatorial females was just a feature of fashionable life. Causing trouble for their male relatives had become an excuse for anything. Mothers regarded it as a duty to educate daughters to be rebellious. Daughters revelled in it, throwing themselves at gladiators, joining queer sects, or becoming notorious intellectuals. By comparison, the vices open to boys seemed tame.

Even so, running off to live with an informer was an act more shocking than most. Helena Justina had good taste in men, but she was an unusual girl. Sometimes I forgot how unusual.

I stopped at a street corner, caught by an occasional need to check up on her. I had one arm tight around her to protect her from the bustle. She tipped her head to look at me questioningly; her stole fell back from her face, its trimming caught on her earring. She was listening, though trying to free the strands of fine gold wire, as I said, 'You and I lead a strange life. Sometimes I feel that if I cared for you properly I would keep you somewhere more suitable.'

Helena shrugged. She was always patient with my restless attempts to make her more conventional. She could take pomposity, if it came as a near relative to a cheeky grin. 'I like my life. I'm with an interesting man.'

'Thanks!' I found myself laughing. I should have expected her to disarm me, but she still caught me unawares. 'Well, it won't last for ever.'

'No,' she agreed solemnly. 'One day you will be a prim middle-rank bureaucrat who wears a clean toga every day. You'll talk of economics over breakfast and only eat lettuce for lunch. And I'll have to sit at home with my face in an inch-thick flour pack, forever checking laundry bills.'

I controlled a smile. 'Well that's a relief. I thought you were going to be difficult about my plans.'

'I am never difficult, Marcus.' I swallowed a chortle. Helena slipped in thoughtfully, 'Are you homesick?'

I probably was, but she knew I would never admit to it. 'I can't go home yet. I hate unfinished business.'

'So how are you proposing to finish it?'

I liked her faith in me.

Luckily I had put arrangements in hand for resolving at least one commission. Pointing to a nearby house wall, I showed off my cunning device. Helena inspected it. 'Congrio's script is getting more elaborate.'

'He's being well taught,' I said, letting her know I realised who had been improving him.

Congrio had drawn his usual poster advertising our performance of *The Rope* that evening. Alongside it he had chalked up another bill:

HABIB

301

(VISITOR TO ROME)
URGENT MESSAGE: ASK FOR FALCO
AT THEATRE OF HEROD
IMMEDIATE CONTACT IS
TO YOUR DEFINITE ADVANTAGE

'Will he answer?' asked Helena, a cautious girl.

'Without a doubt.'

'How can you be so sure?'

'Thalia said he was a businessman. He'll think it's a promise of money.'

'Oh well done!' said Helena.

LIV

The specimens called Habib who asked for Falco at the
theatre were varied and sordid. This was common in my line
of work. I was ready for them. I asked several questions they
could answer by keen guesswork, then slipped in the
customary clincher: 'Did you visit the imperial menagerie on
the Esquiline Hill?'

'Oh yes.'

'Very interesting.' The menagerie is outside the city by the
Praetorian Camp. Even in Rome not many people know that.
'Don't waste my time with cheating and lies. Get out of here!'

They did eventually catch on, and sent their friends to try
'Oh no' as the answer to the trick question; one spectacularly
blatant operator even attempted to delude me with the old
'Maybe I did, maybe I didn't' line. Finally, when I was starting
to think the ploy had failed, it worked.

On the third evening, a group of us who had suddenly
become very interested in helping out with the costumes were
stripping off the female musicians for their half-naked
starring roles in *The Girl from Mykonos*. At the crucial
moment I was called out to a visitor. Torn between
pulchritude and work, I forced myself to go.

The runt who might be about to help me with Thalia's
commission was clad in a long striped shirt. He had an
immense rope girdle wrapped several times about his
unimpressive frame. He had a lazy eye and dopey features,
with tufts of fine hair scattered on his head like an old bedside
rug that was fast losing its grip on reality. He was built like a
boy, yet had a mature face, reddened either by life as a
furnace stoker or some congenital fear of being found out in
whatever his routine wrongdoing was.

'I suppose you're Habib?'

'No, sir.' Well that was different.

'Did he send you?'

'No, sir.'

'Are you happy speaking Greek?' I queried drily, since his conversation did seem limited.

'Yes, sir.'

I would have told him he could drop the 'sir', but that would have left us staring in silence like seven-year-olds on their first day at school.

'Cough it up then. I'm needed on stage for prompting.' I was anxious to see the panpipe girl's bosom, which appeared to be almost as alarmingly perfect as the bouncing attributes of a certain rope dancer I had dallied with in my bachelor days. For purely nostalgic reasons I wished to make a critical comparison. If possible, by taking measurements.

I wondered if my visitor had just come to cadge a free ticket. Obviously I would have obliged just to escape and return to the theatre. But as a hustler he was sadly slow, so I spelled it out for him. 'Look, if you want a seat, there are still one or two at the top of the auditorium. I'll arrange it, if you like.'

'Oh!' He sounded surprised. 'Yes, sir!'

I gave him a bone token from the pouch at my belt. The roars and whoops from the theatre behind us told me the orchestra girls had made their entrance. He didn't move. 'You're still hanging around,' I commented.

'Yes.'

'Well?'

'The message.'

'What about it?'

'I've come to get it.'

'But you're not Habib.'

'He's gone.'

'Gone where?'

'The desert.' Dear gods. The whole damn country was desert. I was in no mood to start raking through the sands of Syria to find this elusive entrepreneur. In the rest of the world there were vintages to sample, rare works of art to accumulate, fine foods to cadge off rich buffoons. And not far from here there were women to ogle.

'When did he go?'

304

'Two days ago.'

My mistake. We should have omitted Canatha.

No. If we had omitted Canatha, Canatha would have turned out to be where the bastard lived. Destiny was against me as usual. If the gods ever did decide to help me out, they would mislay their map and lose themselves on the road down from Mount Olympus.

'So!' I took a deep breath and started off again with the brief and unproductive dialogue. 'What did he go for?'

'To fetch his son back. Khaleed.'

'That's two answers to one question. I haven't asked you the second.'

'What?'

'What's his son's name?'

'He's called Khaleed!' wailed the red-faced drip of rennet plaintively. I sighed.

'Is Khaleed young, handsome, rich, wayward and utterly insensitive to the wishes and ambitions of his outraged parent?'

'Oh, you've met him!' I didn't need to. I had just spent several months adapting plays that were stuffed with tiresome versions of this character. Nightly I had watched Philocrates shed ten years, put on a red wig, and stuff a few scarves down his loincloth in order to play this lusty delinquent.

'So where is he being a playboy?'

'Who, Habib?'

'Habib or Khaleed, what's the difference?'

'At Tadmor.'

'*Palmyra?*' I spat the Roman name at him.

'Palmyra, yes.'

He had told me right then. That really was the desert. The nasty geographical feature of Syria that being a fastidious type I had sworn to avoid. I had heard quite enough stories from my late brother the soldier about scorpions, thirst, warlike tribesmen, deadly infections from thorn prickles, and men raving as their brains boiled in their helmets from the heat. Festus had told a lurid tale. Lurid enough to put me off.

Perhaps we were talking about entirely the wrong family.

'So answer me this: does your young Khaleed have a girlfriend?'

The dope in the shirt looked guarded. I had stumbled on a scandal. Not hard to do. It was the usual story after all, and in the end he admitted it with the usual intrigued glee. 'Oh yes! That's why Habib has gone to fetch him home.'

'I thought it might be! Daddy does not approve?'

'He's furious!'

'Don't look so worried. I know all about it. She's a musician, one with a certain Roman elegance but about as high-born as a gnat, completely without connections, and penniless?'

'That's what they say . . . So do I get the money?'

'Nobody promised any money.'

'The message for Habib then?'

'No. You get a large reward,' I said, loftily giving him a small copper. 'You have your free ticket to see the half-naked dancers. And thanks to you inflicting this scandalous story on my delicate earlobes, I now have to go to Palmyra to give the message to Habib myself.'

ACT THREE : PALMYRA

Late summer at an oasis. Palm and pomegranate trees cluster tastefully around a dirty-looking spring. More camels are wandering about as a disreputable caravan arrives upon the scene . . .

SYNOPSIS: *Falco*, a cheeky low-life character, appears in the gracious city of Palmyra with a troupe of *Travelling Players*. He discovers that *Sophrona*, a long-sought runaway, is having an affair with *Khaleed*, a rich ne'er-do-well whose father is furious; Falco will have to resort to trickery if he is ever to sort things out. Meanwhile danger threatens from an unexpected quarter as the drama on-stage becomes more lifelike than the players had bargained for . . .

LV

My brother Festus was right about the dangers. But Festus
had been in the Roman legions, so he had missed a few quaint
customs. For instance, in the desert everything is based on
'hospitality' to strangers, so nothing comes free. What Festus
left out were little matters like the 'voluntary contribution' we
found ourselves needing to make to the Palmyrenes who
offered us their 'protection' across the desert. It would have
been fatal to cross without an escort. There were rules. The
chief man in Palmyra had been charged by Rome to police the
trade routes, paying for his militia from his own well-stuffed
coffers as befitted a rich man with a civic conscience. The
chief man provided the escort, therefore, and those who
enjoyed the service felt obliged to show immense gratitude.
Those who rejected the service were asking to be set upon.

The regular protection squads were waiting for us a few
miles north of Damascus, where the road divides. Helpfully
loafing at the wayside, as soon as we took the right-hand turn
for Palmyra they offered themselves as guides, leaving us to
work out for ourselves the penalty for refusing. On our own
we would make an easy target for marauding tribesmen. If the
tribesmen didn't know we were there, the rejected escort
would soon point us out. This protection racket must have
operated in the desert for a thousand years, and a small
theatre group with unwieldy baggage was unlikely to thwart
the smiling tradition of blackmail. We paid up. Like everyone
else, we knew that getting to Palmyra was only one part of our
problem. Once there, we wanted to be able to come back.

I had been to the edge of the Empire before. Crossed the
boundary, even, when I had nothing better to do than risk my
life in a foolish mission. Yet as we headed eastwards deep into
Syria, I had never experienced quite such a strong feeling that
we were going to stare out at unknown barbarians. In Britain
or Germany you know what lies over the frontier: more

Britons or Germans whose nature is just a touch too fierce to conquer and whose lands are just too awkward to enclose. Beyond Syria, which itself becomes a wilderness a mere fifty miles inland, lie the unconquerable Parthians. And beyond them roll legendary tracts of unexplored territory, mysterious kingdoms from which come exotic goods brought by secretive men and borne on strange animals. Palmyra is both the end of our Empire, and the end of the long road leading towards us from theirs. Our lives and theirs meet face to face in a market that must be the most exotic in the world. They bring ginger and spices, steel and ink, gemstones, but primarily silk; in return we sell them glass and Baltic amber, cameo gemstones, henna, asbestos and menagerie animals. For a Roman, as for an Indian or Chinaman, Palmyra is as far as you can ever go.

I knew all this in theory. I was well read, within the limits of a poor boy's upbringing, though one with access to dead men's libraries when they came up in my father's auctions. Moreover, I had brought with me a strikingly well-read girl. There had never been limits on what Helena's father could provide for her. Decimus Camillus had always allowed her to ask for literary works (in the hope that once she had grabbed the new scroll box and devoured it in an evening he might saunter through the occasional scroll himself). I knew about the East because my own father studied the luxury trade. She knew because she was fascinated by anything unusual. By pooling our knowledge, Helena and I were forewarned of most things we encountered. But we guessed before we ever started that mere theory might not be enough preparation for Palmyra in reality.

I had persuaded the company to come with us. Hearing that finding Sophrona had suddenly become a possibility, many were curious. The stagehands and musicians were loath to let me leave them so long as our killer remained on the loose. The long desert haul offered us one last chance to drive him out from under cover. So, by a large majority, Chremes' cherished plan to trot sedately up to Emesa had been overturned. Even the giant watermills on the Orontes and the famous decadence of Antiochia failed to match the lure of the empty desert, the exotic silk markets, and a promise of solutions to our mysteries.

I was no longer in doubt that I was finding solutions. I had obtained an address in Palmyra for the businessman whose son had absconded with the water organist. If I found her, I was confident I would also find some way of restoring her to Thalia. It sounded as if Habib was already hard at that. If he successfully split her from her boyfriend, my offer of her old job back in Rome should come as welcome news.

As for the killer, I was sure I was close to him. Perhaps even in my own mind I had worked out who he was. I had certainly reduced my suspects to two. Whilst I could accept that one of them might have gone unobserved up the mountain with the playwright, I still believed it was impossible for him to have killed Ione. That left only the other, apparently – unless somewhere I could nail a lie.

Sometimes, when we pitched camp among the rolling brown hills where the wind moaned over the sandy slopes so ominously, I sat and thought about the killer. Even to Helena I was not yet ready to name him. But more and more in the course of that journey I was allowing myself to put a face to him.

We had been told it was a four-day trip to Palmyra. That was the time our escort would have taken, by camel, unencumbered by cartloads of properties and the awkward stumbles and accidents of complaining amateurs. For one thing, we insisted on taking our carts. The Palmyrenes had tried strenuously to persuade us to abandon our wheeled vehicles. Our fear had been that this was a ploy to let their comrades pinch the waggons once we had parked them and left them behind. Eventually we accepted that the urgings were genuine. In return for our money they did wish to give a good service. Oxen and mules took far more time than camels to cross the wilderness. They carried less, and were subject to more stress. Besides, as our guides generously pointed out, at Palmyra we faced a punitive local tax on each cart we wanted to take into town.

We said that since we were not trading we would leave our

311

carts at the city perimeter. Our escort looked unhappy. We explained that trying to load a camel with two extremely large stage doorways (complete with doors), plus the revolving wheel of our lifting machinery for flying in gods from the heavens, might be difficult. We made it clear that without our normal transport for our odd trappings we would not go. In the end they shook their heads and allowed us our madness. Escorting eccentrics even seemed to give them a sense of pride.

But their pleas had been sensible. We soon groaned at the slowness of our journey as the waggons toiled along that remote highway in the grinding heat. Some of us had been saved from the painful choice between four days of agony in a camel saddle or four days of increasing blisters leading a camel on foot. But as the journey dragged on, and we watched our draught animals suffering, the swifter choice looked more and more like the one we should have made. Camels conserved moisture by ceasing to sweat – surely their only act of restraint in regard to bodily functions. Oxen, mules and donkeys were as drained of energy as we were. They could manage the trip, but they hated it, and so did we. With care, it was possible to obtain sufficient water to exist. It was salty and brackish, but kept us alive. To a Roman this was the kind of living you do only to remind yourself how superior existence in your own civilised city is.

The desert was as boring as it was uncomfortable. The emptiness of the endless dun-coloured uplands was broken only by a dun-coloured jackal slinking off on private business, or the slow, circling flight of a buzzard. If we spotted a distant flock of goats, tended by a solitary figure, the glimpse of humanity seemed surprising among the barrenness. When we met other caravans the escorting cameleers called out to each other and chattered excitedly but we travellers hunched in our robes with the furtive behaviour of strangers whose only common interest would be complaints about our escorts – a subject we had to avoid. There were glorious sunsets followed by nights ablaze with stars. That did not compensate for the days spent winding headgear ever more tightly against the stinging dust that was blown in our faces by an evil wind, or the hours wasted beating our boots against rocks or shaking out our bedding in the morning and evening ritual of the scorpion hunt.

It was when we reckoned we were about halfway that disaster struck. The desert rituals had become routine, but we were still not safe. We went through the motions of following advice given to us by local people, but we lacked the instinct or experience that give real protection.

We had drawn up, exhausted, and were making camp. The place was merely a stopping-point beside the road to which nomads came to sell skinfuls of water from some distant salt marsh. The water was unpalatable, though the nomads sold it pleasantly. I remember a few patches of thorny scrub, from which fluttered a startingly coloured small bird, some sort of desert finch, maybe. Tethered at odd points were the usual unattended solo camels with no obvious owner. Small boys offered dates. An old man with extremely gracious manners sold piping-hot herbal drinks from a tray hung on a cord around his neck.

Musa was lighting a fire, while I settled our tired ox. Helena was outside our newly erected tent, flapping rugs as Musa had taught her to do, unrolling them one at a time from our baggage, ready to furnish the tent. When the disaster happened she spoke out not particularly loudly, though the stillness and horror in her voice reached me at the waggon and several people beyond us.

'Marcus, help! A scorpion is on my arm!'

LVI

'Flick it off!' Musa's voice was urgent. He had told us how to smite them away safely. Helena either could not remember or was too shocked.

Musa leapt up. Helena was rigid. In one hand she still clutched the blanket it must have skuttled from, terrified even to relax her fingers. On her outstretched forearm danced the ominous black creature, half a finger's length of it, crab-like, its long tail reared in an evil curl. It was viciously aggressive after being disturbed.

I covered the ground between us on legs of lead. 'My darling – '

Too late.

It knew I was coming. It knew its own power. Even if I had been standing at Helena's elbow when it rushed out of hiding I could never have saved her.

The tail came forwards over its head. Helena gasped in horror. The sting struck down. The scorpion immediately dropped off.

Hardly a beat of time had passed.

I saw the scorpion run across the ground, darting rapidly like a spider. Then Musa was on it, screaming with frustration as he beat at it with a rock. Over and over came his furious blows, while I caught Helena in my arms. 'I'm here – '

Not much use if she was being paralysed by a fatal poison. 'Musa! Musa! What must I do?'

He looked up. His face was white and appeared tear-stained. 'A knife!' he cried wildly. 'Cut where it stung. Cut deep and squeeze hard – '

Impossible. Not Helena. Not me.

Instead I pulled the blanket from her fingers, supported her arm, cradled her against me, tried to make time jump back the few seconds that would save her from this.

314

My thoughts cleared. Finding extra strength, I wrenched off one of my bootstraps, then fastened it tightly as a tourniquet around Helena's upper arm.

'I love you,' she muttered urgently, as if she thought it was the last time she would ever be able to tell me. Helena had her own idea of what was important. Then she thrust her arm against my chest. 'Do what Musa says, Marcus.'

Musa had stumbled to his feet again. He produced a knife. It had a short, slim blade and a dark polished hilt bound with bronze wire. It looked wickedly sharp. I refused to think what a priest of Dushara would use it for. He was trying to make me take it. As I shrank from the task, Helena now offered her arm to Musa; he backed away in horror. Like me he was incapable of harming her.

Helena turned quickly to me again. Both of them were staring at me. As the hard man, this was down to me. They were right, too. I would do anything to save her, since more than anything I was incapable of losing her.

Musa was holding the knife the wrong way, point towards me. Not a military man, our guest. I reached over the blade and grasped the worn hilt, bending my wrist downwards to stop him slicing through my hand. Musa let go abruptly, with relief.

Now I had the knife but had to find my courage. I remember thinking we should have brought a doctor with us. Forget travelling light. Forget the cost. We were in the middle of nowhere and I was going to lose Helena for want of proper expertise. I would never take her anywhere again, at least not without someone who could surgically operate, together with a massive trunk of apothecary's drugs and a full Greek pharmacopoeia . . .

While I hesitated, Helena even tried snatching at the knife herself. 'Help me, Marcus!'

'It's all right.' I sounded terse. I sounded angry. By then I was walking her to a roll of baggage where I made her sit. Kneeling alongside I held her close for a moment, then kissed her neck. I spoke quietly, almost through my teeth. 'Listen, lady. You're the best thing in my life, and I'll do whatever I have to do to keep you.'

315

Helena was shaking. Her earlier strength of will was now fading almost visibly, as I took control. 'Marcus, I was being careful. I must have done the wrong thing – '

'I should never have brought you here.'

'I wanted to come.'

'I wanted you with me,' I confessed. Then I smiled at her, so her eyes met mine, full of love, and she forgot to watch what I was doing. I cut twice across the mark on her arm, making the two cuts cross at right angles. She let out a small sound, more surprise than anything. I bit my lip so hard I broke the skin.

Helena's blood seemed to dash everywhere. I was horrified. I still had work to do, extracting what I could of the poison, but at the sight of those bright red gouts welling up so fast I felt uneasy. Musa, who had no part in the action, fainted clean away.

LVII

Squeezing the wound had been hard enough; staunching the blood proved frighteningly difficult. I used my hands, always the best way. By then people had come running. A girl – Afrania, I think – was handing me ripped cloths. Byrria was holding Helena's head. Sponges appeared. Someone was making Helena sip water. Someone else gripped my shoulder in encouragement. Urgent voices muttered together in the background.

One of the Palmyrenes came hurrying up. I demanded if he carried an antidote; he either failed to understand, or had nothing. Not even a spider's web to salve the wound. Useless.

Cursing myself again for lack of forethought, I used some general ointment that I always carry before binding up Helena's arm. I told myself the scorpions in this area might not be fatal. The Palmyrene seemed to be jabbering that I had done well with my treatment. That made me think he must reckon it was worth trying. He was nodding madly, as if to reassure me. Swallowing my panic, I tried to believe him.

I heard the swish of a broom as someone angrily swept the dead scorpion out of sight. I saw Helena, so pale that I nearly cried out in despair, struggling to smile and reassure me. The tent cleared suddenly. Unseen hands had rolled down the sides. I stood back as Byrria started helping Helena out of her blood-soaked clothing. I went out for warm water and a clean sponge.

A small group were quietly waiting by the fire. Musa stood in silence, slightly apart from them. Someone else prepared the bowl of water for me. Once again I was patted on the back and told not to worry. Without speaking to anyone I went back to Helena.

Byrria saw that I wanted to look after Helena alone; she discreetly withdrew. I heard her voice, chivvying Musa. Something in my head warned me that he might be needing attention.

317

While I was washing her, Helena suddenly started to collapse from the loss of blood. I laid her down and talked her back to consciousness. After a while I managed to get a clean gown over her head, then made her comfortable with cushions and rugs. We hardly spoke, conveying everything we felt by touch.

Still white-faced and perspiring, she watched me cleaning up. When I knelt down beside her she was smiling again. Then she took my hand and held it against the thick pad of bandages, as if my warmth were healing.

'Does it hurt you?'

'Not badly.'

'I'm afraid that it will.' For some time we stayed there in complete silence, gazing at one another, both now in shock. We were as close as we had ever been. 'There will be scars. I couldn't help it. Oh my darling! Your beautiful arm . . .' She would never be able to go bare-armed again.

'Lots of bangles!' murmured Helena practically. 'Just think what fun you're going to have choosing them for me.' She was teasing, threatening me with the expense.

'Lucky stroke!' I managed a grin. 'I'll never be in a quandary what to bring you for your gift at Saturnalia . . .' Half an hour beforehand I had never expected us to share another winter festival. Now she was somehow convincing me that her tenacity would bring her through. The fast, painful throb of my heart settled back to nearly normal as we talked.

After a moment she whispered, 'Don't worry.'

I would have a lot more worrying to do yet.

She stroked my hair with her good hand. Occasionally I felt her tugging gently at the worst tangles amongst the un-combed curls that she had always said she loved. Not for the first time I vowed that in future I would keep myself barbered, a man she could be proud to be seen talking to. Not for the first time I dropped the idea. Helena had not fallen in love with a primped and pungent man of fashion. She had chosen me: a decent body; just enough brains; jokes; good intentions; and half a lifetime of successfully concealing my bad habits from the women in my life. Nothing fancy; but nothing too dire either.

318

I let myself relax under her fingers' familiar touch. Soon, through calming me, she put herself to sleep.

Helena still slept. I was crouching beside her with my face in my hands when a noise at the tent's entrance roused me. It was Musa.

'Can I help, Falco?'

I shook my head angrily, afraid he would waken her. I was aware that he picked up his knife, hesitantly taking it from where I had dropped it. There was one thing he could do, though it would have sounded harsh and I managed not to say so. A man should always clean his own knife.

He disappeared.

A long while later it was Plancina, the panpipe-player, who came to look in on us. Helena was still drowsing, so I was called outside and fed a huge bowl of the stagehands' broth. Even in the most isolated places, their cauldron was always put on the boil as soon as we stopped. The girl stayed to watch me eat, satisfied with her good deed.

'Thanks. That was good.'

'How is she?'

'Between the poison and the knife cut, only the gods can help her now.'

'Better sprinkle a few pints of incense! Don't worry. There's plenty of us ready to help pray for her.'

Suddenly I found myself in the role of the man with a sick wife. While I was nursing Helena Justina, all the other women in our party would be wanting to act like my mother. Little did they know that my real mother would have knocked them aside and briskly taken charge while I was left with only drink and debauchery to keep me occupied. Still, Ma had had a hard lesson in men, being married to my pa. I didn't have to wonder what my mother would have done with Plancina; I had seen Ma put to flight plenty of floozies whose only social error was being too sympathetic towards me.

'We've been talking to the escorts,' Plancina told me confidentially. 'These things are not fatal in this country. But you'll have to be careful about infection in the wound.'

319

'Easier said than done.'

Many a fit adult had been terminally stricken after what seemed a minor accident. Not even imperial generals, with the full panoply of Greek and Roman medicine at their disposal, were immune to an awkward graze or septic scratch. Here we were surrounded by sand and dust, with grit working its way everywhere. There was no running water. Indeed there was barely water enough to drink, let alone to clean wounds. The nearest apothecaries must be in Damascus or Palmyra. They were famously good – but days away.

We were talking in low voices, partly to avoid disturbing my lass as she slept, partly from shock. By now I was desperately tired and glad of somebody to talk to.

'I'm hating myself.'

'Don't, Falco. It was an accident.'

'It should have been avoidable.'

'Those little bastards are everywhere. Helena just had terrible luck.' Since I was still looking glum, Plancina added with unexpected sympathy, 'She was more careful than anybody else. Helena did not deserve this.'

I had always taken the panpipe-player for a sassy piece. She had a loud mouth, a ferocious turn of phrase, and liked to wear skirts that were slashed from hem to armpit. On a Spartan maiden dancing her way around a redware vase this daring fashion looks the height of elegance; in real life, on a plump little wind-instrument-player, the effect was simply common. I had had her down as one of those girls who have an immaculately presented face, with nothing behind the eyes. But like most girls, dashing men's misconceptions was what she did best. Despite my prejudice, Plancina was extremely bright. 'You notice people,' I commented.

'Not as dumb as you thought, eh?' She giggled good-humouredly.

'I always took you for the clever one,' I lied. It came out automatically; I had been a carefree womaniser once. You never lose the knack.

'Clever enough to know a few things!'

My heart sank.

For an informer, talking privately like this in the lee of quite

320

a different situation can sometimes produce evidence that turns over the whole case. Plancina seemed all too eager for an intimate chat. On a better day I would have seized the chance.

Today I had totally lost the will to proceed. Solving mysteries was the last thing I wanted to bother with. And so, since Destiny is an awkward slut, today she had brought the evidence to me.

I managed to avoid groaning. I knew that Plancina was going to talk to me about Heliodorus or Ione. All I wanted was to wish them, and their killer, at the bottom of the Middle Sea.

If Helena had been sitting out here she would have kicked me for my lack of interest. I spent a few moments reflecting dreamily on the wonderfully curved ankle with which she would lash out – and her power to inflict a memorable bruise.

'Don't look so miserable!' Plancina commanded.

'Give it a rest! I'm heartbroken. I'm off duty tonight.'

'Might be your only chance.' She was bright all right. She knew how fickle witnesses can be.

This reminded me of a game I used to play in the army with my old friend Petronius: speculating which we liked better, bright girls who just looked stupid, or stupid ones who looked passable. On the whole neither kind had looked at either of us when we were twenty, though I used to pretend that I did all right and I reckon he had conquests I never knew about. He certainly turned into a sly reprobate later.

Shock must have plunged me into homesickness. I was off again into a reverie, now wondering what Petronius would have to say about me letting Helena get hurt like this. Petro, my loyal friend, had always agreed with the general view that Helena was far too good for me. As a matter of course he took her part against me.

I knew his views. He thought I was completely irresponsible taking a woman abroad, unless the woman was dismally ugly and I stood in line for a huge legacy if she was struck down by pirates or plague. According to what he called good old-fashioned Roman rectitude and I called blind hypocrisy, Helena should have been locked up at home with a twenty-stone eunuch as bodyguard, and only permitted to venture outside if she was going to see her mother and was accompanied by a trustworthy friend of the family (Petro himself, for example).

'Do you want to talk or not?' Plancina virtually yelled, growing indignant at my day-dreaming.

'I was always the type who liked to run away,' I muttered, fumbling the old repartee to the surface.

'Kiss and flee?'

'Then hope to get caught and kissed again.'

'You're no fun,' she complained. I had lost the knack after all. 'I don't think I'll bother.'

I sighed gently. 'Don't be like that. I'm upset. All right – what are you telling me?'

'I know who he was,' Plancina admitted in a hollow tone. 'The bastard! I know who Ione was favouring.'

I let the fire leap a few times. Some moments do need savouring.

'Were you and Ione friends?'

'Close as crumbs on a loaf.'

'I see.' This was a classic. The two girls had probably vied bitterly for menfriends, but now the survivor was going to split on the villain. She would call it loyalty to her dead friend. Really it was simple gratitude that it was Ione who had picked the wrong man. 'Why are you only telling me this now, Plancina?'

Maybe she looked abashed, or maybe she was just brazen. 'It's nice and quiet and dark. I've got an excuse to snuggle up outside your tent and look as if I'm just consoling you.'

'Very cosy!' I commented, in a gruff mood.

'Get off, Falco. You know the situation. Who wants to end up very wet and absolutely dead?'

'Not in the desert,' I carped tetchily. 'This bastard likes to drown people.'

'So what's it worth?' Plancina asked frankly.

I feigned shock: 'Is this a request to negotiate?'

'It's a request to be paid! You're an informer, aren't you? Don't you people offer cash for information?'

322

'The idea', I explained patiently, 'is that we obtain facts by our skill and cunning.' I left out theft, fraud, and bribery. 'Then in order that we can make a living, other people pay *us* for those facts.'

'But it's me that knows the facts,' she pointed out. Not the first woman I had encountered who had brilliant financial acumen even though she never went to school.

'So what facts are we discussing, Plancina?'

'Are you getting paid to find the killer?' She was persistent, this one.

'By *Chremes*? Don't be silly. He calls it a commission, but I know that louse. No. I'm doing this out of my superlative moral sense.'

'Drop dead, Falco!'

'Would you believe civic duty then?'

'I'd believe you're a nosy bastard.'

'Whatever you say, lady.'

'What a ghoul!' Plancina was fairly good-humoured with her insults. I reckoned she was intending to come clean without an argument. She would not have broached the issue otherwise.

There is a ritual in these exchanges, and we had reached the nub at last. Plancina pulled down her skirt (as far as this was possible), picked her nose, stared at her fingernails, then sat up to tell me all she knew.

LVIII

'It was one of them clowns,' she said.

I waited for more. Gradually I ceased expecting it. 'Is that your story?'

'Oh, you want the dirty details?'

'I'd like some, at any rate. Don't shock me; I'm a shy floret. But how about, which one of them it actually was?'

'Gods, you don't want much, do you?' she muttered darkly. 'You're supposed to be the informer. Can't you work it out?'

I thought she was playing me up. It was time for *me* to shock her. 'Maybe I can,' I said dourly. 'Maybe I already have.'

Plancina was staring at me. I saw a look of panic and fascination cross her face. Then she shivered. She dropped her voice abruptly, even though we had already been talking quietly. 'You mean you know?'

'You mean you don't?' I returned. A neat turn of phrase, though it meant nothing.

'Not which one,' she admitted. 'It's horrible to think about. What are you going to do?'

'Try and prove it.' She made a face, stretching the fingers of both hands suddenly. She was afraid of what she had stumbled into. 'Don't fret,' I said calmly. 'Your Uncle Marcus has jumped in piles of donkey shit before. Nobody will have to know you said anything, if that's worrying you.'

'I don't like the idea of meeting them.'

'Just think of them as men you're stringing along. I bet you can do that!' She grinned, with a flash of wickedness. I cleared my throat. 'All I need is whatever you do know. Tell me the story.'

'I never said anything because I was scared.' All her confidence was evaporating. That did not necessarily mean she had nothing useful to say. The ones to watch are those who come bursting with definite answers. 'All I really know is that Ione was having a fling with both of them.'

'Where does Afrania fit into this? I thought she was Tranio's pet?'

'Oh yes! Afrania would have been livid. Well that was why Ione was doing it; to put one over on Afrania. Ione thought she was a silly cow. And as for Grumio . . .' Plancina's flood of recollections trailed off for some reason.

'What about him? Did he have another girlfriend too?'

'No.'

'That's a short answer. Is there a long explanation?'

'He's not like the others.'

This surprised me. 'What are you saying? He really likes men? Or he doesn't know how to get on with women?' I stopped short of the more disgusting alternatives.

Plancina shrugged helplessly. 'It's hard to say. He's good company; they both are. But none of us like to get involved with Grumio.'

'Trouble?'

'Nothing like that. We all reckon he never has much time for it.'

'For what?' I asked, innocently.

'You damn well know what!'

I conceded that I knew. 'He talks about it.'

'That means nothing, Falco!' We both laughed. Then Plancina struggled to enlighten me. 'He probably is normal, but he never bothers much.'

'Too conceited?' I guessed.

'That's it.' I swear she was blushing. Some girls who give the impression they are ready for anything are strangely prudish in conversation. She made herself try to elaborate: 'If you had anything to do with him, you'd feel he would be sneering at you behind your back. Then if he did anything, he wouldn't want to enjoy it.' No good at it either, probably.

'That's interesting.' Discussing another man's impotence – or even his indifference – was outside my sphere. I remembered that the night I went to dinner with Chremes and Phrygia I had seen Plancina herself being entertained at the Twins' tent. 'You've had dealings with the clowns yourself. I saw you drinking with them both one night at Abila – '

'Drinking is all there was. I got talked into it by another girl. Phrosine has her eye on Tranio.'

'Popular fellow! So you drew the straw for Grumio?'

'Not likely! I went home. I remember what Ione used to say about him.'

'Which was?'

'If he could do it, and if he did enjoy it, nobody else got any fun.'

'Sounds as if Ione had some practice.' I asked how she had come to know such intimate details if Grumio rarely involved himself in sex.

'She liked a challenge. She went after him.'

'So what exactly was the situation there?' I recapped. 'Ione was sleeping with both Tranio and Grumio, Tranio on the side, and Grumio perhaps under protest. And were there plenty of others?'

'No one important. She'd stopped bothering with the rest. This is why I said it must be one of the clowns. She told me she had her hands full, what with trying to get at Tranio without Afrania noticing, and then having to use all her tactics to lure Grumio into anything. She said she was ready to chuck it all up, go back to the village she came from in Italy, and vamp some dumb farmer into marriage.'

'A lesson to you,' I commented. 'Don't wait too long to retire, Plancina.'

'Not in this bloody group!' she agreed. 'I haven't been any help, have I?'

'Don't think that.'

'But you still don't know.'

'I know enough, Plancina.' I knew I had to work on the clowns.

'Be careful then.'

I thought little of her warning when she gave it. I watched her leave, carrying the soup bowl she had brought me. Then, with the eerie ability the clowns had to turn up just when they were on my mind, one of them came sauntering to my tent.

326

It was Grumio. On my guard, I was ready for most things, though not for what was about to transpire. I was certainly not ready to accuse him of anything. My bets were still on Tranio anyway.

Grumio parried with a few casual questions about Helena and then asked, 'Where's Musa?' He sounded so casual I knew that it mattered.

'I've no idea.' I had forgotten about him. Maybe he was being entertained by Byrria.

'That's interesting!' exclaimed Grumio, knowingly. I had a feeling of being teased and spied upon, as if I were being set up for one of the Twins' practical jokes. Taking advantage of a man whose much-loved girlfriend had been stung by a scorpion would be just like them. I even felt anxious in case another attempt had been made on Musa's life.

Deliberately showing no further interest, I swung myself to my feet and made as if I were going in to see Helena. Grumio failed to enlighten me. I waited until he left. With a sense of unease I called Musa's name. When there was no answer, I lifted the flap on his part of our shared tent.

It was empty. Musa was not there. Nothing was there. Musa, with all his meagre property, had gone.

I had believed him to be homesick, but this was ridiculous.

I stood, unable to take in what was happening, staring at the bare ground in the empty tent. I was still there when footsteps hurried up behind me. Then Byrria brushed against me as she pushed me aside to look.

'It's true!' she exclaimed. 'Grumio just told me. There's a camel missing. And Grumio thought he saw Musa riding off back the way we came.'

'Alone? Across the desert?' He was a Nabataean. He would be safe, presumably. But it was incredible.

'He had talked about it.' I could tell the girl was unsurprised.

Now I was feeling really grim. 'What's going on, Byrria?' Whatever their strange relationship, I had had the impression that Musa might confide in her. 'I don't understand!'

'No.' Byrria's voice was quiet, less hard than usual, yet

strangely dull in tone. She seemed resigned to some dire
fatality. 'Of course you don't.'

'Byrria, I'm tired. I've had a terrible day, and my worries
about Helena are nowhere near over yet. Tell me what has
upset Musa!'

I realised now that he had been upset. I recalled his
anguished face as he beat the scorpion to death in such a
frenzy. I remembered it again later, when he came to offer
help – help I had curtly refused. He had looked withdrawn
and defeated. I was not an idiot. It was a look I didn't want to
see, but one I recognised.

'Is this because he's fond of Helena? It's natural, when we
have lived so closely as friends.'

'Wrong, Falco.' Byrria sounded bitter. 'He was *fond* of you.
He admired and hero-worshipped you. He had much deeper
feelings for Helena.'

Stubbornly I refused to accept what she was saying. 'He
didn't have to leave. He was our friend.' But I was long
accustomed to Helena Justina attracting followers. Helena's
devotees came from some strange walks of life. The very top,
too. A quiet, competent girl who listened to people, she
attracted both the vulnerable and those with taste; men liked
to think they had privately discovered her. Their next mistake
was discovering that privately she belonged to me.

As I stalled, Byrria reacted angrily: 'There was no room for
him! Don't you remember today when you were looking after
Helena? You did everything, and she wanted only you. You
know he would never have told either of you how he felt, but
he could not bear being no use to her.'

I breathed slowly. 'Don't go on.'

Finally, too late, our misunderstandings unravelled. I
wondered if Helena knew. Then I remembered the night we
had entertained Byrria. Helena would never have joined me
in teasing either Musa or Byrria if she had understood the
situation. The actress confirmed it, reading my thoughts: 'He
would have died of shame if she had ever found out. Don't tell
her.'

'I'll have to explain where he is!'

'Oh you'll do it! You're a man; you'll think up some lie.'

328

The wrath with which the girl had just spoken was typical of her contempt for all things masculine. But her earlier bitterness brought another thought to me: 'And what about you, Byrria?'

She turned away. She must have been able to hear that I had guessed. She knew I meant no harm to her. She needed to tell somebody. Unable to prevent herself, she admitted, 'Me? Well what do you think, Falco? The only man I could not have – so naturally I fell in love with him.'

My own heart ached for the girl's distress, but frankly I had far worse on my mind.

I found out that Musa had already been gone for hours. Even so, I would probably have ridden after him. But with Helena lying so ill, that was impossible.

LIX

Despite my efforts to keep the poison from entering her bloodstream, Helena soon had a high fever.

There was a small Roman garrison at Palmyra, I knew. Another we had left behind at Damascus. Either might contain somebody with medical knowledge. Even if not, the troops would have tried out the local physicians and would be able to recommend the least dangerous to consult. As an ex-soldier, and a Roman citizen, I was ready to use my influence to beg for help. Most frontier garrisons were an abusive bunch, but mentioning that Helena's father sat in the Senate should encourage the career-conscious. There was always a chance, too, that among the battered legionaries I might find some ex-British veteran I knew.

I reckoned we needed a doctor as soon as possible. At first, it had not seemed to matter which way we went; soon I wished we had turned back to Damascus. That was nearer to civilisation. Who could say what we were heading towards instead?

Helena lay helpless. Even in lucid moments she hardly knew where she was. Her arm gave her increasing pain. She desperately needed rest, not travel, but we could not stop in the wilderness. Our Palmyrene guides had adopted that annoying trait in foreigners: looking deeply sympathetic whilst in practice ignoring all my pleas for help.

We pressed on, with me having to do all the driving now that Musa had decamped. Helena never complained – quite unlike her. I was going frantic over her fever. I knew how badly her arm hurt, with a burning pain that could be caused by the cuts I had had to make, or by something worse. Every time I dressed the wound it looked more red and angry. To kill the pain I was giving her poppy juice, in melted honey drinks since I distrusted the water. Phrygia had produced some henbane to supplement my own medicine. For me, the sight of Helena so drowsy and unlike herself was the worst part. I felt she was going a long way from me. When she slept, which was most of the time, I missed not being able to talk to her properly.

People kept coming up, as if to check on us. They were kind, but it meant I could never sit and think. The conversation that stays in my mind most clearly was another involving Grumio. It was the day after the accident, in fact. He turned up again, this time in a most apologetic mood.

'I feel I let you down, Falco. Over Musa, I mean. I should have told you earlier.'

'I could do with him,' I agreed tersely.

'I saw him ride off, but hardly thought he could be leaving you permanently.'

'He was free to come or go.'

'Seems a bit odd.'

'People are.' I may have sounded grim. I was feeling drawn. After a hard day on the desert road, with no hope of reaching the oasis yet at the dire pace we were travelling, I was at a low ebb.

'Sorry, Falco. I guess you're not feeling talkative. I brought you a flagon, in case it helps.'

It was welcome. I felt obliged to invite him to stay and share the first measure with me.

We talked of this and that, of nothing in particular, and of Helena's progress or lack of it. The wine did help. It was a fairly ordinary local red. Petronius Longus, the Aventine's wine expert, would have likened it to some off-putting substance, but that was just him. This was perfectly palatable to a tired, dispirited man like me.

Recovering, I considered the flagon. It was a handy size, about right for a packed lunch if you were not intending to do any work afterwards. It had a round base covered in wickerwork, and a thin, loosely plaited carrying string.

'I saw one like this at a scene I'll not forget.'

'Where was that?' asked Grumio, disingenuously.

'Petra. Where Heliodorus was drowned.'

Naturally the clown expected me to be watching him, so

331

instead I stared into the fire as if gloomily remembering the scene. I was alert for any twitches or sudden tensions in him, but noticed none. 'These are about the most common kind you can get,' he observed.

It was true. I nodded easily. 'Oh yes. I'm not suggesting it came from the same vintner, in the same basket of shopping.' All the same, it could have done. 'There's something I've been meaning to ask you, Grumio. People have been wishing on me the idea that Heliodorus was killed because of his gambling habits.'

'You asked Tranio about it.' I was interested to hear they had conferred.

'So I did. He lost his temper,' I mentioned, now turning a calm stare on him.

Grumio cradled his chin, looking reflective. 'I wonder why that could be?' He spoke with the light twist of malice I had heard from him before. It was hardly evident – could have been an unfortunate mannerism – except that one of the times I had heard it was when he was entertaining the crowd at Gerasa by hurling a knife at me. I remembered that rather clearly.

I stayed calm. 'The obvious reason is he had something to hide.'

'Seems a bit *too* obvious, though?' He made it sound like a question I should have thought of for myself.

'There has to be some explanation.'

'Maybe he was afraid you had found out something that looked bad for him.'

'That's a good thought!' I replied brightly, as if I had been incapable of it myself. We were sparring here, each pretending to be simple. Then I let a growl slink back into my voice. 'So tell me about you and your tentmate playing dice with the playwright, Grumio!'

He knew there was no point denying it. 'Gambling's not a crime, is it?'

'Nor is having a gambling debt.'

'What debt? Playing was just a lark from time to time. We soon learned not to bet seriously.'

'He was good?'

'Oh yes.' There was no hint that Heliodorus might have cheated. Sometimes I wonder how gambling sharks get away with it – and then I talk to an innocent minnow, and realise.

Tranio might know that Heliodorus had weighted his dice; I had wondered about that when I talked to him. So now I considered the interesting prospect of Tranio perhaps keeping this information from his so-called friend. Just what *was* the relationship between these two? Allies covering up for each other? Or a pair of jealous rivals?

'So what's the big secret? I know there must be one,' I urged him, putting on my frank, successful-informer air. 'What's Tranio's beef?'

'Nothing big, and not a secret.' Not now, anyway; his friendly tentmate was about to land him in it without compunction. 'What he was probably loath to tell you was that once, when he and I had been having an argument, he played with Heliodorus while I was off on my own – '

'With a girl?' I too could be disingenuous.

'Where else?' After my chat with Plancina, I didn't believe it. 'Anyway, they were in our tent. Tranio needed a forfeit and placed something that wasn't his, but mine.'

'Valuable?'

'Not at all. But as I felt like having a wrangle I told him he had to get it back from the scribe. Then, you know Heliodorus – '

'Actually, no.'

'Oh well, his reaction was typical. The minute he thought he had something important he decided to keep it and taunt Tranio. It rather suited me to keep our clever friend on tenterhooks. So I let on that I was mad about it. Tranio went spare trying to put things right, while I hid a smile and got my own back watching him.' One thing for Grumio; he possessed the full quota of the comedian's natural streak of cruelty. By contrast, I really could imagine Tranio taking the blame and becoming distraught.

'Maybe you should let him off now, if he's sensitive! What was the pledge, Grumio?'

'Nothing important.'

'Heliodorus must have believed it was.' So must Tranio.

'Heliodorus was so dedicated to torturing people, he lost

333

touch with reality. It was a ring,' Grumio told me, saying it with a slight shrug. 'Just a ring.'

His apparent indifference convinced me he was lying. Why should he do that? Perhaps because he didn't want me to know what the pledge really was . . .

'Precious stone?'

'Oh no! Come on, Falco. I had it off my grandfather! It was only a trinket. The stone was dark blue. I used to pretend it was lapis, but I doubt if it was even sodalite.'

'Was it found after the playwright died?'

'No. The bastard had probably sold it.'

'Have you checked with Chremes and Phrygia?' I insisted helpfully. 'They went through the playwright's stuff, you know. In fact we discussed it and I'm sure I remember them owning up quite freely that they had found a ring.'

'Not mine.' I thought I detected just a faint trace of irritation in young Grumio now. 'Must have been one of his own.'

'Or Congrio might have it –'

'He hasn't.' Yet according to Congrio, the clowns had never asked him properly about what they were looking for.

'Tell me, why was Tranio afraid to tell me about this missing pledge?' I asked gently.

'Isn't that obvious?' A lot of things were obvious, according to Grumio. He looked remarkably pleased with himself as he landed Tranio in it. 'He's never been in trouble, certainly not connected with a murder. He overreacts. The poor idiot thinks everyone knows he had a row with Heliodorus, and that it looks bad for him.'

'It looks far worse that he hid the fact.' I saw Grumio's eyebrows shoot up in a surprised expression, as if that thought had not struck him. Somehow I reckoned it must have done. Drily, I added, 'Nice of you to tell me!'

'Why not?' Grumio smiled. 'Tranio didn't kill Heliodorus.'

'You say that as if you know who did.'

'I can make a good guess now!' He managed to sound as if he were chiding me with negligence for not guessing myself.

'And who would that be?'

That was when he hit me out of the blue: 'Now that he's

334

skipped so suddenly,' suggested Grumio, 'I should think that the best bet is your so-called interpreter!'

I was laughing. 'I really don't believe I heard that! *Musa?*'

'Oh, he really took you in, did he?' The clown's voice was cold. If young Musa had still been here, even innocent, I reckon he would have panicked.

'Not at all. You'd better tell me your reasoning.'

Grumio then went through his argument like a magician consenting to explain some sleight of hand. His voice was level and considered. As he spoke, I could almost hear myself giving this as evidence before a criminal judge. 'Everyone in the company had an alibi for the time Heliodorus was killed. So maybe, unknown to anyone, he had an outside contact at Petra. Maybe he had an appointment with somebody local that day. You say you found Musa in the close vicinity; Musa must have been the man you had followed from the High Place. As for the rest – it all follows.'

'Tell me!' I croaked in amazement.

'Simple. Musa then killed Ione because she must have known that Heliodorus had some private connection in Petra. She had slept with him; he could have said. Again, the rest of us all have alibis, but wasn't Musa in Gerasa on his own that night for hours?' Chilled, I remembered that indeed I had left him at the Temple of Dionysus while I went off to make enquiries about Thalia's organist. I didn't believe he had been to the Maiuma pools in my absence – but nor could I prove that he had not.

With Musa no longer here, I could never ask him about it either.

'And how do you explain Bostra, Grumio? Musa being nearly drowned himself?'

'Simple. When you brought him into the company, some of us thought him a suspicious character. To deflect our suspicion, he took a chance at Bostra, jumped into the reservoir deliberately, then made up a wild claim that someone shoved him in.'

'Not the only wild claim hereabouts!'

I said it, even though I had the inevitable feeling that all this

335

could be true. When someone throws such an unlikely story at you with such passionate conviction, they can overturn your common sense. I felt like a fool, a bungling amateur who had failed to consider something right under my nose, something that ought to have been routine.

'This is an amazing thought, Grumio. According to you, I've spent all this time and effort looking for the killer when the plain fact is I brought him with me all along?'

'You're the expert, Falco.'

'Apparently not . . . What's your explanation for the scam?'

'Who knows? My guess is Heliodorus was some sort of political agent. He must have upset the Nabataeans. Musa is their hit man for unwelcome spies – '

Once again I laughed, this time rather bitterly. It sounded weirdly plausible.

Normally I can resist a clever distraction. Since there certainly was one political agent amongst us, and he was indeed now acting as a playwright, Grumio's solemn tale had a lurid appeal. I really could envisage a scenario in which Anacrites had sent more than one disguised menial into Petra – both me and Heliodorus – and The Brother had schemed to deal with each of us in turn, using Musa. Helena had told me Musa was marked for higher things. Maybe all the time I had been patronising his youth and innocence, he was a really competent executioner. Maybe all those messages to his 'sister' deposited at Nabataean temples were coded reports to his master. And maybe the 'letter from Shullay' he kept hoping to receive would not have contained a description of the murderer, but instructions for disposing of me . . .

Or rather, maybe I should lie down quietly, with sliced cucumber cooling my forehead, until I got over this lunacy.

Grumio rose to his feet with a demure smile. 'I seem to have given you a lot to think about! Pass on my regards to Helena.' I managed a wry nod of the head, and let him go.

The conversation had been devoid of clowning. Yet I was still left with the sinking sensation that somehow the joke was on me.

Very neat.

Almost, as the grim jokester Grumio himself would have said, too obvious to be true.

LX

I was dismal now. It felt like a nightmare. Everything appeared close to reality, yet was hugely distorted.

I went in to see Helena. She was awake, but flushed and feverish. I could tell by looking at her that unless I could do something, we were in serious trouble. I knew she could see I had problems I wanted to talk about, but she made no attempt to ask. That in itself was a depressing sign.

In this mood, I was hardly expecting what happened next.

We heard a commotion. The Palmyrenes were all exclaiming and shouting. It did not sound as though raiders had set upon us, but my worst fears leapt. I rushed out of the tent. Everyone else was running, all in the same direction. I felt for my knife, then left it down my boot so I could run faster.

At the roadside an excited group had clustered around a particular camel, a new arrival whose dust was still creating a haze above the road. I could see the beast was white, or what they call white in a camel. The trappings looked brighter than usual and more lavishly fringed. When the crowd suddenly spilled outwards so I had a clearer view, even to my untutored eye this was a fine creature. A racing camel, plainly. The owner must be a local chief, some rich nomad who had made several fortunes from myrrh.

I was losing interest and about to turn back when somebody yelled my name. Men in the crowd gesticulated to some unseen person who was kneeling at the camel's feet. Hoping this might be Musa returning, I walked up closer. People fell back to let me through, jostling close behind again as they tried to see what was happening. With bruised heels and a bad temper I forced my way to the front.

On the ground beside the splendid camel, a figure wrapped in desert robes was searching in a small roll of baggage. Whoever it was stood up and turned to me. It was definitely not Musa.

337

The elaborate head-dress was pushed back from a startling face. Vivid antimony eye paint flashed while earrings as big as the palm of my hand rattled out a joyous carillon. All the Palmyrenes gasped, awestruck. They dropped back hastily.

It was a woman, for one thing. Women do not normally ride the desert roads alone. This one would go anywhere she wanted. She was noticeably taller than any of them, and spectacularly built. I knew she must have chosen her own camel, with expertise and taste. Then she had cheerfully raced across Syria unaccompanied. If anyone had attacked her, she would have dealt with them; besides, her bodyguard was wriggling energetically in a large bag she wore slung across a bosom that meant business.

When she saw me, she let out a roar of derision, before brandishing a little iron pot. 'Falco, you miserable dumb-head! I want to see that sick girl of yours – but first come here and say a nice hello!'

'Hello Jason,' I responded obediently, as Thalia's python finally forced his head out of his travelling bag and looked around for somebody meek whom he could terrorise.

LXI

There were a lot of frightened men at this gathering, and not all of them were worried about the python.

Thalia shoved Jason unceremoniously back into his bag, then hung it around her camel's neck. With one bejewelled finger she stabbed towards the bag. Slowly and clearly (and unnecessarily), she addressed the assembled nomads: 'Any man who puts a hand on the camel gets seen off by the snake!'

This hardly squared with what she had always assured me about Jason's lovable nature. Useful, however. I could see the Palmyrenes all inclined to my own nervous view of him.

'That's a gorgeous camel,' I said admiringly. 'With a gorgeous rider whom I never expected to meet in the middle of the desert.' It seemed right, however. Somehow I felt more cheerful already. 'How in the name of the gods do you come to be here, Thalia?'

'Looking for you, darling!' she promised feelingly. For once I felt able to take it.

'How did you find me?'

'Damascus is plastered with posters with your name on them. After a few days of desperately dancing for the rent, I spotted one.' That's the trouble with wall posters: easy to write, but nobody ever rubs them out. Probably in twenty years' time people would still be calling at Herod's Theatre trying to touch a man called Falco for cash. 'The theatre gateman told me you'd gone on to Palmyra. Good excuse to get a camel. Isn't he a cracker? If I can get another and race them, he'll wow those front-seat freaks in Rome.'

'Where did you learn to race a camel?'

'Anyone who can do a twirl with a python can manage a ride, Falco!' Innuendo came swimming back with every stride we took. 'How's the poor girlie? Scorpion, wasn't it? As if one nasty creature with a wicked tail on him is not enough for her . . .'

339

I hardly dared ask, but brought out the question: 'How do you know about it?'

'Met that strange fellow – your gloomy priest.'

'Musa?'

'Riding towards me like a death's head in a cloud of dust. I asked if he'd seen you. He told me everything.'

I gave her a sharp look. '*Everything*?'

Thalia grinned. 'Enough!'

'What have you done with him?'

'What I do with them all.'

'The poor lad! Bit tender for you, isn't he?'

'They all are by my standards! I'm still holding out for you, Falco.'

Ignoring this dangerous offer, I managed to extract more details. Thalia had decided that looking for Sophrona was a mission I might not manage. She had taken a whim to come east herself. After all, Syria was a good market for exotic animals; before the racing camel she had already bought a lion cub and several Indian parrots, not to mention a dangerous new snake. She had been earning her way by displays of her famous dance with the big python, Zeno, when she noticed my posters. 'So here I am, Falco, large as life, and twice as exciting!'

'At last. My chance to catch your act!'

'My act is not for faint hearts!'

'All right, I'll skulk out the back and mind Jason. So where's the snake you dance with?' I had never even seen this legendary reptile.

'The big fellow? Following on slowly. Zeno doesn't like disturbance. Jason's more versatile. Besides, when I tell him he's going to see you, he comes over all silly – '

We reached my tent, thank Jupiter.

At the sight of Helena I heard Thalia suck in her breath. 'I've brought you a present, sweetie, but don't get too excited; it's not a new man.' Thalia produced the little iron pot again. 'Small but incredibly powerful – '

'As the altar boy promised!' quipped Helena, perking up. She must have been reading her scroll of rude stories again.

Thalia had already lowered herself to one mighty knee and

340

was unbandaging Helena's wounded arm as gently as if she were tending one of her own sick animals. 'Giblets! Some slapdash butcher made a mess with his cleaver here, sweetheart!'

'He did his best,' Helena murmured loyally.

'To mangle you!'

'Lay off, Thalia!' I protested. 'There's no need to make me out to be the sort of thug who'd knife his girl. Anyway, what's in your magic jar?' I felt obliged to show some caution before my lass was anointed with a strange medicament.

'Mithridatium.'

'Have I heard of that?'

'Have you heard of gold and frankincense? Compared with this they're as cheap as cushion dust. Falco, this potion contains thirty-three ingredients, each one expensive enough to bankrupt Croesus. It's an antidote for everything from snakebites to splitting fingernails.'

'Sounds good,' I conceded.

'It had better be,' growled Thalia, unscrewing the lid with relish, as if it were a potent aphrodisiac. 'I'll spread it all over your lady first – then I'll tell you what you owe me.'

I declared that if mithridatium would help Helena, Thalia could smooth on the stuff an inch thick with a mortar trowel.

'Listen to it!' marvelled Thalia confidentially to her patient. 'Isn't he ridiculous – and don't you just love his lies!'

Helena, who had always found that her spirits rose with any chance of mocking me, was already chortling healthily.

When we drove on towards Palmyra I had Thalia alongside like a spectacular outrider, galloping away in wild loops from time to time to exercise the racing camel. Jason enjoyed a more leisurely journey in a basket in the back of my cart. The Syrian heat had proved almost too much for him. He lay virtually inert, and whenever we could spare any water he had to be bathed.

'My python's not the only reptile in your group,' Thalia muttered furtively. 'I see you've got that know-all comic Tranio!'

'Do you know him?'

'I've met him. Entertaining is a small world when you've been doing it as long as me, and in some funny places too. Tranio used to appear at the Vatican Circus. Quite witty, but thinks far too much of himself.'

'He does a good tug of war. Know his partner?'

'The one with the hair like a pie dish and the sneaky eyes?'

'Grumio.'

'Never seen him before. But that's not true of everybody here.'

'Why, who else do you know?'

'Not saying,' grinned Thalia. 'It's been a few years. Let's wait and see if I'm recognised.'

I was struck by an intriguing possibility.

Thalia's thrilling hints were still engaging Helena and me when our long ride reached its end. We had been driving at night, but dawn had now broken. With the stars long gone and the sun strengthening, our party was weary and longing to break the journey. The road had grown more winding, twisting upwards through more hilly country. The caravan trail finally emerged on to a level plain. We must now be at midpoint between the fertile coast far away on the Mediterranean and the even more remote reaches of the River Euphrates.

Low ranges of mountains ran to the north and behind us, serrated by long dry wadis. Ahead, disappearing into infinity, stretched flat tawny desert covered with rocky scree. To our left, in a stony valley, stood square towers that we later learned were multiple tombs for wealthy families. These kept their lonely vigil beside an ancient track overlooked by the sheltering hills. On the bare slopes, a shepherd on a donkey was herding a flock of black-faced sheep. Closer to, we began to perceive a shimmer of green. We sensed expectation among our nomad guides. I called to Helena. As we approached, the effect was magical. The haze rapidly acquired solidity. The moisture that rose off the saltpans and lakes quickly resolved into fields surrounding large swathes of date-palms and olive and pomegranate trees.

At the heart of the huge oasis, beside an energetic spring

with supposedly therapeutic waters (like Thalia's dance, not for the faint-hearted), stood the famous old nomad village of Tadmor, once a mere camp in the wilderness, but now the fast-growing Romanised city of Palmyra.

LXII

If I say that in Palmyra the revenue officers take social precedence over members of the local government assembly, you will see their preoccupations. A welcoming city, in fact one that welcomed its visitors with a tariff of taxes on goods entering its territory, continued the happy greeting by relieving them of some hefty rates for watering their caravans, and completed the process by exacting a little something for the treasury for every camel, donkey, cart, container or slave that they wished to take back out of the city when they left. What with the salt tax and the prostitution tax, staying there was clear-cut too: the very staples of life were nobbled.

The Emperor Vespasian, a tax collector's grandson, was running Palmyra with a light hand. Vespasian liked to squeeze the fiscal sponge, but his treasury officials had grasped that they had little to teach the efficient Palmyrenes. Nowhere I had ever visited was so concerned to strip all comers of their spending money, or so adept at doing it.

Even so, long-distance traders were coming here with caravans the size of armies. Palmyra sat between Parthia in the east and Rome in the west, a semi-independent buffer zone that existed to enable commerce. Tariffs aside, the atmosphere *was* a pleasant one.

Historically Greek and governed now by Rome, it was packed with Aramaic and Arabian tribesmen who had only recently been nomads, yet it still remembered periods of Parthian rule and looked to the East for much of its character. The result was a mixed culture unlike anywhere else. Their public inscriptions were carved in Greek and a strange script of their own. There were a few massive limestone buildings, constructed on Syrian plans with Roman money by Greek craftsmen. Around these monuments were spread quite large suburbs of blank-walled mud-brick houses through which meandered narrow dirt lanes. The oasis still had the air of a

344

massive native village, but with signs that sudden grandiosity was liable to break out all over the place.

For one thing, the people were unashamedly wealthy and enjoyed showing off. Nothing had prepared us for the brightness of the linens and silks with which every Palmyrene of any standing was adorned. The rich weaves of their cloth were unlike any produced further west. They liked stripes, but never in plain bands of colour. Their materials were astonishing feasts of elaborate brocaded patterns, studded with flowers or other dainty emblems. And the threads used for these intricate weaves were dyed in spectacular varieties of purples, blues, greens and reds. The colours were deep and warm. The hues in the streets were a dramatic contrast to any public scene in Rome, which would be a monochrome of scarcely modulated grades of white, broken only by the vibrant purple bands that designate high status.

The men here would have looked effeminate in Rome. It took some getting used to. They all wore tunics laden with splendidly embroidered braid; beneath were swathed Persian trousers, again richly hemmed. Most men wore straight-sided, flat-topped hats. Female dress consisted of conventional long gowns, covered by cloaks caught on the left shoulder by a heavy brooch. Veils were routinely worn by all women except slaves and prostitutes. The veil, ostensibly protecting the ownership of a strict father or husband, fell from a tiara or turban, and was then left loose as a frame to the face, allowing the owner to manipulate its folds attractively with one graceful hand. What could be glimpsed behind the pretence of modesty were dark curls, chubby chins, huge eyes and strong-willed mouths. The women were broad in the beam and all wore as many necklaces, bangles, rings and hair jewels as they could cram on; no wench with less than six neck-chains could be considered worth talking to. Getting them to talk might be difficult, however, due to the looming presence of jealous menfolk and the fact they all went about with dogged chaperones.

Philocrates did very quickly manage to make the acquaintance of a creature in lavish pleats of azure silk, crushed under eight or nine gold necklaces from which dangled an array of pendants set with pearls and polished glass. Her arms were virtually armoured with metal bracelets. We watched her peep at him entrancingly from behind her veil, only one lovely eye revealing itself. Maybe she was winking. Shortly afterwards we were watching *him* being chased down the street by her relatives.

There was supposed to be a theatre, so while Chremes tried to find it and find out whether rude Roman vagabonds like us could appear there, I set off to discover the missing girl, Sophrona. I had asked Thalia whether she wanted to come with me.

'No. You go and make a fool of yourself first, then we'll put our heads together once you know what the situation is.'

'That's good. I had thought that with you in Syria I was going to lose my fee.'

'You can't lose what you never earned, Falco. The fee is for getting her back to Rome. Don't waste your ink on an invoice until she's off the boat at Ostia!'

'Trust me.' I smiled.

Helena laughed. I touched her forehead, which at long last was cooler. She was feeling much better. I could tell that when she gaily explained to Thalia, 'It's sweet really. Poor Marcus, he likes to convince himself he has a way with girls.'

I leered like a man who should never be allowed out alone; then, feeling fonder than ever of Helena, I set off into town.

I seemed to remember hearing that this Sophrona was a beauteous bit of stuff.

LXIII

It had seemed best to deal with Thalia's task quickly, before Chremes called upon my services as his luckless author. Besides, I was happy to pack in some sightseeing.

If you visit Palmyra, go in Spring. Apart from the cooler weather, April is when they hold the famous processions at the great Temple of Bel. In any other month you get sick of people telling you how wonderful the festival is, with its minstrels, its palanquins of deities, and its lengthy processions of garlanded animals. Not to mention the subsequent blood-letting. Or the breakdown of social order that inevitably follows serious religion. The festival (to be regarded askance by a sober Roman, though it sounded good fun to me) must have been taking place about the time Helena and I were planning our trip. It offers the only chance of seeing open the mighty portals that hold back the public from the triad in the inner sanctuary, so if you like gaping at gods or at fabulous stonework, April is a must. Even then it's a slim chance, due to the secrecy of the priests and the vast size of the crowds.

In August you can only wander around the immense courtyard like a water flea lost in Lake Volusinus, being told by everyone what a treat you missed earlier. This I did myself. I sauntered between the altar and the lustral basin, mighty examples of their kind, then stared sadly at the closed doors in the immensely high and opulently decorated entrance porch. (Carved monolithic beams and stepped merlons, in case you wanted to know.) I had been told that the inner sanctum was an architectural wonder. Not much use for adding tone to your memoirs if it's shut.

The other reason for not going to Palmyra in August is the unbearable heat and brightness. I had walked all the way across town from our camp outside the Damascus Gate. I strolled from the Temple of Allath – a severe goddess

347

guarded by a ten-foot-high lion with a jolly countenance, who sheltered a lithe gazelle – to the far end of town where the Temple of Bel housed the Lord of the Universe himself, plus two colleagues, a moon-god and a sun-god, named Aglibol and Yarhibol. The profusion of deities honoured in this city made the twelve gods of Roman Olympus look a meagre picnic party. As most of the temples in Syria are surrounded by huge open-air courtyards that act as suntraps, each of Palmyra's hundreds of divinities was baking, even inside his darkly curtained-off adyton. However, they were not as hot as the poor fools like me who had risked marching about the city streets.

The sulphurous springs were low in their cistern, the gardens surrounding them reduced to sticks and struggling succulents. The odour of hot therapeutic steam was no match for the pervading wafts of a city whose major imports were heady perfume oils. Brilliant sunlight zinged off the dirt roads, lightly poached the piles of camel dung, then wrapped its warmth around thousands of alabaster jars and goatskin bottles. The mingling fragrances of heated Oriental balms and fine oils choked my lungs, seeped into my pores and hung about the crumples of my robes.

I was reeling. My eyes had already been dazzled by tottering piles of bronze plaques and statues, endless bales of silks and muslins, the deep shine of jade and the dark green glimmer of Eastern pottery. Ivory the size of forest logs was piled haphazardly alongside stalls selling fats or dried meat and fish. Tethered cattle awaited buyers, bellowing at the merchants selling multicoloured heaps of spice and henna. Jewellers weighed out pearls in little metal scales as casually as Roman sweetsellers toss handfuls of pistachio nuts into wrapping cones of remaindered songs. Minstrels, tapping hand-drums, intoned poetry in languages and measures I could not begin to comprehend.

Palmyra is a mighty emporium; it depends on helping visitors secure contracts. In the packed streets even the busiest traders were prepared to stop and hear about my quest. We could understand each other's Greek, just about. Most tried to point me where I should be going. Once I had been marked as a man with a mission, they insisted on helping. Small boys were sent running to ask other people if they knew the address I was looking for. Old fellows bent double over knobby sticks tottered up twisting lanes with me to check possible houses. I noticed that half the population had terrible teeth, and there was a bad epidemic of deformed arms. Maybe the hot springs were not all that medicinal; maybe the sulphuric spring water even caused these deformities.

Eventually, in the centre of town, I found the home of a well-to-do Palmyrene who was a friend of Habib, the man I sought. It was a large villa, constructed with no windows on the outside walls. Entering through a door with an exuberantly carved lintel, I found a cool, rather dark courtyard with Corinthian columns surrounding a private well. A dark-skinned slave, polite, but firm, made me wait in the courtyard while he consulted within several times.

My story was that I had come from Rome (no point pretending otherwise) as a connection of the girl's. Since I hoped I looked fairly respectable, I assumed her boyfriend's parents would be eager to check any faint possibility that their prodigal Khaleed had fallen for someone acceptable. Apparently not: despite my best efforts I failed to acquire an interview. Neither the Palmyrene who owned the house nor his guest Habib appeared in person. No attempt was made to deny that Habib was staying there, however. I was informed that he and his wife were now planning to return to Damascus, taking their son. That meant Khaleed currently lived here too, probably under duress. The fate of his musical pick-up remained unclear. When I mentioned Sophrona, the slave only sneered and said she was not there.

Knowing that I was in the right place, I did what I could, then stayed calm. Most of an informer's work consists of keeping your nerve. My insistent efforts would have caused a commotion. Sooner or later young Khaleed would hear of my visit and wonder what was up. I guessed that even if he had been gated by his parents he would try to contact his lady love.

I waited in the street. As I expected, within half an hour a youth shot outside, glancing back furtively. Once he was sure nobody from the house was following, he set off fast.

He was a short, thickset lad of about twenty. He had a square face with heavy, fly-away eyebrows; they almost met in the centre of his brow, where a tuft of hair grew like a small dark diamond. He had been in Palmyra long enough to be experimenting with Parthian trousers, but he wore them under a sober Western tunic in Syrian stripes and without embroidery. He looked athletic and good-humoured, though not very bright. Frankly, he was not my idea of a hero to run off with – but I was not a daft young girl hankering for a foreign admirer to lure her away from a job she was lucky to have.

I knew Sophrona was daft; Thalia had told me.

The young man kept up a rapid pace. Luckily he was heading west, towards the area where my own party was staying, so I was not too dispirited. I was starting to feel exhausted, though. I wished I had borrowed a mule. Young love may not notice draining heat, but I was thirty-two and ready for a long lie-down in the shade of a date-palm. I wanted a good rest and a drink, after which I might manage to interest myself in a bit of fun with Helena, if she stroked my brow temptingly enough first. Chasing this sturdy playboy soon lost its appeal.

The increasing nearness of my tent beckoned. I was ready to peel off from the breakneck gallop. A fast sprint through the Thirteenth District in Rome is bad enough in August, but at least there I know where the wineshops and public latrines are. This was torture. Neither refreshment nor relief was available. And all in the cause of music – my least favourite performing art.

Eventually Khaleed glanced back over his shoulder, failed to spot me, then picked up even more speed. Turning off the main track, he dashed down a twisting lane between modest little houses where chickens were running freely along with the odd skinny goat. He plunged inside one of the houses. I waited long enough for the youngsters to start panicking, then I dived after him.

Unlike Habib's friend's villa, there was a simple

rectangular doorway in the mud-brick wall. Beyond lay a tiny courtyard: no peristyle columns; no well. There was bare earth. A stool had been kicked over in one corner. Wool rugs hung over an upper balcony. The rugs looked clean, but I sensed the dull odours of poverty.

I followed the anxious voices. Bursting in on the couple, I found Khaleed looking tear-stained and his girl pale but definitely stubborn. They stared at me. I smiled at them. The young man beat his brow and looked helpless while the girl shrieked unpleasantly.

The usual scenario, in my experience.

'So you're Sophrona!' She was not my type. Just as well; she was not my sweetheart.

'Go away!' she screamed. She must have deduced I had not come all this way to announce an unexpected legacy.

She was very tall, taller even than Helena, who sweeps a stately course. Her figure was more scrawny than I had been led to expect, reminding me vaguely of somebody – but certainly not Helena. Sophrona was dark, with straight hair tied fairly simply. She had enormous eyes. They were a mellow brown with immensely long lashes, and could be described as beautiful if you were not too fussy about eyes revealing intelligence. She knew they were lovely, and spent a lot of time gazing up sideways; somebody must once have admired the effect. It failed with me. It made me want to chop up her chin and tell her to stop the deplorable pose. There was no point. No one would ever train her out of it; the habit was too ingrained. Sophrona intended to be pictured one day on her tombstone with this irritating expression, like a fawn with a head cold and a bad case of jitters.

She was about twenty, disreputably unveiled. On her long frame she wore a blue dress, together with ridiculous sandals and too much soppy jewellery (all tiny dangly animals and rings of twisted silver wire worn right on her knuckles). This stuff would be fine on a child of thirteen; Sophrona should have grown up by now. She did not need to grow up; she had the rich man's son just where she wanted him. Playing the kitten had achieved it, so she was sticking with what she knew.

'Never you mind who she is!' cried Khaleed, with spirit. I groaned inwardly. I hate a lad with spirit when he has his arm around a girl I'm intending to abduct from him. If he was already trying to defend her from a stranger whose motives might be perfectly harmless, then prying her free once I had made the situation clear posed even worse problems. 'Who are you?'

'Didius Falco. Friend of the family.' They were complete amateurs; they did not even think of asking me which family. 'I see you're in love,' I told them pessimistically. They both nodded with a defiance that would have been charming, if it had not been so inconvenient. 'I believe I know some of your history.' I had been called in to end unsuitable matches before, so I came prepared with a winning approach. 'Would you mind telling the story, though?'

Like all youngsters with no sense of moral duty, they were proud of themselves. It poured out: how they had met at Thalia's menagerie when Habib had visited Rome, accompanied for educational purposes by his adolescent boy. Khaleed had been cool at first, and obediently went home to Syria with Papa. Then Sophrona had thrown up everything to follow him; boys from rich families appear so romantic. Somehow she made it to Damascus, neither raped nor drowned on the journey. Impressed by her devotion, Khaleed had happily entered into a secret liaison. When his parents found out, the pair ran off here together. Spotted and recognised by his father's friend, Khaleed had been extracted from their love nest and was now about to be dragged home to Damascus, where a suitable bride would be found for him fast.

'Oh how sad!' I wondered whether to bop Khaleed on the head, swing Sophrona over my shoulder, and make off with her. A neat trick, if you can pull it – which I had been known to do with shorter women, on my home territory, when the weather was cooler. I decided against playing the man of action here. That left me to use the more sophisticated skills of a Roman informer: blatant lies.

'I understand your problem, and I sympathise. I think I may be able to help you . . .' The babes fell for it eagerly. I was

352

accepted as the classic clever trickster without needing any alibi for or explanation of my role in Palmyra. I could have been the worst pimp in Corinth, or a foreman recruiting forced labour for a Spanish copper mine. I began to understand why slave markets and brothels are always so full.

I scrounged in my purse for some of the tokens we used when we gave away free seats. I told Khaleed to look out for wall posters advertising a performance by Chremes and company; then to bring his parents as a filial treat. Sophrona was to attend the theatre on the same night.

'What are you going to do for us?'

'Well, it's obvious what you need. Get you married, of course.'

The wild promise could prove a mistake. Thalia would be furious. Even if I could achieve it – most unlikely – I knew Thalia had no intention of seeing her expensively trained product yoked to a brainless boy somewhere at the end of the Empire. Thalia dreamed only of providing Rome with high-class entertainment – entertainment she herself both owned and controlled.

You have to do your best. I needed to gather all the parties together somewhere. On the spur of the moment it seemed the only way to ensure everyone came.

If I could have told them just what kind of night out at the theatre it was going to be, there would have been no doubt they would turn up.

Free tickets wouldn't have been necessary either.

LXIV

It was so late when I returned to camp that Helena and Thalia had despaired of me and were already eating. Chremes and Phrygia happened to be there too. Since they had dropped in casually, the manager and his wife were holding back from tucking in, though I knew Helena would have asked them to help themselves. To spare them the embarrassment of wanting more than they liked to take, I cleaned up all the food bowls myself. I used a scrap of sesame bread to load all the remains into one pot of cucumber relish, which I then kept as my own bowl. Helena gave me a snooty look. Pretending to think her still hungry, I lifted a stuffed vine leaf from my laden dish and set it on a plate for her. 'Excuse fingers.'

'I'm excusing more than that!' she said. She ate the vine leaf, though.

'You have a crumb on your chin,' I told her with mock severity.

'You've a sesame seed on your lip.'

'You've a pimple on the end of your nose – '

'Oh shut up, Marcus!'

The pimple story was untrue. Her skin was pale, but clear and healthy. I was just happy to see Helena with her fever gone, looking well enough to be teased.

'Good day out?' queried Thalia. She had finished her dinner before I arrived; for a big woman she ate sparingly. More of Thalia consisted of pure muscle and sinew than I liked to contemplate.

'Good enough. I found your turtledoves.'

'What's the verdict?'

'She's as exciting as a used floorcloth. He has the brain of a roof truss.'

'Well suited!' quipped Helena. She was surreptitiously fingering her nose, checking on my pimple joke.

'It will be Sophrona who is holding them together.' I could

354

see Thalia thinking that if this were the case, she only had to prise Sophrona off, and her troubles were over.

I reckoned Sophrona would be difficult to loosen from her prey. 'She really means to have the rich boy. I've promised to get them married.' Best to own up, and get the storm over as soon as possible.

A lively commotion ensued amongst the women of my party, enabling me to finish my dinner in peace while they enjoyed themselves disparaging me. Helena and Thalia were both sensible, however. Their indignation cooled rapidly.

'He's right. Yoke them together – '

'– And it will never last!'

If it did last, they would have outwitted us. But evidently I was not the only person here who felt so cynical about marriage that the happy ending was ruled out.

Since one person present was the person I intended to marry as soon as I could persuade her to sign a contract, this was worrying.

Chremes and Phrygia had watched our domestic fracas with a distant air. It struck me they might have come with news of our next performance. If it needed two of them to tell me about the play, that boded harder work than I wanted at this stage of our tour. Since Palmyra was likely to be the end of our association, I had rather hoped for an easier time, zonking the public with some little number I had long ago revised, while I relaxed around the oasis. Even perhaps laying before the punters Helena's perfect modern rendition of *The Birds*. Its neo-Babylonian flamboyance ought to appeal to the Palmyrenes in their embroidered hats and trousers. (I was sounding like some old sham of a critic; definitely time to resign my post!)

With Chremes and Phrygia remaining so silent, it was Helena who brightly introduced the subject of booking a theatre.

'Yes, I fixed something up.' A hint of wariness in Chremes' tone warned me this might not be good news.

'That's good,' I encouraged.

'I hope you think so . . .' His tone was vague. Immediately I began to suspect I would not agree with him. 'There is a little problem – '

'He means a complete disaster,' Phrygia clarified. A blunt woman. I noticed Thalia regarding her sardonically.

'No, no!' Chremes was blustering. 'The fact is, we can't get the civic theatre. Actually, it's not up to our usual standards in any case – '

'Steady on,' I said sombrely. 'Apart from Damascus, we've mainly been playing at holes in the ground with a few wooden benches. This must be pretty rough!'

'Oh I think they have plans to build something better, Falco!'

'Everywhere in Syria has plans!' I retorted. 'In twenty or thirty years' time this province will be a theatrical company's dream of sipping ambrosia on Mount Olympus. One day they'll have perfect acoustics, majestic stage architecture, and marble everywhere. Unluckily, we cannot wait that long!'

'Well, it's typical!' Chremes gave in. He seemed even more despondent than me tonight and set off on a catalogue of miseries: 'We have the same situation everywhere – even in Rome. The performing arts are in a steep decline. My company has tried to raise standards, but the fact is that legitimate live theatre will soon not exist. We'll be lucky if plays are performed as readings by bunches of amateurs sitting round on folding stools. All people want to pay money for nowadays are mimes and musicals. For a full house you have to give them nude women, live animals, and men sacrificed on stage. The only play that is guaranteed success is bloody *Laureolus*.'

Laureolus is that rubbish about the brigand, the one where the villain is crucified in the final act – traditionally a way of creating free space in the local jail by dispatching a real criminal.

Helena intervened: 'What's wrong, Chremes? You normally look on the bright side.'

'Time to face facts.'

'It was time to face facts twenty years ago.' Phrygia was even more gloomy than her hated spouse.

'Why can you not get the theatre?' Helena persisted.

356

Chremes sighed heavily. 'The Palmyrenes are not interested. They use the theatre for public meetings. That's what they *say* anyway; I don't believe it. Either they don't enjoy entertainment or they don't fancy what we're offering. Being rich is no guarantee of culture. These people are just shepherds and cameleers dressed up in lush brocade. Alexander was supposed to have come here, but he must have thought better of it and passed them without stopping. They have no Hellenic heritage. Offering a Palmyrene town councillor the chance to see select Greek or Latin comedies is like feeding roast peacock to a stone.'

'So what now?' I asked when the tirade finally ended. 'Are we all trooping back across the desert to Damascus without speaking a line?'

'If only that were true!' remarked Phrygia under her breath. More than ever she seemed to be nursing some immense grudge. Tonight it was even making her incapable of being constructive about her beloved company.

Maybe that was because after all its vicissitudes, the company was finally cracking up. Chremes turned to me. His bluster was leaving him. 'There was a bit of bother today among the lads and lasses.' At first I assumed he was coming to me for help, in view of my success at turning around the stagehands' and musicians' strike. I was wrong, however. 'The worst is, Philocrates has given notice. Having no stage available here is more than he can take.'

I laughed briefly. 'Don't you mean he's depressed by the lack of available women?'

'That doesn't help!' Phrygia agreed sourly. 'There is some suggestion he's also upset because a certain party accused him of causing past events – '

'The certain party was me,' I admitted. 'Just stirring. He can't have taken it seriously.'

'Don't believe it!' Thalia put in. 'If Philocrates is the dot with the itchy piece and the big opinion of himself, he's shitting elephant plop.' She missed nothing. She had only been with us a few days, but already knew who was a real poser.

'He's not the only one anxious to leave, Falco.' Phrygia

357

sounded ready to give up herself. So was I, come to that. 'A whole mob are demanding their severance pay.'

'I fear the troupe is falling apart,' Chremes told me. 'We have one last night together, however.' As usual he rallied with a flourish, though an unimpressive one. His 'last night' sounded like some grim party where your creditors turn up, the wine runs out, and a bad oyster dramatically lays you low.

'Chremes, you said you had failed to get the theatre?'

'Ah! I try never to fail, Falco!' *I* tried to keep my face neutral. 'There is a small Roman garrison,' Chremes informed me, as if he had changed the subject. 'Not very visible in the neighbourhood, perhaps, though I believe that may be policy. They are here to undertake road surveys – nothing to which the Palmyrenes could take exception.'

'If the roads are heading out to the Euphrates, the Parthians may baulk.' I had answered the political point without thinking. Then I guessed what the manager was saying and I groaned. 'Oh, I don't believe this . . . Tell us the worst, Chremes!'

'I happened to meet one of their officers. He has placed at our disposal a small amphitheatre which the troops have built for themselves.'

I was horrified. 'Dear gods! Have you ever attended a garrison theatre?'

'Have you?' As usual he dodged.

'Plenty!'

'Oh I'm sure we can manage – '

'You're ignoring the little matter of having no front stage,' Phrygia gloatingly broke in, as she confirmed the unsuitable venue Chremes had accepted. 'A performance in the round. No fixed scenery, no exits and entrances, no trapdoors from below, and nowhere to hide the lifting machinery if we want to do flying scenes. Giving our all to an audience of bullies, all screaming for obscenities and supplying them if we don't – '

'Hush!' Helena soothed her. Then her common sense broke through. 'I do see it may be hard to keep soldiers happy for a whole play . . .'

'Torture!' I rasped. 'If they only chuck rocks, we'll be lucky.'

'This is where you come in,' Chremes informed me eagerly.

'I doubt it.' I was planning to load the ox-cart and turn back to Damascus that night. 'I think you'll find this is where I back out.'

'Marcus Didius, listen. You'll be pleased by our idea.' I doubted that too. 'I've discussed this with the company and we all feel that what we need to hold the soldiers' attention is something short, light, dramatic and above all, different.'

'So what?' I asked, wondering why Helena suddenly giggled behind her stole.

Chremes for his part appeared to be blushing. 'So we wondered if you were ready to let us rehearse your famous ghost play?'

That was how my elegant creation, *The Spook who Spoke*, came to receive its sole performance on a hot August evening, in the Palmyra garrison amphitheatre. If you can think of worse, I'd be intrigued to hear it. The soldiers, incidentally, only turned out at all because they had been told one of the support acts was a suggestive snake dancer.

They got more than they bargained for. But then, so did we all.

LXV

One problem we faced was that as a result of all the derision people had poured on my idea, most of the play was not even written. All writers must know that sinking feeling, when the goods are demanded in the firm expectation of a delivery you know is impossible . . . But by now I was so professional that the mere lack of a script left me undeterred. We wanted the drama to have speed and bite; what better than to improvise?

I soon knew that my play would not have to carry the entire evening: Thalia's travelling sideshow had caught up with us.

I first noticed something new when a lion cub appeared in our tent. He was sweet but ungainly, and so boisterous it was frightening. Investigation revealed extra waggons. One of them consisted of two large carts fixed together, on top of which loomed a massive structure shrouded in skins and sheets. 'Whatever's that?'

'Water organ.'

'You haven't got an organist!'

'You're fixing that, Falco.'

I cringed. 'Don't back that bet with money . . .'

Among the new arrivals were one or two seedy characters from Thalia's troupe in Rome. 'My dancing partner arrived too,' Thalia said: the famous snake she called 'the big one'.

'Where is he?'

'In charge of my keen new snakekeeper.' She sounded as if she knew something the rest of us had missed. 'Want to see?'

We followed her to a waggon on the far side of camp. The lion cub gambolled after us. 'What does keeping the snake entail?' Helena enquired politely as we walked, keeping an eye on the cub.

'Catching mice, or anything bigger, then poking them into the basket, preferably still alive. A large python needs a lot of lunch. Back in Rome, I had a gang of lads who brought rats to me. They liked to watch things being swallowed. We had

360

some trouble once when there was a spate of lost cats in the Quirinal lanes. People wondered why their pet pussies kept disappearing . . . Zeno ate a baby ostrich once, but that was a mistake.'

'How can you swallow a whole ostrich by mistake?' I laughed.

'Oh it wasn't a mistake to Zeno!' Thalia grinned. 'Fronto was owner of the circus then. He was livid.' Fronto's menagerie had a history of creatures finding unfortunate meals. Fronto himself had become one eventually. Thalia was still reminiscing: 'Apart from losing the feathers, watching the long neck go in was the worst bit . . . and then we had Fronto creating. We could hardly pretend it hadn't happened, what with the lump slowly gliding head first down inside Zeno, and the legs still sticking out. And of course they don't always do this, but just to make sure Fronto couldn't forget the loss, he spat out the bits that had once been the bones.'

Helena and I were still gulping as we climbed into the waggon.

The light was dim. A large rectangular basket, worryingly knocked about and with holes in it, stood in the back of the cart. 'Bit of trouble on the journey,' Thalia commented. 'The keeper's trying to find the baby a strong new cradle . . .' I refrained from asking what the trouble had been, hoping the damage had resulted from ruts in the desert road rather than delinquent activity from the giant snake. Thalia lifted the lid and leaned in, affectionately stroking whatever the basket contained. We heard a sluggish rustle from deep within. 'That's my gorgeous cheeky darling . . . Don't worry. He's been fed. Anyway, he's far too hot. He doesn't want to move. Come and tickle him under the chin, Falco.'

We peered in, then hastily withdrew. From what we could see of the big sleepy python, he was immense. Golden coils half as thick as a human torso were looped back and forth like a huge skein of loom wool. Zeno filled the basket, which was so big it would take several men to move it. Rough calculations told me Zeno must be fifteen to twenty feet long. More than I wanted to think about, anyway.

'Phew! He must be too heavy to lift, Thalia!'

'Oh I don't lift him much! He's tame, and he likes a lot of fuss, but if you get him too excited he starts thinking he'll mate with something. I saw a snake run up a woman's skirt once. Her face was a picture!' Thalia cackled with raucous laughter. Helena and I smiled bravely.

I had been leaning on a smaller basket. Suddenly I felt movement.

'That's Pharaoh.' Thalia's smile was not encouraging. 'Don't open the basket, Falco. He's my new Egyptian cobra. I haven't tamed him yet.'

The basket jerked again and I sprang back.

'Good gods, Thalia! What do you want a cobra for? I thought they were deadly venomous?'

'Oh yes,' she replied offhandedly. 'I want to liven up my stage act – but he'll be a challenge!'

'However do you manage to dance with him safely?' Helena demanded.

'I'm not using him yet!' Even Thalia showed some wariness. 'I'll have to think about it on the way home to Rome. He's gorgeous,' she exclaimed admiringly. 'But you don't exactly say "Come to Mother!" and pick up a cobra for a cuddle . . . Some operators cut out their fangs, or even sew their mouths up, which means the poor darlings starve to death, of course. I haven't decided whether I'll milk his venom before a performance, or just use the easy method.'

Full of foreboding, I felt obliged to ask: 'What's the easy method?'

Thalia grinned. 'Oh, just dancing out of range!'

Glad to escape, we jumped down from the waggon and came face to face with the 'keen new snakekeeper'. He had his sleeves rolled up and was dragging along one of the company costume trunks, presumably intended as the big python's new bed. The lion cub rushed up to him, and he rolled it over to scratch its stomach. It was Musa. Knowing Thalia, I had half expected it.

Musa looked unexpectedly competent as he dodged the big flailing paws, and the cub was ecstatic.

362

I grinned. 'Surely the last time I saw you, you were a priest? Now you're an expert zookeeper!'

'Lions and snakes are symbolic,' he answered calmly, as if he was thinking of starting a menagerie on the Petra High Place. I did not ask about him leaving us. I saw him glance diffidently at Helena, as if ensuring she was making a good recovery. She still looked pale. I slung an arm around her. I was not forgetting how serious her illness had been. Maybe I wanted to let it be known that any cosseting she needed would come from me.

Musa seemed rather withdrawn, though not upset. He stepped up to the waggon where the snakes were kept and lifted something from a peg in the dark interior. 'Look what I found waiting for me at a temple here, Falco.' He was showing me a hat. 'There is a letter from Shullay, but I have not read it yet.'

The hat was a wide-brimmed, round-crowned, Greek-looking number, the sort you see on statues of Hermes. I sucked air through my teeth. 'That's a traveller's headgear. Have you seen it before – travelling very fast downhill?'

'Oh yes. I think it was on a murderer that day.'

It did not seem the moment to tell Musa that according to Grumio he was the murderer himself. Instead I amused myself remembering Grumio's absurd theory that Musa was some high-powered political agent, sent out by The Brother on a mission to destroy.

Musa applied his contract killer's skills to clearing up a pile of lion dung.

Helena and Thalia set off back to our tent. I dallied behind. Musa, who had been grappled by the cub again, looked up long enough to meet my eyes.

'Helena has recovered, but she was very sick. Sending Thalia with her mithridatium helped a lot. Thanks, Musa.'

He disentangled himself from the fluffy, overactive little lion. He seemed quieter than I had been dreading, though he started to say, 'I want to explain – '

'Never explain, Musa. I hope you'll dine with us tonight. Maybe you'll have good news from Shullay to tell me.' I clapped his shoulder as I turned to follow the others. 'I'm sorry. Thalia's an old friend. We let her have your section of the tent.'

I knew that nothing had ever happened between him and Helena, but I was not stupid. I didn't mind how much he cared about her, so long as he honoured the rules. The first rule was, I did not expose Helena by letting other men who hankered after her live in our house. 'Nothing personal,' I added cheerily. 'But I don't care for some of your pets!'

Musa shrugged, smiling in return as he accepted it. 'I am the snakekeeper. I have to stay with Zeno.'

I took two strides, then turned back to him. 'We missed you. Welcome back, Musa.'

I meant that.

Returning to Helena I happened to pass Byrria. I told her I had been to see the big python, recommended the experience, and said I was sure the keeper would be pleased to show her his menagerie.

Well, you have to try.

LXVI

That night I was sitting outside our tent with Helena and Thalia, waiting for Musa to turn up for dinner. We were approached by Chremes and Davos, together with the long, gawky figure of Phrygia, apparently on their way to dine at one of their own tents. Chremes stopped for a discussion with me about an unresolved problem with my play. As we talked, with me paying as little attention as possible to the manager's fussing, I overheard Phrygia muttering to Thalia: 'Don't I know you from somewhere?'

Thalia laughed gruffly. 'I wondered when you would ask!'

I noticed that Helena applied herself to a tactful chat with Davos.

Phrygia looked tense. 'Somewhere in Italy? Or was it Greece?'

'Try Tegea,' stated Thalia. She had on her sardonic look again.

Then Phrygia gasped as if she had been poked in the side with a spindle. 'I need to talk to you!'

'Well I'll try and fit you in some time,' Thalia promised unconvincingly. 'I have to rehearse my snake dance.' I happened to know she claimed *never* to rehearse her dance, partly because of the danger it entailed. 'And the acrobats need a lot of supervision . . .'

'This is cruelty!' murmured Phrygia.

'No,' said Thalia in a tone that meant to be heeded. 'You made your decision. If you've suddenly decided to change your mind after all these years, the other party deserves some warning. Don't push me! Maybe I'll introduce you after the play . . .'

Chremes had given up trying to interest me in his troubles. Looking frustrated, Phrygia felt silent and allowed her husband to lead her away.

I was not the only one who had overheard the intriguing

snatch of conversation. Davos found some excuse to dally behind, and I heard him say to Thalia, 'I remember Tegea!' I felt Helena kick my ankle, and obediently joined her in pretending to be very busy laying out our meal. As usual Davos was being blunt. 'She wants to find the baby.'

'So I gathered,' Thalia returned rather drily, tipping her head back and giving him a challenging stare. 'A bit late! Actually, it's not a baby any more.'

'What happened?' Davos asked.

'When people give me unwanted creatures, I generally bring them up.'

'It lived then?'

'She was alive the last time I saw her.' As Thalia informed Davos, Helena glanced at me. So Phrygia's baby had been a girl. I suppose we had both already worked that out.

'So she's grown up now?'

'A promising little artiste,' Thalia said grittily. That too was no surprise to some of us.

Seeming satisfied, Davos grunted, then went on his way after Chremes and Phrygia.

'So! What happened at Tegea?' I tackled our companion innocently when the coast was clear. Thalia would probably have said that men are never innocent.

She shrugged, pretending indifference. 'Not a lot. It's a tiny Greek town, just a blot on the Peloponnese.'

'When were you there?'

'Oh . . . how about twenty years ago?'

'Really?' We both knew exactly where the conversation was leading. 'Would that have been about the time our stage manager's wife missed her famous chance to play Medea at Epidaurus?'

At this, Thalia stopped playing at being unconcerned and burst into guffaws. 'Get away! She told you that?'

'It's common currency.'

'Common codswallop! She's fooling, Falco.' Thalia's tone was not unpleasant. She knew most people spend their lives deluding themselves.

'So are you going to give us the real story, Thalia?'

'I was just starting out. Juggling – and the rest!' Her voice dropped, almost sadly. 'Phrygia play Medea? Don't make me laugh! Some slimy producer who wanted to get his hand up her skirt convinced her he could swing it, but it would never have happened. For one thing – you should know this, Falco –Greeks never allow women actresses.'

'True.' It was rare in Roman theatre too. But in Italy actresses had done mime plays for years, a vague cover for striptease acts. In groups like ours, with a manager like Chremes who was a pushover for anyone forceful, they could now earn a crust in speaking parts. But groups like ours never took part in the ancient Greek mainland festivals.

'So what happened, Thalia?'

'She was just a singer and dancer in the chorus. She was drifting about with grand ideas, just waiting for some bastard to con her into believing she would make the big time. In the end, becoming pregnant was a let-out.'

'So she had the baby – '

'That's what tends to happen.'

'And she gave it away at Tegea?'

By now this was fairly obvious. Only yesterday I had seen a tall, thin, slightly familiar twenty-year-old who I knew had spent her childhood fostered out. I remembered that Heliodorus was supposed to have told Phrygia that her daughter had been seen somewhere by someone he knew. That could be Tranio. Tranio had appeared at the Vatican Circus; Thalia had known him there, and he presumably knew her troupe, especially the girls if his current form was indicative. 'I suppose she gave it to you, Thalia? So where is the child now? Could Phrygia need to look in somewhere like Palmyra, I wonder . . .'

Thalia tried just smiling knowingly.

Helena joined in, saying quietly, 'I think we could tell Phrygia who her baby is now, Marcus.'

'Keep it to yourself!' commanded Thalia.

Helena grinned at her. 'Ooh Thalia! Don't tell me you're considering how you can cheat Phrygia.'

'Who, me?'

'Of course not,' I weighed in innocently. 'On the other

367

hand, wouldn't it be a nuisance if just when you'd found your valuable water organist, some tiresome relation popped out of the rocky scenery, dying to tell the girl she had a family, and keen to whisk her off to join quite another company than yours?'

'You bet it would!' agreed Thalia, in a dangerous tone that said she was not intending to let Sophrona meet such a fate.

Musa turned up at that moment, allowing Thalia to shrug off the Phrygia incident. 'What kept you? I was starting to think Pharaoh must have got out!'

'I took Zeno for a swim at the springs; he didn't want to be brought back.'

My mind boggled at the thought of trying to persuade a giant python to behave himself. 'What happens when he gets his own ideas and starts playing up?'

'You grab his neck and blow in his face,' Musa told me calmly.

'I'll remember that!' giggled Helena, glancing teasingly at me.

Musa had brought with him a papyrus, closely written in the angular script I vaguely remembered seeing on inscriptions at Petra. As we sat down to eat he showed it to me, though I had to ask him to translate.

'This is the letter I mentioned, Falco, from Shullay, the old priest at my temple. I had sent to ask him if he could describe the man he saw coming down from the High Place just before we saw you.'

'Right. Anything useful?'

Musa ran his finger down the letter. 'He starts by remembering the day, the heat, the peacefulness of our garden at the temple . . .' Very romantic, but not what I call evidence. 'Ah. Now he says, "*I was surprised to hear somebody descending from the High Place so rapidly. He was stumbling, and falling over his feet, though otherwise light of step. When he saw me, he slowed up and began whistling unconcernedly. He was a young man, about your age, Musa, and also your height. His body was slim. He wore no beard. He wore the hat . . .*" Shullay found the hat later, cast aside behind rocks lower down the mountain. You and I must have missed it, Falco.'

368

I was thinking fast. 'It doesn't add much, but this is very useful! We have six possible male suspects. We can certainly now eliminate some of them on Shullay's evidence alone. Chremes, and also Davos, are both too old and too heavy to fit the description.'

'Philocrates is too small,' Musa added. He and I both grinned.

'Besides, Shullay would certainly have mentioned if the man was quite so handsome! Congrio may be *too* slight. He's so weedy I think if he had seen Congrio, Shullay would have made more of his poor stature. Besides, he can't whistle. That leaves us,' I concluded quietly, 'with only Grumio and Tranio.'

Musa leaned forwards, looking expectant. 'So what are we to do now?'

'Nothing yet. Now I'm certain it has to be one of those two, I'll have to identify which one we definitely want.'

'You cannot interrupt your play, Falco!' Thalia commented reprovingly.

'No, not with a rapacious garrison screaming for it.' I applied a competent expression that probably fooled no one. 'I'll have to do my play as well.'

LXVII

Rehearsing a half-written new play with a gang of cocky subversives who would not take it seriously nearly defeated me. I failed to see their problem. *The Spook who Spoke* was perfectly straightforward. The hero, to be played by Philocrates, was a character called Moschion – traditionally the name of a slightly unsatisfactory youth. You know the idea – trouble to his parents, useless in love, uncertain whether to turn into a wastrel or to come good in the last act.

I had never decided where the action should take place: some district no one ever fancies visiting. Illyria, perhaps.

The first scene was a wedding feast, an attempt to be controversial after all those plays where the wedding feast happens at the end. Moschion's mother, a widow, was remarrying, partly in order to allow Tranio to do his 'Clever Cook' routine and partly to let the panpipe girls wander around deliciously as banquet entertainment. Amidst Tranio's jokes about rude-shaped peppered meats, the young Moschion would be complaining about his mother, or when nobody had time to listen just muttering to himself. This portrait of dreadful adolescence was, I thought, rather finely drawn (it was autobiographical).

Moschion's grumbles were halted by a shock meeting with the ghost of his dead father. In my original concept the apparition was to have popped out of a stage trapdoor; in the amphitheatre, where this effect would be impossible, we planned to tow on various chests and altars. The spook, chillingly realised by Davos, would conceal himself there until needed. It would work, so long as Davos could avoid getting cramp.

'If you do, don't let it show, Davos. Ghosts don't limp!'

'Stuff you, Falco. Order someone else about. I'm a professional.'

Being a writer-producer was hard work.

The ghost accused the widow's new husband of having murdered her old one (himself), leaving Moschion in anguish about what to do. Obviously the rest of the play concerned Moschion's frustrated efforts to get the ghost into court as a witness. In the full-length version, this play was a strong courtroom drama, though the garrison was getting a short farce where Zeus nipped on in the last scene to clear everything up.

'Are you sure this is a comedy?' queried Philocrates haughtily.

'Of course!' I snapped. 'Have you no dramatic instinct, man? You can't have spooks leaping about with lurid accusations in tragedy!'

'You don't have ghosts in tragedy at all,' Chremes confirmed. He played both the second husband and also the funny foreign doctor in a later scene where Moschion's mother went mad. The mother was Phrygia; we were all looking forward to her mad scene, despite Chremes uttering disloyal thoughts that he for one would not be able to spot any difference from normal.

Byrria played the girl. There had to be one, though I was still slightly uncertain what to do with her (man's eternal predicament). Luckily she was used to minimal parts.

'Can't I run mad too, Falco? I'd like to dash on raving.'

'Don't be daft. The Virtuous Maid has to survive without a stain on her character so she can marry the hero.'

'But he's a weed!'

'You're learning, Byrria. Heroes always are.'

She gave me a thoughtful look.

Tranio and Grumio doubled up as various silly servants, plus the hero's worried friends. At Helena's insistence I had even devised a one-line part for Congrio. He seemed to have plans for expanding the speech: a typical actor already.

I discovered that one of the stagehands had been sent to buy a kid, which was to be carried on by Tranio. It was certain to lift its tail and make a mess; this was bound to appeal to the low taste of our anticipated audience. Nobody told me, but I gained the definite impression that if things were going badly Tranio had been ordered by Chremes to cook the cute creature live on-stage. We were desperate to satisfy the raw ranks from the barracks. The kid was only one distraction. There was also to be lewd dancing by the orchestra girls at the start of the evening, and afterwards a complete circus act that Thalia and her troupe would provide.

'It'll do!' Chremes pompously decided. This convinced all the rest of us that it would not do at all.

I wore myself out drilling the players, then was sent away while people practised their stunts, songs and acrobatics.

Helena was resting, alone in the tent. I flopped down alongside, holding her in the crook of one elbow while I stroked her still-bandaged arm with my other hand.

'I love you! Let's elope and keep a winkle stall.'

'Does that mean,' Helena demanded gently, 'things are not going well?'

'This looks like being a disaster.'

'I thought you were an unhappy boy.' She snuggled closer consolingly. 'Kiss?'

I kissed her, with half my mind on it.

'Kiss properly.'

I kissed her again, managing three-quarters of my attention. 'I'll do this, fruit, then that's the end of my glorious stage career. We're going home straight afterwards.'

'That's not because you're worried about me, is it?'

'Lady, you always worry me!'

'Marcus – '

'It's a sensible decision which I made some time ago.' About a second after the scorpion stung her. I knew if I admitted that, Helena would rebel. 'I miss Rome.'

'You must be thinking about your comfortable apartment on the Aventine!' Helena was being rude. My Roman apartment consisted of two rooms, a leaky roof and an unsafe balcony, six storeys above a neighbourhood that had all the social elegance of a two-day-old dead rat. 'Don't let an accident bother you,' she added less facetiously.

I was determined to haul her back to Italy. 'We ought to sail west before the autumn.'

Helena sighed. 'So I'll think about packing . . . Tonight

you're going to sort out Thalia's young lovers. I won't ask how you plan to do it.'

'Best not!' I grinned. She knew I had no plan. Sophrona and Khaleed would just have to hope inspiration would strike me later. And now there was the additional complication of Thalia wanting to hide the facts of Sophrona's birth.

'So, Marcus, what about the murderer?'

That was a different story. Tonight would be my last chance. I had to expose him, or he would never be brought to account.

'Maybe', I reflected slowly, 'I can somehow draw him out into the open in the course of the play?'

Helena laughed. 'I see! Undermine his confidence by affecting his emotions with the power and relevance of your drama?'

'Don't tease! Still, the play is about a murder. It might be possible to work on him by drawing succinct parallels – '

'Too elaborate.' Helena Justina always pulled me up sanely if I was flitting off into some rhapsody.

'We're stuck then.'

That was when she slipped in cunningly, 'At least you know who it is.'

'Yes, I know.' I had thought that was my secret. She must watch me even more closely than I realised.

'Are you going to tell me, Marcus?'

'I bet you have your own idea.'

Helena spoke thoughtfully: 'I can guess why he killed Heliodorus.'

'I thought you might! Tell me?'

'No. I have to test something first.'

'You'll do no such thing. This man is deadly dangerous.' Resorting to desperate tactics, I tickled her in various places I knew would render her helpless. 'Give me a clue then.' As Helena squirmed, trying not to give in, I suddenly eased off. 'What did the vestal virgin say to the eunuch?'

'I'd be willing if you were able?'

'Where did you get that from?'

'I just made it up, Marcus.'

'Ah!' I was disappointed. 'I hoped it might be from that scroll you always have your nose in.'

'Ah!' Helena said as well. She put on a light voice, avoiding particular emphasis. 'What about my scroll?'

'Do you remember Tranio?'

'Doing what?'

'Being a menace for one thing!' I said. 'You know, that night soon after we joined the company in Nabataea, when he came looking for something.'

Helena obviously remembered exactly what I was talking about. 'You mean, the night you came back to the tent tipsy, brought home by Tranio, who annoyed us by hanging about and grovelling in the play box?'

'Remember he seemed frantic? He said Heliodorus had borrowed something, something Tranio failed to find. I think you were lying on it, my darling.'

'Yes, I wondered about that.' She smiled. 'Since he insisted that his lost object wasn't a scroll, I didn't feel I needed to mention it.'

I thought of Grumio telling me that ridiculous story about his lost ring with the blue stone. I knew now I had been right to disbelieve the tale. You would never hope to find so small an item in a big trunk crammed with many sets of scrolls. They had both lied to me about it, but the famous gambling pledge that Tranio gave away to Heliodorus should have been obvious to me long ago.

'Helena, do you realise what all this has been about?'

'Maybe.' Sometimes she irritated me. She liked to go her own way, and refused to see that I knew best.

'Don't mess about. I'm the man of the household: answer me!' Naturally, as a good Roman male, I had fixed ideas about women's role in society. Naturally, Helena knew I was wrong. She hooted with laughter. So much for patriarchal power.

She relented quietly. This was a serious situation, after all. 'I think I understand the dispute now. I had the clue all along.'

'The scroll,' I said. 'Your bedtime read is Grumio's inherited humour collection. His prized family asset; his talisman; his treasure.'

Helena drew a deep breath. 'So this is why Tranio behaves so oddly sometimes. He blames himself because he pledged it to Heliodorus.'

'And this is why Heliodorus died: he refused to hand it back.'

'One of the clowns killed him because of that, Marcus?'

They must both have argued with the playwright about it. I think that's why Grumio went to see him the day he stopped Heliodorus raping Byrria; she said she overheard them arguing about a scroll. Various people have told me that Tranio tackled the bastard as well. Grumio must have been going spare, and when Tranio realised just what he had done, he must have felt pretty agitated too.'

'So what happened at Petra? One of them went up the mountain to make another attempt to persuade Heliodorus to relinquish it, actually meaning to kill him?'

'Maybe not. Maybe things just went too far. I don't know whether what happened was planned, and if so whether both clowns were in on it. At Petra they were supposed to have drunk themselves unconscious in their rented room while Heliodorus was being killed. One of them obviously didn't. Is the other lying absolutely, or was he really made completely drunk by his roommate so that he passed out and never knew his companion had left the room? If so, and the first deliberately held back from drinking to prepare an alibi – '

'Then that's premeditation!' Helena exclaimed.

It seemed to me that if Grumio were the culprit but Tranio still regretted giving away the pledge, that could make Tranio willingly cover for him at Petra, and might explain Tranio's feeble attempt to make Afrania lie about his own alibi at Gerasa. But Grumio had a whole crowd of people to vouch for him when Ione was killed. Had Afrania been lying to me all along, and was Tranio Ione's killer? If so, were events at Petra the opposite way around? Did *Tranio* kill Heliodorus, and *Grumio* cover up?

'This is all becoming clearer, but the motive seems extravagant.' Helena was looking worried for other reasons. 'Marcus, you're a creative artist.' She said it entirely without irony. 'Would you be so upset by losing a batch of rather old material that you would go so far as to *kill* for it?'

'Depends,' I replied slowly. 'If I had a volatile temperament. If the material was my livelihood. If it was *mine* by

375

rights. And especially if the person who now possessed it was an evil-mannered scribe who would be bound to gloat about using my precious material . . . We'll have to test the theory.'

'There's not going to be much opportunity.'

Suddenly I reached the end of my tolerance. 'Ah cobnuts, sweetheart! It's my début tonight; I don't even want to think about this any more. Everything will be all right.'

Everything. My ghost play; Sophrona; finding the killer; everything. Sometimes, even without grounds for optimism, I just knew.

Helena was in a more sober mood. 'Don't joke about it. It's too grave a subject. You and I never make light of death.'

'Or life,' I said.

I had rolled to pin her beneath me, carefully keeping her bandaged arm free of my weight. I held her face between my hands while I studied it. Thinner and quieter since her illness, but still full of searching intelligence. Strong, quizzical eyebrows; fine bones; adorable mouth; eyes so dark brown and solemn they were making me ferment. I had always loved her being serious. I loved the madcap thought that I had made a serious woman care for me. And I loved that irresistible glint of laughter, so rarely shared with others, whenever Helena's eyes met mine privately.

'Oh my love. I'm so glad you've come back to me. I had thought I was losing you – '

'I was here.' Her fingers traced the line of my cheek, while I turned my head to brush the soft skin of her wrist with my lips. 'I knew all that you were doing for me.'

Now that I could bear to think about what had happened with the scorpion, I remembered how one night when she had been tossing with fever she had suddenly exclaimed in a clear voice, '*Oh Marcus!*', as if I had entered a room and rescued her from some bad dream. Straight after that she had slept more quietly. When I told her about it now, she was unable to recollect the dream, but she smiled. She was beautiful when she smiled that way, looking up at me.

'I love you,' Helena whispered suddenly. There was a special note in her voice. The moment when the mood between us altered had been imperceptible. We knew each other so well it took only the faintest change of tone, a slightly increased tension in our bodies lying together. Now, without drama or prevarication, we were both wanting to make love.

Everywhere outside was quiet. The actors were still rehearsing, so were Thalia and the circus performers. Within the tent a couple of flies with no sense of discretion were buzzing about against the hot goatskin roof. Everything else lay still. Almost everything, anyway.

'I love you too . . .' I had told her that, but for a girl with exceptional qualities I did not mind repeating myself.

This time I did not have to be asked to kiss her, and every atom of my concentration was being applied. It was the moment to find the jar of alum wax. We both knew it. Neither of us wanted to disturb the deep intimacy of the moment; neither of us wanted to draw apart. Our eyes met, silently consulting; silently rejecting the idea.

We knew each other very well. Well enough to take a risk.

LXVIII

We did our best to search the soldiers at the gates. We managed to confiscate most of their drink flagons and some of the stones they were planning to hurl at us. No one could stop large numbers of them peeing against the outside wall before entering; at least that was better than what they might do inside later. Syria had never been a fashionable posting; dedicated men applied for frontier forts in Britain or Germany, where there was some hope of cracking foreign heads. These soldiers were little more than bandits. Like all Eastern legions, they turned to salute the sun each morning. Their evening fun was likely to be slaughtering us.

Their commander had offered us military ushers but I said that was asking for trouble. 'You don't control legionaries by using their mates!' He accepted the comment with a curt, knowing nod. He was a square-faced career officer, a sinewy man with straight-cut hair. I remember the pleasant shock of running into someone in authority who realised it would be useful to avert a riot.

We exchanged a few words. He must have been able to see I had a more solid background than scribbling light comedies. However, I was surprised when he recognised my name.

'Falco? As in Didius?'

'Well I like having a reputation, but frankly, sir, I did not expect my fame to have reached a road-building vexillation in the middle of the desert, halfway to bloody Parthia!'

'There's a note out, asking for sightings.'

'A warrant?' I laughed as I said it, hoping to avoid unpleasantness.

'Why that?' He looked both amused and sceptical. 'It's more *"Render assistance; agent lost and may be in difficulty"*.'

Now I really was surprised. 'I was never lost! Whose signature?'

'Not allowed to say.'

378

'Who's your governor in Syria?'

'Ulpius Traianus.'

It meant nothing much then, though those of us who lived to be old men would see his son's craggy mush on the currency. 'Is it him?'

'No,' he said.

'If it's a short-arsed flea called Anacrites from the political bureau – '

'Oh no!' The garrison commander was shocked by my irreverence. I knew what that meant.

'The Emperor?' I had long stopped respecting official secrecy. The commander, however, blushed at my indiscretion.

The mystery was solved. Helena's father must be at the back of this. If Camillus had not heard from his daughter for the past four months, he would wonder where she was. The Emperor, his friend, was not looking for me at all but for my wayward lass.

Oh dear. Definitely time I took Helena home again.

The commander cleared his throat. 'So are you? In difficulty?'

'No,' I said. 'But thanks for asking. Ask me again when we've played to your mob here!'

He did invite Helena to a seat in the tribunal, a nice courtesy. I agreed, because he seemed far too straight to start fingering her, and I reckoned it was the one place a respectable woman would be safe that night.

Helena was furious at being sent out of the way.

The house was full. We drew about a thousand soldiers, a group of Palmyrene archers who had served in Judaea with Vespasian and learned about Roman spectacles, plus a few townspeople. Among them were Khaleed and his father, another short, stumpy Damascene. Facially, they did not much resemble each other, apart from a slight similarity in hairlines. I joked to Thalia, 'Khaleed must take after his mother – poor woman!' Then his mother turned up (maybe they had left left her to park the chariot), and unfortunately I was right: not exactly a model of feminine beauty. We gave them front-row seats, and hoped nothing too hard would be thrown at them by the soldiers behind.

Sophrona had arrived earlier, and I had made her accompany Helena as a chaperone. (We kept the girl out of sight of Thalia, in case Sophrona realised what was planned for her and tried to do another flit.) What did happen, of course, was that the family Habib soon spotted Sophrona in the ceremonial box alongside the garrison commander and Helena, who was in full regalia as a senator's daughter, resplendently dressed in new Palmyrene silk, with bronze bracelets to the elbow. My lady was a loyal soul. As it was my play's first night, she had even brought out a tiara to peg down the necessary veil.

The family were impressed. This could only help. I had not worked out exactly how I would solve their troubles, but after three months submerged in soggy dramas, I was full of crass ideas.

The amphitheatre was small by theatrical standards, and ill-equipped for creating dramatic effects. It had been built for gladiatorial fights and wild-beast shows. There were two gates made from heavy timber baulks at opposite ends of the ellipse. The arena had two arched niches on its longer sides. In one, our stagehands had draped a statue of Nemesis with garlands; the musicians were crouching under her skirts. The other niche was to be used as a refuge for actors exiting. Around the arena ran a wooden protective barrier, several yards high. Above it was a steeply raked bank with tiers of wooden benching. The commander's tribunal, little more than a plinth with a couple of thrones, was on one side.

The atmosphere was vibrant. Too vibrant. The troops were restless. Any moment now they would start setting fire to their seats.

It was time to diffuse the kind of trouble we could not stop by stirring up the audience even more with music and dancing girls. In the tribunal the commanding officer politely let drop a white scarf.

Thalia appeared at my side as I stood in the gateway listening to the orchestra begin its first number.

Afrania and Plancina jostled up, huddling in stoles. They wore head-dresses and Palmyrene veils, but only bells and spangles beneath the stoles. Thalia took Plancina, who was nervous, under her accommodating wing. I talked with Afrania.

'This is the night, Falco!' Within the amphitheatre our girls had been glimpsed. Boots began drumming rhythmically. 'Juno! What a gang of turds.'

'Give them your best; they'll be like kittens.'

'Oh, I reckon they're animals all right.'

Plancina ran on, doing things with a set of castanets it was hard to believe were possible. 'Not bad!' Thalia commented.

Soon Plancina was working up a frenzy of applause with her panpipe dance. She writhed well. Afrania dropped her stole, grabbed her musical instrument, then, while I was still blinking, she bounced out, virtually naked, to join the dance.

'Wow!'

'She'll do herself a mischief with that tibia,' growled Thalia, unimpressed.

Not long afterwards the stagehands started clustering around the gate with the props we would be using for *The Spook who Spoke*. Soon the actors came out from the dressing tent in a tense group. Musa appeared at my elbow.

'Your big night, Falco!'

I was sick of people saying that. 'It's just a play.'

'I have my work too,' he said, rather drily; he was looking after the kid that Tranio was to cook. It struggled valiantly in his arms, trying to run away. Musa also had charge of Philocrates' mule, which was to be ridden in a journey scene. 'And tonight,' he said, with an almost eerie satisfaction, 'we shall identify our murderer.'

'We can try.' His calm attitude disturbed me. 'Domestic livestock seems a comedown for you. Where's the big snake?'

'In his basket,' replied Musa, with the faintest of smiles.

The music ended. The orchestra came off for a drink while the girls raced at speed for the dressing tent. Soldiers poured out for an interval pee, even though we had not planned to allow them an interval. I had been a soldier; I was not surprised.

The actors had seen it all before. They sighed, and stood back from the entrance until the crush had galloped by.

I could see Tranio approaching for his first scene as the busy cook. He looked preoccupied with his coming performance, and I reckoned I might be able to shake him if I asked the right question unexpectedly. I was weighing up my moment to beard him, when Congrio tugged at my sleeve. 'Falco! Falco! This speech I have – ' Congrio's 'speech' was one line; he had to enter as a household slave and announce that the Virtuous Maiden had just given birth. (In plays, virtuous maidens are not *that* virtuous. Don't blame me; this is the tradition of a soiled genre. Your average theatrical juvenile sees rape as his first step to marriage, and for some reason your average comic heroine goes right along with it.) Congrio was still complaining. 'It's boring. Helena Justina told me I can fill it out – '

'Do whatever you like, Congrio.'

I was trying to move away from him. Tranio was standing some distance apart, getting his wig on. Just as I freed myself from Congrio and his maundering anxiety, a gaggle of heavies from the garrison blocked my path. They sized me up. They despised actors, but I was being taken as more promising bait. Evidently I looked tough enough to have my head kicked in.

I had no time to distract them with genial banter. I leapt straight through the group of hooligans, pounding off on a lengthy detour, then, as I swerved back towards Tranio, I ran into a little fellow who was swearing that he knew me: some lunatic who wanted to discuss a goat.

LXIX

'Hello, this is a bit of luck!'

I had been stopped by a tiny chap with one arm cut off at the elbow and a hopeful toothless grin. Being trapped was unusual; normally I'm much too smart for street hustlers. I thought he was trying to sell me something – and I was right. He wanted me to have his goat.

My play was starting. I could hear Ribes playing a delicate introductory melody on the lyre.

Before I could buff aside the man who had stopped me, something made me think again. The loon looked familiar.

His companion seemed to know me too, for it butted me in the kidneys as familiarly as a nephew. It was a brown-and-white-patched billy goat, about waist high, with a sad expression. Both its ears had nervous tics. Its neck had a queer kink.

I knew about this goat. The owner made some hopeless claim that it had been born with its head facing backwards.

'Sorry – ' I tried to make off.

'We met at Gerasa! I've been trying to find you!' the owner piped.

'Look, friend; I have to go – '

He looked downcast. They made a gloomy pair. 'I thought you were interested,' protested the man. The goat had the sense to know I just wanted to escape.

'Sorry?'

'In buying the goat!' Dear gods.

'What made you think that?'

'Gerasa!' he repeated doggedly. A dim memory of viewing his beast for a copper or two in a mad moment came floating back. A more terrible memory – of foolishly discussing the beast with its owner – followed rapidly. 'I still want to sell him. I thought we had a bargain . . . I came looking for you that night, in fact.'

It was time to be blunt. 'You've got the wrong idea, friend. I just asked you about him because he reminded me of a goat I once owned myself.'

He didn't believe me. It sounded weak only because it was the truth. Once, for very complex reasons, I had rescued a runaway nanny from a temple on a seashore. My excuse is, I was living rough (I was doing a job for Vespasian, always prone to leave me short of tavern fees) and any companion had seemed better than none at the time.

I had always been a sentimental type. Now sometimes I let myself indulge in conversations with owners of peculiar goats just to show off my former expertise. So, I had talked to this man in Gerasa. I remembered he had told me he wanted to sell up and plant beans. We had discussed what price he wanted for his quaintly angled exhibit, but I had never had any intention of rejoining the goat owners' guild.

'Look, I'm sorry, but I like a pet who looks you in the eye.'

'Depends where you stand,' the menace persisted logically. He tried to edge me into position behind his billy's left shoulder. 'See?'

'I've got a girlfriend now; she takes all my energy – '

'He draws the crowds!'

'I bet he does.' Lies. As a sideshow the goat was completely useless. He was also nibbling my tunic hem, despite his disability. In fact, the crooked neck seemed to place him more readily in line with people's clothes. The last thing I needed was a series of domestic writs for damaged skirts and togas.

'What was yours called?' demanded the owner. He was definitely mad.

'What? Oh my goat. She didn't have a name. Growing too familiar only leads to heartache on both sides.'

'That's right . . .' The goat owner could tell I understood his problems. 'This is Alexander, because he's great.' Wrong. He was just terrible.

'Don't sell him!' I urged, suddenly unable to bear the thought of them parting. It seemed to me this couple of deadbeats depended on each other more than either realised. 'You need to know he has a good home. If you're going to retire from the road, take him with you.'

384

'He'll eat the beans.' True. He would eat everything. Goats actually tear up plants and shrubs by the roots. Nothing they come near to ever sprouts again. 'You seemed like a good sort, Falco – '

'Don't bet on it.'

'He has his funny ways, but he repays affection . . . Still, maybe you're right. He belongs with me.' I had been reprieved. 'I'm glad I've seen you again; it's cleared my mind.' I pulled Alexander by the ears, almost regretfully. Obviously a connoisseur of quality, he tried to eat my belt.

I was leaving them when the long-faced goat owner suddenly asked, 'That night in Gerasa, did your friend ever find his way to the pools?'

LXX

'What friend?' if we were talking about Gerasa, I didn't need to ask what pools.

I was trying to keep things light, whilst all the time my sense of oppression grew. I hate murder. I hate murderers. I hate running up against the need to name one of them. Very soon now it was going to be unavoidable.

'He was in your company. When I came to offer you the goat, I asked him where you were. He said you'd gone into town, and in return for that he asked me directions to the pools of the Maiuma.'

'What did he look like?'

'Blow me if I know. He had no time to stop; he was dashing off on a camel.'

'Young? Old? Tall? Short? *Can you see him here now?*'

The man looked panicky. Unused to describing people, he was fumbling for anything to say. It was no use pressing him. Not even with one possible murderer – Tranio – standing ten feet from us waiting to go on-stage. The witness was unreliable. Too much time had passed. Now if I offered suggestions he would agree with them instantly to escape his quandary. This loon held the answer to everything, but I would have to let him go.

I said nothing. Patience was my only hope. Alexander was slyly consuming the sleeve of my tunic; seeing it, his owner biffed him between the ears. Striking the goat's head reminded him of something: 'He wore a hat!' I had heard that before.

While I was catching my breath, the goat's owner voluntarily described the Gerasa specimen. 'It was one of them knitted things, with a flopped-over top.'

That was nothing like the wide-brimmed, round-crowned Greek hat that Musa had been sent from Petra by Shullay. But I knew where I had seen this. 'A Phrygian cap? Like the sun-god Mithras wears?'

386

'That's right. One of them long floppy ones.'

Grumio's collection cap.

So Ione's killer was Grumio. I had given him an alibi myself, based on the bad premise that I had seen him several times in the same place. I never dreamt that in between he might have galloped off somewhere else.

Looking back, my confidence had been ridiculous. Of course he had taken a break from his act. He could never have sustained that sparkling performance all night. If he had stood on that barrel for the whole evening, by the time Musa and I returned from the Temple of Dionysus he would have been hoarse and completely exhausted. That had not been his condition when he dragged me up for abuse and the near-fatal 'accident' using my own knife. He had been alert, in control, exhilarated, *dangerous*. And I had missed the obvious.

Grumio had done two turns on the barrel. In between, he had ridden to the pools and killed the girl.

Had he acted alone? And had he killed Heliodorus too? It was hard to work out. My mind was a mess. Sometimes it is better to have twenty suspects than a mere two. I wanted to consult Helena. Unluckily I had trapped her in the commander's private box.

I walked to the arena entrance. Grumio was no longer there. He and Chremes had slipped into the arena ready to make their entrances from one side. They were hiding in one of the niches. Davos was concealed on-stage, ready to pop out as the ghost. The rest of the cast had been waiting for me.

Ribes was still enjoying himself with the lyre. Luckily Syrians liked minstrels. Ribes fancied himself rotten, and since no one had signalled him to end the overture, he was working it up in frenzied improvisation.

Tranio was by the gate. I walked up to him casually. 'You'll be glad to know I found Grumio's ring.'

'His ring?'

'Blue stone. Could be lapis; might just be sodalite . . .' He had absolutely no idea what I was talking about.

'As I thought – he even lied about that!' I grabbed Tranio by the elbow and yanked him closer.

'What's the game, Falco?'

'Tranio, I'm trying to decide whether you're foolishly loyal – or just a complete fool!'

'I don't know what you mean – '

'It's time to stop protecting him. Believe me, he's tried quite happily to implicate you! Whatever you think you owe him, forget it now!'

Other people were listening: Thalia, Musa, many of the cast. Tranio's eyes flickered towards those present.

'Let them hear,' I said. 'We can do with witnesses. Own up. What was the pledge you gave to Heliodorus, then had the row about?'

'Falco, I have to go on – ' Tranio was panicking.

'Not yet.' I gripped his costume by the neck and jerked it tight. He could not tell whether I was really angry, or just playing him along. 'I want the truth!'

'Your play, Falco – '

'Stuff my play.'

For a moment I felt things were getting away from me. Help came from an unexpected quarter: 'The pledge was a scroll.' It was Philocrates who spoke. He really must be worried that he would be blamed for the crimes himself. 'It was Grumio's; his collection of terrible old jokes.'

'Thanks, Philocrates! All right Tranio, you've got some fast answers to provide! First, were you really with Afrania the night Ione died?'

He gave up. 'Yes.'

'Why did you ask her to pretend otherwise?'

'Stupidity.'

'Well that's honest! And were you conscious or in a stupor in Petra the afternoon Heliodorus was killed?'

'Paralytic.'

'What about Grumio?'

'I thought he was the same.'

'Are you certain he was?'

Tranio dropped his eyes. 'No,' he admitted. 'I passed out. He could have done anything.'

388

I let go of him. 'Tranio, Tranio, what have you been playing at? If you are not the killer, why protect the man who was?'

He shrugged helplessly. 'It was my fault. I'd lost him his scroll.'

I would never entirely understand it. But I was a writer, not a performer. A comedian is only as good as his script. A writer never has to grieve too long for lost material. Unluckily for the reading and viewing public, writers can easily rattle off more.

I despaired of Tranio. In the arena Ribes had been covering the unexpected pause with his rapid plectrumming but the audience was tired of it. I could see he was starting to feel desperate as he wondered why Tranio was failing to enter. I took a swift decision. 'We'll have to discuss this later. Get out on-stage. Don't warn Grumio, or you'll be arrested too.'

Released from my furious grip, Tranio pulled on a sparse two-tone wig, then strode in through the gate. Free members of the cast, together with Thalia, Musa and myself, all crowded around to watch.

Looking out at ground level, the elliptical space seemed immense. Musa and Thalia stared at me curiously as I wondered what to do. On-stage, Tranio began carrying on as the hectic cook. He seemed to be safely sticking to his lines. Soon he was berating the less sophisticated Grumio, playing a farm boy who had brought meat for the feast. Chremes rushed on to give them orders, made some jokes about voracious women wanting sex night and day, then rushed off again.

To one side, Philocrates as my hero, Moschion, interjected adolescent bile, sitting on a costume basket covered in a blanket to represent a couch. Davos, the ghost, was concealed in a portable oven. From time to time he leant out to address Moschion – the only person who could 'see' him. The ghost then became worried because Tranio was about to light a fire in the oven: sophisticated stuff. You can see why I had been proud of it. Not that the play mattered to me now. I was about to confront the killer; I had bile in my mouth.

Being set on fire was nothing to what I intended for Tranio

for frustrating my enquiries. As for Grumio, I noted with relish that in provincial locations criminal executions usually take place in the local arena. I glanced up at the garrison commander. I wondered if he held the right to award the death penalty. Probably not. But the governor, Ulpius Traianus, would.

Davos let out a terrific shriek, which most characters on-stage ignored. Clutching the seat of his ghostly robe, he ran off through the gate as if alight. The crowd really loved seeing a character in pain. The atmosphere was excellent.

'Falco, what's going on?' Davos exclaimed. While squashed in the oven he had had more reason than most to notice the long pause before we began.

'Crisis!' I said tersely. Davos looked startled, but evidently realised what sort of crisis it must be.

On-stage, Phrygia and Byrria had appeared from the far gate entrance. They were shooing away the two 'slaves' in order to have a sly chat in the kitchen about young Moschion. Tranio and Grumio ran off, according to my stage directions, in opposite directions; fortuitously, that put them one in each side niche, unable to confer.

Moschion was hiding behind the oven so he could overhear his mother and girlfriend discussing him. It was meant to be a very funny scene. While the women tossed wit around, I breathed slowly to calm down.

Soon, however, the clowns were back on-stage again. Suddenly I began to worry that I had misjudged Tranio. I had made a mistake.

I muttered to Musa, 'This isn't going to work . . .'

I had to choose: whether to stop the performance in mid-scene, or wait. We had a large group of unruly soldiers who had paid for a spectacle. If they were disappointed, we could expect a riot.

My fears were well founded. 'You're going to catch it!' the Clever Cook warned the Country Clown as they bantered on-stage. This was not in the script. 'If I were you I would leg it while you can!'

Davos, quicker-witted than most people, grasped the point and muttered '*Shit!*'

Tranio's exit was back into the side niche, but Grumio came our way. Maybe he thought Tranio had just been improvising lines. At any rate, he was still in character.

Musa glanced at me. I decided to do nothing. In the play, Philocrates was discovered hiding by his mother, had a quarrel with his girlfriend, and was exiled to the country for the usual complicated plot reasons. My drama moved fast.

Philocrates left the stage and arrived among us looking uneasy. I gave him a discreet nod; the play would continue. I noticed Thalia grab Davos by the arm. I saw her mouth in his ear, 'Next time you're on-stage, give that Tranio a thump!'

Musa went forward to hand Grumio the reins of Philocrates' mule, ready for the next scene. Both Philocrates and Grumio had flung on travelling cloaks; it was a very quick costume change. Philocrates as the young master swung on to his mule. Grumio for one was paying little attention to those of us standing around.

Just as they set off back on-stage for a short scene journeying to a farm, Musa stepped forward again to Grumio. Grumio, leading the mule, was on the verge of passing into view of the audience. Quite unexpectedly, Musa rammed a hat upon his head. It was a wide Greek hat with a string beneath the chin. I saw Grumio go pale.

The hat was bad enough. But my faithful accomplice had devised a further trick: 'Don't forget to whistle!' Musa commanded cheerfully. It sounded like a stage direction, but some of us knew otherwise.

Before I could stop him, he clapped the mule on its rump, so it skidded out into the arena, dragging Grumio.

'Musa! You idiot. Now he knows we know!'

'Justice must be done,' said Musa calmly. 'I want him to know.'

'Justice won't be done,' I retorted, 'if Grumio escapes!'

On the far side of the arena, the other gate gaped wide. Beyond it a clear vista of the desert was stretching endlessly.

LXXI

I saw Grumio glance back at us. Unluckily for him, the sturdy figure of Philocrates was holding forth on the mule so there was no chance of bringing the scene to a premature end. Moschion had a lengthy speech about women, which Philocrates enjoyed giving. No wonder. The character was an ignorant bastard; the speech based on himself.

Spinning around, I gripped Davos by his arm. 'I'll need your help. First, Musa! Get around to the end of the amphitheatre, and if it's not too late, slam those gates shut!'

'I'll do that,' said Thalia quietly. 'He's caused enough trouble!' She was a girl for action. She ran for a camel left outside by one of the audience, and within seconds was haring off in a cloud of dust.

'Right, Davos. Go up the back of the arena, and down the steps to the tribunal. Whisper to the commander we've got at least one killer out there, and possibly an accomplice.' I was not forgetting Tranio, currently holed up in a side niche. I had no idea what he might be planning. 'Helena's there. She'll back you up. Tell the man we're going to need some arrests.'

Davos understood. 'Someone will have to fetch that bastard off-stage . . .' Without hesitation, he threw his stage mask at a bystander, stripped off his white ghost's costume, and dropped it over my head. Wearing only a loincloth, he ran off towards the commander. I was given the mask.

I found myself shrouded in long folds of material that flapped strangely on my arms – and in darkness. The ghost was the only character we were playing in a mask. We rarely used them. I knew why the minute I had this one rammed over my face. Suddenly excluded from half of the world, I tried to learn how to look through the hollow eyes, while scarcely able to breathe.

A bothersome presence was grabbing my elbow.

'He's guilty then?' It was Congrio. 'That Grumio?'

'Get out of my way, Congrio. I've got to confront the clown.'

'Oh I'll do that!' he exclaimed. The certainty in his tone carried a familiar echo of Helena's brisk style. He was her pupil, one she had clearly led astray. 'Helena and I have thought up a plan!'

I had no time to stop him. I was still trying to master my costume. Adopting a curious sprint (his idea of great acting, apparently), Congrio raced into the arena ahead of me. Even then I still expected to hear the one line I had written for him: 'Madam! The young lady has just given birth to twins!'

Only he did not say the line.

He was not playing the part I had written him, but the traditional Running Slave: 'Gods above, here's a pickle –' He ran so fast he caught up the travellers on their mule. 'I'm wearing myself out. Moschion turned out of doors, his mother in tears, the roast on fire and the bridegroom furious, and now this girl – hold on, I'll tell you all about the girl when I get round to it. Here's a pair of travellers! I'll stop for a chat with them.'

Then, as my heart sank further than I had ever thought it could, Congrio began to tell a joke.

LXXII

Congrio had climbed up on a model of a rock for a better view. 'Hello down there! You look glum. Would you like cheering up? Here's one I bet you haven't heard.' Philocrates, still on the mule, looked furious. He liked to know where he was with a script, and hated minions anyway. Congrio was unstoppable.

'A Roman tourist comes to a village and sees a farmer with a beautiful sister.'

I noticed that Grumio, who had been about to tug the mule's reins, abruptly stopped, as if he recognised the joke. Congrio was revelling in his new power to hold an audience.

' "Ho there, peasant! How much for a night with your sister?"

' "Fifty drachmas."

' "That's ridiculous! Tell you what, you let me spend a night with the girl and I'll show you something that will amaze you. I bet I can make your animals talk . . . If not, I'll pay you the fifty drachmas."

'Well the farmer thinks, "This man is crazy. I'll string him along and agree to it."

'What he doesn't know is that the Roman has been trained as a ventriloquist.'

'The Roman reckons at least he can have a bit of fun here. "Let me talk to your horse, peasant. Hello, horse. Tell me, how does your master treat you then?" '

' "Pretty well," answers the horse, "though his hands are rather cold when he strokes my flanks . . ." '

As Congrio rambled on, I could just make out through the mask that Philocrates looked stunned, while Grumio was seething furiously.

' "That's wonderful," agrees the farmer, though he isn't convinced entirely. "I could have sworn I actually heard my horse speak. Show me again." '

394

'The Roman chuckles quietly to himself. "Let's try your nice sheep then. Hello, sheep! How's your master?" '

' "Not too bad," says the sheep, "though I do find his hands rather cold on the udder when he milks me . . ." '

Philocrates had assumed a fixed grin, wondering when this unplanned torture was going to end. Grumio still stood like bedrock, listening as if he could not believe it. Congrio had never been so happy in his life.

' "You're convincing me," ' says the farmer.

'The Roman is really enjoying himself now. "I knew I would. I'll do one more, then your sister's mine for the evening. Hello, camel. You're a lovely-looking creature. Tell me – " '

'Before he can go any further, the farmer jumps up furiously. "Don't listen to him! The camel's a liar!" he shrieks.'

Someone else was jumping up.

With a cry of rage, Grumio flung himself at Congrio. 'Who gave it to you?' He meant his scroll of jokes. Helena must have lent it to Congrio.

'It's mine!' The bill-poster was taunting Grumio. He sprang down from the rock and leapt about the stage, just out of reach. 'I've got it and I'm keeping it!'

I had to act fast. Still wearing the ghost's costume, I entered the ring. In the vain hope of making the audience believe my appearance was intentional, I waved my arms above my head and ran with a weird loping gait, pretending to be Moschion's paternal phantom.

Grumio knew the game was up. He abandoned Congrio. Spinning around, he suddenly grabbed Philocrates by one smart boot, gave a wrench of his leg and pulled him off the mule. Not expecting the assault, Philocrates crashed to the ground horribly.

The crows roared with appreciation. It was not funny. Philocrates had fallen on his face. His handsome visage would be ruined. If only his nose was broken, he would be fortunate. Congrio stopped cavorting and ran to him, then pulled him towards the side niche, from which Tranio now emerged, also looking shocked. Together they carried the unconscious actor from the ring. The crowd were thrilled. The fewer cast members left still upright, the more delighted they would be.

Ignoring the rescue of Philocrates, Grumio was trying to mount the mule. I was still stumbling over the long hem of my costume, half blind in the mask. I struggled on, hearing the crowd's bursts of laughter, not only at my antics. Grumio had not reckoned with the mule. As he swung one leg to mount, the animal skittered sideways. The more he tried to reach the saddle, the more it veered away from him.

Amusement soared. It looked like a deliberate trick. Even I slowed up to watch. Hopping in frustration, Grumio followed the mule until they actually came face to face. Grumio turned to approach the saddle again, then the mule twisted, shoved him in the back with its long nose, and knocked him flat. Whinnying with delight at this feat, the mule then galloped from the scene.

Grumio was an acrobat. He had landed better than Philocrates and was on his feet straight away. He turned to follow the mule and escape on foot – just as Thalia had the far gate swung closed against him. Designed for keeping in wild beasts, it was far too tall to climb. He spun back – and met me. Still dressed as the ghost, I tried to fill enough space to block his exit the other way. The gateway behind me gaped open at least twelve feet wide, but members of the company were pressing into it, eager to see the action. They would not let him through.

It was him and me now.

Or rather, it was more than that, for two other figures had emerged. For that last scene in the arena it would be him and me – plus Musa and the sacrificial kid.

Ensemble playing of the finest quality.

LXXIII

I wrenched off the mask. Its flowing grey locks, made from rough horsehair, caught in my fingers. Shaking it free with some violence, I hurled it away.

Blinking in the torchlight, I saw Helena standing up in the tribunal, talking urgently to the commander. Davos was leaping down the steps towards the front, taking the treads three at a time. The Palmyra garrison must have some troops who were not quite the dregs; soon there was a flurry of controlled activity at one end of a row.

A long way behind me, Musa stood with the kid in his arms. He was crazy; a Nabataean; from another world. I could not understand the idiot. 'Back off. Get help!' He ignored my shout.

I gathered the ludicrous folds of the costume and stuffed them in my belt. The crowd suddenly fell so completely silent that I could now hear the flames on the bitumen torches that stood around to light the stage. The soldiers had no idea what was happening, but they knew it was not in the programme. I had a bad feeling that *The Spook who Spoke* was turning into something they would talk about for years.

Grumio and I were standing about fourteen feet apart. Scattered around were various props, mostly items left as hiding places for the ghost: the craggy rock; the beehive oven; a wicker laundry trunk; a couch; a huge ceramic pot.

Grumio was enjoying it. He knew I would have to take him. His eyes were flashing. His cheeks were flushed hectically. He looked drugged with excitement. I should have known all along he was one of those tense, arrogant killers who destroy life coldly and never recant.

'This is the killer from the High Place,' stated Musa, publicly inditing him. The bastard coolly started whistling.

'Give up.' My voice was quiet, addressing Grumio. 'We have evidence and witnesses. I know you killed the playwright

397

because he would not return your missing scroll – and I know you strangled Ione.'

' *"Now she's dead, which takes away some of the problem . . ."* ' He was quoting *The Girl from Andros*. The sheer flippancy enraged me. 'Don't come any closer, Falco.'

He was mad, in the sense that he lacked humanity. In every other sense he was as sane as me, and probably more intelligent. He was fit, athletic, trained to do sleight of hand, keen-sighted. I did not want to have to fight him – but he wanted to fight me.

A dagger was in his hand now. My own knife came from my boot into my grip like a friend. No time to relax, however. He was a professional juggler; if I came too close I was likely to find myself weaponless. I was unarmoured. He, casting aside the cloak from his costume, was at least protected by the leather apron of a stage slave.

He crouched, feinting. I stayed upright, refusing to be drawn. He snarled. I ignored that too. I started circling, weight secretly on the balls of my feet. He prowled too. As we spiralled gently, the distance between us reduced. On the long-benched galleries, the soldiers started a low drumming of their heels. They would sustain the dreadful racket until one of us was done for.

My body felt stiff. I realised just how long it was since I had exercised in a gymnasium. Then he came for me.

The fight was fierce. He had nothing to lose. Hate was his only incentive; death now or later the only possible prize.

One thing was pretty obvious: the garrison enjoyed gladiators. This was better than mere comedy. They knew the knives were real. If someone got stabbed, the blood would not be cochineal.

Any thought that the officer in charge would send men in to help me faded early. There was a group in armour at each gate now, but they were just standing there for a better view. If anyone from the theatre company tried to rush on and assist, the soldiery would hold them back and call it keeping the peace. Their commander would know his best hope of maintaining order was to allow the contest, then either praise me or arrest Grumio, whoever survived. I was not taking bets; nor was the officer, I guessed. Besides, I was an imperial agent. He would expect a certain standard of competence, and if I failed to find it, he probably would not care.

Things began stylishly. Cut and slash. Parry and thrust. Balletic moves. Soon choreographed into the usual panic, heat and mess.

He tricked me. Dismayed, I fled; rolled; threw myself at his feet as he ran at me. He leapfrogged over me and dodged behind the laundry basket. The soldiery roared. They were on his side.

He was safe. I had to be more cautious.

I grabbed the spook's mask and flung it at him. Ever the juggler, he caught the thing and sliced it at my throat. I was no longer there. He spun; glimpsed me, so he thought; felt my knife rip the back of his tunic; but managed to slide out of it.

I pursued. He stopped me with a tornado of whipping strokes. Some bastard in the audience cheered.

I kept my head. I had been the unfavoured man before. Plenty of times. Let him think he had the crowd. Let him believe he had the fight . . . Let him jab me in the shoulder as the ghost's robes untwined around my feet and tripped me up.

I got out of that. With an ungainly clamber I straddled the wicker basket, flopped over it and just found time to thrust the folds of dragging material back in my belt. I stopped thinking pretty thoughts. Stuff strategy. Best just to react.

Stuff reacting. I wanted to finish it.

Grumio suspected the trip had thrown me. He was coming for me. I grabbed his knife arm. The dagger flipped across to his other hand: an old trick, and one I recognised. He stabbed up at my ribs, only to gasp as my knee hit his left wrist and cheated him of his intended blow. Now I was the one who was laughing while he looked stupid and yelled.

Taking advantage of his lapse in concentration, I fell on him. I had trapped him on top of the laundry basket. It lurched wildly as we struggled. I slammed Grumio's arm against the lid. I pinned him to the basketwork. I managed to press my own arm down on to his throat.

He looked thinner, but was as strong as me. I could find no better purchase. I knew that any minute he would fight back and it would be my turn to be hammered. Desperate, I rammed his body against the prop, so the whole basket skidded forwards. We both fell.

Grumio scrambled up. I was coming after him. He hurled himself across the basket as I had done earlier, then turned back. He withdrew the wedge from the clasp and pulled up the lid in my face.

The lid dropped open, on my side. Grumio had dropped his dagger but made no attempt to retrieve it. The thunder of boots from the soldiers stilled. Grumio stood transfixed. We both stared at the basket. There was an enormous snake looking out at Grumio.

The thud of the lid had mobilised the reptile. Even I could tell it was disturbed by the blaze of the torches, the strange setting, the violent shaking it had just experienced. Slithering restlessly, it swarmed out of the chest.

A gasp ran around the amphitheatre. I was gasping myself. Yard after yard of diamond-patterned scales ran from the basket to the ground. 'Keep away!' Grumio yelled at it. No use. Snakes are nearly deaf.

The python felt threatened by the clown's aggression; it opened its mouth, showing what seemed to be hundreds of curved, needle-sharp, backward-pointing teeth.

I heard a quiet voice. 'Stand still.' It was Musa. The keen snakekeeper. He seemed to have known what the chest contained. 'Zeno will not hurt you.' He sounded like some competent technician taking charge.

Thalia had told me pythons do not attack humans. What Thalia said was good enough for me, but I was not taking chances. I remained quite motionless.

The kid, still in Musa's arms, bleated nervously. Then Musa moved steadily past me towards the huge snake.

He reached Grumio. Zeno's tongue flicked rapidly through the side of his mouth. 'He is just taking your scent.' Musa's voice was gentle, yet not reassuring. As if to free himself for dealing with the python, he set down the kid. It leapt forwards. Tottering towards Grumio on fragile legs, it looked terrified, but Zeno showed no interest. 'I, however,' Musa continued quietly, 'already know you Grumio! I arrest you for the murder of the playwright Heliodorus and the tambourinist Ione.' In Musa's hand had appeared the slim, wicked-looking blade of his Nabataean dagger. He was holding it with its point towards Grumio's throat; it was merely a gesture, though, for he was still several feet from the clown.

Suddenly Grumio sprang sideways. He grabbed the kid, and threw it towards Zeno. The kid let out a pitiful bleat of terror, expecting to be bitten and constricted. But Thalia had once told me that snakes in captivity can be choosy. Instead of co-operating, Zeno executed a smooth about-turn. Plainly unhappy, he doubled up on himself with an impressive show of muscle and tried to leave the scene.

The great python sped straight into a group of stage scenery. Hitching strong loops of himself around whatever he encountered, almost deliberately he knocked things flying. The big ceramic jar crashed over, losing its lid. Zeno wound himself around the stage oven, then curled up on top of it, looking superior, as the contraption bowed beneath his enormous weight. Meanwhile, Grumio had gained ground on both Musa and me. He seemed to have a clear run to the exit and began to spring away from us.

From the overturned jar something else emerged. It was smaller than the python – but more dangerous. Grumio stopped in his tracks. I had started to pursue him, but Musa exclaimed and gripped my arm. In front of Grumio there was now another snake: a dark head, a banded body, and as it reared upright to confront him, a golden throat beneath the wide extension of its sinister hood. It must be Pharaoh, Thalia's new cobra. He was angry, hissing, and in full threat display.

'Retreat slowly!' Musa commanded in a clear voice.

Grumio, who was nearly ten feet from the reptile, ignored the advice. He seized a torch and made a sweeping gesture with the burning brand. Pharaoh made what was obviously a mere feint. He expected respect.

401

'He will follow movement!' Musa warned, still unheeded.

Grumio shook the torch again. The cobra let out a short, low hiss, then darted across the whole distance between them and struck.

Pharaoh moved back. Slamming down at body height, he had bitten the leather apron Grumio wore in costume as a slave. The leather must be snakeproof. It would have saved the clown's life.

But his ordeal had not ended. As he was struck that first ferocious blow, Grumio, terrified, staggered and then tripped. On the ground, he instinctively scrabbled to get away. Pharaoh saw him still moving, and rushed forwards again. This time he struck Grumio full on the neck. The downward bite was accurate and strong, followed by a fast chewing movement to make sure.

Our audience went wild. A kill on-stage: just what they had bought their tickets for.

EPILOGUE: PALMYRA

Palmyra: the desert. Hotter than ever, at night.

SYNOPSIS: *Falco*, a playwright, not in the mood to play the hired trickster, finds that as usual he has set everything to rights . . .

LXXIV

Something told me that no one was ever going to ask me what happened about Moschion and his ghost.

Musa and I emerged from the arena badly shaken. We had seen Grumio collapse in shock and hysteria. As soon as the cobra retreated by stages from his vicinity, we crept forward cautiously and dragged the clown to the gates. Behind us the crowd was in uproar. Soon the python was maliciously destroying props while the cobra watched with a menacing attitude.

Grumio was not dead, but undoubtedly he would be. Thalia came over to look at him, then caught my eye and shook her head.

'He'll be gone before dawn.'

'Thalia, should somebody catch your snakes?'

'I don't suggest anyone else tries!'

She was brought a long, pronged implement and ventured into the arena with the bravest of her people. Soon the cobra had been pinned down and reinstalled in his jar, while Zeno rather smugly returned to his basket of his own accord, as if none of the chaos should be blamed on him.

I stared at Musa. Clearly he had brought the python to the arena, ready for Thalia's act after the play. Had it been his idea to take the basket on-stage as a dangerous prop? And had he also known that Pharaoh was in the ceramic jar? If I asked him he would probably tell me, in his straight way. I preferred not to know. There was little difference between what had happened today and subjecting Grumio to the delays of a trial and almost certain condemnation *ad bestias*.

A group of soldiers pulled themselves together. They took charge of Grumio, then, since the commander had told them to arrest all possible culprits, they arrested Tranio too. He went along with a shrug. There was hardly a case to answer. Tranio had behaved unbelievably, but there was no law in the

Twelve Tables against sheer stupidity. He had given away the precious scroll of stories, failed to retrieve it, then allowed Grumio to carry on undetected long after he himself must have known the truth. But if he really thought that his own original mistake equated with Grumio's crimes, he needed a course in ethics.

Later, while we were waiting for the convulsions and paralysis to finish Grumio, Tranio would admit what he knew: that Grumio, acting alone, had lured Heliodorus up the mountain at Petra, making sure no one else knew he had gone there; that Grumio had been walking closest to Musa when he was pushed into the reservoir at Bostra; that Grumio had actually laughed with his tentmate about various attempts to disable me – letting me fall off a ladder, the knife-throwing incident, and even threatening to push me into the underground water system at Gadara.

When Helena and I finally left Palmyra, Tranio would remain in custody, though much later I heard that he had been released. I never knew what happened to him afterwards. It was Congrio who was to become the famous Roman clown. We would attend many of his performances despite those harsh critics at the Theatre of Balbus who dared to suggest that the great Congrio's stories were rather antique, and that somebody should find him a more modern scroll of jokes.

Life would have to alter for several of our companions. When Musa and I first left the arena, Philocrates, in great pain and covered in gore from a glorious nosebleed, had been sitting on the ground waiting for a bone-setter. He looked as if he had a fractured collarbone. His nose, and probably one of his cheekbones, had been broken in his fall. He would never again play the handsome juvenile. I tried to encourage him: 'Never mind, Philocrates. Some women adore a man who has a lived-in face.' You have to be kind.

Once she had ruled out any hope for Grumio, Thalia came to help mop up the drips of blood on this casualty; I swear I heard her trying to negotiate to buy Philocrates' comic mule. The creature would be knocking people over regularly in Nero's Circus when Thalia returned home.

I myself was temporarily in trouble. While Musa and I were hanging on to each other getting our breath back, a familiar voice stormed angrily: 'Didius Falco, if you really want to kill yourself, why not just get run over by a dung-cart like everybody else? Why do you have to attempt your destruction in front of two thousand strangers? And why do I have to be made to watch?'

Magic. I was never so happy as when Helena was berating me. It took my mind off everything else.

'May as well sell tickets for the fight, and help you pay for my funeral – '

She growled, dragging the ghost's costume up and over my head to give me air. But it was a gentle hand that wiped my perspiring brow with her own white stole.

Then we were rushed by the Habib family. They had burst from their seats to tell us what a wonderful evening we had invited them to share – and to stare hard at Helena's lanky chaperone. I left the next part to the women. Helena and Thalia must have planned it in advance, and while Helena was taking her up into the tribunal, Sophrona must have been instructed to go along with it.

Helena hugged the girl, then cried to the Habib family gratefully, 'Oh thank you for looking after her – I've been searching all over for the naughty thing! But now she's found and I can take her back to Rome with me to her proper life. I expect you realised she was from a good family. Such a talented musician, but wicked to run away to be on the stage, of course. Still, what can you expect. She plays the instrument of emperors . . .'

I was choking quietly.

The Habib parents had weighed up the quality of Helena's jewels, some of which she must have been buying quietly from Nabataean caravans and Decapolis markets while my back was turned. They had seen the commanding officer treating her with extreme respect, since he knew that Vespasian himself wanted her whereabouts reported on. Now Khaleed put on a beseeching look. His father was salivating over their apparent good luck. Sophrona herself, like most girls, found she could easily slip into the appearance of being better than she was.

Khaleed's mother suggested that if the girl had to leave Syria, maybe the young couple could be married first. Helena then proposed that Khaleed should spend some time in Rome improving himself among the nobility . . .

'Isn't that nice?' uttered Thalia, with no apparent trace of irony. Nobody but me seemed to entertain any notion that once in Rome the forceful Thalia would persuade Sophrona that her best interests lay not in settling down, but in her public career as an organist.

Discussion was avoided because of a rumpus in the amphitheatre. Denied a full programme, the angry soldiers had started to tear up benches from the ramps.

'Jupiter! Better stop this! How can we distract them?'

'Easy.' Thalia grabbed hold of the young lady. 'Now you're nicely sorted out, Sophrona, you can do something in return. Buck up! I didn't bring it all the way from Rome just to let mosquitoes breed in the water tank . . .'

She signalled to her staff. With a speed that astonished us they lined up around a large low carriage. Calling some of Chremes' stagehands to help them, they wheeled it to the gate, counted three, then ran out across the open space. The audience stilled, and quickly resumed what was left of their seats. The shrouds dropped from the looming item. It was a hydraulus.

When levered off its carriage, the water organ stood over twelve feet high. The upper portion looked like a gigantic set of syrinx pipes, made partly of bronze, partly of reed. The lower part was formed from an ornamental chest to which bellows were attached. One of Thalia's men was pouring water carefully into a chamber. Another was attaching a footboard, a huge lever, and a keyboard.

I saw Sophrona's eyes widen. For a few moments she managed to hide her eagerness, performing a brief pageant of reluctant maidenhood. Helena and the rest of us went along with it and pleaded with her to take the stage. Next minute she was bounding out to give orders to those setting up the instrument for her.

It was obvious that playing the organ mattered. I decided I ought to introduce Sophrona to Ribes. Our moody lyre-player seemed like a young man who might be done a power of good by a girl with wonderful eyes who could talk to him about music . . .

Thalia grinned at Davos. 'Going to help me pump her bellows?' She could make the simplest question sound cheeky. Davos accepted the dubious invitation like a man, even though Thalia had a glint that promised even harder work for him afterwards.

A decent fellow. I reckoned he would cope.

Just as they were about to leave us to provide Sophrona's support on-stage, Phrygia called Thalia back. She had teetered up, her long gangly figure balancing precariously on platform heels. She was waving at the equally tall figure of Sophrona.

'That girl . . .' She sounded anguished.

'Sophrona? She's just a waif I inherited with Fronto's circus.' The narrowing of Thalia's eyes looked unreliable to anyone who wasn't desperate.

'I hoped my daughter was here . . .' Phrygia was not giving up.

'She's here. But maybe after twenty years alone she doesn't want to be found.'

'I'll make everything up to her! I can offer her the best.' Phrygia gazed around wildly. Only one other female in our circle was the right age: Byrria. She snatched at the younger actress hysterically. 'We took you on in Italy! Where were you brought up?'

'Latium.' Byrria looked calm, but curious.

'Outside Rome? Do you know your parents.'

'I was an orphan.'

'Do you know Thalia?'

I saw Thalia wink at Byrria. 'Obviously,' said Thalia quietly, 'I never told your daughter a famous actress was her mother. You don't want girls getting big ideas.'

Phrygia threw her arms around Byrria and burst into tears.

Thalia shot me a look, one of calculation and amazement at what fools would believe when their eyes should tell them different. Then she managed to grab Davos and escape into the arena.

'Everything is going to be wonderful from now on!' Phrygia cried to Byrria. Byrria gave her the doubtful grimace of the usual ungrateful daughter who wants to make her own life.

Helena and I exchanged a glance. We could see the young actress considering what to do as she recognised her amazing luck. Out in the arena, Sophrona had no idea she was being displaced; she was being given plenty of options anyway. Byrria's determination to gain a place in the world had never been in doubt. She wanted a career. If she played along with Phrygia's mistake, she could not only demand good acting parts, but without a doubt she would sooner or later end up in command of the whole company. I reckoned she would be good at that. Loners can usually organise.

What Chremes had told us about the death of live theatre would probably not count. He had been despondent. There was still scope for entertainers, certainly in the provinces, and even in Italy if they adapted to the market. Byrria must know she had been offered the chance of her life.

Chremes, who appeared to need more time than his wife to consider his position, gave Byrria an embarrassed smile, then led Phrygia away to join most of our company, who had collected inside the gate of the amphitheatre. They were eagerly waiting to judge Sophrona's keyboard skills on the fabulous instrument. Byrria dallied behind with Musa, Helena and me. On the whole, I thought Chremes' position was a good one. If he kept his head down he could keep his wife, find himself promoting a popular and beautiful young actress, and probably have peace at home.

Davos, I thought, might soon want to be leaving the company.

If Davos joined forces with Thalia, there seemed a possibility that Sophrona might have lost a mother, but gained a father here today.

I lurched to my feet. 'I'm not a great fan of sonorous music.' Especially after a nerve-racking physical experience. 'Don't let me spoil the fun for anyone else, but if none of you mind, I've had enough of this.' They all decided to come with me back to camp.

We turned away. Helena and I had our arms tightly around one another as we walked, in a sad and contemplative mood. Musa and Byrria were strolling in their normal manner, straight-backed, solemn-faced, side by side in silence and not even holding hands.

I wondered what would become of them. I wanted to think they would now find a quiet corner together and come to terms. Since it was what I would have done myself, I wanted them to go to bed.

Somehow I doubted that would happen. I knew Helena shared my melancholy feeling that we were watching a relationship fail to materialise.

Musa would return to Petra; Byrria would be well known in the Roman theatre. Yet they were obviously friends. Maybe she would write to Musa, and he to her. Maybe I ought to encourage it, one link at least to smooth the path to Nabataean assimilation into the Empire. Cultural contact and private friendship forging bonds: that old diplomatic myth. If he could overcome his urge to run a menagerie, I could see Musa becoming a grand figure in Nabataea. If Byrria became a major entertainment queen, she would meet all the Empire's men of power.

Perhaps one day in the future, when Byrria had exhausted her dreams, they would meet again and it might not be too late.

We had walked some distance. Dusk had long given way to night. Beyond reach of the arena torches we had to pick our way with care. The great oasis was peaceful and mysterious, its palms and olive trees reduced to vague dark shapes; its homes and public buildings lost in their midst. Above our heads a myriad of stars plunged through their endless rota, mechanical yet heart-tugging. Somewhere in the desert a camel brayed its preposterous call, then a dozen others started harshly answering.

Then we all paused, and turned back for a moment. Awestruck, we had reacted to an extraordinary sound. From the place we had left sounded a resonance unlike anything any of us had ever heard. Sophrona was playing. The effect

411

astonished us. If she was Phrygia's true daughter I could see exactly why Thalia wanted to keep the information to herself. Nothing should be allowed to interfere with such a remarkable talent. The public deserves to be entertained.

Around Palmyra, even the beasts in the merchants' caravans had ceased their cacophonous calls. Like us, they stood stock-still listening. The reverberating chords of the water organ rose above the desert, so all the camels were stilled by a wild music that was even more powerful, even louder, and (I fear) even more ridiculous than their own.

FOOTNOTES

Archaeology

The First Century is a patchy period in our knowledge of the
eastern Mediterranean. The Emperors Trajan and Hadrian
took a keen interest in the region, visited it, and initiated
much new town planning. Many spectacular Roman remains
in Jordan and Syria, therefore, including existing theatres,
date from the Second Century. Information about what may
have existed in AD 72 is so sparse that the writer of fiction
must use intelligent invention. The location of some
Decapolis towns has yet to be conclusively established. I have
used the most widely accepted list, choosing the most
convenient of several sites for Dium, and assuming that
Raphana and Capitolias are the same place.

Political History

Nabataea was peacefully annexed by Trajan and became the
Roman province of Arabia Petraia in AD 106. Bostra became
its chief city and the trade routes were shifted east, away from
Petra. This may have been a suggestion from an imperial
agent, possibly one made under a previous emperor and
which Trajan found filed in the Palatine archives.

Literature

Scholars are still hoping to discover a manuscript of *The
Spook who Spoke*. This lost comedy by an unidentified First
Century author (conjecturally identified as M. Didius ?) had
only one recorded stage performance, but is believed by some
to be the prototype for *Hamlet*.

TIME TO
DEPART

For Helen
with thanks for once keeping me alive with Chanel
(and with gin . . .)

ROME: TWO WEEKS IN OCTOBER, AD 72

'It's the City that creates luxury. And out of luxury, inevitably, comes greed, out of greed bursts forth violence, out of violence proliferate all the various kinds of crime and iniquity.'

Cicero

Extract from the Family Tree

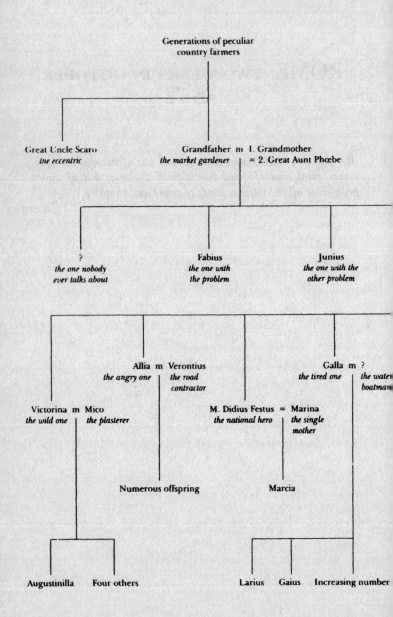

of Marcus Didius Falco

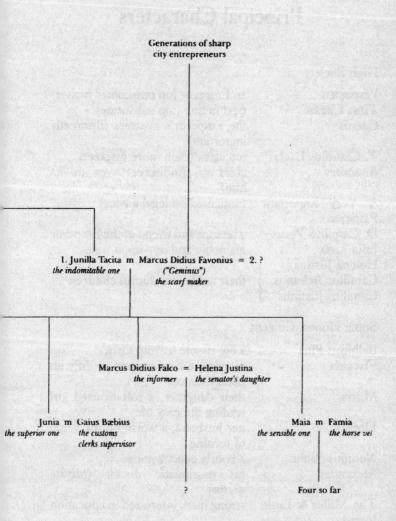

Generations of sharp
city entrepreneurs

1. Junilla Tacita m Marcus Didius Favonius = 2. ?
the indomitable one　　　　　　("Geminus")
　　　　　　　　　　　　　the scarf maker

Marcus Didius Falco = Helena Justina
the informer　　　　*the senator's daughter*

Junia m Gaius Bæbius
the superior one　　*the customs*
　　　　　　clerks supervisor

Maia m Famia
the sensible one　*the horse vet*

?

Four so far

Key: 'm' = Married;
'=' = Not exactly married;
'?' = Unknown, never mentioned in public, or a matter of speculation.

Principal Characters

High Society

Vespasian	an Emperor (no one comes higher)
Titus Caesar	next in line (top substitute)
Caenis	the Emperor's mistress (discreetly important)
T. Claudius Laeta	top clerk (even more discreet)
Anacrites	chief spy (indiscreet even to list him)
A Very Important Patrician	(unnamed on legal advice)
D. Camillus Verus	a senator and friend of the Emperor
Julia Justa	his noble and put-upon wife
Helena Justina Camillus Aelianus Camillus Justinus	their noble and dutiful children

Some Honest Citizens

Balbinus Pius	a big rissole leaving town
Flaccida	his wife, a hard woman in difficult circumstances
Milvia	their daughter, a soft-hearted girl leading the easy life
Florius	her husband, a worm on the verge of turning
Nonnius Albius	a poorly court witness
Alexander	his pessimistic doctor (private sector)
The Miller & Little Icarus	strong men, interested in education
Lalage	refined proprietress of the Bower of Venus
Macra	a young lady at that élite finishing school

| Gaius & Phlosis | two extremely helpful boatmen |

Low Society (Fountain Court)

Lenia	a blushing bride
Smaractus	her bashful groom
Cassius	a baker whose oven may get too hot
Ennianus	a basket-weaver who may be tangling with trouble
Castus	a newcomer, dealing in old junk
An old bag woman	
Nux	a homeless dog looking for a soft touch
Falco	her target (not as tough as he thinks)
A baby	abandoned, also looking for a nice home with kindly folk

Law and Order (all under suspicion)

Marcus Rubella	tribune of the scrupulous Fourth Cohort of vigiles
L. Petronius Longus	enquiry chief in the XIII region
Arria Silvia	his often furious wife
Their cat	(a cohort joke)
Martinus	A deputy (not for long, he hopes)
Fusculus	an expert on rackets
Linus	on detached duty on the *Aphrodite*
Rufina	the reason Linus has detached himself
Sergius	a happy punishment officer
Porcius	a young recruit (unhappy)
Scythax	an optimistic doctor (public sector)
Tibullinus	a centurion of the dubious Sixth Cohort
Arica	his sidekick (certainly needs kicking)

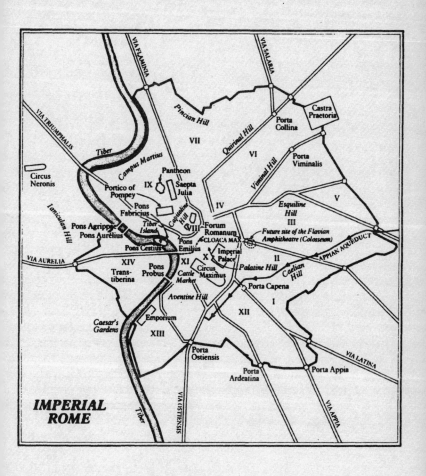

IMPERIAL ROME

Circus Neronis

VIA TRIUMPHALIS

Tiber

Ianiculan Hill

Pons Agrippae
Pons Aurelius

VIA AURELIA

XIV
Transtiberina

Pons Probus

Caesar's Gardens

XIII

Emporium

VIA OSTIENSIS

Tiber

Campus Martius

VIA FLAMINIA

Pincian Hill

VII

Pantheon

IX   Saepta Julia

Portico of Pompey

Pons Fabricius

Tiber Island

Pons Cestius

Pons Emilius

Capitoline Hill

VIII

Forum Romanum

CLOACA MAX.

XI   X   Imperial Palace

Cattle Market   Circus Maximus

Aventine Hill

Porta Ostiensis

Porta Ardeatina

Quirinal Hill

Porta Collina

VI

Viminal Hill

Porta Viminalis

IV

Esquiline Hill

III

Future site of the Flavian Amphitheatre (Colosseum)

Palatine Hill   II   Caelian Hill

Porta Capena

I

XII

VIA SALARIA

Castra Praetoria

V

APPIAN AQUEDUCT

VIA LATINA

Porta Appia

VIA APPIA

I

'I still can't believe I've put the bastard away for good!' Petronius muttered.

'He's not on the boat yet,' Fusculus corrected him. Clearly the Watch's optimist.

There were five us waiting on a quayside. Mid-October. An hour before dawn. A wakening breeze chilled our tense faces as we huddled in cloaks. The day was making itself ready for action somewhere on the other side of Italy, but here in Portus, Rome's new harbour, it was still fully dark. We could see the huge beacon on the lighthouse flaunting itself, with glimpses of tiny figures tending the fire; pale sheets of flame sometimes lit the statue of Neptune presiding over the entrance. The sea god's illuminated torso stood out strangely in our surroundings. Only the scents of old, hardened rope and rotting fish scales told us we were standing on the grand harbour bowl.

We were five honest, respectable citizens who had been waiting all night for a sixth. *He* had never been honest, though like most criminals he had no difficulty passing himself off as respectable. Roman society had always been readily bamboozled by brazen acts. But now, thanks to Petronius Longus, the man and his crimes had been publicly exposed.

We had been waiting too long. Although nobody said it, we were starting to dread that the big rissole would not show.

The lowlife was called Balbinus.

I had been hearing his name as long as I could remember. It had certainly been notorious when Petronius and I had come home from the army six years before. At that time my old tentmate Petro, being a dutiful type who fancied a good salary, had put himself forward as a public officer; I set up in business alone. He was chasing cabbage thieves through the markets while I was picking through clerks' divorces and tracing stolen art. On the face of it we lived in different worlds, yet we stumbled across the same tragedies and heard the same worrying stories on the streets.

Balbinus was renowned throughout our district as one of the dirtiest underworld organisers ever to gild imperial Rome. The area he terrorised included brothels, wharfside warehouses, the back-doubles on the Aventine slopes, the dark colonnades around the Circus Maximus. He ran jostlers and confidence tricksters; prostitutes and cutpurses; cat burglars and marauding gangs of street beggars with fake blind eyes who could soon spot trouble coming. He kept a couple of safe houses for receiving, set up under the cover of straight businesses. Petronius reckoned that the flow of stolen goods into these dens of illicit commerce rivalled the international trade at the Emporium.

Petro had been trying to nail Balbinus for years. Now, somehow, he had managed to set up a capital charge – and go on to secure a conviction despite all Balbinus' efforts to escape using democratic channels (intimidation and bribes). I had yet to hear the full details. Barely back in Rome from what I liked to describe as a confidential diplomatic mission, I had been roped in tonight as a dependable extra and friend.

'He's not going to come now,' I suggested easily, since I knew how stubborn Petro was.

'I'll not risk losing him.'

'Right.'

'Don't niggle me, Falco.'

'You're so conscientious you're tying yourself up in knots. Listen to someone rational: he'll either have left Rome last evening, in which case we would have seen him by now, or he went to bed first. If that's it, he won't arrive for another hour or two. When's the ship due to leave?'

'The minute he gets here, if I have any control over it.'

'With the light,' clarified Fusculus in a quiet tone. I guessed my point about our quarry's arrival had already been made to Petro by his men. Since they knew him too, their reaction to my attempt was restrained. They were hoping he would either listen to a pal, or at least give them some entertainment by losing his temper and thumping me.

'I need a drink,' I commented.

'Stuff you, Falco. Don't try that one.' It was too dark to

428

see his face. All the same, I chuckled; he was weakening.

The trick was not to make an issue of it. I said nothing, and about five minutes afterwards Petronius Longus burst out with an obscenity that I hadn't heard uttered in a public place since we left Britain. Then he growled that he was cold and past caring – and was off to the nearest wine bar for a beaker to console himself.

Nobody chortled. By then we were too relieved that he had given way to gloat over our victory, just as Petro had known we would be. He had a nice sense of timing. Martinus growled, 'Better take the bloody barnacle. It'll be his last chance for a long time.'

So we bawled out to Linus to stop pretending he was a sailor and to come off the ship and have a drink with us.

II

The atmosphere was thick with lamp smoke; hard to see why, as there was a mean supply of lamps. Something crunched under my boot – either an old oyster shell, or part of a whore's broken necklace. There seemed to be a lot of debris on the floor. Probably best not to investigate.

No one else was in the dump. No customers, anyway. A couple of grimy lasses roused themselves slightly when we tramped inside, but they soon got the message and slumped back into sleep. They looked too exhausted even to be curious. That didn't mean they wouldn't be listening in, but we were not intending any loud indiscretions. There was too much at stake.

We cramped ourselves on to benches, feeling stiff and oversized in our outdoor dress. We were all armed, to the point where it was impossible to be discreet when crowding around small tables. If we tried to pretend we were just carrying Lucanian sausage rolls, someone would have his privates shorn off by an awkwardly placed sword blade. We arranged ourselves with care.

The landlord was an unsmiling, unwelcoming coastal type who had summed us up as we crossed his threshold. 'We were just closing.' We must have brought in a suggestion of imminent violence.

'I apologise.' Petronius could have used his official status to insist we were served, but as usual he preferred to try his charm first. His brevity probably screamed 'law and order'. The landlord knew he had no choice. He served us, but made it plain that he hoped we would be leaving quickly. It was too late in the night for trouble.

Well, we agreed with that.

There was tension in all of us. I noticed Martinus, the cocky bantam who was Petro's second in command, took one deep swig of his drink, then kept going to the doorway and staring out. The others ignored him fidgeting. In the end he parked

430

his rather jutting backside on a stool just beyond the threshold, occasionally calling in some remark to the rest, but watching the waterfront. In Petro's troop even the tame annoyance was a decent officer.

Petronius and I ended up at a table to ourselves.

He had strong bonds with his men. He always led from the front. He pulled his weight in routine enquiries and on a surveillance he mucked in as one of them. But he and I had been friends for a long time. Between us were even stronger links, forged from when we had met at eighteen and shared a legionary posting to one of the grimmest parts of the Empire while it was earning dismal fame – Britain, in Nero's time, with the Boudiccan Rebellion as our special treat. Now, although for long periods we often failed to meet, when we did we could pick up straight away, as if we had shared an amphora only last Saturday. And when we entered a wine bar with others it was understood that we two would sit together, very slightly separate from the rest.

Petro gulped his wine, then visibly regretted it. 'Jupiter! You could paint that on warts and they'd fall off by dinner time . . . So how was the East?'

'Wild women and wicked politics.'

'Didius Falco, the world traveller!' He didn't believe a word of it. 'What really happened?'

I grinned, then gave him a neat summary of five months' travelling: 'I got my ear gnawed by a few camels. Helena was stung by a scorpion and spent a lot of money – much of it my father's, I'm delighted to say.' We had brought a quantity of stuff back with us; Petro had promised to help me unload in return for my assistance tonight. 'I ended up in a hack job scribbling Greek jokes for second-rate touring actors.'

His eyebrows shot up. 'I thought you went on a special task for the Palace?'

'The bureaucratic mission rapidly fell through – especially after I found out that Vespasian's Chief Spy had sent a message ahead of me encouraging my hosts to lock me up. Or worse,' I concluded gloomily.

'Anacrites? The bastard.' Petronius had no time for officials, whatever smooth title they dressed themselves up in. 'Did he land you in bad trouble?'

431

'I survived.'

Petronius was frowning. He viewed my career like a kind of blocked gutter that needed a hefty poke with a stick to shift the sludge and get it running properly. He saw himself as the expert with the stick. 'What was the point, Falco? What's in it for Vespasian if he destroys a first-class agent?'

'Interesting question.' In fact there could be several reasons why the Emperor might feel a foreign jail was just the place for me. I was an upstart who wanted social promotion; since he disapproved of informers, the idea of letting me wear the gold ring and strut like a man of substance had always rankled. Most of the time he owed me money for my undercover services; he would love to renege. Then one of his sons had tender feelings towards a certain young lady who preferred to live with me, while I had a long-term feud with the other. Either Titus or Domitian might have asked their pa to dump me. Besides, who really likes a hireling who handles problems with dispatch, then comes back wearing a happy smile and expecting a huge cash reward?

'I don't know why you work for him,' Petronius grumbled angrily.

'I work for myself,' I said.

'That's news!'

'That's the truth. Even if the damned secretariat offers me a straight task with a set fee and vast expenses, I won't consider it. From now on, I stick to private commissions – which was what I had to do after I got shoved in shit in Arabia by bloody Anacrites and his devious games.'

'You're a dope,' Petro answered disbelievingly. 'You can't resist the challenge. One nod from the man in purple and you'll scuttle back.'

I grabbed the flagon and helped us both to more wine. It still tasted like a cure for swine fever. 'Petro, the man in purple didn't try to sell me to a camel trader.'

Whatever I thought of the rank of emperor, Vespasian the man was completely straight. Even Petronius grudgingly allowed the point. 'So it was the spy, Falco. What's the difference?'

'Who knows? But Anacrites thinks I'm rotting in some desert citadel; this could be the lever I'm looking for to show him up. I'll give my travelogue to Vespasian before the spy finds out I'm alive and back in Rome.'

It was good to unload my anger, but there were better things to talk about. 'Come to dinner when we get settled back in – bring Silvia and the girls. We'll have a gathering and tell our gripping travellers' tales.'

'How's Helena?' Petro remembered to ask when I mentioned his own wife and children.

'Fine. And no, we're not married, or planning it; nor quarrelling and planning to separate.'

'Any signs of impending fatherhood?'

'Certainly not!' I retorted, like a man who knew how to handle his private life. I hoped Petro would not notice I was bluffing. 'When I'm honoured, you'll be the first to know . . . Olympus! Talking to you is like fending off my mother.'

'Wonderful woman,' he commented in his aggravating way.

I carried on with a feeling of false confidence. 'Oh yes, Ma's a credit to the community. If everyone on the Aventine was as stiff-backed as my mother, you'd have no work to do. Unfortunately some of them are called Balbinus Pius – about whom you still owe me an explanation or two.'

This time the distraction worked. With a glow of satisfaction Petronius threw back his great head and stretched his long legs under the table. Beaming proudly, he settled down to bring me up to date.

'You realise,' Petro began, with mock-heroic grandeur, 'we're talking about the most vicious, seditious operator in organised crime who ever fixed his claws on the Aventine?'

'And now *you*'ve caught him!' I grinned admiringly.

He ignored the jesting undertone. 'Believe it, Falco!'

I was enjoying myself. Petronius Longus was a stolid, patient worker. I could not remember that I had ever heard him boasting; it was good to see him thrilled by his own success for once.

Inches taller than me to start with, he even seemed to have grown. His quiet manner tended to disguise how powerfully built he was. Slow of step and wry of speech, he could lean on wrongdoers before they even saw him coming, but once Petro

433

applied weight, resistance caved in fast. He ran the watch enquiry team without seeming to exert himself, although as his best friend I happened to know that in private he worried deeply about standards. He achieved the highest. His was a lean, competent squad which gave the public what they paid for and kept the villains on the hop.

He had a calm grip on his domestic life as well. A good Roman: honorific father of three children. He had a small, scathing wife who knew how to make her presence felt, and a much-loved trio of lively little girls. At home he fielded Arria Silvia's sparky temper pretty easily. The children adored him. Even the wife modulated her complaints, knowing she had one piece of fortune that was missing from most marriages: Petro was there because he wanted to be. Both as a family man and as a public officer, he looked easy-going but was utterly reliable.

'Balbinus Pius . . .' he said softly, savouring his triumph.

'Ludicrous name,' I commented. 'Balbinus the Dutiful! As far as I know his only duty is serving himself. Isn't he the mouldy cheese who owns that filthy brothel they call Plato's Academy? And the thieves' kitchens down on the waterside at the back of the Temple of Portunus?'

'Don't speak to me about Plato's. I get a pain in the bladder just thinking about the place. Jupiter knows whose name is scratched on the crumbling title deeds, but you're right, it was Balbinus who had it sewn up. He took a percentage of every transaction in bed, plus whatever the house made on robbing purses or selling "abandoned" boots and belts. Then, as well as his entertainment interests, he had a nice goldsmith's workshop where stolen goblets could be melted down in minutes; several sweatshops that specialised in putting new braid on tunics that "fell off" washing lines; numerous tat stalls in the markets, constantly shifting just when I placed a man in the portico watching them; and a couple of counterfeiting factories. If it stank, he owned it,' confirmed Petro. 'Past tense, though, Falco. One of the bleak facts he has to face today is that a capital conviction means losing all his property.'

'I'm sobbing into my napkin.'

'Don't upset yourself too much – I'm still not certain

we'll net his whole empire. Some of it must be in hidden hoards.'

'I bet! Was he expecting to be put away?'

'He wasn't even expecting to be put on trial! This has taken me months of planning, Falco. There was only ever going to be one crack at him, or he'd be screaming "persecution of a citizen!" and I'd be out of a job. But he didn't believe I'd ever find anybody prepared to prosecute.'

'So, Lucius Petronius, how did you arrange it?'

'Marcus Didius, there was only one way possible. I found somebody even greedier, and even more of a bastard, than him!'

III

Smiling, Petro passed one big hand over his brown hair. He seemed to have been having it styled more snappily. (Well, it was shorter; that was his barber's creative limit.) His other great paw lay lightly at his waist, where the staff of his office was stuck behind a wide, creased leather belt that I remembered him buying from a shifty Celt in Londinium. Otherwise, apart from the flash haircut, he did not trouble to priss himself up like a man of fashion. On duty it was better to be protected by a leather jerkin that might deflect a knife blade and a thick wool cloak which would shrug off the mud if he hurled himself to the pavement when tackling a runaway. His boots had come up hard on quite a few doorframes too by the looks of them.

'So who was the high-principled, public-minded citizen who squealed about Balbinus?' I asked.

'A donkey's turd called Nonnius.'

'Not Nonnius Albius? I thought he was a racketeer himself?'

'He had been. He actually worked with Balbinus, was his chief rent collector. That was what appealed to me.'

'Of course! You needed an insider.'

'No one else could have done it. Nonnius was ideal.'

'But he was a Balbinus boy. How did you sew him up?'

'A sad story.' Petro grinned. 'He's dying. His doctor had just put the frighteners on. Poor old Nonnius is suffering from terminal rot.'

'Something nasty that people don't talk about?'

'Same as his profession!' Petro snarled. Then he told me the story: 'Back in the spring, I just happened to learn that Nonnius had been given notice to quit by his pet medicine man —'

'Happened?' This seemed a nice coincidence.

Petro was in full flow and not to be sidetracked by my scepticism. 'Nonnius gets informed by some pet Aesculapius

436

that he's finished, but the doctor says he'll last longer if he takes care of himself – no worries, lots of pampering – '

'Expensive!' I was beginning to see Petro's reasoning.

'A life of luxury prescribed! So I get to him when he's just reeling from the bad news, I lend a sympathetic ear, then I put it to him he's spent his life running around for Balbinus while that rat lay on a reading couch counting his winnings – and for what? Now seems the time for a spot of levelling ... Since Nonnius has to give up the low life, he soon settles on snatching at the high life to compensate. This appeals to the bastard: taking a litter through the Forum, giving orders to slaves through the window and greeting fawning admirers who are hoping for free gifts. Even more than that, suddenly he loves the idea of robbing Balbinus.'

I laughed shortly. 'The loyalty of thieves! So he was prepared to testify?'

'In return for the traditional reward.'

'You did a deal?'

'All legal. He appeared before Marponius and twittered like a happy song finch. In return, as a successful prosecutor he can seize a proportion of Balbinus' traceable assets. The only disincentive is that he has to help us trace them. But it's well worth his while to hire accountants. Having been on the money-collecting side himself he knows the occasional fellow with a dodgy abacus, imaginative enough to guess where the loot may be hidden.'

'I love it!' I was laughing. We both grabbed more wine, which now tasted almost palatable. 'But Petro, you must have needed to take great care framing the actual charge against Balbinus. What did you throw at him?'

'Murder. The only count that would have worked.'

'Of course. It had to be a capital offence.'

'Right. Anything less and he would only end up with a fine – and however large, a fine wouldn't choke him. He could shed thousands and hardly feel a tickle.'

I didn't say it, but putting Balbinus in court on any charge that left him free in Rome afterwards would have placed Petro himself in a very dangerous position. There was no point dwelling on this feature. He knew all right.

'So who had been topped – and how did you nail Balbinus

for the murder?' I didn't suppose he had actually stuck a
dagger in someone personally. 'Getting blood spots on his
own tunic was never his style.'

'Happy accident,' said Petro. 'It happened at Plato's
Academy.' The brothel we had already mentioned. 'They
specialise in fleecing foreign visitors. Some poor Lycian had
been set up to lose his travelling pouch in the floor-creeping
gag. While the girl was giving him the push-and-shove that
he'd paid for, he made the mistake of noticing a rustle in the
straw. Up he jumps, and discovers the whore's accomplice
just reaching for his money. Instead of making a discreet
complaint to the madam, then leaving the brothel with an
apology and a wiser attitude, this fool puts up his fists and
makes a fight of it. The snatcher was so surprised at the
Lycian's unsporting behaviour that he knifed him on the
spot.'

I whistled. 'Someone should hand out warnings to
innocent travellers! But how did you prove it? Surely the
brothel's mother hen was used to denying all knowledge of
trouble?'

'Oh yes. Lalage's well up to it. I'd never have pinned her
down, and I'm not sure I'd even have fancied tackling her . . .
Thank Jupiter Plato's is on the Sixth Cohort's beat, and I
don't normally have the problem.' I saw his point. The whores
who crowded around the Circus Maximus were as fierce as
lynxes, and Lalage, the madam at Plato's, had a phenomenal
reputation. 'There was a witness,' Petro told me grimly. 'And
for the first time in history it was a witness who managed not
to yell at the scene of the crime. So instead of the usual turn-
up where the witness gets stabbed too, he hid up in the rafters
until he had a chance to run away.'

'Unbelievable.'

'Better yet, one of my men then found him wandering in
shock up on the Hill. He blurted out his tale, and we went
straight to Plato's. The Sixth were nowhere in sight – that's
normal – so we handled it ourselves. We were able to jump
from an alley just as two bouncers were dragging the corpse
out through the back door. That pegged the crime to the
brothel. So for a start, when we went into court half the
Thirteenth-sector Watch had seen Plato's management

438

towing the Lycian to a gutter by the boot-thongs, with Lalage herself holding a lamp. Next we had our witness to narrate the stabbing luridly. *He* was a second Lycian who had been smuggled in by the first one. The pair were hoping to slip the girl a copper and get a double spike half-price.'

I slapped the table. 'Disgraceful! How can you police the city when even the victims are crooks?'

'Falco, I'll live with it! I locked our witness in protective custody, lost the address until he was needed, then produced him at the Basilica in his best tunic to tell how he had trembled in his hiding place and seen all. He identified the prostitute, the madam, and the creeping snatch.'

'Do I know the snatch?'

'A weasel called Castus.'

It meant nothing. I didn't ask if I knew the prostitute, and Petro didn't bother to embarrass anyone by naming her. 'So what about your star witness? What about Nonnius?'

'We were well set up by the time our barrister called him. All Nonnius Albius had to do was to confess his own role as a Balbinus collector, and state that he knew the killer Castus was on the Balbinus payroll. He played his part very prettily – he even produced tallies to show the percentage Balbinus regularly took from stolen purses at the brothel.'

'Good value!'

'A prime witness. Our Lycian had come up with some joyful clinchers, like Castus exclaiming as he stabbed the dead man, "Teach him to argue with Balbinus!" Nonnius then told the jury that all the Balbinus henchmen are routinely ordered to slash if trouble threatens. He had frequently heard Balbinus give those instructions. So we had him for organised crime, profiteering, and conspiracy, resulting in actual death.'

'The jury bought it?'

'Marponius had explained to them that he needed their co-operation if he was to be seen as the judge who cleaned up Rome . . .'

Marponius was the main judge in the murder court. He was keen on his work, and personally ambitious, though not necessarily as blatant as Petronius made out. For one thing, Marponius was not a clever man.

'There were some juicy details,' Petro said. 'I was threatening Lalage with a range of offences against the prostitutes' registration rules, so even she went into court to give evidence on our side.'

'Couldn't Balbinus buy her off?'

'I reckon she's keen to see him take a trip,' opined Petronius. 'Lalage would be quite capable of running Plato's on her own. Maybe things were different once, but nowadays she really doesn't need a king of crime creaming off the top of her income.' He leant back and went on with his usual modesty: 'Oh I had some luck in the timing. Balbinus believed himself untouchable, but there was a new mood in the underworld. People were ready to revolt. I noticed the change before he did, that's all.'

The point was, Petronius Longus *had* noticed. Many an enquiry captain would have had his nose so close to the pavings he wouldn't have spotted the flies on the balcony.

'Take your credit for sniffing the air,' I commanded. 'And then for fixing it!'

He smiled quietly.

'So your jury convicted, and Marponius did his own career some good by handing out a death penalty – I presume the Assembly ratified the sentence. Did Balbinus appeal any further?'

'Straight to Vespasian – and it came straight back: negative.'

'That's something!' I commented. We were both cynics about the Establishment. 'Who signed the chitty?'

'Titus.'

'Vespasian must have approved.'

'Oh yes.' Only the Emperor has the final power of removing life from a Roman citizen, even if the citizen's life smells like a pile of cat's turds. 'I was quite impressed by the quick response,' Petro admitted. 'I don't really know whether Balbinus offered money to officials, but if he tried it he was wasting his time. Things at the Palace seem to be scented like Paestum violets nowadays.' One good result of the new Flavian Caesars. Graft had gone over the balcony with Nero, apparently. Petro seemed confident anyway. 'Well it was the result I wanted, so that's that.'

'Here we are!' I congratulated him. 'Ostia at dawn!'

'Ostia,' he agreed, perhaps more cautiously. 'Marponius gets a free meal at the Palace; I get a scroll with a friendly message from Titus Caesar; the underworld gets a warning – '

'And Balbinus?'

'Balbinus,' growled Petronius Longus bitterly, 'gets time to depart.'

IV

I suppose it is a comfort to us all – we who carry the privilege of being full citizens of the Empire – to know that except in times of extreme political chaos when civilisation is dispensed with, we can do what we like yet remain untouchable.

It is, of course, a crime for any of us to profiteer while on foreign service; commit parricide; rape a vestal virgin; conspire to assassinate the Emperor; fornicate with another man's slave; or let amphorae drop off our balconies so as to dent fellow citizens' heads. For such evil deeds we can be prosecuted by any righteous free man who is prepared to pay a barrister. We can be invited before a praetor for an embarrassing discussion. If the praetor hates our face, or merely disbelieves our story, we can be sent to trial, and if the jury hates us too we can be convicted. For the worst crimes we can be sentenced to a short social meeting with the public strangler. But, freedom being an inalienable and perpetual state, we cannot be made to endure imprisonment. So while the public strangler is looking up a blank date in his calender, we can wave him goodbye.

In the days of Sulla so many criminals were skipping punishment, and it was obviously so cheap to operate, that finally the law enshrined this neat dictum: no Roman citizen who was sentenced to the death penalty might be arrested, even after the verdict, until he had been given *time to depart*. It was my right; it was Petro's right; and it was the right of the murderous Balbinus Pius to pack a few bags, assume a smug grin, and flee.

The point is supposed to be that living outside the Empire is, for a citizen, a penalty as savage as death. Balbinus must be quaking. Whoever thought that one up was not a travelling man. I had been outside the Empire, so my verdict was not quite that of a jurist. Outside the Empire can be perfectly liveable. Like anywhere, all you need to survive comfortably is slightly more cash than the natives. The sort of criminals who can afford the fare in the first place need have no qualms.

So here we were. Petronius Longus had convicted this mobster of heinous crimes and placed him under sentence of death – but he was not allowed to apply a manacle. Today had been set for the execution. So this morning, while the greybeards from the Senate were tutting away over the decay of public order, Balbinus Pius would stroll out of Rome like a lord and set off for some hideaway. Presumably he had already filled it with golden chalices, with rich Falernian to slosh into them, and with fancy women to smile at him as they poured the happy grape. Petro could do nothing – except make damn sure the bastard went.

Petronius Longus was doing that with the thoroughness his friends in Rome would expect.

Linus, the one dressed as a sailor, had been listening in more closely than the other members of the squad. As his chief started listing for me the measures he was taking, Linus slewed around on his bench and joined us. Linus was to be a key man in enforcing the big rissole's exile.

'Balbinus lives in the Circus Maximus district, unluckily –' Petro began.

'Disaster! The Sixth Cohort run that. Have we hit some boundary nonsense? Does that mean it's out of your watch and you can't cover his house?'

'Discourteous to the local troopers . . .' Petro grinned slightly. I gathered he was not deterred by a bit of discourtesy to the slouchers in the Sixth. 'Obviously it's had to be a joint operation. The Sixth are escorting him here – '

I grinned back. 'Assisted by observers from your own cohort?'

'*Accompanied,*' said Petro pedantically. I looked forward to seeing what form this might take.

'Of course you trust them to do the job decently?'

'Does he heck!' scoffed Linus, only half under his breath.

Linus was a young-looking thirty, dressed for his coming role in more layers of tunics than most sailors wear, crumpled boots, a floppy hat his mother had knitted, and a seaman's knife. Below the short sleeves of the tunics his bare arms had a chubby appearance, though none of Petro's men were

443

overweight. Level eyes and a chin square as a spade. I had never met him before, but could see he was lively and keen. A typical Petro recruit.

'So the Sixth carry the big rissole here, then he's handed over to you?' I smiled at Linus. 'How far does this slave-driver want you to go with him?'

'All the way,' answered Petro for himself.

I shot Linus a look of sympathy, but he shrugged it off. 'A lad likes to travel,' he commented. 'I'll see him land the other side. At least the esteemed Petronius says I don't have to shin up rigging on the journey back.'

'Big of him! Where's the rissole going?'

'Heraclea, on the Taurica peninsula.'

I whistled. 'Was that his choice?'

'Someone made a very strong suggestion,' came Petro's dry response. 'Someone who *does* have the right to feed him to the arena lions if he fails to listen to the hint.' The Emperor.

'Someone has a sense of humour then. Even Ovid only had to go to Moesia.'

The world had shrunk since emperors sent salacious poets to cool their hexameters on the lonely shores of the Euxine Sea while other bad citizens were allowed to sail to Gaul and die rich as wine merchants. The Empire stretched far beyond Gaul nowadays. Chersonesus Taurica, even further away on the Euxine than Ovid's bleak hole, had vivid advantages as a dump for criminals: though technically not a Roman province, we did have a trading presence all along its coast, so Balbinus could be watched – and he would know it. It was also a terrible place to be sent. If he wasn't eaten by brown bears he would die of cold or boredom, and however much money he managed to take with him, there were no luxuries to spend it on.

'It's no summer holiday for you either,' I told Linus. 'You'll never get home this side of Saturnalia.'

He accepted the news cheerily. 'Someone needs to make sure Balbinus doesn't nip off the ship at Tarentum.' True. Or Antium, or Puteoli, or Paestum, Buxentum or Rhegium, or Sicily, or at any one of scores of seashore towns in Greece, and the islands, and Asia, that would lie on our criminal's way into exile. Most of these places had an ambiguous form of loyalty towards Rome. Some were run by Roman officials who were only looking for a rest. Many were too remote to be supervised even by officials who liked to throw their weight about. Petronius Longus was rightly distraught about making the penalty stick. Linus, however, seemed to take his responsibility placidly. 'This is my big chance to travel. I don't mind wintering at some respectable town in Bithynia, or on the Thracian coast.' Petro's stooge had looked at a map, then.

'Will you get your lodging paid, Linus?'

'Within the limits,' Petronius uttered sombrely, resisting any frivolous suggestion that Linus might be heading for a spree at the state's expense.

'Anything for a bit of peace!' said Linus. Evidently there was a woman involved.

Well, we were all henpecked. Not that most of us would have entertained four or five months beyond the Hellespont at the worst time of year simply to avoid having our ears battered. Linus could not have mastered the gracious art of sloping off to the public baths for half a day (a set of baths you are not known to frequent).

Martinus appeared in the doorway. He gave Petronius a signal that was barely more than a twitch.

'They're coming! Scram, Linus.'

With a grin I can still remember, Linus slid from his bench. Keyed up for adventure, he was out of the wine bar and off back to the Chersonesus-bound ship while the rest of us were still bringing our thoughts to bear.

We had paid for the wine. We all left the bar in silence. The landlord closed the door after us. We heard him fasten it with a heavy log, pointedly.

Outside the darkness had altered by several shades. The wind freshened. As we regained the quay Fusculus shook a shin that must have had cramp, while we all adjusted our swords and freed them from our cloaks. Nervously we strained to listen for the sound we really wanted to hear above the creaks of ropes and boards, and the plashing of wavelets under buffers, floats and hulls.

We could make out a movement on the harbour road,

though still only faintly. Martinus must have honed his ears for this mission if he had heard something earlier.

Soon the noise clarified and became brisk hoofbeats, then we picked out wheels as well, somewhere in their midst. Almost at once a short cavalcade clattered up, the iron shoes of the horses and mules ringing loud. At the centre was an exceptionally smart carriage of the type very wealthy men own for comfortable summer visits to their remote estates – big enough to allow the occupant to eat and write, or to try to forget being shaken by potholes and to sleep. Balbinus was probably not napping on this journey.

A couple of freedmen who must have decided, or been persuaded, that they could not bear to leave their master hopped off the top and began unloading a modest selection of luggage. Balbinus had lost all his slaves. That was part of stripping him of his property. What his freedmen did now was up to them. Soon they would possess more civic rights than he did – though they might still feel they owed familial debts to the master who had once freed them. Whether they saw it that way would depend on how many times he had kicked them for nothing when they were still slaves.

So far the rissole had remained inside his carriage. It was a heavy, four-wheeled special, all gleaming bright coachwork and silver finials, drawn by two lively mules with bronze snaffles and millefiori enamels on their headbands. The driver enjoyed making play with his triple-thonged whip; the mules took it calmly, though some of our party cantered uneasily when he suddenly cracked the thing above our heads. We were on edge – still waiting for the big moment. Dark curtains across the carriage's windows were hiding the occupant.

Petronius walked forwards to greet the officers of the Sixth watch who had escorted the man from Rome. I stayed at his shoulder. He introduced Arica and Tibullinus, whom he knew. Tibullinus appeared to be the man in charge. He was a truculent, untidy centurion, and I didn't like him much. With them was Porcius, a young recruit of Petro's who had been formally attached to them as an observer. He lost himself among the rest of the Sixth's enquiry team rather rapidly.

While we were going through the formalities, another

couple of horses turned up. Their riders slid down, then they too joined us, openly nodding to Petro.

'What's this?' cried Tibullinus, sounding annoyed, though he tried to hide it. 'Checking up? On the Sixth?'

'Far be it from me to slander the meticulous Sixth!' Petro assured him. He was a devious bastard when he chose. 'Just a couple of lads I told to lend a hand when they'd finished something else. Looks like they only just caught up with you . . .'

Everyone realised his couple of lads had attached themselves to the Sixth and their not-quite prisoner for the whole journey – and that the men of the Sixth had failed to notice they were being tagged. They should have known. It could have been any kind of ambush. We left it at that, before things became too sensitive.

Something was about to happen.

There was a moment's unnatural atmosphere, then everyone straightened and grew watchful. The carriage door creaked as it opened. Then Balbinus emerged.

447

V

Always the same shock: you come face to face with a murderous master criminal, and he looks like a ribbon-seller.

Balbinus Pius was five feet three digits – definitely not tall. He was looking me in the windpipe, and appeared not to notice that most of the officers present overstripped him by almost a foot. He had an oval head; an expressionless face; wavering eyes; an anxious expression that verged nicely on bewilderment. His manner was quiet; no more threatening than a ladybird.

His hunched shoulders held up a dapper white tunic and short grey cloak. The cloak was pinned extremely neatly on the left shoulder by a round gold brooch set with five garnets. He had healthy pink skin. On the top of his head it was visible through the short, thinning down of near-baldness; the bushier stuff above his ears had been lathered with some discreetly piquant lotion. He wore dark grey leather travelling boots. His seal ring was gold, a Greek design of a winged female driving a four-horse chariot. He wore two others for ornament, one set with sapphires and ovals, the other openwork, cut from sheet gold with added granulation. He wore the plain wide gold band of the middle rank. He carried no weapons.

I was annoyed, and so was Petro, that Tibullinus, Arica and some of the other men of the Sixth stepped forwards and shook hands with him, bidding farewell. Words were exchanged. Unable to tolerate it, the rest of us looked away and breathed disapproval. We were reluctant to become part of the conversation. We were resisting being coerced. We had glimpsed the complacency amidst which corruption flowers.

'How can you do that?' Martinus spluttered at Arica; Arica had actually slapped Balbinus on the back, as if he were seeing off his own cousin to the army. Martinus always spoke his mind.

'No harm being polite.' The Sixth had been supervising

Balbinus' movements ever since he went to trial. Contact would have been unavoidable.

The whole group of the Sixth began standing back now that they had delivered the package to us. As soon as he saw them shaking hands with the criminal, Petronius Longus had abandoned any pretence that this was a joint mission. His normal easy-going manner had vanished; I had never seen him so serious. The rest of the climax belonged to him and to the Fourth. Once the Sixth had formally taken their leave, they slunk from the scene.

I said nothing, but I had a sense that Petro's night of triumph had just been spoiled.

The freedmen had taken all the luggage on to the ship. They stayed aboard. We could see sailors assuming their places at the mooring ropes. The captain hovered at the head of the gangplank, impatient to sail now he had the breeze and approaching light. None of us made any attempt to look for Linus. It was best to forget he was there.

The vessel was a roomy merchantman called the *Aphrodite*. Balbinus would be well set up; there was a cabin for the captain and favoured passengers, a latrine hanging over the stern, even a galley where food could be prepared. The *Aphrodite* was half as big again as the ship on which Helena and I had returned from Syria. She needed to be strongly built to make such a long voyage so late in the year.

Now the criminal stood looking hesitant; he seemed uncertain what was expected of him. 'Am I to board?'

His doubt did not last. Petronius Longus appeared in front of him, flanked by Martinus and me. The other squad members clustered close, in a tight circle.

'Just a few formalities.' It was clear that now Balbinus was in the care of the Fourth Cohort there would be no hail-fellow handshaking. 'I've waited a long time, Balbinus,' Petro said.

'No doubt you have done your duty, officer.' The man spoke with reproach. He still seemed like a tunic-braid salesman – one who had just been told to his amazement that his embroidered Egyptian fancies had leaked crimson dye all over ten togas at some swanky laundry. 'I am innocent of the crimes of which I have been accused.'

449

'They all say that,' Petronius complained, addressing the sky in despair. 'Gods, I hate this hypocrisy! A straight villain always respects a straight arrest. He'll shrug and accept that he's caught. But all you self-justifying types have to make out that you cannot believe anyone could so terribly misjudge you. You convince yourselves all that matters in a civilised society is for men like you to continue your businesses without interference from officious sods like us. Sods who don't understand.' Petronius set his jaw so hard I thought I heard his molars crunch. 'Only I do understand!' he sneered. 'I understand what you are all too well.'

This rant had had no effect. Balbinus' eyes, some colour you wouldn't bother to notice, wandered to me. He seemed to realise I was an outsider, and was hoping for some sympathy. 'You had your chance,' I told him, before he could start whining. 'The benefit of a jury trial, in the calm of the Basilica. Six lawyers. A jury of your equals, who heard about your activities without allowing themselves to be sickened. A judge who, even while passing sentence, was polite. Meanwhile outside, market traders still had their takings grabbed by your rampaging street gangs. Near-destitute old women were being tricked out of their savings. Men who dared to resist your hold-up thieves spilled their lifeblood into the gutter. Female slaves were sold into prostitution by angry mistresses after your footpads snatched the shopping money –' Petronius moved slightly. I fell silent.

'Is there anything further you wish to tell me about your business?' Petro's request was formal; a vain hope.

'I am innocent,' Balbinus intoned solemnly.

Petro's sarcasm was milder than I expected: 'Oh, for a moment I thought you were going to surprise me and admit something.'

His men were on edge, wanting to retaliate, wanting something to make them feel good.

Petronius held out his hand, palm upwards. 'You can keep what you stand up in. I need your equestrian ring.'

With automatic obedience, the big rissole pulled off the badge of his lost social status, struggling to wrench it over

450

his first knuckle bone. He looked puzzled again. 'May I have a receipt?'

'No need.' Petro took the small band of gold between finger and thumb as if it offended him. He set it edge up on the top of a bollard, then raised one boot. A full inch of layered oxhide stamped down, studded with iron and moulded by hard usage to intractable curves that echoed the shape of Petro's foot. I knew, through having stumbled over it on many occasions when drunk, that my old tentmate's massive trotter deserved respect.

Petro crushed the ring into a useless twist. Sneering, he handed it back. The state would forego that gold.

'You're enjoying this,' Fusculus tutted, pretending to admonish his chief. Fitted out with a sense of irony, Fusculus must be the sensitive one.

'I enjoy knowing that I'm never going to see this bastard again.'

'Strip him of his rights!' That was Martinus, ever eager for drama and about as sensitive as a dead newt.

Petronius Longus folded his arms. Enjoying this he might be, but he sounded tired: 'Tiberius Balbinus Pius, you stand condemned of capital crimes. The laws of Rome grant you time to depart. That is your only prerogative. You are no longer a citizen. You no longer possess equestrian rank, nor the honours attached to that rank. Your property is forfeit to the Treasury and your accusers. Your wife, children and heirs have no future claims upon it. You shall depart beyond the Empire. You shall never return. If you set foot in any territory governed by Rome, the penalty is death.'

'I am innocent!' Balbinus whined.

'You're grime!' roared Petronius. 'Get on the boat before I forget myself!'

Balbinus shot him a vindictive look, then walked straight to the ship.

VI

Petro and I regained the quay later that morning. We had snatched a few hours' snoring on a bench in a wine bar that was fractionally more friendly than our previous foray. While we were relaxing the scene had changed completely. It was light. The quays were full of people. After a long, nerve-racking night, the hubbub was a shock.

As we hunted for the *Providentia*, which had brought me home from Syria, we could now make out fully the great man-made harbour basin. This was Portus. Claudius had first enclosed the spectacular new mooring that had replaced the old silted-up basin two miles away at Ostia. Nowadays only shallow-draught barges could use the old port. Portus had taken several decades of construction since Claudius sank the first breakwater – a massive ship once used to carry an obelisk for Caligula. That was now the base of a two-hundred-foot mole holding back the weather and carrying the three-storeyed lighthouse whose constant beacon announced from the harbour mouth that this was the centre of world navigation: one hundred and sixty acres of quiet mooring, to which all the Empire's trade came, eager to cough up harbour tax. I had paid my tax like a good citizen, one whose brother-in-law was a customs officer who liked asking unwanted questions. I was now trying to reclaim my goods.

There was more noise than earlier. Workers were already pouring in from Ostia along the road through the market and flower gardens, or via the Claudian canal (which badly needed widening and dredging): clerks, customs inspectors, owners of vessels and goods, all jostling on the jetties with passengers and porters. We were tired, and the scene was unfamilar. Somehow the waterfront turmoil stripped us of our normal authority. Petronius and I were battered and cursed along with every other stranger.

'Sorry for getting you into this,' I told him ruefully. He was taking it well, however. This was by no means the worst pickle

452

we had been in. Balbinus had put us in a gloomy mood; we were glad to forget him. We applied ourselves to commerce like heroes on behalf of my auctioneer father. He irritated all Hades out of me – but he had at least given us a chance to skive at the seaside for a time.

My father's general habit was to cause me trouble. From the day he had run away from home when I was still in the tunic of childhood I had despised pretty well everything he did. I never dealt with him if I could help it, but he had a way of winding himself into my life however hard I tried to avoid it.

He had known better than to ask me to help him make money from my trip to Syria. On hearing of our exotic destination he had commissioned Helena instead. Helena Justina, my girlfriend who had been brought up a senator's daughter, thought Pa was just a likeable scamp. She said I was too hard on him. She wanted us all to be friends; this gave Pa a chance to inveigle her into any devious scheme, especially if he could do it behind my back.

Though he claimed to be destitute (a piteous but fake complaint), my father had managed to dispatch Helena with instructions to get me to Tyre if she could – and with a two-hundred-thousand-sesterces banker's draft. She had a free hand to spend this exorbitant sum. He must have trusted her taste. In thirty years he had never given me such leeway with his private funds.

We had naturally been investing for ourselves as well; no point travelling to one of the Empire's richest markets unless you buy cheap from the caravans. Using Helena's money mainly, plus my own meagre savings, we had laden ourselves with enough bales of silk to dress our entire families like Parthian dancing girls and still have some over to sell. Helena's ex-husband had imported peppers, so we shied off those, but that left plenty of other spices to bring home in casks that hummed with addictive scents. We had purchased Arabian incense and other perfumes. I had acquired a few extras at markets when Helena was not looking. Then finally, just when I believed we were coming home, Helena Justina had coerced me into buying glassware for Papa.

She had made me do the bargaining, though she herself handled a portable abacus with a verve that made the traders

453

sweat. She chose the stock. Helena had a good eye for a flask. Grumbling aside, glass was the desirable commodity. My father knew what he was doing. There were bowls and bottles, jugs and beakers in delicate pinks, metallic greens, sulphurous blues; vases with snakes of molten glass trailing around their elegant throats; tiny perfume flagons like little doves; jugs with furled spouts and fine etching. There was cameo glass, at a price that rivalled the incense. There were even spectacular funeral jars.

All this glass was a serious burden. We had crept home, trembling for the safety of Pa's fragile water sets and dinner bowls. As far as I knew, it was all in one piece when we sailed into Portus on the *Providentia*. All I had to do now was transport it upriver to Rome. If I wanted to remain Helena's private demigod, I had to make sure I did not slip with the bales.

All our own packages had already been taken over to Ostia on mules. I had booked a passage up the Tiber on a barge that was leaving today. Now I was on edge about Pa's damned glass. I did not intend to endure the rest of his lifetime being derided as the son who smashed the equivalent of two hundred thousand pieces of silver. This had to be done right.

Petronius had some sympathy; he was a loyal friend. But he lacked the direct interest I had myself, and I didn't blame him for that. It was hard enough for *me* to interest myself in another man's profit margins. Only Helena's pride in her commission kept me going.

We were having trouble finding transport. We wanted to take the glass to the old harbour using the canal. Some idiot (me) had deemed this the best way. No one would hire us a boat, though. After a couple of hours of fruitless begging Petro left me on the jetty, saying I was to keep looking out for a skiff while he approached the harbour staff and mentioned his official position in a casual manner, hoping to get us fixed up with reliable rowers that way.

He was gone so long I reckoned he must have slipped off for breakfast without me. If I was lucky he might bring me back a squashed roll with a sliver of limp cheese and a quarter of an olive. More likely the rascal would saunter back whistling and say nothing. Great. The glass had been unloaded from the *Providentia* and left on the quay, so I had to stay with it.

I had had enough. I tried to sit on a bollard, but they're never designed to let a backside rest there. While seagulls squawked scornfully I cursed my father to Hades and back, and even muttered about Petronius. I was wasting time here when I had yet to spend a full day back in Rome. Petro's caper with the criminal had robbed Helena and me of a much-longed-for first night together in our own bed. Pa, lounging with his boots on a lamp table, had told me that he was 'a bit too busy' to visit Ostia. So he had left me to reclaim his goods, which had already cost me enough trouble, and on which, if I knew him, he would deny Helena her agent's percentage. Assuming the daft girl had even thought of asking for a percentage in the first place.

I was all set to kick the glass into the harbour when Destiny took pity. A couple of men in a sturdy boat actually hailed me and asked if I wanted my goods ferrying. I was delighted, though after six years as an informer, I naturally viewed the offer with caution.

Adopting a suave manner, I made some enquiries. Luckily they had the right answers: they were members of the rowers' guild, and owned their own craft. They looked like lads who knew their business. Their names, which I insisted on knowing, were Gaius and Phlosis. We agreed a price, and they began loading my precious crates, taking all the care I asked for. There were a lot of crates. When they finished, they had to tell me apologetically that the boat could not take me as well. It did seem pretty low in the water.

Time was running out if I was to catch the barge. Gaius and Phlosis seemed so concerned that I might think they were stealing my collateral, I reluctantly agreed to let them row to Ostia without me while I took one of the regular hired carts. We would meet at the barge; they themselves suggested I didn't pay them until then. This evidence of their honesty clinched the deal.

Tired, and pleased to have sorted myself out without aid from Petro, who could be supercilious about commerce, I was ready to agree to anything sensible. I waved them off.

I was still on the quay, looking around for my friend, when I spotted another skiff. In it I could see Petro, who must have picked up his man Fusculus from somewhere. I waved impatiently. I would now have to explain to the second crew that their services were no longer needed – and if I knew the rules of the Ostian rowers' guild, they would probably demand a disappointment fee.

As I was tapping my toe, Petronius' two rowers suddenly began shouting. Then Petro himself joined in. His boatmen began to row very fast towards Gaius and Phlosis. They tried to speed up. Then, to my amazement, my two handy lads jumped over the side, swam rapidly to the jetty some distance from me, and made off down the quay.

The realisation that I had been caught by a swindle fell on me like a cartload of wet sand.

Next moment I was screaming with anxiety over Pa's cargo of glass. Fortunately the inner harbour was sheltered, so there was rarely a swell, and no large ships were manoeuvring at that moment. The abandoned skiff had rocked wildly when Gaius and Phlosis dived over the gunnels, but it had stayed afloat. It was collected by Petronius, who had stepped across from his own boat, then held the two craft close together so that Fusculus could scramble across too. Petronius could row; he brought my goods slowly back to me while his own boatmen raced to shore. Still yelling, they jumped out and ran after Gaius and Phlosis.

I didn't care about those thieves; I just wanted Pa's treasure. Petronius threw a rope to me, while Fusculus shook his head over my narrow escape. 'You were certainly conned there! A lovely example of the craft-rig,' he informed me knowingly.

'Oh yes?'

'They steal a boat, then prowl the wharves looking for a sucker who has just arrived at the harbour and needs some goods transferred somewhere. Luckily our own two honest fellows recognised the boat. It belongs to a friend of theirs, so they knew your heroes must have pinched it.'

I did not want to hear the depressing details, but I gave him a hand to jump back to dry land. 'You're the expert on low tricks are you, Fusculus?'

456

'Fusculus is a fervent scholar of the underworld,' grinned Petro. Thankfully, he was too good a friend to jeer directly at my mistake.

'Balbinus used to run a gang who specialised in this dodge along the wharves by the Emporium,' Fusculus said. 'You'd be surprised, Falco, how easily tired travellers can be taken in.'

'I'm not surprised at all,' I growled.

The two rowers who had exposed the near-disaster came back, having failed to catch my lads. We unloaded half the glass from the first boat, then got hot and fractious transferring it to the second one so we could spread the weight between the two and hitch a ride ourselves. Petronius, Fusculus and I all stuck with the precious cargo right to the barge at Ostia. Not until I had seen every crate transferred did I feel able to relax again.

Exhausted by our adventures, we lay on deck in the autumn sunlight as slowly the barge started to navigate the shoals, creeping up the muddy Tiber into Rome.

VII

Helena Justina had not heard me come home. She was tying in strands of my climbing rose, a thing of long spindly growth that struggled for water and nourishment on the narrow balcony outside my sixth-floor apartment. For a moment I was able to watch her while she remained quite unaware of me.

Helena was tall, straight-backed, dark-haired, and serious. She was five days from her twenty-fifth birthday. The first time I ran across her, married life in the utmost luxury but with an insensitive young senator had left her bitter and withdrawn. She had just divorced him, and made it plain that anyone else who got in her way could expect to be kicked out of it. Don't ask how I got around the problem – but writing my memoirs promised some fun.

Astonishingly, two years of surviving scandal and squalor with me had softened the hard shell. Maybe it was being loved. Now, as she paused rather dreamily to suck at a thorn in her finger, there was a stillness about her. She looked far away, yet unconscious of her own thoughts.

I had neither moved nor made a sound, but she turned quickly. 'Marcus!'

We embraced. I buried my face in her soft neck, groaning with gratitude for the way her strong, sweet face had lit with pleasure when she realised I was there.

All the same it worried me. I would have to hang a bell inside our entrance door, so nobody else could creep up on her like this. Where we lived was a lawless tenement.

Maybe I needed to find a better place for us.

Helena seemed tired. We were both still drained of energy after travelling home from the East. Coming in and crossing the outer room, I had seen evidence that she must have spent my absence at Ostia unpacking and tidying. My mother or one of my sisters might have dropped in to help, but they fussed around and were likely to have been seen off politely with cinnamon tea and a few tales about our journey. Helena never fussed. She liked to set things just so – and then forget about them.

I pulled her to the rickety wooden bench, which felt even worse than I remembered. Bending down with a curse, I fiddled about with a piece of broken roof tile – which probably meant we had a new leak somewhere – and managed to level up the bench's feet. Then at last we sat quietly together, gazing out across the river.

'Now there's a view!'

She smiled. 'You love coming home, Marcus.'

'Coming home to you is the best part.'

As usual Helena ignored my suggestive gleam – though as usual I could tell she welcomed it. 'Did everything go all right at Ostia?'

'More or less. We got back to Rome about an hour ago. Pa finally managed to show an interest. Once I'd done the hard work he turned up and took charge at the Emporium.' Luckily my father actually lived on the riverbank, below the Aventine cliff and only a step from the wharves. 'He's got the glass, so make sure he pays you an agency fee.'

Helena seemed to smile at my advice. 'Did Petronius do what he wanted? And are you now going to tell me what the fuss was about?'

'He was sending a condemned man into exile.'

'A real villain?' she asked, lifting her bold eyebrows as she caught my surly tone.

'The worst.' Petronius Longus would be horrified at the way I shared such information; I knew he never told his wife anything about his work. Helena and I had always discussed things; for me, the big rissole was unfinished business so long as I was waiting to confide in Helena. 'Balbinus Pius. We saw him on to his ship, and one of Petro's men has gone along undercover to see he doesn't hop ashore prematurely. By the way, I asked Petro and Silvia to dinner once we're straight again. Everything in order here?' I didn't bother looking back at the bare room behind me: a small table, three stools, shelves with a few crocks, pots and beakers, a next-to-useless cooking bench.

'Oh yes.'

For the past few months my sister Maia would have valiantly toiled up the six flights from time to time, making sure for us that no one broke in and that Smaractus, my pig of a landlord, had not tried his usual trick of squeezing extra cash from subtenants if he thought I was not here. Maia had also kept the balcony garden watered and had pinched back the herbs, though she drew the line at controlling the rose. She reckoned I had only planted it to get cheap flowers for seducing girls. All my sisters were naturally unfair.

I took charge of Helena's finger, removing the thorn with adept pressure from one thumbnail. My right hand was habitually caressing the two-month-old scar on her forearm where she had been stung by a scorpion in the Syrian desert.

'I'll be in trouble over your war wound.' Both my own mother and Helena's noble parent would blame me for taking her to such a dangerous province and bringing her back scarred for life . . . And there might be another new situation that would set both our mothers on the alert. Newly home after a whole summer abroad, I did not want to start broaching issues. But I took a slow breath and braced myself. 'Maybe there's worse than that in store for me.'

Helena showed no reaction: so much for being mysterious.

'I think there's something we need to talk about.'

She heard the message in my tone that time. She looked at me askance. 'What's wrong, Marcus?'

Before I was ready I heard myself saying: 'I'm beginning to suspect I'm going to be a father.'

I fixed my gaze on the Ianiculan Mount and waited for her to accept or reject the news.

Helena was silent for a moment, then asked quietly, 'Why do you say that?' There was a very slight rasp in her voice.

'Observation.' I tried to sound nonchalant. 'Matching evidence with probability is my job, after all.'

'Well, I'm sure you're the one who knows!' Helena spoke like an angry householder whose chief steward had just accused a favourite slave of raiding the wine cellar. 'How do you reckon it happened?'

'The usual way!' Now I sounded tetchy. We had only

ourselves to blame. It was a classic failure of contraception – not the alum in wax letting anyone down, but two people failing to bother to use it.

'Oh,' she said.

'Oh, indeed! I'm referring to a certain occasion in Palmyra – '

'I remember the date and time.'

As I feared, she was sounding far from overjoyed. I decided that my consoling hand on the scorpion scar might be unwelcome; I drew back and folded my arms. Once again I gazed out beyond the Tiber to the Ianiculan Hill, where I sometimes dreamed of owning a villa if Destiny ever forgot that I was the one she liked tormenting with hammerblows. My chance of ever becoming a householder in a quiet and spacious home was in fact ludicrously slim.

'I know you have your position in society to think about,' I told Helena, more stiffly than I had intended. 'Your family's reputation, and of course your own.' Unhelpfully, she made no comment. It tipped me into flippancy: 'I'm not asking you to stand by me.'

'I will, of course!' Helena insisted, rather bitterly.

'Better not commit yourself,' I warned. 'When you've had time to think, you may not be too happy about this.'

We were not married. She was two ranks above me. We never would be married unless I could persuade the Emperor to promote me to the middle rank – which had been refused once already. One of the Caesars had turned down my request, even though I had earned quite a few favours from the Palace and my father had lent me the qualifying cash. Humbling myself to take the loan from Pa had been hard; I reckoned the Palace owed me more than favours now.

But the Palace was irrelevant. I was in a fix. Plebeians were not supposed to sleep with senators' female relations. I was not a slave, or I would have been dead meat long ago. There was no husband to be affronted, but Helena's father was entitled to view our crime in the same light as adultery. Unless I was much mistaken about the ancient traditions of our *very* traditional city, that gave him the right to execute me personally. Luckily Camillus Verus was a calm man.

*

461

'So how do *you* feel, Marcus?'

Fortunately my life as an informer had trained me to avoid saying what I felt when it could only lead to trouble.

Helena filled in the gap for herself wryly, addressing the sky: 'Marcus is a man. He wants an heir, but he doesn't want a scandal.'

'Close!' I said it with a smile as if both of us were joking. She knew I was dodging the issue. Applying a serious expression, I altered my story: 'It's not me who has to go through with the pregnancy and the dangers of birth.' Not to mention enduring the extreme public interest. 'What I think takes second place.'

'Ho! That will be a novelty . . . It may not happen,' Helena suggested.

'Looks definite to me.' Helena had been pregnant with a child of mine before, miscarrying before she had even told me. When I found out, I had vowed never to be left out again. Believe me, keeping track had not been easy. Helena was the kind of girl who lost her temper if she felt she was being watched. 'Well, time will show if I'm right.'

'And there's plenty of time,' she murmured. I sat there wondering: time for what?

The child would be illegitimate, of course. It would take its mother's rank – utterly worthless without a father's pedigree to quote as well. Freed slaves stood a better chance.

We could cope with that, if it ever came to it. What was likely to break us, one way or another, would happen to us before the poor scrap was even born.

'I don't want to lose you,' I stated abruptly.

'You won't.'

'Look, I think it's fair to ask what you want to do.'

Helena was frowning. 'Marcus, why can't you be like other men, who don't want to face up to things?' Maybe she was joking, but she sounded serious. I recognised her expression; she was not prepared to think about this. She was not intending to talk.

'Let me say what I have to.' I tried playing the man of the house, knowing this normally only got me laughed at. 'I know you. You'll wait until I leave for the Forum, then you'll worry in private. If you choose a course of action, you'll try to do

462

everything alone. I'll have to come chasing after you, like a farm boy left behind at market when the cart sets off for home.'

'You'll soon catch up,' she answered with a faint smile. 'I know you too.'

I was remembering the little I knew about what she had gone through, on her own, that other time. It was best not to think about it.

Legally, every day I kept her I was robbing her noble father. Once the results of our fling became apparent, Helena would be strongly encouraged to regularise her life. The obvious solution for her family would be a quick arranged marriage to some senator who was either too stupid to notice this, or plain long-suffering. 'Helena, I just want you to promise that if there are decisions to be made, you will let me share in making them.'

Suddenly she laughed, a tense and breathy explosion of dry mirth. 'I think we took our decisions in Palmyra, Marcus Didius!'

The formality cut like a boning knife. Then, just when I thought I really had lost her, she seized me in a hug. 'I love you very much,' she exclaimed – and unexpectedly kissed me.

It was no answer.

On the other hand, when a senator's daughter tells a plebeian that she loves him, the man is entitled to feel a certain low pride. After that it is all too easy to be seduced by the offer of coming indoors for dinner. And there are domestic routines of an even more wicked nature that can be made to follow dinner with a senator's daughter, if you can manage to lure one of these exotic and glorious creatures away from her noble father's house.

VIII

Allowing a woman to sidetrack me was routine. Come the morning I was still resolute. Plenty of ineffectual clerks had hired me to chase after heartless females who were giving them the silly story; I was used to being offered sensual bribes to make me forget a mission.

Of course I never accepted the bribes. And of course Helena Justina, that upright, ethical character, would never try to influence me by shameless means. She went to bed with me that night for the same reason she had always done so: because she wanted to. And the next day, I carried on directly facing up to the situation because that was what *I* wanted.

Helena carried on dodging. I had made absolutely no progress in finding out how she felt. That was fine. Her motives defied prediction. That was why I was in love with her; I was tired of predictable women. I could be persistent. Maybe that was why she was in love with me.

Assuming she really was. A shiver as I remembered our lovemaking last night convinced me – at which point I stopped worrying.

I washed my face, rinsed my teeth, and bit my way into a hard bread roll. Yesterday's; we lived too far from the street to buy fresh loaves for breakfast. I gulped down some of the warm drink I was preparing for Helena. While she sleepily drank hers in bed, I put on a tunic that had spiced itself up with a gay shower of moth holes and renewed acquaintance with a wrinkled old belt that looked as if it had been tanned from the ox Romulus had used to measure Rome. I dragged a comb into my curls, hit a tangle, and decided to keep the relaxed coiffure that matched my casual clothes. I cleaned my boots and sharpened my knife. I counted my small change – a swift task – then transferred the purse to today's belt.

I kissed Helena, following up with a bit of fumbling under the bedsheet. She accepted the playfulness, laughing at me. 'Oh go and flaunt your Eastern tan where the men show off

464

. . .' Today she would readily surrender me to the Forum, the baths, even the imperial offices. She knew that when I had had my fill of the city I would come home to her.

After a short tussle with the outer door, which had taken to sticking, I limped downstairs. I had hurt my toe kicking the doorframe and was cursing gently: home again. Everything as I remembered it.

I was absorbing the familiar experience of the ramshackle apartment block: for five floors angry voices reached me from behind curtains and half-doors. Two apartments per storey; two or three rooms per apartment; two and a half families per dwelling and as many as five or six people to a room. Sometimes there were fewer occupants, but they ran a business, like the mirror-polisher and the tailor. Sometimes one room contained an old lady who had been the original tenant, now almost forgotten amidst the rumbustious invaders to whom Smaractus had sublet parts of her home 'to help her with the rent'. He was a professional landlord. Nothing he did was to help anybody but himself.

I noticed a few more graffiti gladiators chalked on the poorly rendered walls. There was a smell like wet dog mingling with yesterday's steamed cabbage. Stepping down around one dark corner I had a narrow escape when I nearly trod on some child's lost pottery horse-on-wheels, which would have skated my foot from under me and probably left me with a broken back. I put the horse on a ledge, alongside a broken rattle and one tiny sandal that had been there when I left for Syria.

The stairs ended outside in a dim nook under two columns that had once made a portico. The rest of this row of columns had long ago fallen down and vanished; it was best not to think about what was happening to the parts of the building they had been meant to support. Now most of the frontage was open, allowing free encroachment from Lenia's laundry. She had the whole ground floor, which according to her included what passed for a pavement and half the dusty road in Fountain Court. Just now her staff were doing the main morning wash, so warm, humid air hit me as I reached the street. Several rows of soaking togas and tunics hung nicely at face height, ready to slap at anyone who tried to leave the building on lawful business.

I went inside to be neighbourly. The sweet smell of urine, which was used for bleaching togas, met me like an old acquaintance I was trying to avoid. I had not seen Lenia yet, so when someone else shrieked my name she thrust herself out from the steamy hubbub like some disreputable sand beetle heaving its way above ground. She had armfuls of crumpled garments crushed against her flopping bosom, her chin balanced on top of the smelly pile. Her hair was still an unconvincing red; after the sophisticated henna treatments of the East, it looked hideously brash. The damp air had stuck her long tunic to parts of her body, producing an effect that did little for a man of the world like me.

She staggered towards me with an affectionate cry of, 'Look! Something nasty's blown in with the road dust!'

'Aphrodite rising from the washtub, sneezing at the wood ash!'

'Falco, you rat's bum.'

'What's new, Lenia?' I answered breezily.

'Trade's bad and the weather's a menace.'

'That's hardly new. Have I missed the wedding?'

'Don't make me angry!' She was betrothed to Smaractus, a business arrangement. (Each craved the other's business.) Lenia's contempt for my landlord exceeded even' mine, though she had a religious respect for his money. I knew she had carried out a meticulous audit before deciding Smaractus was the man of her dreams. Lenia's dreams were practical. She really intended to go through with it apparently, for after the conventional cursing she added, 'The wedding's on the Kalends of November. You're invited so long as you promise to cause a fight with the nut boys and to throw up on his mother.' I've seen some sordid things, but the idea of my landlord having a mother set me back somewhat. Lenia saw my look and laughed harshly. 'We're going to be desperate for entertainment at this party. The arrangements are driving me mad, Falco. I don't suppose you would read the omens for us?'

'Surely you need a priest?'

Lenia shrieked with outrage. 'I wouldn't trust one of those sleazy buggers! Don't forget I've washed their underwear. I'm in enough trouble without having my omens mucked up

'. . . You're a citizen. You can do it if you're prepared to be a pal.'

'A man's duty is to honour the gods for his own household,' I intoned, suddenly becoming a master of informed piety.

'You're scared of the job.'

'I'm just trying to get out of it.'

'Well, you live in the same building.'

'No one ever told me it meant peering into a sheep's liver for the damned landlord! That's not in my lease.'

'Do it for me, Falco!'

'I'm not some cranky Etruscan weather forecaster.' I was losing ground. Lenia, who was a superstitious article, looked genuinely anxious; my old friendship with her was about to take its toll. 'Oh I'll think about it . . . I told you from the start, woman, you're making a big mistake.'

'I told you to mind your own,' quipped Lenia, in her brutal, rasping voice. 'I heard you were back from your travels – though this is the first time you've bothered to call on me!'

'Having a lie-in.' I managed to beat her to a leering grin.

'Scandalous bastard! Where've you been to this time, and was there profit in it?'

'The East. And of course not.'

'You mean you're too tight to tell me.'

'I mean I'm not giving Smaractus any excuse to bump my rent up!' That reminded me of something. 'This deadly dump is getting too inconvenient, Lenia. I'll have to find somewhere more salubrious to live.'

'Oh Great Mother!' Lenia exclaimed immediately. 'He's pregnant!'

Taken aback by the shrewdness of her guesswork, I blushed – losing any chance of disguising my plight. 'Don't be ridiculous,' I lied as brazenly as possible. 'I know how to look after myself.'

'Didius Falco, I've seen you do a lot of stupid things.' That was true. She had known me since my bachelor days. 'But I never thought you'd be caught out in the old way!'

It was my turn to say mind your own business, and Lenia's to laugh seditiously.

I changed the subject. 'Does your slimy betrothed still own that decrepit property across the court?'

'Smaractus never disposes of a freehold.' He never bothered to redevelop a wrecked tenement either. As an entrepreneur, Smaractus was as dynamic as a slug. 'Which property, Falco?'

'The first-floor spread. What's he call it? *"Refined and commodious self-contained apartment at generous rent; sure to be snapped up."* You with me?'

'The dump he's been advertising on my wall for the past four years? Don't be the fool who does snap it up, Falco. The refined and commodious back section has no floor.'

'So what? My shack upstairs hardly has a roof. I'm used to deprivation. Mind if I take a look at the place?'

'Do what you like,' sniffed Lenia. 'What you see is all there is. He won't do it up for you. He's short of loose change.'

'Of course. He's getting married!' I grinned. 'Old Smaractus must be spending every day of the week burying his money bags in very deep holes in faraway fields in Latium. If he's got any sense, he'll then lose the map.'

I could tell Lenia was on the verge of advising me to jump down the Great Sewer and close the manhole after me, but we were interrupted by a more than usually off-putting messenger.

It was a grubby little girl of about seven years, with large feet and a very small nose. She had a scowling expression that I immediately recognised as similar to my own. She was one of my nieces. I could not remember which niece, though she definitely came from the Didius tribe. She looked like my sister Galla's offspring. They had a truly useless father, and apart from the eldest, who had sensibly left home, they were a pitiful, struggling crew. Someone had hung one of those bull's-testicle amulets around this one's neck to protect her from harm, though whoever it was had not bothered to teach her to leave her scabs alone or to wipe her nose.

'Oh Juno,' rasped Lenia. 'Take her out of here, Falco. My customers will think they'll catch something.'

'Go away,' I greeted the niece convivially.

'Uncle Marcus! Have you brought us any presents?'

'No.' I had done, because all my sisters' children were in sore need of a devoted, uncomplicated uncle to ruin their characters with ridiculous largesse. I couldn't spoil only the

468

clean and polite ones, though I had no intention of letting the other little brats think me an easy touch. Anyone who came and asked for their ceramic Syrian camel with the nodding head would have to wait a week for it.

'Oh Uncle Marcus!' I felt like a heel, as she intended.

'Cut the grizzling. Listen, what's your name – '

'Tertulla,' she supplied, without taking offence.

'What are you after, Tertulla?'

'Grandpa sent me.'

'Termites! You haven't found me then.'

'It's urgent, Uncle Marcus!'

'Not as urgent as scratching your elbow – I'm off!'

'He said you'd give me a copper for finding you.'

'Well he's wrong.' Needing to argue more strongly, I had to resort to blackmail. 'Listen, wasn't yesterday the Ides?' One good thing about helping Petronius at Ostia was that we had missed the Festival of the October Horse – once a savage carnival and horse race, now just a complete mess in the streets. It was also the end of the official school holidays. 'Shouldn't you be starting school now? Why are you loose today?'

'I don't want to go.'

'Tertulla, everyone who has a chance to go to school should be grateful for the privilege.' What an insufferable prig. 'Leave me alone, or I'm telling your grandma you've bunked off.'

My mother was helping with the fees for Galla's children, a pure waste of money. Ma would have stood for a better return gambling on chariot races. What nobody seemed to have noticed was that since I gave my mother financial support, it was *my* cash being flung away.

'Oh Uncle Marcus, don't!'

'Oh nuts. I'm going to.'

I was already feeling gloomy. From the first moment Tertulla mentioned my father I had begun to suspect today might not be all I had been planning. Goodbye baths; goodbye swank at the Forum . . . 'Grandpa's in trouble. Your friend Petronius told him to get you,' my niece cried. Persistence ran in the family, if it involved telling bad news.

Petro knew what I felt about my father. If Pa was in such

trouble Petro reckoned even I would help him out, the trouble must really be serious.

IX

The emporium is a long, secure building close to the Tiber. The barges that creep up from Ostia reach the city with Caesar's Gardens on their left, and a segment of the Aventine district, below the Hill, to their right. Where they meet the left-hand city boundary at the Transtiberina, with a long view upriver towards the Probus Bridge, they find the Emporium lying to their right, a vast indoor market that includes the ancient Aemilian Portico. You can smell it from the water. A blind man would know he had arrived.

Here, anything buildable, wearable or edible that is produced in any province of the Empire comes to be unloaded at the teeming wharves. The slick stevedores, who are renowned for their filthy tempers and flash off-duty clothing, then crash the goods on to handcarts, dump them in baskets, or wheel about with great sacks on their shoulders, ferrying them inside the greatest indoor market in the world. Cynical sales are conducted, and before the importer has realised he has been rooked by the most devious middlemen in Europe, everything whirls out again to destinations in workshops, warehouses, country estates or private homes. The moneychangers wear happy smiles all day.

Apart from a few commodities like grain, paper and spices, which are so precious or are sold in such quantities that they have their own markets elsewhere, you can buy anything at the Emporium. Through his profession, my father was well known there. He no longer involved himself in general sales, for his interest had narrowed to the kind of fine-art trade that is conducted in quieter, highly tasteful surroundings where the purchaser submits to a more leisurely screwing and then pays a more gigantic premium to the auctioneer.

Pa was a character people noticed. Normally I could have asked anybody if they had seen Geminus, and pretty soon someone would have told me which hot-wine stall he was lurking at. I should have been able to find him easily – if only the fierce patrolmen of the Fourth Cohort of vigiles had been letting people in.

The scene was incredible. Nothing like it could ever have happened before. The Emporium lay in the area included by Augustus when he redrew Rome's boundaries because habitation had expanded. I had made the mistake of coming out from the old part through the city walls, using the Lavernal Gate – a spot always busy but today almost impassable. Down in the shadow of the Aventine approaching the Tiber, I had found chaos. It had taken me an hour to force a passage through the people who were clogging up the Ostia Road. By the time I really made it to the wharves beside the river, I knew something highly peculiar must have gone wrong. I was prepared for a scene – though not one evidently caused by my sensible friend Petronius.

It was midmorning. The gates to the Emporium, normally closed at night for security but flung open at first light and kept that way well into the evening, now stood barred. Red-faced members of the watch were drawn up with their backs to the doors. There were a lot of them: five hundred men formed the half-cohort that patrolled the river side of the Aventine. A proportion were dedicated to fire-watching, and with the special dangers of darkness they were mostly on duty at night. That still left ample cover to combat daylight crime. Now, Petronius must have drawn up all the day roster. The line was holding, but I was glad I was not part of it. A huge, angry crowd was milling about insulting the watch and calling for Petro's head. Occasionally a group rushed forwards, and the line of patrolmen had to link arms and face them out. I could see a small cluster at the far end of the building where Porcius was handing out shields from a waggon.

Petro was nowhere in sight. It seemed wise.

With a spurt of anxiety I shoved my way to the front. 'Great gods, what's this? Am I supposed to believe that Petronius Longus, notorious for caution, has suddenly decided to make his name in history as the Man Who Stopped Trade?'

'Shove off, Falco!' muttered Fusculus, who had been trying to argue with four or five score merchants and workmen, many of them foreign and all of them spitting fire.

'Petro sent for me.' It was worth a try.

472

'Petro's not bloody here!' Fusculus told me through bitterly clenched teeth as he pushed back a furious Gallic wine merchant by the simple means of lifting one leg and applying his boot sole firmly to the man's belt buckle. The Fourth Cohort were slightly more sophisticated than others in Rome, but no one argued with them twice. 'Petro's in shit. A Praetorian Guard dragged him off to the Palace to explain this mess.'

'I may as well get back to bed then!'

'You do that, Falco . . .'

The vigiles had their hands full. With so large a crowd, in such an ugly mood, I did not fancy helping them. Luckily they did not demean themselves by asking. I had a let-out anyway, for I heard my name roared by an unmistakable foghorn, and turned to be greeted by my papa. He clapped me in his arms affectionately. This was not his normal greeting, just showing off before a crowd of foreigners. I shook myself free angrily.

'Marcus! Let's get out of this stew – we've things to discuss!'

I had nothing to discuss with my father. I experienced the usual sense of dread.

He hauled me into a more-or-less quiet corner around the back of the old Galban granaries. Needless to say, the corner was in a wine bar. After my exhausting passage through the streets I did not object to that, though in an equal world since he had issued the summons, I would have preferred that he paid the bill. Somehow the chalked piece of tile landed on the table in front of me.

'Oh thanks, Marcus. Your health!'

My father was a sturdy character of sixty-odd, with a greying thatch of marauding curls and what passed for a twinkle in his untrustworthy dark brown eyes. He went by the name of Geminus, though his real name was Favonius. There was no point in the change; that was typical. Not tall, he was still a commanding presence; people who wanted to annoy me said we looked alike. In fact he was heavier and shiftier. His belly supported a money belt whose weight told its own story. His dark blue tunic was now old enough to be used when he was lifting furniture around warehouses, but the wrecked braid on it, still with traces of silver thread, gave a clue to the style he could afford when relaxing socially. Women liked his grin. He liked most things about women. He had run away with a red-haired one when I was a child, after which he and I could hardly exchange a civil word.

'Your mad crony's caused a bit of a pickle!' One of the few paternal routines he still honoured was criticising my friends.

'He would have had his reasons,' I said coldly. I was trying to think of any possible reason for what Petronius had done. 'This can't just be a reprisal because some stallholder forgot to pay his market dues.'

I have to admit, the thought had struck me that maybe Petro was so proud of himself for capturing Balbinus that he had become a power-crazed maniac. This had always been a Roman trait, at the first hint of success to dream of being deified. It seemed unlikely in Petro's case, however. He was so rational he was positively staid.

'Tertulla said you'd spoken to him,' I prodded.

'Oh you've seen Tertulla? That little mite needs looking after. You're her uncle. Can't you do something?'

'You're her grandfather! Why me?' I felt myself going hot. Trying to instil a sense of duty into Father, who had already abandoned one generation, was hopeless. 'Oh Jupiter! I'll see Galla about it sometime . . . What's the tale here, Pa?'

'Disaster.' My father enjoyed a spot of misery.

'Well, that's clear! Can we be more specific? Does this disaster involve a major defeat for the legions in a prestigious foreign war – or just the lupin crop failing in two villages in Samnium?'

'You're a sarcastic trout! It's this: a gang of robbers burst in last night and cleaned out half the Emporium.' Pa leaned back on his stool watching the effect on me. I tried to look suitably horrified, while still dwelling thoughtfully on my own fancy rhetoric. He scowled. 'Listen, you dozy bastard! They obviously knew exactly what they wanted – luxury items in every case. They must have been watching for weeks, until they knew they could snatch an exquisite haul – then they whipped in, snatched the goods to order, whipped out and vanished before anything was noticed.'

'So Petronius has shut the building while he investigates what happened?'

'I suppose so. But you know him; he wasn't saying. He just looked solemn and closed it.'

'So what *did* he say?'

'Stallholders and wharfingers would be let in one by one, with his man Martinus – '

'Another master of tact!' Martinus, with his high opinion of himself, was especially dour when dealing with the public.

'To make a list of what was missing.' Pa completed his sentence doggedly.

'Well that's fair,' I said. 'Surely those idiots can see that their best chance of getting their property back will be if Petronius knows what to look for?'

'Too subtle,' replied Pa with the famous flashing grin that had laid barmaids on their backs from here to the Flaminian Gate. It only caused irritation in me.

'Too organised!' Petronius had my sympathies. Presumably he had come back from Ostia expecting a short stretch of peace after his Balbinus coup, only to be dragged from bed that very night to face one of the worst heists I could remember, in the most important building on his patch. Instead of enjoying a glorious rest as a community hero, he now faced working at full stretch for months. Probably with nothing to show at the end: it sounded as if this robbery had been scrupulously planned.

One aspect was still niggling me. 'Just as a matter of interest, Pa – why did Petronius tell you to send for me?'

My father put on his reliable look – always a depressing portent. 'Oh . . . he reckoned you might help me get back my glass.'

He had slipped it in as delicately as a fishmonger filleting a mullet.

'They stole your glass?' I could not accept this. 'The glass Helena bought for you? That I nursed all the way back from Syria?' I lost my temper. 'Pa, when I left it with you, you told me you were carting the whole lot straight back to the Saepta!' The Saepta Julia, up by the Plain of Mars, was the jewellery quarter where Pa had his office and warehouse. It was very well guarded.

'Stop roaring.'

'I will not! How could you be so damned careless?'

I knew exactly how. Traipsing to the Saepta with a waggon would have taken him an hour or two. Since he only lived two minutes from the Emporium he had gone home and put his feet up instead, leaving the glass that we had nursed so carefully to look after itself for the night.

Pa glanced over one shoulder and lowered his voice. 'The Emporium should have been safe enough. It was just temporary.'

'Now it's temporarily lost!' There was something shifty about him. My lava eruption checked in midflow. 'I thought you said this lift was planned? That they knew just what they were going for? How could anybody know that you had half a treasury in Syrian dinnerware, coincidentally brought home by me that very evening and locked up there for only one night?'

Pa looked offended. 'They must have found it by chance.'

'Oh donkey's balls!'

'There's no need to be coarse.'

I was doing worse than that: I was taking a stand. 'Now listen, Pa, let's get something straight. This loss is your affair. I don't want to hear any nonsense like you'll not pay Helena because you never took delivery – '

'Stuff you!' scoffed Pa. 'I'd never cheat that girl, and you know it.' It was probably true. He had a sickening respect for Helena's rank, and a wild hope she would make him a grandfather of senators one day. This was not the moment to tell him he was halfway home on that one. In fact, that was when I started hoping we would have a girl. 'Look son, I know how to shrug off a reverse. If the glass is gone for good I'll have to carry the loss and keep smiling. But after you buzzed off last night, I looked through the boxes. It was beautiful quality – '

'Helena can pick out a tasty jug.'

'Too right. And I'm damned if I'll let it go without a fight. I want you to help track it down for me.'

I had already worked out what he wanted. I had my answer ready too: 'I have to earn. I'll need a fee. I'll need expenses.'

'Oh we can come to some arrangement,' murmured Pa in his airy fashion. He knew Helena would be so upset when she heard this that I would probably end up searching for him for free. He also knew that finding stolen art was my speciality, so he had come to the best man. Other people would be after my services too. Pa had got to me first, before anyone else who had suffered losses today – anyone who might actually pay me – could claim my time.

I downed my wine, then shoved the bill across the table pointedly. If he was paying my expenses he could start with the one for entertaining him. 'I'm off then.'

'Beginning already?' Pa had the grace to look impressed. 'Do you know where to look?'

'That's right.' Well, I knew how to lie well.

In fact, I had only one plan at this stage. Petronius Longus had been hauled to the Palace by the imperial guard. He was in grave trouble. After all the times he had criticised the way I carried out my own work, I could stand watching him squirm. I was off to see how he tried to convince the Emperor that he knew what he was doing.

Besides, Petro was my oldest friend. There was a risk he was about to lose his job for today's action. If I could, I would help him bluff his way out of that.

X

I marched up the Clivus Victoriae to the old Palace of Tiberius, where the bureaucrats still had their offices.

Petronius Longus was sitting on a bench in a corridor. He had been there long enough to start looking worried. His face was pale. He was leaning forwards with his knees apart, staring at his upturned palms. I saw him twitch as I arrived. He pretended to look suave. I thumped his shoulder and berthed alongside.

'Lucius Petronius – the man who brought Rome to a standstill!'

'Don't harass me, Falco!'

'Don't fidget. I'm here to back you up.'

'I can manage.'

'Well you can manage to get yourself into a fix.'

'I don't need a nursemaid.'

'No, you need a friend at court.' He knew I was right.

'You've been there, I take it, Falco? What's going on now?'

'Fusculus is keeping the crowds penned out. Porcius is distributing riot shields. I didn't see Martinus. Pa told me the gist of last night's disaster.'

'He lost that glass of yours, he says.' Petro knew my father well enough to allow for possible deception. I was unperturbed by the insult to the family name. It had never stood high, least of all in respect of Papa. 'They were a sharp crowd of thieves, Falco. I don't like the smell of it. Geminus lost his glass; we know that was quality. Calpurnius was deprived of a huge haul of porphyry that also only came in yesterday. Someone else lost ivory.' I wondered what, if anything, was special about goods landed yesterday. 'Martinus is collecting full details, but we can see the losses are serious.'

'I thought the Emporium was guarded at night?'

Petro growled in the back of his throat. 'All hit over the head and laid out in a line like dead sardines, tied up and gagged.'

478

'Neat. Too neat?' I queried thoughtfully. 'An inside job, maybe?'

'Possibly.' Petro had thought of it. 'I'll work some of the guards over. When I get the chance.'

'If!' I grinned, reminding him that his position was about to be tested. 'This could be your big chance to meet the Emperor.'

'I've met him.' Petro was terse. 'I met him with you, Falco! On the famous occasion when he offered you a fortune to keep quiet about a scandal but you opted for the high moral ground and threw away the cash.'

'Sorry.' I had not forgotten refusing the fortune, merely that Petro had been there watching me play the fool. I had made the mistake of uncovering a plot that impinged too closely on the imperial family; struck by an urgent need to protect his son Domitian, Vespasian had rashly promised me advancement, a ploy he now regretted, probably. It had been pointless in any case, given that I had turned the offer down in a high-handed manner. 'Nobody buys my silence.'

'Hah!' Petronius knew the only loser had been myself.

Suddenly a chamberlain slid out through a curtain and gave Petro the nod.

I stood up too. 'I'm with him.' The official had recognised me. If he thought I was trouble he was too well groomed to let it show.

'Didius Falco,' he greeted me smoothly. The two Praetorian Guards flanking the doorway gave no sign of hearing what was said, but I knew they would now let me pass inside without tying my arms in a Hercules knot. I had no wish to approach anyone of regal status looking flustered after a fight. I knew, even though we were not in the right part of the Palace, that we were about to meet regality: hence the Praetorians.

Petronius had shot towards the curtain the minute he was signalled. Before he could object I stepped past him and entered the audience chamber. He grabbed the curtain and bounced in after me.

Petronius would have been expecting an office, one full of people perhaps, but all with the kind of status he felt free to ignore. I heard him utter something, then cut it off short. It was a lofty room full of scribes. But there was one other, very particular occupant. Petro choked. Even though I had warned him, he had not seriously expected that he would meet the Emperor.

Vespasian was reclining on a reading couch, glancing over a note tablet. His craggy face was unmistakable; he had certainly not bothered to demand a flattering portrait when he approved the new coin issue.

There was no pomp. The couch was against a side wall, as if it had been placed there for casual visitors. The whole impression was that the lord of the Empire had just dropped in and made himself at home in someone else's cubbyhole.

Centrally, there was the long table, covered with scrolls and piles of tablets. Secretaries were stationed there with their styli. They were scratching away very fast, but the speed was unforced. A young slave, smart though not particularly handsome, stood quietly near the Emperor, a napkin over one arm. In fact Vespasian was pouring his own drink – half a cup, just to wet his whistle. He left it on a bronze pedestal so that he was free to stare at us.

He was a big, easy-going, competent character. An organiser, he had the direct glance of a blacksmith, with the country-born arrogance that reminded me of my grandfather. He knew what he believed. He said what he thought. People acted on what he said. They did it nowadays because they had to, but people had been jumping when Vespasian barked since long before he was Emperor.

He had held all the civil magistracies and the highest military ranks. Every post in his career through the *cursus honorem* had been screwed out on merit and in the face of Establishment prejudice. Now he held the final post available. The Establishment was still prejudiced against him, but he need not care.

He wore the purple; it was his entitlement. With it he had neither wreath nor jewels. For him the best adornment of rank was acute native intelligence. That was aimed at us. An uncomfortable experience.

'Falco! What are you doing here, and who's your big bodyguard?'

I walked forwards. 'I act as his guardian actually, sir.' Petronius, annoyed at my joke, followed me; I shoved him to the front. 'This is my friend Lucius Petronius Longus, whom you want to see: the enquiry captain of the Aventine sector in the Fourth Cohort of the vigiles. He's one of the best – but he's also the happy fellow who shut the Emporium today.'

Vespasian Augustus stared at Petronius. Petronius looked self-conscious, then thought better of it and stared boldly at the floor. It was marble; a tasteful acreage in black and white. The tesselations had been laid by a sharp tiler.

'That took nerve!' commented the Emperor. Petronius looked up again, and grinned slightly. He would be all right. I folded my arms and beamed at him like a proud trainer showing off his best gladiator.

'I apologise for any inconvenience, sir.' Petronius always sounded good. He had a mellow voice and a calm delivery. He gave a trustworthy impression. That explained his success with civic selection boards, and with women.

'Apologies may not be enough,' replied Vespasian. Unlike selection boards and women, he could spot a rogue. 'How do you know Falco?'

'Colleagues from the Second Augusta, sir.' Our legion was one Vespasian himself had once led. Both Petro and I allowed ourselves a certain cockiness.

'Really.' The Second had disgraced itself since Vespasian's day. Regretfully, we all let the subject drop. 'You two work in different areas now.'

'We both strive for law and order, sir.' A bit too pious, I thought. Petro could get away with it perhaps, since Vespasian had not known him long. 'Which is what I was doing today after the robbery at the Emporium.' Petronius liked to gallop straight to the point. The concept of first being weighed up through friendly chatter was so alien to his blunt nature that he was rushing the interview.

'You wanted to assess the damage before people trampled everywhere.' Vespasian could assimilate information swiftly; he rapped out the explanation as if it were obvious. I saw Petro flush slightly. He now realised he had plunged in too fast. Given our relative positions in this conversation, forcing the pace was rude. Being rude to an Emperor was the first step to having a lion sniff your bum. 'Why', asked the Emperor coolly, 'could you not have made the merchants responsible for alerting you to their losses in due course? It is in their own interests to provide the information. They will want you to retrieve the stolen goods. So why cause a riot?'

Petronius looked alarmed. He had done things his own way. It was a way that would work, so he had not bothered with alternatives. Alternatives tend to be messy. Just thinking about them wastes time.

'Closing the market sounds crude,' he admitted. 'I was thinking ahead, sir. It was clear we were dealing with a highly organised gang. They had already made fools of everyone involved with security at the Emporium.' He paused. Vespasian quietly indicated that he could go on. Petro got into his stride: 'My immediate reaction was that the raid was so well done they wouldn't stop there. We'll see them again — either at the Emporium, or elsewhere. At this moment they have the advantage of me. I need all the facts – and I need them rapidly. Today I had to discover everything I could about the methods used – how they had identified the goods in advance, for instance. This was no ordinary robbery. The haul was exceptional, and I prophesy big trouble in Rome.'

Without actually answering the original question, Petronius Longus had managed to put the situation in context. He came out of it well, too. I knew it was bluff, but he looked like a man who was planning well.

'You expect a repetition of today?'

'I fear it, sir.'

The Emperor leant forwards suddenly. 'Were you expecting *this*?'

Petronius did not flinch from the fierce question. 'No, sir. But I had felt *something* might happen.'

'Why?'

'A power vacuum has been created in the criminal fraternity.'

'How? Oh, Balbinus Pius of course. You were responsible for that.'

This time Petro was startled. He had not realised that the tablet which Vespasian had been reading when we entered would have been his brief from the secretariat: a swift summary of events today, an account of Petro's career, a résumé of the Balbinus case, even polite suggestions for handling this interview.

I stepped in: 'Petronius Longus is too modest to regale you with his success, sir. He was indeed the officer who convicted Balbinus. He found an opportunity to do it, and he saw matters through. He's too good a man to stop there. He thought ahead, and considered the effect on Rome.'

Vespasian gave no sign of having heard me, though he certainly had. He looked at Petro, who was quite capable of sliding out of this. While I burbled, he had already marshalled his thoughts: 'Sir, I realised the size of the Emporium heist meant there would be political implications.'

'*Political?*' We had the Emperor's full attention. He himself had stepped into a power vacuum when he wrested the throne from the various contenders and settled in to remedy the oddities of Nero's reign and the devastation of the ensuing civil war. He had yet to prove himself. He was working hard, but the benefits of good government take longer than the ravages of bad to become apparent. His grasp on power was still precarious.

I suggested dryly, 'Robbery on a grand scale casts doubt upon the government's effectiveness, sir.'

'No, it casts doubt on the effectiveness of the watch!' retorted the Emperor.

Petronius was visibly annoyed with me. 'Sir, it will cause grumbles, I realise. But I take this theft as a signal. It was very bold. Some element is declaring open war – '

'On whom?' rapped the Emperor. 'You? Me?'

'On the watch, certainly,' Petro replied slowly. 'On the state by implication. And probably on other major thieves. Given that context, I should say that it is likely to involve more than one city sector – '

'That's beyond your scope!' Vespasian had an old-fashioned regard for the limits of office. Immediately he reined Petro in: 'That calls for a co-ordinated strategy.'

'Yes, sir,' agreed Petronius, looking meek. 'I was of course intending to alert my cohort tribune and the Prefect of the City, sir.' The lying shark!

Vespasian thought about it. 'I'd better see your tribune. I'd

483

better see them all.' He gave a slight nod to some sideliner in a white tunic. This silent, virtually invisible official was more than just a secretary. Notes were being made briefly on a tablet, but these were the notes of a man taking instructions. He knew the first rule of administration: always cover yourself. 'Conference. After lunch. Warn Titus.' The Emperor spoke offhandedly, though both Petro and I had a sense of starting far more than we had bargained for. He turned back to us. 'That still leaves the riot to diffuse. What do you suggest?'

Knowing that the man who starts a riot rarely thinks about how he will stop it, I thought best to offer ideas myself. 'You could mollify the discontent to some degree by announcing compensation, sir.'

'*Compensation?*'

I had done it now. I had used a naughty word.

XI

'Thanks a lot, Falco!'

We were back on the bench in the corridor. The chamberlain who shepherded visitors was looking curious. The white-tunic-clad official strode off. Vespasian's mention of lunch told us that the 'few minutes' we had been told to wait would be several hours. Petronius was furious. 'Well if that was helping, thanks, Falco! Thanks to you mentioning money, the poor old buffer's had to rush to his bedroom for a quiet lie-down!'

'Forget it,' I assured Petro. 'Vespasian's famously tight, but he won't faint at the mere mention. If he hates our suggestion he'll say no.'

'*Your* suggestion,' Petro inserted. I ignored it.

We were silent for a while, mulling over events past and recent. 'What in Hades have you got me into here?' Petro grumbled.

'At some point later, when we want to be having our dinner, we'll find ourselves advising a committee on the fine points of managing crime.'

'I just want to get back to my case.'

'This could be the most promising assignment of your life.'

'Stuff it,' Petro growled.

It was in fact lunch time when things started to happen. First the white tunic came and collected us. He wanted to pick our brains. We allowed it, but made sure we shared his lunch.

He introduced himself as Tiberius Claudius Laeta. Evidently a Palace freedman of great status, he had possession of a room that was twice as big as my whole apartment. There, when Vespasian didn't need a minion to push around, the good Laeta could sit and pick his nose. There, too, persons of lesser status brought him trayloads of sustenance.

'Nice!' we said.

'It's a living,' he replied. There was only one winecup but Petro quickly found a couple of dusty extras hidden behind some scroll boxes. The clerk tried to look impressed with our initiative as, smiling like happy new cronies, we poured his flagon for him. Since the wine was free, it proved good enough even for Petro. Laeta raised his cup to us, looking pleased to have company. Being top clerk, which he obviously was, can be a lonely life. 'So! I gather you're Falco, one of Anacrites' men?'

'I'm Falco,' I answered patiently. 'I'm my own man.'

'Sorry. I understood you worked for the bureau that we don't talk about.'

'I have worked for the Emperor. I found the rewards unrealistic, and I don't plan any more.'

'Ah!' The good Laeta managed to say this with an air of discretion, while implying that whatever bureau *he* served was scheming to put the Chief Spy on the rim of a live volcano and give him a big shove. 'Maybe you would find it more rewarding working for us.'

'Maybe,' I said, fairly peacefully. If it upset Anacrites, I would consider anything.

Claudius Laeta gave me a considered stare, then turned to Petronius. Petro had been stolidly putting away a platter of cold artichoke hearts. As his attention was demanded by our host, I myself started on Laeta's dish of anchovies. 'And you are Petronius Longus, of the Aventine Watch?' Petro nodded, still chewing. 'Do set me straight about the vigiles. I confuse them with the Urban Cohorts . . .'

'Easily done.' Petronius filled him in politely. Replete, he leant back on a stool and gave Laeta his lecture for new recruits: 'This is how law and order works in Rome. Top of the heap you have the Praetorian Guard; Cohorts One to Nine, commanded by the Praetorian Prefect, barracked at the Praetorian Camp. Fully armed. Duties: one, guarding the Emperor: two, ceremonial swank. They are a hand-picked élite, and full of themselves. Next in line and tacked on to them are Cohorts Ten to Twelve, known as the Urbans. Commanded by the Urban Prefect – a senator – who is basically the city manager. Routinely armed with sword and knife. Their unofficial job description is *to repress the mob*.

Duties officially: to keep the peace, keep their ears open, and keep the Urban Prefect informed of absolutely everything.'

'Spying?' Laeta queried dryly. 'I thought Anacrites did that?'

'He spies on them while they're spying on us,' I suggested.

'And at the bottom,' Petro continued, 'doing all the real work, you have the vigiles, commanded by the Prefect of the Vigiles. Unarmed, but run on military lines. Seven cohorts, each led by a tribune who is an ex-chief centurion; each with seven centuries who do the foot patrols. Rome has fourteen administrative regions. Each cohort looks after two. Duties: everything those flash bastards at the Praetorian Camp won't lower themselves to touch.'

'So in the Aventine Watch you cover the Twelfth and Thirteenth regions?'

'Yes. We're the Fourth Cohort.'

'And your tribune is?'

'Marcus Rubella.' Petro rarely spoke of the tribune, whom he cordially dismissed as a legionary has-been who should have stuck to square-bashing.

'An equestrian?'

'Bought it with his discharge grant. Almost enough rank now to be a master criminal,' Petro replied dryly, thinking of Balbinus Pius.

'And the main role of the vigiles is fire-watching?'

'*One* role.' Petro hated to be thought of as a mere fireman. 'Yes, but since that involves patrolling the streets at night, when most crimes are committed, our remit expanded. We apprehend street thieves and housebreakers, round up runaway slaves, keep custodians of tenements and warehouses up to the mark. We spend a lot of effort controlling the baths. Clothes stealing is a big problem.'

'So you remain a proletarian squad?' Laeta was falling into the administrator's trap of obsession with titles and rank.

'We are freedmen and honest citizens,' snarled Petro, clearly not amused.

'Oh quite. And what's your own position?'

'Casework,' said Petro. 'I head the enquiry team for the Thirteenth district. The foot patrols pound the pavements, sniffing for smoke and apprehending wrongdoers if they meet

487

them face to face. They're competent for basic tasks like thrashing householders who let stoves fall over. But each cohort has an officer like myself with a small team of agents doing house-to-house searches and general follow-up. Two, in fact, one per district. Between us we trace the stolen goblets and investigate who hit the barmaid over the head with a plank.'

'Reporting to the tribune?'

'Partly. We do a lot for the Prefect's office as well. Any case where more than a public whipping is called for has to go forward to him. The Prefect has a full staff, including a registrar for various lists of undesirables, and an interrogation officer –'

'He carries out the torturing?'

'We find brute force can be counterproductive,' Petro replied: the official disclaimer.

I laughed bitterly. 'Tell that to a hard case who has just had his privates squeezed in the little back room!'

Petronius chose not to hear me.

'So . . .' Laeta moved on. 'Tell me your anxieties about the Emporium raid. Your theory is that we have an organised and daring gang moving in on the city centre? I'd like to know how much of Rome is threatened.'

'Who can say?' Petronius knew better than to give neat summaries. Criminals don't follow neat rules. 'I'd reckon all the central watches ought to be put on alert.'

Laeta made a note. 'So what is your assessment of the threat?'

'They are aiming at commodities,' Petro answered confidently. 'It will be wharves and stores – not, I think, the general food markets. This affects the Thirteenth region mainly, but also the Eleventh and Twelfth, which include some specialist warehouses. I doubt if the granaries are vulnerable.'

'Why not?'

'With the state corn dole for the poor and the rich living off grain from their own estates, where's the scope for a black market? The bastards might take a swipe at the paper warehouse on the Quirinal. The Saepta Julia will also be a target. The jewellers should be warned.' Laeta was absorbing all this assiduously.

He had a warm almond omelette under a cover, so we divided that up into three for him and shared it round. Soon the food tray was empty.

Laeta then excused himself. We were allowed to put our feet up in his luxurious bolt hole until required.

'This is a right mess, Falco!' Petro tested the flagon but we had already drained it. 'I don't want a bunch of amateurs all over my patch.'

'Don't burst your pod. It was you who made yourself out to be a master of criminal intelligence.'

'Hercules Victor! How was I to know a passing thought would be turned into an issue, with secretaries running around like rabbits and a full intersectional conference on major crime being thrown together the same day?'

I grinned at him kindly. 'Well, you've learned something useful here: keep your thoughts to yourself!'

Rooting amongst the scroll boxes, I discovered a slim alabastron of red wine that Laeta had already unbunged and half drunk on some previous occasion. We unbunged it again and helped ourselves. I replaced the container just where I had found it, so Laeta would not think we had been prying amongst his personal stuff.

We took it in turns to nod off.

Instinct told us when to rouse ourselves. This we had learned primarily while watching for moustachioed Britons to jump out from broom bushes. In fact, the Britons had never jumped us. But the instinct had proved useful for warning us of bad-tempered centurions who didn't think it was funny if the footsloggers on guard duty happened to lean against a parapet to discuss whether the Greens were having their best season ever in the chariot races at home. At any event, when Claudius Laeta bustled back to fetch us, we were neither leaning nor dozing, but had washed our hands and faces in a bowl that a flunkey had brought for Laeta's use, then combed our hair like a couple of swanks going to a party, and sat ourselves up like men who could be relied upon.

'Ah there you are . . .' Laeta gazed around his room nervously, as if he expected to find vandalism. 'The old man's gone across to his own quarters. We'll have to make the trip to the Golden House.'

I smiled. 'Lucius Petronius and I would welcome a stroll in the fresh air.'

Laeta looked worried a second time, as if he was wondering what we had been up to that could necessitate a breather.

Nero had set out his Golden House across the whole of central Rome. Via a garden that filled the entire valley of the Forum, he had linked the old Palace of the Caesars to a new complex completed for him by masters of architectural innovation and decor. Our conference was held in the new part. I had seen it before. It still made me gasp.

To reach it, we had come down from the Palatine, through the cool, guarded cryptoporticus, and walked across the eastern end of the Forum, past the Vestals' House and the Sweating Fountain, then around the mess that had recently been the Great Lake dominating the country gardens that Nero had created in the bowl of the Palatine and Esquiline hills. The lake was now a gigantic hole where Vespasian had inaugurated his promised amphitheatre. On the Oppian crest beyond it still stood Nero's fantastic palace. It was too opulent for the new Flavian dynasty, who had restrained good taste, yet too costly and too exquisite to pull down. To build another palace when Rome itself lay in ruins would look a worse extravagance than Nero's. So Vespasian and his sons were living here. At least they could blame their mad predecessor.

Claudius Laeta led us through a maze of marble-clad entrance halls and tall, intensely decorated corridors. I think we were in the east wing; the west seemed to be the private quarters. Guards nodded Laeta past, and he found his way with ease. To a stranger, the Golden House was deliberately bewildering. Rooms and passageways succeeded one another in a seemingly random profusion. The eye was dazzled with gilt and the gleam of the finest polished marble; the brain was bemused by twists and turns; the ear was assaulted by the continual music of water in fountains and cascades. Petronius stumbled into me as he tried to stare up at the minutely painted ceilings while Laeta hurried us along. Finally we took a dart to the left, glimpsed an apsidal hall, whipped past

490

another room, and stepped into the famous fabulous octagonal dining room.

In Nero's day people came here for orgies; just our luck to arrive when times had changed and the best we could get was a crime conference.

The room was full of light. There was an open aspect to the south, with a heart-stopping view that we would not be gazing at. There was a theatrical cascade (turned off). There were curtained side rooms in which scenes of revolting debauchery had once occurred (now empty). Above our heads had been the legendary revolving ivory ceiling that had showered gifts down upon lucky diners (dismantled; no presents for us).

Already assembled were Vespasian and his elder son, Titus, seated on thrones. Petronius would like the thrones. He approved of formality. Titus, a younger version of his father but with a jolly hint of chubbiness, gave me a pleasant nod; I showed my teeth politely. Calm administrators were handing them last-minute briefs.

Other officials were just arriving with us. Summoned from their lunches were both the Urban Prefect, who thought he ran the city, and the Prefect of the Vigiles, who really did the work. Each had a fleet of office minions who were shuttled into the side rooms. To speak up for them (since they kept themselves unencumbered by practical knowledge), the prefects had brought all seven tribunes of the vigiles cohorts, including Rubella, the Fourth Cohort's own top man, to whom Petro was supposed to report any problems before they became public. Rubella had brought a paper cone of sunflower seeds, which he continued to munch surreptitiously. Despite Petro's scorn, I thought he looked pleasingly human.

Present, though not named in the record, was Anacrites the Chief Spy.

'Falco!' His light eyes flickered nervously as he realised that I was alive, and deep in this unexpected enterprise. He did not ask how I had enjoyed his Eastern fiasco. When I was ready I would report to Vespasian personally, and my comments would be unrestrained by loyalty to the man who sent me there.

'Excuse me,' I answered coldly. 'I'm presenting a report . . .'

Claudius Laeta must have overheard, for he waved Petro and me up close to him; his position was nearest the Emperor. On Vespasian's behalf he was chairing the meeting. What was said is, of course, confidential. The minutes ran to half a closely written scroll. In confidence, of course, what happened was:

The regular officials conducted business briskly. They were held up sometimes by tribunes holding forth on personal theories that had nothing to do with the issue and were sometimes incomprehensible (unminuted). Once or twice a prefect ventured a trite remark (paraphrased succinctly by the secretary). Petronius Longus gave a clear account of his belief that with the removal of Balbinus some new crime lord had seized the initiative. (This, pretty well verbatim, took up most of the record.) Petro had moved in the course of that morning from a man who was talking his way out of trouble to one who looked a contender for a laurel crown. He took it well. Petronius had the right sceptical attitude.

I found myself being consulted by Vespasian as his expert on life in the streets; I managed to produce some ideas that had a ring of good sense, though I forsaw problems explaining later to Helena Justina exactly what I had said.

Anacrites was suddenly asked by Titus what his professional intelligence team had noticed. He offered nothing but waffle. His team was useless, unaware of pretty well everything that . went on in Rome. The Urban Prefect gleefully stepped in and pretended *his* spies had spotted worrying signs of unrest. Asked to be more specific, he was soon floundering.

It took two hours of debate before the Emperor was satisfied. The problem – if it existed – was to be tackled with energy (though no extra men would be drafted in). The Prefect of the Vigiles would co-ordinate a special investigation, reporting to the Urban Prefect, who would report to Titus Caesar. Petronius Longus, reporting to Rubella, reporting to the Prefect of the Vigiles, would identify the Emporium thieves, then evaluate whether they were a one-time strike or a more widespread threat. He had the right to advise any cohort tribune of a perceived danger in a particular sector, and all had a duty to assist him if required.

Anacrites was allocated no activity, though as a courteous gesture Titus said it was assumed the intelligence network would 'keep a watching brief'. We all knew this traditional phrase. It meant they were to keep out of the way.

As an exceptional measure only (this was heavily stressed by Vespasian), compensation would be offered to those traders at the Emporium who had lost goods last night, so long as their names appeared on the official list. Martinus had brought this for Petronius, sent in via a flunkey. Vespasian, who knew how to dodge fiddles, told a copy clerk to duplicate the list for him immediately.

I found myself assigned as a supernumerary officer, to work alongside Petronius. As usual with meetings, I came away not entirely clear what I was supposed to do.

493

XII

'So Marcus, you went out for a quiet stroll up and down the Forum,' mused Helena, passing a platter of cheese savouries to Silvia. 'By the time you came home, there was a major epidemic of crime, an imperial commission, and both of you hearty fellows had become special-enquiry officers?'

'Beats shopping for radishes,' I commented, though since we had guests, I had done that too. A householder has to be versatile.

'Working together will be nice for them,' remarked Arria Silvia. Petro's wife was petite and pretty. A bright, dainty girl with ribbons binding her hair, she was the kind I had once thought I wanted – until Petro acquired Silvia. She had a habit of stating the obvious; I suppose he found it comforting. They had been married for about seven years, and with three children to secure them in affection (or whatever it was), the union looked likely to last. I had therefore decided to put aside my reaction to Silvia. Which was that she brought me out in a rash.

Helena seemed able to get along with her, though their friendship lacked the warmth that I had noticed flowering naturally between Helena and my sister Maia, for instance. 'I hope you two won't quarrel,' Helena said to me, smiling quietly. The shrewd one, mine. Whether or not he recognised what she meant, Petronius did not respond but went out to the balcony, where he lifted up his eldest daughter so she could pee into one of my pots of bulbs. This would probably kill them but I said nothing. He was a competent, un-complicated father. A lesson to all of us.

I had the other two girls on my lap, playing with toys we had brought them. We were a happy party, stuffed with food and still enjoying a fine wine Petronius had donated from his extensive collection. Petro and Silvia had spent the early evening with us, laughing over stories of our travels in Syria. Friends do so love to hear about you suffering from ghastly climates, crooked moneychangers, and intense pain from poisonous arachnids. Saves them going on holiday themselves.

There had been so much to say about the scorpion nipping Helena and other lively memories that she and I had managed to avoid mentioning the one item that Silvia would think important: that we too might become a family.

I won't say Helena and I were sneakily pleased to keep it a secret. It was too much of an issue; we were not ready to laugh about it. But we were close enough friends for Helena to let me see her wry expression as Silvia prattled cheerfully about her own little girls. Silvia was hinting that it was about time Helena started to feel jealous yearnings. Eventually I caught Helena's eye privately and winked at her. Silvia saw me do it. She shot a mock-scandalised look at Petronius, thinking I was being amorous. Petro pretended, as usual, that he had no idea at all what was going on.

The wink remained as a moment of stillness between Helena and me.

The women were taking a greater interest in our new task than either Petro or I wanted. Silvia had realised that Helena Justina was used to more free consultation than Petronius allowed her. She plunged in, picking over issues as tenaciously as she had earlier torn apart her chicken wings in peppered wine sauce.

Petronius and I had been allies for a long time. While Silvia speculated, we just talked quietly among ourselves.

'I want you to come over the road later, Petro. There's a property Smaractus is offering on the market. It's a dump, but a better one than this if it was done up a bit.'

'*Done up a bit?*' Petro squinted at me as if he had just caught me stealing wine jars from caupona counters. 'Will Smaractus invest in improvements?'

'No, but I'm determined to find another place for us, even if I have to renovate a wreck myself.'

'I've not heard about this!' said Helena, taking one of Petro's girls from me. The other scampered off to play on the balcony. 'Shouldn't I be the one to inspect the real estate?'

'And why can't you find another landlord?' Silvia put in.

I grinned at Helena. 'The person who needs to inspect it is the kind associate who will be helping me install the new windows and floorboards!'

'Forget it!' exclaimed Petro, looking appalled.

'You're a good carpenter.'

Helena laughed. 'And he *was* a good friend!'

'I'm going to have my hands full with this initiative against the Emporium thieves,' said Petronius firmly. Sometimes he would help out in my crazy schemes; sometimes he didn't want to know. I let it drop. He was too stubborn to change his mind.

'So why has our bijou niche here lost its charm after so long?' Helena asked with the air of a Fury lightly fingering her scourge.

'I'm getting old. My legs are hating the stairs.' My beloved gave me a very sweet smile that meant I was toying with serious trouble.

'You should try it with three children hanging round your neck!' Silvia's remark was too close for comfort; I was dreading it with just one, particularly on Helena's behalf in the long months before our shrimp was born. I could already hear helpful relatives suggesting she should live somewhere more accessible, hoping that would be the first step to her leaving me for good.

Presumably Helena realised why I wanted a better billet. She leant back on her stool, cradling Tadia, and gave me a long stare. It was a challenge to tell Petro and Silvia the situation we were in. I returned the stare but stayed silent.

'Now doesn't Helena look good holding a baby!' Silvia rebuked me, clearly not even suspecting the truth. I had denied it to Petro, and he must have passed this on. Feeling mild pangs of guilt on his behalf, I condescended to survey Helena. She was wearing blue, with a tasteful row of bracelets covering her scarred arm, and silver earrings on which I had squandered a week's earnings one day in Palmyra just because I knew she was enjoying herself travelling the world with me.

She did look good. She looked healthy, calm and sure of herself. As she gripped the child – who was trying to fling herself to the floor to see if landing hard on boards would hurt – Helena's big brown beautiful eyes sent me another dare.

I stayed calm. I never let Silvia see how much she annoyed me. And I tried not to let Helena discover how her challenges made me feel jittery. 'The first time I ever saw Helena she was holding a child.'

'I don't remember that.'

'The British procurator's daughter.'

'Oh, Aunt Camilla's eldest!' She did remember now; her blush told me. 'Flavia.'

'Flavia!' I agreed, grinning at her. I could see she had recalled the scene: a polite family group, educated after-dinner people discussing whether it might rain the next day, then I prowled in, newly landed in the province, flexing my class prejudice and intending to break bones if anyone offered me any pleasantries.

'What was *he* doing?' giggled Silvia.

'Scowling,' replied Helena patiently. 'He looked as if a Titan had just stepped on his foot and crushed his big toe. I was staying with nice people who had been very kind to me, then this hero turned up, like Milo of Croton looking for a tree to split with his fist. He was exhausted, miserable and exasperated by his work – '

'Sounds normal!'

'But he still managed to be rude to me.'

'The lout!'

'In a way that made me want to – '

'Go to bed with me?' I offered.

'Prove you wrong!' Helena roared, still hot-headed at the thought.

When I met her in Britain she had thoroughly overturned me: I had started out believing her stuck-up, strict, ill-humoured, uncharitable and untouchable; then I fell for her so hard I was barely able to believe my luck when she did go to bed with me.

'And what were you after, Falco?' Silvia was half hoping for a salacious answer.

I wanted Helena as my partner for life. That was too shocking to mention to a prim little piece like Silvia. I reached for the fruit bowl and savagely bit a pear.

'We're still waiting to hear about this task you two have for the Emperor!' Making Silvia change the subject was simplicity itself. If you ignored one remark she came out with something different. That did not mean you liked it better.

I saw Petro frown slightly. We both wanted to let things ride. We still had to manoeuvre for position, and we didn't need women helping us.

'Which of you is taking the lead in this venture?' Helena asked curiously. She could always find really awkward questions.

'I am,' said Petro.

'Excuse me!' I had wanted to sort this out privately with him, but we were now trapped. 'I work independently. I don't take orders from anyone.'

'I'm head of the special enquiry,' said Petro. 'You'll have to work with me.'

'My commission comes direct from Vespasian. He always gives me a free hand.'

'Not in my district.'

'I hadn't foreseen any conflict.'

'You hadn't been thinking then!' muttered Helena.

'There's no conflict,' Petronius said calmly.

'Oh no. It's all pretty clear. You intend to be planning the work, giving the orders and leading the team. That leaves me sweeping the office.'

Suddenly he grinned. 'Sounds fair – and I suppose you're competent!'

'I can wield a broom,' I agreed, though I was conceding nothing.

'We can work something out,' Petronius murmured airily.

'Oh we can operate in tandem. We've been friends for a long time.' That was why it was impossible for either of us to be in sole charge, of course. Helena had seen that immediately.

'Of course,' confirmed Petro, with the briefest of smiles.

Nothing was settled, but we left it at that to avoid a furious argument.

XIII

Fountain Court on a quiet October evening had its usual soiled and sultry charm. A faint pall of black smoke from the lampblack ovens drifted languidly five feet above the lane looking for passers-by with clean togas or tunics to smudge. Amidst its acrid tang lingered scents of sulphur from the laundry and rancid fat frying. Cassius the baker had been making veal pies earlier – with too much juniper by the smell. Above us people had hung bedding over their balconies, or sat there airing their fat backsides over a parapet while they shouted abuse at members of their family hidden indoors. Some idiot was hammering madly. A weary young girl staggered past us, almost unable to walk under the weight of the long garlands of flowers she had spent all day weaving for dinner parties in louche, wealthy homes.

A thin scruffy dog sat outside Lenia's, waiting for someone soft-hearted it could follow home.

'Don't look,' I commanded Helena. I took her hand as we crossed the dusty street to ask Cassius to give us the key to the empty apartment.

Cassius was a genial fellow, though he had never deigned to notice that Helena Justina was attached to me. He sold her loaves, at more or less reasonable prices; he chucked me the occasional stale roll while we swapped gossip. But even when Helena appeared in his shop with her noble fist grasped in mine, Cassius gave no acknowledgement that he was addressing a couple. He must regard us as unsuitable; well, he was not alone. I thought we were unsuitable myself – not that that would stop me.

'Ho, Falco!'

'Got the key for upstairs?'

'What idiot wants that?'

'Well, I'll have a look – '

'Hah!' chipped Cassius, as if I had dared to suggest one of his whole grain crescent baps had a spot of mould.

Refusing to be put off, we made him go for the key, which had been abandoned for so long he had lost it somewhere behind a mountain of sacks in his flour store. While we waited for him to track down the nail he had hung it on, I hunted for interesting crumbs in the bread roll display baskets, and grinned at Helena.

'It's right, you know. You looked quite at home that time I saw you with Aelia Camilla's little girl. A natural!'

'Flavia was not my child,' said Helena, in a cold voice.

Cassius came back, armed with an iron key the size of a ratchet on some dockyard winding gear. Being nosy, he made sure he kept hold of it and came with us up the dilapidated stone steps beside his shop. Not many of the treads were completely broken away; if you kept near the wall it was almost safe. Using both hands, Cassius struggled to turn the key in a rusted lock. Failing, we discovered the easiest way in was to push open the back edge of the door and squeeze through the matted spiderwebs that had been acting as hinges.

It was very dark. Cassius boldly crossed to a window and threw back a shutter; it dropped off in his hand. He cursed as the heavy wood crashed to the floor, leaving splinters in his fingers and grazing his leg on the way.

'Frankly,' Helena decided at once, 'this seems a bit too elegant for us!'

It was out of the question. Deeply depressed, I insisted on seeing everything.

'Who lives upstairs, Cassius?'

'No one. The other apartments are even worse than this. Mind you, I saw some old bag woman poking round this afternoon.'

Disaster. The last thing we needed was vagrants for close neighbours. I was trying to become more respectable.

Huge sheets of plaster hung away from the wall slats, which themselves bowed inwards alarmingly. The floors dipped several inches every time we trod the boards, which we did very delicately. The joists must have gone. Since the floor joists should have been tying the whole building together, this was serious. All the internal doors were missing. So, as Lenia had warned me, was the floor in the back rooms.

'What's that down there?'

'My log store,' said Cassius. True. We could see the logs through his ceiling. Presumably when Cassius was loading his oven, sometime before dawn, anyone upstairs would hear him rolling the logs about.

The place was derelict. We would not be asking for a lease from Smaractus. Cassius lost interest and left to tend his leg, which was now bleeding badly. 'Is this your dog down here, Falco?'

'Certainly not. Chuck a rock at him.'

'It's a girl.'

'She's still not mine – and she's not going to be!'

Helena and I stayed, too dispirited to shift. She gazed at me. She knew exactly why I was looking at property, but unless she acknowledged being pregnant, she could not discuss my project. For once, I had the upper hand.

'Sorry,' I said.

'Why? Nothing's lost.'

'I was convinced this dump had been on the market so long I could walk in and pay Smaractus in old nuts.'

'Oh, he'd be delighted to find a tenant!' Helena laughed. 'Can we mend it? You're very practical, Marcus – '

'Jupiter! This needs major building work – it's far beyond my scope.'

'I thought you liked a challenge?'

'Thanks for the faith! This whole block should be torn down. I don't know why Cassius sticks it. He's risking his life every day.' Like much of Rome.

'At least we could get fresh bread,' Helena pretended to muse. 'We could reach down through the floor for it without getting out of bed ...'

'No, we can't live above a bakery. Apart from the fire risk – '

'The oven is separate, in the street.'

'So are the mills, with a damned donkey braying and the endless rumble of grinding querns! Don't fool about, lady. Think of the cooking smells. Bread's fine, but when Cassius has baked his loaves he uses the ovens to heat offal pies in nasty gravy for the entire street. I should have thought of that.'

Helena had wandered to the window. She stood on tiptoe,

leaning out for the view, while she changed the subject: 'I don't like this trouble between you and Petronius.'

'There's no trouble.'

'There's going to be.'

'I've known Petro a long time.'

'And it's a long time since you worked together. When you did, it was back in the army and you were both taking orders from somebody else.'

'I can take orders. I take them from you all the time.'

She chortled seditiously. I joined her at the window and caused a diversion, trying to nudge her off balance. She slipped an arm around me to save herself, then kept it there in a friendly fashion while we both looked out.

This side of Fountain Court was lower down the hillside than where we lived, so we were almost opposite the familiar streetside row of lockups: the stationery supplier, the barber, the funeral parlour, small pavement businesses in a gloomy colonnade below five storeys of identical apartments, some overpaid architect's notion of thoughtful design. Few architects permit themselves to live in their own tenements.

'Is that our block?'

'No, the one next door.'

'There's a letting notice, Marcus.'

'I think it's for one of the shops on the ground floor.'

Helena's sharp eyes had spotted the kind of street graffiti you usually ignore. I walked her downstairs and across the road to check up. The chalked advertisement was for a workshop. It called itself 'well-set-out artisan premises with advantageous living accommodation', but it was a damp booth with an impossible stairway to a disgusting loft. It's true there was a small domestic apartment attached, but the two-room tenancy was for five years. Who could say how many offspring I might have accidentally fathered by that time, and how much space I should be needing to house them all?

Shivering, I let Helena lead me out to Fountain Court. The scruffy dog had found us again, and was staring at me hopefully. She must have worked out who was the soft one.

Since the barber had no customers we dumped ourselves pessimistically on two of his stools. He grumbled briefly, then went indoors for a lie-down, his favourite occupation anyway.

'You know we can live anywhere,' Helena said quietly. 'I have money – '

'No. I'll pay the rent.'

As a senator's daughter she owned far less than her two brothers, but if she allied herself with anyone respectable there was a large dowry still kicking around from her previous failed marriage, plus various legacies from female relations who had spotted her special character. I had never let myself discover the exact extent of Helena's wealth. I didn't want to upset myself. And I never wanted to find myself a kept man.

'So what are we looking for?' She was being tactful now. Refraining from comment on my proud self-respect. Naturally I found it maddening.

'That's obvious. Somewhere we don't risk scum breaking in. Where perverts who come to see me about business won't make trouble for you. And more space.'

'Space for a cradle, and seats for all your sisters when they come cooing over the item in it?' Helena's voice was dry. She knew how to soften me up.

'More seats would be useful.' I smiled. 'I like to entertain.'

'You like to get me annoyed!'

'I like you in any mood.' I ran one finger down her neck, just tickling the skin beneath the braid on her gown. She lowered her chin suddenly, trapping my finger. I thought about pulling her closer and kissing her, but I was too depressed. To provide a public spectacle you need to be feeling confident.

From her position with her head tucked down, Helena was looking across Fountain Court. I felt her interest shift. Gazing at the sky, I warned the gods: 'Watch out, you loafers on Olympus. Somebody's just had a bright idea!'

Then Helena asked in the curious tone that had so often led to trouble, 'Who lives above the basket shop?'

The basket-weaver occupied a lockup two along from Cassius the baker. He shared his frontage with a cereal-seller – another quiet trade, and fairly free of smelly nuisances. Above them rose a typical tenement, similar to ours and with the same kind of underpaid, overworked occupants. There was no letting sign, but the shutters on the first-floor

503

apartment were closed, as they always had been to my knowledge. I had never seen anybody going in.

'Well spotted!' I murmured thoughtfully.

Right there, opposite Lenia's laundry, we could have found our next home.

XIV

The basket-weaver, a wiry gent in a tawny tunic whom I knew by sight, told us the apartment above him belonged to his shop. He had never occupied the upstairs because he only bunked temporarily in Fountain Court. He lived on the Campagna, kept his family there, and intended to retire to the country when he remembered to stop coming to town every week. The rooms above were in fact impossible to live in, being filled up with rubble and junk. Smaractus was too mean to clear them out. Instead, the idle bastard had negotiated a reduced rent. It suited the basket-weaver. Now it suited me.

Helena and I peered in warily. It was very dark. After living on the sixth floor, anywhere near ground level was bound to be. No balcony; no view; no garden, of course; no cooking facilities. Water from a fountain a street away. A public latrine at the end of our own street. Baths and temples on the Aventine. Street markets in any direction. My existing office within shouting range across the lane. It had three rooms – a gain of one on what we were used to – and a whole array of little cubbyholes.

'Pot stores!' cried Helena. 'I love it!'

'Cradle space!' I grinned.

Smaractus, my landlord, was a person I avoided. I lost my temper just thinking about that fungus. I had intended to discuss matters peacefully with Lenia, but I foolishly chose a time when her insalubrious betrothed had dropped in with a wine flagon.

I refused to drink with him. I'll take a free tipple from most people, but I'm a civilised man; I do discriminate. Below the line I drew in those days lay unrepentant murderers, corrupt tax-gathers, rapists, and Smaractus.

Luckily I knew I made him nervous. There had been a time he always brought two gladiators from the gym he ran whenever he risked his neck in Fountain Court; with Lenia to

505

defend him from aggrieved tenants he had taken to dispensing with the muscle. A good idea; poor Asiacus and Rodan were so badly nourished they needed to conserve their strength. The big daft darlings would never stagger into the arena after a day fighting me. For Smaractus I was a difficult proposition. I was lean and hard, and I hated his guts. As I crossed the threshold I heard his voice, so I had time to apply what Helena called my Milo of Croton look.

'Falco is going to read the sheep's liver at the wedding for us!' Lenia simpered, incongruously playing the eager young bride. He couldn't have been there for more than a few minutes but she was well into the wine. Who could blame her?

'Better watch out!' I warned him. He realised that if I took the augury this might be a double-edged favour. A bad omen could ruin his happiness. A *really* bad omen, and Lenia might back out before he got the ring on her, depriving him of her well-filled strong-boxes. Being sick on his mother as Lenia had asked me was nothing to the fun I could have with a co-operative ewe.

'He's nice and cheap,' said Lenia to him, as if explaining why I seemed a good idea. I was on her side too, though we refrained from mentioning that. 'I see the little dog's found you, Falco. We call it Nux.'

'I'm not taking in a stray.'

'Oh no? So when did you change your attitude?'

Smaractus muttered that I lacked experience as a priest, and I retorted that I knew quite enough to pontificate on *his* marriage. Lenia shoved a winecup into my hand. I shoved it back.

With the business formalities over, we could get down to cheating each other.

I knew Smaractus would try to swing some fiddle if he heard we were the basket-weaver's subtenants. One way out was to avoid telling him. Unfortunately, now he was betrothed to Lenia he was always littering up the neighbourhood; he was bound to spot us going in and out. This needed care – or blatant blackmail. To start with I ranted at him about the dilapidated rooms above Cassius. 'Somebody's going to tell the aediles that place is a danger to passers-by, and you'll be

ordered to demolish the lot before it falls in the street!'
Smaractus would do anything to avoid pulling down a
property because by law he would have to replace it with
something equal or better. (The idea of making more money
from higher rents afterwards was too sophisticated for his
mouldy old sponge of a brain.)

'Who would stir up trouble like that?' he sneered. I smiled
courteously, while Lenia kicked his foot to explain what I was
getting at. He would be limping for a week.

'Wasn't it you I saw talking to the trug-seller?' Lenia asked
me. You couldn't squeeze a pimple in Fountain Court
without three people telling you to leave yourself alone.

'I'm going to help him clear out his upper floor.'

'Why's that?' demanded Smaractus suspiciously.

'Because I'm a kind-hearted fellow.'

I waited until he was about to explode with curiosity, then I
told him what I had just agreed with the cane-weaver: I would
clear out the apartment and in return live there rent-free.
Once we moved in I would keep an eye on the lockup when it
was closed, allowing the weaver greater freedom to buzz off to
his family.

Smaractus was nonplussed by this news. The word 'rent-
free' was not in a landlord's vocabulary. I explained what it
meant. He then used some phrases that proved what I had
always suspected: he had been brought up by runaway
trireme slaves in an unlicensed abattoir.

'I'm glad you approve,' I told him. Then I left, while he was
still choking on his wine.

XV

Next morning I presented myself at the Aventine Watch. The Fourth Cohort had its tribunal headquarters in the Twelfth region, the Piscina Publica, which most people deemed more salubrious. Alongside the HQ was a station house for the foot patrols, where their fire-fighting equipment was stored. To cover their other patch, the Thirteenth region, they had a second station house, to which Petronius bunked off whenever possible. That was where he kept an office staffed by his casework team of plain-clothes enquiry agents and scribes. They had a lockup for people who were caught in the act by the foot patrols or who sensibly chose to confess as soon as challenged, plus a room for more detailed questioning. It was small, but had interesting iron devices hung on all the walls. And there was just space to get a good swing with a boot.

Fusculus was outside the office, helping an old woman compose a petition. They had a bench in the portico for local people who came with complaints. The duty clerk, a lanky youth who never said much, leaned down and worked grit out of his left sandal while Fusculus very patiently went through the procedure for the crone: 'I can't write it for you. Only you know the facts. You want to start off: *To Lucius Petronius Longus, chief enquirer of the Thirteenth region* . . . Don't worry. The scribes will put that bit automatically. *From* . . . Then say who you are, and tell us details of your loss. *On the Ides of October*, or whenever it was – '

'Yesterday.'

Fusculus kicked the clerk into action. *'The day after the Ides, there was stolen from me . . .'*

'A bedcover.' The woman had caught on rapidly, as they do when they have persuaded some handsome young fellow to work for them. 'By a street gang who removed it from my balcony. In Conch Court, off Armilustrum Street.'

'Worth?' Fusculus managed to squeeze in.

'A denarius!' She was probably guessing.

'How long had you had it?' demanded Fusculus suspiciously. 'What was this treasure made of?'

'Wool! The most serviceable wool. I'd had it twenty years – '

'Put: *worth a dupondius*! Then the usual formula: *I therefore request that you give instructions for an enquiry into the matter* . . .'

As the clerk began to write, Fusculus nodded me indoors. He was a round, happy fellow, about thirty-five years and a hundred and eighty pounds. Balding on top, the rest of his hair ran around his skull in horizontal ridges. It had remained dark, and he had almost black eyes. Though rotund, he looked extremely fit.

'If you're after Petro, he'll be in later. He went out with the night patrol,' Fusculus announced. 'He's convinced there will be another gigantic raid. Martinus is on duty. He's gone back to the Emporium to check on some things.'

'I can wait.' Fusculus grinned slightly. Most people didn't bother with Martinus. 'So what's on, Fusculus?'

'Seems pretty quiet. The day patrol is out looking into a possible theft from the Temple of Ceres. We've got scratchers doing statues at the Library of Asinius – '

'Scratchers?'

'Lifting off the gilding. Then a tanner's allegedly poisoning the air by the Aqua Marcia. Normally it's poisoning the water . . . Anyway, we can get him for noxious smells and shift his workshop to the Transtiberina, but somebody's got to go there and actually sniff the air while he's working. Street fight by the Trigeminal Gate – be over by the time the lads can get down the Clivus Publicus. Three apparently responsible citizens have laid separate reports of seeing a wolf by the Temple of Luna.'

'Probably a large cat,' I suggested.

'On the usual form it will turn out to be a small, timid tabby!' chortled Fusculus. 'Escaped bears and panthers we pass straight on to the Urban Cohorts – well, at least those bastards are armed. And we let them catch senators' sons' pet crocodiles that have escaped from the rainwater tank. But a "wolf" we usually have a look at. Just in case it's suckling heroic twins, you know.'

'Oh, you'd want to be in on the action then!'

'Right! More boringly, we have an abandoned dead horse in the Cattle Market forum which will have to be cleared with fire-breaking tackle. Meanwhile we've got a bunch of runaway slaves in the lockup waiting for owners to collect them. There are also two careless householders for me to interview. They were picked up by the fire-watchers last night for allowing fires or smoke in their premises. The first-timer will be let off with a warning; another has been dragged in before, so *he* has to prove it was an accident or he'll be thrashed.'

'Who does that?'

'Sergius!' said Fusculus gleefully. I had met Sergius. He enjoyed his work. 'Then we've a third would-be arsonist in the cell who is definitely on his way.'

'On his way?'

'To the Prefect. He's a stupid sod of a jeweller who constantly leaves unattended lamps swinging in the breeze in his colonnade.'

'So what'll he get?'

'A hefty fine. I'm taking him over to headquarters to be processed. Maybe you'd better come with me. Rubella wants a welcoming word.' Rubella was the Fourth's tribune.

I grinned. 'Am I going to enjoy this?'

'What do you think?' twinkled Fusculus. As he collected his cudgel, the arsonist and some official notes about the prisoner's misdemeanours, he continued filling me in. Obviously he was a thoughtful type, and one who enjoyed lecturing. 'Apart from all that, it's work as normal – which means not doing it because of more urgent priorities. We have an ongoing investigation of a secret religion that will have to be delayed *again* because of the new task, as will our long-term granary fire-protection programme, our anti-toga-theft campaign at the baths, and keeping up the lists of undesirables.'

'What undesirables are these?' I asked, curious about what kind of degenerate earned a formal state record.

Fusculus looked rather shy. 'Oh well, you know we have to assist the aediles with their registers. Bars and brothels.'

'Somehow, Fusculus, I don't think bars and brothels were what you meant!'

510

'Mathematicians and astrologers,' he confessed. I looked faintly surprised. 'Anyone who leans towards the occult or magic has a question mark over them in the public-order stakes. Philosophers especially.'

'Oh, flagrantly seditious!'

'So I'm told. I'm not saying we believe the principle, Falco, but we like to be ready in case the Emperor demands a purge. Under Nero it was Christians. That's eased off lately, so we can go back to actors.'

'Disgusting degenerates!' I did not reveal that I had just spent three months working with a theatrical troupe. 'Who else?'

'Greek shopkeepers.'

'Now that's a new one. What's wrong with them?'

'They keep their booths open night and day. It's reckoned unfair on the locals. That can lead to trouble, so we keep lists to tell us quickly who to lock up when a row flares and dung starts being hurled about.'

Somehow I didn't suppose he kept matching details of the local businessmen who complained.

'I'm sure it's a relief to all honest citizens to know you stay vigilant!' Sarcasm was breaking through as I sensed there was more. 'And is there anybody else who threatens public order so badly you keep them under surveillance and maintain their names on secret lists?'

'Informers,' Fusculus admitted, looking resigned.

XVI

Rubella was still eating sunflower seeds.

He looked about fifty. Must have been, to have put in a full stint in the legions. He had been a chief centurion; that takes sticking power as well as a clean nose. Once he would have been about my level socially. Twenty years had pushed him on: promotion the whole way in the legions, discharge with honour, and buying himself into the middle rank. Now he commanded a thousand men; poor quality, it's true – the vigiles were ex-slaves for the most part – but if he continued to dodge disasters he could aspire to the Urban Cohorts, and maybe even the Praetorian Guard. Rubella was made – though he had spent his whole useful life getting there.

He was big physically; quiet; not tired by life. His grey hair was still close-cropped in the military manner, giving him a tough appearance. His strength was enough to move an ox aside merely by leaning on it. The knowledge soothed him. Rubella took the world at his own pace. He was utterly composed.

Fusculus introduced me. Rubella forced himself to pause between the seeds. 'Thanks for coming over. I like to induct new attachments personally. Welcome to the squad, Falco.'

The tribune's welcome was deceptive. Like Petro, he didn't want me near the squad. He seemed friendly, but it was a barely concealed front. I was an outsider. Uninvited. Liable to uncover private grief.

Some officials would have made me talk about my work for the Emperor. Rubella must have been told of my past career. He might have picked it over, full of prejudice and seeking to belittle me. Instead he ignored that side completely: a worse insult.

'You're an old colleague of Petronius'.'

'We go back ten years.'

'Same legion?'

'Second Augusta. Britain.'

'A good man,' said Rubella. 'Absolutely straight . . .' His

mind seemed somewhere else. 'I've been having a talk with Petro about this task with the gangsters. He suggested I assign you to looking up some past history.'

I noticed the subtle way Rubella had put himself in charge of allocating duties. Clearly it wouldn't just be Petro and me haggling over the booty. Rubella wanted in. Any moment I expected the Prefect of the Vigiles to put an oar in the stream too. Then there was probably the Fourth Cohort's interrogation officer – Petro's immediate superior – to contend with. And no doubt each of the seven cohort centurions thought himself top man on the Aventine. If I wanted work, I would have to grapple for it.

'Past history?' I asked, giving nothing away. If a client paid I would look up birth certificates or wills, but it was not my favourite activity.

'You have skills we should be using.' I noticed his dismissive tone. I had plenty of skills available. Informing needs rugged persistence, intelligence, intuition and hard feet. 'Attention to detail,' Rubella selected.

'Oh dear. I feel like a rather plain barmaid when offered as a chat-up line, "*I like you, you're different from the other girls . . .*" '

Rubella stared at me. Apparently he had as much sense of humour as a centipede. He couldn't take an interruption either. 'Petro doesn't agree, but I think we should send you to meet Nonnius.'

'The nark who used to work with Balbinus? The rent-collector whose testimony put the big rissole away?'

'We have an excuse to intervene. The man is involved with tracing Balbinus' assets – '

'Oh I'm thrilled!' I was annoyed. I let it show. 'So while there's juicy work on the streets, I'm to be sitting with an abacus playing at audits!'

'No. There already is an auditor.' He had failed to notice I was ready to explode. 'A priest from the Temple of Saturn is representing the state's interest.'

He could represent the Establishment on this enquiry too, if blinking at profit-and-loss columns was supposed to be my fate. 'I can contribute something more useful than spotting a few dodgy figures on a balance sheet!'

'I hope so! You were assigned to us with a reputation, Falco. You'll want to sustain the myth.' Rubella was smiling now. He could. All he had to do was munch endless seeds in his official throne of office while minions scurried in the dust. He knew he had riled me; he was openly enjoying it. 'Do I detect a problem with rank? I bet when you were in the army you hated your centurion!'

'I don't expect he liked me much either.' Aware of the goad, I came under control at once. Maybe he was trying to pack me back to the Palace with a complaint that I was uncooperative. If he imagined he could shed me before we had started, tough. I wasn't intending to play.

Rubella walked away from the fight. Barely pausing, he reiterated, 'Past history, yes. If we believe that the gangsters who robbed the Emporium have dropped into a hole that formed after Balbinus was removed, maybe we should have a look at what existed before the hole.'

The man made sense. My mind leapt, and I threw in quickly: 'Whoever ploughed the Emporium was lined up and waiting to go. Balbinus had only taken ship the night before. Someone could hardly wait to announce there was a new criminal regime.'

'They were effective,' Rubella commented. His manner was restrained. He looked like a cook who hopes the pudding will get stirred if he just stands gazing at the bowl.

'They knew how to get things done,' I agreed. 'Maybe it is someone from the Balbinus organisation – maybe even Nonnius himself.'

'That's an interesting suggestion,' Rubella murmured, apparently taking no interest at all.

Suddenly I quite liked being given Nonnius to tackle. I said I would visit him at once; Fusculus offered to come with me and effect the introductions.

At the door I paused. Rubella was busy opening a new cone of sunflower seeds. 'Tribune, a question. How much am I allowed to say to Nonnius?'

He looked back at me almost dreamily. 'Anything you like.'

'He turned state evidence. Doesn't that mean he gets treated with circumspection?'

'He's a hardened criminal,' said Rubella. 'He knows the

numbers on the dice. Balbinus has been safely put away. Nonnius is no use to the state now, not unless he comes up with further evidence. If he helps you, you may feel it is appropriate to behave respectfully. If not, feel free to trample his toes.'

'Fine.' I could trample toes. I could even be respectful if the situation really warranted. I had one more question. It concerned another sensitive area. 'Does Petronius know that I'm being given a wider brief than he suggested?'

'You can tell him when you see him,' said Marcus Rubella, like a man who really did not know he had just put the lid down on a very old friendship. He was still smiling benignly as I shut the door.

He could be one of those dark types who like to pretend they never lift a digit, while all the time they have a swift comprehension of events, a warm grasp of human relationships, and an incisive grip on their duties in public life. He could be loyal, trustworthy and intelligent.

On the other hand, he could be just as he appeared: a lazy, carefree, overpromoted swine.

XVII

Nonnius lived in the Twelfth region – about two streets from
Helena Justina's father. Which proves that money can buy
you respectable neighbours – or a house next door to
criminals. It was no better than where I lived. The criminals
in the Capena Gate sector just happened to be richer and
more vicious than the ones in Fountain Court.

The senator was a millionaire; he had to be. This was the
rough-and ready qualification for the job. Well, nobody
needs exorbitant talents like judgement, or even a sense of
honour, to vote in an assembly three times a month. But
possessing a million is useful, I'm told, and the Camillus
family lived comfortable lives. Helena's mother wore her
semiprecious jasper necklace just to visit her manicurist.

Nonnius Albius had been chief rent-runner for a master
criminal. The qualifications for *his* job were simple:
persistence and a brutal temperament. For employing these
over thirty years of violent activity he had earned the right to
live in the Capena Gate area, just like a senator, and to own
his own freehold, which in fact many a senator has mortgaged
away. His house, which looked modest but was nothing of the
kind, had a subdued portico, which carefully refrained from
drawing attention to itself, where callers had to wait while a
growling porter who had only peered at them through a fierce
iron grille took news of their arrival indoors.

'It's like visiting a consul!' I marvelled.

Fusculus looked wry. 'Except that Nonnius' bodyguards
are better groomed and more polite than consuls' lictors tend
to be.'

There were stone urns with well-watered laurel bushes
just like those at Helena's father's abode. Clearly the
topiary-tub supplier at the Capena Gate didn't care who his
customers were.

'What did you make of Rubella?' queried Fusculus as we
still tapped our boot heels in the unobtrusive portico while

the porter went off to vet us. 'A bit of a complicated character?'

'He has a secret sorrow.'

'Oh! What's that, Falco?'

'How would I know? It's a secret.'

Petro's team had investigated too many inarticulate inadequates. None of his lads could spot a joke coming. 'Oh, I thought you were in on something.'

'No,' I explained gently. 'I just get a deep sexual thrill from speculating wildly about people I have only just met.'

Fusculus gave me a nervous look.

Nonnius was, as everybody knew, a dying man. We could tell it was true because when we were let in we found him lying on a reading couch – but *not* reading – while he slowly ate a bowl of exquisite purple-bloomed plums. These were the hand-picked fruits, weeping unctuous amber, that are sent to console invalids by their deeply anxious friends. Perhaps thinking of your friends laying out silver by the purseload takes your mind off the pain.

The bowl they were in was a cracker too: a wide bronze comport two feet across, with three linked dolphins forming a handsome foot and with sea-horse handles. The bowl was far too heavy for a sick man to lift, so it was held for Nonnius by an even-featured eight-year-old Mauretanian slave-boy in a very short, topless tunic with gold fringes all around the hem. The child had gilded nipples, and his eyes were elongated with kohl like a god on an Egyptian scarab. My mother wouldn't have taken him on even to scrub turnips.

Nonnius himself had a lean face with an aristocratically hooked nose, big ears and a scrawny neck. He could have modelled for a statue of a republican orator. In the old Roman manner he had features that could be called 'full of character': pinched lips, and all the signs of a filthy temper if his dinner was late.

He was about sixty and pretty well bald. Despite being so poorly he had managed to shave; to make it more bearable his barber had aided the process with a precociously scented balsam. His tunic was plain white, but scrupulously clean. He wore no gems. His boots looked like old favourites. I mean,

517

they looked as if they had already kicked in the kidneys of several hundred tardy payers, and were still greased daily in case they found a chance of kicking more. Everything about him said that if we annoyed him, the man would cheerfully kick *us*.

Fusculus introduced me. We had fixed a story: 'Didius Falco has a roving commission, in a supervisory capacity, working alongside the public auditor.'

Nobody believed it, but that didn't matter.

'I'm sorry to learn you're off colour,' I mouthed sympathetically. 'I may need to go through some figures eventually, but I'll try to limit the agony. I don't want to tire you – '

'You being funny?' Nonnius had a voice that sounded polite, until you noticed threads of a raw accent running through it. He had been brought up on the Tiber waterfront. Any semblance of culture was as incongruous as a butcher calmly discussing Heraclitus' theory of all things being in a state of eternal flux just as he cleavered the ribs of a dead ox. I knew one like that once; big ideas, but overprone to making up the weight with fat.

'I was told you had to take it easy . . .'

'Raiding Balbinus' accounts seems to have given me a new lease of life!' It could just have been the desperate jest of a genuine deathbed case. I was trying to decide if the bastard was really ill. Nonnius noticed, so he let out a pathetic cough. The exotic slave child rushed to wipe his brow for him. The tot was well trained in more than flirting his fringes, apparently.

'Is the Treasury man helping you?' I asked.

'Not a lot.' That sounded like most Treasury men. 'Want to see him?' Nonnius appeared perfectly equable. 'I put him in a room of his own where he can play with the balls on his abacus to his heart's content.'

'No thanks. So what's the score so far?' I tossed at him unexpectedly.

He had it pat: 'Two million, and still counting.'

I let out a low whistle. 'That's a whole bunch of radishes!' He looked satisfied, but said nothing. 'Very pleasant for you,' I prompted.

'If I can get at it. Balbinus tried to lock it in a cupboard out of reach.'

518

'Not the old "present to wife's brother" trick?'

He gave me a respectful gleam. 'Haven't come across that one! No: "dowry to daughter's husband".'

I shook my head. 'Met it before. I took a jurist's advice and the news is bad: you can't touch the coinage. So long as the marriage lasts it has passed away from the family. Title to the dowry goes with the title to the girl. The husband owns both, with no legal responsibility to the father-in-law.'

'Maybe they'll divorce!' sneered the ex-rent-collector, in a tone that suggested heavy whacks might be used to end the marriage. Once a muscleman, always a thug.

'If the dowry was big enough, love will triumph,' I warned. 'Cash in hand tends to make husbands romantic.'

'Then I'll have to explain to the girl that her husband's an empty conker shell.'

'Oh I think she must have noticed that!' Fusculus put in. He glanced at me, promising to elaborate on the gossip later.

I saw Nonnius looking between us, trying to work out how Fusculus and I were in league. None of the vigiles wore uniforms. The foot patrols were kitted out in red tunics as a livery to help them force a right of way to the fountains during a fire, but Petro's agents dressed much as he did, in dark colours with only a whip or cudgel to reveal their status, and with boots that were tough enough to serve as an extra weapon. They and I were indistinguishable. I wore my normal work clothes too: a tunic the colour of mushroom gravy, a liverish belt, and boots that knew their way around.

The room was full of working boots. There were enough soles and studs to subdue a crowd of rioting fishmongers in five minutes flat. Only the slave boy, in his embroidered Persian slippers, failed to match up to the rest of us.

'What's your background?' Nonnius demanded of me, bluntly suspicious.

'I'm an informer basically. I take on specials for the Emperor.'

'That stinks!'

'Not as much as enforcing for organised crime!'

I was pleased to see he did not care for me standing up to him. His tone became peevish. 'If you've finished insulting me, I've got enough to do chasing my stake from the Balbinus case.'

519

'Stay busy!' I advised.

He laughed briefly. 'I gather your "roving commission" will not include helping me!'

I wanted to tackle the area that Rubella had called past history; the one that had big implications for the future. 'I need to rove in other directions.'

'What do you want with me?'

'Information.'

'Of course. You're an informer! Are you buying?' he tried brazenly.

'Not from a jury fixer!'

'So what are you looking for, Falco?' Nonnius asked, ignoring the insult this time as he tried to startle me.

I could play that game. 'Whether it's you who master-minded the Emporium heist.'

It failed to nettle him. 'I heard about that,' he said softly. So had most of Rome, so I couldn't accuse him of unnatural inside knowledge. Not yet anyway. I was starting to feel that if he *had* been involved, handing him over to justice would give me great pleasure. I had a distinct feeling that he knew more than he ought. But crooks enjoy making you feel that.

'Somebody could hardly wait for Balbinus to leave town,' I told him. 'They snatched the inside lane of the racecourse – and they want everyone to know who's driving to win.'

'Looks that way,' he agreed, like a convivial friend humouring me.

'Was it you?'

'I'm a sick man.'

'As I said earlier,' I smiled, 'I'm very sorry to hear that, Nonnius Albius . . . I've been away. I missed your famous court appearance, so let's run over a few things.'

He looked sulky. 'I said my piece and I'm finished.'

'Oh yes. I heard you're quite an orator – '

At this point Fusculus, who had been watching with amused patience, suddenly cracked with anger and had to butt in: 'Get a grindstone and sharpen up, Nonnius! You're a committed songbird now. Tell the man what he needs to know!'

'Or what?' jeered the patient, showing us the ugly glower that must have been forced on countless debtors. 'I'm dying. You can't frighten me.'

520

'We all die,' Fusculus replied. He was a quiet, calm philosopher. 'Some of us try to avoid being hung up in chains in the Banqueting Chamber first, while Sergius gives his whip an airing.'

Nonnius was hard to terrify. He had probably devised and carried out more excruciating tortures than we two innocents could even imagine. 'Forget it, shave-tail! That's the frightener you use for schoolboys filching oysters off barrows.' He glared at Fusculus suddenly. 'I know you!'

'I've been involved in the Balbinus case.'

'Oh yes, one of the Fourth Cohort's brave esparto-grass boys!' This was the traditional rude nickname for the foot patrols, after the mats they were issued with for smothering blazes. Used of Petro's team, who thought themselves above firefighting, it was doubly rude. (All the worse because the esparto mats were regarded as useless anyway.)

I managed to break in before things got too hot. 'Tell me about how the Balbinus empire worked.'

'A pleasure, young man!' Nonnius decided to treat me as the reasonable person in our party in order to show up Fusculus. The latter settled back again, quite content to simmer down. 'What do you want, Falco?'

'I know Balbinus was the uncrowned king of rat thieves and porch-crawlers. He ran small-time crime as an industry and had drop shops on every street corner to process the loot. I haven't even mentioned the brothels or the illicit gaming houses yet – '

'He could run an estate,' Nonnius conceded, with visible pride at being an associate.

'With your help.' He accepted the smarm. I choked back my disgust. 'It was more than stealing scarves from washing lines, however.'

'Balbinus was big enough to have carried off the Emporium raid,' Nonnius agreed. 'Were he still in Rome!'

'But sadly he's travelling . . . So who might have inherited his talent? We'll take it that you personally have retired to lead a blameless life.' Nonnius allowed that lie too. 'Were there any other big boys in the gang who could be showing a flash presence now?'

521

'Your sidekick ought to know names,' Nonnius sneered nastily. 'He helped close down the show!'

Fusculus acknowledged it with his normal grace, refusing to lose his temper this time. 'They all had cheap nicknames,' he said quietly to me, before running off one of his competent lists: 'The Miller was the most sordid; he did the killings. The more brutal, the more he liked it. Little Icarus thought he could fly above the rest, the joke being that he was a complete no-hoper. Same for Julius Caesar. He was one of those madmen who think they're an emperor. Laurels would get the blight pretty quickly on his greasy head. The others I knew were called Verdigris and the Fly.'

We looked at Nonnius for confirmation; he shrugged, pretending at last to be impressed. 'Clever boy!'

'And where are they all now?' I asked.

'All gone to the country when the trial came off.'

'Quiet holidays in Latium? You reckon that's true?' I put to Fusculus.

He nodded. 'Minding goats.'

Petro would have kept tabs on them as far as possible. 'So, Nonnius, those were the centurions, and now they're living in rural retirement like a legion's colony of veterans ... Who were the big rivals to your dirty group?'

'We did not allow rivals!'

I could believe that.

There was no need to press the point. Better to think about the other criminal gangs after we left him. I sensed that Nonnius was taking a gloating delight in my interest in the rivals – who undoubtedly existed, even though Balbinus Pius must have done his best to strong-arm them out of his territory. I saw no need to gratify the rent-collector's pernicious taste for making trouble.

'We'll be in touch,' I said, trying to make it sound worrying.

'Don't wait too long,' leered Nonnius. 'I'm a sick man!'

'If the Fourth want you, we'll find you in Hades,' Fusculus chortled. A pleasant threat, which somehow carried a darker tone than his mild, cheery nature led one to expect. Petronius knew how to pick his men.

Fusculus and I left then, without bothering to make contact with the Temple of Saturn auditor.

XVIII

When we returned to the station house Petronius had just come in. At the same time his deputy, Martinus, had gone off duty, so Petro was in an affable mood. In our absence the day patrol had brought in two suspected lodging-house thieves, and a man who kept an unleashed dog that had bitten a woman and a child (the 'suspected wolf' from the Temple of Luna). Petro told Fusculus to do the interrogations on these.

'What, *all* of them, chief?'

'Even the dog.'

Fusculus and I exchanged a grin. It was his punishment for palling up with me. Petronius wanted to keep me on a very tight rein – one that could be personally jerked by him.

'And you can stop smirking!' he snarled at me. 'I've seen Rubella. I know you're setting up special little escapades that I haven't agreed to!'

Looking innocent, I made sure I told him how friendly my chat with his tribune had been, and how I had been given a free hand to interview Nonnius.

'Bastard,' Petro commented, though it was fairly automatic. 'You're welcome to the rent-collector. I warn you, he's a snake nesting in a midden heap. Be careful where you shove your garden fork.' He relaxed. 'What did you think of Rubella?'

Assessing the tribune seemed to be a cohort obsession. It's the same anywhere that has a hierarchy. Everyone spends a lot of time debating whether their supervisor is just an ineffectual layabout who needs a diagram in triplicate before he can wipe his backside clean – or whether he's so poisonous he's actually corrupt.

'Snide,' I said. 'Could be more dangerous than he looks. He can make a sharp judgement. It was like being interviewed by a crap fortune-teller. Rubella chewed some magic seeds, then informed me that as a legionary I didn't like my centurion.'

Petro feigned an admiring look. 'Well he was right there!' We both laughed. Our centurion in the Second Augusta had been a brutal lag named Stollicus; both Petro and I were constantly at loggerheads with him. Stollicus reckoned we were a pair of unkempt, unreliable troublemakers who were deliberately ruining his own chances of promotion by dragging down his century. *We* said he marked down our personnel reports unfairly. Rather than waiting to find out after twenty years of failing to make centurion ourselves, we manufactured invalidity discharges and left him to it. Last I heard he was tormenting the local populace in Nicopolis. Interestingly, he was still a centurion. Maybe we really had been successful in blighting his life. It was a pleasing thought.

'Your honourable tribune spoke as if it were a promise to find out who our centurion was, and ask.'

'He loves handing out some hint of blackmail that sounds like a joke but might not be,' scoffed Petro.

'Oh well,' I teased. 'At least he won't have any trouble tracing Stollicus. He will have already found him once, to ask about you!'

Thinking about our military careers we were silent for a moment, and allies again. Perhaps, being more mature now, we wondered whether it might have been wiser to placate the official and salvage our rights.

Perhaps not. Petronius and I both believed the same: only crawlers get a fair character reference. Decent characters don't bother to argue. For one thing, the truly decent know that life is never fair.

Changing the subject, Petro asked, 'Did you get anywhere with Nonnius?'

'No. He swears the Emporium raider isn't him.'

'Hah! That was why,' Petro explained, fairly mildly, 'I myself wasn't going to bother to visit him.'

'All right. I just thought I'd been assigned here to volunteer for the embarrassing jobs, so I might as well get on with one.'

'*Io!* You're going to be a treasure.'

'Oh yes. You'll be asking for a permanent informer on the complement . . . So what lying ex-mobster do you reckon we should tackle next?'

Petro looked thoughtful. 'I've had Martinus doing the

rounds of the other big operators. They all deny involvement, of course. The only hope is that one of them will finger the real culprit out of spite. But Martinus can handle that. Why should we upset ourselves? The only trouble is he's slow. Martinus reckons never to break into more than a decorous stroll. Asking three gang warlords where they were on a certain Thursday night will take him about five weeks. But left to himself he'll tell us in due course if anything has an abnormal whiff.'

'You trust him?'

'He has a reasonable nose – with expert guidance from his senior officer!'

'So while he's sniffing villains extremely cautiously, what do we two speedy boys get up to? Investigating the races?'

'Depends . . .' Petro looked whimsical. 'Do you see this as an office job, or will you take a mystery assignment that could ruin your health and your reputation?'

'Oh the office job for me!' I lied. If I had realised what mystery assignment he meant, I might have stuck to this joke.

'That's a pity. I thought we could go visiting my auntie.' A very old euphemism. Petronius Longus did not mean his Auntie Sedina with the big behind and the flower stall.

'A brothel?'

'Not just any old brothel.'

'Ooh! A *special* brothel!'

'I do have my standards, Marcus Didius! You don't have to come with me – '

'True, you're a big lad.'

'If Helena wouldn't like it – '

I grinned gently. 'She'd probably want to come too. The first time I slept with Helena Justina we'd been to a brothel earlier that night.'

Petronius snorted disapprovingly. 'I didn't know Helena Justina was that kind of girl!' He thought I had been implying she had once been one of those senatorial stiffs who descend on bawdy-houses for a thrill.

'We were just passing through . . .' Calling his bluff could be easy. 'Oh get wise. Helena could have been a vestal virgin if she hadn't met her heart's delight in me.' I shook my head at him. He winced. I didn't worry him by mentioning the rest of the story. 'So where is this palace of delight you're luring me to? The dives in the Suburra where the practices are ancient and the whores positively mummified? The out-of-town cabins where runaway slaves solicit travellers for a bit of brass? Or the lousy dens of push-and-shove in the deeply plebeian Patrician Street?'

'Home ground. Down by the Circus.'

'Oh Jupiter! You can catch something just thinking about those filthy holes.'

'Shut your brain off then. You get by without thinking often enough . . . We've had a hard morning. I thought we deserved an afternoon of exotic entertainment with the exquisite Lalage!'

'I'll buy you lunch first,' I offered promptly. Petro accepted, agreeing with me that we needed to build up our strength before we went.

XIX

We had entered the Eleventh region. It was outside Petro's area, although he said it was unnecessary to make a courtesy call on the Sixth Cohort, who patrolled here. His was the career in public service, so I let him decide. I could tell he didn't like the Sixth. He was enjoying the fact we had sneaked into their patch privately, on the excuse of our special task.

Most prostitutes around the Circus Maximus are pavement-crawlers and portico practitioners. They hang about during and after the races, preying on men whose appetites for excitement have been aroused by watching arena crashes. (Or men who have just come out hoping to waste money and don't fancy any of today's track runners.) Some of these women give themselves an air of moral rectitude by parading near temples, but the trade is the same: up against a wall, with the penalties of theft, a guilty conscience, and disease.

The brothel known as Plato's Academy offered a few advantages. At Plato's, unless you were a nice boy who liked clean bedding, you could at least do the deed horizontally. Theft and the scald were still hazards. Your conscience was your own affair.

Petronius and I carried out a reconnoitre of Plato's. I won't say we were nervous, but the place did have a lush reputation even by Roman standards. We wanted to be sure of ourselves. We walked to the Circus, scowled at the dark-eyed girls who hooted lewd suggestions after us from the colonnades, and ventured into a maze of lanes at the south end of the hippodrome. We stationed ourselves at a streetside drink stall opposite. While we decorated the marble with cups of the worst wine I had sunk in Rome for several years, I risked some chilled peas. Petro asked for brains; excitement had always made him go peculiar.

The peas were completely tasteless. The brains didn't look as if they had ever been up to much either, even allowing for the fact that calves don't devise encyclopedias. Whatever they tasted like, something made Petro say gloomily, 'There's a rumour Vespasian wants to ban the sale of hot food in the streets.'

'Well that'll solve one of life's great dilemmas: to go hungry or get the runs.'

'The latrine-keepers are hopping with worry.'

'Well they're always on the go.'

The chat was meant to divert the stallholder whilst we sized up our destination.

Officially Plato's appeared, from a very faint painted sign above the lintel, to be called the Bower of Venus. Depressed cherubs swinging on garlands at either end of the sign attempted to reinforce the dainty-sounding message. To reassure tourists who had been recommended in the vernacular, a larger chalked banner gave its common name at eye level, just alongside a stone Priapus with a horrible erection, for those who either could not read or were in too much of a hurry to stand about deciphering mere lettering. On the opposite side of the doorway another slogan announced, *Come and Get What Every Man Wants*, with a graphic doodle which made it plain that this did not mean a modest woman, an unexpected legacy, and a tranquil life. For all but the tragically short-sighted, there could be no doubt which trade was carried on within the drab-looking premises.

There was a lumbering oak door, propped open with two staves. It looked too slumped on its hinges to be closed. No doubt it never was.

This portal was barely a couple of yards from us, diagonally up the dirty street. Through it marched a regular line of last-time-before-recall soldiers, straight-off-the-ship sailors, slaves, freedmen, and small businessmen. Some of the sailors felt obliged to make a bit of noise. An occasional character who looked like an olive-oil salesman or corn chandler's understeward had the grace to appear furtive and only slipped inside at the last moment. Most men just strode in clinking their coins. Even while we were eating, one or two we already recognised strode back out and carried on in the same direction as if they had merely stepped inside to say hello to their old mothers. Business at Plato's must be matter-of-fact and brisk.

'I suppose there's a difference,' Petro commented in his dark, philosophical voice, 'between men who come because it's not allowed, and those who come because it is.'

'I'm not with you.'

'One kind who buy it actually get a thrill from the guilt. That's not Plato's trade. Around here, you purchase a whore in between picking up a chicken for supper and putting your boots in at the cobbler's to have a strap mended.'

'Daily shopping!' I was feeling silly. 'Do you think the madam lets you feel the girl first, to convince yourself she's ripe?'

He dug me in the ribs. 'We're like recruits again, wondering what went on in the *canabae* outside Isca fort!'

I could not quite tell whether my old comrade Lucius Petronius thought this comparison was reprehensible, or a positive hoot. 'I think I know what went on in the *canabae*,' I said gravely. 'I'll explain it to you some day, when you've got a lot of listening time.' This time I sidestepped and managed to avoid his elbow before it had a chance to cause a bruise.

We were so near to the open doorway we could hear the bargaining as customers arranged their treats. The bug-eyed foreigners were obvious. So were the Roman goldfinches, men with too many sesterces in their purses, picked like flowers in the Forum by affable pimps; they had been lured here to be gulled, fleeced, and if possible heavily blackmailed. Otherwise it was impossible to tell which of the crumpled tunics who entered were straightforward customers, which wanted to defy the anti-gambling laws with a few games of soldiers, and which were small-time members of the criminal underworld gathering to exchange news of likely homes to burgle.

Not many women were visible in the vicinity.

'Too busy?' I speculated.

'Their conditions of employment don't encourage popping out for a length of hair-ribbon.' Petro meant the prostitutes at Plato's were slaves.

We had finished our lunch. We paid, leaving a meagre tip. It was what the barman expected, but he roused himself to spit with disgust after us. Petro said over his shoulder, 'Do that again, and you'll lose your food licence.' The man retorted something we could not quite catch.

We crossed the street, and glanced at one another. We had a justifiable job to do, but inevitably felt like conspirators.

'If my mother gets to hear of this, I'm blaming you.'

'Falco, it's not your mother you should be worried about.'

He was wrong about that, but it was no time to block the entrance arguing. We went in.

A flaunty piece in the scarlet toga that was the strict legal badge of her trade was taking the money and fixing the arrangements. It was not a requirement that the toga should be vermilion and make her blaze like a corn poppy, nor that she wear it within the brothel; this lady liked to defy the law by obeying it with too much flourish. None of the other girls we glimpsed inside were in togas, though in fact most of them were not wearing many of their clothes – if they possessed any. The doorkeeper was watched over by a hound-dog male whom she sensibly ignored. He couldn't have bounced a feather ball, let alone a determined rioter. Having a dozy protector did not seem to cause her much anxiety. She looked like a girl with a good uppercut.

'Afternoon, boys. I haven't seen you before. I'm Macra and I'm here to see you enjoy yourselves.' It was the kind of aggressive sales talk I dread.

'He's Falco, I'm Petronius, and we're with the vigiles,' announced Petronius immediately. I had been wondering how he would handle that aspect.

'We're always pleased to see the hornets . . .' She must have been chosen for her manners, though her tone managed a sneer. Her eyes sharpened slightly as she weighed up what we expected. We could see her deciding we were definitely not foot patrol. Nor were we Sixth Cohort, the regulars for this district, whom she was bound to know. She had soon worked out *Prefect's office, or tribunal staff*, from which she made the inevitable smooth transferral to *troublemakers*. Clearly a young lady of some initiative, her reaction was: *Find out what they want, and humour them*. 'This is a decent house, with all clean young girls. I can choose you something a bit special,' she offered. 'We like to do business with the forces of law and order.' Her gaze flickered to the hound dog. Even we could see he was supposed to run for reinforcements at this point, but he was no help.

'Something special,' repeated Petronius thoughtfully.

On the assumption he was welcoming the offer, Macra cheered up. 'As it's your first time being entertained here, it will be on the house. May I recommend Itia. She's a lovely creature, a freeborn girl who normally only works on private hire. One at a time suit you? For both together we would have to make a small charge, I'm afraid.'

'Freeborn?' asked Petro. 'So you can tell me which aedile she's listed with, and her registration number?' Any freeborn woman who wished to shed her reputation could work as a prostitute, so long as she formally declared her profession and put herself outside the reach of the adultery laws.

As soon as Petro's attitude became clearer, Macra kicked the sleepy bouncer, who condescended to show an interest. He stood up.

'Sit down,' said Petronius pleasantly. The man sat down again.

Macra took a very deep breath. 'If you scream I'll knock your head off,' said Petro, still in a level tone. 'I can't abide loud noises. We're here to see Lalage.'

Macra managed to defer screaming. 'Lalage is engaged at the moment.' It would be her stock rejoinder. The madam is never available.

'Don't panic. We're not asking to query a bill.'

'Very funny! Is she expecting you?' Another tactic.

'She's a brothel-keeper,' said Petro. 'Her whole life must be spent expecting questions from the law! Do you want fish pickle on it? Stop stalling. There's no point.'

'I shall go and enquire,' the girl informed him pompously. 'Kindly wait just here.'

'No. You'll take us,' Petronius corrected. 'Hit the grit.' She pretended not to know the expression. '*Walk, Macra!*'

With a curse she didn't much bother to muffle the girl led us in, swinging her hips in a parody of a seductive dance. Artfully untidy tangles of black hair swished on her bare shoulders. Her heels clattered loudly. She was grimy, and not very pretty, though she did have a certain style.

We passed a series of dim cubicles. Crudely obscene pictures above the doors made a feeble attempt at suggesting erotic art. The grunts we overheard were far from high culture. One customer was washing himself from a ewer, so minimal hygiene must be provided for. There were cloak pegs and a sign to the latrine.

A small slave boy with a trayful of flagons dashed past us and dived into a room like an inn's refectory, where low-class men were crouched about tables either gambling or conspiring. Petro half-heartedly started to investigate, but the door swung across behind the slave and he gave up. Maybe it was just the weekly meeting of the chicken-feed suppliers' guild.

Up narrow steps we found a corridor with doors to larger rooms for higher-paying customers. We could hear a tabor being thumped, and smell insidious smoke. By now we had realised that Plato's was much more extensive than its street frontage suggested. It also provided for a varied clientele. I reckoned there were probably other ways in and out of it too.

The odour of burning bay leaves gave way to imitation frankincense. I coughed slightly, and Petronius grimaced. Further on Macra led us through a veritable banqueting hall. It had a sunken floor; Jove knows what orgies were carried out there. Tired flower petals still lay squashed on the steps. There was a statue of two entwined figures who appeared to have more than two full sets of procreative organs, though as we said afterwards, we might have been misled by some scraps of left over garland and the fact that a stone goat was also participating.

The corridor grew darker. From a room at what must have been the farthermost end of the building came sounds of an unexpectedly professional flute. Macra knocked, then kept the half-open door against her hip so we could not see past her. With a rapid apology she relayed who we were. A woman's voice swore briefly, then said, 'I'm sorry for the intrusion. Look after him nicely please, Macra.'

There was an angry movement. A half-naked teenage-girl flautist pushed past Macra and vanished. Then a magistrate we could not fail to recognise walked out.

He did not deign to greet us. Petronius gave an ironic

salute, and I squeezed against the wall so as not to dirty His Honour's purple stripes as he rushed by. The Very Important Patrician ignored these courtesies. Maybe that was because he was famous for his devotion to a cultured, highly connected, slightly older (but immensely wealthy) wife.

Macra sneered at us and flung open the door, releasing natural daylight amid curious wafts of violets and hydromel. She twirled off after the magistrate. We walked in to meet Lalage.

She had the face of a once very beautiful woman, painted so thickly you could hardly detect the sweetness it still carried. She wore a yellow silk gown, which she was casually readjusting after most of it had been removed to allow access to an oiled and perfumed body that made two honest citizens gulp. Her headdress contained Oriental pearls an empress would die for; her necklace was of mixed sapphires and amethysts; her arms were sheathed in bracelets of Greek gold filigree. Her eyes were angry. She did not welcome us to her establishment, or offer us a glass of the strong honeyed wine.

The notorious Lalage had a scar on her delicate left ear. It brought back nostalgic memories. She was pretending to be an elegant Oriental courtesan, but I knew exactly where this precious pullet came from. I had met her before.

XX

'Will this take long?' Her voice had all the fluting charm of pebbles in vinegar cleaning out a blackened skillet. 'We're expecting guests.'

'Lycians, maybe?' asked Petronius.

'You've got a nerve.' She was still pinning folds of her dress, more interested in how it draped than in dealing with us. 'This had better be good,' she snapped, looking up abruptly. 'Luckily we'd finished, or I'd kill you for interrupting that customer. He's my best client.'

'Who gets a personal service,' Petro commented.

'He knows this is where he'll receive the best!' smirked Lalage. I noticed her giving us a thorough squint: Petronius solid, tough and hostile; me less tall, but just as tough and even more disparaging.

'Left his lictors at home, did he?' I asked, in an offensive tone. I was referring to the mighty man's state-employed bodyguard; they were supposed to escort him everywhere, showing the axes and rods that symbolised his power to chastise. Or as Petro used to say, symbolising what a big donkey he was.

'We're looking after the lictors.'

'I bet! Lictors usually know how to park their rods,' I said.

'A man should always take his lictors, Marcus Didius,' Petro reproved me gravely.

'Oh true, Lucius Petronius,' I corrected myself formally. 'Leaving your lictors at home is the right way to make the wife suspicious.'

'And he's a magistrate, so he must be a clever man! He'll know how to bluff the old broomstick he left at home in his atrium. Besides, I expect the lictors only keep quiet about his habits, provided they get theirs – '

'Spare me the comedy!' Lalage interrupted. She swung her bare feet to the floor and sat up on the edge of her couch, an ornate affair with bronze curlicues all over it, dripping with

534

cushions of the type that are described as 'feminine'. I could think of several women who would shove Lalage out of a window and fling her tasselled and pleated pink fripperies after her – not so much for moral reasons, but in disgust at her decor.

With a shimmer and tinkle of jewellery, she folded her fine arms and waited.

Petronius and I had deliberately stood at opposite ends of the room so she had to turn her head to face whoever was speaking. In more fragile company it was a tactic to cause alarm. I suspected Lalage had had plenty of practice in dealing with two men at once. Still, we went through the routine, and she let us play.

'We need to ask you some questions,' Petro began.

'Don't you mean *more* questions? I thought the damned business with the Lycians was all sorted out.' She assumed we had come about the murdered tourist whose death had formed the basis of the Balbinus trial.

'This is not about the Lycians.'

'Afraid I can't help you then.'

'Afraid you'd better. Do you want a raid?' Petronius asked. 'I dare say we could find a few kidnapped minors working your cubicles. Or unlicensed freeborns. Are you absolutely certain you comply scrupulously with the hygiene regulations? Is any food being supplied on the premises? If so, are you licensed for hot meals? Who *exactly* were those shady characters Falco and I saw huddled downstairs?'

Petronius tended to stick stolidly to his remit, but this could take poking with a fancier baton. 'How about a scandal?' I chimed in. 'Senior magistrate named; society divorce ensues; shocked officials say they have seen nothing like it since Caligula's excesses. That should make a few entries in the *Daily Gazette*!'

'Good for trade,' Lalage shrugged. Annoyingly, she was right. Such a story might limit her upper-class clients for a while but others would flock. She decided to defy Petro. 'Anyway, you work in the Thirteenth. This is the Eleventh; it's out of your jurisdiction. I'm not going to be raided,' she assured him serenely. 'The Bower of Venus has an excellent relationship with the local boys.'

Petro's voice grated. 'Excellent as tar!'

'They look after us very prettily.'

'I'm not the Sixth Cohort. I don't take oily handshakes, and I don't want half an hour with a dubious haybag on one of your flea-ridden blankets – '

'Of course you don't. You're a hero and your cohort's incorruptible! Something more select?' Lalage then rasped at Petro, with an affected attitude. 'Does the most excellent sir have interesting tastes?'

'Shut it, Lalage!'

'Juno! Have I just met the one and only member of the vigiles who's not on the take?'

Petro ignored it. We were not investigating graft. If anyone tackled that problem, it would need more than two agents, and they would want to be wearing Scythian chain mail. 'Hear my words. I'm not touting for a free tickle, and you're in danger of finding the brothel closed down and yourself back as a paviour again.'

'I was *never* a streetwalker!' the madam exclaimed with true horror.

I took a turn in the conversation. 'This is the real business,' I warned her. 'Unless we get co-operation, you'll find yourself making an appearance before the eagle's beak!'

'Nice oratory. So what's the catch?'

'Be clever. My colleague's easily upset.'

She turned lustrous eyes on me. Her manner altered. She had had fifteen years of practice and I felt my breath falter. 'So what about you?' she murmured.

'He has a very respectable girlfriend,' Petronius shot in rapidly.

'Oh I see! Why keep a pig and honk yourself?' Her eyes never left me. If I looked at her, the pressure was serious, and if I stared back, I could no longer see Petro. This was where separating ourselves at two ends of the room could leave one of us vulnerable. Lalage knew how to make feeling vulnerable seem exciting. She was still relaying the promising smile, and I was freely admiring the act. She had once been a genuine looker. She was soiled, but still attractive. Well-worn glory has its own allure. Virginity's a bland commodity.

The skirmish was brief, however. 'You seem to be a man of taste,' she said.

'I like to bask at my own fire.' I liked rather more than that, and what suited my taste was not sold by the hour. My girl could never be bought.

Lalage dropped the subject, though not without a sneer. 'Well thanks for making it sound like an apology!'

'Aventine etiquette.'

She gave me a sharper look, but I chose to pretend I had said nothing significant. She still did not know what I was hinting; she had seen too many men to remember who I was. I felt her lose interest – leaving me with a strong sense of unfinished business.

Unexpectedly she spun back to Petro: 'I haven't got all day! What do you want?'

She was using our own separation routine; letting one relax, then trying to catch him off guard. Petro managed to avoid being thrown. His chin came up, but he turned it into a surly gesture by sweeping back his straight hair with one hand, like a dandy who didn't reckon on letting a mere woman make him jump. 'To discuss the Emporium heist.'

'Oh that was a loud one!' She rolled her eyes. They were still very beautiful: wide-set, large, dark as a winter evening, and melting with suggestiveness. Personally, I liked eyes with a more subtle challenge. But Lalage had nice eyes.

Petronius had noticed them, though only a close friend would know it. 'Yes, they're talking about it everywhere – but nobody's whispering who did the dirty deed.'

'Who do you think did it?' Lalage asked, pretending to flatter him.

'I haven't time to waste thinking. I want names.'

She tried the innocent-little-woman trick: 'Well what makes you believe I might know anything about thieves?'

Petro's temper was running short now. His teeth had locked. 'You mean, apart from the fact that your downstairs parlour is full of sneaks who follow funerals to rob the mourners, door-knock thieves who work the rush-the-porter game, balcony-crawlers, basement rats, and that little runt who hangs the fake fly in people's faces, then slits their purse thongs while they're brushing it away?'

537

I was impressed. We had only glimpsed the trading room for a moment. Petro must have sharp eyes. He certainly knew the streets.

And I knew him. I recognised the signs: he felt uneasy with the location and was working up to dragging Lalage over to his station house. If she had been a well-bred schoolgirl who had never spoken to a public official he might have stood a chance. But he ought to realise what a fool he would look, trying to put an arm lock on a glittering saffron butterfly who would shriek abuse at him all the way to the Aventine. Arresting a brothel madam is never discreet.

'Are you talking raids again?' Lalage laughed. She knew he had lost his grip enough to give her the upper hand.

'He knows better,' I assured her. 'By the time we can bring the espartos in, the joint will be clean. Macra probably gave the word straight after she finished massaging your magistrate.'

'Well I do hope she was thorough,' grinned the madam shamelessly. 'A person of his status doesn't expect to be hustled!'

It seemed to me it was time the man was hustled out of office. Rome would never be cleaned up if every time Petronius brought a mugger to court the bad character could smile at a judge who had shared the ewer where he washed his privates after his Tuesday-afternoon binge. The fellowship of Plato's had insidious tentacles. In fact that was only one aspect of our visit today that had an aura of ambidextrous ethics. The smack of sticky payments seemed to be lurking everywhere.

Lalage's diversion failed. Petronius Longus was strictly unamused. 'Who's your landlord now?' he sprang on her. 'Who runs this place since Nonnius did his singing from the high twig and Balbinus Pius took a sail?'

'What sort of a question's that?'

'Well it's not about who has decorating rights under your building tenancy. Who's the mighty man behind you, Lalage?'

'I don't go in for boys' stuff.'

'Stifle the innuendo! Who's giving Plato protection? We proved in court that Balbinus used to cream off his percentage, so who skims Plato's now?'

538

'Nobody. Who needs it? I'm running everything myself.'

It was what we already suspected. Petronius screwed the corner of his mouth. 'This had better be honest gen.'

'Who needs a man?' scoffed Lalage lightly. 'I had it up to here with the old system. Balbinus demanded an exorbitant cut, then I was constantly giving presents to Nonnius to stop him breaking up the furniture – all in return for a supposed service we never saw. Any trouble had to be sorted out by my own staff. What happened when the Lycian blew away was typical – we tried to clear up ourselves. I was doing the hard work, and Balbinus was just milking the business. That's over. The only commerce I'm interested in now is when men are paying me!'

'Someone will try to take over his position,' Petronius insisted.

'Let them try!'

'If it hasn't happened yet, now Balbinus has left Rome you'll meet with pressure eventually. When it happens, I want to know.'

'Sorry,' she answered acidly. 'You're in the same bumboat as all my customers: you'll get what you pay for – and no more!'

'That's closer to what I call a bargain,' Petronius responded, in his normal, level tone. 'For the big item, I'll be buying.'

She heaved her bosom, setting up ripples of light from the jewellery. The effect was less worrying than the eye trick, but highly professional. 'How much?'

'What it's worth. But I don't want shoddy goods or fakes.'

'You don't want much.' The last comment was amiable bluster. They had reached the real centre of the discussion; the terms were understood and more or less accepted by both sides. Whether that meant Lalage would ever produce any information was another matter.

'Bring me the name I need, and you won't regret it. You'll find me at the station house in the Thirteenth,' Petro announced politely.

'Oh go away,' she sneered, addressing me as if her patience with him had run out. 'And take the Big Unsusceptible with you!'

539

We were leaving. I turned back at the last moment to add a courtesy of my own. Giving the famous whore a generous smile, I said, 'I'm glad to see your ear healed up!'

While she and Petronius were thinking about it, I grabbed him by the elbow and we fled.

XXI

We emerged unscathed, though I for one wanted to head for the nearest respectable bathhouse.

'What was the crack about the lug, Falco?'

I just grinned and looked mysterious.

The place seemed much emptier than when we arrived. News spreads.

The girl Macra was standing back at the outside door. She looked edgy, but when she saw we were leaving peacefully she relaxed. As we passed her I heard a young child's cry. Macra noticed my surprise. 'Things happen, Falco!'

'I thought you were organised in places like this.' Some brothels were *so* organised, their expertise had led to them operating as neighbourhood abortionists.

'Losing a baby's illegal, isn't it, officer?' Macra gurgled at Petronius. He looked tense. We all knew it would be a long time before anyone bothered to take a prostitute to court for this. The unborn are protected if there's a legacy in it; the unborn with shameless mothers have few rights.

'Like to see around the nursery?' the girl then offered Petro. There was a distinct undertone of offering him a prepubertal titbit. He declined in silence, and she giggled. 'You're a hard man to tempt! Maybe I'll have to come and see you in your station house.'

'Maybe I'll show you the cell!' Petro growled in annoyance. A mistake.

'It's a promise!' Macra shrieked. 'We know a client in the vigiles who does *amazing* things with chains during "interviews".'

Petronius had had enough. He took out his note tablet formally: 'And who would that be?'

'Well do you believe,' she leered at him, 'his name seems to just escape me . . .'

'You're a lying little flirt,' Petronius told her, fairly

pleasantly. He put away the note tablet. We stepped out into the street with her jibes ringing along the narrow passage at our backs.

'So that's a brothel!' Petro said, and we both nudged each other, grinning at an old joke from the past.

We had hesitated, lacking plans. We should not have laughed. Laughing on a brothel doorstep can lead to disaster. Never do it before you have taken a careful look in both directions down the street.

Somebody we knew was coming towards us. Petro and I were already helpless. It was too late to make off discreetly; *far* too late to look less like guilty men.

Approaching down the narrow lane, crying loudly, was a little girl with big feet and a dirty face. She was seven years old, in a tunic she had outgrown months ago; with it she wore a cheap glass bracelet that a kind uncle had brought her from abroad, and an extravagant amulet against the evil eye. The evil eye had not been averted; the child was being dragged along by a small, fierce old lady with a pinched mouth who had an expression of moral outrage even before she spotted us. Spot us she did, of course, just as we two emerged like utter layabouts from Plato's Academy.

The little girl was in deep trouble for playing truant. She was glad to see anyone else she could drag down to Hades with her. She knew we were exactly the distraction she needed.

'There's Uncle Marcus!' She stopped crying at once.

Her jailer stopped walking. Petro and I had been reprobates in our youth, but nobody in Rome knew that. Petro and I had not been stupid. We were reprobates abroad.

We had just blown our cover. My niece Tertulla stared at us. She knew that even bunking off school after her grandma had pinched and scraped to pay for it failed to match our disgrace. We knew it too.

'Petronius Longus!' cried the old lady in frank amazement, too horrified even to mention me. Petro was renowned as a good husband and family man, so this disaster would be blamed on me.

'Good afternoon,' murmured Petro shyly, trying to pretend

542

he had not been chortling, or if he had it was only because he had just heard a *very* funny but perfectly tasteful story about an aspect of local politics. With great presence of mind he embarked upon explaining that we could not make ourselves available to escort people to a safer neighbourhood, owing to a message he'd just received about a crisis over at the station house.

At the same moment a flying figure whom I recognised as my fraught sister Galla came hurrying down the lane crying, 'Oh you've found the little horror!' Galla spent half her life oblivious to what her children might be getting up to, and the rest in guilty hysterics after somebody stupid had told her.

'I found more than that!' came the terse reply, as a pair of unmatchedly contemptuous eyes finally fixed themselves on me.

There was nowhere to hide.

'Hello, Mother,' I said.

XXII

Ouch!

XXIII

When I walked into my apartment I found someone standing in the doorway from the balcony. Her dark hair shone in the sunlight behind her; she had left its warmth immediately she heard my footfall.

She was full of grace and serenity. She wore a simple dress in blue, with a late October rosebud in a pin on the top seam. If she had used perfume, it was so discreet that only the favoured fellow who kissed her neck would be aware of it. A silver ring worn on her left hand showed her loyalty to whoever he was. *She* was everything that a woman should be.

I gave her a courteous nod.

'People will be racing to tell you,' I said, 'that Petronius and I spent an hour in a brothel near the Circus Maximus this afternoon. It's famous for offering disgusting services as bribes to the vigiles. We were witnessed coming out nudging each other guiltily, and with happy grins.'

'I know,' she said.

'I was afraid of that.'

'I dare say!'

The slender links of one bracelet slipped over her fine wrist as she lightly held a scroll. Her feet were bare. She, who should have been cushioned on swan's-down amidst some great man's marble colonnades, had been reading in the warm sun, high above the squalor of the Aventine where she lived with me.

I selected a cool and formal tone. 'People overreact sometimes. I was with Petro when he reached his own house and couldn't make his wife answer the door. A neighbour shoved her head through a shutter and bawled, "*She's taken the children to her mother's and your dinner's been thrown at the cat.*" I had to help him pick the lock. He loves that cat; he insisted on going in to look for it.'

She smiled. 'Every hero should have a tragic flaw.' I

happened to know she didn't care for cats. I suspected she despised heroics too.

I thought it best to maintain a serious approach. 'Despite his pleading, I felt unable to escort him to fetch Arria Silvia from her mother's lair.'

'Did you leave him by himself then?'

'He was all right. He had his cat . . .' Something caught in my throat. 'I wanted to make sure you were still here.'

'I'm here.'

'I'm glad.'

It was mid-afternoon. I had been as quick as possible, but I had gone to bathe. Now I was clean. Every inch of me was oiled and scraped, but I felt as if I walked in grime.

'Were you worried?' I asked.

Her dark eyes were fixed on me with a steadiness my heart was failing to match. 'I do worry when I hear you're in a brothel,' she told me in a low voice.

'I worry when I go into a brothel myself.' For some reason, I suddenly felt clean again. I smiled at her with special warmth.

'You have to do your work, Marcus.' There was a shade of resigned amusement lurking deep in Helena Justina's gaze. It seemed to me she had deliberately placed it there. While she waited for me she had taken her decision: either we could fight, and she would only end up feeling more wretched than when she started, or she would make it be like this. 'So what did you think of the brothel?' she asked quietly.

'It was a dump. They didn't have a monkey. I wouldn't take a senator's daughter near the place.'

'The monkey in the one we ran through was a chimpanzee,' she reminded me. Her tone was serious, but the seriousness was a joke.

Sometimes we did fight. Sometimes, because she wanted me too badly to use reason, I could make her quarrel bitterly. Other times, the intelligence with which she handled me was breathtaking. She set trust between us like a plank, and I just walked straight across.

I could see a very faint twist at the corners of her mouth. If I chose to do it now, with merely a look in my eyes I would be able to make her smile.

I crossed the room. I came right up to her and took her by

546

the waist. A slight colour stained her cheeks, echoing the unopened rose pinned to her dress. As I had suspected, the perfume was there for somebody who knew her well enough to come close enough to treat her tenderly. Not many had ever had that privilege. I breathed slowly. A whisper of cinnamon crept over me, not just any perfume, but one I particularly liked. It was fresh, only recently applied.

I let myself enjoy looking at her for a while. She enjoyed herself letting me drown gently in old memories and new expectations. I must have dropped my hand without intending it. I felt her fingers entwine in mine. I drew up both our hands and held hers hard against my chest.

The room was silent. Even the street noise beyond the balcony seemed far away.

Helena leaned forward and brushed my mouth with a kiss. Then, with no flutes or incense or sticky wines, without needing to negotiate a price, without even needing words, we went to bed.

XXIV

By the time consciousness reasserted itself, my sister Galla
had told my sister Junia, who had rushed to relate the tale to
Allia, who – since she could no longer exclaim with Victorina,
who was dead – told Maia. Maia and Allia normally did not
get on, but this was an emergency; Allia was almost last in the
queue and she was bursting to amaze somebody with news of
my latest offence. Maia, who alone amongst them had a
conscience, first decided to leave us alone with our trouble.
Then, since she was a friend to Helena, she set off for our
apartment to make sure nobody had left home over it. Had
rapid action been necessary, Maia would have comforted
anyone she found sobbing, then rushed out to look for the
runaway.

While she was still on her way to us, I was rousing myself.
'Thank you.'
'What for?'
'The sweet gift of your love.'
'Oh that!' Helena smiled. I had to close my eyes, or I would
have been in bed with her until nightfall.

Then she asked me, wanting answers this time, about our
visit to Plato's Academy. I rolled over on my back, with my
arms behind my head. She lay with her cheek against my
chest while I told her my impressions, ending with the fact
that I had known Lalage long ago.

Helena laughed at the story. 'Did you tell her?'
'No! But I left a few hints to worry her.'

Helena was more interested in the results of our official
enquiries: 'Did you believe her when she claimed she was going
to resist having the place "protected" by a male criminal?'

'I suppose so. To call her competent would be an
understatement! She can run the brothel and easily beat up
anyone who tries to interfere.'

'So maybe,' suggested Helena, 'she was telling you more
than you think.'

548

'Such as?'

'Maybe *she* would like to take over where Balbinus left off.'

'Well we've agreed she wants to run her own empire. Are you suggesting something more?'

'Why not?'

'Lalage control the gangs?' It was an alarming thought.

'Think about it,' said Helena.

I was silent, but she must have known I always took her suggestions seriously. Grumpily I accepted this one, though it was against my will. If we could say Nonnius Albius had stepped into the space left by his former chief, things would be much simpler both to prove and to put right. If we needed to consider newcomers, let alone women, the affair assumed unwelcome complexity.

Wanting to make sure I had listened, Helena sprang up excitedly, leaning over me on her elbows. Then I noticed her expression change. With a sudden mutter she turned away out of bed and left me. She scampered next door, and I heard her being sick.

I followed, waited until the worst was over, then put an arm around her and sponged her face. Our eyes met. I gave her the look of a man who was being more reasonable than she deserved.

'Don't say anything!' she commanded, still white-lipped.

'Wouldn't dream of it.'

'It can't be something we ate at dinner disagreeing with me, because we forgot to have any dinner.'

'Just as well, apparently.'

'So it seems you were right,' she admitted, in a neutral voice.

Then Maia's voice exclaimed from the door, 'Well congratulations! It's a secret, I dare say.'

'Unless you tell somebody,' I answered, biting back a curse.

'Oh trust me!' smiled Maia, deliberately looking unreliable.

She came in, a neat, curly-haired woman wearing her good cloak and nicest sandals so she could make a real occasion of simpering at the trouble I had caused. 'Put her on the bed and lie her flat,' she advised. 'Well this is it!' she chirped at Helena helpfully. 'You've really done it now!'

'Oh thanks, Maia!' I commented as Helena struggled upright and I started clearing up.

Helena groaned. 'Tell me how long this is going to last, Maia.'

'All your life,' snarled Maia. She had four children, or five if you counted her husband, who needed more looking after than the rest. 'Half the time you're lying down exhausted, and the rest you just wish you could be. As far as I can tell it goes on for ever. When I'm dead I'll come back and tell you if it improves then.'

'That's what I was afraid of,' Helena answered. 'First the pain, and then your whole life taken over . . .'

They both seemed to be joking about it, but there was a real edge. Helena and my youngest sister were on very friendly terms; when they talked, especially about men, there was a fierce undertone of criticism. It made me feel left out. Left out, and thoroughly to blame.

'We can have a nurse,' I offered. 'Helena my darling, if it makes you feel better, I'll even set aside my principles and let you pay for her.'

This piece of piety did not soothe the situation. I decided it was time to go out. I put up the excuse of emptying the rubbish pail, grabbed it and sauntered downstairs whistling, leaving the pair of them to enjoy themselves grumbling. I wasn't going far. I would use up the rest of the evening at the new apartment on the other side of Fountain Court. Having a second home to escape to began to seem a good idea.

I felt shaken. Faced with definite evidence that I was becoming a father, I needed to be alone somewhere so I could think.

I had chosen a good moment. The basket-weaver hailed me with news that a man he knew who hired out carts was bringing one round for me, something he had volunteered when I talked to him previously. The cart could only be driven here at night because of the vehicle curfew, and as I would be keeping it for a few days while I cleared the property, arrangements were required. I wanted to use the cart as a temporary rubbish skip. For this to work we had to put it up on blocks and take the wheels off, or someone was bound to make off with it. That was no easy task. Then we had to manhandle the wheels inside the weaver's shop and chain them together for added security. My troubles had only just started. In the short time that the weaver, the carter and I were in the shop making the wheels safe, some joker stowed half a woodwormy bed frame and a broken cupboard in the skip.

We dragged them out and towed them a few strides further, leaving them outside the empty lockup on the other side of the road, so the aediles would not make us (or anybody who knew us) pay for clearing the street. Luckily Maia came down at that point, so I told her to send her eldest boy and I'd give him a copper or two to act as a guard.

'I'll send him tomorrow,' Maia promised. 'You can have Marius when he's finished school, but if you want a watchman earlier in the day you'll have to pinch one of Galla's or Allia's horrible lot.'

'Marius can miss a few lessons.'

'He won't. Marius *likes* school!' Maia's children were encouragingly well behaved. Since I felt disinclined to bring more vandals and loafers into the world, this cheered me up. Maybe, despite all the evidence I saw daily in Rome, parenthood could work out well. Maybe I too could father a studious, polite little person who would be a credit to the family. 'Put a cloth on top overnight. Famia reckons that makes a skip invisible.'

Famia, her husband, was a lazy swine; trust him to realise people are so idle they would rather lose a chance of dumping their waste in someone else's bin than apply a bit of exertion uncovering the container first.

Maia hugged me rather unexpectedly. In our large family she was the only one younger than me; we had always been fairly close. 'You'll make a wonderful father!'

I pointed out that there were a great many uncertainties before ever I got that far.

After Maia left I started hauling debris from the first-floor apartment. The weaver, who told me his name was Ennianus, assured me he would love to be some help but apparently he had a bad back that not many people knew about. I said it was lucky that selling baskets didn't call for much bending and lifting, then he shambled off.

I didn't need him. I rolled my tunic sleeves up to my shoulders and set to like a man who has something disturbing to forget about. Although autumn had arrived, the nights were still light long enough for me to put in an hour or two of heavy work. The whole first-floor apartment was crammed with dirty old junk – though I came across no dead bodies or other unpleasant remains. It was hard work, but could have been much worse.

Smaractus must have let his handymen use this place sometimes as a materials store. There were half-buckets of good nails lurking under the warped scaffold boards and bits of mangled joist timber. One of his halfwits had left behind a perfectly decent adze that would find a welcome place in my own toolbag. They were a feckless lot. Dustsheeting had gone mouldy through being folded up while wet. Pulleys had rusted solid. Paint had gone hard in uncovered kettles. They never took home an empty wine flask or filthy food wrapper if they could stuff it under the unusable tangles of hoisting rope. There were unopened sacks of substances that had set like rock so it was impossible to identify the contents; nothing was labelled, of course. Smaractus never bought from a regular builders' merchant, but acquired oddments from contractors who had already been paid once by some innocent house-holder who had never heard of demanding to keep spare materials.

I cleared one room and used it to store any stuff I could reclaim. By the end of the evening I had made good headway and felt pleased with my work. One more stint would reduce the apartment to a shell, then Helena and I could start thinking about what was needed next. I had not found many bad mending jobs to do. The decor would probably be a pleasure to tackle once I had braced myself to start. Living in the kind of hovels I did, I had never had much call to be a dado and fresco man so this would be something new. Everywhere needed a furious scrubbing, but it struck me that while I was attached to the Fourth Cohort I might be able to wangle help from the fire-fighters to bring the water in . . .

On my final trip down to street level I found I had been donated an old bench and a soaking-wet counterpane in my rubbish skip. I turfed them out, then covered the skip, and roped it too. I went to the nearest baths to cleanse myself of dust and sweat, mentally adding sweet oil and a strigil to the list of things I would bring across next time I came to work. After I rinsed the dirt from my hair, I also added a comb to the list.

It was dark when I made my way back up Fountain Court. I felt tired but satisfied, as you do after hard labour. My muscles were stretched, but I had relaxed at the baths. I felt on top of life. Playing the thorough type, I stepped over to look under the cover and check my skip again.

In the gloom I nearly didn't see what was there. If I had still been tipping rubbish in, I would not have noticed a thing. That was somebody's intention. Rome being the city it is, whoever put the young baby in the cart meant him no good. He was cute, and gurgling trustingly, but a baby who gets dumped by his keeper does not easily acquire another – not unless he is grabbed by a woman who is purposely watching the middens in case someone abandons an unwanted newborn. Nobody in Fountain Court felt that desperate. Whoever ditched this little one had left him to die. They would not have expected anybody else to pick him up and take him home.

Since it was me who found him, that was what I did.

XXV

'Only you could do this!' Helena groaned.

'Your lucky day!' I told the babe. 'Here's a nice lady who only wants to cuddle you. Listen to me. She's a pushover for big brown eyes and a showy grin – '

'This is no good, Marcus.'

'Very true. I'm determined to be firm. I'm not allowing other people's unwanted goods in my rubbish skip. I paid for it, and I've got plenty of clutter to shift for myself – '

'Marcus!'

'All right, but once I picked him up and took him out, what was I supposed to do? Lay him down in the gutter and just walk off?'

Helena sighed. 'Of course not.'

'He'll have to find himself a berth somewhere. This is just a temporary reprieve.' It had a callous ring.

I noticed Helena made no attempt to come and take the child. He stared at me, as if he realized this could be the big tricky moment in his life. He was quite a few months old, enough to take notice of his surroundings anyway.

He looked healthy. His hair, which was dark and slightly curled, had been trimmed neatly. He wore a proper little tunic, in white, with embroidery at the neck. He had been wearing it much longer than he should, however. That kind of babywear usually belongs to families where the children are changed regularly, almost certainly by a nurse; this baby had not been cleaned up, perhaps for days. He was soiled and sore. I was handling him gingerly.

'Poor little fellow needs a bath.'

'I'll find you a big bowl,' snorted Helena. She was definitely not going to help.

'Luckily you've come to a home where the women are fierce but the men understand it's not your fault,' I told him. When I talked, he hardly seemed aware of me. I tickled his chin, and he did condescend to wave his feet and hands about.

He was a very quiet baby. Something about him was too subdued. I frowned, and Helena, who had by then brought me a bowl of warm water, looked at me closely the way she did when she thought I was drawing conclusions. 'Do you think he has been mistreated?'

I had lain him on his back on a tunic on the table while I took the clothes off him. He was not afraid of being handled. He was plump, a good weight. There were no bruises or unhappy marks on him.

'Well, he looks unharmed. But there's something odd,' I mused. 'He's too old, for one thing. Unwanted babies are abandoned at birth. This lost mite must be nearly a year old. Who keeps a child so long, looks after him, grows fond of him – and *then* carefully pushes him under a canvas in a rubbish skip?'

'Someone who knows it's *your* skip!' suggested Helena dryly.

'How could they? I only got it tonight. And if they wanted me to find him, why wait until I'd finished work, covered it up, and could not be expected to look inside again? I only found him by accident. He could have died of exposure or been gnawed by rats or anything.'

Helena was examining a loose cord around his neck, a twisted skein of coloured material. 'What do you think this is? It's very fine thread,' she said, unravelling it partially. 'One of the strands could be gold.'

'He's had an amulet probably. But where's it gone?'

'Too valuable to throw away with the child!' Helena Justina was growing angry now. 'Some person felt able to abandon the baby – but made sure they kept his bulla.'

'Perhaps they removed it because it might have identified him?'

She shook her head sadly, commenting, 'This never happens in stories. The lost child always has a jewel very carefully left with it so years later it can be proved to be the missing heir.' She softened slightly. 'Maybe his mother cannot keep him, but has preserved his amulet as a memento.'

'I hope it breaks her heart! We'll make sure we keep his tunic,' I said. 'I'll get Lenia to wash it, and I'll ask her if any of the laundry girls have seen it before. If they have they are bound to remember the embroidery.'

'Do you think he's a local baby?'

'Who knows?'

Somebody knew. If I had had more time, I might have traced his parents, but the rubbish-skip babe had picked the wrong moment to be dropped on me. Working with Petronius on the Emporium heist was going to take up all my energies. In any case, finding parents who don't want their babies is a dead-end job.

I had done the child a favour, but in the long run he might not thank me for it. He had been found in a district so poor that we who lived there could hardly keep ourselves alive. On the Aventine, three times as many children died in infancy as those who survived, and many of the survivors grew up with no life worth speaking of. There was little hope for him, even if I did find somebody to take him in. Who that could be I had no idea. Helena and I had our own troubles; at this stage we were certainly not available to foster unknown orphans. There were too many children already in my family. Although no member of the Didius clan would be made to suffer this child's fate, finding space for an extra who had no claim on us was inconceivable.

We could sell him as a slave, of course. He wouldn't be overjoyed about that.

The baby seemed to like being washed. The sensation appeared to reassure him, and when Helena allowed her guard to slip and started a gentle splashing game, he seemed to know he was expected to chuckle and play along with her. 'He's not a slave's baby,' I observed. 'He's already been among feckless time-wasters who throw water all over the room!'

Helena let me haul him out, though she did find a towel to dry him on. He must have decided that now he could start in with the serious demands: food preferably. We had patted him all over, allowing him a few more tickles on the way, and rolled him in a stole while we thought about where we could stow him safely overnight. Then the babe decided to assert himself and began roaring.

Unluckily for Helena, that was the moment when the Palace slave arrived to ask me to an urgent confidential meeting with the Emperor's eldest son.

I managed not to grin as I kissed Helena tenderly, apologised for bunking off – and left her to cope.

XXVI

Rome was full of litters taking the wealthy out to dinner. It was, therefore, also full of harshly squabbling voices as the slaves carrying the litters vied for road space with the heavy carts delivering necessities that were now permitted to enter the city. Flutes and harps occasionally tweedled above the havoc. Around the temples and courts in the Forum I noticed the good-time girls, the night moths, already hovering. There seemed to be more than usual. Maybe I had prostitutes on the brain.

I was being taken to the Golden House. The slave made enquiries at the marble-clad entrance while Praetorians gave us nasty looks. I was led in to the west wing, the private apartments where I had never been before. Once past the Guards, there was a quiet atmosphere. It was like entering a friendly home, though one with sumptuous embellishments.

Titus was in a garden. The state bedrooms were all designed to face across the Forum valley, with views that would once have included the Great Lake and which now took in the building site of the Flavian amphitheatre. Behind them, decorously lit with outdoor lamps, lay this private, interior court. It was dominated by an immense porphyry vase but also contained select pieces of statuary chosen to delight Nero. The planting was tasteful, the topiary pristine, the seclusion divine.

The Emperor's heir and colleague was sitting with a woman who must have been nearly forty years older than him. Since he was a handsome man in his thirties who was currently unmarried, my imagination leapt wildly. She couldn't be his mother; Vespasian's wife was dead. The Chief Vestal Virgin would be a regular visitor at the Palace, but this elderly biddy wasn't dressed as a vestal. They had been talking together pleasantly. When he saw me being brought through the colonnade, Titus began rising as if he meant to excuse himself for our discussion, but the woman held out a hand to prevent him. He then kissed her cheek before she herself rose and left him. This could mean only one thing.

Her name was Caenis. She was Vespasian's freedwoman mistress. As far as I knew, Caenis did not interfere in politics, although any woman whom Vespasian had cherished for forty years and whom Titus treated respectfully must have the potential for enormous influence. The freedwoman was a scandal waiting to happen, but the cool glance she gave me said that scandal stood no chance.

As she passed me, I stood aside meekly. Her intelligent gaze and upright carriage reminded me of Helena.

'Marcus Didius!' Titus Caesar greeted me like a personal friend. He had noticed me looking at his noble father's not so noble ladyfriend. 'I was telling Caenis your story. She was listening very sympathetically.'

I was pleased the Emperor's mistress found details of my life entertaining, though I noticed that Titus had not introduced us so the lady could award me a bag of gold, a kindly word, and my heart's desire.

'Are you well?' Titus was asking, as if my health were of major significance to world events. I said I was. 'And how is the splendid daughter of the excellent Camillus?'

Titus Caesar had in the past looked at Helena as if he found her as attractive as I did. This was one reason why she and I had been spending time abroad, in case he decided his famous fling with the Queen of Judaea was completely doomed and looked around Rome for a replacement. While Helena would make a perfect substitute for a beautiful, spirited and slightly naughty royal, this would leave me bereft and with little hope that Queen Berenice would fancy me as a quid pro quo. So I was resisting a swap. I thanked him for asking, then made damn sure he knew the truth: 'Helena Justina is fit, flourishing – and doing me the immeasurable honour of carrying my heir.'

If he drew an unexpected breath, he disguised it well. 'I congratulate you both!' Titus Caesar had the knack of sounding as if he meant exactly what he said.

'Thank you, sir,' I replied, a mite sombrely.

There was a small pause. Titus gazed at the dimly visible topiary. I restrained any urge to feel smug. Putting one over on the Emperor's elder son was not clever. Everyone knew Titus had a very pleasant temperament, but he could also have me sent down to Hades by the short route.

'This will be a difficult time for you, Falco. Is there anything I can do to assist?'

'I don't think so, sir. I did once make Helena and her parents a rather rash promise to improve myself socially and marry her – but your brother tells me the equestrian rank is to be kept select, and I am not the right material.'

'Domitian said so?' Titus appeared unaware of it. I didn't blame him. Rome was full of eager self-improvers; he could not expect to keep daily track of all of us. However, it might have been sensible to watch the ones that his family had kicked in the teeth.

'Obviously, you will not wish to overrule your brother, sir.'

'Oh obviously not,' Titus agreed, though I detected exasperation that his brother had chosen to antagonise me. He was publicly loyal to Domitian, but his private opinion might be interesting. 'So you have been having a bad time lately? I discover you went to Nabataea, on the state's behalf, and encountered difficulties?'

'There was no difficulty with Nabataea,' I told him. 'Only with the shark who sent me there.'

'Anacrites! I'd like to hear your side of the story sometime,' Titus offered in a friendly tone. That left me worrying exactly what side of the story Anacrites had already told. I said nothing. Titus had known me long enough to realise when I was angry. Sometimes complaints have more effect if you make people sweat. 'My father would welcome a report – if you will consider it.' I love to see a prince pleading. 'We do need a confidential assessment of the situation in the desert.'

I smiled. Without a word, I produced a slim scroll from my tunic. Helena, smart girl, had not only forced me to write up my findings, but tonight she had guessed that I might find occasion to hand in my homework. This way Anacrites took no credit. He would not even know what I had said.

'Thank you,' said Titus gently, balancing the scroll between his well-manicured fingers. 'You always serve us well, Falco. Both my father and I have a high opinion of your judgement and trustworthiness.' In fact they hated informers, and only used me when desperate. This must be leading somewhere. 'Do you want to tell me about the problems you encountered?'

It was an invitation to land Anacrites in mule dung. Needless to say I took the sophisticated option: sheer stupidity. 'It's not important, Caesar. I survived.'

'I think it is important.' Titus was acknowledging that spies receive speedy justice in hostile foreign kingdoms. 'You were sent incognito and somebody accidentally exposed you.'

'Deliberately exposed me,' I corrected in a mild tone.

'Do you want an enquiry into that?'

'Best not find out,' I sneered. 'Anacrites is too dangerous to dismiss. Better for him the telling demotion: say, conducting a very long survey of ordering procedures for sanitary materials in the public-works domain.'

Titus had always privately enjoyed my cynicism. He ran both hands through his neat hair. 'Falco, why is it when I talk to you I always end up wondering whether I can stand the pace?' He knew why. He was the Emperor's son, and would be Emperor himself. Few people would ever again offer him a decent argument.

'I'm a sterling debater, Caesar.'

'And modest!'

I produced a gracious shrug. 'And the only kind of fool who'll risk offending you.' He accepted it, and laughed.

'And have you been paid for your work?' Titus then asked narrowly. Whatever Vespasian and he wanted from me next must be spectacularly unpleasant.

'Please don't trouble yourself. When the omens are right for the accounts clerks I shall draw my standard fee, Caesar.'

'There will be an addition,' Titus remarked.

'That's most kind.' I was convinced something big was coming.

The pleasantries had been cleared away. Titus admitted that there was a reason why I had been summoned at night, without any record-takers present. He said the matter was confidential and sensitive; I could have guessed both. However, I had not guessed what I was being asked to undertake. And when I knew, I hated it.

*

561

'What I am going to say to you must remain a complete secret. Nobody – *nobody*, Falco, however close to you – is to be told what we discuss.'

I nodded. You commit yourself to this kind of nonsense like a lamb. That's the trouble with secrets. Until you know what they are, how can you tell whether your ethical element approves of them?

'Marcus Rubella,' Titus began crisply, 'is a recent appointment to the tribunate of the vigiles.' Quite so. Vespasian's man. The city cohorts must be reckoned to be fairly loyal, since even while his predecessor and rival, Vitellius, had ruled Rome, Vespasian's brother Sabinus had been Prefect of the City. Sabinus, a popular man trying to keep the peace in impossible times, inspired lasting respect. To reinforce that, officers throughout the civil institution in Rome were now, like those in the legions, being changed as the new Emperor handed out rewards and replacement where applicable.

'I met Rubella,' I said conversationally.

'I know that,' Titus said. A bad feeling was already creeping over me.

'Seemed an interesting character.'

Titus smiled. 'That must be some kind of cautious shorthand – Rubella said much the same about you.' So, since interviewing me only that morning, Marcus Rubella, the tribune of Petro's cohort, had been talking to Titus. Another evil sensation hit me somewhere in the lower gut.

'This is rather unpleasant,' Titus explained inexorably. 'Rubella is disturbed about the low level of ethics amongst his men.'

Of course I had seen it coming, but I drew a harsh breath. 'Rubella thinks the *Fourth* accept bribery?'

'Does that surprise you, Falco?'

'I know one of them,' I confessed.

'I am aware of that.'

'I know him well.'

'And?'

And I could not stomach the suggestion that Petro might even be under suspicion. 'It's impossible.' Titus was waiting for me to elaborate. 'The man I know, my friend Lucius Petronius, is an impeccable character. You saw him at the meeting yesterday; you must have judged his quality. He is the man who has just expelled from Rome a major criminal. Balbinus Pius would never have been brought to justice without him.'

'True. Were it not for that,' Titus said, 'he would be under a cloud with the rest, and there would be no question of asking you to assist us. We are assuming that Petronius Longus need not feature in Rubella's concern. However, Petronius must not be made aware of our enquiries until he is formally ruled out, and perhaps not even then.'

'This stinks,' I said. 'You want me to spy on the Fourth – '

'Not only them,' Titus broke in. 'Your special assignment is to involve any relevant regions of the city. What Rubella has reported about his own cohort may apply elsewhere – his may not even be the worst problem. I want you to take a close look at any cohort you come into contact with.'

That was better. I had already gathered from Petro a feeling that some of the rest were much less choosy in their habits than his own team. But if I was not allowed to tell him what I was doing, it would be difficult to pry this kind of information from him. If I was underhand and he found out later, he would be outraged. Rightly so.

'Sir, this could damage my most valued friendship.'

'I apologise if so. But I believe you are capable of handling it.' Oh thanks! 'You were selected as particularly suitable. In fact, we have been awaiting your return from the East.'

I managed a grin. 'So that was how you found out where I was!' Nice thought: the great ones wanting me for something else – and Anacrites having to own up that he had probably disposed of me. How happy they must all have been when my boots touched Italy again. 'The Fourth Cohort trust me, sir. Because of my friendship with their enquiry captain.'

'Exactly,' Titus insisted. 'This is a far better disguise than if Rubella put in a special agent, someone who would inevitably be identified as Rubella's man.'

'Very convenient!' I saw his point; that only made it worse. 'And is the graft Rubella suspects a general problem, or does it relate somehow to the Emporium heist?'

'Rubella thinks it may be relevant. The robbery occurred so swiftly after the criminal Balbinus left Rome.'

'Jupiter! It's a mess if he's right.'

'Rubella's a good officer. You will need to take extreme care, Falco.'

'Do you trust Marcus Rubella?' I shot at Titus unexpectedly.

'Rubella is a known commodity.' He accepted my suspicion indulgently. 'We trust him as much as we trust you, Falco.'

If that was a joke, it was in bad taste.

'If you will do this – ' Titus began to say, but I was so angry with the mission that I cut him short.

'Don't make promises,' I snarled, remembering how his brother Domitian had done me down when I asked for a just reward. 'I've had them before. I'll do the job. I'll do it well if I can.' Better me than some idiot from the spy network. 'Whatever you think of informers, rewarding me would be a sign of respect for my reliability, which you say you value. Maybe one day you will think about that, but in any case, I have to ask you this, Caesar: if as a result of this distasteful assignment I end up in a back alley with a knife in my ribs, I hope at least you will remember my family.'

Titus Caesar inclined his head in agreement. He was known as a romantic. He must have understood which member of my family I meant. Maybe, since he really was a romantic, he even had some idea of her distress if she ever lost me.

He was famous for his courtesy, so we had to end with further pleasantries. I slid mine in first: 'Please convey my regards to your father, sir.'

'Thank you. It must be Helena Justina's birthday soon,' Titus offered in return. He liked to remind me that he knew when Helena's birthday was. One year he had even tried to inveigle himself into the family festivities.

'The day after tomorrow,' I said firmly, as if it was in my every thought.

'Do congratulate her from me.'

I forced my teeth into a show of gratitude.

I had not forgotten her birthday. Nowadays I even knew the date myself. For once I had managed to buy her a rather fine present. I had been trying not to think about that. Added to

the various complex tasks that had been laid on me since I
returned to Rome, it was one problem too many.

Helena's present had been hidden amongst the Syrian
glass that was stolen from my father in the Emporium heist.

565

XXVII

The streets were quieter, and dark. There was a chill in the air at night as autumn made its presence felt. I would have welcomed a cloak, though mainly it was what Titus had said that caused my shivering.

I had to cross the Forum, negotiate the Palatine, and climb the Aventine. I walked steadily, keeping away from doorways and glancing down any alleys that I passed. I stuck to streets I knew. Where there was space for more than one person I went straight up the centre of the road. When I heard anybody who must realise I was there I made sure my tread was confident. If the other person did not appear to have noticed me, I kept quiet.

I had a lot to think about. Domestic events alone were enough to take up all my energy: a pregnant girlfriend who still had to decide how she wanted to react; her family; my family. Then there were the hours of work I needed to put in on the new first-floor apartment; my friend Lenia's wedding, in which I was expected to participate as a convivial priest; and now the baby I had discovered in my skip. Just sorting out the foundling might take a week – a week I didn't have to spare for him.

Somehow, too, I had to find a replacement birthday gift for Helena. I was short of cash (partly because I had spent so much on the now stolen original). There was an obvious solution, but it was one that niggled me: I would have to ask Pa to find me a tasteful antique in his warehouse, one he was prepared to let me buy at cost. For Helena he would probably do it – and for Helena, so would I without quibbling – but the process would be horrible. I felt tense just imagining what I would have to go through in the bargain with Pa.

And now Titus had asked me to break faith with Petronius. I hated this. I was also angry that I was supposed to be on my own with it. The only person who would know anything about my filthy task was the tribune Marcus Rubella, and he was not the type I chose for consoling little chats. But even if I wanted it, seeking him out was impossible. If I tried nipping into the tribune's office to mull over my findings, all sorts of rumours would immediately start.

Luckily I could talk to Helena. Although Titus had forbidden me to tell anyone about this, one exception could not be overruled. Whatever the jokes about keeping wives in ignorance, a Roman expected his domestic partner to bear his children, keep the store-cupboard keys, quarrel with his mother, and, if required, to share his confidence. The fact that Brutus failed to confess to Porcia what he was planning on the Ides of March just shows you why Brutus ended up as dead mutton at Philippi.

Helena and I had always shared thoughts. She told me about feelings nobody would imagine she had. I rarely told her my feelings, because she guessed them anyway. I discussed my work. Openness was our pact. Neither Titus nor Vespasian could interfere with that.

I had plenty of company on the streets that night. A couple of times I noticed groups of dubious characters huddled around the folding doors of lockup shops. Once there were scuffles above me as climbers scaled balconies on their way to upstairs burglaries. A woman called out, offering her services in a voice that reeked of dishonesty; having passed by in silence, I spotted her male accomplice in the next lane, hanging about waiting for her to bring a client for him to beat up and rob. A shadowy figure slipped from the back of a moving delivery cart, carrying a bundle. Slaves escorting a rich man's litter were sporting ripped tunics and black eyes, having been mugged despite their sticks and lanterns.

All normal. Rome was itself. No livelier than usual. Eventually I heard the tramp of the vigiles' foot patrol; someone in the shadows laughed at the sound dismissively.

There were still lamps in the laundry. The slurred voices of Lenia and Smaractus were arguing dismally: all normal there, too. I reached in through a shutter to steal a light, then called goodnight, scaring the pair witless. They were too drunk to do much. Lenia cursed, but I was already heading up the stairs before they could try to lure me indoors to ramble about their wedding plans. I was not in the mood for a long wrangle about what colour sheep to sacrifice. I was not in the mood for Smaractus: end of tale.

The lamp helped me avoid obstacles. Smaractus ought to have provided light if he wasn't intending to keep the stairs clear of toys and rubbish. As I mounted the stairs, my useless, sestercius-grubbing, dupondius-pinching landlord became the focus of my entire catalogue of frustrations and anxieties. If he had appeared in person, I would have knocked his head off . . .

Movement in a corner attracted my eye. I reached for my knife, then decided a rat was about to tear out past me and got ready to boot it. The shuffle subsided; it was probably the mongrel Lenia called Nux. The scrawny bundle of misplaced hopefulness whimpered once, but I carried on upstairs.

When I reached home, I saw that Helena Justina must be in bed. A dim taper provided a glow by which I found the skip baby in a basket that looked as if it came from Ennianus across the road. Helena had tucked the child up safely; somehow she must have fed him too, for he was placid, though whimpering slightly. I picked him up and took him out to the balcony to say goodnight to Rome. He smelt clean now, and slightly milky. He had a little burp on my shoulder; I joined in with a nicely controlled belch, showing him how to do it properly.

After I put him back I noticed a bowl of cold fish and lettuce left on the table for me. I ate, pouring myself a cup of water. I blew out his taper to save the baby from fire, then found my way in darkness to my own bed.

Helena must have been asleep, but she stirred as I crawled in beside her. Somehow she realised how deeply disturbed my talk with Titus had made me. She held me while I told her the story, and calmed me down as I started to rant.

'Why do I always have to get the filthy jobs?'

'You're an informer. Finding unpleasant information is what you do.'

'Maybe I'm tired of being despised. I'm tired of being a fool to myself. Maybe I should change my work.'

'To do what?' Helena murmured, in a reasonable tone. 'Do you see yourself selling purses or plucking ducks?'

'I hate women who reprove me with their sensible attitude when I'm trying to curse madly!'

'I know you do. I love you even when you hate me. Go to sleep,' she said, wrapping herself around me so I could no longer jump about in the bed. I sighed, submitting to her good sense. About three breaths later I dropped off into a heavy slumber. In my dreams I knew that Helena Justina was lying awake, worrying for me over what I had to do.

By that time the first victim would already have been tortured and murdered, and his body dumped.

XXVIII

Petro's whistle woke me from the street. Within the apartment it was still dark.

We had been friends so long he could rouse me even from outside and six flights down. I knew it was him. When I dragged myself to the balcony parapet and looked over, he was standing below with one of the foot patrol. I could tell from the top of his head that he was cursing me for taking so long to appear. I whistled back and he glanced up. He waved urgently. I didn't stop to shout questions, but ran down to him, pulling on clothes as I went.

'Morning, Petro. No problem with your cat, I hope?'

He growled. 'Stollicus was right, Falco! You're an irritating, insolent, dozy dog.'

'Stollicus just misunderstood my charm. What's up?'

'Body in the Forum Boarium. Sounds like problems.'

I let my curiosity ride. In the time it had taken me to come downstairs, Petro and the foot patroller had already strolled impatiently halfway along the lane. The three of us walked briskly to the end of Fountain Court, then hurried downhill, picking up Fusculus from his house. Petro must have banged on his door on the way to collect me and he was waiting for us, rotund and unreasonably bright for the time of day.

'Morning, chief. How's the cat?'

'Fusculus, I'm not in the mood.'

Neither Fusculus nor the vigilis who was with us grinned. Petro's men knew how to irritate a senior officer without needing to smirk.

At the end of the Clivus Publicus we saw Martinus emerging from his tenement, summoned by another member of the vigiles. 'Don't ask about the cat,' warned Fusculus. Martinus lifted a wry eyebrow in a significant fashion and said nothing in a way that drove Petro mad. Martinus *was* allowed a grin, since he had had to forgo the joke. Petronius, who had the longest legs amongst us, lengthened his stride so the rest of us were forced to step out.

It was barely dawn. The pale light, empty streets and our echoing footfalls increased the air of urgency. We came down past the Temple of Ceres into the damp grey mist along the river.

'Why does this always happen before I've had my breakfast?' Petro grumbled.

'They dump the corpse in the dark, then the dawn patrol discovers it at first light,' Martinus explained. Petronius had not needed him to say this. Martinus went in for pedantry. As a result Petronius went in for thinking that Martinus needed to be washed out with a violent enema.

It crossed my mind that I could do Petro a favour by naming his deputy as a bribe-taker and having him removed. In fact, if my interest in truth had inclined to the inaccurate, I could have wreaked havoc in the watch. I could finger anyone I took against; it would be hard to disprove. Even though none of them knew the position, I felt sour.

'Petro, they do it on purpose, to stop you enjoying your morning ... Do we know who this dumped corpse is?' I asked.

Petronius glanced back at the patrolman who had been with him at Fountain Court. 'Not yet,' Petro said. He seemed to be keeping something back.

'Who found the remains?'

'One of the Sixth's patrols. It's in their patch.' That explained Petro's restrained attitude. He kept his counsel in front of men from another cohort. But he did condescend to mutter, 'There seems to be a connection with the Emporium.'

We had reached the scene of the crime – or at least where the victim had ended up. Our pace slowed and we left further questions to answer themselves.

The Forum Boarium lies in the Eleventh region, immediately below the Capitol, between the river and the starting-gate end of the Circus Maximus. It is part of the Velabrum. Once the marsh where Romulus and Remus were supposedly found by the shepherd, it has a long history. There must have been a landing place and a market here since long before Romulus grew up and identified the Seven Hills as an ideal development site. The rectangular Temple of Portunus marked the ancient use as a harbour of the riverbank between the Aemilian and Sublician bridges. The diminutive round Temple of Hercules Victor was later, a cute initiative in marble that dated from the time when shrines started to become decorative and, according to my grandfather, morals declined.

The meat market had its own decidedly off-putting flavour. Owing to the presence of the body it had not yet been set up for the day, which made it appear even shabbier. There was a mess of hurdles everywhere. I never liked walking through it, for the putrid smell of drying animal blood always hung about. The disgusting odour filled the air this morning so strongly I felt sick.

Right in the centre of the area a small group of fire-watchers were conversing in a huddle near a body on the ground. Further away a couple of street-sweepers stood gawping, leaning on flat-headed brooms. Market traders, kept back from their normal business, hung about talking in low voices, some of them warming their hands around little cups of hot spiced wine. The first arrivals of cattle were jammed in a pen on the river-side. They were lowing with distress; maybe they sensed even more trouble than the slaughter that awaited them.

We walked across to the corpse. The vigiles drew back and watched us as we looked down at their find. The two who had come to fetch us joined their colleagues. As they let officers take charge of their discovery they were wary, and dis-believing of our so-called expertise. We inspected the body in silence. It was a bad experience.

We were looking at a man, age indeterminate, probably not young. He lay on his front, with arms and legs neatly outstretched like a starfish – not the attitude of any accidental death. We could see at once that he had been tortured. He was barefoot, wearing what might once have been a white tunic. The tunic was almost completely soaked in blood. Its material also bore signs of what seemed to be scorching. There were marks of a thrashing on his calves. His arms were

572

badly bruised and had been slashed with knives. People with perverted natures had really enjoyed themselves here, and their victim must have died slowly.

We could see nothing above the neck. At some point during his terrible adventure last night, his head had been crammed inside a large bronze pot. The pot was still on the corpse.

XXIX

Martinus made a loop of his neckscarf. He bent over the victim and pulled it up an arm, then dragged at the corpse until one shoulder twisted and the body turned over. The metal pot scraped piercingly on grit. There was less blood on the front of the tunic, but a great deal of dirt, as if the body had been dragged about face down. The pot stayed in place, wedged on by a cloak shoved inside. If the man had not been dead when they covered his head, he must have been suffocating while they tortured him.

Petronius strode over to the vigiles. 'How did you find him?'

'On our last round,' said their leader, stressing that it was now time they went off duty. 'We came upon him just where he is.'

'Had you been around here earlier?'

'When our shift started. He wasn't here then. We hadn't been back during the night. We check the temples for vagrants, but apart from that we don't get much to do in the Boarium. The smell of dead meat puts off courting couples.'

'Dear, dear!' Petronius tutted to me. 'Lovers are becoming so fastidious . . .'

The patrolman gave him a sideways look, then continued sombrely: 'There's nothing to pinch, and nothing to go up in smoke. So if there's no one about we forget it. We've got plenty of worse trouble spots.'

'This is the Eleventh region. What made you come for me?'

'The pot.'

'The pot?'

'A list was circulated to all the cohorts yesterday: things to watch for from that robbery. Anything we spotted being disposed of, you were the special contact name.' The patrolman grinned slightly. He had very stained teeth. 'Nobody mentioned that the funeral urns might be full!'

Petro's face set. He rarely joked about murder. 'You're

referring to the Emporium losses? Was a pot like this on the list?'

The man Petro was talking to stared at him pityingly. 'I seem to remember "Etruscan bronze vessels: set comprising jugs, ladle, suspension hooks, and *double-handled wine bowl*, sir!'

'Right!' said Petronius, managing to sound crisp. 'Well spotted, lads.'

He came back to us. We had been standing in silence, listening in. He checked with Martinus in a low voice, 'Was stuff like this on our list?'

Martinus shrugged. 'Could be. I only drew up the list. You know how many items were on it. I didn't know I was meant to learn it off by heart.' Sensing his chief's disapproval, he had second thoughts. 'Maybe. Could well have been.'

Petro turned to me. 'You're the antiques expert, Falco. Is this Etruscan?'

He really needed Pa to discuss bronzes. I walked to the top of the corpse's head and viewed the item more or less the right way up. It was a large, open-topped bowl, with two handles as the patrolman said, each fixed with two attachment plates and cast with satyrs' heads in relief. Handsome. Probably robbed from a tomb. My father would adore it; my mother would call it 'too good to use'.

'It looks extremely ancient. One thing I do know,' I conceded. 'This is a highly valuable pot. I personally would not stuff even my favourite granny into it.'

Petronius looked at me. 'Who would abandon something like that, Falco?'

'Someone who knew what it was worth. Upending our friend in the pot was a statement: we killed him because of the robbery – and here's an item to prove the point.'

'What point?' asked Fusculus.

Petro supplied it: 'We're the big boys now.'

Martinus pondered, 'So who's the man who wasn't quite big enough? The man in the pot?'

I poked at the handsome crater, attempting to remove it with the toe of my boot. No luck. Like a naughty child egged on by an even naughtier brother, this corpse had ended up completely stuck. I had been jammed in a pot myself once.

575

Remembering could still raise panic. I had had to be worked loose using cold water and olive oil. I could still hear my ma soothing me quietly while she eased my ears out – and feel the great whack she had given me as soon as I was free.

At least with a dead man there was no need to mess about being gentle on the ears.

I squatted on my haunches, grabbed the two handles and twisted off the vase. I threw it aside, letting it ding heavily across the blood-soaked pavings. My father would have yelled in horror, and no doubt the owner would complain loudly about the dents I had caused. But I felt no twinge of conscience. It had been used in the torture of a human being. Its beauty was soiled. Its price had slumped.

The idea of touching the corpse made us all recoil. Gingerly I tugged away the cloak from around the dead man's head.

In fact, apart from discoloration, the face was unmarked. We recognised him instantly. If he had been wearing his boots instead of being barefoot, I would probably have known him earlier. It was Nonnius Albius.

XXX

Petronius took charge in his quiet, resigned way.

'Martinus, you're the king of the stolen-property list. Take the nice Etruscan wine bowl to its owner to identify. Maybe you should wash off the blood a bit first. I need sensible answers. Don't give him a chance to get hysterical.'

'I'll have to go to the station house and look up who owns it.' Martinus could be bone idle.

'I don't care how you set about the job,' Petro said, restraining himself.

'What if the man wants his bowl back?' asked Fusculus, to calm things.

Petro shrugged. 'Suits me. I can't see us needing to use it as evidence. If it could answer questions I'd put it on a stool and start wheedling, but I reckon the pot's a hostile witness . . .'

He fell silent, though at first he pretended not to notice that a new group of figures were marching into the square. Fusculus groaned quietly. I recognised Tibullinus, the centurion from the Sixth Cohort whom I had not much taken to. He must have been told about the body. He and his sidekick, Arica, came briskly across, flanked by a small honour guard. They folded their arms and stood watching us with a cocky air.

Petro forced himself to look up and gave Tibullinus a brief nod. 'Your patch, but it's one for us – direct bearing on the post-Balbinus enquiry. The pot comes from the Emporium haul, and the victim was my chief suspect.'

'Looks like poor old Nonnius,' Tibullinus remarked to Arica. Arica tutted in mock-tragic style. Making a deliberate survey of all his wounds, they sucked their teeth; then they grinned. Tibullinus viciously kicked an arm straight. They had a callousness that the men of the Fourth lacked. While Petro's group had no tolerance for a gangster's enforcer while he was alive, they still showed grim respect for his mangled body.

577

Then I overheard Martinus say openly to Arica, 'Some people are going to be grieving that they've lost their paymaster!' It was a jibe, though I could not tell from his tone whether his feelings were jealous or reproving.

Arica and Tibullinus barely glanced at one another. It was Petro who seemed angry, and who brushed the comment aside. 'I assume you're happy for me to take this one on.' His colleagues made a theatrical show of standing aside for him. It may have been accidental, but Petronius then virtually turned his back on them. He gave orders in a low voice: 'Fusculus, get some help and shift the remains. I don't want the whole city talking about this. If it's meant to cause public comment, I'm going to disappoint them. Whip it out of sight. Nab one of the hurdles and carry him to the station house for the time being. Maybe Scythax could take a look. He might be able to tell us something about what went on – though it's fairly obvious.'

Petro seemed too tense for comfort. I noticed the Sixth, having made their presence known like generals on a battlefield, were now melting from the scene. Petro started relaxing as soon as they left.

'Who's Scythax?' I put in.

'A medico attached to our patrols.' The vigiles always had doctors on the squad; they looked after the patrolmen, whose work led to frequent injuries, and when there were bad fires or building collapses they tended civilian victims at the scene. 'Falco, I think you and I should go to the victim's home. Martinus, if you are going to the station house, send a detachment to meet us at the Nonnius place. I'll have to search it, and probably guard it afterwards. Mind you, Rubella won't be happy to allow us the men . . .'

Mention of Rubella made me go quiet.

On the way to the Capena Gate we bought bread rolls and munched as we walked. Luckily sight of a corpse always stopped Petro wanting to talk. He must have assumed I was reacting the same way.

We strolled the length of the Circus on the north side, then around its end under the Appian and Marcian aqueducts. As we emerged from their shadow, shopkeepers were unlocking their booths and washing the pavements. There were some decent residential streets but they were interspersed with rougher ones. Interestingly, it was an area of mixed jurisdiction by the vigiles. The First region, which we were just entering, was looked after by the Fifth Cohort, yet we were quite near to the Twelfth region, which as part of the Aventine came under the Fourth. We were also very close to the much seedier quarter where Plato's Academy lurked. That was in the Circus Maximus region, the Eleventh, and like the Forum Boarium it was prowled by the Sixth Cohort.

'Petro, does the fact that three different groups of vigiles are responsible for this triangle have any bearing on the crime that's rife?'

'Probably,' he said. I could not tell him that according to Rubella criminality occurred amongst the vigiles themselves.

'Do you work closely together?'

'Not if we can help it.'

'Any reason?' I was hoping there would be one.

'I've enough to do without wasting effort on "inter-cohort co-operation"!' Petro sneered.

'Strikes me the cohorts all have different characters?'

'Right. The Fifth are dull, the Sixth are bastards, and as you know, we in the Fourth are unsung heroes with a mature and efficient approach!'

I just hoped I could show that that was the truth.

I took a deep breath. 'Are Tibullinus and Arica on the take?'

'Probably,' said Petro shortly. Something in his manner made me reluctant to ask more.

As we neared the street we wanted, a familiar figure hailed me.

'Marcus!'

'Quintus! I heard you were back from Germany. Oh this is good. Petro, let me introduce you to Camillus Justinus.'

Justinus was Helena's younger brother, a slight, boyish lad of twenty-odd. Today he was in civilian dress – a pristine white tunic and rather casually draped toga. The last time I saw him he had been in tribunal uniform, in the army on the Rhine. I myself had been there on a mission for Vespasian, one Justinus had joined in, acquitting himself bravely. I knew he had been recalled and was now expected to work through the stages of upper-class civilian life, probably ending in the Senate when he reached twenty-five. Despite that, I liked him. We embraced like brothers, and I chaffed him about his position.

'That's right. I've been brought back home to be a good boy, and to start planning to cadge votes.'

'Don't worry. The Senate's a doddle. All you have to do is learn to say, "Gods, what a stench!" every time you appear in a crowd, while keeping your teeth bared in a friendly smile in case any of the plebs can lip-read.'

'Well, it's a few years away yet . . .' Justinus sighed. 'I was hoping to see you. I think I'm in love with an actress.'

Petro and I turned to one another and groaned.

'Why do the young always have to make the old mistakes?' I asked. Petro shook his head sadly. Petro and I had been friends with a few stage performers in our day, but now we had responsibilities. (We were too old, too cynical, and too careful with our cash.)

'I think you may know her – ' Justinus tried.

'Very probably!' exclaimed Petronius, as if it was nothing to be proud of. Since getting married, he had turned highly self-righteous. I suspected it was a deliberate pose. He hadn't really changed.

'Quintus, don't ask me any favours to do with entertainers! I'm in enough trouble with your family.'

Justinus slipped into his infectious grin. 'That's true – and heading for more! If I see you I am to invite you and Helena to dinner on her birthday. Tomorrow,' he spelt out annoyingly. That reminded me about my lost birthday present problem, and I cursed to myself. 'What you don't know', continued Helena's favourite brother, 'is that someone else has come home from abroad. Somebody who doesn't take kindly to having his sister living with an informer, and who keeps describing in tortuous detail what he would like to do to you.'

'Aelianus?'

'Aelianus.' The other brother, whom I had never met but already disliked. His views on me were plain too; he had written them to his sister with great acrimony. The distress he had caused Helena was more than I could think about.

'Looks as if we're heading for a wonderful evening!' I commented.

Quintus Camillus Justinus, an odd soul who happened to believe I was quite good for his sister, gave me a formal salute. 'You can, of course, rely on my unstinted support, Marcus Didius!'

'Oh thanks!' I said.

He would make a good politician: it was a blatant bribe. So now I had to find time to introduce a senator's son to an actress, then watch him ruin his previously immaculate reputation in a scandalous love affair. No doubt afterwards I would be expected to help this young man tour the city trying to win votes.

Petronius and I were admitted to the Nonnius house by the porter as soon as we shouted our arrival. He seemed relieved that we had turned up to take charge. He came out to greet us carrying a temporary screen and watched us examine the front door, which had been battered open last night so efficiently that little of it now remained. 'They came in a cart with a ram on it. A pointed tree trunk mounted on a frame. They pulled it back on a sling, then let go – it crashed right through.'

Petro and I winced. This was real siege warfare. No house in Rome would be safe from such artillery – and only a daring gang would risk taking that kind of illegal weapon openly through the streets.

The house was silent now. Nonnius had been unmarried and had no known relatives. With him gone, domestic management would come to a full stop.

We walked about unhindered, finding few of the slaves who had been in evidence the last time I visited. Maybe some had run away, either eager to be free or simply terrified. In strict law, when a man was murdered, his slaves were subjected to statutory torture to make them identify his murderer. Any who had denied him assistance would be punished severely. If he was murdered in his own house, his slaves were bound to be the first suspects.

The porter was the most helpful. He freely confessed that strange men had come to the house after dark, had broken

581

down the door suddenly and violentiy, and rushed past him. He had hidden in his cubicle. Sometime later the men had left. A long time after that he had ventured out. He learned from the others that Nonnius had been dragged away.

None of the other slaves would admit to having seen what was done to their master. At last we found the little Negro who had been his personal attendant; the child was still hiding under a bedroom couch, crazy with fear. He must know the truth, but we got nothing from him but whimpering. Some of the cohort had turned up by then, brought here by Fusculus. Petronius, not unkindly, put the child in the charge of one of them and ordered him to be brought to the station house.

'Put a blanket or something around him!' Petro's lip curled in distaste at the little black boy's fluttery skirt and bare, gilded chest. 'Try and convince him we're not going to beat him up.'

'Growing soft, chief?'

'He's palpitating like a run-down leveret. We'll get nothing if he drops dead on us . . . Now let's do a regular search.'

We drew some conclusions from the search. Nonnius had been in bed. Boots were in the bedroom, thrown in different directions, and tunics lay on a stool. The bed stood askew, as if it had been jerked violently; its coverlet had fallen half on the floor. We reckoned he had been surprised and snatched while asleep, or at least only partly awake. Whether he was alive or dead when they took him from the house was debatable, though Petronius decided on him being still alive. There was only a small amount of blood on the bedclothes and the floor – not enough to have been caused by the mass of wounds we had seen on the body.

We should probably only ever find out where they had taken him if somebody confessed. We might never know. What had happened to him in the hour or so that followed his abduction we could all imagine clearly. Most of us preferred not to think about it.

XXXI

As we were leaving the Nonnius mansion someone else made the mistake of trying to arrive. We were keyed up in investigating mode, and surrounded him. He was a lean fellow in a smart white tunic, carrying a leather satchel.

'May we look in the bag, sir?' The man handed it over to Fusculus with a rather dry expression. It was full of tweezers, spatulas and stoneware medicine jars. 'What's your name?'

'Alexander. I am the householder's doctor.'

We relaxed, but our humour was harsh. 'Well he won't need you now!'

'The patient has suffered a fatal dose of being beaten up.'

'Terminal knife wounds.'

'Irreversible death.'

'I see,' commented the doctor, no doubt thinking of his lost fees.

Petronius, who had not spoken to him before this, said, 'I respect your relationship with your patient, but you will understand my enquiries are very serious. Did Nonnius say anything to you in confidence that might tell us who may have done this?' To judge from his careful phrasing, Petro had had trouble extracting information from doctors.

'I don't believe he did.'

'Well you are free to go then.'

'Thank you.'

Something about the man's manner was oddly restrained. He seemed hardly surprised to have lost his patient in this appalling way. Perhaps that was because he knew what line of business Nonnius had been in. Or perhaps there was another cause.

'There was something peculiar there,' I suggested, as we all walked back to the patrol house.

'He's a doctor,' Petro assured me calmly. 'They're always peculiar.'

If I had not known him better I might have thought

583

something in Petro's own manner seemed oddly restrained too. In view of my special investigation for Titus, I wanted Petronius to behave in ways I understood.

At the station house Petro's young assistant, Porcius, was in deep trouble with a woman. Luckily for him she was extremely old and not worth creating a fuss about. It was another stolen-bedcover case; somebody was going around with a hook on a stick targeting ancient dames who were too bent to chase after a thief. Porcius was trying to write a report for this one; we could see he would be helpless for the rest of the morning unless rescued.

'See the clerk,' Petro told her curtly.

'The clerk's a dozy mule!' She must have been here before. 'This nice young man is looking after me.'

Porcius was a new recruit. He was desperate to arrest as many wrongdoers as possible, but had no idea of how to dodge time-wasters. Petro was unimpressed. 'This nice young man has more important things to do.'

'See the clerk, please,' muttered Porcius, looking embarrassed.

Indoors we found a nasty scene: a large boulder was lying in the centre of the floor, along with the broken shutter it had been thrown through last night and the wreckage of a stool. Petro sighed, and said to me, 'As you see, sometimes the locals chuck worse things at us than cabbages.'

'They poked some brassica stalks through the cell air hole too,' Porcius told him. 'People round here do seem to think we're short of greens.'

'Well next time forget charitable deeds for grannies, and try to find out who hates the vigiles!'

'That's easy,' grinned Fusculus, rolling the boulder towards the door. '*Everyone* does.'

He roared for the foot patrol to stop counting their esparto mats in the firefighting equipment store and come to remove the debris from indoors.

Trying to regain Petro's approval, Porcius announced nervously, 'One of the centurions had been sitting just where it landed, but luckily he'd just gone for a pee. It would have killed him otherwise.'

584

Petronius, who had merely been frowning with annoyance, checked slightly. 'Right. This looks bad. Fusculus, put the word around the whole cohort: keep alert. We could be in for a dangerous time.'

Frowning, he turned into the small room he used for interrogations, only to find two of the foot patrol's most recent prisoners. One of them was shouting and throwing himself about, nearly throttling himself with the giant ring chained around his neck. The other stayed sullenly silent, a middle-class fire offender who was pretending this was all a nightmare from which a smart lawyer would extract him, probably with compensation for insult and slander. (I could tell from Petro's irritated expression the man was probably right.) With them, huddled on a bench, was the minute black slave from the Nonnius house.

Petro fumed at the chaos. 'Shut up!' he bawled abruptly at the half-mad drunken man who was shouting; surprised, the fellow obeyed instantly. 'Fusculus, start asking questions and see if we can let these prisoners go. Unless they're hard nuts, we need the space. Porcius, get Fusculus to tell you what we know happened to Nonnius Albius, then I want you to take this little lad somewhere quiet and make friends with him. If you can deal with indignant grannies, you can handle terrified tots. Win his confidence, then find out what he saw when his master was attacked. He's not arrested, but if he witnessed anything useful I'll want him put somewhere very safe after he's talked.'

Since there was nowhere else private, Petro and I went out for a conference at the chophouse just across the street.

'So what do you think, Falco?'

I chewed a stuffed vine leaf, trying not to think about its consistency and taste. This job promised an endless parade of lukewarm, stand-up food taken squashed against the cracked counters of unhygienic foodshops. Petro did not come from a family that provided lunch baskets. When we were in the legions, he was always the one who never hid spare marching bread in his tunic, though he soon learned to pinch mine. I spat out a rough bit. 'It looks as if the Emporium robbery may have been organised by Nonnius – and that somebody else has punished him rather publicly for daring to think big.'

We both considered that, eating gloomily.

'Alternatively – ' I offered.

Petro groaned. 'Knowing you, I might have known the easy answer wasn't enough. Alternatively?'

'Nonnius had nothing to do with the raid. Some swine just thinks it would be convenient if the Emporium do was *blamed* on him to take the heat off them.'

'Bit stupid,' argued Petro. 'So long as Nonnius was alive he was a suspect. Now when these others do a raid, they've no cover and I'll be sure it's them.'

'If you ever find out who they are.'

'I love a chirpy optimist.'

'Helena thinks we should be looking at Lalage for the Emporium.'

Petronius laughed dismissively, then fell silent. Helena Justina's wild ideas had a way of turning themselves over in your head so they soon seemed completely rational. I myself had stopped even thinking they were wild. I had known her to be right too many times.

Petro tried looking at me as if I were daft either to share information with my girlfriend, or to indulge her mad suggestions. Eventually this palled too. 'Suppose that was right, Falco. Suppose Lalage did want to take over running the gangs. Why would she kill Nonnius?'

'She hated him. She had scores to settle. He had leaned on her too heavily when he was collecting for Balbinus. And then he left her with the problem when the Lycian was murdered at Plato's. Besides, if she is ambitious, maybe Nonnius guessed that and tried to apply pressure. He could have blackmailed her and demanded a cut. Since he'd already squealed once in court, he was a formidable threat; he only had to say he would inform on her too. She'd know he could very well mean it.'

'True.'

We were both uneasy. There was not enough to go on. We could only speculate. And although we were both good at making the facts fit in a situation, there was always the unexpected waiting to confound us. Like me, Petro had probably lost count of the times he had found out that the facts he had been working on for months were only marginal. The final story could be wildly different from any theories he had so carefully pieced together.

'Want any more to eat?'

I shook my head. 'No thanks. I had to leave without even saying good morning to Helena. If nothing else turns up, I'll be going home for lunch. Won't you?'

'Suppose so.'

My question had been ironic. I knew Petro always ignored lunch. He went home for dinner with his children in the evening, and sometimes he slipped off if there was a definite household job to do, like mending a window. He enjoyed carpentry. Otherwise, Petronius Longus was the type whose domestic life ran smoothest when he stayed out part of the night with the patrols, then lingered at the station house most of the day on follow-up. This applied most of all when Arria Silvia was furious with him for some reason.

I grinned. 'Thought you might need to feed the cat again.' He refused to rise.

It was still too early for lunch. A wise man doesn't stroll home halfway through the morning as if he has nothing else to do. He allows time for the cheese and olives to be bought and set out on the table, then he comes in looking as if he has made a special effort to fit in being with his family.

We discussed what we could do. Other than plug away with routine questioning, the answer seemed to be, not much. 'I really hate this part,' fretted Petro. 'Just sitting back, waiting for a tribe of rats to spring something.'

'They'll make a mistake in the end.'

'And how many have to suffer in the meantime?' He felt responsible.

'We both know it will be as few as you can make it. Listen, Rubella wanted me to check up on the Balbinus background in case anything was relevant to what's going on now.' At my mention of Rubella, Petro scoffed, though in a fairly routine manner. He had no particular grouse. He just hated officers.

He would hate Rubella rather more personally if he ever found out that thanks to him I was spying on the cohort for suspected graft.

I tried again. 'What about the Balbinus men?'

Petro answered this one quite calmly. 'As far as I know, Little Icarus, the Miller and all the rest of the mob are still out of Rome. Lying low. I have a pet squealer who lets me know their movements. I can nose him out and check, but if they had been seen in the city he would almost certainly have come to sell me the information.'

'When I interviewed Nonnius there was mention of the Balbinus family, which sounded interesting.'

Again Petro favoured me with a short bark of laughter. 'The wife's a mean bitch. Flaccida.'

'And there's a daughter?'

'The lovely Milvia! Their only child. She had education and culture lavished on her – a classic case of crooks with too much money trying to better themselves through their offspring.'

'Brought up like a vestal. So did she go to the bad?' I asked dryly. I had seen that happen.

'Funnily enough, not apparently. Milvia turned out as innocent as rosebuds – if you believe her version. She claims she never knew what her papa did for a living. She's been married off to an equestrian who had some money of his own – one Florius, son of a minor official. Florius never intended himself to be better than anyone. He goes to the races most of the time. I don't think he's ever been known to do anything else.'

'So he's not involved in criminal activities?'

'Other than having more money to bet with than anyone deserves, no.'

'There was a large dowry then.'

'Probably,' said Petro. 'Balbinus kept the details obscure. Suffice it to say, Milvia and Florius live in style, apparently having little to do with each other but both content to stick it out in harness. This leads me to suppose there is cash which they want to keep their hands on.'

'Fascinating. I might go and see these colourful folk.'

'I thought you might.'

Petronius would probably have come with me but just then a messenger from Rubella hurried up. Since Nonnius had been a judicial informer of some importance, his sudden death had caused questions from on high. Rubella wanted Petronius at the cohort headquarters to prepare a report.

Petro growled. 'This is how crimes go unsolved! Instead of asking painful questions of villains, I spend my time helping Rubella make up lies. Falco, if you're wandering among the Balbinus set, you ought to have a witness with you. I can't spare anyone just now. Wait until this afternoon and I'll find someone.'

'I don't need a nanny.'

'Take a witness!' he growled. 'With this bunch it's policy.'

'Is that why Fusculus made sure he came with me when I went to see Nonnius?'

'Fusculus is a decent, well-trained agent.'

Trained to interfere with me, apparently. Annoyed, I found the thought of cheese and olives reasserting itself. 'Well if I have to wait for a minder, I'll nip off home. Send whoever it is to Fountain Court, will you?'

'You're getting soft!' he snorted.

I wanted to explain that Helena was pregnant, but it seemed too soon after I had so firmly denied it. With yet more guilt depressing me, I left him to pacify his tribune while I sauntered off to see my girl.

XXXII

A small, serious figure greeted me as I turned into Fountain Court.

'Uncle Marcus! May Mercury god of the crossroads ever watch over you!'

Only Maia's eldest boy, Marius, ever sounded off so formally. He was a good-looking, extremely solemn little person, eight years old and completely self-possessed.

'*Io*, Marius! I was not expecting you until after afternoon school. Are you particularly fond of me, or just very short of money for pastries?'

'I've organised a rota for you. Cornelius will be on guard duty this afternoon, then Ancus. You should pay me, and I'll do the sharing out.' Maia had made all her children excellent foremen. Both I and my rubbish were in safe hands. But his mind appeared to be somewhere else. 'We have a crisis,' he announced, as if I were a partner in disaster. Marius believed in the sanctity of personal relationships: I was family; I would help.

The best help to offer was the sacred art of spotting trouble and bunking off the other way. 'Well I'm very busy on official business. But I'm always available if you need advice.'

'I'm afraid I'm heading for a row,' confessed Marius, walking with me towards the apartment. 'I expect you would like me to tell you what has transpired.'

'Frankly, Marius, one more problem and I'll buckle.'

'I rather hoped I could rely on you,' he said gloomily. Short of bopping him on the head with a baton and sprinting for cover, I was trapped.

'You're a hard master! Have you ever thought of becoming a bailiff?'

'No, I think I shall be a rhetoric teacher. I have the mind for it.'

Had he not borne his father's eyes (in a less bleary vision), I might have wondered whether Marius had been found under

590

the parapet of a bridge. Still, maybe young sobersides would grow up and fall in love with a tinker's by-blow, then run off to be a harp player.

I doubted it. Full of calm assurance, Marius saw the pitfalls of eccentricity and had simply turned his back on them. Sad really. The mind he spoke of with such respect deserved a more colourful fate.

We had reached the laundry. 'I'm going up, Marius. If you've something to tell me, this is the moment.'

'Tertulla's disappeared again.'

'Why fret? It happens all the time. Anyway, your grandma's taken her in hand.'

'It's true. This time I'll get the blame for it.'

'Nobody could possibly blame you for Tertulla, Marius. She's your cousin, not your sister, and she's beyond help. You're not responsible.' I wondered if he knew he had been supposed to be named Marcus, after me. When his father was sent to register his birth, Famia had dropped into several wine bars on the way to the Censor's Office, then he had misread the note Maia had sent him out with. This would have been bad enough once, but he had repeated his triumph when he registered his second son as Ancus instead of Aulus. When Maia gave birth to her daughters she dragged herself to the Censor's with him and made sure things were done right.

'Uncle Marcus, I think I'd better tell you what has happened.' The sight of a child confiding his problems was too much. Marius must have been relying on this, the cunning brat.

I sighed. 'You ought to be at home having your dinner.'

'I'm frightened to go.'

He didn't look very frightened, but it was unlike him to say it. 'Walk upstairs with me then.'

'Tertulla hasn't run away. She's too scared of Grandma. Grandma put me in charge of seeing her to school. It was really annoying. And then I was supposed to march her to lunch at her mother's house – '

'So she did go to school in the morning?'

'No, of course not!' scoffed Marius impatiently, scuttling after me around the third bend. 'She skipped off as soon as we arrived, but she promised to meet us all outside after lessons.'

591

'So what happened?'

'She never showed up. I think something bad has happened. I need you, Uncle Marcus. We'll have to conduct a search.'

'Tertulla's a minx and she's forgotten the time. She'll turn up.'

Marius shook his head. He had the same curls as me and Pa, yet somehow managed to make his look neat. I ought to ask him for hairdressing tips sometime. 'Look, Uncle, I have an interest in this problem since I shall be blamed for losing her. If you agree to search, I'll help you.'

'I don't agree!' I told him cheerfully. We had reached the apartment; I led him indoors. 'But I don't agree with a future rhetoric teacher being made a scapegoat for one of Galla's rascals either. Now here's Helena – '

'Oh good!' exclaimed Marius, with no attempt to disguise his relief. 'Somebody who will know what we should do!'

Helena came in from the balcony. She was carrying the skip baby. I grinned approvingly, but it was my nephew who risked his neck. Maia must have been talking at home about our own impending family because as soon as Marius saw the baby he shrieked, 'Oh goodness, Helena! Has Uncle Marcus brought you one in advance to practise on?'

She was not pleased.

XXXIII

I did not wait for Petro's promised agent to come with me to see the Balbinus relatives. My domestic cares were so pressing it seemed necessary to leave home as soon as I had swallowed lunch. I did take a witness, however.

'I miss you, Marcus,' Helena had complained.

This was an aspect of living together that had always worried me. Born into a class where the women spent their days surrounded by scores of slaves and visited by flocks of friends, Helena was bound to feel isolated. Senators' daughters were offered no other respectable daytime occupation than taking mint tea together, and though many preferred to forget being respectable and hung around gladiators, Helena was not that type. Living with me in a sixth-floor apartment must be frightening – especially when she often woke up to find I had rushed out without leaving a note of my plans. Some girls in this position might get too friendly with the janitor. Luckily Smaractus had never provided one. But if I wanted to keep her, I would have to produce some other option.

'I miss you too.' It sounded glib.

'Oh yes? And that's why you have deigned to come home?'

'That, and I have to wait to be supplied with a witness.' A thought struck me. 'You could take notes and listen as well as some silly coot from the vigiles.' She looked surprised. 'Wear a plain dress and no necklaces. Bring a stylus, and don't interrupt. I hate a secretary who talks smart.'

So Helena came with me. She was not one for staying at home with the domestic cares either.

It suited me to start investigating without one of Petro's minders lurking at my elbow, breathing my air, then reporting everything I did straight back to him. It certainly suited me to be out with my lass – more like leisure than work.

We sent Marius home to Maia's, telling him to confess his loss of Tertulla and to promise that if the girl was still missing

593

this evening Helena and I would organise a search from Fountain Court. Marius looked happier about owning up. He knew nobody would thump him once I was involved; they would rather wait for a chance of thumping me. We made him take the skip baby to his mother's for the afternoon. It was leading a busy life. Helena had found a wet nurse to feed it sometimes, while in between it went to Ma's house to be weaned on the gluey polenta that had produced my sisters, me and numerous sturdy grandchildren.

'Your mother agrees with me; there's something odd about the baby,' Helena said.

'You'd seem odd if you found yourself abandoned in a rubbish skip on the Aventine. Incidentally, I met Justinus this morning. He's in love with an actress, but I'll try to cure him of it. We are invited to a birthday dinner with your parents. I'm to have the extreme pleasure of being introduced to Aelianus.'

'Oh no!' cried Helena. 'I wanted my birthday to be fun!'

I always enjoyed discovering that relationships in patrician homes were as terrible as those in my own low family.

'There will be fun,' I promised. 'Watching your mother trying to be polite to me while your father hankers to nip off and hide in his library, your friendly brother nags me to teach him flirting with floosies, and your nasty brother flicks sauce in my eye should provide hours of jollity.'

'You go,' Helena urged despondently. 'I think I'll stay at home.'

Flaccida, the Balbinus wife, lived in a gorgeous gem of town architecture just south of the Circus Maximus, at the Temple of Ceres end. It was a rare residential block in the Eleventh district – well placed for the crime empire Balbinus had run along the Tiber waterfront. It lay in the lee of the Aventine but on a piece of land that was patrolled, along with the racecourse itself, not by Petro's cohort but by the Sixth.

At least, Flaccida was living there this week. A huge notice advertised that the spread was for sale; confiscated straight after the trial verdict. Flaccida would be moving house soon.

Indoors, everything echoed. The place was virtually empty, and it was not done for stylish effect. Only the fixed assets remained to show the opulent lifestyle master criminals enjoy: ravishing yardages of mosaic floor, endless perspectives in top-quality wall painting, meticulously plastered ceilings, fascinating shell grottoes that housed well-maintained fountains. Even the birdbaths were gilded.

'Nice place!' I remarked, though for me the columns were too massive and the artwork too frenetic.

'It was nicer when it was full.'

Flaccida was a short, thin woman, a blonde of sorts, about forty-five. From twenty strides away she would have looked fabulous. At six feet she showed signs of a troubled past. She wore a gown in material so fine its threads were tearing under the weight of its jewelled fastenings. Her face and hair were a triumph of cosmetic attention. But her eyes were restless and suspicious. Her mouth set in a hard, straight line. Her hands seemed too big for her arms. Size mattered here. On both wrists she wore bangles that were trying too hard to tell people how much they cost, and on her fingers two full rows of high-budget rings.

Naturally Flaccida was giving us the eyeball. I reckoned we would pass: whereas Helena had dressed down for the occasion, I had dressed up. Smartness always helps in gaining access to the houses of the wealthy. Anyone with a clean face is acceptable to thugs.

I wore my best white tunic, newly laundered, and even a toga, which I knew how to handle with an air. A recent shave and a faint splash of pomade announced status, a bold lie. A money purse clinked on my belt and I was flaunting my great-uncle's massive obsidian finger ring. Helena had followed me quietly. She was also in white, a straight gown with sewn sleeves and a plain woollen belt. She usually fixed her hair very simply, and she wore no jewels today apart from one insignificant silver ring that she never took off. Some might imagine her a slave. I tried to view her as a highly trained freedwoman inherited from an aunt. Helena herself seemed quite at ease, without being explained away.

I found a bland smile. 'I am working closely with Marcus Rubella, the tribune of the Fourth Cohort of vigiles.'

'So you're in the Prefect's Office?' Flaccida's voice had a smoky rasp that came from a misspent life in ill-lit places.

'Not really. I normally represent a more senior outfit . . .' Leaving it vague was easy. Half the time I didn't know who I was working for myself. 'I have some news to break, and I need to ask some questions.'

She pinched her mouth, but did gesture me impatiently to a seat. Her movements lacked grace. She dumped herself on a couch while I took its partner. They were handsome pieces in silver, with winged griffin armrests and sinuous backs, but they looked slightly too small for the room. We had found Flaccida in one more-or-less furnished salon, though as I settled in I noticed bare curtain rods. Shadowed lines on the wall showed where display shelves had been removed. Dark marks on the ceiling spoke of candelabra, though there were none now.

Helena had perched on the other end of my couch, with a note tablet on her knees. 'My assistant may take a few notes,' I informed Flaccida, who replied with a gesture of indifference. Interesting that she accepted Helena's presence so readily.

'What's this about?'

'Your husband, partly.'

'My husband is abroad.'

'Yes, I met him briefly as he was leaving. So how will you manage? I notice the house is up for sale.'

'I shall be living with my daughter and son-in-law.' Her tone was dry enough to elicit any sympathy we could find for her. She was still too young for that option. She was neither a widow nor divorced. Moving in with the youngsters was not going to work. Something about her manner suggested she would not even try to co-operate.

'Your daughter must be a great comfort,' I said. Without meeting her, I felt sorry for the girl.

'Get on with what you came for,' Flaccida snapped. 'What's the news you mentioned? Has somebody died?' Watching for any reaction, I told her it was Nonnius Albius. 'That traitor!' She said it fairly quietly. I happened to catch Helena's eye, and reckoned she thought that Flaccida had already known.

'I suppose you're glad to hear it?'

'Correct.' She was still speaking in a flat tone. 'He ruined my life.'

I decided not to waste my breath mentioning all the people whose lives had been ruined by the crime empire her husband had run. 'Nonnius was murdered, Flaccida. Do you know anything about it?'

'Only that I'd give whoever did it a laurel wreath.'

'He was tortured first. It was very unpleasant. I could tell you the details.'

'Oh I'd like that.' She spoke with a disturbing mixture of contempt and enjoyment. I found myself wondering whether Flaccida would herself be capable of ramming a wine bowl on a man's head and having the rest of him mutilated while he choked. She sat very still, scrutinising me through half-closed eyes. It was easy to imagine her presiding over horror.

Various pale maids were sitting in on the interview. A rapid scan indicated that most were undernourished, several had bruised arms, and one bore the remnants of a black eye. Flaccida's immaculate coiffure had been achieved with a level of violence that would not disgrace a gladiators' training school.

'Were you aware what kind of business your husband ran?'

'What I know is my affair.'

I kept trying. 'Have you seen any of the men who used to work with him recently? The Miller? Little Icarus? Julius Caesar, and that lot?'

'No. I never mixed with the work force.'

'Is it true they are all out of Rome?'

'So I heard. Driven out by the vigiles.'

'So you cannot say if any of them were behind the recent theft from the Emporium?'

'Oh, was there a theft?' cooed Flaccida, this time scarcely concealing her prior knowledge. The raid had certainly not been announced in the *Daily Gazette* as a national triumph, but word had galloped around the bathhouse circuit the same day. Flaccida was just giving us the routine false innocence of a regular villain.

'A big one. Someone who wants to be *very* big must have organised it.' Flaccida herself, for instance. If she had done it, though, she knew better than to signal the fact. I wondered how she would react to the notion of a female rival. 'Do you know Lalage?'

'Lalage?'

'Keeps the brothel called Plato's Academy.' Helena, who had not previously heard the popular name for the Bower of Venus, stifled a giggle. 'She's a business contact of your husband's.'

'Oh yes. I think I've met her.' They were probably best friends, but Flaccida would never admit it under official questioning. She would lie, even if there was no reason to do so. Lying was her way of life.

'Do you think Lalage might be trying to take over where your husband was forced to leave off?'

'How should I know? You'd better ask her.'

'Oh I've done that. She knows how to lie as well as you.' I changed tack wearily: 'Let's start again. Nonnius Albius, your husband's one-time associate, turned him in. It could be suggested that now your husband has left the Empire, you may be acting as his agent of revenge against Nonnius.'

This charge, though unproven, could go straight into the mouth of a prosecutor in a court of law. Flaccida started fighting back seriously. 'You have no right to make such suggestions to an unsupported woman.' Legally this was true. A woman had to have a male representative to speak for her in public. The answer was well rehearsed too. Not many women I knew would raise that objection. But not many of my associates needed to shelter behind the law.

'Quite right. I apologise.'

'Shall I strike the question from the record?' Helena interrupted demurely.

'I shouldn't think it matters, since the lady has not answered it.'

Helena smiled gently at my anger. She suggested, in a way that sounded straightforward but was actually sceptical, 'Perhaps Flaccida has a guardian acting for her now her husband is away?'

'I have a guardian and a battery of barristers, and if you want to ask questions about the business,' barked Flaccida, using the word 'business' as if the family were engaged merely in carving cameos or in scallop fishing, 'you can go through the proper procedures.'

'Make an appointment?' I grinned, but my tone was bitter.

'Send a prior written list of queries to some pompous toga who charges me five hundred just to tell me you cannot comment? Expect a writ for slander if I mention this discussion in public? Find myself barred from the Basilica Julia on some frivolous charge? Discover no one in the Forum wants to talk to me? Lose my clothes every time I go to the bath, find my mother's rent has been put up threefold, receive a summons from the army board of deserters, have mule dung shovelled into my doorway?'

'You've done this before,' smiled Flaccida. She was quite blatant.

'Oh I know how intimidation by the powerful works.'

'Lucky for you, you didn't tell me what your name is!'

'The name's Falco.' I could have used an alias. I refused to be dragged down to the level of fear these operators used. If they wanted to humiliate me, they would have to find me first. My normal clients were sadder and seedier; I was not well known amongst major criminals.

'And who's your friend?' This Flaccida was nasty work. It was a threat against Helena – and not a subtle one.

'No one you should tangle with,' I answered coolly.

'Unusual to see an official with a female scribe!'

'She's an unusual scribe.'

'I assume you sleep with her?'

'So long as it doesn't affect her handwriting . . .' I rose. 'I'm not intending to bother you further. I don't like wasting effort.'

'I don't like you,' Flaccida told me frankly. 'Don't harass me again!'

I said to Helena, 'Make a note that the wife of Balbinus Pius refused to answer routine questions, then described polite enquiry by a civil investigator as "harassment".'

'Get out!' sneered the more-or-less blonde.

In some circles the women are more fearsome than the men.

XXXIV

'Oh you really made a mess of that!' Helena Justina was furious with me. 'Is that how you normally conduct interviews?'

'Well, yes. With slight variations.'

'For instance, sometimes people throw you out right at the start?'

'Sometimes they never even let me in,' I admitted. 'But it can be easier than that was.'

'Oh? Sometimes the women are all over you?'

'Naturally a handsome lad like me gets used to asking questions while fending off attention.'

'Don't fool yourself. She slaughtered you!' growled Helena.

'Oh I wouldn't say that. But what a hard-faced hag! At least she gave us the full flavour of life among the big-time crooks: lies, threats, and legal bullying.'

We were standing in the street outside Flaccida's house, having a warm set-to. I didn't mind. Arguing with Helena always cheered me up. So long as she thought I was worth fighting, life still held some hope.

'You learned nothing from her, but you told her all the lines of enquiry you're pursuing – plus the fact you can't prove *any* of them! This is no good at all,' Helena continued crossly. 'We'll have to go and see the daughter. We'll have to go fast, before the mother sends to warn her, and when we get there, leave the talking to me this time!'

Investigating with Helena as my partner was wonderful fun. I gave way gracefully and we marched off to see the girl.

Milvia and her gambling husband, Florius, lived pretty close to her parents' house. Perhaps that was how Balbinus had come to notice the young equestrian on whom he had foisted his daughter. At any event, this house was even larger and more elaborate than the one where Flaccida had seen us off.

That probably meant we should expect an even more rapid dispatch here.

The husband was out. The girl saw us. She was about twenty, dark, sharp-faced, very pretty. Nothing at all like either of her parents. She was dressed in an extremely expensive gown of deep purple silk weave, with panels of silver-thread embroidery. None too practical for eating pears in a sloppy honey sauce, which was what she was doing. Somehow I doubted whether young Milvia had ever worried about a laundry bill. Her jeweller was more tasteful than her mother's; she was decked out in a complete set of antique Greek gold, including a neat little stephane on her crisply curled hair.

She saw us without any chaperone, so I could not check whether the maids who wielded the curling tongs in this mansion had to endure being thrashed if they misplaced a ringlet. Milvia had a bright, intelligent expression that suggested she could manage staff by guile. Or bribe them, anyway.

Taking charge firmly, Helena proffered a smile that would polish sideboards. 'I do apologise for bothering you – you must have lots to do. This is Didius Falco, who is conducting enquiries on behalf of an important committee. He'll be sitting here quietly while we have our chat, but you don't need to worry about him. It was thought that you might prefer to be interviewed by a woman, so that's why I'm here.'

'Anything I can do to help!' promised the bright-eyed, innocent daughter of gangsters, as if she was agreeing to assist in raising a subscription for a new shrine to Juno Matrona.

'Well, perhaps I can just make sure that I'm clear on one or two details . . . You're Balbina Milvia, daughter of Balbinus Pius and Cornella Flaccida, now married to Gaius Florius Oppicus?'

'Ooh that's me!' Apparently it was a great delight for little wide-eyes to find herself so well documented.

'Of course,' said Helena kindly, 'your recent family difficulties are known. It must have been a shock to discover the serious charges against your father?'

The pretty face clouded; the sweet mouth pouted slightly. 'I don't believe it,' Milvia protested. 'It's all lies made up by wicked enemies.'

601

Helena spoke in a low, stern voice. 'I wonder how you think your father made such enemies, though?' The girl shuddered. 'We cannot help our relations,' Helena sympathised. 'And sometimes it's hardest for those who are closest to see the truth. I know this from personal experience.' Helena had had an uncle who dabbled in treason, not to mention the husband she divorced, who had been a maniacal social menace. 'I understand that your father did ensure *you* had a perfect upbringing. I'm sure your husband thinks so too.'

'Florius and I are very close.'

'That's wonderful.' As this conversation proceeded I was more and more glad it was not me being obliged to maintain a sickly expression in the face of so much mush. I reckoned the girl was a complete sham. So long as she kept up the act consistently, it would be difficult to prove, however. 'My dear, you're clearly a credit to Rome, and I'm sure,' smiled Helena serenely, 'I can rely on you to help our enquiries . . .'

'Oh I'd love to be of use,' lilted the creditable citizen, stroking the lovely skirts that had been acquired for her with the proceeds of theft and extortion. 'Unfortunately, I know nothing at all about anything.'

'You may know more than you think!' Helena informed her decisively. 'Let me just ask a few questions, and we'll see.'

'Oh whatever you want.'

I personally wanted to upend the innocent protester over a knobbly log and thrash a conscience into her. Helena restrained herself. 'Let's think about your father's associates, Milvia. I'm sure you won't know this, but Nonnius Albius, who used to be your father's chief assistant, has just been found dead in rather ugly circumstances.'

'Oh goodness!'

'Have you seen Nonnius, or heard anything about him, since your father's trial?'

'Oh no!' burbled the dainty one.

'But you did know him?'

'He was a kind of uncle to me when I was small. I still can't believe the terrible things he's supposed to have done. And I can't believe he meant to go into court and make up those stories about Papa. His illness must have affected him. As

602

soon as he did it, I knew neither Mama nor I could ever meet him again. Mama hates him.'

'Yes, she told us that.' Somehow Helena made it sound as if she thought Flaccida and Nonnius must have been having a torrid affair. Whether little Milvia was receptive to this much irony seemed doubtful, but I was enjoying myself. 'Now,' Helena continued strictly, 'I want to ask you about some of the other members of your father's business. What can you tell me about people called Little Icarus and – who else is there, Falco?'

'The Miller, Julius Caesar – no relation, I'm told – and a couple of thugs called Verdigris and the Fly.'

'Ooh, I don't know any of them!' I knew from Petro that Balbinus used to run his empire from home; the thugs I mentioned must have been in and out of his house all the time. Milvia was either lying, or very dim indeed. 'They sound horrible – '

'They are,' I said tersely.

Milvia turned to Helena, looking flustered and seeking protection. 'Tell him I don't have anything to do with such people.'

'She doesn't have anything to do with such people,' Helena told me dryly. Milvia had the grace to look worried that her interrogator was so unmoved. Helena Justina possessed natural politeness (when she chose to employ it). Underneath she was shrewd and tough. Normally it was me she liked to screw to the floor with the toughness; watching her tackle someone else made a pleasant change. I had to admit she was doing it well – even though the answers were disappointing. 'Tell me now,' Helena continued relentlessly, 'have you ever met a rather exotic businesswoman called Lalage?'

'I don't think so. What business is she in?'

'She keeps a brothel.' Helena's voice was calm.

'Oh no!' shrieked the shocked moppet. 'I've never met anyone like that!'

'Neither have I,' said Helena reprovingly. 'But one ought to be aware that such places and people exist.'

'Especially', I interjected, 'when such places have funded one's education and stocked one's dowry chest! If she denies knowledge of rents from brothels, ask Balbina Milvia where she thinks her family's money came from?'

Helena gave Milvia a questioning look, and the girl muttered, 'From some kind of trade, I suppose.'

'Very good. From selling stolen property, and percentages on prostitution.'

'Excuse me, Falco.' It was Helena's interview; I subsided quietly. 'Is trading your husband's background?' Helena queried thoughtfully.

'I believe his father was a tax-farmer.'

I nearly burst out laughing. For the first time ever, I felt tax-farming was a clean occupation.

'And what does Florius do?' asked Helena.

'Oh Florius doesn't need to work.'

'That must be nice for him. How does he spend his time, Milvia?'

'Oh this and that. Whatever men do. I don't need to set spies on him!'

'Why? Don't you care?' I challenged her. 'He might be with women.'

She blushed prettily. 'I know he's not. He's socialising with his menfriends.'

'Any chance the menfriends he's so pally with might be criminals?'

'No.' Again Milvia threw an anguished appeal at Helena, as if she hoped for protection from my unjust accusation. 'Florius goes to the baths, and the races, and he talks with people in the Forum, and looks at art in the porticoes – '

'Nice!' I said. It did not preclude a career in crime as well. All those activities were routine features of Roman life – and all could provide ideal cover for organising a major network in the underworld.

'So Florius is a man of the world,' mused Helena. 'A man of affairs.' Florius kept his hands clean while he spent what his own forebears had earned and what his wife with the nasty relations had brought him in return for sharing his respectability. He sounded a typical middle-class parasite.

'Who is your father's heir?' I asked abruptly.

'Oh goodness, I have no idea!' Thanks, Milvia. Well up to standard.

At that point a slave entered bearing a salver on which were presented the young lady's mid-afternoon tipple and the

604

dainty bronze cup she was to drink it from. Milvia handed over her empty fruit bowl (a heavy gilt item with finely chased bacchanal scenes). The maid poured her a dash of rich-looking red wine, headily infused with spices that clogged the strainer that filtered them. Cold water was added from a glass jug. We were invited to join her, but we both refused. Helena drank only with me; I never drank with other women when Helena was present. I also hated to have my wine thinned down so much.

'What a wonderful water jug!' cried Helena, who rarely commented on chattels when we visited strangers' homes.

'Do you like it?' Milvia grabbed it from the tray, poured the contents into a vase of flowers, and handed it to Helena. 'Do accept it as a present!'

The offer was so spontaneous I found it hard to think she was bribing us. The maid looked unsurprised. Balbina Milvia must be one of those girls who showered over-expensive gifts on everyone she came into contact with. The only child of people who moved in a restricted and secretive circle, a circle from which she herself had been shielded, she probably found it hard to make acquaintances. Her husband had little to do with her. Their social life was no doubt limited. If we could have believed she was genuinely ignorant of her father's world, we might have felt quite sorry for the girl.

Even I managed a smile as Helena turned to show me the beautiful jug. 'You're very generous. This is a fine piece. Did you buy it in Rome?'

'A family friend gave it to my husband.'

'Somebody with excellent taste. Who was that?' I kept my voice light as I took the article from Helena.

'Oh just a well-wisher. I don't know his name.'

'Won't your husband mind you giving it away?'

'He didn't seem to like it much. We haven't had it long,' replied Milvia.

About two days, I reckoned. I decided not to press the point until I had consulted Petronius, but sooner or later guileless little Milvia would have to supply the well-wisher's name. When Petro saw what she had handed over so gaily, he would probably want to search her house for more – and it would not be because he admired her choice of wineware.

What I was carefully holding was a delicate glass water jug in a translucent white, around which trailed fine spirals of dark blue; it had a twisted, twin-thread applied handle and a neat, pinched spout.

'Very fine,' Helena repeated. 'I should say that it was Syrian, wouldn't you, Marcus Didius?'

'Undoubtedly.' I could say more. Unless it was a double, this was one of the pieces Helena had bought at Tyre for my father; one taken in the Emporium raid.

I would not normally have permitted a stranger to make a present to Helena Justina. On this occasion there was no argument. We took the jug away with us.

XXXV

'Well, that's how to do it,' Helena preened herself, as we walked back over the Aventine towards Fountain Court.

'I'm deeply impressed! If I had only approached the mother with your conciliatory line, who knows what luxuries we might have acquired for the home!' I made the idea of a present from Flaccida sound disgusting.

Helena ducked under a row of buckets hanging in a shop portico. 'I admit our discovery was an accident. I'm not unreasonable.'

'You're a gem.'

'Well I prised out more information than you did.'

'You got no information, Helena! The mother refused to help us; the daughter batted her fine lashes, promised to give us anything we asked for, but then denied any knowledge to give. Different tactic; same useless results.'

'She seems genuine, Marcus. She cannot have known the water jug was stolen.'

'She cannot have known it was stolen from *us*!' I corrected. I sounded like some old pedantic Roman paterfamilias. Helena skipped down a kerbstone and laughed at me.

I couldn't skip. I was carrying the stolen jug.

While Helena repaired to Maia's to collect our abandoned baby and check whether Tertulla had turned up again, I took the glassware to the station house and exhibited the gorgeous thing. Petro weighed it in his great paw while I sweated pints in case he dropped it. 'What's this?'

'A present from Milvia. Last time I saw this, it belonged to Pa.'

'You've questioned Milvia? That's quick. I only just sent Porcius over to your house.'

'I work fast,' I said smoothly, not telling him I took my own witness. 'The girl claims she and Florius had it as a "gift from a well-wisher".'

'Believe her?'

'I stopped believing girls when I was about fourteen.'

My old friend was not a man who rushed in without preparation. He thought this through carefully. 'The glass jug was one Geminus had stolen. Now it's been found with Milvia and Florius, but we don't know how it came there – '

'It's always possible sweet little Milvia acquired it legitimately,' I pointed out. 'An innocent purchase, or genuine gift.'

'Don't annoy me, Falco! But it might be all she has.'

'I hope not. There was a matching beaker set,' I remembered bitterly.

Petro carried on doggedly, now instructing his men: 'I don't want to force the issue and bungle it, but I do want to see what else they've got. What we'll do is conduct house searches of all the major criminals, then we'll add in Flaccida and Milvia. We'll go in as if it was a routine result of the Emporium raid. We'll probably net a few interesting trophies anyway, so it won't be wasted. Falco won't be there. We won't mention Milvia's water jug at this stage.'

'That sounds sensible. There's been time for the raiders to share out the loot, but I'd assumed most of it would go for sale.'

'Falco's right,' Petro conceded. 'We'll raid a few hot-property shops at the same time.' Turning to Martinus he added, 'Try to find out what new receivers have opened up recently, so we don't miss any.'

'Keep your eyes peeled for one item that is not on your theft list,' I said gloomily. 'It's gold, and it cost a fortune, believe me!' I described Helena's birthday present carefully while they all listened with expressions of rapt attention – all of them mocking my extravagance. 'It was among Pa's load of glass, but he won't have mentioned it to Martinus because he didn't know I had hidden it.'

'Bribe for a mistress?' enquired Fusculus, looking innocent.

'Birthday gift for Helena. I've got a day to find it – or pay up twice.'

'Why not explain to Helena and hope to find the original soon?' Petro suggested. 'That girl is strangely understanding where you're concerned.'

'Helena is not the problem. I have to come up with something, and it has to be spectacular so her damned family don't sneer. Her mother for one will be expecting me to let Helena down.'

'Oh it's the *mother* he's trying to impress!' Petro murmured wickedly to Fusculus.

Fusculus sagged his jaw into a sorrowful grimace. 'Explain to the man, chief – the mother *never* comes around!'

Since I was not needed for the searches I left Petro and Fusculus shaking their heads over my predicament while I set off on errands of my own. The jug stayed at the station house, which was just as well or it might have ended up in pieces before the day ended.

I called at my father's house, knowing he would be at the Saepta Julia. That suited me. I left messages with his domestic staff saying we had recovered one of his Syrian treasures, and explaining about my need for a gift for Helena. Now Pa would know it was her birthday; he would try to inflict himself on us to celebrate, but as we were promised at her parents' house we could escape that. Leaving, I popped in at Mother's. She was out too, but I made sure a nosy neighbour saw me so word would reach Ma. Brilliant. I had made duty calls on both my parents, without the trouble of seeing either.

Back to Fountain Court. I waved at Cassius, noticing that somebody had suddenly taken over the ground-floor shop lease opposite his bakery, the one Helena and I had looked at briefly before we spotted our preferred new abode. Some sort of mixed hardware was now being offered for sale from the lockup, though I didn't take note of what. My own new let, which I ran up to and inspected by daylight, was looking as if we could make something respectable of it. At street level, the skip had lost several items to desperate scavengers, but I had gained little more; I was winning on that. I now felt like a juggler who was keeping the balls in the air. Overconfident, I made the mistake of letting Lenia see me as I crossed to walk upstairs.

'Falco! We need to discuss arrangements!'

'Like, how can you be persuaded to jilt the bridegroom?'

'You never give up.'

'I don't want to find myself in two months' time being

harassed to suggest grounds for divorce so you can claw your dowry back. Getting evidence on Smaractus will be more sordid than anything I've ever had to do.'

'He's just a colourful character,' Lenia sulked.

'He's a disaster.'

'He just needs to settle down.'

'In a dung heap,' I said.

After that I was allowed to leave without discussing the auguries at all.

I took the stairs at a cheerful pace, pausing only to instruct the stray dog called Nux not to follow me up. She was a tufty mongrel in several colours, with limpidly soulful eyes. Something about her big furry paws and her whiskery face had a dangerous appeal. I sped off fast to discourage her.

By now it was well into the afternoon, so everywhere was fairly quiet in the lull after siesta and before the mens' baths grew busy. The apartments I passed sounded more peaceful than they were sometimes; fewer screaming children, fewer distressed adults. The smells seemed less obnoxious. I could almost convince myself that though the building was shabby and overcrowded, its landlord did deserve a chance at normal life ... This was no good. Being dragged in to act at the nuptials was shaking my cynical view. I knew what it was: playing the priest for Lenia and Smaractus was making me feel responsible for their future wellbeing.

Cursing, I leapt up the stairs on the fourth and fifth flights several at a time. I wanted to leave the laundry and its crazy proprietress behind as fast as possible. At the top I slowed. An automatic instinct for caution led me to silence my steps.

Somebody else was making a noise, though. As I reached the final landing I heard a man shouting anxiously. Then Helena screamed, 'No! Oh no!'

I crossed the landing in two strides. The door stood open. I shot through it, out of breath from the stairs yet ready for anything.

The voice I had heard belonged to Porcius, Petro's young recruit. He was holding up one hand, trying to calm the situation. It was well beyond him. Two ugly brutes whose violent intentions were unmistakable had invaded the apartment, probably not long before I arrived. One leering thug, a huge collection of sinew, was laughing at Porcius as the lad tried to reason with him. The other man was menacing Helena; he was holding our rubbish-skip baby by his tiny wrists and swinging him backwards and forwards like a pegged napkin on a windy washing line.

'I'm not Falco, and that's not their child!' Porcius attempted valiantly.

From the doorway I roared, '*I'm Falco!*'

The giant spun to face me, a terrifying prospect. I had pulled out my knife, but I had to drop it. The small man had hurled something at me. I dropped my knife because I had to catch his missile – and I had to catch it right: the bastard had thrown the babe at me.

XXXVI

I caught him and turned him upright. The baby was screaming but I didn't think he had broken any bones or been crushed. Still, he wanted everyone to know he was outraged. Without letting my eyes give away my intentions, I tried frantically to think of somewhere I could put him down. The only place was the table; I could not get to it.

Fighting for time, I tried to calm the atmosphere. 'Good afternoon!' I saluted the unknown visitors. 'Are you melon-sellers, or just passing financiers trying to interest us in a favourably priced loan?' The two bullies stared. A jest was my only weapon now; they looked unimpressed. Meanwhile the skip baby grabbed me around the throat in a stranglehold, but he did stop crying. 'I'm afraid you must leave,' I continued hoarsely. 'My doctor has advised me against acid fruit, and we're a household that avoids debt on religious grounds.'

'You're Falco!' It was the small man who owned the voice. The brain it went with must be a slow one. His voice was harsh; his tone arrogant. His friend didn't need to talk. The large fellow only had to stand there pulling and clicking his finger joints in order to contribute to this conversation quite successfully.

I managed to loosen the babe's grip and snatched some air. 'What do you want?'

'A word.' I could tell what they really wanted was to kick me in the ribs. The smaller man spat deliberately into a dish of newly peeled boiled eggs. These were very unpleasant people. Helena seethed, and he grinned at her.

He was exceptionally small. Not a dwarf; perfectly proportioned, but a good foot less than average. A statue would not have revealed his problem, but not even his mother would want to commission a statue of this villain. They could afford it, though, judging by the torque-style bracelets on his upper arms. And he wore signet rings so solid they were more like growths than jewellery.

'Who sent you?'

'You don't need to know.'

'I'll find out.' I glanced at Helena. 'Something tells me, love, that somewhere today we upset someone!'

'You're upsetting us!' the first man commented.

'And you're going to back off!' growled the wide man. His voice rumbled deeply, rich with the remembered pleasure of torturing people who ignored what he said. Shaved hair and unclean skin were his badges of toughness. Massive shoulders were bursting through the strained skeins of a worn-out tunic. He liked to show his teeth in a neat white rectangle when he talked. He nearly filled the room.

'Back off what?' I answered pleasantly. 'Exactly which group of uncompromising social misfits have you been sent to represent?'

I saw Helena close her eyes in despair, thinking this the wrong attitude. Apologising meekly would have done no better, and I knew it. The men had come to terrorise us; they would not leave until they saw us cowering. They would enjoy inflicting pain. With a pregnant woman, an innocent rookie and a baby to answer for, my main interest was making sure it was me they chose to damage.

There were two of them and three of us, but we were outranked in power. There seemed no way I could get us out of this, yet I had to try. I would have liked to tackle the small man first, but there was no space to move; my scope for action was limited.

I said, 'I think you should leave.' Then I passed the baby to Porcius and squared up as the wide man came for me.

It was like being tackled by an altar stone on legs. Like a marble slab full in the guts, he caught me in a wrestling hug. His grip was unbearable, and he was not even trying yet.

The baby screamed again. The small man spun around to Helena. He grabbed her. Porcius slipped the child out onto the balcony, then he jumped on Helena's attacker from behind and tried to pull him off. Porcius was yelling, which might have brought help, had any one of my fellow tenants been the type to notice murder happening. They were deaf. We had to sort this out ourselves.

The others skirmishing did slightly distract my man. I

forced my elbows outwards just enough to get my hands down low. I used the squeeze. I used both hands. The wide man's face creased into an angry grimace, but my attempt to pestle his privates had no other visible effect. I was for it. He lifted me off my feet merely by expanding his chest. He would have raised me overhead, but the room was too small. Turning slowly, he prepared to crash me against a wall instead. I glimpsed Porcius staggering backwards; he had yanked the small man away from Helena. They fell against us; the wide man changed his mind about making wall decoration out of me; Porcius and his captive bounced off again.

The wide man kept his hold, but swung me back the other way. Now I was to be a weapon; he was intending to attack Porcius using me as a battering ram.

Suddenly Helena grasped a hot pan of broth from the cooking bench. She upended the vessel over the small man so that the scalding liquor flowed down his face and neck.

Porcius saw her coming; he let go and sprang back just in time. The small man became a shrieking mess. The wide one shifted his grip on me. He seemed genuinely troubled by his friend's cries of agony. I was fighting back now. I was doing everything right. It was hopeless – like trying to mould set concrete with bare hands.

Porcius rushed back, punched the small man a few times, then he and Helena started battering the fellow to chase him out of doors, Helena now trying to brain him with the pan's red-hot iron base. He was still yelling, and trying to get away. Somehow he found my fallen knife. Next minute he was crouching and making vicious feints with the blade. Helena and Porcius pressed back against the balcony door. Even scalded and trying to pluck boiling-hot lentils from his tunic neck, he was dangerous.

I was in deep trouble. Every move I made brought me closer to asphyxiation. I pushed the heel of one hand beneath the wide man's chin, forcing his head back as far as possible. He pulled a face like a demonic mask, but continued to crush me. My other arm seemed useless; he had badly mauled it. I started losing consciousness.

Then I was aware of other people rushing up the stairs outside. Helena was crying out for help. I heard tramping feet. Suddenly something flew through the air to fasten itself on the great arm that was crushing my head. The wide man yelled and tried to shake himself free; I slid to the floor. My saviour was Nux, her jaws clamped on my attacker, though she still growled loudly.

The room filled up with shrieking women. The small man dropped the knife; I grabbed it. I lurched to my feet. Without waiting, I plunged my knife into the side of the wide man's neck. It was a poor blow. There was no time to aim, and he was too large to stop with one stab wound anyway. But it hurt. The blood gushed – always worrying.

'You're dead!' I snarled (though I doubted it). He brushed at the cut like a man swatting wine flies – one-handed, because the dog Nux was still hanging on to his other arm with rigidly clenched jaws. The more he hurled her about, the more fiercely the creature clung on.

A boy slipped through the crush – my nephew Marius. He leapt for the balcony and let out a piercing whistle. 'Up here, officers – and be quick!' He was apparently calling down to a troop of vigiles.

It was all too much. A landing full of extra witnesses – my mother, sister Maia, and Marius – was unwelcome even to our visitors. There was no space for beating anyone up properly. And now Marius had summoned further help. The two of them decided that if the vigiles were coming up they had better rush down. With a mighty effort, the wide one forced the dog's jaws apart and flung her to the floor.

'Be wise, idiot!' he shouted at me. Then both men took a run for the door (chased by the little dog, barking ferociously). They barged past Ma and Maia, and thundered downstairs.

Porcius grabbed the dog by its neck fur and dragged her in as he slammed the door. Nux flung herself against it, still trying to chase the villains. Now tearful, Marius threw himself on me. 'There, there! They've gone now, Marius.'

'When they reach ground level they'll realise I was whistling at thin air.'

When they reached ground level they would be exhausted. One was covered in blood, even if his wounds were far from fatal. The other was quite seriously scalded. 'Trust me, they've gone. You were a brave boy.'

'They'll be back,' commented Ma.

'Not tonight.'

We took precautions, then we men started clearing up while the women exclaimed over the incident. I thanked the recruit for his help. 'You're a bright lad, Porcius! Where did Petro discover you?'

'I was a cold-meat-seller's son.'

'Wanted to clean up society?'

'Wanted to get away from pickled brains!'

Helena had brought in the baby from his refuge on the balcony. She passed him to me; I jiggled him comfortingly, using one arm, though I soon handed him to Ma, for reasons of my own. As his screaming subsided, I watched Helena anxiously. Her face was white, but she seemed calm as she swept her hair up tidily and refixed two side combs just above her ears. We two would talk after the rest had left.

As I felt my body surreptitiously, checking for permanent damage, I noticed Ma staring at Helena. There was nothing to suggest Helena was feeling bilious, but Ma's face tightened. Sometimes she piped up at once when she recognised a secret; sometimes it pleased her more to keep quiet. I winked at Helena. Ma said nothing. She didn't know we knew she knew.

Helena looked around the disordered room. Catching her eye, the little dog leapt straight into her arms, licking her frantically. As a jumper it could have won a crown at the Olympic Games.

'I am not adopting a dog,' I tried instructing them both sternly.

Helena still clutched the mad bundle of fur. The dog was full of life. Well, she was now she saw a chance of worming her way into a cosy home. 'Of course not,' Ma said, finding a space to sit down and recover. 'But the dog seems to have adopted you!'

'Maybe you could train her to guard your clothes at the baths,' suggested Porcius. 'We get a lot of theft. It can be very embarrassing to come out naked and find your tunic's gone.'

'Nobody pinches old rags like the tunics I wear!'

Ma and Maia were fussing over Marius. Glad to have someone even younger to look down on, Porcius chucked his chin. 'You're a quick thinker, Marius! If your uncle's still in this business when you grow up, you could make him a fine assistant.'

'I'm going to teach rhetoric,' insisted Marius. 'I'm grooming my brother to work with our uncle.'

'Ancus?' I laughed at the way I was being set up. 'Will he be any good?'

'He's useless,' Marius said.

Life's a basket of eggs; I invariably pick out the one that's cracked.

Ma and Maia had arrived at a lucky moment, but now I had time to think about it I knew there must be a reason, one I didn't like. 'Thanks for interrupting the festivities, but what brought you? Don't tell me Tertulla's still lost?' They nodded, looking grim. Maia reminded me I had promised to organise a search party, and gave me the fabulous news that most of my brothers-in-law – a crass gang of idlers and idiots – would be turning up shortly to assist. I groaned. 'Look, she's always running off. I've got enough on at the moment. Does a naughty child call for all this fuss?'

'She's seven years old,' Maia rebuked me. In silence we all thought about the brutal assaults that could be inflicted on a child.

'Something's happened.' Mother pursed her lips. 'If you can't help us, perhaps you can suggest what the rest of us can do?'

'I'll help!' I snarled.

'Oh you're busy. We don't want to trouble you!'

'I said I'll help!'

Porcius looked curious. 'Is this something for the vigiles?'

'Missing child.'

'We've had a lot of those lately.'

'Do they turn up?' I asked.

'They seem to. The parents arrive in hysterics demanding house-to-house investigations, then they come in again looking sheepish, and saying the little one was just at Auntie's, or out looking for excitement . . .' That would have sorted the issue, had he not gone on to report, 'Petro did think there might be a pattern, but we've never had time to look into it.'

I said, 'Anyone who kidnaps Tertulla will hand her back pretty quick.'

'Don't joke,' retorted Helena, beating Maia to it by half a breath.

Sighing, I promised to draw up a regular plan for searching. To start with, Helena and my sister could prepare a description for the vigiles. We might as well involve the patrols.

I would have showed more enthusiasm, but I was trying to hide the fact I was in pain and next to panicking myself. My left arm still hung limp. I was afraid I had suffered permanent harm from the wide man. Porcius finally noticed my distracted air. 'Oh Falco! You've been nadgered – something's up with your collarbone.'

I raised an eyebrow. That was still working anyway. 'You a medical man?'

Porcius said, 'Recognising damage was the first part of our training in the vigiles.'

Helena was upset, mostly because she herself had failed to notice my disablement. Porcius told her he would fetch Scythax, the cohort doctor, to look at me. Suddenly I was being treated like an invalid. When Helena went into the bedroom for a blanket to wrap me in, I told Porcius in a low voice that we ought to have followed the intruders and tried to discover who they were.

Porcius looked dismayed, but then he smiled. He was tall, well built in a youthful way, and had a rosy glow beneath his outdoor tan. Helping out in the fight, he seemed to have gained confidence. 'I think I know who they were,' he assured me. 'I haven't met them before, but I bet those two were the Miller and Little Icarus.'

I was right. I had offended someone – someone I should have left alone. The problem with Tertulla might have to wait. This was far more serious.

XXXVII

Porcius went off to fetch Scythax and report to Petronius the bad developments.

Porcius and I had exchanged a few thoughts: 'If you're right, and I have every confidence in your judgement, Porcius – ' he blushed happily – 'we now know that some of the Balbinus men are back in Rome. That probably means they all are.'

'That makes them suspects for the Emporium raid,' offered the young recruit. A fast thinker. Good material. Even in the aftermath of a fight he was piecing together the evidence.

I was thinking myself. 'Interviewing Lalage, I was with Petro as a member of the cohort. She has no reason to single me out for special treatment. Apart from Nonnius – who's out of it – the Balbinus females are the only people I've visited on my own. The fact that it's the Miller and Little Icarus who were sent to put me off does point to this being in the family.' I was convinced this had happened because I had asked too many questions of Flaccida and Milvia. The speed with which they had tracked me down was worrying. I kept that to myself. 'Maybe we can forget the other gangs. Maybe Petro cut the head off the Balbinus organisation but the body's still active. We'll have to find out who's running it now, Porcius.' For the safety of my household, we needed to find out fast.

'Do you really think it could be the wife or the daughter, Falco?'

'Or the son-in-law. I haven't met him yet.'

'Or Lalage,' Helena put in, refusing to give up her theory. 'She could easily have taken over the services of the Miller and company.'

Porcius and I exchanged a surreptitious glance. Face it: it was easier for us to accept that the Balbinus organisation had been hijacked by his deadboat thugs themselves than that it was masterminded by women. Even women as hard-baked as Flaccida and Lalage.

619

Neither Porcius nor I were intending to say this to Helena Justina. She came from the same stern mould that had produced the warrior-queen Tanaquil, Cornelia, Volumnia, Livia, and other tough matrons who had never had it mentioned to them that they were supposed to be inferior to men. Personally I like women with ideas. But you have to be genteel when you're teaching a recruit about life on the streets.

'The Miller and Little Icarus can't be very bright,' Helena said. 'They were frightening, but if they have sneaked back to Rome to run the show they ought to lie low, not draw attention to themselves. Flaccida struck me as clever enough to realise that.'

'Right! So we're back with Lalage as the queen of intelligent activity!' I smiled at her.

Or with somebody we had not thought of yet.

Scythax came quickly. Porcius had made it to the station house in one piece. I had warned him to keep his eyes peeled when he hit street level. He must have told his story with some urgency, for the physician was with us by return. Porcius came back with him, to show him the right house. Petro had sent two members of the foot patrol as guards too. He had recognised the danger I was in.

Scythax was a brusque Oriental freedman who seemed to suspect malingering. This was understandable. The vigiles patrol-men were always trying to dodge off sick; given the dangers of their work, no one could blame them. Scythax expected people to cry ouch as soon he entered a room; he viewed 'headaches', 'bad backs' and 'old knee trouble' with little patience. He had heard it all before. To get sympathy from Scythax you had to produce a bright red rash or a hernia: something visible or proddable.

He did concede that my shoulder and arm were genuinely out of action. He was delighted to inform me the shoulder joint was merely dislocated. His treatment would be to manipulate it back into place.

He did this. 'Manipulate' had sounded a gentle enough word. In fact the manoeuvre involved working on me with a brute force that the Miller would have been proud of. I should have realised that when Scythax told Helena and Ma to grip my feet so I couldn't kick out, while Porcius was to throw himself on my chest with all his weight. Scythax immediately attacked me, bracing his foot against the wall as he leaned back and pulled.

It worked. It hurt. It hurt a lot. Even Ma had to sit down fanning herself, and Helena was openly in tears.

'There's no fee,' Scythax condescended amiably.

My mother and my girlfriend both made comments that seemed to surprise him.

To smooth over the angry atmosphere (since he really had mended my shoulder), I managed to gasp, 'Did you see the body the patrol brought in this morning?'

'Nonnius Albius?'

'You know of him?'

Scythax peered at me rather wryly, packing away his equipment. 'I keep abreast of the cohort's work.'

'So what did you think?'

'What Petronius Longus suggested: the man had been tormented, mostly while he was still alive. Many of the wounds were not fatal in themselves. Somebody had inflicted them to cause pain – it looked like punishment. That fits his position as a squealer who had betrayed his chief.'

And it called for the same list of suspects as the people who might have taken over afterwards: the Balbinus women, the other gang members, and Lalage.

'He was very ill,' I mentioned, as the doctor reached the door. 'Were you able to tell what might have been wrong with him?'

Scythax reacted oddly. An expression that could almost have been amusement crossed his face, then he said, 'Nothing much.'

'He was supposed to be dying!' Helena exclaimed in surprise. 'That was the whole reason Petronius was able to persuade him to give evidence.'

'Really?' The freedman was dry. 'His doctor must have been mistaken.'

'His doctor's called Alexander.' I was already growing suspicious. 'I met him at the house. He seemed as competent as any other Aesculapius.'

'Oh Alexander is an excellent doctor,' Scythax assured me gravely.

'Do you know him, Scythax?'

I was prepared for rivalry, or professional solidarity, but not for what I learned instead: 'He is my brother,' said Scythax.

Then he smiled at us like a man who was far too long in the tooth to comment, and left.

I caught the eye of Petro's impressionable recruit. His mouth had dropped open as he worked out, slightly slower than I did, the implication of the cohort doctor's last remark. I said softly, 'That's a lesson to you, Porcius. You're working for a man who is not what he seems. I'm talking about Petronius Longus. He has a mild-mannered reputation – behind which lurks the most devious, evil-minded investigation officer anywhere in Rome!'

XXXVIII

Maia was the kind of organiser generals love. She had put terror into the men of our family. Their response to her instructions to converge on Fountain Court to search for little Tertulla was mindless obedience; even Marius, the dedicated scholar, had abandoned his grammar homework. I was impressed. My brothers-in-law arrived all at once – all except the water boatman, Lollius. He was the missing child's father. It was too much to expect that creep to take an interest. Not even Galla, his wife, ever expected any support from Lollius.

The other four were bad enough. What a gang! In order of my sisters' seniority, they were:

Mico. The unemployed, unemployable plasterer. Pasty-faced and eternally perky. He was bringing up five children on his own, now his wife Victorina had died. He was doing it badly. Everyone felt obliged to say at least he was trying. The children would have stood more chance of surviving if he sailed off to Sicily and never came back. But Mico defended his useless role like a fighter. He would never give up.

Verontius. Allia's treasure. A shifty, untrustworthy road contractor who smelt of fish pickle and unwashed armpits. You would think he had been heaving shovels all day long when all he really did was codge together contracts. No wonder he sweated. The lengths he went to to defraud the government were tortuous. A glance at Verontius looking half-asleep and guilty was enough to explain all the potholes in the Via Appia.

Gaius Baebius. Utter tedium. A ponderous customs-clerk organiser who thought he knew it all. He knew nothing, especially about home improvements, a subject on which he liked to expound for hours. Gaius Baebius had brought Ajax, his and Junia's spoiled, uncontrollable watchdog. Apparently some clown had decided Ajax could sniff one of Tertulla's shoes, then trace her movements. Gaius and Ajax arrived in a lather of paws and untidy black fur, then we had to lock Nux in my bedroom to stop Ajax attacking her (he already had a history of violence).

Famia. Maia's darling was the best of the bunch, though I have to report Famia was a slit-eyed, red-nosed drunk who would have regularly cheated on Maia if he could have found the energy. While she brought up their children, he whiled away his life as a chariot-horse vet. He worked for the Greens. I support the Blues. Our relationship could not and did not flourish.

Everyone milled around noisily to start with. Some of the brothers-in-law looked as if they had hoped we would give up the idea of a search and all sit down with an amphora. Helena disabused them crisply. Then we had the inevitable jokes about the skip baby, mostly suggesting he was some unfortunate relic of my bachelor past. I dealt with that one. There was one good side to my male relations. Since they were married to my sisters, they had all learned to be swiftly subdued by sarcasm.

As there was no one else at home to look after the children (except his old mother, who had gone to play dice tonight at a caupona by the Temple of Isis), Mico had brought his three youngest. These unpleasant mites had to be kept amused, given copious drinks, and protected from Gaius and Junia's dog.

'He loves children!' protested Gaius Baebius, as Ajax strained at the flimsy string on his collar and tried to reduce Mico's family to something he could bury under Gaius' home-built sun-yourself pilastered breakfast patio. Then Ajax was offered a shoe, so he could do his stuff as a tracker. He just worried the shoe, thinking it was a dead rat. Gaius Baebius blustered about, looking embarrassed and blaming everyone else.

Helena took charge, supported by young Marius. They gave each brother-in-law a sector to search, and ordered them to question shopkeepers and locals whether anyone had seen Tertulla earlier that day; then they organised my various nephews to act as runners if any information were found.

'You coming, Falco?'

'Marcus has been gated.' Helena made out that I had been

seriously wounded that day. I know how to look pale in a crisis; I had been in the army for seven years. The mob dispersed without me. Gaius took his watchdog. Mico's children clung to their father and left with him. Silence descended. Helena started spooning porridge into the skip baby. It would be a long, messy process. I went into my bedroom for a quiet lie-down. I wanted to think about the interesting information that the physician who had told Nonnius Albius he was dying had lied to him, and that that physician just happened to have a brother working in the public sector – alongside Petronius.

As soon as I stretched out, easing my sore arm, Nux jumped straight on the end and settled as if she thought it was her role in life to sleep on her master's bed.

'Stop warming my feet. I'm not your master!'

Nux opened one eye, put out a long pink tongue, and wagged her tail enthusiastically.

XXXIX

The brothers-in-law took their time. They had probably all
met around the corner and gone into a wine shop to relax.

It gave me an opportunity to walk over to the new
apartment and carry on with its clearance. My sore arm made
work difficult but Helena had come to help. Even with a
couple of guards loitering on the stairs, there was no way I
intended leaving her alone. Not now the vicious Balbinus
mob knew where we were.

Nux trotted happily after us. I shut her out, but we could
hear her lying right outside the door, snuffling under it as she
waited for me to re-emerge.

'She adores you!' Helena laughed.

'It won't do her any good.'

'The hardhearted hero! Still,' Helena was smiling, 'you
once took that defensive attitude with me.'

'Nonsense. I was the one slavering outside doors, begging
you to let me in.'

'I was frightened of what might happen if I did.'

'So was I, lady!'

I was grinning at her. I had never quite lost that quick
thump of the heart whenever I thought where our relationship might be taking us.

We had to open the door to carry out the last of the rubbish,
so then the dog got in. I was forced to whistle her after me,
rather than leave an untried animal alone with the skip babe.
Between the two of them they had me in knots.

As we worked I discussed with Helena my theory about
Nonnius being set up by Petronius.

'Was that illegal, Marcus?'

'Doubt it.'

'Entrapment?'

'Nonnius was the fool to believe his physician, that's all.'

'What if he had found out? Presumably when he failed to

626

die of his "fatal" disease, he would eventually have realised the diagnosis was at fault.'

'He couldn't complain. Had he lived, he would have been enjoying his share of the Balbinus estate as a direct result.'

'He's a clever man, your friend Petronius.'

'The quiet ones are the worst,' I said.

While we were still in our new lodging Petro himself turned up to inspect how much damage the Miller and Icarus had wreaked on me. He started out anxious, but once he had looked me over his broad face became happier. 'So you're off our necks for a while, Falco? How will long will the convalescence be?'

'Forget it! Here, lug down this bale to the skip for me.' He complied obligingly while I enjoyed myself playing the man in charge. 'What your investigation needs is brainwork; there's nothing wrong with my head.'

Trotting down to the skip he pulled a face as if he was questioning that, so when he passed me I thumped him with my good arm to prove I could still be active; then I laid into him with jibes about how he had put one over on Nonnius. He merely smiled in his annoying way.

'Has Silvia come home again yet?' Helena called down after us.

'Oh yes.'

He seemed surprised she asked. I could imagine how he had talked himself out of trouble and won Silvia round. Petronius had had years of practice in softening up his angry wife.

Returning upstairs for more rubbish, Petro changed the subject. 'Was Porcius any use in the scrap?'

'Perfectly adequate. A sound one, I'd say.'

'Bit raw.' Petro rarely complimented his men until he had thoroughly tested them. Though he wanted to hear good news about the lad, his voice carried a doubtful tone.

'He seems impressed by his senior officer's deviousness!'

Once again Petronius carried on as if he had no idea what I meant. He glanced around the apartment, which was now almost clear. 'This place is better than your usual standard but it's filthy, Falco. Helena can't live here.'

'All it needs is a good scrub,' Helena demurred loyally.

I dug Petro in the ribs. 'As a friend, you might offer the foot patrols to help bring the water up.'

Petro barked with scornful laughter. 'If you want a favour from the bloody fire-fighters, you'll have to ask them yourself!'

He had found the stuff that I had salvaged from Smaractus' workmen, and dived in with a whoop. Immediately he started sorting out wood nails and pieces of good timber. When it came to carpentry, he was a worse scavenger than I was.

'Just take anything you want!' I snorted, grabbing back a pair of metal pincers.

'Thanks, Falco!'

'Petro, did Porcius tell you about Marcus' missing niece?' Helena broke in as we rummaged on the floor. 'We are having to think she may have been abducted. Is it true this has happened other times?'

'We've had a spate. I thought there was something in it because they were all from wealthy families.' Petro grinned. 'With due respect to the Didius clan, this must be un-connected!'

'Pa has cash,' I pointed out tersely.

'Your father's not exactly known for family loyalty. I wouldn't hold out any chances for the kidnapper who tried squeezing Geminus. Be fair. Can you see him coughing up a ransom for one of your sisters' horrors?'

'Maybe.' Or maybe not.

'Most of the other lost sprats were sweet little moppets. Parents would gladly pay to get them back. Plus one baby lifted from a very exalted cradle, finally said to have been *merely taken by a nurse to show to a friend.*'

'Believe it?'

'No.'

'Were you allowed to interview the nurse?'

'Of course not. We might have actually learnt something!'

'And every single child turned up?'

'Apparently.'

'Were there any leads we could follow?'

'Only that the cases were all south of the Circus. I checked, but none of the other cohorts were having the same stuff happening. I tried working out a theory that somebody who normally hangs around the Aventine and wouldn't be noticed was snatching. The parents refused to co-operate, so I was in the dark and let it slide. I have enough to do.'

Helena murmured thoughtfully, 'Would you be prepared to tell me some of the parents' names?'

'You're not intending to see them!' Petro waited for a denial, but received none. 'Are you going to allow this, Falco?' His attitude to women was as traditional as mine was relaxed. The odd thing was, his surly paternalism had always done him more good – at least until I met Helena. Petro couldn't compete with that.

I grinned. 'I draw the line at her questioning suspects.' This overlooked the fact that I had taken her with me to assist that very afternoon. A dangerous gleam lit Helena's soft eyes. 'But there's no harm in her visiting respectable victims.'

'Oh thanks!' muttered Helena. Definitely *not* a traditionalist.

'It's highly irregular,' complained Petronius.

He was weakening. Helena Justina had one great advantage over us: she could approach snooty families on equal terms; she was probably superior to most of them. We could see how her mind was working, but she politely told us anyway: 'I can say I begged their addresses because we are desperate about our own missing child. If they believe I am asking as a private individual, they may just confide more than they were prepared to tell the vigiles.'

Petro abandoned resistance. 'Going to play the distraught mother?'

Helena gave him a straight look. 'Good practice, Petro. I'll be hysterical for real reasons soon enough.'

He glanced at me. I shrugged. 'Yes, it's true. I would have told you.'

'Oh really? What you actually told me was some lie about this not happening!' He made as if to leave in a huff, but at the last moment picked up the skip baby, who had been reclining like a pharaoh on a sack of old rags. Petro, the dedicated father of three, leant against the outside doorframe, showing off his expertise. The babe, tolerant as ever, accepted that big tough men are full of soppy talk. 'Hello, cheeky fellow, what are you doing with these two eccentrics?'

I was just explaining that when I wasn't being thumped by desperadoes I was trying to find the babe's guardians for him when Martinus arrived in Fountain Court. From our first-floor landing we saw him before he spotted us. Initially Petronius ducked back indoors, pretending to hide. Across the lane Martinus started jabbering something to Lenia. Seeing the slowcoach Martinus in a hurry changed Petro's mind.

He went out onto the steps and whistled. Nux barked at him loudly. Lenia shouted abuse across the street. Heads shot out of windows to gape. Passers-by stopped in their tracks. Casual shoppers listened brazenly. This was the Fourth Cohort at its discreet, efficient best; soon the whole Aventine would know what was up. Any chance of solving the problem by using an element of surprise was lost before we even heard what the problem was.

Martinus turned towards us. Excitedly the deputy shouted his message: there had just been a heavy raid – in broad daylight – by a gang who had ransacked the goldsmiths in the Saepta Julia. The size of the haul, the speed of the attack, and the efficiency of the robbers bore marked similarities to the raid at the Emporium. The Seventh Cohort were in charge, but Petronius was expected to attend.

Petro had run down almost to the street before he cursed and remembered he was still holding the skip baby. He leapt back three steps at a time with his long, spider's legs, shoved the child into my arms, then hared off again. I passed the baby to Helena, instructed Nux to stay and guard them, then set off after Petronius.

I was wearing the wrong boots for hurrying, but I had no intention of missing this.

XL

There was much less commotion at the Saepta than we had
seen at the Emporium. Goldsmiths are a more secretive lot
than merchants. They were wary of making a fuss about their
stock even after it had been wrenched from them. None of
them wanted to confess, especially to each other, exactly what
they possessed let alone what they had lost. They merely
stood around the ground floor and the upper balcony looking
deeply glum.

Petronius made sure he reminded them that Vespasian had
said he was compensating the Emporium merchants as an
exceptional measure. The goldsmiths had been warned to
take care, Petro declared. If they had failed to secure their
premises despite the formal notification of a need for extra
vigilance, they would have to stand the loss.

This went down like a gladiators' strike at a five-day
festival. Hoping to avoid inflated claims, Martinus started
trooping around the jewellers to make up another of his lists.
Maybe the Emperor would agree token compensation after
all. More likely he would confine himself to issuing a strict
reprimand to the Prefect of the Vigiles for neglecting to
prevent another robbery. The Prefect would take it out on the
tribune of the Seventh Cohort, who was responsible for the
Saepta, and on Marcus Rubella, tribune of the Fourth, who
was in charge of the special initiative for catching the gang.
Rubella would land on Petronius like a barrel of bricks from a
great height.

I absorbed the size of the raid, which was phenomenal.
That was all I needed to know. The next stage of action would
be routine: taking endless details and asking questions of
hostile witnesses whose information would probably prove
pointless. Spotting my father, I dragged him into his office.
'There's enough grief here! Let's keep out of the way.'

Pa had lost nothing this time. The robbers had stormed
through the building swiping jewels and precious metalwork.

They had had a strict menu of items to lift. Furniture and fancy lamps were off their agenda. Pa looked miffed.

'No bloody taste!'

'Be grateful, you villain.'

'I like to put it about that my stuff is desirable.'

'Any connoisseur of mock-marble tables with one foot missing can see yours are up with the best! Any collector who wants twenty identical statuettes of a muse on Mount Helicon – one or two with chipped noses – will come rushing straight here . . . Did you get my message?'

'Some garbled jabbering from my steward.'

Pa's steward was perfectly competent, as I happened to know. Like Pa's stock, his staff turned out to be better quality than you thought at first glance. I reiterated patiently, 'We found one of the glass jugs.'

'Oh?' He could hardly force himself to express an interest. I knew why it was. He would rather claim the Emperor's compensation, cash in hand, than enjoy owning and selling the treasures we had taken so much trouble to bring home. He made me furious.

'You give me a pain in the brain, Pa! What about what I said about a present for Helena?'

'That was a gorgeous piece you got her.'

'You mean you found it?' I was beside myself.

'I had a very good look at the glass in the boxes that first night. I thought I told you.'

'Then I wish you'd taken it out and kept it safe for me!'

'How was I to know it was a present for Helena?'

'It was wrapped up in one of my old tunics. You should have realised.'

'I thought you were secreting away a bribe for some fancy bit.'

'Oh for heavens' sake! I hate to flirt and fornicate.'

'Jupiter, that's new!'

'Don't judge me by your own low behaviour!' I felt so annoyed with him I could not bear to stay and haggle over a replacement, even though I needed a present by the next morning. With a brief curse – my usual salutation – I brushed aside Pa's offer of a drink and stormed off home.

*

632

By the time I returned to Fountain Court it was dark. I put aside my anger; I had to give my attention to keeping alert. A loose chicken scuttled across my feet in a panic, frightening me too. There were the usual feeble lamps flickering like extremely tired glow-worms on the porches of the bakery, the basket shop and one or two others. Only the funeral parlour was ablaze with cheerful strings of lights; offering a brilliant welcome was their idea of comforting the bereaved. In one deeply shadowed doorway two figures were locked together; hard to see whether it was a pair of lovers steadfastly taking their pleasure or a mugger throttling a victim. In keeping with the traditions of our area, I did not enquire. I had once helped a youth who was being raped by a carter, only to have him steal my purse while his attacker was giving me a black eye. Not a set-up; just a typical Aventine reward for my overfriendliness.

I was walking up the laundry side of the lane, which was normally quieter. This brought me to the ground-floor lockup alongside the barber's, the set of rooms that had previously been advertised to let. The new tenants had made fast work of moving in. There was a dim lantern with a dirty horn shutter swinging from an awning support, by the light of which I could make out masses of intriguing stuff for sale. A faint chalked sign above the entrance now advertised: *The Lumber Room: Bargains Aplenty and Gifts Full of Charm.*

This was my last hope of acquiring a birthday present for the girl I adored. Even better, I could possibly get something cheap. I had nothing to lose, so I rapped on a cauldron hanging by the doorway, and went in.

XLI

If you liked jumble, it was a wondrous glory hole. As soon as I squeezed in through the folding doors, which had been nearly closed, I knew this was the sort of cavern that cried out for half a day's perusal. It all looked extremely casual. There were enough mixed sacks of pictures and crocks to give the impression the proprietor had lost any chance of knowing his stock – holding out the tantalising hope of unsuspected valuables for which the sharp-eyed browser could offer a copper, intending to sell on to a more discerning dealer at twenty times the price. My father always called these places rubbish dumps; his disdain only made me like them more.

By the light of a few tiny oil lamps I tried to familiarise myself. Dust filled the air. There was a smell which I recognised from the house sales my father organised after people had died, that faintly upsetting aroma of old things newly disturbed. The confined space was very warm. From the rear of the building came a succession of muffled noises, not quite domestic in character.

I brushed through a strung-up cascade of belts, some with extraordinary buckles. Then I nearly stepped on a dismantled chariot wheel. Sandals and boots were knotted on ropes like onions. They bulged on the walls amidst hookfuls of skillets and drainers that hung in colonies like shellfish on a groyne. Around my feet were teetering piles of bowls and platters. To reach the gloom where the counter groaned under mounds of cloth items – old clothes and household drapes, apparently – required steering a path through the tableware; huge baskets of ironmongery that leant against the serving island, keeping you at a distance. Little stands dripped bead necklaces. Caskets stood open to show off glittering finger rings. There were bronze flagons, black metal cups that could well clean up into silver, and an astonishing candelabra that reached the roof.

I wondered where the proprietor got his stuff. On the off chance, I kept an eye out for Syrian glass.

A figure emerged suddenly from the rear, making me jump. He looked flustered and suspicious, as if I had invaded a shop that was really closed for the night. I stuck one thumb in my belt and applied an unthreatening air.

'Evening. This is quite a collection! I bet you don't even know what you've got.' It was intended as a compliment; he took it as an insult, I could see.

The man was slight and seedy-looking. I had seen this type in many a dark boothful of paraphernalia before. I never know how they live. They never seem to want to part with any goods from their untidy selection, and if you bring anything to offer for sale, they despise that too.

This one had lanky strings of hair covering his ears, though the dome of his head was bald. His skin was like old cheese rind, the sort at which even sparrows turn up their beaks when you find it behind a cupboard and throw it out. He looked insignificant. I tried to tell myself he was a pent-up ball of energy and intelligence. I failed.

'Mind if I look around?'

He condescended to allow it, but appeared about as happy as if I had told him I represented the aedile in charge of licences. 'Anything special you're looking for?' he forced himself to demand. He definitely had the gloom of a man whose credentials were being checked – one who knew he had not paid the right bribes to be in the clear.

'I'll know it if I see it.'

I wanted to browse; he just wanted me to leave. The fact that he stood there watching meant that things which had once looked attractive rapidly lost their interest. I started noticing chips and dents the minute I picked up an item, then I felt embarrassed about putting it straight down. He had no idea how to sell. Even if he suspected I was an evening opportunist looking for goods to lift, he could have watched me without letting it show. Anyone would think I had slouched in with a hook on a stick or a large swag bag.

I lost myself for a long time in a basket of handles, brackets and hinges. Eventually I straightened up. 'Do you sell any decent-quality jewellery?'

'I don't have much in stock at the moment.' He meant, if any ever came in he sold it straight on to a specialist jeweller who could present it on a pretty display and charge more. 'My partner reclaims precious metal, and we have a good craftsman who can make it up into anything you want. We could commission you a piece.'

'In gold?'

'Oh yes.'

'Would you guarantee the purity?'

'All our work goes out with a certificate.'

Anyone who 'reclaims' metal can probably forge documents too, but it sounded a reasonable offer. That only made me feel more worried. This was a prime opportunity for them to pinch the materials, if I supplied any, or for me to pay a lot of money for work that entirely lacked artistry.

'What's your name?'

'Castus.'

'Maybe we can do business, Castus.'

I hated the normal class of jeweller. I hated their prices and the stuck-up way they sneered at me. I really would have liked to give some smaller firm a chance. But Helena was special. Feeling like a louse, I promised to decide more clearly what I wanted and come back later with instructions. Then I left the shop. Poor Castus obviously knew I was just a time-waster.

Back at home, Helena was in bed. I knew pregnant women have to rest a lot. When I suggested this, Helena retorted that she had just decided I was an unreliable wanderer it was no use waiting up for.

I sat on the edge of the bed, holding the skip baby, who had been awake when I came in. He gazed back with his normal, quiet, trusting expression. I had a bad conscience about this one. I kept forgetting him. I kept forgetting my niece Tertulla too. There was madness on the Aventine, a two-way traffic in youth. Some children were being abandoned; some were being snatched. I tried to make a connection, but nothing jumped out at me.

I pushed Nux off the end of the bed; she crept closer along the floor, and since she was shy of fussing me while I was acting stern, she licked the baby's foot instead.

'That's a good sign.' Helena smiled.

'She's good with children!' We both giggled, thinking of

Gaius Baebius making this wild claim as he fought to hold his struggling hound, Ajax.

Helena told me the brothers-in-law had achieved nothing in the search for little Tertulla (no surprise). The last sighting of her must have been soon after Marius had left her, in a street only two away from Fountain Court. Gaius Baebius had offered to come again tomorrow to continue searching. He and Junia had no children of their own, but he was a good-hearted soul. That had never made him easier to like.

I sighed. Trying to think what I could do about this, I stretched on top of the coverlet alongside Helena. I was still holding the babe. Next thing, the damned dog started creeping up over the edge too, one paw at a time. There was hardly room for all of us. At this rate we would need a bigger bed.

Tertulla might have to wait. She had been missing most of the day, and we were now into the night. I knew what that meant. I was perfectly aware of the dangers she might be in. She was certainly frightened. She might be hurt. Or dead. But without a lead to follow, I had little chance of doing anything.

I was her uncle. I was head of her mother's household, since Pa was an absconding scoundrel and the child's own father was a complete deadbeat whom even Galla threw out whenever possible. It was my role to find the child. Dear gods, I hated this kind of responsibility.

'Let me try,' Helena urged, snuggling up to me. 'I'll speak to the parents of the other so-called missing children. Marcus, you can't do everything.'

I turned my head and gazed at her sadly. 'You're beautiful!'

'What's that for?' She was suspicious at once. 'What's happened?'

I closed my eyes wearily. This had to be confession time. 'I can't do anything right. I bought you a wonderful present for once – and it's been stolen from me.'

'Oh no! Oh my darling.'

'It was marvellous. Something I'd probably never be able to better.' I was really depressed. 'I've been trying to replace it, but I can't find anything I like as much.'

'Ah Marcus . . . It doesn't matter. Come to bed properly.'

637

'I didn't want to have to tell you this.'

'It's not your fault.'

'I'm supposed to be catching the bastards. I thought I'd get it back.'

'You will,' she said. I loved her faith, but it was terrifying. Helena put her arms around me. I began to feel drowsy straight away. That was no good. I had too much to worry about. If I dozed I would have bad dreams. I might as well just stay awake and ruin my chances of sorting out anything by making myself completely exhausted for tomorrow.

Tomorrow was going to be a difficult day. 'Helena Justina, what are we going to tell your mother when she asks you what you had from me?'

'I shall just smile mysteriously and say it's a secret.'

Helena's mother would take this for a salacious reference to the child we were expecting. Once she knew of it. 'Well what, if it isn't too much to ask, are we going to tell your mother about starting a family?'

'Don't worry.'

'I do worry. I've bungled enough things. I'd like to handle this with decorum and tact.'

'I'll tell her that was my birthday present.' Exactly as I feared: *'He's made me pregnant. What more do you want?'*

What a wonderful household. A hopeless informer, a girl he should not be living with, a strange little foundling baby, and a dog I didn't want. And somehow between the four of us, we were trying to solve half the conspiracies in Rome.

By next morning there was another crime for us. During the night Alexander, the doctor who had told Nonnius he was dying, was found by the watch lying in his open surgery. The place was a wreck and he was surrounded by scattered instruments and spilled medicines. His throat had been cut with one of his own scalpels. Various disgusting experiments had been perpetrated on him first. His brother, Scythax, the Fourth Cohort's medico, happened to be out with the night patrol that came across the corpse.

XLII

Helena's birthday. My poor girl loyally spent her time trying to find my lost niece. She set about interviewing all the Aventine householders who had reported missing children. Gaius Baebius had turned up just as I was myself leaving home, so I found a piece of rope in my skip to tie Ajax to a pillar in the laundry portico, then arranged with Gaius that he would stick close to Helena. It was protection for her, something I could not spare time to provide myself, and kept him out of trouble too.

Lenia bawled something angrily about the dog.

'Leave off, Lenia. If I'm to provide your augury, you owe me a favour or two.'

'Don't push your luck, Falco! Seems to me you're using this as an excuse to behave like a complete tyrant.'

'Don't underestimate the lies I'll have to make up.'

'If you feel like that I'll find somebody else.'

'I wish you would.'

Nobody else would do it, we both knew. Every lockup shopkeeper in Fountain Court had already given himself a hernia laughing at the thought of me having to suffer under the sacrificial veil.

Dear gods. That was another problem: I would have to acquire a headdress to parade in at the altar on the wedding day.

'Gaius Baebius, you look like a man with a sense of duty. Have you got a priest's veil?'

'Of course,' smirked my brother-in-law. Trust him. What a pious operator. How could even Junia have married him? (Answer: for his customs salary. Do not ask me, however, how a placid lump like Gaius ever married a spiteful stick like her.) 'Marcus Didius, I am hoping to be elected to the college of the Augustales soon.'

Official religion. Oh spare me, Gaius! 'Excellent fellow! And thanks for the loan of your bonce sheet,' I cried, setting

639

off in the opposite direction from Helena and him at a fast pace. I could see him looking puzzled; Helena would explain. If I knew Gaius Baebius, lending me his head veil would make him think he had the right to attend Lenia's nuptials. Things were looking up. He and Junia were bound to bring their dog; Ajax was their child substitute, treated as one of the family. Maybe Ajax could be trained to bite the bride's beloved. Maybe, if the gods were *very* kind, they would give me time to train Ajax myself.

Walking to the station house, I enjoyed myself thinking of fierce canine teeth being sunk into my landlord's most personal assets on his wedding day.

I already knew how my own day would be unfolding. Fusculus had called at the apartment early to break the news of the doctor's murder. He said Petro had been up half the night pursuing investigations into the Saepta thefts. When he heard of Alexander's murder he had given up and gone home to grab a hasty nap. The plan was for us all to meet at midmorning in order to tackle the new disaster after the crew had rested and were fresh.

This gave me a couple of hours to spare. Time for serious preparations: I went to the gymnasium and put in some wrestling and weapons practice. Given the grim state of Rome it seemed a good idea.

I had forgotten about my shoulder. That very promptly sent me out of the gym and into the massage room.

'You're full of flab,' complained Glaucus the proprietor, who acted as my personal trainer whenever I allowed him access.

'Get me into condition then.'

'In *half an hour*, Falco?'

'Half an hour is all I have.'

'You're slow, you're weak, you're dopy. It's going to take me months to undo this. I hope you're not planning anything dangerous in the near future.'

'Just tackling a gang of vicious murderers. And mind it, man! I had a dislocated shoulder poked back yesterday.'

'Jupiter, Juno and Minerva! I presume', moaned Glaucus sarcastically, 'somebody also landed some heavy blows to the soft part of your head?'

I do like to approach threatening situations with such warm encouragement.

Petronius Longus was in a filthy mood. 'What in Hades is wrong with these bastards? Can't they give us time to run ourselves into the ground on one job before they have to jump up like flea-bitten rabbits? Time was you could rely on growing thoroughly depressed with your first case before some cluck decided to throw the next at you . . .'

He was just ranting. I could understand why.

He had Scythax in the interrogation room. The poor man was so deeply in shock he seemed drunk. Every few minutes he wandered out muttering a confused suggestion, or asking the same question he had put to us three times already. 'What did they think they were achieving? Why did they have to torture him? Why, oh why?'

'Revenge, Scythax. Porcius, make yourself useful. Go in there and sit with him.'

'Just talk to him,' counselled Fusculus in a low voice. 'Or if he talks about his brother, just nod and listen.'

As the nervous recruit obediently led the grief-stricken man indoors again, Petro covered his face briefly. 'I can't send him home. Oh gods on Olympus, Falco! What a mess. He lived with his brother. He'll go mad in those surroundings. Besides, these bastards may be looking for Scythax too.'

'The patrol couldn't hold him back,' Fusculus told me. 'The door was ajar. As soon as Scythax saw the situation, he was in like an arrow, howling and covered with blood himself. They had a terrible time dragging him away from Alexander and getting him back here. He still keeps trying to return to the surgery.'

Everyone present was white-faced. There was plenty to do, but they were sitting together in the patrol house, impotent. They saw violence daily; hideous death far too frequently. This had struck too close. This affected one of them. This – though nobody had yet mentioned it – was something their own work had caused. Alexander *might* have been attacked by a deranged patient, but we all thought this was directly related to his false diagnosis of Nonnius Albius.

We spent a day trying to make sense of it. First we all said there was no point going to look at the surgery – or no point *all* of us going. We all went. It seemed a gesture of respect. We had to force ourselves to see what the man had endured. Petronius imposed it on himself as a punishment. Some of the others made it serve as an apology. I went because I knew from experience that if you don't, you never stop worrying whether there was some clue you could have spotted if you had been there. We badly needed evidence. The squad was so shaken up that any clues there were might easily be missed or misinterpreted.

Young Porcius was the only one who actually vomited. The scene knocked back his composure completely; there was nothing for it but to send him to the station house to sit with Scythax again. By the end of the day the youngster was a gibbering wreck, but we had too much else to think about. He was given sympathy, but no one could nursemaid him.

'The chief's heartbroken,' Martinus muttered at me. Even he had lost all his cockiness.

'I've never seen him so bad,' Fusculus agreed dolefully.

I was his friend. They all seemed to want to tell me about Petro's distressed state. I could hardly bear it. I needed nobody to tell me. He was as foul-tempered as I had ever seen him – except once, during the Boudiccan Rebellion in Britain. He was older now. He knew more obscene words, and more painful ways to take out his anger on people nearby.

I would have hauled him out for a drink, but the mood he was in he would have stayed knocking it back until he passed out or killed himself.

By the afternoon we had exhausted ourselves asking questions. Several innocent householders had gone off to complain to the Prefect's Office about the way they had been pushed around and bawled at. Nobody had seen or heard anything suspicious, either last night or the previous day. Nobody knew anything. Nobody wanted to know. Everyone had caught a whiff of gangster involvement. Everyone was terrified.

We all believed the same people had killed both Alexander and Nonnius. Even that simple fact was hard to prove. The evidence denied it. One victim had been abducted; one was killed at home. One was a declared informant; the other had been sensibly discreet. The methods used were completely different. The message sent out seemed less flagrant the second time. Apart from the fact both murders happened at night – like most crimes in Rome – only the violence inflicted was common to both. Only instinct and experience convinced us we were right to link the two deaths. But it all made sense if we decided that Nonnius had been killed as an act of revenge for betraying Balbinus, and Alexander had died because someone found out it was him telling Nonnius he was dying that had led to that villain's 'reform'.

The public baths were opening by the time the investigation broke up for the day. The scent of wood smoke on the damp October air gave an autumnal gloom and added to our melancholy mood. We were no further forward. There was a sense that we would spend this coming night waiting for more deaths. We were losing. The villains had all the dice running for them.

With a set face, Petronius ordered the body's removal – to an undertaker this time, not the station house, where the dead man's distraught brother was still being looked after. He then arranged for members of the foot patrol to be brought in to clean up and leave the surgery neat. Fusculus volunteered to oversee that. He seemed to need something to fill his time. Petro thanked him, then sent the rest home.

I saw Petronius to his house. He said almost nothing as we walked. I left him at his door. His wife let him in. She glanced at his drawn features, then her chin went up, but she made no comment. Maybe she even gave me a half-concealed nod. Arria Silvia loved to rant, but if ever Petro looked beaten she rushed to protect him. So Silvia took over, and I was not needed. As the door closed, leaving me alone in the street, I felt momentarily lost.

It had been a terrible day. I had seen Rome's underbelly, smelt the matted filth beneath the ravening wolf. It was nothing new, but it forced me to face the lack of hope that lives alongside crime. This was the true face of the Caesars' marble city: not Corinthian acanthus leaves and perfect gilt-lettered inscriptions, but a quiet man killed horrendously in the home and workplace he shared with his brother; a vicious revenge thrust on the one-time slave who had learned a respected profession then repaid his freedom and citizenship with a single act of assistance to the law. Not all the fine civic building programmes in the world would ever displace the raw forces that drive most of humankind. This was the true city: greed, corruption and violence.

It was dusk as I made my way to Fountain Court. My heart lay heavy. And for me, the day was nowhere near over yet. I still had to put on a smile and a toga – then go out to dinner with my girlfriend's family.

XLIII

Once we got past the porter, who had always viewed me like a door-to-door lupin-seller who was aiming to snatch silverware, it was an occasion to remember. The hosts were so considerate that guests felt free to behave badly. Helena Justina's birthday, in the consulship of whoever it was, laid the foundation for many happy years of family recrimination. For once, it was not my family involved.

Being a mere private citizen, my manners were the best on display. As soon as I escorted Helena from the carrying chair I had grudgingly hired, I turned to find her mother right behind me waiting to knock me aside and embrace the birthday girl. I kissed the matron's cheek (smoothly oiled and scented) with grave formality. She was a tall woman who had not expected me to tackle her, so the manoeuvre required dexterity. She was even more surprised than I was.

'Julia Justa, greetings and thanks. Twenty-five years ago today you gave the world a great treasure!' I might not be the ideal son-in-law, but I knew how to press a rather nice soapstone casket of balsam into a lady's receptive hands.

'Thank you, Marcus Didius. What a pretty speech.' Julia Justa was a mistress of elegant hypocrisy. Then her expression froze. 'Why,' queried Helena's mother icily, 'is my daughter carrying a child?' Helena had brought the skip babe.

'Oh Marcus found him in a rubbish skip!' cried Helena Justina breezily. 'But there's another child I'm carrying that you'll want to hear about.'

This was hardly the tact and decorum I had tried to plan. On the other hand, nobody could say that it was my fault.

I had a side bet with the Fourth Cohort that the night would end with women in tears and men losing teeth. (Or the other way round.) Before we even crossed the threshold there was some jostling for position among the female element.

Helena's mother wore leaf-green silk with an embroidered

stole; Helena wore not merely silk, but a fabulous cloth from Palmyra woven in multiple patterns of purple, brown, deep red and white. Helena's mother wore an expensive parure of golden scrolls and droplets set with a clutch of evenly matched emeralds; Helena wore an armful of bangles, and absolutely enormous Indian pearls. Helena's mother was scented with highly refined cinnamon perfume, the one Helena herself often wore; Helena tonight wore a few vivid dabs of a precious liquor containing frankincense. She also had the gracious air of a daughter who had won.

We men were in white. We started in togas, though we soon flung them off. Helena's father had his fond, faintly cautious expression. Her brother Aelianus boasted a scowl and a Spanish belt. I had been smartened up until I felt like a whole guild of shoemakers on their big day out.

Justinus had failed to appear that night. Everyone knew he must be mooning around Pompey's Theatre. 'He won't forget,' his mother assured us as she led us indoors. He might. (The actress might be exceptional, and she might choose tonight to notice him.) Helena and I gulped, then prayed for him.

While the women rushed away to share urgent news, I was led off for a predinner winecup with the Senator (honeyed mulsum, strictly traditional; makes you feel sick without letting you get drunk). Camillus Verus was shrewd and intelligent, with a diffident manner. He did what was necessary, and didn't waste effort on the rest. I liked him. It mattered to me that he should be able to tolerate me. At least he knew the strength of my feelings for Helena.

The Camillus family were certainly patrician when viewed from my own perspective, though there were no consuls or generals in their ancestry. They were rich – though their wealth was in land and my father probably owned far more portable collateral. Their house was spacious and detached, a lived-in town villa with water and drainage but rather tired decor. Lacking expensive works of art, they relied on old-fashioned features for domestic tranquillity. Tonight the courtyard fountains were splashing merrily, but we needed more than that to cool the air as the Senator introduced me to his elder son.

Aelianus was two years younger than Helena, two years older than Justinus. He looked much like his father – sprouting straight hair and slightly stooped shoulders. More chunky than Justinus and Helena and heavier-featured, he was less good-looking as a result. His abysmal manners were a patrician cliché. Luckily I had never expected a senator's son to approve of me. That was fine; it let me off trying to like him.

'So you're the man who's been pushing my young brother's career along!' exclaimed Aelianus.

Nearly a decade his senior, and worth ten times more in useful qualities, I refused to agitate myself. 'Quintus has a warm personality and a fine intellect. People like him, and he's interested in everything – naturally such a man stands no chance in public life! Unlike you, I'm sure.' Well done, Falco; an insult, but nicely ambiguous.

Young Justinus stood every chance, in fact. But I don't stir up trouble; close relatives can usually find enough things to be jealous about.

'And did you get him interested in the theatre too?' his brother sneered.

It was the Senator himself who said, 'He selects his own hobbies – like all of you.' That had to be a fatherly dig; I sat back and wondered what dubious activities the pious Aelianus liked. If he gave me any trouble, this would be something to find out.

'Let's hope my brother's hobby doesn't last – or my sister's either!'

There were now so many stars alongside Justinus' name on the army list, a scandal might just make him appear more intriguing to the public. I refrained from saying that. Aelianus had completed his own military service rather dully, then a year as a governor's unpaid aide-de-camp in Baetica had failed to give him lustre. On the other hand, none of that had been his own fault. Luck stepped around me pretty smartly too, so I said kindly, 'Don't be jealous. Your brother was just in the right province, at the right time.'

'And of course he knew you!'

Again there was an unpleasant, scornful note. Aelianus was naïve enough to expect me to flare up. Instead his father said mildly, 'That was indeed fortunate. When Marcus was sent on one of his peculiarly demanding missions, your brother was able to join him.'

'Did you approve of that?' Aelianus demanded accusingly. 'I've heard what Justinus got up to in Germany was damned dangerous.'

'I didn't know until it was over,' Camillus replied honestly.

The young man was bursting with outraged dignity. 'There are things we ought to get straight.' The Senator and I glanced at one another, then let him get on with it. He needed to make a racket. That was easier than arguing. 'This man is a common informer.' I noticed he found it impossible to use even my formal name. 'The situation with my sister is damaging our family.' He meant that it might reflect on his own career.

The Senator looked annoyed. Whatever he thought about his finely bred daughter absconding with a piece of rough cheese, he always put the best face on it. 'Falco is an imperial agent. He has the confidence of the Emperor.'

'But Vespasian hates informers.'

I laughed. 'Except when he needs them.'

The younger Camillus was still sounding off pompously. 'I have seen no public recognition of the role of "imperial agent". It carries no official title or salary. And as I understand it, although there was once talk of a substantial reward, it has failed to materialise!'

I made an effort to avoid reacting. I had promised Helena not to involve myself in conversations that might end with my fist shattering her brother's jaw.

Camillus Senior looked embarrassed. 'Falco's work is necessarily secret. Don't be offensive to our guest.' He tried gamely to change the subject: 'You look in good form, Marcus. Travel suits you.'

'You should see me in my Palmyrene trousers and embroidered hat . . .' I sighed. Chitchat on Oriental matters would dodge the problem but not solve it. 'Your son is quite right, Senator. I *was* promised social advancement, and it *has* been refused.'

Camillus must have heard about it from Helena. As a member of the Establishment he seemed to feel personally responsible. He scratched his nose; light gleamed on a workaday garnet signet ring. 'It's a misunderstanding, Marcus. It can be resolved.'

'No, Domitian Caesar gave me a very clear ruling, and when I discussed the matter with Titus last week he was unable to change that.'

'Titus told me,' answered the Senator. 'Rulings do tend to become immutable if they involve denying just rewards!' His sense of humour was always refreshingly dry. 'Well, tell me if I can help . . . I gather you're working on the law-and-order issue at present?' So much for keeping the post-Balbinus investigation confidential.

'Yes, I'm on the special commission.'

Camillus noticed my dark mood. 'Not enjoying it?'

'Mixed feelings; mixed loyalties.' The conversation had shifted. The Senator and I were talking at a level that now excluded Aelianus. I went back to one aspect of what Camillus had said: 'I'm asking myself how much of my personal chat with Titus Caesar he passed on, sir? Has he pre-empted a private discussion I intended to have with you?'

Camillus smiled, waving a hand in acceptance of the fact that he had been told he was to be a grandfather by someone other than me. 'I realised Titus was being premature.'

'I'm sorry for it. You know how things work, sir.'

'You had to seize your opportunity,' he agreed. Well, for Helena's sake he would want me to have tried. Our relationship stayed easy. 'Are you pleased?' he asked. I let a grin answer him. Then we both stopped looking so delighted, as like dutiful men we both considered the perils to Helena.

'I still think something can be sorted out for you, Marcus.' Vespasian, like any good Roman, had his private clique of friends who advised him; the Senator was one of them, once close, and still consulted. It could be made to work on my behalf – if I could accept having strings pulled. The senator knew my feelings about that. 'Will you let me speak to the old man?'

'Better not.' I smiled. Even with his personal interest, it was gracious of him to offer. But I had to do this myself. 'My new assignment is a complex one. Let's see the results before I call in imperial favours!'

'Maybe you'd better leave my sister alone then,' Aelianus grappled himself back into the discussion even though unsure of its content.

'I note your advice,' I said pleasantly. Suddenly I was too angry to carry on fielding his jibes. 'I'm sorry you're distressed. I can see it must have been difficult, coming home from abroad to find that the respectable family you had left behind was now tainted with scandal.' He began to speak. I stabbed the air with my finger. 'The scandal I mean has nothing to do with your sister. I refer to the sad mess which brought me into contact with the Camilli in the first place, when various of your noble relations – now fortunately dead – engaged in a treasonous attempt of staggering ineptitude! Camillus Aelianus, before you embark on public life I suggest you ask your father to explain just how much the Emperor allowed to be covered up.'

The jaw of the not so noble Aelianus had dropped open. Clearly he had not realised I knew about his family's near-disgrace.

'Excuse me,' I apologised briefly to his father, for I normally tried not to mention all this.

'Was the cover-up organised by you?' Aelianus was catching on. But now he assumed Helena Justina had been presented to me in return for my silence.

'My job is to expose things. Still, I'm glad we had this opportunity to clear the air ... Philosophical insights are traditionally brought to light by men drinking at a symposium.' Trying to improve the atmosphere, I raised my cup.

Aelianus glowered at me. 'What exactly do you do, Falco?' Sometimes I wondered that myself.

'Nice of you to ask this time, before condemning me! I do what's needed – what nobody else is able or willing to tackle.'

'Do you kill people?' He had no finesse.

'Not regularly. It's too much trouble making my peace with the gods afterwards.'

I avoided looking at the Senator. He was sitting very silent. The last time I remembered killing a man, it was a thug who attacked Helena on her father's own doorstep. Camillus saw me do it. But there were other deaths, closely connected to that, which the Senator and I never talked about.

'It's a glorious thought,' Aelianus was still sneering. 'Some dogged lone operator attempting to right society's wrongs without praise or pay!'

'Pure foolishness,' I agreed briefly.

'Why do it?'

'Oh, the hope of gain.'

'Strength of character?' The family irony had not entirely bypassed Aelianus.

'You've found me out. I'm a soft touch for ethical actions.'

'And it's a short cut to the women too?'

'The very best of them . . . You'd better grit your teeth. I know I've found a good one, and I'm here to stay. My relationship with your sister is permanent. And you're going to be an uncle to an informer's son or daughter by next spring!'

Aelianus was still spluttering with disgust when Julia Justa and Helena sailed back to join us.

XLIV

Repairing to the dining room enabled me to lighten the mood with tasteful praise for a recent repaint (heavy stuff, black dadoes and perspectives in deep red and gold). They must have been taken in by a contractor who dreamed of decorating Oriental tombs.

The Senator's wife declared coolly that we would dine now, without Justinus. She showed no particular emotion after her conversation with Helena about our coming baby; she must have been prepared for it. So much so that she had taken over the skip orphan as if to accustom herself to playing with a child she would rather avoid. Her sole concern now was to get through the celebration without embarrassment. The noble Julia had the suffering air of a woman who was doing her best even though everyone around her seemed determined to ruin her carefully planned day.

She had a fine sense of decency. I made sure I stepped forwards and handed her kindly to her dining couch. In return, Julia Justa politely insisted that I took the couch next to her. I was assuming the air of a guest who was a *very* close family friend. One reason I did this was to annoy Aelianus by letting him think he had been superseded – in his own home and in front of all the slaves and family freedmen and -women – by his sister's unsuitable lover flagrantly adopting the role of a respected son-in-law.

I managed to maintain the fraud of gravitas right up until I caught Helena's eye. I lost control when she winked at me.

Food and wine always help. Besides, it was Helena's birthday, and we were people who all loved her. (Even her tense brother must have cared for her as much as his own right to a scandal-free public life.)

The food was probably better than that normally served in that cash-strapped household. I was particularly taken by the lobster dumplings, which came in the first course along with

Colymbadian olives and various pork nuggets. Helena and I managed to put in a fair ration of travellers' tales concerning food, enabling us to sidestep the dubious theatrical aspect of our tour in Syria. The centrepiece of the main course was a small whole boar in nut sauce, a dish which I freely admitted rarely featured in the cook's repertoire at my own house.

'We don't often have it here!' admitted the Senator, helping me to a vintage that I described as 'suave'.

'Don't you mean smooth?' Aelianus was still trying to be caustic even when he had the bright blue stains of peas indigo spilt down his tunic. I had already pointed this out, while passing on my tip that worldly diners refuse titbits served in squid's ink.

'No, I mean warm and sophisticated with a cynically dangerous undertone that may trip some of us down stairs before the night's up.'

'Are you a connoisseur, Falco?'

'No, but I drink with one. I know the rhetoric,' I said, warning him off if he meant to indulge in snobbery. 'My friend Petronius Longus can convincingly distinguish between Falernian from the hilltops, the middle slopes and the plain. I can't, though I'm always pleased to let him serve me samples as he tries to train my palate . . . His dream is to get hold of some vinum Oppianum.'

Aelianus was sufficiently tipsy to admit his ignorance: 'What's that?'

'It was a legendary year, named after the consul, of course: Oppianus, the man who killed Gaius Gracchus.'

'Why, that must be nearly two centuries old!' exclaimed the Senator. 'If he finds any, try to get me a taste!'

'It may happen. According to Petronius the vintage was so good stocks were hoarded and they occasionally surface.'

'Would it be drinkable?' Helena asked.

'Probably not. A buff like Petro would gulp down the sludge, and get drunk on the mere cachet.'

'Buffs don't gulp,' she laughed, correcting me. 'Buffs breathe, savour, mull, then compete at producing flowery descriptions – '

'And get very sick.'

The Senator laughed, enjoying our repartee. 'Try this,

Marcus. It's Guaranum, only produced in a very small quantity from the ridge above Baia, where the air must be salty, the earth sulphurous, and the grapes encouraged by the happy screams of the girls being seduced by gigolos in the bathing spa.'

'Oh really Decimus!' mouthed Julia Justa, though her goblet was out for a refill. She graciously received her wine from her husband then returned her attention to the skip babe, whose quiet demeanour in public had endeared him to her. She was shaking his rattle, a pottery pig with pebbles inside that Helena had bought from a market stall.

'Oh Mama!' Aelianus shuddered. 'He could have come from anywhere.'

Angry, I had to bury my nose in my cup. Luckily the Guaranum was rich and full-bodied, a consoling wine.

'His clothes were fine quality. We think he came from a good home,' Helena countered coldly. 'Not that that's important; the child is lost, and something must be done for him.' Her mother, who had known Helena long enough, deftly ignored the implication that something should be done by the Camilli.

'If his home was as good as all that,' Aelianus persisted, 'there would be a public outcry from the people he was stolen from.'

'I doubt it!' his mother said abruptly. She moved the rattle, first shaking it to one side, then bringing it in front of the child's face. We watched him react by waving his hands. Helena's mother was an intelligent woman. She had spotted what even mine had missed. The babe did not respond until the rattle actually came into his view. Then Julia Justa told us crisply, 'His family may have lost him deliberately. This baby is deaf!'

I dropped my head, covering my eyes. If he was deaf at birth, he would be dumb too. He was damned. People would write him off as an idiot. There was no chance of finding him a civilized home.

'Jupiter, Falco!' Aelianus crowed. 'Whatever are you going to do?'

'Oh do stop sniping!' His mother turned on her couch back

654

to the table. 'Marcus will produce an apt, elegant solution. Marcus always does.' It was difficult to tell whether she was reproving her son, or grumbling about me.

I raised my winecup to the lady and watched Helena frowning over the child's sad plight. We were two ticks away from giving him a home ourselves.

I was saved by a distraction. The useless door porter had let a drunk into the house. A tall, shyly attractive young man wandered into the dining room, crashing into a side table on his way: Quintus Camillus Justinus had finally shown up.

Blinking in the lamplight, he bent to kiss his mother, not a good thought. He then tickled the sole of Helena's foot, causing her to kick out wildly. She caught Aelianus a nasty blow on the ear as he sat up to say something insulting. With the intense care of the far from sober, Justinus placed two packages before his sister, then made a sudden lunge and kissed her too. Helena biffed him away.

Impervious to atmosphere, Justinus regained his balance like a tightrope walker, then staggered around the couches and threw himself on the empty one alongside me. I braced myself as he flung an arm across my shoulders. 'Marcus! How are you surviving the party?' He was beyond help.

I made soothing noises while Helena sent me urgent signals to feed him. Since it was me he would throw up on, I had an interest in limiting his intake.

'Sorry, I'm a trifle tardy. I've been in the Saepta looking for a gift.'

My heart sank even further. '*Where* at the Saepta?' I already had glimmerings of why young Justinus was late and drunk tonight.

'Oh you'll know, Falco! I was wandering, then I saw a name I recognised and introduced myself ... A wonderful auctioneer,' Justinus told his brother. Aelianus was grinning: the son whose sins still lay undiscovered watching the debauched noisily sink himself. I absorbed the ominous news that it was my not-so-wonderful pa who had been filling up the golden boy.

Helena broke in brightly, 'We missed you! Sweetheart, is this my gift?'

'The small one,' Justinus enunciated clearly. 'A bijou from your devoted brother.'

'Thank you very much.'

'The large heavy item is sent to you with compliments from my excellent friend Didius Geminus.'

'Is that,' jeered Aelianus, 'the man who gave you so much wine?'

'My father,' I snapped. Julia Justa's face had frozen. I pressed on feebly, 'Didius Geminus likes his customers in a weak state. I counsel you, Aelianus, against tippling with an auctioneer. As you see, your brother now needs a quiet lie-down – and the gods only know what he's spent!'

'Very reasonable,' Justinus burbled happily. He at least had taken my advice. He was lying down. Unhappily, it was in the sweetmeat display.

We left him there. It seemed kindest.

Helena tried to look jolly as she unwrapped her brother's gift. It was an extremely attractive mirror, decorated in Celtic style with magnificent swirls and curlicues of foliage. She examined her face in it, trying to forget her younger brother's condition.

'And your father has sent Helena a present too, Marcus!' Julia Justa was much cheered by thinking the Didius family knew about buying off would-be relations. Helena obediently unwrapped it.

'My father thinks a lot of Helena,' I said weakly.

That was evident. Pa had sent her a highly superior (wincingly expensive) jewel casket. Not too big – nothing brash – but a beautiful example in cedarwood. Every corner had elaborate bronze fittings, there were miniature feet, a neat fastener, and a perfect lock with a swinging escutcheon.

'Oh the darling!' Oh the bastard. He had completely ignored my own predicament. Not even a word of apology.

It seemed a moment for toasts. Wine was being poured by slaves who wanted a chance to crane at the young mistress's gifts. Various hairpin pots and tweezer sets were also being proferred by ancient slaves who had once nursed her. 'Happy birthday!' exclaimed Helena's father, who for all his air of innocence knew how to cash in on a good mood.

Helena had found the casket key on a skein of wool. Even the key was a delight, a tiny three-pronged fancy set into a

656

finger ring. 'There's a note inside for you, Marcus.' She tossed across a scrap of recycled scroll. I did not wish to communicate with Pa; I pretended to glance at it, then I burnt it on a handy lamp.

Helena delved inside the box, deep in its handsome interior. I was in two minds to glide off somewhere, pretending to look for the latrine. Manners won; I bit a pastry instead. Honey oozed down my chin.

I saw Helena's face change. There must be more; the amazing box had contents. My heart started bumping angrily. She began lifting something out and immediately I realised what it was. Unexpected gold scintillations flickered on the casket's lid. Light fluttered like butterflies over her skin. Helena exclaimed in astonishment, 'Oh!' Then she lifted an object of breathtaking beauty.

Around the table silence fell.

Slowly, as if terrified she would damage something, Helena placed her gift on the table. Light still glittered from a hundred minutely teased pieces of gold. Helena turned to me. Everyone else was looking at her present. I didn't need to. My concern was watching her.

It was a crown. It was very old. It was Greek. It had once been a prize at some classical games, in the era when athletes were perfect in both body and mind. It was composed of exquisitely suspended leaves and acorns, held on gold wires so delicate they trembled merely in the air. Among the glittering twigs that formed it crouched perfectly shaped insects, and a small golden bee perched over the clasp.

Helena's mother tried to pull herself together. 'Oh Helena Justina, I am not sure you should accept this . . .' Her voice faltered. 'Marcus, you have an extremely generous father.'

There was no doubting the reproof: it was too much. The common Didii had behaved crassly. From a mere relative of a purely unofficial son-in-law, such a gift was gross.

I smiled at Helena gently. Her soft dark eyes were full of tears. She knew. She was touching her little finger to one iridescent cicada as it hid beneath an oak leaf, caressing it as gently as if it were a newborn baby's cheek. 'Pa has his moments,' I told her quietly. 'He has style, and taste, and as your mother mentions, he can be extremely generous.

Thoughtful too. He's obviously gone to a lot of trouble to find exactly the right box.'

'The crown is wonderful,' she said.

'You're a wonderful girl.'

'She cannot possibly accept it,' insisted her mother, more firmly.

I raised an eyebrow. 'Well, can you, fruit?'

Helena Justina smiled at me. She paid no attention at all to her family, but suddenly they understood.

The moment, which had become precious and tender, disintegrated with a lurch. Quintus had roused himself, his face lightly dusted with honey and cinnamon. 'Marcus, a message. Your father says sorry he made you sweat. He had to get the crown back from the man he had sold it to.' What an unspeakable degenerate. Justinus burbled on as I ground my teeth. 'There won't be any comeback – Geminus told the silly bastard he was retrieving it because he'd just seen on a vigiles listing that it's stolen property . . .'

Well thank you, Pa!

Helena giggled. Some members of her family may have found that unexpected. She said to me gravely, 'I wonder, purely from commercial interest, whether your father screwed as much out of the silly bastard as some other seller had already squeezed from you?'

'Probably not. The disreputable Damascan whose retirement in comfort I've assured, could see I was buying out of love.'

I stood and raised my winecup formally, calling upon everyone to join in my toast. 'According to the Damascan, this crown was once a prize in the Nemean Games. A prize worthy only of the finest, my darling.'

Her noble family had the grace to murmur agreement, pretty well spontaneously. We drank to Helena Justina in the robustly acceptable Guaranum that her father had saved to celebrate her special day. 'Helena Justina, daughter of Camillus Verus and heart's joy of Didius Falco, greetings on your anniversary!'

'Happy birthday, Helena,' cried Julia Justa. After which, since she could not reach her daughter, whose dining couch was too far from her, the noble matron shed a seemly tear, then turned on her scented elbow and kissed me.

XLV

It was a night to remember, but once we returned to our own apartment I had to drag myself back to the real and sordid world.

The two watches of the Fourth Cohort must have spent those hours of darkness prowling the violent Aventine Hill, expecting to meet horror again. I knew Petronius would be out with them at least part of the time. Martinus, his deputy, would bestir himself to cover another section of the night watch. Fusculus would be there as well. One or other of them might take Porcius, the recruit. Sergius, their man with the whip who enjoyed his job, would be along somewhere looking for careless householders to thrash – and hoping to try his talents on a killer. I had a good idea that if they ever found out who had murdered the brother of Scythax, someone would simply disappear off the streets. The Fourth were in a mood for rough justice. Maybe that was why, when I found I could not sleep, instead of walking out to join them in their grim patrol I stayed at home in bed.

Eventually my restlessness disturbed Helena.

'Hush, you'll wake the baby.'

'Not this one, love.'

'Then you'll wake the dog.'

The dog, who was squashing my feet again, shuffled to reinforce the point. 'Watch yourself, furry! One false move and I'll turn you into bootliners.'

Winding herself into my arms more closely, Helena lay silent. I knew her well enough to hear her thoughts working; well enough to know what thoughts they were. 'Your mother's right. When we have time to give to the babe, we'll find him a home.'

Unconvinced, Helena went on quietly worrying.

I tried again. 'Don't fret. The baby's safe here. Let's worry about Tertulla. Tell me how you got on today with Gaius

659

Baebius. How many parents did you manage to talk to? Any success?'

'Not much.' In a low voice Helena recounted her adventures. 'There are five families on the list which Petronius gave me. I managed to speak to someone at four of the houses. Only one refused me entry altogether; they are extremely superior.'

'Why do they live on the Aventine then?'

'They must have lived here since they looked down their noses at Romulus.'

'Well if anyone can tweak those noses, it's you! What about the rest?'

'I saw one mother personally. She met me in a room on her own, as if she did not want anyone to know. But even then she just hissed angrily that it was all sorted out now. She was sorry for our troubles, but could not involve herself.'

'Was she frightened?'

'Very, I should say.'

'It fits. Kidnappers tend to say don't go to the law or we'll be back. Did she let you see the child?'

'Oh absolutely not! At two other houses I ran into a reception committee of slaves – polite but distant, and no help. At the fourth house the mother refused to see me, but I happened to meet a nursemaid. As I was being seen out by a steward she was taking the child for a walk.'

'What age was the child?'

'A three-year-old boy. I followed his nurse from the house, and inveigled her into conversation as we went down the street. She was horrified to hear of another case, and let me engage her sympathy. She admitted the boy had been taken away – on a similar walk, so she was escorted everywhere now by slaves. That meant they were breathing down our necks and I only had a short opportunity to talk to her. Her story was quite helpful, and it confirm's Petro's theory as far as it goes. The child was snatched when her back was turned, as she bought something at a garment shop. She turned around seconds later and little Tiberius had vanished. There was complete panic in the household overnight; the vigiles were informed, as we know; the father also had all his slaves out combing the streets. Then next day everything abruptly

660

cooled down. The nurse was never told why. The child's parents became withdrawn and secretive. There was a great deal of tension in the household, but the street searches were ended. She thinks the family banker visited.'

'That's significant.' Lucky too; the father could as easily have arranged a ransom with the banker in the Forum, and we would have missed this. 'It's a useful detail. How was little Tiberius returned?'

'The father went out with the banker, and came home carrying the child. The household were informed that someone had found him by accident. Afterwards they were discouraged from gossiping. That was all I could learn.'

'It's enough. Was the child old enough to talk about what happened?'

'He looked a dim little overfed soul. I suppose he can talk, but we'd never be allowed to get at him, especially now. There's a close guard kept, and the escort soon became twitchy about me conversing with the nurse. I was lucky to find out what I did – and lucky Gaius Baebius had the sense to keep out of the way.'

'The great pudding.'

'He means well, Marcus. He's terribly concerned about Tertulla, and very angry that her own father has never put in an appearance to look for her.'

'This must be the first time one of my brothers-in-law despises another even more than I do! All right, so Gaius Baebius can't choose a wife or a watchdog, but he has a heart of gold. Anyone who'll beat his head against a wall trying to complain about Lollius deserves a laurel wreath. Is he coming to help you tomorrow? Are you intending to tackle the fifth house again?'

'Gaius is scheduled for shift work at Ostia. Yes, I'll try the last family a second time.'

'Not on your own.'

'I wasn't intending that. These are the snooty ones. This time I'm taking Mother's litter and a train of Father's slaves. I'll experiment with announcing myself more formally as a woman of respectable background.'

Helena had spoken seriously, intent on her task. Trusting

her good sense and flair, I could afford to be frivolous. 'Try wearing your Greek crown!'

She chortled. Then Helena Justina set about thanking me for her antique treasure from Damascus in a way that cleared my mind of most of its troubles, and eventually let me find peace and sleep.

If we needed confirmation that a kidnap gang was active, it came first thing next day. We were still at breakfast. Light footsteps scuffed the stairs outside, then, while I was wondering whether to grab a bread-roll knife in case the Miller and Little Icarus had returned, young Justinus bowled in.

We relaxed.

'Quintus! Greetings, you bibulous rascal!'

'Falco, there's been a terrible mistake!'

'Drinking with my father always is. Cool off. Your purse is deep enough; you'll get over it.'

He looked sheepish. 'I think I've endured enough reproaches.'

'I bet.'

'There's been a misunderstanding, one that concerns you.'

'What's new?'

'No, listen,' he burst out excitedly. 'We owe you an apology.'

'I'm all ears, Quintus.'

Then he told us that while we had been dining at the Camillus house last night a strange messenger had called. He brought a note, which the Senator's secretary took in and read. Since there was a family party in progress, the secretary dealt with it himself. The note asked for money for the return of the child; the child's name was unfamiliar to the scribe. He angrily sent the messenger away, and only when the strange story was mentioned this morning had Camillus Verus realised the truth. Luckily we had been talking about Tertulla during our visit.

'Jupiter! At least we can tell Galla she's probably alive. But what a cheek! Helena Justina, someone has been trying to put pressure on your father to ransom my niece!' As if our relationship did not entail enough embarrassments.

Needless to say, no clues had been retained. The ransom note had been thrust back at the seedy messenger; there was no useful description of the man; and nobody had watched to see which way he went after he was turned out of the house. Maybe the kidnappers would try again. Maybe they would have the sense to approach Helena Justina or me. Maybe they would lose patience, and just hand Tertulla back.

Maybe.

XLVI

At the thirteenth-sector patrol house moods were as dour as mine. It had been a quiet night on the Aventine. A normal one, anyway. Apart from eighteen house fires, arson in a grain warehouse, a rash of burglaries, several street fights related to the festival of the Armilustrium, three suicides dragged from the Tiber, and two more angry women whose nicely airing counterpanes had been stolen from balcony parapets, nothing had disturbed the peace.

I told Petro what we had discovered about the kidnaps, and he told me what I could do with my news.

'Don't fob me off. Tertulla is an official case, Petro. Galla demands an enquiry.'

'She's on our daily list.'

'Damn the list. This needs a vigorous follow-up.'

'Give me a name or a suspect house and I'll send in men.'

'It's someone with good information. It's someone who knows enough to connect my ghastly sister's snotty truant with the fact that my girlfriend comes from a family with status.' Not enough information, however, to realise that the illustrious Camilli had no spare cash.

'They could have heard it at any barber's or breadshop.'

'Are you sure? Someone out on the streets knows more than Helena's father's secretary does. He sent the runner away!'

'I presume you've made sure next time he'll put a leg ring on the messenger and pass him to us.'

'She's a seven-year-old girl. She ought to be a priority.'

'My priority is set by Rubella. My priority is eliminating the gangs.'

His scowl told me different. Petro had fathered girls himself. He knew all the doubts and dreads when a female child went missing. He quietened down, told me Helena had done splendidly over questioning the other families, and remarked that I didn't deserve her. With her help, and now

664

the attempt to involve her father, at least we knew what was going on.

'That's no consolation to my sister, and you know it!'

Petro promised that as soon as he had time he would look into it. As things were, he would never have time. We both knew that.

There had been no more raids and no more murders. That was a relief – yet it meant we had no more to go on. Petronius and the squad were back with the dire, depressing task of flogging once more through old evidence. Worrying at empty details. Trying to tease an extra ounce of significance from useless facts.

'Where's the black boy?' Petro demanded suddenly. 'The Nonnius slave?'

'With Porcius.'

'Then where's Porcius?'

Porcius was summoned from fending off counterpane victims. He came into the interrogation room nervously. He must have known Petro was the calmest man on the Aventine, but he could sense short temper tingling in the air like the night before a blinding storm.

'I thought I told you to make friends with the squealer's attendant?'

'Yes, chief. I'm doing it.'

'Well?'

'He's very timid, chief.'

'I don't care if he wets himself every half-hour. Mop him dry and keep up the pressure. I want to know what he saw.'

'He talks a lot of gibberish, chief.'

'We can find a translator if he lacks Latin – '

'It's not his Latin – '

'Don't nit-pick. Porcius, this is Rome. We can find a trustworthy translator for any language in the world.'

'Chief, he's just terrified.' Like himself, Porcius could have said.

'So he's no use? I don't accept it. Surely if he was hiding right under the couch where we found him he could have glimpsed a few feet. Did he hear anything said? Can he not suggest how many abductors came to the house? Were *they* talking any foreign languages?'

Porcius blinked a bit, but pulled himself together. He must have acquired some feeling of responsibility for the tiny slave who had been placed in his care. Now he tried standing up to Petro – not a good idea. 'Chief, I'm working on him. I've got a plan to lure him into talking usefully. He was brave enough the night it happened, actually; he must have gone into shock afterwards. He loved his master. He was loyal. So far I've found out that when Nonnius was taken, the boy ran after the group who grabbed him – '

Listening from the sidelines, I felt myself wince. Petronius Longus leapt to his feet. Already under stress, he picked up the last sentence and broke into a froth. 'What's this? I don't believe I heard you!'

Porcius realised his error and stopped.

Petronius had needed an outlet for his frustration. The well-meaning recruit made an easy target. Petro was beside himself. 'How long have you been holding this information, Porcius? Are you looking for early retirement? We have dead men and stripped buildings all over Rome, and you're prancing about like a circus horse "working on" the only witness! Get this straight: if you serve in this cohort's investigation unit, you're in a team, a team headed by me. You don't bury yourself in private schemes, you report every detail – relevant or irrelevant – to your colleagues and to me!'

'You'll burst something,' I muttered.

'Stuff you, Falco!' The interruption had calmed him slightly. Even so he slammed his hand against the wall. It must have hurt. 'Porcius, don't stand there buckling like a bale of felt. I want to hear exactly what the slave has told you – every detail – and you'd better be fast. After that I'm going to hang you from the Probus Bridge by your boot-thongs just low enough to drown you slowly when the tide comes in!'

He was still so angry he had to do something more vigorous. It was either hit Porcius or break the furniture. He seized a stool and flung it splintering against the door.

There was a long silence. The entire station house grew still. The normal ranting of victims pleading for urgent enquiries and the racket from last night's prisoners abruptly stopped. The prisoners thought some suspect was being hurled around a cell. They thought they might be next.

Porcius had his eyes closed. He knew if anyone got pounded it was going to be him.

Fusculus and Martinus, who were tough nuts, appeared in the doorway looking openly curious. I commented gently, 'What with the seating that's broken by flying boulders thrown in by your neighbours and the bum-props you destroy yourselves, the Fourth's office equipment bill must be rocketing these days.' Petronius, red in the face and ashamed of the lapse, fought to calm down.

Porcius, to his credit, did not waver. He was white as ash. I could see his knuckles shining as he gripped his fists beside his tunic seams. He had just been bawled at and attacked by a man who was famous for never losing his temper. He knew Fusculus and Martinus were playing about behind him, pretending to give his achievement admiring looks.

He took a deep breath. 'The slave boy saw Nonnius being dragged into a house.'

I watched my old friend forcibly restrain himself. 'Tell me about it,' said Petronius, ominously quiet.

'He doesn't know whose dwelling it was. He was a house slave. Normally he hardly ever went out.'

'But we found him the next day in his master's place. If he had followed the abductors, how had he got home again?'

'He says he wandered about for hours then found his way back by accident. When we arrived to investigate he had only just reached home. The front door had been smashed to pieces, so he crept inside without anybody seeing him.'

'Right. So go back to the moment it first happened. He witnessed the abduction. What exactly did he see?'

'He was sleeping in a side-room and ran out when he heard the noise. He then saw Nonnius dragged from his bedroom by several men. At that point Nonnius was gagged with something like a scarf. He was rushed out of the house, and marched through the streets. He was taken into this other house. The lad hid outside for a long time, then saw a body dragged out backwards by the feet. That was when he panicked. He guessed it must be his master. He was so afraid that he ran away.'

'He didn't see the body dumped in the Forum Boarium?'

'He says not,' declared Porcius.

'Believe him?'

'Yes. My guess is that if he had known where the body ended up we'd have found him crying beside it instead of back at home.'

Petronius Longus folded his arms. He threw back his head, staring at the stained daub of the patrol house roof. Porcius managed to remain silent while his chief pondered. Martinus, Fusculus and I exchanged looks.

Petronius lowered his gaze and applied it to the stricken recruit.

'So you discovered all this in the course of your independent plan to "lure" the witness into telling more. Now we're all going to help you resolve things, Porcius. So tell us – what exactly was your plan?'

'I thought,' Porcius gulped miserably, 'I could attempt to get the slave boy to identify the house where Nonnius was killed. I thought, so as not to confuse him by going through a lot of streets, I could put him in a closed carrying chair and take him to a selection of likely spots – show him the homes of specific suspects.'

'I see.'

As Petronius glared at their unhappy young colleague, Fusculus risked chirping, 'So what's the plan now, chief?'

'Pretty obvious,' snapped Petro. 'We put the black child in a carrying chair and show him suspects' homes! Our young colleague may be irresponsible, but his idea has a certain charm. Where's the boy, Porcius?'

'I'll fetch him – '

'No. Fusculus will fetch him. You'll tell Fusculus where he has to go.' This distrust of Porcius seemed hard. Petronius strode from the room before anyone could attempt to arbitrate.

Porcius appealed to me for sympathy: 'I thought it was a good idea!'

I clapped him on the shoulder. 'Don't worry about it. But on this case, protect your back, Porcius. Don't bother having big ideas.'

Fusculus started sauntering off; he turned back and

beckoned slowly to Porcius, who scuttled after him. Martinus stayed grinning at me.

'Resignation time?' I asked, nodding after the anguished figure of the recruit.

'Who knows? Nice lad,' Martinus told me. 'Sends all his pay home to his mother, doesn't play around with women, doesn't leer at the male scribes, doesn't have smelly feet or tell bad jokes, turns up for his shift on time. Seems absolutely nothing wrong with him.'

'Oh right!' I remarked, pretending to catch on at last. 'I can see he was never going to fit in with this cohort!'

I was joking, but the angry scene had left a bad feeling. The pressure was on now. I would hate to think any part of the Fourth might be cracking up. Especially the part that Petronius Longus ran – and most of all Petronius himself.

The Nonnius slave was taken to see the houses of a couple of big gang leaders, which at least served to eliminate rivals to the Balbinus empire; he recognised none of them. He was shown Plato's Academy; still nothing. He was then asked to look at the lovely homes of Flaccida and Milvia. He saw Milvia's first, and wasn't sure. He made up his mind the minute we let him out of the chair at Flaccida's.

He was eight years old, still in shock, and incoherent with fright. There was no way we could have used his evidence in court, even if the law had allowed it. As it was, we could only quote him if we extracted his story under torture. Petro decided not to try. One glimpse of Sergius wielding the red-hot forceps and this fragile soul was likely to drop off his twig.

There were plenty of problems with the boy's story. A barrister would tear it to shreds. Nonnius had been taken away not by Flaccida herself, but by a group of men, none of whom we could yet identify. The slave boy could give no descriptions. Petronius was in no position to make arrests. But for our own purposes, although we could not *prove* Flaccida had been involved in anything, at least we knew: Nonnius Albius had been murdered at her house. Work on the case had begun to simplify at last.

'So what are you going to do?' I asked Petro as we walked back towards the patrol house. 'Interview Flaccida?'

'You said you did that, Falco.'

'I wasn't able to make her sweat. It was before we had a lead on the Nonnius death. I couldn't frighten her with a witness.'

'Neither can I.' Petronius was a realist.

'So you leave her bust up on its pedestal?'

He stopped on a street corner, stretching his neck. He rubbed one hand all around inside the neck of his tunic, as if the hem was causing a rash. What irritated Petro was something else. He hated to see criminals getting away with a crime.

'The bust can keep its station – but I'll chuck a few stones at it. Flaccida's the one to work on, though we need something indirect. Forget Nonnius. I'll nail Flaccida for him one day. And I'll nail her for Alexander too, though as yet don't ask me how.' I could see he had made up his mind. 'We've made an advance on the murders. Let's go back to the Emporium and Saepta thefts, Falco. Let's see if we can trace your father's pretty Syrian glass.'

I had known him long enough to recognise which approach he was planning. 'You reckon our brothel prank is now safely forgotten and you can drag me off on some new escapade.'

'Exactly. Comb your hair for once, Falco. You and I are going to spend the afternoon chatting like dangerous degenerates with lovely little Milvia!'

670

XLVII

Milvia was at home. This confirmed my previous impression that she led a lonely life. It seemed she rarely went out. Still, staying in this afternoon had brought the lucky girl the pair of us.

'I'm getting too old for this,' I joked as Petro and I waited for her to be told her good fortune. No doubt she wanted to jump into her nicest frock.

'You've forgotten how. Just follow my lead.'

We sat up and tried looking like sober citizens as Milvia tripped through the door.

She seemed delighted to see us. When she rushed in, all pleated white stoles and dainty ribbons, I had forgotten quite what a pretty girl she was. This was certainly more pleasant than exchanging barbs with that hard nut her mother. Of course we did not place too much faith in Milvia; in our time, Petronius and I had been flattered then dumped in a midden by plenty of round-eyed, honest-looking girls.

When we asked her again about the glass flagon, she told the same tale: a present from someone to Florius. Petronius demanded a sight of her household shelves. 'But you have looked at them!' Milvia cried wonderingly.

'I'd like to look again.' Petronius Longus could manage to sound as stern as if he were inspecting an unauthorised standpipe on an aqueduct, yet with a subtle hint of approving comment on a woman's physique. What a dog.

Milvia was worried. This was good. Milvia would complain to her mother; Flaccida, not having been here, would find that very disconcerting. Flaccida would wonder why Milvia had been singled out for an extra visit, and what dangerous hints Milvia might have given away.

'Falco is going to take a look with me this time.'

'Oh you're the nice one!' Milvia obviously remembered me. Petronius gave me a cheesy grin, then dug me sharply in the small of the back as we marched to the kitchen.

671

For about an hour we gravely surveyed miles of expensive tableware on shelves, in cupboards, displayed formally on buffets, or tucked tidily into niches. Redware and lead glaze, glass and gilded metalware. It was all in sets, and the sets were meant for civic banquets of fifty people or so. It made a poor comparison with the wonky shelf of bowls Helena and I owned at Fountain Court – barely enough for a quiet one-course supper for two people, especially if they were entertaining a foundling and a hungry new dog.

There was no glass that I recognised. Since the house had already been searched by the Fourth Cohort, I expected no surprises. I gave Petro the headshake several times, but he seemed in no hurry to leave. He smiled at Milvia, who had been showing off the household goods herself. 'Let's return to the salon and get some details straight . . .'

We trooped back and sat down. It was a decorous room in whites, greens and blues, but I hate Egyptian summerhouse furniture that looks so light the legs may snap if you wriggle. Its pert young owner was not my kind of girl either. Once I had liked the ones who smile a lot and look admiring, but I had grown up since then. I was starting to feel alone in this sophisticated attitude.

Petro had on his stubborn look. Milvia was unreliable, but just the kind of bright-eyed puppet Petro always wanted to discuss the weather with. The whole situation took me back ten years. It was like trying to drag him out of a British meadmaker's hovel once the biddy in charge had swung her golden plaits at him. As always I was at a loss how to deal with it. When he was in this mood tutting and mentioning other social engagements would only make him linger. I had already dragged his wife into the conversation, in some forced context to do with tureens. Any more would just make me sound like a surly prude.

I would not have minded, but as an informer I was the one who had always had to fight off a reputation for chasing women.

'Nice room!' smiled Petronius, glancing around. He was very relaxed. He spoke in a kindly, reassuring tone, and Milvia smiled back at him.

672

'Watch out,' I muttered. 'He'll try to sell you mediocre frescoes if you show an interest.'

Milvia giggled at me. 'You two are not like law officers at all!'

'Is that right?'

Petronius smirked at me, then set about some genuine work. 'So. Let's just get this straight. The flagon you gave to Didius Falco – '

'I gave it to his charming colleague, actually. Is the glass flagon what your enquiries have all been about?'

'Charming colleague, Falco?' Petro asked.

'Helena,' I owned up. Well, it wiped off his smirk.

'After all, I had been talking to her mostly,' Milvia carried on.

'Had you really?'

'We all have our methods,' I told Petro.

'The flagon,' Petro began again with Milvia, looking dangerous.

'Was brought home by my husband.'

'Was brought home by Florius. Florius had it from?'

'From somebody he knows.'

'A mysterious benefactor. Have you asked him who?'

'Why should I? He seemed rather vague.'

'Does Florius keep things to himself?'

'Not particularly.'

'Do you and your husband discuss his daily business?'

'No, not much.' Milvia glanced down at her lap, aware how her answer could be interpreted.

'That's very sad,' Petronius Longus commented sombrely.

'Don't be snide,' I said.

'It was a straight comment.'

'There's nothing wrong!' Milvia cried defensively.

'But you're not close,' Petro decided, looking pleased about it.

'We are perfect friends.'

'And some other friend of Florius gives him expensive gifts.'

There was a small pause.

Milvia looked from Petronius to me and back again. 'You *are* proper law officers.'

673

'If you're honest that won't worry you. Was it a woman?' I enquired. There was no point now being soft on her. It was possible, if her marriage mattered to her, that we had just destroyed it in a couple of suggestive remarks. Even if Florius was as chaste as dew we might have ruined the relationship. Suspicion is an evil ingredient in any match.

'Could your husband be taking gifts from a woman?' I pressed Milvia again.

'I didn't think so.'

'But could he have been?'

'That was not the impression he gave me. Did you have any particular woman in mind?' Milvia managed to riposte proudly.

'No. But no doubt now you will ask Florius.' That came from Petronius.

'I think,' Milvia decided more firmly than I would have expected, 'if you want to know, you should ask Florius yourself.'

Petronius smiled quietly. 'I shall do that.'

But Florius was not at home.

Petronius was now in a tenacious mood. Nothing would put him off until he traced the flagon right back from its arrival in this house to when I first left the glass with Pa at the Emporium. When we came out of the house he told me he intended to return there that evening to tackle Florius in person. I naturally started making arrangements to come with him, but he reckoned that unnecessary. Florius, apparently, was viewed by the watch as a soft custard; a witness would be superfluous.

'Hah! Don't come the innocent – I know what that means, you gigolo!'

Petro graciously suggested that instead of spreading slander I could devote some time to the search for my niece.

In fact I went to the Temple of Castor baths, where I gave a couple of useful hours to exercise with Glaucus. My shoulder still felt delicate, but I managed to work on the rest. I wanted to be fit. I felt we were starting to twist the tensioning cord on the whole enquiry now. I could tell Petronius shared some of this feeling, though if his idea of getting fit was a romantic interlude, he was welcome to Milvia.

We were both on the alert, with that special edge that only comes when action is just around the corner. Neither Petro nor I were the least prepared for what actually happened next.

XLVIII

When I reached the apartment I found we had visitors who were guaranteed to undo all the benefits of my bath and training session. I had walked in before I realised, or I would have turned tail quietly and fled. Too late: I found Helena talking in subdued tones to my brother-in-law Gaius Baebius. Gaius had brought along my sister Junia. I immediately noticed they had left their dog Ajax at home. The absence of Ajax warned me of trouble. I assumed something dire had been discovered in connection with Tertulla, but there had been no further news; the trouble Gaius Baebius was bringing turned out to be worse.

Everyone had been waiting for me. It was lucky Petronius and I had not decided to bathe together and have a long session in a wine bar. (For some unusual reason Petro had not even wanted a drink.)

In the apartment the atmosphere was strained. Junia had the skip baby across her bony knees; Helena was telling her his story, as a polite way of filling in time. Gaius Baebius, sitting upright with a superior expression, was dressed in a toga. Not even this peculiarly formal character had ever been known to don traditional dress before calling at Fountain Court.

'Gaius! What are you all wrapped up like a parcel for? And why are you here anyway? I was told you were working at Ostia.'

A worrying thought struck me that Gaius and Junia might want to foster the skip babe. It was nothing so simple, though finding out took willpower.

'I went to Ostia this morning,' Gaius said. That explained nothing. Yet somehow he managed to give his routine trip to work a resonant significance.

I sighed and gave up. Persuading Gaius Baebius to tell a five-minute tale normally took about three days.

I hung my cloak on a peg, flopped on the floor (since all the

676

seats were taken), grabbed the baby from Junia and started playing with him and Nux.

'Marcus!' said Helena, in a light, warning voice.

'What's up?' I immediately stopped playing camels with the babe, though Nux had less sense and carried on pretending to hunt me like a wild boar. This dog would have to be put through a course on domestic etiquette. Maybe a better solution would be to get rid of the dog. (Maybe Gaius and Junia would like to foster *her*.)

'Marcus, Gaius Baebius has to visit an official. He wants to ask if you'll go with him.'

'Well, I just wondered if you could tell me the name,' Gaius demurred, as I was fending off the crazy dog.

'Whose name?'

'The tribune of the Fourth Cohort of the vigiles.'

'Marcus Rubella. He's a misery. Don't have anything to do with him.'

'I need to. The customs force have a report to make.'

'In full formal dress? What's up, Gaius? Is this something sensitive?'

On reflection it had to be, if those plodders in the taxation force had sent a supervisor back to Rome before the end of his shift. Gaius Baebius was also clearly disturbed by his task.

I stood up and straightened my tunic. I gave Junia the baby to hold again. Helena quietly squashed along a bench, leaving me room to perch on the end of it close to Gaius. That big wheat pudding was sitting on a stool, so he was lower than me. It made him vulnerable to stern treatment. Gaius knew that. He was looking uncomfortable.

I tapped him on the knee and lowered my voice into friendly cajolement. 'What's the game, Gaius?'

'It's a confidential matter.'

'You can tell me. Maybe I already know. Is it graft?'

He looked surprised. 'No, nothing like that.'

'One of the inspectors made a nasty discovery,' interrupted Junia.

My sister Junia was an impatient, supercilious piece. She had a thin face, a skinny frame, and a washed-out character to match. She wound her black hair into tight plaits pinned around her head, with stiff little finger-long ringlets in front

677

of her ears and either side of her neck. This was all modelled on a statue of Cleopatra: a big joke, believe me.

Life had disappointed Junia, and she was firmly convinced that it could not possibly be her own fault. In fact, between her terrible cooking and her resentful attitude, most of what went wrong could be easily explained.

She always treated her husband – in public anyway – as if supervising customs clerks stood on a par with the labours of Hercules, and was better paid. But his ponderous conversational style must drive her wild. Now she snorted and took charge of him: 'An inspector in pursuit of unpaid harbour tax looked into a boat and found a dead man. The corpse was in a bad condition but it carried an identification tag. Gaius Baebius has been specially selected to bring it to Rome.' Junia spoke as if the trusty Gaius had flown here on winged sandals in a gilded helm.

My heart took an unpleasant lurch. 'Show Marcus, Gaius,' Helena urged as if she had already managed to see it.

What he unwrapped cautiously from a piece of cloth was a simple bone disc. Gaius held it out to me on the cloth, reluctant to touch it. It looked clean. I picked it up between my fingertips. A nerve in my wrist gave an involuntary twitch.

It had a round hole at the top, through which were threaded two entwined leather strings. One of them was broken. The other still held in its knot. On one side of the disc were the letters COH IV. They were very neat, centrally set, with that telling gap which showed the last two letters were the numeral four. Around the rim in smaller letters was the word ROMA followed by a spacing mark, then PREF VIG. I turned the disc over. More untidily scratched on the back was one masculine name. It was a name I knew.

My face had set. 'Where's the body, Gaius?'

Gaius must have recognised the dark tone in my voice. 'They're bringing it from Ostia.' He cleared his throat. 'We had a problem persuading a carter.'

I shook my head. I could work out how many days the body might have been lying at the port. The filthy details I did not want to know.

It was clearly a matter of pride to have identified the disc and to be drawing official notice as promptly as possible.

Customs like to think they are as sharp as fencing nails. Even so, my brother-in-law must have had mixed feelings even before he saw me. Officials stick together. A blow against one arm of the public service dismays them all. Always a lover of a crisis but aware of the implications, Gaius murmured, 'Is this bad, Falco?'

'As bad as it could be.'

'What's happened?' demanded Junia.

I ignored her. 'Was the man drowned, Gaius?'

'No. Thrown into the keel of an old barge that had been stuck on the silt for months. One of our lads noticed footprints on a mudbank, and thought he might have uncovered some smuggling. He had a bad fright. There were no hidden bales, just this: a corpse hidden out on the barge. Whoever dumped him probably thought no one would ever go out there to look.'

'You mean it made a safer hiding place than the ocean, which might have washed the corpse ashore?'

'Looked as if the fellow had been strangled, but it was hard to tell. Nobody wanted to touch the body. We had to, of course,' Gaius added hastily. 'Once discovered it couldn't be left there.' Nice to know that in the customs realm the highest standards of public hygiene ruled.

'Was the disc actually on the corpse?'

Something in Gaius' manner made me wish I had not asked. He flushed slightly. Customs have their moments. Screwing money from reluctant importers they have to face plenty of aggravation, but it usually stops at shouting and obscenities. Holding back a shudder he confirmed the worst. 'We spotted the thongs. I'm afraid the disc had been rammed in the poor fellow's mouth. It looked as if in the process of killing him, someone had tried to make him eat it.' I swallowed air. In my mind I was seeing a boyish, cheery face with bright eyes and an enthusiastic grin. Gaius enquired, 'Is anyone missing?'

'No one the cohort knew was lost.'

'So was he one of theirs then?'

'Yes.' I was terse. I stood up again. 'I knew him briefly. This is very important, Gaius – for the cohort and for Rome. I'll come with you to see Rubella.'

I refolded the cloth gently around its significant contents. Gaius put out his hand to take it back, but I closed my fist too fast for him.

We found Marcus Rubella at the cohort headquarters. I was surprised. It was by then the hour when most people were thinking about relaxation and food. Mentally I had had Rubella listed as the type who worked set hours – the minimum he could get away with. I had imagined he would slide out with his oil flask and strigil, bidding his clerks farewell the minute the bathhouse stokers started thrusting wood into their stoves. I thought he probably left his work behind him then, and kept a clear mind all through dinner and his recreation hours.

But he was alone in the office, a still, brooding presence, staring at documents. When we first walked in he barely reacted. When I told him there was trouble he opened a shutter, as if to see the problem more clearly. For a brief moment he seemed the type who faced up to things after all.

Gaius Baebius relayed his story, prompted by me when he tried to slow down. Rubella made no fuss. Nor did he decide on any action, beyond some comment that he would write in sympathy to the family. Maybe he liked to brood first – or more likely he just loved to let events roll forwards without throwing in his own spear.

'Any idea where Petronius Longus is, Falco?'

I had a good idea, and I preferred to keep it private. 'He's following up an interview. I can track him down.'

'Good.' This was the sunflower-seed eater, neutral and standing well back. 'I'll leave it to you to tell him then.' Thanks, tribune!

Gaius Baebius and I left the building. With the usual difficulty I managed to shed my brother-in-law, who always liked to cling on when he was not wanted. As the streets grew darker, I walked sombrely from the Twelfth sector, where the Fourth had their headquarters, and down the hill to the Circus side of the Aventine. I could hear gulls squabbling over the Tiber wharves. They must always be there, but tonight I noticed them with resentment. Tonight was not the time to be reminded of the sea.

Everywhere seemed full of excited parties going out to dinner. Horse-faced women shrieked. Crass men chivied their trains of slaves to trot along faster. All shopkeepers looked malevolent. All passers-by had the air of would-be thieves.

A meek porter admitted me to Milvia's elegant house. I was told Florius was still out. No one seemed perturbed by it, even though respectable householders normally show up at home in the evening. If he was going out to dinner he ought at least to change his tunic – and some wives would expect to be taken along. No one had much idea when they might expect him back either. It seemed routine. Warily I asked whether an officer of the vigiles had visited that evening, and was told he was talking to Milvia in private.

As I feared. Another allegedly respectable husband was marauding off the leash. Petronius Longus could behave like a real boudoir bandit.

I was shown once more into the salon with the thin-legged Egyptian furniture. No one else was there. The house seemed very quiet, with not much going on. The whole time I was there Milvia, the young lady of the house, failed to appear.

I waited. After a few minutes Petronius walked in. He was wearing a green tunic that I had last seen the night he and Silvia dined at our apartment. He had bathed and changed, but there was no special odour of unguents. I might have been wrong; this was hardly the debonair adulterer at work. He looked perfectly normal – calm, steady, utterly the man in charge. My abrupt appearance here gave him some warning. We were such close friends he immediately knew far more than I had done when I set eyes on Gaius Baebius.

But I would still have to tell him.

'What's up, Falco?' Petro's voice was quick and light.

'You won't like this.'

'Can things get worse?'

'A lot worse. Tell me, do all members of the vigiles carry identity tags?'

He stared, then took from a pouch on his belt a small bone counter, exactly like the one from Ostia. He let me examine it. On the face was the symbol COH IV, surrounded by ROMA and PREF VIG. On the reverse, being a neat, systematic character, Petro had scratched in full his three names.

681

'You don't wear it?'

'Some do. I don't like cords around my neck – villains can grab at them and throttle you.' Well he was right about that.

I gave him back his tag. Then I took from my tunic the other disc, handing it over in silence. By then he was expecting sorrow. His face had set into melancholy hollows. He turned the bone and read the name: LINUS.

Petronius sat on one of the delicate couches, leaning fowards, knees apart, hands clasped between them, holding the disc. I told him what had happened, as far as the customs force had worked it out. When I finished I walked over to a folding door and stood staring out at a garden while Petro absorbed the facts and tried to cope.

'This is my fault.'

I had known he would say that. It was nobody's fault, but taking the blame was the only way Petronius could handle his grief.

'You know that's wrong.'

'How can I get them, Falco?'

'I don't know. Look, we can't even start yet; there have to be formalities. Rubella is going to write a letter of sympathy to the relations, but you know what that will sound like.' We had both seen how officialdom informs bereaved families of death.

'Oh dear gods! That isn't any good.' Petronius roused himself. 'I'll have to go. I'll have to tell his wife.'

'I'll come with you,' I said. I hardly knew Linus, but I had met him once and even the brief memory affected me. I was involved.

Petro made no move yet. He was still struggling. 'I'm trying not to think about what this means.'

He spoke the name on the tablet he was cradling so gently. Linus. Linus, the young, keen undercover man whom Petro had placed on the ship that had supposedly taken the condemned criminal Balbinus into exile.

The death of Linus at Ostia must strongly imply that Balbinus Pius never went. In reality the ship must have dropped off passengers at the harbour mouth. Either then, or very shortly afterwards, Petro's agent was dead.

IL

Normally I liked widows. They are women of the world, often without guardians, and frequently adventurous. This one was different. She did not know she was a widow yet.

Her name was Rufina. She admitted us both with a hint of a simper, then offered us wine, which we refused.

'Greetings, chief!'

Rufina looked about thirty-five, at any rate older than Linus. She dressed smartly, though her jewellery consisted merely of coloured beads strung on wires. There was no spare meat on her. She was not as pretty as she tried to act. Her manner was brash and ingratiating in a way I could only just tolerate, given what I knew.

'This is about time, I must say. I hoped you would be dropping in sometime. He's famous for being conscientious,' she giggled at me. I felt ill. She crossed her knees, showing ankles and toes beneath the hem of her gown. 'Have you brought me news of my husband?' Things were already unbearable. She managed to make the reference to having a husband seem even more saucy than the previous comment about Petro calling on her while Linus was away.

Petronius closed his eyes briefly. 'Yes.'

I glanced around. Linus and Rufina lived in a third-floor back-of-building apartment that appeared to have just two rooms. They had made no attempt to redecorate what came with their lease; the usual landlord's dirty plasterwork, ornamented with half-hearted scrolls of red carried out by a painter who had two patterns and could only do one of those properly. With relief I realised there was no evidence of children in the house.

The furniture was sparse. There was a loom in one corner. Rufina was a home-worker, though the state of the weaving – with an untidy straggle of wools in a basket on the floor and loose loom weights scattered everywhere – suggested she approached it lethargically. From a wall niche two household

gods, the lares and penates, dominated the room. The
dancing figures were in bronze with a very dark patina, rather
heavier and more ornate than the rest of their owners' lifestyle
called for.

'It's very naughty of you to take Linus from me for months,
you know.'

Petronius said nothing.

Doubt fluttered across Rufina's face. 'What are you telling
me, chief?' She was a vigiles wife. She must have spent most
of her married life half-prepared for an official visit of this
kind.

When Petronius told her what had happened she screamed
so loudly we heard doors of other apartments opening in the
outside corridor. At first she pretended she would not believe
it, then, amid racking sobs and wild exclamations, she
launched into the vilification that Petronius had dreaded.

'You should never have made him do it!'

'Linus volunteered.'

Rufina howled. 'He was afraid of you!'

It seemed more likely he was afraid of his own home life. I
could vaguely remember Linus suggesting he had wanted to
leave Italy for some peace. It seemed to me things could have
been worse. Still, in relationships small habits can soon
multiply into monumental grievances. 'He wanted the
adventure,' Petronius told the wife patiently. I could see he
was badly shaken by the violence of Rufina's hysteria. 'He was
eager to travel.' Not that he managed it.

'Oh Linus, Linus! Oh my darling! Whatever am I going to
do?'

'The cohort is ready to support you all it can. The tribune
will be writing you a letter – '

'Will I get compensation?'

That was better. It came out smart as a crack of artillery.
Petro could deal with that. 'I believe there will be a modest
award, enough to give you a small pension. Linus was a good
officer killed in the state's service – '

'Small!'

'Of course nothing can really replace him.'

'Small, you say! He deserved better. I deserve better for
acting as his only solace while he did his cruel job!'

'We all deserved better than to lose Linus.'

We were achieving little, and as soon as it seemed decent we prepared to leave. Rufina then thought of more embarrassment to hurl at us: 'Where is he now?'

'Not in Rome yet,' Petronius rapped back swiftly. He had gone very pale. 'You don't want to see him. Rufina, don't try!'

'He's my husband! I want to hold him in my arms one final time. I want to know what they did to him – '

Petronius Longus raised his voice so harshly he stopped her. 'Remember Linus as he was! What they are bringing to Rome is a six-day-old corpse that has been lying in the open. It's not him, Rufina. It's not your husband; it's not the friend and comrade who served under me.'

'How do I know it is really Linus then? There might have been a mistake.'

I put in weakly: 'Petronius Longus will ensure there has been no mistake. Don't upset yourself on that point. He will do what is needed; you can rely on him.'

That was when the widow suddenly crumpled up. With a small gurgle of pathetic grief she fell into Petro's arms and sobbed. She was taller than the girls he liked comforting, older, and her nature was much harder. But he never flinched, and he held her firmly while she wept. I managed to find a neighbour to take over, then we slunk away.

When the carter brought the body to the Ostia Gate, Petro and I were there waiting for it. The customs people had found an undertaker to provide a lidded coffin; Linus came home sealed in state like some general who had died on an intercontinental campaign. But before we passed him on to the funeral arrangers we had brought to the gate with us, my friend Lucius Petronius wrapped a scarf around his face, then insisted that the coffin lid be raised so he could identify his man formally.

As Petronius had warned Rufina, after six days in the sun and salty air this body bore little resemblance to his bright, cheerful, fearless volunteer. The corpse was wearing the sailor's disguise we recognised. It was the right build. The features looked correct. Taken with the identification-tag evidence, we accepted that this was Linus.

Balbinus had taken a stupid risk. He must have been so eager to regain land that he couldn't wait until the *Aphrodite* left the coastal shallows and found deeper waters where a corpse could be safely pushed overboard and lost. So he brought Linus back to land with him. Someone – the freedmen we had seen leave with him, perhaps – must have helped. Then Balbinus or others had killed Linus, and abandoned his body in a casual manner that was unbelievably arrogant.

I stayed alongside Petronius while he grieved, then I dealt with transferring the coffin. When the grumbling Ostian carter had removed his vehicle and the coffin had been carried away by officers of the vigiles' funeral club, we two walked back from the Ostia Gate. Once in our nostrils, the smell of putrefaction stayed cloyingly with us. In silence we found our way to the riverbank.

It was now dark. We had the complicated mass of buildings forming the granary area and the Emporium complex on our left, and the Probus Bridge along on the right, lit by dim lamps. Occasional figures crossed the bridge. We could hear the Tiber shifting, with splashes that could be fish or rats. Across the water, donkey hooves sounded sharply on a road in the Transtiberina. A breeze made us bury our chins deeply in our cloaks, though the air was humid and we were more depressed than cold.

There was no easy way to end this night. Already I felt ominous portents of how it might turn out for me.

'Do you want to go for a drink?'

Petronius did not even answer me.

I should have left him then.

We continued to stare across the river for some time. I tried again. 'There's nothing you can do and it's not your fault.'

This time he roused himself a little. 'I'm going to the patrol house.'

'You're not ready for that yet.' I knew him better than he knew himself. People never want to hear that happy news.

'I have to tell my men Linus is dead. I want them to hear it from me.'

'Too late,' I said. 'Rumour will have rushed straight to

686

them long ago. We've spent more hours on this than you realise. You've lost track of time. On the Aventine this is old news. The whole cohort already know.' I reckoned at least one cohort member knew about this before we did. A fact to which Lucius Petronius still seemed oblivious.

'This is nothing to do with you, Falco. This concerns me and my men.'

I felt the full drag of disaster now. He wanted a quarrel. He needed a bad one. It could have been anyone who caught the eruption, but I was his best friend so I was the rash man who had stayed at hand.

'You're not ready to see them,' I told him again. 'There is a situation you have to think about carefully first.'

'I know what needs to be done.'

'I don't believe you do.'

Somewhere in the remote distance we heard the trumpet. After our years in the legions our brains took it in, though we were too absorbed to react. In the Praetorian Camp a watch had changed. I could no longer tell which stretch of the night we were in now. Normally I always knew, even if I awoke from heavy sleep. Now the darkness seemed quite different, the city's noise unlike itself. Events had been moving at an unnatural pace. Emotions had blurred everything. Dawn might be several hours or merely minutes away from us.

At my side I was aware of Petronius giving me more attention. Patiently I explained. I knew we were unlikely to stay friends.

'This job started out as unpleasant, but it's filthy now. You have to accept that fact before you make a move, or you're going to get it wrong, Petro. There are two issues – '

'What issues?' he burst out angrily.

'Linus' death throws up two stinking problems.' Both seemed self-evident to me. They remained invisible to him.

'Falco, I have a heart full of grief, there are urgent things I need to do, and it's just not clever to hold me back for some piddling irrelevancy.'

'Listen! First, you've got the whole black business of Balbinus Pius. You can leave that one to creep up and depress you slowly if you like, but let's not delude ourselves. Linus must have been killed to stop him reporting that Balbinus

687

came off the *Aphrodite* pretty well while we were waving him goodbye across the harbour. There are enormous implications: the man is still here. He never left. Balbinus is in Rome. He probably fixed the raid on the Emporium and he hit the Saepta Julia. He killed Nonnius. He killed Alexander. He killed Linus too, of course. Jove only knows what he's planning next.'

Petronius would face it – and deal with it – but not now. He stirred restlessly. I put a hand on his arm. His skin was hot, as if his blood raced in turmoil. His voice was perfectly cold. 'What else?'

'Balbinus knew who had to be killed. Somebody betrayed Linus.'

He answered me at once. 'It's not possible.'

'It happened.'

'Nobody knew.'

'Think how he died! His identity tag was thrust between his teeth. Some swine was making a point that his true role had been exposed. Linus himself had to face up to the fact he had been spotted. He must have died knowing he had been betrayed. You can't refuse to acknowledge it, for his sake, Petro!'

Petronius rounded on me, full of hate. 'Do you think I would have put him in that position? We were dealing with power and money at their most vicious. If I could have hidden him on that ship without letting him even know himself that he was there I would have done! How can you suggest I gave no thought to the risks? Do you think I would send an unprotected agent on that trip without ensuring no one in Rome was in a position to let him down?'

'Your men all knew.'

'*My men?*' He was livid. 'My own team, Falco! I'm not talking cohort; I don't mean the bloody foot patrols! The only ones who knew I had sent a spy with Balbinus were my own, personally hand-picked investigation team.'

I hated saying it, but I had to: 'I'm sorry. One of your hand-picked babies has gone wrong. One of them must be on the take.'

He did not explode immediately. Still, I knew he was deaf to

688

my arguments. There was nothing for it but to carry on talking quietly, as if we were having some sort of rational conversation: 'I know they're special. I see it's going to hurt. I can understand you if you say you've thought about this possibility, that you've considered it in a sensible manner and found evidence to clear them all. But a young man who didn't deserve it is dead. Somebody told Balbinus who he was. Lucius Petronius, I'm just amazed that you won't even entertain the obvious.'

It was no good. Even years of friendship could not carry us through this. I heard his voice change; he demanded in a ghastly tone, 'You know something. What are you telling me?'

'There's graft among the cohorts.'

'Oh nothing new!' Petro raged at me scornfully.

'All right. This is absolutely confidential: I'm on a special task.'

'*Another?*'

'That's right. Investigations are being planted around Rome like crocuses in an orchard. I'm under secret orders to find and label which of the vigiles are accepting hand-outs – '

Petronius was horrified. 'You're spying on the Fourth.'

'Oh do me a favour! I'm spying on everything that moves. There's nothing particular about the Fourth. I had hoped to leave them out of it.'

'Not according to what you've been saying to me tonight.' That was when I knew I had really lost him. 'I should have known: informers and law officers never mix. Your motives are far too grimy. Get out of my sight, Falco.' He meant it, I knew.

'Don't talk rot.'

'Don't speak to me! Take your filthy suspicions somewhere else. Balbinus is mine; he always was. I'll get him. I don't need help from you. I don't want to see you at the patrol house – I don't want to find you on my patch at all!'

There was nothing else for it. I left him and went home. The Emperor might like to think he had commissioned me for a confidential investigation, but Petronius Longus was the real force on the Aventine, and he had thrown me off the case.

L

There was very little time now. As soon as the body of Linus came home, we had lost our only advantage: that Balbinus had to lie low. Now he had much less to lose. Although he would have to remain in hiding, he could act much more freely. He faced the death penalty when we caught him, but he was so full of arrogance he probably thought he could evade capture. He was planning to rule Rome from some extravagant hiding place.

One thing he would want to do would be to carry on his campaign of vengeance against those who had brought him to justice. There was no doubt about it. Extreme peril threatened Petronius Longus. Apart from hating him for the court case, Balbinus would know Petro would be looking for him. Recapturing the big rissole was now Petro's sole task. Preventing him must be his enemy's chief goal. That, more than anything, was why I felt there was so little time to act.

I had had to tell Helena that I was persona non grata with the vigiles. For one thing she would soon notice me loafing at home instead of rushing out to crises. I had to explain the reason as well.

'Oh Marcus, this is terrible. I was so afraid it would happen . . . Will Petronius tell his men that you have been looking for corruption?'

'He's bound to tell his own team.'

'That means . . .' Helena paused. 'The one who betrayed Linus will find out what your task is.'

'Don't worry.'

'It looks dangerous for you as well as for Petro.'

'Love, this investigation was always dangerous.'

'Are you carrying on with it?'

'Yes.'

'How are you going to manage if Petronius won't see you?'

'He'll calm down.'

Seeing that I did not intend to discuss the quarrel further,

690

she stopped talking. One thing I liked about Helena was that she knew when not to pry. She had her own interests, which helped. Then if she ever did want to fight, she liked to blow up nonsense out of nothing. Things that were really important could be handled more sensibly.

Over breakfast, she seemed rather quiet. Maybe that was my fault. Even warm honey was failing to soothe me; I had had hardly any sleep and felt like sludge in the Great Sewer. I noticed Helena neither ate nor drank. That made me feel worse. She was pregnant, and I was ignoring it. The more bravely she endured her plight, the more guilt made me grouse.

'Are you still being sick?' She just shrugged. I had been decreed too busy to be kept informed. Dear gods, I wanted this trouble to be over so I could attend to my own life. 'Listen, if I want to be companionable and concerned, you might try helping!'

'It's all right. You're a man. Just be yourself.'

'That's what I was doing. But I can probably be boorish, callous and insensitive if you prefer.'

'I'll bear with you while you're learning to do it.' She smiled. Suddenly she was winsome again.

I refused to be charmed. 'Don't worry. I learn quickly.'

Helena Justina restrained herself, plainly making allowances for the tetchiness that had followed my falling out with my best friend. This only made me more angry, but she found a new subject to talk about: 'I haven't had a chance to tell you, Marcus. Yesterday when I came home another message about Tertulla was pinned in a bag on the door. And this . . .' She reached to a shelf and produced a gold object. I recognised the overflown bulla that my sister Galla had hung around her daughter's neck, the amulet which was supposed to protect Tertulla from the evil eye. Its powers had been sorely overtaxed. Now some fool had sent the useless thing to me.

'So they're telling us this is genuine. What are they asking me to cough up?' Even to my own ears I still sounded gruff.

'A thousand sesterces.'

'Do you happen to know what they asked from your father?' Helena looked apologetic. 'Ten thousand.'

'That's all right. When they come down to a hundred I might consider it.'

'You're all heart, Marcus!'

'Don't worry. I suspect they know they grabbed the wrong child this time. There's no money, but they don't want to lose face.'

'If they reduced the price once they may be weakening,' Helena said. 'They seem like amateurs. People who knew what they were doing would pile pressure on us, then keep asking for more and more.'

'I don't belittle the situation, but we may as well not panic. Are there any instructions in the message?'

'No just the price they want.' She was so reluctant to bother me she had not even let me see the message. Luckily I could trust Helena to tell me anything relevant. It was a relief to let her handle this. Even though I was in a filthy mood, I managed to feel some gratitude.

'We'll hear from them again, I'm sure. Sweetheart, if I'm too busy, do you think you can watch for the next contact?'

'Does that mean I should stay at home?' Helena sounded doubtful.

'Why? Have you an appointment to hear an epic poem in sixteen scrolls?'

'Certainly not. I did want to try that other house where a child is supposed to have been taken.'

'No luck yesterday?'

'I was told the woman was not at home.'

'True, or a fable?'

'I couldn't tell. Since they were being polite they implied I could try another time, so I shall make sure I do.' She looked thoughtful. 'Marcus, when the amulet was left there, I found myself thinking about the skip baby. Remember, he had a broken thread around his neck. Maybe it's a kidnap victim too. These people I haven't managed to see yet were supposed to have lost a baby. It was reported by the child's nurse. Maybe they will listen to me if I can tell them he's been found.'

Suddenly I experienced a huge pang of regret that she and I were not working together. I reached for her hands. 'Would it help if I came with you?'

692

'I should say not.' Helena smiled at me. 'With due respect, Marcus, at the house in question an informer would be someone to eject. I'm trying to cross the private bastions of a very important magistrate.'

A thought struck me. 'What's his name?'

Helena told me. My lawyers advise me not to mention it; I don't want a libel action. Besides, men like that get enough publicity.

I laughed throatily. 'Well, if you can use the information, I last saw the most excellent personage in question having his fancy tickled by a high-class prostitute.'

She looked worried, and then perhaps offended. One of the reasons I had always loved her so dearly was that Helena Justina was absolutely straight. The idea of blackmailing a man who was entitled to wear the purple toga to show his distinction would never cross her mind.

'Which brothel was it, Marcus?'

'I promise I've only been in one you know about – Plato's Academy.'

'That's interesting,' said Helena. She was trying to make it significant.

I knew that game. I had been in the enquiry business longer than she had. I let her dream.

LI

Mentioning Plato's had given me an idea.

Reluctant to work on my own if it proved unnecessary, I did take myself first to the Thirteenth-district patrol house to see if Petro would acknowledge me. Neither he nor any of his team were there. When I tried to go in, a couple of fire-fighters appeared. They seemed not to know about my job tracing grafters, but someone had ordered them not to admit me. I tried to look unimpressed by their surly behaviour, though I confess it shook me.

I realised afterwards that Petronius and his men would be attending the funeral of Linus. The patrolmen must have thought it odd that I had not gone myself.

Had Petro and I not quarrelled I would have paid my own respects. It seemed better to avoid causing trouble, so I honoured the dead man privately. He was young and had seemed straightforward. He deserved a better fate.

I walked down to the Circus, made my way to Plato's, and with more skill than I had applied at the patrol house, I talked my way inside. An expert informer is not easily thrown. I even managed to get myself taken straight to see Lalage.

It was still early morning and not much seemed to be happening. The brothel was in a lethargic mood. Just a few local clients indulging on their way to their employment, and at the time I arrived, mostly leaving. The corridors were empty; it could have been a lodging house, except that at certain points stood mounds of wilting garlands or neatly stacked empty amphorae waiting to be taken out. There was some general cleaning with mops and sponges going on, but quietly. The night shift needed their sleep, presumably.

Lalage herself must have been snatching a rest between clients. Since a prostitute works on her back – well, often horizontally – Lalage's idea of a rest was not to relax on a reading couch with a Virgilian eclogue, but to climb up

694

steps and replenish the oil in a large icon ceiling light.

'I know,' I grinned. 'You can't trust slaves to do anything.'

'Slaves here have other duties, with my customers.' She swayed slightly, nearly going off balance as she tilted her jug against the last lamp. The effect was decorously erotic, though probably unintentional. I stepped closer and prepared to place a steadying hand on her backside, though when she managed to remain upright modesty stayed my helpful paw. 'You're Falco, aren't you?'

'Fame at last.'

'Notoriety,' she answered. Something in her manner told me this might be the kind of notoriety I could do without.

'In the wrong quarters? I had a visit from the Miller and Little Icarus. Do you know that pair?'

'Nasty. I barred them.'

'I'm not surprised. I've seen your respectable clients . . .' She did not react. It would take a determined niggler to worry Lalage. 'My two visitors came to threaten me. Obviously my name is being mentioned in rougher circles than I like.' I was trying to obtain some sign that she was in contact with the Balbinus gang; her response was completely negative.

I offered a wrist to lean on as she descended from her perch, oil flask on the drip. She stepped down, brushing against me with a firm body warm through a single layer of finely woven cloth. 'And what does the notorious Marcus Didius want with me?'

'Marcus? That's informal! When I called with Petronius, I don't believe we got on first-name terms. Has someone well informed been talking, or might you and I be old friends?'

Lalage gave me the full benefit of those wonderful eyes. 'Oh hardly!'

'I'm crushed! By the way, you can stop flashing the peepers. They're lovely, but it's too early in the morning for me – or not early enough. I like a roll in the sheets instead of breakfast, but I like it with a woman who has been in my arms all night.'

'I'll put that in our scroll of client's preferences.'

'I'm not enrolled as a client.'

'Want to negotiate terms?'

'Sorry, can't afford it. I'm saving up to go to philosophy school.'

'Don't bother. You ramble on enough, without paying to be taught.'

She was still too close for comfort. I resisted manfully. We fought eye to eye; she must have known I was afraid she would manhandle me. The hairs on my neck were standing as stiff as a badger's bristles. It was hard to look tough when every nerve was screaming to me to protect my assets from assault – but the assault never came. For a brothel queen Lalage was surprisingly delicate.

'I want to negotiate a truce,' I croaked. She received the news with a chortle, but waved me to a couch with her. Breathing more freely, I perched on the far end. She tipped her head back, surveying me. She had a long, smooth neck, today unadorned by jewellery. Her eyelashes swept down and up again with the strength and fluid grace of trireme oars.

I sighed gently. 'Stop acting up like Thaïs. Your name's Rillia Gratiana. Your parents used to keep a stationer's shop on the corner of Dogfish Court.'

She did not deny it. Nor did she encourage me. Appealing to old memories would be no help. 'I keep this brothel, Falco. I do it well. I run the girls, I control the clients, I organise salty entertainments; I keep the ledgers and I obtain the necessary licences; I pay the rent, and I pay the grocery bills; when I have to I even sweep the stairs and lance the doorman's boils. This is my life.'

'And the past is irrelevant?'

'Not at all. My parents gave me all my local knowledge and commercial acumen.'

'Do you still see them?'

'They died years ago.'

'Want to know how I know all about you?'

'Don't bother. You're an informer. Even if you tell me some sob story, I won't be impressed.'

'I thought a brothel was the place men told the truth about themselves?'

'Men never tell the truth, Falco.'

'Ah no, we don't know what truth is . . . So can I call on fellow feeling?'

'No,' she said. That was even before she remembered how she came by her wounded ear. She was clearly not thinking about it, though seeing the scar again, I felt a warm sense of nostalgia.

We were both professionals. For different reasons we were attuned to the surges of communication – in my case talk, in hers the other thing. A cycle in this conversation had exhausted itself. By mutual agreement we gave up and relaxed.

I would have said neither of us had given any ground in the repartee stage, but then Lalage started playing with the clasp of a bracelet fretfully. Maybe she was weakening. (Maybe the arm decoration just had a tricky hook and loop.) 'So what do you want?' she asked again.

'To give you a word from a friend.'

'Oh?'

'You're driving me mad with that thing. Take it off and I'll mend it.' Surprised, she gave up trying to fix the bracelet and tossed it in my lap. It was a gorgeous bauble: fine gold scrollwork in sections, holding pale emeralds. Expensive, but ruined by the usual trashy clasp. 'Got some tweezers?' She provided me with a handsome set, six or seven assorted toiletry tools on a ring. 'Jewellers are stupid bastards.' I was working on a bent piece of gold wire that needed to be reshaped. 'They spend hours of labour on the fancy parts, but begrudge a decent hook. That should hold. If you like the piece, get a new fastener.' I held out my hand for her arm. When I had replaced the bracelet on her scented wrist, I kept hold of her. My grip was friendly, but inescapable. She made no attempt to break away; prostitutes know when to avoid hurting themselves. I looked straight at her. 'Balbinus is in Rome.'

Her fine eyes narrowed. It was impossible to tell whether she was hearing this for the first time, or merely wished me to think so. Her mouth pursed. 'That's bad news.'

'For everyone. Have any vigiles been to see you?'

'Not since you and your long friend.' I felt I could believe her when she was being factual. That could be a trick, of course.

'You can see the implications?'

'Not exactly. Balbinus is condemned. What can he do, Falco?'

697

'Quite a lot, it seems. The Fourth Cohort have been busting themselves trying to work out who was trying to replace him – when all the time nobody was. Everything that's happened lately could be down to him.'

'Like what?'

'The Emporium raid, and the one at the Saepta. The deaths. You have presumably heard about the deaths?'

'Whose deaths are these?' she murmured, deliberately provoking me.

'Don't come it.'

There was no visible hardening; she remained the polite courtesan. But she said, without any change of tone, 'If you don't want to pay for mauling me, would you mind letting go of my wrist?'

I gave her a stare, then opened my hand abruptly, fingers splayed. She waited a beat, then took back her arm.

'I want to talk about Balbinus,' I said.

'And I don't.'

I looked at her carefully, seeing past the elegant attire, the fine paintwork on her eyelids and lashes, the allure of the gorgeous body. There were tiny lines and dark patches around those languorous, limpid brown eyes. 'You're tired. The brothel's very quiet this morning too. What's up, Lalage? Having to work overtime at nights? Why's this? Someone squeezing you? Can it be that the profit margins of the Bower of Venus are being reduced by having to pay a managing director's fee again?'

'Take a jump in the river, Falco.'

'I'm surprised. I thought you enjoyed your independence, lass. I must admit, I respected you for it. I can't believe Balbinus just turned up and asked for a cut, and you gave it to him!'

'Don't even think it. I wouldn't give him half an as if he was bursting for the lavatory. Balbinus can't pressure me these days. He's condemned. If he's in Rome he'll have to stay in hiding, or he's for it.'

'Execution,' I agreed. Then I challenged her: 'So you're not concealing him on the premises?'

She laughed.

I decided to accept her version. I had believed her when

698

she talked of running the brothel without a protector. 'You still ought to take an interest,' I warned. 'Someone must be helping him, but if it's not you, you fall into the other category.'

'And what's that, Falco?'

'His enemies.'

There was a pause. Lalage had always been intelligent, top of the class when she went to school; I happened to know that. Finally she rasped, 'You're talking about deaths again.'

'Nonnius Albius,' I confirmed. She must have known about his killing. 'And the doctor who convinced Nonnius he was dying, the one who frightened him so much he felt prepared to turn Balbinus in. That was wrong, incidentally. The vigiles had set him up.'

I was hoping to shock her into making revelations but it was Lalage who surprised me. She laughed again, though somewhat bitterly. 'Not entirely,' she said. Enjoying the thrill of seeing me startled, she stretched as gracefully as a panther; the action was automatic, not meant to be enticing, but I had to control myself. She smiled wryly. 'It would only have been a set-up if Nonnius hadn't known about it.'

'What do you mean?'

'Nonnius realised all along that the Fourth Cohort had sent that doctor to lie to him.'

Luckily Petronius Longus was no longer speaking to me, so I would be spared having to tell him this depressing news.

699

LII

'It's old history,' Lalage confessed. 'What's the difference now Nonnius is dead? Who cares?'

'Balbinus cares!' I rapped back tersely. 'And so should you.'

'I don't see it.'

'You will when a gang of killers bursts in one night, and drags you off by the hair.'

'I'll wear a wig for a few days . . .' Flippancy was not her style. She knew her limits and it did not last. 'This is a brothel. I thought you would have noticed that! We have a system to keep out hooligans.'

'Jupiter, I've seen your security! Macra busy counting the money, and a half-asleep hangdog who dies if you raise your voice to him? Nonnius had an armoured door. They broke in with artillery; it was a military raid.'

'Well thanks. Now I know what we have to be ready for.' She was unimpressed. She stretched her leg, dangling her sandal from a lithe instep. The footgear had a light sole but a substantial upper, the kind that is completely cut out in one piece of leather, then its myriad thongs tied up on top. Not a walking shoe, but that would not have troubled her. What troubled me was that it was being dangled from a very pretty foot.

Her blasé attitude heated me more, but in a different way. 'What's the matter with you, Lalage? Balbinus has perpetrated revenge killings on at least two people who brought him to trial. I was abroad at the time, but I understood Nonnius was not his only old associate to help the prosecution. You also gave evidence.'

'I was pressurised.'

'By Petronius Longus.'

'That's the bastard's name.'

'Call me simple, but it seems to me that helping to convict him puts you next on Balbinus' shopping list of corpses, Lalage.'

'You're simple.' She knew exactly what she was saying when she returned slyly, 'I can think of one person who may be ahead of me.' She meant Petronius. I hoped she could not see me going cold.

'He's a big lad, and avoiding villains is his job. He can take his chance. There is still a serious risk to you.'

'I can deal with it.'

'The oldest lie in the world, Lalage! History is littered with the corpses of fools who gurgled, "I'm different. I can keep out of the way!" Or have you bought him off?' I was angry as the thought struck me. 'One of the vigiles has been murdered too. Are you responsible for that? Did you betray Linus?'

'I've never even heard of him.' She spoke calmly. I wanted to believe her.

'Have you seen Balbinus recently?'

'No.'

'He must need a bolt hole. Has he asked to hide up here?'

'That again! Don't make me laugh, Falco.'

'What about his men? Little Icarus and the Miller? Do you let them come here?'

'I told you, they're barred, the lot of them.'

'And none of the old gang have been in touch with you? What about Balbinus himself?'

'No.' It sounded like a lie. I watched her notice me thinking that. 'Balbinus is a shark.' Her voice was hard. 'Believe me, Falco, he knows that he's met his match in me. I'm stronger than him, and if he wants to survive in Rome he'd better leave me alone. What – an exile who has returned in secret? He's a fool. He doesn't stand a chance.' She was talking too much now. This was not like Lalage. She still had the wide-open gaze of a whore who was lying. The trouble with whores is they look like that all the time, even when spouting truths like vestal virgins.

'And what about Nonnius? How in Hades did you know he saw through Alexander's tale?'

'Alexander is the doctor?'

'Was.'

'Oh, was! Failed to diagnose his own condition, didn't he? Well I know, Falco, because the whole thing was arranged by Nonnius and me. Don't worry your little head with the details, but when Petronius sent his man with the fake story, Nonnius didn't believe him. He wasn't stupid. He could tell he wasn't ill.'

'So he made enquiries and found out that the doctor who was saying he was dying had a brother in the watch?'

'He was a rent-collector, Falco. He could easily add up! He told me about it. He was just laughing at first because the whole idea seemed ridiculous, but I saw how we could use it. We wanted to be rid of Balbinus. I was after sole charge of the brothel, and Nonnius intended to run all the rest. We planned it together.'

'Nonnius called Alexander back?'

'He had a lot of fun pretending to be terrified, and then convinced your friend the way was clear to clean up Rome.'

'What about the dead Lycian?'

'He was killed here at Plato's.'

'I know that.' I was thinking fast. She had to be telling me that the Lycian's murder was deliberate. 'It was a fix? The weasel who did the stabbing was sent in purposely?'

'No, Castus didn't need encouraging. He was a Balbinus plant. He used to hang around here and report back how things were. I didn't tell him anything; I knew how he would react if we could get a fight going. The girl was in on it, though. I didn't want her telling Castus to calm down when the row flared up.'

'They still work here?'

'Only the girl.'

She was horribly calm. She and Nonnius actually had the Lycian traveller killed so the watch could discover it 'by accident', and so that they could provide evidence which Lalage could be 'coerced' into giving in court.

I realised Lalage would never admit this formally, and hearing it today could prove fatal for me. The mood had become dangerous. I was deep within this place. No one knew I was here. If she decided to have me killed like the Lycian, I would be seriously stuck. I tried changing the subject. 'Once Balbinus was supposed to have sailed away, was it Nonnius who organised the Emporium raid?'

'I've no idea. Once the court case was over, I didn't want to know anything about the street-gang side.'

702

'Really? I wondered whether you and Nonnius had been scheming together because you were having an affair?'

Genuine amusement rocked her. 'Only a man would imagine women conduct their businesses on the basis of love.'

'You were no admirer of Nonnius?'

'No.' She did not bother to insult him.

'You told me once you hated him – and yet now you say you conspired together over the court case.'

'So? I loathed him, but I could still use him.'

'You've told a lot of lies. Why suddenly start telling the truth about Nonnius?'

'Because he's dead. As soon as I heard that, I guessed Balbinus had returned. You should have known too,' she taunted.

'We thought Flaccida murdered Nonnius.'

'Oh I bet she had a hand in it. The word on the streets is that it happened in her house. They say she was there gloating. They say she herself rammed that pot on his head.'

'A spirited witch!' My lip curled. 'Is Balbinus at the house?'

'I doubt it. He's not stupid. That's the first place the vigiles will look.' She clearly meant they *were* stupid, or at least predictable.

'Well, thanks for all this. It's good of you to co-operate.'

'If you hadn't realised Balbinus was here in Rome, I was going to tell you myself.'

She had not done so, though.

I stood up. For a moment I half expected her to prevent me leaving. I was guarding against an attack, and this time not the erotic sort.

'You frightened of something, Falco?' She understood men. It was her trade.

'No, but you should be. Balbinus is back. You helped get him condemned. He'll be looking for you.'

'Oh, I don't think I need to worry!' She definitely meant it. I was wondering why. She rose, graciously acknowledging my departure as she supplied one possible reason in a scornful tone: 'Balbinus won't be in Rome for long.' The smile she gave me was the sweetest available in her wide repertoire – as dangerous as a draught of aconite. 'Balbinus won't even be *alive*, will he? Not now you're looking for the man!'

I told her there was no need to be sarcastic, then I saluted the lady respectfully and took my leave.

Nonnius had hoped to take over the crime empire, but Nonnius was dead. I wondered who Lalage imagined would step in once Balbinus was settled for good. I wondered who she hoped to see running things then.

She was competent and ambitious. And Lalage, as I knew from many years ago, had always been a very clever girl.

LIII

There was no chance that Petronius would welcome me with almond cakes if I came with my new information. Hearing that his ploy had been seen through by Nonnius would only make him flare up again. What was the point of harassing him? He knew Balbinus was back; he could work out for himself his own personal danger. All I had learned for certain was some unpleasant background relating to the court case. Lalage had implied she had some mysterious hold over Balbinus, but it could be bluff. If not, it was still too nebulous to be useful.

Nonetheless I felt I had gained a better grip on the situation. The main thing now was to find Balbinus Pius. I decided to risk my neck and tackle Flaccida. Too late: when I reached her house at the other end of the Circus, the vigiles were already there. I must have spent longer in the brothel than I realised. (Not the first man to be in that predicament.) The funeral of Linus was over now. Petronius had obviously come straight from it, with barely time for the ritual purification, in order to lead a search party at the Balbinus house.

Flaccida was standing white-faced and rigid in the street, surrounded by the few slaves she had been left for personal use. No one had been arrested, but members of the foot patrol were strategically placed so that interested passers-by (of whom there were many) were being held back away from her. Despite precautions, Flaccida must have managed to send word to her daughter because while I was there Milvia came scuttling up looking flustered. She was promptly corralled with her mother. Her house would be the next target.

I also reckoned Balbinus would not be found in either mansion. Petronius presumably knew that too, for I could see him leaning casually in a portico with his arms folded. When he looked over and spotted me, I made sure I was sitting against a wall chewing my thumb in a similarly relaxed pose. I heard him give an order to have the street cleared of gawpers, so I left of my own accord.

It would be easy to let this situation deteriorate until it became even more personal. Searching for Balbinus was already feeling like some grim competition between Petro and me. That could be an advantage if it sharpened us up. But it was equally likely to jeopardise our hopes of capturing the criminal.

I went to see Marcus Rubella.

'There's been a development. Petronius has declared me out of bounds at the patrol house, and he refuses to communicate.'

'I was warned that having you two together would mean trouble.' That sounded as if it came from our old centurion, Stollicus.

'That's rubbish!' I retorted irritably.

Rubella was watering his inkwell and scraping the innards with a stick – the usual useless procedure for trying to get a decent mix. He possessed a fancy desk set: silver inkpot, stylus rack, sand tray, nib knife and sealing-wax lamp. It looked like a gift. Maybe somebody was fond of him. It wasn't me.

'Do you want to be taken off the enquiry, Falco?' He knew this had thrown me. 'Are you prepared to tell Titus you're ditching it?' This was a vicious man. Sympathetic staff management was not in his armoury.

'I can't afford that. I need his goodwill. I came to see you because I hoped you might be able to mediate.'

Rubella looked at me as though I was a cockroach crawling up his favourite stool. 'Mediate?'

'Sorry. Did I slip into a rare Etruscan dialect? Try arbitrate.'

'You're asking me to calm Petronius Longus down?'

'Subtle.'

'Fly off a crag, Falco.'

'No use?'

'I value life too dearly.'

'You won't try.'

'He's your old tentmate.'

'I don't find him in a nostalgic mood, unfortunately. Well it seems I'll be acting alone.' That was what I had wanted, though not this way. I told Rubella what I had learned from Lalage; he thanked me, in his dry manner, for handing him the task of telling Petro how Nonnius Albius had played with him. 'Rubella, since Petronius won't be using my valuable talents, I'm available to take instructions directly from you.'

'I like a man who co-operates. Well now, what nugget can I find for you? Petronius is in charge of finding Balbinus.'

'I can help with that.'

'No. I don't want your paths crossing until your feud is worked out.'

'I'll keep out of his way.'

'Yes.' Rubella gave me his slow, untrustworthy smile. 'That's best.' He meant, he was making sure of it. 'As I said, Petronius is looking for the escapee. What I'd like you to take on is tracing the goods stolen from the Saepta and the Emporium.' Before I could protest at this menial role, he added smoothly, 'Following up the raids may be another way to find a trail to Balbinus. Besides, you have connections in the fine-art world. You seem ideal for this job – much better than anyone on my own staff.'

Always a sucker for personal flattery, I heard myself agree to it. 'Do I get men to assist?'

Rubella flattened the stubs of his close haircut with one hand; it must have felt like abrading his palm with pumice stone. 'I don't see that you'll need any initially. If you are on to something, come straight to me for backup.'

I had heard that before. I knew I would be searching for the stolen goods on my own. If I found them, I would be a solitary hero timidly approaching whichever giant was hoarding them and asking if he could please hand them over and explain himself . . . I started planning further visits for exercise at my local gymnasium.

I was ready to leave when the tribune raised his chin more than usual. 'Do I take it that you are still pursuing the request to identify corrupt officers?'

'Certainly. I'm looking all the time.'

'That's interesting. You report to me on that, I think.'

707

'What are you getting at?'

'Linus was an unfortunate loss. I've been at the funeral; I noticed you didn't go to it . . .' I let that ride. 'I've been waiting,' said Rubella, with an insinuating sneer, 'for you to tell me that there must be a maggot in the Fourth Cohort's enquiry team.'

I managed to keep my voice quiet, though I may have flushed. 'I thought you suspected a maggot all along. I thought that was why Titus brought me in!' We clashed eye to eye. Neither achieved supremacy. The sooner I stopped working with Marcus Rubella, the happier I would be. 'Petronius Longus will be reporting on the traitor who betrayed Linus when we have discovered who it is.'

'You told him there was a traitor?'

Not even I as Petro's close friend could pretend that Petro had been aware of it. 'It seemed best for me to warn him that he needs to be careful whom he trusts, so I did discuss the subject with him last night before we parted company.'

'I suppose that's why you quarrelled?' The reason was between the two of us. Rubella glared. 'He and I have also spoken.' Relief. Petro had faced the issue. Petro had even come clean with his tribune. I wondered whether he had asked for an interview of his own accord, or whether Rubella – who was undeniably sharp in his dour way – had realised there had been an error and had insisted they discuss what had gone wrong. 'No thoughts on it?' Rubella tried.

I was not inclined to share them. 'I'm standing back. Petronius Longus wants to sort it out internally.' I knew that without having any contact with him.

'I have agreed his approach. He'll review events surrounding the failed attempt to send Balbinus into exile. Then he'll interview the entire team individually.' For a moment I experienced the odd feeling that whatever Petro or I said to Rubella would make its way to the other. It was like conversing through an intermediary to save face. Maybe the damned tribune understood men after all. Maybe he could arbitrate.

'Keep me informed,' he concluded, as if confirming it.

Then the hypocrite wished me luck (hoping I would fall flat on my face of course) and I took myself off to apply my special gifts to the world of stolen luxuries.

Rubella had given me the lists of stolen property. I had a quick glance at the endless details of six-foot-high Etruscan terracotta stands and bowls, ancient Athenian red-figure, gilt and jewellery, porphyry and ivory. Then, to deal with two commissions at once, I started with the piece I knew: Papa's glass jug.

There was one character involved in this saga whom nobody else seemed to be considering. So I pulled my cloak around my shoulders and decided to meet Florius.

I had to find him first.

LIV

My brother-in-law Famia, Maia's treasure, prided himself on being a man with contacts. It was rubbish. Famia's contacts were one-legged jockeys and liniment-sellers who drank too much. He was a vet, working for the Greens. Their pathetic choice of horse doctor may account for the fact that as a chariot team they stink.

Famia was no stranger to flagons of non-vintage grape juice himself. He had a florid face with puffy eyes. Maia fed him well and tried to keep him neat, but it was hard work. He favoured a long tunic the colour of estuary mud, over which went a filthy leather apron and a belt from which hung curious tools, some of which he had devised himself. I had never seen him use a single one of them on a sick animal.

I found him sitting on a barrel at the stables, talking to some visitors. A lame horse waited patiently. It appeared to know it stood no chance of attention this week if it had to depend on Famia. Hung on the wall behind it was an impressive selection of harness rings and roundels, blacksmiths' hammers and pliers, and hippo shoes.

'What ho, Falco! I hear you slipped up with your fancy piece?'

'If that's a coarse reference to my impending father-hood –'

'Don't be stupid. I presume Helena will be getting rid of it.'

'That so? I like to be kept up to date, Famia. Thanks for telling me!'

'Well, that's the impression Maia gave me anyway.' Realising he was likely to get thumped, he sniffed and backed off. Famia simply could not believe that a senator's daughter would carry an informer's child. I had long given up any attempt to hack a path through the dark undergrowth of his social prejudice. He wasn't worth trying to talk to sensibly.

The bastard had upset me. No use denying it.

*

It was too much to hope Famia knew Florius, but since Florius was a gambling man Famia must know someone else who did. Prising the information out of him gave me indigestion for the rest of the day. He enjoyed being difficult.

It took me most of the afternoon. A long stream of undesirable characters whom Famia had suggested I consult finally ended with a snooty ex-charioteer who kept a training stable near the Plain of Mars. His office was full of the silver crowns he had won when he himself raced, but somehow lacked the odour of real money that I associate with retired champions, most of whom are nearly millionaires. Famia had hinted darkly there was some scandal attached to him, though needless to say he then sent me in there without saying what. Maybe the fellow tried to diddle on the slave tax when he bought his drivers, and had been found out. Many a hopeful setting up a new business assumes the fiscal rules don't apply to him. Catching them out works wonders for the Treasury's income from fines.

One reason it was so difficult to trace Florius was that it turned out he supported the Whites. 'The *Whites*?' I was incredulous. No wonder he was elusive. Nobody in Rome supports the Whites. Even the Reds are less unpopular. A man who supported the Whites could well wish to remain invisible.

The ex-charioteer thought he might be seeing Florius later. Naturally he viewed me with suspicion. People never entertain the thought that an informer might be tracing folk for a good reason, such as to bring them news of an unexpected legacy. I was interpreted as trouble. It was quite likely Florius would be warned of my visit and advised to avoid me. Determined to better him, I pretended to go along with it, said I'd call back in an hour, and concealed myself in a wine bar to await developments. At least I got a drink.

The racing snob went out in his cloak almost immediately. I gulped down my tipple and followed him. He met Florius at the Pantheon, obviously a regular rendezvous. I stood back, but neither was keeping watch for trouble. Shading my eyes against the glitter of the gold tiles on the domed roof, I observed them without them even once looking in my direction. They had a short chat together, fairly unexciting and perhaps even routine business, then the charioteer strolled off again. Florius sat among the forest of columns in Agrippa's confrontational portico. He appeared to be working out figures on a note tablet. I walked across the open area in front of the temple, then slid up to talk to him.

Florius was a mess. He was a shapeless lump, too heavy for his own good and unkempt with it. His baggy tunic had spots of dried fish pickle down the front. It was untidily hooked up over his belt, from which hung a fat hide purse so old its creases were black and shiny and stiffened with use. His boots had been handsome knee-highs once, but their complex thongs were mud-splashed and needed grease. His feet were badly mis-shapen with corns; the thick toenails had been hacked short, apparently with a meat knife. His brown hair looked as if it had been cuts in tufts by several barbers over several days. He wore his equestrian ring, plus a haematite seal and a couple of other heavy gold lumps. This was hardly for personal adornment; his fingernails were ferociously bitten, with ragged cuticles. His hands looked in need of a wash.

This neglected bundle received my greeting without alarm. He put away his notes, which looked like details of form. (I craned for a look, hoping they would be lists of stolen goods; nothing so obvious.) He was sharp enough in his obsession; as I had approached the temple I had seen him scribbling away with his stylus so rapidly that in minutes his little squiggly figures filled a whole waxed board. I determined not to ask him about racing. He was clearly one of those mad devotees who would bore you to death.

A gusty wind had driven a sharp rain shower over the Plain, so I suggested we take shelter. He clambered to his feet and we strolled inside the temple, passing the statues of Augustus and Agrippa in the vestibule. Though I rarely entered the Pantheon, it always had a calming effect on me. The gods looked out peacefully from their niches in the lower drum while clouds covered the open circle in the roof.

'Wonderful building,' I commented. I liked to reassure my subjects with some casual chat – a few pleasantries about the beauty of concrete before suggesting that they had better talk

712

or I'd tear their liver out. 'They say it's the first piece of architecture that was designed from the inside outwards instead of the other way. Don't you think the proportions are perfect? The height of the dome is exactly the same as its diameter.' Florius took no notice. That did not surprise me. The Pantheon would have needed four legs and a bad-tempered, pockmarked Cappadocian rider before Florius raised a flicker of interest. 'Well! You're a hard man to catch up with, I must say!' He looked nervous. 'Your friend seemed to be protecting you. Have you been bothered by any unwelcome visitors?'

Florius cleared his throat. 'What do you want?' He had one of those light, overcheerful voices that always sound un-reliable.

'I'm Didius Falco. A special investigator working on your father-in-law's case.'

He exclaimed in considerable anguish, 'Oh no!'

'Sorry, does this bother you?'

'I don't want anything to do with it.'

I took a chance. 'I sympathise. When you discovered what kind of family had tricked you into marriage, you must have felt really trapped.' He said nothing, but made no protest, 'I've come to you because I realise you're different.'

'I don't know anything about what my father-in-law does.'

'Have you seen him?' I asked pleasantly.

'Oh don't get me into this!' he pleaded.

'You have? How long ago was that?'

'Five or six days ago.' Interesting. It was only a week since we put the big rissole aboard the *Aphrodite* at Ostia. Florius had spoken without intending to co-operate, but now he decided to ditch Balbinus anyway. 'I'm not supposed to tell anyone.'

'Of course not. It's very unfair of him to put pressure on you this way.'

'Oh I wish he'd just go away.'

'I hope he will do soon. We're working on it hourly.'

'Oh?' Florius seemed puzzled. 'I must have misunder-stood. I thought you said you were a special investigator. But you're with the vigiles?'

'Can it be that you don't think the vigiles are pursuing matters energetically?'

713

'My father-in-law reckons they do what he likes,' he answered flatly.

That was bad news for Rome. I was supposed to be looking into this. Rubella would be overjoyed. I broached the issue carefully: 'Look. This is just between us.' He looked grateful for the confidence. A simple soul. 'The vigiles are themselves the subject of a probe at the moment. Obviously I cannot be too specific, but my role includes reviewing them . . . Perhaps you can help.'

'I doubt it!' The great booby just wanted to hide his head in a sack.

'I don't suppose Balbinus mentioned names?'

'No.'

'Did he say anything about his escape from the ship?'

'The ship he was supposed to leave on? No.'

'Can you tell me what he wanted with you?'

'He only wanted me to tell him how Milvia was. He's very fond of her. Actually, he wanted me to tell her he was home again, but I refused.'

'If he's so close to her, why didn't he come to your house?'

'He was afraid people might be watching it.'

'Does Milvia know he's here in Rome?'

'No. I don't want her to know. She's my wife, and I want to keep her out of all this. He doesn't understand.'

'Oh he wouldn't, Florius. He's been a villain all his life. His wife is as bad. They wanted Milvia to have a respectable place in society, but that doesn't mean they really think there is anything wrong with their own way of life.'

'Well it's made them rich enough!' snapped Florius.

'Oh quite. Do you know where I can find Balbinus?'

'No. He just appeared one day. I used to spend time in the Portico of Octavia; he found me there. So now I come here just to get away from him.'

'I'm very glad to hear your attitude.' There was no harm in putting pressure of our own on him. 'It's wise, Florius. I expect you realise your position could be awkward. There are people who keep saying you may work with Balbinus in some kind of partnership.'

'That's nonsense!' His fists were clenched. I sympathised. Innocence can be hard to prove. 'I answered all their

714

questions before the trial happened. They assured me there would be no more trouble.'

'Of course . . . Going back to Balbinus being here now, is there a system set up for you to contact him?'

'No.' Florius was exasperated. 'I don't want to contact him; I want to forget he exists! I told him not to bother me again.'

'All right. Calm down. Let me ask you something different. Was it Balbinus who gave you the glass water jug, the one all the fuss has been about?'

'Yes.'

'He approves of you then?'

'No, he thinks I'm nothing. It was a present for Milvia.'

'Did you tell her that?'

'No. I took the damned thing home, then I had to be vague about it. I don't want her to know he's here. I don't want him to give her gifts paid for from his illegal activities.'

'Pardon me, but you and Milvia seem to have a strange relationship. I've been trying to meet you at your house, but you're never there. You hate your wife's family, and you seem to have little to do with her, yet you stay married. Is this for purely financial reasons? I thought you had money of your own?'

'I do.'

'Are your gambling debts exorbitant?'

'Certainly not. I've been very successful.' He might support the Whites, but clearly he did not bet on them – unless he bet on them losing. But no one would give him long odds. 'I'm just about to buy a training stable of my own.'

I whistled jealously. 'So what's with Milvia?'

He shrugged. Complete disinterest. Amazing.

I gave him a stern look. 'Take my advice, young man!' He was about my own age, but I was streets ahead of him in experience. 'Either get a divorce, or pay some attention to your wife. Be businesslike. A racing trainer wants to impress the punters. You can't afford to have whiffs of scandal sullying your name. People you depend on will just laugh at you.'

Forgetting that people would know he had a father-in-law who was a condemned extortionist and murderer, Florius fell for the domestic threat. 'Milvia wouldn't – '

715

'She's a woman; of course she would. She's a pretty girl who's very lonely. She's just waiting for a handsome piece of trouble to walk in and smile at her.'

'Who are you talking about?' It would have been tough talk, had he not been less worked up than a scallop basking open on a sandbank. Pardon me; scallops lead lives of vivacious incident compared with Florius.

'It's hypothetical.' I was terse. 'Let's stick with your father-in-law. It sounds to me as if you have a very strong interest in helping the officials discover him. To start with, you can assist me. I was enquiring into the glassware. It is stolen property – ' Florius groaned. He was a man in a nightmare. Everything he heard about the Balbinus family – including my instructions about his wife – made him more anxious. 'I don't suppose Balbinus made up a story about where he got it from?'

'He didn't have to make it up,' said Florius, sounding surprised. 'I was with him at the time.'

'How come?'

'He kept insisting he wanted to send a present to my wife. He made me go with him to buy something.'

Taking a hostile witness to a receiver's lockup sounded strangely careless for a king of crime. I was amazed. 'Balbinus *bought* his gift? Where from?'

'A place in the Saepta Julia.'

It was still raining, but the Saepta lies right alongside the Pantheon. I dragged Florius across the street and into the covered market. I made him show me the booth where the jug had been purchased. Almost as soon as we reached it, the eager proprietor hurried out to greet us, clearly hoping his previous customer had come back for more. When I stepped into view, the atmosphere cooled rapidly.

I told Florius to go. He already had a jaded view of life. I didn't want him more upset. And I did not want any strangers present when I spoke my mind about the glass to its slimy, seditious retailer. All our efforts to follow up the Syrian water jug had been a waste of time. It had no bearing on the Balbinus case. The 'stolen' glass had never been lost. All I was pursuing here was a sleazy compensation fraud – one to which I was myself inextricably linked.

'Hello, Marcus,' beamed the dealer, utterly unabashed as usual.

I answered in my blackest tone, 'Hello, Pa.'

'That crown of yours was a gorgeous bit of stuff. I can make you a fortune if you want to sell. I had one customer who was interested – '

'Who actually bought it, you mean?'

'I told him Alexander the Great had worn it once.'

'Funnily enough, that's one of the ludicrous stories the original salesman tried out on me. You're all the same. Though not all of you steal from your own sons and go in for blatant fraud!'

'Don't be unkind.'

'Don't make me livid. You bastard, you've got some explaining to do.'

Frankly, now I knew the 'loss' of the glass was just another example of my father on the fiddle, I did not want to hear any more. 'Ah Marcus, settle down – '

'Stop warbling. Just describe the man who came here with the limp lettuce leaf who was just with me – the man who bought the glass water jug.'

'Balbinus Pius,' answered Pa.

'You know that thug?'

'Everyone knows him.'

'Do you know he's an exile case?'

'I heard so.'

'Why didn't you report seeing him?'

'He was buying; I don't throw trade away. I knew someone would be on to him eventually. That great po-faced lump of a friend of yours, presumably . . . Come in for a drink,' invited my father cheerily.

Instead I left.

717

LV

As I strode angrily home I felt edgy. For one thing I had ringing in my ears various sly protestations from Pa – mighty claims that he had meant no harm (oh that old story!), and bluster that he would never have accepted compensation illegally . . . To be descended from such a reprobate filled me with bile.

There was more to my sense of unease than that. Maybe I was growing jumpy. The knowledge that Balbinus was here and apparently flourishing, despite all the law's efforts, depressed me bitterly. What was the point in anything if criminals could do as they liked and go where they pleased, and laugh at verdicts so blatantly?

The city felt unfriendly. A cart raced around a corner, causing walkers and pigeons sipping at fountains to scatter; it must be breaking the curfew, for dusk had only just fallen and there had hardly been time for it to have reached here legitimately from one of the city gates. People pushed and shoved with more disregard than ever for those in their path. Untethered dogs were everywhere, showing their fangs. Sinister figures slunk along in porticoes, some with sacks over their shoulders, some carrying sticks that could be either weapons or hooks for stealing from windows and balconies. Groups of uncouth slaves stood blocking the pavement while they gossiped, oblivious to free citizens wanting to pass.

An irresponsible girl backed out of an open doorway, laughing. She banged into me, bruising my forearm and making me grab for my money in case it was a theft attempt. I roared at her. She raised a threatening fist. A man on a donkey shoved me aside, panniers of garden weeds crushing me against a pillar that was hung dangerously with terracotta statuettes of goggle-eyed goddesses. A beggar stopped blowing a raucous set of double pipes just long enough to cackle with mirth as a white-and-red-painted Minerva cracked me across the nose with her hard little skirt. At least

718

being pressed back so hard had saved me from the bucket of slops that a householder then chose to fling out of a window from one of the dark apartments above.

Insanity was in Rome.

When I reached Fountain Court the familiar scents of stale flatfish, gutter water, smoke, chicken dung and dead amphorae seemed positively civilised. At the bakery, Cassius was lighting a lamp, meticulously trimming its wick and straightening the links on its hanging chain. I exchanged greetings with him, then walked up on that side of the street to say a few words to Ennianus, the basket-weaver who lived below my new apartment. He had supervised removal of the skip. I borrowed a flat broom and swept some loose rubbish up the gulley so it was outside a house whose occupants never spoke to us.

I was still talking to Ennianus when I spotted Lenia taking tunics down from a line across the laundry's frontage. I turned my back, hoping to avoid being hailed for a boring discussion of her wedding, now only ten days away. She must have missed me; her eyes were never good. Either that or she had finally given up any hope of cajoling me into sympathy. I had no energy to spare for people who ought to know better, who dragged aggravation down on themselves. Rome was too full of trouble for me to face her tonight.

There was more trouble than I realised. When Ennianus grinned and told me it was safe to face the street again, I saw two men walking past the barber's shop. I knew I recognised them, though at first I could not remember why.

'Who are those two, Ennianus?'

'Never seen them here before.'

I felt I had a grievance against them. So I broke off my chat with the basket-weaver and quietly followed them.

As they walked I applied my subtle knowledge of the world to deducing what I could about them. From behind, they were ordinary, empty-handed punters, about the same height as each other, and the same build. They wore brown sleeveless tunics, belted with old rope by the look of it, unexceptional boots, no hats or cloaks. They must be outdoor types.

They were walking with purpose, though not hurrying.

719

These were not loafers just looking for fun in the city. They had a fixed destination, though they lost themselves on the way. They led me along on the Aventine summit towards the riverside, then discovered the crag and had to find a path down. They did not know Rome – or at least they were strangers on the Hill.

Eventually they hit the Clivus Publicus. They carried on downhill past the Temple of Ceres, then, when they reached the bottom near the Circus Maximus, they had to buy a drink at a streetside stall so they could ask directions from the proprietor. They next turned along the Circus and began walking its length; clearly they should have come down off the Hill in the other direction, towards the twin aqueducts and the Capena Gate.

We were in an area which had featured frequently in my life the past few days: that part of the Eleventh region which bordered the Circus. At one end lay the Forum Boarium, where the body of Nonnius Albius had been left on the pavement in the stink of animal blood. Along the valley of the Circus ran a narrow finger of land where stood the lavish houses inhabited by Flaccida and Milvia. Then, at the other end, were the cluster of dingy, unattractive streets which included Plato's Academy.

By the time we had gone that far, I felt unsurprised that the brothel should be where my two men were heading. I was also certain they were rogues. I could prove it: I had recalled where I first saw them, though it was not in Rome. Their names – their working names anyway – were Gaius and Phlosis. They were the pair of fake boatmen at Ostia who had tried to relieve me of my father's glass before I brought it to Rome for that other great fraud to try stealing it from himself.

I watched them enter the brothel, greeting the girl on the door as if they knew her. They could have been clients, visitors to Rome who had had Plato's recommended by a friend. That was my assumption until I realised the girl had let them enter without money changing hands.

There was no doubt Lalage had customers who kept monthly accounts here. However, the kind of men who were so favoured would not be lowlifes from the waterfront, but trusted people like the Very Important Patrician who came

720

with lictors in tow. Gaius and Phlosis were here in some other, very different, context. And from the doorkeeper's friendly attitude, even if they had got lost on the Hill, down here at Plato's the incompetent couple were regular visitors.

I wondered whether to follow them in. I was in the wrong condition for adventures tonight. I was tired. It had been a hectic week, packed with incident, and I knew my concentration was slipping. Besides, Plato's was a huge warren; nobody knew I had come here tonight, and if I went inside I had no idea what I would be going into.

The situation was far too dangerous. For once, discretion won.

LVI

I needed help with this. I needed someone who would be tough if we ran into trouble, someone trained to carry out surveillance properly. If my hunch was correct, I had stumbled across something major. It would be hazardous. It needed the vigiles. The person I really should take this evidence to was Petronius Longus. Well, that was impossible.

I could ask Rubella. Pride – pride and the fact that if I was wrong I could be merely watching a couple of paltry sneak thieves enjoying themselves at a brothel – determined me to take this forwards unofficially.

There were practical problems. I did need a partner. I wanted to subject the brothel to all-day surveillance, with the possibility of tailing some of its visitors as they came and went. I wondered whether I could risk using one of my nephews. But with Tertulla still missing I knew all the young Didii were being marched to school in convoys and supervised by anxious mothers. There was no way I could cream one off without an angry rumpus flaring up. Besides, even I could see this work was too dangerous.

Still desperate, I faced the fact that if Petronius would not help me what I needed was one of his men. With luck, whoever I picked would not be the happy sneak who had betrayed Linus.

As chance had it, on my way back up the Aventine I ran into Fusculus. He would have been ideal. Fusculus was fascinated by the world of small-time criminals, an expert on specialist dodges. He would be full of ideas on why a set of cargo raiders from Ostia might have come to Rome. It was he himself who had inspired my belief that Gaius and Phlosis might have serious significance: I remembered that after my own close shave with the stolen boat at Portus, he had told me Balbinus Pius used to run a whole gang of craft-rig thieves along the wharves in Rome. Maybe these two were part of his old network. Maybe it was Balbinus who had brought Gaius and

722

Phlosis here. Maybe that meant the brothel was being used to run his empire now. It looked like that good old ruse, a cover joint.

When I fell into step beside him Fusculus growled, 'Get lost, Falco!'

Presumably Petronius had been unable to confide in any of his men the fact that one of them was a traitor. He needed to identify the bad apple first. So I could not call on that to justify my role in working for their tribune. 'Settle down. So Petro's told you all that I'm a management nark. He says I betrayed his friendship to spy on you – and naturally you simple souls all think that's terrible.'

'I don't want to know you, Falco.'

'What beats me, Fusculus, is how if you're all in the clear you can take the attitude that anyone trying to oppose corruption has to be your enemy.'

'You're poison.'

'Wrong. What you mean is, he's your chief, so even if he wants to play the silly ass you'll stick by him to protect your promotion chances. You would all do better starting a whip-round to buy Lucius Petronius a new brain.'

Fusculus told me to get lost again, and this time I did.

I felt sour. Nobody likes being hated.

Luckily there was one person left whom I could safely call upon. Someone sufficiently experienced for my purposes. Someone who was hated too.

I knew where he lived: back again on the opposite side of the Hill, by the Clivus Publicus. The Fates were enjoying themselves tonight. I marched my weary feet there again, and fortunately found that he was not yet out on night patrol. It was as I thought. Petro always took the busy first shift. He left the later, quieter one to Martinus his deputy.

It was late. I came to the point. I had been hoping to avoid telling him all my suspicions, but I soon saw that the best plan was to throw the big idea at him: 'How's the hunt for Balbinus going? Not well. Of course not; he's too clever. But I think I've got a lead. I'd take it to Petronius, but since he wants to play soft, I'll have to do the surveillance alone. Maybe once I can demonstrate how the Balbinus empire now operates

723

undercover at Plato's, Petro will want to join in. Maybe I won't give him the chance. I could keep all the glory – me and whoever shares my trouble . . .'

Martinus did not fail me. He was overjoyed at being asked to help. Well I knew why: he thought it was his great chance to do Petro down.

I told him what I had seen at Plato's, and what I reckoned we might see if we watched the place. 'Does Rubella know about this, Falco?'

'I'm not at liberty – '

'Don't get pious! I know what that means.'

I considered for a moment. 'He doesn't know, but we shall have to tell him. You can't go missing from the official team.'

'I'll see Rubella,' Martinus suggested. 'If he goes along with this, he can fix it. He can say he's sending me to some other cohort. The chief won't be the least surprised. It's more or less traditional that as soon as you're stretched beyond endurance on a really major case, your best man gets filched to look for brooch thieves in some disgusting bath-house in another watch's patch.'

I had no doubt that the axiomatic secondment would be easy to arrange. Whether Martinus was the Fourth Cohort's 'best man' could brook more argument. That didn't matter. The pompous self-satisfied article was good enough for what I wanted. Martinus would love to spend all day just sitting in a food stall waiting for nothing much to happen. As long as I could be in a different food stall at the opposite end of the alley, I didn't care how tedious he was.

When I finally made it back there for the second time that night, Fountain Court lay in complete darkness. No one there wasted lamp oil providing light for muggers and porch-crawlers to go about their dirty work. I steeled myself and trod quietly, keeping to the centre of the lane. As I walked past the bakery I thought I heard a shutter creak above my head. I looked up, but could see nothing. The apartment above the bakery, the one with half its floor missing, could hardly have been let and all the storeys above it were supposed to be even more derelict. Once beside the laundry I looked back again to make certain, but nothing moved.

Climbing the endless steps to my apartment I should have felt more confident. I was now on my own territory. That situation can be deadly dangerous. You relax. You assume the problems of night-time in Rome are over. You know too much to be really observant. Your ears stop listening for unnatural sounds. You can easily be rushed by some unexpected watcher who is lurking in the pitch dark halfway up the stairs.

But nobody attacked me. If anyone lay in hiding, I never noticed. I reached my own door, opened it stealthily, and soon stood indoors.

There were no lights here either, but I could feel the familiar presence of my furniture and possessions. I could hear the breathing of Helena, of the unwanted mongrel who had adopted us, and the skip baby. Nothing else. Nothing more sinister. Everyone within these two rooms was safe. They had lived through the day even without me to guard them, and now I was home.

I said quietly, 'It's me.'

The dog thumped its tail, but stayed under the table. The babe said nothing, but he could not have heard. Helena half roused herself as I climbed into bed, then came into my arms, warm and drowsy. We would not talk tonight. I stroked her hair to put her back to sleep again, and within a short period I drifted into sleep myself.

Out in the streets the foot patrols would be marching, on the search for fires and loiterers. Somewhere Petronius Longus also kept watch, hearing in the sharp October air endless rustles and creaks of evil at work, but never the certain footfall of the man he sought. In the restless pulse of the city lone thieves crept over windowsills and balconies, conspirators plotted, off-duty gangs drank and swore, lechers grabbed and fumbled, hijackers held up delivery carts, organised robbers ransacked mansions while bleeding porters lay bound in corridors and frightened householders hid under beds.

Somewhere, in all probability, Balbinus Pius was dreaming peacefully.

LVII

One day might be enough. It could certainly be enough to make me look a fool. If we watched the brothel all day and there was no discernible criminal activity, my name would be bog weed. Whether I wanted to skulk around longer looking for a chance to apprehend Gaius and Phlosis for annoying me at Ostia would be up to me. Martinus would curse me and storm off to tell the entire cohort what incompetent, aggravating blocks of wood informers were, and how he had been taken in.

On the other hand, if there was enough toing and froing of known members of the Balbinus gangs to suggest a link with his empire, I would be justified. Not a hero, but entitled to swank at the bathhouse. It would be a pleasant change.

Martinus and I arrived at dawn. We began by sitting in a doorway like runaway slaves. Later a sad thermopolium was opened by a creaky woman who spent ages dabbling around the floor with a flat-headed broom and a bucket of grey water. We watched her desultory efforts at wiping down counters, then she fidgeted about with her three shelves of cups and flagons, emptied some blackened pots into her counter holes, and stood a few amphorae crookedly against a wall.

We ambled up. We told her we were foxing – watching the streets for 'opportunities', illegal ones being understood. She seemed neither surprised nor shocked by this notion. Martinus engaged in brief negotiations, coins chinked into her apron pocket, and we were encouraged to park ourselves indoors on tall stools. There we could look as if we were picking at olives while we watched Plato's. We bought a dish of something in cold dark gravy. I left most of mine.

Things were very quiet to begin with. Despite my good intentions I ended up staying in the same bar as my assistant (stalwartly ignoring the fact that he seemed to assume *I* was helping *him*). The only other food stall was the one where Petro and I had sat when we first eyed up the brothel before

726

visiting Lalage, a place where we had shown ourselves to be law-and-order men. Today I wanted to pass for ordinary street grime.

I could just about trust Martinus to blend in. He must have been forty, so older than Petronius, the chief he was longing to elbow aside. As far as I knew he had remained unmarried, and though he talked about women his relationships were quiet incidents in a fairly ordered life. He had straight brown hair, cut neatly across the forehead, heavily shaded jowls and a dark mole on one cheek. He seemed too boring to arouse comment.

As the morning passed we started to see typical activity – locals visiting Plato's routinely. It seemed a long time since I had groaned over this with Petro, though when I bothered to work out the time scale (needing mental entertainment) I realised it was only five days ago. In those five days Rome had descended from a city where you were wise to keep your eyes open into one of complete lawlessness.

'Here we go!' Martinus had spotted suspects. From the brothel emerged three figures; a thin man in sky-blue tunic with an intelligent face and a scroll dangling from his waist, and two companions, one plump, one pockmarked, both inconspicuous. We had not seen them going in that morning; they must have been at Plato's overnight.

'Know them?' I asked quietly.

'The one in blue is a Cicero.' I lifted an eyebrow. 'A talker, Falco. He engages the attention of men drinking in wine bars, then keeps them laughing at his stories and jokes while the other two rob them.'

Martinus drew out a tablet, and stylus, then began making notes in firm square Latin lettering. As the day progressed, his writing was to shrink as the tablet rapidly filled up. To make us more unobtrusive, he later produced a pocket set of draughts, glass counters in black and red that he kept in a small leather bag. We set out a board, drawn in gravy on the marble. To look authentic we had to play for real, worse luck. I hate draughts. Martinus was an intelligent player who enjoyed his game. In fact he was so keen it would have been insulting to fake it, so I had to join in properly and attempt to match his standard.

'You should practise, Falco. This is a game of skill. It has parallels with investigation.' Martinus was one of those pretentious board-game philosophers. 'You need mental agility, strength of will, powers of bluff, concentration – '

'And little glass balls,' I remarked.

The morning continued without much incident, though we did see a limping man whom we reckoned must be on the 'wounded soldier' racket and another whom Martinus had once arrested for hooking cups off drink stall shelves. He ignored the Oily Jug, our perch. At lunch time a whole parade of men who appeared to be legitimate customers were crowding to the brothel when my companion stayed his hand just at the moment of capturing my last viable counter. 'Falco! There go a real couple of gangland educators!'

I didn't need him to point out the enforcers. Emerging from Plato's for a midday stroll were the Miller and Little Icarus. 'I know them. Those are the pair who tried acting as rough masseurs to me. They must be living there.'

'Seeing two from the old Balbinus set-up gives us enough to mount a raid, Falco.'

'You sure? We have to be certain we land the big one.'

'If he's there.'

'If he isn't there all the time, I reckon he comes visiting.' Before we did anything rash I wanted to watch for an evening and night at least. Martinus made no attempt to demur. He was not stupid – far from it. The bastard was a champion draughts player.

In the afternoon three more seedy characters caught our attention as they emerged. We decided they were low-life. There was a flash type in punched sandals and a niello belt, a broken-nosed hearty who kept kicking kerbstones, and a weed who came out scratching his head as if a whole herd of little lodgers were bothering him. I felt itchy just looking.

'Fancy stretching your legs?' I asked. Martinus swept up his glass counters in an instant and we set off to trail the trio. We both had to go. One man can't follow three.

For a nicely brought-up Aventine boy it was a real eye-opener. First two of them joined the squash in an elbow joint, pretending to buy a stuffed-vine-leaf lunch while they worked through the customers with a skill that left me

728

gasping. When someone went to pay for a flagon too early, found his purse gone and caught on to them, out they ran like eels. The third man was loafing on the doorstep as if unconnected; he misdirected the robbed man, who pelted down the wrong street while our friends met up together and mooched off the other way. We never saw them cleaning out the purses they had lifted, but we noticed the empty pouches flipped into a cart.

We split up to walk on either side of the street for a while, still tailing the three. They were now heading for the Forum. It was at its busiest, all the temple steps crowded with moneychangers and salesmen, and the spaces around the rostra packed. Our mark with the overactive lice paused to kick and rob a drunk near the House of the Vestals. The crunch of his boot going in symbolised all that was vicious in the Balbinus gangs.

They moved on through the press of fishwives and bread-sellers, 'sampling' rolls, sausages and fruit as the fancy took them, never paying for any of it. One was a real reacher, adept at leaning across shop counters to grab money or goods. In the end we could bear to watch no longer, not without arresting them. That might alarm the brothel; we had to hold back. They were tackling the Basilica Aemilia, the main centre of commerce in Rome, which was cluttered with itinerant sellers and tacky stalls; plenty of scope for our boys to spend a lucrative hour.

Incensed, Martinus and I walked back into the Forum. We took a breather in the shade of the Temple of the Divine Julius, reflecting on our researches so far.

'Those three were sharp little movers. What you've uncovered has Balbinus' seal stamped all over it,' Martinus commented. He seemed depressed.

'What's up? Do you think we're wasting our time taking on the gangs?'

'You never wipe out thieves, Falco. If we put those three in a cell, someone else will be along, aiming to relieve diners of their purses while they're licking out their bowls.'

'If you think that, why do this job at all?'

'Why indeed!' He sighed bitterly. I said nothing. I knew this mood was a hazard of life in the vigiles. I had known Petro long enough.

Sometimes the pressure and danger, and the sheer weight of despair, caused one of them to resign. The others became even more unsettled for a while. But normally they moaned a lot, got paralytic with an amphora, then carried on. Given their lousy pay and harsh conditions, plus the traditional indifference of their superiors, complaint seemed understandable.

Martinus was now watching passers-by. His arms were crossed on his chest and his fat backside was thrust out in his habitual way. His large eyes were taking in everything. I remembered that when we were waiting for Balbinus at Ostia it was Martinus who had stayed twitching at the door of the tavern, and how timely had been his warning of the escort's approach. Here in the Forum, although his thoughts seemed to be upon disheartened philosophy, he had spotted the vagrant who was drunk as a vintner's carthorse weaving a determined course towards two highly snooty types in togas outside the Julian courts. He had noted the slaves fooling about, including the one who had pinched another's inkpot and hidden it in his tunic with a genuine intent to steal. He had seen the old woman crying and the girl who did not realise she was being followed home. His gaze had finally settled on the group of young boys loitering on the steps of the Temple of Castor and Pollux, youths who were clearly looking for trouble though probably not yet committed to a life of crime.

'Of course it's a job,' he mused. 'Fresh air and mental challenges. At least when you get hit on the head it's no surprise. There's a routine, if you like that, but scope to use your initiative. You have wonderful colleagues to insult you day and night. Plus the joy of knowing everyone else thinks you're just a fireman and despises you. I haven't doused a flame in fifteen years.'

'You've been on enquiries most of your career?'

'Must be thought to have the knack,' he replied dryly.

He had the cynical tone of a man who knew all superiors were incapable of judgement or man management. This could have made him vulnerable. But somehow I felt that Martinus was too easy-going to complicate his existence by taking bribes. He was too lazy to bother, Petro would say.

'So what do you reckon we do now?' I asked. Naturally I had my own ideas. I was convinced the brothel had been made the new centre of the Balbinus organisation.

'We need to know if Balbinus is inside Plato's.'

I agreed so far. 'Or if not, when they are expecting him.'

'So we need an inside man,' Martinus said.

I glanced at him uneasily. 'You mean one of us?'

'Jupiter, no! Unless,' he grinned, 'you fancy volunteering?'

'If that's the plan, I fancy a long vacation on a pig farm in Bruttium!'

Martinus shook his head. 'We need a single-handed worker. One who looks bent enough to be accepted without comment, but who has no real allegiance to the Balbinus mob.' He pointed a long finger at a pickpocket who for the past half-hour had been patiently working the crowds. 'There's one I know. He'll do.'

We walked across to the unobtrusive pouch-snatcher and waited until he bumped into his next victim. Martinus instantly laid a hand on his shoulder, and just as quickly the man darted off. 'Drop him, Falco!'

I knocked the snatcher's legs from under him, and Martinus sat down hard on his ribs. We tossed the purse back to the victim, who blinked in surprise, then looked at us as if he feared we were setting him up for some really complicated con. Sighing, Martinus waved him away.

We stood the pickpocket upright and grinned at him.

LVIII

'Listen, Claudius – '

'Me name's Igullius!'

He was a runt. I myself would never have let him nick my purse; I would not have let this ill-favoured, pathetic creature stand near enough to me to finger it. 'His name's Igullius. Write it down, Martinus!' Martinus fetched out his note tablet and wrote it down. First, however, he courteously checked the spelling.

This pickpocket had a greasy face and oily hair. His breath was coming in short, frightened pants. It informed us that his breakfast had included hard-boiled eggs; his lunch was a garlic stew. The flavouring had been generous and was now pervading all the pores of his unhealthy skin.

Martinus and I stepped back. Igullius wondered if he dared make a run for it. We glared. He stayed put. Martinus explained like a kindly uncle that it was necessary for him to submit to a search.

Igullius was wearing a natural wool toga which Martinus lifted off him, using the tips of his fingers as if he thought he might catch plague. Somewhat to our surprise we found nothing in its folds. Igullius looked self-righteous. We surveyed what was left of him: battered boots and a rather wide-necked tunic, fastened tightly round his midriff by a nipped-in belt that was nearly bisecting him.

'Take off your belt,' I commanded.

'What for?'

'So I can thrash you with it, if you don't get a move on.' I sounded like a watch captain. Sometimes you have to lower yourself to obtain a result.

With a filthy look, Igullius hoicked in his rib-gripper and let the clincher off its notch. Purses tumbled from beneath his tunic with a melodious clink. One bounced on his kneecap, causing his leg to kick. 'Ooh look, Falco, it's snowing denarii!'

'I'll see you,' the pickpocket replied defiantly as Martinus tweaked at the tunic in case there was more.

'I don't take.' The answer from Martinus came out sweetly and calmly. Igullius probably failed to realise this was the Forum Romanum district, whereas we were from the Aventine. The First Cohort ought to be in charge here, though typically none had been visible anywhere for the past hour. Martinus stooped, gathering the booty. 'The game's up, Igullius. You're going to climb the tree; we'll crucify you.'

'I never did nothing.'

Martinus shook a couple of purses in his face. 'We'll have to discuss that. Falco, let's take him to a private room somewhere.'

'Oh no!' Sheer terror now gripped our captive. 'I'm not going in any ceil with you!' Martinus had never intended taking him to the Fourth's patrol house; apart from the fact we did not want to involve Petronius, we were too far away. But the mere hint caused an extreme reaction. Somebody somewhere in the cohorts had a formidable reputation.

In fright Igullius made a sudden break. I grabbed him and wrapped his arms around his back, holding him fast. Martinus was stuck with the flavoursome breath, but carried on bravely. 'You stink and you steal. Give me one good reason to go easy on you, Igullius!'

The pickpocket had been in the streets long enough to know what was required. 'Oh Jupiter! Well what have I got to do?'

'Co-operate. But you'll like it,' we told him. 'We're going to give you the money to go with a prostitute!' We turned the pickpocket round, took an arm each, lifted him over a screever who was begging on the pavement with a piteous message, then marched him down the Sacred Way.

As we crossed the Via Nova into the shadow of the Palatine I noticed Tibullinus, the centurion of the Sixth. We had seen him at Ostia, and he had turned up when we were looking at the corpse of Nonnius. Tibullinus was too closely involved in events to let him notice us here. I gave Martinus the nod. Alert, he took the point. But Tibullinus was patrolling the Palatine in a style that seemed to suit him – laughing and joking with fellows he recognised. He did not see us.

*

We took our new acquaintance back to the Oily Jug. This time we were more brisk with the woman. She had two choices – either to spend the next couple of days with a friend somewhere, or to pass them in a cell. Once again this threat worked miracles. She decided she had a sister who was longing to see her, and fled from our watching post.

Training Igullius was tiresome. We used the kind method, only thumping him when his eyes glazed. 'That building over there is called the Bower of Venus – '

'That's Plato's.'

'Have you been there?'

'Of course.' He was possibly bluffing, but he wanted to appear a smart man about town.

'Well Plato's may be under new management, but we're not interested in the brothel itself. There's a phoenix in Rome. A person who is supposed to be banished has come home again.' Maybe Igullius knew. He was already pale. 'His name is Balbinus Pius. Some of his men are hanging out in Plato's. Maybe he's there too. Maybe he's just hiring rooms for them. But if he visits his troops, we want to know. You see how it is, Igullius. You're going in, you're going to recognise a friend, or make a new one if you have to, but however you do it you're going to sit in a corner keeping quiet until you can come out and tell us a date and time when Balbinus will be available for interview.'

'Oh give me a chance, Falco! I'm dead if I try that.'

'You're dead if you don't,' smiled Martinus. He enjoyed playing the cruel executioner.

I took a hand again. 'Now settle down, Igullius. We know you're not entirely bad, so we're giving you this fine job opportunity. You're going to be our undercover man. And to compensate your loss of earnings from your regular work, we'll find you a big ex gratia at the end of the day.'

'How about paying some in advance?'

'Don't be stupid,' said Martinus. 'We're in the vigiles. We have to remember public accountability.'

Igullius tried one last desperate wriggle. 'That place is full of hard men. They'll spot a weed in the garden straight away.'

'You've been there before, according to you. You'll have to

734

make sure you blend in,' I said callously. 'You're perfectly capable. Anyone who can slide up and sneak purses even though he has breath that can be smelled at twenty paces can merge into a nest of mostly stupid criminals.'

We gave him the price of a whore to start him off convincingly, then pushed him on his way.

Success came fast. Igullius was back in a couple of hours, nipping across the street like a startled cat. Whatever he learnt had left him panic-stricken. He fell into the thermopolium, then threw himself behind the counter with his head in his hands.

'Oh you bastards! Don't make me go back again.'

'That depends,' sneered Martinus. 'What have you got for us?'

'I've got what you asked for, and I'm not getting any more!'

I found him a drink to calm his hysteria. He gulped down the wine, which I knew was disgusting, as if he had just crawled out of a six-day sandstorm in an arid zone. 'Control yourself. You're safe now. What was your girl like?'

'All right . . .' Easily sidetracked! Martinus and I leaned on the counter watching him. Crouching at our feet, he managed to slow his breath.

'I think he's there! I'm sure he is!'

'Not visible, presumably?' Martinus asked.

'I didn't see him. I mean, I didn't see anyone who looked that big a character.'

'Big? Don't believe it,' I snarled. 'Balbinus is just a flea.'

Igullius continued, talking fast as if he wanted to get this over. 'The place is humming. I've never been in a barn with such a live atmosphere. I saw half a dozen faces, I mean *serious* faces. There's one big room – ' He shook, unable to spit it out. That sounded like the cavernous hall Petro and I had glimpsed. It had been full of small-timers then, but when I pressed the trembling Igullius for details he described a real thieves' kitchen with mobsters nesting openly.

I stared at Martinus. 'Something's changed. It sounds as though Balbinus has taken over and made the place his own. Igullius, was there any mention of Lalage?' He shook his head. 'Well if you've been there before, is the brothel business being run the same as usual?' This time he nodded.

While I was pondering, Martinus tried screwing more useful facts from our eavesdropper, though to little effect. I sat in silence. We certainly could not send him straight back into Plato's this afternoon or it would arouse the suspicions of the girl on the door. Martinus decided that Igullius could be let off and dismissed.

'I want my money then.'

Martinus was looking at me unhappily. I realised he lacked the authority to pay over the kind of reward we had promised, and he was even too straight to hand back the purses Igullius had stolen in the Forum (which is what I would have done, given this was a crisis). Instead, Martinus was forced to remove the back block from his note tablet and write out a chit. 'Take this to the patrol house – tomorrow!' he said sternly. That would give him some grace before Petronius found out.

The pickpocket snatched the warrant, then found his feet and scurried off.

I continued thinking. It looked as if Lalage had lied to me – no surprise at all.

I did not believe she was running the crime empire from Plato's herself. Lalage was not so stupid as to do that openly.

They were still working for the old regime. After all Lalage's claims about seizing her independence, it was hard to accept that she had caved in and allowed Balbinus Pius to take over her premises. That he might even be hiding up there seemed incredible.

She would not do it. Either he had removed her – in which case I doubted that the brothel would be running as smoothly as usual –or Lalage had some ploy in hand. That boded ill for Balbinus. But it might help us.

As Martinus and I continued our vigil we abandoned casual chat – and draughts. That suited me. It also stopped his overblown raving about men who played board games being suitable to pit their wits against major criminals. Removing Balbinus from Rome called for a sudden rush with a sharp weapon, not cerebral guile.

It already felt like a long day and I reckoned we were

heading for a big night exercise. We found some stale bread
to gnaw on. We had a drink. Indigestion set in cruelly.

Towards the evening we started feeling tense. Something
was going on. Men, singly or in twos or threes, walked up to
the brothel. They appeared in the street as quietly as bats.
Making their way inside, they might have been bound for a
party with their workplace dining club. If so, they were
dressed less smartly than most colleages going out for a bash.
Also, they were being asked to pay a hefty ticket price: 'That's
boodle, or I'm a baby!' Martinus had identified our first
definite sack of swag – a bedcover knotted at the corners,
from within which came the charming chink of stolen
silverware.

We both knew what we were watching. I had discussed this
when I first tried to involve the deputy, and now as the early
dusk fell I was being proved right. The starlings were
roosting. All the day shifts were closing and their operators
were reporting in with their take. Cashing up: making their
way here with their takings from all the corners of the
Aventine, the waterfront and the Forum. The snatchers and
grabbers, the confidence tricksters and bluffers, the
strangling muggers, the dirty alley girls with thugs for
minders, the robbers of drunks and schoolchildren, the mobs
who held up ladies' litters, the thieves who beat up slaves. It
was mainly money that was pouring in. Saleable goods would
be passed to receiving shops or metal furnaces. I had to slip
out to a stationer's to buy more wax tablets as Martinus had
run out of space to note down all the criminals he knew.
There were many more we could not identify – or not yet.
Most of them left again shortly after arrival, clearly lighter of
baggage.

We had to decide what to do. 'Balbinus could have an
accountant working at Plato's. A sidekick who just keeps the
ledgers and pays off the workmen.'

'What would you do, Martinus, if your most trusted
collector had been Nonnius Albius, and he put you away?'

'I'd do the reckoning myself after that.'

'I bet he agrees! If so, then he's in there.'

'He's in there, Falco. Now he is. But if I was him, I'd move
about.'

'So you're saying let's nab him before he hops?'

'Don't you agree?'

Of course I agreed – but I wanted to go in there in strength. In particular I wanted Petronius among us. It was partly old loyalty. But more than that, if I was going into Plato's knowing it was full of evil men and hoping to find the worst of all calmly sitting there with a glass in his hand and an abacus, then I wanted someone at my back I could trust.

'So is it a jump?' Martinus demanded impatiently. From his tone it was clear that if I declined tonight, he would not continue to work with me. I could live without his draughts game, but not with whatever chaos he might wreak if he started working on his own.

'It's a jump if Rubella will give us some backup.'

Even Martinus, with his high opinion of his own quality, could not consider a raid at Plato's with just the two of us. He went off to consult his tribune. I had to stay on watch. Things were so lively we no longer dared to leave together in case we missed something.

I sat there for some time. I had taken one of the spare noteblocks, and was drawing a map of the brothel based on what I remembered from my two visits. One thing I knew was that the place was very large. It occupied at least three storeys, each with numerous corridors. It had probably grown from a single house, taking in those either side as success enabled expansion. Although there was one main door, we had noticed that some of the gangsters knocked and were admitted to a more innocent-looking hole in the wall: they had a family entrance for criminals. In the other direction was a similar house door, much less used. Women occasionally slipped in and out. Once one emerged with two small children: it must be the prostitutes' private exit. Not many had freedom to come and go. I wondered where that would place them in a fracas with the law.

Sometimes the prostitutes received their own visitors. All were women. I made up some pretty reasons for these intriguing social calls. Some involved special entertainers who lived elsewhere but were hired in. Some involved the sort of tales adolescents tell each other about high-class ladies working in brothels for high-spending favoured clients.

738

Some of my theories were purely daft. Then two women called whose behaviour convinced me I knew what sometimes happened behind that private door.

They had come in a litter. It waited for them at the corner. They climbed out slowly, looking up and down the narrow street. Their skirts were long and full, their heads muffled in quite heavy cloaks. After a brief hesitation they straightened up and marched arm in arm to the mysterious door. Well-heeled sandals clipped the pavement. One of them rapped, so loudly I could hear it. Soon there was a furtive conversation with an inmate and the two women went inside.

Of course I knew what I was witnessing. A girl with money had got into trouble with a lover. Taking a friend for support, she had come to the brothel in order to end her problem with the aid of the abortionist. The Bower of Venus was bound to possess one.

I could have lived with that. Desperate people are entitled to risk their lives if it seems less harsh than the alternative.

What made me sick was that despite their caution I recognised those women. One was short and sturdy with a self-confident walk; one taller and straight-backed. The first was my sister Maia. And the other was Helena.

739

ILX

They were in there for a long time. I wanted to rush in after them. Instead I remained at my post, brooding horrendously.

When they came out, it was hurriedly. The door slammed behind them. They took a few quick steps, then stood in heated discussion. I strode across to them.

'Oh gods, not still hanging around brothels!' Maia shrieked.

'Oh you're here!' exclaimed Helena, with what sounded like relief. Her tone was urgent, tense, yet ill-fitting the situation I had been conjuring up.

I was staring at Helena as she hugged her cloak around her. The girl I had loved – no; did love. With my sister, the only one I had been able to tolerate. 'I'm on surveillance.'

Helena compressed her mouth slightly. I realised I had hardly seen her for the past two days. This morning I had left the house before she woke. Only a dirty tunic on the back of the door would have told her I came in last night.

'Helena, I'm doing what's important. You know that.'

'No I don't know!' She actually stamped her foot. 'I have not seen you to talk to since the day before yesterday. I *wanted* to talk to you – '

'I realise that.' Something was wrong here. Helena knew it too. We looked at each other in some trouble. My face seemed to have turned to wood. Anxiety and irritation jostled in hers. I croaked, 'Are you all right?'

'We were very frightened, but it's better now.'

'Are you hurt?'

'It wasn't like that.'

It was Maia who understood first. Quick-witted and caustic, she had interpreted my clenched fists. She rammed her cloak back abruptly, so her dark curls jumped up. Her eyes were flashing. 'Juno Matrona! Helena Justina, this unforgivable bastard thinks you've just had a bodkin job!'

'Oh thanks, Maia.' Everything took a very nasty lurch. 'Always there with the fine and fluent phrase!'

740

'How could you, brother?'

I felt sick. 'Something Famia said.'

'I'll kill him!' Maia grated through her teeth. 'Then I'll kill you for believing him!' While Helena still looked bewildered, my sister stormed off, yelling back, 'I'll take Galla, I'll leave you the chair. Give my brother a good kicking, then for all our sakes, Helena, *talk to him*!'

I closed my eyes while the world rocked.

'We've commandeered a place to watch from. Will you come inside?'

'Is that an apology?' Helena was starting to appreciate she had the right to feel insulted. I could see a faint gleam in her huge brown eyes that meant she was enjoying power. Dimly, at the corner of my vision, I was aware of Maia dragging my sister Galla from the litter and marching her away.

'What in Hades is Galla doing here with you?' I stormed. Then I warned feebly, 'You gave me a bad fright. I'm in no condition to be whipped.' Helena was staring at me. She looked tired and despondent. Presumably I had contributed to that. I hung my head. I was ready to try any tricks. 'I love you, Helena.'

'Trust me then!' she snapped. Then she softened and offered her cheek for a formal kiss of greeting; I gave her a meek peck. As I drew back her face changed, crumpling slightly as if everything was becoming too much for her. 'Oh stop being stupid and hold me tight!' she cried.

Reprieve.

'Actually,' she said, once I had hugged her fiercely and taken her indoors, 'I was trying to *save* a child.' I received the rebuke like a man, hiding my wince. 'The people who have Tertulla sent another message yesterday –'

'Yesterday?'

'I wanted to discuss it, Marcus; you gave me no chance!' Apprehensive and annoyed with myself, I managed to signal yet another apology. Even I was growing bored with being abject. Helena growled, then herself owned up, 'I decided I must do something, for the child's sake.'

'Note the calm manner in which I hear this news, Helena.'

'Full credit for an understanding nature.' She could tell I was boiling over with anxiety.

'So instead of alerting the vigiles, you brought a couple of female bodyguards and came to ransom the child yourself?'

'What choice did we have?'

'Knowing the address they work from, Petro could have mounted a raid.'

'They would have hidden the child and denied all knowledge. I'm not some frightened magistrate; I was going to report them once we had got Tertulla back.'

I kept my voice level. 'So you gave them the money and of course they kept the bargain?' I had seen no sign of Tertulla.

Helena shook her head despondently. 'No. I kept the money. They told me she's not there.'

'They were lying. They realised you're a tough customer who will land them in court.'

'I don't think so. They wanted the money. They were annoyed themselves. They say Tertulla must have run away. They can't find her anywhere. I did believe them; they even let us search – '

I was horrified. 'In the brothel?'

We were both silent for a while. Bravery had always been Helena's strongest quality, but I knew what she must have undergone. Since she had escaped unscathed, there was no point screaming over it. 'The Fates only know where Tertulla has got to. Are you angry, Marcus?'

'No, but dear gods, it's my turn now to be held tight!'

Time was passing. In the city streets a new, more bustling mood took over as the evening activity began. Men had bathed. The sleek and the sleazy were leaving their homes and their places of business. This lane was growing darker; not many lamps ever burned around here.

I would have to send Helena home soon. Now we had settled down, I was enjoying our short time together. I needed her. Being alone with Helena refreshed me. Even in a tense situation I could open up, be frank, put aside the caution that must always be present with anyone else. While I was on duty with Martinus, I had to disguise my own intentions and to stalk his ambition. With Helena I soon felt clear-headed again.

742

'I suppose,' I ventured thoughtfully, 'you didn't see a man with a balding pate and self-deluding eyes, who looks as if he sells embroidery that will fall apart?'

'I tried to avoid the men.' I bet plenty of men stared at her.

'Oh good! A girl who ignores brothel etiquette.'

'Do you want me to go back and try to spot this man?' she asked. Always keen for adventure. The thought made me sweat with anxiety.

Luckily my stomach gave an enormously loud rumble. I confessed how little I had eaten that day. Helena Justina decided that although looking in the brothel for Balbinus would be a boon to the state, it had been superseded by her domestic responsibilities. She marched off to buy me some food.

As I ate, Helena was adding details to the map I had drawn. Martinus came back while I was still working through her lavish supplies, but I continued to munch without a conscience. Martinus had been missing so long I had a good idea the deputy had shamelessly found himself a full dinner before he visited Rubella. 'So what's the tribune going to do for us?'

'Bad news, Falco. Rubella's sole interest is the fact that this street lies in the Sixth Cohort's empire.'

'He wants to bring them in? That's ridiculous. I don't trust the Sixth.'

'Well, Rubella intends to discuss things with the Prefect before he'll authorise a raid – '

'Rubella's a fool.'

'His plan is to go in tomorrow.'

'That's a plan I'd like – if it was tonight.'

Helena was still sitting quietly at my side. 'What about Petronius?' she asked.

'Oh hadn't you heard?' Martinus looked quite cheerful, so I knew it would be bad news. 'He's off watch. There was an attack on the patrol house yesterday night. The fire-watchers were all out on a false alarm, but the chief was in there working. Someone rammed the joint with the old "runaway cart" trick – a cart full of rocks and rubble. Brought down half the doorway, but the back part of the building stood up to it and Petronius escaped injury. Rubella reckons it was a direct

743

attempt to get the chief. He thinks Balbinus was behind it, so he's declared Petro sick and sent him to the country.'

'He won't take kindly to that.'

'He handed in his resignation.'

'Oh Jupiter!' For a calm man, my friend could do some pig-headed things.

Martinus grinned. 'Rubella broke the tablet in half and handed it straight back.' The tribune had some sense then. But it meant tackling Plato's without our best man. 'While I was on the Aventine I did speak to a few of the lads,' hinted the deputy.

'What does that mean?'

'Sergius and four or five others may be along later.'

'*Four or five?* Out of the question,' I replied at once. 'We can't go into Plato's without saturation coverage. Tell them not to bother.'

'Tell them yourself!' retorted Martinus. He sounded petulant. Then someone tapped discreetly on the counter and I found myself looking into the ridiculously handsome face of the whip man, Sergius. He had a long head, with a strong nose and chin, and flashing, even teeth. He was staring at Helena; she fixed her attention on counting the olive stones I had left after my repast.

Events were moving faster than I liked. They were out of control. With a thug like Balbinus that could have fatal results.

Behind Sergius were several other men from the Fourth. At least now I knew that Petro had been sent on a goat-grazing holiday I could forget that they might have sneaked here in some mood of disloyalty to him. They were defying Rubella; I could allow that.

What I would not accept was any kind of crackbrained exercise against orders, without planning or backup, and really without a full reconnaissance. I was determined to resist Martinus on this. Not that my common sense came to anything. The lads, as he called them (though they were large, fit and ugly apart from Sergius), had piled into the Oily Jug like schoolboys invading a pastry shop. I was groaning and trying to say goodbye to Helena, so it was Sergius who spotted the development. He hissed, and quickly snuffed our lamp.

I heard the noise he had noticed. Two pairs of feet walking briskly in concert, accompanied by the disturbing chinks of heavy chains. They came from the direction of the Circus. The feet stamped with a cheerful energy in thick-soled, businesslike boots.

The men those feet carried so purposefully were known to most of us. They were Tibullinus and Arica, the centurion and his sidekick from the Sixth – two upstanding officers whom we all believed were taking bribes. They were marching into Plato's like conquering hunters, carrying on their shoulders a long pole of spoils. Suspended from the pole in chains was a male figure I recognised.

'Oh gods!' murmured Martinus. 'I forgot to tell him we're the Fourth. He's gone and taken his damned chitty to the Sixth.'

The trussed man was Igullius. He looked alive – but only just.

'*Scatter!*'

I heard my voice without expecting it. Somehow I made them all jump from the Oily Jug before the two men from the Sixth came out again to look for us. We managed to whip out of sight around a corner just in time, and heard a commotion as a group from the brothel turned over the dump we had left. Helena had had the sense to bring the still-warm bowl from which I had eaten my food. Tibullinus must have thought Martinus and I had gone home much earlier. They gave up after a short time, and retreated back to Plato's.

We were still there, however. And naturally there was just one thought on the rash deputy's mind: 'They've got Igullius. If they don't know our plans already, he'll soon squeal to them. We have no time. Balbinus will be leaving any minute.'

'Helena – '

Helena turned and banged the map we had drawn against my chest. Her voice was taut. 'Don't apologise again. I don't want the last thing I remember to be you saying you were sorry. Oh don't explain. I know!' she raged. 'You've lost your surprise; you have no support; no one knows if the man you want is even in the brothel – but *you're going in!*'

745

LX

I took charge.

I passed the map around quickly and told them to get in without fuss, then disperse through the building fast. Forget thieves. Forget hard men. Forget even Tibullinus and Arica. Say nothing and hit no one, unless there was no choice. Save Igullius if it were possible, but keep filtering through towards the top and the back and the farthermost rooms of the brothel until we found Balbinus Pius.

'What then?'

'Yell your head off for the rest of us.'

I like to keep plans simple. At least when this went wrong there would be only a minor body count. Only seven of us were going in.

We slipped inside in ones and twos. Paid the tally and winked at the doorkeeper.

'I'm Itia, and I'm here to see you enjoy yourselves.'

'Thanks, Itia.'

'Are you being joined by friends tonight?'

'Just a few.'

'Maybe we'll give you a discount then.'

I was right. The brothel side of the business was reserving its position. But I did not imagine our discount would take the form of help.

I had gone in first. I walked quickly but with a casual manner. I went straight past the ground-floor rooms, the cloak pegs and the washing facilities. There was a louder hum of masculinity than on previous times I had visited. From the big room where conspirators gathered came a full-throated wave of men drinking and talking. I did not look in. He would not be there, amongst the throng.

The place was already warm and hazy with lamp oil and taper smoke. Further on it seemed quiet. Once, something attracted attention. I stepped into a room and found normal

746

commerce in action. The girl was in the saddle. I quipped, 'Glad to see you're on top of things!' and whipped the door shut on them.

Reaching stairs I started climbing. At the landing I paused to listen. Behind me all sounded normal. No shouts of alarm. Martinus and the others must so far be undiscovered. It would not last.

Still no sign of Tibullinus and Arica. I opened more doors, more gently this time. I found either empty rooms or flesh trade of one kind or another. More kinds than I had ever heard of in fact, though I had no time to make detailed notes.

The brothel seemed busy, but not in flourishing party mode. No one stopped me. No one even challenged my presence. Balbinus would have guards, the Miller for instance. I would have to get past them; I had not even seen them yet.

The longer I was in there, the more urgent became my feeling that I needed to escape. I had come so far that if anything went wrong, fighting my way out would be impossible. I had been a spy scouting in hostile citadels many times before, but then I had stood some chance of disguising my identity. I was too well known here. Helena had been right. We were probably walking into a trap. My skin crawled as I began to feel the certainty that someone was fully expecting me.

There was a faint odour of incense in the air. I thought I recognised my location. I hit a wider corridor, where I remembered that the rooms were grander, though I felt no need to investigate now. I could hear music. I discerned light, and laughing voices. My stride increased. At the last moment memory failed me and without warning I crashed into the large room with the sunken entertainment area where Petro and I had reckoned orgies might be staged. I pulled up short, facing the certainty that something grossly pornographic had either been enacted in the recent past or was about to take place. As the braziers wreathed, burning an exotic fuel, the atmosphere hit me in the gullet; the inescapable message was that nobody who entered here would want to plead he was too honest to participate.

Candelabra stood all around the upper seating bank.

Garlands of roses and other musky flowers coiled and writhed from every surface. There was a small band of musicians idly tuning up: a hand drum, panpipes, tambourines and a curled flute. The musicians wore pleasingly friendly expressions and diagonal wisps of seethrough drape. A smiling man in satyr's costume approached – the full gear of hairy trousers, goat hooves, highly visible naked working parts. His face, with its paint and fragile smile, was a disturbing contrast to the prominent masculine attribute. He gestured a welcome to me with a dreamy air. In the centre of the floor four exquisite young girls, none of them older than fifteen, were performing warm-up stretches with a languid grace that spoke all too strongly of the nature of their act. They wore no clothes, even before their tableau commenced.

On the outer rim, men waited. Some tasted wine; others prodded at the serving staff or picked their teeth.

Opposite me stood the doorway that led to Lalage's rooms. There was another door. Either side of it were two long torches thrust into waist-high urns, blazing with a sweet odour of something akin to applewood. Before it lay an irregular, striped mat, the skin of some dead carnivore. To one side an extremely muscular man was chatting up a stripling who was holding a bronze ewer.

The music started. The audience stirred with a low ripple of lecherous anticipation. My eyes went automatically to the floor area. It was time to leave or be seduced. I had made my choice.

I walked around the edge of the room, as if searching for a space to sit. As I came to the door with the braziers I was keeping my eyes fixed on the slow and intricate patterns being wrought by the gleaming bodies of the quartet of girls. All around me were the heated faces of men looking shy while they fervently hoped we would soon reach that moment when a member of the acrobatic display would call for a volunteer from the audience.

It was certainly better than watching a grizzled Egyptian in a long nightgown performing 'Where's my snake?'

I stared with the same eagerness as the rest of them, despite myself hoping to be shocked by the writhing hot properties. I was still staring as I leaned on the bronze ram's-head door handle and backed quickly through the door.

748

I closed it as I turned. It was solid and ornate, muffling the music instantly. Whatever I had entered was pitch-black. A short distance away I could hear a shuffling noise, joined at one point by a metallic clink. Could this be Igullius?

I slipped the door ajar again and reached out for one of the Dioscuri torches. The brief inflow of light from the entertainment room gave me a second's warning. I sensed movement. Spinning back, I flung the torch to the right. Then from the left came a noisy snake of heavy chain, thrown by an expert who lassoed me and then dragged it tight. My torch had crashed onto a mosaic floor. By its quaking light Tibullinus the centurion flung another chain across the room so Arica could help hold me.

I had one chance. My arms were pinioned with bruising force. I threw myself backwards, jerking the second chain so that Arica fell off balance as he was catching it. Pain seared my arms and my spine jarred badly. Arica dropped towards me. I had both feet up ready, and kicked into him with all my might.

Not hard enough. He yelled, but staggered upright. The bastard must have ribs like iron. As for me, I was on my back now, trapped in a mesh of links that Tibullinus was threshing tauntingly. Arica relieved his hurt feelings by stamping on my face. I managed to roll aside, but his great boot creamed down my scalp alongside one ear, tearing off skin and hair. They pulled me around the floor, knocking into the torch, though it failed to ignite me. There were enough restraints on me to subdue a maddened elephant. As I fought to resist, I roared out a name or two when I could, hoping help would come. I should have known better. My own name is Didius Falco and help for me is the last gift the Olympian gods toss down.

In the end my dead weight must have tired them. I lost track of the kicks I had received. They lashed me up and attached part of the cold knotwork to a pillar. Tibullinus produced his centurion's vinewood stick, and amused himself by describing in picturesque terms what he would do with it. I pretended to be a pervert and slavered eagerly. If he came near enough at least I could spit on him.

Again, no such luck. They knew there were others with me. They promised a feast of torture later, then left with an

749

appearance of urgency. Not long afterwards the fallen torch spluttered and went out.

I was in despair, but worse followed. How long I lay in the dark with my arms going numb I cannot say. It must have been an hour or so. There had to be time for Helena Justina to rush to the Aventine and take action she thought appropriate. The person she sent here had to start searching for *me*, and Tibullinus had to find and overpower *him*. By the time the door opened, I had heard the musicians in the room outside drive themselves into a frenzy – matched no doubt by the girls and their customers. I had also wasted considerable effort calling out to the exhausted company after the noise died down. Whatever their perverted tastes, they had no interest in a shackled man.

Then the door cracked open. Tibullinus did not bother bringing light into the room. He flung his captive headlong, gave him a good kicking, chained him up, spoke his usual attractive oration, and marched out again.

'Brisk,' I said into the familiar darkness. 'Though comforting in its warm predictability.'

My new companion groaned. Maybe he was suffering from being kicked. Maybe he was just happy to be sharing his captivity with me.

After a few moments he recovered himself sufficiently to break out into banter. 'This is the last time.' His voice was hoarse. He forced himself to have a rest. 'This is the last time, Falco.' I laid my head against the pillar behind me and sighed reflectively. 'Next time you're in deadly danger, I'll stay at home and stroke the cat.'

'Thank you,' I said, inserting a quiet note of humility which I knew would drive him wild. 'I'm touched at you coming to assist me – though it's not much use if you get yourself trussed up as well. But thank you, Lucius Petronius, my loyal friend.'

LXI

Time passed.

Something dangerous was happening to my arms. I mentioned it to Petro. He was not so tightly shackled as me, probably because he had been chained up only after being knocked downstairs, hammered, and hit into the middle of next week with a large vase. He had not had my opportunities for increasing the torque by wild acrobatics. He expressed kind concern for my predicament, followed by the logical question of what did I expect him to do about it?

More time passed.

'Petro, where are your men?'

'What men? When Helena Justina had finished berating me, I ran straight here.'

'Wonderful.'

'Anyway, how could I call for reinforcements? I'm not here. I've been sent to the country.'

'You didn't go.'

'You bet I didn't. Not once I heard you'd cajoled that fool Martinus into some disastrous scheme.'

'Well I'm glad you're here,' I told him warmly.

'Go to Hades,' he instructed, though in the tone of a friend.

After a while I said, 'I heard about the attempt to get you.'

'Stupidity.'

'Balbinus is not stupid. He knows you're the one he should worry about.'

'You're right. I should have expected trouble.' Petronius agreed to discuss it. His personal danger had been preying on his mind, and there was no one else with whom he could share his thoughts. His wife Silvia would have run amok in distress, and presumably Rubella thought imposing temporary exile showed sufficient sympathy. 'The false fire alarm was a set-up, of course. Someone knew I was working late that night.'

'Any ideas?' I enquired, with caution.

'Someone in the team. Whoever set up Linus, presumably.' The merest change in his voice acknowledged at last that I had been right about the cohort containing a traitor.

'Know who it was?'

'I've had suspicions for some time. I haven't tackled the issue yet.'

There was a silence. He did not tell me the name of his suspect. Well that was fine. Nor did I tell him mine.

'So,' I exclaimed brightly. 'Why were you working late? Reports?'

'No. While you and Martinus were playing hide-and-seek in a chop shop, some of us had work to do. Well, Rubella's idea of it. I've been caged up with the Temple of Saturn auditor – you know, the one who was working on the confiscation of the Balbinus estate.'

'Anything useful emerge?'

'Not unless you want to split your sides at the news that Plato's Academy is a lease Balbinus had laundered. This henhouse had been given away as part of his daughter's dowry. So its landlord is wimpy Florius.' We laughed.

Probably Florius had never realised. He would not be the first clean-living, self-righteous equestrian whose portfolio, unbeknown to him, was bursting with legendary brothels and cover joints.

I shifted. It was agonising. I was yearning to escape. 'When you got here, did you see Martinus, Sergius and the rest?'

'Martinus was hustling out some half-dead pickpocket – an informant, I presume.'

'Igullius?'

'If you say so. I didn't see the others.' Petro's voice was clipped. 'And if they had any sense they'd make damn sure they weren't near me to be seen.'

Tibullinus must have left the door on the catch. A draught had blown it ajar slightly. All noises had ceased in the entertainment room now, as though the night must be well over. The audience and performers had gone home. Well, they had slunk off somewhere more private anyway.

Nobody else had been brought to join us. Maybe that meant the others from the troop had found nothing of interest; maybe they had abandoned us. Typical of Martinus, Petro commented. I said nothing. In view of my presuming on his deputy's disloyalty, I was treading with care.

Tread was the wrong word. I could hardly move. Any attempt was torture. My flesh had swollen and my arms felt as though they would never work again. I tried various ways of manipulating my body, but there was only one that permitted any kind of relief. So, if only to help my bruised feelings, I let out a mighty belch.

Then a small female voice outside the door whimpered, 'Uncle Marcus, is that you?'

I heard a sharp intake of breath from Petro. Keeping down hysteria as much as possible, I managed to sound like an uncle who had a pocket full of honeyed dates. 'Tertulla! Goodness, you'll be my favourite niece for this. Tertulla, pick up one of those big torches. Make sure you don't touch the flaming part, then bring it in to us . . .'

'I don't want to play this game.'

'But come in and say hello to us,' Petronius said. 'Anyway, we haven't told you yet what the game is.'

There was a pause that made me ache with irritation, then a squeak, then the door widened and in came a frightened little figure. She wore a dress that even her mother would disapprove of. She was dirty and exhausted, but she had the mournful air that told us she was terrified of being in trouble yet now wanted to go home. If we promised her a big enough bribe – for instance, protection against her distraught mother – Tertulla might be on our side.

LXII

Petronius Longus had always possessed a special smile, which he kept for certain situations when whatever he was planning did not require my presence. Now I learned that with this smile, subtly applied while talking quietly in that slow and friendly manner, Petronius could make a woman forget entirely that she did not want to co-operate. It was probably practice. He was, after all, the father of three little girls.

Somehow Petronius engaged Tertulla in the game of unwinding the chains that trussed him, then he and she together worked for a much longer time on the vicious cat's cradle that had been pinioning me.

He jerked my arms up and down. 'Does this hurt?'

'Ow! Yes.'

'That's good,' he said. 'You've still got some nerves left.'

The entertainment room was deserted. Its floral decor had suffered a pounding. Behind the large obscene statue of the peculiar group intertwining, we spotted a window. It led onto a roof, which gave onto the street. I had to admit that my arms were unlikely to take weight yet; the pain was excruciating as the blood came back. So it was Petro who carefully lowered himself outside, who prayed that the tiles would hold him, and then dropped to the ground. Tertulla needed no encouragement to trust herself to the open if this wonderful man would catch her. Now his fervent devotee, she was soon out of there and jumping into his arms. I had had to grab her dress to hold her back until Petronius was standing in place.

We had agreed it was time to be sensible. I waited until I saw Petronius hoist my niece in his arms and lope away. He would carry the child to safety, then come back with reinforcements – this time convincing the sober Rubella that the Sixth Cohort had no sensibilities we needed to respect. Left alone, I too would be sensible. I would just wait quietly out of sight.

754

As soon as he had gone I tossed that thought aside, and crossed to the doorway which would take me to Lalage's room.

It was all very quiet. I knocked gently, in case she was engaged in work of a sensitive nature, then I ventured in.

She was standing opposite, against a curtain. She appeared to be alone. Though she had not replied to my knocking, I was welcomed in with a deliciously courteous wave of one arm. The room was deeply scented with its usual perfumes. Lalage was wearing the bracelet I had mended. Her gown was of glowing golden silk, so fine it both covered and expressly described the magnificent womanhood beneath. Straight-backed and bejewelled, this fabulous creature had come a long way from the girl I had once known. I was angry and battered, but I warmed to her dangerous magic.

'Marcus Didius! Why do I feel that I should have expected you? Welcome to my bower.'

I paused, staring around. There could be no one behind the curtain. It was attached to a rod that would allow it to be drawn modestly to hide a bed in an alcove I had never seen before. Maybe it was her own bed. Even prostitutes have to sleep. Maybe once she lay flat just to dream, a prostitute of her calibre earned the luxury of privacy.

The curtain was now gathered up in a tasselled cord against the wall. Nobody was concealed there, as I said. It was not clear why Lalage continued standing there. But she did, erect as a javelin, with one slim hand catching on to the embroidered folds. Her fingers were buried so deeply in the material I could not see whether she was wearing rings.

I folded my arms. The air in this place was alive with danger of all kinds tonight. My eyes wandered to all the furniture, continuing until I was satisfied. I could see floor space beneath the bed in the niche, and also under the couch where she normally sat. Tables, stools, display shelves, all looked innocent. No windows. The ceiling was solid plaster, no rafters to crouch in. I searched the walls for doors; none visible. The frilled rose-coloured fittings were too flimsy to hide a fugitive.

Lalage smiled. 'Done like a professional.'

'We all have skills. I know how to use mine.'

'Are you working tonight, Falco?'

'Afraid so.' I knew that tonight we were on equal terms. I permitted myself a rueful grin, which she took up with a quiet incline of her head. 'Where is he?' I asked in a low voice.

'Not here. He fled.'

'Are you prepared to explain?'

'Do I need to?' Her voice was arch. 'The big villain was so powerful he conquered and swept me aside. Balbinus took over the establishment, while I languished helplessly.'

I had to laugh. 'I don't believe that!'

'Thank you.' Her eyes were bright though her sigh seemed weary. 'You have good manners, Falco. In addition to a desirable body, attractive intelligence, and gorgeous eyes.'

'You're playing with me.'

'Oh we all have skills!'

'Where is he?' I asked again stubbornly.

'Gone to a place where he holes up. He's probably in disguise. His hideaway is on the Aventine. I don't know where. I was trying to find out for you.'

'Not for me.'

'For myself then. The plan – oh yes, there was a plan, Falco – was that I pretended to be terrified of what he would do to me for speaking against him in court. I let him use the brothel, so that I knew where he was.'

'If you're claiming to be helping, why did you not call in the vigiles as soon as he arrived?'

'Here? The contemptible Sixth?'

'You could have contacted Petronius. He's straight. He told you he would buy the information if required.'

'It was not for sale.' I believed that. If Lalage chose to betray anyone, it would be for her own reasons. Reasons she felt were strong enough to put the whole contract outside mere commerce. Selling was what she did with herself. She would do something else with her enemies.

'So what has gone wrong, Lalage?'

'You mostly.' She said it with diffidence, as if sorry to be involving me. 'Tibullinus told him tonight that you were outside watching Plato's. Balbinus blamed me.'

'It was nothing to do with you!'

756

'Does it matter?' She closed her eyes briefly. It was a shadow of her alluring glance, but almost too slight to count. I glimpsed a woman for some reason pushed beyond her normal strengths. She almost looked ill. 'Anyway, Balbinus left at once. I ordered Tibullinus and Arica to get out as well – so that's us finished here.'

'Don't worry about them. Tibullinus and Arica – and the entire Sixth Cohort if needs be – will be under a judicial review for corruption in the near future.'

'I'll believe it when I see it, Falco. Better hop off quick. They're still in service, and I reckon they will be coming back with their whole cohort.'

'What about you?'

'Don't worry about me.'

I was worrying about something else. The curtain hanging above her began to pull away from its fixings. A small shower of plaster dust scattered on her hair. Instead of letting go of the material, she held on more tightly.

'Oh Jupiter, girl – '

I leapt forward with my arms open and caught Lalage against my heart.

The curtain rod collapsed. She had dragged it from the wall with her weight as she tried to support herself. I managed to buff aside the pole with my shoulder. The cloth engulfed us for a moment, then fell to the floor.

Lalage crashed forwards onto me. My knees bent as I braced myself. She suppressed a cry, then I stood there aghast, clutching her under the armpits and trying not to yell. Deep in her back was a knife blade. Once I looked over her shoulder I was seeing blood everywhere – soaking her gown, pooling the floor, staining the curtain now draped around her feet.

She was still alive. The gods know how. 'Ah, Falco . . . Sorry about this. Balbinus of course – in case you're too shy to ask. How will you put me down?'

'Well, not on your back for certain. You're the expert in fancy positions. What do you suggest?'

'Have to be on top . . .'

'You're enjoying the situation.'

'Always a game girl . . .'

'Well I realise some of your finer clients would pay a lot for this.'

I had sunk on one knee. Bringing her with me, I managed to lower her carefully. Then there was only one thing for it. I had to stretch out on the floor myself, balancing on one elbow and holding Lalage above me in my arms. That way, I could keep her weight off the knife. She laid her head against my collarbone with the small contented smile of a sleepy child.

'Oh this is nice.'

'I'll get help.'

'No, stay with me, Falco.'

'I'm doing you no good. It's ridiculous.'

'Just be patient. It'll be over soon. How like a man!'

'I must be tired today. Not at my best . . .'

She was smiling. For some hideous reason I was smiling myself. 'Ask me questions, Falco. Take the chance.' She was right. I ought to be demanding last-minute information. Not indulging in crass witticisms while she lay dying in my arms.

'It doesn't matter any more.'

'Why should I die for nothing? I told you about Balbinus. Listen, who was that young officer you asked me about?'

'Linus,' I forced out obediently.

'Linus. I can tell you how Balbinus found out about him being on the ship – Tibullinus and Arica.'

'They're damned for it then. Did he tell you who told them?'

'Someone in another cohort. A youngster they got friendly with . . .' She was fading. People always say the eyes glaze over, but Lalage's were so bright it broke my heart. 'I wanted to ask you – '

She began but never finished. I thought I knew what she might have been wondering. When I pulled out the knife and turned her over gently, I touched the scar that still strikingly marred her ear. I straightened her limbs and her clothing, then partly covered her in the rich material of the curtain. Although she lay upon the floor, she looked as stately and comely as any queen in a mausoleum.

Stumbling to my feet, I crossed to her couch and sat. For a moment I stayed there remembering. Rillia Gratiana: the astonishingly pretty daughter of the snooty stationer, whose first day at school had been on the Ides of October, twenty-five years ago. A day that had been turned into a local scandal when a small boy who was frightened she was going to steal his school fees had reacted just a little too quickly and found his snarling teeth had met female flesh long before he was ready to cope with girls.

I wanted to tell her. I had been wanting to tell her ever since that day when we were seven: biting her ear had been an accident.

Well it was too late now.

LXIII

The commotion burst out as I made my way downstairs. Things had been quiet, so much so that I even entertained the wild hope that Balbinus might still be in the brothel, convinced that by murdering Lalage he had secured his hiding place.

It had been *too* quiet. At some point during my long captivity with Petro, all the lads who came in with me had been rounded up and locked away. No one could believe so few of us had invaded the place, so a protracted search must have ensued. Goodness knows how many outraged males had their evening of delights interrupted by Tibullinus, Arica, or the bunch of thugs who had been secretly living there. The annoyance of these mere customers was ignored – a highly misplaced piece of arrogance.

Enraged at losing money, Plato's customers became a defiant lot. Lalage would never have denied their push-and-shove in this outrageous way. Promising them refunds only produced a sullen crowd at the door, half of them still in their undertunics as they went on hoping for entertainment. After an hour of haggling with Macra, the inevitable happened: by some process of natural democracy a leader emerged. He roused the rest, then led them back into the brothel for a tiff.

Their first action was to find Sergius and the lads, and set them free. Sergius explained the position, and naturally made it plain (with a wink) that his duty to the public compelled him to advise the disappointed customers to run for home. As I may have remarked, Sergius was a big, handsome fellow whose main talent was thrashing folk. He only had to be thinking about this to give others the idea. A wink from Sergius was enough to turn Plato's normally furtive customers into marauding Gauls.

When I came down a fierce battle had broken out spontaneously all over two floors of the brothel. If I wanted to get through to the outer door there was nothing for it but to join in.

I wound my belt round one hand with the buckle end free, and grabbed a torch in the other fist. Flailing viciously, I drove a path down the remaining stairs through people grappling untidily. It was unclear who was what. I ran the gauntlet of a corridor full of half-clothed screaming women, then met a faceful of what I hoped was washing water from a crazy man who was giggling repeatedly in a high-pitched monotone.

The main action surged within the large, refectory-like room. It was a sea of madly working limbs and tousled heads. One fellow singled me out. He had a tapered waist and shoulders so wide he looked as if he had been hung up like a tunic with a pole through its sleeves: a gymnasium freak. It did him no good. Without waiting for his carefully rehearsed approach, I kicked him below the belt, banged the stub of my torch down hard on his neck as he doubled up, and flung him back into the scrum. Across the room, Sergius grinned. I had no time to grin back, for someone else ran at me with a stool, legs first. I snatched one of the legs and yanked it aside, going in with my elbow and knee.

The girls who worked here were clustering together, some hanging in the doorways of the refectory. A small group rushed in with bigger ideas, spitting, chucking trays and cups about, pinching, scratching, and pulling hair. I could not tell which side they supported – perhaps any that enabled them to get even with men for once. One mighty dark-skinned amazon chose to come at me, huge breasts thudding as she ran. The charge petered out, to my relief, and she sank her teeth into my hand. I grabbed her nose and twisted it hard until she let go.

Two of the lads were working well together, knocking criminals out in a well-co-ordinated routine. But elsewhere others were suffering. We were greatly outnumbered. We soon ran out of both energy and flair. There was a thunder along the main corridor. Prostitutes raced past screeching. Martinus came into the room backwards, using crossed broom-handles to fend off three or four attacking heavies. Behind him, laughing as they chose victims to slaughter, were the Miller and Little Icarus.

761

The small snarling form of Icarus hurtled straight at me. I grabbed an unconscious street villain by the shoulders of his tunic and used his body to block the impetus. Icarus had a knife. Well, it might be illegal, but I'm the kind of law-abiding citizen who fully expects to meet the other sort, so I had one as well. Sparks flew as we clashed hasp to hasp. I gripped his spare wrist with my free hand and banged against his knife arm to break the deadlock of our weapons. Then Martinus sent one of his own attackers flailing into Icarus. I disarmed him and knocked him over. He was still kicking, but after living in a Smaractus tenancy, I knew how to stamp on beetles.

As soon as Icarus gave up and just prayed that he could die now, I tried to help my comrades. The Miller was mashing bodies left and right; Sergius had been crowded into a corner by some street slime, but was keeping the honours even. Martinus was down; he was covered in blood, though still jabbing with his brooms. Identifiable customers were thin on the ground. Our chance had gone. We were facing a massacre. At that moment I saw in the doorway the bemused-looking figure of the Very Important Patrician who had been Lalage's best customer, hot for an evening of exotic massage with the sinuous proprietress.

No one could have told him Lalage was dead; only I knew. The magistrate (to allude to him with courteous vagueness) was finding it hard to comprehend that his gilded boots had stepped into the dark outer suburbs of Hades. As usual, he was followed by his lictors. They were shrewd men, trained to spot trouble two streets away. They grasped what was happening at once.

Martinus muttered, 'Oh gods. Do us all a favour, Falco — march the marble-prancer out of here before he knows what's happening!'

I had no need to bother. Macra, bright girl, was already wheeling him off somewhere. The lictors, having gaped at the blithe anarchy before them, rushed up the corridor after him, already forming into a protective phalanx. Well, all except one rushed off. *He* had spied the Miller, who at that moment was raising a table above his head with the aim of squashing Sergius like a rabbit beneath a wine-cart wheel. With a roar of delight the lictor unfastened the gold ribbon on his bundle of rods. Then he hooked out an axe.

To those of you who may have wondered, I can now reveal that the axe in a lictor's ceremonial bundle is a real one – and sharp. The honed edge glittered briefly. The lictor had only had time to grip his weapon by the far end of its handle, but he knew what to do. He swung low. He swung his axe in a wide, beautiful half-circle like a scythe. He swung to cut the Miller off at the ankles . . . I looked away.

I never saw what happened to the lictor. I reckon he escaped. I doubt if he wanted any credit: there was a man who had truly enjoyed himself.

The omens suddenly grew more bleak for us. Tibullinus and Arica had returned with a century of men. They were fresh, and they were mean. They burst in ready to kill us all. For a few hairy moments Tibullinus and his patrolmen squared up to clear the party. I managed to scramble across the wet, bloody floor towards Sergius, who was smashing down shutters at a window. The other lads forced their way through to us, dragging Martinus. Opposite, the two narrow doorways both filled with ugly vigiles. Any criminals who could move were dragging themselves aside to leave room for these heroes from the Sixth to charge. We lined up to do our best. The shutters would serve us as weapons. Maybe one or two of us could climb out to the street. There were more troops in the street, however – we could hear that.

Someone said something to Arica. He passed it on to Tibullinus. Next minute the two doorways were empty, and so was the outer corridor. Girls rushed past again, this time in the other direction, jostling to reach the street door. We stood feeling abandoned, then we tore outside after them.

We fell out into a streetfight. It looked like some crazy public-service exercise. There were vigiles everywhere. They were fighting each other. Suddenly I realised that in their midst were Petronius, Fusculus and Porcius. These were not the Sixth Cohort attacking themselves, but the Sixth being set upon by the Fourth. Nothing like it had happened since the civil wars.

A man adept in violence crashed across the street towards me. He was locked in a hold with Tibullinus, a hold of painful

763

illegality. As I winced, stepping back to give him space, he broke a bone somewhere in the centurion with a horrendous crack, then put in a punch like a pile-hammer. Tibullinus lay still. His assailant stood up. He jerked his chin up derisively as if despising the weak opposition.

Across the road, Petronius clung in the doorway of the Oily Jug, catching his breath. He grinned at me wryly. The vanquisher of Tibullinus looked at both of us.

'Nice work,' I said. I meant it too.

Whatever we thought of him, Marcus Rubella had come good.

The turmoil continued. It was a head-to-head conflict of the foot patrols now; I stood back, near the tribune, and watched. Then I glimpsed through the fighting that Petro had someone with him. He was talking to Porcius.

The lad looked confused. He was shaking his head vigorously. Even though not a word was audible I knew what I was witnessing: my old friend had chosen this moment of grief and commotion to put his raw recruit through a disciplinary interview.

I knew why. Petronius had remembered the time when Balbinus Pius, awaiting sentence and his legal right to exile, was under house surveillance by the Sixth Cohort. He had been guarded by Tibullinus and Arica, whom we now knew were in his pocket. An officer of the Fourth had been assigned to them as an observer. That man was among the party, led by Tibullinus and Arica, that had brought Balbinus to Ostia. Presumably that officer had known Linus would be on watch once Balbinus joined his ship. The observer had been Porcius.

Petronius must have been suspicious for some time. This explained why he had been so hard on the recruit; why, too, when he needed the little black slave Porcius had been looking after, Petro had been so insistent it was Fusculus who fetched the child, protecting the witness against 'accidents'. It explained why Petronius had lost his temper so badly with Porcius.

He was angry again now.

I saw Martinus and Fusculus conferring as they kept

764

Petronius under scrutiny. They too had worked out what was going on. Marcus Rubella, completely expressionless, stood at my side with his arms folded, watching them all. Ex-centurions are the hardest men you can meet. When Martinus and Fusculus began walking grimly towards Porcius and their chief, Rubella and I both turned and left the scene.

LXIV

For days Rome revelled in the stories: how down in the Eleventh region fighting had broken out among the vigiles, leaving several dead and many sorely hurt. It had been necessary for a Very Important Patrician, horrified by the breakdown of order, to send one of his own personal lictors to the Praetorian Camp to call out the Urban Cohorts, who, with the advantage of being armed to the teeth, speedily put down the riot. The Very Important Patrician was reputed to have composed a scroll for the Emperor denouncing the lax discipline of the foot patrols, the astonishing complacency of their officers, and the possibility that the whole event had been orchestrated by undesirable republican elements in the vigiles in order to distract attention from some sinister web of public-service fraud . . .

My contacts said that the Emperor was delighted to be supplied with the great man's views, though Vespasian was already taking action on the basis of another report that had been slapped in fast by Marcus Rubella and the official anti-corruption team.

Crushed by this rebuff, the Very Important Patrician had adopted a new interest. He was now devoting himself to opposing obscenity and reforming prostitutes. Obviously this meant he would have to force himself to survey brothels personally. Some of us thought this had its hilarious side.

The Sixth Cohort were to be broken up and re-formed under new officers. Their tribune and several centurions had resigned. Petronius Longus was delighted by this because Martinus was now devoting all his efforts to trying to get promoted into one of the vacant postings in the Sixth. Martinus was of the opinion that his talents for relaxed enquiry and demonic draughts would fit in well in the prestigious Palatine and Circus Maximus regions. Like a decent superior, Petronius was strongly supporting his bid to have these talents recognised.

The Fourth Cohort had been formally reprimanded by Rubella for running wild. They had been confined to their patrol houses overnight to calm them down. This had the useful side benefit of allowing Rubella to visit each station and ensure that the official story of their incursion into another cohort's district was understood by all. Luckily most civilians were unable to distinguish between one cohort and another anyway.

Among the dead, the Fourth had lost one of their youngest officers, Porcius. The burial club was to provide him with a basic funeral, though his tribune had to tell the family that regretfully his short time in service, and other factors, meant that no claim for compensation could be allowed.

Official annoyance about the disturbance had been mitigated by the night's other results. Arrested at the brothel called the Bower of Venus were an astonishing number of criminals. It was estimated that tracing and returning stolen property recovered would take the vigiles three months. So many runaway slaves had been rounded up that the Prefect of the Vigiles held a special all-day session for owners wanting to reclaim them (those owners, that is, who were prepared to give house room to a sullen slave who had been exposed to bad company at Plato's). The power of a notorious organised gang had been broken. Among the street operators rounded up were every kind of hustler, cat burglar and cudgel boy, and in addition there was evidence of a kidnap racket operated by some of the prostitutes.

The main evidence of this pin-money racket had been provided by Helena Justina. There was one intriguing aspect that we did not make public: Helena had obtained a confession that the baby I found in the rubbish skip had been stolen by the girls. One of the hags at Plato's had realised he was deaf. When his family refused to ransom him, he was taken up on the Aventine and dumped there by a one-time doorman at the brothel. Macra told us this was the man who did all their snatching – Castus, who had also stabbed the Lycian when Lalage and Nonnius were setting out to betray Balbinus Pius. Castus no longer worked at the brothel; he had been a Balbinus stooge, and Lalage had sent him packing after the trial. He had been apprehended and was awaiting his turn for detailed questioning.

767

Helena Justina knew who the stolen baby's family were. The last people on the list had finally spoken to her: they denied that they had ever had a baby, let alone that the child was missing, even though a frightened nurse had originally reported it. And who were these forgetful parents? None other than a certain Very Important Patrician and his well-connected, extremely wealthy wife. According to gossip the woman was now pregnant again. Helena and I had decided not to insist on restoring their son to them. We did not even tell them he had been identified.

The famous brothelkeeper at the Bower of Venus had been discovered dead. As a result the authorities believed that one of Rome's most sordid bordellos might now lapse into decline. (Not everyone shared this fond hope.) Its landlord had promised to take action, anyway.

I had met Florius standing outside Plato's Academy with a long scroll in his hand. He had been informed by the Prefect of the Vigiles that this was one of his properties. Horrified, he told me that he had called for a full list of the sites he had acquired with Milvia's dowry. Obviously, as a decent equestrian he would now inspect the estate, and do everything possible to clean it up.

There was only one failure amongst all this fervent reform. We had scoured the brothel, and other places named to us by arrested criminals. Nowhere had we found any trace of Balbinus Pius.

Petronius and the Fourth Cohort spent all their time searching Rome for him. Balbinus had lost his empire. His wife and daughter were under surveillance. He had no regular income, though we knew all too well he would never lack funds. Petro looked hard at any property where he was known to have had connections, but if he had any sense he would take out a lease anonymously somewhere else. He could be anywhere. He could even by now have left Rome altogether. All the ports and all the provincial governors had been notified, but he could have slipped away to anywhere in the known world. Lalage had warned me he would have adopted a disguise.

For days the search continued. I helped, whenever I was

768

free from the eternal writing of reports. I also spent a great deal of time at the gymnasium, trying to get in shape. For one thing, it was my belief that the big rissole would never leave Rome, which was his natural territory. If we cornered him, it would be highly dangerous. In addition, I needed all my strength for a domestic event: on the day before the Kalends of November, Helena and I, Petro, his wife and children, his enquiry team, my family and many of my relatives were going to a wedding.

It had been planned for the Kalends, but at the last minute my mother took charge of the chaotic arrangements. Her first action was to change the date. She pointed out to Lenia that it is regarded as unlucky to marry on the first day of a month. Lenia burst into tears, then plumped for the last day of October instead.

Some of us thought that for marrying Smaractus the unlucky day would have been far more appropriate.

Two days before the Kalends, I was going crazy trying to obtain a cheap white sheep. All it had to do was behave nicely while I cut its throat and skinned it – a task which as a town boy I viewed with distaste, though for Lenia's sake I would grimly go through with it. She wanted all the trimmings. Auguries, and the bit where the bride and groom sit together on the sheepskin – the sheepskin that I had to provide. Yes, I had to skin it neatly because everybody would be watching, and I also had to keep the blood off so none marred the bride's highly expensive wedding gear.

Those with an aptitude for logistics will have worked out that to avoid disaster it was necessary to choose and purchase my animal the day before it was needed. I could not risk ending up as the wedding priest who had nothing to sacrifice. Having bought it, I then had to find somewhere to keep the thing.

Maia made Famia agree it could go to the Greens' stable. The laundry yard would have been a more sensible overnight billet, but by then Lenia had become hysterical at the thought of any action that might bring bad luck. I could have stowed the woolly one with a neighbour, but I was afraid I would wake to the tantalising scent of roast mutton with garlic and rosemary.

I had to take the sheep to the stables myself. And on the morning of the wedding, I had to cross the city to fetch her back. I made a nice little lead for her. I felt like a clown. From the Plain of Mars to the top of the Aventine is a damned long way.

On the way home I decided to stop at the Temple of Castor baths, so I would be sweet-smelling and ready to put on my clean outfit. As a gesture to Lenia I took the sheep through with me and washed her as well. For some reason Glaucus was horrified. Don't ask me why. There was nobody important there in the morning, and I had paid her entrance fee.

Returning home I ran into turmoil as young women rushed around trying to deck the laundry with garlands while old crones sat sipping strong drinks and discussing other people's bowel problems. The facade on Fountain Court had been hung with elaborately painted sheets. The doorway was almost impenetrably blocked with a prickly fringe of branches and flowers. Unlit torches lining the street outside were crying out to be sabotaged by passing youths.

The whole neighbourhood had been disrupted by this ridiculous fling. Lenia and Smaractus had taken to heart the dictum that a good wedding should advertise itself. The back yard of the laundry was being used for huge bonfires, already slowly roasting various whole beasts. Fountain Court was full of delivery men and curious onlookers. As a temporary measure the unhappy couple were even using the empty apartment above the bakery, the one I had rejected summarily. There they had stored the amazing number of presents given to them, together with little parcels of sweets that would be bestowed on guests (in return for their ordeal, no doubt) and the nuts which Smaractus would fling to any onlookers watching the torchlight procession (as a symbol of fertility: dreadful thought). Smaractus was coming to live at the laundry after the marriage, so for one night they were even using the place opposite as a token 'bridegroom's house'. Workmen had mended the floor and installed a bed.

Since the bride had no relations to support her she had borrowed most of mine. I met my mother and Maia staggering in with the bloodless offering (a dry piece of ritual bakery) and the wedding cake. This gross item, oozing fried almonds and warmly redolent of wine, had been baked by Ma, apparently using a fish kettle the size of a small shark.

'Get your fingers out of there!' As Ma whacked me for picking off crumbs to taste, I dived indoors with the useless hope that I might find a quiet corner to tie up the sheep. 'That's right. Stop sneaking around looking for trouble to cause. Pay your respects to the bride.'

I found a woman I didn't recognise. Lenia, who normally looked like a sack of turnips, was neatly dressed in the traditional rough-woven gown and orange slippers, with a big fat Hercules knot or her girdle prominent under her bust.

771

Her raging hennaed hair had been tamed by determined female friends, divided with partings into seven clumps, braided tightly over wooden fillets, crowned with a garland of glossy leaves and flower petals, and topped with the traditional flame-coloured veil. The veil was turned back so that her friend Secunda, frowning with concentration, could complete the task of outlining her eyes with a sooty cosmetic. To go with the dramatic elegance she was adopting an expression which mingled a simper with haughtiness. I guessed that wouldn't last.

'Oh rats, here's a bad omen on legs!' roared the immaculate vision.

'Got your distaff ready?'

'Give over, Falco. Maia's gone to find me one.'

'What, a bride who doesn't own her own? Does Smaractus realise he's getting an incompetent housewife?'

'He knows he's got a brilliant businesswoman.'

'I'm not sure about that!' I grinned at her. 'Rumour has it you're spending the wedding night in that run-down wreck of an apartment above Cassius. Can this be wise? What couple wants to be holding back in case the floor gives way beneath the nuptial bed?'

'He's shored it up.'

'What are we talking about?'

'Oh go and jump in a cesspit, Falco!'

'Now that's enough insults. This is the moment when you have to lay aside childish things.'

'Oh good. It can be the last I see of you then . . .'

I showed her the sheep, gave her a congratulatory kiss that had her reaching for a napkin to wipe her face, then bounded cheerily upstairs.

There were a few hours to go yet. In the peace of my own apartment I lay on my bed, pretending to lull myself into a contemplative mood for the augury. Helena appeared and stretched alongside for a rest. 'Hmm, this is nice.' I put one arm around her. 'Maybe I'll get pregnant myself. I'd like lying around all day.'

'We could compare notes of our symptoms. You wouldn't like being sick, though.'

A silence fell. After a moment Helena rolled over so she

772

could look at me. She held my face between her hands, inspecting the half-healed physical scars from my recent ordeal at the brothel. Though she said nothing, her expression was concerned. She understood that beneath the facade of merriment my real mood was dark. Always the first to sense depression in me, she also knew what was wrong: we had cleansed Rome of plenty of dross, but the task remained unfinished. We had swept up shoals of criminal life, and purged corruption in at least one cohort of the vigiles; I myself had even received a hefty fee for doing it. I ought to have been feeling pleased with myself.

How could I, though? Balbinus had escaped. He was dangerous. He was still out there plotting. Given time, he would revive his empire. He would go for Petronius, and maybe for me. Nothing would have changed.

The death of Lalage had had a disturbing effect on me too.

When Helena had read my thought to her own satisfaction, she kissed me gently, then settled down again. We lay close, both awake. The familiar sound of her quiet breathing calmed me. Her contentment became infectious. Her steady enjoyment of my presence worked its magic, filling me with amazement that she had chosen to be mine.

'I'm sorry, my love. I have not been with you enough lately.'

'You're here now.'

'Tomorrow I'm going to start painting the new apartment.'

'We need to clean it first.'

'Trust me. It's to be done tonight. I've struck a bargain with some of the vigiles.'

'But it's the wedding! Had you forgotten?'

'Sole reason for choosing today! I can see two advantages, Helena my darling. If I hate the wedding,' which seemed highly likely, 'I can run off to assist the floor-washers. Or if the wedding seems too good to miss, I can stay with the celebrations and avoid getting my feet wet.'

'You're incorrigible,' said Helena, with a warm mixture of admiration and mockery.

We lay still again. Up here near the sky I could feel quite cut off from the noise and press in the streets. I would miss that.

'Are we giving Lenia a wedding present?'

'A nice set of snail picks,' said Helena. For some reason I found that hilarious.

'I hope you didn't buy them from Pa?'

'No, from that second-hand gift shop down the street. It's got a lot of well-made horrors in terrible taste – just right to embarrass a bride.'

I refrained from mentioning that I had nearly bought her own birthday present there.

A few minutes later our soothing interlude was disturbed by visitors. I went out from the bedroom first, Helena following more slowly. Junia and Gaius Baebius glared at us as if they assumed we had been indulging in dalliance. There was no point protesting that we had merely been talking. 'What do you two want?' I saw no reason to pretend to be delighted that my sister had deigned to climb the stairs.

'Gaius has brought you his priestly veil.'

'Oh yes, thanks, Gaius.'

Without being invited, Junia and Gaius plonked themselves on the best seats. Helena and I found space on a bench, deliberately snuggling up like lovers to embarrass them.

'I hear you're pregnant!' Junia announced with her customary verve.

'That is correct.'

'Was it an accident?'

'A happy one,' Helena said stiffly.

I glanced at her. She refused to meet my eye. Helena Justina had accepted the situation but was not allowing anyone to gloat. I turned back to my sister with a shameless grin.

'What about the other little one?' asked Junia. She coloured slightly. 'You can't be wanting him as well?'

I felt Helena's hand grip mine abruptly. Gaius Baebius rose and walked to the basket where the skip baby lay dribbling. He lifted out the child. I noticed that Gaius held the baby with the care of a man who was unused to children, yet his grip was firm and although he was a stranger the babe accepted him. He walked back to Junia, who was not quite ready to approach us with whatever she had come to say.

'You two ought to be getting married now,' she instructed us instead.

774

'What for?' I asked. My intention to marry Helena had immediately sprouted rose-pink wings and flown off the balcony.

'Oh it's a decent institution,' Helena protested teasingly. 'A husband must maintain his wife.'

I handed her an apple from the fruit bowl. 'A husband is permitted to chastise his wife if she shows him too little reverence.'

Helena biffed me on the chin. 'Each party has the right to the society of the other,' she chortled. 'I haven't seen much of that lately!'

Junia's face was set. Her voice was tense. 'Gaius and I have been talking about this baby, Marcus.' She had a knack of sounding as if she was informing me she knew I had been pinching pastries behind our mother's back. Gaius continued to stare at the deaf babe (who dribbled back at him thoughtfully). Becoming more confident, Gaius wiped dry the dribble. My sister carried on talking: 'He needs a home. In view of his difficulty, he needs a rather special one. Obviously he cannot remain with you and Helena. Of course you are kind-hearted, but your home life is chaotic and when your own child is born there will be too much competition for your love. He needs people who can look after him more devotedly.'

She was monstrous. She was arrogant and rude – but she was right.

'Gaius and I are prepared to adopt him.'

This time Helena and I could not look at each other. We had had him for two weeks now. We did not want to let him go.

'What about Ajax?' I quavered weakly.

'Oh don't be ridiculous, brother! Ajax is just a dog.' Poor old Ajax. Yesterday this would have been blasphemy. 'Besides, Ajax loves children.'

'For lunch,' I muttered, while Helena pretended not to hear.

Junia and Gaius were assuming that once their sensible suggestion had been voiced we must have gratefully agreed to it. Of course we had. The child would be given every possible advantage. Apart from the comfortable home that my

775

brother-in-law's customs salary ensured, whatever I thought of my sister I knew that she and Gaius would dote on the babe. Both would make every effort to help him communicate.

'Is his parentage known?' Gaius found his voice now.

I opened my mouth to supply the glorious details. 'No,' said Helena at once. 'We tried, but it has been impossible to find out.' I took her hand. She was right. She and I could always break the news if necessary. Otherwise, better for him and everyone if there was no chance of recrimination, no danger of false hope.

'I expect you've grown very fond of him,' said Junia in a kindly tone. This strange softening upset me more than anything. 'You'll be very welcome to see him again, any time you like.'

Helena managed to disguise the hysterical giggle in her voice. 'Thank you very much. Have you decided on a name for him?'

'Oh yes.' For some reason Junia had gone red again. 'It seems only right in view of who found him – we're going to call him Marcus.'

'Marcus Baebius Junillus,' confirmed my brother-in-law, gazing proudly at his new son.

LXVI

In case the sight of me veiled as a priest failed to cause a sufficient sensation, I had decided to attend Lenia's wedding in my Palmyrene suit. Frankly, there were not many other occasions in Rome where a decent man could appear in purple and gold silk trousers, a tunic embroidered all over with ribbons and florets, cloth slippers appliquéd with tulips, and a flat-topped braided hat. To complete the picture, Helena had even found me a filigree scabbard containing a ceremonial sword, a curiosity we had bought from a travelling caravan in Arabia.

'I wanted an auspex,' complained Lenia. 'Not King Vologaeses of the bloody Parthians.'

'In Palmyra this is modest streetwear, Lenia.'

'Well in Rome it stinks!'

The ceremony began a little late. When the bridegroom's friends delivered him, they were staggering and yodelling; unnerved by his coming ordeal, he was so drunk we could not stand him up. As the ritual demands, a short verbal exchange took place between the bride and groom.

'You bastard! I'll never forgive you for this –'

'What's the matter with the woman?'

'You've ruined my day!'

Lenia then retired to sob in a back room while the guests helped themselves to amphorae (of which there were many racks). While Smaractus was sobered up by his mother and mine, we all started gaily catching up. Members of the public had learned that there was a free-for-all, and found excuses to call at the laundry. Members of the wedding party, who were not paying the bill for refreshments, greeted them with loud cries of friendship and invited them in.

When Petronius arrived things were humming along warmly. It was late afternoon, and there were hours to go yet. After he and his family had finished laughing at my dramatic attire, Helena suggested we all went out for a meal in a decent

777

chophouse to give us strength for the long night ahead. Nobody missed us. On our return, there was still nothing much happening, so Petronius jumped up on a table and called for quiet.

'Friends – Romans – ' This address failed to please him for some reason, but he was in a merry mood. As well as the wine we had drunk with our dinner, he had brought a special alabastron of his own. He and I had already sampled it. 'The bride is present – '

Lenia had been elsewhere in fact, still weeping, but she heard the new commotion and rushed straight out, suspicious that her wedding was being sabotaged.

'The groom', proclaimed Petro, 'is practising for his nuptials and having a short lie-down!' Everyone roared with delight, knowing that Smaractus was now unconscious in a laundry basket; he must have found himself more wine and was completely out of it. Petro adopted an oratorical stance. 'I have consulted among those with legal knowledge – my friend Marcus Didius, who has frequently appeared in court, my colleague Tiberius Fusculus, who once trod on a judicial praetor's toe – '

There were impatient cries. 'Get on with it!'

'We are agreed that for a marriage to be legal the bridegroom need not be present in person. He may signify consent through a letter or a messenger. Let's see if we can find someone who can tell us Smaractus consents!'

It was his mother who betrayed him. Annoyed by his continuing indisposition she jumped up and shouted, 'I'll answer! He consents!' She was a fierce little body about as high as my elbow, as round as a tub of oysters, with a face like a squashed sponge and flashing black eyes.

'What about you?' Petronius asked Lenia.

Fired by her previous success, my landlord's mother screamed out hilariously, 'I'll answer for her too. She consents as well!'

So much for the exchange of vows. Petro swayed and fell off the table, to be caught safely by merrymaking strangers. A hubbub arose again, and it was clear we were in for much longer delays before I could impose enough order to begin the sacrifice and augury. Being in no hurry, I went out and across the street to inspect what was happening in my new rooms.

A group of patrolmen were sitting in the apartment discussing whether rats were more dangerous than women. I concealed my irritation, added a few philosophical comments, then offered to show them where the nearest fountain was. They picked up their buckets fairly agreeably (the fee they had negotiated with me was, to put it mildly, adequate) and followed me down to the street. I told them the way, but I stayed in Fountain Court. I had seen someone I knew.

He was standing down by the barber's, an unmistakable, untidy lump. He had a bundle of scrolls, and was writing notes against one of them. When I came up, I could see the same intense concentration on his face and the same little squiggly lettering that I had seen once when I interrupted him outside the Pantheon making detailed comments on racehorses. It was Florius. Across the street, detailed to tail him everywhere in case he was contacted by his father-in-law, stood Martinus; he had stationed himself by the baker's, pretending he could not decide which loaf to choose. He looked an idiot.

'The barber's is closed, Florius. We have a wedding locally. He wore himself out this morning snipping the guests.'

'Hello, Falco!'

'You remember me.'

'You gave me advice.'

'Did you follow it?'

He blushed. 'Yes. I'm being friendly to my wife.' I tried not to speculate what form his friendliness might take. Poor little Milvia.

'I'm sure your attentions will be happily received. Let me tell you something else: whatever trouble it causes, don't let your mother-in-law come to stay in your house.'

He opened his mouth, then said nothing. He understood exactly what I meant about Flaccida.

I was curious. At the same time, I was beginning to feel I knew what he would answer when I asked, 'So what brings you here to Fountain Court?'

He gestured to the scrolls he was holding under his elbow. 'The same as when I saw you at that brothel the other day. I have decided I ought to go around and take a look at all the properties which Milvia and I were given as her dowry.'

I folded my arms. Together we stared at the place he had been inspecting. 'You own the whole block up to the roof?'

'Yes. Most of the rest of this street belongs to another man.' Smaractus. 'There are domestic tenants on the upper floors. This small shop was leased out recently, but it's not open and I cannot make anyone reply.'

He was talking about the cave of delights that offered second-hand 'Gifts of Charm'. The place where I had declined to buy Helena a birthday present, though where she had found a refined set of eating tools to give Lenia as her wedding gift. I had seen the snail picks now: they were bronze, big heavy spoons with pointed ends, probably from the fine workshops of central Italy. I had a similar set myself, though of more refined design. Lenia's looked like consular heirlooms, but were sold to us extremely cheaply. I knew what that could mean.

'Don't knock any more.' Florius looked surprised by my sharp tone. 'Wait here. I'll fetch someone.'

Back at the wedding Maia had arrived. Her sons Marius and Ancus and Galla's son Gaius sat lined up on a bench, ready to act as the three escorts when the bride went in procession to her new husband's house. Marius was looking cross; he probably knew the torchlight procession would be an occasion of rude songs and obscene jokes: not his style. Gaius was pretty sullen too, but that was just because Maia had insisted the young scruff should be clean. Ancus, who was only five, just sat there with his ears sticking out and wished he could go home.

I waved to them, then found Petro. 'Sober up!'

Without a word, and without revealing that he was sloping off, he slid out with me. We walked back down the street to the jumble shop. My heart was knocking. I began to wish I had drunk less. When we reached Florius he straightened up slightly at the sight of Petro; Petro gave him a polite official nod.

I explained to Petro what the problem was. He listened like a man whose concentration needed help. I recounted my visit to the shop when it was open, describing the kinds of items I had seen. His initial disinterest gradually faded. 'Are you suggesting what I'm thinking, Falco?'

'Well, booths of old clutter are everywhere, and some of them probably contain the odd thing that was bought in a legitimate sale, but they are ideal cover for receiving. One reason I'm suspicious is that I saw Gaius and Phlosis, those two boat thieves, in our street not long ago. I now think they may have been up here to hand in swag they'd pinched. And there's something else, Petro: the man who ran this joint was called Castus.'

Petronius made the link far quicker than I had done: 'Same as the weasel who stabbed the Lycian at Plato's.' He was no longer as drunk as he seemed.

'Exactly. That Castus was a Balbinus man. He had been booted out by Lalage but he was still helping the girls who ran the kidnap scheme. My niece Tertulla was snatched very near here. And I found the baby in my skip just along the street.'

'Castus was one of the men we arrested at the brothel,' said Petro. 'In view of his past history the Prefect has kept him in close custody. Which explains why there is no one here.' He screwed up his mouth. 'Of course,' he went on reflectively, 'I'm spending my time checking over all the places we know that had links to Balbinus. I haven't finished the dowry properties. I'm kicking myself.'

I said quietly, 'I told you what Lalage reckoned: Balbinus was living "somewhere on the Aventine".'

Petronius took a deep breath, flexing his wide shoulders. Then he shook his head like an athlete trying to concentrate before a big race. 'Jupiter, I should have been sober for this!' He signalled to Martinus and ordered him to fetch Fusculus from the wedding. At that moment my helpers came back from the fountain, so they were summoned too. They set down their buckets carefully and began to size up the shop. Florius asked us what was happening. Petro looked grave. 'Let's say that as a concerned landlord whose tenant may have done a bunk, I assume you would like us to break in?'

'Try not to do any damage,' protested Florius at once. As a

781

landlord he was learning fast. Then he paled. 'What are you expecting to discover?'

'Loot,' I said. 'Stolen goods. Everything from luxuries robbed at the Saeptā Julia and flagons pinched from food shops right down to all the bedcovers old ladies have been losing from their balconies recently. And if I'm right about how the premises have been used, I think we'll find a foundry at the back where precious metal has been melted down.'

'And your father's glass?' enquired Petro dryly.

'Oh Lucius Petronius, I have to tell you honestly – I fear not!'

'Do I need to be here?' Florius was feeling nervous.

'Better slide off home.' Petronius gave him a kindly pat on the shoulder. 'I don't like to see trouble in a family; you'd best not be involved. One of the items I'm now hoping to recover is your missing father-in-law.'

Florius looked more interested. 'Can I help?' Clearly the worm had turned. From being a passive victim of Milvia's parents, he was now eager to see Balbinus recaptured. In view of the situation, with Balbinus under a death sentence if he was found on Roman soil, that meant mild-mannered Florius was longing for rather more than a mere arrest. The keen glint in his eye said he knew very well what recapture meant.

We broke in at a rush. The vigiles are trained to smash their way into buildings during fires. Even without their heavy equipment they can go through a door without raising a sweat. Making Florius wait outside, Petronius, Martinus, Fusculus and I followed the patrol straight in. We marched through the premises without stopping to investigate. It was evident, once you viewed the place as a possible receiving shop, that it was packed with items of interest – and I don't just mean potential Saturnalia gifts. As I had suspected, beyond the curtain at the back lay a cold furnace and plenty of encrusted crucibles.

'A melting pot – and they've been painting the Emperor's picture for him too!' Fusculus held up a mould for counterfeit coins.

We searched the shop, and the attached living quarters. Then we left a guard and searched every apartment upstairs, breaking into any where nobody replied when we knocked.

We disturbed a lot of people doing things they would have preferred to keep private, but we did not discover any trace of Balbinus Pius.

'Ah well. Just have to keep looking.' Petronius managed to sound neutral. But I knew his true feelings. Hope had been raised for a moment. The disappointment that followed was twice as acute as our gloom before. 'I'll get him,' said Petro quietly.

'Oh yes.' I thumped him on the shoulder. 'You'd better. Old friend, there's still a nasty chance that he's hoping to get you!'

We walked down to the street. We gave Florius the news that his wife's father was still at large, told him to report anything suspicious, and watched him leave. Martinus sauntered after him, still pretending to be unobtrusive.

I had a dark sensation as Florius loped off with his scrolls and stylus. The thought of him so carefully researching his father-in-law's property made me wonder if one day he might want to research other aspects of the Balbinus empire too. Clearly he meant to expand his business interests. He had told me he wanted to start a racing stable, and I already knew from Famia that the partner Florius had chosen had an off-colour reputation. Why stop there? His wife came from a notorious criminal family. Florius had never seen any need to abandon her once he realised this. Maybe I had just witnessed the beginning of another depressing cycle in the endless rise and fall of villains in the underworld.

Well, it should take him a few years yet to establish himself.

LXVII

I was in disgrace. Back at the wedding Lenia had called for her augury to be taken. This was the ceremony I had promised to supervise. Nobody could find me. Nobody knew where I was. It was, of course, considered untenable to proceed without the inspection of a sheep's liver. Respectable people would be shocked. Luckily the imperturbable Gaius Baebius had seized upon my absence and stepped into the breach.

'Oh I'm sure you did it better than I would have done, Gaius!'

And at least the head veil fitted him.

'He gave me some very nice promises,' said Lenia sniffily.

'I had never realised that Gaius Baebius was such a liar!' Helena whispered. Gaius explained to me very soberly that as part of his preparations for trying to join the priestly college of the Augustales, he had been taking lessons on sheep-skinning.

The bride was by now ensconced on her neatly hacked-off sheepskin, side by side with the slumped form of her husband, newly removed from the laundry basket. She was gripping his hand, not so much to symbolise union as to stop him falling onto the floor. A friend of Smaractus' was going around trying to get up ten witnesses for the contractual tablets, but most of the guests tried to wriggle out of this duty and privilege with weak excuses such as they had inadvertently left their seals at home. Nobody wanted to be blamed if the marriage failed, or be called upon to help sort out the dowry afterwards.

We all decided we had suffered enough and wanted our presents. This meant sending the bridegroom over the road to get them. It was obvious we would only get him over there once, so we combined this trip with sending him to sing the Fescennine verses (a raucous litany that nobody sober could remember, let alone your average bridegroom). Soon he was

784

lighting the torches along the route for the bride's procession. Somebody supplied him with his fire and water for welcoming Lenia to his home. Smaractus revived enough to cry loudly that she could go to Hades for all he cared. Lenia had in fact gone to the lavatory, or the divorce could have been ratified that very day.

We kept the bride's procession short. This seemed wise because by then the bride herself was drunk as well as tearful. With no mother of her own from whose arms she could be dragged protesting, Lenia, overcome by a last-minute realisation of her stupidity, decided to cling to Ma instead. Ma told her to stop messing everyone about. Heartlessly jovial, we hauled Lenia away and set her up in proper fashion, with Marius and little Ancus taking her hands while Gaius gingerly carried the whitethorn torch ahead of them. Her veil had slipped and she was limping, as in her left shoe was one of the traditional coins she must take to her husband. 'As if I hadn't given him enough already!'

It had grown dark enough to lend some mystery. A hired flautist came to lead the happy throng. Throwing nuts and yelling, we all jogged up one side of Fountain Court, then danced inelegantly back again, tripping on the nuts. Children woke up and became really excited. People hung out of upstairs windows, watching and cheering. The night was still and the torchlight flickered handsomely. The air, on the last day of October, was chill enough to sober us slightly.

We reached the bakery. Jostling up the narrow outer stairs, I joined the group of delirious attendants who pulled the bride up the last few steps to the nuptial rooms. Smaractus appeared in the doorway, with one of his friends loyally propping him up from behind. He managed to cling on to his ritual torch-and-water vessel while Lenia spilled oil down her dress as she made an attempt to anoint the doorframe in the time-honoured way. Petronius and I braced ourselves, then linked hands under her backside and heaved her indoors.

Smaractus rallied abruptly. He saw Lenia, leered horribly, and made a sudden grab. Lenia proved a match for him. She let out a shriek of salacious delight and lunged for him.

Appalled, Petronius and I made a break for the outside and left hurriedly. Most of the other attendants followed us. Any tradition of witnessing what happened in that nuptial bed was too ghastly to contemplate. Besides, the remaining wine was in the laundry across the road.

The street was packed with singing revellers. It took single-minded desperation (and thirst) to force a passage through. We made it as far as the laundry's garlanded doorway. We found Arria Silvia shrieking to Petro over the noise that she was taking their young daughters home to bed. She asked if he was going with them, and of course he said yes but not yet. Helena, looking wan, told me she was going up to our apartment. I too promised to follow my dear one 'very soon' – as the old lie has it.

Something made us look back across the road. Lenia had run out onto the first-floor landing, waving her arms about. Her veil flapped wildly and her gown was half off. A raucous cheer rose from the crowd. Lenia shouted something and raced back in.

It was dark. There was plenty of smoke from the torches. Almost immediately the distraught bride reappeared in the doorway of the nuptial home. People had quietened down, most of them looking for something to drink. Lenia spotted Petronius and me. In a voice like a grindstone she shrieked to us: 'Help, help, you bastards! Fetch the vigiles! The bed's collapsed and the apartment is on fire!'

786

LXVIII

Guests who had been prepared to fill the street when there was hope of free food and liquor found a sudden urge to go home quietly once they realised they might be asked to form a bucket chain. Others made sure they didn't help us, though they still hung around in doorways having a good gape.

The smell of real smoke had become apparent. Lenia had vanished again back into the first-floor apartment with a wild cry of 'My wedding presents! My husband! Help me get them out!' It was clear that the presents were to be given priority.

There was one saving feature: as soon as someone cried 'Fire!', out from my own new apartment came a group of vigiles. My Fourth Cohort helpers were soon spotted by the excellent Petronius and chivied into action. They smartened up immediately. Someone went running to the patrol house for equipment, the rest were ordered straight into the laundry where there was a well and plenty of water carriers too. Petro and I then raced across to see what we could do for the disrupted bridal group.

Lenia was scuttling about the outer room, uselessly gathering armfuls of gifts. We shoved her outside, fairly roughly for fire has to be taken seriously; things could end up worse than she realised. In the second room we were met by a pitiful sight: the nuptial bed, complete with exotic purple coverlet, had crashed partway through the floor. My landlord, even more dishevelled than usual, was clinging on to one corner in terror. He was afraid to move a muscle in case the bed slipped completely and fell into the bakery store below. That was where the fire was, started when in the midst of his uncontrollable passion for Lenia, Smaractus had pounded his bride so heavily that the props beneath the floor had given way. A bridal torch had then rolled across the collapsing floor and fallen through the jagged hole onto the baker's well-dried logs.

'Dear gods, Smaractus, we never knew you were such a hot lover!'

'Shut up and get me out of here!'

Below us we could already hear battering as the vigiles tried to break into the bakery. Petro and I began to cross towards Smaractus, but the boards lurched beneath us too dangerously. We had to stay where we were, trying to calm the stricken bridegroom while we waited for helpers with proper equipment. At first the smoke seemed slight enough and we were not too worried. A pillow slid slowly across the tilting bed, then tumbled down into the fire, showing what could happen to Smaractus. He squealed. He was looking dangerously warm. Petronius started bellowing for help.

A setback occurred. Instead of dousing the fire immediately, the vigiles allowed themselves to be lured from their duty by the tragic spectacle of a heartbroken bride: I won't say Lenia offered bribes to them, but overcome by good nature (or something) they came galloping upstairs to save her precious wedding gifts. By the time more help arrived and operatives started flinging water and mats over the logs in Cassius' store, lively flames were at work. Upstairs with us Smaractus was now screaming as the mattress he was clutching caught light from the flames beneath. That was when Petro and I really started worrying.

Luckily a centurion with sense turned up, bringing more men with grappling hooks, axes and mattocks. A party below us were clearing space in the log store, although one side of it was now raging with fire. Before they were forced back, the landlord's prop was replaced beneath the bed, along with poles they had brought themselves, to give him more security until someone could rescue him. Ordered to this task, vigiles pressed past Petronius and me, at last working with speed and efficiency. They flung a huge espartograss mat across the room and commanded Smaractus to throw himself onto it. Just in time, he obeyed. They hauled. We helped. We dragged him clear at the very moment the flames shot up through the floor and devoured the bed. We all leapt back into the outer room, and heard the floor fall in accompanied by a huge roar of fire and sparks.

The blaze went racing up the walls. Smaractus had collapsed. He was picked up as if he were light as a leaf and rushed outside. A terrific gust of heat and smoke rushed through the building. Petro and I found ourselves coughing. The foul-tasting smoke was so thick it was difficult to find the door. As we fell outside, covering our mouths and retching, a member of the vigiles ran up the stairs, axe in hand, gesturing upwards.

'Who lives in the other apartments?'

'No one. They're even more derelict than this one.'

'Quick then. Get out of here!'

We all staggered down to street level, relieved to be out of it.

A syphon party came running up, towing their pumping engine. They forced a passage into the laundry, and soon there were more buckets being passed out at a fast pace. More foot patrols arrived. When Petronius found his breath, he began organising these into crowd control, gradually moving the sightseers back. A recruit with a bucket went up the street, dousing the wedding torches. We had enough light now without them. A ballista was dragged to the corner, though it got stuck trying to turn into the narrow lane. Smaractus saw it, panicked, and began wandering about drunkenly, threatening to sue if anyone made a firebreak by knocking down any other buildings owned by him. He was so much of a nuisance, the vigiles arrested him for failing to keep fire buckets, interfering with their duties, and (just to make certain) arson with his bridal torch.

The fire was now being contained, but with difficulty. One problem was the outer stairs. They had been rickety to start with, and the weight of heavy patrolmen thundering up in gangs with their buckets proved too much. The broken stonework gave way, luckily without too much damage to the fire-fighters. Petronius rushed forward to help them, and was knocked flat by a blazing shutter as it fell from above. I raced to pull him clear. At least he was conscious. Two patrolmen took charge of him, flapping cloths to give him air and checking him for broken bones. They knew their stuff.

I saw Cassius, standing with his arms folded, glumly watching the loss of his premises. Leaving Petro for a moment, I went over to commiserate.

'Could have been worse. You could have been in there asleep.'

789

'Not with Lenia and Smaractus pounding all Hades out of the ceiling! But thanks, Falco.' I had turned away. 'By the way,' asked the baker, 'has anyone checked the upper floors?'

'Nobody lives there, do they?'

'I've seen an old woman going up a few times. Could be a new tenant – Smaractus will lease anything. Or a vagrant.'

'Dear gods. Any idea whereabouts she snuggles down?'

'Who knows?' Cassius shrugged, too absorbed in his own problems.

I stepped across to the centurion to warn him there might be a person trapped. At the same moment he noticed for himself: two floors up a shutter opened, and through the smoke we glimpsed a frightened face.

The vigiles had brought up ladders after the stairs collapsed. Without a word the centurion and I ran for a spare one, praying it would be long enough. We dragged it forwards and raised it below the right window. It barely reached the ledge. Whatever was in there had disappeared. We yelled, but there was no response.

The centurion swore. 'We'll make a bridge from across the street.' I had seen them do that, raising and lowering ladders on ropes to form a dangerous crossing point. Sooner them than me.

But it would take time to organise. There was nothing for it. The centurion had turned away to give orders. While his back was turned I sprang onto the lower rungs of our own ladder and started up.

I was wearing the wrong clothes for this. The thin material of my Palmyrene suit shrivelled into little burnt holes every time sparks hit me. I kept on the hat, in the vague hope that it would protect my hair from being set alight. Below me I heard gasps as people realised what was happening.

I arrived below the window and shouted, but nobody appeared. Carefully I climbed higher. I reached up and managed to get one arm over the sill. Then it was necessary to climb with mere toeholds, knowing I had little chance of making my way back again. I pulled myself up, got halfway through the window, and felt the ladder move away from the wall. I let it fall back.

Now I was stuck clinging to the window. No choice but to

go in. With a supreme effort I scrambled inside, falling headlong. I stood up, testing the floor beneath me nervously.

'Is anyone there?'

The room was full of smoke. It had seeped up from the two blazing storeys beneath, finding its way thickly through cracks and crannies in the ill-maintained building fabric. The air felt hot. The floor beneath my Syrian slippers burned the soles of my feet as if its underside must be smouldering like red-hot cinders. At any moment everything around me could explode into an inferno.

In the back of this apartment fire broke through. The noise was appalling. Walls and floors cracked open. Flames roared up as they gave way. Light flickered wildly through an open door.

Now I saw a human figure. Someone crouched in a far corner. Shorter than me of course. Flowing female drapes. The head tightly wrapped against the smoke.

To calm any feminine fears I tried jovial reassurance: 'Madam, you need to get out of here!' I strode across. I was all set to do a shoulder hoist, though I was not sure where to turn with the burden afterwards.

Then I saw the glint of a knife. It was no time for being soft on frightened virginity. With a hard blow of my wrist I knocked the blade to the floor. A foot kicked out frantically. Alert for the knee-in-the-groin defence, I glanced downwards ready to protect myself. Beneath the flounced hem of a matronly skirt lashed a dark grey leather travelling boot – on a foot as big as mine. It was a boot I seen before somewhere – the quay at Ostia. This was Balbinus Pius.

I wrenched aside the stole. A hand was grabbing for my throat. I banged that upwards with my forearm. He ought to have used my surprise, but he was still fumbling at his disguise. He underestimated the threat. If Petronius had stumbled in here, Balbinus would really have gone for him; Petro would be dead. I was safer. Balbinus had not bothered to remember me.

But I knew him. I drew my Arabian blade. The scabbard was pure decoration; the weapon was vicious. I set the point straight against his ribs and rammed home the sword.

I heard my voice grating, 'Time to depart, Balbinus!' But he was already dead.

LXIX

Something crashed against the window. From far away across the street I could hear shouts. Wiping and sheathing my sword, I staggered to the sill. On the opposite side of the lane, which was fortunately narrow, the vigiles had somehow raised a ladder, balancing it precariously on a balcony parapet their side and lowering one end to where I was. If I could find the courage, I could now crawl to safety across the full width of Fountain Court. It was no time for debate. Fire was sweeping through the apartment behind me. I took off and threw out my slippers (which had been quite expensive), then I checked that my end of the ladder was stable and set off for the other side.

I made it. Let's leave it at that. There is only one way to scramble for your life across a bowing wooden ladder two storeys above the ground, and it has to be undignified. The moment when Petronius leant out from the opposite balcony and grabbed me was one of the best of my life.

We exchanged glances. Petronius saw there was blood on my tunic, but that I had no visible wounds.

'Where's the crone you went to rescue?'

'I stuck my sword in her.' He did not ask why. I think he guessed. 'It was Balbinus.'

'That's the last time I work with you. You've stolen my case!'

'I owe you one,' I acknowledged.

'Tell me he's dead. I want to hear the words.'

'He's dead,' I answered, seeing it again. Then I was sick. The vigiles blamed the smoke.

With arms across each other's shoulders, Petro and I staggered down to street level. In the lane we discovered Helena, clutching my discarded slippers. She must have watched my feat with the ladder. Just as well I didn't know.

Helena was white and trembling, but she managed to

sound cheerful: 'Bad news, I'm afraid. In the confusion poor Lenia lost track of her wedding presents and some rotter's swiped the lot.'

Well there you are. That's Rome all over. Organised crime never lies down for long.

Time for someone to compose a petition to the enquiry chief of the vigiles.

could hear her. "Her arms I'm afraid in the cold, the best
I can... you know all her mother has... and some other
kind of... boy..."

"Reddish? I saw him," Bay's flower slowly changed across
from Do down the edge...

"That I can... not N... not... patient h... has to say
that of his waking..."

A DYING LIGHT
IN CORDUBA

In Memory of
Edith Pargeter

Romans, in or out of Rome

M. Didius Falco	a frantic expectant father; a hero
Helena Justina	a thoroughly reasonable expectant mother; a heroine
D. Camillus Verus	her father, also quite reasonable, for a senator
Julia Justa	her mother, as reasonable as you could expect
A. Camillus Aelianus	bad-tempered, self-righteous, and up to no good
Q. Camillus Justinus	too sweet-natured and good to appear
Falco's Ma	who may be spooning broth into the wrong mouth
Claudius Laeta	top clerk, and aiming higher
Anacrites	Chief Spy, and as low as you can get
Momus	an 'overseer'; the man who spies on spies
Calisthenus	an architect who stepped on something nasty
Quinctius Attractus	a senator with big Baetican aspirations
T. Quinctius Quadratus	his son, a high-flyer grounded in Baetica
L. Petronius Longus	a loyal and useful friend
Helva	a short-sighted usher who can look the other way
Valentinus	a skilful gatecrasher; on his way out
Perella	a mature dancer with unexpected talents
Stertius	a transport manager with inventive ideas
The Baetican Proconsul	who doesn't want to be involved
Cornelius	ex-quaestor of Baetica; leaving the scene hastily
Gn. Drusillus Placidus	a procurator with a crazy fixation on probity
Nux	a dog about town

Baeticans, out of and in Baetica

Licinius Rufius	old enough to know there's never enough profit?
Claudia Adorata	his wife, who hasn't noticed anything
Rufius Constans	his grandson, a young hopeful with a secret
Claudia Rufina	a serious girl with appealing prospects
Annaeus Maximus	a community leader; leading to the bad?
His Three Sons	known as Spunky, Dotty and Ferret; say no more!
Aelia Annaea	a widow with a very attractive asset
Cyzacus senior	a bargee who has barged into something dubious?
Cyzacus junior	an unsuccessful poet; paddling the wrong raft?
Gorax	a retired gladiator; no chicken!
Norbanus	a negotiator who has fixed a dodgy contract?
Selia	an extremely slippery dancer
Two musicians	who are not employed for their musical skills
Marius Optatus	a tenant with a grievance
Marmarides	a driver whose curios are much in demand
Cornix	a bad memory
The Quaestor's clerk	who runs the office
The Proconsul's clerks	who drink a lot (and run the office)
Prancer	a very old country horse

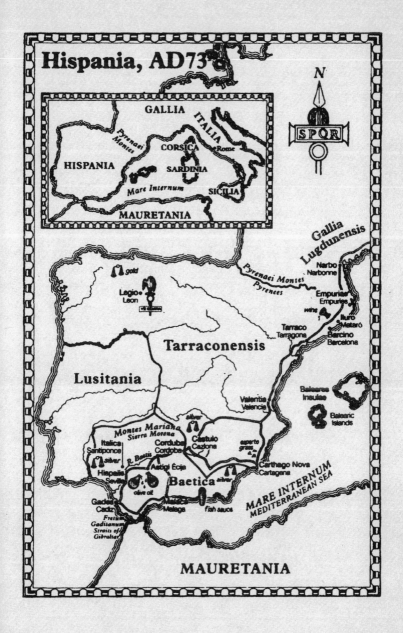

Hispania, AD73

GALLIA

ITALIA

Pyrenaei Montes

HISPANIA

CORSICA

Rome

SARDINIA

Mare Internum

SICILIA

MAURETANIA

N

SPQR

Gallia Lugdunensis

gold

Pyrenaei Montes
Pyrenees

Narbo
Narbonne

Legio
Leon

Empuriae
Empuries

wine

Iluro
Mataró

Tarraco
Tarragona

Barcino
Barcelona

Tarraconensis

Lusitania

Valentia
Valencia

Baleares
Insulae

Balearic
Islands

Montes Mariana
Sierra Morena

silver

Italica
Santiponce

Corduba
Cordoba

Castulo
Cazlona

esparto
grass

silver

R. Baetis

Astigi Écija

Carthago Nova
Cartagena

Hispalis
Sevilla

Baetica

silver

olive oil

Gades
Cadiz

Malaca
Malaga

fish sauce

MARE INTERNUM
MEDITERRANEAN SEA

*Fretum
Gaditanum
Straits of
Gibraltar*

MAURETANIA

PART ONE:
ROME

AD73: beginning the night of 31 March

Cordobans of any status surely sought to be as Roman as the Romans themselves, or more so. There is no evidence of a 'national consciousness' in the likes of the elder Seneca, although there was presumably a certain sympathy among native sons who found themselves in Rome together ...

Robert C. Knapp, Roman Cordoba

I

Nobody was poisoned at the dinner for the Society of Olive Oil Producers of Baetica – though in retrospect, that was quite a surprise.

Had I realised Anacrites the Chief Spy would be present, I would myself have taken a small vial of toad's blood concealed in my napkin and ready for use. Of course he must have made so many enemies, he probably swallowed antidotes daily in case some poor soul he had tried to get killed found a chance to slip essence of aconite into his wine. Me first, if possible. Rome owed me that.

The wine may not have been as smoothly resonant as Falernian, but it was the Guild of Hispania Wine Importers' finest and was too good to defile with deadly drops unless you held a *very* serious grudge indeed. Plenty of people present seethed with murderous intentions, but I was the new boy so I had yet to identify them or discover their pet gripes. Maybe I should have been suspicious, though. Half the diners worked in government and the rest were in commerce. Unpleasant odours were everywhere.

I braced myself for the evening. The first shock, an entirely welcome one, was that the greeting-slave had handed me a cup of fine Barcino red. Tonight was for Baetica: the rich hot treasurehouse of southern Spain. I find its wines oddly disappointing: white and thin. But apparently the Baeticans were decent chaps; the minute they left home they drank Tarraconensian – the famous Laeitana from northwest of Barcino, up against the Pyrenees where long summers bake the vines but the winters bring a plentiful rainfall.

I had never been to Barcino. I had no idea what Barcino was storing up for me. Nor was I trying to find out. Who needs fortune-tellers' warnings? Life held enough worries.

I supped the mellow wine gratefully. I was here as the guest of a ministerial bureaucrat called Claudius Laeta. I had followed him in, and was lurking politely in his train while trying to decide what I thought of him. He could be any age between forty and sixty. He had all his hair (dry-looking brown stuff cut in a short, straight, unexciting style). His body was trim; his eyes were sharp; his manner was alert. He wore an ample tunic with narrow gold braid, beneath a plain white toga to meet Palace formality. On one hand he wore the wide gold ring of the middle class; it showed some emperor had thought well of him. Better than anyone yet had thought of me.

I had met him while I was involved in an official enquiry for Vespasian, our tough new Emperor. Laeta had struck me as the kind of ultra-smooth secretary who had mastered all the arts of looking good while letting handymen like me do his dirty work. Now he had taken me up – not due to any self-seeking of mine, though I did see him as a possible ally against others at the Palace who opposed promoting me. I wouldn't trust him to hold my horse while I leaned down to tie my boot thong, but that went for any clerk. He wanted something; I was waiting for him to tell me what.

Laeta was top of the heap: an imperial ex-slave, born and trained in the Palace of the Caesars amongst the cultivated, educated, unscrupulous orientals who had long administered Rome's Empire. Nowadays they formed a discreet cadre, well behind the scenes, but I did not suppose their methods had changed from when they were more visible. Laeta himself must have somehow survived Nero, keeping his head down far enough to avoid being seen as Nero's man after Vespasian assumed power. Now his title was Chief Secretary, but I could tell he was planning to be more than the fellow who handed the Emperor scrolls. He was ambitious, and looking for a sphere of influence where he could really enjoy himself. Whether he took backhanders in the grand manner I had yet to find out. He seemed a man who enjoyed his post, and its possibilities, too much to bother. An organiser. A long-term planner. The Empire lay bankrupt and in tatters, but under Vespasian there was a new mood of reconstruction. Palace servants were coming into their own.

I wished I could say the same for me.

'Tonight should be really useful for you, Falco,' Laeta urged me, as we entered a suite of antique rooms in the old Palace. My hosts had an odd choice of venue. Perhaps they obtained the cobwebbed imperial basement at cheap rates. The Emperor would appreciate hiring out his official quarters to make a bit on the side.

We were deep under Palatine Hill, in dusty halls with murky histories where Tiberius and Caligula once tortured men who spoke out of turn, and held legendary orgies. I found myself wondering if secretive groups still relived such events. Then I started musing about my own hosts. There were no pornographic frescos in our suite, but the faded décor and cowed, ingratiating retainers who lurked in shadowed archways belonged to an older, darker social era. Anyone who believed it an honour to dine here must have a shabby view of public life.

All I cared about was whether coming tonight with Laeta would help me. I was about to become a father for the first time, and badly needed respectability. To play the citizen in appropriate style, I also required much more cash.

As the clerk drew me in I smiled and pretended to believe his promises. Privately I thought I had only a slim hope of winning advancement through contacts made here, but I felt obliged to go through with the farce. We lived in a city of patronage. As an informer and imperial agent I was more aware of it than most. Every morning the streets were packed with pathetic hopefuls in moth-eaten togas rushing about to pay attendance on supposedly great men. And according to Laeta, dining with the Society of Baetican Olive Oil Producers would allow *me* to mingle with the powerful imperial freedmen who really ran the government (or who thought they did).

Laeta had said I was a perfect addition to his team –

807

doing what, remained unclear. He had somehow convinced me that the mighty lions of bureaucracy would look up from their feeding bowls and immediately recognise in me a loyal state servant who deserved a push upwards. I wanted to believe it. However, ringing in my ears were some derisive words from my girlfriend; Helena Justina reckoned my trust in Laeta would come unstuck. Luckily, serious eating in Rome is men's work so Helena had been left at home tonight with a cup of well-watered wine and a cheesy bread roll. I had to spot any frauds for myself.

One thing was completely genuine at the Baetican Society: adorning their borrowed Augustan serving platters and nestling amongst sumptuous garnishes in ex-Neronian gilt comports, the food was superb. Peppery cold collations were already smiling up at us from low tables; hot meats in double sauces were being kept warm on complex charcoal heaters. It was a large gathering. Groups of dining couches stood in several rooms, arranged around the low tables where this luxurious fare was to be served.

'Rather more than a classic set of nine dinner guests!' boasted Laeta proudly. This was clearly his pet club.

'Tell me about the Society.'

'Well, it was founded by one of the Pompeys –' He had bagged us two places where the selection of sliced Baetican ham looked particularly tempting. He nodded to the diners whose couches we had joined: other senior clerks. (They mass together like woodlice.) Like him they were impatiently signalling to the slaves to start serving, even though people had still to find places around other tables. Laeta introduced me. 'Marcus Didius Falco – an interesting young man. Falco has been to various trouble-spots abroad on behalf of our friends in intelligence.' I sensed an atmosphere – not hostile, but significant. Internal jealousy, without doubt. There was no love lost between the correspondence secretariat and the spies' network. I felt myself being scrutinised with interest – an uneasy sensation.

Laeta mentioned his friends' names, which I did not

bother to memorise. These were just scroll-shufflers. I wanted to meet men with the kind of status owned by the great imperial ministers of olden days – Narcissus or Pallas: holding the kind of position Laeta obviously craved himself.

Smalltalk resumed. Thanks to my ill-placed curiosity I had to endure a rambling discussion of whether the Society had been founded by Pompey the Great (whom the Senate had honoured with control of *both* Spanish provinces) or Pompey the rival of Caesar (who had made Baetica his personal base).

'So who are your members?' I murmured, trying to rush this along. 'You can't be supporting the Pompeys now?' Not since the Pompeys fell from grace with a resounding thud. 'I gather then that we're here to promote trade with Spain?'

'Jove forbid!' shuddered one of the high-flown policy-formers. 'We're here to enjoy ourselves amongst friends!'

'Ah!' Sorry I blundered. (Well, not *very* sorry; I enjoy prodding sore spots.)

'Disregard the name of the Society,' smiled Laeta, at his most urbane. 'That's a historical accident. Old contacts do enable us to draw on the best resources of the province for our menu – but the original aim was simply to provide a legitimate meeting ground in Rome for like-minded men.'

I smiled too. I knew the scenario. He meant men with like-minded politics.

A *frisson* of danger attended this group. Dining in large numbers – or congregating in private for any purpose at all – was outlawed; Rome had always discouraged organised factions. Only guilds of particular merchants or craftsmen were permitted to escape their wives for regular feasting together. Even they had to make themselves sound serious by stressing that their main business was collecting contributions for their funeral club.

'So I need not really expect to meet any substantial exporters of Spanish olive oil?'

'Oh no!' Laeta pretended to look shocked. Someone

809

muttered to him in an undertone; he winced, then said to me, 'Well, sometimes a determined group of Baeticans manages to squeeze in; we do have some here tonight.'

'So thoughtless!' another of the scroll-pushers sympathised drily. 'Somebody needs to explain to the social élite of Corduba and Gades that the Society of Baetican Olive Oil Producers can manage quite well without any members who actually hail from southern Spain!'

My query had been sheer wickedness. I knew that among the snobs of Rome – and freed slaves were of course the *most* snobbish people around – there was strong feeling about pushy provincials. In the Celtic faction, the Spanish had been at it far longer than the Gauls or British so they had honed their act. Since their first admission to Roman society sixty or seventy years ago, they had packed the Senate, plucked the plum salaried jobs in the equestrian ranks, conquered literary life with a galaxy of poets and rhetoricians, and now apparently their commercial tycoons were swarming everywhere too.

'Bloody Quinctius parading his retinue of clients again!' muttered one of the scribes, and lips were pursed in unison sympathetically.

I'm a polite lad. To lighten the atmosphere I commented, 'Their oil does seem to be high quality.' I collected a smear on one finger to lick, taking it from the watercress salad. The taste was full of warmth and sunshine.

'Viscous gold!' Laeta spoke with greater respect than I anticipated from a freedman discussing commerce. Perhaps this was a pointer to the new realism under Vespasian. (The Emperor came from a middle-class family, and he at least knew *exactly* why commodities were important to Rome.)

'Very fine – both on the food and in the lamps.' Our evening was being lit with a wide variety of hanging and standard lights, all burning with steady clarity and, of course, no smell. 'Nice olives, too.' I took one from a garnish dish, then went back for more.

'Didius Falco is famous for political analysis,' commented Laeta to the others. News to me. If I was famous for anything it was cornering confidence tricksters and kicking the feet from under criminals. That, and stealing a senator's daughter from her lovely home and her caring relatives: an act which some would say had made me a criminal myself.

Wondering if I had stumbled on something to do with Laeta's motive for inviting me, I carried on being reverent about the viscous gold: 'I do know your estimable society is not named after any old table condiment, but a staple of cultured life. Olive oil is any cook's master ingredient. It lights the best homes and public buildings. The military consume vast quantities. It's a base for perfumes and medicines. There's not a bath-house or athletic gymnasium that could exist without oily body preparations –'

'And it makes a failsafe contraceptive!' concluded one of the more jolly stylus-shovers.

I laughed and said I wished I had known that seven months ago.

Feeling thoughtful, I returned my attention to the food. Plainly this suited the others; they wanted outsiders to keep quiet while they showed off. The conversation became encoded with oblique references to their work.

The last speaker's remark had me grinning. I could not help thinking that if I passed on the stylus-shover's suggestion Helena would scoff that it sounded like making love to a well-marinaded radish. Still, olive oil would certainly be easier to obtain than the illegal alum ointment which we had intended to use to avoid starting a family. (Illegal because if you took a fancy to a young lady who was of the wrong status you were not supposed to speak to her, let alone bed her – while if your fancy was legal you had to marry and produce soldiers.) Olive oil was not cheap, though there was plenty available in Rome.

There was a suitably Hispanic theme throughout the meal. This made for a tasty selection, yet all with a similar presentation: cold artichokes smothered in fish-pickle sauce from the Baetican coast; hot eggs in fish-pickle sauce with

811

capers; fowl forcemeats cooked with fish-pickle and rosemary. The endives came naked but for a chopped onion garnish – though there was a silver relish dish of you-guessed-it placed handily alongside. I made the mistake of commenting that my pregnant girlfriend had a craving for this all-pervasive *garum*; the gracious bureaucrats immediately ordered some slaves to present me with an unopened amphora. Those who keep frugal kitchens may not have noticed that fish-pickle is imported in huge pear-shaped vessels – one of which became my personal luggage for the rest of the night. Luckily my extravagant hosts lent me two slaves to carry the dead weight.

As well as the deliciously cured hams for which Baetica is famous, the main dishes tended to be seafood: few of the sardines we all joke about, but oysters and huge mussels, and all the fish harvested from the Atlantic and Mediterranean coasts – dory, mackerel, tuna, conger eel, and sturgeon. If there was room to throw a handful of prawns into the cooking pot as well, the chef did so. There was meat, which I suspected might be dashing Spanish horse, and a wide range of vegetables. I soon felt crammed and exhausted – though I had not so far advanced my career an inch.

As it was a club, people were moving from table to table informally between courses. I waited until Laeta had turned away, then I too slipped off (ordering the slaves to bring my pickle jar), as if I wanted to circulate independently. Laeta glanced over with approval; he thought I was off to infiltrate some policy-moulders' network.

I was really intending to sneak for an exit and go home. Then, when I dodged through a doorway ahead of my bearers and the *garum*, I crashed into someone coming in. The new arrival was female: the only one in sight. Naturally I stopped in my tracks, told the slaves to put down my pickle jar on its elongated point, then I straightened my festive garland and smiled at her.

812

II

She had been swathed in a full-length cloak. I like a woman
well wrapped up. It's good to ponder what she's hiding and
why she wants to keep the goodies to herself.

This one lost her mystery when she bumped into me. Her
long cloak slithered floorwards, to reveal that she was dressed
as Diana the Huntress. As definitions go, 'dressed' was only
just applicable. She wore an off-one-shoulder little gold
pleated costume; one hand carried a large bag from which
emerged a chink of tambourine clackers while under her
spare armpit were a quiver and a silly toy hunting bow.

'A virgin huntress!' I greeted her happily. 'You must be the
entertainment.'

'And you're just a big joke!' she sneered. I bent and
retrieved her cloak for her, which allowed me to peruse a
shapely pair of legs. 'You're in the right place to get kicked
somewhere painful!' she added pointedly; I straightened up
fast.

There was still plenty to look at. She would have come up
to my shoulder but was wearing cork heels on her natty hide
hunting boots. Even her toenails were polished like alabaster.
Her smooth, extremely dark skin was a marvel of depilatory
care; she must have been plucked and pumiced all over – just
thinking about it made me wince. Equal attention had been
lavished on her paintwork: cheeks heightened with the purple
bloom of powdered wine lees; eyebrows given super-
definition as perfect semicircles half a digit thick; lids glowing
with saffron; lashes smothered in lampblack. She wore an
ivory bangle on one forearm and a silver snake on the other.
The effect was purely professional. She was nobody's
expensive mistress (no gemstones or filigree) and since
women were not invited tonight, she was nobody's guest.

She had to be a dancer. Her physique looked well fleshed

813

but muscular. A shining swatch of hair, so black it had a deep blue sheen, was being held back from her brow in a simple twist which could be rapidly loosened for dramatic effect. She had both hands posed with a delicacy that spoke of practice with castanets.

'My mistake,' I pretended to apologise. 'I had been promised a Spanish dancer. I was hoping you were a bad girl from Gades.'

'Well, I'm a good girl from Hispalis,' she countered, trying to sweep past me. Her accent was crisp and her Latin abrasive. But for the Baetican theme of the evening it might have been hard to place her origins.

Thanks to my trusty amphora I was keeping the doorway well blocked. If she squeezed through, we were going to be pleasantly intimate. I noted the look in her eye, suggesting that one wrong move in confined conditions and she was liable to bite my nose off.

'I'm Falco.'

'Well, get out of my way, Falco.'

Either I had lost my charm, or she had sworn a vow to avoid handsome men with winsome smiles. Or could it be she was worried by my big jar of fermented fish entrails?

An oldish man with a cithara stepped from a room across the corridor. His hair was grizzled and his handsome features had dark, Mauretanian colouring. He took no interest in me. The woman acknowledged his nod and turned after him. I decided to stop and watch their performance.

'Sorry; private room!' she smirked, and closed the door smack in my face.

'Absolute nonsense! The Baetican Society has never encouraged plotting in smoky corners. We don't allow private parties here —'

It was Laeta. I had dallied too long and he had followed me. Overhearing the girl turned him into the worst kind of clerk who knows it all. I had stepped back to avoid getting my elegant Etruscan nose broken, but he pushed right past me intent on barging after her. His overbearing attitude almost made me decide against going in, but he had drawn me back into his orbit once more. The patient slaves wedged my amphora on its point against the doorframe and we sailed into the salon where the rude girl was to do her dance.

As soon as my eyes wandered over the couches I realised that Laeta had lied to me. Instead of the high-class world governors he had led me to expect, this so-called select dining club admitted people I already knew – including two I would have crossed Rome on foot to avoid.

They were reclining on adjacent couches – which was worrying in itself. The first was my girlfriend's brother Camillus Aelianus, a bad-mannered, bad-tempered youth who hated me. The other was Anacrites, the Chief Spy. Anacrites loathed me too – mainly because he knew I was better than him at the work we both did. His jealousy had nearly had lethal results, and now if I ever had the chance I would take great delight in tying him to a spit on the top of a lighthouse, then building a very large signal fire under him and setting light to it.

Maybe I should have left. Out of sheer stubbornness I marched straight in after Laeta.

Anacrites looked sick. Since we were supposed to be colleagues in state service he must have felt obliged to appear polite, so beckoned me to an empty place beside him. Instead of reclining myself I signalled the slaves to put my amphora to bed there with its neck on the elbow-bolster. Anacrites hated eccentricity. So did Helena's brother. On the next couch, the illustrious Camillus Aelianus was now simmering with fury.

This was more like it. I grabbed a cup of wine from a helpful server, and cheered up dramatically. Then ignoring them both I crossed the room after Laeta, who was calling me to be introduced to someone else.

III

As I caught up with Laeta, I had to make my way through an odd roomful. I had hoped I would have no reason to take a professional interest tonight, but my suspicions of the Chief Secretary's motives in inviting me had kept me on the alert. Besides, it was automatic to size up the company. Whereas Laeta had first led me among a hardcore group of regular eaters and drinkers, these men seemed almost like strangers who had reclined together just because they spotted empty couches and were now stuck with making a night of it. I sensed some awkwardness.

I could be wrong. Mistakes, in the world of informing, are a daily hazard.

This salon had always been designed as a dining room – the black and white mosaic was plain beneath nine formal, matching, heavyweight couches, but boasted a more complex geometric design in the centre of the floor. Laeta and I were now crossing that square, where the low serving tables were currently set but the dancer would be performing in due course. We were approaching a man who occupied the pivotal position like some grand host. He looked as if he thought he was in charge of the whole room.

'Falco, meet one of our keenest members – Quinctius Attractus!'

I remembered the name. This was the man the others had complained about for bringing in a troupe of real Baeticans.

He grunted, looking annoyed with Laeta for bothering him. He was a solid senator in his sixties, with heavy arms and fat fingers – just the right side of debauchery, but he obviously lived well. What was left of his hair was black and curly and his skin was weathered, as if he clung to old-fashioned habits: prowling his thousand-acre vineyards in person when he wanted to convince himself he stayed close to the land.

Maybe his collateral lay in olive groves.

I was clearly not obliged to make conversation, for the senator showed no interest in who I was; Laeta himself took the lead: 'Brought another of your little groups tonight?'

'Seems an appropriate venue for entertaining my visitors!' sneered Quinctius. I agreed with the man in principle, but his manner was off-putting.

'Let's hope they will benefit!' Laeta smiled, with the serene insolence of a bureaucrat making a nasty point.

Not understanding the sniping, I managed to find amusement of my own. When I first came in Anacrites had been enjoying himself. Now when I looked back in his direction I could see he was lying straight and very still on his couch. His strange light grey eyes were veiled; his expression unreadable. From being a cheerful party guest with slicked-back hair and a meticulous tunic, he had become as tense as a virgin sneaking out to meet her first shepherd in a grove. My presence had really tightened his screw. And from the way he was staring – while pretending not to notice – I didn't think he liked Laeta talking to Quinctius Attractus like this.

I quickly glanced around the three-sided group of couches. It was easy to spot the Baetican interlopers whose invasion had annoyed Laeta's colleagues. Several men here had a distinct Hispanic build, wide in the body and short in the leg. There were two each side of Quinctius, forming the central row in the most honoured position, and two more on the side row to his right. They all wore similar braid on their tunics, and dinner sandals with tough esparto rope soles. It was unclear how well they knew one another. They were speaking in Latin, which fitted the prosperous weave of their garments, but if they had come to Rome to sell oil they seemed rather restrained, not displaying the relaxed confidence that might charm retailers.

'Why don't you introduce us to your Baetican friends?' Laeta was asking Quinctius. He looked as if he wanted to tell Laeta to take a one-way trip to the Underworld, but we were all supposed to be blood-brothers at this dinner, so he had to comply.

The two visitors on the right-hand row, introduced rapidly and rather dismissively as Cyzacus and Norbanus, had had their heads together in close conversation. Although they nodded to us, they were too far from us to start chatting. The nearer pair, those on the best-positioned couches beside Quinctius, had been silent while Laeta spoke to him; they overheard Laeta and the senator trying to outdo one another in urbane unpleasantness, although they hid their curiosity. An introduction to the Emperor's Chief Secretary seemed to impress them more than it had done the first two. Perhaps they thought Vespasian himself might now drop in to see if Laeta had tomorrow's public engagement list to hand.

'Annaeus Maximus and Licinius Rufius.' Quinctius Attractus named them brusquely. He might be patron to this group, but his interest in them hardly took a paternal tone. However he did add more graciously, 'Two of the most important oil producers from Corduba.'

'*Annaeus!*' Laeta was in there at once. He was addressing the younger of the two, a wide-shouldered, competent-looking man of around fifty. '– Would that make you a relative of Seneca?'

The Baetican assented with a head movement, but did not agree the connection with enthusiasm. That could be because Seneca, Nero's influential tutor, had ended his famous career with an enforced suicide after Nero grew tired of being influenced. Adolescent ingratitude at its most extreme.

Laeta was too tactful to press the issue. Instead he turned to the other man. 'And what brings you to Rome, sir?'

Not oil, apparently. 'I am introducing my young grandson to public life,' answered Licinius Rufius. He was a generation older than his companion, though still looked sharp as a military nail.

'A tour of the Golden City!' Laeta was at his most insincere now, feigning admiration for this cosmopolitan initiative. I wanted to crawl under a side table and guffaw. 'What better

818

start could he have? And is the lucky young man with us this evening?'

'No; he's out on the town with a friend.' The Roman senator Quinctius interrupted with ill-concealed impatience. 'You'd best find a perch, Laeta; the musicians are tuning up. Some of us have paid for them, and we want our money's worth!'

Laeta seemed satisfied that he had made his mark. He had certainly annoyed the senator. As we picked our way back across the room through the slaves who were lifting the food tables in order to clear a central space, Laeta muttered to me, 'Unbearable man! He throws his weight about to a degree that has become quite unacceptable. I may ask you, Falco, to help me with my endeavours to deal with him ...'

He could ask as much as he liked. Keeping members of dining societies in order was not my work.

My host had not yet finished bopping upstarts on the nob. 'Anacrites! And who amongst our refined membership has deserved *your* attentions?'

'Yes, it's a working supper for me –' Anacrites had a light, cultured voice, about as unreliable as a dish of over-ripe figs. I felt bilious as soon as he spoke. 'I'm here to watch you, Laeta!' To do him justice, he had no fear of upsetting the secretariats. He also knew when to thrust his knife in quickly.

Their warfare was pretty open: the legitimate administrator, who dealt in manipulation and guile, and the tyrant of the security forces, who used blackmail, bullying and secrecy. The same force drove them; both wanted to be the dunghill king. So far there was not much difference between the power of a well-honed damning report on first-quality papyrus from Laeta, and a snide denunciation whispered by the spy in the ear of the Emperor. But one day this conflict was bound to reach a head.

'I'm quaking!' Laeta insulted Anacrites by using nothing worse than sarcasm. '– Do you know Didius Falco?'

'Of course.'

'He should do,' I growled. Now it was my turn to attack the

819

spy: 'Anacrites may be disorganised, but even he rarely forgets occasions when he sends agents into hostile territory, then deliberately writes to let the local ruler know to look out for them. I owe this man a great deal, Laeta. But for my own ingenuity he might have had me tied out on a rock in the Nabataean desert for all the crows of Petra to pick clean my bones. And in the case of unwelcome visitors I don't believe the cruel Nabataeans bother to kill you first.'

'Falco exaggerates,' Anacrites smirked. 'It was a regrettable accident.'

'Or a tactical ploy,' I returned coolly.

'If I was at fault, I apologise.'

'Don't bother,' I told him. 'For one thing you're lying, and for another, it's a pleasure to continue hating your guts.'

'Falco is a wonderful agent,' Anacrites said to Laeta. 'He knows almost everything there is to know about tricky foreign missions – and he learned it all from me.'

'That's right,' I agreed mildly. 'Campania, two years ago. You taught me all the mistakes and bungles. All the ways to upset local sensitivities, trample the evidence and fail to come home with the goods. You showed me that – then I went out and did the job properly. The Emperor still thanks me for learning to avoid your mistakes that summer!'

Laeta took a turn: 'I'm sure we all profit from your mutual past relationship!' He was letting Anacrites know I was working for him now. 'The entertainment is starting,' Laeta smiled in my direction. The general noise in the room had dropped in response to signs of impending action from the dancer. Laeta patted me on the shoulder – a gesture I found highly annoying, though I made sure Anacrites did not see me react. 'Stay and enjoy yourself, Falco; I'd like to hear your opinion in due course ...' It was obvious he was not talking about the musicians. He wanted Anacrites to think something was going on. Well, that suited me.

Only two vacant couches remained, at each end of the side rows on opposite sides of the room. I had decided my preference, but just at that moment someone beat me to it. It was a man I found hard to place – a fellow in a subdued oatmeal tunic, about my age. He dropped on to the couch as if it had been his place previously and was soon leaning on his elbows to watch the dancer, with his muscular legs sprawled behind him. He had an old scar down one forearm and bunioned feet that had done their share of tramping pavements. He spoke to no one but appeared sociable enough as he tossed grapes into his mouth and grinned at the girl who was about to perform.

I grabbed a wine refill to brace myself, then took the final couch – the one which was already partially occupied by my amphora of fish-pickle, alongside Anacrites.

IV

There were two musicians, both with that deep black North African skin. One played the cithara, fairly badly. The other was younger and with more menacing, slanted eyes; he had a hand drum. He pattered on it in a colourful manner while the girl from Hispalis prepared to thrill us with the traditional gypsy display. I gave Anacrites a pleasant smile that was bound to annoy him as we waited to marvel at the suppleness of her hips. 'Diana looks hot stuff. Have you seen her before?'

'I don't believe so ... What's our Falco been up to then?' I hated people who addressed me in that whimsical way.

'State secret.' I had just spent a winter delivering subpoenas for the lowest class of barrister and helping out as an unpaid porter at my father's auction house. Still, it was fun pretending that the Palace harboured a rival spy network, one run by Claudius Laeta over which Anacrites had no control.

'Falco, if you're working for Laeta, my advice is watch your back!'

I let him see me chuckle then I turned back to the dancer. She was giving us a few teasing poses with her golden bow and arrow: standing tiptoe on one foot with the other kicked up behind her while she pretended to shoot at diners, so she could lean back and show off her half-bared chest. Since this was Rome, it was nothing to cause a riot. Well, not unless any respectable equestrian went home and described her little Greek costume too graphically to his suspicious wife.

'I've been talking to young Camillus.' Anacrites had leaned across to whisper in my ear. I made a violent scratching movement as if I thought a beetle had landed on me. I just missed blinding him. He popped back on to his couch.

'Aelianus? That must have tried your patience,' I said. Just the other side of Anacrites Helena's angry brother was making sure he avoided my eye.

'He seems a promising young character. It's clear that he doesn't care for you, Falco.'

'He'll grow up.' The spy should have learned by now there was no future in baiting me.

'Isn't he your brother-in-law or something?' It was casually offensive.

'Or something,' I agreed calmly. 'What's he doing here? Don't tell me he heard there would be top men from the bureaucracy, and he's trying to worm his way into a sinecure?'

'Well, he's just back from Baetica!' Anacrites loved being obscure.

I loathed the thought of Helena's hostile brat of a brother hobnobbing here with the spy. Maybe I was getting over-excited, but the scenario had a whiff of plots being hatched against me.

The girl from Hispalis was now well into her routine, so conversation ceased. She was showy, but not outstanding. Dancing girls are a thriving export from southern Spain; they all seem to train in the same terpsichoreal school, one where the movement-coach needs retiring. This wench could roll her eyes, and various other parts of her anatomy. She threw herself about the floor as if she wanted to polish the whole mosaic with her wildly swinging hair. Once you've seen one snappy lass bent over backwards with her clackers in a frazzle, the attention may start wandering.

I was looking around. The room contained a disparate group. The world-weary, middle-class-looking pair of Baeticans on the other row of couches were as unreceptive as me to the girl's efforts; they still muttered among themselves. Quinctius Attractus, who had claimed to be paying for this, leaned on his elbow looking full of himself for the benefit of the more patrician pair of visitors either side of him. They watched politely, though the elder in particular looked as if he would normally be too aesthetic to indulge in this kind of show. All the Baeticans looked so polite it had to be forced, and I wondered why *they* thought they had been favoured here. Anacrites, the professional state meddler, appeared perfectly at home, though I could not believe Quinctius Attractus had intended him to join the group. Then there was Aelianus, too young to be a member of the dining club in his own right. Who had brought him? And who was the man in the oatmeal tunic at the end of the opposite row from me, who enjoyed himself in that seemingly sociable manner — yet actually spoke to nobody?

I nudged Anacrites. 'Who's that fellow?'

He shrugged. 'Probably a gatecrasher.'

The dancer ended a set, twanging away an arrow for real. It hit young Aelianus, who squeaked as if it packed more force than her toy bow suggested. She then let off a shower, most of which found a mark, causing me to make a note that if anybody died later of a slow poison, I would know who to pull in for questioning. As she retired for a breather she indicated, with eyes full of sluttish promise, that Camillus Aelianus could keep his pretty arrow as a souvenir.

I slid upright, walked around Anacrites, and deliberately seated myself on Aelianus' couch, forcing the brat to salute me. 'Oh you're here, Falco!' he said rudely. He was a thickset though physically undisciplined lad, with straight floppy hair and a permanent sneer. He had a younger brother who was both better looking and more likeable. I wished it were Justinus here tonight.

I fingered the arrow as if Aelianus were a schoolboy with some illegal toy. 'This is a dangerous memento. Better not let your parents find it in your bedroom; favours from performing artistes can be misconstrued.' I liked to worry him with threats that I might blacken his name in the way he always tried to blacken mine. My reputation had never existed, but he would be standing for election to the Senate soon, and had something to lose.

He snapped the arrow in two: an impolite gesture, since the girl from Hispalis was still in the room, talking to her musicians. 'She's nothing special.' He sounded sober as well as bored. 'She's relying on saucy eyes and a scanty outfit; her technique's very basic.'

'That so?' I know a snake dancer who says people only watch for the dress – or lack of it. 'So you're a connoisseur of Spanish choreography?'

'Anyone is, who has done a tour in the province,' he shrugged offhandedly.

I smiled. He must have known his youthful experience in peaceful Baetica would not impress an imperial agent who had specialised in working at the Empire's trickiest boundaries. I had crossed them too, when a risk was needed. 'So how did you enjoy Hispania?'

'Well enough.' He did not want to have to talk to me.

'And now you're placing your expert knowledge at the disposal of the Society of Baetican Olive Oil Producers! Do you know the ones over there with Quinctius Attractus?'

'Slightly. I was friendly with the Annaeus lads in Corduba.'

'What about the grandson of Licinius Rufius? He's here in Rome at the moment.'

'I believe so.' Aelianus was certainly not intending to discuss his friends. He could hardly wait to be rid of me.

'I gather he's out on the town tonight – I would have thought you would have been there.'

'I'm here instead! Do you mind, Falco; I want to see the dancer.'

'Nice girl,' I lied. 'I had a pleasant chat with her.'

It misfired: 'Of course; you must be going short,' Aelianus suggested unpleasantly. 'With my sister in her condition.' How Helena and I lived was our own affair. I could have told him that sharing our bed with several months of unborn offspring had not impeded a healthy lovelife, but merely set greater challenges. 'So now you're upsetting Helena by scurrying after entertainers. If anyone tells her maybe she will miscarry.'

'She won't!' I snapped.

I had just spent six months trying to reassure Helena (who had in fact lost one child in pregnancy, though her brother may never have been told of it). Now it was hard work convincing her that she would give birth safely and survive the ordeal. She was terrified, and I was not much happier myself.

'Maybe she'll leave you!' he speculated eagerly. That had always been a possibility.

'I see you really have her interests at heart.'

'Oh, I'm happy to see her with you. I think when I stand for the Senate I'll make my election platform denouncing your relationship – I'll be a man of such traditional rectitude I even criticise my own sister –'

'You won't succeed,' I told him. He might. Rome loves a pompous bastard.

Aelianus laughed. 'No; you're probably right. My father would refuse to finance the election.' Camillus Verus, father of my beloved and of this poisonous young ferret, always looked like an uncomplicated old buffer, but evidently Aelianus was sharp enough to realise that their parent loved Helena and understood that I did too; however much he regretted our relationship, the senator knew he was stuck with it. I had a sneaky idea he was quite looking forward to having a grandchild too.

'Jupiter, you must be really gloating, Falco!' Helena's brother's bitterness was even worse than I had realised. 'You've jumped up from nowhere and seized the only daughter of a patrician house –'

'Cobnuts. Your sister was glad to fly off her perch. She needed rescuing. Helena Justina did her duty and married a senator, but what happened? Pertinax was a disaster, a traitor to the state, who neglected and mistreated her. She was so miserable she divorced him. Is that what you want? Now she's with me, and she's happy.'

'It's illegal!'

826

'A technicality.'

'You could both be accused of adultery.'

'We regard ourselves as married.'

'Try that in the Censor's court.'

'I would. No one will take us there. Your father knows Helena made her own choice, and she's with a man who adores her. There is no moral objection the senator can make.'

Across the room the dancing girl with the limited technique shook out her waist-length hair. She seemed to know how to do that. I realised she had been watching us quarrelling. It gave me an uneasy qualm.

To end the fight I stood up, preparing to return to my own couch. 'So, Camillus Aelianus, what does bring you among the revered Society of Baetican Olive Oil Producers?'

The angry young man calmed down enough to boast: 'Friends in high places. How did you get in, Falco?'

'Much better friends, in even more select positions,' I told him crushingly.

Settling back the other side of Anacrites came almost as a relief. Before he tried to have me killed we had been able to work together. He was devious, but like me he had lived. He enjoyed a good wine, he was in control of his barber, and he had been known to crack the occasional joke against the Establishment. With an emperor who liked cost-cutting and hated too much security, Anacrites must be feeling beleaguered. He wanted me, for one, well out of his way. He had tried to discredit me, and he had planned to get me executed by a tricky foreign potentate. But even now, I knew where I was with him. Well, I knew it as much as you ever could with a spy.

'What's this, Falco? Is my young friend from the noble family pursuing vindictive claims against you?'

I said his young friend was about to get his nose pulled off. Anacrites and I resumed our usual hostility.

Gazing up, I fixed my eyes on a lamp. Burning with the

clear, odourless flame of fine Baetican oil, it was in gleaming bronze and the shape of a flying phallus. Either this rude vessel was swinging more than it should, or the whole room had begun to manoeuvre in some swooning routine ... I decided I had reached my full capacity for Barcino red wine. At the same moment, as so often happens, a slave poured more into my cup. I sighed and settled down for a long night.

I must have had yet more drink later, though I cannot provide a catalogue. As a result, nothing of interest happened – not to me, anyway. Others no doubt threw themselves into risk and intrigue. Someone presumably made an assignation with the dancer from Hispalis. It seemed the kind of party where traditional customs would be observed.

I left when the atmosphere was still humming. Nobody had noticeably fallen out, and certainly at that stage there was nobody dead. All I recall of my final hour are some tricky moments trying to shoulder my amphora; it was half as high as me and immovable to a man in my condition. The young fellow in the oatmeal tunic from the other row of couches was also collecting his cloak; he seemed relatively sober, and helpfully suggested I roust out some more slaves to lug the cumbersome container home for me on a carrying pole. I suddenly saw the logic of this. We exchanged a laugh. I was too far gone to ask his name, but he seemed pleasant and intelligent. I was surprised he had been at the dinner all on his own.

Somehow my legs must have found their way from the Palatine to the Aventine. The apartment where I had lived for some years was six floors up in a dismal tenement; the slaves refused to come up. I left the amphora downstairs, tucked out of sight under a pile of dirty togas in Lenia's laundry on the ground floor. It was the kind of night where my left foot set off in one direction and met my right one coming back. I have no recollection of how I persuaded them to co-operate and find their way upstairs.

Eventually I awoke from troubled blackness to hear the

distant cries of market stallholders and the occasional clonk of a harness bell. I realised the activity in the streets below had been disturbing me for some time. It was the first day of April and the outdoor street life was hectic. Watchdogs were barking at chickens. Cockerels were crowing for the fun of it. Day had dawned – quite a few hours ago. On the roof tiles outside a pigeon cooed annoyingly. Light, with a painful midday intensity, streamed in from the balcony.

The thought of breakfast marched into my brain automatically – then receded fast.

I felt terrible. When I squirmed upright on the saggy reading couch where I had flung myself last night, one look around the apartment made everything worse. There was no point calling out to Helena, not even to apologise. She was not here.

I was in the wrong place.

I could not believe I had done this – yet as my head throbbed it seemed all too plausible. This was our old apartment. We did not live here any more.

Helena Justina would be in our new home, where she would have waited for me all last night. That's assuming she had not already left me on the grounds that I had stayed out partying. A fact which any reasonable woman would interpret as meaning I had stayed out with another girl.

V

There was a dark first-floor apartment on the shady side of Fountain Court. At first glance the shady side looked superior, but that was only because the sun failed to light the decay that encased all these buildings like a mouldy crust. Shutters peeled. Doors sagged. People frequently lost heart and stopped paying their rent; before the landlord's muscle-bound assistants beat them up as a penalty, they quite often died in misery of their own accord.

Everyone who lived here was trying to leave: the basket-weaver with the street-level lock-up wanted to retire to the Campagna, the upstairs tenants came and went with a rapidity that said much about the facilities (that is, that there were none) while Helena and I, the weaver's sub-tenants, dreamed of escaping to a plush villa with piped water, a boundary of pine trees, and airy colonnades where people could hold refined conversations on philosophical subjects ... Anything, in fact, would be better than a three-room, small-dimensioned let, where the spitting and swearing totters who lived in the upper storeys all had a right of way past our front door.

The front door had been stripped and planed down, ready for new paint. Inside, I squeezed down a corridor full of stored items. The first room off it had bare walls and no furniture. The second was the same, apart from an unbelievably obscene fresco painted straight opposite the entrance. Helena was spending much time doggedly scratching off the lewd copulating couples and the coarse satyrs in garish hyacinth wreaths and panpipes who lurked behind laurel bushes while they ogled the scene. Obliterating them was slow work and today all the wet sponges and scrapers lay abandoned in a corner. I could guess why.

I walked further down the corridor. Here its newly

nailed floorboards were firm beneath my feet. I had spent hours getting them level. On the walls hung a series of small Greek plaques with Olympic scenes, Helena's choice. A niche seemed to be awaiting a pair of household gods. Outside the final room lay a red and white striped rug which I didn't recognise; on it slept a scruffy dog who got up and stalked off in disgust when I approached.

'Hello, Nux.'

Nux farted quietly, then turned round to survey her rear with mild surprise.

I tapped the lintel gently, and opened the door. Part of me hoped the usual occupant had gone out for a stroll.

There was no reprieve. She was there. I should have known. If she went out without me I had ordered her to take the guard dog. She was not in the habit of obeying my instructions, but she had become fond of the hound.

'Hello, brown eyes. Is this where Falco lives?'

'Apparently not.'

'Don't tell me he's run off to become a gladiator? What a swine.'

'The man is grown up. He can do as he likes.' Not if he had any sense.

Routinely, Falco's new office had been furnished as a bedroom. Informing is a sordid job and clients expect to be shocked by their surroundings. Besides, everyone knows that an informer spends half his time giving his accountant instructions how to cheat his clients, and any spare moments seducing his secretary.

Falco's secretary was lying against the pleasant scallop-shell bedhead reading a Greek novel. She doubled as Falco's accountant, which might explain her disillusioned manner. I did not attempt to seduce her. A tall, talented young woman, her expression hit me like a sudden gulp of snow-chilled wine. She was draped in white, with fine dark hair, loosely pinned up with ivory side combs. On a small table beside her lay a manicure set, a bowl of figs, and a shorthand copy of yesterday's *Daily Gazette*. With these she occupied her time while awaiting the master's return.

831

This had left her copious spare capacity for inventing whiplash retorts.

'How are you?' I enquired, tenderly checking up on her condition.

'Angry.' She enjoyed being frank.

'That's bad for the baby.'

'Leave the baby out of this. I hope to shield the baby from knowing it has a father who is a degenerate stop-out whose respect for his home life is as minimal as his courtesy to me.'

'Nice talking, Demosthenes! – Helena, my heart, you *are* angry!'

'Yes, and it's bad for you.'

'I do have an explanation.'

'Don't make me tired, Falco.'

'I've tried to produce something lucid and witty. Want to hear?'

'No. I'll be happy with your shrieks of grief as a posse of soldiers marches you away.'

'I made a stupid mistake, fruit. I had too much to drink and went home to the wrong house.'

'Lucid,' she smiled weakly. 'Though only witty in the sense that it's ludicrous ... Whose house?' Suspicion dies slowly.

'Ours. Over the road. Whose did you think?' I jerked my head in the direction of my old apartment.

Helena had always taken the line that she hated half the things I did – yet chose to believe that I told her the truth. In fact I did. She was too shrewd for deceit. In sudden relief she dropped her face in her hands and burst into tears. It was involuntary, but the worst punishment she could have chosen to whack me with.

I reflected sadly on the fact I was still half drunk and bound to have the ghastly breath to prove it. Rubbing one hand over my chin, I met relentless stubble. Then I crossed the room and gathered my poor cumbersome darling into my arms, taking the opportunity to slide my own body alongside her on the bed.

832

I had reached the point of comforting Helena just in time. I needed to get horizontal. The ravages of the night before would have had me keeling over otherwise.

We were still there, collapsed in a comfortable mound, about an hour later. Helena had been holding me and staring at the ceiling. I was not asleep, just slowly recovering.

'I love you,' I gurgled eventually, to take her mind off whatever dark thoughts held her transfixed.

'You do know when to splash out on a romantic phrase!' She gripped me by the bristled chin and stared into my bleary eyes. A girl of great courage, even she went slightly pale. 'Falco, your raffish good looks are the worse for wear.'

'You're a charitable woman.'

'I'm a fool!' she frowned. Helena Justina knew she had let herself be lured into caring for an unsatisfactory lowlife who would only bring her sorrow. She had convinced herself she enjoyed the challenge. Her influence had already refined me, though I managed to conceal the evidence. 'Damn you, Marcus, I thought you had been carried away by the excitement of your orgy and were lying in the lap of a dancing girl.'

I grinned. If Helena cared enough for me to be upset there was always hope. 'There *was* a dancing girl at the party but I had nothing to do with her. She was got up as Diana in a fraction of a costume. Spent her time leaning backwards so you could look right down –'

'At your foodbowl, if you were sensible!'

'Exactly,' I assured my beloved.

She gave me a fierce hug; by accident I let out a revolting belch. 'Then I thought you had been set upon and were bleeding in a gutter somewhere.'

'Just as well it didn't happen. I was carrying a valuable quantity of top-quality liquamen, which I managed to pinch from the party as a gift for my lady love, whose pregnancy has given her insatiable cravings for the most expensive kind of sauce.'

'My unerring good taste! As a bribe, it's virtually enough,' she conceded. Always fair.

'It's a whole amphora.'

'That's the way to show your remorse!'

'I had to borrow two slaves to drag it home.'

'My hero. So is it from Baetica?'

'The label on the shoulder says Gades.'

'Sure it's not just cheap old Muria?'

'Do I look like a second-class tunnyfish salesman? Entrails of prime mackerel, I promise you.' I had not tested the *garum* but the boast seemed safe. Given the high standard of food at the dinner, the condiments were bound to be excellent. 'Am I forgiven, then?'

'For not knowing where you live?' she jibed pointedly.

'Yes, I'm suitably embarrassed.'

Helena Justina smiled. 'I'm afraid you will have to face quite a lot more embarrassment. You see, Marcus my darling – I was so worried by your non-appearance that I rushed out at first light to see Petronius Longus.' Petronius, my best friend, was not above sarcasm when it came to my escapades. He worked as an enquiry officer in the local watch. Helena gurgled prettily. 'I was distraught, Marcus. I insisted he get the vigiles to look everywhere for you ...'

Helena assumed the demure expression of a girl who intended to enjoy herself, knowing I was condemned to suffer in a very public manner. She did not need to continue. Everyone on the Aventine would have heard that I disappeared last night. And whatever lies about my drunken return I tried telling, the true story was bound to come out.

834

VI

Luckily Petronius must have had enough to do chasing real villains. He had no time to come looking for me.

I spent my morning in modest domestic pursuits. Sleeping. Asking for headache remedies. Giving attention to the selfless woman who had chosen to spend her life with me.

Then a distraction turned up. We heard a man who was hot and fractious arriving on the outer stairs. We ignored the noise until he burst in on us. It was Claudius Laeta: he seemed to expect rather more ceremony than the quiet stare he received from both of us.

I had got myself bathed, shaved, massaged, combed, dressed in a clean tunic, revitalised with several pints of cold water, then further nourished with a simple meal of lightly cooked cucumber in eggs. I was sitting like a decent householder at my own table, talking to my own woman and politely allowing her to select whatever subject she liked. The chat was undemanding because Helena had her mouth full of mustcake. She had bought it for herself that morning, half suspecting I would turn up eventually with some disgraceful tale. There had been no suggestion of offering me any.

So we sat, decorous and peaceful after lunch, when a man with a commission I didn't want or care for burst into our home: for an informer, this was a normal event. I greeted him resignedly. Luckily we had our temporary table in the room without the obscene plasterwork. I took my time fetching another seat from a cubbyhole. I knew whatever Laeta had come to say would be burdensome.

Laeta sat down. Here, in a low street on the turbulent Aventine, the great man was well out of his fishpond. Like a grounded carp he was gasping, too. I never told anyone my new address, preferring to let trouble go to the old one. He must have stomped up the six flights to my room across the road, then stumbled down them all again before Lenia at the laundry (who had callously watched him going up) drawled out that I also leased an apartment over the basket shop opposite. He had vented his curses on the ox-wagon driver who had knocked him down as he was crossing Fountain Court.

'Perhaps Marcus Didius can advise you on suing the driver?' murmured Helena, with the refined patrician mockery which was the last thing he could cope with in his present indignant state.

I introduced her formally: 'Helena Justina, daughter of Camillus Verus, the senator; he's a friend of Vespasian, as I expect you know.'

'Your wife?' quavered Laeta, alarmed by the incongruity and trying not to sound surprised.

We smiled at him.

'What's the problem?' I asked gently. There had to be a problem, or a high-class official would not have dragged himself here, especially without an escort.

He cast a wild glance towards Helena, meaning I should get rid of her. Not easy. Not easy, even if I had wanted to. Quite impossible while she was two months away from giving birth and shamelessly exploiting it: groaning with restrained discomfort as she settled into her wicker arm-chair with her tired feet on her personal footstool. She folded her stole around herself and smiled at Laeta again – then continued with the remains of her cake. He was not worldly enough to suggest he and I went out to a wine bar, so Helena prepared to listen.

As she licked her long fingers I watched her wicked brown eyes survey the top clerk. He was sweating badly, partly from his hike up to my old eyrie and partly from agonies of awkwardness here. I wondered what Helena made of him. In fact, I wondered what I really made of him myself.

'Did you enjoy the dinner, Falco?'

'Excellent.' Years of encouraging difficult clients had taught me to lie smoothly. I seemed to have a prospective client here. Well, I had already turned down people who were more important than him.

'Good; good ... I need your help,' he confessed.

I raised an eyebrow as if that sordid idea had never crossed my mind. 'What can I do for you?'

This time Laeta turned to Helena directly. 'Perhaps you have some weaving you want to attend to?' He was persistent, yet had the sense to make it sound like a joke in case she still refused to budge.

'Afraid not.' She waved her arm around the empty room. 'We're still waiting for the loom to be delivered.'

I grinned. Helena Justina had never promised me the traditional attributes of a good Roman wife: reclusive social habits, a submissive demeanour, obedience to her male relatives, a big fat dowry – let alone home-woven tunics. All I got was bed and banter. Somehow I still ended up convinced that I had it better than the old republicans.

Laeta stopped fidgeting. He fixed his gaze on me as if to make my eccentric companion invisible. 'I need assistance from someone who is totally reliable.'

I had heard that before. 'You're saying the job is dangerous!'

'This could bring you large rewards, Falco.'

'That old song! This is work of an official nature?'

'Yes.'

'And is it official as in "just between friends", official as in "a highly placed person whose name I won't mention needs this", or official as in "the highly placed person must never know about it and if you get in trouble I'll deny I've ever heard of you"?'

'Are you always so cynical?'

'I've worked for the Palace before.'

Helena cut in, 'Marcus Didius has risked his life on public service. His reward has been slow payment, followed

837

by a refusal of social promotion even though it had previously been promised him.'

'Well, I know nothing of your past employment terms, Marcus Didius.' Laeta knew how to blame other departments. A natural. 'My own secretariat has an unblemished record.'

'Oh good!' I jeered. 'Yet my enthusiasm for your bureau's clean habits doesn't mean I accept the job.'

'I have not told you what it is,' he twinkled.

'By Jove; no you haven't! My curiosity is bursting.'

'You're being satirical.'

'I'm being rude, Laeta.'

'Well, I'm sorry you take this attitude, Falco –' There was an unspoken hint of regret that he had honoured me with his invitation to the oil producers' party. I ignored it. 'I had been told you were a good agent.'

'Good means selective.'

'But you refuse my work?'

'I'm waiting to hear about it.'

'Ah!' He assumed an expression of huge relief. 'I can promise I shall take personal responsibility for the payment of your fees. How much are we talking about, by the way?'

'I'll fix the terms when I accept the work – and I'll only accept if I know what it is.'

There was no escape. He looked uncomfortable, then he came out with it: 'Someone from our dinner last night has been found badly beaten in the street.'

'Then you must call for a surgeon and inform the local cohort of the watch!'

I avoided looking at Helena, aware she was newly anxious on my own behalf. If I had known we had to talk about people being beaten up, I would have whipped Laeta out of doors as soon as he arrived.

He pinched his mouth. 'This is not for the watch.'

'What makes a late-night street mugging peculiar? Home-going revellers are always being attacked.'

'He lives at the Palace. So he wasn't going home.'

'Is that significant? Who is this man?'

I should have worked out the answer, if only from the high status of my visitor and his unhealthy excitement. Yet it was quite unexpected when Laeta informed me with an air of panache: 'Anacrites, the Chief of Intelligence!'

VII

'*Anacrites?*' I laughed briefly, though not at the spy's misfortune. 'Then the first question you should be asking is whether I did it!'

'I did consider that,' Laeta shot back.

'Next, the attack may be connected to his work. Maybe, unknown to you, I'm already involved.'

'I understood that after he landed you in trouble on your Eastern trip, the last thing you would ever do is work with him.'

I let that pass. 'How did he get himself beaten up?'

'He must have gone out for some reason.'

'He wasn't going home? He actually lives at the Palace?'

'It's understandable, Falco. He's a free man, but he holds a sensitive senior position. There must be considerations of security.' Laeta had clearly given much thought to the luxury Anacrites had fixed up for himself: inter-service jealousies were seething again. 'I believe he has invested in a large villa at Baiae, but it's for holidays – which he rarely takes – and no doubt his retirement eventually –'

Laeta's obsession with his rival's private life intrigued me – as did the amazing thought that Anacrites could somehow afford a villa at ultra-fashionable Baiae. 'How badly is he hurt?' I butted in.

'The message said he might not live.'

'Message?'

'Apparently he was discovered and rescued by a house-holder who sent a slave to the Palatine this morning.'

'This man identified Anacrites how?'

'That I don't know.'

'Who has checked Anacrites' condition? You have not seen him?'

'No!' Laeta seemed surprised.

I restrained myself. This was looking like a mess. 'Is he still with the charitable private citizen?' Silence confirmed it. 'So! You believe Anacrites has been knocked about, and possibly murdered, by somebody or some group he was investigating. Official panic ensues. You, as Chief of Correspondence – a quite separate bureau – become involved.' Or he involved himself, more likely. 'Yet the Chief Spy himself has been left all day, perhaps without medical attention, and in a place where either he or the helpful citizen may be attacked again. Meanwhile nobody from the official side has bothered to find out how badly Anacrites is hurt, or whether he can speak about what happened?'

Laeta made no attempt to excuse the stupidity. He linked the fingertips of both hands. 'Put like that,' he said, with all the reasonableness of an important official who had been caught on the hop, 'it sounds as if you and I should go straight there now, Falco.'

I glanced across at Helena. She shrugged, resigned to it. She knew I hated Anacrites; she also knew that any wounded man needs help from someone sensible. One day the body bleeding in the gutter might be mine.

I had a further question: 'Anacrites runs a full complement of agents; why are they not being asked to see to this?' Laeta looked shifty; I dropped in the real point: 'Does the Emperor know what has occurred?'

'He knows.' I could not decide whether to believe the clerk or not.

At least Laeta had brought an address. It took us to a medium apartment on the south end of the Esquiline – a once notorious district, now prettied up. A famous graveyard which had once possessed a filthy reputation had been developed into five or six public gardens. These still provided a venue for fornication and robbery, so the streets were littered with broken wine jugs and the locals walked about with their heads down, avoiding eye contact. Near the aqueducts some pleasant private homes braved it out.

On the first level of living quarters in a four-storey block, up a cleanly swept stair which was guarded by standard bay trees, lived a fusspot bachelor architect called Calisthenus. He had been trapped at home all day, unwilling to leave a mugging victim who might suddenly revive and make off with his rescuer's collection of Campanian cameos.

Laeta, with unnecessary caution, refused to identify himself. I did the talking: 'I'm Didius Falco.' I knew how to imbue that with authority; there was no need to specify what post I held. 'We've come to carry off the mugging victim you so kindly took in – assuming he is still alive.'

'Just about, but unconscious still.' Calisthenus looked as if he thought he deserved our official attention. I contained my distaste. He was a thin, pale weeping willow who spoke in a tired drawl. He implied he had great ideas preoccupying him, as if he were a grand temple designer; in reality he probably built rows of little cobblers' shops.

'How did you come across him?'

'Impossible to avoid: he was blocking my exit.'

'Had you heard any disturbance last night?'

'Not specially. We get a lot of noise around here. You learn to sleep through it.' And to ignore trouble until they could not step over it.

We reached a small closet where a slave normally dossed down. Anacrites was lying on the meagre pallet, while the slave watched him from a stool, looking annoyed that his blanket was being bled on. The spy was indeed unconscious. He was so ill that for a second I found him unrecognisable.

I spoke his name: no response.

There was a cloth in a bowl of cold water; I wiped his face. His skin was completely drained of colour and felt icily moist. The pulse in his neck took careful finding. He had gone somewhere very far away, probably on a journey that would have no return.

I lifted the cloak covering him, his own garment presumably. He still wore last night's reddish tunic held together along all its seams with padded braid in dark berry colours. Anacrites always swanked in good stuff, though he avoided garish shades; he knew how to mix comfort with unobtrusiveness.

There were no bloodstains on the tunic. I found no stabbing wounds nor general signs of beating, though he did have identical bad bruises on both his upper arms as if he had been fiercely grabbed. The side of one shin had a small cut, new and about a digit long, from which ran a dried trickle of blood, thin and straight as a dead worm. No serious wounds accounted for his desperate condition until I drew back another cloth. It had been placed at the top of his head, where it formed a wad pressed against his skull.

I peeled it off gently. This explained everything. Someone with unpleasant manners had used Anacrites as a pestle in a very rough mortar, half scalping him. Through the mess of blood and hair I could see to the bone. The spy's cranium had been crushed in a way that had probably damaged his brain.

Calisthenus, the droopy architect, had reappeared in the doorway. He was holding Anacrites' belt; I recognised it from last night. 'He was not robbed. There is a purse here.' I heard it clink. Laeta grabbed the belt and searched the purse, finding just small change in normal quantities. I didn't bother. If he hoped to discover clues there, Laeta had never dealt with spies. I knew Anacrites would carry no documents, not even a picture of his girlfriend if he had one. If he ever carried a note-tablet he would have been too close even to scratch out a shopping list.

'How did you know he belonged in the Palace, Calisthenus?'

Calisthenus handed me a bone tablet, the kind many officials wear to impress innkeepers when they want a free drink. It gave Anacrites a false name which I had heard him use, and claimed he was a palace secretary; I knew that disguise too, and presumably so did whoever at the Palace received the architect's message.

'Was anything else with him?'

'No.'

I lifted the Chief Spy's lifeless left wrist, splaying the cold fingers on mine. 'What about his seal ring?' I knew he wore one; he used it to stamp passes and other documents. It was a large chalcedony oval engraved with two elephants entwining trunks. Calisthenus again shook his head. 'Sure?' He was growing indignant as only an architect can (all that practice bluffing out overspent estimates and expressing disbelief that clients expect a house that looks like what they asked for ...) 'No disrespect, Calisthenus, but you might have thought the ring would cover any costs you incurred in tending the victim?'

'I can assure you —'

'All right. Settle down. You have rescued an important state servant; if it does impose any financial burden, send your invoice to the Palace. If the ring turns up it should be returned straight away. Now if your boy can run out for a litter, my colleague here will take this poor fellow away.'

Laeta looked put out that I assigned him to babyminding, but as we watched Anacrites being loaded into a hired chair for what could be his last journey anywhere, I explained that if I was being asked to work on the problem I had best nip off and start. 'So what is required, Laeta? You want me to arrest whoever bopped him?'

'Well, that would be interesting, Falco.' In fact Laeta sounded as if apprehending the villain was his least concern. I began to wonder if it was wise to let him escort the wounded spy back to the Palatine. 'But what investigation do you think Anacrites was working on?'

'Ask the Emperor,' I instructed.

'Vespasian is unaware of any major exercise that could be relevant.' Did that mean the Emperor was being kept in ignorance — or simply that the intelligence network had no work? No wonder Anacrites always gave the impression he feared compulsory retirement was lurking just around the corner.

'Have you tried Titus?' The Emperor's elder son shared

844

the business of government. He happily involved himself in secrets.

'Titus Caesar had nothing to add. However, it was he who suggested bringing in your good self.'

'Titus knows I won't want to tangle with this!' I growled. 'I told you: interview Anacrites' staff. If he was on to something, he will have had agents out in the field.'

Laeta was frowning. 'I have been trying, Falco. I cannot identify any agent he was using. He was very secretive. His record-keeping was eccentric to say the least. All the named employees on his bureau's roll seem very low-grade runners and messengers.'

I laughed. 'No operative who worked for Anacrites would be high class!'

'You mean he couldn't choose good people?' Laeta seemed pleased to hear it.

Suddenly I felt angry on the damned spy's behalf. 'No, I mean that he was never given any money to pay for quality!' It did raise the question of how his own villa at Baiae had been acquired, but Laeta failed to spot the discrepancy. I calmed down. 'Look, he was bound to be secretive; it comes with the job. Olympus! We're talking about him as if he were dead, but that's not so, not yet –'

'Well, no indeed!' Laeta muttered. The litter-bearers were maintaining their normal impassive stare straight ahead. We both knew they were listening in. 'Titus Caesar suggests we ensure no news of this attack leaks out.' Good old Titus. Famous for flair – especially, in my experience, when organising cover-ups. I had helped him fix a few of those.

I looked Laeta firmly in the eye. 'This could have something to do with the dinner last night.'

Reluctantly he admitted, 'I was wondering about that.'

'Why was it you invited me? I had the feeling there was something you wanted to discuss?' He pursed his lips. 'Why were you keen to have me meet that senator?'

'Only my own general impression that Quinctius Attractus is getting above himself.'

'Might Anacrites have been investigating Attractus?'

'What reason could he have?' Laeta would not even admit that Anacrites might have noticed the man's behaviour just as he did.

'Spies don't have to have legitimate reasons; that's why they are dangerous.'

'Well, somebody has made this one quite a lot less dangerous, Falco.'

'Perhaps,' I suggested nastily, 'I should be asking whether *you* got on with him badly.' Since I knew better than to expect a sensible answer, I turned my attention back to the spy himself.

I wondered whether it would have been better to leave Anacrites discreetly at the house of Calisthenus, paying the architect to have the sick man nursed and to keep quiet about it. But if someone really dangerous was about, the Palace would be safer. Well, it ought to be. Anacrites could be the victim of a straightforward palace plot. I was sending him home to be looked after – that nasty ambiguous phrase. Maybe I was sending him home to be finished off.

Suddenly I felt a surge of defiance. I could see when I was being set up as the booby. Laeta loathed the spy, and his motives towards me were ambiguous. I didn't trust Laeta any more than Anacrites, but whatever was going on, Anacrites was in deep trouble. I had never liked him, or what he represented, but I understood how he worked: knee deep in the same middenheap as me.

'Laeta, Titus is right. This needs to be kept quiet until we know what it's about. And you know how rumours fly at the Palace. The best solution is to put Anacrites somewhere else where he can die in peace when he decides to go; then we can choose whether or not to announce it in the *Daily Gazette*. Leave everything to me. I'll carry him to the Temple of Aesculapius on Tiber Island, swear them to secrecy, but give them your name to inform you of developments.'

Laeta thought hard, but submitted himself to my plan.

Telling him that I had a few ideas of my own to pursue, I waved him off.

I then examined the doorway where Anacrites had been found. It was easy to see where and how he had been hurt; I discovered an ugly clump of blood and hair on the house wall. It was below chest height; the spy must have been bent over for some reason, though he carried no marks of any blow that would have doubled him up. I looked around, covering some distance, but found nothing significant.

The wounded man had been propped in a chair long enough; I told the bearers to come along with him. I did walk them to Tiber Island where I unloaded Anacrites and dismissed the chair. Then, instead of depositing the sick man amongst the clapped-out abandoned slaves who were being cared for at the hospital, I hired another chair. I led this one further west along the riverbank in the shadow of the Aventine. Then I took the unconscious spy to a private apartment where I could be sure of his good treatment.

He might yet die of last night's wound, but no one would be allowed to help him into Hades by other means.

VIII

Though I was a man on a charitable mission, my greeting
was not promising. I had dragged Anacrites up three flights
of stairs. Even unconscious he made trouble, buckling me
under his weight and tangling his lifeless hands in the
handrail just when I had got a good rhythm going. By the
time I arrived upstairs I had no breath to curse him. I used
my shoulder to knock open the door, a worn item that had
once been red, now a faded pink.

A furious old biddy accosted us. 'Who's that? Don't drag
him in here. This is a peaceful neighbourhood!'

'Hello, Mother.'

Her companion was less blunt and more witty. 'Jove, it's
Falco! The little lost boy who needs a tablet round his neck
to tell people where he lives! A tablet he can consult himself
too, when he's sober enough to read it –'

'Shut up, Petro. I'm giving myself a hernia. Help me lie
him down somewhere.'

'Don't tell me!' raged my mother. 'One of your friends
has got himself in trouble and you expect me to look after
him. It's time you grew up, Marcus. I'm an old woman. I
deserve a rest.'

'You're an old woman who needs an interest in life. This
is just the thing. He's not a drunk who fell under a cart,
Ma. He's an official who has been cruelly attacked and until
we discover the reason he has to be kept out of sight. I'd
take him home but people may look for him there.'

'Take him home? That poor girl you live with doesn't
want to be bothered with this!' I winked at the unconscious
Anacrites; he had just found himself a refuge. The best in
Rome.

Petronius Longus, my big grinning friend, had been
lounging in my mother's kitchen with a handful of almonds

848

while he regaled Ma with the now famous finish of my big
night out. Seeing my burden his mood quietened, then
when he helped me shove Anacrites on a bed and he
glimpsed the damage to the spy's head, Petro's face set. I
thought he was going to say something but he buttoned his
lip.

Ma stood in the doorway, arms folded; a small, still
energetic woman who had spent her life nurturing people
who didn't deserve it. Olive black eyes flicked over the spy
with flashes like signal torches announcing an international
disaster. 'Well, this one won't be a lot of trouble. He's not
going to be here long!'

'Do your best for the poor fellow, Ma.'

'Don't I know him?' Petronius mumbled in a low voice
to me.

'Speak up!' snapped Ma. 'I'm not deaf and I'm not an
idiot.'

Petronius was frightened of my mother. He replied
meekly, 'It's Anacrites, the Chief Spy.'

'Well, he looks like a nasty dumpling that should have
been eaten up yesterday,' she sneered.

I shook my head. 'He's a spy; that's his natural attitude.'

'Well, I hope I'm not expected to work some miracle and
save him.'

'Ma, spare us the quaint plebeian cheerfulness!'

'Who's going to pay for the funeral?'

'The Palace will. Just take him in while he's dying. Give
him some peace from whoever is trying to get him.'

'Well; I can do that,' she conceded grumpily.

I come from a large feckless family, who rarely permit
themselves to perform deeds of kindness. When they do,
any sensible conscious man wants to run a fast marathon in
the other direction. It gave me a grim pleasure to leave
Anacrites there. I hoped he came round and got thoroughly
lectured – and I hoped that when it happened I would be
present to watch.

I had known Petronius Longus since we were both

849

eighteen. I could tell he was holding back like a nervous bride. As soon as we could, we edged to the door, then bidding Ma a fast farewell we were out of the apartment like the naughty schoolboys she reckoned we both still were. Her derogatory cries followed us downstairs.

Petronius knew I realised there was something he was bursting to say. In his usual aggravating way he kept it to himself as long as possible. I clamped my teeth and pretended not to be wanting to knock him into the copper shop opposite for keeping me on tenterhooks.

'Falco, everyone's talking about a body the Second Cohort found this morning.' Petro was in the Fourth Cohort of vigiles, lording it over the Aventine. The Second were his counterparts who covered the Esquiline district.

'Whose body's that?'

'Looked like a street attack; happened last night. Man had his head stove in, in a remarkably violent manner.'

'Rammed against a wall, perhaps?'

Petro appraised my suggestion. 'Sounds as if it could have been.'

'Know anybody friendly in the Second?'

'I thought you'd ask that,' Petro replied. We were already making headway on the long route back to the Esquiline.

The Second Cohort's guardhouse lies on the way out to the Tiburtina Gate, close to the old Embankment which carries the Julian Aqueduct. It is situated between the Gardens of Pallentian and the Gardens of Lamia and Maia. A bosky spot – much frequented by elderly grubby prostitutes and persons trying to sell love potions and fake spells. We burrowed in our cloaks, walked quickly, and discussed the races loudly to reassure ourselves.

The Second Cohort were in charge of the Third and Fifth regions: some routine squalor, but also several large mansions with tricky owners who thought that the vigiles existed solely to protect them while they annoyed everyone else. The Second patrolled steep hills, run-down gardens, a

big chunk of palace (Nero's Golden House) and a prestigious public building site (Vespasian's huge new amphitheatre). They faced some headaches, but were bearing up
like Stoics. Their enquiry team were a group of relaxed
layabouts whom we found sitting on a bench working out
their night-shift bonus pay. They had plenty of time to tell
us about their interesting murder case, though perhaps less
energy for actually solving it.

'Io! He took a knock all right!'

'Bang on the knob?' Petro was doing the talking.

'Cracked open like a nut.'

'Know who he is?'

'Bit of a mystery man. Want a look at him?'

'Maybe.' Petronius preferred not to be that kind of
sightseer, until it was unavoidable. 'Can you show us the
scene of the mugging?'

'Sure! Come and see the happy fellow first ...'

Neither of us wanted to. Blood is bad enough. Spilt
brains we avoid.

Luckily the Second Cohort turned out to be an outfit
with caring methods. While they waited for someone to
come forward and claim the victim, they had slung his body
in a sheet between two laundry poles, in the shed where
they normally kept their fire engine. The pumping machine
had been dragged out to the street where it was being
admired by a large group of elderly men and small boys.
Indoors, the corpse lay in a dim light. He had been neatly
arranged and had his head in a bucket to contain leakage.
The scene was one of respectful privacy.

I did not enjoy looking at the body. I hate becoming
introspective. Life's bad enough without upsetting yourself
drawing filthy parallels.

I had seen him before. I had met him briefly. I had talked
to him – *too* briefly, perhaps. He was the cheerful lad at the
dinner last night, the one in the oatmeal tunic who kept his
own council in a diffident manner while watching the
dancer Attractus had hired. He and I had later shared a
joke, one I could not even now remember, as he helped me

851

round up some slaves to shoulder my amphora of fish-pickle.

The victim was about my own age, build and body-weight. Before some thug split his skull apart he had been intelligent and pleasant; I had had the impression he lived in the same world as me. Although Anacrites had pretended not to know who he was, I wondered if that had been a lie. An uneasy feeling warned me the dead man's presence at the dinner would turn out to be relevant. He left the Palatine at the same time as me. He must have been killed very soon afterwards. Whoever attacked him may well have followed us both from the Palace. He went off alone; I had been escorted by two hefty slaves with my amphora.

A nagging premonition suggested that had I also been unaccompanied, the body in the firefighters' shed could well have been mine.

IX

Petronius and I made a cursory survey of the corpse, trying to ignore the head damage. Once again we found no other significant wounds. But a stain on the sheet which was cradling the body made me lift his right leg. Behind the knee I discovered a torn flap of skin – little more than a scratch, though it had bled freely because of its location, and it must have stung when he acquired it.

'Petro, what do you make of that?'

'Snagged himself on something?'

'I don't know ... Anacrites also had a cut leg for some reason.'

'You're scavenging, Falco. It's nothing.'

'You're the expert!' That always worried him.

The Second Cohort had ascertained that the dead man's name was Valentinus. It had only taken a few moments of asking around locally. He had rented lodgings on the Esquiline, just ten strides from where somebody had battered him to death.

The neighbour who identified the body had told the Second that Valentinus had lived alone. His occupation was unknown. He had gone out and about at different hours and quite often received callers of various kinds. He went to the baths, but avoided temples. He had never been any trouble to his neighbours. He gave no signs of enjoying himself much, nor had he ever been arrested by the vigiles. Until the night he died, he had always taken care of himself.

The Second led us to his apartment, which they had previously searched. It was a two-room fourth-floor lease in a dark tenement. Its furnishings were sparse but neat. The inner room held his bed, a couple of tunics dumped on a bench, his spare boots, and a few unrevealing personal items. The outer room contained a table, his smart red gloss food bowl, his winecup with a jocular message, his stylus and string-bound note tablet (clean of useful information), and a hook with his cloak and hat. Each room was lit by one high window, too far away to see out.

Petronius and I took a sombre look around while the Second Cohort members tried not to show that they resented us checking their work. We found nothing remarkable, nothing to identify the man or his occupation. Even so, to me the style of his living quarters was depressingly familiar.

Then, as we were all trooping out again, I stopped. Light from our lantern happened to fall on the doorpost outside the apartment. There, somebody some years ago had drawn a neat pictogram of a single human eye. I knew the faded symbol. It's a sign informers use.

Petro and I stared at each other. Looking more keenly for clues, I noticed that although the doorlock appeared innocuous its fine bronze lion-headed key, which the Second had taken from the body, showed that instead of the common pin-tumbler fastener that most people use, Valentinus had invested in a devious iron rotary lock, which would be difficult to pick or force without the proper key. Then, crouching near ground level, Petro spotted two tiny metal tacks, one knocked into the door itself, one in the frame. A classic tell-tale: tied between the tacks had been a human hair. It had been broken, presumably when the Second first entered.

'No offence, lads, but we'd better think about this again,' said Petro, looking virtuous.

He and I went back inside. Quietly and carefully we searched the room afresh, as if Valentinus had been a pal of ours. This time the Second watched us in fascination while we took the place apart.

Under the bed, lashed to its frame, we found a sword capable of quick release by pulling one end of a knot.

Although the windows looked out of reach, if you dragged the table to one, or climbed on the upended bench below the other, you could stretch outside and discover that somebody had banged in a couple of useful hooks. One had an amphora of good Setinum red wine hung up to warm in the sunlight; the other, through which a lithe man might just wriggle, had a stout rope neatly rolled up but long enough to reach a balcony roof on the storey below. Under most of the floorboards lurked nothing of interest, though we did find some letters from his family (parents and a cousin, who lived a few miles from Rome). We discovered no money. Like me, Valentinus probably kept a bankbox in the Forum, with its access number stored securely in his head.

One floorboard in the bedroom actually had nails with false heads. It came up quite smoothly when you pulled it up by way of a knot, waggled your fingers underneath the wood and released a specially constructed bar that pivoted aside. Built under the board was a small, locked wooden compartment. Eventually I located the key, concealed in a hollow carved under the seat of the stool in the outer room. In his secret box the dead man had kept spare, succinct notes about his work. He was a neat, regular record-keeper. We already knew that: Valentinus' hat had been double lined; inside it Petronius had found expense sheets of a type I knew all too well.

Some work that the dead man did, probably from necessity, was just the kind of dreary intrigue I often had to carry out myself for private clients. The rest was different. Valentinus had been more than an informer, he was a spy. He was claiming for many hours spent on surveillance. And although there were no names for the people he had been recently watching, the latest entries on his claim sheet were all codenamed 'Corduba'. Corduba is the capital of Romanised Baetica.

We reckoned we knew who had commissioned this work. One of the expense claims from his hat had already been

stamped and approved for payment. The stamp was a large
oval, featuring two elephants with entwined trunks: Anacrites'
chalcedony seal.

X

Petronius left me in the Forum. The task was mine now. Facing up to it with my usual compulsion and stamina, I went home to bed.

Next day, striking while some impetus was with me, I walked back to the Forum, up through the Cryptoporticus where the scoffing Praetorians knew me well enough to admit me after a few threats and jeers, then into the old Palace. I had no need of Claudius Laeta to advise me who to interview or to smooth the way. I possessed other contacts. Mine were probably no more reliable than the devious correspondence chief, but I was attached to them on the usual perverse grounds that make you trust men you have known for some time even when you suspect that they lie, cheat and steal.

Momus was a slave overseer. He looked as healthy as a side of condemned beef and as dangerous as an escaped gladiator on the run. His eyes were moist with some infection, his body was scarred, his face was a fascinating grey shade as if he had not been outside for the past decade. Being an overseer was something he no longer worked at very hard; he left the rituals of slave market, placement, whipping and bribe-taking to others.

Momus now held some nebulous position at the Palace; in effect, he was another spy. He did not work for Anacrites. He did not care for Anacrites either. But in a bureaucracy every employee has to have another officer who reports on him to his superiors. Anacrites was attached to the Praetorian Guard but worked directly to the Emperor, so he was judged by Vespasian himself when it came to matters of reprimand or reward. Both Anacrites and I believed Momus to be the nark who told the Emperor what he should think of the Chief Spy's work. That meant

Anacrites despised and loathed him, but it made Momus a friend of mine.

I told him the Chief Spy had been seriously hurt. It was supposed to be a secret but Momus already knew. I guessed he had also heard that Anacrites was supposed to be hidden away at the Temple of Aesculapius on Tiber Island – but maybe he had not yet found out that the victim was really laid up on the Aventine with Ma.

'Something funny's going on, Momus.'

'What's new, Falco?'

'This attack is supposed to relate to intelligence work. Nobody even knows what Anacrites was investigating. I'm trying to track down his agents, or records of what he's been involved with –'

'You'll have a job.' Momus enjoyed disheartening me. 'Anacrites is like an Athenian vote machine.'

'That's a bit subtle for me.'

'You know; it's a gadget to prevent nobbling. When they used open jars fistfuls of votes used to go astray. So now the voters put balls in the top of a closed box; they wiggle down inside and then the election results pop out at the bottom. No fraud – and no fun, either. Trust the bloody Greeks.'

'What's this to do with Anacrites?'

'People pile information into his brain and if he's in the right mood he farts out a report. In between, everything is locked up.'

'Well, it looks as if the next person he blows a report at could be Charon the ferryman.'

'Oh dear, poor Charon!' sneered Momus, with the cheery expression of a man who was just thinking that if Anacrites had sailed away on the decrepit punt to Hades, he might immediately apply for Anacrites' job. Some state employees love to hear about a colleague's premature demise.

'Charon's going to be busy,' I commented. 'Villains have been cracking spies' heads all over the Esquiline. There was also a pleasant lad who used to do surveillance work.'

'Do I know him, Falco?'

'Valentinus.'

Momus let out a snarl of disgust. 'Oh Jupiter! Dead? That's terrible. Valentinus who lived on the Esquiline? Oh no; he was class, Falco. He must have been the best snuffler Anacrites used.'

'Well, he's not on the staff roll.'

'Better sense. He stayed freelance. Self-employed. I used him myself sometimes.'

'What for?'

'Oh ... tracking down runaways.' The alleged overseer looked vague. I reckoned whatever Momus used Valentinus for would give me a queasy stomach. I decided not to know.

'Was he good?'

'The best. Straight, fast, decent to deal with, and accurate.'

I sighed. More and more this sounded like a man I would have liked to share a drink with. I could have made friends with Valentinus last night at the dinner, if I had only realised. Then maybe if we had rolled out of the Palace together like cronies, events might have turned out differently for the freelance. Together we might have fought off his attackers. It could have saved his life.

Momus was eyeing me up. He knew I had an interest. 'You going to sort this out, Falco?'

'It looks like a murky fishpond. Reckon I stand a chance?'

'No. You're a clown.'

'Thanks, Momus.'

'My pleasure.'

'Don't enjoy yourself too much with the hard-hitting insults; I may prove you wrong.'

'Virgins might stay chaste!'

I sighed. 'Heard anything about any dirty goings-on in Baetica?'

'No. Baetica's all sunshine and fish-sauce.'

'Know anything about the Society of Olive Oil Producers, then?'

'Load of old belchers who meet in the basement and plot how they can straighten out the world?'

'They didn't seem to be plotting last evening, just stuffing their faces. Oh, and most were trying to ignore a group of genuine Baetican visitors.'

'That's them!' grinned Momus. 'They pretend to love anything Hispanic – but only if it can be served on a dish.' I gathered that the Society was officially deemed innocuous. As usual, Momus knew more about it than a slave overseer should. 'Anacrites got himself voted into the club so he could keep an eye on them.'

'Was political scheming likely?'

'Piddle! He just liked feeding at their well-filled manger.'

'Well, as anarchists they didn't look very adventurous.'

'Of course not,' scoffed Momus. 'I haven't noticed the world being straightened out, have you?'

There was not much else Momus could tell me about Anacrites or Valentinus – or at least nothing he was prepared to reveal. But with his knowledge of the unfree workforce he did know which usher had been running the dinner for the Society. While I was at the Palace I looked out this man and talked to him.

He was a lugubrious slave called Helva. Like most palace types he looked oriental in origin and gave the impression he misunderstood whatever was being said to him, probably on purpose. He had an official job, but was trying to improve himself by sucking up to men of status; the Baetican Society members obviously saw him as a soft touch to be sneered at and put upon.

'Helva, who did the organising for this exclusive club?'

'An informal committee.' Unhelpful: clearly he could see *my* status did not call for an ingratiating style.

'Who was on it?'

'Whoever bothered to turn up when I insisted someone tell me what was wanted.'

'Some names would help,' I suggested pleasantly.

'Oh, Laeta and his deputies, then Quinctius Attractus –'

'Is he an overweight senator who likes holding court?'

'He has interests in Baetica and he's the big mover in the Society.'

'Is he Spanish by origin?'

'Not the slightest. Old patrician family.'

'I should have known. I understood the Society's real links with Hispania are defunct and that members try to deter provincials from attending?'

'Most do. Attractus is more enlightened.'

'You mean, he sees the Society as his personal platform for glory and he likes to suggest he can work wonders in Rome for any visitors from Spain? Is that why he hogs a private room?'

'Well, unofficially. Other members annoy him by barging in.'

'They think he's someone to annoy, do they?'

It looked to me as if Attractus, and possibly his Baetican friends, had been under observation – probably by both Anacrites and his agent. Was Anacrites suspicious of something they were up to? Did Attractus or the Baetican group want to wipe him out as a result? It looked all too obvious if they were the attackers. They surely must realise questions would be asked. Or was Attractus so arrogant he thought the attacks could be got away with?

Needing to think about that, I went back to my original question. 'Who else organises events?'

'Anacrites –'

'*Anacrites?* He never struck me as a dinner party planner! What was his role?'

'Be reasonable, Falco! He's a spy. What do you think his role is? On rare occasions when he exerts himself, he causes upsets. He really enjoys carping about the guests other members bring. *"If you knew what I knew, you wouldn't mix with so-and-so ..."* All hints, of course; he never says why.'

'Master of the non-specific insult!'

'Then if ever I upset him he'll query the accounts for the previous party and accuse me of diddling them. The rest of the time he does nothing, or as little as possible.'

'Did he have anything special to say about yesterday?'

'No. Only that he wanted space for himself and his guest in the private room.'

'Why?'

'Usual reason: it was bound to offend Attractus.'

'And the spy's guest was Valentinus?'

'No, it was the senator's son,' said Helva. 'The one who just came back from Corduba.'

'*Aelianus?*' Helena's brother! Well, that explained how Aelianus had wheedled his way in – on the tunic tail of the Chief Spy. Unhealthy news.

'I know the family – I didn't realise Anacrites and Aelianus were on such good terms.'

'I don't suppose they are,' Helva remarked cynically. 'I expect one of them thought the other would do him some good – and if you know Anacrites you can bet which way the benefit was supposed to flow!'

It left an unanswered question. 'You knew who I meant when I mentioned Valentinus. Who brought him last night?'

'No one.' Helva gave me a narrow look. He was trying to work out how much I knew. All I had to do now was work out what dubious situation I was reckoned to know *about*, and I could press him hard. Until then I was likely to miss something important.

'Look, was Valentinus an official member of the Society?' Helva must have known I could check up; he reluctantly shook his head. 'So how much money did he slip you to let him in?'

'That's a disgusting suggestion; I'm a reputable state servant –'

I named the sum that I would have offered and Helva in his gloomy-faced way told me I was a mean bastard who gave bribery a bad name.

I decided to appeal to his better nature, if he had one. 'I don't suppose you've heard – Anacrites has been badly hurt.'

'Yes, I heard it's a big secret.'

Then I told him that Valentinus was actually dead. This time his face fell. All slaves can spot serious trouble. 'So this is bad, Helva. Time to cough, or it will be the Guards you have to talk to. Had Valentinus paid you to admit him to any previous dinners?'

'Once or twice. He knew how to behave himself. He could fit in. Besides, I had seen Anacrites wink at him so I assumed it was something I was supposed to allow.'

'How did he wangle himself a place in the private room?'

'Pure skill,' said Helva, frowning with admiration. 'He picked up one of the Baeticans as they arrived in the lobby and sauntered in chattering to him.' I knew the trick. A few minutes discussing the weather can admit you to many private parties. 'Quinctius Attractus was not officially supposed to reserve that room for himself. If there were free places anyone could take them.'

'So he didn't object to Valentinus?'

'He couldn't. Any more than he could complain about being landed with Anacrites. They took their couches among his party as if it were a coincidence, and he had to put up with it. Anyway, Attractus is not observant. He was probably so busy getting hot under the tunic about Anacrites, he never noticed Valentinus was there too.'

I wondered if the blinkered senator had noticed me.

I asked Helva about the entertainment. 'Who booked the musicians?'

'I did.'

'Is that routine? Do you pick the performers yourself?'

'Quite often. The members are only really interested in food and wine.'

'Is there always a Spanish dancer?'

'It seems appropriate. She's not really Spanish, incidentally.' Just like most 'Thracian' gladiators, 'Egyptian' fortune-tellers, and 'Syrian' flute players. Come to that, most of the 'Spanish hams' bought at food markets were previously seen skipping around pig farms in Latium.

'She? Is it always the same one?'

'She's not bad, Falco. The members feel reassured if they recognise the entertainment. They don't watch her much anyway; they only care about their food and drink.'

'Attractus was boasting he paid for her. Is that usual?'

'He always does. It's supposed to be a generous gesture – well, it shows he's rich, and of course he gets to have the dancing performed first wherever he's dining himself. The other members are happy to let him contribute, and his guests are impressed.'

He told me the girl's name was Perella. Half an hour later I was bracing myself to square up to the immaculate body that I had last seen in hunting gear.

I had a slight surprise. I was expecting to meet the dashing Diana with the blue-black hair who had elected to be so rude to me. To my surprise Perella, who was supposed to be the dancer who performed regularly at the Society of Olive Oil Producers of Baetica, was a short, stout, surly blonde.

XI

'Blonde' was putting it kindly. She had hair the texture of mule fodder and about the same shade. It looked as if she styled it once a month then just poked in more bone pins when ends worked loose. You could see why independent-minded pieces of the fantastic coiffure might want to make a break for freedom. The high-piled construction looked as if she was keeping three white mice and her dowry in it.

Lower down, the scenario improved somewhat. I won't say she was tasty, but her person was clean and tidy. As a chaste, ethereal moon goddess she would be a disaster, though as a companion in a wine bar she might be cracking good fun. She was of an age where you could rely on her having had a fair old amount of experience – in almost anything.

'Oh! Am I in the right place? I'm looking for Perella. Are you her friend?'

'I'm her!' So Perella was definitely the wrong dancer. She was putting out a smile that she meant to be winsome: wrong assumption, but I could cope with that. 'What might you be looking for, centurion?'

'Chaste conversation, sweetheart.' She knew better than to believe it. Her outlook on society was mature. 'The name's Falco.' It meant nothing to her, apparently. Well, sometimes it was best if my reputation had not gone before me. Critics can be uncouth. 'I expect you'd like my credentials. Do you know Thalia, the snake dancer at Nero's Circus?'

'Never heard of her.' So much for my guaranteed entrée to the world of Terpsichore.

'Well, if you knew her, she'd vouch for me.'

'As what?' asked the dancer, pointedly.

'As an honest man on an important quest with a few simple queries to put to you.'

'Such as?'

'Why wasn't a luscious piece like you dancing at the dinner for the Society of Baetican Oil Producers two nights ago?'

'Why do you ask?' leered Perella. 'Were you there hoping to watch me – or were they only letting in the rich, handsome ones?'

'I was there.'

'I always told them they had a slack door policy.'

'Don't be cruel! Anyway, you're a regular. What happened to you that night?'

Getting tough actually softened her up. 'Don't ask me,' she confided in a cheerful tone. 'The message just came that I was not wanted so I stayed in and put my feet up.'

'Who sent you the message?'

'Helva presumably.'

'No. Helva still thinks you did the act. He told me to ask you about it.'

Perella squared up, looking angry. 'Then somebody's messed me about!'

The thought crossed my mind that Helva himself might have decided to employ a higher-class dancer and that he had been scared of telling Perella – but then he would hardly have sent me along here to give him away. 'Who was it came to warn you off, Perella? Can you give a description?'

'No idea. I never took any notice of him.' I waited while she scanned her memory, a slow process apparently – though I did wonder if she was considering whether she wanted to tell me the truth. She looked older than a dancer should, with coarser skin and bonier limbs. Close to, these performers are never as refined as they appear when in costume. 'Dark fellow,' she said eventually. 'Had a few years on him.' Sounded like one of Diana's tame musicians.

'Seen him before?'

'Not to remember.'

866

'And what exactly did he say?'

'That Helva apologised, but the bloody Baetican trough-nuzzlers had decided not to have music.'

'Any reason?'

'None. I thought either the new Emperor had put his foot down about them using the rooms for enjoying themselves, or they had run out of money and couldn't find my fee.'

'They looked a well-packed lot.'

'Mean, though!' replied Perella, with feeling. 'Most of them spend the whole time moaning how much the dinners cost them; they wouldn't have entertainers at all. There's a swank who pays –'

'Quinctius Attractus?'

'That's him. He usually pays up, but it takes several tries to get it and there's never a sniff of a tip!'

'So he could decide to hire his own girl, if he wanted to?'

'The bastard could,' Perella agreed sourly.

'Would he bother to tell Helva?'

'No. He's a nob. He doesn't understand about organisation. He wouldn't think of it.'

'And would the girl be able to get in without Helva noticing that she wasn't you?'

'Helva's so short-sighted you have to get an inch from his nose before he can see who you are. Anyone who rattled a tambourine would sail straight in.'

So there had been a set-up. It came as no surprise that the so-called 'good girl from Hispalis' was not as good as she pretended. In my experience good girls never are.

Perella had nothing more to tell me. I was left with a loose end: unknown entertainers had deliberately muscled in and taken the usual dancer's place. They knew enough to use Helva's name in a convincing fake message. Knew it, or had been told what to say. Were they specifically booked by Attractus, or did he just accept that Helva had acquired them? And why? I would be asking the senator, but somehow I guessed in advance that tracing the lovely Diana and her two dark-skinned musicians would be next to impossible.

They could have been sent to the dinner by Anacrites. They could have been infiltrated by someone outside (a jealous would-be member of the dining club, perhaps?). Or they could have come of their own accord. They might have nothing at all to do with the attacks on Anacrites and Valentinus. Even though circumstances had made them look suspicious, they might simply be struggling performers who had failed to persuade Helva to give them an audition, and who then used their initiative.

But I told Perella she had been trounced by a very slick rival, and probably one who had had more than Spanish dancing in mind. Perella shoved a couple of new hairpins into her tumbling scarecrow coiffure, and gave me an unfathomable look. She threatened to 'sort' the girl from Hispalis. She sounded as if she meant it too. I left her my address in case she had any success.

'By the way, Perella, if you do meet this girl be careful how you tangle with her. It looks as if she was involved in a killing that night – and in a nasty attack on the Chief Spy.'

Perella went white. 'Anacrites?'

As she stood staring I added, 'You'd do best to avoid her. Finding this one is a job for an agent – and a good one at that.'

'And you reckon you're up to it, Falco?' Perella asked drily.

I gave her my best smile.

I was not yet ready for another conversation with Laeta, so I escaped from the Palace, ran some domestic errands, then went home to Helena for lunch. Fried anchovies in a plain wine sauce. Unassuming but tasty.

Helena told me I had received a message of my own that morning. It was from Petronius. He had found out something useful: I went straight out after eating, taking Helena with me for the exercise, and also Nux in the vain hope that while the scruffy hound was careering around in circles we might lose her somewhere. Petro was at home, off duty. Helena went off with his wife while Nux and I found my old crony in the yard at the back, doing woodwork.

'This is for you, Falco. I hope you're grateful.'

'What is it – a small coffin or a large brooch box?'

'Stop playing the fool. It's going to be a cradle.' Nux jumped in to try it. Petro turfed her out again.

'It's going to be a good one then,' I smiled. That was true. Petro enjoyed carpentry and was skilled at it. Always methodical and practical, he had a decent respect for wood. He was making a bed where eventually the sturdy unborn one who was already kicking me in the ribs every night would be safe; it had half-moon rockers, a knob to hang a rattle on, and a canopy over the pillow end. I felt touched.

'Yes, well; it's for the baby, so if your lousy behaviour makes Helena Justina leave you, this cradle will have to go with her.'

'I doubt it,' I scoffed. 'If she flits she'll leave the baby behind.' Petronius looked horrified, so I carried on appalling him: 'Helena only likes children when they are old enough to hold adult conversations. The bargain is, she'll carry my offspring and give it birth but only on condition I'm there to defend her from the midwife and that afterwards I bring it up myself until it's old enough to pay its own tavern bills.'

Petronius gave me a piercing stare; then he laughed weakly. 'You maniac! I thought you were serious ...' He lost interest, which saved me having to disillusion him with the news that I meant what I said – and so did Helena. 'Listen, Falco, I've come up with some evidence for you: the Second must want to redeem their reputation after missing all that stuff in Valentinus' apartment. They went back to the crime scene this morning and did a hands and knees creep.'

I joined him in chuckling at the thought of his luckless colleagues enduring stones in the kneecap and backache. 'Anything turn up?'

'Could be. They want to know if we think this is relevant –'

Petronius Longus placed a small item on his sawing bench. I blew the road dust off it, then sighed quietly. This was relevant enough to identify the attackers: it was a small golden arrow, as neat as a toy but dangerously sharp. On its tip was a rusty stain that was probably blood. Remembering the small leg wounds carried by both Anacrites and Valentinus, I guessed that both victims had been surprised by being shot in the calf from behind. The toy arrow would sting enough to bother them, then when they stooped to investigate they were rushed, grabbed, and run hard against a nearby wall.

Helena Justina had come out behind us, unnoticed. 'Oh dear!' she exclaimed, ever one with the unwelcome insight. 'I suppose that belonged to your mysterious Spanish dancer. Don't tell me it's just been found in a compromising position at the scene of a crime?'

Gloomily we confirmed it.

'Ah, never mind, Marcus,' Helena then chivvied me kindly. 'Cheer up, my love! You ought to have lots of fun with this – it looks as though somebody is setting you up against a beautiful female spy!'

Naturally I retorted that I was not in the mood for clichés – though I have to admit my heart took an uneasy lurch.

XII

There was no chance of interviewing the girl from Hispalis. I didn't even know her name – or her alias. If she was sharp she would have left Rome. Smirking, Petronius Longus promised to place her description on his list of wanted suspects. He offered to subject her to a personal interrogation. I knew what that meant.

I told him not to exert himself; I would probe her secrets myself. Petronius, who believed that men with pregnant wives were bound to be looking for extra-domestic exercise, twinkled wisely and promised to inform me the minute the beauteous Diana came his way. At this point Helena said coldly that she would take herself home.

I went to see Quinctius Attractus.

When a case involves a senator, I always start at the top. I don't mean this was a step towards clearing up uncertainties. Not at all. Interviewing a member of Rome's revered patrician order was likely to introduce pure chaos of the kind that is believed by some philosophers to comprise the outermost limits of the eternally whirling universe: a vortex of limitless and fathomless darkness. In short, political ignorance, commercial deceit, and blatant lies.

Even provincials among you will deduce that M. Didius Falco, the intrepid informer, had posed questions to senators before.

You'll spot this too: I went to see Quinctius Attractus to get any whirling vortex straight out of the way.

Once I had managed to impress the doorkeeper with my rank – well, once I had slipped him half a denarius – I was allowed to step inside away from a sharp April wind that was darting through the city streets. Attractus lived in an imposing house, groaning with art torn from more ancient and more refined civilisations than our own. Egyptian turquoise and enamel vied for space with Thracian gold and Etruscan bronze. Pentellic marble crowded his corridors. Forests of plinths bore up porphyries and alabasters. Racks bowed beneath uncatalogued rows of vases and craters, against which lolled unmounted wall plaques and fabulous old armour which must have been plundered from many famous battlefields.

Quinctius Attractus condescended to come to his public rooms to meet me. I remembered the heavy build and weathered country countenance from two nights ago; today I was being given the full urban look – the statesman putting an invisible peg on his nose so he could follow the old Roman tradition and be nobly at home to the unwashed.

Our interview was hardly private. In every archway lurked a toga-twitcher just itching to dart out and pluck straight a pleat. They kept him perfect. His boot-thongs were aligned. His sparse curls gleamed, rigid with pomade. If a finger-ring slipped sideways a lithe slave nipped forwards to straighten it. Every time he walked three paces his purple-striped garments all had to be realigned on his wide shoulders and fat arms.

If I hated this parade when he first came to receive me, I felt utter frustration once he started to talk. It was all condescension and empty guff. He was the type who liked to lean back slightly, gazing above his companion's head, while intoning nonsense. He reminded me of a barrister who had just lost a case, coming out into the Forum knowing he will have to face a tricky interview. I said I had come to discuss the Oil Producers' dinner – and he seemed to be expecting it.

'The Society – oh, it's just a meeting place for friends –'

'Some of the friends met very nasty accidents afterwards, senator.'

'Really? Well, Anacrites will vouch for us all –'

'Afraid not, sir. Anacrites has been badly hurt.'

'That so?' One of his flapping footmen found it necessary

to rush up and straighten a thread of fringe on a heavily decorated tunic sleeve.

'He was attacked the night of the dinner. He may not survive.'

'I'm shocked.' Checking the fall of his toga, he looked as if he had just heard about a minor skirmish between locals in some remote area. Then he noticed me watching and his fleshy jowls set for a ritual senatorial platitude: 'Terrible. A sound man.'

I swallowed it whole, then tried to fix the slithery senator to a firm base: 'Were you aware that Anacrites was the Chief Spy?'

'Oh certainly. Bound to. You can't have a man like that attending private functions unless everybody knows what his position is. Men would wonder. Men wouldn't know when it was safe to speak freely. Be a shambles.'

'Oh? Does the Society of Baetican Olive Oil Producers often discuss sensitive issues, then?' He stared at my effrontery. I hadn't finished yet: 'You're telling me the Chief of Intelligence was openly invited to join your group, in order to suborn him? I'm willing to bet you allowed Anacrites membership without the indignity of subscription fees!' A nice life, for a spy who was gregarious.

'How formal is this?' Attractus demanded suddenly. I knew the type. He had assumed that his rank gave him immunity from questioning. Now I was being nasty, and he couldn't believe it was happening. 'You say you're from the Palace – do you have some kind of docket?'

'I don't need one. My commission is from the highest quarters. Responsible people will co-operate.'

Just as suddenly he changed attitude again: 'Ask away then!' he boomed – still not seriously expecting I would dare.

'Thank you.' I controlled my temper. 'Senator, at the last assembly of the Society for the Olive Oil Producers of Baetica you dined in a private room with a mixed group, including several Baeticans. I need to identify your visitors, sir.' Our eyes met. 'For elimination purposes.'

The old lie proved sufficient, as it usually does. 'Business acquaintances,' he guffed with an offhand air. 'See my secretary if you must have names.'

'Thanks. I have the names; we were introduced,' I reminded him. 'I need to know more about them.'

'I can vouch for them.' More vouching! I was used to the fine notion that the slightest trade connection made for complete blood-brotherhood. I knew how much faith to place in it too.

'They were your guests that evening. Was there any special reason for entertaining those particular men that particular night?'

'Routine hospitality. It is appropriate,' mouthed Quinctius sarcastically, 'that when senior men from Baetica visit Rome they should be made welcome.'

'You have strong personal connections with that province?'

'I own land there. I have a wide range of interests, in fact. My son has just been appointed quaestor to the province too.'

'That's a fine honour, sir. You must be proud of him.' I didn't mean the compliment, and he didn't bother acknowledging it. 'So you take the lead in encouraging local business interests in Rome? You're a *proxenos*.' The handy Greek term might impress some people, but not Attractus. I was referring to the useful arrangements all overseas traders make to have their interests represented on foreign soil by some local with influence – a local who, in the good old Greek tradition, expects them to grease his palm.

'I do what I can.' I wondered what form *that* took. I also wondered what the Baeticans were expected to provide in return. Simple gifts like the rich produce of their country – or something more complex? Cash in hand, perhaps?

'That's commendable, sir. Going back to the dinner, Anacrites was also present. And a couple of others, including myself.'

'That may be so. There were spare couches. I had intended to take my son and a friend of his, but that kind of occasion can be too stiff for the young so they were excused.'

'One guest was Camillus Aelianus, the son of Vespasian's friend Verus.'

'Oh yes. Back from Corduba. Straightforward lad; knows what he's doing.' Quinctius was just the sort to approve of that pompous young bigot.

'Perhaps you remember one other man. I need to identify what he was doing there – reclining on the right-hand end couch, opposite Anacrites – quiet fellow; hardly spoke. Did you know him?'

'Never even noticed him.' Thirty years in politics made it impossible for me to tell whether Quinctius Attractus was honest. (After thirty years in politics, almost certainly he was not.) 'What's his significance?'

'Nothing any more: the man is dead.' If he had anything to do with killing Valentinus, he was good; he showed complete indifference. 'And finally, may I ask if you knew the entertainers, sir? There was a girl who danced, with a pair of Libyan-style accompanists – I believe you paid their fee. Did you know them personally?'

'Certainly not! I don't mingle with tarts and lyre-players.'

I smiled. 'I meant, did you book them for the dinner specially, sir?'

'No,' he said, still contemptuous. 'There are people to do that. I pay for the musicians; I don't need to know where they come from.'

'Or know their names?'

He growled. I thanked him for his patience. Still playing the big man in Baetica, he asked me to report any developments. I promised to keep him informed, though I had no intention of it. Then, since he had mentioned that I might, I went to see his secretary.

Correspondence and record-keeping at the house of Quinctius Attractus was conducted by a typical Greek scribe in a tunic almost as neat as his master's. In a clean little office, he catalogued the senator's life in curious detail. A cynic might wonder whether this implied that the senator feared he might one day be called to account. If so, he must be very worried indeed. Any tribunal investigating Quinctius was going to expire under the weight of written evidence.

'The name's Falco.' The scribe made no move to note me down but he looked as if he would later list me under *'Visitors: Uninvited, Category: Dubious'*. 'I'm enquiring about the senator's guests at the last dinner for the oily Baeticans?'

'You mean the Society of Olive Oil Producers?' he corrected humourlessly. 'I have details, certainly.'

'His honour says you will tell me.'

'I shall have to confirm that.'

'You do so then.'

I sat on a stool among racks of locked scroll boxes while the slave disappeared to check. Don't ask me how I know that the boxes were locked.

When he came back his manner was even more pedantic, as if he had been told I was trouble. He unlocked a silver box and removed a document. I was not allowed to crane over his shoulder, but I could see the script. It was a perfect, neutral cursive hand that could not have changed since he first learned to copy by rote.

He read out five names: *'Annaeus Maximus, Licinius Rufius, Rufius Constans, Norbanus, Cyzacus.'* Then he corrected himself: 'No; Rufius Constans was not at the dinner. He is the grandson of Licinius. He had gone to the theatre, I understand, with my master's son.' That almost sounded as if he were reciting something somebody had drummed into him.

'How old are these two lads?'

'Quinctius Quadratus is twenty-five. The Baetican boy looks younger.' Hardly adolescents then. The younger Quinctius would have just been elected to the Senate if he was to be a provincial quaestor as his father had boasted.

'Is the senator a stern father? Was he annoyed by them bunking off to a play?'

'Not at all. He encourages their friendship, and their independence. They are both promising young men.'

I grinned. 'That fine phrase can mean they are promising to cause trouble!' The secretary gazed at me coldly. He had never been trained to gossip. I felt like a slug spotted taking a stroll across a particularly elegant dish of dressed salad. 'The Baetican visitors make an interesting list. We have an Annaeus – presumably from the same Corduban family as the famous Senecas?' I had picked that up from Laeta at the dinner. 'And who else? A couple of men from the provincial merchant class? What can you tell me?'

'I cannot give personal information!' he cried.

'I don't need to know who slept with a flute girl or the state of their impetigo! Why were they welcome guests of a Roman senator?'

Looking distasteful the slave squeezed out: 'My master is a very important figure in Baetica. The first of those I mentioned, Annaeus and Licinius, are large landholders in Corduba.' Those would be the favoured pair who had been dining either side of Attractus at the dinner. 'The last two are businessmen from further south, involved with transportation, I believe.'

'Norbanus and Cyzacus?' The two who kept their heads down, conversing among themselves. Lower-class – perhaps even ex-slaves. 'They are shippers?'

'So I understand,' agreed the secretary, as if I was making him swear an oath to undertake physical torments and huge financial expense on behalf of an extremely bad-tempered god.

'Thank you,' I answered heavily.

'Is that all?'

'I need to interview these men. Are they staying here?'

'No.'

'Can you give me the address of their lodging in Rome?'

'They *were* staying here,' admitted the cautious Greek reluctantly. 'All of them left Rome very early today.'

I raised an eyebrow gently. 'Really? How long had they been with you?'

'Just a few days.' The secretary made an effort not to look uncomfortable.

'How many is a few?'

'About a week.'

'*Only a week?* Isn't their decision rather sudden?'

'I could not say.' I would have to ask the house steward if I wanted precise details of the Baeticans' original booking – but private informers are not given access to the domestic staff in a senator's house.

'Is it possible to interview the senator's son?'

'Quinctius Quadratus left for Corduba as well.'

'Was that planned?'

'Of course. He is taking up his new provincial post.'

I could not fault the newly fledged quaestor – but how many provincials, especially men of status, would make a long sea trip to Rome then skip for home almost immediately, without fully enjoying the sights, exploring the possibilities for social advancement, and making sure they stayed away long enough to make those at home believe they had conquered Roman society?

As tourists their behaviour was highly suspicious. They might as well have left behind a wall plaque telling me these gadfly Corduban businessmen were up to no good.

XIII

That night I took Helena to the refined Capena Gate district to dine at the large, slightly faded villa which had been her family home. It was time her mother had another chance to rage at her about the poor arrangements we were making for the baby's birth and upbringing. (Julia Justa had a well-rehearsed script on this subject.) And I wanted to see her father. I like to keep my senators in sets.

As usual, before my official meeting I made sure that Helena's papa and I had conspired so our stories would match. I found Decimus Camillus Verus at the baths we both frequented. He was a tall, stooping figure with thinning, spiked hair, who already looked hunted even before I invited myself to dinner and explained that I now required him to play the heavy father to one of his rebellious sons.

'This is imperial business. I need to interview Aelianus. I'm telling you in advance so you can make sure he'll be there!'

'You overestimate my paternal authority, Marcus.'

'You're a Stoic!' I grinned and explained the situation. Then I gave Camillus a stiff bout of swordplay to make him feel even more despondent, and we parted friends.

His attitude to me, whom many in his place would have loathed, was open and amiable: 'I have no objection to you providing me with grandchildren, Marcus. A new generation is my one hope of getting someone on my side!'

'Oh *I'm* with you, senator!' In fact we both knew his relationship with me (like mine with his daughter) was the main reason the illustrious Camillus had a hard time at home.

Neither of the young Camillus brothers, Aelianus and

Justinus, were at dinner. They were bright fellows in their early twenties brought up to have moderate habits – so naturally they were out on the town. As a sober citizen of thirty-three, approaching the grave honour of Roman fatherhood, I tried not to look as if I wished I were out there with them.

'Is Justinus still keen on the theatre?' Their youngest rascal had taken up leering after actresses.

'They both like to keep me worried!' Camillus senior reported drily. He kept his troubles close to his chest. 'Aelianus has promised to return in an hour.' Immediately I noticed his wife working out that he and I must have discussed this subject previously.

'At least he knows *where* his home is!' Julia Justa had a tart version of Helena's sarcasm. She was a handsome, hard-done-by woman, like her daughter, with fierce intelligence and liquid brown eyes. Maybe Helena would end up like this. Helena herself stabbed at her bowl of shrimp dumplings, looking morose. She knew what was coming.

Her mother took a deep breath, in a way that was familiar to me. I had a mother too. The views of these two women from distinctly different backgrounds were tragically similar, especially in regard to me. 'You look as if you are about to rush away with acute diarrhoea, Marcus Didius,' smiled the noble Julia through thin lips. She understood men. Well, she was married to one, and had produced two more.

'I wouldn't dream of insulting the wonderful banquet before us!' It was a workaday spread, in fact, for the Camilli were struggling against the dire financial troubles that afflict hereditary millionaires. Still, flattery seemed wise.

'Someone has to ensure that my daughter is fed.' A certain kind of woman always goes for the self-righteous in insults.

'Cobnuts!' Helena contributed. It was perhaps injudicious to use a phrase she had clearly picked up from me. 'With donkey bells on them!' she added – an embellishment of her own.

'I don't believe I know that expression, Helena.'

'The nuts are mine,' I admitted. 'I take no credit for the bells.' To Helena I said, 'If word's going around that I starve you, I'll have to buy you a pork rissole on the way home and insist that you eat it in public.'

'Cobnuts again. You never let me do anything scandalous.'

'Please be serious!' her mother retorted. After a day hard at work, I felt too tired to respond politely and Julia Justa seemed to sense my weakness. On first hearing the news of our forthcoming child her reaction had been muted, but since then she had had six months to brood. Tonight she had opted for the full lecture. 'I simply feel there are things we all ought to face up to, since it does look as if Helena will be carrying her child to term. This time,' she added unnecessarily, as if to have had one miscarriage was somehow Helena's fault. 'I had hoped to see you married before this, Helena.'

'We *are* married,' said Helena stubbornly.

'Be sensible.'

'Marriage is an agreement between two people to live together. Marcus and I have clasped hands and agreed.'

'It's plain you have done more than that –' Julia Justa tried appealing to me, pretending she thought I was more reasonable: 'Marcus, help me out!'

'It is true,' I mused, 'that if I went before the Censor and was asked "*To the best of your knowledge and belief, and by your own intention, Didius Falco, are you living in a valid state of marriage?*" I should bravely answer "*Yes, sir!*" '

The senator smiled and engaged in a bit of private commentary. 'I love that "*to the best of your knowledge and belief*"!' His own wife received this very coolly, as if she suspected some hidden jibe.

'Formalities are not required,' growled Helena. 'We don't need an augury because we know we are going to be happy –' It sounded more of a threat than a promise. 'And we don't need a written contract to tell us how our affairs will be unwound if we part, because we won't ever

881

separate.' Actually we didn't need a contract because there was nothing financial to unwind. Helena possessed money but I refused to touch it. I had none, which saved a lot of fuss. 'Just be grateful we are sparing Papa the expense of a ceremony and the burden of a dowry. Times will be hard if he is to put both of my brothers into the Senate –'

'I doubt that will occur,' her mother replied bitterly. She decided not to specify why, though it was obviously our fault: bringing the family into disrepute.

'Let's be friends,' I said quietly. 'I'll do my best to acquire greater status, and when I'm a suave equestrian counting beans on my farm in Latium and fiddling my taxes like respectable people do, we'll all wonder what the fuss was about.'

Helena's father was keeping quiet. He knew his daughter was not the problem nowadays. It was his sons he needed to watch. Without extremely careful treatment Justinus was likely to end up entangled with an actress (specifically illegal for the son of a senator) while my current enquiries were beginning to suggest that Aelianus was involved in an intrigue that could be both dangerous and politically disastrous. He had told his father nothing about it – a bad omen in itself.

Luckily at that point a slave brought a message that Aelianus had come home. His father and I were able to escape to the study to interview him. By the rules of convention Helena Justina would remain with her mama.

Well, she would do until she lost her temper. That might happen fairly soon. I overheard her mother asking, 'How are your bowels, Helena?' I winced, and fled after her papa. He had already skipped out of it. For a senator, he was a wise man.

XIV

Three of us were seated together, like an intellectual symposium. Lack of space in the small, scroll-filled room made civilised reclining impossible. Letters, accounts and intriguing works of literature were piled all around us in teetering stacks. If challenged about his untidiness (as he regularly was by his wife) Decimus Camillus Verus would say that he knew exactly where everything was. One of his likeable characteristics: in truth he could have had no idea.

The senator and I were both upright on his reading couch. Aelianus had squeezed on to a stool which his father's secretary occupied in the daytime. While he fiddled with a pot of pens, a bust of Vespasian stared down from a shelf above him, as if our eminent Emperor were checking that the young man's neck was clean.

This son and his father looked fairly alike. They had matching strong eyebrows, though the boy was more thickset. He was also surly where his father was mild-mannered. It was a phase of youth – unfortunately a phase which could lose him the chance of making useful friends. There was no point telling him that. Being critical of his social skills was the certain way to rush him into making life's fatal mistakes.

'I don't have to talk to you, Falco!'

'It's advisable,' his father chastised him briefly.

I kept my voice quiet. 'You can talk to me informally here – or you can be sent for a full grilling on the Palatine.'

'Is that a threat?'

'Senators' sons don't get beaten up by the Praetorian Guard.' I made it sound as if they could be, when someone with my clout requested it.

Aelianus glared. Maybe he thought that if he had been anybody else's son I would have taken him to a wine bar

883

and enjoyed a much more easygoing chat without involving his family. Maybe he was right.

'What's this about?' he demanded.

'One man dead and another close to Hades. A strong Baetican connection, and an unhealthy whiff of conspiracy. Your presence at the last Olive Oil Producers' dinner in close company with one of the victims now needs accounting for.'

He went pale. 'If I have to explain myself I want to see someone more senior.'

'Of course,' I agreed. 'I'll just point out that asking for special treatment makes you sound like a man in trouble. People with nothing to hide give their evidence to the regular official.'

'And that's you?' He was being careful now.

'It's me. Orders from the top.'

'You're trying to implicate me in something.' Dear gods, he was truculent. And I hadn't even started yet.

'Actually I want to clear you.'

'Just answer the questions,' his father instructed patiently.

Hoping for filial obedience, I tried greater formality: 'Camillus Aelianus, how did you come to know Anacrites, and why did he take you to that dinner as his guest?'

'Why don't you ask him?' Useless. Well, I was somebody's son. I should have known the odds on obtaining filial obedience were short.

'Anacrites has been attacked – and by thugs who killed one of his agents the same night. He's been taken to a place of safety, but he's likely to die. I need to find out very quickly what is going on.' I remembered how long it had been since I dumped the spy on my mother. It was time to make dutiful enquiries – or to relieve her of the corpse.

The senator leaned towards me anxiously. 'Are you saying *Aulus* may have been in danger that night?' Aulus must be his elder son's personal name. One which the young chap was unlikely to invite me to use.

Unless Aelianus had been dabbling in something far

bigger than I gave him credit for, I could not believe professional killers would bother with him. 'Don't worry, senator. Presumably your son is an innocent bystander.' I thought the bystanding innocent looked leery, in fact. 'Aelianus, did you realise your dinner host was the Emperor's Chief Spy?'

The young man seemed chastened. 'I understood something of the sort.'

'What was your connection with him?'

'Nothing really.'

'Then how did you come to meet him?'

He did not want to tell me, but admitted, 'I had been sent to him with a letter when I returned from Corduba.'

His father looked surprised. Forestalling his interruption, I asked, 'Who wrote the letter?'

'It's confidential, Falco.'

'Not any more!' his father snapped briskly. He wanted to know about this as much as I did. Though he appeared so easygoing, Camillus had old-fashioned views on a father's rights. The fact that none of his children agreed with him was just a father's usual hard luck.

'It was from the quaestor,' Aelianus replied irritably.

'Quinctius Quadratus?'

He looked surprised at my knowledge. 'No, his outgoing predecessor. Cornelius had just heard that his father is sending him on a trip to Greece before he has to come back to Rome. Since I *was* coming back, he gave the thing to me.'

We were talking about the young finance officer in charge of collecting taxes for Rome. 'A provincial quaestor would normally correspond with the Chief Secretary, Claudius Laeta.' His letters would travel via the *cursus publicus*, the imperial post service. It was quick, secure, and reliable. 'So why send something to Anacrites, and why entrust it to you? You were friendly with this Cornelius?'

'Yes.'

'If he wanted it entrusted to safe hands, was this letter very sensitive?'

'Presumably. Don't ask me what was in it,' Aelianus continued triumphantly, 'because it was heavily sealed and I had strict instructions to deliver it unopened straight to the Palatine.' Very convenient.

'Were you present when Anacrites read it?'

'He asked me to wait in another office.'

'And then what was his reaction?'

'He came in and invited me to the Baetican dinner as if to thank me for its safe delivery.'

I changed the subject: 'If you knew the outgoing quaestor, do you know Quinctius Quadratus too?'

'What's that got to do with anything?'

'He had been meant to attend the dinner as well. His father had booked him a place – but he went to the theatre instead.'

'I leave the theatre to my brother!' Aelianus sneered self-righteously.

'Do you know Quadratus?' I repeated.

'Slightly,' he then admitted. 'He was in Corduba last autumn – preparing himself to bid for the Baetican quaestorship I imagine, though he never came clean at the time. I had a disagreement with him about some work his people did on my father's estate. Now we don't particularly get on.'

'And besides, you had cornered yourself an invitation from a mighty official? Being noticed by Anacrites would be something to brag about!'

Aelianus gave me a nasty look. 'Have you finished, Falco?'

'No,' I snapped back. 'We need to discuss your time in Corduba. Your father sent you out there to gain experience, and you were working informally in the proconsul's office –'

'I was never privy to policy meetings,' Aelianus took pleasure in telling me.

'No. It would be an unusual office if the governor's young staff actually noticed what was going on.' While he was here, and under parental supervision, I determined to

886

pick his brains. 'There were some top Baeticans dining with Quinctius Attractus at the dinner. I presume you knew most of them?'

'Provincials?' Aelianus sounded hurt at being associated with foreigners.

'Given that men of Hispanic origin fill a third of the Senate that you yourself are trying to join, snobbery is short-sighted. I assume you know who they were! I'm interested in this group: Annaeus Maximus, Licinius Rufius, someone called Norbanus and another called Cyzacus.'

'Annaeus and Rufius are leading citizens of Corduba.'

'Big in olive oil production?'

'Annaeus has the largest estate. Licinius isn't far behind.'

'Is there rivalry between the landowners?' his father put in.

'Only mild jostling.' This was better. When he co-operated, Aelianus was a useful witness. The best kind: he liked showing off. He lacked the dry wit of other members of his family, but had grown up with their analytical attitude. He was, moreover, a great deal more intelligent than he wanted to allow himself to be. 'The producers all compete to obtain the highest yield and quality, and to demand the best prices, but in general there is a good community spirit. Their main obsessions are getting rich, then demonstrating their wealth by way of luxurious houses, benefactions in the community, and holding local magistracies and priesthoods. Long-term, they all want to buy positions in Rome if possible. They take pride in anyone from Corduba being successful, because that increases the status of all.'

'Thanks,' I said, rather surprised at his sudden fluency.

'What about the other two names Falco mentioned?' enquired the senator, who was taking a keen interest.

'Cyzacus is from Hispalis. He runs a fleet of barges; upriver at Corduba the Baetis is too narrow for big vessels, so bargees take the amphorae downstream. I knew him by sight, but that's all.'

'Not a producer himself?'

'No, he just collects. And Norbanus is a negotiator.'

'Negotiating what?' I asked.

Aelianus gave me a pitying look. 'Negotiating anything, but mostly space on the ocean-going ships that pick up the amphorae of oil once they are assembled at Hispalis. He's a Gaul.' The young man was dismissive.

'So everybody hates him!'

'Well, even provincials need someone else to despise, Marcus.' The senator joked, while his son merely looked superior.

'I'm getting a picture of a happy flock of middlemen,' I commented. 'The estate owners produce the oil, then the bargemen take it downstream to an entrepôt – that's Hispalis – after which negotiators find it space in ships to take it abroad. So producers, bargemen, negotiators, and ship-owners are all expecting their cut. This is before any retailers in the Emporium and the Roman markets get their sticky fingers on the amphorae. If all these chancers are creaming off profits, no wonder we pay nice prices.'

'It's no worse than any other commodity.' Camillus Verus was a fair man.

'Except that oil carries the highest premium. It's a commodity everybody needs, from the Emperor down.' I turned back to Aelianus. 'So what is your evaluation of the commercial situation?'

He shrugged. 'Olive oil is increasingly important. Production in Baetica is rising steeply. It's rapidly overtaking the traditional sources in Greece or Italy. That's partly because from Spain it's easy to send it north to meet the huge demand in Gaul, Britain and Germany, as well as dispatching it direct to Rome. It's fine quality for emollient usages – and the taste is reckoned to be special too. The producers in Baetica are lucky men. There are fortunes to be made.'

'A star product.' I looked him in the eye. 'And what's the scope for funny business?'

888

'I don't know what you mean, Falco.'

'Price-fixing, for example,' I specified crisply. Once I started considering how many amphorae of olive oil were being shipped around the Empire, I realised that millions of sesterces were involved. 'Cornering the market and withholding supplies – The usual pretty tricks of commerce are what I mean!'

'I wouldn't know.' Now he had shown us that his time in the governor's office had at least taught him to give a sensible briefing, I reckoned he was being disingenuous.

I had no more to ask. His father let Aelianus go. The young man said he was off out again; Decimus told him to stay indoors, though he did not make too much of giving the order, in case Aelianus disobeyed.

Just as he reached the doorway I called out, 'One more thing!' He made the mistake of stopping. 'You carried the mysterious letter to Anacrites with you. How did you travel to Rome? By sea or land?'

'By sea.'

'That's a week's journey?' He nodded, and I gave him a pleasant grin. 'So tell me, *Aulus* –' He finally noticed I was not being friendly. 'What exactly did you read in the letter when your curiosity broke and you picked the seal?'

To his credit, Aulus Camillus Aelianus managed not to blush. He knew when he was rumbled. He sighed, thought about it, then slowly admitted the truth: 'It was a reply to a request from Anacrites to the proconsul for a report on the stability of the oil market. The quaestor had assessed the situation, and answered on the lines of what I told you earlier: that olive oil is going to be very big business.' Aelianus braced himself then added honestly, 'He also confirmed what you suggested, Falco – that there might be some scheming locally in Corduba. A possible cartel to rig and control the price of oil. He felt it was at an early stage, and could be contained.'

'Did he name names?'

'No,' said the noble Aelianus, rather quietly. 'But he said

889

that the proconsul had asked him to mention that enquiries had not been welcome. He felt the situation could become dangerous for everyone involved.'

XV

Without speaking, the senator and I walked slowly through the house in search of our womenfolk. It was dusk, on one of the first fine nights of the year. Passing through a folding door that gave access to the garden we dabbled our fingers in a hiccuppy fountain then joined Julia Justa who was reclining under a portico, eating grapes. She regarded us in silence. She could certainly pluck fruit from its stem in a telling manner: she was a woman with burdens, and we two men were contributors to her grief.

The senator had learned how to live with reproach; he surveyed the roses on his sagging trelliswork, apparently oblivious. I stayed on my feet, close to a pillar, with my arms folded. On the other side of the colonnade, which was dimly lit by oil lamps, I could see Helena Justina. She had separated from her mother for some reason (one I could guess) and was picking dead leaves from a huge urn of neglected agapanthus. I watched, waiting for her to look across and notice me.

Lately she had become withdrawn, lost even to me in the concerns of her pregnancy. She moved carefully now, with her back slightly arched for balance. She spent a lot of time being busy on her own, engaged in tasks I never really knew about. We were still close; I had, for instance, been favoured with full details of all the physical problems which her mother kept mentioning. I had myself scoured apothecaries for cures, and had my head bitten off for bringing them home.

Helena still told me her private thoughts. I knew she wanted the baby to be a girl (and I knew why). I also knew that if one more person asked if she was hoping for a boy, she was likely to knock them down and jump on their heads. She was heartily sick of being nagged. And the main

891

reason she was starting to lose her temper was that she was afraid. I had promised to stay near and share everything with her, but she reckoned when it came to it I would find an excuse to escape. Everyone we knew believed I would let her down.

The senator sighed, still in contemplation of our conversation with his son. 'Marcus, I would be happier if neither you nor Aelianus were in contact with the palace spy network.'

'So would I,' I agreed sombrely. 'Anacrites has given me plenty of aggravation. But he has given me work too – and I need that. Don't worry. Anacrites is in no condition to trouble Aelianus again. Even if he makes a miraculous recovery I reckon I can handle him.' The gods knew, I had had enough practice. The senator must have heard details of my long enmity with the Chief Spy – and we both thought it was Anacrites who had intervened with the Emperor's son Domitian to ensure I was refused promotion socially. That had been a personal blow to the Camilli. They wanted me to make equestrian rank, in order to protect Helena's good name.

'In general, Marcus, how do you see the Chief Spy's role?'

'Interesting question. On a descending curve, I should say. Anacrites is devious, but he's not as efficient as he ought to be and he works with a historical disadvantage: his team has always been small, and his line of command is through the Praetorian Guard. So his theoretical task, like that of the Praetorians, is limited to acting as the Emperor's bodyguard.' Of course that now included providing protection for Vespasian's two sons, Titus and Domitian.

'I think the whole show is due for a shake-out,' the senator said.

'Be disbanded?'

'Maybe not. Both Vespasian and Titus hate the idea of being emperors who openly pay for trumped-up evidence to destroy their political enemies. Vespasian won't change,

892

but Titus might want a tougher organisation – and Titus is already commander of the Praetorians.'

'Are you telling me you know something, sir?'

'No, but I can sense a mood among the palace staff that there will soon be scope for men who offer to help Titus achieve his ends. He's a dasher; he wants everything yesterday –'

I knew what that meant. 'By the quickest means – legal or not! That's bad news. We don't want to go back to the old state-employed informers. The network that was so notorious under Tiberius and Nero – little more than torturers in basement prison cells.'

Decimus was mulling this over gloomily. He was an old crony of Vespasian, and a shrewd judge of a situation. His advice mattered. 'Marcus, it's your world. If there is a power struggle, I suppose you may want to involve yourself –'

'I'd prefer to run fast the other way!' I was thinking about the implications. 'Rivalries already exist,' I confirmed, thinking of the open antagonism between Anacrites and Laeta that I had witnessed at the dinner. 'Anacrites has been tussling with just the kind of clever bureaucrat who might suggest to Titus that he should develop a new agency, one with a fuller remit, which could answer directly to Titus himself – In any case, Anacrites is seriously wounded. If he dies there will be a scuffle among people who want his old job.'

'Who's the bureaucrat?'

'Laeta.'

The senator, who naturally knew the correspondence chief, shuddered distastefully.

I felt I was myself already being used as a patball between Laeta and Anacrites. This was the kind of situation where the general good – for instance the smooth running of the Spanish olive oil trade – could be overturned in the pursuit of some disastrous administrators' feud. And it was a situation where Rome could, yet again, end up in the grip of sinister forces who ruled by torture and infamy.

*

893

It was at this point that Julia Justa, who had been sitting with us in silence as a respectable matron ought to when her male relatives debate world issues, decided she would exert her rights. She waved to Helena, signalling her to come over and join us.

'I would prefer to keep Aelianus right out of this,' her father carried on. 'I'm beginning to be sorry I ever sent him out to Spain. He seemed a bit raw; the governor was a friend; it looked like an ideal opportunity. My son could see administration working, and I had bought a new estate on the River Baetis which needed organising.' Helena Justina had condescended to notice her mother waving and was coming around the portico. Decimus continued, 'Of course he's inexperienced –' I had realised what was coming. 'I could still use a friend to look at the estate.' Sensing that I preferred her not to overhear, Helena sped up and reached us. By that time her father was unstoppable: 'The oil problem in that quaestor's letter sounds like something a man like you could clear up in a matter of weeks if you were out there on the spot, Marcus!'

Julia Justa fastidiously removed a grape pip from her elegant lip. Her voice was dry. 'Well, it's not as if he's needed here. Having babies is women's work!'

I didn't stop to look at Helena's expression: 'Baetica is off-limits. I promised Helena I would be here when the child is born. It's more than a promise; it's what I want.'

'I'm only surprised you don't suggest taking her with you!' her mother sniffed.

This was unfair when I had already taken the decent line. Helena Justina's smile was dangerously quiet. 'Oh, taking me away to Baetica is out of the question!' she said.

That was when I knew for sure that Baetica was where I would be when I let Helena down.

XVI

'I kept him alive,' snarled my mother. 'You never said I was expected to make him sensible as well. If I know men, he never was.' She glanced at Helena, whose eyes gleamed warmly in agreement.

Apparently Anacrites was now lurching in and out of consciousness. He could yet lurch the wrong way and die. Once I would have been glad. Now the bastard had made me feel responsible. Meanwhile, whenever he opened his eyes, Ma pulled his mouth open too and spooned in chicken broth.

'Does he know where he is?'

'Not even *who* he is. He doesn't know anything.'

'Has he spoken?'

'Just mumbles like a hopeless drunk.'

There could be a reason for that. 'Are you giving him your brothers' wine?'

'Only a dribble.' No wonder he wasn't lucid. Uncles Fabius and Junius, who shared a farm when they were not trying to tear each other's throats out, produced a harsh red Campagnan rot-gut with a kick that blew the wax out of your ears. A goatskin or two was enough to lay out a whole cohort of hard-living Praetorians.

'If he can survive that, you must have saved him!'

'I never know what you've got against your uncles,' grumbled Ma.

I loathed their awful wine, for one thing. I also thought the pair of them were illogical, moody clowns.

Helena and I inspected the invalid. Anacrites looked unpleasantly pale, and already much thinner. I could not tell whether this was one of his conscious phases or not. His eyes were nearly closed, but not quite. He made no attempt to speak or move. Calling his name caused no reaction.

'Ma, I've found out more about what's been going on and I've decided it's too dangerous keeping him. He's part of the Praetorian Guard; I reckon they can be trusted to look after one of their own. I've spoken to a centurion I know, and Anacrites is going to be taken into the safety of the Praetorian Camp. A man called Frontinus will turn up and whisk him away secretly. Then don't mention to anybody that you had him here.'

'Oh I see!' complained Ma, highly affronted. 'Now I'm not good enough!'

'You're wonderful,' Helena soothed her. 'But if his attackers find out where he is, you're not strong enough to fend them off.' Actually, if I knew my mother she would have a damned good try.

Helena and I sat with Anacrites for a while, so Ma could have a rest. My mother's idea of having a rest was to gather five shopping baskets and rush out to the market, pausing only to shower Helena with rude comments on her appearance and dark advice on managing her pregnancy. I watched Helena bite her tongue. Ma scuttled off. If she met any of her witchy cronies, which was quite likely, she would be away for hours. This made a mockery of us coming to visit her, but was typical in my family. At least it prevented quarrels. I knew we had just narrowly avoided yet another one.

Anacrites, Helena and I now had the apartment to ourselves. Without Ma whirling to and fro it felt unnaturally quiet. She had stashed the invalid in a bed that had belonged at various times to my elder brother and me. Sometimes when we were boys we had shared it, so this had been the scene of much lewd talk and a multitude of ludicrous plans – plans that were now doomed to be forever unfulfilled. I left home, and ended up as an informer. My brother was dead. Before he was killed in Judaea Festus had dossed here on trips home from the army. The gods only know what scenes of surreptitious debauchery our little room had seen then.

It seemed odd to be here with Helena. Odder still that the familiar old bed, with its rickety pine frame and twisted webbing, now possessed a brown chequered cover that I did not recognise and a spanking new pillow. Before long my eyes were sending messages that had Anacrites not been inconveniently in possession I would have grabbed Helena and renewed my own acquaintance with the bed ...

'Don't push your luck,' murmured Helena, with what I hoped was shared regret.

Since there was no hope of persuading Anacrites to contribute usefully, the choice of conversation was ours. It was the morning after our dinner at the Camillus house. I had reported the latest facts to Helena, but we were still chewing over the story.

'Someone's been stupid,' I said. 'There may be a commercial conspiracy in Corduba. Presumably Anacrites and his man were attacked in a feeble attempt to deter investigation. The way that group of Baeticans left Rome immediately afterwards certainly makes it look as if they knew something about it. But our officials are aware of whatever's going on; Claudius Laeta can take whatever steps he thinks necessary from this end. He's made himself acting Chief Spy, apparently. It's his decision. I'm certainly not going out there.'

'I see,' replied my beloved, ever queen of the unexpected. 'There is nothing to discuss then.' Her brown eyes were thoughtful; that tended to precede trouble. 'Marcus, you do realise that you may have had a lucky escape the night of the dinner and the attacks?'

'How would that be?' I made an attempt to act the innocent.

'You're known as an imperial agent, and you had been talking to Anacrites. I expect you also found a reason to meet the beautiful dancing girl –' I pished. Helena carried on regardless. 'And you spoke to Valentinus. You were probably seen doing that, then when you both left the dinner at the same time, it must have looked like more than coincidence. But unlike Anacrites and Valentinus you didn't leave the Palatine alone. You came home to Fountain Court with two palace slaves, carrying your *garum* jar. Perhaps if it hadn't been for them you would have been set upon too.'

'I had thought of that,' I admitted. 'I didn't want to worry you.'

'I *was* worried.'

'Well, don't brood on it. This must be the first recorded incidence of a man having his life saved by an amphora of fish-pickle.'

Helena was not laughing. 'Marcus, you're involved whether you want to be or not.'

We were silent for a while. Anacrites seemed to be fading right before my eyes. I felt a surge of anger again. 'I'd like to get whoever murdered Valentinus.'

'Of course you would, Marcus.'

'Fellow feeling.'

'I know.'

Helena Justina always spoke her mind and let me know exactly where I stood. If there was any chance of an argument she set about it briskly. Sounding meek was worrying. It meant she might be planning some big surprise.

'Helena, I'm not going to let these killers get away with it. If they are still in Rome —'

'They won't be,' said Helena.

She was right. I had to swallow it. 'Then I'll be wasting my time as usual.'

'Laeta will ask you to be the man who goes to Baetica.'

'Laeta can go red in the face and burst a blood vessel.'

'Laeta will make the Emperor or Titus order it.'

'They'll be ordering trouble then.'

She gazed at me sombrely. 'I think you ought to be prepared to go to Spain.'

Helena's offer seemed out of the question — and yet straight away I began to wonder if it might be feasible.

We believed we had nearly two months before the baby would be born. I did a rapid calculation: a week lost on the journey out, plus several days to travel inland to Corduba. Ten more days for returning home. In between, another week should be ample to identify and assess the personnel involved and tackle a solution ... Oh yes. Easy to go, do the job, and come home just in time to put down my luggage on the doormat and receive the newborn baby into my arms from a smiling midwife who had just finished tidying its proud and happy mama ...

A fool could convince himself that it would work, provided nothing went wrong. But I knew better. Travelling always takes longer than you hope. And things always go wrong.

It was far too tight. And what if the baby came early anyway? Apart from outfacing the oil cartel conspirators – something which hardly interested me, though that was what would make the state provide my fare – where in this ludicrous timetable was there any allowance for tracing Diana and her murderous musicians?

'Helena, thanks for the offer, but be sensible. Just because everyone else assumes I'm planning to bunk off and abandon you doesn't mean they are right!'

'I'm coming with you,' she told me. I knew that tone of voice. This was no mere suggestion. Being bossed and bullied by relatives was irritating her too much. Helena had decided to abscond from Rome.

It was at that moment that Anacrites opened his eyes and stared at me vaguely. By the looks of him his body was giving up and his black soul was on the ferryboat to Hades. His mind was just about still here, however.

I told him bitterly, 'I've just been informed I have to sail to Baetica on this dead-end job of yours!'

'Falco ...' he croaked. What a compliment. He might not have known who *he* was, but he recognised me. I still refused to spoon-feed the bastard with broth. 'Dangerous woman!' he moaned. Maybe it was apropos of nothing, though it sounded like fair comment on my chosen partner in life.

He faded out again. Well, enigmas are what you expect from spies.

Helena Justina ignored him. 'Don't mention to your mother that we're going,' she instructed me.

'And don't you tell yours either!' I retorted nervously.

PART TWO:
BAETICAN SPAIN – CORDUBA

AD73: mid April

The trader I consider to be an energetic
man, and one bent on making money; but
it is a dangerous career and one subject to
disaster. On the other hand it is from the
farming class that the bravest men and the
sturdiest soldiers come, their calling is
most highly respected, their livelihood is
most assured and is looked on with the
least hostility, and those who are engaged
in that pursuit are least likely to be
disaffected.

Cato the Elder

XVII

'You pay me by the mile,' said the carriage-hire man.

I didn't believe it. That would mean at the end of our hiring period I just had to lie to him about how far I had driven. He was an ex-legionary. How could he be so innocent?

'What's the catch?' I asked.

He grinned, appreciating that I had at least had the courtesy to query the system, instead of jumping in with intent to cheat. 'No catch.'

The hireman was a wide-shouldered former footslogger whose name was Stertius. I was unsure what to make of him; my mission was making me distrust everyone. This man owned a commercial transport business in the southern Baetican port of Malaca – mainly ox-wagons collecting amphorae of fish-pickle from all along the coast to bring them to port, but also gigs, carts and carriages for travellers. It would be an ideal cover if he engaged in espionage; he would see everyone who came and went. He had been in the Roman army; he could easily have been recruited by the legions to work for Anacrites; even Laeta could have coerced him somewhere along the line. Equally, local loyalty could put him firmly in league with the men I had come to investigate – or the dancing girl.

Helena sat down on our mound of baggage in the quiet, unobtrusive manner of a woman who was making a point. We had been sailing for a week, then landed in the wrong place so we now had a lengthy trip by road ahead of us. She was very tired. She was sitting in the hot sun. She did not need me dragging out what ought to have been a straightforward commercial transaction. She stroked Nux as if the dog were her only friend.

I still felt queasy from the ocean. It was possible to travel the entire way from Rome to Gades overland if you had the time to spare. Someone like Julius Caesar who wanted to show up well in his memoirs took pride in reaching Hispania without crossing water. Most people with interesting lives to lead preferred the quicker sea trip, and Helena and I were not in a good state for forced marches anyway. So I had agreed to take a boat. Getting this far was torture for anyone like me who could be seasick just looking at a sail. I had been groaning all the way, and my stomach was still not sure it had returned to land. 'I'm dazed. Explain your system.'

'You pay me what I freely admit is a hefty deposit.' Stertius had the typical sardonic air of an old soldier. He had retired from the army after decades in north Africa, then crossed the Straits to Spain to start his business. Up to a point I trusted him commercially, though I was beginning to fear he was the type who enjoys himself inflicting arcane mysteries on helpless customers. 'If you don't use up your allocation, I'll give you a rebate. If you overrun, of course, I'll have to charge you more.'

'I'm taking the equipage to Corduba.'

'As you wish. I'll be giving you Marmarides as your driver –'

'Is that optional?' I was facing enough unknowns. The last thing I wanted was to be saddled with someone else's employee.

'It's voluntary,' grinned the hireman. '– In the legionary sense!' It was compulsory. 'You'll get on with him fine. He's one of my freedmen. I've trained him well, he's a natural with horseflesh and he has a good temperament.' In my experience that meant he would be a maniacal driver who let the mules get the staggers and tried to knife his customers. 'Marmarides will bring the carriage home when you've finished. He'll tell you the mileage price at the end.'

'He'll just tell us? Excuse me!' Baetican commercial practice seemed to have its extraordinary side. 'I'm sure the amiable Marmarides has your absolute trust, but I like the right to query costs.'

I was not the first suspicious Roman to land in Malaca. Stertius had a well-worked-out routine for technical quibbles: he crooked one finger knowingly, then led me to the rear of the sturdy two-wheeled, two-mule carriage which I was attempting to lease. Its iron-bound wheels would bounce painfully on the track to Corduba, but the passenger compartment had a leather cover which would protect Helena from rough weather, including hot sun. Nux would enjoy trying to bite the wheels.

Stertius bent over one axle hub. 'I bet you've never seen one of these before,' he claimed proudly. 'Look, centurion: this commodious vehicle that I'm letting you have at negligible rates is fitted with an Archimedes hodometer!'

Dear gods, he was a mechanical enthusiast. A flywheel-and-twisted-rope man. The kind of helpful character who asks for a drink of water then insists on mending your well-tackle that has been out of use for three generations. He was almost certainly building himself a complete siege warfare catapulta in the garden of his house.

The wheel hub over which we were crouched in the dust had been fitted with a single-tooth gear. Every rotation of the carriage wheel caused this gear to engage with a flat disc set vertically at right angles above it, which was cut into numerous triangular teeth. Each wheel rotation moved the disc on by a notch, eventually operating a second gear which in turn moved on a second disc. That one, which was horizontal, had been drilled with small holes, upon each of which was balanced a smooth pebble. Every operation of the top disc moved up a new hole, allowing a pebble to drop through into a box below, which Stertius had secured with a fierce padlock.

'The top disc rotates one hole for every four hundred revolutions of the carriage wheel – which takes one Roman mile!'

'Amazing!' I managed to utter. 'What beautiful workmanship! Did you construct this yourself?'

'I do a bit of metalwork,' Stertius admitted shyly. 'I can't think why these are not fitted as standard on all hired vehicles.'

I could. 'Wherever did you get the idea, Stertius?'

'Road-building with the Third Augusta in bloody Numidia and Mauretania. We used something like it for measuring accurate positions for the mileposts.'

'Amazing!' I repeated feebly. 'Helena Justina, come and look at this; it's an Archimedes hodometer!'

I wondered how many more colourful eccentrics I was doomed to meet in Baetica.

'There's just one thing that has to be understood,' Stertius warned me as Helena dutifully dragged herself over to inspect his mileage measurer. 'You'll find Marmarides can turn his hand to most things, but he won't deliver babies!'

'That's all right,' Helena assured him, as if we were a couple who had plans for all contingencies. 'Didius Falco is a Roman of the traditional, hardy type. He can plough his fields with his left hand, while his right delivers twins. At the same time he can spout a finely phrased republican oration to a group of senatorial delegates, and invent an ode in praise of the simple country life.'

Stertius gave me an approving look. 'Handy, eh?'

'Oh, I do my best,' I answered, with traditional Roman modesty.

XVIII

It took nearly a week's driving to Corduba. Stertius had charged us a deposit based on a main journey of a hundred and twenty-five Roman miles. I reckon he was accurate. He must have checked it already with his miraculous hodometer. I guessed that crazy man had measured every road in Baetica, and he owned marked-up itineraries to prove it.

Nobody of status ever went the way we did. I had not planned it myself. Once we had chosen the sea trip there were further options available. One sailing route went north of Corsica then came south hugging the coast of Gaul and Tarraconensis; it was famous for shipwrecks. The alternative nipped between Corsica and Sardinia; provided we didn't run aground on either island and fall into bandits' eager hands it had appeared a better bet. It probably was for most people, though not those prone to emptying their stomach at the first ripple of a wave.

What most folk did then was to sail right past Malaca to Gades, and take a boat up the grand River Baetis. I had decided against that for excellent reasons: I wanted to disembark as soon as possible. I also planned to arrive in Corduba in an unexpected manner that would bamboozle my Baetican suspects. So I had pored over route-charts and picked out my landfall on the eastern coast at Carthago Nova, proposing then to drive along the Via Augusta, the main inland highway through southern Hispania. This formed the final link of the great Via Herculana; it was supposedly the immortal hero's route across Europe to the Gardens of the Hesperides, imbued with romantic associations as the pathway to the ends of the earth. Better than that, it would be a fast paved road with well-equipped mansios.

Another reason for my choice was Carthago Nova itself –

the centre of esparto grass production. My mother, to whom I owed a belated bribe for nursing Anacrites, had supplied me with a more than usually detailed list of presents to bring home, including baskets, mats and even sandals for her numerous grandchildren. A decent Roman lad respects his ma.

Mine would be unsurprised to discover that I had failed her. She would have to make do with a few jars of *garum* from Malaca, for the captain of our vessel had unexpectedly decided the winds were wrong for the landing he had previously promised.

'He's an idiot! I should have found out earlier —'

'How could you?' asked Helena. 'He would never have admitted *"Yes, your honour; I'm an idiot."*'

By the time I realised, he had sailed right past Carthago Nova and was halfway to Gades. He seemed pretty pleased with himself. I forced him to put in at Malaca. From here a road to Corduba did exist, though not a good one. It would be shorter than coming all the way west from Carthago, but the grim quality of the road would probably use up the extra time. Time was just what I could not afford.

Once in the carriage we started well enough, but the level plain with a few dry, pointy little hills quickly gave way to barren grey slopes speckled with sparse vegetation and creased by dry watercourses. Soon we met a range of hills with almost vertical crags; although we traversed them without incident, I had some bad moments riding on top with Marmarides as we passed slowly through the landscape of deep ravines and precipitous rocks. Further inland, the unpopulated countryside changed again to gently rolling ground. We came to the first olive trees, their gnarled trunks rising from low sprigs of greenery, set out with good spaces between them in the stony soil. In the richer, redder ground that came later the olives were interspersed with blocks of fruit trees, grain, or vegetable fields.

Settlements, or even farms, were few. There were

mansios, of a meagre kind, where the innkeepers all looked astonished to have their bare little rooms inspected by a senator's daughter in an advanced state of pregnancy. Most expected Romans to be travelling with an entourage. Most Romans would indeed ensure they took a bustle of friends, freedmen and slaves. We found it easiest to pretend we had lost our escort temporarily.

There was no point trying to bluff Marmarides, of course. He knew we were without companions, and it afforded him much amusement. 'You come to Baetica for a nice summer holiday, lord?'

'That's right. I'm hoping for a sun-drenched spell in an esparto rope hammock. As soon as I can, I'll be stretched out under an olive tree with the dog at my feet and a jug of wine.'

Stertius must have picked him up in North Africa; he was as black as the Baetican olives. I tried to forget I was distrusting everyone I met and accept him as a welcome addition, though I wished he had been as broad as his master (Stertius was built like a bacon pig). Marmarides had a neat slim build, whereas I wanted a type who went into a fight smiling, and came out of it five minutes later having wrung the oppositions' necks.

Our driver's face creased into satirical wrinkles and he laughed at us breathily. 'Stertius reckons you're a government agent, and your lady's been sent abroad to have her baby in disgrace!'

'I see you're frank talkers in Baetica.'

'You want any help with your agenting?' he offered hopefully.

'Forget it. I'm just a loafer on holiday.'

Marmarides burst out laughing again. Well, I like a man who is happy in his work. That's more than I was.

Some of the mansio landlords seemed to believe we were carrying out a trick accommodation survey on behalf of the provincial quaestor. I let them think it, hoping to improve the quality of supper. Hoping in vain.

The landlords' fears derived from their resentment of

bureaucracy. Maybe this meant they thought the quaestor made an efficient job of checking their returns. I could not tell whether it implied that Roman financial management worked well here generally, or whether it was a specific comment on Cornelius, the young friend of Aelianus who had just left his post. Presumably Quinctius Quadratus, the new boy, had yet to make his mark.

'Helena, tell me about your father's estate.' I had seized the advantage of a smooth patch of road on one of the occasions when I was riding inside the carriage with her.

'It's quite small, just a farm he bought when he thought of sending Aelianus to Baetica.' Camillus senior owned the statutory million's worth of land in Italy which was his qualification for the Senate, but with two sons to equip for the high life he was trying to create a bigger investment portfolio. Like most wealthy men he aimed to distribute his spare holdings among the provinces in order to avoid suffering too much in times of drought or tribal revolt.

'Aelianus lived on the estate?'

'Yes, though I expect he enjoyed the high life in Corduba whenever possible. There's a villa rustica where he was supposed to spend his spare time quietly – if you believe that.' Helena had of course been brought up to respect her male relatives – a fine Roman tradition which all Roman women ignored. 'Aelianus found a tenant who now occupies part of the house, but there will be room for us. The farm is a little way inland of the river, in olive-growing country, though I'm afraid it's typical of my dear papa, that he bought through an agent who palmed him off with very few olive trees.'

'It's a dud?'

'Well, there are almonds and grain.' Nuts and feed were not going to turn the Camilli into tycoons.

I tried not to let any insult to her noble father's acumen show; Helena was deeply fond of him. 'Well, Spanish grain is the best in the Empire apart from African or Italian. And what else is wrong with this agricultural gem your father

910

acquired? He said you would tell me about some problems he wants me to look into.'

'Papa was being cheated over the olive oil pressing. That was why Aelianus took on a tenant. Using an overseer of our own wasn't working. This way Papa receives a fixed rent, while the man with the lease is responsible for whether he makes a profit or not.'

'I hope we're not having to share accommodation with one of your brother's friends!'

'No, no. The man had fallen on hard times somehow and needed a new farm. Aelianus decided he was honest. I don't suppose he knew him personally; can you imagine my brother sharing a drink with a farmer?'

'He may have had to lower his snooty standards in the provinces.'

Helena looked sceptical about that. 'Well, what I do know is that this man – whose name is Marius Optatus – volunteered to point out that Papa was being cheated in some way. It sounds as if Aelianus brushed his advice aside – but then had the sense to check, and found it was right. Remember my father had entrusted him with seeing that the estate was running properly. It was the first time Aelianus had such a responsibility, and whatever you think of him he did want to do well.'

'I'm still surprised he listened.'

'Maybe he surprised himself.'

An honest tenant sounded unlikely, but I wanted to believe it. If I could report back to Camillus Verus that his son had at least put in a good man to work the estate, that suited me. Whereas if the tenant proved a bad one, I had agreed to sort things out – one more claim on my hard-pressed time.

I'm no expert on big villa economy, though I had been partly brought up on a market garden so I should be able to spot gross bad practice. That was all Helena's father required. Absentee landlords don't expect to make vast profits from remote holdings. It is their estates on the

911

Italian mainland, which they can tour in person every year, that keep the rich in luxury.

Something was on Helena's mind. 'Marcus, do you trust what Aelianus told you?'

'About the farm?'

'No. About the letter he brought home.'

'It looked as though he was coming clean. When I told him what had happened to the Chief Spy and his agent your brother seemed to realise he was in deep trouble.' Back in Rome I had tried to find the letter, but Anacrites' papers were in too much disarray. Sight of it would have reassured me, and even if Aelianus had told me the truth I might have learned further details. Laeta had had his own staff search for it, without success. That could just mean Anacrites had devised a complicated filing system – though whenever I had visited his office his scheme seemed to consist of merely throwing scrolls all over the floor.

The road had become rough again. Helena said nothing while the carriage lurched over the uneven pavings. The northward cross-country road to Corduba was not exactly a marvel of engineering, precision-built by the legions in some mighty politician's name, and intended to last for millennia. The regional council must have charge of this one. Public slaves occasionally patched it up well enough to last through the current season. We seemed to be travelling when the work gang were overdue.

'Aelianus must also have realised,' I added when the carriage stopped jolting, 'the first thing I would do – whether I had to correspond from Rome or whether I came here myself – was to ask the proconsul's office for their side of the correspondence. In fact I'm hoping to discuss the whole business with the proconsul himself.'

'I had a go at him,' Helena said. She still meant Aelianus. I felt sorry for her brother. Helena Justina could have been a cracking investigator had it not been impossible for respectable women to converse freely with people outside their family, or to knock on strangers' doors with nosy requests. But I always felt a mild pang of resentment when

912

she took the initiative. She knew that, of course. 'Don't fret. I was careful. He's my brother; he wasn't surprised I cornered him.'

If he had told her anything worthwhile I would have heard about it before now. So I just grinned at her; Helena grabbed at the carriage frame as we were flung forward by a violent bounce. I braced my arm across in front of her for protection.

Just because Aelianus was her brother did not mean I intended to trust him.

Helena squeezed my hand. 'Justinus is going to keep prodding him.'

That cheered me up. I had shared time abroad with her younger brother. Justinus looked immature, but when he stopped mooning after unsuitable women he was shrewd and tenacious. I had great faith in his judgement too (except of women). In fact there was only one problem: if Justinus discovered anything, sending correspondence to Spain was highly unreliable. Helena and I would probably be home again before any letter could arrive. I was out here on my own. Not even Laeta would be able to contact me.

Changing the subject Helena Justina joked, 'I hope this won't be like our trip to the East. It's bad enough finding corpses face down in water cisterns; I don't care for the idea of plucking a preserved one from a vat of olive oil.'

'Messy!' I grinned.

'And slippery too.'

'Don't worry; it won't happen.'

'You were always over-confident!'

'I know what I'm talking about. It's the wrong time of year. Harvest starts in September with the green olives, and is over in January with the black. In April and May the presses stand still and everyone is chipping away at weeds with hoes, spreading manure made from last year's squelched olive pulp, and pruning. All we'll see will be pretty trees with jolly spring flowers hiding tiny fruit buds.'

'Oh, you've been reading up!' Helena scoffed. Her

913

teasing eyes were bright. 'Trust us to come at the wrong time of year.'

I laughed too – though it was exactly the right time for some things: in spring the labour-intensive work of tending the olive trees was at its least demanding. That could be when the olive-owners found the time to scheme and plot.

The closer we got to the great oil-producing estates south of the River Baetis, the more my unease grew.

XIX

There is a fine tradition that when landowners arrive
unexpectedly on their lush estates they find the floors
unswept for the past six months, the goats roaming free in
the vineyard eating the new young fruits, and grooms
asleep with unwashed women in the master's bed. Some
senators stop in the next village for a week, sending
messages of their imminent arrival so the cobwebs can be
sponged down, the floosies persuaded to go home to their
aunties, and the livestock rounded up. Others are less
polite. On the premise that having their names on a five per
cent mortgage from the Syrian lender in the Forum gives
them right of possession, they turn up at dinnertime
expecting hot baths, a full banquet and clean apartments
with the coverlets already folded down for their accompanying forty friends. They at least get to publish fine literary
letters full of satirical complaints about country life.

We had no one to send ahead as a messenger and we
were sick of inns, so we pressed on and turned up
unannounced, quite late in the day. Our appearance caused
no visible panic. The new tenant had passed the first test of
his efficiency. Marius Optatus didn't exactly welcome us
with fresh roses in blue glass bud vases, but he found us
seats in the garden and summoned a passable julep jug,
while he ordered curious servants to prepare our rooms.
Nux scampered off after them to choose a good bed to sleep
on.

'The name's Falco. You may have heard Aelianus railing
about me.'

'How do you do,' he answered, omitting to confirm
whether or not he had been told I was a reprobate.

I introduced Helena, then we all sat around being polite

and trying not to show that we were people with nothing in common who had been thrown together unavoidably.

Helena's father had bought himself a traditionally built Baetican farmhouse almost alongside the nearest road. It had mud-brick foundations below wooden panels; the arrangement was one long corridor with reception rooms at the front and more private accommodation behind them. The tenant lived in rooms along one side of the corridor, with views over the estate. The other rooms, which flanked a private garden, were supposed to be set aside for the Camilli if ever any of them visited. This part had been left unused. Either the tenant was scrupulous – or he had been warned to expect visitors.

'You're being extremely gracious!' I was cheering up now I had been told that the amenities included a small but functioning bath suite, slightly separate from the house. 'With young Aelianus barely off the premises you must have imagined you were safe from further inspection for at least twenty years.'

Optatus smiled. For a Spaniard he was tall, very thin, rather pale, with a foxy face and bright eyes. Among the Balearic mix of curly Iberians and even more shaggy Celts, all of whom were stocky and short, he stood out like a thistle spike in a cornfield. He looked a few years older than me, mature enough to run a workforce yet young enough to have some hopes in life. A man of few words. Silent men can be simply bad news at a party – or dangerous characters. Before we even fetched the baggage in I felt there was something about him I needed to investigate.

Supper was a simple affair of salt tuna and vegetables, shared with the house slaves and our driver Marmarides, in the old family tradition. We all ate in a long, low kitchen at the back of the house. There was local wine, which seemed good enough if you were tired, and if you added enough water to make the old woman who prepared meals and the lamp boy (who were staring fixedly) think you vaguely respectable. But afterwards Helena suggested I invite

Optatus to share a glass of a more refined Campanian I had brought with me. She declined the wine, but sat with us. Then while I, with my fine sense of masculine decorum, tried to keep the conversation neutral, Helena recovered from her weariness enough to start interviewing her father's tenant.

'My brother Aelianus says we had great good fortune in finding you to take on the estate.' Marius Optatus gave us one of his reserved smiles. 'He mentioned something about you having had some bad luck – I hope you don't mind me asking?' she added innocently.

Optatus had presumably met people of senatorial rank (not including Helena's brother, who was too juvenile to count), but he would rarely have dealt with the women. 'I had been rather ill,' he hedged reluctantly.

'Oh, that I didn't know! I'm so sorry – was that why you had to find a new estate? You were farming hereabouts before, weren't you?'

'Don't be grilled if you don't want to be,' I grinned, helping the man to a modest top-up of wine.

He saluted me with his cup and said nothing.

'I'm just making polite conversation, Marcus,' Helena protested mildly. Optatus wouldn't know she had never been the kind of girl who bothered with idle chat. 'I'm a long way from home, and in my condition I need to make friends as quickly as possible!'

'Are you intending to have the baby here?' Optatus asked, rather warily. He was probably wondering whether we had been dispatched abroad to have it in secret and hide our disgrace.

'Certainly not,' I retorted. 'There is a battery of antique nursemaids at the Camillus house all anxiously awaiting our return to Rome – not to mention the crabby but very cheap old witch who once delivered me, the highly exclusive midwife Helena's mother places her faith in, my younger sister, Helena's second cousin the Vestal Virgin, and phalanxes of interfering neighbours on all sides. It will cause a social scandal if we fail to use the birthing chair

917

which helped Helena's noble mama produce Helena and her brothers, and which has been purposely sent to Rome from the Camillus country estate –'

'But you'll gather most of Rome disapproves of us,' Helena quietly inserted into my satire.

'How true,' I said. 'But then I find myself increasingly disapproving of most of Rome ... Optatus, in case you're wondering, you should treat Helena Justina as the noble daughter of your illustrious landlord, though you may pray to the gods that I whisk her away before her lying-in. You can treat me how you like. I'm here on some urgent official business, and Helena was too spirited to be left behind.'

'Official business!' Optatus had found a sense of humour. 'You mean my new landlord Camillus Verus has not sent you out in a hurry to see whether his youthful son has unwisely signed a lease with me? I was intending to rush out at dawn to make sure the cabbage rows are straight.'

'Aelianus was satisfied you know how to farm,' said Helena.

I backed her up: 'He said you had informed him his father was being cheated.'

A shadow briefly crossed the tenant's face. 'Camillus Verus was losing a lot of the profits from his olive trees.'

'How was that?'

Optatus' face darkened even more. 'Several ways. The muleteers who take the skins of oil to the Baetis were stealing from him outright; they needed to be supervised. The bargemen on the river were also somehow miscounting when they stowed his amphorae – though they try to do that to everyone. Worst was the lie he was being told about how much oil his trees were yielding.'

'Who was lying?'

'The men who pressed his olives.'

'How can you be sure?'

'I knew them. They are from my ex-landlord's personal estate. Camillus Verus does not own his own press here. Millstones are very expensive and the number of trees does not justify it. Better if a neighbour contracts to do the work. My ex-landlord's family used to do it, on an amicable basis – but when your father bought his estate the good relationship was abandoned.'

I sucked my teeth. 'And how would Camillus, thousands of miles away in Rome, ever have known he was being misled? Even when he sent Aelianus, the boy would have been too inexperienced to realise.'

Optatus nodded. 'But I found out. My father and I had always lent workers to help our landlord at harvest, then his workers used to come to help us in turn. So my own people were present when the Camillus fruit was crushed. They told me of the fraud.'

'Does this have anything to do with why you lost your own farm?' Helena put in suddenly.

Marius Optatus placed his winecup on a stool, as if refusing to be lulled into any confidence by the drink – or by our offer of friendship either, if I was any judge. 'There were two reasons why I was asked to leave. Firstly, I was a tenant, as my family had been there for many years.'

'It was hard to lose?' Helena murmured.

'It was home.' He was terse. 'I lost my mother some years ago. Then my father died. That gave my landlord an excuse to alter our arrangement. He wanted the land back for himself. He declined to sign a new tenancy with me.' He was only just managing to remain calm. 'The second reason of course was my disloyalty.'

'When you told Aelianus that my father was being cheated?' That would not have made him popular with anyone. Optatus had chosen the outsider, not the local community. Fatal, wherever you live.

'People had been hoping to make money from Camillus.'

'Deceiving a foreigner is always a good game,' I said.

'And how did your ex-landlord manoeuvre you out?' Helena enquired.

'Unluckily that was when I fell ill. I had a fever on the brain. I should have died.' There was deep unhappiness behind this story. I rather thought the worst of it would never be told. 'There was a long period while I was too weak to do anything. Then I was ousted from my land on the pretext that it had been badly neglected; I was a bad tenant.'

'Harsh!'

'I had certainly not expected it. I stand by what I did – and had I not been ill, I would have argued the issue. But it's too late now.'

'Did nobody defend you?' Helena demanded indignantly.

'None of my neighbours wanted to become involved. In their eyes I had become a troublemaker.'

Helena was furious. 'Surely once you had recovered everyone could see you would run things properly again?'

'Everyone who *wanted* to know the truth,' I said. 'Not a landlord who was keen to end the tenancy. And besides, in that situation it's sometimes best to accept that goodwill has broken down.' Optatus agreed with me; I could see he wanted to end the discussion.

Helena was still too angry. 'No, it's monstrous! Even at this late stage you should take your landlord before the regional council and argue for reinstatement.'

'My ex-landlord,' Optatus replied slowly, 'is an extremely powerful man.'

'But disputes can be heard before the provincial governor.' With her deep hatred of injustice, Helena refused to give in.

'Or the quaestor if he is sent to the regional court as the proconsul's deputy,' Optatus added. His voice was tight. 'In Corduba that usually happens. The quaestor spares his proconsul the business of hearing pleas.'

Remembering that the new quaestor was to be Quinctius Quadratus, the son of the senator I had met and disliked in Rome, I was losing my confidence in the regional rule of law. 'The quaestor may be young, but he is a senator-elect,' I argued, nevertheless. Not that I had ever felt any awe for senators–elect. Still, I was a Roman abroad and I knew how to defend the system. 'When he stands in for his governor he ought to do the job properly.'

'Oh, I'm sure he would!' Optatus scoffed. 'Perhaps I should mention, however, that my previous landlord is called Quinctius Attractus. I should be making my petition to his son.'

Now even Helena Justina had to see his point.

XX

I wanted to know Optatus better before I discussed anything with political overtones, so I yawned heavily and we went to bed. He had described some lively local disputes and crookedness. Still, that happens everywhere. Big men stamp on little men. Honest brokers stir up their neighbours' antagonism. Incomers are resented and regarded as fair game. Urban life seems to be noisy and violent, but in the country it's worse. Poisonous feuds fester behind every bush.

Next day I persuaded Optatus to tour the estate with me. We set off to inspect the olive trees that all the fuss was about, while Nux gambolled wildly around us, convinced that our walk was for her sole benefit. She had only ever known the streets of Rome. She tore about with her eyes mere slits in the wind, barking at the clouds.

Optatus told me that along the Baetis, especially running west toward Hispalis, were holdings of all sizes – huge estates run by powerful and wealthy families, and also a variety of smaller farms which were either owned or leased. Some of the big holdings belonged to local tycoons, others to Roman investors. Camillus Verus, who was perennially short of cash, had bought himself a pretty modest one.

Though small, the place had potential. The low hills south of the Baetis were as productive in agriculture as the mountains to the north of the river were rich in copper and silver. Camillus had managed to obtain a good position, and it was already clear his new tenant was putting the farm to rights.

Optatus first showed me the huge silo where grain was stored underground on straw in conditions that would keep it usable for fifty years. 'The wheat is excellent, and the land will support other cereal crops.' We walked past a bed

922

of asparagus; I cut some spears with my knife. If my guide noticed that I knew how to select the best, how to burrow down into the dry earth before making my cut, and that I should leave a proportion for growing on, he made no comment. 'There are a few vines, though they need attention. We have damsons and nuts –'

'Almonds?'

'Yes. Then we have the olive trees – suffering badly.'

'What's wrong with them?' We stood under the close rows, running in an east–west direction to allow breezes to waft through. To me an olive grove was just an olive grove, unless it had a chorus of nymphs tripping about in windblown drapery.

'Too tall.' Some were twice as high as me; some more. 'In cultivation they will grow to forty feet, but who wants that? As a guide, they should be kept to the height of the tallest ox, to allow for picking the fruit.'

'I thought olives were shaken down by banging the trees with sticks? Then caught in nets?'

'Not good.' Optatus disagreed impatiently. 'Sticks can damage the tender branches that bear the fruit. Falling can bruise the olives. Hand-picking is best. It means visiting every tree several times in each harvest, to catch all the fruit when it is exactly ripe.'

'Green or black? Which do you favour for pressing?'

'Depends on the variety. Pausian gives the best oil, but only while the fruit is green. Regia gives best from the black.'

He showed me where he was himself stripping back the soil to expose the roots, then removing young suckers. Meanwhile the upper branches were being severely pruned to reduce the trees to a manageable height.

'Will this harsh treatment set them back?'

'Olives are tough, Falco. An uprooted tree will sprout again if the smallest shred of root remains in contact with the soil.'

'Is that how they can live so long?'

'Five hundred years, they say.'

'It's a long-term business. Hard for a tenant to start afresh,' I sympathised, watching him.

His manner did not alter – but it was pretty restrained to start with. 'The new cuttings I have planted this month in the nursery will not bear fruit for five years; it will take at least twenty for them to reach their best. Yes; the olive business is long-term.'

I wanted to ask him about his old landlord Attractus, but I was not sure how to tackle it. Last night, with supper and wine inside him, he had shown his feelings more freely, but this morning he had clammed up. I am the first to respect a man's privacy – except when I need to extract what he knows.

In fact he saved me the trouble of opening the discussion.

'You want me to tell you about the Quinctii!' he announced grimly.

'I'm not harassing you.'

'Oh no!' He was working himself up well. 'You want me to tell you how the father did me down, how I suffered, and how the son gloated!'

'Is that how it was?'

Optatus took a deep breath. My quiet attitude had relaxed him too. 'Of course not.'

'I didn't think so,' I remarked. 'If we had been talking about an obviously corrupt action you wouldn't have stood for it, and other people would have come out on your side. Whatever pressure the Quinctii applied to make you leave, you must have felt that technically, at least, they had the law on their side.'

'I'm not the man to judge what happened,' Marius Optatus said. 'I only know I was helpless. It was all achieved very subtly. I felt, and still feel, a deep sense of injustice – but I cannot prove any wrongdoing.'

'The Quinctii had definitely decided that they wanted you out?'

'They wanted to expand their own estate. The easiest way, and the cheapest, of course, was to kick me off the

924

land that my family had been improving for several generations and take it over themselves. It saved them buying more ground. It saved them clearing and planting. I couldn't complain. I was a tenant; if I gave them cause, ending the contract was their right.'

'But it was harsh, and it was done badly?'

'The father was in Rome. His son dealt with me. He doesn't know.' Optatus shrugged, still almost with disbelief. 'Young Quinctius Quadratus watched me leave with my bed, and my tools, and my saltbox – and he really did not understand what he had done to me.'

'You call him young,' I rasped. 'He has been given charge of all the financial affairs of this province. He's not a child.'

'He is twenty-five,' Optatus said tersely.

'Oh yes! In his year.' Quadratus had achieved the quaestorship at the earliest possible date. 'We're in circles where golden youths don't expect to hang about. They want their honours now – so they can go on to grab more!'

'He's a shooting star, Falco!'

'Maybe somebody somewhere has a sharp arrow and a long enough reach to bring him down.'

Optatus did not waste effort on such dreams. 'My family were tenants,' he repeated, 'but that had been our choice. We were people of standing. I was not destitute when I left the farm. In fact,' he added, becoming quite animated, 'it could have been worse. My grandfather and father had always understood what the situation was, so every last wooden hayfork that belonged to us was inventoried on a list. Every yoke, millstone and plough. Every basket for straining cheese. That gave me some satisfaction.'

'Did Quadratus try to haggle about what you could take with you?'

'He wanted to. I wanted him to try it –'

'That would be theft. It would have destroyed his public face.'

'Yes, Falco. He was too clever for that.'

'He is intelligent?'

925

'Of course.'

They always are, those golden boys who spend their lives destroying other people.

We strolled to the nursery where I inspected the tiny sprouts, each standing in a hollow to conserve moisture and with a windbreak made from an esparto sack for protection. Optatus was carrying out this task himself, though of course he had workers on the estate including slaves of his own. While we were there he puddled in his precious nurselings with water from a barrel, stroking their leaves and tutting over any that looked limp. Seeing him fuss, I gained some sense of his grief at losing the farm where he grew up. It did not improve my opinion of the Quinctius family.

I could tell he wanted to be rid of me. He had been polite, but I had had my ration. He walked me back to the house formally, as if ensuring I was off the scene.

We stopped on the way to look into some outbuildings, including one where olives that were stored for domestic consumption were kept in amphorae, packed in various preparations to preserve them through winter. While we were engrossed, disaster struck. We arrived at the small garden area in front of the main building just as Helena was trying to catch Nux. The dog rushed towards us ecstatically, with what appeared to be a twig in her mouth.

Optatus and I both immediately knew what it really was. I cursed. Optatus let out a wild cry. He seized a broom and began trying to smash it down on the dog. Helena squealed and stepped back. Loosing off a smothered protest, I managed to grab the culprit, picking up Nux by the scruff of her neck. We jumped out of reach of Optatus. With a hard tap on the nose I prised the trophy from Nux, who compounded her crime by scrabbling free again and leaping about yapping and pleading with me to throw the thing for her. No chance!

Optatus was white. His thin frame went rigid. He could hardly speak for anger — but he forced the words out:

'Falco! Your dog has torn up the cuttings in my nursery bed!'

Just my luck.

Helena captured Nux and carried her off to be scolded, well out of sight. I strode back to the churned-up plant nursery, with Optatus stalking at my heels. Nux had torn up only one tree, in fact, and knocked a few others over. 'I'm sorry; the dog likes chasing things, big things mainly. At home she's been known to frighten vintners delivering wine amphorae. She has simply never been trained to be loose on a farm ...'

Scuffing earth flat quickly with the side of my boot, I found the damage much less than it could have been. Nux had been digging, but most of the holes had missed the little trees. Without asking, I found where the rescued cutting belonged and replaced it myself. Optatus stood by in fury. Part of me expected him to snatch the twiglet from me; part knew he was shrinking from it as if the dog had contaminated his treasure.

I picked off the damaged leaves, checked the stem for bruising, redug the planting hole, found the support stake, and firmed in the little tree in the way my grandfather and great-uncle had taught me when I was a small boy. If Optatus was surprised that a street-pounding Roman knew how to do this, he showed nothing. His silence was as bleak as his expression. Still ignoring him, I walked quietly to the water barrel and fetched the jug I had seen him use earlier. Carefully I soaked the plant back into its old position.

'It's gone limp, but I think it's just sulking.' I arranged its sackcloth windbreak, then I stood up and looked straight at him. 'I apologise for the accident. Let's look on the bright side. Last night we were strangers. Now everything's changed. You can think me an inconsiderate, wantonly destructive townee. I can call you an oversensitive, agitated foreigner who is, moreover, cruel to dogs.' His chin came up, but I wasn't having it. 'So now we can stop sidestepping: I'll tell you the unpleasant political nature of the work

I'm really sent here to do. And you,' I said clearly, 'can give me a true assessment of what's wrong in the local community.'

He started to tell me which plot in Hades I could go and sink my roots in. 'Perhaps first of all,' I continued pleasantly, 'I should warn you that I came to Corduba to investigate two matters: one involves a scandal in the oil market – and the other is murder.'

XXI

I had managed to strike Optatus dumb, which was no mean feat. When normally silent types do decide they are bursting with indignant exclamations, they tend to be unstoppable. But on a quiet sunlit slope among the timeless dignity of olive trees, murder sounds a powerful word.

'Falco, what are you talking about?'

'One man dead, possibly two of them, in Rome. And it looks as if somebody from Baetica arranged it.' That night I had dinner at the Palace seemed a long way off, yet the thought of Anacrites lying pallid and still and almost a stranger to himself came clearly to mind. Even more vivid was Valentinus' corpse: that young man so like myself, lying in the dim light of the Second Cohort's engine house.

Marius Optatus looked disgusted. 'I know nothing of this.'

'No? Then do you know two big landowners called Licinius Rufius and Annaeus Maximus? When I was introduced to them they set themselves up as honest men of high renown – but they were in doubtful company that night, and after the attacks they behaved very oddly themselves. Then what about a *scapharius* called Cyzacus? Well, when was a bargee to be trusted? A *navicularius* called Norbanus? He's a Gaul, I believe, and a shipping negotiator into the bargain, so you don't have to pretend to like him. When I met them all these fellows were dining with someone you certainly do know – a certain Roman senator called Quinctius Attractus! In Rome he's regarded as a big bean in Baetica, though in Baetica you may prefer your legumes home-grown. He's regarded by *me* as a very suspicious character.'

'Attractus has for some time been inviting groups of

people to visit him in Rome,' Optatus agreed, blinking with amazement at my angry speech.

'Do *you* think he's up to no good?'

'After my experience of him as a landlord, I'm bound to think that – but I'm prejudiced, Falco.'

'I'll ask you something different then. You're a bachelor, I gather; I don't suppose you have any lithe girlfriends in Hispalis who might just have returned abruptly from a trip to Rome?'

Optatus looked po-faced. 'I know nobody from Hispalis.'

'You'd know this one again if you saw her; she's a dancer – just bursting with talent of one kind or another.'

'There must be thousands of girls who dance, but most of them have gone to Rome –'

'With their fee paid by Attractus? And a habit of leaving their props behind at the scenes of bloody crimes?'

I had been going too fast for a countryman. 'Who are you?' Optatus demanded in apparent bewilderment. 'What are these people from Baetica to you? What harm are you bringing them?'

'The harm has been done,' I retorted. 'I saw the corpse, and the dying man too. Now I'm looking for the killers, at the request of Titus Caesar – so if you're honest, Marius Optatus, you will help me with my task.'

The tall, pale figure beside me began to recover his equanimity. Crouching down on one knee he firmed in the disturbed cutting to his own satisfaction. There was nothing wrong with the way I had replanted it, but I stood unmoved while he left his own scent on the damned thing.

He stood up. He had become more serious than ever. Brushing soil from his long hands he stared at me. Enduring the fascinated gaze was routine work for an informer and I remained relaxed. I could stand hostile scrutiny. 'So what do you see?'

'You know what you are, Falco.'

'Do I?'

'You arrive like a naïve tourist.' Optatus had assumed a critical voice to which I was no stranger. He had stopped regarding me just as a rather raffish Roman in a patched tunic. He had realised he hated what I did. 'You seem inoffensive, a mere joker, a lightweight. Then people notice that you are a watcher. You have a stillness which is dangerous. You carry a sharp knife, hidden in your boot; you cut asparagus like a man who has used that knife for many unpleasant tasks.'

My knife had certainly hacked some bad meats, but he wouldn't want to know about that. 'I'm just a joker.'

'You tell jokes, while unknown to your listener you are measuring the quality of his conscience.'

I smiled at him. 'I am the Emperor's agent.'

'I have no desire to know of this, Falco.'

'Well, that's not the first time a prude told me my presence tainted his air.'

He stiffened, then accepted the rebuke: 'You will say that your work is necessary, I realise that.'

I clapped him gently on the shoulder, to reassure him if possible. He himself seemed like an innocent abroad. According to my famous worldly experience, that probably meant he was a devious swine, and setting me up.

We began walking towards the house again, along a dry track where even so early in the year the soil smelt hot and dusty. The red Baetican earth had already stained my boot-leather. It was pleasant weather. Just the kind of day when the men who were plotting the olive oil cartel were probably riding out on fine Spanish horses to each other's estates, refining their plans.

'Optatus, I mentioned some names. Tell me about them. I need to know how the men I saw in Rome relate to each other and to their fine friend Attractus.'

I watched him struggle with fastidious dislike of the topic. Some people are eager to gossip, but a few unusual souls do find discussing their neighbours distasteful. These are the ones who are best value to an informer. They are offended by offers of payment, and better still they tell the truth.

931

'Come on, Marius! You *must* know the Corduban oil tycoons. The Annaeii are one of the most prominent families in Corduba. Annaeus Maximus ought to carry top weight in Baetica. He's from the family of the Senecas; we're talking about extraordinary wealth.'

'This is true, Falco.'

'Since it's public knowledge, there is no need to be coy. So what about Licinius Rufius?'

'Not so grand a family.'

'Any senators?'

'No, but their time must come. Licinius himself is elderly but he has worked to become important in Corduba and he intends to build a dynasty. He is extremely ambitious for his two grandchildren, whom he brought up when their parents died. The young man should do well –'

'Local priesthoods and magistracies?'

'Rufius Constans is bound for Rome, Falco: it is a distinct and separate career.' I gathered Optatus slightly disapproved.

'Doesn't the one lead to the other?'

'That is not how it works. In the provinces you have to make a choice. Think of the Annaei whom you mentioned: the elder Seneca was a leading citizen and famous author and bibliographer, yet he remained socially obscure. Of his three sons, the first went straight into a senatorial career in Rome and achieved prominence, the next became an equestrian first, also in Rome, and only entered the Senate when he showed the promise that was to make him a major figure. The youngest son remained all his life in Corduba.'

'As the Annaei nowadays all choose to do?'

'There is no disgrace in provincial life, Falco.'

'Rome has its moments too,' I commented. 'So going back to the other man's grandson, Rufius Constans – This young man, a jewel of Baetican high society, is in his early twenties and to promote him his grandfather took him off to Rome recently?'

'I heard so.'

'He enjoys the theatre, I'm told!'

'Is that significant?'

'I didn't think so when I heard it – but he went with your new provincial quaestor. If the younger generation are so friendly, their elders may be nuzzling up to each other too.'

'People here tend to keep Roman landowners like Attractus at arm's length. He has hardly ever been here.'

'But they go to Rome at his invitation? Maybe he helps them with the fare. Then they arrive, eager to see the Golden City, flattered by the attention of a man with influence. Clearly he *does* have influence – he's the type who can get the Senate to vote a particular provincial post to his son.'

'You think his visitors become open to persuasion?'

'He may be offering just what they want: for instance patronage for the Rufius grandson – and did you say there's a girl in that family?'

'Claudia Rufina is expected to marry my ex-landlord's son.' Optatus never mentioned his dispossessor by name if he could avoid it. Nor the quaestorly son. 'I trust Licinius, Falco. For instance, I shall be sending the olives from this estate to his presses next autumn, so we don't get cheated elsewhere. Of the others you mentioned,' he went on crisply, trying to blot out mention of his own troubles, 'Norbanus is a shipping negotiator, as you said. He buys and sells space in the ocean-going craft that come upriver as far as Hispalis. I have met him, but I don't know him well. My family used someone else.'

'Any reason for not using him?'

For once Optatus smiled. 'Ours was a remote cousin.'

'Ah!'

'Norbanus, however, is the most well known. He is chief of the guild of negotiators at Hispalis. He also has his own office at Ostia, in the port of Rome.'

'He's well-to-do, then. And Cyzacus must be top man among the Baetis bargees?'

'You have heard of Cyzacus?'

'You mean, how do I know he's the tribal chief? I worked

it out. Attractus appears to go for the most prominent men. So how do they all get on together? Norbanus and Cyzacus seemed to be deep in gossip. Are the two estate owners close drinking cronies too?'

'Shippers and landowners exist in mutual contempt, Falco. Cyzacus and Norbanus would have been lucky to get anybody else to speak to them. They and the producers spend most of their lives trying to mislead each other about prices or complaining about late deliveries, or how the oil has been handled ... As for Annaeus and Licinius, they are in the same business as each other, so they are rivals in earnest.' That was good news. Wedges might be inserted here. This is how conspiracies are toppled by agents who know how. We find a cosy clique, which has internal rivalries, and we nimbly cause dissent. 'One difference is, the Annaeii came from Italian stock many years ago, the very first Roman settlers here. The Rufii are of pure Spanish origin and have ground to make up.'

'I see you have plenty of local snobberies!'

'Yes, people who have vital interests in common do love to despise one another for grand reasons.'

'Tell me, what makes the two olive growers hate each other? Is it purely commercial jostling?'

'Oh, I think so. There is no deadly quarrel,' Optatus told me rather wryly, as if he assumed I thought provincial towns were hotbeds of family feuds and intriguing sexual jealousy. Well, no doubt they had their fun, but making money took precedence. On the other hand, in my work, when people denied the existence of strong emotions, it was usually a prelude to finding corpses with knives in their backs.

We had reached the villa rustica. I could hear Nux barking, probably in protest because Helena had locked her up. I made my retreat before Optatus could remember his heartache over the torn-up tree.

XXII

Corduba sits on the north bank of the River Baetis, overlooking a fertile agricultural plain. Marmarides drove Helena and me there the next day. Where the navigable water petered out into spongy pools and channels we crossed a bridge, made of stone, which everyone claimed replaced one that Julius Caesar had built. Even in April the river was virtually fordable at this point.

Corduba has an old local history, but had been founded as a Roman city by Marcellus, the first Roman governor of Spain. Then both Caesar and Augustus had made it a colony for veteran soldiers, so Latin was the language everyone now spoke, and from that staged beginning must have come some of the social snobberies Optatus had described for me. There were people with all sorts of pedigrees.

Even while it was being colonised the district had a turbulent history. The Iberian landmass had been invaded by Rome three hundred years ago – yet it had taken us two hundred and fifty to make it convincingly ours. The numerous conflicting tribes created trouble enough, but Spain had also been the entry route for the Carthaginians. Later it made a fine feuding ground for rivals every time prominent men in Rome plunged us into civil war. Corduba had repeatedly featured in sieges. Still, unlike most large provincial centres I had visited, mainly on the frontiers of the Empire, there was no permanent military fort.

Baetica, which possessed the most natural resources, had yearned for peace – and the chance to exploit its riches – long before the wild interior. At home in the Forum of the Romans was a golden statue of Augustus set up by wealthy

Baeticans in gratitude for his bringing them a quiet life at last. How quiet it really was, I would have to test.

We passed a small guardhouse and crossed the bridge. Beyond lay stout town walls, a monumental gate and houses built in the distinctive local style of mud walls topped with wood; I discovered later the town had a prominent fire brigade to cope with the accidents that endanger timber buildings in close-packed urban centres where lamp oil is very cheap. They also boasted an amphitheatre, doing well according to a rash of advertising placards; various bloodthirsty-sounding gladiators were popular. Aqueducts brought water from the hills to the north.

Corduba had a mixed, cosmopolitan population, though as we forced a passage through the twisting streets to the civic centre we found the mixture was kept strictly separate – Roman and Hispanic areas were neatly divided by a wall running west to east. Notices carved on wall plaques emphasised the divide. I stood in the forum, labelled as Roman, and thought how odd this strict local schism would seem in Rome itself, where people of every class and background are thrust up against each other. The rich may try to keep apart in their mansions, but if they want to go anywhere – and to be anyone in Rome you must be a *public* man – they have to accept being buffeted by the garlic-eating hordes.

I had a good idea that in Corduba both the elegant Roman administrators and the aloof, inward-looking Baeticans would soon find themselves in a close pact on one subject: disapproval of me.

Like all decent tourists we had made our way first to the forum. It was in the northern sector. As soon as we enquired for directions I learned that the governor's palace was back down by the river; distracted by talking to Helena, I had let myself be driven past it. Helena and Marmarides, who were keen to see the sights, went off to explore. Helena had brought a town plan left behind by her brother. She would show me any decent landmarks later.

I was obliged to register my presence with the proconsul of Baetica. There were four judicial regions in this sun-drenched province – Corduba, Hispalis, Astigi and Gades. I knew therefore that there was only a one in four chance of finding the governor at home. Since the Fates regard showering me with disappointment as a good game of dice, I expected the worst. But when I presented myself at the proconsular palace, he was there. Things were looking up. That didn't mean I could get the mighty man to meet me.

I set myself a pleasant wager: seeing how soon I could wangle an official interview. I tried to make my approach subtle, since there was an obvious need for secrecy. A simple request fell flat. Producing a tablet with the dignified seal of Claudius Laeta, Chief of Correspondence to the Emperor, obtained mild interest among the flunkies, who must have written Laeta's name on a few thousand dreary communiqués. One neatly cropped fellow said he would see what he could do then ducked out into a corridor to discuss his last night's wine consumption with a friend. I put on the bleak expression auditors wear when tasked to eliminate excessive staff numbers. Two other relaxed lads put their heads together and worked out their order for lunch.

There was only one thing for it. Dirty tactics.

I leaned against a side table and whittled my nails with my knife. 'Don't hurry,' I smiled. 'It's not going to be easy informing the proconsul his great-grandfather has finally died. I wouldn't have minded the job, but I'm supposed to explain about the old blighter changing his will, and I just don't see how I can do that without mentioning a certain little Illyrian manicurist. If I'm not careful we'll be getting into the business of why his honour's wife didn't go to the country as instructed, and then the ding-dong with the charioteer will slip out. Jove knows they should have kept it quiet but of course her doctor talked, and who can blame him when you hear where the proconsul's spare epaulettes were sewn –' Both the flunkey in the corridor and his friend stuck their heads slowly round the door to join the others staring at me goggle-eyed. I beamed at them. 'Better not say any more, even though it is all over the Senate. But you heard it from me first! Remember that when the drinks are being got in ...'

I was lying of course. I never socialise with clerks.

The first young person dashed off, zipped back rather breathless, then shunted me into the presence. The proconsul was looking surprised, but he didn't know he had become a celebrity. His loyal scroll-pushers would be clustered outside the door, applying winecups to the lacquered panels in the hope of overhearing more. Since the personage in charge sat on his dais under some purple curtains at the far end of a room which seemed the length of a running stadium, our mundane discussion of trade issues would be out of earshot of the gossips with their ears on fire. There were still a few scribes and cup-bearers attending the mighty man, though; I wondered how to get rid of them.

The proconsul of Baetica was a typical Vespasian appointee: he looked like a pig-farmer. His tanned face and ugly legs would not have counted against him when he was chosen to sit here on an ivory seat between the dusty set of ceremonial rods and axes, below the rather tarnished and tired gold eagle. Instead Vespasian would have noted his illustrious career – bound to include commanding a legion and a stint in a consulship – and would also have marked the shrewdness behind the man's intent hooded eyes. Those eyes watched me approach down the lengthy audience chamber, while a brain as sharp as a Pict's hatchet was summing me up just as fast as I was evaluating him.

His was a post that needed a strong grip. It was only three years since two Hispanic provinces played their part in the legendary Year of the Four Emperors: Tarraconensis in backing Galba, then Lusitania in supporting Otto. Galba had actually stood for emperor while still a provincial governor, using the legions of his official command to uphold his claim. This caught on, as bad ideas do: Vespasian eventually used the same ploy from Judaea.

Afterwards he had to take firm action in Hispania. He reduced the Spanish legions from four to one – a fresh one – and even before I met this man I was sure the proconsul had been chosen for his allegiance to Vespasian and all that the new Flavian emperors stood for. (Those of you in the provinces may have heard that your new Roman governors are selected by a lottery. Well, that just shows how magically lotteries work. They always seem to pick out the men the Emperor wants.)

Hispania had lost its chance of glory when Galba slipped off the throne after only seven months and Otto barely lasted three; they were past history in Rome. But the rich estate- and mine-owners of Corduba had been among Galba's allies. Here there could still be dangerous tingles of resentment. Needless to say, outside the massive walls of the administrative palace, the town had appeared to be going about its business on this bright southern morning, as if setting up emperors carried no more world importance than a small scandal to do with amphitheatre ticket sales. Yet maybe among the olive groves ambitions still seethed.

'What's the news on the Palatine?' The proconsul was blunt. He had been working in informal dress – a bonus of life in the provinces – but seeing me in my toga he slid into his surreptitiously.

'I bring you cordial greetings from the Emperor, Titus Caesar, and the Chief of Correspondence.' I handed over a scroll from Laeta, introducing me.

He didn't bother to unseal it. He was not a man for etiquette. 'You work for Laeta?' He managed to restrain a humph. Secretariat employees would be rare visitors – and unwelcome ones.

'I was sent here by Laeta – well, he signed a docket for my fare. There's an interesting situation at home, sir. The Chief Spy has been nastily knocked on the head, and Laeta has assumed some of his responsibilities. I was chosen to come out because I have what we'll call diplomatic experience.' Calling myself an informer tended to explode ex-generals and ex-consuls into unsavoury bouts of flatulence.

The proconsul absorbed my story and sat up slightly. 'Why send you?'

'Expediency.'

'Good word, Falco. Covers a wealth of donkey dung.' I started to like the man.

'More like pulped olive manure,' I said.

He got rid of his staff.

Achieving an interview was one thing. In the lustrous halls of power I often ended up dissatisfied. Like eating a meal in a bad mansio in Gaul.

We quickly established that I had an official mission, for which the proconsul did not wish to be responsible. He had an official mission too. Since he represented the Senate and I represented the Emperor, our interests did not necessarily collide. It was his province; his role took precedence. That was preserving good relations with the local community.

I described the attacks on Anacrites and Valentinus. The proconsul looked politely regretful about the Chief Spy and merely dismissive of the fate of an unknown underling. He denied knowing any dancers from Hispalis too, and looked annoyed that I had asked. However, he did suggest that the local aediles in her home town might have the murderous Diana on their lists of licensed entertainers; to find out I would have to go to Hispalis.

He told me I could count on him for full support – although due to the Emperor's wish to reduce provincial expenditure, no resources could be allocated to assist me. That was not unexpected. Luckily I pay for my own boot-leather, and I could charge Laeta for necessary bribes.

I requested comments on the local personnel. The proconsul said I was the expert: he would leave judgements to me. I deduced that he was a frequent dinner guest in at least the more upper-class suspects' homes.

'Obviously the export of olive oil is a major trade which Rome intends to safeguard.' And obviously it was the proconsul's place to sum up. I was only the expert; I bit my tongue. 'If there *were* to be an attempt to influence prices unfavourably, Falco, we would have to stamp on it severely. The consequences for the home market, the army, and the provincial outlets would be appalling. However, I don't want to upset sensitivities here. You must do what you have to, but any complaints and you'll be bumped out of my province faster than you can breathe.'

'Thank you, sir.'

'Is that all?'

'Just a minor point, sir.' I usually manage to call them 'sir' a few times. The shrewd ones are never fooled. 'You had some correspondence with Anacrites recently, but it's lost in his coded filing library. I'd like permission to see the documents at your end.'

'Financial subject. My quaestor was the official point of contact.'

'That would be Cornelius? I gather it was time for him to move on – had he discussed the issue with you?'

'In general terms.' I gained the subtle impression this was only one of a myriad of topics on meeting agendas, and that the proconsul could not bring to mind the salient facts. But then he seemed to change his mind. 'Are you the agent Anacrites warned us he was sending?' That was a development I had not known about.

'No; Laeta took me on, after Anacrites was put out of action. Valentinus, the man who was killed in Rome, looks the likeliest person to have been sent by the Chief Spy. I assume no one else has turned up?'

'No one has made contact.'

'Then we can assume I'm doing the job now.'

The proconsul decided to be frank with me. 'Well, to clear your passage: Anacrites wrote to query whether the olive oil market was stable. I've been in the business long enough to assume that meant he suspected it was not; he would not have expressed an interest otherwise. I had Cornelius review the situation urgently.'

'He could be trusted?'

'Cornelius was reliable.' He seemed about to add something on that topic, but instead went on, 'There did appear to be restiveness, the kind of mood in the business community that is hard to define and harder still to tackle. I was unhappy, certainly. We sent a report. The response was that an agent would be coming out at once.' I wondered if the reason Anacrites had left the Palace after the dinner I attended was to meet Valentinus and order him to make a trip to Corduba.

'Thank you; that's clear, sir. From all I've heard, you'll be missing Cornelius. He sounds a useful deputy. And now you've had an unknown quantity wished on you, I hear – Will the new quaestor now be taking over the oil cartel issue, sir?'

I had kept my expression neutral, but I let the proconsul see me watching him. Since the new lad in charge of financial matters was the son of a man who appeared to be piping the tune for the oil producers, this could become delicate.

'My new officer is unfamiliar with the subject,' stated the proconsul. It sounded as if he was warning me not to alert young Quinctius. I felt reassured.

'I believe he's in Corduba already?'

'He came in and had a look around the office.' Something sounded peculiar. The proconsul looked me straight in the eye. 'He's not here at the moment. I gave him some hunting leave. Best to let them get it out of their system,' he told me drily, like a man who had had to train a long procession of administrative illiterates.

I thought his real meaning was different. The proconsul would have had little choice about his new officer. The appointment of Quinctius Quadratus would have been lobbied by his influential father and fixed up by the Senate. The Emperor had the right of veto but to use it would be a mark of disfavour, one which the Quinctius family had not openly deserved. 'I met his father in Rome,' I said.

'Then you will know Quinctius Quadratus comes to us

with fine recommendations.' There was not a flicker of irony.

'Certainly his father carries weight, sir.'

I was hardly expecting a proconsul to damn a fellow senator. It didn't happen either. 'Tipped for a consulship,' he commented gravely. 'Would probably have got it by now if there hadn't been a long queue for rewards.' After coming to power Vespasian had been obliged to offer honours to his own friends who had supported him; he had also two sons to be ritually made magistrates every few years. That meant men who had thought they were certainties for honours were now having to wait.

'If Attractus does get his consulship he'll be in line for a province afterwards,' I grinned. 'He could yet take over from you, sir!' The great man did not find it a joke. 'Meanwhile the son is expected to go far?'

'At least as far as hunting leave,' the proconsul agreed more jovially. I felt he quite enjoyed having kicked out the young Quinctius, even though it could only be temporary. 'Luckily, the office runs itself.'

I had seen offices that allegedly ran themselves. Usually that meant they were kept steady by one wizened Thracian slave who knew everything that had happened for the past fifty years. Fine – until the day he had his fatal heart attack.

Hunting leave is an ambiguous concept. Young officers in the provinces expect a certain amount of free time for slaying wild animals. This is normally granted as a reward for hard work. But it is also a well-known method for a pernickety governor to rid himself of a dud until such time as Rome sends out some other dewy-eyed hopeful – or until he himself is recalled.

'Where can we contact you?' asked the great man. He was already shedding his toga again.

'I'm staying on the Camillus Verus estate. I expect you remember his son Aelianus?' The proconsul signalled assent, while avoiding comment. 'The senator's daughter is here at present too.'

'With her husband?'

943

'Helena Justina is divorced – widowed too.' I could see him noting that he would have to meet her socially, so to avoid the agony I added, 'The noble Helena is expecting a child shortly.'

He gave me a sharp look; I made no response. Sometimes I tell them the situation and stare them out. Sometimes I say nothing and let someone else gossip.

I knew, since I had picked it open and read it, that my letter of introduction from Laeta – as yet unopened on the proconsul's side table – gave a succinct description of our relationship. He described the senator's daughter as a quiet, unassuming girl (a lie which diplomatically acknowledged that her papa was a friend of the Emperor). I won't say what he called me, but had I not been an informer it would have been libellous.

XXIII

The flock of scribes scattered like sparrows as I emerged. I winked. They blushed. I screwed out of them directions to the quaestor's office, noting that my request seemed to cause a slight atmosphere.

I was greeted by the inevitable ancient slave who organised documents in the quaestor's den. He was a black scribe from Hadrumetum. His will to subvert was as determined as that of the smoothest oriental secretary in Rome. He looked hostile when I asked to see the report Cornelius sent to Anacrites.

'You'll remember inscribing it.' I made it clear I understood how delicate the subject matter had been. 'There will have been a lot of fuss and redrafting; it was going to Rome, and also the material was sensitive locally.'

The inscrutable look on the African's face faded slightly. 'I can't release documents without asking the quaestor.'

'Well, I know Cornelius was the authority on this. I expect the new fellow has had a handover, but the governor told me he hasn't been granted his full authority yet.' The scribe said nothing. 'He came in to meet the proconsul, didn't he? How do you find him?' I risked.

'Very pleasant.'

'You're lucky then! A baby-faced brand-new senator, working abroad, and virtually unsupervised? You could easily get one who was arrogant and boorish —'

The slave still did not take the bait. 'You must ask the quaestor.'

'But he's not available, is he? The proconsul explained about your new policy in Baetica of screwing poll tax out of wild boars! His honour said if you had taken a copy of the letter you should show me that.'

'Oh, I took a copy! I always do.'

Relieved of responsibility by the proconsul's authority (invented by me, as he may well have guessed), the quaestor's scribe at once started to hunt for the right scroll.

'Tell me, what's the word locally on why Anacrites first took an interest?' The scribe paused in his search. 'He's the Chief Spy,' I acknowledged frankly. 'I work with him from time to time.' I did not reveal that he was now lying insensible in the Praetorian Camp. Or already ashes in a cinerary urn.

My dour companion accepted that he was talking to a fellow professional. 'Anacrites had had a tip from somebody in the province. He did not tell us who. It could have been malicious.'

'It was anonymous?' He inclined his head slightly. 'While you're finding the report Cornelius wrote I'd be grateful for sight of the original enquiry from Anacrites too.'

'I was getting it. They should be linked together ...' Now the scribe was sounding abstracted. He was already looking worried, and I felt apprehensive. I watched him once more search the round containers of scrolls. I believed he knew his way around the documents. And when he found that the correspondence was missing, his distress seemed genuine.

I was starting to worry. When documents go missing there can be three causes: simple inefficiency; security measures taken without a secretariat's knowledge; or theft. Inefficiency is rife, but rarer when the document is highly confidential. Security measures are never as good as anyone pretends; any secretary worth his position will tell you where the scroll is really stowed. Theft meant that somebody with access to officialdom knew that I was coming out here, knew why, and was removing evidence.

I could not believe it was the new quaestor. That seemed too obvious. 'When Quinctius Quadratus was here, did you leave him alone in the office?'

'He just looked around from the doorway then rushed off to be introduced to the governor.'

'Does anyone else have access?'

'There's a guard. When I go out I lock the door.' A determined thief could find a way in. It might not even take a professional; palaces are always rife with people who look as if they have the right of entry, whether they do or not.

When I calmed the scribe down I said quietly, 'The answers I want are known by your previous quaestor, Cornelius. Can I contact him? Has he left Baetica?'

'His term ended; he's going back to Rome – but first he's travelling. He's gone east on a tour. A benefactor offered him a chance to see the world before he settles down.'

'That could take some time! Well, if the junketer's unavailable, what can you remember from the scrolls that are lost?'

'The enquiry from Anacrites said hardly anything. The messenger who brought it probably talked to the proconsul and the quaestor.' He was a scribe. He disapproved. He liked things safely written down.

'Tell me about Cornelius.'

The scribe looked prim. 'The proconsul had every confidence in him.'

'Lots of hunting leave, eh?'

Now he looked puzzled. 'He was a hardworking young man.'

'Ah!'

'Cornelius was very worried,' the scribe continued doggedly. 'He discussed things with the proconsul, though not with me.'

'Was that usual?'

'It was all so sensitive.'

'He dictated the report to you though. What did it say?'

'Cornelius had concluded that people might want to inflate the price of olive oil.'

'More than general overcharging?'

'Much more.'

'Systematic fixing?'

947

'Yes.'

'Did he name names?'

'No.'

'Still, he thought that if action was taken quickly the cartel could be nipped in the bud?'

'Did he?' asked the scribe.

'It is a customary phrase. I was told that was his verdict.'

'People are always repeating wrong statements that are supposed to be in reports,' said the scribe, as if the very untidiness of the habit upset him. Something else was annoying me: Camillus Aelianus had apparently lied to me about this point.

'So Cornelius felt the situation was serious? Who was supposed to act on it?'

'Rome. Or Rome would order action by us – but they preferred to send their own investigator. Isn't that why you are here?'

I smiled – though the fact was, with Anacrites out of it and Laeta so untrustworthy, I had no idea.

XXIV

There was no hope of further help: today was a public holiday. Informers work loose hours and try to ignore such things, but everyone else in the Empire realised that this was eleven days before the Kalends of May – the big spring festival. The governor's palace had been working for a couple of hours, following the fine tradition of pretending that state business is too important to stop. But now even the palace was closing down, and I had to leave.

After walking uphill again, I found Marmarides in a tavern; I left him there. Helena was moping in the basilica entrance in the forum, looking at plans for a spanking new Temple of the Imperial Cult; she was clearly bored and it was time to remove her before she tried chalking faces on the Corinthian columns in the elegant design elevations. Ceremonies were about to start in any case.

I slipped my hand around hers and we walked slowly down the flight of steps among increasing crowds, Helena being careful to keep her balance. Reaching street level we dodged acolytes with incense-sprinklers as they gathered for a sacrifice.

'That looked a zippy new hexastyle portico they're going to build for the Imperial Cult!'

'When you start spouting architecture, I know you're in trouble,' she said.

'I'm not in trouble – but somebody soon will be.'

She gave me a sceptical look, then made some dry comment about the crisp modelling of the proposed temple's capitals. I said I wondered who would pay for this fine community monument. The citizens of Rome, perhaps, through exorbitantly priced olive oil.

I told Helena today's events as we found a space in the piazza, to view whatever was about to happen. Corduba is set on rising ground, the older part with a maze of narrow streets which come up from the river, its houses close set to keep out the hot sun. These byways lead uphill to the public buildings where we now were. Helena must have surveyed the small forum pretty well while she was waiting for me, but the festival pageantry revived her. 'So the proconsul has given you permission to operate in his territory. You're looking, without much hope, for a dancing girl who kills people –'

'Yes, but I imagine somebody hired her to do it.'

'For which your group of suspects are the Baeticans you saw at the dinner: Annaeus, Licinius, Cyzacus and Norbanus. Optatus told us Quinctius Attractus has been making overtures to other people too –'

'He would have to. Price-rigging only works if all the producers band together.'

'But the ones who were in Rome when Valentinus was killed have made themselves suspects you have to concentrate on.'

'It could be just their hard luck that they got themselves tangled up in a killing. But yes; it's those I'm after.'

Helena always considered every possibility: 'I suppose you don't think the dancing girl and her accomplices could be ordinary thieves whose method is to size up guests at parties then rob the rich ones as they stagger home drunk?'

'They didn't pick the rich ones, sweetheart; they jumped the Chief Spy and his agent.'

'So you definitely think the attacks are linked to what's going on in Baetica?'

'Yes, and showing that the Baetican visitors were involved in the attacks will not only do right by Valentinus, but ought to discredit the whole conspiracy.'

Helena grinned. 'It's a pity you can't talk to the much-admired Cornelius. Who do you think has paid for his "chance to see the world before he settles down"?'

'A gold-laden grandpa I expect. Types in those posts always have them.'

'The proconsul sounds very suspicious of the new

incumbent. Surely that's unusual? The lad hasn't even started yet.'

'It confirms that his father is regarded as a bad influence in Baetica.'

'The proconsul would be too tactful to libel Attractus of course ...'

'He was! I could tell he dislikes the man, though – or at least he dislikes the kind of pushiness Attractus represents.'

'Marcus, since Attractus himself isn't here you may be forced to have a look at his son. Have you brought your hunting spears?'

'Jupiter, no!' I had brought a sword for protection, though. 'Given the chance to pursue wolves around a wild peninsula with my old friend Petronius I'd jump – but the quaestor will have gone on a rich idiots' trip. If there's one thing I can't stand it's a week of camping in a forest with a group of braying bastards whose idea of fun is sticking javelins into beasts that thirty slaves and a pack of vicious hounds have conveniently driven into nets.'

'And no women,' Helena nodded, apparently sympathetically.

I ignored the jibe. 'Too much drink; too much noise; half-cooked, half-warm greasy meat; and listening to boasts and filthy jokes.'

'Oh dear! And you the refined, sensitive type who just wants to sit under a thorn bush all day in a clean tunic with a scroll of epic poetry!'

'That's me. An olive tree on your father's farm will do.'

'Just Virgil and a sliver of goat's cheese?'

'Seeing we're here, I'd better say Lucan; he's a Corduban poet. Plus your sweet head upon my knee, of course.'

Helena smiled. I was pleased to see it. She had been looking tense when I found her at the basilica but a mixture of banter and flattery had softened her.

We watched a pontifex or flamen, one of the priests of the imperial cult, make a sacrifice at an altar set up in the open forum. A middle-aged, portly Baetican with a jolly expression, he wore a purple robe and a pointed, conical hat. He was attended by assistants who were probably freed slaves, but he himself flashed the equestrian ring and was a citizen of social solidity. He had probably held a senior military post in the legions, and maybe a local magistracy, but he looked a decent jolly soul as he rapidly cut a few animals' throats, then led out a fitful procession to celebrate the Feast of the Parilia, the lustration of the flocks.

We stood respectfully in the colonnade while the troop of civic dignitaries squashed by, on their way to the theatre where a day of fun would take place. The procession was accompanied by some worried sheep and a skipping calf who clearly had not been told he was to form the next sacrifice. Persons who were pretending to be shepherds came past with brooms, supposedly for sweeping out stables; they also carried implements to light fumigatory fires. A couple of public slaves, clearly fire watchers, followed them with a water bucket, looking hopeful. Since the Parilia is not just any old rustic festival but the birthday of Rome, I bit back a surge of patriotic emotion (that's my story). A personification of Roma armed with shield and spear and a crescent moon on her helmet, swayed dangerously on a litter midway down the line. Helena half turned and muttered sarcastically, 'Roma Resurgans is rather perilous on her palanquin!'

'Show some respect, bright eyes.'

An official statue of the Emperor teetered before us and nearly toppled over. This time Helena obediently said nothing, though she glanced at me with such a riotous expression that while the wobbly image of Vespasian was being steadied by its bearers I had to pretend a coughing fit. Helena Justina had never been a model for perfect sculptural beauty; but in a happy mood she had life in every flicker of her eyelashes (which were in my opinion as fine as any in the Empire). Her sense of humour was wicked. Seeing a noble matron mock the Establishment always had a bad effect on me. I mouthed a kiss, looking moody. Helena ignored me and found another tableau to giggle at.

Then, following her line of sight, I spotted a familiar

952

face. One of the broad burghers of Corduba was sidestepping the shepherds as they wrestled with a wilful sheep. I recognised him at once, but a quick check with someone in the crowd confirmed his name: Annaeus Maximus. One of the two major oil producers at the dinner on the Palatine.

'One of those puffed-up dignitaries is on my list. This seems a good opportunity to talk to a suspect ...'

I tried to persuade Helena to wait for me at a streetside foodshop. She fell silent in a way that told me I had two choices: either to abandon her, and see her walk away from me for ever (except perhaps for a brief return visit to dump the baby on me) – or else I had to take her along.

I attempted the old trick of holding her face between my hands, and gazing into her eyes with an adoring expression.

'You're wasting time,' Helena told me quietly. The bluff had failed. I made one more attempt, squashing the tip of her nose with the end of my finger while smiling at her beseechingly. Helena bit my playful digit.

'Ow!' I sighed. 'What's wrong, my love?'

'I'm starting to feel too much alone.' She knew this was not the moment for a domestic heart-to-heart. Still, it never is the right time. It was better for her to be abruptly honest, standing beside a flower stall in a narrow Corduban street, than to bottle up her feelings and end up badly quarrelling later. Better – but extremely inconvenient while a man I wanted to interview was scuttling away amongst the ceremonial throng.

'I do understand.' It sounded glib.

'Oh do you?' I noticed the same frowning and withdrawn expression Helena had been wearing when I found her outside the basilica.

'Why not? You're stuck with having the baby – and obviously I can never know what that's like. But maybe I have troubles too. Maybe I'm starting to feel overwhelmed by the responsibility of being the one who has to look after all of us –'

'Oh, I expect you'll cope!' she complained, almost to

herself. 'And I'll be poked out of the way!' She was perfectly aware it was her own fault she was stuck on her feet in a hot noisy street in Baetica.

I managed a grin, then followed it with a compromise: 'I need you! You've been summing up my job for me pretty accurately. How about being poked on to a seat at the theatre next to me?' I gave her my hand again, and we hurried together the way the procession had gone. Fortunately I possessed skills which most urban informers lack. I am an expert tracker. Even in a completely strange city I know how to trace a Parilia procession by following the newly deposited animal dung.

My experiences in Baetica already warned me that when I caught up with the priest and magistrates I might detect an equally pungent smell.

I hate festivals. I hate the noise, and the wafts of lukewarm pies, and the queues at the public lavatories – if you can even find one open. Still, coming to Corduba on the Parilia could prove useful as a study of town life.

As we hurried through the streets, people went about their business in a pleasant mood. They were short and stocky, vivid evidence of why Spanish soldiers were the Empire's best. Their temperament seemed level too. Acquaintances greeted each other with a relaxed style. Women were not accosted. Men argued over kerbside space for tying up wagons in a lively, but non-violent way. Waiters in wine bars were friendly. Dogs yapped, then soon lost interest. All this seemed everyday behaviour, not some holiday truce.

When we reached the theatre, we found events were unticketed because the religious stuff was public and the dramatic scenes had all been paid for by the decurions, members of the town council; they, the Hundred Men, had the best seats, of course. Among them we picked out Annaeus Maximus again, and from his position he was a duovir, one of the two chief magistrates. If Corduba was typical, the Hundred Men controlled the town – and the duovirs controlled the Hundred Men. For conspirators, that could be very convenient.

Annaeus was the younger of the two landowners I had met in Rome, a square-faced Spaniard with a wide girth, giving me maybe fifteen or twenty years. Coughing slightly in the wafts of incense as the pontifex prepared to slaughter the calf and a couple of lambs, Annaeus was the first to rush forward to greet the governor. The proconsul had arrived direct from his palace, escorted by lictors. He was wearing the toga I had seen him in, not a military breastplate and cloak; ruling the senatorial provinces was a purely civic office.

In fact his role, we soon saw, was as a figurehead on somebody else's ship. The cream of Corduba had welcomed him as an honorary member of their own tightly knit top-notch Baetican club. He sat on his throne in the centre of the front rows of seats around the orchestra, flanked by well-dressed families who gossiped and called out to each other – even shouting to the pontifex in mid-sacrifice – as if the entire festival was their own private picnic.

'It's sickening!' I muttered. 'The Roman proconsul has been swallowed up by the ruling families, and he's become so much a part of the local clique it must be hard for him to remember that the Roman treasury pays his salary.'

'You can see how it is,' Helena agreed, only a little more mildly. 'At every public occasion the same few men are in charge. The same faces cluster in the best positions. They're terribly rich. They're completely organised. Their families are linked intimately by marriage. Their ambitions may clash sometimes, but politically they are all one. Those people in the front-row seats run Corduba as their hereditary right.'

'And in Gades, Astigi and Hispalis it's going to be the same – some of the faces will match too, because some of the men will be powerful in more than one place. Some must own land in several areas. Some will have taken rich wives from other towns.'

We fell silent for the sacrifice. In acquiring foreign

955

provinces, the plan was to assimilate local gods into the Roman pantheon, or simply add them to it if people liked to keep lots of options. So today at the Parilia ceremony two Celtic deities with unintelligible names received a lavish sacrifice, then Jupiter was allowed a slightly weedy lamb. But the Baeticans had been wearing Roman dress and speaking Latin for decades. They were as Romanised as provincials could be. And like the patricians of Rome, keeping a rigid grip on local politics through a small group of powerful families came as naturally as spitting.

'You can see it all,' I muttered to Helena. 'I bet the governor goes to all their private dinner parties, then when he holds a reception, this same crowd fills out the guest-list. These folk will be at the Palace every week, munching dainties and sipping free wine. No one else gets a look in.'

'If you live here, and belong to the charmed circle, you have to hob-nob with the same suffocating group continually.' That tedium was never going to afflict a dusty pleb like me – and Helena would have lost her own invitation the minute the proconsul read Laeta's letter about me.

'I'm just surprised the old man was as frank as he was!' I muttered.

Helena looked worried. 'Do you regret making yourself known to him?'

'No; I represent Laeta; I had to report in. It's safe; the proconsul is one of Vespasian's men. But now I've seen what social obligations he has, I'll hold back from contact again.'

The dramatic performances began. These consisted of brief scenes or tableaux which had been decreed suitable for public show on an occasion of organised celebration. There was little content, and less humour. I had seen more exciting theatre; I had even written a better play myself. No one was going to wet themselves with outrage here.

We watched dutifully for some time. I had been in the army; I knew how to endure misery. Eventually Helena wilted and said she wanted to go home. 'I can't see any

956

point in waiting. Annaeus will never talk to you in the middle of all this.'

'No; but since he's a duovir he has to keep a house within a mile of the town. He's bound to be there this evening. I could visit him then.'

Helena looked depressed and I was not pleased at the thought of hanging around town all afternoon until my man made himself available. Still, I needed to tackle him about the cartel and see if I could establish a link between him and the dancing girl.

Helena and I left the theatre, amazing the doorkeeper who thought we should have been engrossed in the drama. We rousted out Marmarides, who still seemed fairly sober, and I told him to drive Helena home. I would find my own transport back tonight or tomorrow – another prospect that made me glum. Riding home on a hired mule after dark through unknown roads can be disastrous.

I went with them as far as the bridge over the Baetis. 'I'll make a bargain,' Helena declared. 'If I go home quietly and let you stay on your own to investigate Annaeus, then I'm going to go over to the Licinius Rufius estate tomorrow and make friends with his granddaughter.'

'Find out if she can dance!' I chortled, knowing that the wealthy family she came from would be scandalised if she did.

The bridge at Corduba is three hundred and sixty-five paces long, one for every day of the year. I know, because I counted as I marched miserably back.

To fill in time I went to investigate the shipping offices of the bargees, in the vague hope of interviewing my other suspect, Cyzacus. All the wharfside huts were locked. A bleary-eyed man fishing off a jetty said the offices were closed for the festival, and that they would be for the next three days.

957

XXV

Later that day, after a few enquiries, I left by the northwestern gate. Annaeus Maximus owned a lovely home outside the town walls, where he could plot the next elections with his cronies and his wife could run her salon for other elegant socially prominent women, while their children all went to the bad. Beyond the cemetery lining the route out of town lay a small group of large houses. An enclave of peace for the rich – disturbed only by the yapping of their hunting dogs, the snorting of their horses, the rioting of their children, the quarrelling of their slaves and the carousing of their visitors. As town houses go, the Annaeus spread was more of a pavilion in a park. I found it easy to identify – lit throughout, including the long carriage drive and surrounding garden terraces. Fair enough. If a man happens to be an olive oil tycoon, he can afford a lot of lamps.

The clique we had seen at the theatre were now assembling for a dinner party at this well-lit house with garlanded porticos and smoking torches in every acanthus bed. Men on splendid horses were turning up every few minutes, alongside gilded carriages which contained their over-indulged wives. I recognised many of the faces from the front rows at the theatre. Amidst the coming and going I also met the shepherds from the Parilia parade; they may indeed have been here for ritual purification rites in the stables, though I thought it more likely they were actors who had come to be paid for their day's work in town. There were a few shepherdesses among them, including one with hugely knowing dark brown eyes. Once I would have tried to put a light of my own into eyes like that. But I was a responsible father-to-be now. Besides, I could never take to women with straw in their hair.

I made myself known to an usher. Baetican hospitality is legendary. He asked me to wait while he informed his master I was here, and as the whole house was pervaded by delicious cooking smells I promised myself I might be offered a piquant dish or two. There was bound to be plenty. Excess breathed off the frescoed walls. However, I soon learned that the Cordubans were as sophisticated as Romans. They knew how to treat an informer – even when he described himself as a 'state official and associate of your neighbour Camillus'. 'Associates' received short commons in Corduba – not so much as a drink of water. What's more, I had to wait a damned long time before I got noticed at all.

It was evening. I had set out from town in the light, but the first stars were winking over the distant Mariana mountains when I was led outside to meet Annaeus Maximus. He had been mingling with his guests on one of the terraces, where they were soon to hold an outdoor feast, as is traditional at the Parilia. The supposed shepherds had really been setting fire to sulphur, rosemary, firwood and incense in at least one of the many stables so the smoke would purify the rafters. Now heaps of hay and straw were being burned on the well-scythed lawns, so that a few by now extremely tired sheep could be compelled to run through the fires. It's hard work being a ceremonial flock. The poor beasts had been on their trotters all day, and now they had to endure being ritually lustrated while humans stood around being sprinkled with scented water and sipping bowls of milk. Most of the men had one eye out for the wine amphorae, while the women kept flapping their hands about, in the vain hope of preventing their fabulous gowns being imbued with lustral smoke.

I was kept well back in a colonnade, and it wasn't to protect me from the sparks. The invited guests began to seat themselves for the feast out amongst the regimented topiary, then Annaeus stomped up to deal with me. He looked annoyed. Somehow I have that effect.

'What's this about?'

959

'My name is Didius Falco. I have been sent from Rome.'

'You say you're a relative of Camillus?'

'I have a connection –' Among snobs, and in a foreign country, I had no qualms about acquiring a respectable patina by shameless usage of my girlfriend's family. In Rome I would have been more circumspect.

'I don't know the man,' Annaeus snapped. 'He's never ventured out to Baetica. But we met the son, of course. Knew my three boys.'

The reference to Aelianus sounded gruff, though that could be the man's normal manner. I said I hoped Helena's brother had not made himself a nuisance – though I wished he had, and that I was about to hear details I could use against him later. But Annaeus Maximus merely growled, 'High spirits! There's a daughter who's got herself in trouble, I heard?' News flies round!

'The noble Helena Justina,' I said calmly, 'should be described as high-minded rather than high-spirited.'

He stared at me closely. 'Are you the man involved?'

I folded my arms. I was still wearing my toga, as I had been all day. Nobody else here was bothering with such formality; provincial life has some benefits. Instead of feeling civilised, being overdressed made me hot and slightly seedy. The fact that my toga had an indelible stain on its long edge and several moth-holes did not help.

Annaeus Maximus was viewing me like a tradesman who had called with a reckoning at an inconvenient time. 'I have guests waiting. Tell me what you want.'

'You and I have met, sir.' I pretended to stare at the bats swooping into the torchlight above the laughing diners' heads. I was really watching him. Maybe he realised. He appeared to be intelligent. He ought to be. The Annaei were not country bumpkins.

'Yes?'

'In view of your reputation and your position I'll talk straight. I saw you recently in Rome, at the Palace of the Caesars, where you were a guest of a private club who call themselves the Society of Olive Oil Producers of Baetica.

Most neither own olives nor produce oil. Few come from this province. However, it is believed that among your own group the oil industry in Hispania was the topic under discussion, and that the reason is an unhealthy one.'

'That is an atrocious suggestion!'

'It's realistic. Every province has its own cartel. That doesn't mean rigging the price of olive oil is something Rome can tolerate. You know how it would affect the Empire's economy.'

'Disastrous,' he agreed. 'It will not happen.'

'You are a prominent man, Annaeus. Your family produced both Senecas and the poet Lucan. Then Nero left you with two enforced suicides because Seneca had been too outspoken and Lucan allegedly dabbled in plots – Tell me, sir, as a result of what happened to your relatives, do you hate Rome?'

'There is more to Rome than Nero,' he said, not disputing my assessment of his family's reduced position.

'You could be in the Senate; your financial position entitles you.'

'I prefer not to move to Rome.'

'Some would say it was your civic duty.'

'My family have never shirked our duty. Corduba is our home.'

'But Rome's the place!'

'I prefer to live modestly in my own city, applying myself to business.' If Seneca, Nero's tutor, was renowned for his dry Stoicism and wit, his descendant had failed to inherit this. Maximus became merely pompous: 'The oil producers of Baetica have always done business fairly. Suggesting otherwise is scandalous.'

I laughed quietly, unmoved by the feeble threat. 'If there is a cartel, I'm here to expose the perpetrators. As a duovir – and a legitimate trader – I assume I can count on your support?'

'Obviously,' stated the host of the feast, making it plain he was now returning to the singed meats at his open-air barbecue.

'One more thing – there was a dancer at that dinner; she came from this area. Do you know her?'

'I do not.' He did look surprised at the question, though of course he would deny a connection if he knew what she had done.

'I'm glad to hear it,' I said coldly. 'She's wanted for murder now. And tell me, why did you leave Rome so abruptly?'

'Family troubles,' he shrugged.

I gave up, without obvious results, but feeling I had been touching nerves. He had remained too calm. If he was innocent I had insulted him more than he had shown. If he was truly ignorant of any conspiracy, he ought to have been excited to discover that one existed. He ought to be shocked. He ought to be outraged that maybe some of the well-clad guests at his own table tonight had betrayed the high standards he had just proclaimed for Baetican commerce. He ought to be afraid that they had offended Rome.

Without doubt, he knew a cartel was being brokered. If Annaeus did not himself belong to it, then he knew who did.

As I was leaving I saw what his family troubles must be. While their elders were only just sitting down to their banquet, the younger generation were rushing off to places unknown and habits unseemly. If the three Annaeus sons had been friends of Aelianus, he must have enjoyed a jolly time in Baetica. They were various ages, but of a similar mentality: as they set off riding out from the stables when I began my own slow walk to the front of the house, they galloped either side of me, coming closer than I found comfortable, while they whooped and whistled and chided each other loudly for not flattening me properly.

A young woman who might be their sister was also leaving the house as they raced off down the drive. She was a self-assured piece in her mid-twenties, wrapped in a furred stole. She was wearing more pearls and sapphires than I had ever seen layered on a single bosom – too many,

962

in fact, to let you see what kind of bosom it was (though it looked promising). She was waiting to enter a carriage from which emerged the head of a man about the same age as her. He was indecently handsome. He was cheering a younger male, very drunk already, who had rushed out from the carriage to be violently ill on the mansion's immaculate steps. Corduba at festival time was the place to be.

I might have asked for a lift in the carriage, but I did not fancy being thrown up on. To her credit, as I passed her the daughter did warn me to watch where I stepped.

Unfed, unwatered, and unlustrated, I turned away and set off wearily back towards Corduba. There was no chance of returning to the Camillus estate tonight. I needed to find myself a lodging where the owner was still sober and had a bed to offer despite the festival crowds. Before that I would have to flog through the dark countryside that lay beyond the Annaeus property, back to the even darker streets of the town, passing the cemetery on the way. I am not afraid of ghosts – but I don't care for the hideous real-life characters who lurk among the tombs of a necropolis at night.

I walked steadily. I folded my toga, as well as you can fold a cumbersome ellipse, then slung it over one shoulder. I had gone beyond the reach of the torches, though I had pulled one up and stolen it. I was finding my way along the track back to town, concentrating on my thoughts about the day. I did not hear anyone following, even though I stayed alert to the possibility. But I certainly felt the sharp stone that flew out of nowhere and smacked into the back of my neck.

XXVI

Instinct wanted me to slap my hand on the pain, and to bow my head. Damn instinct. I wanted to stay alive.

I spun around. I drew my sword. In Rome carrying a weapon is illegal – but here that did not apply. All Romans know the provinces are hotbeds of banditry. All Romans on holiday or foreign service go armed.

Ironically my sword, an unofficial relic of my five years in the army, was a short stabbing blade made from the finest Spanish steel.

I listened. If there were more than one assailant out there I could be in deep trouble. Was this how Anacrites and Valentinus had felt when the arrows stopped them in their tracks?

Nobody rushed me. There was only silence, however hard I listened.

Had I imagined it? No; there was blood on my neck. At my feet lay the culprit stone, large and pointed like a flint. There was no mistake. I picked it up; it also had my blood on it. I tucked it into the pouch at my belt. Well, I was enjoying myself in a foreign province; I was bound to want a souvenir.

Sometimes in the country yokels let fly with missiles. Sometimes in the city idiots hurl tiles and bricks. It is a territorial gesture, an act of defiance when strangers pass. I did not believe that was what had just occurred.

I rammed my torch into soft ground at the edge of the track and moved away from it. Letting the toga slide down to my elbow, I wound the cloth around my forearm so it could act as a shield. With the torch alight I was still providing a target, but I preferred to risk that than to douse the flame and plunge myself into darkness in the middle of

964

strange countryside. I strained my ears, shifting position continually.

Eventually, when nothing happened, I pulled up the torch again and searched around in circles. On either side of the track lay olive groves. In the dark they were full of hazards, though these were purely natural. Weeding hoes lay waiting to be stepped on, their handles all set to spring up and break my nose. Low branches were ready to crack my brow. For all I knew the groves contained courting couples who might turn nasty in a wild provincial manner if I interrupted them in mid-fumble. I was about to give up when I stumbled into a disorientated sheep.

The animal was very tired. It must belong to the lustral flock. Then I remembered the shepherdess with the interesting eyes. I had seen her before. She had looked very different in her sophisticated little gold costume as Diana, but even smothered in sheepskin I ought to have recognised the girl.

Keeping my sword out, I walked back grimly to the Annaeus house. Nobody attacked me again — which was odd. Why hadn't the dancer tried to kill me out there on the track?

Fired up by annoyance at myself as much as anything, I made a formal complaint. This time, with blood trickling down my neck, I was given a better welcome. I kept making a fuss until Annaeus Maximus reluctantly ordered a search for the girl. The chief shepherd, who was still there with most of his accomplices, was summoned to respond to my accusations.

Annaeus seemed taken aback by my story. According to him, most of the group were well known to everyone, actors from the local theatre. They routinely earned extra money by providing assistance with civic rituals. This was better than allowing real shepherds to get big ideas, I could see that. Naturally the man then claimed this particular girl was a stranger to him.

The leader of the actors turned up, still dressed as the

chief shepherd and emitting a belch after his supper. He confessed he had employed a few extras to pad out the parade today. This included the shepherdess with the big brown eyes (whom he rather clearly remembered). She had presented herself when he was auditioning; he had no idea where she came from, though her name was supposed to be Selia. He said she wasn't local, though by that he merely meant she did not come from the immediate confines of Corduba; Hispalis would still be a possibility. I had just let the killer of Valentinus slip right through my fingers. And needless to say, all the slaves Annaeus had sent out to look for her came back empty-handed.

'I'm sorry.' The actor appeared pretty genuine. 'Next time I'll ask for references.'

'Why?' I scoffed bitterly. 'Do you think she'd admit she was up to no good? Anyway – are you constantly being offered the services of undulating women?'

He looked shamefaced. 'No,' he mumbled. 'Though that was the second one this week.'

'And what was the first one like?'

'Older, though she could dance better.'

'Why didn't she get the job instead of Selia, then?'

'She wasn't from around here.' Trust a local to take precedence. He looked even more ashamed, then rallied with his big excuse: 'Well, Selia was thoroughly professional; she even brought her own sheep!'

'She's abandoned it now!' I retorted. She was a professional killer – and if she could claim a whole sheep, whoever was paying her expenses must be allowing her a substantial daily rate.

966

XXVII

I spent the night at the Annaeus house. The notables let me feed at their table (well, their tenants' table). They loaned me an empty cell in their slaves' barracks. It was near the well, so I even managed to get something to wash my wounded neck – and there was all I could wish for to drink. What civilised people. Next morning their steward sent me away on a very slow horse which he said I could borrow indefinitely since its useful life had run out. I said I would report my gracious treatment by the Annaei to the Emperor. The steward smiled, openly showing his contempt.

The three sons had come home at dawn. I met them thundering in as I rode away. On principle they left me in a cloud of dust again, though the initiative had gone out of them to some extent and they were all looking faintly tired. As far as I knew the daughter was still out. Women have more stamina.

The Camillus estate lay bathed in sunlight when I finally rode back. As I expected, Helena had already followed up her promise to go over to the Licinius Rufius spread and pursue the next suspect for me. Marmarides, looking annoyed at having his nose put out of joint, told me Marius Optatus had driven her.

It gave me time to bathe and change my tunic, then to hang around the kitchen until the cook found me the kind of nourishing breakfast certain old women like to lay before an honest young man who is known to have fathered an almost-born baby and who clearly needs his strength built up. As I enjoyed the food, she cleaned my cut neck with a thyme wash and stuck on some sort of salve. Needless to say, its main ingredient was olive oil.

Helena returned to find me still being pampered. She

grabbed me by the scruff of the neck and inspected the damage. 'You'll live.'

'Thanks for the loving concern.'

'Who did it?' I winked; she took the point. We walked outside to the shady area of garden near the house, where a bench was placed under a fig tree on a wall. There, safe from being overheard, I told her about the shepherdess. Helena winced. 'You think this pageant queen all bundled up in smelly wool is the "dancer from Hispalis"?'

I did not want to say I had definitely recognised her, since that gave a false impression of me gawping too keenly at women. 'Striking down men from behind certainly seems to be her trademark. But Anacrites and Valentinus were then rammed against walls. Apart from the fact that there were none available last night, if it *was* Selia, she made no attempt to follow up.'

'Maybe she relies on her two musicians to do the dirty work, and didn't have them with her.'

'Then what was the point of the stone? It seemed random – more like a warning than anything.'

'Marcus, if the stone had hit you on the head, would you have been killed?' Sparing Helena's feelings, I said no. It certainly could have done more damage. But stone-throwing takes a good aim.

'Don't worry. What it's done is put me on my guard.' Helena frowned. 'I do worry.'

So did I. I had been struck by a recollection of Anacrites mumbling 'dangerous woman' when I said I was coming to Baetica. I now realised it was not Helena he had meant. He too must have been warning me – about his assailant.

To lighten the atmosphere I related my experience with Annaeus Maximus. 'I gained some insight into his attitude. His family is in a political trough. He is socially crippled by what happened to Seneca. Undeserved or not, the taint has lingered. Wealth alone might recapture the family's old lustre, but they've clearly lost heart too. Maximus certainly does not want a career in Rome, though he doesn't seem to mind being the big boy around here. Still, the Annaei are yesterday's heroes, and now it all depends whether running Corduba will be enough for them.'

'Will it?'

'They are not stupid.'

'What about the younger generation?' Helena asked.

'Running wild with great panache.' I described what I had seen of the sons and the jewel-clad daughter.

Helena smiled. 'I can tell you about the daughter – including where she stayed last night!'

I pricked up my ears. 'Scandal?'

'Nothing like it. Her name is Aelia Annaea. She was at the Licinius Rufius house. Despite the alleged feud between their families Aelia Annaea and Claudia Rufina, the other fellow's granddaughter, are good friends.'

'How sensible you women are! And so you met both of them today?'

'Yes. Claudia Rufina is quite young. She seems genuinely good-natured. Aelia Annaea is more of a character; the bad girl enjoys knowing that her papa would hate her to accept hospitality from Licinius when the two men aren't speaking.'

'What does Licinius feel about it?'

'I didn't meet him.'

'Aelia sounds a bundle of trouble. And if Licinius encourages her to upset her father, he sounds a wicked old man.'

'Don't be a prig. I liked Aelia.'

'You always like rebels! What about her little friend?'

'Much more serious. Claudia Rufina yearns to endow public buildings and earn a statue in her honour.'

'Let me guess: the Annaea babe is pretty –'

'Oh, you thought so?' Helena asked quickly; she had not forgotten me saying that I had seen Aelia Annaea at her home last night.

'Well, she's rich enough to get herself admired for her necklaces, and she's polite,' I corrected myself. 'Honestly, I hardly noticed the girl ... Nice sapphires!'

'Not your type!' Helena sneered.

'I'll decide my type, thank you! Anyway, she was being picked up by someone last night; I bet she's betrothed to the handsome god I saw in the carriage when she went off. I suppose the Rufius poppet with the commendable social ambitions will be very plain —'

Helena's eyes were bright. 'You're so predictable! How can you ever judge human nature when you're so bound up in prejudice?'

'I get by. Human nature makes people fall into distinct pigeonholes.'

'Wrong!' Helena said crisply. 'Claudia is just rather serious.' I still reckoned Claudia Rufina would turn out to be plain. 'The three of us had a civilised chat over a refreshing tisane. And you're wrong about Aelia Annaea too.'

'How's that?'

'She was happy and light-hearted. Nobody has burdened her with a future husband of any kind, least of all a good-looking untrustworthy one.' Helena Justina had never liked handsome men. So she claimed, anyway. There must have been some reason why she chose to fall for me. 'She was overdressed in jewellery, but wore nothing like a betrothal ring. She is very direct. If the situation called for it, she would have asked for one.'

'The arrangement may not be public knowledge yet.'

'Trust me; she's not spoken for! Claudia Rufina, on the other hand, was sporting a heavy bracelet of garnets, which cannot be to her taste (she told me she collects ivory miniatures). The awful bracelet looked just the thing a man would grab at a goldsmith's for a girl he feels obliged to present with a formal gift. Expensive and horrible. If she does ever marry the man who gave it to her, she will be obliged to treasure it for a lifetime, poor soul.'

I found myself smiling. Helena herself was dressed simply, in white, with hardly any extra decoration; while pregnant she found wearing jewellery uncomfortable. She unconsciously fingered a silver ring which I had given her. It was a plain design with its love message hidden inside. It represented the time I had suffered as a slave in a silver mine in Britain. I hoped any comparison she was making with Claudia Rufina's gift was favourable.

I cleared my throat. 'Well, did you meet any male hangers-on today?'

'No, but there was talk of "Tiberius", who was thought to be at the gymnasium. He sounds like the man you saw. If he's good-looking enough to irritate you, he's also bound to be crazed on sports.'

'Because he's handsome?' I chortled. In fact having seen him I agreed he must be a handball lout. The man I saw had a thick neck and probably a brain to match. When he chose a wife he would be looking at the size of her bust and wondering how readily she would let him run off to exercise or hunt.

The thought of hunting made me wonder if his formal name was Quinctius.

'The youth you saw being sick on the steps was probably Claudia's brother.'

'The lad who was taken to Rome with the Baetican group?'

'He never appeared this morning. He was still in bed. I heard distant groans that were supposed to be him with a wine-headache.'

'If the handsome dog is after Claudia I bet there's a scheme to marry her brother to her best friend Aelia.' I was always a romantic.

Helena was scathing: 'Aelia Annaea would eat a young lad for lunch!' She seemed well disposed towards both girls, but I could tell Aelia Annaea was the one who really appealed to her.

I scowled. 'There's not much to gain from courting the young people. It's the old men who run Corduba. From what I saw last night that's wise; their heirs look thoroughly overindulged: bored girls and bad young men.'

'Oh, they're just rich and silly,' Helena demurred.

Her trip to the Licinius house had cheered her up since yesterday. Her mother's highly expensive midwife had advised me to keep her mind occupied for these last few weeks – though the woman probably did not expect Helena to be gallivanting about Baetica.

'So what's your verdict, my darling? Have we decided these young creatures just have too much spending cash and too little parental supervision – or are the brats up to no good?'

'I don't know yet, Marcus. But I'll find out.'

I stretched lazily. 'You should enjoy yourself more. A good long bathe is what I recommend. If you whistle loudly while you're steaming, Optatus and I will keep out of the way.'

Helena Justina patted her bulge and told the child-in-waiting that if she had as many baths as its father suggested the baby would be washed away. Sometimes I wondered if Helena saw through my schemes. It would be like her to have found out exactly what the midwife had told me – and to disobey deliberately.

'So I've seen the gem-encrusted Aelia. What's Claudia Rufina like?'

'Neat, smart, and rather shy,' said Helena. 'She has a rather big nose which she unfortunately accentuates by tilting back her head then looking at people over it. She needs a *tall* husband – which is interesting, Marcus, because from the way Marius Optatus insisted on driving me today instead of Marmarides, I'd say he has a yen for Claudia! When we got there he vanished to discuss farming with the old man, but I swear he only wanted to go so he could offer greetings to the girl.'

I raised my eyebrows. Naturally I disapproved of unions that broke barriers. 'Unless I've misunderstood the rules of Baetican etiquette I reckon Optatus is risking it!'

'He's a free man,' Helena reminded me snootily. 'Anyway, when did the fact that a girl was unsuitable ever stop a man taking a chance?'

I grinned at her.

At that point we shelved the discussion because Optatus himself came out into the garden. He was splitting his sides over the decrepit horse I had brought home, and said he hoped I had not paid out money for it; I assured him it was a virtual gift from the gracious Annaei. Marius Optatus gravely replied that the Annaei had always been renowned for their generosity.

I noticed a whiff of smoke and burnt rosemary hanging around his work clothes. It would not surprise me if he was the serious sort who quietly cleansed his stables each Parilia with a private lustration made in genuine reverence. The sober tenant seemed like a dedicated farmer with no space in his life for frivolity. But once I had started to see him as a ladies' man, eyeing up the handsome dowry of a neighbour's rather big-nosed granddaughter, anything could be possible.

XXVIII

Helena had invited Claudia Rufina to return her call, but the social rules dictated there should be a short lapse of time first. Our young neighbour was probably dying to inspect Helena's paramour, but the poor thing would have to wait to see my friendly face. Meanwhile I decided to see her grandfather; now I had met Annaeus I needed to compare the rivals soon before I ended prejudiced either for or against the one just because I met him first. Since the Rufius family had had one visit from us today, Helena told me I should wait until tomorrow. It gave me an afternoon loafing about. That suited me.

'You'll like their house,' Helena giggled, for reasons she refused to divulge.

I rode over the next morning on my borrowed horse. His name was allegedly Prancer. It must have been given to him a long time ago. I think he wanted to be a botanist. His notion of a canter was a decorous sidle, slow enough to inspect every dockleaf on the way.

The Licinius Rufius estate lay comparatively close, though (given my mount) not as near as I would have liked. This was mainly because of a large number of intervening olive groves which belonged to someone else. Marius Optatus had warned who it was: his ex-landlord, Quinctius Attractus. I surveyed the senator's holding with great interest. He was happily ostentatious. After the olive groves I had to pass his fields of flax, his market gardens, his vineyards, his pig farm and his wheat.

When I did reach the Rufius villa, I saw what Helena Justina had meant: the family had embarked on a truly brave improvement programme. It was easy to see where the money for it came from: once I had entered a gateway

974

with their name on a column I had ridden through at least a couple of miles of well-aged olive trees, grand monsters with several trunks growing from stocks with huge circumferences; these were clearly only a fraction of the whole estate. I had passed a working area where they had not one but two oil-presses. Even more significant was the fact that they actually owned their own kilns for making amphorae. This estate, which ran on until it bordered the river, was obviously near enough to water transport at Corduba not to need to use mules for carrying the oil down for shipment. (The estate roads were in fact immaculate.) The kilns were five in number; alongside them were rows of bricks drying in the sun awaiting their turn to be home-fired too.

In an area the builders were using as their yard, I spotted the youth I had last seen being ill at the Annaeus house. He must be the grandson, as we had guessed. He was wearing a brilliant tunic in broad stripes of red and murex purple, a garment that shouted loudly that his family could afford the best. He was helping a bailiff decide something with a carpenter who had a new window-frame on a trestle. Young Rufius looked barely into his twenties, awake though perhaps not yet fully alert. Still, he was the one holding the building plan, his relations with the workmen sounded pleasant, and he did appear quite confident discussing the chart. I went past without making myself known and left Prancer under an oak tree; it did not seem worthwhile tethering him.

The house made me gulp.

It had once been a modest Baetican country villa, like the one on the Camillus estate – a short axial design based on a single corridor, with a very basic suite of reception rooms and small cubicles for private use on either side. But this was no longer enough for people who clearly thought themselves the rising stars in Corduba.

The whole building was scaffolded. The roof was off. A second storey was being raised on top. Some of the walls were being torn down so their traditional construction could be replaced with Roman concrete faced with the type of bricks I had seen being made in the yard. A massive entrance portico had been stuck on the front, complete with marble steps and columns the full height of the new roof. The Corinthian order had arrived in Baetica in a big way. These capitals were fabulously carved riots of acanthus leaves – though one had unfortunately been dropped. It lay where it had fallen, split in two. Work on the entrance had come to a standstill, presumably while the masons went into a corner to think up a good story to explain the accident. Meanwhile the entire ground plan of the house was being expanded to twice or three times its original area. To my astonishment, the family were still living in the old core of the house while the work went on.

When I asked for Licinius Rufius, the first person who came to greet me was his wife. She found me in the new vestibule, gawping at some gigantic paintings of Alexander the Great's campaigns. I was wondering whether I dared explore the huge internal peristyle garden which had been expanded from an original courtyard into a wonder of imported marble colonnades and topiary lions, beyond which I could just see a monumental dining room still under construction.

An elderly, upright woman, Claudia Adorata's centrally parted grey hair was held in a low bun in the nape of her neck with a circle of crystal pins. She was swathed in saffron linen and wore a fine necklace of twisted gold wires, with agate, emerald and rock crystal stones in a complex setting that resembled a butterfly. 'Excuse the mess!' she apologised, reminding me of Ma. Maids had decorously followed her into the echoing atrium, but when she saw I looked fairly tame she clapped her hands and sent them scurrying back to their looms. Their work must have been well impregnated with building dust.

'Madam, I salute your courage and initiative!' I grinned candidly.

It appeared the old lady had no notion of why I had come. We mentioned Helena, and the Camillus family, which seemed enough to gain me admittance. She said her husband was out on the estate but had been summoned to meet me. While we waited, she offered a tour of the renovations. Since I try to be polite to ancient dames, I said obligingly that I was always glad of a chance to pick up ideas. The crude apartment that Helena and I were renting in Rome would have been beyond this lady's comprehension. I was not even sure she realised that I was the father of the noble Helena's child.

By the time Licinius Rufius appeared his wife and I were sitting beside the new fishpond (the length of the house), exchanging gardening notes on the new Campanian roses and Bithynian snowflake bulbs, and taking warmed wine from bronze goblets like a pair of old friends. I had admired the five-room bath-house with its complicated heating system, special dry heat box, and exercise area; praised the half-finished but pleasing black and white mosaics; envied the new kitchen suite; taken the name of the fresco painter who ornamented the summer and winter dining rooms; cooed over the space where the library was to be; and expressed suitable disappointment that I could not view the suite of upstairs bedrooms because the stairs had not been built.

Now we were seated on an expensive set of folding chairs, placing our drinks on a matching collapsible table, covered with a fine Spanish linen tablecloth. These had been set out for us on a small paved patio which had an astounding vista of a fashionable apsidal grotto at the end of the pool, where a twinkling glass mosaic of Neptune enthroned amidst a lot of writhing sea creatures was surrounded by a heavy border of sea-shells. No doubt the Baetican murex industry had helped provide the shells.

Delicate probing had ascertained that Claudia Adorata described her family's financial position as 'comfortable'.

There was a reason for the sudden renovation campaign. She and her husband were creating a glorious backdrop for the anticipated achievements of their much-loved grandchildren, the youth in particular. His handle was Gaius

Licinius Claudius Rufius Constans, which would make a long and ornamental honorific inscription when his fabulous deeds came to be celebrated in his native town one day. Clearly the Senate in Rome must be keeping a chair warm for him, and it was hoped he would eventually rate a consulship. I tried to look impressed.

Claudia told me she and her husband had brought up the two grandchildren since they were orphaned at an early age. Their mother had died a few weeks after producing the young male prodigy; their father, himself the only son and heir, had lasted another three years then caught a fever. The two tots had become their grandparents' consolation and hope for the future – as dangerous a situation as young people could ever find themselves in. At least they had money in indecent quantities to help them through it. On the other hand, having so much money so young could make their situation even more dangerous.

Licinius Rufius strode out through the fug of dust, washing his hands in a silver bowl held by a slave who had to scamper after him. He was wide-set but not overweight, with a heavy face and a shock of crinkled hair that shot off to one side. Of an older generation than Annaeus Maximus, he remained firm on his feet and dynamic. He greeted me with a knuckle-crushing handshake, then took one of the chairs, flattening its cushion and causing the delicate legs to bow. He helped himself to black olives from a fancies dish, but I noticed he did not take wine. Perhaps he felt more cautious than his wife about my motives. Claudia Adorata herself smiled, as if she felt reassured now he was in charge, then she slipped away.

I too picked up some of the olives. (They were superb quality, almost as lush as the finest from Greece.) Eating allowed us both a short pause to do some sizing up. Licinius would have been viewing a thoughtful character in a plain green tunic and a graded Roman haircut, clearly displaying the traditional virtues of honesty, uprightness, and personal modesty. I saw an elderly man with an inscrutable expression, whom I decided I would not trust one jot.

XXIX

From the beginning I felt that, unlike his wife, Licinius Rufius knew *exactly* why I had come to Baetica. He let me pass some idle remarks about the mad scale of his home improvements, but soon the conversation shifted to agricultural matters, which would lead to the real subject of my interview. We never mentioned the magic word 'cartel', though it was always our point of reference. I began frankly: 'I could say I'm checking over the family estate for Decimus Camillus – but actually my trip out here has an official purpose –'

'There was a rumour of an inspector from Rome,' Rufius answered readily. Oh yes. Well, why pretend? News that Anacrites had planned to send an agent, and that I for one was actually here, would have been leaked from the proconsul's office – and possibly confirmed to all his Baetican friends by the proconsul himself.

'I am hoping to talk to you about oil production, sir.'

'Obviously Baetica is the place for that!' Licinius made it sound as though I was just on a mild fact-finding survey, instead of investigating a vicious conspiracy where agents had had their heads smashed in. I could feel the old man taking over. He was used to sounding off with his opinions. Thinking they know it all is a habit of rich men who build up large outfits of any kind.

'I've been discussing some figures with Marius Optatus at the Camillus estate,' I interrupted as quickly as I could. 'He reckons there may be as many as five million olive trees and a thousand oil presses in the River Baetis hinterland. An owner of standing like yourself could possess maybe three thousand *acti quadrati* – say eight or ten centuries of land?'

He nodded but made no comment, which almost

certainly meant he owned more. That was a massive area. There used to be an old system of measurement which we all learned at school, where two *acti* equalled a 'yoke', and two yokes were a 'hereditary area' – that's the amount of land that was supposed to suffice for one person in the frugal republican days. By that reckoning the average oil magnate in Baetica could support seven hundred and fifty people – except that the old method of measurement would have been when farming merely consisted of barley, beans and cabbages for domestic consumption, not a luxury export crop like olive oil.

'What's an average yield per century?'

Licinius Rufius was offhand. 'Depending on the soil, and the weather that year, between five and six hundred amphorae.' So the typical plot we had been talking about would produce between four and five thousand amphorae per year. That would buy a whole forest of Corinthian columns, plus a fine public forum for their owner to endow.

'And how is my young friend Optatus?' Rufius smoothly changed the subject.

'Bearing up. He told me a little about his misfortunes.'

'I was delighted when he took his new tenancy,' the old man said in a tone of voice I found irritating, as if Marius Optatus were his pet marmoset. From what I had seen of Optatus, he would not accept being patronised.

'The way he lost the old one sounds hard. Do you think he had bad luck, or was he sabotaged?'

'Oh, it must have been an accident,' Licinius Rufius exclaimed – as if he knew damn well it had not been. He was not going to support accusations against a fellow landowner. Quarrelling with colleagues is a bad business move. Encouraging victims never brings in cash.

Licinius had sounded fairly sympathetic, but I remembered Optatus' bitterness when he told me the locals had refused to become involved in his quarrel with his ex-landlord. I took a chance. 'I gather Quinctius Attractus conducts business in a pretty ruthless manner?'

'He likes to be firm. I cannot argue with that.'

'It's a long way from the benevolent paternal style that we Romans like to consider traditional. What's your opinion of him personally, sir?'

'I hardly know the man.'

'I don't expect you to criticise a fellow producer. But I would suppose someone as shrewd as you would have firmed up *some* conclusions after being the man's guest in Rome and staying at his house!' Licinius was still refusing to be drawn so I added coldly, 'Do you mind if I ask who paid your fare?'

He pursed his lips. He was a tough old bastard. 'Many people in Baetica have been invited to Rome by Attractus, Falco. It's a courtesy he extends regularly.'

'And does he regularly invite his guests to help him corner the oil market and drive up prices?'

'That is a serious accusation.'

Rufius was sounding as prim as Annaeus when I interviewed him. Unlike Annaeus he did not have the excuse of guests to drag him away so I was able to press him harder: 'I make no accusations. I'm speculating – from my own, maybe rather cynical standpoint.'

'Do you have no faith in human ethics, Didius Falco?' For once, the old man seemed genuinely interested in my reply. He was now staring at me so closely he might have been a sculptor trying to decide if my left ear was a fraction higher than my right.

'Oh, all business has to be based on trust. All contracts depend on good faith.'

'That is correct,' he declared autocratically.

I grinned. 'Licinius Rufius, I believe all men in business want to be richer than their colleagues. All would happily cheat a foreigner. All would like the running of their own sphere of commerce to be sewn up as tight as a handball, with no uncontrollable forces.'

'There will always be risk!' he protested, perhaps rather drily.

'The weather,' I conceded. 'The health of the business-man, the loyalty of his workers. War. Volcanoes. Litigation. And unforeseen policies imposed by the government.'

'I was thinking more of the fickleness of consumers' taste,' he smiled.

I shook my head, tutting gently. 'I forgot that one! I don't know why you stay in the business.'

'Community spirit,' he laughed.

Talking to Licinius Rufius resembled the overblown jollity of a military dining club the night the pay-chest came – when everyone knew the sesterces were safely in camp, but the distribution would happen tomorrow so nobody was drunk yet. Maybe we two soon would be, for Rufius seemed to feel he had led me astray from my purpose so successfully he could now afford to clap his hands for a slave to pour him wine. I was offered more, but declined, making it plain I was only waiting for the nervous waiter to remove himself before I continued the interview. Rufius drank slowly, surveying me over the rim of his cup with a confidence that was meant to beat me down.

I dropped my voice abruptly. 'So I met you in Rome, sir. We both dined on the Palatine. I then called on you at the Quinctius house, but you had gone. Tell me, why did you leave our splendid city so suddenly?'

'Family ties,' he replied, without pausing.

'Indeed? I gather your colleague Annaeus Maximus suddenly developed pressing family ties too! And the bargeman, I suppose – and the negotiator from Hispalis! Forgive me, but for men of affairs you all seem to have made that long journey without enough forward planning.'

I thought I saw him check, but the reaction was slight. 'We had travelled to Rome together. We travelled home in one group too. Safety, you know.' For the first time I detected a slight impatience with my questions. He was trying to make me feel like a lout who had abused his hospitality.

'I'm sorry, but your departure looks suspiciously hur-ried, sir.'

'None of us ever intended a long stay in Rome. We all wanted to return home for the Parilia.' Very rustic! And he had dodged a direct answer with the glibness of a politician.

'And of course this had nothing to do with Quinctius Attractus trying to promote a cartel?'

Licinius Rufius stopped answering me so smoothly.

We stared at each other for a few beats of time.

'There is no hoarding or price-fixing in Corduba!' His voice rasped so harshly it startled me. He sounded extremely angry. His protest could be genuine. He knew why I had come here though, so he had had time to prepare a convincing show of outrage. 'There is no need for it. There is plenty for everyone. The olive oil trade is now flowering in Baetica as never before –'

'So once the trees are planted you can all just sit back and watch the fortunes flowing in! Tell me this then, sir: why did that group of you really decide to visit Rome?'

I saw him regain control of himself. 'It was a normal business voyage. We were renewing ties with our agents in Ostia and exchanging goodwill with our contacts in Rome. This happens all the time, Falco.'

'Oh yes. Nothing unusual at all – except that the night your main contact entertained you all in the Palace of the Caesars, two men who had been in the same dining room were later brutally attacked!'

I could see he was forcing himself not to react. He chose to try and bluff it out: 'Yes, we heard about that just before we left.'

Twitching an eyebrow, I asked gently, 'Oh? And who told you this, sir?'

Rufius belatedly realised he had walked into trouble. 'Quinctius Attractus.' A neat dodge, since Quinctius had enough importance in Rome to be well informed about everything.

'Really? Did he tell you who told him?'

'He heard it at the Senate.'

'He could well have done,' I smiled, 'only the dinner for

984

the Society of Olive Oil Producers of Baetica was held on the last night of March. The Senate goes into recess from the beginning of April to the middle of May!'

Licinius almost gave away the fact that he was struggling now: 'Well, I cannot say where he heard it. He is, after all, a senator and hears all the important news before most of Rome –'

'It was never news,' I corrected him. 'An order had been given on the highest authority that the attacks should not be made public. You people left the very day afterwards. At that time only a handful of people on the Palatine – a very small group in the intelligence service and Titus Caesar himself – knew that killers had been at work.'

'I think you underestimate the importance of Quinctius Attractus,' answered Licinius.

There was another short silence. I sensed a worrying force behind his words. Ambitious men like Attractus always do carry more weight than they deserve.

Licinius felt a gloss was necessary: 'The fact that we had dined with two men who died was, Falco, as you are suggesting, one of the other reasons my colleagues and I took our leave. The incident sounded a little too close for comfort. We decided Rome was a dangerous city, and I confess we fled.'

He struck me as a man who would not normally run away from a spot of civic disorder.

Natural curiosity about the tragedy gripped him. He leaned forwards and murmured in a confidential tone, 'Did *you* know these two men?'

'I know the one who is not dead.'

I spoke it very gently, leaving Rufius to wonder which one had survived; how well I knew him; and what he had managed to say to me before I left Rome.

I might have taken things further, though I doubt I would have been any more successful. In any case, it was my turn to be called away unexpectedly. An uproar disturbed us, then almost immediately a slave came running to tell me I had better come quick because my borrowed horse Prancer had wandered through the new entrance portico, and into the gracious peristyle garden with the beautiful topiary. Prancer's yearning for foliage was insatiable, and he had lost all discretion. By the time he was spotted many of the clipped trees had ceased to look so elegant.

The Rufii coped with this accident in a terribly good-natured manner and assured me the lions would grow again. They just scoffed when I offered to pay for the damage. We all joked merrily that it was an act of revenge from their rivals the Annaei who had lent me the horse.

They could afford to replace the boxtrees and I couldn't, so I thanked them quietly for their generous attitude – then Prancer and I left, as fast as I could make him trot.

XXX

Helena Justina had very few clothes on. Any ideas this might have given me were soon banished by the fact that she smelt like a salad.

'I see you're marinading the child!'

Calmly she continued to massage neat olive oil into her stomach. 'Apparently this will ease my stretched skin – and if there's any over I can pour it on our lunch.'

'Wonderful stuff. Want any help rubbing it in?'

Helena waved a Baetican redware jug at me. 'No.'

'Well, it should do you good.'

'I'm sure! Like using oil in dough; perhaps I'll be more flexible, and with a moist crust ...' Helena loved to collect interesting lore, but often had a hard time taking it seriously.

I threw myself on a couch and settled down to watch. Stricken with an odd quirk of modesty, Helena turned her back. 'Was there ever a more useful substance?' I mused. 'Olive oil prevents burns from blistering and it's good for your liver, it stops rust in iron pots, and preserves food; the wood makes bowls and it flames well in a fire –'

'In this country the children are weaned on a porridge made from olive oil and wheat,' Helena joined in, turning back to me. 'I've been talking to the cook. Baetican midwives smother a new mother with oil to help slide the baby out.'

I chortled. 'And then they present the happy father with a little dressed onion to name!'

'I'm giving Nux a spoonful a day to try to improve her coat.'

Hearing her name, Nux looked up from a rug where she had been sleeping and thumped her tail enthusiastically. She had fur like rough turf; around her unpleasant extremities it stuck together in impenetrable clumps. 'Nothing will improve Nux's coat,' I said regretfully. 'She really needs a complete shave. It's time you broke the news to her that she'll never be a pampered lapdog. She's a smelly street scruff, and that's it.'

'Give Marcus a nice lick for loving you so much!' Helena cooed at the dog, who immediately roused herself and jumped straight on the middle of my chest. If this was a clue to what kind of subversive mother Helena Justina intended to be, I was heading for more trouble than I'd thought. As I fended off a long, frenzied tongue, Helena disarmed me by suddenly saying, 'I like it here. It's peaceful in the countryside and nobody harangues us about our situation. I like being on my own with you, Marcus.'

'I like it here too,' I grunted. It was true. Were it not for the baby and my fixed intention to return Helena to our mothers' care in time for them both to supervise the birth, I could have stayed here for months. 'Maybe we should emigrate to some far province away from everyone.'

'You belong in the city, Marcus.'

'Perhaps. Or perhaps one day I'll set up home with you in some villa in a river valley – choose your spot.'

'Britain!' she quipped wickedly. I returned to my original dream of a town house above the Tiber with a garden on a terrace with a view across to Rome.

Helena watched me as my thoughts idled romantically. She must know my situation was so disappointing all hope seemed pointless and all plans looked doomed. Her eyes sparkled in a way that made me push the dog aside. 'Marcus, another thing the cook told me is that a diet rich in oil makes women passionate and men softer.'

I held out my arms to her. 'We can easily test that!'

XXXI

Helena was asleep. Off guard and helpless, she looked more tired than when she knew I was checking up on her. I told myself some of her present exhaustion reflected my rampant skills as a lover, but her drawn face was starting to worry me.

I should never have let her travel so far. Bringing her to Baetica was stupid. I had no real hope of finishing my task before the baby arrived. The past two days had convinced me of what I should have known from the first: none of the suave local dignitaries was likely to admit what was going on. Exposing the conspiracy would take halfway to for ever – and finding 'Selia', the dancing girl who liked attacking agents, might be impossible.

I had to allot more time to Helena, though I needed to balance this carefully with letting her help in my work; it tired her nowadays more than she wanted to admit. Another man with a different woman might have kept work and home separate. For us there was no choice. Helena became distant and unhappy if I left her out of a problem. If I encouraged her to help me, she tore in wholeheartedly – but was it wise? If not, how could I dissuade her? This was how we had first come to know one another and her interest was unlikely ever to diminish. Besides, now I was used to it I relied on her help.

As if she sensed my thoughts, she awoke. I watched the relaxed expression on her face alter to suspicion that I was up to no good.

'Don't squash the baby,' she murmured, since I was lolling all over her.

I roused myself and prepared to get up. 'I'm taking advantage while I still can. You know Roman children expect to start barging their parents aside from the moment they're born.'

'Oh, it will bully you all right,' Helena laughed. 'You'll spoil this baby so much it will know it can do as it likes with you ...' Behind the banter she was looking concerned. I was probably frowning, thinking yet again that somehow we had to get it born first. Alive.

'Maybe we ought to investigate a midwife in Corduba, fruit. Just in case anything starts happening early –'

'If you will feel happier.' For once she seemed prepared to accept advice. Maybe that was because it was me talking. I liked to think I could handle her – though from the first hour I met her I had realised that with Helena Justina there was no hope of issuing instructions. She was a true Roman matron. Her father had tried to create in her a meek, modest partner to some all-knowing male. But her mother's example of quiet contempt for the opposite species was just as traditional, so Helena had grown up forthright, and doing just as she liked. 'How did you progress with Licinius Rufius?' she asked sweetly.

I started pulling on tunics. 'We were gossiping like foster-brothers until Prancer took to munching his clipped trees.'

'Any results?'

'Oh yes, he cut them down to size –' Helena threw a boot at me. 'All right, seriously: Rufius takes the line that hoarding oil and fixing prices would be unnecessary. He says there is plenty for all. Like Annaeus he feigns shock at the suggestion that any upright Corduban businessman would be so greedy as to plot a cartel.'

Helena slid on to the edge of the bed beside me so she too could dress. 'Well, you're used to being considered a crude slanderer of men with crystal consciences – and you're also used to proving them villains in the end.'

'Whether these two have actually joined the conspiracy I wouldn't like to say – but someone has definitely asked them about it. I'm convinced the issue was discussed when they went to Rome.'

'Would Annaeus and Rufius be particularly important in setting up a price ring?' Helena wondered, slowly combing her hair.

While she was trying to wind up a chignon, I tickled her neck. Being a rascal always helped me to think. 'I bet they would. Annaeus is a duovir, for one thing; he carries clout in Corduba. Consider him first: from a great Hispanic family with extraordinary wealth. He could perhaps feel he's above corrupt business ideas. He might even feel too much loyalty to Rome.'

'Or too much to lose!' Helena commented.

'Exactly. But still he's tinged with disgrace that was not of his making; he now belongs to a family of enforced outsiders – and he has his sons to think about. He looks a disaffected rebel in the making. Add to that his huge influence on the local political scene, and if I was recruiting for a cartel, I'd certainly be after him.'

'He may just prefer to opt out,' Helena argued. 'His family have seen what happens to schemers. He may want the quiet life.' I conceded the point as she pouted thoughtfully. 'What about Rufius?'

'Different: a new man. Driven by ambition for his grandchildren,' I said. 'If he joins in, it will be because he wants a short route to power and popularity. If a price ring is set up, it would suit him to be known as the man who started it; other members would more readily support him in pushing his grandson. So I shall have to decide: is he honest or crooked?'

'What do you think?'

'He looks honest.' I grinned at her. 'That probably means he's a complete crook!'

At last Helena managed to lean away from me long enough to skewer her hair with an ivory pin. She lurched upright and went to our bedroom door to let in Nux; I had shut out the dog earlier because she was jealous if we showed each other affection. Nux scampered in and shot under the bed defiantly. Helena and I smiled and sneaked out, leaving Nux behind.

'So what now, Marcus?'

'Lunch.' An informer has to honour the priorities. 'Then I'm going back to Corduba to see if I can roust out Cyzacus, the bargee. He's not a damned shepherd; he can't have a load of flocks to fumigate. I don't believe his office is really closed up for three days on account of the Parilia.'

I rode in on the horse, slowly. So slowly I started dozing and nearly fell off.

The bargee's office *was* still closed. I failed to find anyone who knew where his private house was. Another afternoon of my precious time was wasted, and I could see there was little point returning here for at least another day.

While I was in Corduba, I seized advantage of Helena's agreement and sought out a midwife. For a stranger in town, this was fraught with difficulties. My sisters back in Rome, who were keen on sensational stories, had already scared me with wild tales of crazy practitioners who tried shaking out babies using physical force on the mother, or their hopeless assistants who tied the poor woman in labour to the top of the bed, then lifted the foot in the air and dropped it suddenly ... My eldest sister had once had a dead baby dismembered in the womb; none of the rest of us had ever quite recovered from hearing the details over nuts and mulled wine at our Saturnalia gathering.

I walked to the forum and asked various respectable-looking types for advice, then I double-checked with a priestess at the temple who laughed drily and told me to see somebody quite different. I suspect it was her mother; certainly the dame I eventually visited looked seventy-five. She lived down a lane so narrow a man with decent shoulders could hardly squeeze through it, but her house was tidy and quiet.

I sniffed at her to see if she had been drinking and I squinted at her fingernails to make sure she kept her hands clean. Without actually seeing her in action, that was all I could do; by the time I did test her methods, it would be too late.

She asked me a few questions about Helena, and told me dourly that as she sounded a bonny girl she would probably have a large baby, which of course might be difficult. I hate professionals who cover themselves so obviously. I asked to see the equipment she used, and was readily shown a birthstool, jars of oil and other unguents, and (very quickly) a bagful of instruments. I recognised traction hooks, which I supposed could be used gently to pull out living children; but then there was also a set of metal forceps with two hideous rows of jagged teeth along its jaws, which I guessed from my sister's old story must be for crushing skulls to remove them in pieces when all else had failed and a stillbirth became inevitable. The woman saw me looking sick.

'If a child dies, I save the mother if I can.'

'Let's hope it won't come to that.'

'No; why should it?' she replied calmly. There was a small sharp knife for cutting birth-cords, so maybe the old dame did manage to produce infants intact occasionally.

Somehow I escaped on terms which left us free to send for the midwife if we needed her, though I had omitted to tell the woman where we stayed. Helena could decide.

I was so disturbed I lost my way and left by the wrong city gate. White pigeons fluttered as I passed. Needing to think, I led Prancer along the track outside the town walls which would bring me to the river. The bright day mocked my gloomy mood. Poppies, borage and daisies raised their heads beside the way, while pink oleanders crowded against the ramparts and plunged down towards the river which I eventually reached. I was on the upstream, totally unnavigable side, where the low marshy ground looked as if it never flooded. Meandering streams dawdled among tracts of firmer land which supported wild tangles of undergrowth and even large trees where birds that looked like herons or cranes nested. Other significant winged creatures – maybe falcons, or hoopoes – occasionally swooped fast among the foliage, too far away to identify properly.

Nearer to me midges swarmed, and above them were

993

swallows. Less idyllically, a dead rat lay in a cart rut, complete with its phalanx of flies. Further on I came to a group of public slaves; I won't call them workmen. One was dancing, two took their ease on stools, and four more leaned against the wall while they all waited for the stonecutter to carve the sign that said they had completed a repair today. Not long afterwards I came to the bridge.

The afternoon was a waste of time, and my visit to the midwife had failed to reassure me. Feeling more tense than ever, I rode back to the estate. Evening was falling on the distant Mariana mountains, and I wanted to be with my girl.

XXXII

The next day turned out to be slightly more productive, though I began it gloomily.

Tormented by my thoughts about Helena and the baby, I tried clearing my mind by helping Marius Optatus on the estate. He was spreading manure that morning, which I found appropriate. I reckon he could see the mood I had worked myself into, but in his usual way he said nothing, just handed me a rake and let me work up a sweat among his slaves.

I could not ask his advice. In the first place he was a bachelor. Besides, if any of his slaves overheard us they were bound to join in the conversation with colourful country lore. The last thing an expectant Roman father needs is a bunch of rural types cackling at his anxieties and telling him to sacrifice expensive animals to invisible woodland deities at some Celtic shrine in a grove guarded by a stone lion.

I would have paid for a kid and for a priest of the Imperial Cult to deal with it too, if I had thought it would do Helena any good. But the only gods I ever had faith in are the faceless kind who come in dark hoods with sinister downturned torches, looking for new clients to introduce to the Underworld.

I was close to madness. I admit it. Anyone in my position who had paid attention to the high rate of mother and infant mortality would be just as bad.

About the time the slaves were starting to hint that Optatus should signal a break for a cup of posca and an apple – in fact while they were making loud jokes about what a dour-faced overseer he was – the boy from the house came out to inform him visitors had called. Optatus merely nodded to show he had received the information. I leaned on my rake and questioned the lamp-boy, who said we had been favoured by Claudia Rufina and her friend Aelia Annaea.

Optatus still doggedly carried on working as long as he could. His attitude intrigued me. He would not stop work for women – even if Helena was right and he hankered after one of them. He was the first man I had ever met who appeared to have perfectly normal inclinations yet who would rather spread manure.

Eventually, when the slaves' mutters of rebellion did force a halt, he and I handed over to a foreman and walked back to the house. We then had to wash rather thoroughly, but the young women seemed determined to wait until we both appeared; they were still talking to Helena in the garden when we finally emerged.

As Optatus and I walked outside to the sun-drenched garden we heard giggling: the result of allowing three women to gossip together for an hour with a jug of what passed for herbal tea. All three would have described themselves as quiet creatures with serious outlooks. Optatus may have believed it. I knew better.

Claudia Rufina, the girl I hadn't seen before, must have been older than her brother. She looked just over twenty – easily marriageable, especially since she had a huge dowry and was part-heiress to a man of some age. The girl should have been snapped up by now. Her head lifted, and she stared at me with solemn grey eyes over the big nose Helena had previously described. She was a sturdy young lady with a worried expression. Perhaps it was caused by constantly seeing the world at an angle.

Her friend had mastered the feminine trick of appearing serene. I recognised Aelia Annaea from seeing her at her father's house, though today she was not quite so plastered in gems. At close quarters she was a little older than I had first thought, and several years older than Claudia; she looked much more of a challenge too. She had a fine-featured, very delicate face with clear skin and hazel eyes which missed absolutely nothing that went on.

This trio looked like an exposition of the architectural orders. If Helena was Ionian with her smooth wings of hair pinned aloft with sidecombs, then Aelia Annaea inclined to the Doric severity of a neat pediment of brown hair fixed dead square upon her small head; young Claudia, in Corduban modernist fashion, had allowed a maid to inflict on her a Corinthian flourish of ringlets. Our two visitors were the kind of close friends who went out together in same-colour dresses – blue, today; Claudia in light-hearted aquamarine and Aelia more subdued in a deep squid-ink shade. Helena wore white. All three women were enjoying themselves making constant small gestures: adjusting their stoles, preening their hair, and rattling their bracelets (of which there were enough to stock a market stall).

I sat down with Marius Optatus. Though we had washed, we retained a close memory of the smell of manure so we tried to keep still and limit how much we exuded. I picked up the jug, and found it empty. I was not surprised. I had already noticed a plate which must once have been piled high with sesame cakes; it too had been thoroughly cleaned up, except for a few seeds. When the talk is of fashion tips, the munching gets serious.

Optatus greeted everyone with a silent nod. Helena introduced me.

'Have you come to Baetica on business, Marcus Didius?' enquired Aelia Annaea disingenuously. I reckoned she had overheard enough from her grumbling relatives at home to know just what my position was. This was a young lady who picked up all the news.

'It's no secret,' I answered. 'I'm the hated agent who has been sent from Rome to poke his nose into the olive oil business.'

'Oh, what's the reason for this?' she responded lightly.

I just smiled, trying to look like a dumbcluck who would be satisfied with any tale her untrustworthy papa wished to hand me.

997

'We had heard there was somebody coming from Rome.' Claudia was the serious one, utterly straightforward: the type who had never realised that when a delicate question had been posed it was perfectly permissible to keep quiet. Especially if your grandpapa might have something to hide. 'My grandfather thought it was somebody else.'

'Someone else in particular?' I asked, smiling again.

'Oh, a strange old woman who had approached him asking questions when he was out in the fields one day. He actually wrote to your father about it, Aelia!'

'Did he?' Aelia Annaea was too clever to tell Claudia to shut up; it would only draw attention to her tactlessness.

'Well, that was a surprise!' Catching my curious expression Claudia explained, 'Everyone was amazed to find them corresponding. Grandpapa and Annaeus Maximus usually avoid each other if they can.'

'An old feud?'

'Just professional rivalry.'

'That's sad!' I grinned. 'I was hoping for a hot tale of seething envy and passion. Was there no stolen land? No favourite slavegirls raped on riverbanks? No runaway young wives?'

'You read the wrong poetry,' said Helena.

'No, love; I read the law reports!'

Marius Optatus said nothing, but chuckled to himself. He was not much help with repartee. I was perfectly prepared to handle three women at once, but an occasional respite would have been useful; in fact, this situation called for my rascally friend Petronius.

'What happened to the old biddy?' I enquired of Claudia.

'She was shooed away.'

Aelia Annaea had been watching me. She was thinking herself a match for any undercover agent – especially one investigating openly. I winked at her. She was no match for that.

Apropros of nothing Helena asked, 'So were you both acquainted with my brother?'

Oh, of course, squeaked both wenches, in enthusiastic

tones. Past acquaintance with Aelianus would be their public reason for making much of Helena, a new face (with a Roman hairstyle, and perhaps bringing a scroll of Roman recipes). Apparently Aelianus had been a jewel of Corduban society (these were very polite young women). At least, he had been a close friend of Claudia's brother, Rufius Constans, and of Aelia's three brothers, who must all have owned impressive formal names in the Roman style, but whom she called Spunky, Dotty and Ferret.

What all the male juveniles had in common, it emerged, was that they were close cronies of Tiberius.

'Tiberius?' asked I, like a wide-eyed novice.

'Oh, you must know Tiberius!'

'I'm afraid I don't have that honour. Tiberius who?'

'Tiberius Quinctius Quadratus,' stated Marius Optatus suddenly. 'In my house he has one or two less polite names.'

'Your ex-landlord's son?'

'Our admired new quaestor, Falco.'

His intervention had darkened the tone of the conversation. He looked as if he wanted to cause trouble. Aelia Annaea tried to soften the atmosphere: 'Well, what can one say about Tiberius, except that he is charming?'

Helena said quietly, 'Don't you just hate charming men? I always think charm is a certain clue to a man you shouldn't trust.'

'This one is also extremely good-looking,' I supplied. 'If he's the hero I saw the other night collecting you from your father's house, Aelia Annaea?' She acknowledged it.

'Oh, he has everything!' muttered Optatus jealously. 'A distinguished father in a prominent position, a winning way, political promise, and the good opinion of everyone he comes into contact with.' I saw young Claudia compress her lips slightly. She was embarrassed by his anger; her young friend merely looked resigned.

I pretended to know nothing about him. 'Is this paragon new to the area?'

'The family's Roman of course,' Optatus answered

bitterly. 'But we know him well already. The Quinctii have large tracts of land. Quadratus has spent time in the district before, and we'll be seeing even more of him now he holds his official post.'

I beamed at the two young ladies. 'I take it he's related to Quinctius Attractus, the senator your father and grandfather stayed with in Rome just recently?' This time even Claudia had the sense merely to answer with a vague nod and smile. If they knew the visit to Rome was significant, somebody seemed to have told them not to discuss it with me. 'I met Attractus myself. What a coincidence.'

'You'll meet his son too,' growled Optatus. 'Don't worry about missing that treat, Marcus Didius. He's everywhere, is Tiberius.' The two young ladies had fallen silent; fending off difficulties with Optatus had now gone beyond their control.

'I heard he was off hunting,' I said.

'He's hanging around Corduba enjoying himself,' replied Marius. 'I heard the proconsul told him he wasn't to show his face in the office any more than strictly necessary.'

He was wanting to argue with somebody, so I gave him his money's worth: 'I reckon you're being hard on the new quaestor. From the glimpse I had, he seemed a gifted lad.'

'Oh, he's wonderful,' breathed Claudia.

'Young lady, do I detect a blush?' I quipped. She obliged me, though it earned me a black look from Helena, who had already decided to support a romance for Optatus with Claudia. I refused to take the hint from my beloved, and carried on, 'Claudia Rufina, your grandparents were telling me their plans for your brother's career – Rome, and so forth. They must have high hopes for you too. Does that include a handsome dowry to share with some promising star?'

This time Helena actually kicked me. Too late. While she squinted a reminder about Marius Optatus harbouring a tenderness for Claudia, his expression remained decidedly neutral. But a sudden frosty tension told me three different

1000

women were cursing me and wondering how to be kind to him.

Claudia, the least adept, answered my question in her usual serious and strictly accurate way: 'My grandfather has not discussed anything with me –' It sounded as though Licinius Rufius had actually told her it was too soon for public comment.

Helena Justina leaned forward and tapped my wrist with the herbal tea strainer. 'Marriage isn't everything, Marcus!' She turned to Aelia Annaea. 'I remember when my former husband first asked for me. I was young; I thought it was my duty to accept him. But I can recall feeling very angry that he had placed me in the position where I felt obliged to have him just because he was the one who had asked.'

'I think I understand that,' Aelia Annaea responded. Then, somewhat to the surprise of both Helena and me, she mentioned that she had been married herself, then after three years and no children she had been very recently widowed. Something in her tone implied she had no plans to repeat the experience.

'Was your marriage happy?' Helena asked in her forthright way.

'I had nothing to complain about.'

'That sounds rather qualified.'

'Well, I could never in conscience have requested a divorce.'

'And yet?' asked Helena, smiling.

'And yet, Helena!' Aelia Annaea had probably not talked like this before. We watched the young widow surprising herself: 'To be honest, when my husband died I felt I had been given another chance in life.' Her eyes sparkled wickedly. 'I do enjoy myself now. A widow has a different status. For a year at least, I shall have a certain independence –' She stopped, as if we might disapprove of what she was saying.

'Why only a year?' Helena growled.

Aelia looked rueful. 'That's about as long as a woman with a fortune can expect to hold out against the hordes of people who want to suggest ways she can invest it with them!'

Claudia Rufina certainly looked shocked now. Helena turned to her kindly: 'Don't listen to us crabby things! You should just try to feel sure that you share common bonds with your husband.'

'Love?' asked Claudia, rather defiantly.

Helena laughed. 'Well, that might be stretching it.'

'Love is a luxury!' I joined in the teasing. 'But you don't need to demand anything excessive – a shared fondness for chariot races, or a keen interest in sheep-breeding can be a wonderful basis for at least four or five years together.'

Torn between Helena's advice and my flippancy, Claudia looked puzzled. I noticed Marius Optatus had been listening to all this and apparently watching both girls with curious interest. Apart from his one brief outburst he had said hardly anything, yet seemed quite content to sit here as one of the party.

I said gently to our two visitors, 'Your friend Tiberius sounds fascinating. I think I'd like to meet this young man!'

They agreed that I must do so, then with one accord they jumped up from their seats and decided that they really had to leave.

I stayed behind alone while they were being seen off. I wanted to think about the 'strange incident' when an old biddy (or a young dancer, well disguised?) had tried to talk to Claudia's grandfather.

XXXIII

Optatus tried to vanish for the rest of the afternoon. I had obviously upset him somehow, but he was useless as a sulker: he had the kind of stubborn nature that refused to let him miss his meals. At dinner he was there again, a silent presence. Helena and I talked to Marmarides our driver about going into Corduba next day. We let Optatus work his way through half a loaf of farm-baked bread, a bowl of preserved olive salad and some smoked sausage from the hanging rack above the hearth. Then he drank a whole jug of water from the dolium, and sat and picked his teeth.

Helena moved away from the bench at the table, needing space for two. With a slight sigh she eased herself into a chair near the hot water cauldron on the cooking bench. I put one leg up on the bench, twisting to look at our friend. I was still eating; I had more appetite than him.

'Something struck me today,' Helena put in from her chair beside the cooking bench. 'Those two young women called the Quinctius son charming. They were not just saying it because he had flirted with them prettily; they meant that everybody thinks he is wonderful.'

'Everyone except you,' I suggested to Marius Optatus. I would be the second exception, if I came up with my usual reaction to jumped-up lads in administrative posts.

'Don't answer if you don't want to, Marius,' Helena said. 'We are all living in the same house, and there are rules of good manners.'

She had sensed what was the matter, and he finally broke his silence in reply. 'What you do is horrible, Falco.'

I pulled through my teeth a piece of sausage skin that was too tough to eat. 'How have I offended you?'

'I think you must offend everyone.'

'Close!' I took a spill from a vase that stood with the saltbox on the table. Everyone in Rome has been fed that myth about Hispanians cleaning their teeth with their own urine, so I was glad to find that in this villa rustica they had heard of using a sharp bit of stick. Never believe what you read. Half the time it has just been copied by a pig-ignorant hack from some previous author's bogus scroll.

Optatus pushed away his bowl and swung out from the table. In the measured pace of life in the country he took a small pottery lamp, carried it to an amphora, filled a jug from the larger container, filled the lamp from the jug, brought it back to the hearth, lit his toothpick from the embers, lit the lamp wick, placed the light on the table and stood there thoughtfully. His actions alerted the lamp-boy to go about his task of lighting the rest of the house, and the cook to collect crockery to wash. Marmarides caught my eye, then went out to feed the carriage mules. People were now moving about freely in the kitchen, and our discussion took on a more informal tone.

'The Annaei and Licinii Rufii are my friends,' he complained. 'I grew up with them.'

'Would that be with the boys – or the girls?' I asked pointedly. 'Which am I not allowed to approach in my work, Marius?' He made no answer, so I added quietly, 'Aelia Annaea *certainly* knew exactly what our conversation was about – and I really don't believe I took advantage of Claudia.' Optatus resumed his place at the table at last, his tall shadow wavering on the kitchen wall as he sat down. 'They both know my role; I told them quite freely. If those two young ladies have made a pet of Quinctius Quadratus, they are both mature enough to take the consequences.'

'I don't see what this has to do –'

'His father is heavily implicated in a probable conspiracy. I think we can guess that deliberate influence was used to get the son his posting as quaestor. The Quinctii are building themselves a dangerous powerbase in Baetica. If I end up nailing Attractus, his son is almost certain to be disgraced at the same time. The son *may* be an innocent tool of a devious father, but that quaestorship makes him look a willing participant in the master plan. Even if he's as pure as snow, he's stuck with how it looks – though from what you told me about the way he kicked you out of your tenancy, "pure" is not the word to use.'

Optatus was brooding on his personal problems. 'They will not succeed in their ambitions.' At least he was talking again. 'People here don't welcome their interference. People will resist them; I will do so myself. When I have money, I will buy land of my own. If I cannot achieve it myself, at least my descendants will be equal to the Quinctii.'

'You've already been saving!' Helena guessed acutely. 'You're mulling over a plan!'

'You could marry into an estate,' I suggested. 'That would help.' He looked at me, affronted. 'Marius Optatus, you are well respected in the local community. All sorts of people regard you kindly. Set your sights high.'

'You are advising me from experience?' He sounded barbed.

I said, 'A man should go for the girl he wants, my friend.'

Helena was looking worried. 'She might not always be available!'

'She might be,' I retorted. I pretended to be unaware of any feelings Optatus had. 'Take Claudia Rufina, for example – you could say the signs are all there that she's earmarked for the fabulous quaestor "Tiberius". But will it ever happen? I suggest it's unlikely. He comes from an old Italian family. The Quinctii are certain to look for a bride from the same patrician *Roman* background. Making money from the provinces is one thing. Making an alliance is another.'

On reflection, Helena backed me up: 'It's true. If you took a census of the men in the Senate, you'd find the Spaniards are married to Spanish women, the Gauls to Gauls – and the Romans to their own kind. So, Marcus, that's why nothing is being said openly about Claudia and the quaestor?'

'Nothing ever will be. The Quinctii aren't buying. Having met Claudia's grandfather, I'd call him shrewd enough to see it.'

'The girl could be hurt by this,' Helena frowned.

'Only if she's daft enough to fall in love with the charmer. I dare say she may be, but it need not be irretrievable. Well, there you are!' I exclaimed to Optatus. 'A nice rich girl who may soon have a heartache, and be going spare in the marriage market!'

He took it well. 'Thanks, Falco!' He managed a grin and I knew we were friends again. 'But maybe Claudia Rufina isn't nice enough or rich enough!'

Helena and I both beamed at him. We do like to manipulate a man who stands up for himself.

Optatus was still niggling about the way I had to work. 'I was taking you to task, Falco.'

'About what I do?'

'For all I know, when we converse in this friendly fashion, you are laying traps even for me!'

I sighed. 'Rest assured. If there is a conspiracy, by the time the Quinctii started trying to arrange their cartel, you were on very bad terms with them. Only men who look amenable are invited on their friendly trips to Rome. Let's be fair to the Quinctii though; they may be honest as daisies.'

'So you like to be fair!' he observed drily.

'I've been caught out too many times! But I don't believe you were ever invited to join any price-fixing; you disapprove too strongly of corrupt practices.'

Maybe I was being stupid. Maybe Marius Optatus was so utterly disgruntled by what had happened to him that *he* was the moving spirit behind the plot Anacrites had wanted to investigate. He had just told us he was saving hard and harbouring ambition. Perhaps I had been underestimating his importance here.

1006

'I'm flattered,' said Optatus. 'So you will concentrate your efforts on the young ladies' handsome friend, Falco?'

'The charming Tiberius does pose one fascinating puzzle. If the Quinctii are villains, they appear to have everything well sewn up. But even so, the proconsul has sent Quinctius Quadratus on hunting leave.'

'So what, Falco? He is a sporting type. He loves hunting; in a young man of promise that goes down well.'

I smiled wisely. 'In a young man who has just started a major public role, this phrase has other connotations. He's not hunting at present, is he?'

'He's enjoying himself in every way.'

'Quite. Flirting with Aelia Annaea and Claudia. What a bastard.'

'And he is influencing their brothers,' Optatus told me. 'Particularly young Rufius Constans; Quadratus has made himself the boy's mentor.'

'That sounds unfortunate! But listen: I was telling you about hunting leave; you have to be aware of the subtleties here. In the army it's called "being sent up country". In civic life it's a different term, but same result: your quaestor is not actually expected to hunt. He can loaf on his father's estate, attend the gymnasium, entertain women – whatever he likes, just so long as he doesn't show his face. The fact is, at least temporarily, the proconsul has shoved this twinkling star out of the way.'

Optatus looked pleased. He immediately saw that for the Quinctii and their ambitious plans this could be a disaster. The Senate might have been bought and the Emperor bamboozled, but here the proconsul had a mind of his own. Against all the odds, not everything was going right for Quinctius Attractus and his son. Apparently there was a black mark on a list somewhere, against the name of Tiberius Quinctius Quadratus.

Maybe Laeta had sent me to Baetica to be the man who turned the mark into a line drawn right through the name.

'What happens now, Falco?'

'That's easy,' chortled Helena sleepily from her place

1007

beside the fire. 'Marcus has the kind of job he likes: he has to find a girl.'

'In order to disgrace one or both of the Quinctii,' I explained quietly, 'I have to link them to Selia, the dancing girl from Hispalis I mentioned to you before. She helped get a man killed in Rome – and someone almost certainly hired her.'

For once it was Optatus who laughed. 'I told you before! You won't find many of those girls in Baetica; they all sail off to make their fortunes in Rome!'

Well, that was good. It should be easier to identify the one who had sneaked back to Spain.

'Mind you ...' mused Optatus, as if he had had a thought he rather liked, 'I ought to be able to introduce you to someone else – Quinctius Quadratus.' I raised an eyebrow at the suggestion. He smiled. 'Falco, you need to meet people and sample some entertainment in Corduba. I know where to find it.'

'One of the boys, eh?' I tried hard to believe it, though it was difficult to see him as a ringleader at a bachelors' night out.

'In there with the best of them,' he claimed.

'So what disreputable scheme do you have in store for us?'

'I've heard that Annaeus Maximus is going to visit his Gades estate. The last time he left Corduba – when he went to Rome to see Quinctius Attractus – his sons held a party where so much damage was caused they were forbidden to invite their friends home again.'

'I saw them in passing the other night. Nice lads!'

Optatus grinned. 'I've also heard that the minute Maximus leaves for Gades, Spunky, Dotty and Ferret will be defying their parents and holding open house again!'

Every parent's nightmare. Once I would have been delighted. Now I found myself wondering whether poor Annaeus Maximus could somehow be warned to take his cellar keys to Gades. I knew why I felt so dispirited: one day there would be out-of-control young persons throwing up in my own Attic vase collection. One day it would be my polished sandalwood table that some little drunken idiot decided to dance upon while wearing her sharpest-heeled shoes.

Then as I glanced at Helena (who was regarding me rather quizzically) I felt able to view coming events at the Annaeus house with greater complacency: after all, my own children would be brought up well. With model parents, they would love us and be loyal. They would heed our prohibitions and follow our advice. My children would be different.

XXXIV

This job was taking longer than I wanted – like most of my work. At least it was civilised. I was more accustomed to being compelled to get drunk during long waits in seedy wine bars, and joining in the occasional fight with a bunch of roughs in the kind of location you don't let your mother know about.

Next day it was back to Corduba, determined this time to force a meeting with Cyzacus, the bargee I had seen being dined out by Quinctius Attractus back in Rome. Helena Justina came with me. She pretended my constant trips had made her suspect I was keeping a light woman somewhere, but it turned out that when we had driven in together on the Parilia Helena had discovered a manufacturer of purple dye, the expensive juice extracted from murex shells that is used for top-rank uniforms. While I had been chatting to the proconsul she had ordered a quantity of cloth. Now she said she wanted my company – though it was also a chance to pick up her bargain.

'Sweetheart, I hate to be pedantic but nobody in either of our families is an army commander, let alone a candidate for emperor!' I wondered if she was making wild plans for our baby. Political ambition in Helena was a terrifying prospect. Helena Justina was the kind of girl whose wild plans came into effect.

'Bought here, the stuff is so reasonable, Marcus. And I know just who wants it!' I would never match her in deviousness: Helena intended to offer the purple material at cost to the Emperor's mistress when we went home. She reckoned that if all the stories of frugality (otherwise called meanness) in Vespasian's household were true, the lady Caenis would leap at this chance to kit out Vespasian, Titus Caesar, and the sprog Domitian in really cheap imperial

1010

uniforms. In return, there might be a chance that Vespasian's darling, strongly encouraged by *my* darling, would put in a good word for me to him. 'It's more likely to work than smarming around your friend Laeta,' Helena sneered.

She was probably right. The wheels of empire turn on barter. After all, that was why I was spending the end of April flogging around Corduba.

I had managed to persuade Helena to meet the midwife I had interviewed. She screwed out of me what had happened during my own introduction. 'So that's what upset you!' she muttered darkly, grabbing my hand in a rather fierce manner. She must have noticed I came back from town the day before yesterday in a bad mood. Her promise to have a look at the woman herself lacked conviction, I thought.

I was now very familiar with the sluggish River Baetis, its sudden petering out at the sixteen-arch bridge, and the lazy wheeling of marsh birds above the wooden wharf with its collection of rough and ready sheds. At last there were signs of activity, though the riverside was not exactly heaving with life.

Marmarides parked our carriage in a tree-shaded area where stakes had been set up for tethering wagons and mules. It was a beautiful morning. We all walked slowly to the water's edge. Nux trotted happily alongside, thinking she was in charge of the party. We passed a large character who was crouching down talking quietly to a clutch of choice African fowl as he put together a new hen-house. Far out, a man was crouched in a small raft with a fishing line, with the air of having found a good excuse to sleep in the sun.

A barge which had been motionless at the wharf for three days to my knowledge now had its covers off; looking down into it we could see rows of the distinctive globular amphorae in which oil was transported long distances. They were packed several deep, each balanced between the necks of the previous layer, with reeds stuffed among them to prevent movement. The weight must have been enormous, and the sturdy barge had sagged low in the water.

Cyzacus' office – a shed with a stool set outside it – was open today. Not much else had improved.

Presumably once harvest time started in September the action here would be hectic. In spring, nothing much happened for days on end, unless a convoy of copper, gold or silver happened to come down from the mines in the Mariana mountains. Left in charge during this dead period was a run-down, rasping runt with one leg shorter than the other and a wine jug clamped under his arm. Nux barked at him once loudly, then when he turned and stared at her she lost interest and confined herself to blinking at clouds of midges.

'Cyzacus here?'

'No chance, legate!'

'When's he due?'

'You tell me.'

'Does he ever show his face?'

'Hardly ever.'

'Who runs the business?'

'I reckon it runs itself.'

He was well trained. Most useless lags who pretend to be watchmen feel compelled to tell you at length how pitiful the management is and how draconian are their own employment terms. Life was one long holiday for this reprobate, and he didn't intend to complain.

'When was the last time you saw Cyzacus down on the wharf?'

'Couldn't tell you, legate.'

'So if I wanted to ask someone to arrange to ship a large load down to Hispalis, say, I wouldn't ask for him?'

'You could ask. It wouldn't do you any good.'

I could tell Helena was losing her temper. Marmarides, who nursed the fond idea that what he called agenting was tough work with interesting highlights, was beginning to look openly bored. Being an informer is hard enough, without subordinates who expect thrills and quaking suspects.

'Who runs the business?' I repeated.

The lag sucked his teeth. 'Well, not Cyzacus. Cyzacus has pretty well retired nowadays. Cyzacus is more what you'd call a figurehead.'

'Somebody must sign the invoices. Does Cyzacus have a son?' I demanded, thinking of all the other men involved in the conspiracy.

The man with the wine jug burst out laughing, then felt the need to take a hefty swig. He was already obstinate and awkward. Soon he would be obstinate, awkward, and drunk.

When he stopped chortling he told me the story: Cyzacus and his son had fallen out. I should have known, really. I fell out with my own father, after all. This son had run away from home – the only oddity was what he had run off to do: Spain produced the Empire's best gladiators. In most towns boys dream of upsetting their parents by fighting in the arena, but maybe in Spain that's the sensible career that they rebel against. At any rate, when Cyzacus junior had his blazing row with Papa and left home for ever with just a clean tunic and his mother's hoarded housekeeping, *he* ran off to be a poet.

'Well, Hispania has produced a lot of poets,' said Helena quietly.

'It's just a different way of messing me about,' I snarled at the watchman. 'Now look here, you great poppy: I don't want a tragic ode, I want the man in charge.'

He knew the game was up. 'Fair enough. No hard feelings –' My feelings should have been obvious. Then he told me that when Cyzacus senior was disappointed by his boy's flight to literature, he adopted someone more suitable: someone who had been a gladiator, so he had nothing to prove. 'Now he has Gorax.'

'Then I'll speak to Gorax.'

'Ooh, I don't advise it, legate!'

I asked what the problem was and he pointed towards

1013

the large man we had seem earlier engaged in building a hen-house: Gorax had no time for visitors because of his chickens.

Helena Justina gave up on my investigation and said she would go into town for her purple cloth. Marmarides escorted her back to the carriage, reluctantly because he knew the name Gorax: Gorax had once been famous even as far as Malaca, though now he was retired.

Never one to shrink from challenges, I said chickens or no chickens, he would have to speak to me.

I approached quietly, already having second thoughts. He was covered in scars. What he lacked in height he made up in width and bodyweight. His movements were gentle and he showed no wariness of strangers: if any stranger looked at him the wrong way Gorax could just wrap him around a tree. Gorax must have been a gladiator who had known what he was doing. That was why, after twenty bouts in the arena, he was still alive.

I could see the big fellow was really enjoying himself, building his chickens a house. I had been told by the watchman that Gorax had a girlfriend who lived downstream near Hispalis; she had given him the poultry, to provide a safe hobby while he was away from her. It seemed to have worked; he was clearly entranced by the birds. The great soft-hearted lunk looked completely absorbed by his pretty cockerel and three hens as they pecked up maize.

They were finer than common barnyard poultry, special guineafowl so delicate they begged to be fussily hand-reared. Neat, dark-feathered birds, with bare heads and bony helmet crests, all speckled like fritillaries.

As I tentatively approached him, he stood up to stare at me. He might have been willing to allow a polite interruption, especially if I admired his pets. But that was before he glanced around his little flock and noticed that only two of the precious hens were here. The third had wandered off along the wharf towards the tethered barge – where she was about to be spotted by Nux.

XXXV

The dog let out quite a tentative yip when she first noticed the hen. For a single drumbeat, Nux pondered in an amiable fashion whether to make friends with the bird. Then the hen saw Nux and fluttered up on to a bollard with a frantic cluck. Delighted, Nux sprang into the chase.

As the dog began to rush towards the little hen, the huge gladiator dropped the hammer with which he had been nailing up a perch. He pounded off to save his pet, holding another bird under his arm. I sprinted after him. He naturally had the turn of speed a fighter needs to surprise an unwary opponent with a death-thrust. Oblivious, Nux sat down on her tail and had a meditative scratch.

Marmarides had been lurking by the carriage, unwilling to leave with Helena while I was talking to the famous Gorax. He saw the fun start. I glimpsed his slight figure running our way. Three of us were converging on the dog and the hen – though it was doubtful whether any of us would reach them in time.

Then the stunted watchman, still clutching his wine, began dancing about on the wharf. Nux thought it was a game; she remembered the hen and decided to fetch it for him. Marmarides whooped. I gulped. Gorax shrieked. The hen squawked hysterically. So did the other one, squashed against the mighty chest of Gorax. Nux barked again ecstatically and jumped at the hen on the bollard.

Flapping its wings (and losing feathers) the endangered fowl flew off the bollard, and scooted along the wharf just ahead of Nux's eager nose. Then the stupid thing took off and flapped down into the barge. Gorax rushed at Nux. She had been up on the edge of the planking having a bark at the hen but with a heavyweight bearing down on her, yelling obvious murder, the dog leapt straight after the hen.

The hen tried to flutter up off the barge again but was terrified of the watchman peering down and calling obscene endearments. Nux floundered amongst the necks of the amphorae, paws flailing.

I jumped off the quayside on to the barge. It was basic – no features to grab. I had no time to judge my footing, so one end of the boat swung out suddenly into the stream as I landed. Gorax, who had been about to step aboard himself, slipped on the thwart as the tethered end bumped the quay unexpectedly; he crashed to the deck with one leg overboard. Landing on his chest, he crushed the hen he had been carrying. From his expression, he knew he had killed it. I teetered wildly, trying hard to keep my balance since I could not swim.

Marmarides skidded up the quay and chose a target. He gave the watchman a shove, so the befuddled fool tipped straight into the river. He started screaming, then gurgling. Marmarides had a change of heart and plunged in after him.

Gorax had let out a whine as he cradled the dead bird, but he dropped it as Nux scrabbled closer to the one that was still flapping. Gorax went for the dog, so I aimed at the fowl. We collided, lost our footing on the amphorae, and caused a nasty crack of pottery underfoot. The ex-gladiator had gone through one and was ankle-deep in broken pot. As he struggled to extricate his leg the container broke again, so he was up to his knee, with oil sloshing everywhere. To regain his balance he grabbed at me.

'Ooh, be gentle!'

Unlikely! I had a swift glimpse of his gullet as he let out a wild cry. Even his tonsils were terrifying. I thought he was going to bite off my nose, but just then a refined voice cut through the racket saying, 'Leave it out, Gorax! You're frightening the fish away!'

Gorax, all obedience, dragged his leg out of the smashed amphora, trailing blood and golden oil. Then he sat down on the edge of the barge and held the dead fowl on his massive knee, while tears streamed down his face.

'Thanks!' I said quietly to the newcomer. I grabbed Nux with one hand, and made my way carefully to the river side of the barge, where a thin man who was propelling a raft with a pole had stuck his head above the deckline to see what was going on. I crouched and offered a handshake. 'The name's Falco.'

'Cyzacus,' he said.

I managed to keep my temper. 'You're not the man I was introduced to by that name in Rome!'

'You must mean Father.'

'Apollo! You're the poet?'

'I am!' he responded, rather tetchily.

'Sorry; I thought you had left home.'

'I did,' said Cyzacus junior, punting his raft around to the wharfside with some competence.

'You wield a mean oar, for a man of literature.' Clamping the dog under my arm, I had regained the wharf. After Cyzacus tied up his raft I reached down and helped him spring up on to the jetty.

He had a slight body and a few whiffs of hair, amongst which was actually a stylus shoved behind his ear. Maybe the fishing was a cover for writing a ten-volume magisterial epic to glorify Rome. (Or maybe like my Uncle Fabius he was the crazy type who liked to note down descriptions of every fish he caught – date, weight, colouring, time of day, weather, and bait used on the hook ...) He did look like a poet, saturnine and vague, probably with no sense about money and hopeless with women. He was about forty – about the same as his adopted brother Gorax. There appeared to be no animosity between them, for Cyzacus went to console the big hulk, who eventually shrugged, tossed the dead hen into the river, and came back on to the wharf cooing over the live one fondly while it tried to fly away. He had simple emotions and a short attention span; perfect in the arena, and probably just as useful sorting out wholesalers who wanted to hire space on the barge.

'He organises the loads,' Cyzacus told me. 'I keep the records.'

'Of course, a poet can write!'

'There's no need for cheek.'

'I'm just fascinated. You went to Rome?'

'And I came back,' he said shortly. 'I failed to find a patron. Nobody came to my public readings; my scrolls failed to sell.' He spoke with much bitterness. It had never entered his head that wanting to be famous for writing was not enough. Maybe he was a bad poet.

I wasn't going to be the man who pointed this out, not with Gorax standing beside him looking immensely proud of his creative business partner. An ex-gladiator's brother is entitled to respect. The two were about the same height, though the big one filled about three times the space of the other. They looked totally different, but I already sensed there were closer bonds between them than between most real brothers who have grown up squabbling.

'Never mind,' I said. 'The world has far too many tragedies and almost enough satires. And at least while you're dreaming on a raft on the River Baetis you'll be spared too many crass interruptions to your thoughts.' The failed poet suspected I was ragging him, so I went on quickly, 'I was just explaining to Gorax when the fracas blew up, your father and I met at a very pleasant dinner in Rome.'

'Father does the trips abroad,' Cyzacus junior confirmed.

'What was it? Making contacts?'

Cyzacus and Gorax exchanged looks. One thought himself intellectual and one was a beaten-up punchbag – but neither was dumb.

'You're the man from Rome!' Cyzacus told me in a sour voice.

Gorax snarled. 'We were expecting you.'

'I should hope you were. I've been here three times!' I bluffed it out. 'The office has been closed.'

They exchanged looks again. Whatever they told me, I

could see it would be a concocted story. Somebody had already primed them to be difficult.

'All right,' I confided in a friendly fashion. 'Corduba seems a town that has no secrets. I don't know how closely you work with your old man, but I need to ask him about the oil business.'

'Father stays in Hispalis,' the true son said. 'That's where the guild of bargees have their headquarters. He's a big man in the guild.' He looked pleased with himself for this unhelpfulness.

'I'd better go down to Hispalis, then,' I retorted, undeterred. Once more I noticed the two brothers shifting nervously. 'Is this load on the barge going downriver soon? Can I hitch a ride?'

They did tell me when the barge would be leaving; they were probably relieved to let their father deal with me. From what I remembered, he had looked a tougher proposition. Gorax even offered to let me go to Hispalis on the barge for free. This was one of the perks of informing. People I interviewed often seemed glad to pay my fare to send me on to the next person, especially if the next person lived a hundred miles away.

'It must be slightly inconvenient for the bargees,' I suggested, 'having so much trade from Corduba, when your guild is set up at Hispalis?'

The poet smiled. 'It works. At Cyzacus et Filii we see ourselves as go-betweens in every sense.'

I smiled back at the pair of them. 'Many people have told me that Cyzacus et Filii are the most influential bargemen on the Baetis.'

'That's right,' said Gorax.

'So if the oil producers were banding together to further their trade, your firm would be in there too, representing the guild of bargees?'

The younger Cyzacus knew full well I was referring to the proposed cartel. 'The bargees and the oil producers tend to stick firmly to their separate interests.'

'Oh, I must have got it wrong then; I understood your

father went to Rome to be part of some negotiations for a new system of price banding?'

'No, he went to Rome as part of a visit to the guild's offices at Ostia.'

'I see! Tell me, does your father have any connections with dancing girls these days?'

They both laughed. It was perfectly genuine. They told me their parent had not looked at a girl for fifty years, and with the innocence of loyal sons they really believed it, I could tell.

Then we all had to stop sidestepping as our attention was claimed by a desperate cry. Still down in the river, my driver Marmarides was floating on his back in an approved Roman legionary manner (which he must have learned in the service of his master Stertius), gripping the watchman under the chin to keep his head above water, while the watchman clutched his wine jug and they both waited patiently for somebody to throw them down a rope.

XXXVI

My social life was looking up. I was acquiring a full calendar, what with Optatus promising me japes among the bachelors of Corduba, and my free ticket down the Baetis.

Had the elder Cyzacus been the sole reason for visiting Hispalis I might have dropped him as a suspect to interview, but there was also the negotiator Norbanus, who arranged ocean-going shipping from the downstream port. I might even trace the elusive and murderous 'Selia' – assuming that the fake shepherdess who chucked the stone at me had used her real name. Hispalis posed a problem, however. On my mapskin it looked a good ninety Roman miles away – as the raven flies. The River Baetis appeared to meander atrociously. That could mean anything from a week to a fortnight floating down to do interviews that might add absolutely nothing to my knowledge. I could not afford to waste so much time. Every day when I looked at Helena Justina I was struck by anxiety.

Cyzacus and Gorax had almost certainly wanted to make me waste time for no good reason. If those two managed to put a government agent out of action for a fortnight by trapping him on a very slow barge miles away from anywhere, they would feel proud of themselves. They were protecting their father, not realising how urgently I wanted to trace the dancer and that if I did go to Hispalis she would be my main quarry. I felt sure their father must have reported full details of the dinner, though whether he had told them anything about the attacks afterwards would depend on how much he trusted them. Clearly the poet's time in Rome, while it failed to make him a famous man of letters, had taught him to be a thoroughgoing Celtiberian pain in the backside.

I had now interviewed two suspects, Annaeus Maximus

and Licinius Rufius. There were two more in Hispalis, assuming I ever made it there. Yet another pair could well be implicated, even though they had ducked out of the dinner on the Palatine: young Rufius Constans and the Quinctius son. They had both been in Rome at the right time. Optatus reckoned Quinctius Quadratus exerted a bad influence on Constans – though until I met Quadratus and judged him for myself I had to allow for some prejudice in his ex-tenant. Yet the wary Greek secretary at the house of Quinctius Attractus who first told me that the two young men had bunked off to the theatre had been very reluctant to give me details. Neither the youngsters themselves nor their whereabouts had seemed important to the enquiry then. Now I was not so sure.

This was one avenue I would be able to pursue immediately, for Optatus had established that the three Annaei were holding their party only a couple of evenings later. Through old channels of communication he had obtained a ready invitation for the pair of us. Young Rufius was trying not to offend his grandfather by openly fraternising with rivals, so he was pretending to visit us that evening and we were taking him. Marmarides would drive us, and later bring home any who had managed to remain sober. Helena seemed to be remembering the last time I went off without her, when I could not even find the right way home afterwards. She saw us off with an intense sniff of disapproval. Apparently Claudia Rufina was taking the same attitude; she stayed at home with their grandparents, though she seemed very fond of her brother and had sportingly agreed not to give him away.

I myself took a conscious decision that evening not to wear anything that might show stains. Optatus had dressed up; he was in a suavely styled outfit that made excellent use of the famous Baetican cinnabar dye, a rich vermilion pigment, complemented by heavily formal black braid on the neck and shoulder seams. With this came an incongruous set of antique finger-rings and a faint waft of balsam around his carefully shaved jowls. It all gave him an air of being up to no good. Even so, he was outshone by the youth.

This was my first real encounter with Rufius Constans. We were all just in tunics – no ceremony in the provinces – and his was the finest quality. I was barely neat; Optatus had on his best. Rufius Constans could well look down on both of us. In his casually worn white linen, his gleaming niello belt, his shaped calfskin boots and even a torque (Jove!), he was far more comfortable in his clothes; he had coffers full at home. So here was a rich lad with high aspirations, setting off for a night among friends, beautifully turned out – yet he was jumpy as a flea.

Constans was pleasant-looking, nothing more. His nose, set in a young, unformed face, was a weak shadow of his sister's but there was something of her in the way he peered shyly at the world. At twenty or so, I felt he had not yet decided his ethical position. He seemed unfinished, and lacking the weight he would need for the élite public career his proud grandfather had charted for him. Maybe I was feeling old.

'I've been meaning to ask you,' I tackled the young man casually, 'how did you enjoy the theatre?'

'What?' He had a light voice and restless eyes. It may be that any lad of twenty who finds himself knee to knee in a jolting carriage with an older man who has a lively reputation may automatically look shifty. Or perhaps he had something to hide.

'I nearly met you during your trip to Rome with your grandfather. But you and Quinctius Quadratus decided to go to the theatre instead.' Was it my imagination or did the playgoer look hunted? 'See anything good?'

'Can't remember. A mime, I think. Tiberius took me drinking afterwards; it's all a blur.'

It was too early in the night to turn nasty on him. I smiled and let the lie go past. I felt convinced it *was* a lie. 'You want to be careful if you go out on the town in Rome. You could get mugged. People are getting beaten up on the streets all the time. You didn't see any of that, I suppose?'

'Oh no.'

'That's good.'

'I'm sorry I missed the chance of meeting you,' Rufius added. He had been brought up to be polite.

'You missed some excitement too,' I said.

I did not say what, and he displayed no curiosity. An exceptional young fellow, apparently.

I felt sour. I was still thinking about the dead Valentinus, and even about Anacrites, when the carriage pulled up at the smart out-of-town Annaeus residence.

Lucius Annaeus Maximus Primus, Lucius Annaeus Aelius Maximus, and Lucius Annaeus Maximus Novatus (to honour Spunky, Dotty and Ferret officially) knew how to throw a bash. Money was no object, and neither was taste. They had the household slaves scampering about with great vigour. It was all much more exciting than the stultified jollifications I had seen here at the Parilia festival. Released from parental authority, our hosts were being themselves, and a hilarious trio they were. I was glad they weren't my boys.

They had bought up every garland of flowers in Corduba. Their father's frescoed house smelt like all the gardens of ancient Tartessos, its air thick with pollen, a nightmare for sensitive noses. To add to the lamp smoke, the floral scents and the all-pervading aromatic odours of young bodies given unaccustomed hours of grooming, the lads had devised an Egyptian theme for the evening. It involved a few home-made dog-headed gods, some wicker snakes, two ostrich-feather fans, and cones of scented wax which new arrivals were instructed to wear on their heads: as the heat of the party rose so the cones would melt, giving everyone a bitter aura of Pharaonic myrrh and impossibly matted hair. I made sure I lost mine.

Word had gone around all the baths and gymnasiums in town that the three great lads were holding a party. The news had spread like foot-fungus. The seediest youths of the city had suddenly muttered to their parents that they were going over to a friend's house, being careful not to specify which friend. All over Corduba parents were now vaguely wondering where their pallid offspring had scuttled off to, and why there was such a reek of breath-freshening pastilles. Inadequate teenage owners of large personal allowances, mostly with skinny shoulders and pustular skin, had been waiting weeks for this night. They were hoping it would make men of them; the only certainty was that it would make them bilious.

Girls had come too. Some were nice, though their reputations might not last the evening. Some were slightly soiled to begin with and would be horrendous by the time they had swallowed several jugs of unwatered wine and had their frocks pulled off behind laurel bushes. Some were clearly professionals.

'It's worse than I expected, Falco,' Optatus confessed.

'You're getting too old to take it?'

'I feel like a bad-tempered grandfather.'

'You're not entering into the spirit.'

'Are you?' he huffed defiantly.

'I'm here to work.' That made me wonder: what was Marius Optatus here for? He had some ulterior motive, I was sure of it.

Optatus and I were the eldest men there. At least ten years separated the Annaeus sons. Primus, the eldest, might be almost our age, but his youngest brother was not yet twenty, and Fortune had arranged it that he was the one with the most friends. This largest group coalesced first, though all they did was to mill around trying to find food, drink or sinful women; they were stuck with the stuff in cups and bowls because they did not know how to recognise the other. We worried them. (They worried me.) We belonged to a wholly different generation. They all slipped by us, avoiding contact, because they thought we were somebody's parental police.

A second party had developed in the cellar, to which friends of Dotty, the middle son, zoomed with a sense of purpose which would quickly leave them. They despised food, and had probably tried women, but were all betrothed to sweet, virginal girls (who were currently behind bushes with other young men). Suspicions that they were being deceived, and that life would only bring them more of the same, made the middle son's cronies a brooding, cynical group. Optatus and I exchanged a few witty thoughts with them, before we moved on.

Spunky, who would be known to posterity and the Censor as the honourable Lucius Annaeus Maximus Primus, was pretending to be grown up. He had retreated from the noise and debauchery to his father's elegant library. It was a quiet upper room with a splendid balcony which gave views across the ornate gardens. There he and a few jaded companions were pulling scrolls from their pigeonholes, examining them satirically, then tossing them into a heap on the floor. An amphora had made a vicious ring on a marble side table. Another had been knocked over after uncorking, so some spirited soul had pulled down a curtain to mop up the mess. How thoughtful. I was pleased to see they were not all bad.

Optatus told me that this Annaeus, unlike his two younger brothers, was actually married, though to a girl so young she remained with her parents while he simply enjoyed the income from her dowry and pretended he was still safe from responsibility. He was a plump-faced, solidly built young Baetican, whose amiable nature made him instantly forgive me for being the man he and his brothers had shoved about (twice) the last time I visited their palatial home. He greeted Optatus like a lost lamb. Optatus seemed genuinely friendly towards him.

Rufius Constans, though rather young for this group, had already made his way here. I thought he coloured up when I first walked through the door, and after I found myself a place to squat he seemed to edge away as far as possible. Wine was being splashed around at that point, so maybe he just wanted to avoid the spillage. Slaves were serving, but they looked extremely nervous. When the guests wanted more, they bawled for it loudly; if nobody came soon enough they grabbed the jugs for themselves, deliberately missing their cups when they poured.

I had been among this type before. It was a long time since I had found them amusing. I knew what to expect. They would sit around for hours, getting pointlessly drunk. Their conversation would consist of bloody-minded politics, coarse abuse of women, boasting about their chariots, then making exaggerated assessments of their wealth and the size of their pricks. Their brains were no bigger than chickpeas, that's for sure. I won't speculate on the rest.

Several scions from other families were among this group. They were introduced to me at the time, though I reckoned there was no real need to remember them. These would be the chubby heirs to all the fine folk Helena and I had seen at the Parilia, the tight little section of snobs who ran everything in Corduba. One day these would be the snobs themselves. There would come a time for most of them when a father would die, or they married, or a close friend was killed very young; then they would move silently from being crass young idiots to being the spit image of their staid fathers.

'Bollocks!' muttered a voice beside me in the chaos.

I had thought I was next to Optatus, but when I turned it was another who had joined us without introductions. I knew who he was. I had seen him here before, collecting Aelia Annaea, and since then I had learned that he was Quinctius Quadratus.

At close quarters familial resemblance to his father was clear. He had a thick thatch of black crinkled hair, muscular arms, and a lordly expression. He was tanned, hirsute and strong-featured. Sporting and popular. Possessed of ease and happy arrogance. He wore a white tunic with broad purple stripes and had even put on his scarlet boots, things I had rarely seen in Rome: he was a senator-elect, and new enough to want to be seen in every detail of the historic uniform. I was looking at the recently appointed financial controller of Baetica. Even though the proconsul was unhappy with his assignment here, Quadratus himself was

1027

flaunting it. So I already knew one thing: he had no official tact.

The cause of his exclamation was not a spot of mind-reading, but an uncouth response to a scroll which he had plucked from the library columbarium. I couldn't read the title. He sneered, rolled it up very tightly, then stuffed it into the neck of an empty wine vessel like a plug.

'Well, well,' I said. 'They told me you were charming and gifted, but not that your talents extended to instant crits of literature.'

'I can read,' he answered lazily. 'I say, I don't believe we've met?'

I viewed him benignly. 'The name's Falco. And of course I know who you are, quaestor.'

'There's no need to be formal,' he assured me in his charming way.

'Thanks,' I said.

'Have you come out from Rome?'

'That's right,' I replied for the second time that night. 'We nearly bumped into each other there recently, but I hear you were at the theatre instead. The last dinner for the Society of Baetican Olive Oil Producers?'

'Oh, them!' he replied offhandedly.

'What was the play? Any good?'

'A farce, I think.' Rufius Constans had pretended it was a mime. 'So-so.' Or not. He paused. He knew what I was doing here. 'Is this an interview?'

'Great gods, no,' I laughed, reaching for more wine. 'I'm bloody well off duty tonight, if you don't mind!'

'That's good,' smiled Tiberius Quinctius Quadratus, quaestor of Baetica. He was off duty too, of course. The proconsul had arranged that.

1028

XXXVII

The room was squashed, and noisy with brash young idiots' chatter. What was more, they were about to amuse themselves playing the ancient Greek game of *kottabos*. Spunky, who would have made a good crony for the Athenian reprobate Alcibiades, had been given the apparatus for his birthday – an aptly chosen gift from his younger brothers. Clearly nobody had told him that *kottabos* explains why the Greeks no longer rule the world.

For refined readers of this memoir who will certainly never encounter it, *kottabos* was invented by a group of uproarious drunks. You have a tall stand, with a large bronze disc suspended horizontally halfway up. A small metal target is balanced on the top of the stand. The players drink their wine, then flick their cups to expel the dregs. They aim to make the flying lees hit the target so it falls off and hits the lower disc with a noise like a bell. All the wine they flick splatters the room and themselves.

That's it: a little gem from the wise, wonderful people who invented the classic proportions of sculpture and the tenets of moral philosophy.

By mutual consent Quadratus and I took wine and cups to drink it from, then we moved out smartly to the balcony. We were the mature ones here. We were men of the world. Well, he was a Roman official, and *I* was a man of the world. So we drew apart to give ourselves space to spread a bit. (It's hard to fulfil your potential as a man of the world when your knees are jammed under a reading couch and a murex-merchant's nephew has just belched in your ear.) Optatus, who was talking earnestly to young Constans, raised his winecup wryly as I stepped over him, following my smart new pal.

We *were* going to be pals, that was obvious. Quadratus was accustomed to being friendly with everyone, apparently. Or maybe his father had warned him I was dangerous and should be disarmed if possible.

The night air was cool and perfect, barely touched by the scent of the torches which flickered on the terraces below. Occasional shrieks reached us from crude horseplay among the adolescents. We sat on the marble balustrade, leaning against pillars, and drank Baetican white and the fresh air in equal measure.

'So, Falco – Baetica must be a change from Rome?'

'I wish I had more time to enjoy it.' There is nothing like a fake polite chat to bring on my apoplectic tic. 'My wife's expecting. I promised to take her home for the birth.'

'Your wife? She's the sister of Camillus Aelianus, isn't she? I didn't know you were actually married.'

'There's a theory that marriage consists of the decision by two people to live as man and wife.'

'Oh, is there?' His reaction was innocent. As I expected, he had been educated by the best tutors – and he knew nothing. He'd be a magistrate one day, laying down laws he had never heard of to people whose lives in the real world he would never understand. That's Rome. City of glorious tradition – including the one that if the landed élite can bugger up the little man, they will.

'Ask any barrister.' I could be pleasant too. I grinned at him. 'Helena and I are conducting an experiment to see how long it takes the rest of Rome to admit the fine theory holds good.'

'You're very courageous! So will your child be illegitimate?' He wasn't carping, just curious.

'I had assumed so – until it struck me that if we regard ourselves as married, how can it be? I'm a free citizen and I'll register it proudly.'

Quinctius Quadratus whistled quietly. After a while he said, 'Aelianus was a good lad. One of our set. The best.'

'Bit of a lively character?'

Quadratus chuckled. 'He lost his rag over you!'

'I know.'

'He'll be all right when he finds his feet.'

'Good to hear.' Young men with weak spots are always keen to assess others. The quaestor's patronising tone almost made me defend Aelianus. 'Lad about town?' I suggested, hoping for dirt.

'Not as much as he liked to think.'

'A bit immature?'

'Cock shy.'

'That won't last!'

We poured more wine.

'The trouble with Aelianus,' the quaestor confided dismissively, 'is he can't judge his length. The family's poor as Hades. He's aiming for the Senate with absolutely no collateral. He needs to make a rich alliance. We tried to set him up with Claudia Rufina.'

'No good?' I prompted neutrally.

'He wanted more. His idea was Aelia Annaea. I ask you!'

'Too old for him, presumably?'

'Too old, too sharp, too aware of what she's got.'

'And what's that?'

'A quarter of her papa's estate when he passes on – plus the whole of her husband's property.'

'I knew she was widowed.'

'Better than that. She had the good taste to be widowed by a man with no close family. There were no children and no co-heirs. He left her everything.'

'Wonderful! How much was "everything"?'

'A whopping tract of land – and a small gold mine at Hispalis.'

'She seems a nice girl!' I commented, and we laughed.

'The Annaeus lads look like a boisterous bunch.'

'Just the job,' cackled Quadratus. He libelled his friends without a second thought: 'Thick as curd cheese, and just as rich!'

That seemed to sum up Spunky, Dotty and Ferret well enough for my purposes.

'What's your reaction to young Rufius?' I asked, hoping that his protégé at least would attract some approval.

'Oh, Jupiter, what a waste!'

'How's that?'

'Haven't you noticed? All that energy being squandered on making him something, but he's just not up to it. There's some decent cash in the family, but Constans is never going to use it properly.' He defined everything in monetary terms. It grew wearisome for a man like me, with virtually nothing in the bank.

'You don't think he will be the success his grandfather wants? Won't he make it to Rome?'

'Oh, he can be bumped into the posts, of course. Licinius Rufius can afford to get him whatever he wants. But Constans will never enjoy it. He doesn't command much attention here, and the sharks in Rome will swallow him. He can't take Grandpa along to give him authority.'

'He's young. He could grow into it.'

'He's just a raw Spanish ham that's not been smoked enough. I try,' Quadratus declared. 'I show him a thing or two when I can.'

'I expect he looks up to you.'

A sudden grin split the handsome face. I had disturbed the smooth, bland, utterly plausible exterior and the result was a shock. 'Now you're pissing yourself laughing at me!' He said it without malice. His candour in discussing his friends had had a tone I didn't care for, but he knew how and when to turn the conversation. He seemed modest now. People were right to compliment his charm.

'Someone told me, Quadratus, you were about to exchange contracts with the Rufius girl yourself?'

He gave me a level stare. 'I couldn't comment. My father will make any marriage announcement in due course.'

'Not ready yet?'

'You have to get it right.'

'Oh yes; it's an important decision for anyone.'

'There are personal issues – and I must think of my career.'

I had guessed correctly. He would never be paired off in Baetica.

'Tell me about yourself, Falco.'

'Oh, I'm nobody.'

'Bull's testicles!' he said crudely. 'That's not what I heard.'

'Why, what have you heard?'

'You're a political drain-cleaner. You do missions for the Emperor. There's some rumour about you sorting a problem in the British silver mines.' I said nothing. My work in Britain was known only to a very close circle. It was highly sensitive. Records of the mission had been burned, and however important the quaestor's father thought himself in Rome, Attractus ought not to have known about it. If he really did, that would alarm the Emperor.

My experience in the mines at Vebiodunum, disguised as a slave, was one I never talked about. Dirt, vermin, beatings, starvation, exhaustion, the filthy overseer whose kindest punishment was to strangle the culprit while his only notion of reward was an hour of enforced buggery ... My face must have changed. Quadratus was unobservant, however.

My silence did not make him stop to think. It merely offered another opportunity to show off what somebody had told him. 'Don't you specialise in mineral rights, Falco? I thought you looked keen when I mentioned Aelia Annaea's legacy. You're in the right province. There's iron, silver, copper and gold in huge quantities. A lot of it's at Corduba – I have to know all this stuff for my work,' he explained.

'The *aes Marianum*,' I answered steadily. 'That's the famous copper mine at Corduba that produces the fine ore for all Roman bronze coins. Tiberius wanted to bring it under state control. He had the millionaire who owned it,

Sextus Marius, thrown off the Tarpeian Rock on the Capitol.'

'How come?'

'Accused of incest.'

'That's disgusting.'

'It was a trumped-up charge.' I smiled. I nearly added that nothing changes – but the dumb optimist in me hoped that with Vespasian's arrival it might have done.

'You amaze me, knowing all that, Falco!'

'I collect information.'

'For professional reasons?'

'I'm an informer. Stories are the material of my trade.'

'I'll have to be careful, then,' Quadratus grinned. 'My father's on the Senate committee that runs the mint mines.'

That gave me an unpleasant feeling: Quinctius Attractus trying to dabble one more sticky finger in Baetica. Fortunately there was an imperial procurator actually in charge of the *aes Marianum* mine. He would be an equestrian, a career official whose only concern would be doing the job right for his own sake. The other side of government: and not even the Quinctii could interfere with that.

'The Senate committee, eh?' It fitted the pattern. Attractus wanted influence in every sphere of this province. Getting a place on the committee would have been easy, given his strong local interests. 'I'm surprised your family aren't involved in mineral production.'

'Oh, we are,' laughed young Quadratus. 'There's a silver mine that's run by a society at Castulo. My father shares the franchise; he's a leading member of the Society. I'm standing in for him while I'm out here. We have our own copper mine too.'

I should have known.

'I'm surprised you have the time for personal work,' I cut in coolly. I had let him run until I felt I knew him, but his time was up. 'A quaestorship is not an easy ride.'

'I'm not really worked in yet.'

'So I gather.'

1034

His face did not alter. He had no idea what those in the know would think of him being given hunting leave before he had even started. How could he? He was a raw egg in bureaucracy. He probably thought the proconsul had done him some kind of favour. Favours are what people like him expect. Duties don't come into it.

'Of course there's a lot of responsibility,' he declared. I put on my sympathetic face and let him talk: 'I reckon I can handle it.'

'The Senate and the Emperor must believe you can, quaestor.'

'Of course there are well-established routines.'

'And permanent employees who are used to doing the work.'

'There will still be some tricky decisions to take. They'll need me for those.'

The po-faced scribe from Hadrumetum whom I had met at the proconsular palace would be able to cope with any decisions the quaestor was supposed to put his name to.

I served Quadratus more wine. My own cup still sat brimful on the balustrade. 'What's in your remit?' He shrugged vaguely. These lads are never sent to their provinces with a proper brief; I summarised the quaestor's role for him: 'Apart from deputising for the proconsul in the lawcourts, there's collection of property taxes, provincial poll tax, port taxes, inheritance tax, and the state percentage on manumission of slaves. Hispania's huge. Baetica may not be the biggest province, but it's the richest and most populous. The sums you oversee must be significant.'

'It's not real money, though.'

I disagreed. 'It's real enough to the merchants and heads of household who have to cough up!'

'Oh, it all comes out of their budget ... From my point of view it's just figures. I'm not obliged to get my hands dirty counting coins.'

I refrained from saying I was surprised he could even count. 'You may never touch the dosh, but you've been entrusted with a full range of headaches: *"the collecting, disbursing, safeguarding, managing and controlling of public funds".'*

Quadratus was taking the flippant line. 'I suppose the records will come to me and I'll approve them – or I'll alter them if they don't fit,' he giggled. He showed no sense of responsibility. I was struck by the horrific possibilities for embezzlement. 'Let's face it, Falco – I have a title and a seal, but in reality I'm impotent. I can't alter the way things are run. Rome is fully aware of that.'

'You mean because your stint in the post is only a year?'

He looked surprised. 'No, because that's just how things are.'

This was the rotten side of government. Enormous power was placed at the disposal of an untried, overconfident young man. His only superior here was the hard-pressed governor who had a full complement of legislative and diplomatic work himself. If the salaried officials who really ran the provinces were corrupt, or if they simply lost heart, here was an outpost of the Empire which could fall apart. With a brash and completely unprepared master placed over them, who could blame them if they did lose heart?

Something like that had happened in Britain over a decade earlier. I was there. I knew. The Icenian Revolt was brought about by a combination of indifferent politicians, overbearing armed forces and ill-judged financial control. This had alienated the local populace, with results that were sheer murder. Ironically, a major catalyst for trouble had been the sudden withdrawal of loans by Seneca – the big name from Corduba.

'I see what they mean about you,' Quadratus said suddenly. I wondered who 'they' were, who had been briefing him about me. He wanted to know how good I really was at my job – and how dangerous.

I quirked up an eyebrow, enjoying his unease as he went on, 'You sit drinking your wine just as pleasantly as anyone. But somehow I don't reckon you're thinking "This is a

1036

palatable vintage, if a little sweet." You're in another world, Falco.'

'The wine has its moments. Baetica suffers from too much wind from the south; it troubles the grapes.'

'Jove, you know everything! I do admire that. I really do —' He really did. 'You're a complete professional. That's something I'd like to emulate.' He might — but not if it meant he had to work on my pay, eating gritty bread and paying too much rent for a hovel in a lousy tenement.

'You just have to be thorough.' I couldn't be bothered with his sham flattery, or his ignorance of conditions in the real world.

'So what's on your mind, Falco?'

'Nothing changes,' I said. 'Lessons are constantly put before us — and are never learned.'

Quadratus was still game, though his speech was becoming slow. I had drunk much less. I had no taste for it. I had lost my taste for philosophy too.

Below in the garden dim figures rushed about, engaged in some dubious form of hide-and-seek. It required neither skill in the chase nor subtlety in claiming the prize. I watched for a moment, feeling my age, then turned back to the quaestor. 'So what, Tiberius Quinctius Quadratus, are you intending to do as quaestor to prevent the formation of an oil cartel in Baetica?'

'Is there one?' he asked me, suddenly as wide-eyed as the second-rate virgins who were squealing among the clipped myrtles on the terraces below.

XXXVIII

I stood up to leave. I clapped his shoulder, and handed him the jug of wine. 'Enjoy your evening.'

'What cartel?' he slurred, much too solemnly.

'The one that can't possibly exist in this respectable province where the businessmen are so ethical and the officials perform their duties to the highest standards of probity!'

I stepped back into the heated room indoors. There was wine everywhere. The illustrious Spunky and his cronies were roaring with laughter, looking shiny and much redder in the face. They had reached the happy stage of dying with mirth at their own silliness. Marius Optatus had disappeared somewhere. I didn't blame him, though since we were sharing a carriage it was somewhat inconvenient. He had probably found a bailiff and was discussing the fine details of making chestnut withy baskets. His interests were so practical.

'Grand party!' I applauded my host. He looked pleased. 'Is your sister here?'

'Locked in her bedroom pretending not to know it's going on!'

Maybe Aelia Annaea would welcome some refined masculine company. It had to be worth a try.

When I clambered over the revellers and out into the corridor, I left behind whoops of determined foolishness. I had noticed one poor soul already lying prone beside a cabinet of curios with his eyes tightly closed in misery. His capacity must be no bigger than a gnat's. By my reckoning they were all less than an hour from being sick over the balcony. There would be one or two who could not crawl that far. It boded ill for my host's father's porphyry vases

1038

and his silk-covered ivory-ended reading couch. His collected works of Greek men of letters had already been well trampled by flailing boots and his Egyptian carpet was being rolled up to make a swat in a game of 'Human Fly'.

Sticking my thumbs in my belt I moved carefully through the groups of rich children dangerously rollicking. This was not an occasion to reassure a father whose first offspring was only weeks from birth. Annaeus Maximus could have picked a better month to visit his Gades farms.

As I rather expected I learned nothing else that helped my mission, only that the town house of the Annaei covered two floors, was exquisite though slightly old-fashioned in décor, and possessed every amenity. I found a large number of beautifully appointed bedrooms, some occupied, though not by people who wanted my staid company. Becoming morose, I wandered down a staircase, stepping over various young ladies without partners who were sitting on the marble treads getting piles while they bemoaned the stupidity of Corduban boys. I concurred with their view, though perhaps not for the same reasons; what's more, I had my doubts about some of the girls.

The ground floor comprised the normal public rooms and peristyles of a large, showy home. The rude huts of their forefathers had been transformed by the modern Annaei into high temples where they could act as patrons to the less well-off. It was meant to impress; I allowed it a few astonished gasps.

There was a full bath-house suite, where some luckier young ladies were being repeatedly thrown by young men into the heated swimming pool; they squealed a lot then struggled out and ran back to be thrown in again. No one had drowned yet. In the attached ball-park a lively group thought it good fun to dress up a nannygoat in a garland of flowers and the robes which the important householder wore when he officiated as a priest. I greeted them serenely, then passed on into the covered arcade which led to the garden area.

This was more peaceful, apart from occasional troops of youths who galloped through it in a jiggling human daisy-chain. Turning away from the main terrace, where the merrymaking among the topiary looked more lewd than I could contemplate, I was heading for an ivy-covered gazebo, lit by torches. There were two figures conversing; they looked rather like Optatus and the gracious Aelia, sister of our three jolly hosts. Before I could reach them I was stopped by a pair who were stock-still on the gravel path, locked in a desperate, motionless embrace. They were about sixteen; she thought she might be losing him, whereas he held her with the calm, reassuring air of a faithless swain who knew it had already happened.

Touched, I started doubling back to avoid disturbing their poignant and ultimately pointless idyll. Then I bumped into Marmarides. He was coming to find me to ask permission to borrow the carriage; he had become embroiled with a group of young creatures who were fascinated by his African appearance. Just by asking him the question, I had embroiled myself too: 'I suppose they want to know about your Aethiopian potency!' He looked embarrassed but did not deny that his female admirers had the usual curiosity about his personal equipment. 'Does this happen to you often?'

'Oh, all the time, Falco! My master Stertius lives in terror he'll be called to account when some citizen complains that I'm responsible for his lady having a dark child. The only reason I was allowed to come with you is that he reckoned yours was long past the dangerous stage!'

'Oh thanks! I wish I was back home with her now.'

'I can take you, easy.'

'We'd better deal with your supporters' club first. At least we may save a couple of young women from debauchery tonight!'

That was debatable, but I wanted an excuse to escape. Marmarides could have just dumped his admirers — but decent men don't, do we? He had promised to drive two of them home to Corduba before they got into trouble with their parents (or some such tale). I said I would leave at the same time. There would be no room for Optatus or Constans, but I could protect Marmarides from assault on the journey into Corduba, we could ditch the dames safely, then he could leave me in a tavern where I could have a quiet bite to eat while he went back to collect our comrades. Providing food of any substance lacked glamour for our hosts; they had omitted it.

We shoved a couple of the shrieking women inside the carriage; they were probably demure little things when sober, though drink had robbed them of all taste. I climbed up on top with Marmarides and we set off fast before our passengers could thrill themselves by swarming out to join us. When our mules reached the gate at the end of the long entry drive, we had to swerve madly; we passed a much larger piece of coachwork, drawn by two fiery horses and driven by a set-faced groom in livery. As we went out it was coming in.

'Keep going!' I grinned. 'Marmarides, I rather think that Annaeus Maximus has remembered what happened the last time he left his boys at home unsupervised.'

XXXIX

We found where the girls lived and persuaded them to go in quietly; we used the shameless trick of mentioning the return of Annaeus Maximus and warning them that that angry father would soon be talking to their own parents.

'Spunky, Dotty and Ferret are in big trouble! Best to nip indoors looking innocent and pretend you never went anywhere.' I could just hear some pert little minx in the distant future trying this one out on me. I could just see me too, willing myself to believe the lie ...

My plan to have supper alone seemed churlish now; we went back together to try to extricate Optatus and young Constans, if possible before they were publicly linked with the row. Approaching the town house we met a string of chastened youngsters being marched home in the custody of Annaeus' slaves. These were the walking wounded. Up at the house others who could not stagger had been collected up and laid out neatly in a colonnade. We gathered that parents had been sent for. We also sensed that it had not been done out of malice – but as a sensible precaution in case any of these stupid children had actually poisoned themselves with too much wine.

Of Spunky, Dotty and Ferret I saw no sign. Nor were their father and mother visible, though the slaves mopping up the battlefield were doing it very quickly and efficiently, with downcast eyes. The master's physician, overseeing the row of unconscious young bodies, was fiercely purse-lipped. There was no longer an amphora in sight.

We could find neither Optatus nor Constans. In the end we went home, before the oil in the carriage lamp ran out.

Helena Justina was still up, quietly writing letters to Rome.

I sat on the floor at her feet and hugged her. 'Dear gods, I'm sick of other men's sons! I hope mine's a daughter!'

As if to confirm it, the baby kicked me soundly in the face. 'She's got huge hooves!' Helena muttered, after crying ouch herself.

'She'll be a darling ... Listen, I'm establishing the rules now – boy or girl, it doesn't go out to visit friends without permission, without an escort of extremely prissy slaves, and without me personally going to fetch it home not more than an hour after it departs our house.'

'Very wise, Marcus. I'm sure this will work wonderfully.'

Helena laid down her pen on a side table and closed the inkwell gently. She ran her fingers through my curls. I pretended not to notice, while I let myself relax. Too large now to be flexible, instead of bending down to me as she once would have done, she kissed the tip of her finger and touched my brow consolingly. 'What's the matter, you poor tired, miserable soul? Didn't you enjoy the party, then? What went wrong with your boys' night out?'

'They were too rough for me. I had a depressing experience talking to the fabled quaestor, who is the last word in moral toughness – if you think fluff is tough. Then the hosts' parents came home unexpectedly – a scheme I shall follow myself when our limb gets old enough. I scarpered. I couldn't find the other two –'

'Constans came back,' she told me.

'The night is full of surprises. How did he find his way?'

'The quaestor brought him.'

'That's commendable!'

'Charming,' she agreed.

'You don't like him?'

'I deeply distrust charm. Even so, I let him share the guest room where he had deposited the snoring Constans.'

'So Quadratus is not beyond redemption?'

'He seemed appalling. He apologised in a well-spoken voice. He introduced himself politely, then praised my brother Aelianus. I loathed him instinctively. But it was very late.'

'Are they in the same bed?' I asked, wondering.

'No.'

'It's not like that then!'

'He seems to treat young Constans as an immature lad who needs an older friend.'

'*Really* charming!'

'So we are supposed to believe,' said Helena.

It was then that Marius Optatus reappeared. He had walked much of the way, apparently. 'I was looking for you, Falco!' he stormed tetchily.

'I looked for you too – honestly! I'd seen you hob-nobbing with Aelia Annaea so I thought that since she owns her own gold mine you were in there doing yourself some good!'

'Was Claudia Rufina at the party, Marius?' asked Helena sympathetically.

'No,' he said. Presumably that was one reason for his short temper.

'He was too wrapped up with Aelia,' I teased. 'The man has no loyalty.'

'Probably talking about Claudia,' retorted Helena.

Optatus had no sense of humour this evening. He was white with tiredness, and irritation too. 'I did my best for you, Falco, and in return you stole the transport and stranded me!'

'Why, what did you do?'

'I found out that Dotty and his merry selection of friends were –'

'In the cellar?'

'Yes.'

'Soaking up all Papa's choice imported Falernian?'

'Yes.'

'Putting the world to rights like depressed witches when half the coven's failed to show – Yes?'

'– And watching a dancing girl,' said Marius.

*

Helena Justina gripped me by the shoulders and removed me from my cosy position. I sat up with my arms around my knees. Helena demanded, 'Marius Optatus, would this be a dancing girl Marcus has seen before?'

'How should I know?' He was still angry, though being polite to Helena. 'I could not find Falco to compare points of similarity! I had decided to accost the girl myself, but then Annaeus Maximus came home and the row started. In the chaos the dancer slipped away somewhere; that was understandable. Clearly you had done the same,' he sneered at me. 'I wanted to leave myself, but I thought I should try and find out about the girl for you –'

'You've taken to undercover work! What was she like?' I inserted quickly. 'Loose-limbed, gorgeous and with luxurious black hair?'

'She was nothing of a looker – but she could certainly dance.'

That was a surprise. I must have been even more drunk than I remembered at the dinner for the Society of Olive Oil Producers of Baetica. I had thought Diana was fairly personable but her repertoire lacked skill. Aelianus had also said she had her limitations. Maybe we were right; maybe Optatus took the uncritical view. For some men, if a woman has very few clothes on and is signalling that the rest might come off with modest encouragement, that's enough. 'Marius, Baetica is full of women wielding tambourines to make a quick denarius. Why did you decide this one was significant?'

'Dotty told me she had been asking curious questions. She wanted to know where his father was. He reckoned she was making sure there was no chance of parental displeasure – wrong, as it turned out.'

'She's a decent dancer, yet she was tantalising teenagers?'

'Most dancers are short of money,' he corrected me frostily.

'Was she dancing in a costume?'

'She was dancing in an immodest shift, Falco. That is

1045

what young men expect.' The stern Marius had reached the
sarcastic stage.

'I wonder how they found her? Is some sort of directory
of dubious entertainers kept at the Temple of the Capitoline Triad, perhaps? I don't suppose the young Annaei
were able to consult the aedile's list; the aedile would have
gone straight to their papa.'

'Please don't be facetious, Falco. Dotty was taking the
credit for hiring her.'

'My good Marius, you've been working hard.'

'Don't bother to thank me! Dotty said that she had heard
about the party and presented herself, offering to perform.
He did not know where she came from.' She must be
hanging around Corduba – and she must have her ear to
the ground.

'Rich young men have all the luck.'

'I expect she charged a gigantic fee,' chided Helena.

'Rich young men don't feel the pain.'

'Anyway –' Optatus deflated and confessed with a sigh, 'I
know this is not the girl you want, Falco. Dotty was
perfectly frank. He knew of Selia – she is familiar to all
those young men, apparently. They don't care that she is
not the most perfect dancer – she has other attractions that
compensate. Dotty hadn't been able to hire her this evening
because she is supposed to have returned to Hispalis. He
did say the older one, the one they did have there, had been
trying to find out what other dancers he knew.'

'Did he own up to her that he had wanted Selia instead?'

'He's an oil producer's son, Falco! He's much too cute to
do that.'

While I was wondering whether the appearance of a
second dancer was just coincidence, Helena decided to
confess about the two young disasters who were asleep in a
guest bedroom. Optatus was furious.

However, he calmed down next day, thanks to a jape we
two devised. The quaestor and Constans had arrived at our
house the night before riding together on a highly bred
horse which they had stolen from the Annaeus stable. We

solemnly promised to return it for them before there was a hue and cry. Then I sent them off back to their own homes on a special horse of my own.

'His name's Prancer. You have to check him or he dashes away. Hold on tight in case he bolts.'

'Thanks, Falco.' Quadratus had already realised he was the butt of a joke. 'But this leaves you without a mount —'

'I will find Marcus Didius a horse,' grinned Optatus pleasantly. 'You keep that one — with our compliments!'

XL

Where next?

I was glad Optatus had offered me a decent mount. I had run out of options in Corduba, and badly needed to visit Hispalis. According to the middle Annaeus, that was where Selia would be found. She had always been my prime target.

Had events been different, Helena and I would have enjoyed a slow boat ride together as offered by Cyzacus and Gorax. We had first come to know one another well on a trip across Europe which had included journeys by river. Ever since those long weeks falling in love we had adored water transport; we were nostalgic types. This time though, time was against us.

There was a good road all along the Baetis – the Via Augusta which travelled to Gades. If dispatch-riders of the imperial post with urgent missives could gallop fifty miles a day, I could certainly try to match them. I would use the horse our friend produced for me and ride into Corduba, then I would call at the governor's palace and demand that he give me authority to use the stables and lodges of the *cursus publicus*. Two days there; two days back; plus however long it took me to interview Cyzacus senior and Norbanus, then to search for the dancing girl.

While I executed this fantastic feat of logistics, Helena could wait on the estate, sleeping mostly. That was what she needed now.

Helena Justina pointed out quietly that I hate horses. I said I was a professional. I thought she hid a smile.

I had been up at dawn so I was at the Palace waiting when the clerks first strolled into their offices discussing last night's drinking bout. They had barely got on to how many stairs they had fallen down when they found me, looking brisk. My previous visit had left me a hero. There was no need to see the proconsul; these lads were mine to command. My scandalous stories about their master, invented or not, had worked: clerks are always longing for somebody to brighten up their lives.

Permits to use the *cursus publicus* are not readily available. They have to bear the Emperor's personal signature; that's their validation. Governors of provinces are supplied with a finite number, which they are supposed to use only in the proper circumstances. Prissy ones actually write home to check whether they are following the rules. But the clerks of the proconsul of Baetica decided that their man would approve one for me, without being put to the trouble of knowing he had done it. Nice lads.

I usually go on foreign missions already equipped with my own pass. I had not thought about it this time, and neither had Laeta – assuming he possessed the authority to give me one. I had been trying not to think about Laeta. But when I did, I asked the clerks whether he had become the official point of contact for intelligence issues.

'No, it's still supposed to be Anacrites, Falco.'

'Isn't that typical! I left Anacrites on his deathbed. He must have been formally replaced by now.'

'Well, nobody tells us – unless Rome's decided to leave a corpse in charge!'

'Believe me, lads, you won't notice any difference if they replace the Chief Spy with a stiff.'

'Suits us!' they giggled. 'We hate getting letters from him. The old man always goes on the rampage because he can't understand what Anacrites is on about. Then if we send for clarification we get the same message back, only not just in cypher; all the references are changed to code names as well.'

'How about Laeta? Have you noticed an increase in the volume of messages from him? More urgent signals, perhaps?'

'No more than usual. He can't use signals.'

'Why? No entitlement?'

'He writes too much. The beacon flares can only send one letter at a time; it's too slow for long documents.' Too inaccurate as well; you need night-time, with exactly the right visibility, and even then every time a message is transmitted between watch-towers there is a risk that the signallers may misread the lights and pass along gobbledegook. 'Laeta sends scrolls, always via the dispatch-riders.'

'No sign of him having new responsibilities, then?'

'No.'

'I don't suppose he's bothering to enquire after me?'

'No, Falco.'

There was something I wanted to check up on. I gazed at them in a frank and friendly manner. 'I'm asking because if Anacrites is laid up or dead, there may be changes on the Palatine ... Listen, you know how I came out to Baetica with a letter for the proconsul saying I was a man on a secret mission?' They were bound to know; there was no harm in sharing the confidence. 'The old man told me you had already been asked to note the presence of another person nobody talks about?' They glanced at each other. 'I'm getting worried,' I told them, lying well. 'I think an agent might have gone missing. With Anacrites lying prone we can't find out who he had in the field.'

More obvious looks were now being exchanged. I waited. 'Letters of introduction from the Chief Spy's office carry the top security mark, Falco.'

'I know. I use it myself.'

'We are not allowed to read them.'

'But I bet you do!'

Like lambkins they agreed: 'Just before you came Anacrites sent one of his coded notes. It was his normal nutter's charter: the agent would not be making contact officially – yet we were to afford full facilities.'

'I bet you thought that was about me.'

'Oh no.'

'Why not?'

'The agent was a woman, Falco.'

'Well, you'll enjoy facilitating her!' I had grinned, but I was groaning inside.

Anacrites *ought* to have been planning to send out Valentinus. He was definitely working on the case and Momus, my crony at the Palace, had told me Valentinus had been the best agent Anacrites used. Why send a female? Well, Valentinus was a freelance, his own master. Perhaps he had refused to work abroad. That surprised me though. All I knew of him – not much, admittedly – had suggested he was a calm, efficient type who would not balk at anything. Most people welcome the offer of a free long-distance trip.

Surely even Anacrites hadn't fallen for the old belief that respectable businessmen like the oil producers of Baetica were likely to be seduceable? The ones I had met might possibly be so – but they were too long in the tooth to be blackmailed about it afterwards.

Maybe I had been living with Helena Justina for too long. I had grown soft. My natural cynicism had been squeezed out. I had forgotten that there will always be men who can be lured into pillow confessions by a determined dancing girl.

Just as I left I asked another question: 'What do you think about the new quaestor? What are your views on Quadratus?'

'A bastard,' my allies assured me.

'Oh go on. A quaestor is always a bastard; that's how they're defined. Surely he's no worse than the rest of them? He's young and jumped-up – but you've seen it all before. A few months with you showing him how the world works and he'll be all right, surely?'

'A double bastard,' the lads reiterated solemnly.

One thing I always reckon in the marbled halls of bureaucracy is that the best assessments of personalities come from the clerks they kick.

I went back and sat down. I laced my fingers and leaned my chin on them. First the proconsul had taken the initiative to show he entertained doubts about Quadratus,

1051

and now these characters openly despised him without giving him a trial. *'Tell me!'* I said. So being obliging friends of mine, they did.

Quinctius Quadratus was not entirely clean. His personal record had preceded him to Baetica, and although it was confidential (*because* it was), it had been pored over by the secretariat: there was a bad story, one that Quadratus would find hard to shake off in his future career. On his route to the Senate in his late teens he had served as a military tribune. Posted to Dalmatia he had been involved in a messy incident where some soldiers attempting to reinstate a bridge on a flood-swollen river had lost their lives. They could have waited until the torrent abated, but Quadratus ordered them to tackle the job despite the obvious risk. An official enquiry had deemed the affair a tragic accident – but it was the kind of accident whose details his old commanding officer had bothered to pass on personally to the proconsul who was just inheriting Quadratus in a new civil post.

So there really was a black mark against his name.

Shortly afterwards, I had finally reached the corridor when I noticed some early arrivals queuing for an interview with the proconsul. A scribe who must be senior to the other men – because he had sauntered in even later and with an even worse air of being weighed down by a wine headache – had been waylaid by two figures I recognised. One was the elderly oil magnate, Licinius Rufius, the other his grandson Rufius Constans. The youth was looking sullen; when he spotted me he seemed almost afraid.

I overheard the senior clerk say the proconsul would not be available that day. He gave them some good reason; it was not just a brush-off. The old man looked irritated, but was accepting it reluctantly.

I nodded a courteous greeting to Licinius, but with a long hard ride ahead of me I had no time to stop. I took the road to Hispalis with problems cluttering my mind.

Most puzzling was the female agent Anacrites had

intended to send to Baetica. Was she the 'dangerous woman' he had been muttering about? Then *where* was she? Had he ever actually given her orders? When Anacrites was attacked, had she stayed in Rome without further instructions? Or was she here? Here perhaps even on her own initiative? (Impossible; Anacrites had never employed anyone with that much gumption.)

The female agent had to be identified. Otherwise *she* might be the dancer I was pursuing. I might have drawn all the wrong conclusions about Selia. She could have been at the dinner as backup for Anacrites and Valentinus; she could be innocent of the attacks; she could have dropped her arrow in the street during a meeting with them; the wounds on the two men could have had some other cause. If so, what was she up to now in Corduba? Had she been dressed as a shepherdess at the Parilia parade in order to follow up the cartel? Had she then disguised herself as an old woman to try and interview Licinius Rufius? Were she and I all along working for the same ends? — Well then, who was the real attacker of Valentinus and Anacrites?

The other possibility was that Selia was as dangerous as I had always thought – and that some other woman was in Baetica on the Chief Spy's behalf. One I had not encountered yet. Very likely the dancer Dotty had hired for the party. Some lousy fleabag Anacrites used, who was dogging my steps and liable to get in my way. That was the most likely. And it made me livid. Because maybe somebody at the Palace *knew* we were both out here – in which case why in Hades was it necessary? Why, when Helena Justina needed me, was I wasting my own time and duplicating effort?

I dismissed the idea. The Palace might be well capable of keeping agents in the dark, but under Vespasian double payment was never sanctioned where a single fee would do. So that meant there were two different offices actively involved. Laeta had sent me out, unaware that Anacrites had someone else in the field. Our objectives might be similar – or absolutely different. As I homed in on Selia, somebody else with conflicting orders could be doing the same. And in the long run, as I had suspected right from the night of the dinner on the Palatine, I myself would probably end up suffering: the hapless victim of a palace feud.

There was nothing I could do. Communications with Rome took too long to query this. I had to set off for Hispalis and do my best. But all the time I had to watch my back. I risked finding out that another agent had got there first and all my efforts were redundant. Somebody else might take the credit. Somebody else might earn the reward.

I could find no answers. Even when I had puzzled over the questions until I was sick of them there was still one more which might or might not be related, a new question that I had just left behind in Corduba. Why had Licinius Rufius wanted an interview with the proconsul? What had brought an elderly gentleman into the city so early in the morning, with his grandson morosely in tow?

PART THREE:
HISPALIS: CORDUBA: MONTES MARIANA

AD73: May

What difference does it make how much is laid away in a man's safe or in his barns, how many head of stock he grazes or how much capital he puts out at interest, if he is always after what is another's and only counts what he has yet to get, never what he has already? You ask what is the proper limit to a person's wealth? First, having what is essential, and second, having what is enough.

Seneca

XLI

Three mornings later I was sitting in a foodshop in Hispalis. Every muscle ached. I had blisters in obnoxious places. My brain was exhausted too.

Hispalis was growing hot. By midsummer this would be one of the most fiercely baked little towns in the Empire. Midsummer was closer than I dared contemplate. Weeks before then the child I had rashly fathered would be born. It could be happening while I was here. I could be breaking all my heartfelt assurances to Helena. The baby might have been born already without me. I could be a condemned man.

I felt like one, as I positioned my backside with extreme caution on the bench of this quiet place near the southwestern gate, within smell of the quays. The silence suited me. Eating bad food in an empty bar felt like home. For a moment I could imagine I was giving myself bellyache with a limp salad, somewhere on the crest of the Aventine. I was still enjoying the memory when the tambourinists arrived. Spotting a stranger they sidled up to try their luck with a noisy serenade. I would have left, but my stiffened limbs did not want to be disturbed.

Anybody who has lived in Rome has learned to ignore even the most vigorously orchestrated pleas from beggars. I had already set myself with my back to the wall, to avoid having my purse lifted from behind. I became resolutely deaf. Eventually someone who lived in a house next door threw open a shutter and screamed at the minstrels to lose themselves. They moved a few doorways up and stood there muttering. The shutter slammed. I kept chewing on rather tough lettuce.

This was supposed to be the third town in Baetica, after Corduba and Gades. My route had brought me in from the east, along with the aqueduct. Staggering under the town gate on the Corduba road last night, exhausted, I had ridden straight down the main street and discovered a modern civic forum complete with meeting-house, courts and baths: all people needed to dabble in the mire of local politics and justice, then wash off the stench afterwards. This morning I crawled out from the mansio, bleary-eyed and bilious, and soon found the original republican forum, with elderly temples and a more serene atmosphere, now too small for this thriving town. Further on towards the river was a third, extremely large piazza, the most busy of all, where commercial life hummed. Here the baths were bigger than in the forum, since there was more cash to build them, and the porticos were more packed. Money-changers had their stalls set out soon after dawn. Not long after that the throngs of distributors, merchants, shippers and other speculators started to appear. I had soaked in the atmosphere until I felt at home. Then I found this backstreet bar. I had been over-confident in my choice.

When more street musicians hove in sight, I paid the bill (pleasingly cheap). I took the last of my bread and smoked ham, and ate as I walked. I headed out of town to the river. Here the Baetis was broad and tidal. Its banks were crowded with jetties made from hewn stone blocks, and noisy with boatmen and porters. Everywhere were negotiators' offices. Everywhere cargoes were being transferred from barges to deep-sea vessels, or vice versa. Substantial fortunes were being made from commodities which nobody here would be using and nobody here had produced. Oil, wine, cloth, minerals from the interior mines, and cinnabar were being shipped in quantities. It was a middleman's dream.

Returning from the waterside hubbub, I discovered the clubhouse of the guild of bargees near the commercial square. A few permanent fixtures were already there; they probably lived in the clubroom – and they were certainly the bargees who did least work. I learned that the elder

Cyzacus was not there today. They spoke with a note of jealousy, and said he lived out at Italica.

'He's in demand a lot lately! What's making him so popular?'

'I can't answer that. I have never really met the man – who else wants him?'

'Someone we'd prefer to you! Someone a lot prettier.'

'A woman?' It came as no surprise. And it irritated me intensely. Trust Anacrites to lumber me. Trust one of his minions to spoil the show before I had the chance to survey the ground. But I was working for Laeta (much as I distrusted him) and I felt determined not to stand back and give Anacrites a free run. The only time Anacrites had employed me direct, he dumped me and tried to kill me. I would never forget that. 'So does Cyzacus come into Hispalis for meetings with lissom girls?'

'Not him. The old bastard comes into Hispalis to tell the rest of us what's what!' I gathered they viewed him as a leisured degenerate who thought himself above them.

I knew what that meant. Cyzacus really was the best. He had worked hard all his life. He had sons who still ran his business for him successfully. He won all the contracts because people could rely on him. He devoted effort to the affairs of the guild. Meanwhile these grumpy layabouts who liked to start lunching immediately after they finished breakfast sat about here playing Soldiers and drinking posca, and steadfastly complained.

'*Was* his girlfriend lissom – or long in the tooth?'

They cackled with grainy laughter, and I could get no sense out of them.

I had a good idea why Cyzacus might prefer the quiet life in Italica. I found out how to get there, then moved on to my next task.

Norbanus, the Gallic negotiator who arranged shipping space, occupied a majestic office right on the commercial square. People from whom I asked directions told me where it was, sneering openly. Nobody likes foreigners who

1059

demonstrate how successful they are. It was clear from his wide portals, carpeting of polychrome mosaic, statuettes on marble tripods, and neatly dressed office staff that Norbanus knew all there was to know about making money from other people's goods.

The staff were neat, but just as sleepy as subordinates anywhere once the master goes out. Because he was a Gaul, many of his menials were family. Their response was pretty Gallic. They excitedly discussed my question concerning his whereabouts amongst themselves for a long time, then one admitted with extremely formal wording that he wasn't here. They could have told me in a few words right at the start, but Gauls like the embroidery of debate. Urbanity for them means an impression of superior breeding – coupled with a barbarian yearning to swipe off your head with a very long sword.

I asked when Norbanus might be returning. They gave me a time that I felt was just a put-off. We all shook hands. They were smooth; I stayed polite. I ground my teeth in private. Then, having no option, I left.

It was death to my blisters, but I walked back to the mansio, claimed a new horse, and set off across the river to ride the five miles to Italica.

XLII

Founded by Scipio as a colony of veterans, Italica boasted itself the oldest Roman town in Hispania. Before that the happy Phoenicians had known it, and the ancient tribes of Tartessos had made it a playground when the shepherds, who had already exploited wool as far as possible, learned that their land possessed great mineral wealth and eagerly took to mining. Set on slightly hilly ground, with an open aspect, it was a very hot, dusty cluster – relieved by the presence of a grandiose complex of baths. Those who lived to be old men would know this dot in the provinces as the birthplace of an emperor. Even when I was there the rich used it as a hideaway, separated from Hispalis by just sufficient distance to make Italicans feel snooty.

There was a theatre, and a good amphitheatre too. Everywhere was spattered with plinths, fountains, pediments and statuary. If there was a bare space on a wall, someone erected an inscription. The wording was lofty. Italica was not the kind of place where you find a poster from the guild of prostitutes pledging their votes to some deadbeat in the local elections.

In the strict grid of well-swept streets near the forum I found mansions that would not disgrace the finest areas of Rome. One of them belonged to Cyzacus. I was not allowed in, but I could see from the doorstep with its matched pair of standard bay trees that the entrance corridor was painted richly in black, red and gold, and that it led to a sumptuous atrium with a pool and gorgeous fresco-panelled walls. This was elegant public space for the patron's reception of his clients – but informers did not qualify.

Cyzacus was out. His steward told me quite agreeably. Cyzacus had been driven into Hispalis to meet a friend at the bargees' guild.

I was running around to no purpose here. The day was slipping away. This was the kind of work every informer dreads. The gods know it was appallingly familiar to me.

I went to the baths, felt too fretful to enjoy them, spurned the gymnasium, had a bowl of almond soup with enough garlic to ensure nobody spoke to me again for a week, then I returned to Hispalis myself.

XLIII

The bargees' clubhouse was a large bare room, with tables
where the layabouts I had seen that morning were still
dicing. With midday more members had come from the
wharves to eat. Food was brought in from a thermopolium
next door. It was probably bought at special rates, and
looked good value; I reckon they got their wine for free.
The atmosphere of comradeship was of the quiet kind. Men
entering nodded to those present, and some sat down
together; others preferred to eat alone. Nobody challenged
me when I started looking around.

This time I found them: Cyzacus and Norbanus, two
familiar faces from a month ago at the Baetican dinner on
the Palatine. Sitting at a table in a corner, looking as deep
in gossip as the last time I saw both of them. It seemed like
their regular venue, and they looked like customary
daytime debauchers. They had already finished their lunch.
From the piles of empty bowls and platters it had been
substantial and I guessed the wine jug would have been
replenished several times.

My arrival was timely. They had reached the point of
slowing down in their heavy meal. Where diners at a formal
feast might now welcome a Spanish dancer to whistle at
while they toyed with the fresh fruit, these two pillars of
Hispalis commerce had their own diversion: me.

Cyzacus was a dapper, slightly shrunken old feather-
weight, in a slimline grey tunic over a long-sleeved black
one. He was the quiet, better-mannered partner in what
seemed an unlikely pair. He had a hollow, lined face with
an unhealthy pallor, and closely clipped white hair. His
bosom pal Norbanus was much heavier and more untidy,
pressing folds of belly up against the table edge. His fat
fingers were forced apart by immense jewelled rings. He too

was a mature vintage, his hair still dark, though with wings of grey. Several layers of chin sported dark stubble. He had all the physical attributes that pass for a jolly companion – including a painfully raucous personality.

I slumped on a bench and came to the point: 'The last time we met, gentlemen, I was at home and you were the visitors. We were dining, though.' I cast my eyes over the empties, with their debris of fish skeletons, chewed olive stones, stripped chicken wings, oyster shells, bay leaves and rosemary twigs. 'You know how to produce an impressive discard dish!'

'You have the advantage,' Norbanus said. He sounded completely sober. Feasting was a way of life for these men. He had already buried his snout in his cup again, making no attempt to offer a drink to me.

'The name's Falco.'

They did not bother to make eye contact, either with one another or with me: they had known who I was. Either they really remembered being introduced on the Palatine, or they had worked out that I was the none-too-secret agent investigating the cartel.

'So! You're the respected master bargeman Cyzacus, and you're the notable negotiator Norbanus. Both men with sufficient standing to be entertained in Rome by the eminent Quinctius Attractus?'

'The eminent crawler!' Norbanus scoffed, not bothering to keep his voice down. Cyzacus gave him an indulgent glance. The negotiator's contempt was intended not just for the senator; it embraced all things Roman – including me.

'The eminent manipulator,' I agreed frankly. 'Myself, I'm a republican – and one of the plebs. I'd like to hope the senator and his son might have overstretched themselves.' This time they both stilled. I had to look closely to spot it, though.

'I've been talking with *your* sons,' I told the bargee. There was no way young Cyzacus and Gorax could have communicated with their papa in the three days since I saw them; I was hoping to make him worry what they might have said.

'Nice for you.' He did not disconcert so easily. 'How are my boys?'

'Working well.'

'That makes a change!' I was in a world of rough opinions and plain speaking, apparently. Even so I felt this wary old man would not leave his boys in charge of business upstream at Corduba unless he really trusted them. He had taught them the job, and despite the ruck they must have had when the natural son went off to dabble with poetry, nowadays the three of them worked closely together. The two sons had struck me as loyal both to each other and to their father.

'Cyzacus junior was telling me about his literary career; and Gorax had his mind on some chickens. They explained to me how when I saw you in Rome you were there to talk tough about exports.'

'I was there as a guest!' Cyzacus had the manner of a meek old chap whose mind was wandering. But he was defying me. He knew I could prove nothing. 'Attractus invited me and paid for it.'

'Generous!'

'Bottomless purse,' cackled Norbanus, indicating that he thought the man a fool. I gained the welcome impression that these two had cynically accepted the free trip without ever intending to be coerced. After all, they were both in transport; they could certainly go to Rome whenever they wanted, for virtually nothing.

'It strikes me that much as Attractus may admire your wit and conversation, to pay out fares and offer hospitality in his own fine home – all of which I gather he has done on more than one occasion for different groups of Baeticans – might suggest that the illustrious codger wants something?'

'Excellent business sense,' Norbanus grinned.

'And a sharp eye for a deal?'

'He thinks so!' Another insult tripped lightly off the Gallic tongue.

1065

'Maybe he wants to be the uncrowned king of Baetica.'

Norbanus was still sneering: 'Isn't he that already? Patron of Corduba, Castulo and Hispalis, representative of the oil producers in the Senate, linchpin of the copper mines –'

Talking about mines depressed me. 'What part of Gaul are you from?'

'Narbo.' This was close to Tarraconensis though outside Hispania. It was a major entrepôt in southern Gaul.

'You specialise in shipping olive oil? Is that just to Rome?'

He snorted. 'You can't have much idea about the market! A lot of my contracts are bound for Rome, yes; but we're shipping thousands of amphorae. We cover the whole of Italy – and everywhere else. The stuff goes in all directions – up the Rhodanus in Gallia Narbonensis, to Gaul, Britain and Germany; I've done shipments straight across the Pillars of Hercules to Africa; I've sent it as far as Egypt; I've supplied Dalmatia, Pannonia, Crete, mainland Greece and Syria –'

'*Greece*? I thought the Greeks grew their own olives? Weren't they doing it for centuries before you had them here in Baetica?'

'Not got the taste. Not so mellow.'

I whistled quietly. Turning again to Cyzacus I said, 'Expensive business, exporting oil. I gather the price starts going up as soon as they funnel it into the amphorae?'

He shrugged. 'The on-costs are terrible. It's not our fault. For instance, on the journey down from Corduba we have to pay port taxes every single time we stop. It all gets added to the bill.'

'That's after your own profits have been taken out. Then Norbanus here wants his percentage, and the shipper too. All long before the retailer in Rome even has a smell of it.'

'It's a luxury item,' Cyzacus replied defensively.

'Luckily for all of you in Baetica it's an item in universal use.'

'It's a very wonderful product,' Norbanus put in drily, in a holy voice.

'Wonderfully profitable!' I said. I had to change the subject. 'You're a Gaul. How do you get on with the producers?'

'They hate my guts,' Norbanus admitted proudly. 'And it's mutual! At least they know I'm not some bloody interloper from Italy.'

'Speculators!' I sympathised. 'Coming out to the provinces from Rome solely because they can get away with low cash inputs, then drain off huge profits. Bringing their alien work practices. If they ever come out here in person, clinging together in tight little cliques – always planning to go home again once their fortunes are made ... Attractus is a prime example, though he seems to want more from it than most. I know about his olive estate and his mineral mine – what interests does he have in Hispalis?'

'None,' Cyzacus said, disapprovingly.

'He built the baths near the wool market,' Norbanus reminded him. Cyzacus sniffed.

'Didn't it go down well?' I asked.

'The people of Baetica,' Cyzacus informed me, sucking in his thin cheeks, 'prefer to be honoured with benefactions from men who were born here. Not outsiders who want to impress for their personal glory.'

'Where does that leave you as a Gaul?' I demanded of Norbanus.

'Stowing my money in a bankchest!' he grinned.

I looked at them both: 'But you two are friends?'

'We dine together,' Cyzacus told me. I knew what he meant. These were two dedicated men of commerce. They could exchange public hospitality on a regular basis for years on end, yet I doubted if they had ever been to each other's houses, and once they retired from business they might never meet again. They were on the same side – cheating the oil producers and forcing up prices for the eventual customers. But they were not friends.

This was good news. On the face of it the men Quinctius

Attractus had invited to Rome last month shared a common interest. Yet several kinds of prejudice divided them – and they all loathed Attractus himself. The bargees and negotiators tolerated each other, but they hated the olive producers – and those snobs on their grand estates shared no common feeling with the transport side.

Was this antagonism strong enough to prevent them all forming a price ring? Would their shared distrust of a Roman interloper dissuade them from joining him? Had Attractus miscalculated the lure of money? Might these hard-nosed operaters reject him as a leader? Might they reckon there was sufficient profit to be made from oil, and that they were perfectly capable of squeezing out the maximum gain without any help from him – and without any obligation to him afterwards?

'You know why I'm here,' I suggested. Both men laughed. After the size of meal they had eaten all this hilarity could not be good for them. 'There are two reasons. Attractus has drawn attention to himself; he is thought to be a dangerous fixer – and I'm looking into ways of fixing him.' The two men glanced at each other, openly pleased he was in trouble. 'Of course,' I said gravely, 'neither of you has been approached to take part in anything so crooked as a cartel?'

'Certainly not,' they agreed solemnly.

I smiled like a pleasant fellow. 'Reputable businessmen would want nothing to do with such villainy?'

'Of course not,' they assured me.

'And you would immediately report such an approach to the authorities?' I dropped the pose: 'Don't bother to insult me by answering that!'

Old Cyzacus was picking his teeth, but behind the ensuing grimace he may have looked offended that I had just accused them of lying. Liars are always very sensitive.

Norbanus continued to be as unhelpful as possible. 'Is there a cartel, Falco? If so, good luck to it!' he declared. Then he spat on the floor. 'Tcha! They'll never do it – the bloody producers couldn't organise themselves!'

I leaned my elbows on the table, linking my fingers and surveying the reprobates over my hands. I tried ingratiating myself: 'I think you're right. I've seen them in Corduba. They spend so much time making sure they don't get missed off the guest-list for the next soirée with the proconsul, they can't manage much else.'

'All they care about,' Norbanus growled, 'is taking a turn as duovir and sending their sons to ponce about in Rome spending money – wasting their capital!' he added, as if failure to thrive as an investor was an unforgivable offence.

'So don't you think Attractus managed to lean on them?'

Cyzacus took an interest: 'He could lean until he fell over. The producers would never do anything risky.'

'And what about you two?' I challenged. This only produced contemptuous smiles. 'All right. You've been frank with me, so I'll return the compliment. I have to report to the Emperor. I'm going to tell Vespasian that I am convinced there is a cartel being mooted. That Attractus is the prime mover. And that all the men who were seen dining with him at the Society of Olive Oil Producers' dinner at the end of March have assured me they were horrified and that they spurned the idea. Well, you wouldn't want to be indicted with him before the court of conspiracy, would you?'

'Let us know if you get him there,' Norbanus said drily. 'We'll all come and cheer.'

'Perhaps you'd like to help me form a case? Perhaps you'd like to give evidence?'

Neither even bothered to reply. And I didn't bother offering another free fare to Rome on the strength of future assistance. They would not appear in court. Rome has its own snobberies anyway. A couple of foreigners engaged in transportation – however flourishing their businesses – would be despised. I needed to subpoena the estate owners at least. Land counts. Land is respectable. But to indict a senator with a long Roman pedigree even Annaeus and Rufius would not be enough. The Quinctii would walk, unless I could produce witnesses of their own social weight. And where were they?

I was glad I had spoken to these two in person, despite the long trip. I did feel their story carried weight. Their assessment of the producers matched my own. Norbanus and Cyzacus seemed too self-reliant to follow the lead of an entrepreneur from the political world – and too capable of making money on their own account. Not that I could ever rely on this: if the men Attractus had summoned to Rome had leapt at his suggestion, they were hardly likely to tell me. Price-fixing works on subtlety. Nobody ever admits it is happening.

I was leaving. 'I said there were two reasons why I came to Baetica.'

Cyzacus stopped wielding his toothpick. 'What is the other one?' For a vague old man, he responded well.

'It's not pleasant. The night you dined on the Palatine a man was killed.'

'Nothing to do with us.'

'I think it was. Another man, a high official, was seriously wounded. He may be dead too. Both victims were at the dinner. Both were in fact dining with Attractus – which means he's implicated, and as his guests so are you. Somebody slipped up that night – and it won't go away.' This was a long shot. I was hoping that if the Baeticans were unconnected with the attacks, they would turn in the real perpetrator to absolve themselves.

'We can't help you,' said Norbanus. So much for that pious hope.

'Oh? Then why did you leave Rome so fast the next day?'

'Our business was concluded. Since we turned down his offer, we all thought it would be presuming on the senator's hospitality to remain.'

'You've just admitted that an offer *was* made,' I pointed out. Norbanus grinned evilly.

The excuse for leaving could be true. Staying at the

Quinctius house after refusing to play the Attractus game could have been embarrassing. Besides, if they hated the plan, they might want to escape before Attractus tried putting on more pressure. And if they had said no, then they heard about the murder and suspected it was connected with the cartel scheme, they were bound to flee.

'It looks bad,' I returned sombrely. 'A sudden departure straight after a killing tends to appear significant in court. Part of my work includes finding evidence for barristers, and I can assure you that's the sort of tale that makes them gloat and think of massive fees.'

'You're making wild accusations,' Norbanus told me coolly.

'No.'

My simple reply for once caused silence.

Cyzacus recovered himself. 'We offer our sympathy to the victims.'

'Then perhaps you would like to help. I need to find a girl who comes from Hispalis. In delicate official parlance: we think she may have important information relating to the deaths.'

'She did it?' Norbanus sneered crudely.

I smiled. 'She was at the dinner, dancing for Attractus; he claims he doesn't know her though he paid her fee. You may have recognised her; her name's Selia – probably.'

To my surprise they made no quibble about it: they knew Selia. It was her real name. She was a local girl of moderate talent, struggling to make a career where all the demand was for dancers from Gades. (Gades dancers had organised a closed shop on the entertainment circuit ... it had a familiar ring.) Cyzacus and Norbanus remembered seeing Selia at the dinner on the Palatine; they had been surprised, but assumed she had finally made the big breakthrough in Rome. Recently they had heard she was back in Hispalis, so they assumed it came to nothing.

I stared Cyzacus in the eye. 'Just how well do you know her? Would Selia be the lovely who came here looking for you recently?'

'Girls like Selia are not welcome at the bargees' clubroom,' he maintained.

'So she never found you?'

'That's right,' he answered with a cool glare that suggested he was lying again, but that I would extract no more.

Patiently I explained why I was asking: 'There's another woman going around asking questions about this business. They're both trouble. I need to know which is up to what. Your fellow members implied that the girl who came here was a looker – but their standards may be more flexible than mine.' The daytime skivers playing dice looked as if anything in a dress would make them salivate. 'So was it Selia or not?'

'Since I never saw her,' sneered Cyzacus, 'I can't say.'

He and Norbanus were closing up on me, but when I asked the most important question they did know the answer and they told me straight away: they gave me directions to where Selia lived.

XLIV

I walked back to the quays, needing to rid my mind of other men enjoying a long convivial lunch – which they called doing business. I hated my work. I was tired of working alone, unable to trust even the people who had commissioned me. This was a worse case than usual. I was sick of being a plaything in the pointless bureaucratic feud between Laeta and Anacrites.

If Helena had been here, she would have made me feel ludicrous by appearing to sympathise – then suggesting that what I wanted was a new job as a cut-out-fringe sewer in the suede-purse market, with a stall on the Via Ostiana. Just thinking about it made me grin. I needed her.

I found myself staring at the shipping. More boats than I would have expected had plied their way through the straits of Hercules and into the broad gulf at the start of the Atlantic Ocean, past Gades, past the lighthouse at Turris Caepionis, and up the wide estuary of the Baetis to reach Hispalis. Huge merchantmen from all around the Inner Sea were here, and even deep-sea ships that ventured around the outer edge of Lusitania to make landfall in North Gaul and Britain by the hard route. They lined the wharves; they jostled in the channel. Some were anchored out in the river, for lack of space on the quays. There was a queueing system for the barges that came down from Corduba. And this was April, not even the olive harvesting season.

It wasn't April. May had arrived. Some time this month, unavoidably, Helena would produce our child. While I stood here dreaming she might even be having it ...

Now I had Selia's address. Even so, I was in no hurry to go chasing there. I was thinking about this just as carefully as a man who finally made a successful move on a girl who had been playing hard to get – and with the same mixture of excitement and nerves. I would be lucky if the worst that happened was acquiring a slapped face.

Before I could tackle the dancer, I had to prepare myself. Brace myself. She was a woman; I could handle her. Well, I was a man so I assumed I could; plenty of us have been caught out like that. She might even be on my side – if I had a side. The evidence in Rome said Selia was a killer. It might be wrong. She might work for Anacrites. If she did, someone else must have attacked Valentinus and him – unless the Chief Spy was even more behind with approving expenses for his agents than usual. That would be typical, though not many of his deadbeats responded by trying to crack his skull.

If Selia was in the clear I still had to identify the real killer. That was a very big unknown.

Whatever the truth – and being realistic, I thought she *was* the killer – this woman knew I had come to Baetica; she would be waiting for me. I even considered approaching the local watch and asking for an escort, an option I rejected out of sheer Roman prejudice. I would rather go alone. But I had no intention of just strolling up to her door and asking for a drink of water like an innocent passer-by. One wrong move and the dangerous lady might kill me.

I must have been looking grim. For once the Fates decided that I was so pessimistic I might give up this job altogether and deprive them of a lot of fun. So for the first time ever they decided to offer me a helping hand.

The hand was ink-stained and nail-bitten, attached to a weedy arm which protruded from a shrunken long-sleeved tunic with extremely ragged cuffs. The arm hung from a shoulder over which was slung a worn satchel; its flap was folded back for easy access and I could see note-tablets inside. The shoulder served as a bony hanger for the rest of the tunic, which came down below the knees of a short, sad-looking man with pouchy eyes and uncombed hair. Every dry old thong of his sandals had curled back on itself

1074

at the edges. He had the air of being much rebuffed and cursed. He was clearly ill-paid. I deduced, even before he confirmed the tragedy, that he worked for the government.

'Is your name Falco?' I shook the inky hand cautiously as a sign that it might be. I wondered how he knew. 'I'm Gnaeus Drusillus Placidus.'

'Pleased to meet you,' I said. I wasn't. I had been half-enjoying myself remembering Selia as I prepared myself to visit her house. The interruption hurt.

'I thought you would be coming downriver to speak to me.'

'You knew I was here?' I ventured cautiously.

'The quaestor's clerk told me to look out for you.' The old black slave from Hadrumetum; the one who had lost the correspondence with Anacrites — or had it lifted from him.

'He didn't tell me about you!'

The man looked surprised. 'I'm the procurator,' he cried importantly. 'I supervise the port taxes and export tax.' My enthusiasm still failed to match his. In desperation he lowered his voice and hissed, 'It was me who started this!'

I nearly let myself down completely by asking 'Started what?' But his urgency and the way he looked over his shoulder for eavesdroppers explained everything.

'It was you!' I murmured discreetly, but with the note of applause the man deserved. 'You were the sharp-eyed fellow who first wrote to Anacrites, sounding the alarm!'

XLV

I was looking at him keenly now. Still an unimpressive experience. I would like to complain that he behaved officiously, but he was just perfectly straight. Nobody likes a government official they cannot moan about.

We walked nearer to the water, deliberately looking casual. As a procurator he would have an office, but it would be stuffed with staff from the cache of public slaves. They would probably look honest – until the day when it counted. What he and I had to discuss could be the big secret they were all waiting to sell.

'What's your history?' I asked. 'You're not from Baetica? You sound Roman to me; you have the Palatine twang.'

He was not offended at the question. He was proud of his life, with reason. 'I am an imperial freedman. From Nero's time,' he felt obliged to add. He knew I would have asked. Palace freedmen are always judged by the régime when their career took off. 'But that does not affect my loyalty.'

'Anyone who struggled to serve the state under Nero will welcome Vespasian with a huge sigh of relief. Vespasian knows that.'

'I do my job.' It was a statement I believed.

'So how did you reach this position?'

'I bought my freedom, worked in commerce, earned enough to be granted equestrian rank, and offered myself for useful posts. They sent me here.' He had the kind of record I ought to pursue myself; maybe if I had been born a slave I might have managed it. Instead pride and obstinacy got firmly in my way.

'And now you've stirred up quite a controversy. What's the smell that you don't like?'

1076

He did not answer immediately. 'Hard to say. I nearly did not make a report at all.'

'Did you discuss it with anyone?'

'The quaestor.'

'Cornelius?'

He looked shocked. 'Who else?' Clearly the *new* quaestor was not an alternative.

'Decent?'

'I liked him. No side. Did the job — you can't often say that!'

'How did Cornelius get along with the proconsul?'

'He was the chosen deputy, in the old-fashioned way. They had worked together before. He was the senior tribune when the old man had a legion. They came out as a pair. But now Cornelius needs a career move. He wants to show his face in the Senate. The old man agreed to release him.'

'After which he had to take whatever he was sent as a replacement! But I heard Cornelius hasn't gone back to Rome? He's travelling.'

An angry expression passed over Placidus' face. 'Cornelius going on his travels is all part of the nasty smell!' That was intriguing. 'Rome would have been too convenient, wouldn't it? He could have made the report on our problem himself.'

'What are you telling me, Placidus?'

'Cornelius *was* going back. He *wanted* to go back.'

'Keen?'

'Highly excited.' One of those. A careerist. I kept my face neutral. On the lower rung of the public service ladder, Placidus was a careerist himself. 'He was ready for politics. He wanted to get married too.'

'A fatalist! So where exactly is he?' I demanded, with a sinking feeling. For some reason I felt he was about to say the young man was dead.

'In Athens.'

Once I recovered from the unexpected answer I asked, 'What's the attraction in Athens?'

1077

'You mean apart from art, history, language and philosophy?' asked Placidus rather drily. I had an idea he was the type of cultural dreamer who would adore a trip to Greece. 'Well, Cornelius didn't care much for those, in fact; he wasn't the type. Someone in Rome just happened to have an unused ticket on a ship from Gades to Piraeus; he spoke to Cornelius' father and offered free use of it.'

'Generous! Cornelius senior was delighted?'

'What father would turn down the chance of getting his son to the University like that?'

Well, mine, for one. But mine had long ago realised that the more I learned – about anything – the less control he had over me. He never lavished art, history, language or philosophy upon me. That way he never had to face me faking gratitude.

But I could sympathise with Cornelius; he would have been trapped. No senatorial career comes cheap. Nor does marriage. To preserve good relations at home he had to go along with whatever embarrassment his parent well-meaningly bestowed on him – just because some acquaintance at the Curia had smiled and offered it. My own father was an auctioneer. He could recognise a bribe coming five miles away. Not all men are so adept.

'So poor Cornelius only wanted to rush home to govern people, but he's stuck with a present that he would far rather dump – and he has his papa happily telling him it's a chance in a lifetime and he should be a grateful boy? Placidus, can I guess the name of his benefactor? Someone Cornelius did not want to write a nice thank-you letter to? Can the name of Quinctius Attractus be dropped into this conversation without causing a misfit?'

'You've thrown a six, Falco.'

'I've thrown a double, I think.'

'You know how to play this game.'

'I've played before.'

We stared at the river gloomily. 'Cornelius is a very sharp

young man,' said Placidus. 'He knows that a free trip always costs something.'

'And what do you think this one will cost?'

'A great deal to consumers of olive oil!'

'Through Cornelius not mentioning his disquiet about the upcoming situation in Baetica? I suppose he couldn't argue with his father who was far away in Rome. He couldn't risk writing a letter explaining, because the subject was too sensitive. So he's forced to take the ticket – and once he goes, he's obligated to the Quinctii.'

'I can see you have done your research,' said Placidus, thoroughly miserable.

'Can I get the timing straight? You and Cornelius became anxious about the influence of the Quinctii when?'

'Last year when his son came out to Baetica. We knew there must be a reason and Cornelius guessed Quadratus was aiming to replace him in the quaestorship. At the same time Attractus was first starting to invite groups to Rome.'

'So Quadratus may have warned his father that Cornelius might make adverse comments when he was debriefed by the Palace at the end of his tour? The Quinctii decided to delay him, while they consolidated their position. And when the unwanted cultural holiday arose, Cornelius gave in but you decided to take action?'

'I wrote a note.'

'Anonymously?'

'Official channels were too dangerous. Besides, I did not want to land Cornelius with an enemy in Rome. He had always supported me.'

'Was this why you approached Anacrites and not Laeta?'

'It seemed appropriate to involve the intelligence group.'

Involving Anacrites was never appropriate, but one had to work with him to see it. 'What happened next? Anacrites wrote back formally and asked the proconsul to investigate – so he handed the job straight to Cornelius? Won't that turn out awkward for him anyway?'

'He could say he had no choice. Once there was an instruction from Rome, Cornelius was bound to follow up.

Still, we made sure his answering report was conveyed discreetly.'

I laughed briefly. 'I know! Whoever decided to send that report with Camillus Aelianus?'

'He was friendly with Cornelius.'

I shook my head. 'And with another young man too! Aelianus read the report and I have a nasty feeling he passed on the contents to exactly the wrong person.'

Placidus paled. 'Quinctius Quadratus?'

I nodded. Placidus hit his palm against his head. 'I never thought!'

'It's not your fault. Young Quadratus is everywhere. Clearly it runs in the family.'

We considered the situation like men of affairs. We looked grave; our talk was measured; we stared hard at the water, pretending to count fish.

'Being involved in many spheres of provincial life is not a crime, of course,' Placidus commented.

'No, but at some point being over-busy speaks for itself. A good Roman only flaunts himself if he's trying to get the populace to support him in a ballot – and even then he tries to look as if he hates putting himself forward.'

'You picture a man I could vote for, Falco!' he cried admiringly. He was being ironic. So was I, come to that.

'And I'm *not* picturing Attractus. Everything he does has the smack of personal ambition and family gain.'

'But the situation is not being ignored,' Placidus tried to console himself.

'That's no guarantee of action. You learned your job on the Palatine. You know how things work. It's a difficult one.'

'You are asking me to provide evidence?'

'And you're going to tell me there is none?'

He shrugged wearily. 'How do you prove these things, Falco? Businessmen talk among themselves. If they are plotting to force up prices, only they know. They are hardly likely to tell me or you. Half of the smalltalk will be innuendo anyway. And if challenged, they will deny it all, and look outraged at the suggestion.'

'You sound as if you had done ten years as an informer,' I told him sadly.

His tone became more embittered. 'Obtaining information is easy, Falco! A bit of cheap charm and a few bribes will do the trick for you. You want to try a job where you're taking money from people. That's the hard life!'

I grinned. I was starting to like him. Well, I had the same rule for state officials as I had always had with women: once the situation started getting friendly it was time to leave.

'Just one more thing, Placidus — I had no luck when I tried to see the original correspondence. There seem to be two versions. Am I right that in his report Cornelius told Anacrites you suspected a cartel was being set up, but it was at an early stage and could be contained?'

Placidus frowned slightly. 'I didn't see the actual letter.'

'But?'

'But that's not quite what he and I agreed.'

'Which was?'

'Plans for price-rigging seemed to be at an early stage, certainly — but we were extremely concerned that because of the key personnel and their influence in Baetica, containment would be *very difficult!*'

XLVI

The procurator was seriously upset. 'You just can't tell, can you? Cornelius and I had agreed the exact opposite of what you say was reported in! I would have sworn Cornelius was absolutely straight. And I would have banked on the proconsul to back him –'

'Calm down –'

'No, I won't! It's too bad, Falco. Some of us really try to do a decent job, but we're thwarted at every turn!'

'You're jumping to conclusions, friend. The wrong ones, I think.'

'How can that be?'

'Two reasons, Placidus. First, I never saw any of the letters, so this is just hearsay. And second, while the report from Cornelius was in the custody of Camillus Aelianus, maybe he let it be tampered with.'

'*Tampered with*? You mean, forgery?'

'I realise such words are odious to a conscientious man.'

'And Aelianus, you say?'

'Don't be misled by his sweet smile.'

'He's just a lad.'

'He's twenty-four. A careless age.'

'I heard he was some relative of yours?'

'He'll be my first child's uncle in a matter of weeks. That does not mean I shall trust him to rock the cradle unsupervised. He may have been a friend of the upright Cornelius, but he was also thick with the young Annaei – a disreputable crowd. Until they quarrelled over a situation on their fathers' estates, he rode with Quinctius Quadratus too. You know this group?'

'Young fellows, some away from home, loose in a provincial capital and looking for a riot. Too much drinking; a lot of athletics and hunting. They're just

1082

wanting thrills – particularly if they think their elders won't approve. Quadratus had them dabbling with the cult of Cybele –'

'That's an Eastern religion!'

'Brought here by the Carthaginians. There is a temple in Corduba. At one stage they were all going there, then Annaeus Maximus stopped his sons, the proconsul made some sour remarks to Cornelius, and it tailed off.'

'I expect they had second thoughts,' I said gravely, 'when they heard about the castration rites!'

Placidus laughed.

'Tell me more about Quadratus – he was out here last year?'

'His father sent him, allegedly to supervise their estate.'

'Including the eviction of tenants whose faces didn't fit!'

At my sharp retort, Placidus looked purse-lipped. 'There was some trouble, I gather.' He was being cautious. I signalled that I had heard the full story. He then said, with a bluntness that seemed uncharacteristic, 'Quinctius Quadratus is the worst kind, Falco. We've had them all. We've had them rude and over-confident. We've had debauched young tyrants who live in the brothels. We've had fools who can't count, or spell, or compose a sentence in any language, let alone in correspondence-Greek. But when we heard that Quadratus had been wished on us as quaestor, those of us in the know nearly packed up and left.'

'What makes him so bad?'

'You can't pin him down. He looks as if he knows what he is doing. He has success written all over him, so it's pointless to complain. He is the sort the world loves – until he comes unstuck.'

'Which he may never do!'

'You understand the problem.'

'I've worked with a few golden boys.'

'High-flyers. Most have broken wings.'

'I like your style, Placidus. It's good to find a man who doesn't mind sticking his head over the rampart when everyone else is cowering. Or should I say, everyone except the proconsul? Despite everything, Quadratus is on hunting leave, you know.'

'I didn't! Well, that's one bright spot. His father's influence made the appointment look staged: the proconsul hates anything that looks off-colour.'

'Quadratus may have a black smudge against his name,' I hinted, remembering what the proconsul's clerks had told me about the dead soldiers in Dalmatia. 'Then a query about the family's role from Anacrites does not exactly help him maintain a glowing aura – somebody worked a flanker to be proud of,' I commented.

Placidus beamed. 'Terrible, isn't it?'

'Tragic! But you're stuck with him unless he or his father, or both if possible, can be discredited. That's my job. I'm part-way there. I can finger them as ringleaders when the cartel was being mooted last month in Rome – though I can't put up witnesses. Of course they were both on the spot. Even young Quadratus had finished his agricultural clearances and gone home again to triumph in the Senate elections and the jobs lottery.'

'Yes. He must have known Cornelius wanted to give up his post; he and his father somehow manoeuvred the quaestorship into their own hands. From here, it looks difficult to see why Rome fell for it.'

'The greybeards in the Curia would approve. The family had interests here. The Emperor may have assumed the proconsul would be delighted by his catch.'

'The proconsul soon told him otherwise. He was livid!' Placidus muttered. 'I heard about it from Cornelius.'

It sounded as though this proconsul liked breaking rules: he could spot a wrong move coming – and he was not afraid to dodge it. Not afraid of telling Vespasian he was annoyed, either. He was exceptional among men of his rank. No doubt he would live down to my expectations eventually, but at the moment it looked as though he was doing his job.

I returned to the main problem: 'I'll be fair to Aelianus. Assume he meant no harm. He arrived in Rome with the report for Anacrites, all full of the importance of his mission. He was bursting with it, and could simply have boasted to the wrong friend in Rome. He may not have realised the Quinctii were involved.'

'Did Cornelius tell him what the sealed letter said?' Placidus scowled.

'Apparently Cornelius used some discretion. Of course that only excited the lad's curiosity; Aelianus confessed to me he read the report.'

Placidus was raging again: 'Oh, I despair of these young men!'

I smiled, though it took an effort. Pedants irritate me. 'At risk of sounding like a ghastly old republican grandfather, discipline and ethics are not requirements for the *cursus honorem* nowadays ... With or without the connivance of Aelianus, someone altered the report. Even with that done, they knew Anacrites would be taking it further. They decided to stop him. The results were disastrous. Somebody killed the agent who was on surveillance when the oil producers came to Rome – and they made a brutal attack on Anacrites too.'

'Dear gods! Is Anacrites dead?'

'I don't know. But it was a serious misjudgement. It drew attention to the plot, rather than burying it. The investigation wasn't stopped, and won't be now.'

'If they had kept their heads,' Placidus philosophised, 'nobody could have proved anything. Inertia would set in. Cornelius has left; Quadratus is installed. He can't be left on hunting leave for ever. The financial affairs of this province are under his sole control. For myself, I expect every hour to be recalled to Rome, due to some quiet manipulation by the tireless Quinctius Attractus. Even if I stay on, anything I say can easily be dismissed as the ravings of an obsessive clerk with cracked ideas about fraud.'

'You know how the system operates,' I complimented him.

'I should do. It stinks – but gods alive, it rarely involves the murder of state servants!'

'No. That was arranged by somebody who *doesn't* know.' Somebody inexperienced. Someone who lacked the patience and confidence to wait and let the inertia Placidus mentioned creep insidiously through the state machine.

Placidus was frowning. 'Why are you so vague about the report, Falco? There ought to be copies of everything filed by the quaestor's clerk.'

'He tried to find it for me. Gone missing.'

'Why did you think that was?'

'Stolen to hide the evidence? Quinctius Quadratus is the obvious suspect. I'm only surprised he knew his way around the office.'

'I bet he doesn't,' Placidus retorted sourly. 'But he will one day. Maybe it wasn't him. Maybe the documents have been removed by someone else to stop him seeing them!'

'Who do you suggest?'

'The proconsul.'

If that was true, the bastard could have told me he had done it.

Placidus took a deep breath. When governors of provinces have to start prowling offices, censoring records in order to deceive their own deputies, order has broken down. Governors of provinces are not supposed to know how the filing system works (though of course they have all held lowly posts in their youth). Allowing them to fiddle with scrolls opened up frightening avenues. This was all filthier and more complex than Placidus had thought. 'So what now, Falco?'

'A tricky piece of reconnaissance.'

I explained about finding the dancer. The procurator did not know her, or was not aware of it if he did. He expressed a theory that men may watch, but do not learn the names of girls who entertain. Obviously his past life had been more innocent than mine.

'And where does she fit in, Falco?'

'I found evidence that she and her African musicians carried out the attacks in Rome on Anacrites and his man.'

'What did she have against them?'

1086

'Nothing personal, probably. I imagine that somebody paid her. If I find her I'll try to make her tell me who it was. And if his name happens to be one of those we have been discussing, you and the proconsul will be happy men.'

I told him the address the two shipping tycoons had given me. Placidus said he believed it was a dangerous area of town – though inspired by the excitement of our conversation, he decided he would come along with me.

I let him. I believed he was straight, but I do have my standards; he was still a man who held a salaried government post. If I got into trouble with Selia and needed a decoy, I would cheerfully throw him to her as bait.

XLVII

Every town and city has its unhappy quarter. Hispalis
might be a thriving hub of commerce, a producer of
sculptors and poets, and a regional capital, but it too had
potholed lanes where thin, dark-eyed women dragged
screaming toddlers to market while very few men were in
evidence. I could guess that the missing masculine element
were all loafers or thieves, or had died of a wasting disease.
Maybe I was prejudiced. Maybe I was just nervous. And
maybe I was right to be.

Where the girl lived proved hard to find. There was no
point asking directions. Even if anyone knew her, they
would conceal it from us. We were too smart and too well-
spoken – at least I was. Placidus looked pretty down-at-
heel.

'This is a bad place, Falco!'

'Surprise me. At least with two of us, we can watch our
backs in two directions.'

'Are we watching for anything in particular?'

'Everything.'

It was now late afternoon. The people of Hispalis were
taking a lengthy siesta, much needed in the terrific heat of
midsummer. The narrow lanes were quiet. We walked in
the shade and trod softly.

Eventually we identified a lodging house, slightly larger
and less grim than its surroundings, which appeared to
match the directions Cyzacus and Norbanus had given me.
A fat, unhelpful woman on a wonky stool peeling a cabbage
into a chipped bowl agreed grumpily that Selia lived there.
We were allowed up to knock on her door. She was out.

We went down and sat in what passed for a foodshop
opposite. There appeared to be little to eat or drink, but a
waiter was gambling furiously with a friend. He managed to

break off long enough to ask us to wait until they finished the next round, after which he scribbled hasty sums on a piece of board, collected the dice again ready, then dashed together two beakers of something lukewarm and cut us two chunks from a loaf, before he and his pal reabsorbed themselves in their game.

Placidus carefully wiped the rim of his cup with the hem of his sleeve. I had learned to toss down a draught without touching the container. There would not be much point in hygienic precautions if the liquor itself was contaminated.

'This is a fine way to do work, Falco!' my companion sighed, settling in.

'If you want it, the job's yours.'

'I don't know if I'm qualified.'

'Can you sit in a bar doing nothing half the day, while you wait for a girl who wants to beat your brains out?'

'I can sit and wait – but I don't know what I'm supposed to do once she arrives.'

'Keep well out of the way,' I advised.

I was beginning to regret bringing him. The neighbourhood was too dangerous. We were getting into serious trouble, and Placidus did not deserve it. Neither did I perhaps, but at least I had some idea what to expect and it was my job.

These tiny streets with cramped dwellings had neither piped water nor sewerage. Ill-defined gutters in the stony tracks between hovels served to take away waste. In bad weather they must be atrocious; even in sunlight they stank. Depression was all around. A pitifully thin goat was tethered to a stick in the foodshop yard. Flies zoomed at us in angry circles. Somewhere a baby cried mournfully.

'You're not by any chance armed, Placidus?'

'You're joking; I'm a procurator, Falco! – Are you?'

'I brought a sword to Hispalis; I didn't expect to get this close to the girl, so I left it at the mansio.'

We were badly positioned. We had come to the only place where we could stop and wait, but the alley outside was so narrow and winding we could see little of it. The few people who passed all stared at us hard. We sat tight, trying not to look as if our chins were barbered, and trying not to speak when anyone could overhear our Roman accents.

There were several battered lock-ups facing the path. One contained a man whittling at crude pieces of furniture; the rest were closed up, their doors leaning at odd angles. They looked deserted, but could just as well be in fitful use; any artisans who worked in this area were sad men with no hope.

After a while the waiter's friend left and two giggling girls arrived. They sat on a bench and did not order anything, but ogled the waiter who now had time to enjoy the attention. He had extremely long eyelashes; Helena would have said it was from batting them at women. After a short time the girls suddenly scuttled off, then a wide-bodied, bandy-legged man who could have been their father turned up and looked the waiter over. He left too, with nothing said. The waiter cleaned his fingernails with the knife he had used to cut our pieces of bread.

A redhead was walking past outside; she gave the waiter a faint smile. I have a strong aversion to redheads, but this one was worth looking at. We were seated below her line of sight, so we could peruse the goods unobtrusively. She was a girl who made the best of herself: a well-filled soft green tunic above thongy shoes, earrings of cascading crescents, a chalk-white face highlighted with purplish colouring, eyes lengthened and widened with charcoal, and elaborate plaits of copper-coloured hair. Her eyes were particularly fine. She walked with a confident swagger, kicking the hem of her skirt so her jingling anklets showed. She looked as though for the right reward she might show off the ankles they decorated, plus the knees and all the rest.

She also looked unlike anyone I had ever seen – though her best feature was that set of rolling brown eyes which did seem familiar. I never forget a shape either, however differently it may be trussed and decorated when I see it a second time. When the girl vanished somewhere opposite I found myself quietly finishing my drink. I said unexcitedly to Placidus, 'I'm going across to check on Selia again. You stay here and keep my seat warm.'

Then I hooked my thumbs casually in my belt and strolled over to the lodging house.

XLVIII

The fat woman had gone. Nobody was about.

The building occupied a long, narrow plot running away from the street. It was arranged on two floors either side of an open-roofed passageway, then widening into a small terminal courtyard with a well in it. This was sufficiently confined to keep out the sun at hot times of year. At intervals pots were hung on the walls, but the plants in them had died from neglect.

The girl lived on the upper level over the yard, where there was a rickety wooden balcony which I reached by an uneven flight of steps at the far end. Outside her door was a pulley arrangement to facilitate drawing up water. There were wet dripmarks on the balcony rail. A shutter now stood open, one which I remembered had been firmly closed before.

I walked around the balcony the long way, that is on the opposite side from Selia's room. I trod easily, trying not to let the planking creak. When I came back to the part above the entrance passageway a bridge crossed the gap; I guessed nobody used it much for the whole thing sagged worryingly beneath my weight. I moved on gently to her room. She had killed, or tried to kill, two men, so she had thrown away her right to modesty: I went straight in and didn't knock.

The red wig lay on a table. The green tunic hung on a hook. The dancer was naked apart from a loincloth. As she turned to stare at me angrily, she made an appealing sight.

She had one foot on a stool and was anointing her body with what I took to be olive oil. When I stepped through the doorway she deliberately carried on doing it. The body that received the attention was well worth pampering. The spectacle nearly made me forget what I was there for.

1092

'Well, don't be formal! Treat my place as your own!' She threw back her head. Her neck was long. Her own hair, which was an ordinary brown, had been pinned in a flat coil, close against her head. Her body was hard to ignore.

I cast a rapid glance around the place: one room, with a narrow bed. Most of the clutter was on the table, and it was predominantly female stuff. Occasional eating implements were jumbled in among the hairpin pots, cream jars, combs and perfume vials.

'Don't be shy; I've seen nudity before. Besides, we're old friends.'

'You're no friend of mine!'

'Oh come,' I remonstrated sadly. 'Don't you remember me?'

She did pause, with one palm held flat to the oil flask. 'No.'

'You should do. I'm the man who went home from the Society of Olive Oil Producers of Baetica safely in one piece – because I had acquired a large amphora of fish-pickle, with two slaves to carry it.'

She put her foot down on the floor. Her hand still moved slowly upon her gleaming skin, and as she massaged in the oil it was extremely difficult not to stare. She appeared not to notice that she was transfixing me. But the care with which she oiled her breasts told me she knew all right.

I waited calmly. When she jumped for the meat-knife that lay among the cosmetics pots I grabbed at her wrist. It would have been perfectly effective, had she not been so slippery.

IXL

Luckily for me the wrist I had seized was much smaller than my own; somehow I had encircled it. I felt her bones twisting in my grip and the knife flashed wickedly, but her weapon hand stayed held fast. It wouldn't last. Her all-over lubrication made her impossible to restrain for long.

I kept her at arm's length as she kicked out. Dancers have legs to reckon with. She was strong, but I had the advantage. Barging her shin with mine, I forced her to move back against the wall, making sure the corner of the table bruised her thigh. I banged her arm on the wall to shake the knife free. Spitting, she kept her grip on it. I thought of heaving her off, to spin her round and thrash her back into the wall, but she was so well oiled I would lose my hold. I smashed her elbow on the wall again. She gasped, and struggled to break free.

Her free hand cast behind me, grabbing at a soapstone pot to brain me with. There was no choice. I try hard to avoid naked women who are not my own property, but I had to protect myself. I went in close, throwing my body hard against hers then turning in my shoulder so I could break her hold on the knife two-handedly. This time I did it. The blade clanged to the floor. Instantly she went limp, then flexed herself violently. Her arm escaped from my grip.

I still had her pinned against the wall, but her writhing body was so slippery it was like trying to clutch a live fish. I brought up one knee and stopped her reaching the knife again. She squirmed away from me, dropped to the floor, scuttled under the table, then stood up and tilted it. Vases and boxes crashed to the ground, in a hail of broken glass, coloured powders, and thick scents. It didn't stop me, and dropping the heavy table lost her the second it took me to leap forwards and grab her by the only part I could circle with both hands: her throat.

'Keep still or I'll throttle you until your eyes pop out!' She thought about fighting. 'Believe me!' I warned again, kicking out with one foot to free it from a tangle of cheap jewellery. To reinforce the message I was squeezing hard. She was choking. I was out of breath. She saw her situation was desperate. She stood still. I felt her jaw clench as she gritted her teeth, no doubt vowing to say nothing and bite me if she could.

'Well, this is intimate!' Her eyes told me what I could do with myself. I was aware of her hands twitching, ready to go for me. I tightened my grip. She saw sense. 'Now why is it that when I end up in the arms of beautiful girls with no clothes on they are always trying to kill me?' Her response was a look full of hatred; well, the question had been rhetorical. While she glared, I suddenly wrenched her around so her back was against me and I felt less vulnerable to frontal attack. I kept one arm tight across her throat; with the other hand I was reaching for the knife that I kept down my boot. That improved the situation. I let her see what it was. Then I tucked the tip under one of her ribs so she could feel how sharp the blade was.

'Now we're going to talk.'

She made some sort of angry gurgle. I increased my pressure on her windpipe and she fell quiet again. I edged her over to the table that she had conveniently cleared, then I pushed her face down. I was lying on top of her. This possessed some attractions, though I was too preoccupied to enjoy it. Holding down women is nearly impossible; they're too supple. The gods know how rapists manage it – well, they use terror, which on Selia had no effect. I tweaked my knife against her well-oiled side. 'I can scar you for life, or just kill you. Remember that.'

'Damn you.'

'Is Selia your real name?'

'Get lost.'

'Tell me who you work for.'

1095

'Anyone who pays.'

'You're an agent.'

'I'm a dancer.'

'No, Spanish dancers come from Gades. Who sent you to Rome?'

'I can't remember.'

'This knife advises you to try.'

'All right; kill me with it then.'

'Very professional! Believe me, real dancers give in much more easily. Who asked you to perform at the dinner that night?'

'I was the official entertainment.'

'That was Perella. Stop lying. Who paid you for what you and your two cronies did afterwards?'

'The same person.'

'Oh, you admit you committed murder then?'

'I admit nothing.'

'I want his name.'

'You want your balls hacked off with a disembowelling knife!'

I sighed. 'I'm sorry you're taking this uncooperative attitude.'

'You'll be more than sorry, Falco.' She was probably right there.

'Now listen! You may have killed Valentinus, but you underestimated what a thick skull Anacrites had. Simply cracking the Chief Spy's head will have worse consequences than killing him outright.'

'You're never working for Anacrites?' She sounded surprised.

'You did leave him with a slight headache; he was allowed sick leave for a day or two. So you're right. Anacrites is not commissioning. I'm working for a man called Laeta –' I thought I felt her start. 'Keep still, I said.'

'Why?' jeered Selia. 'What are you worried about?'

'Not a lot. I'm a professional too. Crushing a beautiful naked female on a table has its lighter side – but on the whole I like my women right side up, and I certainly like them affectionate.'

'Oh, you're all heart!'

'A complete softie. That's why you're face down against a plank of wood covered in bruises, and my knife's in your ribs.'

'You're an idiot,' she told me. 'You don't know anything about the mess you're in. Hasn't it struck you that I'm working for Claudius Laeta – just like you!'

That sounded all too plausible. I preferred not to consider it. There was no immediate need to do so: we both abandoned comparing notes on our devious employer. Two things happened. I was unaware of lessening my grip on the dancer, yet somehow she wriggled suddenly and slithered sideways away from me. Then somebody else seized hold of my hair from behind and pulled me backwards in excruciating pain.

L

'I thought you would never get here!' the girl snarled angrily.

Whoever had hauled me upright had me bowed over backwards with a torsion as tight as the throwing sling on a rock-hurling artillery mule. Once I realised, I began to react. Hair grows again. I wrenched my head free. I must have left behind a good handful of my bouncing curls, but now I could move. My eyes streamed, but I was bucking and thrashing. Of course he snatched at my wrist in the same way that I had previously grabbed Selia to make her drop her own knife; he was behind me so I closed my elbow against my side, resisting him.

Blows rained on my spine and kidneys, then I heard somebody else entering the room. The girl meanwhile was rubbing her bruises and finding a tunic as carelessly as if the rest of us were just flies buzzing around the window-frame. Her bodyguards could do the work now.

I had managed to twist free. I jerked around so I could see my assailants: the two dark-skinned musicians from the dinner on the Palatine. It was the elder who had attacked me; he was wiry enough, and full of malice and energy. The other, more youthful, was burly, well-muscled and mean-eyed. I was in deep trouble. These were the men who had smashed in the head of Valentinus and left Anacrites for dead. I was fighting for my life.

'Sort him out!' Selia ordered. She had pulled some clothing over her head, but left it around her neck. She had paid these toughs sufficient to be sure they would kill for her. They looked as if they would enjoy it too. So much for the refining effect of music. Apollo was a thug, according to these two.

It was too small a room to contain four of us. We were

close enough to smell each other's breath. Impetuously Selia herself went for my knife arm, grabbing hold and biting me. The others plunged at me too and with three to contend with in such a confined space, I was soon overpowered. Selia took possession of my knife. Her assistants each had me brutally by an arm; they were turning to rush me forwards against the farther wall when the girl complained, 'Oh not in here!' A person of taste: she shrank from having my brains spread over her living space.

As they manhandled me towards the door I grunted in annoyance, 'Just tell me this, Selia — if we're both working for Laeta why in Hades does he want you to remove me?' I ignored the two brutes, who for a moment stopped bundling me out.

'You're in my way,' Selia responded offhandedly.

'Only because I don't know what's going on!' I was stalling. This group had killed. In no circumstances were they on the same side as me. 'Anyway, you take too many risks!'

'If you say so.'

'The Parilia!' I reminded her. 'You should have been lying low, not showing your face.'

'Oh yes?'

'And I went to a daft lads' party afterwards where everyone knew you had gone home to Hispalis. You leave too many tracks. I found you — and so can anyone.'

The heavies again started dragging me out, but Selia halted them with a raised hand. 'Who's looking?' she demanded.

At least I was collecting my strength. The longer I could hold off any final battering, the more hope of escape. I ignored Selia's question. 'If you really are a home-loving Hispalis girl, however did Laeta discover you?'

'I went to Rome, for someone else. I'm a dancer. I went to Rome to dance.'

'So it wasn't Laeta who sent you to that dinner in your little Diana costume, then?'

'Find out, Falco!'

'Did Laeta order you to attack Anacrites and his man?'

'Laeta gives me a free hand.' I noticed it wasn't an answer.

'You're in trouble,' I warned her. 'Don't trust Laeta to support you if the water heats up too much in his own pot.'

'I trust no one, Falco.' She had pulled down her dress and was calmly applying new paint to her face. She stroked it on with a spatula, swiftly and thickly. Before my eyes she was turning back into the archetypal Spanish castanet girl (the one who only exists in men's dreams); the blue-black hair she wore for dancing for Romans had been combed out on a stand. When she bent forwards and pulled it on the effect was as dramatic as when I saw her on the Palatine.

'I hope Laeta paid you. You won't see a sestertius if you're living out here.'

'I've been paid,' she said, perhaps glancing at the heavies to reassure them she would look after them too.

'So what in the name of Olympus is Laeta trying to do?'

'You tell me.'

'Discredit Anacrites? Take over the spy's work?'

'Looks like it.'

'Why does he need two of us?'

'One wasn't good enough.'

'Or wasn't ever meant to be! You mean Laeta's used me as a noodle – and he's using you to hamper me!'

'An easy game, Falco!'

'Easier than playing around with palace politics. But you're lying anyway. Laeta knows Anacrites is a cheap buffoon who could be put out of action with a bit of simple intrigue. Cracking heads wasn't necessary. Laeta's not vicious. He's not crude. He's quite clever enough to outwit Anacrites, and depraved enough as a bureaucrat to enjoy finessing him. Laeta wants a classic power struggle. He wants Anacrites alive, so he *knows* he has lost the game. Where's the art, otherwise?'

'You're just delaying,' Selia said. 'Get him out of here!'

I shrugged and made no attempt to cause trouble. The two musicians walked me on to the balcony. Just outside I

1100

glanced behind and said calmly to the older one on my left, 'She's calling you.'

He turned back. I threw myself forwards and spun my shoulder hard. The man on my right was pitched straight over the balcony.

The other yelled. I kneed him impolitely. He folded up; I chopped down on his neck with a double fist. He crumpled to the ground and I kicked him in the ribs until he lay still.

Below in the courtyard I had heard the crash and a cry as the first man landed. It was only one floor down, so he might still be mobile. There were confused sounds which I could not interpret, but by then Selia had rushed out.

First she flung a tambourine, edge on. I parried with my arm, but it cut my wrist. I hauled up the man at my feet and held him as a human shield while she then threw a knife – mine. He flung himself aside, dragging me. The blade clattered on the boarding, then with me cursing it tumbled over the edge.

The girl came at us; I barged the man into her. She dropped another weapon, then suddenly muttered something and ran towards the stairs. Her groaning bodyguard came back to life enough to grab the new weapon. It was the kind of cleaver girls who live alone keep in their rooms to shorten flower stems, hack up pig carcasses and discourage lovers from leaving early. I'd be afraid to have one in the house.

He set about me again, keeping himself between me and the girl. It was her I wanted; we all knew that.

I managed to dodge the swooping blade. Then I let off a high kick, flummoxed him, and shoved him backwards. I set off around the balcony, sprinting lightly on my toes. I was going the long way, the way I had first come to Selia's room.

The elderly fellow was tougher than he looked. I could hear him chasing after me. At the passageway bridge I slowed my steps. He was gaining, which made him pound harder to catch me. Once across, I turned back just in time

1101

to see the bridge give way. With a crack of splitting timber, the musician fell through. The wood was not rotten, just too flimsy for its intended purpose. He was left dangling, trapped between the broken planking. Blood dripped from his wounds where he was impaled on huge splinters of wood. When he tried to move he screamed.

To save time, I flipped over the balcony, clung to the rail, lowered myself as far as possible then dropped. I had just missed the well. (I had forgotten about that.) Neat work, Falco.

In the courtyard to my astonishment I found Placidus, fighting the other bodyguard, who was limping and nursing a broken arm from his fall. Placidus was keeping him under control, though only just. The procurator himself had a long gash in his side. My dagger, which had fallen from the balcony, lay near them, still bloody.

'The girl –' Placidus gasped, as I took over and stopped his opponent with a well-aimed kick. I got one arm around Placidus and leaned him on the well. 'I could have handled this one –' If he was a freedman now, he had been a slave once. Even in the imperial palace that meant a sordid early life. He knew how to take care of himself. 'I just didn't expect her. The girl slashed me before I could square up to her –'

'She got away?' I asked, retrieving my knife. He nodded disconsolately. I was peeling back his tunic gently to reveal the wound. 'Save your strength. Don't talk. We've caught these two gruesome characters anyway.' I was annoyed about losing Selia, but I did not let it show.

Placidus had put himself out for me. He looked pleased with his success, but he had paid a dangerous penalty. His wound was deep and nasty. 'What's the damage, Falco?'

'You'll live – though once the pain sets in you're going to know all about this.'

'Ah well, the scar should be interesting.'

'I can think of easier ways to excite rumours!'

'I'll be all right. You go after the girl.'

If we had been anywhere respectable I would have done.

I could not abandon Placidus in this seedy area where the dancer might have friends. A crowd was gathering. They were silent and still; I would not trust them. No one offered assistance but at least nobody tried to interfere.

I made the man with the limp stand up and walk ahead of me with my knife against his back. Supporting the procurator with my free arm, I slowly set off on a difficult trip to find the nearest guardpost of the local watch.

Fortunately it was not too far. Rather than have Placidus faint at their feet, folk did give us directions. The glare I gave them persuaded them to tell us right.

We limped there safely. My prisoner was locked in the cell. Officers went off to bring in his companion. Placidus was carefully stretched out, bathed and bandaged; at first he protested volubly, then he suddenly passed out and made no more fuss. I led a search that lasted the rest of the day, but Selia had slipped away somewhere. I am a realist. She could have gone in any direction, and would be miles from Hispalis by now.

At least I knew something about her. She had lied about most of it, but sinister patterns were emerging. Events had moved on. Suspects had laughed at me and beaten me up, but I had sized up the opposition – including the man who had commissioned me.

If her claim to be working for Laeta was right, Selia and I took our wages from the same soiled hands. I had no real job; I could not rely on being paid. On these terms I was not even sure I wanted to be.

It was time to return to Corduba. I badly needed to discuss all this with Helena. And if she agreed, I could ditch the whole filthy business and go home to Rome.

LI

I rode back to Corduba even faster than I had come. I was
glad I was not journeying in July or August, but even so the
weather was uncomfortable enough to remind me this was
the hottest part of Spain. Around me, covering the alluvial
plain to the south of the River Baetis, lay the finest olive
groves in Baetica. For oil rather than fruit, maybe the best
olives in the world. Beyond the river even in the baking sun
all the hills were green. Trees and shrubs flourished. I was
crossing a bowl of abundant fertility, yet my mood
remained grim.

For one thing, I was worried about Helena. There was
nothing I could do about that. At least I was on my way
back to her.

And I now had a new problem. I had not told poor
Placidus, who was in enough misery with his wound, but
what I had learned from the dancer filled me with dread. If
Selia really had been working for Laeta, the attacks in
Rome made one kind of sense: I was involved in a power
struggle – as I had all along suspected – between two arms
of palace officialdom. It looked darker and more bloody
than I would have expected, but it was internal.

Whatever was going on here in Baetica might not matter
to anybody back in Rome. The oil cartel could merely be
the excuse Laeta and Anacrites used to perpetuate their
rivalry. Or Laeta had used it on his own. Much as I loathed
Anacrites, he was beginning to look like an innocent victim.
He might have been just doing his job, decently attempting
to protect a valuable commodity. Perhaps he was unaware
of the threat from Laeta. When I saw them together at the
dinner they had sparred verbally, but there was no sense
that the spy suspected Laeta might actually be preparing to

pick him off. Him and his best agent – a man I reckoned I would have liked.

I could walk away from the palace intrigue – but the dead Valentinus would continue to haunt me.

The scenario stank. I was furious that I had ever become involved. Helena's father had warned me that whatever was happening among the Palatine magnates would be something to avoid. I should have known all along how I was being used. Well, of course I did know, but I let it happen anyway. My mission was a bluff – if Laeta hired Selia to attack Anacrites, he must have brought me in merely to cover his own tracks. He could pretend publicly that he was searching for culprits, though all he wanted was power. He must have believed I would fail to find Selia. Maybe he even supposed I would be so entranced with the importance of investigating a provincial cartel, I would forget to look for her at all. Did he hope I would be killed off in the attempt? Well, thanks, Laeta! Anacrites at least would have shown greater faith in my tenacity.

Perhaps instead Laeta wanted *me* to kill *Selia*, because she would know how he came to power.

As for the quaestor and his bumptious senator father, they looked like mere adjuncts to this story. I could only warn the Emperor that Quinctius Attractus was assuming too much power in Baetica. The proconsul would have to deal with Quadratus. I was treading on sliding scree, and I could risk nothing more. No informer accuses a senator of anything unless he is sure of support. I was sure of nothing.

I decided I did not want Claudius Laeta to acquire more power. If Anacrites died, Laeta could take over his empire; once in charge, whether he was bothered about the price of olive oil looked doubtful to me. I had heard for myself how Laeta was obsessed with the trappings of success with which Anacrites had surrounded himself: the suite in the Palace of the Caesars, the villa at Baiae. Laeta's personal ambition looked clear enough. And it relied on undetected manoeuvring. He certainly would not want me popping up

1105

in Rome to say *he* had paid Selia to eliminate Anacrites. Vespasian would never stand for it.

Maybe I would have to use this knowledge to protect myself. I was perfectly prepared to do so, to secure my own position – yet dear gods, the last thing I really wanted at this point in my life was a powerful politician nervous about what I might know.

I would have to fight him ruthlessly. It was his own fault. He was leaving me no choice.

I spent two days riding hard with muscles that had already ached and a brain that swam. I was so tired when I reached the mansio at Corduba I nearly fell on to a pallet and stayed there overnight. But I needed to see Helena. That kept me on my feet. I recovered the horse Optatus had lent me to come into town, and forced myself to stay upright on it all the way home to the Camillus estate.

Everything looked normal. It was dark, so the watchdogs set up a hectic yammering at my approach. When I led the horse to the stable a slave appeared to look after him, so I was spared that. The slave looked at me shiftily, as most villa rustica staff do. Without a word, I left my baggage roll and limped slowly to the house.

Nobody was about. A few dim lamps lit the corridor. I was too weary to call out. I went to the kitchen, which was where I expected to find everyone. Only the cook and other house-slaves were there. They all froze when I appeared. Then Marius Optatus broke in through another door opposite.

He was holding a leash; he must have been to investigate what had disturbed the dogs. His face was grey, his manner agitated even before he saw me.

'Falco, you're back!'

'What's wrong?'

He made a vague, helpless gesture with the hand that held the dog-leash. 'There has been a tragic accident –'

I was already on my way, running like a madman to the room I shared with Helena.

LII

'Marcus!'

She was there. Alive. Larger than ever; still pregnant. Whole. Sound.

I fell to my knees beside the chair as she struggled to rise and took her in my arms. 'Oh dear gods ...' My breath rasped in huge painful gulps.

Helena was crying. She had been crying before I crashed into the room. Now instead she was calming me, holding my face between her hands, her light rapid kisses on my eyes both soothing and greeting me.

'Optatus said there had been an accident –'

'Oh my darling! It's neither of us.' She laid my hand upon the unborn child, either to comfort me or herself, or to give the baby notice that I was home again. It seemed a formal, archaic gesture. I tickled the child and then kissed her, both with deliberate informality.

'I should bathe. I stink and I'm filthy –'

'And half dead on your feet. I had a feeling – I've ordered hot water to be kept for you. Shall I come and scrape you down?'

'That's more pleasure than I can cope with ...' I rose from my kneeling position beside her wicker chair. 'Stay and rest. But you'd better tell me about this accident.'

'Later.'

I drew a finger across her tear-stained cheek. 'No, now.'

Helena said nothing. I knew why she was being stubborn. I had left her. Something terrible had happened, which she had had to cope with on her own, so now I had lost my rights.

We gazed at one another quietly. Helena looked pale, and she had her hair completely loose, which was rare for her. Whatever had happened, part of her unhappiness was because she had been alone here without me. Well, I was home now.

In the dim light of a single oil lamp, Helena's eyes were nearly black. They searched my face for my own news, and for whatever I was feeling towards her. Whenever we had been apart there was this moment of readjustment; the old challenge was reissued, the new peace had to be reaffirmed.

'You can tell me I shouldn't have gone away – but do it after you explain what's been happening.'

She sighed. 'You being here wouldn't have changed anything. There has just been a terrible accident. It's young Rufius,' she told me. 'Rufius Constans. He was working on an oil press on his grandfather's estate when one of the quernstones slipped and crushed him. He was alone when it must have happened. By the time somebody found him he was dead.'

'Yes, that's a dreadful thing to have happened ...' Constans had been young and full of promise; I felt bitterly depressed. Helena was expecting my next reaction. I tipped my head on one side. 'He was alone? Nobody else was with him?'

'No, Marcus,' she replied softly. I knew that, trained by me to be sceptical in every situation, she had already spent time wondering, just as I was doing now. 'No; I can see what you are thinking. But there is no possibility of mischief.'

'No special crony lending Constans a hand with the oil press?'

'No. Quinctius Quadratus was out of action; I can vouch for that myself.'

I took her word. I was too tired to concern myself with how she knew.

I held out my hand and now she let herself take it. 'Have you been fighting?' Helena could always spot the damage.

'Just a few knocks. Did you miss me?'

'Badly. Was your trip useful?'

'Yes.'

1108

'That makes it all right then.'

'Does it? I don't think so, love!' Suddenly unable to bear being apart from her, I tightened my grip to pull her up from the chair. 'Come and wield a strigil for me, sweetheart. I'll never reach my own back tonight.'

We had edged around my guilt and her withdrawal. Helena Justina held herself against me for a moment, her soft cheek pressed to my stubbled one, then she took my arm, ready to walk with me to the bath-house. 'Welcome home,' she whispered, and I knew she meant it now.

LIII

The bath-house at the villa was designed for hardy old
republicans. I won't say it was crude, but if anyone
hankered for the unluxurious days of dark, narrow bathing
places with mere slits for windows, this was ideal. You
undressed in the cold room. Unguents were stored on a
shelf in the warm room, which was certainly not very warm
at night; you got up a sweat by vigorously shaking an oil jar
to try to dislodge the congealed contents.

A single stoker kept the fire alight and brought water in
buckets. He had gone for his supper but was summoned
back. Since the bath was reserved for Optatus, Helena and
myself, plus any visitors, he seemed glad of a rare chance to
show off his skills. We needed him this evening. The
promised hot water had been used up by someone else.

'That's just typical!' Helena stormed moodily. 'I've had
three days of this, Marcus, and I'm ready to scream.'

I was stripping, very slowly. I hung my foul togs on my
favourite hook, tossing aside a blue tunic that had been left
by some previous bather. Nobody was in evidence now,
which was just as well. Helena insisted on kneeling to
unstrap my boots for me. I helped her upright, then kept
hold of her. 'What's the matter, fruit?'

She took a deep breath. 'I have about four different
events to relate; I've been trying to keep them neatly
arranged in my mind –'

'You're so organised!' I threw back my head, smiling at
the anticipated luxury of listening to Helena. 'A lot has
been happening? You mean Constans?'

'Oh …' Helena closed her eyes. The young man's death
had affected her profoundly. 'Oh Marcus, I was with his
sister and Aelia Annaea when the news was brought; I feel
I'm part of it.'

1110

'But you said it was an accident. Truly?'

'It had to be. I told you; he was alone. It was such a shock. Everyone is very distressed. His sister is so young. I have not seen his grandparents, but we've all been imagining how distraught they must be –' She stopped, and suddenly became weepy again. Helena rarely gave way like that.

'Start from the beginning,' I said, stroking her neck.

Taking a lamp, we walked through a heavy door into the so-called warm room. This part of the bath-house was deadened to sound by the thickness of its walls, though somewhere at the far end of the hotter room I could hear vague shovelling sounds as the slave began replenishing the fire; the rattling and bumping noises travelled through the floor. Helena Justina rested on the low ledge against one wall as I worried a flask to extract a few dribbles of oil. She had presumably bathed once today, so she retained her undertunic modestly and forwent the full cleansing procedure.

She linked her hands and began rather formally: 'The first thing, Marcus, was that I had a letter from home – from my brother Justinus.'

'The lad! How is he?'

'Still in love with his actress.'

'It's just a crush.'

'So it's dangerous! Well, he's been working hard on Aelianus anyway, which he complains cost him a lot of drinks. Aelianus is feeling terribly guilty; his friend Cornelius, the one who wrote the famous secret dispatch, has written from Athens telling Aelianus not to talk about it to anyone called Quinctius.'

'But Aelianus had already done that?'

'Apparently.'

'He told me he fell out with Quadratus when your father was being cheated over the oil pressing.'

'Well, quarrels don't last among lads. But Aelianus now says he and Quadratus did meet in Rome, though it wasn't

a success. Their row in Baetica had soured the friendship so
by the time of that dinner it had cooled permanently.'

'Too late!'

'I'm afraid so. Justinus has found out that Aelianus has
been bottling up a disaster. Before he went to the Palace, he
had had the report with him at the Quinctius house. He left
it with his cloak, and when he collected it the seal looked
different. He picked it open again – as he confessed to you,
he had actually read it once – the second time the letter had
been altered to give a quite different assessment of how
serious the cartel was.'

I nodded. 'So either Quadratus or his father Attractus
deliberately tried to underplay the situation. Did Aelianus
challenge his pal?'

'Yes, and that was when they quarrelled again. Then
Aelianus was frightened that he couldn't alter the scroll any
more without making a thorough mess of it, so he just
handed it in to Anacrites and hoped everything would be all
right.' Helena sucked her lip. 'I have strong views on
Quadratus – which I'll come to next!'

'How has he been annoying you?'

'He'll annoy you too, because we've been landed here
with the dreadful bull-necked, spoiled-brat, insensitive rich
girls' delight "Tiberius" himself.'

'*Here?*'

'It's your fault.'

'Naturally!' I know my place. Helena was clearly furious;
I kept hold of the oil flask in case she let fly with it. 'Even
though I was a hundred miles away?'

'Afraid so.' She had the grace to grin at me. I put down
the oil flask. Helena Justina had a smile that could freeze all
my capillaries. Our eyes met, a glance that was rich with
feeling and memory. Only friends can exchange so much,
so rapidly. 'It was because of your horse, Prancer.'

'Prancer belongs to Annaeus Maximus.'

'And you lent him to Quadratus and Constans. Quadratus brought him back.'

'I told him not to.'

1112

'Well, isn't that just like him?' Her voice grated. 'And now the irritating creature has come to stay here, where everyone loathes him, and he's using all the bath water! – If I challenge him about it he will apologise so politely I'll want to hit him with an oven hook. I can't prove that he does it deliberately, but he makes life a trial from morning to night for everyone around him.'

I tutted. 'He has to be a villain. I'll prove it yet! – But Helena, my heart, you still haven't told me: why has this social woodlouse become our guest?'

'Your horse threw him. He has hurt his back.'

'I won't hear another word against Prancer: the horse has taste!' I cried.

Growing too cold, we both stepped into wooden-soled clogs and braved the steam of the hot room. Helena took a bronze strigil and started scraping me down while I braced my aching limbs against her steady strokes. I could take as much of that as she was prepared to indulge me with, especially now that her mood had softened up.

'So Quadratus is bedridden?'

'No such luck. He can shuffle about. Everywhere Optatus and I try to go, he appears, making himself agreeable.'

'That's disgusting!'

'He decided it was courteous to take an interest in my pregnancy. He keeps asking questions I don't want to think about. He's worse than my mother.'

'The man's a complete lout. Worse than a girl's mother? That's as low as he can get! By the way, how is your pregnancy?'

'Don't bother, Falco. When you try to take an interest, I know it's all fake.'

'You know I'm a fake you can trust.'

'You're the fake I'm stuck with, anyway ..'

She looked tired. I pried the curved strigil from her hand and took over ridding myself of sweat, oil and filth. Then we both sank on to the wooden bench to endure what else we could of the heat. Helena collected the damp strands of her hair and wound them into a clump, holding the weight off the back of her neck.

'Marius Optatus could go out in the fields and olive groves, but I've been stuck with our unwanted guest. I had to talk to him. I had to listen too – unendingly. He is a man. He expects to hold the floor. What he has to say is banal, humourless and predictable. He expects admiration in inverse proportion to content, of course.' I was chortling. I loved to hear Helena condemning somebody else.

'Has he made advances to you?' I demanded suspiciously. I knew how I would react if I had Helena Justina to myself for days.

'Of course not.'

'He's an idiot then!'

'He regards me as a mother-goddess, I believe. He pours out his heart to me. His heart is about as interesting as a burned cinnamon bun.'

'Has he admitted he's a bad boy?'

'He doesn't know,' said Helena, summing him up with furious clarity. 'Whatever he does, he never even thinks about whether it's right or wrong.'

I sucked my lower lip. 'No fascinating hopes and joys? No undetected talents?'

'He likes hunting, drinking, wrestling – with opponents who are not too professional – and telling people about the future he has planned.'

'He told me how good he was going to be as quaestor.'

'He told me the same,' she sneered. 'I expect he tells everyone.'

'I expect some are impressed.'

'Oh lots would be,' she agreed readily. 'People think mere self-confidence equates to nobility.'

She fell silent for a moment. '*I'm* confident,' I mentioned, since she was obviously thinking it.

'You're confident for good reason. And when that's inappropriate you're filled with doubt. What Quinctius Quadratus lacks is judgement.'

We were again silent. The slave had done his duty with a will, and the room quivered with steam now. Wetness streamed over my forehead from the hair flattened on my head. I scooped water from a basin and threw it over my face and chest. Helena was looking very flushed. 'You've had enough,' I warned her.

'I don't care. I'm just so pleased to be with you, to be talking to you.'

It was too hot to touch another person, but I took her hand and we exchanged a slippery embrace.

'Why do we hate him?' I mused after more reflection. 'What has he really done? Other people think he's wonderful.'

'Other people always will.' Helena had clearly had plenty of time to evaluate the hero.

'He's likeable.'

'That's what makes it so bad; he could be worthwhile, but he's chosen to waste his potential. We hate him because he is bound for success, which he doesn't deserve. He is an empty shell, but that will not prevent him rising.'

'His underlings will buoy him up.'

'And his superiors will avoid the effort of reporting his inadequacy.'

'He'll introduce stupid procedures and make terrible decisions, but by the time the results show he'll have moved on up the ladder and be wreaking havoc somewhere else.'

'And he will never be called back to answer for his mistakes.'

'It's the system. The system is rotten.'

'Then the system must be changed,' said Helena.

Left to myself I would have sunk into a heavy sleep, but I managed to rouse us both enough to wash in the warm pool. 'So what's the story of poor young Constans?'

'I told you most of it.'

'You were with Aelia Annaea?'

'Tolerating Quadratus was becoming too much. Optatus

took to finding excuses to ride into Corduba. Aelia and Claudia came to rescue me; we sneaked off in the Annaeus carriage, and then we spent the day at Aelia's house.'

'This was today?'

'Yes. Then this afternoon a desperate message came for Claudia Rufina to rush home because of the tragedy. Her brother had been working on the estate; I think maybe there had been some trouble about the life he had been leading – that party you went to with Aelia's brothers has had its repercussions throughout the neighbourhood. Anyway, Rufius Constans had promised to reform himself. Hard work was his way of showing it.'

'What caused the accident?'

'New stones had been delivered for an oil press, and he went to inspect them. Nobody thought he would attempt to move them on his own. When he failed to return for lunch with his grandmother a servant was sent out, and he was found dead.'

'An accident,' I repeated.

'Nobody else had been there. As for Quinctius Quadratus, he was here; we all know it. Without question he is unable to ride. He could never have got to the Rufius estate. Besides, why would he harm his young friend?'

I shook my head, unable to suggest an answer. Then I did say, 'I saw Rufius Constans before I left. He and his grandfather were at the proconsul's palace, trying to gain an interview.'

Helena looked at me. 'Intriguing! But you cannot ask Licinius Rufius what they were doing there. He and his wife will be heartbroken over their loss. So much was invested in Constans.'

'And so much wasted,' I agreed, in my most republican mood.

'They had probably gone to ask the proconsul for support in advancing the young man's career!'

That was not how it had looked to me. The old man had been too urgent in his manner, and the boy too sullen-faced.

1116

Because of the cramped layout of the bath-house, we had to return through the warm room to reach what passed for a cold plunge. It was in a kind of cupboard to one side, built off the cold room with the cloak-hooks. Even before we pulled back the curtain which concealed the pool, I had an inkling of something suspicious. Then Helena Justina exploded. 'Oh really! I don't believe this thoughtlessness!'

I did. Somebody had bathed in the small pool so vigorously they had swooshed almost all of the water out on to the floor. Before I squashed down on the sitting ledge and splashed myself as best I could to cool down in the remnants, I glanced back into the outer room. There were wet footprints everywhere, and the blue tunic I threw on the bench had now disappeared. Whoever had used the cold water must have been lurking in the pool when Helena and I first entered. Whoever it was could have overheard all we said. Luckily the thick doors to the warm rooms would prevent sound emerging once we had passed through them.

Frankly, if it had been Quadratus eavesdropping, I found it hard to care.

I was pretty well incapable of movement now. When I struggled from the pool, dripping sporadically, Helena had to find a towel and dry me down herself.

'So are you going to tell me your own adventures, Marcus?'

'Oh, mine are just horses, wine, men's talk, and women in their boudoirs getting undressed.' Helena raised her eyebrows and I thought it best to produce a rapid, lightly censored version of my time in Hispalis. She was not best pleased with the part about Selia, I could tell. Being an informer had taught me to recognise growling and grinding of teeth.

'Bad news, Falco.'

'I won't have that! I protest I'm innocent.'

'I think you made up the whole story.' She had guessed that I had pruned it. 'What a puzzle your dancer is! Is she

1117

the killer? Is she seeking the killer for Laeta? Will her ravishing figure distract you from your family loyalties? Will she beat you up again? Or will she just beat you at your own game?'

I tried not to wince as Helena moved to buff up certain lower regions that preferred softer treatment. 'Spare me the exotic massage ... A procurator called Placidus has a dagger gash that proves what she wanted. Selia was not after my body, unless it was dead. I beat up her guards and captured them; they will stand trial before the proconsul on the basis of a report I've left with the vigiles about that night in Rome. I was supposed to stay — material witness — but I waved my pass from Laeta and pleaded urgent secret work.'

'Dry your own feet please,' said Helena. 'I'm too large to reach —'

'You're adorable. Better than a Syrian bodyslave —'

'When have you been cosseted by a bodyslave?'

'They fling themselves on me all the time. Beautiful girls with terrific hands, and slinky boys with very long eyelashes ...'

Helena's chin came up. 'There's one more thing I haven't told you yet. The cook told me that while I was resting one day a woman came here looking for you.'

'Selia?' Was she pursuing me?

'It can't be,' Helena informed me coolly, drying her own hair. 'This one was here three days ago, Falco — when according to you, you were pinning the unclad Selia to a cosmetics table in Hispalis. I had not realised you were so sought-after.'

'Oh gods! You know what this means: I'm not just being beaten up by one female agent — Anacrites' special charmer wants her turn as well!'

I was so depressed that Helena relented. She kissed me, fairly gently. Then she took me by the hand again, and led me away on stumbling feet to bed.

LIV

Grief-stricken women seem to make beelines for informers. It must be our comforting manner.

'You have to help me!' wailed Claudia Rufina.

I was very tired. Normally I could mop tears, straighten a mourning veil, and stop hiccups by giving a sudden shock by way of loud noises, cold keys down the cleavage, or an unexpected pinch on the backside. Today I just sighed.

'Of course he will!' Helena soothed the distressed young lady. 'Marcus Didius is deeply sorry about what happened to Constans; he will help you if he can.'

I had been left to sleep in, but still felt like a half-stuffed cushion. After days in the saddle my spine, and all the parts attached to it, were on fire. I needed to be placed in the tender care of my trainer Glaucus and his fiendish masseur from Tarsus, but they were many hundreds of miles away in Rome, and a great deal of the distance between us was sea.

Worse, when I had crawled into the kitchen this morning the breakfast which the aged cook had lovingly prepared for me had been devoured by Quadratus. Of course the old dear rushed to bring me another plateful, but it was not the same. So let's be literal about this: my mood was absolutely foul.

I held up a hand like a masterful orator. Claudia Rufina fell silent, though Helena sniffed; she hated sham.

'Helena Justina is correct about the deep sympathy I feel towards you and your family. Nothing can mitigate the untimely death of a promising youth with the Empire at his feet.' And so much money, I thought. I was extremely tired. My mood was truly low.

'Thank you,' said Claudia, catching me out by responding with dignity.

'You are a sensible young woman and I believe you will respect frankness.' I was not normally this rough. I noticed Helena's eyebrows shoot up. Guilt increased my bad temper. 'Excuse me if this sounds harsh: I came to Hispania on a difficult mission. I received no assistance – no assistance at all – from the dignitaries of Corduba, including your own family. I have still to solve a murder in Rome, and write a long report on certain commercial matters here. I have to condense my efforts into far too little time, in order to be able to return to Italy before Helena Justina gives birth.' We all glanced at Helena; by now she looked so large it seemed likely we were expecting twins. 'Claudia Rufina, this is no moment for me to take on a private commission, especially when it's fairly clear we're discussing a very sad accident.'

'Besides which,' muttered Helena, 'Marcus has had his breakfast eaten by that young man of whom everyone thinks so highly.'

'Tiberius?' Claudia was looking down that unfortunate nose of hers. She still seemed drawn to the handsome and eligible quaestor – yet her expression had a closed look, as if her attitude might be changing.

'Yes, Tiberius!' Helena's smile was like the benign glance of a sibyl just before she prophesied universal war.

'Oh,' said Claudia. Then she added in her serious way, 'I came in Grandfather's carriage. Would you like me to take Tiberius away?'

'That would be extremely kind,' Helena answered. 'You see, I am being frank too today.'

'It's no trouble,' replied Claudia quietly. 'I would like a chance to talk to him anyway.' That was when I started worrying about Claudia.

I was surveying our visitor more gently. She wore a dark veil, though she had it thrown around her casually as if a maid had persuaded her at the last minute. She had left the maid at home, travelling to see us set-faced and quite alone. Her gown was the blue one I had seen before, less neatly cinched in. Her hair was dressed as normal in a tight, plain style that emphasised the large shape of her nose. As a wealthy heiress she ought to be enjoying herself in elaborate funeral drapes pinned together with onyx jewellery. Instead she could be genuinely abstracted by grief.

'I think we'll send Tiberius home in our own carriage,' I disagreed.

Helena looked annoyed. She was dying to be rid of him. 'Marcus, Claudia Rufina said she wishes to speak to him.'

'What about, Claudia?' I asked crisply.

Claudia looked me straight in the eye. 'I want to ask him where he was when my brother died.'

I looked straight back. 'He was here. He is too badly hurt to ride. When he first took his fall, Helena Justina insisted that a doctor look at him. We know his injury is disabling.'

Claudia's eyes dropped. She looked miserable and confused. She did not think of asking us why anyone should doubt that Quadratus had been hurt, or why we had already taken trouble to work out for ourselves that he had an alibi. She might have an inkling of our own doubts about him, but she still shrank from the full implications.

Helena linked her hands on her stomach. 'Tell us why you came to see Marcus Didius.'

'He investigates,' Claudia declared with a proud tone. 'I wished to hire him to discover how Constans was killed.'

'Don't you believe what you have been told about it?' I asked.

Once again Claudia defied me with her stare. 'No, I don't.'

I ignored the drama. 'Does your grandfather know that you have come to me?'

'I can afford to pay you!'

'Then be businesslike and answer the question I asked.'

Claudia was growing up almost before our eyes. 'My grandfather would be furious. He forbids any discussion of what happened. So I didn't tell him I was coming here, or why.'

I quite liked her in this mood. She was young and spoiled, but she was taking the initiative. Helena had noticed my change of expression, and she was looking less critical. As gently as I could, I explained to the girl, 'Look – people come to me all the time claiming that their relatives have died in suspicious circumstances. They are usually wrong about it. Most people who die unnaturally have been killed by close members of their family, so I don't get asked for help because they're hiding the truth. When I am asked to investigate I almost always discover that the person died because their time was up, or in an honest accident.'

Claudia Rufina took a deep, slow breath. 'I understand.'

'It will be hard to face losing Constans, but you may just have to accept that he is tragically gone.'

She was struggling to seem reasonable. 'You won't help me.'

'I didn't say that.' She looked up eagerly. 'Something brought you here today when you ought to have been grieving, and comforting your grandmother. Something troubled you sufficiently to drive you from home on your own; I take that seriously, Claudia. Tell me why you feel suspicious.'

'I don't know.' She blushed. At least she was honest. That was a rare treat in a client.

I had spent large amounts of time dealing with women who were holding back in one situation or another. I waited. I could tell Helena Justina thought I was being over-stern. I was just far too tired to be messed about.

Claudia Rufina glanced at Helena for encouragement then said firmly: 'I believe my brother was murdered. There is a reason, Marcus Didius. I think Constans knew something about what you are investigating. I believe he intended to reveal what he knew, so he was killed to stop him talking to the authorities.'

There were a number of questions I might have gone on to ask her, but just as she had finished speaking Tiberius Quinctius Quadratus (in a fetching blue tunic that I last saw in the bath-house) tapped on the door politely – in case we were discussing anything private – then as we all fell abruptly silent he strolled into the room.

1122

LV

He went straight to the girl. Considering he had admitted to me that the public were wrongly convinced he would marry her, it might have been kinder to keep his distance. But he was murmuring shock and regret. Then as Claudia collapsed in tears, he stooped over her chair, holding one of her hands and with his other arm gently around her hunched shoulders.

Young men are not normally so good with the bereaved. Maybe Helena and I were wrong about him. It is possible to take against someone, then continue to loathe them out of pure prejudice. Maybe Quadratus was a perfectly well-meaning lad, with a kind heart ...

On the other hand, Claudia had not been crying until he spoke to her.

Claudia struggled to calm herself. She brushed away the tears and leaned forwards to free herself from the young man's solicitous embrace. 'Tiberius, I want to ask you something –'

I interrupted her. 'If and when Quinctius Quadratus is required to answer questions, I'll deal with it.' The girl caught my eye and fell silent. I wondered whether he noticed she might now have doubts about his probity.

Quadratus straightened up, remembering to put a hand to his sprained back. He was rather pale. His good looks were strong enough to take it. His physique was too sturdy for him to look anything other than bouncingly fit. 'Falco, it's perfectly obvious you believe I have done wrong somewhere. I would like to answer your questions and clear things up!' Very good. Spoken like an innocent man, in fact.

'I have nothing to ask you, quaestor.'

'You always use my title as if it were an insult ... I wish to have these suspicions removed!'

'You are not under suspicion.'

'That is clearly untrue.' He sounded so pained a court would free him on the spot. Juries love a man who goes to the trouble of bad acting. 'This is all so unjust, Falco. It seems I cannot move in Baetica without incurring censure. Even the proconsul seems disinclined to work with me – I suppose he thinks I was appointed through influence, not on merit. But is it my fault if my family has strong connections with Baetica? I was as qualified for this quaestorship as any man in Rome!'

'That is perfectly true,' I declared. So it was. Idiots with no sense of ethics are elected to the Senate every day. Some of them are bound to get dumped in important financial posts. 'But be lenient,' I teased him. 'You do meet the occasional eccentric governor who criticises his quaestor on the grounds that the lad has read Plato's *Academy* yet can't tell which way up an abacus should stand.'

Quadratus was letting himself get snappy: 'There are very competent people to do the sums, Falco!' True. And just as well, when the man who should be making decisions on the basis of those sums was unable to understand what the figures meant or whether his staff had fiddled them – and when he had told me he did not think there was any point in trying anyway. Quadratus ran his hands through his fine head of hair, looking troubled. 'I have done nothing wrong.'

I smiled. 'Criminals say that every day. It makes life very hard for innocent men: all the good speeches are used up.'

Quadratus frowned. 'So where does that put me?'

I assumed an expression of surprise. I was enjoying myself. It was time to force the issue too: 'Doing your job, I suggest.' If my doubts about Laeta's purely personal interest were right, there was no point expecting him to pursue the Quinctii once he had snatched Anacrites' position. I may as well give this one a chance to damn himself in office. 'Why not prove the proconsul wrong?

You came to Baetica to fill the quaestorship. The efficient management of your function is the best way to demonstrate your quality. Just tell him hunting's lost its allure, and you're back in harness. Either he'll accept it with good grace, or he'll have to dismiss you and you can go to Rome to fight your case officially.'

He looked at me as if I had just revealed the secrets of eternity. 'By Jove, I will! You are right, Falco!' He beamed. The transformation had been slick. No longer the suffering accused, he was so used to his family brazenly grabbing whatever they wanted, he now burst with confidence that he could force the proconsul to act as he desired. The coming confrontation might be more interesting than Quadratus realised. 'So you're not hounding me, after all?'

I smiled. Let him think that. 'First, quaestor, I shall place my carriage at your disposal to return you to your father's estate.'

'Of course; you must be sick of me. I'm sorry to be a burden. I've been looked after splendidly!'

'Think nothing of it,' smiled Helena.

'But I can't possibly take your carriage.'

'Well, you can't ride Prancer again.'

'That demon! I ordered Optatus to put him down –'

'Prancer does not belong to Optatus,' I interposed coldly. 'His owner is Annaeus Maximus, and his current trustee is me. He threw you; that is what horses do. You were hurt; that was your risk when you mounted him. I'm no horseman, but Prancer never gave me any trouble. Maybe you upset the beast.'

Swift to back off, he answered quietly, 'As you say, Falco.' Then he turned to Claudia Rufina. 'If I'm leaving, I can easily take you home at the same time.'

'I wouldn't hear of it,' I told him. If Rufius Constans had known something about the cartel, whoever wanted him silenced might wonder if he had talked about it to Claudia. If Claudia was correct in thinking her brother had been murdered, then she herself needed to be guarded – even from suspects with firm alibis. I was not having her left alone with the son of the man who was running the cartel. 'Quadratus, you need to travel the shortest way, for the sake of your sprained back. Helena and I will escort Claudia in her grandfather's carriage –'

'Maybe Tiberius would be more comfortable in that one,' suggested Claudia suddenly. 'It has a seat that can be pulled out flat so he can lie at full stretch.'

I accepted the arrangement. Helena and I would escort Claudia in our own carriage. We would be going by way of the scene of the accident – though I did not tell the charming Tiberius that.

LVI

We all set out together in a procession of two carriages, but
I had instructed the Rufius driver to maintain a dead slow
speed, in order to protect the wounded gentleman. That
enabled Marmarides to move ahead and lose them. I felt
better after that, even though for much of the journey we
were driving through the spreading fields of the Quinctius
estate. I had ridden on top with Marmarides, leaving the
women together, though Helena told me afterwards they
had made a silent couple, with Claudia Rufina staring
numbly into space. She had probably run out of energy and
been overtaken at last by shock.

The scene of the young man's death had been marked by
a portable altar. It stood at the roadside, so nobody could
pass without taking note of the tragedy. On the slab stood
flowers, bowls of oil, and wheaten cakes. A slave we found
slumbering in the shade of a chestnut tree was supposed to
be on guard at the sad shrine.

I remembered the place. The Rufius oil presses were in a
yard before the main house; it was attached to what would
have been the original farm, a villa rustica in an older style
that had been abandoned when the family became prosperous and opted for a larger, more lavish and urban home.
The old house was probably now occupied by bailiffs and
overseers, though in the daytime it was normally deserted
as they were all out in the fields and olive groves. That was
how it must have been yesterday when young Rufius came
out here.

I jumped down quickly as Marmarides pulled up. The
main estate road ran through this yard. Marmarides made
the mules wheel and parked the carriage on the shady side,
where a horse was already tethered; I patted the animal as I
went past and found its flanks warm from a recent ride. A

flock of white geese came strutting towards me menacingly, but the slave who was guarding the shrine took a stick and drove them away.

There were various outbuildings into which I glanced: stables and plough stores, a wine cellar, a threshing floor, and finally the oil production area. This was roofed, but the wall that faced the yard comprised huge folding doors, presumably to allow access for carts; in summer they were left standing open.

Two rooms were used for oil production, which was normal on most farms. The outer one contained two presses, as well as vats let into the floor. Here there was no sign of Constans' death. The vats would be used for ladling out the pressed oil, allowing it to rest and separate from its other liquid as many as thirty times. Giant ladles were hung on the walls, along with a large quantity of esparto bags. I was examining these when somebody ducked in through the arch from the adjacent room and said at once, 'Those are used to hold the pulp as it is pressed.'

It was Marius Optatus. Having seen his horse outside I was expecting him, though I wondered what in Hades he was doing here. He went on quietly, 'About twenty-five or thirty bags are piled up, with metal plates between them occasionally to hold them firm –' He gestured to the further room from which he had come. 'Constans died in there.'

Behind me in the yard I could hear Helena and Claudia dismounting slowly from the carriage, Helena trying to delay the girl so I would have time to view the scene alone. Optatus heard them too and looked concerned at their presence. I stepped into the yard and called to Helena to stay outside. Then I followed Optatus into the inner room.

Light struggled to infiltrate through slits in the north-facing walls. I stood for a moment, accustoming my eyes to the half-dark of the small room. A faint rich smell remained from last year's olives. The confined space was quiet, though we could hear the remote sounds of voices from the yard. The boy's body had been removed. It looked as if everything else had then been abandoned as it was.

'This is where the first crushing takes place,' Optatus explained. 'The fruit is picked, and carried in deep baskets to the farm. It is washed, sorted, and stored in heaps on a sloping floor for a couple of days. Then it comes here for malaxation. The olives are crushed in this mill, to form a rough pulp, evenly mixed. After that they go next door for the oil to be pressed out.'

The crushing mill consisted of a large circular stone tank, into which whole fruit would be dumped. A central column was supposed to support heavy wooden arms which ran through the centres of two vertical hemispherical stones; these were kept slightly apart from each other by a strong rectangular box into which the wooden arms were fixed. It was plated with metal and formed part of the pivotal machinery which turned and supported the grinding stones.

'Poles are attached through each stone,' Optatus explained in his steady, unemotional way. 'Two men walk around the vat and turn the poles slowly, churning the fruit.'

'So it's not quite the same as grinding corn?'

'No; cornmills have a conical base and cup-shaped upper stone. This is the opposite – a basin into which the stone rollers fit.'

'They move quite loosely?'

'Yes. The aim is to bruise the olives and free the oil, to make a slippery paste. But you try to avoid breaking the stones; they taste bitter.'

We fell silent.

The old worn grinders were propped against a wall, one flat side out, one convex, both stained dark purple and badly misshapen. Pale new concrete had been used to improve the basin. One new stone stood within it in position, already fixed upright to the central pivot though it was held fast on blocks. Both stones had been supplied with brand new turning poles, their wood still white from the adze.

'You see, Falco,' my companion continued levelly, 'the roller fits fairly loosely. In use the pole acts merely as a lever to move the stone around in the vat. The stones revolve almost of their own volition, due to the pressure of the fruit.' Although the grinder still had wedges beneath it, he leaned on it to show me there was free play. Leverage on the pole would move the stone and tumble the olives against the sides of the basin, but not so tightly that the kernels were split.

I sighed. I fingered a collar, fitting tightly around the pole. 'And this washer – which I presume is adjustable – is fixed here on the outside to keep the stone on?'

'It should be.' Optatus was grim.

'Then I suppose I can work out what happened to the boy.'

'You will!' Presumably Optatus had already thought through events, and did not like the result.

The second grinding-stone lay on the ground. A pole had been partly thrust through it, but then smashed by a fall. Even in the dim light I noticed dark marks on the earth floor next to the stone; they looked like dried blood.

'So what do you reckon?' I asked Marius.

'The new grinders arrived two days ago but Licinius Rufius had not yet made arrangements for fitting them. I asked at the house, and apparently he intended to instruct the stonemasons who have been working on his new portico to do this job.'

'Why didn't he?'

'He had had a dispute with them about a column they broke, and they had walked off the site.'

'That's probably true. I saw the broken column when I was here before.'

'Constans seems to have decided to surprise and please his grandfather. All he had said to anyone, however, was that he was coming over to inspect the new rollers before the bill from the supplier was authorised. Dear gods, Falco,

1130

if I had known his mind I would have helped him myself! I do wonder if he came over to ask me – but I had gone into Corduba to escape from Quadratus ...'

'So they say he was alone – yet here we have the first new stone, already hauled into position.'

'I have talked to the workers, and none of them was involved.'

'This was some job to tackle! Rufius looked a sturdy lad, but he cannot possibly have moved the weight on his own.'

'No, Falco. That is why I rode over here today; I just cannot believe what is being said about this accident. It would take at least two men to manoeuvre and fix these grinding-stones – preferably four.' The concern in our tenant's voice convinced me his motives were genuine. Like me, he was a practical man. The flaws in the story had astonished and dismayed him so much he had had to see for himself.

'So what is the fixing procedure, Marius? Each stone has to be lifted into the basin – I presume you get it upright with a fulcrum, and use ropes to heave it in?' I glanced around. Now my eyes were more used to the light, I could make out discarded equipment.

Optatus confirmed how difficult the task would be: 'It's heavy work, but raising the stone in the basin is really the easy part. Then the grinder has to be held upright, raised off the bottom, and wedged.'

'To set it into position? It churns above the base of the tank?'

'Yes. Setting the height takes strength.'

'And courage! You would know if a stone like that rolled over your toe.'

'Or fell on your chest,' growled Marius, thinking of what happened to young Rufius. 'First you decide the position. Then somebody has to climb up and straddle the centre pivot to aim the pole into its fixing on the column – I have done that, Falco, and unless you get lucky immediately, it leads to some raw cursing. The man who is to guide the end into position soon hates the man who pushes the pole through the stone. Making a fit is very difficult. You have to give clear directions – which your partner naturally gets wrong.'

Optatus painted a neat picture of the joys of teamwork. I wished I could see him trying to organise a couple of my brothers-in-law in some simple household task.

'Maybe Rufius and his helper quarrelled … Rufius must have been the one on the ground.'

'Yes. The stone slipped, and fell out on him,' Optatus agreed. 'The estate workers told me they found him on his back with his arms outstretched, and the grinding-stone right on top of him. It had caved in his chest, and crushed his stomach too.'

I flinched. 'Let's hope he died at once.'

'He could not have lasted long. Even if the stone had been lifted straight off him, he would never have survived.'

'The point,' I said sourly, 'is whether he could have avoided being crushed in the first place.'

Optatus nodded. 'I inspected the pole, Falco.' He bent over it to show me. 'Look, the cap has not been fitted. It looks as if very few wedges were being used to position the stone in the basin either; whoever was doing this job must have been a complete amateur –'

'Rufius was very young. He may never have seen rollers installed before.'

'It was madness. Unplanned, unthinking incompetence. The grinding-stone would have been wobbling around on the lever, very hard to control. Once it started to lean out at an angle, the man on the ground might have jumped out of the way if he was quick, but more likely he found its weight too much to resist.'

'Instinct might have made him try to support the stone longer than he should, especially if he was inexperienced. Jupiter, it's ghastly – Wouldn't his friend up above heave on the top rim to pull the stone upright again?'

Optatus was blunt: 'Maybe this "friend" pushed the stone out instead!'

'You're leaping ahead – But that would explain why the "friend" vanished afterwards.'

Optatus became more than blunt; he was angry. 'Even if it really was an accident, the friend could have got the stone off Constans afterwards. He would still have died in agony, but he need not have died alone.'

'Some friend!'

A noise alerted us, too late perhaps, to the fact that Marmarides had just led in Helena and Claudia. Claudia's expression told us she had heard what Marius said.

Optatus straightened up at once and went to the girl. He placed both hands on her shoulders and kissed her forehead. The action was brisk and he released her immediately. Claudia gave him a half-smile, and unlike when Quadratus swamped her with condolences she did not burst into tears again.

Optatus explained in a few words what we had been discussing. 'There is no doubt; Constans cannot have done this work alone. Somebody – as yet unidentified – was here helping him.'

'Somebody killed him.' Claudia's voice was now eerily controlled.

I had to intervene. 'It could have been a terrible accident. But whoever was here *must* have seen your brother badly hurt, and yet they simply abandoned him.'

'You mean he need not have died? He could have been saved?' A high note of hysteria showed how Claudia's mind was racing.

'No, no. Please don't torture yourself with that thought. Once the stone slipped and fell on him his wounds would have been too severe.' As I spoke to her, Marius put a hand on her arm and shook his head, trying to persuade her to believe it. Now Claudia did begin to cry, but instead of comforting her himself Marius looked embarrassed and steered her to Helena. As a lover he lacked useful instincts.

Helena held the girl close to her, kissed her, and then

asked me, 'Marcus who do we think this missing companion was?'

'I'd happily name one person!' Marius snarled.

'We know you would – but Quinctius Quadratus has an unshakeable alibi: the bastard couldn't ride. Even if his young pal Constans had gone over to our estate to fetch him, he would still need to get home again after the accident. How are you suggesting he did that?' Optatus was silent, reluctantly conceding the point.

'Call it murder, not an accident!' insisted Claudia, breaking free from Helena's arms.

'I won't do that, Claudia,' I said patiently, 'until I can either provide evidence, or make somebody confess. But I give you my word, I will do all I can to discover what happened, and if it really was murder, whoever was responsible will be made to pay.'

Claudia Rufina made a visible effort to control her emotions. The young girl was brave, but she was close to breaking point. At a signal from Helena I quietly suggested we leave the scene of the tragedy and take her on to her grandparents' house.

LVII

The great half-finished house lay silent. The builders had been dismissed and the estate workers kept to their quarters. Frightened slaves flitted among the pillars indoors. Time had stopped.

The body of Rufius Constans had been raised on a bier in the atrium. Extravagant branches of cypress decorated the area. A canopy darkened what should have been a space filled with sunlight, while smoking brands caused visitors to choke and rub their streaming eyes. The young man awaited burial swathed in white, smothered with garlands, reeking of sweet preservative oils. Busts of his ancestors watched over him. Laurel wreaths which he had never managed to earn for himself had been placed on tripods to symbolise the honours his family had lost.

Marius and I exchanged glances, wondering if one of us could keep watch while the other climbed up to inspect the body. The possible gains were not worth the risk of discovery. We chose to avoid the howls of outrage.

In an adjacent reception room Licinius Rufius and his wife were seated, completely motionless. Both were clad in black. Both looked as if they had neither slept nor eaten since they learned of their grandson's death. Neither showed much interest in the fact we had brought back their granddaughter, though they seemed to be pleased that the rest of us had come to share their grief. The atmosphere was stultifying. I sympathised with their tragedy, but I was still weary and short-tempered after my long journey to Hispalis. I could feel my patience ebbing fast.

Chairs were produced. Claudia sat down immediately with her hands folded and her eyes downcast, resigned to her duty. Helena, Marius and I took our places more uneasily. There was a good chance we could all imitate statues for the next three hours and not hear a word spoken. I was angry, and I felt such passivity would not help.

'This is the most terrible tragedy. We all realise how deeply you are suffering.'

A slight reaction passed over the grandfather's face, though he made no attempt to reply to me.

'Will you come to the funeral?' Claudia Adorata, the old lady, asked me in a hushed voice. She belonged to that group of women who seek their comfort in formal events. Marius and I both agreed to go; I had already decided with Helena that she should excuse herself. Nobody would thank us if she caused a disturbance by giving birth in the middle of the drawn-out obsequies.

I had to speak out: 'Licinius Rufius, Claudia Adorata, forgive me for raising unwelcome issues. I speak as a friend. It has been established that somebody who has not come forward must have been with your grandson when he died. The situation needs to be looked into.'

'Constans is gone,' Licinius dragged out. 'There is no point. You mean well,' he conceded in his autocratic way.

'I do, sir. I respect your wish for privacy —' I knew it remained possible that the young man's death had been a sad — but avoidable — accident. I kept my voice calm and respectful. 'I would like to speak to you in private; it concerns the safety of your granddaughter.'

'My granddaughter!' His eyes flew to me, and met a cool reception.

No doubt Claudia Rufina would be smothered with attention after the funeral, but at the moment she was not being granted her due. The old man was sufficiently formal to stop discussing her in what amounted to a public situation, so he stared at me, but then indicated I could follow him to another room. Claudia herself made a swift movement as though she wanted to assert herself and come with us, but Helena Justina shook her head surreptitiously.

Licinius sat. I stood. It gave him status; I did not need it.

'I'll be brief. Your grandson may have died because of a bungled task, or it may have been more than an accident. Perhaps that only matters if you want to know for your own peace of mind. But I saw you and Constans at the proconsul's palace; I have drawn my own conclusions about why you took him there. I strongly believe there are people who will not have welcomed Constans speaking out – and they will be feeling relieved now he has been silenced.'

'You said you wished to speak about my granddaughter, Falco.'

'This does affect her. Will you tell me what Constans knew?'

'I have nothing to say on that subject.'

'If Constans was aware of something illegal – perhaps the cartel I discussed with you recently, or maybe something even more serious – then you should consider the position very carefully. I knew them only a short time, but it seemed to me that Constans and Claudia were very close.'

'Claudia Rufina is deeply upset –'

'It's worse than that. She may be in danger. Other people, those who had an interest in your grandson's silence, may now be wondering whether Constans told his sister what he knew.'

Licinius Rufius made no remark, but he was listening to me much less impatiently.

'Don't lose them both!' I warned.

The girl was not my responsibility. Her grandfather possessed ample means for ensuring her protection. I had seeded his mind, anyway. He rose, looking gruff though on principle. He hated to acknowledge that anyone else knew better.

As he started to leave the room he turned to me with a faint smile. 'Your skills seem limitless.'

'Not at all. I cannot, for instance, lure you by any method I know into discussing the proposed cartel.'

At last he allowed me to mention it, though he still sang the old refrain: 'There is no cartel.'

1137

'I may even end up believing that.' I smiled. 'Try this, sir: a group of you, chosen for your prominence in the business world, were invited to Rome by an influential senator. A suggestion was made which you rejected out of hand. Then somebody – not necessarily the senator himself – made a stupid mistake. It became known that the Chief Spy was showing interest in your group. Somebody lost his head and arranged a couple of murderous attacks. The rest of you recognised a dangerous bungle, one which only drew attention to the unpalatable plan. You left Rome fast.'

'Convincing,' Licinius Rufius commented coolly. He was now walking slowly, as if due to his age and his bereavement. This would allow us a certain period of discussion before we rejoined our companions.

'Then I turned up here, suggesting you were all still in the thick of the conspiracy ... Actually, sir, I've changed my mind: those of you who were important enough to run a cartel are well placed, by your very prominence in the oil-producing world, to ensure fair prices. You could be the people who take a stand *against* price-rigging.'

'I told you that was my view, Falco.'

'Olive oil is a rich commodity? There will be enough for everyone?'

Licinius Rufius gripped my arm and stared at me keenly. 'What's more, because the product has universal applications, including large consumption by the army, we producers should take care. Otherwise the whole industry may be taken over and state-controlled.'

'Just as corn is! You are a man of sense – as well as probity.'

We now reached the intriguing situation where it was Rufius who wanted something from me. He had stopped again. We were standing in a corridor. He seemed much more frail than when I first met him, though I hoped it was temporary. I could not press him to a seat, for there were none. I just had to hope I could squeeze him before the old chap collapsed.

'When I was in Rome, Falco, one of the arguments that

1138

was put to us was this: somebody at the Palace is extremely eager to assume the state control I mentioned. It was suggested that we all get together in a position of strength –' a position which sounded like the cartel to me – 'Then we could resist that move –'

'By bribing the official?' I asked calmly.

He bridled, but replied, 'Was that a reasonable suggestion?'

'You mean, would it work? Only if there was nothing more subtle in the official's mind.'

'Is there?'

'I don't know. If we're talking about a particular official, then anything is possible. He has great power – and a mind like a Cretan labyrinth. Were you told his identity?'

'No. Do you know who it is?'

'I can guess.' Claudius Laeta was the name that floated through my mind. I could still hear him gloating *Liquid gold!* when he and I were discussing olive oil.

Rufius was watching me closely: 'If the threat of state control comes true –'

'As far as I know, sir, that is not current policy.' I had seen a useful lever. Whatever Laeta might be intending, I had my own ideas about how I would report on Baetica once I returned to Rome. It was not necessarily Laeta who would be my first contact. After all, on other missions I had been received in private by the Emperor himself.

'Licinius Rufius, I am not empowered to make promises. But if I were putting forward official proposals, I might say that the oil producers of Baetica seem to me a responsible body of men who should be allowed to run their own industry.' It would be cheap at least. Vespasian liked any system that cost the Treasury nothing. 'Hispania has been a Roman province for a long time. We are not discussing some untrustworthy backwater full of savages in skins. And maybe it's time the Spanish provinces were thought about more carefully.'

'In what way, Falco?'

'I can think of a number of provisions that Vespasian

might consider. Granting wider rights of citizenship. Improved status for Romanised towns. Greater encouragement for Hispanians who wish to partake in the Senate or who qualify for equestrian posts in Rome.'

'Would he do these things?'

'All I can say is that, unlike others, Vespasian listens to advice.' And he knew the power of social bribes.

'You are very close to him, I think?'

'Not close enough for my own sake, sir!' I grinned.

I was still determined to extract his grandson's secret if I could. 'You won't talk about Constans. I accept that, sir —' His protest died, fairly quietly. Perhaps his resolve was softening. 'May I just ask you again about your visit to the proconsul?'

Licinius Rufius sighed. He breathed deeply and slowly. I let him take his time. 'Falco, I had a long discussion with my grandson after the party given by the sons of Annaeus Maximus.'

'You were angry with him for going to the party without telling you?'

'To start with. That became a minor matter. I sensed he was in serious trouble. He was afraid of something. He told me there had been a dancer at the party who was asking questions. It was rather confusing —'

'There are *two* dancers,' I explained.

'So it seems. All I ever persuaded Constans to say was that he had political information involving one of them.'

'Not the one at the Annaeus party?'

'I think not. There was another girl Constans and his friends had known, a local entertainer. I dread to think what class of girl —'

'Not a very good dancer,' I told him.

'You know of her?'

'Her name is Selia; she comes from Hispalis.' She had tried to kill me three days ago; I kept that to myself. 'What's the story with Constans?'

'He had been involved in hiring her once. I cannot imagine how it came about; my grandson was a quiet lad —'

Light was dawning. 'I think it was Quadratus who wanted her hired – but he had gone back to Rome for the Senate elections. So he wrote and asked Constans to organise this girl from Hispalis to dance at that dinner we all went to on the Palatine?'

'Something like that.' Licinius was trying to avoid telling me. He had failed to appreciate how important it was. 'It sounds perfectly harmless. My grandson paid her fare and appearance fee – though, as you know, he didn't even attend. It's annoying, and a waste of money, but young people do far worse things. Frankly, I could not understand why Constans became so exercised about it.'

'And how did this come to light, sir?'

'Annaeus Maximus had ridden over here after his sons' drinking party.'

'To complain about Constans being a guest?'

'No. Maximus came to warn me that his lads had seen fit to allow in a dancer.'

'*Warn* you, sir?'

'The dancer had been asking questions – it is presumably the same woman who had already accosted me. She is taking an interest in what happened when we went to Rome. Well, you must know who I mean! She's asking much the same as you, Falco; Annaeus and I presume you are working with her. She has been hanging around Corduba for weeks.'

'I can see how that would have alarmed you all!' I avoided comment on the suggestion that I was part of some joint enquiry team. 'And how did this frighten Rufius Constans?'

'What upset him, and made me persuade him to appeal to the proconsul, was that the dancer who performed for the Annaei had also been asking questions about the other girl. One of the Annaeus boys had then told her that it was Constans who paid for Selia's trip to Rome. On learning that, for some reason, my grandson became hysterical.'

I could have told him the reason. Perhaps it was better to leave Licinius merely puzzled than to say that Selia's performance in Rome had included murder. Rufius Constans had been her paymaster. I could not believe he had known what he was doing. It seemed much more likely the poor boy was someone's dupe. But it looked bad – and had probably seemed worse to him. It would be easy to suggest that it had been Rufius Constans who panicked and paid Selia to start crashing inconvenient enquirers into Roman walls. My own view was that he was too immature to do that. However, his precise role called for examination, as the boy must have realised.

I could imagine his thoughts when he heard his grandfather and Annaeus Maximus – two men who were normally barely on speaking terms – anxiously discussing government enquiry agents, then revealing that one official had been told how Selia and Constans were linked. He probably thought he was about to be arrested – and so he should have been, both to protect him as a witness and to allow time to question him. Frankly, if he were still alive, I would be arresting him myself.

LVIII

We made a slow and thoughtful journey back to the Camillus estate. I travelled in the carriage this time, and told Helena of my talk with the grandfather. Helena was feeling very tired but still had strength to worry about the bereaved family. 'Something needs to be done for poor Claudia.'

'What's her problem? I think she's seen through Quadratus.'

'Quadratus may think much more of her though, now she's the sole heiress!'

I grinned. 'I wouldn't worry. Claudia may have become a fortune-hunter's dream – though I'm sure her grandpapa is up to the situation. Anyway, as you said yourself once, the Quinctii will be looking for a bride with seven consuls in her pedigree and an ancestry she can trace on copper tablets all the way to the Seven Kings of Rome.'

'Meanwhile Claudia,' said Helena, 'harbours serious ideas of using her inheritance to make endowments in the local community. She wishes to make her life as a female benefactress to Corduba – and now that she'll inherit the entire family fortune, she'll be even more determined.'

'Commendable! Still, she's not averse to men.'

'No,' Helena agreed. 'She is a good young woman with a fine character. She has been well brought up. She is honest, direct, serious, and loyal to those she loves. She ought to be head of her own household; she will make a chaste, intelligent partner and an admirable mother.'

I knew my girl. 'That's a set speech! What exactly are you planning, fruit?'

'She could be married with a clause in her dowry that says large sums are supplied for the comfort of her husband

1143

and any children – but that Claudia Rufina is to have a fixed annual amount to devote to the community.'

'Married to whom, my darling?'

'How about someone from a rising senatorial family who are *not* snobbish about background, but who would be happy to offer their position and refinement –'

'In return for her glittering collateral?'

'Oh, don't be crude, Marcus!'

'It was your idea,' I pointed out.

'She already knows Aelianus,' mused Helena.

'Of course she does,' I answered, thinking how much pleasure it would give me to shackle that young man to a serious girl with a rather large nose whose funds he was forced to respect.

Helena looked pleased with herself. 'She's a nice girl. Marius Optatus may not be too pleased with me, but I think I'm going to invite Claudia to Rome. Obviously she cannot stay with us –' No; our cramped, ill-decorated apartment was not the place to entertain a fabulous olive oil heiress. 'So I shall have to ask Mother to take her instead!'

'Well, I'm sure she'll conquer Rome with ease, my love – and her fortune should conquer your brother! Just give me a chance to clear up the residue of events from her own brother's disastrous visit to the Golden City first.'

Our house was quiet and subdued that evening. Nobody took much enjoyment in dinner, and we dispersed quickly afterwards. I was sitting alone in the garden, trying to shape my thoughts into some sort of order, when Marmarides coughed.

'Something is not right with the carriage, Falco.'

'That seems fairly typical of Baetica! Do you need a part fixed?' My heart sank. As I remembered his employer, the ex-legionary Stertius, his invention and prowess with machinery had far excelled mine.

'There is a difficulty with the hodometer,' Marmarides confessed.

Well, that was no more than I expected. Over-elaborate

gadgets always go wrong. In fact if I come anywhere near them, even simple ones, their rivets snap. 'Do you want me to have a look at it?'

'Later, perhaps.'

To my surprise Marmarides deposited his slight figure on my bench then produced a bundle of note-tablets from a pouch at his belt. He opened one or two; they were covered with slanting figures in a big, careful hand. Every line began with the name of a place. Some were dates.

'What's this, your travel diary?'

'No; it's yours, Falco.'

'Are you writing my memoirs for me, or auditing my expense claims?'

Marmarides laughed his jovial laugh. Apparently I was a crack wit. Then he laid his tablets open on his knee and showed me how every time we took a trip in the carriage he listed it, with the date and the new mileage. When we came to make a final reckoning of how much I owed Stertius, the driver would be able to demonstrate our usage of the vehicle exactly, should I venture to disagree with his reckoning. Plainly his master Stertius thought of everything. Stertius must have dealt with argumentative types before.

'So what's up?'

'Today you went over to the Rufius house, stopped on the way where we all talked about the young man being killed, then I drove you home. Now it is evening. I feed the mules, clean the carriage, and sit down with my little stylus to make up the record.'

'And?'

'The miles don't fit, Falco.'

My first reaction was bored incomprehension. 'Well, if you're slightly out I won't have a seizure. I can trust you on one or two discrepancies – Mind you, Helena Justina keeps my accounts and she's more precise.'

'Falco, how far do you think it is to the Rufius house?'

'Four or five miles?'

'So don't you see, Falco?'

1145

'I'm very tired still from my trip to Hispalis –'

'This line here,' Marmarides explained stubbornly, pointing to his last written note, 'is my count for your last trip that I know about – when Helena and you went into Corduba and you interviewed Cyzacus and Gorax. The day we all had a fight on the riverbank.'

'I'll never forget. You fell in. I thought I would have to compensate Stertius for drowning his freedman ... So now you have to add a new line about today?'

'I go to the hodometer and count the pebbles that remain.'

'And you notate this column?' I indicated the final row, where the figures diminished with each entry.

'That's what doesn't fit. From the day you went to Corduba to now, there are twice as many miles as I expect.'

'You allowed for the return journey?'

'Oh yes. The miles the carriage has travelled since Corduba,' Marmarides told me with a beaming smile, 'are enough for a journey to the Rufius house, there and back – then there and back a second time!'

I was impressed. It was immediately apparent what Marmarides meant. 'This is your big chance to solve something for me,' I said.

He beamed. 'You talked about how the man with the bad back could have gone to help the young one fix the grinding-wheel. He could have gone in your carriage, Falco.'

I was keeping calm. 'In agenting you have to work out everything, and make sure there can be no mistake. I thought Helena was out in the carriage that day? I thought she went with Aelia Annaea to her house?'

'No,' he said. 'Aelia Annaea came to visit in her own carriage, and Helena Justina left with her.' Marmarides had really thought this through. 'Marius Optatus went into Corduba, but he used an ox-wagon.'

'So our carriage was in the stable?' He nodded. 'The slaves were all in the fields and wouldn't see much,

Marmarides. The farm is near the road, so anyone could drive off without drawing attention ... Did you happen to notice whether the mules had been out? Were they sweating at all?'

Marmarides looked sheepish. 'I never looked, Falco.' Then he cheered up, able to exonerate himself. 'I was not here. After Helena Justina left, I hitched a ride with Optatus to Corduba.'

'What did you want in Corduba?'

He just grinned. There was a woman in this somewhere, and I decided not to explore it. Since neither Helena nor I had been here there could be no objection. It also gave Optatus an alibi. 'All right. You observed Quinctius Quadratus with his bad back during the time that he was here. If he couldn't ride, do you think he would have been able to drive a two-mule carriage a short way?'

'Probably. He would not have been much use as a partner in a heavy lifting job though, Falco.'

'Whoever was partnering Constans was certainly no good, we know that.'

If it was Quadratus, maybe he did not let the stone fall deliberately. Maybe his back just gave out. Maybe the boy's death was a genuine accident — one that should never have happened, caused by bungling incompetence. It was cowardly of Quadratus not to own up to his part in the stupidity, but it was not a criminal act.

So perhaps the worst that had happened that day was that Quadratus got bored — or maybe Constans, panicking about Selia, had appealed for his advice. For one reason or another Quadratus went to see his dear friend Constans. Then two young men who should have known better got together and decided to do a job for which they were poorly qualified. The work was too hard for them. Quadratus was unfit; the grinding-stone fell on poor Constans. Quadratus was the elder and should have behaved more responsibly. That would make him the more reluctant to admit he had been there. Besides, he must have been badly shocked by what happened.

1147

'We have to be sure,' Marmarides decided firmly. He had picked up a few phrases from me, apparently. 'You must come with me to the stables and we will re-count the pebbles that are left in the hodometer. Then you will have firm evidence.'

He was in charge. So we walked over to the stables, crouched down at the back of the carriage and inspected the Archimedes hodometer. Marmarides counted the pebbles that remained on the upper gear wheel. Sure enough, there were several less than there should have been according to his notes: a rough count of the missing mileage confirmed that it would equal two trips to the Rufius estate: there and back for Quinctius Quadratus, plus our own drive out and back today.

Solemnly we made a note on the tablet, explained our deductions, and both signed as witnesses.

LIX

The funeral took place next day. There were no distant relatives to summon, and Baetica is a hot locality.

The necropolis which the wealthy Cordubans used lay nearest to us on the south of the city, this side of the bridge. Naturally it presented the best aspect. The wealthy did not inter their smart relations among the middle class or paupers, least of all with the gladiators in their multiple columbarium outside the western gate. Across the river from the noise of the town each family possessed a gracious mausoleum, lining the important road that passed through to the fertile plain and the sun-drenched slopes of their rolling olive groves.

I did wonder why they didn't build their tombs in complete privacy on their own land instead of crowding into a necropolis which was passed daily by carriages and carts. Maybe people who socialise madly in life know their dead will still want friends to mingle with in the afterlife.

The Rufii had not yet become so extravagant as the family who had constructed a miniature temple complete with Ionic columns around a little portico. Grandeur would come, no doubt. For the moment theirs was a simple brick-built, tile-roofed edifice with a low doorway. Within the small chamber was a series of niches containing ceramic urns. Wall plaques already commemorated the parents, son and daughter-in-law of Licinius Rufius. These were sombre enough, though nothing to the new panel planned for the grandson. We were shown a maquette, though the real thing would provide half a year's work for the stonemason. The text began, *'O woe! O lamentation! Whither shall we turn?'* and ran on for about six grim lines: longer than I could force myself to read. Sloths like me were soon

provided with assistance, for Licinius gave an oration on a
similar basis which lasted so long my feet went numb.

Everyone was there. Well, everyone who owned half a
million upwards, plus Marius Optatus and myself. For the
rich, it was just an extra social occasion. They were
arranging dinner-party dates in undertones.

Only one notable person was missing: the new quaestor
Quinctius Quadratus. His sprained back must be still
inconveniencing him. Absenting himself looked amiss,
however, since he had been the dead young man's close
friend.

The proconsul had deigned to be brought over in a litter
from his praetorium. As we all stumped around trying to
fill in time while the corpse heated up in the cemetery oven,
his honour found time for a muttered word with me. I had
been looking for someone to share a joke about whether
they used the embers in the oven to warm hot pies for the
mourners afterwards – but with him I confined myself to a
reverent salute.

'What do you make of this, Falco?'

'Officially – a young lad who foolishly attempted a job
for which he was unqualified while trying to please his
grandfather.'

'And between ourselves?'

What was the point of condemning Constans now? 'Oh
... just a regrettable accident.'

The proconsul surveyed me. 'I believe he tried to see me,
when I had gone out to Astigi ...' This was not an
invitation to speculate on the reason. 'A statue is to be
erected in the civic forum, I understand.'

'It's all work for the stonemasons, sir.'

We did not discuss my mission; well, I never expected
to.

The women had clustered in a huddle. I was in a mood for
avoiding them. I expressed my formal sympathy to Licinius
in the routine handshake line. Optatus made himself more
agreeable; I saw him among the Annaei at one point. Then

1150

he came back and whispered, 'Aelia Annaea asked me to tell you that Claudia wishes to speak to you privately. Licinius must not know.'

'Maybe her friend can arrange something –'

I might have given more precise instructions but just at that moment a hurried messenger came from Helena, asking me to return to her at once.

LX

It was a false alarm.

I sat with Helena, holding her hand, and we both said nothing. The pains which had frightened her seemed to be coming to nothing, but the next occasion could well be different. We were safe today, but seriously alarmed. We had run out of time.

A couple of hours passed. As we began to relax again, we pretended we were both sitting silent in the garden purely in order to enjoy each other's company.

'Marcus, nothing is happening. You can leave me if you want.'

I stayed where I was. 'This could be my last chance for the next twenty years to enjoy an afternoon in the sun completely alone with you. Savour it, my love. Children make it their sole ambition to interrupt.'

Helena sighed gently. The earlier excitement had left her subdued and shocked.

After a while she murmured, 'Don't pretend to be dozing under the fig tree. You're planning things in your head.'

I was in fact mentally packing bags, consulting maps, debating the virtues of sea against land travel – and trying to reconcile myself to absconding from Baetica with my task only half done. 'You know what I think. There's no time to waste. I want to go home now.'

'You think it's too late already! It's my fault,' she shrugged. 'It was my idea to come to Baetica.'

'Everything will be all right.'

'You know how to lie!'

'And you know how to joke – It's time to leave. Good time, I hope. Anyway, I'm coming with you.'

'You're wonderful!' Helena said. Sometimes she almost

1152

sounded as though she trusted me. 'I love you, Didius Falco. One of the reasons is that you pursue a cause relentlessly.'

'Well! And I thought it was because I had momentous brown eyes and a body you want to grab ... So you really think I'm looking for a chance to bunk off after some villain and let you down.'

'No,' she retorted, with her old spirit. 'I think you're lusting after a set-to with some half-naked female spy!'

'Oh discovery! No; let's be honest. You're bound to be annoyed to find I've ended up tangling with devious female agents – but you can count the peas in a pod. You know it's not my fault there seem to be women everywhere – but you think I'm spinning out the job in Hispania purely because I want an excuse to avoid being with you when you start producing the child. I'm famous for breaking promises. I know that.'

'No,' said Helena patiently. 'You're famous for finishing what you start.'

'Thanks! Now I've started on fatherhood – So we are going home?'

The fight seemed to go out of her. 'I'll do what you decide, Marcus.'

That settled it. If Helena Justina was being meek, the poor girl must be terrified. I took a manly decision: I was not up to reassuring a woman in the last stage of her pregnancy. I needed my mother; I needed Helena's mother too. We were going home.

Marius Optatus came riding back shortly, and I told him of my decision. He had the grace to look sad at losing us. Immediately afterwards a carriage appeared, bearing Aelia Annaea and young Claudia. There were some sturdy outriders who made themselves at home in our kitchen; Licinius Rufius must have heeded my advice about protecting the girl.

'Marius told us Helena might be having the baby. We said we were coming to help –'

1153

'Just a twinge,' said Helena. 'I'm sorry to be such trouble –'

They looked disappointed. My feelings were more mixed. I wished it was all over, though I was dreading the event. Helena's eyes met mine, full of tolerance. The requirement to be sociable with our visitors would be good for both of us. But our afternoon together had brought us very close. Those moments of deep, private affection stayed with us as powerfully as if we had spent the time making love in bed. In fact our mood may have communicated itself, for both Marius and Aelia Annaea looked at us rather quizzically.

Since the others had just come from a funeral they needed space to settle their own emotions. They had the customary mixture of anticlimax and revival. The dead young man had been sent to his ancestors; the living could pursue daily routines again. They were tired after the ceremony, but the immediate pressure of grief had been eased, even for Claudia.

Helena ordered mint tea. That's always good for covering any awkwardness. No one has time for anything but finding space to put the strainer and making sure they don't slurp from their beaker or drop crumbs from their almond cake.

I was still sitting close to Helena; Claudia was placed at my other hand so she could tell me whatever she had come about. Marius Optatus seated himself with Aelia, all set to pretend to admire the lily tubs if anything too scandalous was being discussed.

We progressed through the necessary ritual. I apologised for rushing off. Fuss was made of Helena. There was a swift review of the funeral, including the size of the turnout, the quantity of the garlands, the affecting style of the eulogy, and the comfort of knowing that the departed was in peace. I thought Constans had left behind a little too much unfinished business for that, but in the hope that his sister might be intending to right some of it, I was prepared to extend some charity to the lad.

Claudia reached the point where she felt she could talk to

me. She squirmed. She blushed. I tried to look encouraging. 'Marcus Didius, I have something to tell you,' she finally blurted out. 'I have to confess that I have not been telling the truth!'

I was leaning forwards, trying to look happy drinking from a dainty terracotta bowl. I stirred my mint tea with a tiny bronze spoon, flipping out a leaf on to the ground.

'Claudia Rufina, since I became an informer I have talked to many people who have told me one thing – only to realise they should have been saying something else.' Sometimes, in wild moments, I longed for a witness who would break the pattern and surprise me by croaking – under pressure of conscience or perhaps my own fingers squeezing their neck a little too tightly – that they were sorry to cause me extra work but they had mistakenly given me *accurate* answers. No doubt adding that it was quite unlike them, a moment of sheer madness, and they didn't know what came over them ...

'You are not the first person who ever changed their mind,' said Helena softly.

The girl was still hesitating. 'It is better to have the truth in the end,' I stated pontifically, 'than never to learn it at all.'

'Thank you, Marcus Didius.'

There was no point being cruel to her. I could have said, sometimes truth that emerges *so* late in the day is too late to help. But I'm not that kind of dog.

'This is very difficult.'

'Don't worry. Take your time.'

'My grandfather has forbidden me to talk about it.'

'Then we won't mention this conversation to him.'

'Constans told me something – though he made me promise never to reveal it to anyone.'

'You must believe it's important, or you wouldn't be here now.'

'It's horrible.'

1155

'I thought it might be. Let me help you: has it to do with some violent events in Rome?'

'You know!' I needed her to tell me. Finally she forced herself to come out with it: 'When my brother was in Rome he was involved in killing somebody.'

That was more than I expected. All the others were keeping silent and still. I too handled the situation as calmly as possible. 'My dear, you cannot change what Constans did. It's best to tell me exactly what you know. What I most need to hear is who else was involved? And what exactly happened?'

'It was to do with the plan to regulate olive oil.' Regulate was a nice new word.

'Did your brother give you details of the plan?'

'Tiberius and his father were in charge. My grandfather and some other people had gone to Rome to discuss it, though they all decided not to become involved.'

'Yes, I know that. So be assured your grandfather is safe; he retains his position as an honourable citizen. Now I want to talk about what happened in Rome, Claudia. Your brother was there; he was of course a very close friend of the younger Quinctius? Quadratus was older; they were like patron and client. I already know that your brother, at the request of Quadratus, had arranged a special dancer to appear at a dinner where the olive oil plan was being discussed.'

'Yes.'

'Your brother and Quadratus did not attend that dinner. Is this what you want to tell me? Did Constans tell you where they were instead?'

'They stayed away from the dinner — because of what was going to happen.' Claudia's voice was now barely a whisper. 'There had been a discussion in the Quinctius house about certain officials who were aware of the plan and taking too close an interest. The father —'

'Quinctius Attractus.'

'He said those people had to be stopped. I think he meant just pay them some money to go away, but Tiberius thought it wouldn't work. His plan was to hire someone to attack them instead.'

'Just to frighten them, perhaps?' I suggested.

Claudia, who had been staring into her lap, now looked up at me. She was a straightforward girl. 'Marcus Didius, I don't believe we should pretend. They were meant to be killed.'

'Who carried out the attacks?'

'The dancer, and some men who helped her.'

'Were your brother and his friend there?'

'How did you know?' I just raised a rueful eyebrow; Claudia steeled herself and finished her story: 'Quadratus persuaded my brother to be present – first when he hired the people to do it. Then – this is the gruesome part – they both hid in the shadows that night and watched as the first man was killed. My brother was horrified and ran away. Quadratus went with him. They got drunk somewhere, and later went home and pretended they had been to the theatre.'

I replaced my cup on the table in front of us. The tray wobbled; Helena reached out quietly and adjusted it.

'So Quinctius Quadratus and Rufius Constans were present during one of the attacks. Do you know which one?'

'No.'

'Did either of the young men strike the victim at all?'

'Not as far as I know. Not Constans, I am sure of it.'

I linked my fingers, still trying to sound calm. 'Thank you for telling me, Claudia. Is that everything?'

'That is all my brother told me. He was hysterical about it. I helped persuade him to go with Grandfather to admit everything to the proconsul – but they weren't able to have an interview. What should I do now?'

'Nothing,' I said. One step at a time. I might later want to ask her to consider becoming a court witness, but there were difficulties about calling a woman, especially one of refined birth. Somebody male had to speak for her; it always weakened the case.

Helena glanced at me. She had realised that her plan to invite Claudia to Rome might be doubly useful now. We could get the girl there without antagonising her grandfather, then maybe ask Claudia to make a statement for the investigating judge, even if she was never called into court.

'Have I done the right thing?'

'Yes. Go home now, Claudia. I shall have to interview Quadratus, but I won't tell him where I learned my information. You need not even tell your grandfather you talked to me, unless you feel you want to.'

'So everything is all right!'

Nothing was all right. But we called for her carriage and her armed guards, then we sent her home.

Dawn is the classic time to surprise a villain, though I never know why. You run a great risk that his doors are locked. While you are kicking them in he wakes up in a sweat, realises what is happening, and gets his sword out ready to run you through.

It was still early evening. I decided to tackle Quadratus at once.

Aelia Annaea stayed behind with Helena. Marius Optatus came with me. We took his strongest male slaves, plus Marmarides. I strapped on my sword. The others were armed with whatever came to hand, mostly rakes and sticks.

The Quinctius estate was much like others I had visited, though it bore signs of the absentee landlord at his most astute: abundant flocks, tended by the fewest possible shepherds, and secondary cereal crops growing below the olive trees. Everything looked in respectable condition. Moneymakers don't neglect their land. Believe me, there was a great deal of land.

The house had charm and character. Thick walls to keep it cool in summer and cosy in winter. Vine-clad pergolas leading to statues of coy maidens. A separate bath-house. A terrace for airy exercise. It spoke of wealth, yet wealth possessed by an honest country family. Long harvest lunches taken with the tenantry. Girls with pink cheeks and boys who were keen on horseflesh. Life lived with a constant supply of fresh fodder and an old earthenware jug of home-produced wine always ready to hand.

Amazing. Even their damned house lied.

We told the escort to wait quietly but to rush in like ravening wolves if we signalled them. In the event even bringing them proved unnecessary. Quadratus was not there. He had listened when I advised him to take up his job as quaestor. The same day he came home from staying with us he had packed some note-tablets, taken a litter and a pack-mule, a personal bodyslave, clean tunics and a mapskin of the area, then he had told his servants he was going on a surprise tour of the Corduba mines. The procurator whose job was to look after them, and who was probably perfectly competent since he had been appointed by Vespasian, would not be too happy at an unannounced official visit. Nor was I, come to that.

Our trip to the estate was not entirely fruitless. I sensed that the staff there had almost been expecting me. They were surly and clearly nervous, and eventually one of them told me they had just been about to send over to fetch me from the Camillus farm when I turned up anyway. Somebody had left a message on the Quinctius premises, a message personally addressed to me. I could tell from the slaves' expressions I was not going to like it, even before they led me and Marius to the stable where this mysterious missive had been scrawled on a hitching post.

All it said was *For Falco*, followed by a neat pictogram of a human eye.

Lying on the straw below the drawing was the dancing girl called Selia. She was dressed in outdoor clothes, including a wide-brimmed travelling hat tied on over her own loosely knotted brown hair. She was dead. Her skin felt cold, though her limbs were still limp. She had been killed quickly and neatly by pressure to the neck. It was clearly carried out from behind before she realised what was happening. She had been lying here for a few hours. Unless

Quadratus had sneaked back unobserved, the killing certainly happened after he had left for the mines. I could not believe he did it. The method was too professional.

If somebody was killing agents who had worked for Laeta, that could well mean they would now try to kill me.

LXI

Even before I explained what had just happened at the Quinctius estate, Helena Justina had lost the idyllic tenderness she displayed towards me earlier. She was cool. I did not blame her but I could have coped better with solicitude. We were in the garden again. I had hardly even started to discuss what I planned to do next, but we were close to quarrelling.

'Not the mines, Falco!'

'Just think of it as a tour of the local industry.'

'That's what you were going to say, I suppose – had Marius Optatus not told me the whole truth before you could stop him!'

'I don't lie to you.'

'You hold things back – if you believe you can get away with it!'

'I'm a man, Helena. I have to try. I tell myself I'm protecting you.'

'You're annoying me,' she snarled.

I said nothing. Pleasing honesty had failed: time to keep quiet.

'Marcus, I'm in an impossible position now! I don't want you to go – but I don't want you to stay with me unwillingly, just because of my condition; I won't be made an excuse. You'd never forgive me afterwards – maybe I wouldn't forgive myself! Besides, I know just how badly you feel about the mines. You suffered all the torments of Hades once in a silver mine; it's too much for you to volunteer this time.'

'I won't be digging for ore again. All I need to do is to apprehend Quadratus and haul him back to face a trial. But you're right. I'm not irreplaceable. Someone else can go.'

Helena frowned. 'You think anyone else will bungle it.'

'I don't care.'

'Of course you care. And I care too!'

Helena's passionate belief in justice was one of the reasons I first fell for her. Single-minded girls are always dangerous. A man can float along for years being cynical and flippant, then some fierce tyrant (who happens to have the advantages of a sweet mind, a delicious expression and a body that is crying out to be entwined with his) sneaks under his defences; next thing he finds himself taking a stand on some issue he would once have crept away from, simply to impress the girl.

'I am about to be a father. That is my sole priority.'

'Oh Didius Falco, you have so many priorities you need an abacus to count them. You always did. You always will.'

'Wrong. You're going home, Helena – and I'm staying with you.'

'Wrong yourself. You have to finish your work.' She had made up her mind now. 'I hate it, but that's the only way. You know I can't bear to see you nobly pretending not to fidget, while all the time you're in agony because the bastard has got away.'

'I will not break my promise to you.'

'I release you from it – temporarily. Marcus, I don't complain. You never pretended to be other than you are, and I never dreamed of reforming you. I love your persistence, though you know how hard it is for me just now ... Go and find him, and arrest him. Then dear gods, Marcus –' There were tears she could not resist. 'Please promise that as fast as you can you will come back to me.'

Tomorrow was the Nones of May. I could still remember clearly that hot night last August in Palmyra which was probably when our baby was conceived. May was only six days old. The child might not be born until the end of the month. I told myself there was still just time to do it all. I told Helena, and hugged her. While she tried not to cry so much that I wouldn't endure it, I in turn kept her close against me so she would not see the gaunt expression on my own face.

1162

I was starting to hate this garden. Helena must have stayed here when we went over to the Quinctius place, as if she was worried that just moving indoors might start the pains again and cause the birth to begin. Her anxiety only increased mine.

While I had been absent Aelia Annaea had kindly kept Helena company. She was still here. When Marius Optatus foolishly created a crisis by confessing that he thought I was now intending to ride after Quadratus, Aelia had quickly drawn him off the scene for a walk in the orchard while Helena tore me to shreds. Aelia seemed to be waiting around to give us the support of a friend when we reached our decision.

Now she walked back to us, leaving Marius. He mooned in the background, as if he had been given definite orders to wait. Aelia Annaea was quiet, but brisk. Owning a gold mine gives a woman distinct confidence. I liked her, perhaps almost as much as Helena did.

She drew up a folding chair, left from our polite afternoon with Claudia. Smiling, she surveyed our present mood. 'So everything is settled.'

I scowled unhappily. 'Are you asking us, or telling us?'

Helena dried her eyes. 'Careful, Aelia. Marcus hates bossy women.'

'That must be why he lives with one!' Rich widows can be very provocative. I had suffered clients like this – before I learned to turn them down. She grinned at me. 'Well, I have come to offer suggestions, that is all.'

Helena and I both gazed at Aelia; we must have looked pretty wan-faced.

'Marcus Didius has to find Tiberius.' Even now from habit Aelia retained the informal use of his name. 'Helena, if you intend returning to Rome, I think you should start out gently straight away. I have been discussing this with Marius, and I'm going to talk to Claudia. Claudia is very unhappy at home. I think she would like to accept your kind invitation to visit Rome.'

'I haven't actually asked her –'

'No, but I will! It will be hard to leave her grandparents so soon after her brother's death, but if she waits she'll never go. The excuse will be that she is accompanying you, Helena; you will obviously need help on the journey. So!' Aelia Annaea was direct and well organised. 'While Falco goes after the fugitive, you can travel very slowly by road. I'm going to come with you myself as far as the Tarraconensis coast. Claudia will be with us too. We shall take my carriage, which is spacious and comfortable, and I will return in it afterwards. This fellow –' She indicated me – 'can ride after us as soon as he is ready, then take you home by sea.'

Helena looked troubled. 'Marcus may have to attend a court case.'

'No,' I said. 'If there's a court case it will be in Rome.' There were special arrangements for senators-elect. Quadratus would have to be taken back home. There were probably even more interesting arrangements when two different branches of government service had concerned themselves with the crimes. Those arrangements probably featured provisions for silencing me.

'So!' Aelia Annaea exclaimed again brightly. 'What do you think?'

I took and kissed her hand. 'We think you're wonderful.'

'Thank you,' said Helena, clearly very relieved. 'Aelia, would you enjoy a visit to Rome yourself?'

Aelia Annaea looked a little mysterious. 'No, I don't think so at the moment, Helena. I may be busy doing something here in Corduba.' She proudly accepted credit for her solution to our own problem, then stood up again, presumably ready to take her leave of us. Since she had originally come with Claudia I asked, 'Is Marius Optatus intending to arrange some transport for you?'

'I expect so.'

'Would you like me to speak to him?'

'No, don't worry. Marius and I are on good terms.'

She smiled. Even without the jewels which normally

1164

weighed her down, she was a fine young woman, the more so when she felt cheerful and pleased with herself. Her veil fell back; her hair was loose for the funeral and the softened effect made her look even more appealing. She turned away and walked back to Marius, a slim figure with a firm step.

I was intending to find Marmarides, to tell him that our ways must finally part, thank him, and settle up for the carriage. First, I finally persuaded Helena to go indoors. She rose, a little stiff from sitting so long, her shape thoroughly awkward nowadays. I walked with her, taking her slowly to her room. Then, while she was washing her face in a basin, I went to the shutter and quietly opened it. I whistled under my breath; Helena came to look out with me.

Marius Optatus and Aelia Annaea were standing together under an almond tree. They were fairly close, talking quietly. Aelia was probably explaining her scheme for taking Helena to the coast. She had removed her veil and was twirling it casually from one wrist. Marius held on to a bough above his head; he looked even more relaxed. From his attitude, I suspected Marius was harbouring masculine plans.

He spoke. Aelia responded, perhaps rather pertly, for she tilted up her chin. Then Marius slipped his free arm right around her waist and drew her to him while they kissed. It seemed a popular move with Aelia. And when Marius slowly let go of the almond bough to embrace her even more closely, it seemed that his love for the lady's gold mine might actually be slightly less important than the love he felt for her.

LXII

I told myself it was not going to be like the last time. Mines are simply places where ores are produced. In that respect they are no different from glass factories or pig farms. Or even olive groves. There was no reason for me to start sweating with terror simply because I had to visit one or two mines. Time was short. I would not be staying. A couple of questions to ascertain the location of Quadratus – whether he was there, or had already called there, or whether the local foreman had heard he was on his way. Then all I had to do was say a nice hello to him, present him with the evidence, extract his confession, and lead him off. Simple, really. I should be feeling confident.

I could not help remembering what happened to me that other time. Something I hate to talk about. A nightmare to endure, then a cause of other nightmares for decades afterwards.

It had been my first mission for the Emperor. Britain. A province I had served in earlier. I thought I knew everything. I thought I would have everything under control. I was proud, cynical, efficient as an eagle stripping carrion. The first thing that happened was that I met a wild, contemptuous, patrician young divorcee called Helena and long before I noticed it, she had knocked every certainty of the previous thirty years from under me. Then I was sent undercover to the mines. For reasons that had made sense to everybody else, I was sent in disguised as a slave.

In the end it was Helena Justina who rescued me. She would not be doing that again. The last time her crazy driving of a pony cart had almost scared me more than all my sufferings in the silver mine as she raced me to a hospital before I died of exposure and cruelty; now she was herself being carried at a delicate pace along the Via Augusta to Valentia and then north towards a port called Emporiae. From there I would be taking her by sea around the southern coast of Gaul – a route that was famous for storms and shipwrecks, yet the quickest way back home.

Three years. Nearly three years I had known her now. I had changed and so had she. I liked to think I had mellowed her. But she had mellowed herself to begin with, when she let herself feel concern for a man she had at first heartily despised. Then I had found myself falling too. I recognised my fate; I plunged straight in. Now here I was, riding up into the hills of another mineral-rich province, older, mature, responsible, a seasoned state official: still stupid enough to take on any task, still put upon, still losing more than I ever gained.

It would not be like the last time. I was more fit and less fanatical. I distrusted too many people, including those who had sent me here. I had a woman and a baby to care about. I could not take risks.

I had visited the proconsul to tell him my intentions. He listened, then shrugged, then told me I seemed to know what ought to be done so he would not interfere. Same old routine. If it worked out well, he would want all the credit; if I got into difficulties, I was on my own.

The proconsul's staff, who did seem to have decent orders about helping me in my mission, had supplied me with a set of mules. Even better, I had been given a map, and what must be the briefing on mineral deposits that they prepared for the proconsul when he took up his post. From it I learned in detail what I had previously tried to avoid knowing.

Whereas the silver mines of Britain had proved to be disappointing, the landmass of Hispania was blessed with enormous riches. There was gold, gold in fabulous quantities. It had been estimated that the great state-owned mines of the northwest produced as much as twenty thousand pounds of gold every month; they were protected by the

1167

sole legion in the province, the Seventh Gemina. Besides gold there was silver, lead, copper, iron and tin. In Baetica there were old silver mines at Carthago Nova, silver and copper mines near Hispalis, gold mines at Corduba, cinnabar at Sisapo, silver at Castulo; in the ore-laden Mariana mountains – to which I had been told Quinctius Quadratus was heading – there were hundreds of shafts producing the finest copper in the Empire and an extravagance of silver too.

A few older mines remained in private hands, but the Emperor was easing out individual ownership. Most of these establishments were now under government control. A procurator administered the sites; contractors or local mining societies could take a lease on identified shafts on payment of a hefty sum and a proportion of the minerals they produced. Presumably the keen new quaestor imagined he had tripped off on his scenic tour in order to audit the procurator. Unlike his cowardly action in abandoning Rufius Constans under the weight of a grinding-stone, questioning the rule of a high-powered imperial career officer was decidedly brave. I myself was not even looking forward to telling the procurator – if I met him first – that Quadratus had devised such a plan. He might be a senator-elect, and the proconsul's deputy, but compared with the man he was venturing to spy on he was a mere temporary figurehead. Any ferret-faced freedman with equestrian status in a salaried post would wrap the quaestor round a scroll baton and send him home at the bottom of the next dispatch-rider's pouch.

I had to find Quadratus before this was done. I wanted him in one piece, pristine and unrolled.

I had crossed the river at Corduba. My journey would take me into the long line of gentle hills that had been a constant backdrop to our stay. In a gentle arc from west to east they closed off the Baetis valley on its north side, stretching from Hispalis to Castulo, and were pockmarked with mineral works almost all the way. Tumbling rivers with wriggling lakes ran through the hills. Transhumance paths, the ancient drove-roads for moving cattle every season, crisscrossed the terrain. I moved up into cooler air, amongst oak and chestnut trees.

I travelled light, camping out if it was more convenient, or begging a night in a contractor's hut where I could. There were two roads going east from Corduba. I was all too conscious that while I took the upper route through these pleasant hills, Helena Justina was travelling the lower, along the river parallel with me. While I was constantly nipping up byways to ask after Quadratus at isolated workings, she made a steadier progress not too far away. I could almost have signalled the carriage.

Instead here I was, miserable as death, barely in contact with humanity. I hated it when the stubbly speculators only produced morose grunts for me; I hated it more when they were hungry for gossip and wanted to delay me for interminable chats. I ate cheese and hard biscuit; I drank mountain stream water. I washed if I felt like it, or not if I felt perverse. I shaved myself, never a success. It was worse than the army. I was surly, solitary, famished and chaste.

In the end I realised Quadratus was not bothering with the smaller individual mines. Only the big show would do for the famous Tiberius; he must have gone straight to the huge silver mine with its complex of hundreds of shafts let to numerous contractors, which lay at the far eastern end of the mountain range. He probably travelled by way of the river road, and stayed in decent mansios. Still, he would not be as desperate as I was, and he lacked the verve and efficiency to cover as much ground. I might yet head him off.

It was a cheering hope. It kept me going for half a day. Then I knew I had to face the kind of scene I had sworn to avoid for ever, and I felt myself break into a sweat.

It was the smell that turned my stomach first. Even before the appalling sights, that sour odour of slaves in their filth made me want to retch. Hundreds worked here. Convicted criminals who would slog it out until they died; it was a short life.

I could hardly bear to enter the place, remembering how I too once laboured to hew out lead-bearing rocks with inadequate tools on a pitiful diet amidst the most sordid cruelty. Chained; flogged; cursed; tortured. The hopelessness of knowing there was no relief from the work and no chance of escape. The lice. The scabs. The bruising and the beatings. That overseer, the worst man I had ever met, whose mildest thrill was buggery, and his biggest triumph watching a slave die in front of him.

I was a free man now. I had been free then – only enslaved from choice and for an honourable motive, though there are no grades of degradation on a chain-gang in a silver mine. Now I stepped down from a sturdy horse, a self-assured man with position in the world. I had rank. I had a formal commission with an imperial pass to prove it. I had a wonderful woman who loved me and I was fathering a little citizen. I was somebody. The mine perimeter was guarded, but when I announced myself I was called 'legate' and provided with a polite guide. Yet when that smell hit my gut I was nearly thrown back to three years ago. If I relaxed, I would be a trembling wreck.

I was led through a busy township in the shadow of mountains of slag. As we passed the cupellation furnaces, the smog and the ceaseless dints of the hammers left me almost demented. I seemed to feel the ground trembling under my boots. I was told how here the shafts reached over six hundred feet deep. The tunnels chased seams of silver underground for between three and four thousand feet. Deep down below me the slaves worked, for it was daylight. There are rules. No mine may work at night. You have to be civilised.

Below ground there would be huge polished mirrors to reflect the bright sunlight from above; beyond the reach of the sun the slaves carried clay lamps with vertical handles. Their shift lasted until the lamps ran out; never soon enough. The lamps used up the air and filled the tunnels

with smoke. Amongst this smoke the slaves toiled to free
the lumps of ore, then carried the backbreaking weight of
esparto bucketfuls on their shoulders in a human chain. Up
and down from the galleries, using short ladders. Pushing
and shoving in lines like ants. Coughing and perspiring in
the dark. Relieving themselves when they had to, right
there in the galleries. Near-naked men who might never see
daylight for weeks on end. Some endlessly trudged tread-
mills on the huge waterwheels that drained the deepest
shafts. Some struggled to prop up the galleries. All of them
coming a little closer every day to an inevitable death.

'Stunning, isn't it?' enquired my guide. Oh yes. I was
stunned.

We came to the procurator's office. It was manned by a
whole battery of supervisory staff. Men with flesh on their
bodies and clothes on their backs. Clean-skinned, well-
shaven men who sat at tables telling jokes. They picked up
their salaries and enjoyed their lives. Visiting overseers
cursed and complained as they took their breaks above
ground, while they boasted about pacifying new convicts
and keeping the old hands at their hard work. The
supervising engineers, silent men scribbling inventive
diagrams, worked out new and astonishing achievements to
be turned into reality underground. The geometrists, who
were responsible for finding and evaluating the seams of
silver, completed dockets in between putting their feet up
and telling the most obscene stories.

It was a room where people constantly came and went;
nobody took any notice of a newcomer. Arcane discussions
were going on, occasionally heated though more often
businesslike. Huge movements of ore and endless shipments of ingots were being organised through this office. A
small army of contractors was being regulated here, in
order to provide a vital contribution to the Treasury. The
atmosphere was one of rough and ready industry. If there
was corruption it could be scandalous and on a massive
scale, as I had proved in another province. But we had had
a new emperor for two years since then, and somehow I

1171

doubted that more than harmless fiddling went on here. The profits were enough to cushion greed. The importance of the site ensured that only the best staff appointments were approved. There was an unmistakable aura of watchfulness from Rome.

It did not include supervision by the quaestor, apparently.

'Oh yes, Quadratus was here. We gave him the grand sightseeing tour.'

'What? *"This is an ingot; here's an Archimedes screw"* – then sending him down the deepest shaft on a wobbly ladder and suddenly blowing out the lamps to make him shit himself?'

'You know the score!' the procurator beamed admiringly. 'Then we bluffed him with a few graphs and figures, and booted him out to Castulo.'

'When was this?'

'Yesterday.'

'I should catch up with him, then.'

'Want a look around our system first?'

'Love to – but I need to get on.' I managed to make my refusal sound polite. Seen one, you've seen them all.

Castulo would be a day's ride away. Quadratus himself had told me his father had interests there, in the tight little mining society which had tied up all the mineral rights for a radius of twenty miles or more. The mining sites were smaller than here, but the area was important. Some of the wealthiest men in Hispania were making their fortunes at Castulo.

I nearly escaped without incident. I had left the office and was looking for my guide. Apparently he worked on the principle that if he got you in, you could find your own way out while he sloped off for a gossip with a friend.

Then a man came towards me. I recognised him immediately, though he did not know me. A big, shapeless bully, just as sly as he was merciless. He seemed heavier than ever, and shambled with even more threat in his ugly gait. His name was Cornix. He was the slave overseer who had once made a habit of singling me out for torture. In the end he had nearly killed me. Of all the pig-ignorant debauched thugs in the Empire he was the last man I would ever wish to see.

I could have walked right by him; he would never have realised that we had met before. I could not help my start of recognition. Then it was too late.

'Well! Well! If it isn't Chirpy!' The nickname froze my blood. And Cornix was not intending me any favours when he leered, 'I've not forgotten I owe you one!'

LXIII

He had two beats of time to reduce me to a jelly, but he missed his chance. After that it was my turn.

I had made a bad mistake with Cornix once: I had escaped his clutches and publicly humiliated him. The mere fact that I was alive today was because in my time as a slave I had continually outwitted him. Since I had been shackled, starved, despairing, and close to dying at the time, it was all the more commendable.

'I'm going to smash in your head,' he told me, in the same old sickening croak. 'And after that, we'll really have some fun!'

'Still the tender-hearted giant! Well, well, Cornix ... Who let you out of your cage?'

'You're going to die,' he glowered. 'Unless you've got a girl to rescue you again?'

This kind of delay – with its attendant danger – was the last thing I could afford. The girl who had once rescued me was heading for the coast, in a condition where she sorely needed me.

'No, Cornix. I am alone and unarmed, and I'm in a strange place. Obviously you have all the advantages.'

I was being too meek for him. He wanted threats. He wanted me to defy him and force him to fight me. One or two people were already watching. Cornix was yearning for a big display, but it had to be my fault. He was the kind of rowdy who only picked on slaves, and then covertly in corners. His official role was as a tough manager who never put a foot wrong. In Britain his superiors had been told the truth eventually, and it must be due to me that after the shake-up I organised there he had had to roam abroad to find himself a new position. Just my luck he had found it here.

'I'm glad we've had this little chat,' I said very quietly. 'It's always good to renew acquaintance with an old friend!'

I turned away. My contempt was iron-hard and just as cold. Refusing to antagonise the bastard was the surest way to achieve it. There were tools and timber everywhere. Unable to bear my forbearance Cornix grabbed a mining pick and came after me. That was his mistake.

I too had sized up possible weapons. I caught up a shovel, swung it, and banged the pick from his grip. I was angry, and I had no fear. He was out of condition and stupid, and he thought he was still dealing with someone utterly exhausted. Three years of exercise had given me more power than he could cope with. He soon knew.

'You have two choices, Cornix. Give up and walk away — or find out what pain means!' He roared with rage and rushed me with his bare hands. Since I knew where Cornix liked to put his snag-nailed fingers, I was determined not to let him get in close. I used my knee, my fists, my feet. I released more anger than I even knew I had, though dear gods, I had lived with the memories long enough.

The ruck was short. It was nasty. Slowly his oxen brain realised more was called for than he generally had to use. He began to fight harder. I was enjoying the challenge, but I had to be careful. He possessed brute strength, and he had no qualms about how he used his body. I was staving him off with punches and kicks when he bore down on me and grappled me. His roars and the familiar smell of him were churning me up. Then I broke free for a moment. Someone else took a hand. A bystander I had hardly noticed stepped forward adroitly, and passed me a gallery prop. The rough-hewn round timber weighed something terrible, though I hardly felt it. I swung the pole at chest height, with all my force. It felled Cornix with a pleasing crack of broken ribs.

'Oh nice! I learned that from you, Cornix!'

I could easily have brought the timber down on his skull. Why sink to his level? Instead, I raised the prop above my head and crashed it down across his shins. His scream sang sweetly in my ears. When I left he would never be able to follow me.

Suddenly I felt a lot better about a lot of things.

I turned to thank my rescuer and had a shock. For the second time I had escaped that brute's clutches through intervention of a female kind.

I knew I had seen her somewhere, though she lacked the kind of beauty that my brain catalogues. She was of an age where her age had ceased to matter, though clearly full of spirit and energy by the way she had helped me out. She looked nothing, just a dumpling you could see selling eggs on a market stall. She wore a brown outfit with extra swaddlings in unbleached linen, topped by untidy swags of straw-like hair emerging from a scarf. A battered satchel was slung across a bosom that wouldn't raise excitement in a galley-slave who had just set foot on land for the first time in five years. Eyes of an indeterminate colour were surveying me from a face as lively as wet plaster. She showed no reserve about being here on a site that seemed otherwise exclusively for men. Most of them had not even noticed her.

'You saved my life, madam.'

'You were coping. I just threw in some help.'

'We must have met before.' I was still gasping. 'Remind me of your name?'

She gave me a long stare. While I blinked back at her she stretched out one pointed shoe, and drew a sign in the dust with her toe: two curved lines with a smudge in between them. A human eye.

'I'm Perella,' she said matter-of-factly. Then I remembered her: the surly blonde who had originally been booked to dance for the entertainment of the Olive Oil Producers of Baetica.

LXIV

Without another word we turned away from the procurator's office, leaving Cornix writhing on the ground. No one made a move to help him. Wherever he went he was a man with enemies.

Perella and I walked right through the mine environs to the gate where I had left my mules. She had a horse. She mounted without help. I swung up with an element of slickness too. For once.

We rode single file – me leading – down the one-way road from the settlement towards the major cross-country route through the Mariana mountains. When we reached a suitable quiet spot I signalled and reined in.

'I've been dodging another Spanish dancer, name of Selia. Nice little mover with castanets, and even better with a cleaver in her hand. She won't be titillating men any more though – or murdering them either. She's learning new dance steps in Hades. All the breath's been squeezed out of her.'

'You don't say!' Perella marvelled. 'Persons unknown, would that be?'

'I believe so.'

'Better keep it that way.'

I let her see me looking her over. She was bundled up like a wet cheese. I could not see a weapon. If she carried one it could be anywhere. Her satchel, perhaps. But if she killed Selia, she had adequate skills even without weapons.

'I'm not after you, Falco.'

'You've been trying to track me down.'

'Only when I had a moment. You dodge about a lot. Falco, if we're intending to have a cosy chat we could get down and sit under a tree.'

1177

'Far be it from me to refuse to exchange sweet nothings with a woman in a wood!'

'You don't look happy on a mule.'

Apt, though I was not sure I wanted to be cosy with Perella; still, she was right about me hating life in the saddle. I dismounted my mule. Perella jumped off her horse. She unwound a large sturdy shawl which formed one layer of her garments and spread it on the ground. Equipped for everything. Obviously if I wanted to vie with such a specialist I would have to improve myself.

We placed ourselves side by side like lovers on a picnic rug: lovers who had not known each other very long. Midges started to take an interest immediately.

'Well, this is nice! All we need is a flagon of wine and some rather stale rolls, and we can convince ourselves we're a couple of skivers enjoying a holiday.' I could see Perella was not one for light-hearted quips. 'Last time I saw you I believed you were a regular dancer who had lost an engagement due to trickery. You never told me you were employed by the Chief Spy.'

'Of course I didn't tell you. I'm a professional.'

'Even so, eliminating the beauteous Selia just because she pinched your dinner-date seems to be taking your rivalry too far.'

The woman regarded me with those mud-coloured eyes. 'What makes you think I killed her?'

'It was very neat. *Professional*.' I lay back with my hands folded under my head, gazing up through the oak tree boughs. Bits of leaf flittered down and tried to land in my eyes, while I felt that old forest dampness starting to seize up my joints. Going home to hold conversations sensibly in wine bars became an attractive thought.

She sighed, squirming on the rug so she could still see me. 'Too flash, that Selia. So painted up that everywhere she went she was unmissable.'

'Good intelligence agents know how to blend in, eh? Like informers! So the flash lass has had her lamp snuffed out by the decent working girl?'

1178

Perella still managed not to admit it. 'Her time was up. I reckon the young fool quaestor had sent for her from Hispalis to finish you off, Falco.'

'I owe somebody a thank-you then.'

She showed no interest in my gratitude. 'My bet is, Selia thought he was losing his nerve and she intended to do for him as well. If he talked she would have been in trouble.'

'Letting her remove Quadratus would have solved a problem.'

'If you say so, Falco.'

'Well, let's be practical. Apart from whether it's likely anyone can persuade a judge to try him, when any judge in Rome is liable to have his inclination to do so suborned by large gifts from Attractus – somebody has to catch the bastard first. You're chasing round the mines now, and so am I. I'm definitely looking for Quadratus, and you're either after him – or me.'

She turned around and grinned at me.

'What was the game?' I asked in a dangerous voice. 'You've been lurking around all my suspects – Annaeus, Licinius, Cyzacus – they've all had a visitation. I gather you even made a trip to see me.'

'Yes, I got to most of them ahead of you; what kept you dawdling?'

'Romantic mentality. I like to admire the scenery. You may have got to them first, but most of them talked to me for longer.'

'Learn anything?' she jeered.

I ignored it. 'You knew I was official. Why not make contact? We could have shared the work.'

Perella dismissed my quibbles as mere prissiness. 'Making contact with you took second place! Until I decided whether I could trust you I didn't want to give you any clue who I was or what I was there for. I nearly managed to get to you the night of the Parilia.'

'Was it you who hurled that rock at me?'

'Just a pebble,' she smirked.

'Then why make yourself invisible afterwards?'

'Because unbeknown to you, Quadratus was lurking up ahead.'

'He had left in a carriage with two others.'

'He'd stopped it, pretending he wanted to throw up. The girl –' Aelia Annaea – 'was distracted, looking after the youth, who really *was* chucking his heart up. Quadratus had walked back slowly along the track as if he was getting some air, but it looked to me as if he was expecting somebody. That was why I flung the stone, to stop you before you blundered into him. I thought he was waiting for a meeting with Selia; I wanted to overhear what they said.'

'I never saw you and I never saw him.'

'You never saw Selia either! She was creeping up behind. In fact, Falco, the only one who wasn't hiding in the dark from you that night was Selia's sheep!'

'Did Selia make contact with Quadratus?'

'No, the girl in the carriage called out and he had to go off with her and the youth.'

'I thought it might have been you dressed up as the shepherdess?' I suggested. No chance of that: Perella could not compete with the dead girl's glorious brown eyes.

She laughed. 'No fear. Can you imagine trying to get Anacrites to sign an expenses chit for the hire of a sheep?'

So she still thought he was in operation, then.

'Let's talk about Rome,' I suggested. 'Double dealing is afoot; that's clear. It's in both our interests to explore who's doing what to whom, and why two thoroughly reasonable agents like ourselves have ended up in the same province on two different missions involving the same racket.'

'You mean,' mouthed Perella, 'are we on the same side?'

'I was sent by Laeta; I'll tell you that for nothing.'

'And I was not.'

'Now that raises an interesting question, Perella, because I had worked out you were a staffer for Anacrites – but the last time I saw him he was lying in my mother's house with

1180

the fare for the ferrymen to Hades all ready in his outstretched paw.'

'The Praetorians have got him in their camp.'

'I arranged that.'

'I saw him there.'

'Oh, so I'm dealing with a girl who mingles with Guardsmen. Now that's a *real* professional!'

'I do what I have to.'

'Spare my blushes; I'm a shy boy.'

'We all work well together.' That's usually a pious lie.

'How fortunate,' I said. Still, the intelligence service was attached to the Guard. 'Did the Praetorians tell you he was with them?'

'I tracked him down myself, after you told me he had been beaten up. It was hard going, I admit. In the end I came to ask you where he was –' I remembered giving her my address. 'You'd just left Rome, but someone put me on to your mother. She didn't tell me where he was, but she had a big pot of soup bubbling, and I guessed it was for the invalid. When she went out with a basket, I followed her.'

'Ma's still taking Anacrites broth?' I was amazed.

'According to the Praetorians she regards him as her responsibility.'

I had to think about that. 'And when you took your own bunch of flowers to his sickbed, exactly how was your unlikeable superior?'

'As tricky as ever.' This was a shrewd lady. 'He croaked and moaned as sick men always do. Maybe he was dying. Maybe the bastard was rallying and fighting back.'

'And Ma's still nursing him? I don't believe it! In the Praetorian camp?'

'The Praetorians are great lumps of slush. They adore the maternal virtues and such old-fashioned tripe. Anyway, Anacrites is safe with them. If he survives he'll think your mother's wonderful.'

I experienced a swooning dread that I would go home to Rome and find my mother married off to the Chief Spy. Never fear; she would have to divorce Pa first. They would never sort out arrangements while neither was on speaking terms.

'And you talked to Anacrites? What did he say?'

'Nothing useful.'

'How like him!'

'You saw the state he was in. It was only a couple of days after you left.'

'So who sent you here?'

'Own initiative.'

'Do you have the authority?'

'I do now!' Perella laughed, fished down inside her satchel and held something up for me to see. It was a seal ring; rather poor chalcedony; its cartouche showing two elephants with entwined trunks. 'Selia had it. I found it when I searched her. She must have stolen it when she clonked Anacrites.'

'You searched her?' I enquired politely. 'Would that be before or after you squeezed very hard on her pearly throat?' I received a sideways look. 'I knew the ring was missing, Perella. Knowing Anacrites, I assumed he heard Selia and her heavies creeping up behind him, so he swallowed it to safeguard public funds.'

Perella liked that. After she finished laughing she spun the ring in the air, then threw it as far as possible across the road and into a copse opposite. I applauded the action gently. I always enjoy a rebel. And with Selia dead, the ring was no longer useful evidence. 'I'll tell Anacrites you've got it, Falco. He'll be on at you about it for the next fifty years.'

'I can live with that. What are you doing here?' I demanded again.

Perella pursed her mouth and looked sorrowful. I was still trying to reconcile in my mind that this dumpy fright in her frumpish wrappings was a highly efficient agent — not just a damsel in a short dancing frock who listened in at dinners to earn herself a few denarii, but a woman who worked alone for weeks on end, who travelled, and who when she felt like it mercilessly ended lives.

'What's going on, Perella?'

1182

'Did you know Valentinus?' she asked.

As her voice took a lower note, I felt a chill. For a second I
was back in the Second Cohort's fire engine house, with
Valentinus swinging stiffly in a hammock and that gruesome bucket beneath his head to catch his blood. 'Hardly. I
met him once, at that dinner; I really missed my chance to
talk to him. The second time I saw him he was dead.'

'He was a nice lad.'

'He seemed so to me.'

'We had worked together a few times. Anacrites had us
both on the Baetican case. It was all mine to begin with, but
Quinctius Attractus must have twigged that we were on to
him, and he arranged for me to be pushed out by that girl.
So Valentinus had to do duty that night instead of me.
When he was killed, I decided to follow up. I owed him
that. Well, Anacrites too. He does his job in his own way –
and it's better than the alternative.'

'Claudius Laeta?'

Perella let her eyes narrow. 'Obviously I have to watch
my step, Falco – I know you're thick with him.'

'He paid my fare, but I'm not in his pocket.'

'You're independent normally?'

'Freelance. Like Valentinus. That's why I wasn't weeping when I found Selia dead. I recognised your pictogram
too – Valentinus had one on his apartment door ... I gather
you share my sceptical attitude to Laeta?'

Perella hunched her shoulders. She was choosing her
words carefully. The result was a colourful character
appraisal, the kind he would not want to have read to the
Emperor at birthday bonus time: 'Laeta's a cheating,
dabbling, double-dealing, swindling, jumped-up clerk.'

'A gem of the secretariat,' I agreed with a smile.

'It was Laeta who told Quinctius Attractus I was keeping
an eye on the Society; I'm pretty sure of it. You know
what's going on among the palace bureaux?'

'Laeta wants to discredit Anacrites. I hadn't realised he
was stirring the pot so actively, but the word is he wants to

get the spy network disbanded so he can take over. The hidden power in the Empire. The watcher we love to fear.'

'You could get a job with him, Falco.'

'So could you,' I retorted. 'Decent operatives never lack work. There are too many duds out there messing up chances; the new work rosters will contain ample spaces. Laeta would welcome both of us. But do we want to embrace his slimy charms, Perella? It's still our choice.'

'I'll probably stick with the dog I know.'

'If he survives. And if his section survives too.'

'Ah well.'

'I'll work for myself as usual.'

'Well, we both know where we are, then!' she smirked.

'Oh yes. Under a tree in a wood in Baetica without a lunch basket.'

'You're a misery, Falco.'

We seemed to be talking frankly – not that I trusted her any more as a result. Nor did I expect Perella to trust me.

'If I level with you, Falco, can I expect the same favour?' I screwed out a half-hearted shrug. 'I came to Baetica for two reasons,' she announced. 'I wanted to see Selia get it – but most of all, I'm going to sort this cartel nonsense and get the solution marked up as a credit to the spies' network.'

'Outwit Laeta?'

'And you too, if you're on his side, Falco.'

'Oh, I was sent to block the cartel too; I think it's a dead duck now.' I gave her a far from modest grin. 'I dropped a few suggestions in a few relevant ears, so I'm taking credit for suppressing it!'

Perella frowned. 'You'd do better to take a laxative!'

'Too late. Give up. It's fixed. Now there's just young Quadratus. He's crazy and out of control – just the right material for the Palace to use in its cover-up of the real mess. What Rome needs is a juicy patrician scandal to fill up the *Daily Gazette*; that's always good for taking the heat off the government. Putting Quadratus out of action on

1184

grounds of unspeakable misdemeanours caused by foolish youth allows the big men to escape with their pride intact.'

Perella scoffed quietly. 'There is a problem I don't think you realise.'

'You mean the noble Quadratus belongs to a rich and ancient family? Do you think he'll dodge the indictment?'

'Who knows? I mean, the cartel was never just a scheme set up by a few notables in Baetica for their personal gain,' Perella said. I thought she was referring to Attractus. He certainly wanted to rule far more than the cartel. Then I stayed quiet. Something in her tone was far too ominous. 'Laeta wants the cartel too, Falco.'

'Laeta does? Well, I discovered a reason for that. He's suggesting to the oil producers that he intends the industry to become state-controlled. Attractus is trying to bribe him into keeping quiet.'

'I thought Laeta had another plan,' Perella mused. 'Oh, if the oil market comes under state control, he certainly wants to be the man in charge – who creams off the golden froth for himself.'

'It wouldn't surprise me. First he would have to persuade the Emperor to take over the industry and provide state funds for running it.'

'I can think of a way he would manage that.' Perella was enjoying her superior knowledge.

'All right, you've lost me.' I could be frank. I was dying with curiosity.

'Laeta really wants the oil market cornered; he wants it for the Emperor.'

LXV

I gulped discreetly. Immediately she said it I could see there might be an appeal. Yes, Vespasian wanted to go down in history as an honest servant of the state. But yes too, he was notoriously personally mean.

He came from a middle-class family, Sabine farmers turned tax collectors: hardworking, intelligent folk on their way up — but with never enough money to run on fair terms with the old patrician families. He and his elder brother had clawed their way through the Senate to the highest posts, always in comparative poverty, always having to mortgage last year's gains in order to move on to the next magistracy. When Vespasian, having made it to consul somehow, was awarded the governorship of Africa, his brother had been compelled to fund him — and while he was there in his exalted position, Vespasian became a legend: for what? For acquiring a monopoly in the supply of salted fish …

Why should he change? He inherited empty coffers from Nero. He had the new man's zeal to make his mark. Grabbing the market in a staple commodity could still be the Emperor's dream. He ruled the Empire now, but he was just as short of funds for the business of government and probably just as eager for cash in hand himself.

'There could be various ways this would work for Laeta,' I suggested slowly. 'The most basic is the one I mentioned — a local cartel is set up, stage-managed by Attractus, and Laeta agrees that the state will allow it to exist provided he gets a large personal bribe. The next stage, more sophisticated, is that he exerts even more pressure; he says the cartel will only be allowed to continue if *the Emperor* gets a huge percentage of the profits.'

'That's what I thought,' said Perella. 'Both of those

1186

needed Anacrites wiped out. He was trying to stop the cartel.'

'Such a simple soul! Wiping out Anacrites has an additional bonus for Laeta: *he* can then take over the spies' network.'

'So you agree with me. That's it?'

'I think Laeta might be toying with even more elaborate plans. For one thing, I can't see him staying happy with Attractus as prime mover in the cartel. This probably explains why he hired me to expose the conspiracy: he specifically complained about Attractus getting above himself. So let's assume what he really wants from me is to remove Attractus. But what then happens to the cartel?'

Perella was rushing ahead. 'Suppose the cartel is made public, and it's banned – and the estates of the conspirators are all confiscated. That would attract Vespasian!'

'Yes, but what would happen? We're not talking about another Egypt here. Augustus was able to grab Egypt, capture its wonderful grain, and not only accrue huge profits for himself but gain power in Rome by controlling the grain supply and using it for propaganda, with himself as the great benefactor ensuring the poor are fed.'

Vespasian had actually shown that he appreciated the value of the corn supply by sitting in Alexandria during his bid for the throne, and tacitly threatening to keep the grain ships there with him until Rome accepted him as emperor. Would he contemplate a similar move with oil? If so, would it actually work?

'So why can't the same thing happen with Baetican oil, Falco?' Perhaps after all Perella belonged to the active type of agent, rather than the puzzle-solving kind. She was adept at strangling her rivals, but lacked a grasp of political functions. In the complex web of deceit where we were now stuck, she would need both.

'Baetica is already a senatorial province, Perella. This is going to be the problem. It may be why, in the end, nothing will ever happen. Anything in Baetica that's officially taken over, confiscated, or otherwise state-controlled will simply benefit the Treasury. For the Emperor that would hardly be a disaster; the Senate's control of the Treasury is nominal and he himself could use the money for public works, sure. But the olive oil is never going to be a monopoly in his personal control, and he'll get no personal credit for producing an oil dole for the populace. No; better for him that whatever happens is underhand. That way there may be profits.'

'So you're saying, Falco, the ideal result for Laeta is to destroy Anacrites, destroy the Quinctii – and yet keep the cartel?'

'Apparently!' I could see how it might be organised too. 'I bet Laeta will propose something like this: in Rome the estate owners, and anyone else in the trade who joins in, will all become members of the Society of Olive Oil Producers of Baetica as a cover for their operations. The Society will then make large personal gifts to the Emperor – and smaller, but still substantial ones to Laeta of course. It will look like the kind of ingratiating behaviour that's officially allowed.'

'So what can you and I do about this?'

'It all depends,' I said thoughtfully, 'whether Vespasian has been informed of the devious plan.' Remembering earlier conversations with Laeta I reckoned he would not yet have shared his ideas with the Emperor. He would want to be sure his proposals would work. It would suit Laeta to complete the scheme, then present it to his imperial master as a working proposition. He was assured of the credit then. While the cartel was being set up, Laeta could keep open an escape route in case anything went wrong. If that happened he could fall back on the straightforward move, holding his hand from personal involvement and gaining his credit by exposing the plot. But if everything went well, he could produce the more elaborate scheme for his imperial master with a splendid – though secret – secretariat flourish.

He would always have kept a secondary plan to cover snags. Me finding out too much, for instance, on the way to

1188

removing Attractus. So he had hired and kept Selia paid up, in case he wanted to eliminate me.

He had made at least one serious miscalculation: for this plan to work, the oil producers themselves had to want a cartel. If they sneakily took the honest route, Laeta would be nowhere.

The other problem would be if Vespasian decided that *he* preferred to keep his hands clean now that he was an emperor.

'Anacrites had seen what was going to happen.' Perella was still talking. 'He always reckoned Laeta wanted to put the cartel in place, then offer it to the Emperor as his bargaining piece. Laeta's reward will be power – a new intelligence empire, for a start.'

'It's cunning. He will demonstrate that Anacrites has simply blundered in and threatened the success of a lucrative scheme – failing in his dumb spy-like way to grasp the potential for imperial exploitation. Laeta, by contrast, exhibits superb speculative nous, proving himself the better man. He is also loyal – so hands his idea to a happy and grateful Emperor.'

Perella looked sick. 'Pretty, isn't it?'

'Disgusting! And you're telling me before Anacrites received his head damage he was on to all this?'

'Yes.'

'I've been told it was Quinctius Quadratus who lost his nerve and arranged for Anacrites to be beaten up. Is there any possibility that Laeta himself really organised the thugs?'

Perella considered. 'He could be evil enough to do it – but apparently when he heard what had happened he went green with shock. He's a clerk,' she said cruelly. 'I expect he hates violence!'

'He did look flustered when he came to me about it.'

'Maybe it finally struck him that he was messing with something more dangerous than scrolls.'

1189

'That hasn't made him back down from the general plan,' I commented.

'No. You said it right, Falco. Everything depends on whether Vespasian has been told all this. Once he knows, he'll love it. We'll be stuck with it.'

'So what was Anacrites intending to do to thwart Laeta's scheme?'

'What I'm still doing,' she returned crisply. 'The spies' network will produce a report saying *"Look! People were planning to force up olive oil prices; isn't it scandalous?"* Then we show that we've stopped the plot. If enough people know, we force the Emperor to agree publicly that it was corrupt and undesirable. We get the praise for discovering the project, and for ending it. Laeta has to back off – from the cartel, and from us.'

'For now!'

'Oh, he'll be back. Unless,' remarked Perella in a tone Laeta would not have cared for, 'somebody wipes him out first!'

I drew in a long breath then let it out again, whistling to myself.

I had no opinion on whether Anacrites or Laeta was best for running the intelligence service. I had always despised the whole business, and only took on missions when I needed the money, even then distrusting everyone involved. Taking sides was a fool's game. With my luck, whichever side I ended up on would be the wrong one. Better to extract myself now, then wait to see what developed. Watching the two official heavyweights slogging out their rivalry might even be amusing.

I was growing stiff, sitting on the ground. I stood up. The woman followed, gathering up her shawl then shaking it to dislodge twigs and leaves. I was once again struck by how short, stout and apparently unlikely as a spy she was. Still, she didn't look like a dancer, yet everyone who had seen her perform said she could do that.

'Perella, I'm glad we pooled our knowledge. We underlings have to work together!'

'So we do,' she agreed – with a pinch-lipped expression
that told me how she distrusted me just as freely as I did
her. 'And are you still working for Laeta, Falco?'

'Oh, I'm working for justice, truth and decency!'

'How noble. Do they pay well?'

'Pitifully.'

'I'll stick with the network then!' We had walked to our
animals. Perella flung the shawl across her horse's back
then leaned on the saddle before leaping up. 'So who goes
after Quadratus?'

I sighed deeply. 'I'd like to; I hate that young bastard –
but Perella, I'm really stuck now. He's gone in entirely the
wrong direction – back west towards Corduba. I've sent my
girl to the east coast and I ought to go after her.'

She looked surprised. My tenacity must be more famous
than I thought. 'You don't mean that, Falco!'

'I don't have much choice! I want to corner Quadratus,
but I don't want to face Helena – let alone her enraged
family – if I slip up and let anything happen to her. Her
family are important. If I upset them, they could finish me.'

'So what then, Falco? Aren't you the man to take a
chance?'

Irritated, I picked at a tooth, pausing for anguished
reflection. 'No, it's no good. I'm going to have to leave you
to take the credit. Anacrites' group needs the kudos, and I
just haven't the time to follow in the direction Quadratus
has gone. I've found out what you need to know. You saw
me at the silver mine? They told me at the supervisor's ·
office that he had been there yesterday. He let them know
he was going back to look at the mines near Hispalis.'

'And you can't do it?'

'Well, it's impossible for me. That's the wrong way. I'll
have to give up on him. I've simply run out of time. My
lady is about to pop a baby, and I promised to put her on a
ship so she can get to a good Roman midwife. She's gone
on ahead and I'm supposed to be following.'

Perella, who may even have seen Helena looking huge at the Camillus estate in Corduba while I was in Hispalis, snorted that I had better be sharp, then. I gave her the customary scowl of a man who was ruing his past indiscretions. Then I swung up on to my mule again. This time it was I who managed it gracefully, while Perella missed and had to scramble.

'Need a hand?'

'Get lost, Falco.'

So we parted in different directions, Perella going west. I meanwhile took the road to the east at a gentle pace, pretending I was headed for the Tarraconensis coast.

I was. But first, as I had always intended, I would be visiting the mines at Castulo.

LXVI

This time fear had no hold on me. Old anxieties surged around as they always would do, but I was in control.

I found the quaestor very quickly. Nobody could mistake that handsome, wholesome appearance. He was standing, talking to a contractor; the other man looked grateful for my interruption and positively scampered off. Quinctius Quadratus greeted me with warmth, as if we were old dice-playing friends.

This was not one of the great underground workings, but virtually open-cast. We had met at the head of an entry to a seam, more of a cleft in the side of a slope than a real shaft. Below us open tunnels had been carved out like long caves with overhanging roofs. The constant chipping of picks reached our ears. Slaves were clambering up and down an ungainly wooden ladder, ribs showing, all skinny limbs and outsize bony elbows, knees and feet. They carried the sack-like sagging weight of ore-baskets on their shoulders in a jostling chain while Quadratus posed like a colossus at the top of their route, quite unaware that he was positioned in their way.

He had made no attempt to hide from me. In his eyes there could be no reason for him to act the fugitive.

'Do you want to talk indoors, quaestor?'

'It's pleasant here. What can I do for you?'

'A few answers, please.' I would have to pose extremely simple questions. His brain had the consistency of a slab of lead. I folded my arms and talked in a straightforward way like a man he could trust. 'Quinctius Quadratus, I have to put to you some charges which you will see are immensely serious. Stop me if you consider anything is unfair.'

'Yes, I will.' He looked meek.

'You are believed to have been the sole mover, or to have

assisted, in tampering with an official report on corruption which had been written by your predecessor Cornelius; you altered it significantly while the document was at your father's house after being taken there by Camillus Aelianus.'

'Oh!' he said.

'You have also been accused of inveigling Rufius Constans – a minor who was under your influence – into supplying a dancer to the Society of Olive Oil Producers of Baetica. The girl subsequently attacked and killed an imperial agent, a man called Valentinus, and seriously wounded Anacrites, the Chief Spy. The charge is that you incited Rufius to join you in hiring the dancer to do the killings, that you took him with you when you arranged this, and that with him you hid in the shadows and witnessed the first murder. You then got drunk, and later lied about where you had been that night. Rufius Constans confessed everything to a witness, so there will be full corroborative testimony.'

'That's a tough one,' he said.

'There is evidence that you were with Rufius Constans when he was crushed under a grinding-stone, and that you then abandoned him alone with his injuries.'

'I should not have done that,' he apologised.

'I possess physical proof that you took my carriage to visit him. I ask you to tell me whether or not you engineered the apparent accident?'

'Ah!' he responded quietly. 'Of course it was an accident.'

'The dancing girl Selia has been found strangled at your father's estate near Corduba. Do you know anything about that?'

Quadratus looked shocked. 'I do not!'

Well, I believed that.

'There are those who believe you are unsuitable to be quaestor, though you will be glad to know that in my opinion mere ineptitude is not an indictable offence.'

＊

1194

'Why would I want to do these things you mention?' he asked me in a wondering tone. 'Is there supposed to have been some personal advantage to me?'

'Financial motives have certainly been suggested. I'm prepared to be persuaded most of it was caused by complete irresponsibility.'

'That's a hard verdict on my character!'

'And it's a poor excuse for murder.'

'I have a good explanation for everything.'

'Of course you have. There will always be excuses – and I believe you will even convince yourself that the excuses are true.'

We were still standing at the top of the exit from the seam. Quinctius moved aside abstractedly as a chain of slaves began to climb out via the ladder, each with his head down as he carried a basket of newly hewn rocks. I signalled the quaestor to walk further off with me, if only to give the poor souls room, but he seemed rooted to the spot. They managed to get past him somehow, then another lot descended the ladder, most of them going down like sailors, with their backs to the rungs and facing out.

'Thank you for your frankness, Falco.' Quadratus ran his hand through that mop of luxuriant, smartly cut hair. He looked troubled, though perhaps only by the necessity to interrupt his self-appointed mission to inspect these mines. 'I shall consider what you have said very carefully, and provide an explanation for everything.'

'Not good enough. These are capital charges.'

He was still standing there, a sturdy, muscular figure with a bland expression but a pleasing, good-looking face. He had everything that makes a man popular – not merely with women, but with voters, strangers, and many of his peers. He could not understand why he failed to win over his superiors. He would never know why he did not impress me.

'Can we discuss this later?'

'Now, Quadratus!'

Apparently he did not hear me. He was smiling faintly.

He stepped towards the wooden ladder and began to descend. Ever incompetent, he had followed the method used by the more practised slaves – facing outwards instead of first turning around to give himself a proper hold.

I had done nothing to alarm or threaten him. I can say that faithfully. Besides, there were plenty of witnesses. When his heel slipped and he fell, it was just as he said of what happened to Rufius Constans – an accident, of course.

He was still alive when I reached him. He had crashed down on to a ledge, and then fallen another ladder's height. People rushed up and we made him comfortable, though it was clear from the first he would not be recovering. In fact we left him where he was and it was soon over. He never regained consciousness.

Because a man has to stick to his personal standards, I stayed with him until he died.

PART FOUR:
BARCINO

AD73: 25 May

In some parts of the city there are no longer
any visible traces of bygone times, any
buildings or stones to bear witness to the
past ... But the certainty always remains
that everything has happened here, in this
specific space that forms part of a plain
between two rivers, the mountains and the
sea.

Albert Garcia Espuche,
Barcelona, Veinte Siglos

LXVII

From Castulo to the northern coast is a long, slow haul, at least five hundred Roman miles. It depends not just on which milepost you start counting from, but where you want to end up – and whether where you do end up is the place where you wanted to be. I had shed my spare mule then used my official pass for the *cursus publicus* and took it in fast stages, like a dispatch-rider – one who had been charged to announce an invasion by hordes of barbarians, or an imperial death. After several days I hit the coast at Valentia. I had come pretty well half way; then it was another long trek north with the sea on my right hand, through one harbour town after another, right past the provincial capital at Tarraco at the mouth of its great waterway, until at length I was due to reach Iluro, Barcino and Emporiae.

I never got as far as Emporiae, and I'll never see it now.

At every town I had stopped to visit the main temple, where I demanded to know if there was a message. In this way I had traced Helena, Aelia and Claudia from place to place, encouraged by confirmation of their passing through ahead of me – though I noticed that the brief dated messages were all written by Aelia Annaea, not Helena herself. I tried not to worry. I was closing on them fast, so I convinced myself our journeys would coincide at Emporiae as planned. Then I could take Helena safely home.

But at Barcino, the message was more personal: Claudia Rufina was waiting for me on the temple steps.

Barcino.

The one place on that heart-breaking, back-breaking journey that sticks in my mind. All the others, and the

1199

previous long cross-country and coastal miles, were obliterated from my memory the instant that I saw the girl and realised she was weeping into her veil.

Barcino was a small walled town in the coastal strip, a pausing place on the Via Augusta. It was built in a circlet of hills near the sea, in front of a small mountain that was quarried for limestone. An aqueduct brought in water; a canal carried the sewage away. The area was rural; the hinterland was divided into regular packets of land, typical of a Roman settlement that had started life as a military veterans' colony.

Wine-growing was the local commercial success, every farm possessing its kilns for making amphorae. Laeitana: the wine I had last drunk at the dinner for the Olive Oil Producers of Baetica. Wine export thrived so well the town had an official customs post on a bridge beside one of its rivers. The harbour was notoriously terrible, yet because of its handy location on the main route to Gaul, then onwards to Italy, the port was well used. Low breakers rolled unthreateningly on the beaches beyond the inlet. I could have cheerfully taken ship to Rome from here with Helena, but the Fates had another plan.

I had ridden in through the southeastern gate, a triple entrance set in the middle of the town wall. I took the straight road to the civic centre, past unpretentious two-storeyed houses, many of which had a section devoted to wine production or handicrafts. I could hear the trundle of corn- and olive-mills, with occasional bleats from animals. I never thought that my journey would be ending here. I was now so close to Emporiae, which I had planned to use as our staging post; it seemed ridiculous that anything should intervene so late in the journey. I believed we were going to make it.

I reached the forum, with its modest basilica, tempting foodshops, and an open area dedicated to honorary monuments. It was here I saw Claudia. She was leaning against one of the fine local sandstone Corinthian columns in the temple, anxiously looking out for me.

1200

My arrival had made her hysterical – which did nothing for my own peace of mind. I calmed her down enough to let her blurt out what had happened: 'We stopped here because Helena was about to have the baby. We were told they had a decent midwife – though it seems she has gone to deliver twins on the other side of the mountain. Aelia Annaea has rented a house and she's there with Helena. I came to find you if you arrived today.'

I tried in vain to compose myself. 'What are the tears for, Claudia?'

'Helena has gone into labour. It's taking far too long, and she's exhausted. Aelia thinks the baby may have too big a head –'

If so, the child would die. And Helena Justina would almost certainly die too.

Claudia led me as fast as possible to a modest town house. We rushed in through a short passage to reach an atrium with an open roof and a central pool. A reception room, dining room and bedrooms led off it; I could tell at once where Helena was because Nux was lying at full stretch outside the bedroom, with her nose pressed right against the crack under the door, whining pitifully.

Aelia's rental was clean and would have been prepossessing, but it was full of strange women, either clamouring dolefully – which was bad enough – or doing routine needlework as if my girl's suffering merely called for attendance by the civic sewing circle. A new spasm of agonising pain must have come over Helena, for I heard her crying out so dreadfully it shocked me to the core.

Aelia Annaea, ashen faced, had met us in the atrium. Her greeting was merely a shake of her head; she seemed quite unable to speak.

I managed to croak, 'I'll go to her.'

At least this male forwardness silenced a few of the wailing women. I was weary and hot, so as I passed I rinsed my face in the atrium pool – another sacrilege, apparently.

The needles had stopped stabbing, while the hysteria increased.

I scooped up Nux, whose only reaction to me was a slight tremble of her tail. All she wanted was to reach Helena. So did I. I dumped the whining dog in Aelia's arms then I grasped the door handle. As I stepped inside, Helena stopped screaming just long enough to yell at me, 'Falco, you bastard! How could you do this to me? — Go away; go away; I never want to see you again!'

I felt a wild surge of sympathy with our rude forefathers. Men in huts. Men who really were capable of anything. Men who had had to be.

Behind me Aelia gasped, 'Falco, she can't do it; she's too tired. The baby must be stuck —'

It was all out of control. Helena looking ghastly as tears mingled with perspiration on her face; Aelia wrestling with the frantic dog; strange women fluttering uselessly. I let out a roar. Hardly the best way to regain calm. Then, infuriated by the noise and fuss, I seized a broom, and with wide sweeps at waist height I cleared the room of women. Helena sobbed. Never mind. We could panic and suffer just as well on our own; we could manage without interruptions from idiots. I strode to the door after them. Aelia Annaea was the only sensible one present so I rapped out my orders to her:

'Olive oil and plenty of it!' I cried. Adding thoughtfully, 'And warm it slightly, please.'

EPILOGUE

To L. Petronius Longus, of the IV Cohort Vigilorum, Rome:

Lucius Petronius, greetings from the land of the Laeitana vintage, which I can assure you lives up to its reputation, especially when drunk in quantity by a man under stress. I solved the Second Cohort's killing (see coded report, attached: the cross-hatch stands for 'arrogant bastard' but in the prefect's copy it should be translated as 'misguided young man'). For the time being I am delayed at this spot. As you no doubt surmise, it's a girl. She's beautiful; I think I'm in love ... Just like the old days, eh?

Well, old friend, anything you can do three times, I can manage at least once. Here's another report, which with any luck you will *not* be reading in the Forum in the *Daily Gazette*:

> *Hot news just in from Tarraconensis! Word reaches us from Barcino that the family of a close associate of the Emperor may have a reason to celebrate. Details to follow, but rumours that the baby was delivered by the father while the mother yelled 'I don't need you; I'll do it myself, just like I have to do everything!' are believed to exaggerate. M. Didius Falco, an informer, who claims he was present, would only comment that his dagger has seen a lot of action, but he never thought it would end up cutting a natal cord. The black eye he acquired while attempting to ministrate has already calmed down. His finger was broken entirely by accident, when the noble lady grabbed his hand; relations between them are perfectly cordial and he has no plans to sue ...*

Helena and I both feel completely exhausted. At the

moment it seems as if we'll never recover. Our daughter is showing signs of her future personality; she closes her eyes on the crisis and goes fast to sleep.

ACKNOWLEDGEMENTS: RESEARCH

While writing this book I learned of the death of Sam Bryson, who once gave me a practical demonstration of how Falco might thwart an assailant coming at him with a knife. We acted this out in a restaurant, which may have slightly surprised other people who were dining at the time ...

Neither the books I have plundered nor the archaeology I have cribbed will ever be listed as formal sources, because the Falco series is fiction, and meant purely to entertain. But even apart from librarians, authors and tour guides whose job it is, people have always been generous with their interest and help; this seems an occasion to mention just a small sample – for instance, Sue Rollin for reassurance on the Decapolis, Mick McLean for a list of metals that I *will* use one day, Janet for steering me to hypothecs, Oliver for the rude joke about the camel, and Nick Humez for the even ruder song (with tune). I have to thank Sally Bowden who not only published me first, but then thoughtfully brought up her son to be an archaeologist – and Will Bowden, who enabled a trip to the Domus Aurea, and doesn't turn a hair when asked if a descent into the sewers might be possible ... Staff at London Zoo Reptile House were enormously helpful about snakes; then Bill Tyson described what a scorpion bite is really like ...

For this particular story, I relied heavily on Janet Laurence who selflessly handed over all her own notes on olive oil, and Robert Knapp who responded most kindly to a request from a complete stranger for a copy of his authoritative book on Roman Corduba, not to mention Señor José Remesal Rodrigez, who sent me his papers on the Baetican oil trade without even being asked. Most devoted of all must be Ginny Lindzey, who catalogued for me every detail of Jonathan's birth, and the accidental damage to Jeff during Tobin's – only to have this sacrificed to the editorial pencil ...

And as usual thank you Richard, who walks the streets, eats the meals, pours the drink, keeps the tone masculine, carries the fish, photographs the dog, rehearses the fights (and other technically difficult scenes), and inspires the best lines.

PRAISE FOR LINDSEY DAVIS

'With the passing of Ellis Peters the title Queen of Whodunnit is temporarily vacant. Lindsey Davis is well suited to assume it and she is funnier than Peters . . . it is all so enjoyable' *The Times*

Silver Pigs
'Following the blood-stained trail of silver ingots to Britain in AD70 is Marcus Didius Falco, the private eye with the Roman nose. He's the wise-cracking, toga-fumbling hero of a sizzlingly original thriller' *Mail on Sunday*

Shadows in Bronze
'Another rendolent dip into corruption in Vespasian's Rome . . . original and delightful' *Sunday Times*

The Iron Hand of Mars
'Lindsey Davis doesn't merely make history come alive she turns it into spanking entertainment, and wraps it around an intriguing mystery. She is incapable of writing a dull sentence.' *Peter Lovesey*

Poseidon's Gold
'Fast moving, funny and full of atmosphere' *Mail on Sunday*

Last Act in Palmyra
'Several cheers for Lindsey Davis . . . Great fun' *The Times*

Time to Depart
'Non-stop action, excitements and astonishments – a real cracker' *Good Book Guide*

A Dying Light in Corduba
'Highly readable, funny and colourful'
Times Literary Supplement

The Course of Honour
'Like reading Pliny rewritten by Raymond Chandler'
Sunday Times

ODE TO A BANKER

In the long hot Roman summer of AD74, Marcus Didius Falco, private informer and spare time poet, gives a reading for his family and friends. Things get out of hand as usual. The event is taken over by Aurelius Chrysippus, a wealthy Greek banker and patron to a group of struggling writers, who offers to publish Falco's work – a golden opportunity that rapidly palls. A visit to the Chrysippus *scriptorium* implicates him in a gruesome literary murder so when Petronius Longus, the over-worked vigiles enquiry chief, commissions him to investigate, Falco is forced to accept.

Lindsey Davis' twelfth Falco novel wittily explores Roman publishing and banking, two fields with striking contemporary resonance and rich sources of satire. The trail leads from the jealousies of authorship and the mire of patronage, to the darker financial world, where default can have fatal consequences . . .

BODY IN THE BATH HOUSE

AD75. As a passion for home improvement sweeps through the Roman Empire, Marcus Didius Falco struggles to deal with Gloccus and Cotta, a pair of terrible bath house contractors whose slow progress and bad workmanship have been causing him misery for months. They finally finish their contract, but leave Falco and his father with a ghastly smell from a hypocaust and some guesome site debris . . .

Far away in Britain, King Togidubnus of the Atrebates tribe is planning his own makeover. His huge new residence (known to us as Fishbourne Palace) will be spectacular – but the sensational refurbishment is behind time and over budget, its labour force is beset by 'accidents', corrupt practices are rife, and everyone loathes the project manager. The frugal Emperor Vespasian is paying for all this; he wants someone to investigate. Falco has a new baby, a new house, and he hates Britain. But his feud with Anacrites the Chief Spy has now reached a dangerous level, so with his own pressing reasons to leave Rome in a hurry, he accepts the task.

A thousand miles from home, with only his family to support him, he starts restoring order to the chaotic building site. Then, while he searches the feuding workforce for Gloccus and Cotta, he realises that someone with murderous intentions is now after him . . .